By R.A. Salvatore

The Icewind Dale Trilogy
The Crystal Shard
Streams of Silver
The Halfling's Gem

The Dark Elf Trilogy
Homeland
Exile
Sojourn

The Cleric Quintet
Canticle
In Sylvan Shadows
Night Masks
The Fallen Fortress
The Chaos Curse

Legacy of the Drow
The Legacy
Starless Night
Siege of Darkness
Passage to Dawn

Paths of Darkness
The Silent Blade
The Spine of the World
Servant of the Shard
Sea of Swords

The Hunter's Blades
The Thousand Orcs
The Lone Drow
The Two Swords

Paths of Darkness

THE SILENT BLADE

✦

THE SPINE OF THE WORLD

✦

SERVANT OF THE SHARD

✦

SEA OF SWORDS

R.A. Salvatore

PATHS OF DARKNESS
COLLECTOR'S EDITION

©2004 Wizards of the Coast, Inc.

Cover art by Daren Bader
Original Hardcover Edition First Printing: February 2004
First Trade Paperback Printing: September 2005
Library of Congress Catalog Card Number: 2003111901

9 8 7 6 5

ISBN: 978-0-7869-3995-4
620-96480740-001-EN

U.S., CANADA,	EUROPEAN HEADQUARTERS
ASIA, PACIFIC, & LATIN AMERICA	Hasbro UK Ltd.
Wizards of the Coast, Inc.	Caswell Way
P.O. Box 707	Newport, Gwent NP9 0YH
Renton, WA 98057-0707	GREAT BRITAIN
+1-800-324-6496	Save this address for your records

Visit our web site at www.wizards.com

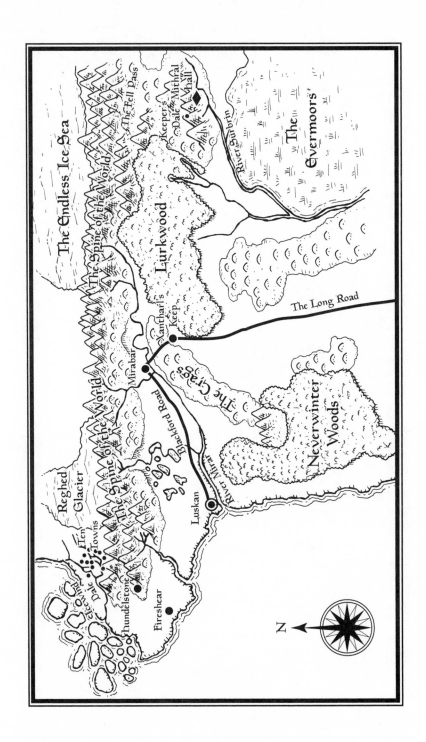

THE
SILENT BLADE

Prologue

Wulfgar lay back in his bed, pondering, trying to come to terms with the abrupt changes that had come over his life. Rescued from the demon Errtu and his hellish prison in the Abyss, the proud barbarian found himself once again among friends and allies. Bruenor, his adopted dwarven father, was here, and so was Drizzt, his dark elven mentor and dearest friend. Wulfgar could tell from the snoring that Regis, the chubby halfling, was sleeping contentedly in the next room.

And Catti-brie, dear Catti-brie, the woman Wulfgar had come to love those years before, the woman whom he had planned to marry seven years previously in Mithral Hall. They were all here at their home in Icewind Dale, reunited and presumably at peace, through the heroic efforts of these wonderful friends.

Wulfgar did not know what that meant.

Wulfgar, who had been through such a terrible ordeal over six years of torture at the clawed hands of the demon Errtu, did not understand.

The huge man crossed his arms over his chest. Sheer exhaustion put him here in bed, forced him down, for he would not willingly choose sleep. Errtu found him in his dreams.

1

And so it was this night. Wulfgar, though deep in thought and deep in turmoil, succumbed to his exhaustion and fell into a peaceful blackness that soon turned again into the images of the swirling gray mists that were the Abyss. There sat the gigantic, bat-winged Errtu, perched upon his carved mushroom throne, laughing. Always laughing that hideous croaking chuckle. That laugh was borne not out of joy, but was rather a mocking thing, an insult to those the demon chose to torture. Now the beast aimed that unending wickedness at Wulfgar, as was aimed the huge pincer of Bizmatec, another demon, minion of Errtu. With strength beyond the bounds of almost any other human, Wulfgar ferociously wrestled Bizmatec. The barbarian batted aside the huge humanlike arms and the two other upper-body appendages, the pincer arms, for a long while, slapping and punching desperately.

But too many flailing limbs came at him. Bizmatec was too large and too strong, and the mighty barbarian eventually began to tire.

It ended—always it ended—with one of Bizmatec's pincers around Wulfgar's throat, the demon's other pincer arm and its two humanlike arms holding the defeated human steady. Expert in this, his favorite torturing technique, Bizmatec pressed oh so subtly on Wulfgar's throat, took away the air, then gave it back, over and over, leaving the man weak in the legs, gasping and gasping as minutes, then hours, slipped past.

Wulfgar sat up straight in his bed, clutching at his throat, clawing a scratch down one side of it before he realized that the demon was not there, that he was safe in his bed in the land he called home, surrounded by his friends.

Friends . . .

What did that word mean? What could they know of his torment? How could they help him chase away the enduring nightmare that was Errtu?

The haunted man did not sleep the rest of the night, and when Drizzt came to rouse him, well before the dawn, the dark elf found Wulfgar already dressed for the road. They were to leave this day, all five, bearing the artifact Crenshinibon far, far to the south and west. They were bound for Caradoon on the banks of Impresk Lake, and then into the Snowflake Mountains to a great monastery called Spirit Soaring where a priest named Cadderly would destroy the wicked relic.

Crenshinibon. Drizzt had it with him when he came to get Wulfgar that morning. The drow didn't wear it openly, but Wulfgar knew it was there. He could sense it, could feel its vile presence. For Crenshinibon remained linked to its last master, the demon Errtu. It tingled with the energy of the demon, and because Drizzt had it on him and was standing so close, Errtu, too, remained close to Wulfgar.

"A fine day for the road," the drow remarked lightheartedly, but his tone was strained, condescending, Wulfgar noted. With more than a little difficulty, Wulfgar resisted the urge to punch Drizzt in the face.

Instead, he grunted in reply and strode past the deceptively small dark elf. Drizzt was but a few inches over five feet, while Wulfgar towered closer to seven feet than to six, and carried fully twice the weight of the drow. The barbarian's thigh was thicker than Drizzt's waist, and yet, if it came to blows between them, wise bettors would favor the drow.

"I have not yet wakened Catti-brie," Drizzt explained.

Wulfgar turned fast at the mention of the name. He stared hard into the drow's lavender eyes, his own blue orbs matching the intensity that always seemed to be there.

"But Regis is already awake and at his morning meal—he is hoping to get two or three breakfasts in before we leave, no doubt," Drizzt added with a chuckle, one that Wulfgar did not share. "And Bruenor will meet us on the field beyond Bryn Shander's eastern gate. He is with his own folk, preparing the priestess Stumpet to lead the clan in his absence."

Wulfgar only half heard the words. They meant nothing to him. All the world meant nothing to him.

"Shall we rouse Catti-brie?" the drow asked.

"I will," Wulfgar answered gruffly. "You see to Regis. If he gets a belly full of food, he will surely slow us down, and I mean to be quick to your friend Cadderly, that we might be rid of Crenshinibon."

Drizzt started to answer, but Wulfgar turned away, moving down the hall to Catti-brie's door. He gave a single, thunderous knock, then pushed right through. Drizzt moved a step in that direction to scold the barbarian for his rude behavior—the woman had not even acknowledged his knock, after all—but he let it go. Of all the humans the drow had ever met, Catti-brie ranked as the most capable at defending herself from insult or violence.

Besides, Drizzt knew that his desire to go and scold Wulfgar was wrought more than a bit by his jealousy of the man who once was, and perhaps was soon again, to be Catti-brie's husband.

The drow stroked a hand over his handsome face and turned to find Regis.

*   *   *   *   *

Wearing only a slight undergarment and with her pants half pulled up, the startled Catti-brie turned a surprised look on Wulfgar as he strode into her room. "Ye might've waited for an answer," she said dryly, brushing away her embarrassment and pulling her pants up, then going to retrieve her tunic.

Wulfgar nodded and held up his hands—only half an apology, perhaps, but a half more than Catti-brie had expected. She saw the pain in the man's sky blue eyes and the emptiness of his occasional strained smiles. She had talked with Drizzt about it at length, and with Bruenor and Regis, and they had all decided to be patient. Time alone could heal Wulfgar's wounds.

3

"The drow has prepared a morning meal for us all," Wulfgar explained. "We should eat wellbefore we start on the long road."

" 'The drow'? " Catti-brie echoed. She hadn't meant to speak it aloud, but so dumbfounded was she by Wulfgar's distant reference to Drizzt that the words just slipped out. Would Wulfgar call Bruenor "the dwarf"? And how long would it be before she became simply "the girl"? Catti-brie blew a deep sigh and pulled her tunic over her shoulders, reminding herself pointedly that Wulfgar had been through hell—literally. She looked at him now, studying those eyes, and saw a hint of embarrassment there, as though her echo of his callous reference to Drizzt had indeed struck him in the heart. That was a good sign.

He turned to leave her room, but she moved to him, reaching up to gently stroke the side of his face, her hand running down his smooth cheek to the scratchy beard that he had either decided to grow or simply hadn't been motivated enough to shave.

Wulfgar looked down at her, at the tenderness in her eyes, and for the first time since the fight on the ice floe when he and his friends had dispatched wicked Errtu, there came a measure of honesty in his slight smile.

* * * * *

Regis did get his three meals, and he grumbled about it all that morning as the five friends started out from Bryn Shander, the largest of the villages in the region called Ten Towns in forlorn Icewind Dale. Their course was north at first, moving to easier ground, and then turning due west. To the north, far in the distance, they saw the high structures of Targos, second city of the region, and beyond the city's roofs could be seen shining waters of Maer Dualdon.

By mid-afternoon, with more than a dozen miles behind them, they came to the banks of the Shaengarne, the great river swollen and running fast with the spring melt. They followed it north, back to Maer Dualdon, to the town of Bremen and a waiting boat Regis had arranged.

Gently refusing the many offers from townsfolk to remain in the village for supper and a warm bed, and over the many protests of Regis, who claimed that he was famished and ready to lay down and die, the friends were soon west of the river, running on again, leaving the towns, their home, behind.

Drizzt could hardly believe that they had set out so soon. Wulfgar had only recently been returned to them. All of them were together once more in the land they called their home, at peace, and yet, here they were, heeding again the call of duty and running down the road to adventure. The drow had the cowl of his traveling cloak pulled low about his face, shielding his sensitive eyes from the stinging sun.

Thus his friends could not see his wide smile.

4

Part 1

Apathy

Often I sit and ponder the turmoil I feel when my blades are at rest, when all the world around me seems at peace. This is the supposed ideal for which I strive, the calm that we all hope will eventually return to us when we are at war, and yet, in these peaceful times—and they have been rare occurrences indeed in the more than seven decades of my life—I do not feel as if I have found perfection, but, rather, as if something is missing from my life.

It seems such an incongruous notion, and yet I have come to know that I am a warrior, a creature of action. In those times when there is no pressing need for action, I am not at ease. Not at all.

When the road is not filled with adventure, when there are no monsters to battle and no mountains to climb, boredom finds me. I have come to accept this truth of my life, this truth about who I am, and so, on those rare, empty occasions I can find a way to defeat the boredom. I can find a mountain peak higher than the last I climbed.

I see many of the same symptoms now in Wulfgar, returned to us from the grave, from the swirling darkness that was Errtu's corner of the Abyss. But I fear that Wulfgar's state has transcended simple boredom, spilling into the realm of apathy. Wulfgar, too, was a creature of action, but that

7

doesn't seem to be the cure for his lethargy or his apathy. His own people now call out to him, begging action. They have asked him to assume leadership of the tribes. Even stubborn Berkthgar, who would have to give up that coveted position of rulership, supports Wulfgar. He and all the rest of them know, at this tenuous time, that above all others Wulfgar, son of Beornegar, could bring great gains to the nomadic barbarians of Icewind Dale.

Wulfgar will not heed that call. It is neither humility nor weariness stopping him, I recognize, nor any fears that he cannot handle the position or live up to the expectations of those begging him. Any of those problems could be overcome, could be reasoned through or supported by Wulfgar's friends, myself included. But, no, it is none of those rectifiable things.

It is simply that he does not care.

Could it be that his own agonies at the clawed hands of Errtu were so great and so enduring that he has lost his ability to empathize with the pain of others? Has he seen too much horror, too much agony, to hear their cries?

I fear this above all else, for it is a loss that knows no precise cure. And yet, to be honest, I see it clearly etched in Wulfgar's features, a state of self-absorption where too many memories of his own recent horrors cloud his vision. Perhaps he does not even recognize someone else's pain. Or perhaps, if he does see it, he dismisses it as trivial next to the monumental trials he suffered for those six years as Errtu's prisoner. Loss of empathy might well be the most enduring and deep-cutting scar of all, the silent blade of an unseen enemy, tearing at our hearts and stealing more than our strength. Stealing our will, for what are we without empathy? What manner of joy might we find in our lives if we cannot understand the joys and pains of those around us, if we cannot share in a greater community? I remember my years in the Underdark after I ran out of Menzoberranzan. Alone, save the occasional visits from Guenhwyvar, I survived those long years through my own imagination.

I am not certain that Wulfgar even has that capacity left to him, for imagination requires introspection, a reaching within one's thoughts, and I fear that every time my friend so looks inward, all he sees are the minions of Errtu, the sludge and horrors of the Abyss.

He is surrounded by friends, who love him and will try with all their hearts to support him and help him climb out of Errtu's emotional dungeon. Perhaps Catti-brie, the woman he once loved (and perhaps still does love) so deeply, will prove pivotal to his recovery. It pains me to watch them together, I admit. She treats Wulfgar with such tenderness and compassion, but I know that he feels not her gentle touch. Better that she slap his face, eye him sternly, and show him the truth of his lethargy. I know this and yet I cannot tell her to do so, for their relationship is much more complicated than that. I have nothing but Wulfgar's best interests in my mind and my heart now, and yet, if I showed Catti-brie a way that seemed less

8

than compassionate, it could be, and would be—by Wulfgar at least, in his present state of mind—construed as the interference of a jealous suitor.

Not true. For though I do not know Catti-brie's honest feelings toward this man who once was to be her husband—for she has become quite guarded with her feelings of late—I do recognize that Wulfgar is not capable of love at this time.

Not capable of love . . . are there any sadder words to describe a man? I think not, and wish that I could now assess Wulfgar's state of mind differently. But love, honest love, requires empathy. It is a sharing—of joy, of pain, of laughter, of tears. Honest love makes one's soul a reflection of the partner's moods. And as a room seems larger when it is lined with mirrors, so do the joys become amplified. And as the individual items within the mirrored room seem less acute, so does pain diminish and fade, stretched thin by the sharing.

That is the beauty of love, whether in passion or friendship. A sharing that multiplies the joys and thins the pains. Wulfgar is surrounded now by friends, all willing to engage in such sharing, as it once was between us. Yet he cannot so engage us, cannot let loose those guards that he necessarily put in place when surrounded by the likes of Errtu.

He has lost his empathy. I can only pray that he will find it again, that time will allow him to open his heart and soul to those deserving, for without empathy he will find no purpose. Without purpose, he will find no satisfaction. Without satisfaction, he will find no contentment, and without contentment, he will find no joy.

And we, all of us, will have no way to help him.

—Drizzt Do'Urden

Chapter 1

A Stranger at Home

Artemis Entreri stood on a rocky hill overlooking the vast, dusty city, trying to sort through the myriad feelings that swirled within him. He reached up to wipe the blowing dust and sand from his lips and from the hairs of his newly grown goatee. Only as he wiped it did he realize that he hadn't shaved the rest of his face in several days, for now the small beard, instead of standing distinct upon his face, fell to ragged edges across his cheeks.

Entreri didn't care.

The wind pulled many strands of his long hair from the tie at the back of his head, the wayward lengths slapping across his face, stinging his dark eyes.

Entreri didn't care.

He just stared down at Calimport and tried hard to stare inside himself. The man had lived nearly two-thirds of his life in the sprawling city on the southern coast, had come to prominence as a warrior and a killer there. It was the only place that he could ever really call home. Looking down on it now, brown and dusty, the relentless desert sun flashed brilliantly off the white marble of the greater homes. It also illuminated the many hovels, shacks, and torn tents set along roads—muddy roads only

11

because they had no proper sewers for drainage. Looking down on Calimport now, the returning assassin didn't know how to feel. Once, he had known his place in the world. He had reached the pinnacle of his nefarious profession, and any who spoke his name did so with reverence and fear. When a pasha hired Artemis Entreri to kill a man, that man was soon dead. Without exception. And despite the many enemies he had obviously made, the assassin had been able to walk the streets of Calimport openly, not from shadow to shadow, in all confidence that none would be bold enough to act against him.

No one would dare shoot an arrow at Artemis Entreri, for they would know that the single shot must be perfect, must finish this man who seemed above the antics of mere mortals, else he would then come looking for them. And he would find them, and he would kill them.

A movement to the side, the slight shift of a shadow, caught Entreri's attention. He shook his head and sighed, not really surprised, when a cloaked figure leaped out from the rocks, some twenty feet ahead of him and stood blocking the path, arms crossed over his burly chest.

"Going to Calimport?" the man asked, his voice thick with a southern accent.

Entreri didn't answer, just kept his head straight ahead, though his eyes darted to the many rocks lining both sides of the trail.

"You must pay for the passage," the burly man went on. "I am your guide." With that he bowed and came up showing a toothless grin.

Entreri had heard many tales of this common game of money through intimidation, though never before had one been bold enough to block his way. Yes, indeed, he realized, he had been gone a long time. Still he didn't answer, and the burly man shifted, throwing wide his cloak to reveal a sword under his belt.

"How many coins do you offer?" the man asked.

Entreri started to tell him to move aside but changed his mind and only sighed again.

"Deaf?" said the man, and he drew out his sword and advanced yet another step. "You pay me, or me and my friends will take the coins from your torn body."

Entreri didn't reply, didn't move, didn't draw his jeweled dagger, his only weapon. He just stood there, and his ambivalence seemed to anger the burly man all the more.

The man glanced to the side—to Entreri's left—just slightly, but the assassin caught the look clearly. He followed it to one of the robber's companions, holding a bow in the shadows between two huge rocks.

"Now," said the burly man. "Last chance for you."

Entreri quietly hooked his toe under a rock, but made no movement other than that. He stood waiting, staring at the burly man, but with the archer on the edge of his vision. So well could the assassin read the movements of men, the slightest muscle twitch, the blink of an eye, that it was

12

he who moved first. Entreri leaped out diagonally, ahead and to the left, rolling over and kicking out with his right foot. He launched the stone the archer's way, not to hit the man—that would have been above the skill even of Artemis Entreri—but in the hopes of distracting him. As he came over into the somersault, the assassin let his cloak fly wildly, hoping it might catch and slow the arrow.

He needn't have worried, for the archer missed badly and would have even if Entreri hadn't moved at all.

Coming up from the roll, Entreri set his feet and squared himself to the charging swordsmen, aware also that two other men were coming over the rocks at either side of the trail.

Still showing no weapon, Entreri unexpectedly charged ahead, ducking the swipe of the sword at the last possible instant, then came up hard behind the swishing blade, one hand catching the attacker's chin, the other snapping behind the man's head, grabbing his hair. A twist and turn flipped the swordsman on the ground. Entreri let go, running his hand up the man's weapon arm to fend off any attempted attacks. The man went down on his back hard. At that moment Entreri stomped down on his throat. The man's grasp on the sword weakened, almost as if he were handing the weapon to Entreri.

The assassin leaped away, not wanting to get his feet tangled as the other two came in, one straight ahead, the other from behind. Out flashed Entreri's sword, a straight left-handed thrust, followed by a dazzling, rolling stab. The man easily stepped back out of Entreri's reach, but the attack hadn't been designed to score a hit anyway. Entreri flipped the sword to his right hand, an overhand grip, then stepped back suddenly, so suddenly, turning his hand and the blade. He brought it across his body, then stabbed it out behind him. The assassin felt the tip enter the man's chest and heard the gasp of air as he sliced a lung.

Instinct alone had Entreri spinning, turning to the right and keeping the attacker impaled. He brought the man about as a shield against the archer, who did indeed fire again. But again, the man missed badly, and this time the arrow burrowed into the ground several feet in front of Entreri.

"Idiot," the assassin muttered, and with a sudden jerk, he dropped his latest victim to the dirt, bringing the sword about in the same fluid movement. So brilliantly had he executed the maneuver that the remaining swordsman finally understood his folly, turned about, and fled.

Entreri spun again, threw the sword in the general direction of the archer, and bolted for cover.

A long moment slipped past.

Where is he?" the archer called out, obvious fear and frustration in his voice. "Merk, do you see him?"

Another long moment passed.

"Where is he?" the archer cried again, growing frantic. "Merk, where is he?"

13

"Right behind you," came a whisper. A jeweled dagger flashed, slicing the bowstring and then, before the stunned man could begin to react, resting against the front of his throat.

"Please," the man stammered, trembling so badly that his movements, not Entreri's, caused the first nick from that fine blade. "I have children, yes. Many, many children. Seventeen . . ."

He ended in a gurgle as Entreri cut him from ear to ear, bringing his foot up against the man's back even as he did, then kicking him facedown to the ground.

"Then you should have chosen a safer career," Entreri answered, though the man could not hear.

Peering out from the rocks, the assassin soon spotted the fourth of the group, moving from shadow to shadow across the way. The man was obviously heading for Calimport but was simply too scared to jump out and run in the open. Entreri knew that he could catch the man, or perhaps re-string the bow and take him down from this spot. But he didn't, for he hardly cared. Not even bothering to search the bodies for loot, Entreri wiped and sheathed his magical dagger and moved back onto the road. Yes, he had been gone a long, long time.

Before he had left this city, Artemis Entreri had known his place in the world and in Calimport. He thought of that now, staring at the city after an absence of several years. He understood the shadowy world he had inhabited and realized that many changes had likely taken place in those alleys. Old associates would be gone, and his reputation would not likely carry him through the initial meetings with the new, often self-proclaimed leaders of the various guilds and sects.

"What have you done to me, Drizzt Do'Urden?" he asked with a chuckle, for this great change in the life of Artemis Entreri had begun when a certain Pasha Pook had sent him on a mission to retrieve a magical ruby pendant from a runaway halfling. An easy enough task, Entreri had believed. The halfling, Regis, was known to the assassin and should not have proven a difficult adversary.

Little did Entreri know at that time that Regis had done a marvelously cunning job of surrounding himself with powerful allies, particularly the dark elf. How many years had it been, Entreri pondered, since he had first encountered Drizzt Do'Urden? Since he had first met his warrior equal, who could rightly hold a mirror up to Entreri and show the lie that was his existence? Nearly a decade, he realized, and while he had grown older and perhaps a bit slower, the drow elf, who might live six centuries, had aged not at all.

Yes, Drizzt had started Entreri on a path of dangerous introspection. The blackness had only been amplified when Entreri had gone after Drizzt again, along with the remnants of the drow's family. Drizzt had beaten Entreri on a high ledge outside Mithral Hall, and the assassin would have died, except that an opportunistic dark elf by the name of

Jarlaxle had rescued him. Jarlaxle had then taken him to Menzoberranzan, the vast city of the drow, the stronghold of Lolth, Demon Queen of Chaos. The human assassin had found a different standing down there in a city of intrigue and brutality. There, everyone was an assassin, and Entreri, despite his tremendous talents at the murderous art, was only human, a fact that relegated him to the bottom of the social ladder.

But it was more than simple perceptual standing that had struck the assassin profoundly during his stay in the city of drow. It was the realization of the emptiness of his existence. There, in a city full of Entreris, he had come to recognize the folly of his confidence, of his ridiculous notion that his passionless dedication to pure fighting skill had somehow elevated him above the rabble. He knew that now, looking down at Calimport, at the city he had known as a home, at his last refuge, it seemed, in all the world.

In dark and mysterious Menzoberranzan, Artemis Entreri had been humbled.

As he made his way to the distant city, Entreri wondered many times if he truly desired this return. His first days would be perilous, he knew, but it was not fear for the end of his life that brought a hesitance to his normally cocky stride. It was fear of continuing his life.

Outwardly, little had changed in Calimport—the town of a million beggars, Entreri liked to call it. True to form, he passed by dozens of pitiful wretches, lying in rags, or naked, along the sides of the road, most of them likely in the same spot the city guards had thrown them that morning, clearing the way for the golden-gilded carriages of the important merchants. They reached toward Entreri with trembling, bony fingers, arms so weak and emaciated that they could not hold them up for even the few seconds it took the heartless man to stride past them.

Where to go? he wondered. His old employer, Pasha Pook, was long dead, the victim of Drizzt's powerful panther companion after Entreri had done as the man had bade him and returned Regis and the ruby pendant. Entreri had not remained in the city for long after that unfortunate incident, for he had brought Regis in and that had led to the demise of a powerful figure, ultimately a black stain on Entreri's record among his less-than-merciful associates. He could have mended the situation, probably quite easily, by simply offering his normally invaluable services to another powerful guildmaster or pasha, but he had chosen the road. Entreri had been bent on revenge against Drizzt, not for the killing of Pook—the assassin cared little about that—but because he and Drizzt had battled fiercely without conclusion in the city's sewers, a fight that Entreri still believed he should have won.

Walking along the dirty streets of Calimport now, he had to wonder what reputation he had left behind. Certainly many other assassins would have spoken ill of him in his absence, would have exaggerated Entreri's failure in the Regis incident in order to strengthen their own positions within the gutter pecking order.

15

Entreri smiled as he considered the fact, and he knew it to be fact, that those ill words against him would have been spoken in whispers only. Even in his absence, those other killers would fear retribution. Perhaps he didn't know his place in the world any longer. Perhaps Menzoberranzan had held a dark . . . no, not dark, but merely empty mirror before his eyes, but he could not deny that he still enjoyed the respect.

Respect he might have to earn yet again, he pointedly reminded himself.

As he moved along the familiar streets, more and more memories came back to him. He knew where most of the guild houses had been located, and suspected that, unless there had been some ambitious purge by the lawful leaders of the city, many still stood intact, and probably brimming with the associates he had once known. Pook's house had been shaken to the core by the killing of the wretched pasha and, subsequently, by the appointment of the lazy halfling Regis as Pook's successor. Entreri had taken care of that minor problem by taking care of Regis, and yet, despite the chaos imposed upon that house, when Entreri had gone north with the halfling in tow, the house of Pook had survived. Perhaps it still stood, though the assassin could only guess as to who might be ruling it now.

That would have been a logical place for Entreri to go and rebuild his base of power within the city, but he simply shrugged and walked past the side avenue that would lead to it. He thought he was merely wandering aimlessly, but soon enough he came to another familiar region and realized that he had subconsciously aimed for this area, perhaps in an effort to regain his heart.

These were the streets where a young Artemis Entreri had first made his mark in Calimport, where he, barely a teenager, had defeated all challengers to his supremacy, where he had battled the man sent by Theebles Royuset, the lieutenant in powerful Pasha Basadoni's guild. Entreri had killed that thug and had later killed ugly Theebles, the clever murder moving him into Basadoni's generous favor. He had become a lieutenant in one of the most powerful guilds of Calimport, of all of Calimshan, at the tender age of fourteen.

But now he hardly cared, and recalling the story did not even bring the slightest hint of a smile to his face.

He thought back further, to the torment that had landed him here in the first place, trials too great for a boy to overcome, deception and betrayal by everyone he had known and trusted, most pointedly his own father. Still, he didn't care, couldn't even feel the pain any longer. It was meaningless, emptiness, without merit or point.

He saw a woman in the shadows of one hovel, hanging washed clothes to dry. She shifted deeper into the shadows, obviously wary. He understood her concern, for he was a stranger here, dressed too richly with his thick, well-stitched traveling cloak to belong in the shanty town. Strangers in these brutal places usually brought danger.

"From there to there," came a call, the voice of a young man, full of pride and edged with fear. Entreri turned slowly to see the youth, a tall and gangly lad, holding a club laced with spikes, swinging it nervously.

Entreri stared at him hard, seeing himself in the boy's face. No, not himself, he realized, for this one was too obviously nervous. This one would likely not survive for long.

"From there to there!" the boy said more loudly, pointing with his free hand to the end of the street where Entreri had entered, to the far end, where the assassin had been going.

"Your pardon, young master," Entreri said, dipping a slight bow, and feeling, as he did, his jeweled dagger, set on his belt under the folds of his cloak. A flick of his wrist could easily propel that dagger the fifteen feet, past the awkward youth's defenses and deep into his throat.

"Master," the lad echoed, his tone as much that of an incredulous question as an assertion. "Yes, master," he decided, apparently liking the title. "Master of this street, of all these streets, and none walk them without the permission of Taddio." As he finished, he prodded his thumb repeatedly into his chest.

Entreri straightened, and for just an instant, death flashed across his black eyes and the words "dead master" echoed through his thoughts. The lad had just challenged him, and the Artemis Entreri of a few years previous, a man who accepted and conquered all challenges, would have simply destroyed the youth where he stood.

But now that flash of pride whisked by, leaving Entreri unfazed and uninsulted. He gave a resigned sigh, wondering if he would find yet another stupid fight this day. And for what? he wondered, facing this pitiful, confused little boy on an empty street over which no rational person would even deign to claim ownership. "I begged you pardon, young master," he said calmly. "I did not know, for I am new to the region and ignorant of your customs."

"Then you should learn!" the lad replied angrily, gaining courage in Entreri's submissive response and coming forward a couple of strong strides.

Entreri shook his head, his hand starting for the dagger, but going, instead to his belt purse. He pulled out a gold coin and tossed it to the feet of the strutting youth.

The boy, who drank from sewers and ate the scraps he could rummage from the alleys behind the merchant houses, could not hide his surprise and awe at such a treasure. He regained his composure a moment later, though, and looked back at Entreri with a superior posture. "It is not enough," he said.

Entreri threw out another gold coin, and a silver. "That is all that I have, young master," he said, holding his hands out wide.

"If I search you and learn differently. . . ." the lad threatened.

17

Entreri sighed again, and decided that if the youth approached he would kill him quickly and mercifully.

The boy bent and scooped up the three coins. "If you come back to the domain of Taddio, have with you more coins," he declared. "I warn you. Now begone! Out the same end of the street you entered!"

Entreri looked back the way he had come. In truth, one direction seemed as good as any other to him at that time, so he gave a slight bow and walked back, out of the domain of Taddio, who had no idea how lucky he had been this day.

*   *   *   *   *

The building stood three full stories and, decorated with elaborate sculptures and shining marble, was truly the most impressive abode of all the thieving guilds. Normally such shadowy figures tried to keep a low profile, living in houses that seemed unremarkable from the outside, though they were, in truth, palatial within. Not so with the house of Pasha Basadoni. The old man—and he was ancient now, closer to ninety than to eighty—enjoyed his luxuries, and enjoyed showing the power and splendor of his guild to all who would look.

In a large chamber in the middle of the second floor, the gathering room for Basadoni's principle commanders, the two men and one woman who truly operated the day-to-day activities of the extensive guild entertained a young street thug. He was more a boy than a man, an unimpressive figure held in power by the backing of Pasha Basadoni and surely not by his own wiles.

"At least he is loyal," remarked Hand, a quiet and subtle thief, the master of shadows, when Taddio left them. "Two gold pieces and one silver—no small take for one working that gutter section."

"If that is all he received from his visitor," Sharlotta Vespers answered with a dismissive chuckle. Sharlotta stood tallest of the three captains, an inch above six feet, her body slender, her movements graceful—so graceful that Pasha Basadoni had nicknamed her his "Willow Tree." It was no secret that Basadoni had taken Sharlotta as his lover and still used her in that manner on those rare occasions when his old body was up to the task. It was common knowledge that Sharlotta had used those liaisons to her benefit and had climbed the ranks through Basadoni's bed. She willingly admitted as much, usually just before she killed the man or woman who had complained about it. A shake of her head sent waist-length black hair flipping back over one shoulder, so that Hand could see her wry expression clearly.

"If Taddio had received more, then he would have delivered more," Hand assured her, his tone, despite his anger, revealing that hint of frustration he and their other companion, Kadran Gordeon, always felt when dealing with the condescending Sharlotta. Hand ruled the quiet services

18

of Basadoni's operation, the pickpockets and the prostitutes who worked the market, while Kadran Gordeon dealt with the soldiers of the street army. But Sharlotta, the Willow Tree, had Basadoni's ear above them all. She served as the principal attendant of the Pasha and as the voice of the now little seen old man.

When Basadoni finally died, these three would fight for control, no doubt, and while those who understood only the peripheral truths of the guild would likely favor the brash and loud Kadran Gordeon, those, such as Hand, who had a better feeling for the true inner workings, understood that Sharlotta Vespers had already taken many, many steps to secure and strengthen her position with or without the specter of Basadoni looming over them.

"How many words will we waste on the workings of a boy?" Kadran Gordeon complained. "Three new merchants have set up kiosks in the market a stone's throw from our house without our permission. That is the more important matter, the one requiring our full attention."

"We have already talked it through," Sharlotta replied. "You want us to give you permission to send out your soldiers, perhaps even a battle-mage, to teach the merchants better. You will not get that from us at this time."

"If we wait for Pasha Basadoni to finally speak on this matter, other merchants will come to the belief that they, too, need not pay us for the privilege of operating within the boundaries of our protective zone." He turned to Hand, the small man often his ally in arguments with Sharlotta. But the thief was obviously distracted, staring down at one of the coins the boy Taddio had given to him. Sensing that he was being watched, Hand looked up at the other two.

"What is it?" Kadran prompted.

"I've not seen one like this," Hand explained, flipping the coin to the burly man.

Kadran caught it and quickly examined it, then, with a surprised expression, handed it over to Sharlotta. "Nor have I seen one with this stamp," he admitted. "Not of the city, I believe, nor of anywhere in Calimshan."

Sharlotta studied the coin carefully, a flicker of recognition coming to her striking light green eyes. "The crescent moon," she remarked, then flipped it over. "Profile of a unicorn. This is a coin from the region of Silverymoon."

The other two looked to each, surprised, as was Sharlotta, by the revelation. "Silverymoon?" Kadran echoed incredulously.

"A city far to the north, east of Waterdeep," Sharlotta replied.

"I know where Silverymoon lies," Kadran replied dryly. "The domain of Lady Alustriel, I believe. That is not what I find surprising."

"Why would a merchant, if it was a merchant, of Silverymoon find himself walking in Taddio's worthless shanty town?" Hand asked, echoing Kadran's suspicions perfectly.

19

"Indeed, I thought it curious that anyone carrying such a treasure of more than two gold pieces would be in that region," Kadran agreed, pursing his lips and twisting his mouth in his customary manner that sent one side of his long and curvy mustache up far higher than the other, giving his whole dark face an unbalanced appearance. "Now it seems to have become more curious by far."

"A man who wandered into Calimport probably came in through the docks," Hand reasoned, "and found himself lost in the myriad of streets and smells. So much of the city looks the same, after all. It would not be difficult for a foreigner to wander wayward."

"I do not believe in coincidences," Sharlotta replied. She tossed the coin back to Hand. "Take it to one of our wizard associates—Giunta the Diviner will suffice. Perhaps there remains enough of a trace of the previous owner's identity upon the coins that Giunta can locate him."

"It seems a tremendous effort for one too afraid of the boy to even refuse payment," Hand replied.

"I do not believe in coincidences," Sharlotta repeated. "I do not believe that anyone could be so intimidated by that pitiful Taddio, unless it is someone who knows that he works as a front for Pasha Basadoni. And I do not like the idea that one so knowledgeable of our operation took it upon himself to wander into our territory unannounced. Was he, perhaps, looking for something? Seeking a weakness?"

"You presume much," Kadran put in.

"Only where danger is concerned," Sharlotta retorted. "I consider every person an enemy until he has proven himself differently, and I find that in knowing my enemies, I can prepare against anything they might send against me."

There was little mistaking the irony of her words, aimed as they were at Kadran Gordeon, but even the dangerous soldier had to nod his agreement with Sharlotta's perception and precaution. It wasn't every day that a merchant bearing coins from far away Silverymoon wandered into one of Calimport's desolate shanty towns.

* * * * *

He knew this house better than any in all the city. Within those brown, unremarkable walls, within the wrapper of a common warehouse, hung golden-stitched tapestries and magnificent weapons. Beyond the always barred side door, where an old beggar now huddled for meager shelter, lay a room of beautiful dancing ladies, all swirling veils and alluring perfumes, warm baths in scented water, and cuisine delicacies from every corner of the Realms.

This house had belonged to Pasha Pook. After his demise, it had been given by Entreri's archenemy to Regis the halfling, who had ruled briefly, until Entreri had decided the little fool had ruled long enough.

When Entreri had left Calimport with Regis, the last time he had seen the dusty city, the house was in disarray, with several factions fighting for power. He suspected that Quentin Bodeau, a veteran burglar with more than twenty years' experience in the guild, had won the fight. What he didn't know, given the confusion and outrage within the ranks, was whether the fight had been worth winning. Perhaps another guild had moved into the territory. Perhaps the inside of this brown warehouse was now as unremarkable as the outside.

Entreri chuckled at the possibilities, but they could not find any lasting hold within his thoughts. Perhaps he would eventually sneak into the place, just to satisfy his mild curiosity. Perhaps not.

He lingered by the side door, moving close enough past the apparently one-legged beggar, to recognize the cunning tie that bound his second leg up tight against the back of his thigh. The man was a sentry, obviously, and most of the few copper coins that Entreri saw within the opened sack before him had been placed there by the man, salting the purse and heightening the disguise.

No matter, the assassin thought. Playing the part of an ignorant visitor to Calimport, he walked up before the man and reached into his own purse, producing a silver coin and dropping it in the sack. He noted the not-really-old man's eyes flicker open a bit wider when he pulled back his cloak to go to his purse, revealing the hilt of his unique jeweled dagger, a weapon well known in the alleys and shadows of Calimport.

Had he been foolish in showing that weapon? Entreri wondered as he walked away. He hadn't any intention of revealing himself when he came to this place, but also, he had no intention of not revealing himself. The question and the worry, like his musing on the fate of Pook's house, found no hold in his wandering thoughts. Perhaps he had erred. Perhaps he had shown the dagger in a desperate bid for some excitement. And perhaps the man had recognized it as the mark of Entreri, or possibly he had noticed it only because it was indeed a truly beautiful weapon.

It didn't matter.

*   *   *   *   *

LaValle worked very hard to keep his breathing steady and to ignore the murmurs of those nervous associates beside him as he peered deeply into the crystal ball later that same night. The agitated sentry had reported the incident outside, a gift of a strange coin from a man walking with the quiet and confident gait of a warrior and wearing a dagger befitting the captain of a king's guard.

The description of that dagger had sent the more veteran members of the house, the wizard LaValle included, into a frenzy. Now LaValle, a longtime associate of the deadly Artemis Entreri, who had seen that dagger many times and uncomfortably close far too often had used that

21

prior knowledge and his crystal ball to seek out the stranger. His magical eyes combed the streets of Calimport, sifting from shadow to shadow, and then he felt the growing image and knew indeed that the dagger, Entreri's dagger, was back in the city. Now as the image began to take shape, the wizard and those standing beside him, a very nervous Quentin Bodeau and two younger cocky killers, would learn if it was indeed the deadliest of assassins who carried it.

A small bedroom drifted into focus.

"That is Tomnoddy's Inn," explained Dog Perry, who called himself Dog Perry the Heart because of his practice of cutting out a victim's heart fast enough that the dying man could witness its last beats (though none other than Dog Perry himself had ever actually seen this feat performed).

LaValle held up a hand to silence the man as the image became sharper, focusing on the belt looped over the bottom post of the bed, a belt that included the telltale dagger.

"It is Entreri's," Quentin Bodeau said with a groan.

A man walked past the belt, stripped to the waist, revealing a body honed by years and years of hard practice, muscles twitching with every movement. Quentin put on a quizzical expression, studying the man, the long hair, the goatee and scratchy, unkempt beard. He had always known Entreri to be meticulous in every detail, a perfectionist to the extreme. He looked to LaValle for an answer.

"It is he," the wizard, who knew Artemis Entreri perhaps better than anyone else in all the city, answered grimly.

"What does that mean?" Quentin asked. "Has he returned as friend or foe?"

"Indifferent, more likely," LaValle replied. "Artemis Entreri has always been a free spirit, never showing allegiance too greatly to any particular guild. He wanders through the treasuries of each, hiring to the highest bidder for his exemplary services." As he spoke, the wizard glanced over at the two younger killers, neither of whom knew Entreri other than by reputation. Chalsee Anguaine, the younger, tittered nervously—and wisely, LaValle knew—but Dog Perry squinted his eyes as he considered the man in the crystal ball. He was jealous, LaValle understood, for Dog Perry wanted, above all else, that which Entreri possessed: the supreme reputation as the deadliest of assassins.

"Perhaps we should find a need for his services quickly," Quentin Bodeau reasoned, obviously trying hard not to sound nervous, for in the dangerous world of Calimport's thieving guilds, nervousness equalled weakness. "In that way we might better learn the man's intentions and purpose in returning to Calimport."

"Or we could just kill him," Dog Perry put in, and LaValle bit back a chuckle at the so-predictable viewpoint and also at his knowledge that Dog Perry simply did not understand the truth of Artemis Entreri. No friend or fan of the brash young thug, LaValle almost hoped that Quentin would give Dog Perry his wish and send him right out after Entreri.

But Quentin, though he had never dealt with Entreri personally, remembered well the many, many stories of the assassin's handiwork, and the expression the guildmaster directed at Dog Perry was purely incredulous.

"Hire him if you need him," said LaValle. "Or if not, then merely watch him without threat."

"He is one man, and we are a guild of a hundred," Dog Perry protested, but no one was listening to him anymore.

Quentin started to reply, but stopped short, though his expression told LaValle exactly what he was thinking. He feared that Entreri had come back to take the guild, obviously, and not without some rationale. Certainly the deadliest of assassins still had many powerful connections within the city, enough for Entreri, with his own amazing skills, to topple the likes of Quentin Bodeau. But LaValle did not think Quentin's fears well-founded, for the wizard understood Entreri enough to realize that the man had never craved such a position of responsibility. Entreri was a loner, not a guildmaster. After he had deposed the halfling Regis from his short rein as guildmaster, the place had been Entreri's for the taking, and yet he had walked away, just walked out of Calimport altogether, leaving all of the others to fight it out.

No, LaValle did not believe that Entreri had come back to take this guild or any other, and he did well to silently convey that to the nervous Quentin. "Whatever our ultimate choices, it seems obvious to me that we should first merely observe our dangerous friend," the wizard said, for the benefit of the two younger lieutenants, "to learn if he is friend, foe, or indifferent. It makes no sense to go against one as strong as Entreri until we have determined that we must, and that, I do not believe to be the case."

Quentin nodded, happy to hear the confirmation, and with a bow LaValle took his leave, the others following suit.

"If Entreri is a threat, then Entreri should be eliminated," Dog Perry said to the wizard, catching up to him in the corridor outside his room. "Master Bodeau would have seen that truth had your advice been different."

LaValle stared long and hard at the upstart, not appreciating being talked to in that manner from one half his age and with so little experience in such matters, for LaValle had been dealing with dangerous killers such as Artemis Entreri before Dog Perry was even born. "I'll not say that I disagree with you," he said to the man.

"Then why your counsel to Bodeau?"

"If Entreri has come into Calimport at the request of another guild, then any move by Master Bodeau could bring dire consequences to our guild," the wizard replied, improvising as he went, for he didn't believe a

23

word of what he was saying. "You know that Artemis Entreri learned his trade under Pasha Basadoni himself, of course."

"Of course," Dog Perry lied.

LaValle struck a pensive pose, tapping one finger across his pursed lips. "It may prove to be no problem at all to us," he explained. "Surely when news of Entreri's return—an older and slower Entreri, you see, and one, perhaps, with few connections left within the city—spreads across the streets, the dangerous man will himself be marked."

"He has made many enemies," Dog Perry reasoned eagerly, seeming quite intrigued by LaValle's words and tone.

LaValle shook his head. "Most enemies of the Artemis Entreri who left Calimport those years ago are dead," the wizard explained. "No, not enemies, but rivals. How many young and cunning assassins crave the power that they might find with a single stroke of the blade?"

Dog Perry narrowed his eyes, just beginning to catch on.

"One who kills Entreri, in essence, claims credit for killing all of those whom Entreri killed," LaValle went on. "With a single stroke of the blade might such a reputation be earned. The killer of Entreri will almost instantly become the highest priced assassin in all the city." He shrugged and held up his hands, then pushed through his door, leaving an obviously intrigued Dog Perry standing in the hallway with the echoes of his words.

In truth, LaValle hardly cared whether the young troublemaker took those words to heart or not, but he was indeed concerned about the return of the assassin. Entreri unnerved the wizard, more so than all the other dangerous characters that LaValle had worked beside over the many years. LaValle had survived by posing a threat to no one, by serving without judgment whomever it was that had come to power in the guild. He had served Pasha Pook admirably, and when Pook had been disposed, he had switched his allegiance easily and completely to Regis, convincing even Regis's protective dark elf and dwarven friends that he was no threat. Similarly, when Entreri had gone against Regis, LaValle had stepped back and let the two decide the issue (though, of course, there had never been any doubt whatsoever in LaValle's mind as to which of those two would triumph), then throwing his loyalty to the victor. And so it had gone, down the line, master after master during the tumult immediately following Entreri's departure, to the present incarnation of guildmaster, Quentin Bodeau.

Concerning Entreri, though, there remained one subtle difference. Over the decades, LaValle had built a considerable insulating defense about him. He worked very hard to make no enemies in a world where everyone seemed to be in deadly competition, but he also understood that even a benign bystander could get caught and slaughtered in the common battles. Thus he had built a defense of powerful magic and felt that if one such as Dog Perry decided, for whatever reason, that he would be better

those horrible memories. Drizzt crouched low and looked into Wulfgar's pale blue eyes, even if the huge man did not match the gaze.

"Do you remember our first fight?" the drow asked slyly.

Now Wulfgar did turn his stare up at the drow. "Do you mean to teach me another lesson?" he asked, his tone showing that he was more than ready to accept that challenge.

The words stung Drizzt profoundly. He recalled his last angry encounter with Wulfgar, over the barbarian's treatment of Catti-brie those seven years before in Mithral Hall. They had fought viciously with Drizzt emerging as victor. And he recalled his first fight against Wulfgar, when Bruenor had captured the lad and brought him into the dwarven clan in Icewind Dale after the barbarians had tried to raid Ten Towns. Bruenor had charged Drizzt with training Wulfgar as a fighter, and those first lessons between the two had proven especially painful for the young and overly proud barbarian. But that was not the encounter to which Drizzt was now referring.

"I mean the first time that we fought together side by side against a real enemy," he explained.

Wulfgar's eyes narrowed as he considered the memory, a glimpse at his friendship with Drizzt from many years ago.

"Biggrin and the verbeeg," Drizzt reminded. "You and I and Guen-hwyvar charging headlong into a lair full of giants."

The anger melted from Wulfgar's face. He managed a rare smile and nodded.

"A tough one was Biggrin," Drizzt went on. "How many times did we hit the behemoth? It took a final throw from you to drive the dagger—"

"That was a long time ago," Wulfgar interrupted. He couldn't manage to maintain the smile, but at least he did not sink right back into the explosive anger. Wulfgar again found a more even keel, much like his detached, almost ambivalent attitude when they had first started out on this journey.

"But you do remember?" Drizzt pressed, his grin growing across his black face, that telltale twinkle in his lavender eyes.

"Why . . ." Wulfgar started to ask, but stopped short and sat study-ing his friend. He hadn't seen Drizzt in such a mood in a long, long time, even well before his fateful fight with the handmaiden of the demon queen Lolth back in Mithral Hall. This was a flash of Drizzt from the days before the quest to reclaim the dwarven kingdom, an image of the drow in those times when Wulfgar honestly feared that Drizzt's recklessness would soon put him and the drow in a situation from which they could not escape.

Wulfgar liked the image.

"We have some giants readying to waylay travelers on the road," the drow said. "Our pace will be slower out of the dale, now that we have agreed to accompany Master Camlaine. It seems to me that a side jour-ney to deal with these dangerous marauders might be in order."

It was the first hint of an eager sparkle in Wulfgar's eye that Drizzt had seen since they had been reunited in the ice cave after the defeat of Errtu.

"Have you spoken with the others?" the barbarian asked.

"Just me and you," Drizzt explained. "And Guenhwyvar, of course. She would not appreciate being left out of this fun."

The pair left camp long after sunset, waiting for Catti-brie, Regis, and Bruenor to fall asleep. With the drow leading, having no difficulty in seeing under the starry tundra sky, they went straight back to the point where the giant and the wagon tracks intersected. There, Drizzt reached into a pouch and produced the onyx panther figurine, placing it reverently on the ground. "Come to me, Guenhwyvar," he called softly.

A mist came up, swirling about the figurine, growing thicker and thicker, flowing and swirling and taking the shape of the great panther. Thicker and thicker, and then it was no mist circling the onyx likeness, but the panther herself. Guenhwyvar looked up at Drizzt with eyes showing an intelligence far beyond that indicated by her feline form.

Drizzt pointed down to the giant track, and Guenhwyvar, understanding, led them away.

* * * * *

She knew as soon as she opened her eyes that something was amiss. The camp was quiet, the two merchant guards sitting on the bench of the wagon, talking softly.

Catti-brie shifted up to her elbows to better survey the scene. The fire had burned low but was still bright enough to cast shadows from the bedrolls. Closest lay Regis, curled in a ball so near to the fire that Catti-brie was amazed the little fellow hadn't gone up in flames. The mound that was Bruenor lay just a bit further back, right where Catti-brie had said good night to her adoptive father. The woman sat up, then got to one knee, craning her neck, but she could not locate two particular forms among the sleeping.

She started for Bruenor, but changed her mind and went to Regis instead. The halfling always seemed to know. . . .

A gentle shake only made him groan and roll tighter into a ball. A rougher shake and a call of his name only had him spitting curses and tightening even more.

Catti-brie kicked him in the rump.

"Hey!" he protested loudly, coming up suddenly.

"Where'd they go to?" the woman asked.

"What're ye about, girl?" came Bruenor's sleepy voice, the dwarf awakened by Regis's call.

"Drizzt and Wulfgar have gone out from camp," she explained, then turned her penetrating gaze back over Regis.

The halfling squirmed under the scrutiny. "Why would I know?" he argued, but Catti-brie didn't blink. Regis looked to Bruenor for support, but found the half-dressed dwarf ambling over, seeming every bit as perturbed as Catti-brie, and apparently ready, like the woman, to direct his ire the halfling's way.

"Drizzt said that they would return to us, and the caravan, tomorrow, or perhaps the day after that," the halfling admitted.

"And where'd they go off to?" Catti-brie demanded.

Regis shrugged, but Catti-brie had him by the collar, hoisting him to his feet before he ever finished the motion. "Are ye meanin' to play this game again?" she asked.

"To find Kierstaad and apologize, I would guess," the halfling said. "He deserves as much."

"Good enough if the boy's got an apology in his heart," Bruenor remarked. Seemingly satisfied with that, the dwarf turned back for his bedroll.

Catti-brie, though, stood holding Regis roughly and shaking her head. "He's not got it in him," she said, drawing the dwarf back into the conversation. "Not now, and that's not where they're off to." She moved closer to Regis as she spoke, but did let go of him. "Ye need to tell me," she said calmly. "Ye can't be playin' this game. If we're to travel half the length o' Faerûn together, then we're needing a bit o' trust, and that ye're not earning."

"They went after the giants," Regis blurted. He couldn't believe that he had said it, but neither could he deny the logic of Catti-brie's argument nor the plaintive look in her beautiful eyes.

"Bah!" Bruenor snorted, stomping his bare foot—and slamming it so hard that it sounded as if he was wearing boots. "By the brains of a pointed-headed orc-cousin! Why didn't ye tell us sooner?"

"Because you would have made me go," Regis argued, but his voice lost its angry edge when Catti-brie moved right in front of his face.

"Ye always seem to be knowing too much and tellin' too little," she growled. "As when Drizzt left Mithral Hall."

"I listen," Regis replied with a helpless shrug.

"Get dressed," Catti-brie instructed Regis, who just looked back at her incredulously.

"Ye heard her!" Bruenor roared.

"You want to go out there?" the halfling asked, pointing to the black emptiness that was the nighttime tundra. "Now?"

"Won't be the first time I pulled that durned elf from the mouth of a tundra yeti," the dwarf snorted, heading for his bedroll.

"Giants," Regis corrected.

"Even worse, then!" Bruenor roared louder, waking the rest of the camp.

"But we cannot leave," Regis protested, motioning to the three merchants and their guardsmen. "We promised to guard them. What if the giants come in behind us?"

That brought a concerned look to the faces of the five members of the merchant team, but Catti-brie didn't blink at the ridiculous thought. She just kept looking hard at Regis, and at his possessions, including the new unicorn-headed mace one of Bruenor's smithies had forged for him, a beautiful mithral and black steel item with blue sapphires set for the eyes.

With a profound sigh the halfling pulled his tunic on over his head.

They were out within the hour, backtracking to the point where wagon track, giant track, and now drow and barbarian track, intersected. They had much more difficulty finding it than had Wulfgar and Drizzt, with the drow's superior night vision. For even though Catti-brie wore an enchanted circlet that allowed her to see in the dark, she was no ranger and could not match Drizzt's keen senses and training. Bruenor bent low, sniffing the ground, then led on through the darkness.

"Probably get swallowed by waiting yetis," Regis grumbled.

"I'll shoot high, then," Catti-brie answered, holding her deadly bow out. "Above the belly, so ye won't have a hole in ye when we cut ye out."

Of course Regis continued to grumble, but he kept his voice lower, not letting Catti-brie hear clearly so that she could not offer any more sarcastic replies.

* * * * *

They spent the dark hours before the dawn feeling their way over the rocky foothills of the Spine of the World. Wulfgar complained many times that they must have lost the trail, but Drizzt held faith in Guenhwyvar, who kept appearing ahead of them, a darker shadow against the night sky, high on rocky outcroppings.

Soon after the break of day, as they moved along a winding mountain path, the drow's faith in the panther was confirmed as the pair came across a distinctive footprint, a huge boot, along a low and muddy depression on the trail.

"An hour ahead, no more," Drizzt explained, examining the print. He looked back at Wulfgar and smiled widely, lavender eyes sparkling.

The barbarian, more than ready for a fight, nodded.

Following Guenhwyvar's lead, they climbed higher and higher until, above them, the land seemed to suddenly disappear, the trail ending at a sheer cliff face. Drizzt moved up first, shadow to shadow, motioning Wulfgar to follow as he determined the way to be clear. They had come to the side of a canyon, a deep and rocky ravine bordered on all four sides by mountain walls, though the barrier to their right, the south, was not complete, leaving one exit from the valley floor. At first, they surmised that the giant encampment must be down there in the ravine, hidden among the boulders, but then Wulfgar spotted a line of smoke drifting up from behind a wall of boulders on the cliff wall almost directly across the way, some fifty yards from their position.

The third, badly wounded, stayed in a crouch behind the wall, not even daring to creep back the fifteen feet to the cave opening in the wall behind it. Head down, it didn't see the dwarf climb into position on a ledge above it, though it did look up when it heard the roar of a leaping Bruenor.

The dwarf king's axe, buried deep into the giant's brain, sported yet another notch.

Chapter 3

The Unpleasant Mirror

"Well would you do to this one investigate," Giunta the Diviner said to Hand as the man left the wizard's house. "Danger I sense, and we both know who it may be, though to speak the name we fear."

Hand mumbled a reply and continued on his way, glad to be gone from the excitable wizard and Giunta's particularly annoying manner of structuring a sentence, one the wizard claimed came from another plane of existence, but that Hand merely considered Giunta's way of trying to impress those around him. Still, Giunta had his uses, Hand recognized, for of the dozen or so wizards the Basadoni house often utilized, none could unravel mysteries better than Giunta. From simply sensing the emanations of the strange coins Giunta had almost completely reconstructed the conversation between Hand, Kadran, and Sharlotta, as well as the identity of Taddio as the courier of the coins. Looking deeper, Giunta's face had turned into a profound frown, and as he had described the demeanor and general appearance of the one who had given the coins to Taddio, both he and Hand began to put the pieces together.

Hand knew Artemis Entreri. So did Giunta, and it was common knowledge among the street folk that Entreri had left Calimport in pursuit of the dark elf who had brought about the downfall of Pasha Pook, and that the drow was reportedly living in some dwarven city not far from Silverymoon.

Now that his suspicions pointed in a particular direction, Hand knew it was time to turn from magical information gathering to more conventional methods. He went out to the streets, to the many spies, and opened wide the eyes of Pasha Basadoni's powerful guild. Then he started back to the main house to speak with Sharlotta and Kadran but changed his mind. Indeed, Sharlotta had spoken truthfully when she had said that she desired knowledge of her enemies.

Better for Hand that she didn't know.

* * * * *

His room was hardly fitting for a man who had climbed so high among the ranks of the street. This man had been a guildmaster, albeit briefly, and could command huge sums of money from any house in the city simply as a retainer fee for his services. But Artemis Entreri didn't care much about the sparse furnishings of the cheap inn, about the dust piled on the window sills, about the noise of the street ladies and their clients in the adjoining rooms.

He sat on the bed and thought about his options, reconsidering all his movements since returning to Calimport. He had been a bit careless, he realized, particularly in going to the stupid boy who was now claiming rulership of his old shanty town and by showing his dagger to the beggar at Pook's old house. Perhaps, Entreri realized, that journey and encounter had been no coincidence or bad luck, but by subconscious design. Perhaps he had wanted to reveal himself to any who would look closely enough.

But what would that mean? he had to wonder now. How had the guild structures changed, and where in those new hierarchies would Artemis Entreri fit in? Even more importantly, where did Artemis Entreri want to fit in?

Those questions were beyond Entreri at that time, but he realized that he could not afford to sit and wait for others to find him. He should learn some of the answers, at least, before dealing with the more powerful houses of Calimport. The hour was late, well past midnight, but the assassin donned a dark cloak and went out onto the streets anyway.

The sights and sounds and smells brought him back to his younger days, when he had often allied with the dark of night and shunned the light of day. He noticed before he had even left the street that many gazes had settled upon him, and he sensed that they focused with more than a passing interest, more than the attention a foreign merchant might expect. Entreri recalled his own days on these streets, the methods and speed with which information was passed along. He was already being watched, he knew, and probably by several different guilds. Possibly the tavern keeper where he was staying or one of the patrons, perhaps, had recognized him or had recognized enough about him to raise suspicions. These people of Calimport's foul belly lived on the edge of disaster every minute of every day. Thus they possessed a level of alertness beyond anything so many other cultures might know. Like grassland field rats, rodents living in extensive burrow complexes with thousands and thousands of inhabitants, the people of Calimport's streets had designed complex warning systems: shouts and whistles, nods, and even simple body posture.

Yes, Entreri knew as he walked along the quiet street, his practiced footsteps making not a sound, they were watching him.

The time had come for him to do some looking of his own—and he knew where to start. Several turns brought him to Avenue Paradise, a particularly seedy place where potent herbs and weeds were openly traded, as were weapons, stolen goods, and carnal companionship. A mockery of culture itself, Avenue Paradise stood as the pinnacle of hedonism among the underclass. Here a beggar, if he found a few extra coins that day, could, for a few precious moments, feel like a king, could surround himself with perfumed ladies and imbibe enough mind-altering substances to forget the sores that festered on his filthy skin. Here, one like the boy that Entreri had paid in his old shanty town could live, for a few hours, the life of pasha Basadoni.

Of course it was all fake, fancy facades on rat-ridden buildings, fancy clothes on scared little girls or dead-eyed whores, heavily perfumed with cheap smells to hide the months of sweat and dust without a proper bath. But even fake luxury would suffice for most of the street people, whose constant misery was all too real.

Entreri walked slowly along the street, dismissing his introspection and turning his eyes outward, studying every detail. He thought he recognized more than one of the older, pitiful whores, but in truth, Entreri had never succumbed to such unhealthy and tawdry temptations as could be found on Avenue Paradise. His carnal pleasures, on those very few occasions he took them (for he considered them a weakness to one aspiring to be the perfect fighter), came in the harems of mighty pashas, and he had never held any tolerance whatsoever for anything intoxicating, for anything that dulled his keen mind and left him vulnerable. He had come to Avenue Paradise often, though, to find others too weak to resist. The whores had never liked him, nor had he ever bothered with them, though he knew, as did all the pashas, that they could be a very valuable source of information. Entreri simply could not bring himself to ever trust a woman who made her daily life in that particular line of employ.

So now he spent more time looking at the thugs and pickpockets and was amused to learn that one of the pickpockets was also studying him. Hiding a grin, he even changed his course to bring himself closer to the foolish young man.

Sure enough, Entreri was barely ten strides past when the thief came out behind him, walking past and "slipping" at the last moment to cover his reach for Entreri's dangling purse.

A split second later, the would-be thief was off balance, turned in and down, with Entreri's hand clamped over the ends of his fingers, squeezing the most exquisite pain up the man's arm. Out came the jeweled dagger, quietly but quickly, its tip poking a tiny hole in the man's palm as Entreri turned his shoulder in closer to conceal the movement and lessened his paralyzing grip.

Obviously confused at the relief of pressure on his pained hand, the thief moved his free hand to his own belt, pulling aside his cloak and grabbing at a long knife.

Entreri stared hard and concentrated on the dagger, instructing it to do its darker work, using its magic to begin sucking the very life-force out of the foolish thief.

The man weakened, his dagger fell harmlessly to the street, and both his eyes and his jaw opened wide in a horrified, agonized, and ultimately futile attempt at a scream.

"You feel the emptiness," Entreri whispered to him. "The hopelessness. You know that I hold not only your life, but your very soul in my hands."

The man didn't, couldn't move.

"Do you?" Entreri prompted, bringing a nod from the now gasping man.

"Tell me," the assassin bade, "are there any halflings on the street this night?" As he spoke, he let up a bit on the life-stealing process, and the man's expression shifted again, just a bit, to one of confusion.

"Halflings," the assassin explained, punctuating his point by drawing hard on the man's life-force again, so forcefully that the only thing holding the man up was Entreri's body.

With his free hand, trembling violently through every inch of movement, the thief pointed farther down the avenue in the general direction of a few houses that Entreri knew well. He thought to ask the man a more focused question or two but decided against it, realizing that he might have revealed too much of his identity already by the mere hunger of his particular jeweled dagger.

"If I ever see you again, I shall kill you," the assassin said with such complete calm that all the blood ran from the thief's face. Entreri released him, and he staggered away, falling to his knees and crawling on. Entreri shook his head in disgust, wondering, and not for the first time, why he had ever come back to this wretched city.

Without even bothering to look and ensure that the thief continued away, the assassin strode more quickly down the street. If the particular halfling he sought was still about and still alive, Entreri could guess which of those buildings he might be in. The middle and largest of the three, The Copper Ante, had once been a favorite gambling house for many of the halflings in the Calimport dock section, mostly because of the halfling-staffed brothel upstairs and the Thayan brown pipeweed den in the back room. Indeed, Entreri did see many (considering that this was Calimport, where halflings were scarce) of the little folk scattered about the various tables in the common room when he entered. He scanned each table slowly, trying to guess what his former friend might look like now that several years had passed. The halfling would be wider about the belly, no doubt, for he loved rich food and had set himself up in a position to afford ten meals a day if he so chose.

Entreri slipped into an open seat at one table where six halflings tossed dice, each moving so quickly that it was almost impossible for a novice gambler to even tell which call the one at the head of the table was making and which halfling was grabbing which pot as winnings for which throw. Entreri easily sorted it out, though, and found, to his amusement but hardly his surprise, that all six were cheating. It seemed more a contest of who could grab the most coins the fastest than any type of gambling, and all half dozen appeared to be equally suited to the task, so much so that Entreri figured that each of them would likely leave with almost exactly the amount of coins with which he had begun.

The assassin dropped four gold pieces on the table and grabbed up some dice, giving a half-hearted throw. Almost before the dice stopped rolling, the closest halfling reached for the coins, but Entreri was the quicker, slapping his hand over the halfling's wrist and pinning it to the table.

"But you lost!" the little one squeaked, and the flurry of movement came to an abrupt halt, the other five looking at Entreri and more than one reaching for a weapon. The gaming stopped at several other tables, as well, the whole area of the common room focusing on the coming trouble.

"I was not playing," Entreri said calmly, not letting the halfling go.

"You put down money and threw dice," one of the others protested. "That is playing."

Entreri's glare put the complaining halfling back in his seat. "I am playing when I say, and not before," he explained. "And I only cover bets that are announced openly before I throw."

"You saw how the table was moving," a third dared to argue, but Entreri cut him short with an upraised hand and a nod.

He looked to the gambler at his right, the one who had reached for the coins, and waited a moment to let the rest of the room settle down and go back to their own business. "You want the coins? They, and twice that amount above them, shall be yours," he explained, and the greedy halfling's expression went from one of distress to a gleaming-eyed grin. "I came not to play but to ask a simple question. Provide an answer, and the coins are yours." As he spoke, Entreri reached into his purse and brought out more coins—more than twice the number the halfling had grabbed.

"Well, Master . . ." the halfling began.

"Do'Urden," Entreri replied, with hardly a conscious thought, though he had to bite back a chuckle at the irony after he heard the name come out of his mouth. "Master Do'Urden of Silverymoon."

All the halflings at the table eyed him curiously, for the unusual name sounded familiar to them all. In truth, and they came to realize it one by one, they all knew that name. It was the name of the dark elven protector of Regis, perhaps the highest ranking (albeit for a short while!) and most famous halfling ever to walk the streets of Calimport.

"Your skin has—" the halfling pinned under Entreri's grasp started to remark lightheartedly, but he stopped, swallowed hard and blanched as he put the pieces together. Entreri could see the halfling recall the story of Regis and the dark elf, and the one who had subsequently deposed the halfling guildmaster and then gone out after the drow.

"Yes," the halfling said as calmly as he could muster, "a question."

"I seek one of your kind," Entreri explained. "An old friend by the name of Dondon Tiggerwillies."

The halfling put on a confused look and shook his head, but not before a flicker of recognition has crossed his dark eyes, one the sharp Entreri did not miss.

"Everyone of the streets knows Dondon," Entreri stated. "Or once knew of him. You are not a child, and your gaming skills tell me that you have been a regular to the Copper Ante for years. You know, or knew, Dondon. If he is dead, then I wish to hear the story. If not, then I wish to speak with him."

Grave looks passed from halfling to halfling. "Dead," said one across the table, but Entreri knew from the tone and the quick manner in which the diminutive fellow blurted it out that it was a lie, that Dondon, ever the survivor, was indeed alive.

Halflings in Calimport always seemed to stick together, though.

"Who killed him?" Entreri asked, playing along.

"He got sick," another halfling offered, again in that quick, telltale manner.

"And where is he buried?"

"Who gets buried in Calimport?" the first liar replied.

"Tossed into the sea," said another.

Entreri nodded with every word. He was actually a bit amused at how these halflings played off each other, building an elaborate lie and one the assassin knew he could eventually turn against them.

"Well, you have told me much," he said, releasing the halfling's wrist. The greedy gambler immediately went for the coins, but a jeweled dagger jabbed down between the reaching hand and the desired gems in the blink of a startled eye.

54

"You promised coins!" the halfling protested.

"For a lie?" Entreri calmly asked. "I inquired about Dondon outside and was told that he was in here. I know he is alive, for I saw him just yesterday."

The halflings all glanced at each other, trying to piece together the inconsistencies here. How had they fallen so easily into the trap?

"Then why speak of him in the past tense?" the halfling directly across the table asked, the first to insist that Dondon was dead. This halfling thought himself sly, thought that he had caught Entreri in a lie . . . as indeed he had.

"Because I know that halflings never reveal the whereabouts of other halflings to one who is not a halfling," Entreri answered, his demeanor changing suddenly to a lighthearted, laughing expression, something that had never come easily to the assassin. "I have no fight with Dondon, I assure you. We are old friends, and it has been far too long since we last spoke. Now, tell me where he is and take your payment."

Again the halflings looked around, and then one, licking his lips and staring hungrily at the small pile of coins, pointed to a door at the back of the large room.

Entreri replaced the dagger in its sheath and gave a gesture that seemed a salute as he moved from the table, walking confidently across the room and pushing through the door without even a knock.

There before him reclined the fattest halfling he had ever seen, a creature wider than it was tall. He and the assassin locked stares, Entreri so intent on the fellow that he hardly noticed the scantily clad female halflings flanking him. It was indeed Dondon Tiggerwillies, Entreri realized to his horror. Despite all the years and all the scores of pounds, he knew the halfling, once the slipperiest and most competent confidence swindler in all of Calimport.

"A knock is often appreciated," the halfling said, his voice raspy, as though he could hardly force the sounds from his thick neck. "Suppose that my friends and I were engaged in a more private action."

Entreri didn't even try to figure out how that might be possible.

"Well, what do you want, then?" Dondon asked, stuffing an enormous bite of pie into his mouth as soon as he finished speaking.

Entreri closed the door and walked into the room, halving the distance between him and the halfling. "I want to speak with an old associate," he explained.

Dondon stopped chewing and stared hard. Obviously stunned by recognition, he began violently choking on the pie and wound up spitting a substantial piece of it back onto his plate. His attendants did well to hide their disgust as they moved the plate aside.

"I did not . . . I mean, Regis was no friend of mine. I mean . . ." Dondon stammered, a fairly common reaction from those faced with the spectre of Artemis Entreri.

"Be at ease, Dondon," Entreri said firmly. "I came to speak with you, nothing more. I care not for Regis, nor for any role Dondon might have played in the demise of Pook those years ago. The streets are for the living, are they not, and not the dead?"

"Yes, of course," Dondon replied, visibly trembling. He rolled forward a bit, trying to at least sit up, and only then did Entreri notice a chain trailing a thick anklet he wore about his left leg. Finally, the fat halfling gave up and just rolled back to his previous position. "An old wound," he said with a shrug.

Entreri let the obviously ridiculous excuse slide past. He moved closer to the halfling and went down in a crouch, brushing aside Dondon's robes that he could better see the shackle. "I have only recently returned," he explained. "I hoped that Dondon might enlighten me concerning the current demeanor of the streets."

"Rough and dangerous, of course," Dondon answered with a chuckle that became a phlegm-filled cough.

"Who rules?" Entreri asked in a dead serious tone. "Which houses hold power, and what soldiers champion them?"

"I wish that I could be of help to you, my friend," Dondon said nervously. "Of course I do. I would never withhold information from you. Never that! But you see," he added, lifting up his shackled ankle, "they do not let me out much anymore."

"How long have you been in here?"

"Three years."

Entreri stared incredulously and distastefully at the little wretch, then looked doubtfully at the relatively simple shackle, a lock that the old Dondon could have opened with a piece of hair.

In response, Dondon held up his enormously thick hands, hands so pudgy that he couldn't even bring the higher parts of his fingers together. "I do not feel much with them anymore," he explained.

A burning outrage welled inside Entreri. He felt as if he would simply explode into a murderous fit that would have him physically shaving the pounds from Dondon's fat hide with his jeweled dagger. Instead, he went at the lock, turning it roughly to scan for any possible traps, then reaching for a small pick.

"Do not," came a high-pitched voice behind him. The assassin sensed the presence before he even heard the words. He spun about, rolling into a crouch, dagger in one hand, arm cocked to throw. Another female halfling, this one dressed in a fine tunic and breeches, with thick, curly brown hair and huge brown eyes, stood at the door, hands up and open, her posture completely unthreatening.

"Oh, but that would be a bad thing for me and for you," the female halfling said with a little grin.

"Do not kill her," Dondon pleaded with Entreri, trying to grab for the assassin's arm, but missing far short of the mark and rolling back, gasping for breath.

56

Entreri, ever alert, noticed then that both the female halflings attending Dondon had slipped hands into secret places, one to a pocket, the other to her generous waist-length hair, both no doubt reaching for weapons of some sort. He understood then that this newcomer was a leader among the group.

"Dwahvel Tiggerwillies, at your service," she said with a graceful bow. "At your service, but not at your whim," she added with a smile.

"Tiggerwillies?" Entreri echoed softly, glancing back at Dondon.

"A cousin," the fat halfling explained with a shrug. "The most powerful halfling in all of Calimport and the newest proprietor of the Copper Ante."

The assassin looked back to see the female halfling completely at ease, hands in her pockets.

"You understand, of course, that I did not come in here alone, not to face a man of Artemis Entreri's reputation," Dwahvel said.

That brought a grin to Entreri's face as he imagined the many halflings concealed about the room. It struck him as a half-sized mock-up of another similar operation, that of Jarlaxle the dark elf mercenary in Menzoberranzan. On the occasions when he had to face the always well-protected Jarlaxle, though, Entreri had understood without doubt that if he made even the slightest wrong move, or if Jarlaxle or one of the drow guards ever perceived one of Entreri's movements as threatening, his life would have been at an abrupt end. He couldn't imagine now that Dwahvel Tiggerwillies, or any other halfling for that matter, could command such well-earned respect. Still, he hadn't come here for a fight, even if that old warrior part of him perceived Dwahvel's words as a challenge.

"Of course," he replied simply.

"Several with slings eye you right now," she went on. "And the bullets of those slings have been treated with an explosive formula. Quite painful and devastating."

"How resourceful," the assassin said, trying to sound impressed.

"That is how we survive," Dwahvel replied. "By being resourceful. By knowing everything about everything and preparing properly."

In a single swift movement—one that would surely have gotten him killed in Jarlaxle's court—the assassin spun the dagger over and slipped it into its sheath, then stood up straight and dipped a low and respectful bow to Dwahvel.

"Half the children of Calimport answer to Dwahvel," Dondon explained. "And the other half are not children at all," he added with a wink, "and answer to Dwahvel, as well."

"And of course, both halves have watched Artemis Entreri carefully since he walked back into the city," Dwahvel explained.

"So glad that my reputation preceded me," Entreri said, sounding puffy indeed.

"We did not know it was you until recently," Dwahvel replied, just to deflate the man, who of course, was not at all conceited.

"And you discovered this by. . . . ?" Entreri prompted.

That left Dwahvel a bit embarrassed, realizing that she had just been squeezed for a bit of information she had not intended to reveal. "I do not know why you would expect an answer," she said, somewhat perturbed. "Nor do I begin to see any reason I should help the one who dethroned Regis from the guild of the former Pasha Pook. Regis, was in a position to aid all the other halflings of Calimport."

Entreri had no answer to that, so he offered nothing in reply.

"Still, we should talk," Dwahvel went on, turning sidelong and motioning to the door.

Entreri glanced back at Dondon.

"Leave him to his pleasures," Dwahvel explained. "You would have him freed, yet he has little desire to leave, I assure you. Fine food and fine companionship."

Entreri looked with disgust to the assorted pies and sweets, to the hardly moving Dondon, then to the two females. "He is not so demanding," one of them explained with a laugh.

"Just a soft lap to rest his sleepy head," the other added with a titter that set them both to giggling.

"I have all that I could ever desire," Dondon assured him.

Entreri just shook his head and left with Dwahvel, following the little halfling to a more private—and undoubtedly better guarded—room deeper into the Copper Ante complex. Dwahvel took a seat in a low, plush chair and motioned for the assassin to take one opposite. Entreri was hardly comfortable in the half-sized piece, his legs straight out before him.

"I do not entertain many who are not halflings," Dwahvel apologized. "We tend to be a secretive group."

Entreri saw that she was looking for him to tell her how honored he was. But, of course, he wasn't, and so he said nothing, just keeping a tight expression, eyes boring accusingly into the female.

"We hold him for his own good," Dwahvel said plainly.

"Dondon was once among the most respected thieves in Calimport," Entreri countered.

"Once," Dwahvel echoed, "but not so long after your departure, Dondon drew the anger of a particularly powerful pasha. The man was a friend of mine, so I pleaded for him to spare Dondon. Our compromise was that Dondon remain inside. Always inside. If he ever is seen walking the streets of Calimport again, by the pasha or any of the pasha's many contacts, then I am bound to turn him over for execution."

"A better fate, by my estimation, than the slow death you give him chained in that room."

Dwahvel laughed aloud at that proclamation. "Then you do not understand Dondon," she said. "Men more holy than I have long identified the seven sins deadly to the soul, and while Dondon has little of the primary three, for he is neither proud nor envious nor wrathful, he is possessed of an excess of the last four—sloth, avarice, gluttony, and lust. He and I made a deal, a deal to save his life. I promised to give him, without judgment, all that he desired in exchange for his promise to remain within my doors."

"Then why the chains about his ankle?" Entreri asked.

"Because Dondon is drunk more often than sober," Dwahvel explained. "Likely he would cause trouble within my establishment, or perhaps he would stagger onto the street. It is all for his own protection."

Entreri wanted to refute that, for he had never seen a more pitiful sight than Dondon and would personally prefer a tortured death to that grotesque lifestyle. But when he thought about Dondon more carefully, when he remembered the halfling's personal style those years ago, a style that often included sweet foods and many ladies, he recognized that Dondon's failings now were the halfling's own and nothing forced upon him by a caring Dwahvel.

"If he remains inside the Copper Ante, no one will bother him," Dwahvel said after giving Entreri the moment to think it over. "No contract, no assassin. Though, of course, this is only on the five-year-old word of a pasha. So you can understand why my fellows were a bit nervous when the likes of Artemis Entreri walked into the Copper Ante inquiring about Dondon."

Entreri eyed her skeptically.

"They were not sure it was you at first," Dwahvel explained. "Yet we have known that you were back in town for a couple of days now. Word is fairly common on the streets, though, as you can well imagine, it is more rumor than truth. Some say that you have returned to displace Quentin Bodeau and regain control of Pook's house. Others hint that you have come for greater reasons, hired by the Lords of Waterdeep themselves to assassinate several high-ranking leaders of Calimshan."

Entreri's expression summed up his incredulous response to that preposterous notion.

Dwahvel shrugged. "Such are the trappings of reputation," she said. "Many people are paying good money for any whisper, however ridiculous, that might help them solve the riddle of why Artemis Entreri has returned to Calimport. You make them nervous, assassin. Take that as the highest compliment.

"But also as a warning," Dwahvel went on. "When guilds fear someone or something, they often take steps to erase that fear. Several have been asking very pointed questions about your whereabouts and movements, and you understand this business well enough to realize that to be the mark of the hunting assassin."

Entreri put his elbow on the arm of the small chair and plopped his chin in his hand, considering the halfling carefully. Rarely had anyone spoken so bluntly and boldly to Artemis Entreri, and in the few minutes they had been sitting together, Dwahvel Tiggerwillies had earned more respect from Entreri than most would gather in a lifetime of conversations.

"I can find more detailed information for you," Dwahvel said slyly. "I have larger ears than a Sossalan mammoth and more eyes than a room of beholders, so it is said. And so it is true."

Entreri put a hand to his belt and jiggled his purse. "You overestimate the size of my treasury," he said.

"Look around you," Dwahvel retorted. "What need have I for more gold, from Silverymoon or anywhere else?"

Her reference to the Silverymoon coinage came as a subtle hint to Entreri that she knew of what she was speaking.

"Call it a favor between friends," Dwahvel explained, hardly a surprise to the assassin who had made his life exchanging such favors. "One that you might perhaps repay me one day."

Entreri kept his face expressionless as he thought it over. Such a cheap way to garner information. Entreri highly doubted that the halfling would ever require his particular services, for halflings simply didn't solve their problems that way. And if Dwahvel did call upon him, maybe he would comply, or maybe not. Entreri hardly feared that Dwahvel would send her three-foot-tall thugs after him. No, all that Dwahvel wanted, should things sort out in his favor, was the bragging right that Artemis Entreri owed her a favor, a claim that would drain the blood from the faces of the majority of Calimport's street folk.

The question for Entreri now was, did he really care if he ever got the information Dwahvel offered? He thought it over for another minute, then nodded his accord. Dwahvel brightened immediately.

"Come back tomorrow night, then," she said. "I will have something to tell you."

Outside the Copper Ante, Artemis Entreri spent a long while thinking about Dondon, for he found that every time he conjured an image of the fat halfling stuffing pie into his face he was filled with rage. Not disgust, but rage. As he examined those feelings, he came to recognize that Dondon Tiggerwillies had been about as close to a friend as Artemis Entreri had ever known. Pasha Basadoni had been his mentor, Pasha Pook his primary employer, but Dondon and Entreri had related in a different manner. They acted in each other's benefit without set prices, exchanging information without taking count. It had been a mutually beneficial relationship. Seeing Dondon now, purely hedonistic, having given up on any meaning in life, it seemed to the assassin that the halfling had committed a form of living suicide.

Entreri did not possess enough compassion for that to explain the anger he felt, though, and when he admitted that to himself he came to understand that the sight of Dondon repelled him so much because, given his own mental state lately, it could well be him. Not chained by the ankle in the company of women and food, of course, but in effect, Dondon had surrendered, and so had Entreri.

Perhaps it was time to take down the white flag.

Dondon had been his friend in a manner, and there had been one other similarly entwined. Now it was time to go and see LaValle.

Chapter 4

The Summons

Drizzt couldn't get down to the ledge where Guenhwyvar had landed, so he used the onyx figurine to dismiss the cat. She faded back to the Astral plane, her home, where her wounds would better heal. He saw that Regis and his unexpected giant ally had moved out of sight, and that Wulfgar and Catti-brie were moving to join Bruenor down at the lower ledge to the south, where the last of the enemy giants had fallen. The dark elf began picking his way to join them. At first, he thought he might have to backtrack all the way around to his initial position with Wulfgar, but using his incredible agility and the strength of fingers trained for decades in the maneuvering skills of sword play, he somehow found enough ledges, cracks, and simple angled surfaces to get down beside his friends.

By the time he got there, all three had entered the cave at the back of the shelf.

"Damned things might've kept a bit more treasure if they're meanin' to put up such a fight," he heard Bruenor complaining.

"Perhaps that's why they were scouting out the road," Catti-brie replied. "Might it have been better for ye if we went at them on our way back from Cadderly's place? Perhaps then we'd've found more treasure to yer liking. And maybe a few merchant skulls to go along with it."

"Bah!" the dwarf snorted, drawing a wide smile from Drizzt. Few in all the Realms needed treasure less than Bruenor Battlehammer, Eighth King of Mithral Hall (despite his chosen absence from the place) and also leader of a lucrative mining colony in Icewind Dale. But that wasn't the point of Bruenor's ire, Drizzt understood, and he smiled all the wider as Bruenor confirmed his suspicions.

"What kind o' wicked god'd put ye against such powerful foes and not even reward ye with a bit o' gold?" the dwarf grumbled.

"We did find some gold," Catti-brie reminded him. Drizzt, entering the cave, noted that she held a fairly substantial sack that bulged with coins.

Bruenor flashed the drow a disgusted look. "Copper mostly," he grumbled. "Three gold coins, a pair o' silver, and nothing more but stinkin' copper!"

"But the road is safe," Drizzt said. He looked to Wulfgar as he spoke, but the big man would not match his stare. The drow tried hard not to pass any judgment over his tormented friend. Wulfgar should have led Drizzt's charge to the shelf. Never before had he so failed Drizzt in their tandem combat. But the drow knew that the barbarian's hesitance came not from any desire to see Drizzt injured nor, certainly, any cowardice. Wulfgar spun in emotional turmoil, the depths of which Drizzt Do'Urden had never before seen. He had known of these problems before coaxing the barbarian out for this hunt, so he could not rightly place any blame now.

Nor did he want to. He only hoped that the fight itself, after Wulfgar had become involved, had helped the man to rid himself of some of those inner demons, had run the horse, as Montolio would have called it, just a bit.

"And what about yerself?" Bruenor roared, bouncing over to stand before Drizzt. "What're ye about, going off on yer own without a word to the rest of us? Ye thinking all the fun's for yerself, elf? Ye thinking that me and me girl can't be helpin' ye?"

"I did not want to trouble you with so minor a battle," Drizzt calmly replied, painting a disarming smile on his dark face. "I knew that we would be in the mountains, outside and not under them, in terrain not suited for the likes of a short-limbed dwarf."

Bruenor wanted to hit him. Drizzt could see that in the way the dwarf was trembling. "Bah!" he roared instead, throwing up his hands and walking back for the exit to the small cave. "Ye're always doin' that, ye stinkin' elf. Always going about on yer own and taking all the fun. But we'll find more on the road, don't ye doubt! And ye better be hopin' that ye see it afore me, or I'll cut 'em all down afore ye ever get them sissy blades outta their sheaths or that stinkin' cat outta that statue.

"Unless they're too much for us. . . ." he continued, his voice trailing away as he moved out of the cave. "Then I just might let ye have 'em all to yerself, ye stinkin' elf!"

Wulfgar, without a word and without a look at Drizzt, moved out next, leaving the drow and Catti-brie alone. Drizzt was chuckling now as Bruenor continued to grumble, but when he looked at Catti-brie, he saw that she was truly not amused, her feelings obviously hurt.

"I'm thinking that a poor excuse," she remarked.

"I wanted to bring Wulfgar out alone," Drizzt explained. "To bring him back to a different place and time, before all the trouble."

"And ye're not thinkin' that me dad, or meself, might want to be helping with that?" Catti-brie asked.

"I wanted no one here that Wulfgar might fear needed protecting," Drizzt explained, and Catti-brie slumped back, her jaw dropping open.

"I speak only the truth, and you see it clearly," Drizzt went on. "You remember how Wulfgar acted toward you before the fight with the yochlol. He was protective to the point of becoming a detriment to any battle cause. How could I rightly ask you to join us out here now, when that previous scenario might have repeated, leaving Wulfgar, perhaps, in an even worse emotional place than when we set out? That is why I did not ask Bruenor or Regis, either. Wulfgar, Guenhwyvar, and I would fight the giants, as we did that time so long ago in Icewind Dale. And maybe, just maybe, he would remember things the way they had been before his unwelcome tenure with Errtu."

Catti-brie's expression softened, and she bit her lower lip as she nodded her agreement. "And did it work?" she asked. "Suren the fight went well, and Wulfgar fought well and honestly."

Drizzt's gaze drifted out the exit. "He made a mistake," the drow admitted. "Though surely he compensated as the battle progressed. It is my hope that Wulfgar will forgive himself his initial hesitance and focus on the actual fight where he performed wonderfully."

"Hesitance?" Catti-brie asked skeptically.

"When we first began the battle," Drizzt started to explain, but he waved his hand dismissively as if it did not really matter. "It has been many years since we have fought together. It was an excusable miscue, nothing more." In truth, Drizzt had a hard time dismissing the fact that Wulfgar's hesitance had almost cost him and Guenhwyvar dearly.

"Ye're in a generous mood," the ever-perceptive Catti-brie remarked.

"It is my hope that Wulfgar will remember who he is and who his friends truly are," the drow ranger replied.

"Yer hope," Catti-brie echoed. "But is it your expectation?"

Drizzt continued to stare out the exit. He could only shrug.

*　*　*　*　*

The four were out of the ravine and back on the trail shortly after, and Bruenor's grumbling about Drizzt turned into complaining about Regis. "Where in the Nine Hells is Rumblebelly?" the dwarf bellowed. "And how in the Nine Hells did he ever get a giant to throw rocks for him?"

65

Even as he spoke, they felt the vibrations of heavy, heavy footfalls beneath their feet and heard a silly song sung in unison. There was a happy halfling voice, Regis, and a second voice that rumbled like the thunder of a rockslide. A moment later, Regis came around a bend in the northern trail, riding on the giant's shoulder, the two of them singing and laughing with every step.

"Hello," Regis said happily when he steered the giant to join his friends. He noted that Drizzt had his hands on his scimitars, though they were sheathed (and that meant little for the lightning-fast drow), Bruenor clutched tightly to his axe, Catti-brie to her bow, and Wulfgar, holding Aegis-fang, seemed as if he was about to explode into murderous action.

"This is Junger," Regis explained. "He was not with the other band—he says he doesn't even know them. And he is a smart one."

Junger put a hand up to secure Regis's seat, then bowed low before the stunned group.

"In fact, Junger does not even go down to the road, does not go out of the mountains at all," Regis explained. "Says he has no interest in the affairs of dwarves or men."

"He told ye that, did he?" Bruenor asked doubtfully.

Regis nodded, his smile wide. "And I believe him," he said, waggling the ruby pendant, whose magical hypnotizing properties were well known to the friends.

"That don't change a thing," Bruenor said with a growl, looking to Drizzt as if expecting the ranger to start the fight. A giant was a giant, after all, to the dwarf's way of thinking, and any giant looked much better lying down with an axe firmly embedded in its skull.

"Junger is no killer," Regis said firmly.

"Only goblins," the huge giant said with a smile. "And hill giants. And orcs, of course, for who could abide the ugly things?"

His sophisticated dialect and his choice of enemies had the dwarf staring at him wide-eyed. "And yeti," Bruenor said. "Don't ye be forgettin' yeti."

"Oh, not yeti," Junger replied. "I do not kill yeti."

The scowl returned to Bruenor's face.

"Why, one cannot even eat the smelly things," Junger explained. "I do not kill them, I domesticate them."

"Ye what?" Bruenor demanded.

"Domesticate them," Junger explained. "Like a dog or a horse. Oh, but I've quite a selection of yeti workers at my cave back in the mountains."

Bruenor turned an incredulous expression on Drizzt, but the ranger, as much at a loss as the dwarf, only shrugged.

"We've lost too much time already," Catti-brie remarked. "Camlaine and the others'll be halfway out o' the dale afore we catch them. Be rid o' yer friend, Regis, and let us get to the trail."

Regis was shaking his head before she ever finished. "Junger does not usually leave the mountains," he explained. "But he will for me."

"Then I'll not have to carry you anymore," Wulfgar grumbled, walking away. "Good enough for that."

"Ye're not having to carry him anyway," Bruenor replied, then looked back to Regis. "I'm thinking ye can do yer own walking. Ye don't need a giant to act as a horse."

"More than that," Regis said, beaming. "A bodyguard."

The dwarf and Catti-brie both groaned; Drizzt only chuckled and shook his head.

"In every fight, I spend more time trying to keep out of the way," Regis explained. "Never am I any real help. But with Junger—"

"Ye'll still be trying to keep outta the way," Bruenor interrupted.

"If Junger is to fight for you, then he is no more than any of the rest of us," Drizzt added. "Are we, then, merely bodyguards of Regis?"

"No, of course not," the halfling replied. "But—"

"Be rid of him," Catti-brie said. "Wouldn't we look the fine band of friendly travelers walking into Luskan beside a mountain giant?"

"We'll walk in with a drow," Regis answered before he could think about it, then blushed a deep shade of red.

Again, Drizzt only chuckled and shook his head.

"Put him down," Bruenor said to Junger. "I think he's needin' a talk."

"You mustn't hurt my friend Regis," Junger replied. "That I simply cannot allow."

Bruenor snorted. "Put 'im down."

With a look to Regis, who held a stubborn pose for a few moments longer, Junger complied. He set the halfling gently on the ground before Bruenor, who reached as if to grab Regis by the ear, but then glanced up, up, up at Junger and thought the better of it. "Ye're not thinkin', Rumblebelly," the dwarf said quietly, leading Regis away. "What happens if the big damned thing finds its way outta yer ruby spell? He'll squish ye flat afore any o' us can stop him, and I'm not thinking I'd try to stop him if I could, since ye'd be deserving the flattening!"

Regis started to argue, but he remembered the first moments of his encounter with Junger, when the huge giant had proclaimed that he liked his rodents smashed. The little halfling couldn't deny the fact that a single step from Junger would indeed mash him, and the hold of the ruby pendant was ever tentative. He turned and walked back from Bruenor and bade Junger to go back to his home in the deep mountains.

The giant smiled—and shook his head. "I hear it," he said cryptically. "So I shall stay."

"Hear what?" Regis and Bruenor asked together.

"Just a call," Junger assured them. "It tells me that I should go along with you to serve Regis and protect him."

67

"Ye hit him good with that thing, didn't ye now?" Bruenor whispered at the halfling.

"I need no protecting," Regis said firmly to the giant. "Though we all thank you for your help in the fight. You can go back to your home."

Again Junger shook his head. "Better that I go with you."

Bruenor glowered at Regis, and the halfling had no explanation. As far as he could tell, Junger was still under the spell of the pendant—the fact that Regis was still alive seemed evidence of that—yet the behemoth was clearly disobeying him.

"Perhaps you can come along," Drizzt said to the surprise of them all. "Yes, but if you mean to join us, then perhaps your pet tundra yetis might prove invaluable. How long will it take you to retrieve them?"

"Three days at the most," Junger replied.

"Well, go then, and be quick about it," Regis said, hopping up and down and wriggling the ruby pendant at the end of its chain.

That seemed to satisfy the giant. It bowed low then bounded away.

"We should've killed the thing here and now," Bruenor said. "Now it'll come back in three days and find us long gone, then it'll likely take its damned smelly yetis and go down hunting on the road!"

"No, he told me he never goes out of the mountains," Regis reasoned.

"Enough of this foolishness," Catti-brie demanded. "The thing's gone, and so should we all be." None offered an argument to that, so they set off at once, Drizzt purposely falling into line beside Regis.

"Was it all the call of the ruby pendant?" the ranger asked.

"Junger told me that he was farther from home than he had been in a long, long time," Regis admitted. "He said he heard a call on the wind and went to answer it. I guess he thought I was the caller."

Drizzt accepted that explanation. If Junger continued to fall for the simple ruse, they would be around the edge of the Spine of the World, rushing fast along a better road, before the behemoth ever returned to this spot.

* * * * *

Indeed Junger was running fast in the direction of his relatively lavish mountain home, and it struck the giant as curious, for just a moment, that he had ever left the place. In his younger days, Junger had been a wanderer, living meal to meal on whatever prey he could find. He snickered now when he considered all that he had told the foolish little halfling, for Junger had indeed once feasted on the meat of humans, and even on a halfling once. The truth was, he shunned such meals now as much because he didn't like the taste as because he thought it better not to make such powerful enemies as humans. Wizards in particular scared him. Of course, to find human or halfling meat, Junger had to leave his mountain home, and that he never liked to do.

68

He wouldn't have come out at all this time had not a call on the wind, something he still did not quite understand, compelled him.

Yes, Junger had all he wanted at his home: plenty of food, obedient servants, and comfortable furs. He had no desire to ever leave the place.

But he had, and he understood that he would again, and though that seemed an incongruous thought to the not-stupid giant, it was one that he simply couldn't pause to consider. Not now, not with the constant buzzing in his ear.

He would get the yetis, he knew, and then return, following the instructions of the call on the wind.

The call of Crenshinibon.

Chapter 5

Stirring the Streets

LaValle walked to his private suite in the guild house late that morning after meeting with Quentin Bodeau and Chalsee Anguaine. Dog Perry was supposed to attend, and he was the one LaValle truly wanted to see, but Dog had sent word that he would not be coming, that he was out on the streets learning more about the dangerous Entreri.

In truth, the meeting proved nothing more than a gathering to calm the nerves of Quentin Bodeau. The guildmaster wanted reassurances that Entreri wouldn't merely show up and murder him. Chalsee Anguaine, in the manner of a cocky young man, promised to defend Quentin with his life. This LaValle knew to be an obvious lie. LaValle argued that Entreri wouldn't work that way, that he would not come in and kill Quentin without first learning all of Quentin's ties and associates and how powerfully the man held the guild.

"Entreri is never reckless," LaValle had explained. "And the scenario you fear would indeed be reckless."

By the time LaValle had turned to leave, Bodeau felt better and expressed his sentiment that he would feel better still if Dog Perry, or someone else, merely killed the dangerous man. It would never be that easy, LaValle knew, but he had kept the thought silent.

As soon as he entered his rooms, a suite of four with a large greeting room, a private study to the right, bedroom directly behind, and an alchemy lab and library to the left, the wizard felt as if something was amiss. He suspected Dog Perry to be the source of the trouble—the man did not trust him and had even privately, though surely subtly, accused him of the intent to side with Entreri should it come to blows.

Had the man come in here when he knew LaValle to be at the meeting with Quentin? Was he still here, hiding, crouched with weapon in hand?

The wizard looked back at the door and saw no signs that the lock—and the door was always locked—had been tripped, or that his traps had been defeated. There was one other way into the place, an outside window, but LaValle had placed so many glyphs and wards upon it, scattering them in several different places, that anyone crawling through would have been shocked with lightning, burned three different times, and frozen solid on the sill. Even if an intruder managed to survive the magical barrage, the explosions would have been heard throughout this entire level of the guild house, bringing soldiers by the score.

Reassured by simple logic and by a defensive spell he placed upon his body to make his skin resistant to any blows, LaValle started for his private study.

The door opened before he reached it, Artemis Entreri standing calmly within.

LaValle did well to stay on his feet, for his knees nearly buckled with weakness.

"You knew that I had returned," Entreri said easily, stepping forward and leaning against the jamb. "Did you not expect that I would pay a visit to an old friend?"

The wizard composed himself and shook his head, looking back at the door. "Door or window?" he asked.

"Door, of course," Entreri replied. "I know how well you protect your windows."

"The door, as well," LaValle said dryly, for obviously he hadn't protected it well enough.

Entreri shrugged. "You still use that lock and trap combination you had upon your previous quarters," he explained, holding up a key. "I suspected as much, since I heard that you were overjoyed when you discovered that the items had survived when the dwarf knocked the door in on your head."

"How did you get a—" LaValle started to ask.

"I got you the lock, remember?" Entreri answered.

"But the guild house is well defended by no soldiers known by Artemis Entreri," the wizard argued.

"The guild house has its secret leaks," the assassin quietly replied.

"But my door," LaValle went on. "There are . . . were other traps."

Entreri put on a bored expression, and LaValle got the point.

"Very well," the wizard said, moving past Entreri into the study and motioning for the assassin to follow. "I can have a fine meal delivered, if you so desire."

Entreri took a seat opposite LaValle and shook his head. "I came not for food, merely for information," he explained. "They know I am in Calimport."

"Many guilds know," LaValle confirmed with a nod. "And yes, I did know. I saw you through my crystal ball as, I am sure, have many of the wizards of the other pashas. You have not exactly been traveling from shadow to shadow."

"Should I be?" Entreri asked. "I came in with no enemies, as far as I know, and with no intent to make any."

LaValle laughed at the absurd notion. "No enemies?" he asked. "Ever have you made enemies. The creation of enemies is the obvious side product of your dark profession." His chuckle died fast when he looked carefully at the not-amused assassin, the wizard suddenly realizing that he was mocking perhaps the most dangerous man in all the world.

"Why did you scry me?" Entreri asked.

LaValle shrugged and held up his hands as if he didn't understand the question. "That is my job in the guild," he answered.

"So you informed the guildmaster of my return?"

"Pasha Quentin Bodeau was with me when your image came into the crystal ball," LaValle admitted.

Entreri merely nodded, and LaValle shifted uncomfortably.

"I did not know it would be you, of course," the wizard explained. "If I had known, I would have contacted you privately before informing Bodeau to learn your intent and your wishes."

"You are a loyal one," Entreri said dryly, and the irony was not lost on LaValle.

"I make no pretensions or promises," the wizard replied. "Those who know me understand that I do little to upset the balance of power about me and serve whoever has weighted his side of the scale the most."

"A pragmatic survivor," Entreri said. "Yet did you not just tell me that you would have informed me had you known? You do make a promise, wizard, a promise to serve. And yet, would you not be breaking that promise to Quentin Bodeau by warning me? Perhaps I do not know you as well as I had thought. Perhaps your loyalty cannot be trusted."

"I make a willing exception for you," LaValle stammered, trying to find a way out of the logic trap. He knew beyond a doubt that Entreri would try to kill him if the assassin believed that he could not be trusted.

And he knew beyond a doubt that if Entreri tried to kill him, he would be dead.

"Your mere presence means that whichever side you serve has weighted the scale in their favor," he explained. "Thus, I would never willingly go against you."

Entreri didn't respond other than to stare hard at the man, making LaValle shift uncomfortably more than once. Entreri, having little time for such games and with no real intention of harming LaValle, broke the tension, though, and quickly. "Tell me of the guild in its present incarnation," he said. "Tell me of Bodeau and his lieutenants and how extensive his street network has become."

"Quentin Bodeau is a decent man," LaValle readily complied. "He does not kill unless forced into such a position and steals only from those who can afford the loss. But many under him, and many other guilds, perceive this compassion as weakness, and thus the guild has suffered under his reign. We are not as extensive as we were when Pook ruled or when you took the leadership from the halfling Regis." He went on to detail the guild's area of influence, and the assassin was indeed surprised at how much Pook's grand old guild had frayed at the edges. Streets that had once been well within Pook's domain were far out of reach now, for those avenues considered borderlands between various operations were much closer to the guild house.

Entreri hardly cared for the prosperity or weakness of Bodeau's operation. This was a survival call and nothing more. He was only trying to get a feeling for the current layout of Calimport's underbelly so that he might not inadvertently bring the wrath of any particular guild down upon him.

LaValle went on to tell of the lieutenants, speaking highly of the potential of young Chalsee and warning Entreri in a deadly serious tone, but one that hardly seemed to stir the assassin, of Dog Perry.

"Watch him closely," LaValle said again, noting the assassin's almost bored expression. "Dog Perry was beside me when we scried you, and he was far from happy to see Artemis Entreri returned to Calimport. Your mere presence poses a threat to him, for he commands a fairly high price as an assassin, and not just for Quentin Bodeau." Still garnering no obvious response, LaValle pressed even harder. "He wants to be the next Artemis Entreri," the wizard said bluntly.

That brought a chuckle from the assassin, not one of doubt concerning Dog Perry's abilities to fulfill his dream or one of any flattery. Entreri was amused by the fact that this Dog Perry hardly understood that which he sought, for if he did, he would turn his desires elsewhere.

"He may see your return as more than an inconvenience," LaValle warned. "Perhaps as a threat, or even worse . . . as an opportunity."

"You do not like him," Entreri reasoned.

"He is a killer without discipline and thus hardly predictable," the wizard replied. "A blind man's flying arrow. If I knew for certain that he was coming after me, I would hardly fear him. It is the often irrational actions of the man that keep us all a bit worried."

"I hold no aspirations for Bodeau's position," Entreri assured the wizard after a long moment of silence. "Nor do I have any intention of impaling myself on the dagger of Dog Perry. Thus you will show no disloyalty to Bodeau by keeping me informed, wizard, and I expect at least that much from you."

"If Dog Perry comes after you, you will be told," LaValle promised, and Entreri believed him. Dog Perry was an upstart, a young hopeful who desired to strengthen his reputation with a single thrust of his dagger. But LaValle understood the truth of Entreri, the assassin knew, and while the wizard might become nervous indeed if he invoked the wrath of Dog Perry, he would find himself truly terrified if ever he learned that Artemis Entreri wanted him dead.

Entreri sat a moment longer, considering the paradox of his reputation. Because of his years of work, many might seek to kill him, but, for the same reasons, many others would fear to go against him and indeed would work for him.

Of course, if Dog Perry did manage to kill him, then LaValle's loyalty to Entreri would come to an abrupt end, transferred immediately to the new king assassin.

To Artemis Entreri it all seemed so perfectly useless.

* * * * *

"You do not see the possibilities here," Dog Perry scolded, working hard to keep his voice calm, though in truth he wanted to throttle the nervous young man.

"Have you heard the stories?" Chalsee Anguaine retorted. "He has killed everything from guildmasters to battle mages. Everyone he has decided to kill is dead."

Dog Perry spat in disgust. "That was a younger man," he replied. "A man revered by many guilds, including the Basadoni House. A man of connections and protection, who had many powerful allies to assist in his assassinations. Now he is alone and vulnerable, and no longer possessed of the quickness of youth."

"We should bide our time and learn more about him and discover why he has returned," Chalsee reasoned.

"The longer we wait, the more Entreri will rebuild his web," Dog Perry argued without hesitation. "A wizard, a guildmaster, spies on the street. No, if we wait then we cannot go against him without considering the possibility that our actions will begin a guild war. You understand the truth of Bodeau, of course, and recognize that under his leadership we would not survive such a war."

"You remain his principal assassin," Chalsee argued.

Dog Perry chuckled at the thought. "I follow opportunities," he corrected. "And the opportunity I see before me now is one that cannot be ignored. If I—if we—kill Artemis Entreri, we will command his previous position."

"Guildless?"

"Guildless," Dog Perry answered honestly. "Or better described as tied to many guilds. A sword for the highest bidder."

"Quentin Bodeau would not accept such a thing," Chalsee said. "He will lose two lieutenants, thus weakening his guild."

"Quentin Bodeau will understand that because his lieutenants now hire to more powerful guilds, his own position will be better secured," Dog Perry replied.

Chalsee considered the optimistic reasoning for a moment, then shook his head doubtfully. "Bodeau would then be vulnerable, perhaps fearing that his own lieutenants might strike against him at the request of another guildmaster."

"So be it," Dog Perry said coldly. "You should be very careful how tightly you tie your future to the likes of Bodeau. The guild erodes under his command, and eventually another guild will absorb us. Those willing to let the strongest conquer may find a new home. Those tied by foolish loyalty to the loser will have their bodies picked clean by beggars in the gutter."

Chalsee looked away, not enjoying this conversation in the least. Until the previous day, until they had learned that Artemis Entreri had returned, he had thought his life and career fairly secure. He was rising through the ranks of a reasonably strong guild. Now Dog Perry seemed intent on upping the stakes, on reaching for a higher level. While Chalsee could understand the allure, he wasn't certain of the true potential. If they succeeded against Entreri, he did not doubt Dog Perry's prediction, but the mere thought of going after Artemis Entreri . . .

Chalsee had been but a boy when Entreri had last left Calimport, had been connected to no guilds and knew none of the many Entreri had slain. By the time Chalsee had joined the underworld circuit, others had claimed the position of primary assassins in Calimport: Marcus the Knife of Pasha Wroning's Guild; the independent Clarissa and her cohorts who ran the brothels serving the nobility of the region—yes, Clarissa's enemies seemed to simply disappear. Then there was Kadran Gordeon of the Basadoni Guild, and perhaps most deadly of all, Slay Targon, the battle mage. None of them had come near to erasing the reputation of Artemis Entreri, even though the end of Entreri's previous Calimport career had been marred by the downfall of the guildmaster he was supposedly serving and by his reputed inability to defeat a certain nemesis, a drow elf, no less.

And now Dog Perry wanted to catapult himself to the ranks of those four notorious assassins with a single kill, and in truth, the plan sounded plausible to Chalsee.

Except, of course, for the little matter of actually killing Entreri.

"The decision is made," Dog Perry said, seemingly sensing Chalsee's private thoughts. "I am going against him . . . with or without your assistance."

The implicit threat behind those words was not lost on Chalsee. If Dog Perry meant to have any chance against Entreri, there could be no neutral parties. When he proclaimed his intentions to Chalsee, he was bluntly inferring that Chalsee had to either stand with him or against him, to stand in his court or in Entreri's. Considering that Chalsee didn't even know Entreri and feared the man as much as an ally as an enemy, it didn't seem much of a choice.

The two began their planning immediately. Dog Perry insisted that Artemis Entreri would be dead within two days.

* * * * *

"The man is no enemy," LaValle assured Quentin later that same night as the two walked the corridors leading to the guildmaster's private dining hall. "His return to Calimport was not predicated by any desire to reclaim the guild."

"How can you know?" the obviously nervous leader asked. "How can anyone know the mind-set of that one? Ever has he survived through unpredictability."

"There you are wrong," LaValle replied. "Entreri has ever been predictable because he makes no pretense of that which he desires. I have spoken to him."

The admission had Quentin Bodeau spinning about to face the wizard directly. "When?" he stuttered. "Where? You have not left the guild house all this day."

LaValle smiled and tilted his head as he regarded the man—the man who had just foolishly admitted that he was monitoring LaValle's movements. How frightened Quentin must be to go to such lengths. Still, the wizard knew, Quentin realized that LaValle and Entreri were old companions and that if Entreri did desire a return to power in the guild, he would likely enlist LaValle.

"You have no reason not to trust me," LaValle said calmly. "If Entreri wanted the guild back, I would tell you forthwith, that you might surrender leadership and still retain some high-ranking position."

Quentin Bodeau's gray eyes flared dangerously. "Surrender?" he echoed.

"If I led a guild and heard that Artemis Entreri desired my position, I would surely do that!" LaValle said with a laugh that somewhat dispelled the tension. "But have no such fears. Entreri is back in Calimport, 'tis true, but he is no enemy to you."

"Who can tell?" Bodeau replied, starting back down the corridor. LaValle fell into step beside him. "But understand that you are to have no further contacts with the man."

"That hardly seems prudent. Are we not better off understanding his movements?"

"No further contacts," Quentin Bodeau said more forcefully, grabbing LaValle by the shoulder and turning him so he could look directly into the wizard's eyes. "None, and that is not my choice."

"You miss an opportunity, I fear," LaValle started to argue. "Entreri is a friend, a very valuable—"

"None!" Quentin insisted, coming to an abrupt halt to accentuate his point. "Believe me when I say that it would please me greatly to hire the assassin to take care of a few troublemakers among the sewer wererat guild. I have heard that Entreri particularly dislikes the distasteful creatures and that they hold little love for him."

LaValle smiled at the memory. Pasha Pook had been heavily connected with a nasty wererat leader by the name of Rassiter. After Pook's fall, Rassiter had tried to enlist Entreri into a mutually beneficial alliance. Unfortunately for Rassiter, a very angry Entreri hadn't seen things quite that way.

"But we cannot enlist him," Quentin Bodeau went on. "Nor are we . . . are you, to have any further contact with him. These orders have come down to me from the Basadoni Guild, the Rakers' Guild, and Pasha Wroning himself."

LaValle paused, caught off guard by the stunning news. Bodeau had just listed the three most powerful guilds of Calimport's streets.

Quentin paused at the dining room door, knowing that there were attendants inside, wanting to get this settled privately with the wizard. "They have declared Entreri an untouchable," he went on, meaning that no guildmaster, at the risk of street war, was to even speak with the man, let alone have any professional dealings with him.

LaValle nodded, understanding but none too happy about the prospects. It made perfect sense, of course, as would any joint action the three rival guilds could agree upon. They had iced Entreri out of the system for fear that a minor guildmaster might empty his coffers and hire the assassin to kill one of the more prominent leaders. Those in the strongest positions of power preferred the status quo, and they all feared Entreri enough to recognize that he alone might upset that balance. What a testament to the man's reputation! And LaValle, above all others, understood it to be rightly given.

"I understand," he said to Quentin, bowing to show his obedience. "Perhaps when the situation is better clarified we will find our opportunity to exploit my friendship with this very valuable man."

Bodeau managed his first smile in several days, feeling assured by LaValle's seemingly sincere declarations. He was indeed far more at ease as they continued on their way to share an evening meal.

But LaValle was not. He could hardly believe that the other guilds had moved so quickly to isolate Entreri. If that was the case, then he understood that they would be watching the assassin closely—close enough to learn of any attempts against Entreri and to bring about retaliation on any guild so foolish as to try to kill the man.

LaValle ate quickly, then dismissed himself, explaining that he was in the middle of penning a particularly difficult scroll he hoped to finish that night.

He went immediately to his crystal ball, hoping to locate Dog Perry, and was pleased indeed to learn that the fiery man and Chalsee Anguaine were both still within the guild house. He caught up to them on the street level in the main armory. He could guess easily enough why they might be in that particular room.

"You plan to go out this evening?" the wizard calmly asked as he entered.

"We go out every evening," Dog Perry replied. "It is our job, is it not?"

"A few extra weapons?" LaValle asked suspiciously, noting that both men had daggers strapped to every conceivable retrievable position.

"The guild lieutenant who is not careful is usually dead," Dog Perry replied dryly.

"Indeed," LaValle conceded with a bow. "And, by word of the Basadoni, Wroning, and Rakers' guilds, the guild lieutenant who goes after Artemis Entreri is doing no favors for his master."

The blunt declaration gave both men pause. Dog Perry worked through it quickly and calmly, getting back to his preparations with no discernible trace of guilt upon his blank expression. But Chalsee, less experienced by far, showed some clear signs of distress. LaValle knew he had hit the target directly. They were going after Entreri this very night.

"I would have thought you would consult with me first," the wizard remarked, "to learn his whereabouts, of course, and perhaps see some of the defenses he obviously has set in place."

"You babble, wizard," Dog Perry insisted. "I have many duties to attend and have no time for your foolishness." He slammed the door of the weapons locker as he finished, then walked right past LaValle. A nervous Chalsee Anguaine fell into step behind him, glancing back many times.

LaValle considered the cold treatment and recognized that Dog Perry had indeed decided to go after Entreri and had also decided that LaValle could not be trusted as far as the dangerous assassin was concerned. Now the wizard, in considering all the possibilities, found his own dilemma. If Dog Perry succeeded in killing Entreri the dangerous young man who had just pointedly declared himself no friend of LaValle's would gain immensely in stature and power (if the other guilds did not decide to kill him for his rash actions). But if Entreri won, which LaValle deemed most likely, then he might not appreciate the fact that LaValle had not contacted him with any warning, as they had agreed.

And yet LaValle could not dare to use his magics and contact Entreri. If the other guilds were watching the assassin, such forms of contact would be easily detected and traced.

79

A very distressed LaValle went back to his room and sat for a long while in the darkness. In either scenario, whether Dog Perry or Entreri proved victorious, the guild might be in for more than a little trouble. Should he go to Quentin Bodeau? he wondered, but then he dismissed the thought, realizing that Quentin would do little more than pace the floor and chew his fingernails. Dog Perry was out in the streets now, and Quentin had no means to recall him.

Should he gaze into his crystal ball and try to learn of the battle? Again, LaValle had to consider that any magical contact, even if it was no more than silent scrying, might be detected by the wizards hired by the more powerful guilds and might then implicate LaValle.

So he sat in the darkness, wondering and worrying, as the hours slipped by.

Chapter 6
Leaving the Dale Behind

Drizzt watched every move the barbarian made—the way Wulfgar sat opposite him across the fire, the way the man went at his dinner—looking for some hint of the barbarian's mind-set. Had the battle with the giants helped? Had Drizzt "run the horse" as he had explained his hopes to Regis? Or was Wulfgar in worse shape now than before the battle? Was he more consumed by this latest guilt, though his actions, or inaction, hadn't really cost them anything?

Wulfgar had to recognize that he had not performed well at the beginning of the battle, but had he, in his own mind, made up for that error with his subsequent actions?

Drizzt was as perceptive to such emotions as anyone alive, but, in truth, he could not get the slightest read of the barbarian's inner turmoil. Wulfgar moved methodically, mechanically, as he had since his return from Errtu's clutches, going through the motions of life itself without any outward sign of pain, satisfaction, relief, or anything else. Wulfgar was existing, but hardly living. If there remained a flicker of passion within those sky-blue orbs, Drizzt could not see it. Thus, the drow ranger was left with the impression that the battle with the giants had been inconsequential, had neither bolstered the barbarian's desire to live nor had placed any further burdens upon Wulfgar. In looking at his friend now, the man tearing a piece of fowl from the bone, his expression unchanging and unrevealing, Drizzt had to admit to himself that he had not only run out of answers but out of places to look for answers.

Catti-brie moved over and sat down beside Wulfgar then, and the barbarian did pause to regard her. He even managed a little smile for her benefit. Perhaps she might succeed where he had failed, the drow thought. He and Wulfgar had been friends, to be sure, but the barbarian and Catti-brie had shared something much deeper than that.

The thought of it brought a tumult of opposing feelings into Drizzt's gut. On the one hand he cared deeply for Wulfgar and wanted nothing more in all the world than for the barbarian to heal his emotional scars. On the other hand, seeing Catti-brie close to the man pained him. He tried to deny it, tried to elevate himself above it, but it was there, and it was a fact, and it would not go away.

He was jealous.

With great effort, the drow sublimated those feelings enough to honestly leave the couple alone. He went to join Bruenor and Regis and couldn't help but contrast the halfling's beaming face as he devoured his third helping with that of Wulfgar, who seemed to be eating only to keep his body alive. Pragmatism against pure pleasure.

"We'll be out o' the dale tomorrow," Bruenor was saying, pointing out the dark silhouettes of the mountains, looming much larger to the south and east. Indeed, the wagon had turned the corner and they were heading south now, no longer west. The wind, which always filled the ears in Icewind Dale, had died to the occasional gust.

"How's me boy?" Bruenor asked when he noticed the dark elf.

Drizzt shrugged.

"Ye could've got him killed, ye durned fool elf," the dwarf huffed. "Ye could've got us all killed. And not for the first time!"

"And not for the last," Drizzt promised with a smile, bowing low. He knew that Bruenor was playing with him here, that the dwarf loved a good fight as much as he did, particularly one against giants. Bruenor had been upset with him, to be sure, but only because Drizzt hadn't included him in the original battle plans. The brief but brutal fight had long since exorcised that grudge from Bruenor, and so now he was just teasing the drow as a means of relieving his honest concerns for Wulfgar.

"Did ye see his face when we battled?" the dwarf asked more earnestly. "Did ye see him when Rumblebelly showed up with his stinkin' giant friend and it appeared as if me boy was about to be squished flat?"

Drizzt admitted that he did not. "I was engaged with my own concerns at the time," he explained. "And with Guenhwyvar's peril."

"Nothing," Bruenor declared. "Nothing at all. No anger as he lifted his hammer to throw it at the giants."

"The warrior sublimates his anger to keep in conscious control," the drow reasoned.

"Bah, not like that," Bruenor retorted. "I saw rage in me boy when we fought Errtu on the ice island, rage beyond anything me old eyes've ever seen. And how I'd like to be seein' it again. Anger, rage, even fear!"

"I saw him when I arrived at the battle," Regis admitted. "He did not know that the new and huge giant would be an ally, and if it was not, if it had joined in on the side of the other giants, then Wulfgar would have easily been killed, for he had no defense against our angle from his open ledge. And yet he was not afraid at all. He looked right up at the giant, and all I saw was . . ."

"Resignation," the drow finished for him. "Acceptance of whatever fate might throw at him."

"I'm not for understanding." Bruenor admitted.

Drizzt had no answers for him. He had his suspicions, of course, that Wulfgar's trauma had been too great and had thus stolen from him his hopes and dreams, his passions and purpose, but he could find no way to put that into words that the ever-pragmatic dwarf might understand. He thought it ironic, in a sense, for the closest example of similar behavior he could recall was Bruenor's own, soon after Wulfgar had fallen to the yochlol. The dwarf had wandered aimlessly through the halls for days on end, grieving.

Yes, Drizzt realized, that was the key word. Wulfgar was grieving.

Bruenor would never understand, and Drizzt wasn't sure that he understood.

"Time to go," Regis remarked, drawing the dark elf from his contemplation. Drizzt looked to the halfling, then to Bruenor.

"Camlaine's invited us to a game o' bones," Bruenor explained. "Come along, elf. Yer eyes see better'n most, and I might be needing ye."

Drizzt glanced back to the fire, to Wulfgar and Catti-brie, sitting very close and talking. He noted that Catti-brie wasn't doing all of the speaking. She had somehow engaged Wulfgar, even had him a bit animated in his discussion. A big part of Drizzt wanted to stay right there and watch their every move, but he wouldn't give in to that weakness, so he went with Bruenor and Regis to watch the game of bones.

* * * * *

"Ye cannot know our pain at seeing the ceiling fall in on ye," Catti-brie said, gently moving the conversation to that fateful day in the bowels of Mithral Hall. Up to now, she and Wulfgar had been sharing happier memories of previous fights, battles in which the companions had overwhelmed monsters and put down threats without so high a price.

Wulfgar had even joined in, telling of his first battle with Bruenor—against Bruenor—when he had broken his standard staff over the

83

dwarf's head, only to have the stubborn little creature swipe his legs out from under him and leave him unconscious on the field. As the conversation wound on, Catti-brie focused on another pivotal event: the crafting of Aegis-fang. What a labor of love that had been, the pinnacle of Bruenor's amazing career as a smith, done purely out of the dwarf's affection for Wulfgar.

"If he hadn't loved ye so, he'd ne'er been able to make so great a weapon," she had explained. When she saw that her words were getting through to the pained man she had shifted the conversation subtly again, to the reverential treatment Bruenor had shown the warhammer after Wulfgar's apparent demise. And that, of course, had brought Catti-brie to the discussion of the day of Wulfgar's fall, to the memory of the evil yochlol.

To her great relief, Wulfgar had not tightened up when she went in this direction, but had stayed with her, hearing her words and adding his own when they seemed relevant.

"All the strength went from me body," Catti-brie went on. "And never have I seen Bruenor closer to breaking. But we went on and started fighting in yer name, and woe to our enemies then."

A distant look came into Wulfgar's light eyes and the woman went silent, giving him time to digest her words. She thought he would respond, but he did not, and the seconds slipped away quietly.

Catti-brie moved closer to him and put her arm about his back, resting her head on his strong shoulder. He didn't push her away, even shifted so they would both be more comfortable. The woman had hoped for more, had hoped to get Wulfgar into an emotional release. But while she hadn't achieved quite that, she recognized that she had gotten more than she could have rightfully expected. The love had not resurfaced, but neither had the rage.

It would take time.

The group did indeed roll out of Icewind Dale the next morning, a distinction made clear by the shifting wind. In the dale, the wind came from the northeast, rolling down off the cold waters of the Sea of Moving Ice. At the juncture to points south, east, and north of the bulk of the mountains, the wind blew constantly no longer, but was more a matter of gusts than the incessant whistle through the dale. And now, moving more to the south, the wind again kicked up, swirling against the towering Spine of the World. Unlike the cold breeze that gave its name to Icewind Dale, this was a gentle blow. The winds wafted up from warmer climes to the south or off the warmer waters of the Sword Coast, hitting against the blocking mountains and swirling back.

Drizzt and Bruenor spent most of the day away from the wagon, both to scout a perimeter about the steady but slow pacing team and to give some privacy to Catti-brie and Wulfgar. The woman was still talking, still trying to bring the man to a better place and time. Regis rode all the day long nestled in the back of the wagon among the generous-smelling foodstuffs.

It proved to be a quiet and uneventful day of travel, except for one point where Drizzt found a particularly disturbing track, that of a huge, booted giant.

"Rumblebelly's friend?" Bruenor asked, bending low beside the ranger as he inspected the footprint.

"So I would guess," Drizzt replied.

"Durned halfling put more of a spell than he should've on the thing," Bruenor grumbled.

Drizzt, who understood the power of the ruby pendant and the nature of enchantments in general, could not agree. He knew that the giant, no stupid creature, had been released from any spell Regis had woven soon after leaving the group. Likely, before they were miles apart, the giant had begun to wonder why in the world he had ever deigned to help the halfling and his strange group of friends. Then, soon after that, he had either forgotten the whole incident or was angry indeed at having been so deceived.

And now the behemoth seemed to be shadowing them, Drizzt realized, noting the general course of the tracks.

Perhaps it was mere coincidence, or perhaps even a different giant— Icewind Dale had no shortage of giants, after all. Drizzt could not be sure, and so, when he and Bruenor returned to the group for their evening meal, they said nothing about the footprints or about increasing the night watch. Drizzt did go off on his own, though, as much to get away from the continuing scene between Catti-brie and Wulfgar as to scout for any rogue giants. There in the dark of night, he could be alone with his thoughts and his fears, could wage his own emotional wars and remind himself over and over that Catti-brie alone could decide the course of her life.

Every time he recalled an incident highlighting how intelligent and honest the woman had always been, he was comforted. When the full moon began its lazy ascent over the distant waters of the Sword Coast, the drow felt strangely warm. Though he could hardly see the glow of the campfire, he understood that he was truly among friends.

* * * * *

Wulfgar looked deeply into her blue eyes and knew that she had purposefully brought him to this point, had smoothed the jagged edges of his battered consciousness slowly and deliberately, had massaged the walls of anger until her gentle touch had rubbed them into transparency. And now she wanted, she demanded, to look behind those walls, wanted to see the demons that so tormented Wulfgar.

Catti-brie sat quietly, calmly, patiently waiting. She had coaxed some specific horror stories out of the man and then had probed deeper, had

85

asked him to lay bare his soul and his terror, something she knew could not be easy for the proud and strong man.

But Wulfgar hadn't rebuffed her. He sat now, his thoughts whirling, his gaze locked firmly by hers, his breath coming in gasps, his heart pounding in his huge chest.

"For so long I held on to you," he said quietly. "Down there, among the smoke and the dirt, I held fast to an image of my Catti-brie. I kept it right before me at all times. I did."

He paused to catch his breath, and Catti-brie placed a gentle hand on his.

"So many sights that a man was not meant to view," Wulfgar said quietly, and Catti-brie saw a hint of moisture in his light eyes. "But I fought them all with an image of you."

Catti-brie offered a smile, but that did little to comfort Wulfgar.

"He used it against me," the man went on, his tone lowering, becoming almost a growl. "Errtu knew my thoughts and turned them against me. He showed me the finish of the yochlol fight, the creature pushing through the rubble, falling over you and tearing you to pieces. Then it went for Bruenor. . . ."

"Was it not the yochlol that brought you to the lower planes?" Catti-brie asked, trying to use logic to break the demonic spell.

"I do not remember," Wulfgar admitted. "I remember the fall of the stones, the pain of the yochlol's bite tearing into my chest, and then only blackness until I awakened in the court of the Spider Queen.

"But even that image . . . you do not understand! The one thing I could hold onto Errtu perverted and turned against me. The one hope left in my heart burned away and left me empty."

Catti-brie moved closer, her face barely an inch from Wulfgar's. "But hope rekindles," she said softly. "Errtu is gone, banished for a hundred years, and the Spider Queen and her hellish drow minions have shown no interest in Drizzt for years. That road has ended, it seems, and so many new ones lie before us. The road to the Spirit Soaring and Cadderly. From there to Mithral Hall perhaps, and then, if we choose, we might go to Waterdeep and Captain Deudermont, take a wild voyage on *Sea Sprite*, cutting the waves and chasing pirates.

"What possibilities lie before us!" she went on, her smile wide, her blue eyes flashing with excitement. "But first we must make peace with our past."

Wulfgar heard her well, but he only shook his head, reminding her that it might not be as easy as she made it sound. "For all those years you thought I was dead," he said. "And so I thought of you for that time. I thought you killed, and Bruenor killed, and Drizzt cut apart on the altar of some vile drow matron. I surrendered hope because there was none."

"But you see the lie," Catti-brie reasoned. "There is always hope, there must always be hope. That is the lie of Errtu's evil kind. The lie about them, and the lie that is them. They steal hope, because without hope there is no strength. Without hope there is no freedom. In slavery of the heart does a demon find its greatest pleasures."

Wulfgar took a deep, deep breath, trying to digest it all, balancing the logical truths of Catti-brie's words—and of the simple fact that he had indeed escaped Errtu's clutches—against the pervasive pain of memory.

Catti-brie, too, spent a long moment digesting all that Wulfgar had shown to her over the past days. She understood now that it was more than pain and horror that bound her friend. Only one emotion could so cripple a man. In replaying his memories within his own mind, Wulfgar had found some wherein he had surrendered, wherein he had given in to the desires of Errtu or the demon's minions, wherein he had lost his courage or his defiance. Yes, it was obvious to Catti-brie, staring hard at the man now that guilt above all else was the enduring demon of Wulfgar's time with Errtu.

Of course to her that seemed absurd. She could readily forgive anything Wulfgar had said or done to survive the decadence of the Abyss. Anything at all. But it was not absurd, she quickly reminded herself, for it was painted clearly on the big man's pained features.

Wulfgar squinted his eyes shut and gritted his teeth. She was right, he told himself repeatedly. The past was past, an experience dismissed, a lesson learned. Now they were all together again, healthy and on the road of adventure. Now he had learned the errors of his previous engagement to Catti-brie and could look at her with fresh hopes and desires.

She recognized a measure of calm come over the man as he opened his eyes again to stare back at her. And then he came forward, kissing her softly, just brushing his lips against hers as if asking permission.

Catti-brie glanced all around and saw that they were indeed alone. Though the others were not so far away, those who were not asleep were too engaged in their gambling to take note of anything.

Wulfgar kissed her again, a bit more urgently, forcing her to consider her feelings for the man. Did she love him? As a friend, surely, but was she ready to take that love to a different level?

Catti-brie honestly did not know. Once she had decided to give her love to Wulfgar, to marry him and bear his children, to make her life with him. But that was so many years ago, a different time, a different place. Now she had feelings for another, perhaps, though in truth, she hadn't really examined those feelings any deeper than she had her current feelings for Wulfgar.

And she hadn't the time to examine them now, for Wulfgar kissed her again passionately. When she didn't respond in kind, he backed off to arms' length, staring at her hard.

Looking at him then, on the brink of disaster, on a precipice between past and future, Catti-brie came to understand that she had to give this to him. She pulled him back and initiated another kiss, and they embraced deeply, Wulfgar guiding her to the ground, rolling about, touching, caressing, fumbling with their clothes.

She let him lose himself in the passion, let him lead with touches and kisses, and she took comfort in the role she had accepted, took hope that their encounter this night would help bring Wulfgar back to the world of the living.

And it was working. Wulfgar knew it, felt it. He bared his heart and soul to her, threw away his defenses, basked in the feel of her, in the sweet smell of her, in the very softness of her.

He was free! For those first few moments he was free, and it was glorious and beautiful, and so real.

He rolled to his back, his strong hug rolling Catti-brie atop him. He bit softly on the nape of her neck, then, nearing a point of ecstasy, leaned his head back so that he could look into her eyes and share the moment of joy.

A leering succubus, vile temptress of the Abyss, stared back at him.

Wulfgar's thoughts careened back across Icewind Dale, back to the Sea of Moving Ice, to the ice cave and the fight with Errtu, then back beyond that, back to the swirling smoke and the horrors. It had all been a lie, he realized. The fight, the escape, the rejoining with his friends. All a lie perpetrated by Errtu to rekindle his hope that the demon could then snuff it out once again. All a lie, and he was still in the Abyss, dreaming of Catti-brie while entwining with a horrid succubus.

His powerful hand clamped under the creature's chin and pushed it away. His second hand came across in a vicious punch and then he lifted the beast into the air above his prone form and heaved it away, bouncing across the dirt. With a roar, Wulfgar pulled himself to his feet, fumbling to lift and straighten his pants. He staggered for the fire and, ignoring the pain, reached in to grab a burning branch, then turned back to attack the wicked succubus.

Turned back to attack Catti-brie.

He recognized her then, half-undressed, staggering to her hands and knees, blood dripping freely from her nose. She managed to look up at him. There was no rage, only confusion on her battered face. The weight of guilt nearly buckled the barbarian's strong legs.

"I did not . . ." he stammered. "Never would I . . ." With a gasp and a stifled cry, Wulfgar rushed across the campsite, tossing the burning stick aside, gathering up his pack and warhammer. He ran out into the dark of night, into the ultimate darkness of his tormented mind.

Chapter 7
Kelp-enwalled

"You cannot come in," the squeaky voice said from behind the barricade. "Please, sir, I beg you. Go away."

Entreri hardly found the halfling's nervous tone amusing, for the implications of the shut-out rang dangerously in his mind. He and Dwahvel had cut a deal—a mutually beneficial deal and one that seemed to favor the halfling, if anyone—and yet, now it seemed as if Dwahvel was going back on her word. Her doorman would not even let the assassin into the Copper Ante. Entreri entertained the thought of kicking in the barricade, but only briefly. He reminded himself that halflings were often adept at setting traps. Then he thought he might slip his dagger through the slit in the boards, into the impertinent doorman's arm, or thumb, or whatever other target presented itself. That was the beauty of Entreri's dagger: he could stick someone anywhere and suck the life-force right out of him.

But again, it was a fleeting thought, more of a fantasy wrought of frustration than any action the ever-careful Entreri would seriously consider.

"So I shall go," he said calmly. "But do inform Dwahvel that my world is divided between friends and enemies." He turned and started away, leaving the doorman in a fluster.

"My, but that sounded like a threat," came another voice before Entreri had moved ten paces down the street.

The assassin stopped and considered a small crack in the wall of the Copper Ante, a peep hole, he realized, and likely an arrow slit.

"Dwahvel," he said with a slight bow.

To his surprise, the crack widened and a panel slid aside. Dwahvel walked out in the open. "So quick to name enemies," she said, shaking her head, her curly brown locks bouncing gaily.

"But I did not," the assassin replied. "Though it did anger me that you apparently decided not to go through with our deal."

Dwahvel's face tightened suddenly, stealing the up-to-then light-hearted tone. "Kelp-enwalled," she explained, an expression more common to the fishing boats than the streets, but one Entreri had heard before. On the fishing boats, "kelp-enwalling" referred to the practice of isolating particularly troublesome pincer crabs, which had to be delivered live to market, by building barricades of kelp strands about them. The term was less literal, but with similar meaning, on the street. A kelp-enwalled person had been declared off-limits, surrounded and isolated by barricades of threats.

Suddenly Entreri's expression also showed the strain.

"The order came from greater guilds than mine, from guilds that could, and would, burn the Copper Ante to the ground and kill all of my fellows with hardly a thought," Dwahvel said with a shrug. "Entreri is kelp-enwalled, so they said. You cannot blame me for refusing your entrance."

Entreri nodded. He above many others could appreciate pragmatism for the sake of survival. "Yet you chose to come out and speak with me," he said.

Another shrug from Dwahvel. "Only to explain why our deal has ended," she said. "And to ensure that I do not fall into the latter category you detailed for my doorman. I will offer to you this much, with no charge for services. Everyone knows now that you have returned, and your mere presence has made them all nervous. Old Basadoni still rules his guild, but he is in the shadows now, more a figurehead than a leader. Those handling the affairs of the Basadoni Guild, and the other guilds, for that matter, do not know you. But they do know your reputation. Thus they fear you as they fear each other. Might not Pasha Wroning fear that the Rakers have hired Entreri to kill him? Or even within the individual guilds, might those vying for position before the coming event of Pasha Basadoni's death not fear that one of the others has coaxed Entreri back to assure personal ascension?"

Entreri nodded again but replied, "Or is it not possible that Artemis Entreri has merely returned to his home?"

"Of course," Dwahvel said. "But until they all learn the truth of you, they will fear you, and the only way to learn the truth—"

"Kelp-enwalled," the assassin finished. He started to thank Dwahvel for showing the courage of coming out to tell him this much, but he stopped short. He recognized that perhaps the halfling was only following orders, that perhaps this meeting was part of the surveying process.

"Watch well your back," Dwahvel added, moving for the secret door. "You understand that there are many who would like to claim the head of Entreri for their trophy wall."

"What do you know?" the assassin asked, for it seemed obvious to him that Dwahvel wasn't speaking merely in generalities here.

"Before the kelp-enwalling order, my spies went out to learn what they may about the perceptions concerning your return," she explained. "They were asked more questions than they offered and often by young, strong assassins. Watch well your back." And then she was gone, back through the secret door into the Copper Ante.

Entreri just blew a sigh and walked along. He didn't question his return to Calimport, for either way it simply didn't seem important to him. Nor did he start looking more deeply into the shadows that lined the dark street. Perhaps one or more held his killer. Perhaps not.

Perhaps it simply did not matter.

* * * * *

"Perry," Giunta the Diviner said to Kadran Gordeon as the two watched the young thug steal along the rooftops, shadowing, from a very safe distance, the movements of Artemis Entreri. "A lieutenant for Bodeau."

"Is he watching?" Kadran asked.

"Hunting," the wizard corrected.

Kadran didn't doubt the man. Giunta's entire life had been spent in observation. This wizard was the watcher, and from the patterns of those he observed he could then predict with an amazing degree of accuracy their next movements.

"Why would Bodeau risk everything to go after Entreri?" the fighter asked. "Surely he knows of the kelp-enwalling order, and Entreri has a long alliance with that particular guild."

"You presume that Bodeau even knows of this," Giunta explained. "I have seen this one before. Dog Perry, he is called, though he fancies himself 'the Heart.'"

That nickname rang a chime of recognition in Kadran. "For his practice of cutting a still-beating heart from the chest of his victims," the man remarked. "A brash young killer," he added, nodding, for now it made sense.

"Not unlike one I know," Giunta said slyly, turning his gaze over Kadran.

Kadran smiled in reply. Indeed, Dog Perry was not so unlike a younger Kadran, brash and skilled. The years had taught Kadran some

91

measure of humility, however, though many of those who knew him well thought he was still a bit deficient in that regard. He looked more closely at Dog Perry now, the man moving silently and carefully along the rim of a rooftop. Yes, there seemed a resemblance to the young thug Kadran used to be. Less polished and less wise, obviously, for even in his cocky youth Kadran doubted that he would have gone after the likes of Artemis Entreri so soon after the man's return to Calimport and obviously without too much preparation.

"He must have allies in the region," Kadran remarked to Giunta. "Seek out the other rooftops. Surely the young thug would not be foolish enough to hunt Entreri alone."

Giunta widened his scan. He found Entreri moving easily along the main boulevard and recognized many other characters in the area, regulars who held no known connection to Bodeau's guild or to Dog Perry.

"Him," the wizard explained, pointing to another figure weaving in and out of the shadows, following the same route as Entreri, but far, far behind. "Another of Bodeau's men, I believe."

"He does not seem overly intent on joining the fight," Kadran noted, for the man seemed to hesitate with every step. He was so far behind Entreri and losing ground with each passing second that he could have jumped out and run full speed at the man down the middle of the street without being noticed by the pursued assassin.

"Perhaps he is merely observing," Giunta remarked as he moved the focus of the crystal ball back to the two assassins, their paths beginning to intersect, "following his ally at the request of Bodeau to see how Dog Perry fares. There are many possibilities, but if he does mean to get into the fight beside Dog Perry, then he should run fast. Entreri is not one to drag out a battle, and it seems—"

He stopped abruptly as Dog Perry moved to the edge of a roof and crouched low, muscles tensing. The young assassin had found his spot of ambush, and Entreri turned into the ally, seemingly playing into the man's hand.

"We could warn him," Kadran said, licking his lips nervously.

"Entreri is already on his guard," the wizard explained. "Surely he has sensed my scrying. A man of his talents could not be magically looked at without his knowledge." the wizard gave a little chuckle. "Farewell, Dog Perry," he said.

Even as the words came out of his mouth, the would-be assassin leaped down from the roof, hitting the ground in a rush barely three strides behind Entreri, closing so fast that almost any man would have been skewered before he even registered the noise behind him.

Almost any man.

Entreri spun as Dog Perry rushed in, Perry's slender sword leading. A brush of the spinning assassin's left hand, holding the ample folds of his cloak as further protection, deflected the blow wide. Ahead went Entreri, a sudden step, pushing up with his left hand, lifting Dog Perry's arm as he went. He moved right under the now off-balance would-be killer, stabbing up into the armpit with his jeweled dagger as he passed. Then, so quickly that Dog Perry never had a chance to compensate, so quickly that Kadran and Giunta hardly noticed the subtle turn, he pivoted back, turning to face Dog Perry's back. Entreri tore the dagger free and flipped it to his descending left hand, snapped his right hand around to the chin of the would-be killer, and kicked the man in the back of the knees, buckling his legs and forcing him back and down. The older assassin's left hand stabbed up, driving the dagger under the back of Dog Perry's skull and deep into his brain.

Entreri retracted the dagger immediately and let the dead man fall to the ground, blood pooling under him, so quickly and so efficiently that Entreri didn't even have a drop of blood on him.

Giunta, laughing, pointed to the end of the ally, back on the street, where the stunned companion of Dog Perry took one look at the victorious Entreri, turned on his heel, and ran away.

"Yes, indeed," Giunta remarked. "Let the word go out on the streets that Artemis Entreri has returned."

Kadran Gordeon spent a long while staring at the dead man. He struck his customary pensive pose, pursing his lips so that his long and curvy mustache tilted on his dark face. He had entertained the idea of going after Entreri himself, and now was quite plainly shocked by the sheer skill of the man. It was Gordeon's first true experience with Entreri, and suddenly he understood that the man had come by his reputation honestly.

But Kadran Gordeon was not Dog Perry, was far more skilled than that young bumbler. Perhaps he would indeed pay a visit to this former king of assassins.

"Exquisite," came Sharlotta's voice behind the two. They turned to see the woman staring past them into the image in Giunta's large crystal ball. "Pasha Basadoni told me I would be impressed. How well he moves!"

"Shall I repay the Bodeau guild for breaking the kelp-enwalling order?" Kadran asked.

"Forget them," Sharlotta retorted, moving closer, her eyes twinkling with admiration. "Concentrate our attention upon that one alone. Find him and enlist him. Let us find a job for Artemis Entreri."

* * * * *

Drizzt found Catti-brie sitting on the back lip of the wagon. Regis sat next to her, holding a cloth to her face. Bruenor, axe swinging dangerously at his side, pacing back and forth, grumbled a stream of curses. The drow knew at once what had happened, the simple truth of it anyway, and when he considered it, he was not so surprised that Wulfgar had struck out.

"He did not mean to do it," Catti-brie said to Bruenor, trying to calm the volatile dwarf. She, too, was obviously angry, but she, like Drizzt, understood better the truth of Wulfgar's emotional turmoil. "I'm thinking he wasn't seein' me," the woman went on, speaking more to Drizzt. "Looking back at Errtu's torments, by me guess."

Drizzt nodded. "As it was at the beginning of the fight with the giants," he said.

"And so ye're to let it go?" Bruenor roared in reply. "Ye're thinkin' that ye can't hold the boy responsible? Bah! I'll give him a beating that'll make his years with Errtu seem easy! Go and get him, elf. Bring him back that he can tell me girl he's sorry. Then he can tell me. Then he can find me fist in his mouth and take a good long sleep to think about it!" With a growl, Bruenor drove his axe deep into the ground. "I heared too much o' this Errtu," he declared. "Ye can't be livin' in what's already done!"

Drizzt had little doubt that if Wulfgar walked back into camp at that moment, it would take him, Catti-brie, Regis, Camlaine, and all his companions just to pull Bruenor off the man. And in looking at Catti-brie, one eye swollen, her bloody nose bright red, the ranger wasn't sure he would be too quick to hold the dwarf back.

Without another word Drizzt turned and walked away, out of the camp and into the darkness. Wulfgar couldn't have gone far, he knew, though the night was not so dark with the big moon shining bright across the tundra. Just outside the campsite he took out his figurine. Guenhwyvar led the way, rushing into the darkness and growling back to guide the running ranger.

To Drizzt's surprise the trail led neither south nor back to the northeast and Ten Towns, but straight east, toward the towering black peaks of the Spine of the World. Soon Guenhwyvar led him into the foothills, dangerous territory indeed, for the high bluffs and rocky outcroppings provided fine ambush points for lurking monsters or highwaymen.

Perhaps, Drizzt mused, that was exactly why Wulfgar had come this way. Perhaps he was looking for trouble, for a fight, or maybe even for some giant to surprise him and end his pain.

Drizzt skidded to a stop and blew a long and profound sigh, for what seemed most unsettling to him was not the thought that Wulfgar was inviting disaster, but his own reaction to it. For at that moment, the image of hurt Catti-brie clear in his mind, the ranger almost—*almost*—thought that such an ending to Wulfgar's tale would not be such a terrible thing.

A call from Guenhwyvar brought him from his thoughts. He sprinted up a steep incline, leaped to another boulder, then skittered back down to another trail. He heard a growl—from Wulfgar and not the panther—then a crash as Aegis-fang slammed against some stone. The crash was

94

near to Guenhwyvar, Drizzt realized, from the sound of the hit and the cat's ensuing protesting roars.

Drizzt leaped over a stone lip, rushed across a short expanse, and jumped down a small drop to land lightly right beside the big man just as the warhammer magically reappeared in his grasp. For a moment, considering the wild look in Wulfgar's eyes, the drow thought he would have to draw his blades and fight the man, but Wulfgar calmed quickly. He seemed merely defeated, his rage thrown out.

"I did not know," he said, slumping back against the stone.

"I understand," Drizzt replied, holding back his own anger and trying to sound compassionate.

"It was not Catti-brie," Wulfgar went on. "In my thoughts, I mean. I was not with her, but back there, in that place of darkness."

"I know," said Drizzt. "And so does Catti-brie, though I fear we shall have some work ahead of us in calming Bruenor." He ended with a wide and warm smile, but his attempt to lighten the situation was lost on Wulfgar.

"He is right to be outraged," the barbarian admitted. "As I am outraged, in a way you cannot begin to understand."

"Do not underestimate the value of friendship," Drizzt answered. "I once made a similar error, nearly to the destruction of all that I hold dear."

Wulfgar shook his head through every word of it, unable to find any footing for agreement. Black waves of despair washed over him, burying him. What he had done was beyond forgiveness, especially since he realized, and admitted to himself, that it would likely happen again. "I am lost," he said softly.

"And we will all help you to find your way," Drizzt answered, putting a comforting hand on the big man's shoulder.

Wulfgar pushed him away. "No," he said firmly, and then he gave a little laugh. "There is no way to find. The darkness of Errtu endures. Under that shadow, I cannot be who you want me to be."

"We only want you to remember who you once were," the drow replied. "In the ice cave, we rejoiced to find Wulfgar, son of Beornegar, returned to us."

"He was not," the big man corrected. "I am not the man who left you in Mithral Hall. I can never be that man again."

"Time will heal—" Drizzt started to say, but Wulfgar silenced him with a roar.

"No!" he cried. "I do not ask for healing. I do not wish to become again the man that I was. Perhaps I have learned the truth of the world, and that truth has shown me the errors of my previous ways."

Drizzt stared hard at the man. "And the better way is to punch an unsuspecting Catti-brie?" he asked, his voice dripping with sarcasm, his patience for the man fast running out.

Wulfgar locked stares with Drizzt, and again the drow's hands went to his scimitar hilts. He could hardly believe the level of anger rising within him, overwhelming his compassion for his sorely tormented friend. He understood that if Wulfgar did try to strike at him, he would fight the man without holding back.

"I look at you now and remember that you are my friend," Wulfgar said, relaxing his tense posture enough to assure Drizzt that he did not mean to strike out. "And yet those reminders come only with strong will-power. Easier it is for me to hate you, and hate everything around me, and on those occasions when I do not immediately summon the willpower to remember the truth, I will strike out."

"As you did with Catti-brie," Drizzt replied, and his tone was not accusatory, but rather showed a sincere attempt to understand and empathize.

Wulfgar nodded. "I did not even recognize that it was her," he said. "It was just another of Errtu's fiends, the worst kind, the kind that tempted me and defeated my willpower, and then left me not with burns or wounds but with the weight of guilt, with the knowledge of failure. I wanted to resist. . . . I . . ."

"Enough, my friend," Drizzt said quietly. "You shoulder blame where you should not. It was no failure of Wulfgar, but the unending cruelty of Errtu."

"It was both," said a defeated Wulfgar. "And that failure compounds with every moment of weakness."

"We will speak with Bruenor," Drizzt assured him. "We will use this incident as a guide and learn from it."

"You may say to Bruenor whatever you choose," the big man said, his tone suddenly turning ice cold once more. "For I will not be there to hear it."

"You will return to your own people?" Drizzt asked, though he knew in his heart that the barbarian wasn't saying any such thing.

"I will find whatever road I choose," Wulfgar replied. "Alone."

"I once played this game."

"Game?" the big man echoed incredulously. "I have never been more serious in all my life. Now go back to them, back where you belong. When you think of me, think of the man I once was, the man who would never strike Catti-brie."

Drizzt started to reply, but stopped himself and stood studying his broken friend. In truth, he had nothing to say that might comfort Wulfgar. While he wanted to believe that he and the others could help coax the man back to rational behavior, he wasn't certain of it. Not at all. Would Wulfgar strike out again, at Catti-brie, or at any of them, perhaps hurting one of them severely? Would the big man's return to the group facilitate a true fight between him and Bruenor, or between him and Drizzt? Or would Catti-brie, in self-defense, drive Khazid'hea, her deadly sword, deep into the man's chest? On the surface, these fears all rang as preposterous in the drow's mind, but after watching Wulfgar carefully these past few days, he could not dismiss the troublesome possibility.

And perhaps worst of all, he had to consider his own feelings when he had seen the battered Catti-brie. He hadn't been the least bit surprised.

Wulfgar started away, and Drizzt instinctively grabbed him by the forearm.

Wulfgar spun and threw the drow's hand aside. "Farewell, Drizzt Do'Urden," he said sincerely, and those words conveyed many of his unspoken thoughts to Drizzt. A longing to go with the drow back to the group, a plea that things could be as they had once been, the friends, the companions of the hall, running down the road to adventure. And most of all, in that lucid tone, words spoken so clearly and deliberately and thoughtfully, they brought to Drizzt a sense of finality. He could not stop Wulfgar, short of hamstringing the man with a scimitar. And in his heart, at that terrible moment, he knew that he should not stop Wulfgar.

"Find yourself," Drizzt said, "and then find us."

"Perhaps," was all that Wulfgar could offer. Without looking back, he walked away.

For Drizzt Do'Urden, the walk back to the wagon to rejoin his friends was the longest journey of his life.

Part 2

Walking the Roads
of Danger

We each have our own path to tread. That seems such a simple and obvious thought, but in a world of relationships where so many people sublimate their own true feelings and desires in consideration of others, we take many steps off that true path.

In the end, though, if we are to be truly happy, we must follow our hearts and find our way alone. I learned that truth when I walked out of Menzoberranzan and confirmed my path when I arrived in Icewind Dale and found these wonderful friends. After the last brutal fight in Mithral Hall, when half of Menzoberranzan, it seemed, marched to destroy the dwarves, I knew that my path lay elsewhere, that I needed to journey, to find a new horizon on which to set my gaze. Catti-brie knew it too, and because I understood that her desire to go along was not in sympathy to my desires but true to her own heart, I welcomed the company.

We each have our own path to tread, and so I learned, painfully, that fateful morning in the mountains, that Wulfgar had found one that diverged from my own. How I wanted to stop him! How I wanted to plead with him or, if that failed, to beat him into unconsciousness and drag him back to the camp. When we parted, I felt a hole in my heart nearly as profound as that which I had felt when I first learned of his apparent death in the fight against the yochlol.

And then, after I walked away, pangs of guilt layered above the pain of loss. Had I let Wulfgar go so easily because of his relationship with Catti-brie? Was there some place within me that saw my barbarian friend's return as a hindrance to a relationship that I had been building with the woman since we had ridden from Mithral Hall together?

The guilt could find no true hold and was gone by the time I rejoined my companions. As I had my road to walk, and now Wulfgar his, so too would Catti-brie find hers. With me? With Wulfgar? Who could know? But whatever her road, I would not try to alter it in such a manner. I did not let Wulfgar go easily for any sense of personal gain. Not at all, for indeed my heart weighed heavy. No, I let Wulfgar go without much of an argument because I knew that there was nothing I, or our other friends, could do to heal the wounds within him. Nothing I could say to him could bring him solace, and if Catti-brie had begun to make any progress, then surely it had been destroyed in the flick of Wulfgar's fist slamming into her face.

Partly it was fear that drove Wulfgar from us. He believed that he could not control the demons within him and that, in the grasp of those pain-ful recollections, he might truly hurt one of us. Mostly, though, Wulfgar left us because of shame. How could he face Bruenor again after striking Catti-brie? How could he face Catti-brie? What words might he say in apology when in truth, and he knew it, it very well might happen again? And beyond that one act, Wulfgar perceived himself as weak because the images of Errtu's legacy were so overwhelming him. Logically, they were but memories and nothing tangible to attack the strong man. To Wulfgar's pragmatic view of the world, being defeated by mere memories equated to great weakness. In his culture, being defeated in battle is no cause for shame, but running from battle is the highest dishonor. Along that same line of reasoning, being unable to defeat a great monster is acceptable, but being defeated by an intangible thing such as a memory equates with cowardice.

He will learn better, I believe. He will come to understand the he should feel no shame for his inability to cope with the persistent horrors and temp-tations of Errtu and the Abyss. And then, when he relieves himself from the burden of shame, he will find a way to truly overcome those horrors and dismiss his guilt over the temptations. Only then will he return to Icewind Dale, to those who love him and who will welcome him back eagerly.

Only then.

That is my hope, not my expectation. Wulfgar ran off into the wilds, into the Spine of the World, where yetis and giants and goblin tribes make their homes, where wolves will take their food as they find it, whether hunt-ing a deer or a man. I do not honestly know if he means to come out of the mountains back to the tundra he knows well, or to the more civilized south-land, or if he will wander the high and dangerous trails, daring death in an attempt to restore some of the courage he believes he has lost. Or perhaps he will tempt death too greatly, so that it will finally win out and put an end to his pain.

That is my fear.

I do not know. We each have our own roads to tread, and Wulfgar has found his, and it is a path, I understand, that is not wide enough for a companion.

—Drizzt Do'Urden

Chapter 8

Inadvertent Signals

They moved somberly, for the thrill of adventure and the joy of being reunited and on the road again had been stolen by Wulfgar's departure. When he returned to camp and explained the barbarian's absence, Drizzt had been truly surprised by the reactions of his companions. At first, predictably, Catti-brie and Regis had screamed that they must go and find the man, while Bruenor just grumbled about "stupid humans." Both the halfling and the woman had calmed quickly, though, and it turned out to be Catti-brie's voice above all the others proclaiming that Wulfgar needed to choose his own course. She was not bitter about the attack and to her credit showed no anger toward the barbarian at all.

But she knew. Like Drizzt, she understood that the inner demons tormenting Wulfgar could not be excised with comforting words from friends, or even through the fury of battle. She had tried and had thought that she was making some progress, but in the end it had become painfully apparent to her that she could do nothing to help the man, that Wulfgar had to help himself.

And so they went on, the four friends and Guenhwyvar, keeping their word to guide Camlaine's wagon out of the dale and along the south road.

That night, Drizzt found Catti-brie on the eastern edge of the encampment, staring out into the blackness, and it was not hard for the drow to figure out what she was hoping to spot.

"He will not return to us any time soon," Drizzt remarked quietly, moving to the woman's side.

Catti-brie glanced at him only briefly, then turned her eyes back to the dark silhouettes of the mountains.

There was nothing to see.

"He chose wrong," the woman said softly after several long and silent moments had slipped past. "I'm knowin' that he has to help himself, but he could've done that among his friends, not out in the wilds."

"He did not want us to witness his most personal battles," Drizzt explained.

"Ever was pride Wulfgar's greatest failing," Catti-brie quickly replied.

"That is the way of his people, the way of his father, and his father's father before him," the ranger said. "The tundra barbarians do not accept weakness in others or in themselves, and Wulfgar believes that his inability to defeat mere memories is naught more than weakness."

Catti-brie shook her head. She didn't have to speak the words aloud, for both she and Drizzt understood that the man was purely wrong in that belief, that, many times, the most powerful foes are those within.

Drizzt reached up then and brushed a finger gently along the side of Catti-brie's nose, the area that had swelled badly from Wulfgar's punch. Catti-brie winced at first, but it was only because she had not expected the touch, and not from any real pain.

"It's not so bad," she said.

"Bruenor might not agree with you," the drow replied.

That brought a smile to Catti-brie's face, for indeed, if Drizzt had brought Wulfgar back soon after the assault, it would have taken all of them to pull the vicious dwarf off the man. But even that had changed now, they both knew. Wulfgar had been as a son to Bruenor for many years, and the dwarf had been purely devastated, more so than any of the others, after the man's apparent death. Now, in the realization that Wulfgar's troubles had taken him from them again, Bruenor sorely missed the man, and surely would forgive him his strike against Catti-brie . . . as long as the barbarian was properly contrite. They all would have forgiven Wulfgar, completely and without judgment, and would have helped him in any way they could to overcome his emotional obstacles. That was the tragedy of it all, for they had no help to offer that would be of any real value.

Drizzt and Catti-brie sat together long into the night, staring at the empty tundra, the woman resting her head on the strong shoulder of the drow.

The next two days and nights on the road proved peacefully uneventful, except that Drizzt more than once spotted the tracks of Regis's giant friend, apparently shadowing their movements. Still, the behemoth made no approach near the camp, so the drow did not become overly concerned. By the middle of the third day after Wulfgar's departure, they came in sight of the city of Luskan.

"Your destination, Camlaine," the drow noted when the driver called out that he could see the distinctive skyline of Luskan, including the treelike structure that marked the city's wizard guild. "It has been our pleasure to travel with you."

"And eat your fine food!" Regis added happily, drawing a laugh from everyone.

"Perhaps if you are still in the southland when we return, and intent on heading back to the dale, we will accompany you again," Drizzt finished.

"And glad we will all be for the company," the merchant replied, warmly clasping the drow's hand. "Farewell, wherever your road may take you, though I offer the parting as a courtesy only, for I do not doubt that you shall fare well indeed! Let the monsters take note of your passing and hide their heads low."

The wagon rolled away, down the fairly smooth road to Luskan. The four friends watched it for a long time.

"We could go in with him," Regis offered. "You are known well enough down there, I would guess," he added to the drow. "Your heritage should not bring us any problems . . ."

Drizzt shook his head before the halfling even finished the thought. "I can indeed walk freely through Luskan," he said, "but my course, our course, is to the southeast. A long, long road lies ahead of us."

"But in Luskan—" Regis started.

"Rumblebelly's thinkin' that me boy might be in there," Bruenor bluntly cut in. From the dwarf's tone it seemed that he, too, considered following the merchant wagon.

"He might indeed," Drizzt said. "And I hope that he is, for Luskan is not nearly as dangerous as the wilds of the Spine of the World."

Bruenor and Regis looked at him curiously, for if he agreed with their reasoning, why weren't they following the merchant?

"If Wulfgar's in Luskan, then better by far that we're turning away now," Catti-brie answered for Drizzt. "We're not wanting to find him now."

"What're ye sayin'?" the flustered dwarf demanded.

"Wulfgar walked away from us," Drizzt reminded. "Of his own accord. Do you believe that three days' time has changed anything?"

"We're not for knowin' unless we ask," said Bruenor, but his tone was less argumentative, and the brutal truth of the situation began to sink in. Of course Bruenor, and all of them, wanted to find Wulfgar and wanted the man to recant his decision to leave. But of course that would not happen.

107

"If we find him now, we'll only push him further from us," Catti-brie said.

"He will grow angry at first because he will see us as meddling," Drizzt agreed. "And then, when his anger at last fades, if it ever does, he will be even more ashamed of his actions."

Bruenor snorted and threw his hands up in defeat.

They all took a last look at Luskan, hoping that Wulfgar was there, then they walked past the place. They headed southeast, flanking the city, then down the southern road with a week's travel before them to the city of Waterdeep. There they hoped to ride with a merchant ship to the south, to Baldur's Gate, and then up river to the city of Iriaebor. There they would take to the open road again, across several hundred miles of the Shining Plains to Caradoon and the Spirit Soaring. Regis had planned the journey, using maps and merchant sources back in Bryn Shander. The halfling had chosen Waterdeep as their best departure point over the closer Luskan because ships left Waterdeep's great harbor every day, with many traveling to Baldur's Gate. In truth, he wasn't sure, nor were any of the others, if this was the best course or not. The maps available in Icewind Dale were far from complete, and far from current. Drizzt and Catti-brie, the only two of the group to have traveled to the Spirit Soaring, had done so magically, with no understanding of the lay of the land.

Still, despite the careful planning the halfling had done, each of them began doubting their ambitious travel plans throughout that day as they passed the city. Those plans had been formed out of a love for the road and adventure, a desire to take in the sights of their grand world, and a supreme confidence in their abilities to get through. Now, though, with Wulfgar's departure, that love and confidence had been severely shaken. Perhaps they would be better off going into Luskan to the notable wizards' guild and hiring a mage to magically contact Cadderly so that the powerful cleric might wind walk to them and finish this business quickly. Or perhaps the Lords of Waterdeep, renowned throughout the lands for their dedication to justice and their power to carry it out, would take the crystal artifact off the companions' hands and, as Cadderly had vowed, find the means to destroy it.

If any of the four had spoken aloud their mounting doubts about the journey that morning, the trip might have been abandoned. But because of their confusion over Wulfgar's departure, and because none of them wanted to admit that they could not focus on another mission while their dear friend was in danger, they held their tongues, sharing thoughts but not words. By the time the sun disappeared into the vast waters to the west, the city of Luskan and the hopes of finding Wulfgar were long out of sight.

Regis's giant friend, though, continued to shadow their movements. Even as Bruenor, Catti-brie, and the halfling prepared the camp, Drizzt and Guenhwyvar came upon the huge tracks, leading down to a copse of trees less than three hundred yards from the bluff they had chosen as a sight. Now the giant's movements could no longer be dismissed as coincidence, for they had left the Spine of the World far behind, and few giants ever wandered into this civilized region where townsfolk would form militias and hunt them down whenever they were spotted.

By the time Drizzt got back to camp, the halfling was fast asleep, several empty plates scattered about his bedroll. "It is time we confront our large shadow," the ranger explained to the other two as he moved over and gave Regis a good shake.

"So ye're meanin' to let us in on yer battle plans this time," Bruenor replied sarcastically.

"I hope there will be no battle," the drow answered. "To our knowledge, this particular giant has posed no threat to wagons rolling along the road in Icewind Dale, and so I find no reason to fight the creature. Better that we convince it to go back to its home without drawing sword."

A sleepy-eyed Regis sat up and glanced around, then rolled back down under his covers—almost, for quick-handed Drizzt caught him halfway back to the comfort zone and roughly pulled him to his feet.

"Not my watch!" the halfling complained.

"You brought the giant to us, and so you shall convince him to leave," the drow replied.

"The giant?" Regis asked, still not catching on to the meaning of it all.

"Yer big friend," Bruenor explained. "He's followin' us, and we're thinking it's past time he goes home. Now, ye come along with yer tricky gem and make him leave, or we'll cut him down where he stands."

Regis's expression showed that he didn't much like that prospect. The giant had served him well in the fight, and he had to admit a certain fondness for the big brute. He shook his head vigorously, trying to clear the cobwebs, then patted his full belly and retrieved his shoes. Even though he was moving as fast as he ever moved, the others were already out of the encampment by the time he was ready to follow.

Drizzt was first into the copse, with Guenhwyvar flanking him. The drow stayed along the ground, picking a clear route away from dried leaves and snapping twigs, silent as a shadow, while Guenhwyvar sometimes padded along the ground and sometimes took to the secure low branches of thick trees. The giant was making no real effort to conceal itself and even had a fairly large fire going. The light guided the two companions and then the other three trailing them.

Still a dozen yards away, Drizzt heard the rhythmic snoring, but then, barely two steps later he heard a loud rustle as the giant apparently woke up and jumped to his feet. Drizzt froze in place and scanned the area, seeking any scouts who might have alerted the behemoth, but there was nothing, no evident creatures and no noise at all save the continuous gentle hissing of the wind through the new leaves.

Convinced that the giant was alone, the drow moved on, coming to a clearing. The fire and the behemoth, and it was indeed Junger, were plainly visible across the way. Out stepped Drizzt, and the giant hardly seemed surprised.

"Strange that we should meet again," the drow remarked, resting his forearms comfortably across the hilts of his sheathed weapons and assuming an unthreatening posture. "I had thought you returned to your mountain home."

"It bade me otherwise," Junger said, and again the drow was taken aback by the giant's command of language and sophisticated dialect.

"It?" the drow asked.

"Some calls cannot be unanswered, you understand," the giant replied.

"Regis," Drizzt called back over his shoulder, and he heard the commotion as his three friends, all of them quiet by the standards of their respective races but clamorous indeed by the standards of the dark elf, moved through the forest behind him. Hardly turning his head, for he did not want to further alert the giant, Drizzt did take note of Guenhwyvar, padding quietly along a branch to the behemoth's left flank. She stopped within easy springing distance of the giant's head. "The halfling will bring it," Drizzt explained. "Perhaps then the call will be better understood and abated."

The giant's big face screwed up with confusion. "The halfling?" he echoed skeptically.

Bruenor crashed through the brush to stand beside the drow, then Catti-brie behind him, her deadly bow in hand, and finally, Regis, coming out complaining about a scratch one branch had just inflicted on his cherubic face.

"It bade Junger to follow us," the drow explained, indicating the ruby pendant. "Show him a better course."

Smiling ear to ear, Regis stepped forward and pulled out the chain and ruby pendant, starting the mesmerizing gem on a gentle swing.

"Get back, little rodent," the giant boomed, averting his eyes from the halfling. "I'll tolerate none of your tricks this time!"

"But it's calling to you," Regis protested, holding the gem out even further and flicking it with a finger of his free hand to set it spinning, its many facets catching the firelight in a dazzling display.

"So it is," the giant replied. "Thus my business is not with you."

"But I hold the gem."

"Gem?" the giant echoed. "What do I care for any such meager treasures when measured against the promises of Crenshinibon?"

That proclamation widened the eyes of the companions, except for Regis, who was so entranced by his own gem-twirling that the behemoth's words didn't even register with him. "Oh, but just look at how it spins!" he said happily. "It calls to you, its dearest friend, and bids you—" Regis ended with a squeaky "Hey!" as Bruenor rushed up and yanked him

110

backward so forcefully that it took him right off the ground. He landed beside Drizzt and skittered backward in a futile attempt to hold his balance, but tripped anyway, tumbling hard into the brush.

Junger came forward in a rush, reaching as if to slap the dwarf aside, but a silver-streaking arrow sizzled past his head, and the giant jolted upright, startled.

"The next one takes yer face," Catti-brie promised.

Bruenor eased back to join the woman and the drow.

"You have foolishly followed an errant call," Drizzt said calmly, trying very hard to keep the situation under control. The ranger held no love for giants, to be sure, but he almost felt sympathy for this poor misguided fool. "Crenshinibon? What is Crenshinibon?"

"Oh, you know well," the giant replied. "You above all others, dark elf. You are the possessor, but Crenshinibon rejects you and has selected me as your successor."

"All that I truly know about you is your name, giant," the drow gently replied. "Ever has your kind been at war with the smaller folk of the world, and yet I offer you this one chance to turn back for the Spine of the World, back to your home."

"And so I shall," the giant replied with a chuckle, crossing his ankles calmly and leaning on a tree for support. "As soon as I have Crenshinibon." The cunning behemoth exploded into motion, tearing a thick limb from the tree and launching it at the friends, mostly to force Catti-brie and that nasty bow to dive aside. Junger strode forward and was stunned to find the drow already in swift motion, scimitars drawn, rushing between his legs and slicing away.

Even as the giant turned to catch Drizzt as he rushed out behind him, Bruenor came in hard. The dwarf's axe chopped for the tendon at the back of the behemoth's ankle, and then, suddenly, six hundred pounds of panther crashed against the turning giant's shoulder and head, knocking him off-balance. He would have held his footing, except that Catti-brie drove an arrow into his lower back. Howling and spinning, Junger went down. Drizzt, Bruenor and Guenhwyvar all skittered out of harm's way.

"Go home!" Drizzt called to the brute as he struggled to his hands and knees.

With a defiant roar, the giant dived out at the drow, arms outstretched. He pulled his arms in fast, both hands suddenly bleeding from deep scimitar gashes, and then he jerked in pain as Catti-brie's next arrow drove into his hip.

Drizzt started to call out again, wanting to reason with the brute, but Bruenor had heard enough. The dwarf rushed up the prone giant's back, quick-stepping to hold his balance as the creature tried to roll him off. The dwarf leaped over the giant's turning shoulder, coming down squarely atop his collarbone. Bruenor's axe came down fast, quicker to the strike than the giant's reaching hands. The axe cut deep into Junger's face.

Huge hands clamped around Bruenor, but they had little strength left. Guenhwyvar leaped in and caught one of the giant's arms, bringing it down under her weight, pinning the hand with claws and teeth. Catti-brie blew the other arm from the dwarf with a perfectly aimed shot.

Bruenor held his ground, leaning down on the embedded axe, and at last, the giant lay still.

Regis came out of the brush and gave a kick at the branch the giant had thrown their way. "Worms in an apple!" he complained. "Why'd you kill him?"

"Ye're seein' a choice?" Bruenor called back incredulously, then he braced himself and tugged his axe from the split head. "I'm not for talking to five thousand pounds of enemy."

"I take no pleasure in that kill," Drizzt admitted. He wiped his blades on the fallen behemoth's tunic, then slid them into their sheaths. "Better for all of us that the giant simply went home."

"And I could have convinced him to do so," Regis argued.

"No," the drow answered. "Your pendant is powerful, I do not doubt, but it has no strength over one entranced by Crenshinibon." As he spoke, he opened his belt pouch and produced the artifact, the famed crystal shard.

"Ye hold it out, and its call'll be all the louder," Bruenor said grimly. "I'm thinkin' we might be finding a long road ahead of us."

"Let it bring the monsters in," Catti-brie said. "It'll make our task in killing them all the easier."

The coldness of her tone caught them all by surprise, but only for the moment it took them to look back at her and see the bruise on her face and remember the cause of her bad mood.

"Ye notice that the damned thing's not working on any of us," the woman reasoned. "So it seems that any falling under its spell are deservin' what they'll find at our hands."

"It does appear that Crenshinibon's power to corrupt extends only to those already of an evil weal," Drizzt agreed.

"And so our road'll be a bit more exciting," Catti-brie said. She didn't bother to add that in this light, she wished Wulfgar was with them. She knew the others were no doubt thinking the exact same thing.

They searched the giant's camp, then turned back to their own fire. Given the new realization that the crystal shard might be working against them, might be reaching out to any nearby monsters in an attempt to get free of the friends, they decided to double their watches from that point forward, two asleep and two awake.

Regis was not pleased.

Chapter 9

Gaining Approval

From the shadows he watched the wizard walk slowly through the door. Other voices followed LaValle in from the corridor, but the wizard hardly acknowledged them, just shut the door and moved to his private stock liquor cabinet at the side of the audience room, lighting only a single candle atop it.

Entreri clenched his hands eagerly, torn as to whether he should confront the wizard verbally or merely kill the man for not informing him of Dog Perry's attack.

Cup in one hand, burning taper in the other, LaValle moved from the cabinet to a larger standing candelabra. The room brightened with each touch as another candle flared to life. Behind the occupied wizard, Entreri stepped into the open.

His warrior senses put him on his guard immediately. Something— but what?—at the very edges of his consciousness alerted him. Perhaps it had to do with LaValle's comfortable demeanor or some barely perceptible extraneous noise.

LaValle turned around then and jumped back just a bit upon seeing Entreri standing in the middle of the room. Again the assassin's perceptions nagged at him. The wizard didn't seem frightened or surprised enough.

"Did you believe that Dog Perry would defeat me?" Entreri asked sarcastically.

"Dog Perry?" LaValle came back. "I have not seen the man—"

"Do not lie to me," Entreri calmly interrupted. "I have known you too long, LaValle, to believe such ignorance of you. You watched Dog Perry, without doubt, as you know all the movements of all the players."

"Not all, obviously," the wizard replied dryly, indicating the uninvited man.

Entreri wasn't so sure of that last claim, but he let it pass. "You agreed to warn me when Dog Perry came after me," he said loudly. If the wizard had guild bodyguards nearby, let them hear of his duplicity. "Yet there he was, dagger in hand, with no prior warning from my friend LaValle."

LaValle gave a great sigh and moved to the side, slumping into a chair. "I did indeed know," he admitted. "But I could not act upon that knowledge," he added quickly, for the assassin's eyes narrowed dangerously. "You must understand. All contact with you is forbidden."

"Kelp-enwalled," Entreri remarked.

LaValle held his hands out helplessly.

"I also know that LaValle rarely adheres to such orders," Entreri went on.

"This one was different," came another voice. A slender man, well dressed and coifed, entered the room from the wizard's study.

Entreri's muscles tensed; he had just checked out that room, along with the other two in the wizard's suite, and no one had been in there. Now he knew beyond doubt that he had been expected.

"My guildmaster," LaValle explained. "Quentin Bodeau."

Entreri didn't blink; he had already guessed that much.

"This kelp-enwalling order came not from any particular guild, but from the three most prominent," Quentin Bodeau clarified. "To go against it would have meant eradication."

"Any magical attempt I might have made would have been detected," LaValle tried to explain. He gave a chuckle, trying to break the tension. "I did not believe it would matter, in any case," he said. "I knew that Dog Perry would prove no real test for you."

"If that is so, then why was he allowed to come after me?" Entreri asked, aiming the question at Bodeau.

The guildmaster only shrugged and said, "Rarely have I been able to control all the movements of that one."

"Let that bother you no more," Entreri replied grimly.

Bodeau managed a weak smile. "You must appreciate our position . . ." he started to say.

"I am to believe the word of the man who ordered me murdered?" Entreri asked incredulously.

"I did not—" Bodeau began to argue before being cut off by yet another voice from the wizard's study, a woman's voice.

"If we believed that Quentin Bodeau, or any other ranking member of his guild knew of and approved of the attack, this guild house would be empty of living people."

A tall, dark-haired woman came through the door, flanked by a muscular warrior with a curving black mustache and a more slender man, if it was a man, for Entreri could hardly make out any features under the cowl of the dark cloak. A pair of armored guards strode in behind the trio, and though the last one through the door shut it behind him, Entreri understood that there was likely another one about, probably another wizard. There was no way such a group could have been concealed in the other room, even from his casual glance, without magical aid. Besides, he knew, this group was too comfortable. Even if they were all skilled with weapons, they could not be confident that they alone could bring Entreri down.

"I am Sharlotta Vespers," the woman said, her icy eyes flashing. "I give you Kadran Gordeon and Hand, my fellow lieutenants in the guild of Pasha Basadoni. Yes, he lives still and is glad to see you well."

Entreri knew that to be a lie. If Basadoni were alive the guild would have contacted him much earlier, and in a less dangerous situation.

"Are you affiliated?" Sharlotta asked.

"I was not when I left Calimport, and I only recently came back to the city," the assassin answered.

"Now you are affiliated," Sharlotta purred, and Entreri understood that he was in no position to deny her claim.

* * * * *

So he would not be killed—not now, at least. He would not have to spend his nights looking over his shoulder for would-be assassins nor deal with the impertinent advances of fools like Dog Perry. The Basadoni Guild had claimed him as their own, and though he would be able to go and take jobs wherever he decided, as long as they did not involve the murder of anyone connected with Pasha Basadoni, his primary contacts would be Kadran Gordeon, whom he did not trust, and Hand.

He should have been pleased at the turn of events, he knew, sitting quietly on the roof of the Copper Ante late that night. He couldn't have expected a better course.

And yet, for some reason that he could hardly fathom, Entreri was not pleased in the least. He had his old life back, if he wanted it. With his skills, he knew he could soon return to the glories he had once known. And yet he now understood the limitations of those glories and knew that while he could easily re-ascend to the highest level of assassin in Calimport, that level would hardly be enough to satisfy the emptiness he felt within.

He simply did not wish to go back to his old ways of murder for money.

It was no bout of conscience—nothing like that!—but no thought of that former life sparked any excitement within the man.

Ever the pragmatist, Entreri decided to play it one hour at a time. He went over the side of the roof, silent and sure-footed, picking his way down to the street, then entered through the front door.

All eyes focused on him, but he hardly cared as he made his way across the common room to the door at the back. One halfling approached him there, as if to stop him, but a glare from Entreri backed the little one off, and the assassin pushed through.

Again the sight of the enormously fat Dondon assaulted him profoundly.

"Artemis!" Dondon said happily, though Entreri did note a bit of tension creeping into the halfling's voice, a common reaction whenever the assassin arrived unannounced at anyone's doorstep. "Come in, my friend. Sit and eat. Partake of good company."

Entreri looked at the heaps of half-eaten sweets and at the two painted female halflings flanking the bloated wretch. He did sit down a safe distance away, though he moved none of the many platters in front of him narrowing his eyes as one of the female halflings tried to approach.

"You must learn to relax and enjoy those fruits your work has provided," Dondon said. "You are back with Basadoni, so 'tis said, and so you are free."

Entreri noted that the irony of that statement was apparently lost on the halfling.

"What good is all of your difficult and dangerous work if you cannot learn to relax and enjoy those pleasures your labors might buy for you?" Dondon asked.

"How did it happen?" Entreri asked bluntly.

Dondon stared at him, obvious confusion splayed on his sagging face.

In explanation, Entreri looked all around, motioning to the plates, to the whores, and to Dondon's massive belly.

Dondon's expression soured. "You know why I am in here," he remarked quietly, all the bounce having left his tone.

"I know why you came in here . . . to hide . . . and I agree with that decision," Entreri replied. "But why?" Again he let the halfling follow his gaze to all the excess, plate by plate, whore by whore. "Why this?"

"I choose to enjoy . . ." Dondon started, but Entreri would hear none of that.

"If I could offer you back your old life, would you take it?" the assassin asked.

Dondon stared at him blankly.

"If I could change the word on the street so that Dondon could walk free of the Copper Ante, would Dondon be pleased?" Entreri pressed. "Or is Dondon pleased with the excuse?"

"You speak in riddles."

"I speak the truth," Entreri shot back, trying to look the halfling in the eye, though the sight of those drooping, sleepy lids surely revolted him. He could hardly believe his own level of anger in looking at Dondon. A part of him wanted to draw out his dagger and cut the wretch's heart out.

But Artemis Entreri did not kill for passion, and he held that part in check.

"Would you go back?" he asked slowly, emphasizing every word.

Dondon didn't reply, didn't blink, but in the nonresponse, Entreri had his answer, the one he had feared the most.

The room's door swung open, and Dwahvel entered. "Is there a problem in here, Master Entreri?" she asked sweetly.

Entreri climbed to his feet and moved for the open door. "None for me," he replied, moving past.

Dwahvel caught him by the arm—a dangerous move indeed! Fortunately for her, Entreri was too absorbed in his contemplation of Dondon to take affront.

"About our deal," the female halfling remarked. "I may have need of your services."

Entreri spent a long while considering those words, wondering why, for some reason, they so assaulted him. He had enough to think about already without having Dwahvel pressing her ridiculous needs upon him. "And what did you give to me in exchange for these services you so desire?" he asked.

"Information," the halfling replied. "As we agreed."

"You told me of the kelp-enwalling, hardly something I could not have discerned on my own," Entreri replied. "Other than that, Dwahvel was of little use to me, and that measure I surely can repay."

The halfling's mouth opened as if she meant to protest, but Entreri just turned away and walked across the common room.

"You may find my doors closed to you," Dwahvel called after him.

In truth, Entreri hardly cared, for he didn't expect that he would desire to see wretched Dondon again. Still, more for effect than any practical gain, he did turn back to let his dangerous gaze settle over the halfling. "That would not be wise," was all he offered before sweeping out of the room and back onto the dark street, then back to the solitude of the rooftops.

Up there, after many minutes of concentration, he came to understand why he so hated Dondon. Because he saw himself. No, he would never allow himself to become so bloated, for gluttony had never been one of his weaknesses, but what he saw was a creature beaten by the weight of life itself, a creature that had surrendered to despair. In Dondon's case it had been simple fear that had defeated him, that had locked him in a room and buried him in lust and gluttony.

In Entreri's case, would it be simple apathy?

He stayed on the roof all the night, but he did not find his answers.

* * * * *

The knock came in the correct sequence, two raps, then three, then two again, so he knew even as he dragged himself out of his bed that it was the Basadoni Guild come calling. Normally Entreri would have taken precautions anyway—normally he would not have slept through half the day—but he did nothing now, didn't even retrieve his dagger. He just went to the door and, without even asking, pulled it open.

He didn't recognize the man standing there, a young and nervous fellow with woolly black hair cut tight to his head, and dark, darting eyes.

"From Kadran Gordeon," the man explained, handing Entreri a rolled parchment.

"Hold!" Entreri said as the nervous young man turned and started away. The man's head spun back to regard the assassin, and Entreri noted one hand slipping under the folds of his light-colored robes, reaching for a weapon no doubt.

"Where is Gordeon?" Entreri asked. "And why did he not deliver this to me personally?"

"Please, good sir," the young man said in his thick Calimshite accent, bowing repeatedly. "I was only told to give that to you."

"By Kadran Gordeon?" Entreri asked.

"Yes," the man said, nodding wildly.

Entreri shut his door, then heard the running footsteps of the relieved man outside retreating down the hall and then the stairs at full speed.

He stood there, considering the parchment and the delivery. Gordeon hadn't even come to him personally, and he understood why. To do so would have been too much an open show of respect. The lieutenants of the guild feared him—not that he would kill them, but more that he would ascend to a rank above them. Now, by using this inconsequential messenger, Gordeon was trying to show Entreri the true pecking order, one that had him just above the bottom rung.

With a resigned shake of his head, a helpless acceptance of the stupidity of it all, the assassin pulled the tie from the parchment and unrolled it. The orders were simple enough, giving a man's name and last known address, with instructions that he should be killed as soon as it could be arranged. That very night, if possible, the next day at the latest.

At the bottom was a last notation that the targeted man had no known guild affiliation, nor was he in particularly good standing with city or merchant guardsmen, nor did he have any known powerful friends or relatives.

Entreri considered that bit of news carefully. Either he was being set up against a very dangerous opponent, or, more likely, Gordeon had given him this pitifully easy hit to demean him, to lessen his credentials. In his former days in Calimport, Entreri's talents had been reserved for the killing of guildmasters or wizards, noblemen, and captains of the guard. Of course, if Gordeon and the other two lieutenants gave him any such difficult tasks and he proved successful, his standing would grow among the community and they would fear his quick ascension through the ranks.

No matter, he decided.

He took one last look at the listed address—a region of Calimport that he knew well—and went to retrieve his tools.

* * * * *

He heard the children crying nearby, for the hovel had only two rooms, and those separated by only a thick drapery. A very homely young woman—Entreri noted as he spied on her from around the edge of the drapery—tended to the children. She begged them to settle down and be quiet, threatening that their father would soon be home.

She came out of the back room a moment later, oblivious to the assassin as he crouched behind another curtain under a side window. Entreri cut a small hole in the drape and watched her movements as she went about her work. Everything was brisk and efficient; she was on edge, he knew.

The door, yet another drape, pushed aside and a young, skinny man entered, his face appearing haggard, eyes sunken back in his skull, several days of beard on his chin and cheeks.

"Did you find it?" the woman asked sharply.

The man shook his head, and it seemed to Entreri that his eyes drooped just a bit more.

"I begged you not to work with them!" the woman scolded. "I knew that no good—"

She stopped short as his eyes widened in horror. He saw, looking over her shoulder, the assassin emerging from behind the draperies. He turned as if to flee, but the woman looked back and cried out.

The man froze in place; he would not leave her.

Entreri watched it all calmly. Had the man continued his retreat, the assassin would have cut him down with a dagger throw before he ever got outside.

"Not my family," the man begged, turning back and walking toward Entreri, his hands out wide, palms open. "And not here."

"You know why I have come?" the assassin asked.

The woman began to cry, muttering for mercy, but her husband grabbed her gently but firmly and pulled her back, angling her for the children's room, then pushing her along.

119

"It was not my fault," the man said quietly when she was gone. "I begged Kadran Gordeon. I told him that I would somehow find the money."

The old Artemis Entreri would not have been intrigued at that point. The old Artemis Entreri would never even have listened to the words. The old Artemis Entreri would have just finished the task and walked out. But now he found that he was interested, mildly, and, as he had no other pressing business, he was in no hurry to finish.

"I will cause no trouble for you if you promise that you will not hurt my family," the man said.

"You believe that you could me cause trouble?" Entreri asked.

The helpless, pitiful man shook his head. "Please," he begged. "I only wished to show them a better life. I agreed to, even welcomed, the job of moving money from Docker's Street to the drop only because in those easy tasks I earned more than a month of labor can bring me in honest work."

Entreri had heard it all before, of course. So many times, fools—camels, they were called—joined into a guild, performing delivery tasks for what seemed to the simple peasants huge amounts of money. The guilds only hired the camels so that rival guilds would not know who was transporting the money. Eventually, though, the other guilds would figure out the routes and the camels, and would steal the shipment. Then the poor camels, if they survived the ambush, would be quickly eliminated by the guild that had hired them.

"You understood the danger of the company you kept," Entreri remarked.

The man nodded. "Only a few deliveries," he replied. "Only a few, and then I would quit."

Entreri laughed and shook his head, considering the fool's absurd plan. One could not "quit" as a camel. Anyone accepting the position would immediately learn too much to ever be allowed out of the guild. There were only two possibilities: first, that the camel would perform well enough and be lucky enough to earn a higher, more permanent position within the guild structure, and second, that the man or woman (for women were often used) would be slain in a raid or subsequently killed by the hiring guild.

"I beg of you, do not do it here," the man said at length. "Not where my wife will hear my last cries, not where my sons will find me dead."

Bitter bile found its way into the back of Entreri's throat. Never had he been so disgusted, never had he seen a more pitiful human being. He looked around again at the hovel, the rags posing as doors, as walls. There was a single plate, probably used for eating by the entire family, sitting on the single old bench in the room.

"How much do you owe?" he asked, and though he could hardly believe the words as he spoke them, he knew that he would not be able to bring himself to kill this wretch.

The man looked at him curiously. "A king's treasure," he said. "Near to thirty gold pieces."

Entreri nodded, then pulled a pouch from his belt, this one hidden around the back under his dark cloak. He felt the weight as he pulled it free and knew that it held at least fifty gold pieces, but he tossed it to the man anyway.

The stunned man caught it and stared at it so intently that Entreri feared his eyeballs would simply fall out of their sockets. Then he looked back to the assassin, his emotions too twisted and turned about for him to have any revealing expression at all on his face.

"On your word that you will not deal with any guilds again once your debt is paid," Entreri said. "Your wife and children deserve better."

The man started to reply, then fell to his knees and started to bow before his savior. Entreri turned about and swept angrily from the hovel, out into the dirty street.

He heard the man's calls following him, cries of thanks and mercy. In truth, and Entreri knew it, there had been no mercy in his actions. He cared nothing for the man or his ugly wife and undoubtedly ugly children. But still he could not kill this pitiful wretch, though he figured he would probably be doing the man a great service if he did put him out of his obvious misery. No, Entreri would not give Kadran Gordeon the satisfaction of putting him through such a dishonorable murder. A camel like this should be work for first year guild members, twelve-year-olds, perhaps, and for Kadran to give such an assignment to one of Entreri's reputation was surely a tremendous insult.

He would not play along.

He stormed down the street to his room at the inn where he collected all his things and set out at once, finally coming to the door of the Copper Ante. He had thought to merely press in, for no better reason than to show Dwahvel how ridiculous her threat to shut him out had been. But then he reconsidered and turned away, in no mood for any dealings with Dwahvel, in no mood for any dealings with anybody.

He found a small, nondescript tavern across town and took a room. Likely he was on the grounds of another guild, and if they found out who he was and who he was affiliated with there might be trouble.

He didn't care.

*　*　*　*　*

A day slipped by unremarkably, but that did little to put Entreri at ease. Much was happening, he knew, and all of it in quiet shadows. He had the wherewithal and understanding of those shadows to go out and discern much, but he hadn't the ambition to do so. He was in a mood to simply let things fall as they might.

He went down to the common room of the little inn that second night, taking his meal to an empty corner, eating alone and hearing nothing

121

of the several conversations going on about the place. He did note the entrance of one character, though, a halfling, and the little folk were not common in this region of the city. Soon enough the halfling found him, taking a seat on the long bench opposite the table from the assassin.

"Good evening to you, fine sir," the little one said. "And how do you find your meal?"

Entreri studied the halfling, understanding that this one held no interest at all in his food. He looked for a weapon on the halfling, though he doubted that Dwahvel would ever be so bold as to move against him.

"Might I taste it?" the halfling said rather loudly, coming forward over the table.

Entreri, picking up the cues, held a spoon of the gruel up but did not extend his arm, allowing the halfling to inconspicuously move even closer.

"I've come from Dwahvel," the little one said as he moved in. "The Basadoni Guild seeks you, and they are in a foul mood. They know where you are and have received permission from the Rakers to come and collect you. Expect them this very night." The halfling took the bite as he finished, then moved back across the table, rubbing his belly.

"Tell Dwahvel that now I am in her debt," Entreri remarked. The little one, with a slight nod, moved back across the room and ordered a bowl of gruel. He took up a conversation with the innkeeper while he was waiting for it and ate it right at the bar, leaving Entreri to his thoughts.

He could flee, the assassin realized, but his heart was not in such a course. No, he decided, let them come and let this be done. He didn't think they meant to kill him in any case. He finished his meal and went back to his room to consider his options. First, he pulled a board from the inner wall, and in the cubby space between that and the outer wall, reaching down to a beam well below the floor in his room, he placed his fabulous jeweled dagger and many of his coins. Then he carefully replaced the board and replaced the dagger on his belt with another from his pack, one that somewhat resembled his signature dagger but without the powerful enchantment. Then, more for appearances than as any deterrent, he wired a basic dart trap about his door and moved across the room, settling into the one chair in the place. He took out some dice and began throwing them on the small night table beside the chair, making up games and passing the hours.

It was late indeed when he heard the first footsteps coming up the stairs—a man obviously trying to be stealthy but making more noise than the skilled Entreri would make even if he were walking normally. Entreri listened more carefully as the walking ceased, and he caught the scrape of a thin slice of metal moving about the crack between the door and the jamb. A fairly skilled thief could get through his impromptu trap in a matter of a couple of minutes, he knew, so he put his hands behind his head and leaned back against the wall.

All the noise stopped, a long and uncomfortable silence.

Entreri sniffed the air; something was burning. For a moment, he thought they might be razing the building around him, but then he recognized the smell, that of burning leather, and as he shifted to look down at his own belt he felt a sharp pain on his collarbone. The chain of a necklace he wore—one that held several lock picks cunningly designed as ornaments—had slipped off his shirt and onto his bare skin.

Only then did the assassin understand that all of his metallic items had grown red hot.

Entreri jumped up and tore the necklace from his neck, then deftly, with a twist of his wrist, dropped his belt and the heated dagger to the floor.

The door burst in, a Basadoni soldier rolling to either side and a third man, crossbow leveled, rushing between them.

He didn't fire, though, nor did the others, their swords in hand, charge in.

Kadran Gordeon walked in behind the bowman.

"A simple knock would have proven as effective," Entreri said dryly, looking down at his glowing equipment. The dagger caused the wood of the floor to send up a trail of black smoke.

In response, Gordeon threw a coin at Entreri's feet, a strange golden coin imprinted with the unicorn head emblem on the side showing to the assassin.

Entreri looked up at Gordeon and merely shrugged.

"The camel was to be killed," Gordeon said.

"He was not worth the effort."

"And that is for you to decide?" the Basadoni lieutenant asked incredulously.

"A minor decision, compared to what I once—"

"Ah!" Gordeon interrupted dramatically. "Therein lies the flaw, Master Entreri. What you once knew, or did, or were told to do, is irrelevant, you see. You are no guildmaster, no lieutenant, not even a full soldier as of yet, and I doubt that ever you will be! You lost your nerve—as I thought you would. You are only gaining approval, and if you survive that time, perhaps, just perhaps, you will find your way back into complete acceptance within the guild."

"Gaining approval?" Entreri echoed with a laugh. "Yours?"

"Take him!" Gordeon instructed the two soldiers who had come in first. As they moved cautiously for the assassin Gordeon added, "The man you tried to save was executed, as were his wife and children."

Entreri hardly heard the words and hardly cared anyway, though he knew that Gordeon had ordered the extended execution merely to throw some pain his way. Now he had a bigger dilemma. Should he allow Gordeon to take him back to the guild, where he would no doubt be physically punished and then released?

No, he would not suffer such treatment by this man or any other. The muscles in his legs, so finely honed, tensed as the two approached, though Entreri seemed perfectly at ease, even held his empty arms out in an unthreatening posture.

The men, swords in hand, came in at his sides, reaching for those arms while the third soldier kept his crossbow steady, aimed at the assassin's heart.

Up into the air went Entreri, a great vertical spring, tucking his legs under him and then kicking out to the sides before the startled soldiers could react, connecting squarely on the faces of both the approaching men and sending them flying away. He did catch the one on his right as he landed, and pulled the man in quickly, just in time to serve as a shield for the firing crossbow. Then he tossed the groaning man to the ground.

"First mistake," he said to Gordeon as the lieutenant drew out a splendid-looking sabre. Off to the side the other kicked soldier climbed back to his feet, but the one on the floor in front of Entreri, a crossbow quarrel deep into his back, wasn't moving. The crossbowman worked hard on the crank, loading another bolt, but even more disturbing for Entreri was the fact that there was obviously a wizard nearby.

"Stay back," Gordeon ordered the man to the side. "I will finish this one."

"To make your reputation?" Entreri asked. "But I have no weapon. How will that sound on the streets of Calimport?"

"After you are dead we will place a weapon in your hand," Gordeon said with a wicked grin. "My men will insist that it was a fair fight."

"Second mistake," Entreri said under his breath, for indeed, it was a fairer fight than the skilled Kadran Gordeon could ever understand. The Basadoni lieutenant came in with a measured thrust, straight ahead, and Entreri slapped his forearm out to intercept, purposely missing the parry but skittering backward out of reach at the same time. Gordeon circle, and so did Entreri. Then the assassin came ahead in a short lunge and was forced back with a slice of the sabre, Gordeon taking care to allow no openings.

But Entreri had no intention of following through his movement anyway. He had only begun it so that he could slightly alter the angle of the circling, putting him in line for his next strike.

On came Gordeon, and Entreri leaped back. When Gordeon kept coming, the assassin went ahead in a short burst, forcing him into a cunning and dangerous parrying maneuver. But again, Entreri didn't follow through. He just fell back to the appropriate spot and, to the surprise of all in the room, stamped his foot hard on the floor.

"What?" Gordeon asked, shaking his head and looking about, for he didn't keep his eyes down at that stamping foot, didn't see the shock of the stamp lift the still-glowing necklace from the floor so that Entreri could hook it about his toe.

A moment later Gordeon came on hard, this time looking for the kill. Out snapped Entreri's foot, launching the necklace at the lieutenant's face. To his credit, the swift-handed Gordeon snapped his free hand across and caught the necklace—as Entreri had expected—but then how he howled, the glowing chain enwrapping his bare hand and digging a fiery line across his flesh.

Entreri was there in the blink of an eye. He slapped the lieutenant's sword arm out wide. Balling both fists, middle knuckles extended forward, he drove his knuckles simultaneously into the man's temples. Clearly dazed, his eyes glossed over, Gordeon's hands slipped to his sides and Entreri snapped his forehead right into the man's face. He caught Gordeon as he fell back and spun him about, then reached through his legs and caught him by one wrist. With a subtle turn to put Gordeon in line with the crossbowman, Entreri pulled hard, through and up, flipping Gordeon right into the startled soldier. The flipped man knocked the crossbow hard enough to dislodge the bolt.

The remaining swordsman came in hard from the side, but he was not a skilled fighter, even by Kadran Gordeon's standards. Entreri easily backed and dodged his awkward, too-far-ahead thrust, then stepped in quickly, before the man could retract and ready the blade. Reaching down and around to catch his sword arm by the wrist, Entreri lifted hard and stepped under that wrist, twisting the arm painfully and stealing the strength from it.

The man came ahead, thinking to grab on for dear life with his free hand. Entreri's palm slapped against the back of his twisted sword hand quicker than he could even comprehend, then bent the hand down low back over the wrist, stealing all strength and sending a wave of pain through the man. A simple slide of the hand had the sword free in Entreri's grasp, and a reversal of grip and deft twist brought it in line.

Entreri retracted his hand, stabbing the blade out and up behind him into the belly and up into the lungs of the hapless soldier.

Moving quickly, not even bothering to pull the sword back out, he spun on the man, thinking to throw him, too, at the crossbowman. And indeed that stubborn archer was once more setting the bolt in place. But a far more dangerous foe appeared, the unseen wizard, rushing down the hallway, robes flapping, across the door. Entreri saw the man lift something slender—a wand, he supposed—but then all he saw was a tumble of arms and legs as the skewered swordsman crashed into the wizard and both went flying away.

"Have I yet gained your approval?" Entreri yelled at the still dazed Gordeon, but he was moving even as he spoke, for the crossbowman had him dead and the wizard was fast regaining his footing. He felt the terrible flash of pain as a quarrel dug through his side, but he gritted his teeth and growled away the pain, putting his arms in front of his face and tucking his legs up defensively as he crashed through the wooden-latticed window, soaring down the ten feet to the street. He turned his legs as he hit, throwing himself into a sidelong roll, and then another to absorb the shock of the fall. He was up and running, not surprised at all when another crossbow quarrel, fired from a completely different direction, embedded itself into the wall right beside him.

All the area erupted with movement as Basadoni soldiers came out of every conceivable hiding place.

Entreri sprinted down one alley, leaped right over a huge man bending low in an attempt to tackle him at the waist, then cut fast around a building. Up to the roof he went, quick as a cat, then across, leaping another alley to another roof, and so on.

He went down the main street, for he knew that his pursuers were expecting him to drop into an alley. He went up fast on the side of one wall, expertly setting himself there, arms and legs splayed wide to find tentative holds and to blend with the contours of the building.

Cries of "Find him!" echoed all about, and many soldiers ran right below his perch, but those cries diminished as the night wore on. Fortunately so for Entreri, who, though he was not losing much blood outwardly, understood that his wound was serious, perhaps even mortal. Finally he was able to slide down from his perch, hardly finding the remaining strength to even stand. He put a hand to his side and felt the warm blood, thick in the folds of his cloak, and felt, too, the very back edge of the deeply embedded quarrel.

He could hardly draw breath now. He knew what that meant.

Luck was with him when he got back to the inn, for the sun had not yet come up, and though there were obviously Basadoni soldiers within the place, few were about the immediate area. Entreri found the window of his room easily enough from the broken wood on the ground and calculated the height of his hidden store. He had to be quiet, for he heard voices, Gordeon's among them, from within his room. Up he went, finding a secure perch, trying hard not to groan, though in truth he wanted to scream from the pain.

He worked the old, weather-beaten wood slowly and quietly until he could pull enough away to retrieve his dagger and small pouch.

"He had to have some magic about him!" he heard Gordeon scream. "Cast your detection again!"

"There is no magic, Master Gordeon," came another voice, the wizard's obviously. "If he had any, then likely he sold it or gave it away before he ever came to this place."

Despite his agony, Entreri managed a smile as he heard Gordeon's subsequent growl and kick. No magic indeed, because they had searched in his room only and not the wall of the room below.

Dagger in hand, the assassin made his way along the still-quiet streets. He hoped to find a Basadoni soldier about, one deserving his wrath, but in truth he doubted he could even muster the strength to

126

beat a novice fighter. What he found instead was a pair of drunks, laying against the side of a building, one sleeping, the other talking to himself.

Silent as death, the assassin stalked in. His jeweled dagger possessed a particularly useful magic, for it could steal the life of a victim and give that energy to its wielder.

Entreri took the talking drunk first, and when he was finished, feeling so much stronger, he bit down hard on a fold of his cloak and yanked the crossbow bolt from his side, nearly fainting as waves of agony assaulted him.

He steadied himself, though, and fell over the sleeping drunk.

He walked out of the alley soon after, showing no signs that he had been so badly wounded. He felt strong again and almost hoped he would find Kadran Gordeon still in the area.

But the fight had only begun, he knew, and despite his supreme skills, he remembered well the extent of the Basadoni Guild and understood that he was sorely overmatched.

*   *   *   *   *

They had watched those intent on killing him enter the inn. They had watched him come crashing through the window in full flight, then run on into the shadows. With eyes superior to those of the Basadoni soldiers, they had spotted him splayed on the wall and silently applauded his stealthy trick. And now, with some measure of relief and many nods that their leader had chosen wisely, they watched him exit the alley. And even he, Artemis Entreri, assassin of assassins, had no idea they were about.

Chapter 10

Unexpected and Unsatisfying Vengeance

Wulfgar moved along the foothills of the Spine of the World easily and swiftly, sincerely hoping that some monster would find him and attack that he might release the frustrating rage boiling within him. On several occasions he found tracks, and he followed them, but he was no ranger. Though he could survive well enough in the harsh climate, his tracking skills were nowhere near as strong as those of his drow friend.

Nor was his sense of direction. When he came over one ridge the very next day, he was surprised indeed to see that he had cut diagonally right through the corner of the great mountain range, for from this high vantage point all the southland seemed to spread wide before him. Wulfgar looked back to the mountains, thinking that his chances for finding a fight would be much better in there, but inevitably his gaze swung back to the open fields, the dark clusters of forest, and the many long and unknown roads. He felt a pull in his heart, a longing for distance and open expanses, a desire to break the bounds of his boxed-in life in Icewind Dale. Perhaps out there he might find new experiences that would allow him to dismiss all the tumult of images that whirled in his thoughts. Perhaps divorced from the everyday familiar routines he could also find distance from the horrors of his memories of the Abyss.

Nodding to himself, Wulfgar started down the steep southern expanse. He found another set of tracks—orc, most likely—a couple hours later, but this time he passed them by. He was out of the mountains as the sun disappeared below the western horizon. He stood watching the sunset. Great orange and red flames gathered in the bellies of dark clouds, filling the western sky with brilliant striped patterns. The occasional twinkling star became visible against the pale blue wherever the clouds broke apart. He held that pose as all color faded, as darkness crept across the fields and the sky, broken clouds rushing past overhead. Stars seemed to blink on and off. This was the moment of renewal, Wulfgar decided. This was the moment of his rebirth, a clean beginning for a man alone in the world, a man determined to focus on the present and not the past, determined to let the future sort itself out.

He moved away from the mountains and camped under the spreading boughs of a fir tree. Despite his determination, his nightmares found him there.

Still, the next day Wulfgar's stride was long and swift, covering the miles, following the wind or a bird's flight or the bank of a spring creek.

He found plenty of game and plenty of berries. Each passing day he felt as though his stride was less shackled by his past, and each night the terrible dreams seemed to grab a him a bit less.

But then one day he came upon a curious totem, a low pole set in the ground with its top carved to resemble the pegasus, the winged horse, and suddenly Wulfgar found himself vaulted back into a very distinct memory, an incident that had occurred many years before when he was on the road with Drizzt, Bruenor, and Regis seeking the dwarf's ancestral home of Mithral Hall. Part of him wanted to turn away from that totem, to run far from this place, but one particular memory, a vow of vengeance, nagged at him. Hardly registering the movements, Wulfgar found a recent trail and followed it, soon coming to a hillock, and from the top of that bluff he spied the encampment, a cluster of deerskin tents with people, tall and strong and dark-haired, moving all about.

"Sky Ponies," Wulfgar whispered, remembering well the barbarian tribe that had come into a battle he and his friends had fought against an orc group. After the orcs had been cut down, Wulfgar, Bruenor, and Regis had been taken prisoner. They had been treated fairly well, and Wulfgar had been offered a challenge of strength, which he easily won, against the son of the chieftain. And then, in honorable barbarian tradition, Wulfgar had been offered a place among the tribesmen. Unfortunately, for a test of loyalty Wulfgar had been asked to slay Regis, and that he could never do. With Drizzt's help, the friends had escaped, but then the shaman, Valric High Eye, had used evil magic to transform Torlin, the chieftain's son, into a hideous ghost spirit.

They defeated that spirit. When honorable Torlin's deformed, broken body lay at his feet, Wulfgar, son of Beornegar, had vowed vengeance against Valric High Eye.

The barbarian felt the clamminess in his strong hands—hands subconsciously wringing about the handle of his powerful warhammer. He squinted into the distance, staring hard at the encampment, and discerned a skinny, agitated form that might have been Valric skipping past one tent.

Valric might not even still be alive, Wulfgar reminded himself, for the shaman had been very old those years ago. Again a large part of Wulfgar wanted to sprint down the other side of the hillock, to run far away from this encounter and any other that would remind him of his past.

The image of Torlin's broken, mutilated body, half man, half winged horse, stayed clear in his thoughts, though, and he could not turn away.

Within the hour, he stared at the encampment from a much closer perspective, close enough to see the individuals.

Close enough to understand that the Sky Ponies had fallen on hard times. And into difficult battles, he realized, for many wounded sat about the camp, and the overall numbers of tents and folk seemed much reduced from what he remembered. Most of the folk in camp were women or very old or very young. A string of more than two-score poles to the south helped to clear up the mystery, for upon them were set the heads of orcs, the occasional carrion bird fluttering down to find a perch in scraggly hair, poking down to find a feast of an eyeball or the side of a nostril.

The sight of the Sky Ponies so obviously diminished pained Wulfgar greatly, for though he had sworn vengeance on their shaman, he knew them to be an honorable people, much like his own in tradition and practice. He thought then that he should leave them, but even as he turned to go, one tent flap at the corner of his line of vision pushed open and out hopped a skinny man, ancient but full of energy, wearing white robes that feathered out like the wings of a bird whenever he raised his arms, and even more telling, an eye patch set with a huge emerald. Barbarians lowered their gazes wherever he passed; one child even rushed up to him and kissed the back of his hand.

"Valric," Wulfgar muttered, for there could be no mistaking the shaman.

Wulfgar came up from the grass in a steady, determined walk, Aegisfang swinging at the end of one arm. The mere fact that he broke through the camp's perimeter without being assaulted showed him just how disorganized and decimated this tribe truly was, for no barbarian tribe would ever be caught so off guard.

Yet Wulfgar had passed the first tents, had moved close enough to Valric High Eye for the shaman to see him and stare at him incredulously before the first warrior, a tall, older man, strong but very lean, moved to block him.

The warrior came in swinging, not talking, launching a sidelong sweep with a heavy club, but Wulfgar, quicker than the man could anticipate,

131

stepped ahead and caught the club in his free hand before it could gain too much momentum, and then, with strength beyond anything the man had ever imagined, turned his wrist and pulled the weapon free, tossing it far to the side. The warrior howled and charged right in, but Wulfgar got his arm across between himself and the man. With a mighty sweep of his arm, Wulfgar sent the man stumbling away.

All the camp's warriors, not nearly as many as Wulfgar remembered from the Sky Ponies, were out then, flanking Valric, forming a semicircle from the shaman out to the sides of the huge intruder. Wulfgar did turn his gaze from the hated Valric long enough to scrutinize the group, long enough to take note that these were not strong men of prime warrior age. They were too young or too old. The Sky Ponies, he understood, had recently fought a tremendous battle and had not fared well.

"Who are you who comes uninvited?" asked one man, large and strong but very old.

Wulfgar looked hard at the speaker, at the keen set of his eyes, the peppered gray hair in a tousled mop, thick indeed for one his age, at the firm and proud set of his jaw. He reminded Wulfgar of another Sky Pony he had once met, an honorable and brave warrior, and that, combined with the fact that the man had spoken above all others, and even before Valric, confirmed Wulfgar's suspicions.

"Father of Torlin," he said, and gave a bow.

The man's eyes widened with surprise. He seemed as if he wanted to respond but could find no words.

"Jerek Wolf Slayer!" Valric shrieked. "Chieftain of the Sky Ponies. Who are you who comes uninvited? Who are you who speaks of Jerek's long-lost son?"

"Lost?" Wulfgar echoed skeptically.

"Taken by the gods," Valric replied, waving his feathered arms. "A hunting quest, turned to vision quest."

A wry smile made its way onto Wulfgar's face as he came to comprehend the tremendous, decade-old lie. Torlin, mutated into a ghastly and ghostly creature had been sent out by Valric to hunt Wulfgar and his companions and had died horribly on the field at their hands. But Valric, likely not wanting to face Jerek with the horrid news, had somehow manipulated the truth, had concocted a story that would keep Jerek in check. A hunting quest or a vision quest, both god-inspired, might last years, even decades.

Wulfgar realized that he had to handle this delicately now, for any wrong or too-harsh statements might provoke the wrath of Jerek.

"The hunting quest did not last," he said. "For the gods, our gods, recognized the wrongness of it."

Valric's eyes widened indeed, for the first time showing some measure of recognition. "Who are you?" he asked again, a hint of a tremor edging his voice.

132

"Do you not remember, Valric High Eye?" Wulfgar asked, striding forward, and his movement caused those flanking the shaman to step forward as well. "Have the Sky Ponies so soon forgotten the face of Wulfgar, son of Beornegar?"

Valric tilted his head, his expression showing that Wulfgar had hit a chord of recognition there, but only vaguely.

"Have the Sky Ponies so soon forgotten the northerner they invited to join their ranks, the northerner who traveled with a dwarf, and a halfling, and," he paused, knowing that his next words would bring complete recognition, "a black-skinned elf?"

Valric's eyes nearly rolled out of their sockets. "You!" he said, poking his trembling finger into the air.

The mention of the drow, probably the only dark elf any of these barbarians had ever seen, sparked the memories of many others. Whispered conversations erupted, and many barbarians grasped their weapons tightly, awaiting only a single word to begin their attack and slaughter of the intruder.

Wulfgar calmly held his ground. "I am Wulfgar, son of Beornegar," he repeated firmly, focusing his gaze on Jerek Wolf Slayer. "No enemy of the Sky Ponies. Distant kin to your people and to your ways. I have returned, as I vowed I would, when I saw dead Torlin on the field."

"Dead Torlin?" many voices from warriors and those huddled behind them echoed.

"My friends and I did not come as enemies of the Sky Ponies," Wulfgar went on, using what he expected to be the last few seconds of dialogue. "Indeed we fought beside you against a common foe and won the day."

"You refused us!" Valric screamed. "You insulted my people!"

"What do you know of my son?" Jerek demanded, pushing the shaman aside and stepping forward.

"I know that Valric quested him with the spirit of the Sky Pony to destroy us," Wulfgar said.

"You admit this, and yet you walk openly into our encampment?" Jerek asked.

"I know that your god was not with Torlin on that hunt, for we defeated the creature he had become."

"Kill him!" Valric screamed. "As we destroyed the orcs that came upon us in the dark of night, so shall we destroy the enemy that walks into our camp this day!"

"Hold!" shouted Jerek, throwing his arms out wide. Not a Sky Pony took a step forward, though they seemed eager now, like a pack of hunting dogs straining against their leashes.

Jerek stepped out, walking to stand before Wulfgar.

Wulfgar locked his gaze with the man, but not before he glanced past Jerek to Valric, the shaman fumbling with a leather pouch—a sacred bundle of mystical and magical components—at his side.

133

"My son is dead?" Jerek, barely a foot from Wulfgar, asked.

"Your god was not with him," Wulfgar replied. "For his cause, Valric's cause, was not just."

He knew before he ever finished that his roundabout manner of telling Jerek had done little to calm the man, that the overriding information, that his son was indeed dead, was too powerful and painful for any explanation or justification. With a roar, the chieftain came at Wulfgar but the younger barbarian was ready, lifting his arm high to raise the intended punch, then snapping his hand down and over Jerek's extended arm, pulling the man off-balance. Wulfgar dropped Aegis-fang and shoved hard on Jerek's chest, releasing his hold and sending the man stumbling backward into the surprised warriors.

Scooping his warhammer as he went, Wulfgar charged forward, but so did the warriors, and the northern barbarian, to his ultimate frustration, knew that he would get nowhere near to Valric. He hoped for an open throwing path that he might take down the shaman before he, too, was killed, but then Valric surprised him, surprised everybody, by leaping forward through the line, howling a chant and throwing a burst of herbs and powders Wulfgar's way.

Wulfgar felt the magical intrusion. Though the other warriors, Jerek included, backed away a few steps, he felt as if great black walls were closing in on him, stealing his strength, forcing him to hold in place.

Waves and waves of immobilizing magic rolled on, Valric hopping about, throwing more powders, strengthening the spell.

Wulfgar felt himself sinking, felt the ground coming up to swallow him.

He was not unfamiliar with such magics, though. Not at all. In his years in the Abyss, Errtu's minions, particularly the wicked succubi, had used similar spells to render him helpless that they might have their way with him. How many times he had felt such intrusions. He had learned how to defeat them.

He put up a wall of the purest rage, warding every magical suggestion of immobility with ten growls of anger, ten memories of Errtu and the succubi. Outwardly, though, the barbarian took great pains to seem defeated, to hold perfectly still, his warhammer dropping down to his side. He heard the chants of "Valric High Eye" and saw out of the corner of his eye several of the warriors turning in ceremonial dance, giving thanks to their god and to Valric, the human manifestation of that god.

"Of what does he speak?" Jerek said to Valric. "What quest fell upon Torlin?"

"As I told you," the skinny shaman replied, dancing out from the lines to stand before Wulfgar. "A drow elf! This man, seeming so honorable, traveled beside a drow elf! Could any but Torlin have taken the beast magic and defeated this deadly foe?"

"You said that Torlin was on a vision quest," Jerek argued.

"And so I believed," Valric lied. "And perhaps he is. Do not believe the lies of this one! Did you see how easily the power of Uthgar defeated him, holding him helpless before us? More likely he returned because his friends, all three, were slain by powerful Torlin, and because he knew that he could not hope to find vengeance any other way, could not hope to defeat Torlin even with the aid of the drow."

"But Wulfgar, son of Beornegar, did defeat Torlin in the contest of strength," another man remarked.

"That was before he angered Uthgar!" Valric howled. "See him standing now, helpless and defeated—"

The word barely got out of his mouth before Wulfgar exploded into action, stepping forward and clamping one hand over the shaman's skinny face. With frightening power, Wulfgar lifted Valric into the air and slammed him back down to his feet repeatedly, then shook him wildly.

"What god, Valric?" he roared. "What claim have you of Uthgar above my own as a warrior of Tempus?" To illustrate his point, and still with only one hand, Wulfgar tightened the bulging muscles in his arm and lifted Valric high into the air and held him there, perfectly steady, ignoring the man's flailing arms. "Had Torlin killed my friends in honorable battle, then I would not have returned for vengeance," he said honestly to Jerek. "I came not to avenge them, for they are well, all three. I came to avenge Torlin, a man of strength and honor, used so terribly by this wretch."

"Valric is our shaman!" more than one man yelled.

Wulfgar put him down to his feet with a growl, forcing him down to his knees and bent his head far back. Valric grabbed hard onto the man's forearm, crying out, "Kill him!" but Wulfgar only squeezed all the tighter, and Valric's words became a gurgling groan.

Wulfgar looked around at the ring of warriors. Holding Valric so helpless had bought him some time, perhaps, but they would kill him, no doubt, when he was finished with the shaman. Still, it wasn't that thought that gave Wulfgar pause, for he hardly cared about his own life. Rather, it was the expression he saw upon Jerek's face, a look of a man so utterly defeated. Wulfgar had come in with news that could break the proud chieftain, and he knew that if he killed Valric now, and many others in the ensuing battle before he, too, was finally brought down, then Jerek would not likely recover. And neither, he understood, would the Sky Ponies.

He looked down at the pitiful Valric. While he had been contemplating his next move he had inadvertently pushed back and down. The skinny man was practically bent in half and seemed near to breaking. How easy it would have been for Wulfgar to drive his arm down, snapping the man's spine.

How easy and how empty. With a frustrated roar that had nothing to do with compassion, he lifted Valric from the ground again, clapped his free hand against the man's groin, and brought him high overhead. With a roar, he launched the man a dozen feet and more into the side of a tent, sending Valric, skins, and poles tumbling down.

Warriors came at him, but he quickly had Aegis-fang in hand, and a great swipe drove them back, knocking the weapon from one and nearly tearing the man's arm off in the process.

"Hold!" came Jerek's cry. "And you, Valric!" he emphatically added, seeing the shaman pulling himself from the mess, calling for Wulfgar's death.

Jerek walked past his warriors, right up to Wulfgar. The younger man saw the murderous intent in his eyes.

"I will take no pleasure in killing the father of Torlin," Wulfgar said calmly.

That hit a nerve; Wulfgar saw the softening in the older man's face. Without another word, the barbarian turned about and started walking away, and none of the warriors moved to intercept him.

"Kill him!" Valric cried, but before the words had even left his mouth, Wulfgar whirled about and let fly his warhammer, the spinning weapon covering the twenty feet to the kneeling shaman in the blink of an eye, striking him squarely in the chest and laying him out, quite dead, among the jumble of tent poles and skins.

All eyes turned back to Wulfgar, and more than one Sky Pony made a move his way.

But Aegis-fang was back in his hands, suddenly, dramatically, and they fell back.

"His god Tempus is with him!" one man cried.

Wulfgar turned about and started away once more, knowing in his heart that nothing could be further from the truth. He expected Jerek to run him down or to order his warriors to kill him, but the group behind him remained strangely quiet. He heard no commands, no protests, no movement. Nothing at all. He had so overwhelmed the already battered tribe, had stunned Jerek with the truth of his son's fate, and then had stunned them all by his sudden and brutal vengeance on Valric, that they simply didn't know how to react.

No relief came over Wulfgar as he made his way from the encampment. He stormed down the road, angry at damned Valric, at all the damned Sky Ponies, at all the damned world. He kicked a stone from the path, then picked up another sizable rock and hurled it far through the air, shouting a roar of open defiance and pure frustration behind it. He stomped along with no direction in mind, with no sense of where he should go or where he should be. Soon after, he came upon the trail of a party of orcs, likely the same ones who had battled the Sky Ponies the previous night, an easily discernible track of blood, trampled grass, and broken twigs, veering from the main path into a small forest.

Hardly thinking, Wulfgar turned down that path, still roughly pushing aside trees, growling, and muttering curses. Gradually, though, he calmed and quieted, and replaced his lack of general purpose with a short-term, specific goal. He followed the trail more carefully, paying attention to any side paths where flanking orc scouts might have moved. Indeed, he found one such path and a pair of tracks to confirm it. He went that way quietly, looking for shadows and cover.

The day was late by then, the shadows long, but Wulfgar understood that he would have a hard time finding the scouts before they spotted him if they were on the alert—as they likely would be so soon after a terrific battle.

Wulfgar had spent many years fighting humanoids beside Drizzt Do'Urden, learning of their methods and their motivations. His course now was to make sure that the orcs were not able to warn the larger group. He knew how to do that.

Crouched in some brush by the side, the barbarian wrapped pliable twigs about his warhammer, trying to disguise the weapon as much as possible. Then he smeared mud about his face and pulled his cloak back so that it looked as though it was torn. Dirty and appearing battered, he walked out of the brush and started along the path, limping badly and groaning with every step, and every so often calling out for "my girl."

Just a short time later he sensed that he was being watched. Now he exaggerated his limp, even stumbling down to the ground at one point, using his tumble to allow him a better scan of the area.

He spotted a dark silhouette among the branches, an orc with a spear poised for a throw. Just a few steps more, he realized, and the creature would try to skewer him.

And the other was about, he realized, though he hadn't spotted the wretch. Likely it was on the ground, ready to run in and finish him as soon as the spear took him down. These two should have warned their companions, but they wanted the apparently easy kill for themselves, Wulfgar knew, that they might loot the poor man before informing their leader.

Wulfgar had to take them out quickly, but he didn't dare get much closer to the spear wielder. He pulled himself to his feet, took another staggering step along the trail, then paused and lifted his arm and eyes to the sky, wailing for his missing child. Then, nearly falling over again, shoulders slumped in defeat, he turned around and started back the way he had come, sobbing loudly, shoulders bobbing.

He knew that the orc would never be able to resist that target, despite the range. His muscles tensed, he turned his head just a bit, hearing trained on the distant tree.

Then he spun as the long-flying spear soared in. Deftly, with agility far beyond any man of his size, he caught the missile as he turned, pulling it tight against his side and issuing a profound grunt, then tumbling backward into the dirt, squirming, right hand grasping the spear, left tight about Aegis-fang.

He heard the rustle to the side from an angle above his right shoulder as he lay on his back, waiting patiently.

The second orc came out of the brush, scampering his way. Wulfgar timed the move with near perfection, rolling up and over that right shoulder, letting the spear fall as he went. He came up in a spin, Aegis-fang swiping across. But the orc skidded short, and the mighty weapon swished past harmlessly. Hardly concerned, Wulfgar continued the spin, right around, spotting the spear thrower on the tree branch as he came around and letting fly. He had to continue the spin, couldn't pause and watch the throw, though he heard the crunch and grunt, and the orc's broken body falling through the lower branches.

The orc before him yelped and threw its club, then turned and tried to flee.

Wulfgar accepted the hit as the club bounced off his massive chest. In an instant, he held the creature on its knees as he had held Valric, on its knees, head far back, backbone bowed. He pictured that moment then, conjuring an image of the wicked shaman. Then he drove down, with all his strength, growling and slapping away the orc's flailing arms. He heard the crackle of backbone and those arms stopped slapping at him, stabbing straight up into the air, trembling violently.

Wulfgar let go, and the dead creature fell over.

Aegis-fang came back to his grasp, reminding him of the other orc, and he glanced over and nodded, seeing the thing lying dead at the base of the tree.

Hardly satisfied, his bloodlust rising with each kill, Wulfgar ran, back to the main trail and then down along the clear path. He found the orcish encampment as twilight descended. There were more than a score of the monsters, with others likely out and about, scouting or hunting. He should have waited until long after dark, until the camp had settled and many of the orcs were asleep. He should have waited until he could get a better picture of the group, a better understanding of their structure and strength.

He should have waited, but he could not.

Aegis-fang soared in, right between a pair of smaller orcs, startling them, then on to slam one large creature, taking it and the orc it had been talking to down to the ground.

In charged Wulfgar, roaring wildly. He caught the spear of one startled orc, stabbing it across to impale the orc opposite, then tearing free the tip and spinning back, smashing the spear down across the first orc's head, breaking it in half. Holding both ends, Wulfgar jabbed them into either side of the orc's head, and when it reached up to grab the poles, the barbarian merely heaved it right over his head. A heavy punch dropped the next orc in line even as it moved to draw the sword from its belt, and then, roaring all the louder, Wulfgar crashed into two more, bearing them to the ground. He came up slapping and punching, kicking, anything at all to knock the orcs aside—and in truth, they showed more desire to scramble away than to come at the monstrous man.

Wulfgar caught one, spun it about, and slammed his forehead right into its face, then caught it by the hair as it fell away and drove his fist through its ugly face.

The barbarian leaped about, seeking his next victim. His momentum seemed to be fast waning with the passing seconds, but then Aegis-fang returned to his hand, and he wasted no time in whipping the hammer a dozen feet, its spinning head coming in at just the right angle to drive through the skull of one unfortunate creature.

Orcs charged in, stabbing and clubbing. Wulfgar took one hit, then another, but with each minor gash or bruise the orcs inflicted, the huge and powerful man got his hands on one and tore the life from it. Then Aegis-fang returned again, and the orcish press was shattered, driven back by mighty swipes. Covered in blood, howling wildly, thrashing that terrible hammer, the sheer sight of Wulfgar proved too much for the cowardly creatures. Those who could get away fled into the forest, and those who could not died at the barbarian's strong hands.

Mere minutes later, Wulfgar stomped out of the shattered camp, growling and smacking Aegis-fang against the trees. He knew that many orcs were watching him; he knew that none would dare attack.

Soon after, he came into a clearing on a bluff that afforded him a view of the last moments of sunset, the same fiery lines he had seen on that evening on the southern edges of the Spine of the World.

Now the colors did not touch his heart. Now he knew the thoughts of freedom from his past were a false hope, knew that his memories would follow him wherever he went, whatever he did. He felt no satisfaction at exacting revenge against Valric and no joy in slaughtering the orcs.

Nothing.

He walked on through the night, not even bothering to wash the blood from his clothes or to dress his many minor wounds. He walked toward the sunset, then kept the rising moon at his back, chasing its descent to the western horizon.

Three days later, he found Luskan's eastern gate.

Chapter 11

The Battle-mage

"Do not come here," LaValle cried, and then he added softly, "I beg."

Entreri merely continued to stare at the man, his expression unreadable.

"You wounded Kadran Gordeon," LaValle went on. "In pride more than in body, and that, I warn you, is more dangerous by far."

"Gordeon is a fool," Entreri retorted.

"A fool with an army," LaValle quipped. "No guild is more entrenched in the streets than the Basadonis. None have more resources, and all of those resources, I assure you, have been turned upon Artemis Entreri."

"And upon LaValle, perhaps?" Entreri replied with a grin. "For speaking with the hunted man?"

LaValle didn't answer the obvious question other than to continue to stare hard at Artemis Entreri, the man whose mere presence in his room this night might have just condemned him.

"Tell them everything they ask of you," Entreri instructed. "Honestly. Do not try to deceive them for my sake. Tell them that I came here, uninvited, to speak with you and that I show no wounds for all their efforts."

"You would taunt them so?"

Entreri shrugged. "Does it matter?"

LaValle had no answer to that, and so the assassin, with a bow, moved to the window and, defeating one trap with a flick of the wrist and carefully manipulating his body to avoid the others, slipped out to the wall and dropped silently to the street.

He dared to go by the Copper Ante that night, though only quickly and with no effort to actually enter the place. Still, he did make himself known to the door halflings. To his surprise, a short way down the alley at the side of the building, Dwahvel Tiggerwillies came out a secret door to speak with him.

"A battle-mage," she warned. "Merle Pariso. With a reputation unparalleled in Calimport. Fear him, Artemis Entreri. Run from him. Flee the city and all of Calimshan." And with that, she slipped through another barely detectable crack in the wall and was gone.

The gravity of her words and tone were not lost on the assassin. The mere fact that Dwahvel had come out to him, with nothing to gain and everything to lose—how could he repay the favor, after all, if he took her advice and fled the realm?—tipped him off that she had been instructed to so inform him, or at least, that this battle-mage was making no secret of the hunt.

So perhaps the wizard was a bit too cocksure, he told himself, but that, too, proved of little comfort. A battle-mage! A wizard trained specifically in the art of magical warfare. Cocksure, and with a right to be. Entreri had battled, and killed, many wizards, but he understood the desperate truth of his present situation. A wizard was not so difficult an enemy for a seasoned warrior, as long as the warrior was able to prepare the battlefield favorably. That, too, was usually not difficult, since wizards were often, by nature, distracted and unprepared. Typically a wizard had to anticipate battle far in advance, at the beginning of the day, that he might prepare the appropriate spells. Wizards, distracted by their continual research, rarely prepared such spells. But when a wizard was the hunter and not the hunted he would not be caught off his guard. Entreri knew he was in trouble. He seriously considered taking Dwahvel's advice.

For the first time since he had returned to Calimport, the assassin truly appreciated the danger of being without allies. He considered that in light of his experiences in Menzoberranzan, where unallied rogues could not survive for long.

Perhaps Calimport wasn't so different.

He started for his new room, an empty hovel at the back of an alleyway, but stopped and reconsidered. It wasn't likely that the wizard, with such a reputation as a combat spellcaster, would be overly skilled in divination spells as well. That hardly mattered, Entreri knew. It all came down to connections, and Merle Pariso was acting on behalf of the Basadoni guild. If he wanted to magically locate Entreri, the guild would grant him the resources of their diviners.

Where to go? He didn't want to remain on the open street where a wizard could strike from a long distance, could even, perhaps, levitate high above and rain destructive magic upon him. And so he searched the buildings, looking for a place to hide, an encampment, and knowing all the while that magical eyes might be upon him.

With that rather disturbing thought in mind, Entreri wasn't overly surprised when he slipped quietly into the supposedly empty back room of a darkened warehouse and a robed figure appeared right before him with a puff of orange smoke. The door blew closed behind him.

Entreri glanced all around, noting the lack of exits in the room, cursing his foul luck in finding this place. Again, when he considered it, it came down to his lack of allies and lack of knowledge with present-day Calimport. They were waiting for him, wherever he might go. They were ahead of him, watching his every move and obviously taking a prepared battlefield right with them. Entreri felt foolish for even coming back to this inhospitable city without first probing, without learning all that he would need to survive.

Enough of the doubts and second guesses, he pointedly reminded himself, drawing out his dagger and setting himself low in a crouch, concentrating on the situation at hand. He thought of turning back for the door, but knew without doubt that it would be magically sealed.

"Behold the Merle!" the wizard said with a laugh, waving his arms out wide. The voluminous sleeves of his robes floated out behind his lifting limbs and threw a rainbow of multicolored lights. A second wave and his arms came forward, throwing a blast of lightning at the assassin. But Entreri was already moving, rolling to the side and out of harm's way. He glanced back, hoping the bolt might have blown through the door, but it was still closed and seemed solid.

"Oh, well dodged!" Merle Pariso congratulated. "But really, pitiful assassin, do you desire to make this last longer? Why not stand still and be done with it, quickly and mercifully?" He stopped his taunting and launched into another spellcasting as Entreri charged in, jeweled dagger flashing. Merle made no move to defend against the attack, continuing calmly with his casting as Entreri came in hard, stabbing for his face.

The dagger stopped as surely as if it had struck a stone wall. Entreri wasn't really surprised—any wise wizard would have prepared such a defense—but what amazed him, even as he went flying back, hit by a burst of magical missiles, was Pariso's concentration. Entreri had to admire the man's unflinching spellcasting even as the deadly dagger came at his face, unblinking even as the blade flashed right before his eyes.

Entreri staggered to the side, diving and rolling, anticipating another attack. But now Merle Pariso, supremely confident, merely laughed at him. "Where will you run?" the battle-mage taunted. "How many times will you find the energy to dodge?"

143

Indeed, if he allowed the wizard's taunts to sink in, Entreri would have found it hard to hold his heart; many lesser warriors might have simply taken the wizard's advice and surrendered to the seemingly inevitable.

But not Entreri. His lethargy fell away. With his very life on the line all the doubts of his life and his purpose flew away. Now he lived completely in the moment, adrenaline pumping. One step at a time, and the first of those steps was to defeat the stoneskin, the magical defense that could turn any blade—but only for a certain number of attacks. Spinning and rolling, the assassin took up a chair and broke free a leg, then rolled about and launched it at the wizard, scoring an ineffective hit.

Another burst of magical missiles slammed into him, following him unerringly in his roll and stinging him. He shrugged through it, though, and came up throwing. A second, then a third chair leg scored two more hits.

The fourth followed in rapid succession. Then Entreri threw the base of the chair. It was a meager missile that would hardly have hurt the wizard even without the magical defense, but one that took yet another layer off the stoneskin.

Entreri paid for the offensive flurry, though, as Merle Pariso's next lightning bolt caught him hard and launched him spinning sidelong. His shoulder burned, his hair danced on end, and his heart fluttered.

Desperate and hurt, the assassin went in hard, dagger slashing. "How many more can you defeat?" he roared, stabbing hard again and again.

His answer came in the form of flames, a shroud of dancing fire covering, but hardly consuming, Merle Pariso. Entreri noted the fire too late to stop short his last attack, and the dagger went through, again hitting harmlessly against the stoneskin—harmlessly to Pariso but not to Entreri. The new spell, the flame shield, replicated the intended bite of that dagger back at Entreri, drawing a deep gash along the already battered man's ribs.

With a howl the assassin fell back, purposely turning himself in line with the door, then dodging deftly as the predictable lightning bolt came after him.

The rolling assassin looked back as he came around, pleased to see that this time the wooden door had indeed splintered. He grabbed another chair and threw it at the wizard, turning for the door even as he released it.

Merle Pariso's groan stopped him dead and turned him back around, thinking the stoneskin expired.

But then it was Entreri's turn to groan. "Oh, clever," he congratulated, realizing the wizard's groan to be no more than a ruse, buying the man time to cast his next spell.

The assassin turned back for the door but hadn't gone a step before he was forced back, as a wall of huge flames erupted along that wall, blocking escape.

"Well fought, assassin," Merle Pariso said honestly. "I expected as much from Artemis Entreri. But now, alas, you die." He finished by drawing a wand, pointing it at the floor at his feet, and firing a burning seed.

Entreri fell flat, pulling what remained of his cloak over his head as the seed exploded into a fireball, filling all the room, burning his hair and scorching his lungs, but harming Pariso not at all. The wizard was secure within his fiery shield.

Entreri came up dazed, eyes filled with heat and smoke as all the building around him burned. Merle Pariso stood there, laughing wildly.

The assassin had to get out. He couldn't possibly defeat the mage and wouldn't survive for much longer against Pariso's potent magics. He turned for the door, thinking to dive right through the fire wall, but then a glowing sword appeared in midair before him, slashing hard. He had to dodge aside and get his dagger up against the blade to turn it. The invisible opponent—Entreri knew it to be Merle Pariso's will acting through the magical dweomer—came on hard, forcing him to retreat. The sword always stayed between the assassin and the door.

On his balance now, Entreri was more than a match for the slicing weapon, easily dodging and striking back hard. He knew that no hand guided the blade, that the only way to defeat it was to strike at the sword itself, and that posed no great problem for the warrior assassin. But then another glowing sword appeared. Entreri had never seen this before, had never even heard of a wizard who could control two such magical creations at the same time.

He dived and rolled, and the swords pursued. He tried to dart around them for the doorway but found that they were too quick. He glanced back at Pariso. Barely, through the growing smoke, he could see the wizard still shrouded in defensive flames, tapping his fireball wand against his cheek.

The heat nearly overwhelmed Entreri. The flames were all about, on the walls, the floor, and the ceiling. Wood crackled in protest, and beams collapsed.

"I will not leave," he heard Merle Pariso say. "I will watch until the life is gone from you, Artemis Entreri."

On came the glowing swords, slashing in perfect coordination, and Entreri knew that the wizard almost got what he wanted. The assassin barely, barely, avoiding the hits, dived forward under the blades, coming up in a run for the door. Shielding his face with his arms, he leaped into the fire wall, thinking to break through the battered door.

He hit as solid a barrier as he had ever felt, a magical wall, he knew. He scrambled back out of the flames into the burning room, and the two swords waited for him. Merle Pariso stood calmly pointing the dreaded fireball wand.

But then to the side of the wizard a green-gloved disembodied hand appeared, sliding out of nowhere and holding what appeared to be a large egg.

Merle Pariso's eyes widened in horror. "Wh-who?" he stuttered. "Wha—?"

The hand tossed the egg to the floor, where it exploded into a huge ball of powdery dust, rolling into the air, then shimmering into a multicolored cloud. Entreri heard music then, even above the roar of the conflagration, many different notes climbing the scale, then dropping low and ending in a long, monotonal humming sound.

The glowing swords disappeared. So did the fire wall blocking the door, though the normal flames still burned brightly along door and wall. So did Merle Pariso's defensive fire shield.

The wizard cried out and waved his arms frantically, trying to cast another spell—some magical escape, Entreri realized, for now he was obviously feeling the heat as intensely as was Entreri.

The assassin realized that the magical barrier was likely gone as well, and he could have turned and run from the room. But he couldn't tear his eyes from the spectacle of Pariso, backpedaling, so obviously distressed. To the amazement of both, many of the smaller fires near the wizard then changed shape, appearing as little humanoid creatures, circling Pariso in a strange dance.

The wizard skipped backward, tripped over a loose board, and went down on his back. The little fire humanoids, like a pack of hunting wolves, leaped upon him, lighting his robes and burning his skin. Pariso opened wide his mouth to scream, and one of the fiery animations raced right down his throat, stealing his voice and burning him from the inside.

The green-gloved hand beckoned to Entreri.

The wall behind him collapsed, sparks and embers flying everywhere, stealing his easy escape.

Moving cautiously but quickly, the assassin circled wide of the hand, gaining a better angle as he realized that it was not a disembodied hand at all, but merely one poking through a dimensional gate of some sort.

Entreri's knees went weak at the sight. He nearly bolted back for the blazing door, but a sound from above told him that the ceiling was falling in. Purely on survival instinct, for if he had thought about it he likely would have chosen death, Entreri leaped through the dimensional door.

Into the arms of his saviors.

Chapter 12

Finding a Niche

He knew this town, though only vaguely. He'd made a single passage through the place long ago, in the days of hope and future dreams, in the search for Mithral Hall. Little seemed familiar to Wulfgar now as he made his plodding way through Luskan, absorbing the sights and sounds of the many open air markets and the general bustle of a northern city awakening after winter's slumber.

Many, many gazes fell over him as he moved along, for Wulfgar—closer to seven feet tall than to six with a massive chest and shoulders, and the glittering warhammer strapped across his back—was no ordinary sight. Barbarians occasionally wandered into Luskan, but even among the hardy folk Wulfgar loomed huge.

He ignored the looks and the whispers and continued merely to wander the many ways. He spotted the Hosttower of the Arcane, the famed wizard's guild of Luskan, and recognized the building easily enough, since it was in the shape of a huge tree with spreading limbs. But again that one note of recognition did little to guide the man along. It had been so long ago, a lifetime ago it seemed, since he had last been here.

Minutes became an hour, then two hours. The barbarian's vision was turned inward now as much as outward. His mind replayed images of the

147

past few days, particularly the moment of his unsatisfying revenge. The image of Valric High Eye flying back into the jumble of broken tenting, Aegis-fang crushing his chest, was vivid in his mind's eye.

Wulfgar ran his hand through his unkempt hair and staggered along. Clearly he was exhausted, for he had slept only a few scattered hours in three days since the encounter with the Sky Ponies. He had wandered the roads to the west aimlessly until he had spotted the outline of the distant city. The guards at the eastern gate of Luskan had threatened to turn him away, but when he had just swung about with a shrug they called after him and told him he could enter but warned him to keep his weapon strapped across his back.

Wulfgar had no intention of fighting and no intention of following the guards' command should a fight find him. He merely nodded and walked through the gates, then down the streets and through the markets.

He discovered another familiar landmark when the shadows were long, the sun low in the western sky. A signpost named one way Half Moon Street, a place Wulfgar had been before. A short way down the street he saw the sign for the Cutlass, a tavern he knew from his first trip through, a place wherein he had been involved, in some ways had started, a tremendous row. Looking at the Cutlass, at the whole decrepit street now, Wulfgar wondered how he could have ever expected otherwise.

This was the place for the lowest orders of society, for thugs and rogues, for men running from lords. The barbarian put his hand in his nearly empty pouch, fumbling with the few coins, and realized then that this was where he belonged.

He went into the Cutlass half fearing he would be recognized, that he would find himself in another brawl before the door closed behind him.

Of course he was not recognized. Nor did he see any faces that seemed the least bit familiar. The layout of the place was pretty much the same as he remembered. As he scanned the room, his gaze inevitably went to the wall to the side of the long bar, the wall where a younger Wulfgar had set a brute in his place by driving the man's head right through the planking.

He was so full of pride back then, so ready to fight. Now, too, he was more than willing to put his fists or weapons to use, but his purpose in doing so had changed. Now he fought out of anger, out of the sheerest rage, whether that rage had anything to do with whatever enemy stood before him or not. Now he fought because that course seemed as good as any other. Perhaps, just perhaps, he fought in the hopes that he would lose, that some enemy would end his internal torment.

He couldn't hold that thought, couldn't hold any thought, as he made his way to the bar, taking no care not to jostle the many patrons who crowded before him. He pulled off his traveling cloak and took a seat, not even bothering to ask either of the men flanking the stool if they had a friend who was using it.

And then he watched and waited, letting the myriad of sights and sounds—whispered conversations, lewd remarks aimed at serving wenches more than ready to snap back with their own stinging retort—become a general blur, a welcomed buzz.

His head drooped, and that movement alone woke him. He shifted in his seat and noted then that the barkeep, an old man who still held the hardness of youth about his strong shoulders, stood before him, wiping a glass.

"Arumn Gardpeck," the barkeep introduced himself, extending a hand.

Wulfgar regarded the offered hand but did not shake it.

Without missing a beat the barkeep went back to his wiping. "A drink?" he asked.

Wulfgar shook his head and looked away, desiring nothing from the man, especially any useless conversation.

Arumn came forward, though, leaning over the bar and drawing Wulfgar's full attention. "I want no trouble in me bar," he said calmly, looking over the barbarian's huge, muscled arms.

Wulfgar waved him away.

Minutes slipped past, and the place grew even more crowded. No one bothered Wulfgar, though, and so he allowed himself to relax his guard, his head inevitably drooping. He fell asleep, his face buried in his arms atop Arumn Gardpeck's clean bar.

"Hey there," he heard, and the voice sounded as if it was far, far away. He felt a shake then, on his shoulder, and he opened his sleepy eyes and lifted his head to see Arumn's smiling face. "Time for leaving."

Wulfgar stared at him blankly.

"Where are ye stayin'?" the barkeep asked. "Might that I could find a couple who'd walk ye there."

For a long while, Wulfgar didn't answer, staring groggily at the man, trying to get his bearings.

"And he weren't even drinking!" one man howled from the side. Wulfgar turned to regard him and noted that several large men, Arumn Gardpeck's security force, no doubt, had formed a semicircle behind him. Wulfgar turned back to eye Arumn.

"Where are ye stayin'?" the man asked again. "And ye shut yer mouth, Josi Puddles," he added to the taunting man.

Wulfgar shrugged. "Nowhere," he answered honestly.

"Well, ye can't be stayin' 'ere!" yet another man growled, moving close enough to poke the barbarian in the shoulder.

Wulfgar calmly swung his head, taking a measure of the man.

"Hush yer mouth!" Arumn was quick to scold, and he shifted about, drawing Wulfgar's gaze. "I could give ye a room for a few silver pieces," he said.

"I have little money," the big man admitted.

149

"Then sell me yer hammer," said another directly behind Wulfgar. When he turned to regard the speaker he saw that the man was holding Aegis-fang. Now Wulfgar was fully awake and up, hand extended, his expression and posture demanding the hammer's immediate return.

"Might that I will give it back to ye," the man remarked as Wulfgar slid out of the chair and advanced a threatening step. As he spoke, he lifted Aegis-fang, more in an angle to cave in Wulfgar's skull that to hand it over.

Wulfgar stopped short and shifted his dangerous glare over each of the large men, his lips curling up in a confident, wicked, smile. "You wish to buy it?" he asked the man holding the hammer. "Then you should know its name."

Wulfgar spoke the hammer's name, and it vanished from the hands of the threatening man and reappeared in Wulfgar's. The barbarian was moving even before the hammer materialized, closing in on the man with a single long stride and slapping him with a backhand that launched him into the air to land crashing over a table.

The others came at the huge barbarian, but only for an instant, for he was ready now, waving the powerful warhammer so easily that the others understood he was not one to be taken lightly and not one to fight unless they were willing to see their ranks thinned considerably.

"Hold! Hold!" cried Arumn, rushing out from behind the bar and waving his bouncers away. A couple went over to help the man Wulfgar had slapped. So disoriented was he that they had to hoist him and support him.

And still Arumn waved them all away. He stood before Wulfgar, within easy striking distance, but he was not afraid—or if he was, he wasn't showing it.

"I could use one with yer strength," he remarked. "That was Reef ye dropped with an open-handed slap, and Reef's one o' me better fighters."

Wulfgar looked across the room at the man sitting with the other bouncers and scoffed.

Arumn led him back to the bar and sat him down, then went behind and produced a bottle, setting it right before the big man and motioning for him to drink.

Wulfgar did, a great hearty swig that burned all the way down.

"A room and free food," Arumn said. "All ye can eat. And all that I ask in return is that ye help keep me tavern free o' fights or that ye finish 'em quick if they start."

Wulfgar looked back over his shoulder at the men across the way. "What of them?" he asked, taking another huge swig from the bottle, then coughing as he wiped his bare forearm across his lips. The potent liquor seemed to draw all the coating from his throat.

"They help me when I ask, as they help most o' the innkeepers on Half Moon street and all the streets about," Arumn explained. "I been thinking o' hiring me own and keeping him on, and I'm thinking that ye'd fit that role well."

"You hardly know me," Wulfgar argued, and his third gulp half drained the bottle. This time the burning seemed to spread out more quickly, until all his body felt warm and a bit numb. "And you know nothing of my history."

"Nor do I care," said Arumn. "We don't get many of yer type in here— northmen, I mean. Ye've got a reputation for fighting, and the way ye slapped Reef aside tells me that reputation's well earned."

"Room and food?" Wulfgar asked.

"And drink," Arumn added, motioning to the bottle, which Wulfgar promptly lifted to his lips and drained. He went to move it back to Arumn, but it seemed to jump from his hand, and when he tried to retrieve it he merely kept pushing it awkwardly along until Arumn deftly scooped it away from him.

Wulfgar sat up straighter, or tried to, and closed his eyes very tightly, trying to find a center of focus. When he opened his eyes once more, he found another full bottle before him, and he wasted no time in bringing that one, too, up to his lips.

An hour later, Arumn, who had taken a few drinks himself, helped Wulfgar up the stairs and into a tiny room. He tried to guide Wulfgar onto the small bed—a cot too small to comfortably accommodate the huge barbarian—but both wound up falling over, crashing across the cot then onto the floor.

They shared a laugh, an honest laugh, the first one Wulfgar had known since the rescue in the ice cave.

"They start coming in soon after midday," Arumn explained, spit flying with every word. "But I won't be needing ye until the sun's down. I'll get ye then, and I'm thinking that ye'll be needin' waking!"

They shared another laugh at that, and Arumn staggered out the door, falling against it to close it behind him, leaving Wulfgar alone in the pitch-black room.

Alone. Completely alone.

That notion nearly overwhelmed him. Sitting there drunk the barbarian realized that Errtu hadn't come in here with him, that everything, every memory, good and bad, was but a harmless blur. In those bottles, under the spell of that potent liquor, Wulfgar found a reprieve.

Food and a room and drink Arumn had promised.

To Wulfgar the last condition of his employment rang out as the most important.

* * * * *

Entreri stood in an alley, not far from his near-disaster with Merle Pariso, looking back at the blazing warehouse. Flames leaped high above

151

the rooftops of the nearest buildings. Three others stood beside him. They were about the same height as the assassin, a bit more slender, perhaps, but with muscles obviously honed for battle.

What distinguished them most was their ebony skin. One wore a huge purple hat, set with a gigantic plume.

"Twice I have pulled you from certain death," the one with the hat remarked.

Entreri looked hard at the speaker, wanting nothing more than to drive his dagger deep into the dark elf's chest. He knew better though, knew that this one, Jarlaxle, was far too protected for any such obvious attacks.

"We have much to discuss," the dark elf said, and he motioned to one of his companions. With a thought, it seemed, the drow brought up another dimensional door, this one leading into a room where several other dark elves had gathered.

"Kimmuriel Oblodra," Jarlaxle explained.

Entreri knew the name—the surname, at least. House Oblodra had once been the third most powerful house in Menzoberranzan and one of the most frightening because of their practice of psionics, a curious and little understood magic of the mind. During the Time of Troubles, the Oblodrans, whose powers were not adversely affected, as were the more conventional magics within the city, used the opportunity to press their advantage, even going so far as to threaten Matron Mother Baenre, the ruling Matron of the ruling house of the city. When the waves of instability that marked that strange time turned again in favor of conventional magics and against the powers of the mind, House Oblodra had been obliterated, the great structure and all its inhabitants pulled into the great gorge, the Clawrift, by a physical manifestation of Matron Baenre's rage.

Well, Entreri thought, staring at the psionicist, not all of the inhabitants.

He went through the psionic door with Jarlaxle—what choice did he have?—and after a long moment of dizzying disorientation took a seat in the small room when the drow mercenary motioned for him to do so. All the dark elf group except for Jarlaxle and Kimmuriel, went out then in practiced order, to secure the area about the meeting place.

"We are safe enough," Jarlaxle assured Entreri.

"They were watching me magically," the assassin replied. "That was how Merle Pariso set the ambush."

"We have been watching you magically for many weeks," Jarlaxle said with a grin. "They watch you no more, I assure you."

"You came for me, then?" the assassin asked. "It seems a bit of trouble to retrieve one *rivvil*," he added, using the drow word, and not a complimentary one, for human.

Jarlaxle laughed aloud at Entreri's choice of that word. It was indeed the word for "human," but one also used to describe many inferior races, which meant any race that was not drow.

"To retrieve you?" the assassin asked incredulously. "Do you wish to return to Menzoberranzan?"

"I would kill you or force you to kill me long before we ever stepped into the drow city," Entreri replied in all seriousness.

"Of course," Jarlaxle said calmly, taking no offense and not disagreeing in the least. "That is not your place, nor is Calimport ours."

"Then why have you come?"

"Because Calimport is your place, and Menzoberranzan is mine," the drow replied, smiling all the wider, as though the simple statement explained everything.

And before he questioned Jarlaxle more deeply, Entreri sat back and took a long while to reflect upon the words. Jarlaxle was, above all else, an opportunist. The drow, along with Bregan D'aerthe, his powerful band of rogues, seemed to find a way to gain from practically every situation. Menzoberranzan was a city ruled by females, the priestesses of Lolth, and yet even there Jarlaxle and his band, almost exclusively males, were far from the underclass. So why now had he come to find Entreri, come to a place that he just openly and honestly admitted was not his place at all?

"You want me to front you," the assassin stated.

"I am not familiar with the term," Jarlaxle replied.

Now Entreri, seeing the lie for what it was, was the one wearing the grin. "You want to extend the hand of Bregan D'aerthe to the surface, to Calimport, but you recognize that you and yours would never be accepted even among the bowel-dwellers of the city."

"We could use magic to disguise our true identity," the drow argued.

"But why bother when you have Artemis Entreri?" the assassin was quick to reply.

"And do I?" asked the drow.

Entreri thought it over for a moment, then merely shrugged.

"I offer you protection from your enemies," Jarlaxle stated. "No, more than that, I offer you power over your enemies. With your knowledge and reputation and the power of Bregan D'aerthe secretly behind you, you will soon rule the streets of Calimport."

"As Jarlaxle's puppet," Entreri said.

"As Jarlaxle's partner," the drow replied. "I have no need of puppets. In fact, I consider them a hindrance. A partner truly profiting from the organization is one working harder to reach higher goals. Besides, Artemis Entreri, are we not friends?"

Entreri laughed aloud at that notion. The words "Jarlaxle" and "friend" seemed incongruous indeed when used in the same sentence, bringing to mind an old street proverb that the most dangerous and threatening words a Calimshite street vendor could ever say to someone were "trust me."

And that is exactly what Jarlaxle had just said to Entreri.

"Your enemies of the Basadoni Guild will soon call you pasha," the drow went on.

Entreri showed no reaction.

"Even the political leaders of the city, of all the realm of Calimshan, will defer to you," said Jarlaxle.

Entreri showed no reaction.

"I will know now, before you leave this room, if my offer is agreeable," Jarlaxle added, his voice sounding a bit more ominous.

Entreri understood well the implications of that tone. He knew about Bregan D'aerthe being within the city now, and that alone meant that he would either play along or be killed outright.

"Partners," the assassin said, poking himself in the chest. "But I direct the sword of Bregan D'aerthe in Calimport. You strike when and where I decide."

Jarlaxle agreed with a nod. Then he snapped his fingers and another dark elf entered the room, moving beside Entreri. This was obviously the assassin's escort.

"Sleep well," Jarlaxle bade the human. "For tomorrow begins your ascent."

Entreri didn't bother to reply but just walked out of the room.

Yet another drow came out from behind a curtain then. "He was not lying," he assured Jarlaxle, speaking in the tongue common to dark elves.

The cunning mercenary leader nodded and smiled, glad to have the services of so powerful an ally as Rai'gy Bondalek of Ched Nasad, formerly the high priest of that other drow city, but ousted in a coup and rescued by the ever-opportunistic Bregan D'aerthe. Jarlaxle had settled his sights on Rai'gy long before, for the drow was not only powerful in the god-given priestly magics, but was well-versed in the ways of wizards as well. How lucky for Bregan D'aerthe that Rai'gy had suddenly found himself an outcast.

Rai'gy had no idea that Jarlaxle had been the one to incite that coup.

"Your Entreri did not seem thrilled with the treasures you dangled before him," Rai'gy dared to remark. "He will do as he promised, perhaps, but with little heart."

Jarlaxle nodded, not the least bit surprised by Entreri's reaction. He had come to understand Artemis Entreri quite well in the months the assassin had lived with Bregan D'aerthe in Menzoberranzan. He knew the man's motivations and desires—better, perhaps, than Entreri knew them.

"There is one other treasure that I did not offer," he explained. "One that Artemis Entreri does not even yet realize that he wants." Jarlaxle reached into the folds of his cloak and produced an amulet dangling at the end of a silver chain. "I took it from Catti-brie," he explained.

"Companion of Drizzt Do'Urden. It was given to her adoptive father, the dwarf Bruenor Battlehammer, by the High Lady Alustriel of Silverymoon long ago as a means of tracking the rogue drow."

"You know much," Rai'gy remarked.

"That is how I survive," Jarlaxle replied.

"But Catti-brie knows it is gone," reasoned Kimmuriel Oblodra. "Thus, she and her companion have likely taken steps to defeat any further use of it."

Jarlaxle was shaking his head long before the psionicist ever finished. "Catti-brie's was returned to her cloak before she left the city. This one is a copy in form and in magic, created by a wizard associate. Likely the woman returned the original to Bruenor Battlehammer, and he gave it back to Lady Alustriel. I should think she would want it back or at least want it out of Catti-brie's possession, for it seems the two had somewhat of a rivalry growing concerning the affections of the rogue Drizzt Do'Urden."

Both the others crinkled their faces in disgust at the thought that any drow so beautiful could find passion with a non-drow, a creature, by that simple definition, who was obviously *iblith*, or excrement.

Jarlaxle, himself intrigued by the beautiful Catti-brie, didn't bother to refute their racist feelings.

"But if that is a copy, is the magic strong enough?" Kimmuriel asked, and he emphasized the word "magic" as if to prompt Jarlaxle to explain how it might prove useful.

"Magical dweomers create pathways of power," Rai'gy Bondalek explained. "Pathways that I know how to enhance and to replicate."

"Rai'gy spent many of his earlier years perfecting the technique," Jarlaxle added. "His ability to recover the previous powers of ancient Ched Nasad relics proved pivotal in his ascension to the position as the city's high priest. And he can do it again, even enhancing the previous dweomer to new heights."

"That we might find Drizzt Do'Urden," Kimmuriel said.

Jarlaxle nodded. "What a fine trophy for Artemis Entreri."

Part 3

Climbing to the Top of the Bottom

I watched the miles roll out behind me, whether walking down a road or sailing fast out of Waterdeep for the southlands, putting distance between us and the friend we four had left behind.

The friend?

Many times during those long and arduous days, each of us in our own little space came to wonder about that word "friend" and the responsibilities such a label might carry. We had left Wulfgar behind in the wilds of the Spine of the World no less and had no idea if he was well, if he was even still alive. Could a true friend so desert another? Would a true friend allow a man to walk alone along troubled and dangerous paths?

Often I ponder the meaning of that word. Friend. It seems such an obvious thing, friendship, and yet often it becomes so very complicated. Should I have stopped Wulfgar, even knowing and admitting that he had his own road to walk? Or should I have gone with him? Or should we all four have shadowed him, watching over him?

I think not, though I admit that I know not for certain. There is a fine line between friendship and parenting, and when that line is crossed, the result is often disastrous. A parent who strives to make a true friend of his or her child may well sacrifice authority, and though that parent may be

159

comfortable with surrendering the dominant position, the unintentional result will be to steal from that child the necessary guidance and, more importantly, the sense of security the parent is supposed to impart. On the opposite side, a friend who takes a role as parent forgets the most important ingredient of friendship: respect.

For respect is the guiding principle of friendship, the lighthouse beacon that directs the course of any true friendship. And respect demands trust.

Thus, the four of us pray for Wulfgar and intend that our paths will indeed cross again. Though we'll often look back over our shoulders and wonder, we hold fast to our understanding of friendship, of trust, and of respect. We accept, grudgingly but resolutely, our divergent paths.

Surely Wulfgar's trials have become my trials in many ways, but I see now that the friendship of mine most in flux is not the one with the barbarian—not from my perspective, anyway, since I understand that Wulfgar alone must decide the depth and course of our bond—but my relationship with Catti-brie. Our love for each other is no secret between us, or to anyone else watching us (and I fear that perhaps the bond that has grown between us might have had some influence in Wulfgar's painful decisions), but the nature of that love remains a mystery to me and to Catti-brie. We have in many ways become as brother and sister, and surely I am closer to her than I could ever have been to any of my natural siblings! For several years we had only each other to count on and both learned beyond any doubt that the other would always be there. I would die for her, and she for me. Without hesitation, without doubt. Truly in all the world there is no one, not even Bruenor, Wulfgar, or Regis, or even Zaknafein, with whom I would rather spend my time. There is no one who can view a sunrise beside me and better understand the emotions that sight always stirs within me. There is no one who can fight beside me and better compliment my movements. There is no one who better knows all that is in my heart and thoughts, though I had not yet spoken a word.

But what does that mean?

Surely I feel a physical attraction to Catti-brie as well. She is possessed of a combination of innocence and a playful wickedness. For all her sympathy and empathy and compassion, there is an edge to Catti-brie that makes potential enemies tremble in fear and potential lovers tremble in anticipation. I believe that she feels similarly toward me, and yet we both understand the dangers of this uncharted territory, dangers more frightening than any physical enemy we have ever known. I am drow, and young, and with the dawn and twilight of several centuries ahead of me. She is human and, though young, with merely decades of life ahead of her. Of course, Catti-brie's life is complicated enough merely having a drow elf as a traveling companion and friend. What troubles might she find if she and I were more than that? And what might the world think of our children, if ever that path we walked? Would any society in all the world accept them?

I know how I feel when I look upon her, though, and believe that I understand her feelings as well. On that level, it seems such an obvious thing, and yet, alas, it becomes so very complicated.

—Drizzt Do'Urden

Chapter 13

Secret Weapon

"You have found the rogue?" Jarlaxle asked Rai'gy Bondalek. Kimmuriel Oblodra stood beside the mercenary leader, the psionicist appearing unarmed and unarmored, seeming perfectly defenseless to one who did not understand the powers of his mind.

"He is with a dwarf, a woman, and a halfling," Rai'gy answered. "And sometimes they are joined by a great black cat."

"Guenhwyvar," Jarlaxle explained. "Once the property of Masoj Hun'ette. A powerful magical item indeed."

"But not the greatest magic that they carry," Rai'gy informed. "There is another, stored in a pouch on the rogue's belt, that radiates magic stronger than all their other magics combined. Even through the distance of my scrying it beckoned to me, almost as if it were asking me to retrieve it from its present unworthy owner."

"What could it be?" the always opportunistic mercenary asked.

Rai'gy shook his head, his shock of white hair flying from side to side. "Like no dweomer I have seen before," he admitted.

"Is that not the way of magic?" Kimmuriel Oblodra put in with obvious distaste. "Unknown and uncontrollable."

Rai'gy shot the psionicist an angry glare, but Jarlaxle, more than

163

willing to utilize both magic and psionics, merely smiled. "Learn more about it and about them," he instructed the wizard-priest. "If it beckons to us, then perhaps we would be wise to heed its call. How far are they, and how fast can we get to them?"

"Very," Rai'gy answered. "And very. They had begun an overland route but were accosted by giantkind and goblinkin at every bend in the path."

"Perhaps the magical item is not particular about who it calls for a new owner," Kimmuriel remarked with obvious sarcasm.

"They turned about and took ship," Rai'gy went on, ignoring the comment. "Out of the great northern city of Waterdeep, I believe, far, far up the Sword Coast."

"But sailing south?" Jarlaxle asked hopefully.

"I believe," Rai'gy answered. "It does not matter. There are magics, of course, and mind powers," he added, nodding deferentially to Kimmuriel, "that can get us to them as easily as if they were standing in the next room."

"Back to your searching, then," Jarlaxle said.

"But are we not to visit a guild this very night?" Rai'gy asked.

"You will not be needed," Jarlaxle replied. "Minor guilds alone will meet this night."

"Even minor guilds would be wise to employ wizards," the wizard-priest remarked.

"The wizard of this one is a friend of Entreri," Jarlaxle explained with a laugh that made it sound as if it were all too easy. "And the other guild is naught but halflings, hardly versed in the ways of magic. Tomorrow night you will be needed, perhaps. This night continue your examination of Drizzt Do'Urden. In the end he will likely prove the most important cog of all."

"Because of the magical item?" Kimmuriel asked.

"Because of Entreri's lack of interest," Jarlaxle replied.

The wizard-priest shook his head. "We offer him power and riches beyond his comprehension," he said. "And yet he leads us onward as if he were going into hopeless battle against the Spider Queen herself."

"He cannot appreciate the power or the riches until he has resolved an inner conflict," explained Jarlaxle, whose greatest gift of all was the ability to get into the minds of enemies and friends alike, and not with prying powers, such as Kimmuriel Oblodra might use, but with simple empathy and understanding. "But fear not his present lack of motivation. I know Artemis Entreri well enough to understand that he will prove more than effective whether his heart is in the fight or not. As humans go I have never met one more dangerous or more devious."

"A pity his skin is so light," Kimmuriel remarked.

Jarlaxle only smiled. He knew well enough that if Artemis Entreri had been born drow in Menzoberranzan the man would have been among the greatest of weapon masters, or perhaps he would have even exceeded that claim. Perhaps he would have been a rival to Jarlaxle for control of Bregan D'aerthe.

"We will speak in the comfortable darkness of the tunnels when the shining hellfire rises into the too-high sky," he said to Rai'gy. "Have more answers for me."

"Fare well with the guilds," Rai'gy answered, and with a bow he turned and left.

Jarlaxle turned to Kimmuriel and nodded. It was time to go hunting.

*   *   *   *   *

With their cherubic faces, halflings were regarded by the other races as creatures with large eyes, but how much wider those eyes became for the four in the room with Dwahvel when a magical portal opened right before them (despite the usual precautions against such magical intrusion), and Artemis Entreri stepped into the room. The assassin cut an impressive figure in a layered black coat and a black bolero, banded about the base of its riser in blacker silk.

Entreri assumed a strong, hands-on-hips pose just as Kimmuriel had taught him, holding steady against the waves of disorientation that always accompanied such psionic dimensional travel.

Behind him, in the chamber on the other side of the door, a room lightless save that spilling in through the gate from Dwahvel's chamber, huddled a few dark shapes. When one of the halfling soldiers moved to meet the intruder, one of those dark shapes shifted slightly, and the halfling, with hardly a squeak, toppled to the floor.

"He is sleeping and otherwise unharmed," Entreri quickly explained, not wanting a fight with the others, who were scrambling about for weapons. "I did not come here for a fight, I assure you, but I can leave all of you dead in my wake if you insist upon one."

"You could have used the front door," Dwahvel, the only one appearing unshaken, remarked dryly.

"I did not wish to be seen entering your establishment," the assassin, fully oriented once more, explained. "For your protection."

"And what form of entrance is this?" Dwahvel asked. "Magical and unbidden, yet none of my wards—and I paid well for them, I assure you—offered resistance."

"No magic that will concern you," Entreri replied, "but that will surely concern my enemies. Know that I did not return to Calimport to lurk in shadows at the bidding of others. I have traveled the Realms extensively and have brought back with me that which I have learned."

"So Artemis Entreri returns as the conqueror," Dwahvel remarked. Beside her the soldiers bristled, but Dwahvel did well to hold them in check. Now that Entreri was among them, to fight him would cost her dearly, she realized.

Very dearly.

"Perhaps," Entreri conceded. "We shall see how it goes."

165

"It will take more than a display of teleportation to convince me to throw the weight of my guild behind you," Dwahvel said calmly. "To choose wrongly in such a war would prove fatal."

"I do not wish you to choose at all," Entreri assured her.

Dwahvel eyed him suspiciously, then turned to each of her trusted guards. They, too, wore doubting expressions.

"Then why bother to come to me?" she asked.

"To inform you that a war is about to begin," Entreri answered. "I owe you that much, at least."

"And perhaps you wish for me to open wide my ears that you may learn how goes the fight," the sly halfling reasoned.

"As you wish," Entreri replied. "When this is finished, and I have found control, I will not forget all that you have already done for me."

"And if you lose?"

Entreri laughed. "Be wary," he said. "And, for your health, Dwahvel Tiggerwillies, be neutral. I owe you and see our friendship as to the benefit of both, but if I learn that you betray me by word or by deed, I will bring your house down around you." With that, he gave a polite bow, a tip of the black bolero and slipped back through the portal.

One globe of darkness after another filled Dwahvel's chamber, forcing her and the three standing soldiers to crawl about helplessly until one found the normal exit and called the others to him.

Finally the darkness abated, and the halflings dared to re-enter, to find their sleeping companion snoring contentedly, and then to find, upon searching the body, a small dart stuck into his shoulder.

"Entreri has friends," one of them remarked.

Dwahvel merely nodded, not surprised and glad indeed at that moment that she had previously chosen to help the outcast assassin. He was not a man Dwahvel Tiggerwillies wished for an enemy.

* * * * *

"Ah, but you make my life so dangerous," LaValle said with an exaggerated sigh when Entreri, unannounced and uninvited, walked from thin air, it seemed, into LaValle's private room.

"Well done—on your escape from Kadran Gordeon, I mean," LaValle went on when Entreri didn't immediately respond. The wizard was trying hard to appear collected. Hadn't Entreri slipped into his guarded room twice before, after all? But this time—and the assassin recognized it splayed on LaValle's face—he had truly surprised the wizard. Bodeau had sharpened up the defenses of his guild house amazingly well against both magical and physical intrusion. As much as he respected Entreri, LaValle had obviously not expected the assassin to get through so easily.

"Not so difficult a task, I assure you," the assassin replied, keeping his voice steady so that his words sounded as simple fact and not a boast.

"I have traveled the world, and under the world and have witnessed powers very different from anything experienced in Calimport. Powers that will bring me that which I desire."

LaValle sat on an old and comfortable chair, planting one elbow on the worn arm and dropping his head sidelong against his open palm. What was it about this man, he wondered, that so mocked all the ordinary trappings of power? He looked all around at his room, at the many carved statues, gargoyles, and exotic birds, at the assortment of finely carved staves, some magical, some not, at the three skulls grinning from the cubbies atop his desk, at the crystal ball set upon the small table across the way. These were his items of power, items gained through a lifetime of work, items that he could use to destroy or at least to defend against, any single man he had ever met.

Except for one. What was it about this one? The way he stood? The way he moved? The simple aura of power that surrounded him, as tangible as the gray cloak and black bolero he now wore?

"Go and bring Quentin Bodeau," Entreri instructed.

"He will not appreciate becoming involved."

"He already is," Entreri assured the wizard. "Now he must choose."

"Between you and . . . ?" LaValle asked.

"The rest of them," Entreri replied calmly.

LaValle tilted his head curiously. "You mean to do battle with all of Calimport then?" he asked skeptically.

"With all in Calimport who oppose me," Entreri said, again with the utmost calm.

LaValle shook his head, not knowing what to make of it all. He trusted Entreri's judgment—never had the wizard met a more cunning and controlled man—but the assassin spoke foolishness, it seemed, if he honestly believed he could stand alone against the likes of the Basadonis, let alone the rest of Calimport's street powers.

But still . . .

"Shall I bring Chalsee Anguaine, as well?" the wizard asked, standing and heading for the door.

"Chalsee has already been shown the futility of resistance," Entreri replied.

LaValle stopped abruptly, turning on the assassin as if betrayed.

"I knew you would go along," Entreri explained. "For you have come to know and love me as a brother. The lieutenant's mind-set, however, remained a mystery. He had to be convinced, or removed."

LaValle just stared at him, awaiting the verdict.

"He is convinced," Entreri remarked, moving to fall comfortably into LaValle's comfortable chair. "Very much so.

"And so," he continued as the wizard again started for the door, "will you find Bodeau."

LaValle turned on him again.

"He will make the right choice," Entreri assured the man.

"Will he have a choice?" LaValle dared to ask.

"Of course not."

Indeed, when LaValle found Bodeau in his private quarters and informed him that Artemis Entreri had come again the guildmaster blanched white and trembled so violently that LaValle feared he would simply fall over dead on the floor.

"You have spoken with Chalsee then?" LaValle asked.

"Evil days," Bodeau replied, and moving as if he had to battle mind with muscle through every pained step, he headed for the corridor.

"Evil days?" LaValle echoed incredulously under his breath. What in all the Realms could prompt the master of a murderous guild to make such a statement? Suddenly taking Entreri's claims more seriously, the wizard fell into step behind Bodeau. He noted, his intrigue mounting ever higher, that the guildmaster ordered no soldiers to follow or even to flank.

Bodeau stopped outside the wizard's door, letting LaValle assume the lead into the room. There in the study sat Entreri, exactly as the wizard had left him. The assassin appeared totally unprepared had Bodeau decided to attack instead of parlay, as if he had known without doubt that Bodeau wouldn't dare oppose him.

"What do you demand of me?" Bodeau asked before LaValle could find any opening to the obviously awkward situation.

"I have decided to begin with the Basadonis," Entreri calmly replied. "For they, after all, started this fight. You, then, must locate all of their soldiers, all of their fronts, and a complete layout of their operation, not including the guild house."

"I offer to tell no one that you came here and to promise that my soldiers will not interfere," Bodeau countered.

"Your soldiers could not interfere," Entreri shot back, a flash of anger crossing his black eyes.

LaValle watched in continued amazement as Quentin Bodeau fought so very hard to control his shaking.

"And we will not," the guildmaster offered.

"I have told you the terms of your survival," Entreri said, a coldness creeping into his voice that made LaValle believe that Bodeau and all the guild would be murdered that very night if the guildmaster didn't agree. "What say you?"

"I will consider—"

"Now."

Bodeau glared at LaValle, as if blaming the wizard for ever allowing Artemis Entreri into his life, a sentiment that LaValle, as unnerved as Bodeau, could surely understand.

"You ask me to go against the most powerful pashas of the streets," Bodeau said, trying hard to find some courage.

"Choose," Entreri said.

A long, uncomfortable moment slipped past. "I will see what my soldiers may discern," Bodeau promised.

"Very wise," said Entreri. "Now leave us. I wish a word with LaValle."

More than happy to be away from the man, Bodeau turned on his heel and after another hateful glare at LaValle, swiftly exited the room.

"I do not begin to guess what tricks you have brought with you," LaValle said to Entreri.

"I have been to Menzoberranzan," Entreri admitted. "The city of the drow."

LaValle's eyes widened, his mouth drooping open.

"I returned with more than trinkets."

"You have allied with . . ."

"You are the only one I have told and the only one I shall tell," Entreri announced. "Understand the responsibility that goes with such knowledge. It is one that I shan't take lightly."

"But Chalsee Anguaine?" LaValle asked. "You said he had been convinced."

"A friend found his mind and there put images too horrible for him to resist," Entreri explained. "Chalsee knows not the truth, only that to resist would bring about a fate too terrible to consider. When he reported to Bodeau his terror was sincere."

"And where do I stand in your grand plans?" the wizard asked, trying very hard not to sound sarcastic. "If Bodeau fails you, then what of LaValle?"

"I will show you a way out should that come to pass," Entreri promised, walking over to the desk. "I owe you that much at least." He picked up a small dagger LaValle had set there to cut seals on parchments or to prick a finger when a spell called for a component of blood.

LaValle understood then that Entreri was being pragmatic, not merciful. If the wizard was indeed spared should Bodeau fail the assassin, it would only be because Entreri had some use for him.

"You are surprised that the guildmaster so readily complied," Entreri said evenly. "You must understand his choice: to risk that I will fail and the Basadonis will win out and then exact revenge on my allies . . . or to die now, this very night, and horribly, I assure you."

LaValle forced an expressionless set to his visage, playing the role of complete neutrality, even detachment.

"You have much work ahead of you, I assume," Entreri said, and he flicked his wrist, sending the dagger soaring past the wizard to knock heavily into the outside wall. "I take my leave."

Indeed, as the signal knock against the wall sounded, Kimmuriel Oblodra went into his contemplation again and brought up another dimensional pathway for the assassin to make his exit.

LaValle saw the portal open and thought for a moment out of sheer curiosity to leap through it beside Entreri to unmask this great mystery.

Good sense overruled curiosity.

And then the wizard was alone and very glad of it.

* * * * *

"I do not understand," Rai'gy Bondalek said when Entreri rejoined him, Jarlaxle, and Kimmuriel in the complex of tunnels beneath the city that the drow had made their own. He remembered then to speak more slowly, for Entreri, while fairly proficient in the drow language, was not completely fluent, and the wizard-priest didn't want to bother with the human tongue at all, either by learning it or by wasting the energy necessary to enact a spell that would allow them all to understand each other, whatever language each of them chose to speak. In truth, Bondalek's decision to force the discussion to continue in the drow language, even when Entreri was with them, was more a choice to keep the human assassin somewhat off-balance. "It seems, from all you previously said that the halflings would be better suited and more easily convinced to perform the services you just put upon Quentin Bodeau."

"I doubt not Dwahvel's loyalty," Entreri replied in the human Calimport tongue, and he eyed Rai'gy with every word.

The wizard turned a curious and helpless look over Jarlaxle, and the mercenary, with a laugh at the pettiness of it all, produced an orb from an inside fold of his cloak, held it aloft, and spoke a word of command. Now they would all understand.

"To herself and her well-being, I mean," Entreri said, again in the human tongue, though Rai'gy heard it in drow. "She is no threat."

"And pitiful Quentin Bodeau and his lackey wizard are?" Rai'gy asked incredulously, Jarlaxle's enchantment reversing the effect, so that, while the drow spoke in his native tongue, Entreri heard it in his own.

"Do not underestimate the power of Bodeau's guild," Entreri warned. "They are firmly entrenched, with eyes ever outward."

"So you force his loyalty early," Jarlaxle agreed, "that he cannot later claim ignorance whatever the outcome."

"And where from here?" Kimmuriel asked.

"We secure the Basadoni Guild," Entreri explained. "That then becomes our base of power, with both Dwahvel and Bodeau watching to make certain that the others aren't aligning against us."

"And from there?" Kimmuriel pressed.

Entreri smiled and looked to Jarlaxle, and the mercenary leader recognized that Entreri understood that Kimmuriel was asking the questions as Jarlaxle had bade him to ask.

"From there we will see what opportunities present themselves," Jarlaxle answered before Entreri could reply. "Perhaps that base will prove solid enough. Perhaps not."

Later on, after Entreri had left them, Jarlaxle, with some pride, turned to his two cohorts. "Did I not choose well?" he asked.

"He thinks like a drow," Rai'gy replied, offering as high a compliment as Jarlaxle had ever heard him give to a human or to anyone else who was not drow. "Though I wish he would better learn our language and our sign language."

Jarlaxle, so pleased with the progress, only laughed.

Chapter 14

Reputation

The man felt strange indeed. Alcohol dimmed his senses so that he could not register all the facts about his current situation. He felt light, floating, and felt a burning in his chest.

Wulfgar clenched his fist more tightly, grasping the front of the man's tunic and pulling chest hairs from their roots in the process. With just that one arm the barbarian easily held the two hundred pound man off the ground. Using his other arm to navigate the crowd in the Cutlass, he made his way for the door. He hated taking this roundabout route—previously he had merely tossed unruly drunks through a window or a wall—but Arumn Gardpeck had quickly reigned in that behavior, promising to take the cost of damages out of Wulfgar's pay.

Even a single window could cost the barbarian a few bottles, and if the frame went with it Wulfgar might not find any drink for a week.

The man, smiling stupidly, looked at Wulfgar and finally managed to find some focus. Recognition of the bouncer and of his present predicament at last showed on his face. "Hey!" he complained, but then he was flying, flat out in the air, arms and legs flailing. He landed facedown in the muddy road, and there he stayed. Likely a wagon would have run him over had not a couple of passersby taken pity on the poor slob and dragged him into the gutter . . . taking the rest of his coins from him in the process.

"Fifteen feet," Josi Puddles said to Arumn, estimating the length of the drunk's flight. "And with just one arm."

"I told ye he was a strong one," Arumn replied, wiping the bar and pretending that he was hardly amazed. In the weeks since the barkeep had hired Wulfgar, the barbarian had made many such throws.

"Every man on Half Moon Street's talking about that," Josi added, the tone of his voice somewhat grim. "I been noticing that your crowd's a bit tougher every night this week."

Arumn understood the perceptive man's less than subtle statement. There was a pecking order in Luskan's underbelly that resisted intrusion. As Wulfgar's reputation continued to grow, some of those higher on that pecking order would find their own reputations at stake and would filter in to mend the damage.

"You like the barbarian," Josi stated as much as asked.

Arumn, staring hard at Wulfgar as the huge man filtered through the crowd once more, gave a resigned nod. Hiring Wulfgar had been a matter of business, not friendship, and Arumn usually took great pains to avoid any personal relationships with his bouncers—since many of those men, drifters by nature, either wandered away of their own accord or angered the wrong thug and wound up dead at Arumn's doorstep. With Wulfgar, though, the barkeep had lost some of that perspective. Their late nights together when the Cutlass was quiet, Wulfgar drinking at the bar, Arumn preparing the place for the next day's business, had become a pleasant routine. Arumn truly enjoyed Wulfgar's companionship. He discovered that once the drink was in the man, Wulfgar let down his cold and distant facade. Many nights they stayed together until the dawn, Arumn listening intently as Wulfgar wove tales of the frigid northland, of Icewind Dale, and of friends and enemies alike that made the barkeep's hair stand up on the back of his neck. Arumn had heard the story of Akar Kessel and the crystal shard so many times that he could almost picture the avalanche at Kelvin's Cairn that took down the wizard and buried the ancient and evil relic.

And every time Wulfgar recounted tales of the dark tunnels under the dwarven kingdom of Mithral Hall and the coming of the dark elves, Arumn later found himself shivering under his blankets, as he had when he was a child and his father had told him similarly dark stories by the hearth.

Indeed, Arumn Gardpeck had come to like his newest employee more than he should and less than he would.

"Then calm him," Josi Puddles finished. "He'll be bringing in Morik the Rogue and Tree Block Breaker anytime soon."

Arumn shuddered at the thought and didn't disagree. Particularly concerning Tree Block. Morik the Rogue, he knew, would be a bit more cautious (and thus, would be much more dangerous), would spend weeks, even months, sizing up the new threat before making his move, but brash Tree Block, arguably the toughest human—if he even was human, for many stories said that he had more than a little orc, or even ogre, blood in him—ever to step into Luskan, would not be so patient.

"Wulfgar," the barkeep called.

The big man sifted through the crowd to stand opposite Arumn.

"Did ye have to throw him out?" Arumn asked.

"He put his hand where it did not belong," Wulfgar replied absently. "Delly wanted him gone."

Arumn followed Wulfgar's gaze across the room to Delly . . . Delenia Curtie. Though not yet past her twentieth birthday, she had worked in the Cutlass for several years. She was a wisp of a thing, barely five feet tall and so slender that many thought she had a bit of elven blood in her—though it was more the result of drinking elven spirits, Arumn knew. Her blond hair hung untrimmed and unkempt and often not very clean. Her brown eyes had long ago lost their soft innocence and taken on a harder edge, and her pale skin had not seen enough of the sun in years, nor proper nutrition, and was now dry and rough. Her step had replaced the bounce of youth with the caution of a woman often hunted. But still there remained a charm about Delly, a sensual wickedness that many of the patrons, particularly after a few drinks, found too tempting to resist.

"If ye're to be killing every man who's grabbing Delly's bottom, I'll have no patrons left within the week," Arumn said dryly.

"Just push them out," Arumn continued when Wulfgar offered no response, not even a change of expression. "Ye don't have to be throwing them halfway to Waterdeep." He motioned back to the crowd, indicating that he was done with the barbarian.

Wulfgar walked away, back to his duties sifting through the boisterous bunch.

Within an hour another man, bleeding from his nose and mouth, took the aerial route, this time a two-handed toss that put him almost to the other side of the street.

* * * * *

Wulfgar held up his shirt, revealing the jagged line of deep scars. "Had me up in its mouth," he explained grimly, slurring the words. It had taken more than a little of the potent spirits to bring him to a level of comfort where he could discuss this battle, the fight with the yochlol, the fight that had brought him to Lolth, and she to Errtu for his years of torment. "A mouse in the cat's mouth." He gave a slight chuckle. "But this mouse had a kick."

His gaze drifted to Aegis-fang, lying on the bar a couple of feet away.

175

"Prettiest hammer I've ever seen," remarked Josi Puddles. He reached for it tentatively, staring at Wulfgar as his hand inched in, for he, like all the others, had no desire to anger the frightfully dangerous man.

But Wulfgar, usually very protective of Aegis-fang, his sole link to his past life, wasn't even watching. His recounting of the yochlol fight had sent his thoughts and his heart careening back across the years, had locked him into a replay of the events that had put him in living hell.

"And how it hurt," he said softly, voice quavering, one hand subconsciously running the length of the scar.

Arumn Gardpeck stood before him staring, but though Wulfgar's eyes aimed at those of the barkeep, their focus was far, far away. Arumn slid another drink before the man, but Wulfgar didn't notice. With a deep and profound sigh the barbarian dropped his head into his huge arms, seeking the comfort of blackness.

He felt a touch on his bare arm, gentle and soft, and turned his head so that he could regard Delly. She nodded to Arumn, then gently pulled Wulfgar, coaxing him to rise and leading him away.

Wulfgar awoke later that night, long and slanted rays of moonlight filtering into the room through the western window. It took him a few moments to orient himself and to realize that this was not his room, for his room had no windows.

He glanced around and then to the blankets beside him, to the lithe form of Delly amidst those blankets, her skin seeming soft and delicate in the flattering light.

Then he remembered. Delly had taken him from the bar to bed—not to his own, but to hers—and he remembered all they had done.

Fearful, recalling his less-than-tender parting with Catti-brie, Wulfgar gently reached over and put his hand about the woman's neck, sighing in profound relief to find that she still had a pulse. Then he turned her over and scanned her bare body, not in any lustful way, but merely to see if she showed any bruises, any signs that he had brutalized her.

Her sleep was quiet and sound.

Wulfgar turned to the side of the bed, rolling his legs off the edge. He started to stand, but his throbbing head nearly knocked him backward. Reeling, he fought to control his balance and then ambled over to the window, staring out at the setting moon.

Catti-brie was likely watching that same moon, he thought, and somehow knew it to be true. After a while he turned to regard Delly again, all soft and snuggled amidst mounds of blankets. He had been able to make love to her without the anger, without the memories of the succubi balling his fists in rage. For a moment he felt as if he might be free, felt as if he should burst out of the house, out of Luskan altogether, running down the road in search of his old friends. He looked back at the moon and thought of Catti-brie and how wonderful it would be to fall into her arms.

But then he realized the truth of it all.

The drink had allowed him to build a wall against those memories, and behind that protective barrier he had been able to live in the present and not the past.

"Come on back to bed," came Delly's voice behind him, a gentle coax with a subtle promise of sensual pleasure. "And don't you be worrying over your hammer," she added, turning so that Wulfgar could follow her gaze to the opposite wall, against which Aegis-fang rested.

Wulfgar spent a long moment regarding the woman, caretaker of his emotions and his possessions. She was sitting up, the covers bundled about her waist, and making no move to cover her nakedness. Indeed she seemed to flaunt it a bit to entice the man back into her bed.

A large part of Wulfgar did want to go to her. But he resisted, realizing the danger, realizing that the drink had worn off. In a fit of passion, a fit of remembered rage, how easy it would be for him to squeeze her birdlike neck.

"Later," he promised, moving to gather his clothes. "Before we go to work this night."

"But you don't have to leave."

"I do," he said briskly, and he saw the flash of pain across her face. He moved to her immediately, very close. "I do," he repeated in a softer tone. "But I will come back to you. Later."

He kissed her gently on the forehead and started for the door.

"You are thinking that I'll want you back," came a harsh call behind him, and he turned to see Delly staring at him, her gaze ice cold, her arms folded defensively across her chest.

At first surprised, Wulfgar only then realized that he wasn't the only one in this room carrying around personal demons.

"Go," Delly said to him. "Maybe I'll take you back, and maybe I'll find another. All the same to me."

Wulfgar sighed and shook his head, then pushed out into the hall, more than happy to be out of that room.

The sun peeked over the eastern rim before the barbarian, an empty bottle at his side, found his way back into the void of sleep. He didn't see the sunrise, though, for his room had no windows.

He preferred it that way.

Chapter 15

The Call of Crenshinibon

The prow cut swiftly through the azure blanket of the Sword Coast, shooting great fins of water and launching spray high into the air. At the forward rail, Catti-brie felt the stinging, salty droplets, so cold in contrast to the heat of the brilliant sun on her fair face. The ship, *Quester*, sailed south, and so south the woman looked. Away from Icewind Dale, away from Luskan, away from Waterdeep, from which they had sailed three days previous.

Away from Wulfgar.

Not for the first time, and she knew not for the last, the woman reconsidered their decision to let the beleaguered barbarian go off on his own. In his present state of mind, a state of absolute tumult and confusion, how could Wulfgar not need them?

And yet she had no way to get to him now, sailing south along the Sword Coast. Catti-brie blinked away moisture that was not sea spray and set her gaze firmly on the wide waters before them, taking some heart at the sheer speed of the vessel. They had a mission to complete, a vital mission, for during their days crossing by land they had come to learn beyond doubt that Crenshinibon remained a potent foe, sentient and intelligent. It was able to call in creatures to serve as its minions,

179

monsters of dark heart eager to grasp at the promises of the relic. Thus the friends had gone to Waterdeep and had taken passage on the sturdiest available ship in the harbor, believing that enemies would be fewer at sea and far easier to discern. Both Drizzt and Catti-brie greatly lamented that Captain Deudermont and his wondrous *Sea Sprite* were not in.

Less than two hours out from port one of the crewmen had come after Drizzt, thinking to steal the crystal. Battered by the flat sides of flashing twin scimitars, the man, bound and gagged, had been handed off to another ship passing by, heading to the north to Waterdeep, with instructions to turn him over to the dock authorities in that lawful city for proper punishment.

Since then, though, the voyage had been uneventful, just swift sailing and empty waters, flat horizons dotted rarely by the sails of another distant ship.

Drizzt moved to join Catti-brie at the rail. Though she didn't turn around, she knew by the footsteps that followed the near-silent drow that Bruenor and Regis had come too.

"Only a few more days to Baldur's Gate," the drow said.

Catti-brie glanced over at him, noting that he kept the cowl of his traveling cloak low over his face—not to block any of the stinging spray, she knew, for Drizzt loved that feel as much as she, but to keep him in comfortable shade. Drizzt and Catti-brie had spent years together aboard Deudermont's *Sea Sprite*, and still the high sun of midday glittering off the waters bothered the drow elf, whose heritage had designed him for walking lightless caverns.

"How fares Bruenor?" the woman asked quietly, pretending not to know that the dwarf was standing behind her.

"Grumbling for solid ground and all the enemies in the world to stand against him, if necessary, to get him off this cursed floating coffin," the ranger replied, playing along.

Catti-brie managed a slight grin, not surprised at all. She had journeyed the seas with Bruenor farther to the south. While the dwarf had kept a stoic front on that occasion, his relief had been obvious when they had at last docked and returned again to solid ground. This time Bruenor was having an even worse time of it, spending long stretches at the rail—and not for the view.

"Regis seems unbothered," Drizzt went on. "He makes certain that no food remains on Bruenor's plate soon after Bruenor declares that he cannot eat."

Another smile found its way onto Catti-brie's face. Again it was short-lived. "Do ye think we'll be seeing him again?" she asked.

Drizzt sighed and turned his gaze out to the empty waters. Though they were both looking south, the wrong direction, they were both, in a manner of speaking, looking for Wulfgar. It was as if, against all logic and reason, they expected the man to come swimming toward them.

"I do not know," the drow admitted. "In his mood, it is possible that Wulfgar has found many enemies and has flung himself against them with all his heart. No doubt many of them are dead, but the north is a place of countless foes, some, I fear, too powerful even for Wulfgar."

"Bah!" Bruenor snorted from behind. "We'll find me boy, don't ye doubt. And the worst foe he'll be seeing'll be meself, paying him back for slapping me girl and for bringing me so much worry!"

"We shall find him," Regis declared. "And Lady Alustriel will help, and so will the Harpells."

The mention of the Harpells brought a groan from Bruenor. The Harpells were a family of eccentric wizards known for blowing themselves and their friends up, turning themselves—quite by accident and without repair—into various animals and all other manner of self-inflicted catastrophes.

"Alustriel, then," Regis agreed. "She will help if we cannot find him on our own."

"Bah! And how tough're ye thinking that to be?" Bruenor argued. "Are ye knowin' many rampaging seven-footers then? And them carrying hammers that can knock down a giant or the house it's living in with one throw?"

"There," Drizzt said to Catti-brie. "Our assurances that we will indeed find our friend."

The woman managed another smile, but it, too, was a strained thing and could not last. And what would they find when they at last located their missing friend? Even if he was physically unharmed, would he wish to see them? And even if he did, would he be in a better humor? And most important of all, would they—would she—really wish to see him? Wulfgar had hurt Catti-brie badly, not in body, but in heart, when he had struck her. She could forgive him that, she knew, to some extent at least.

But only once.

She studied her drow friend, saw his shadowed profile under the edge of his cowl as he stared vacantly to the empty waters, his lavender eyes glazed, as if his mind were looking elsewhere. She turned to consider Bruenor and Regis then and found them similarly distracted. All of them wanted to find Wulfgar again—not the Wulfgar who had left them on the road but the one who had left them those years ago in the tunnels beneath Mithral Hall, taken by the yochlol. They all wanted it to be as it had once been, the Companions of the Hall adventuring together without the company of brooding internal demons.

"A sail to the south," Drizzt remarked, drawing the woman from her contemplation. Even as Catti-brie looked out from the rail, squinting in a futile attempt to spot the too-distant ship, she heard the cry from the crow's nest confirming the drow's claim.

"What's her course?" Captain Vaines called from somewhere near the middle of the deck.

"North," Drizzt answered quietly so that only Catti-brie, Bruenor, and Regis could hear.

"North," cried the crewman from the crow's nest a few seconds later.

"Yer eyes've improved in the sunlight," Bruenor remarked.

"Credit Deudermont," Catti-brie explained.

"My eyes," Drizzt added, "and my perceptions of intent."

"What're ye babbling about?" Bruenor asked, but the ranger held up his hand, motioning for silence. He stood staring intently at the distant ship whose sails now appeared to the other three as tiny black dots, barely above the horizon.

"Go and tell Captain Vaines to turn us to the west," Drizzt instructed Regis.

The halfling stood staring for just a moment, then rushed back to find Vaines. Just a minute or so later the friends felt the pull as *Quester* leaned and turned her prow to the left.

"Ye're just making the trip longer," Bruenor started to complain, but again Drizzt held up his hand.

"She is turning with us, keeping her course to intercept," the drow explained.

"Pirates?" Catti-brie asked, a question echoed by Captain Vaines as he moved up to join the others.

"They are not in trouble, for they cut the water as swiftly as we, perhaps even more so," Drizzt reasoned. "Nor are they a ship of a king's fleet, for they fly no standard, and we are too far out for any coastal patrollers."

"Pirates," Captain Vaines spat distastefully.

"How can ye know all that?" an unconvinced Bruenor demanded.

"Comes from hunting 'em," Catti-brie explained. "And we've hunted more than our share."

"So I heard in Waterdeep," said Vaines, which was why he had agreed to take them aboard for a swift run to Baldur's Gate in the first place. Normally a woman, a dwarf, and a halfling would find no easy—and surely no cheap—passage out of Waterdeep Harbor when accompanied by a dark elf, but among the honest sailors of Waterdeep the names Drizzt Do'Urden and Catti-brie rang out as sweet music.

The approaching ship showed bigger on the horizon now, but it was still too small for any detailed images—except to Drizzt, and to Captain Vaines and the man in the crow's nest, both holding rare and expensive spyglasses. The captain put his to his eye now and recognized the telltale triangular sails. "She's a schooner," he said. "And a light one. She cannot hold more than twenty or so and is no match for us."

Catti-brie considered the words carefully. *Quester* was a caravel, and a large one at that. She held three strong banks of sails and had a front end long and tapered to aid in her run, but she carried a pair of ballistae, and had thick and strong sides. A slender schooner did not seem much of a match for *Quester*, to be sure, but how many pirates had said the same about another schooner, Deudermont's *Sea Sprite*, only to wind up fast filling with sea water?

"Back to the south with us!" the captain called, and *Quester* creaked and leaned to the right. Soon enough, the approaching schooner corrected her course to maintain her intercepting route.

"Too far to the north," Vaines remarked, striking a pensive pose, one hand coming up to stroke the gray hairs of his beard. "Pirates should not be this far north and should not deign to approach us."

The others, particularly Drizzt and Catti-brie, understood his trepidation. Concerning brute force at least, the schooner and her crew of twenty, perhaps thirty, would seem no match for the sixty of Vaines's crew. But such odds could often be overcome at sea by use of a single wizard, Catti-brie and Drizzt both knew. They had seen *Sea Sprite*'s wizard, a powerful invoker named Robillard, take down more than one ship single-handedly long before conventional weapons had even been used.

"Shouldn't and aren't ain't the same word," Bruenor remarked dryly. "I'm not knowing if they're pirates or not, but they're coming, to be sure."

Vaines nodded and moved back to the wheel with his navigator.

"I'll get me bow and go up to the nest," Catti-brie offered.

"Pick your shots well," Drizzt replied. "Likely there is one, or maybe a couple, who are guiding this ship. If you can find them and down them, the rest might flee."

"Is that the way of pirates?" Regis asked, seeming more than a little confused. "If they even are pirates?"

"That is the way of a lesser ship coming after us because of the crystal shard," Drizzt replied, and then the other two caught on.

"Ye're thinking the damned thing's calling them?" Bruenor asked.

"Pirates take few chances," Drizzt explained. "A light schooner coming after *Quester* is taking a great chance."

"Unless they got wizards," Bruenor reasoned, for he, too, had understood Captain Vaines's concerns.

Drizzt was shaking his head before the dwarf ever finished. Catti-brie would have been, too, except that she had already run off to retrieve Taulmaril. "A pirate running with enough magical aid to destroy *Quester* would have long ago been marked," the drow explained. "We would have heard of her and been warned of her before we ever left Waterdeep."

"Unless she is new to the trade or new of the power," Regis reasoned.

Drizzt conceded the point with a nod, but he remained unconvinced, believing that Crenshinibon had brought this new enemy in, as it had brought in so many others in a desperate attempt to wrest the relic away from those who would see it destroyed. The drow looked back across the deck, spotting the familiar form of Catti-brie with Taulmaril, the wondrous Heartseeker, strapped across her back as she made her nimble way up the knotted rope.

Then he opened his belt pouch and gazed upon the wicked relic, Crenshinibon. How he wished he could hear its call to better understand the enemies it would bring before them.

Quester shuddered suddenly as one of its great ballistae let fly. The huge spear leaped away, skipping a couple times across the water far short of the out-of-range schooner, but close enough to let the sailors aboard her recognize that *Quester* had no intention of parlay or surrender.

But the schooner flew on without the slightest course change, splitting the water right beside the spent ballista bolt, even clipping the metal-tipped spear as it hung buoy-like in the swelling sea. Smooth and swift was its run, seeming more like an arrow cutting the air than a ship cutting the water. The narrow hull had been built purely for speed. Drizzt had seen pirates such as this; often similar ships had led *Sea Sprite*, also a schooner, but a three-master and much larger, on long pursuits. The drow had enjoyed those chases most of all during his time with Deudermont, sails full of wind, spray rushing past, his white hair flowing out behind him as he stood poised at the forward rail.

He was not enjoying this scenario, though. There were many pirates along the Sword Coast well capable of destroying *Quester*, larger and better armed and armored than the well-structured caravel, truly the hunting lions of the region. But this approaching ship was more a bird of prey, a swift and cunning hunter designed for smaller quarry, for fishing boats wandering too far from protected harbors or the luxury barges of wealthy merchants who let their warship escorts get a bit too far away from them. Or pirate schooners would work in conjunction, several on a target, a fleet hunting pack.

But no other sails were to be seen on any horizon.

From a different pouch, Drizzt took out his onyx figurine. "I will bring in Guenhwyvar soon," he explained to Regis and Bruenor. Captain Vaines came up again, a nervous expression stamped on his face—one that told the drow that, despite his many years at sea, Vaines had not seen much battle. "With a proper run the panther can leap fifty feet or more to gain the deck of our enemies' ship. Once there she will make more than a few call for a retreat."

"I have heard of your panther friend," Vaines said. "She was much the talk of Waterdeep Harbor."

"Ye better bring the damned cat up soon then," Bruenor grumbled, looking out over the rail. Indeed, the schooner already seemed much closer, speeding over the waves.

To Drizzt the image struck him as purely out of control; suicidal, like the giant that had followed them out of the Spine of the World. He put the figurine on the ground and called softly for the panther, watching as the telltale gray mist began to swirl about the statue, gradually taking shape.

* * * * *

Catti-brie wiped her eyes, then lifted the spyglass once again, scanning the deck, hardly believing what she saw. But again she saw the truth of it all: that this was no pirate, at least none of the kind she had ever before seen. There were women aboard, and not warrior women, not even sailors, and surely not prisoners. And children! Several she had seen, and none of them dressed as cabin boys.

She winced as a ballista spear grazed the schooner's deck, skipping off a turnstile and cracking through the side rail, only missing a young boy by a hands' breadth.

"Get ye down, and be quick," she instructed the lookout sharing the crow's nest. "Tell yer captain to load chain and take her in her high sails."

The man, obviously impressed with the tales he had heard of Drizzt and Catti-brie, turned without hesitation and started down the rope, but the woman knew that the task for stopping this coming travesty had fallen squarely upon her shoulders.

Quester had dropped to battle sail, but the schooner kept at full, kept its run straight and swift, and seemed as if it meant to smash right through the larger caravel.

Catti-brie put up the spyglass again, scanning slowly, searching, searching. She knew now that Drizzt's guess about the schooner's course and intent had been correct, knew that this was Crenshinibon's doing, and that truth made her blood boil with rage. One, or two, perhaps, would be the key, but where . . .

She spotted the man at the forward rail of the flying bridge, his form mostly obscured by the mainmast. She held her sights on him for a long while, resisting the urge to shift and observe damage as *Quester*'s ballistae let fly again, this time in accord with Catti-brie's orders. Spinning chains ripped high through the schooner's top sails. This sight, this man at the rail, one hand gripping the wood so tightly that it was white for lack of blood, was more important.

The schooner flinched, the ship veering slightly, unintentionally, until the crew could work the ballista-altered sails to put her in line again. In that turn, the image of the man at the rail drifted clear of the obstructing mast, and Catti-brie saw him clearly, saw the crazed look upon his face, saw the line of drool running from the corner of his mouth.

And she knew.

She dropped the spyglass and took up Taulmaril, lining her shot with great care, using the mainmast as a guide, for she could hardly even see the target.

* * * * *

185

"If they've a wizard, he should have acted by now," a frantic Captain Vaines cried. "For what do they wait? To tease us, as a cat to a mouse?"

Bruenor looked at the man and snorted derisively.

"They've no wizard," Drizzt assured the captain.

"Do they mean to simply ram us, then?" the captain asked. "We'll take her down, then!" He turned to yell new instructions to the ballista crews, to instruct his archers to rake the deck. But before he uttered a word a silver streak from the nest above startled him. He spun around to see the streak cut across the schooner's deck, then angle sharply to the right and fly out over the open sea.

Before he could begin to question it another streak shot out, following nearly the same course, except that this one didn't deflect. It soared right past the schooner's mainmast.

Everything seemed to come to a stop, a tangible pause from caravel and schooner alike.

"Hold the cat!" Catti-brie called down to Drizzt.

Vaines looked at the drow doubtfully, but Drizzt didn't doubt, not at all. He put his hand up and called Guenhwyvar—who had moved back on the deck to get a running start—back to his side.

"It is ended," the dark elf announced.

The captain's doubting expression melted as the schooner's mainsail dropped, the ship's prow also dropping instantly, deeper into the sea. Her back beam swung out wide, turning the triangular back sail. She leaned far to the side, turning her prow back toward the east, back toward the far-distant shore.

*   *   *   *   *

Through the spyglass, Catti-brie saw a woman kneeling over the dead man while another man cradled his head. An emptiness settled in Catti-brie's breast, for she never enjoyed such an action, never wanted to kill anyone.

But that man had been the antagonist, the driving force behind a battle that would have left many innocents on the schooner dead. Better that he pay for his failings with his own life alone than with the lives of others.

She told herself that repeatedly.

It helped but a little.

*   *   *   *   *

Certain that the fight had indeed been avoided, Drizzt looked down at the crystal shard once more with utter contempt. A single call to a single man had nearly brought ruin to so many.

He could not wait to be rid of the thing.

Chapter 16

Brothers of Mind and Magic

The dark elf leaned back in a chair, settling comfortably, as he always seemed to do, and listening with more than a passing amusement. Jarlaxle had planted a device of clairaudience on the magnificent wizard's robe he had given to Rai'gy Bondalek, one of many enchanted gemstones sewn into the black cloth. This one had a clever aura, deceiving any who would detect it into thinking it was a stone the wizard wearing the robe could use to cast the clairaudience spell. And indeed it was, but it possessed another power, one with a matching stone that Jarlaxle kept, allowing the mercenary to listen in at will upon Rai'gy's conversations.

"The replica was well made and holds much of the original's dweomer," Rai'gy was saying, obviously referring to the magical, Drizzt-seeking locket.

"Then you should have no trouble in locating the rogue again and again," came the reply, the voice of Kimmuriel Oblodra.

"They are still aboard the ship," Rai'gy explained. "And from what I have heard they mean to be aboard for many more days."

"Jarlaxle demands more information," the Oblodran psionicist said, "else he will turn the duties over to me."

"Ah, yes, given to my principal adversary," the wizard said in mock seriousness.

In that distant room, Jarlaxle chuckled. The two thought it important to keep him believing that they were rivals and thus no threat to him, though in truth they had forged a tight and trusted friendship. Jarlaxle didn't mind that—in fact, he rather preferred it—because he understood that even together the psionicist and the wizard, dark elves of considerable magical talents and powers but little understanding of the motivations and nature of reasoning beings, would never move against him. They feared not so much that he would defeat them, but rather that they would prove victorious and then be forced to shoulder the responsibility for the entire volatile band.

"The best method to discern more about the rogue would be to go to him in disguise and listen to his words," Rai'gy went on. "Already I have learned much of his present course and previous events."

Jarlaxle came forward in his chair, listening intently as Rai'gy began a chant. He recognized enough of the words to understand that the wizard-priest was enacting a scrying spell, a reflective pool.

"That one there," Rai'gy said a few moments later.

"The young boy?" came Kimmuriel's response. "Yes, he would be an easy target. Humans do not prepare their children well, as do the drow."

"You could take his mind?" Rai'gy asked.

"Easily."

"Through the scrying pool?"

There came a long pause. "I do not know that it has ever been done," Kimmuriel admitted, and his tone told Jarlaxle that he was not afraid of the prospect, but rather intrigued.

"Then our eyes and ears would be right beside the outcast," Rai'gy went on. "In a form Drizzt Do'Urden would not think to distrust. A curious child, one who would love to hear his many tales of adventure."

Jarlaxle took his hand from the gemstone, and the clairaudience spell went away. He settled back into his chair and smiled widely, taking comfort in the ingenuity of his underlings.

That was the truth of his power, he realized, the ability to delegate responsibility and allow others to rightfully take their credit. The strength of Jarlaxle lay not in Jarlaxle, though even alone he could be formidable indeed, but in the competent soldiers with whom the mercenary surrounded himself. To battle Jarlaxle was to battle Bregan D'aerthe, an organization of free-thinking, amazingly competent drow warriors.

To battle Jarlaxle was to lose.

The guilds of Calimport would soon recognize that truth, the drow leader knew, and so would Drizzt Do'Urden.

* * * * *

"I have contacted another plane of existence and from the creatures there, beings great and wise, beings who can see into the humble affairs of the drow with hardly a thought, I have learned of the outcast and his friends, of where they have been and where they mean to go," Rai'gy Bondalek proclaimed to Jarlaxle the next day.

Jarlaxle nodded and accepted the lie, seeing Rai'gy's proclamation of some otherworldly and mysterious source as inconsequential.

"Inland, as I earlier told you," Rai'gy explained. "They took to a ship—the *Quester*, it is called—in Waterdeep, and now sail south for a city called Baldur's Gate, which they should reach in a matter of three days."

"Then back to land?"

"Briefly," Rai'gy answered, for indeed, Kimmuriel had learned much in his half day as a cabin boy. "They will take to ship again, a smaller craft, to travel along a river that will bring them far from the great water they call the Sword Coast. Then they will take to land travel again, to a place called the Snowflake Mountains and a structure called the Spirit Soaring, wherein dwells a mighty priest named Cadderly. They go to destroy an artifact of great power," he went on, adding details that he and not Kimmuriel had learned through use of the reflecting pool. "This artifact is Crenshinibon by name, though often referred to as the crystal shard."

Jarlaxle's eyes narrowed at the mention. He had heard of Crenshinibon before in a story concerning a mighty demon and Drizzt Do'Urden. Pieces began to fall into place then, the beginnings of a cunning plan creeping into the corners of his mind. "So that is where they shall go," he said. "As important, where have they been?"

"They came from Icewind Dale, they say," Rai'gy reported. "A land of cold ice and blowing wind. And they left behind one named Wulfgar, a mighty warrior. They believe him to be in the city of Luskan, north of Waterdeep along the same seacoast."

"Why did he not accompany them?"

Rai'gy shook his head. "He is troubled, I believe, though I know not why. Perhaps he has lost something or has found tragedy."

"Speculation," Jarlaxle said. "Mere assumptions. And such things will lead to mistakes that we can ill afford."

"What part plays Wulfgar?" Rai'gy asked with some surprise.

"Perhaps no part, perhaps a vital one," Jarlaxle answered. "I cannot decide until I know more of him. If you cannot learn more, then perhaps it is time I go to Kimmuriel for answers." He noted the way the wizard-priest stiffened at his words, as though Jarlaxle had slapped him.

"Do you wish to learn more of the outcast or of this Wulfgar?" Rai'gy asked, his voice sharp.

"More of Cadderly," Jarlaxle replied, drawing a frustrated sigh from his off-balance companion. Rai'gy didn't even move to answer. He just turned about, threw his hands up in the air and walked away.

189

Jarlaxle was finished with him anyway. The names of Crenshinibon and Wulfgar had him deep in thought. He had heard of both; of Wulfgar, given by a handmaiden to Lolth and from Lolth to Errtu, the demon who sought the Crystal Shard. Perhaps it was time for the mercenary leader to go and pay a visit to Errtu, though truly he hated dealing with the unpredictable and ultimately dangerous creatures of the Abyss. Jarlaxle survived by understanding the motivations of his enemies, but demons rarely held any definite motivations and could certainly alter their desires moment by moment.

But there were other ways with other allies. The mercenary drew out a slender wand and with a thought teleported his body back to Menzoberranzan.

His newest lieutenant, once a proud member of the ruling house, was waiting for him.

"Go to your brother Gromph," Jarlaxle instructed. "Tell him that I wish to learn of the story of the human named Wulfgar, the demon Errtu, and the artifact known as Crenshinibon."

"Wulfgar was taken in the first raid on Mithral Hall, the realm of Clan Battlehammer," Berg'inyon Baenre answered, for he knew well the tale. "By a handmaiden, and given to Lolth."

"But where from there?" Jarlaxle asked. "He is back on our plane of existence, it would seem, on the surface."

Berg'inyon's expression showed his surprise at that. Few ever escaped the clutches of the Spider Queen. But then, he admitted silently, nothing about Drizzt Do'Urden had ever been predictable. "I will find my brother this day," he assured Jarlaxle.

"Tell him that I wish to know of a mighty priest named Cadderly," Jarlaxle added, and he tossed Berg'inyon a small amulet. "It is imbued with the emanations of my location," he explained, "that your brother might find me or send a messenger."

Again Berg'inyon nodded.

"All is well?" Jarlaxle asked.

"The city remains quiet," the lieutenant reported, and Jarlaxle was not surprised. Ever since the last assault upon Mithral Hall several years before, when Matron Baenre, the figurehead of Menzoberranzan for centuries, had been killed, the city had been outwardly quiet above the tumult of private planning. To her credit, Triel Baenre, Matron Baenre's oldest daughter, had done a credible job of holding the house together. But despite her efforts it seemed likely that the city would soon know interhouse wars beyond the scope of anything previously experienced. Jarlaxle had decided to strike out for the surface, to extend his grasp, thus making his mercenary band invaluable to any house with aspirations for greater power.

The key to it all now, Jarlaxle understood, was to keep everyone on his side even as they waged war with each other. It was a line he had learned to walk with perfection centuries before.

"Go to Gromph quickly," he instructed. "This is of utmost importance. I must have my answers before Narbondel brightens a hands' pillars," he explained, using a common expression to mean before five days had passed. The expression "hands' pillars" represented the five fingers on one hand.

Berg'inyon departed, and with a silent mental instruction to his wand Jarlaxle was back in Calimport. As quickly as his body moved, so too moved his thoughts to another pressing issue. Berg'inyon would not fail him, nor would Gromph, nor would Rai'gy and Kimmuriel. He knew that with all confidence, and that knowledge allowed him to focus on this very night's work: the takeover of the Basadoni Guild.

*   *   *   *   *

"Who is there?" came the old voice, a voice full of calmness despite the apparent danger.

Entreri, having just stepped through one of Kimmuriel Oblodra's dimensional portals, heard it as if from far, far away, as the assassin fought to orient himself to his new surroundings. He was in Pasha Basadoni's private room, behind a lavish dressing screen. Finally finding his center of balance and consciousness, the assassin spent a moment studying his surroundings, his ears pricked for the slightest of sounds: breathing or the steady footfalls of a practiced killer.

But of course he and Kimmuriel had properly scouted the room and the whereabouts of the pasha's lieutenants, and they knew that the old and helpless man was quite alone.

"Who is there?" came another call.

Entreri walked out around the screen and into the candlelight, shifting his bolero back on his head that the old man might see him clearly, and that the assassin might gaze upon Basadoni.

How pitiful the old man looked, a hollow shell of his former self, his former glory. Once Pasha Basadoni had been the most powerful guild-master in Calimport, but now he was just an old man, a figurehead, a puppet whose strings could be pulled by several different people at once.

Entreri, despite himself, hated those string pullers.

"You should not have come," Basadoni rasped at him. "Flee the city, for you cannot live here. Too many, too many."

"You have spent two decades underestimating me," Entreri replied lightly, taking a seat on the edge of the bed. "When will you learn the truth?"

That brought a phlegm-filled chuckle from Basadoni, and Entreri flashed a rare smile.

"I have known the truth of Artemis Entreri since he was a street urchin killing intruders with sharpened stones," the old man reminded him.

"Intruders you sent," said Entreri.

Basadoni conceded the point with a grin. "I had to test you."

"And have I passed, Pasha?" Entreri considered his own tone as he spoke the words. The two were speaking like old friends, and in a manner they were indeed. But now, because of the actions of Basadoni's lieutenants, they were also mortal enemies. Still the pasha seemed quite at ease here, alone and helpless with Entreri. At first, the assassin had thought that the man might be better prepared than he had assumed, but after carefully inspecting the room and the partially upright bed that held the old man, he was secure in the fact that Basadoni had no tricks to play. Entreri was in control, and that didn't seem to bother Pasha Basadoni as much as it should.

"Always, always," Basadoni replied, but then his smile dissipated into a grimace. "Until now. Now you have failed, and at a task too easy."

Entreri shrugged as if it did not matter. "The targeted man was pitiful," he explained. "Truly. Am I, the assassin who passed all of your tests, who ascended to sit beside you though I was still but a young man, to murder wretched peasants who owe a debt that a novice pickpocket could cover in half a day's work?"

"That was not the point," Basadoni insisted. "I let you back in, but you have been gone a long time, and thus you had to prove yourself. Not to me," the pasha quickly added, seeing the assassin's frown.

"No, to your foolish lieutenants," Entreri reasoned.

"They have earned their positions."

"That is my fear."

"Now it is Artemis Entreri who underestimates," Pasha Basadoni insisted. "Each of the three have their place and serve me well."

"Well enough to keep me out of your house?" Entreri asked.

Pasha Basadoni gave a great sigh. "Have you come to kill me?" he asked, and then he laughed again. "No, not that. You would not kill me, because you have no reason to. You know, of course, that if you somehow succeed against Kadran Gordeon and the others, I will take you back in."

"Another test?" Entreri asked dryly.

"If so, then one you created."

"By sparing the life of a wretch who likely would have preferred death?" Entreri said, shaking his head as if the whole notion was purely ridiculous.

A flicker of understanding sharpened Basadoni's old gray eyes. "So it was not sympathy," he said, grinning.

"Sympathy?"

"For the wretch," the old man explained. "No, you care nothing for him, care not that he was subsequently murdered. No, no, and I should have understood. It was not sympathy that stayed the hand of Artemis Entreri. Never that! It was pride, simple, foolish pride. You would not lower yourself to the level of street enforcer, and thus you started a war you cannot win. Oh, fool!"

"Cannot win?" Entreri echoed. "You assume much." He studied the old man for a long moment, locking gazes. "Tell me, Pasha, who do you wish to win?" he asked.

"Pride again," Basadoni replied with a flourish of his skinny arms that stole much of his strength and left him gasping. "But the point," he continued a moment later, "in any case, is moot. What you truly ask is if I still care for you, and of course I do. I remember well your ascent through my guild, as well as any father recalls the growth of his son. I do not wish you ill in this war you have begun, though you understand that there is little I can do to prevent these events that you and Kadran, prideful fools both, have put in order. And of course, as I said before, you cannot win."

"You do not understand everything."

"Enough," the old man said. "I know that you have no allegiance among the other guilds, not even with Dwahvel and her little ones or Quentin Bodeau and his meager band. Oh, they swear neutrality—we would have it no other way—but they will not aid you in your fight, and neither will any of the other truly powerful guilds. And thus are you doomed."

"And you know of every guild?" Entreri asked slyly.

"Even the wretched wererats of the sewers," Pasha Basadoni said with confidence, but Entreri noted a hint at the edges of his tone that showed he was not as smug as he outwardly pretended. There was a sadness here, Entreri knew, a weariness and, obviously, a lack of control. The lieutenants ran the guild.

"I tell you this out of admission for all that you did for me," the assassin said, and he was not surprised to see the wise old pasha's eyes narrow warily. "Call it loyalty, call it a last debt repaid," Entreri went on, and he was sincere—about the forewarning, at least—"you do not know all, and your lieutenants shall not prevail against me."

"Ever the confident one," the pasha said with another phlegm-filled laugh.

"And never wrong," Entreri added, and he tipped his bolero and walked behind the dressing screen, back to the waiting dimensional portal.

* * * * *

"You have made every defense?" Pasha Basadoni asked with true concern, for the old man knew enough about Artemis Entreri to take the assassin's warning seriously. As soon as Entreri had left him, Basadoni had gathered his lieutenants. He didn't tell them of his visitor, but he wanted to ensure that they were ready. The time was near, he knew, very near.

193

Sharlotta, Hand, and Gordeon all nodded—somewhat condescendingly, Basadoni noted. "They will come this night," he announced. Before any of the three could question where he might have garnered that information, he added, "I can feel their eyes upon us."

"Of course, my Pasha," purred Sharlotta, bending low to kiss the old man's forehead.

Basadoni laughed at her and laughed all the louder when a guard shouted from the hallway that the house had been breached.

"In the sub-cellar!" the man cried. "From the sewers!"

"The wererat guild?" Kadran Gordeon asked incredulously. "Domo Quillilo assured us that he would not—"

"Domo Quillilo stayed out of Entreri's way, then," Basadoni interrupted.

"Entreri has not come alone," Kadran reasoned.

"Then he will not die alone," Sharlotta said, seeming unconcerned. "A pity."

Kadran nodded, drew his sword, and turned to leave. Basadoni, with great effort, grabbed his arm. "Entreri will come in separately from his allies," the old man warned. "For you."

"More to my pleasure, then," Kadran growled in reply. "Go lead our defenses," he told Hand. "And when Entreri is dead, I will bring his head to you that we may show it to those stupid enough to join with him."

Hand had barely exited the room when he was nearly run over by a soldier coming up from the cellars. "Kobolds!" the man cried, his expression showing that he hardly believed the claim as he spoke it. "Entreri's allies are smelly rat kobolds."

"Lead on, then," said Hand, much more confidently. Against the power of the guild house, with two wizards and two hundred soldiers, kobolds—even if they poured in by the thousands—would prove no more than a minor inconvenience.

Back in the room, the other two lieutenants heard the claim and stared at each other in disbelief, then broke into wide smiles.

Pasha Basadoni, lying on the bed and watching them, didn't share that mirth. Entreri was up to something, he knew, something big, and kobolds would hardly be the worst of it.

*   *   *   *   *

Kobolds indeed led the way into the Basadoni guild house, up from the sewers where frightened wererats—as per their agreement with Entreri—stayed hidden in shadows, out of the way. Jarlaxle had brought a considerable number of the smelly little creatures with him from Menzoberranzan. Bregan D'aerthe was housed primarily along the rim of the great Clawrift that rent the drow city, and in there the kobolds bred and bred, thousands and thousands of the things. Three hundred had accompanied the forty drow to Calimport, and they now led the charge, running wildly through all the lower corridors of the guild house, inadvertently setting off the traps, both mechanical and magical, and marking the locations of the Basadoni soldiers.

Behind them came the drow host, silent as death.

Kimmuriel Oblodra, Jarlaxle, and Entreri moved up one slanting corridor, flanked by a foursome of drow warriors holding hand crossbows readied with poison-tipped darts. Up ahead the corridor opened into a wide room, and a group of kobolds scrambled across, chased by a threesome of archers.

"Click, click, click," went the crossbows, and the three archers stumbled, staggered, and slumped to the floor, deep in sleep.

An explosion to the side sent the kobolds, half the previous number, scrambling back the other way.

"Not a magical blast," Kimmuriel remarked.

Jarlaxle sent a pair of his soldiers out wide the other way, flanking the human position. Kimmuriel took a more direct route, opening a dimensional door diagonally across the wide floor to the open edge of the corridor from which the explosion had come. As soon as the door appeared, leading into another long, ascending corridor, he and Entreri spotted the bombers. There was a group of men rushing behind a barricade, flanked by several large kegs.

"Drow elf!" one of the men shouted, pointing to the open door. Kimmuriel stood across the dimensional space behind the other door.

"Light it! Light it!" cried another man. A third brought a torch over to light the long rag hanging off the top of one keg.

Kimmuriel reached into his mind yet again, focusing on the keg, on the latent energy within the wood planking. He touched that energy, exciting it. Before the men could even begin to roll the barrel out from behind the barricade it blew apart, then exploded again as the burning wick hit the oil.

A flaming man tumbled out from the barricade, rolling frantically down the corridor, trying to douse the flames. A second, less injured, staggered into the open, and one of the remaining drow soldiers put a hand crossbow dart into his face.

Kimmuriel dropped the dimensional door—better to run through the room—and the group set off, rushing past the burning corpse and the sleeping and badly injured man, past the third victim of the explosion, curled in death in a fetal position in the corner of the small cubby, then down a side passage. There they found three more men, two asleep and a third lying dead before the feet of the two soldiers Jarlaxle had sent out to flank.

And so it went throughout the lower levels, with the dark elves overrunning all obstacles. Jarlaxle had taken only his finest warriors with him to the surface: renegade, houseless dark elves who had once belonged to noble houses, who had trained for decades, centuries even, for just this kind of close-quartered, room-to-room, tunnel-to-tunnel combat.

A brigade of knights in shining mail and with wizard supporters might prove a credible enemy to the dark elves on an open field of battle. These street thugs, though, with their small daggers, short swords, and minor magics, and with no foreknowledge of the enemy that had come against them, fell systematically to Jarlaxle's steadily moving band. Basadoni's men surrendered position after position, retreating higher and higher into the guild house proper.

Jarlaxle found Rai'gy Bondalek and half a dozen warriors moving along the street level of the house.

"They had two wizards," the wizard-priest explained. "I put them in a globe of silence and—"

"Pray tell me you did not destroy them," said the mercenary leader, who knew well the value of wizards.

"We hit them with darts," Rai'gy explained. "But one had a stoneskin enchantment about him and had to be destroyed."

Jarlaxle could accept that. "Finish the business at hand," he said to Rai'gy. "I will take Entreri to claim his place in the higher rooms."

"And him?" Rai'gy asked sourly, motioning toward Kimmuriel.

Knowing their little secret, Jarlaxle did well to hide his smile. "Lead on," he instructed Entreri.

They encountered another group of heavily armed soldiers, but Jarlaxle used one of his many wands to entrap them all within globs of goo. Another one did slip away—or would have, except that Artemis Entreri knew well the tactics of such men. He saw the shadow lengthening against the wall and directed the shot well.

* * * * *

Kadran Gordeon's eyes widened when Hand stumbled into the room, gasping and clutching at his hip. "Dark elves," the man explained, slumping in the arms of his comrade. "Entreri. The bastard brought dark elves!"

Hand slipped to the floor, fast asleep.

Kadran Gordeon let him fall and ran on, out the back door of the room, across the wide ballroom of the second floor, and up the sweeping staircase.

Entreri and his friends noted every movement.

"That is the one?" Jarlaxle asked.

Entreri nodded. "I will kill him," he promised, starting away, but Jarlaxle grabbed his shoulder. Entreri turned to see the mercenary leader looking slyly at Kimmuriel.

"Would you like to fully humiliate the man?" Jarlaxle asked.

Before Entreri could respond, Kimmuriel came up to stand right before him. "Join with me," the drow psionicist said, lifting his fingers for Entreri's forehead.

The ever-wary assassin brushed the reaching hand away.

Kimmuriel tried to explain, but Entreri knew only the basics of drow language, not the subtleties. The psionicist's words sounded more like the joining of lovers than anything Entreri understood. Frustrated, Kimmuriel turned to Jarlaxle and started talking so fast that it seemed to Entreri as if he was saying one long word.

"He has a trick for you to play," Jarlaxle explained in the common surface tongue. "He wishes to get into your mind, but only briefly, to enact a kinetic barrier and show you how to maintain it."

"A kinetic barrier?" the confused assassin asked.

"Trust him this one time," Jarlaxle bade. "Kimmuriel Oblodra is among the greatest practitioners of the rare and powerful psionic magic and is so skilled with it that he can often lend some of his power to another, albeit briefly."

"He will teach me?" Entreri asked skeptically.

Kimmuriel laughed at the absurd notion.

"The mind magic is a gift, a rare gift, and not a lesson to be taught," Jarlaxle explained. "But Kimmuriel can lend you a bit of the power, enough to humiliate Kadran Gordeon."

Entreri's expression showed that he wasn't so sure of any of this.

"We could kill you at any time by more conventional means if we so decided," Jarlaxle reminded him. He nodded to Kimmuriel, and Artemis Entreri did not back away.

And so Entreri got his first personal understanding of psionics and walked up the sweeping staircase unafraid. Across the way a concealed archer let fly, and Entreri took the arrow right in the back—or would have, except that the kinetic barrier stopped the arrow's flight, fully absorbing its energy.

* * * * *

Sharlotta heard the ruckus in the outer rooms of the royal complex and figured that Gordeon had returned. She still had no idea of the rout in the lower halls, though, and so she decided to move quickly, to use this opportunity well. From one of the long sleeves of her alluring gown she drew out a slender knife, moving with purpose for the door that would lead into a larger room, with the door of Pasha Basadoni across the way.

Finally she would be done with the man, and it would look as if Entreri or one of his associates had completed the assassination.

Sharlotta paused at the door, hearing another slam beyond and the sound of running feet. Gordeon was on the move, as was another.

Had Entreri gained this level?

The thought assaulted her but did not dissuade her. There were other ways, more secret ways, though the route would be longer. She went to

197

the back of her room, removed a specific book from her bookshelf, then slipped into the corridor that opened behind the case.

*   *   *   *   *

Entreri caught up to Kadran Gordeon soon after in a complex of many small rooms. The man rushed out the side, sword slashing. He hit Entreri a dozen times at least and the assassin, focusing his thoughts with supreme concentration, didn't even try to block. Instead he just took them and stole their energy, feeling the power building, building within him.

Eyes wide, mouth agape, Kadran Gordeon backpedaled. "What manner of demon are you?" the man gasped, falling back through a door into the room where Sharlotta, small dagger in hand, had just come out of another concealed passage, standing along a wall to the side of Pasha Basadoni's bed.

Entreri, brimming with confidence, strode in.

On came Gordeon again, sword slashing. This time Entreri drew the sword Jarlaxle had given him and countered, parrying each slash perfectly. He felt his mental concentration waning and knew that he had to react soon or be consumed by the pent-up energy, so when Gordeon came with a sidelong slash, Entreri dipped the tip of his blade below the angle of the cut, then brought it up and over quickly, stepping under, turning about, and rolling his sword around. He took Gordeon off balance and crashed into the man, knocking him to the floor and coming down atop him, weapon pinning weapon.

*   *   *   *   *

Sharlotta lifted her arm to throw her knife into Basadoni but then shifted, seeing the too-tempting target of Artemis Entreri's back as the man went down atop Kadran Gordeon.

But then she shifted again as another, darker form entered the room. She cocked to throw, but the drow was quicker. A dagger sliced her wrist, pinning her arm to the wall. Another dagger stuck in the wall to the right of her head, then another to the left. Another grazed the side of her chest, and then another as Jarlaxle pumped his arm rapidly, sending a seemingly endless stream of steel her way.

Gordeon punched Entreri in the face.

That, too, was absorbed.

"I do grow tired of your foolishness," said Entreri, putting his hand on Gordeon's chest, ignoring the man's free hand as it pumped punch after punch at his face.

With a thought Entreri released the energy, all of it, the arrow, the many sword hits, the many punches. His hand sank into Gordeon's chest, melting the skin and ribs below it. A rolling fountain of blood erupted, spewing into the air and falling back on Gordeon's surprised expression, filling his mouth as he tried to scream in horror.

And then he was dead.

Entreri got up to see Sharlotta standing against the wall, hands in the air—one pinned to the wall—facing Jarlaxle, who had yet another dagger ready. Several other drow, including Kimmuriel and Rai'gy, had come into the room behind their leader. The assassin quickly moved between her and Basadoni, noting the dagger Sharlotta had obviously dropped on the floor right beside the bed. He turned his sly gaze on the dangerous woman.

"It would seem that I arrived just in time, Pasha," Entreri explained, picking up the weapon. "Sharlotta, thinking the guild house secure, had apparently decided to use the battle to her advantage, finally ridding herself of you."

Both Entreri and Basadoni looked at Sharlotta. She stood impassive, obviously caught, though she finally managed to extract the material of her sleeve from the sticking dagger.

"She did not know the truth of her enemies," Jarlaxle explained.

Entreri looked at him and nodded. The dark elves all stepped back, allowing the assassin his moment.

"Should I kill her?" Entreri asked Basadoni.

"Why ask my permission?" the pasha replied, obviously none too pleased. "Am I then to credit you for this? For bringing dark elves to my house?"

"I acted as I needed to survive," Entreri replied. "Most of the house survives, neutralized but not killed. Kadran Gordeon is dead—never could I have trusted that one—but Hand survives. And so we will go on under the same arrangement as before, with three lieutenants and one guildmaster." He looked to Jarlaxle, then back to Sharlotta. "Of course, my friend Jarlaxle desires a position of lieutenant," he said. "One well-earned, and that I cannot deny."

Sharlotta stiffened, expecting then to die, for she could do simple math.

Indeed Entreri did originally mean to kill her, but when he glanced back to Basadoni, when he looked again upon the feeble old man, such a shadow of his former glory, he reversed the direction of his sword and put it through Pasha Basadoni's heart instead.

"Three lieutenants," he said to the stunned Sharlotta. "Hand, Jarlaxle, and you."

"So Entreri is guildmaster," the woman remarked with a crooked grin. "You said you could not trust Kadran Gordeon, yet you recognize that I am more honorable," she said seductively, coming forward a step.

Entreri's sword came out and about too fast for her to follow, its tip stopping against the tender flesh of her throat. "Trust you?" the assassin balked. "No, but neither do I fear you. Do as you are instructed, and you will live." He shifted the angle of his blade slightly so that it tucked under her chin, and he nicked her there. "Exactly as instructed," he warned, "else I will take your pretty face from you, one cut at a time."

Entreri turned to Jarlaxle.

"The house will be secured within the hour," the dark elf assured him. "Then you and your human lieutenants can decide the fate of those taken and put out on the streets whatever word suits you as guildmaster."

Entreri had thought that this moment would bring some measure of satisfaction. He was glad that Kadran Gordeon was dead and glad that the old wretch Basadoni had been given a well-deserved rest.

"As you wish, my Pasha," Sharlotta purred from the side.

The title turned his stomach.

Chapter 17

Exorcising Demons

There was indeed something appealing about the fighting, about the feeling of superiority and the element of control. Between the fact that the fights were not lethal—though more than a few patrons were badly injured—and the conscience-dulling drinks, no guilt accompanied each thunderous punch.

Just satisfaction and control, an edge that had been too long absent.

Had he stopped to think about it, Wulfgar might have realized that he was substituting each new challenger for one particular nemesis, one he could not defeat alone, one who had tormented him all those years.

He didn't bother with contemplation, though. He simply enjoyed the sensation of his fist colliding with the chest of this latest troublemaker, sending the tall, thin man reeling back in a hopping, staggering, stumbling quickstep, finally to fall backward over a bench some twenty feet from the barbarian.

Wulfgar methodically waded in, grabbing the decked man by the collar (and taking out more than a few chest hairs in the process) and the groin (and similarly extracting hair). With one jerk the barbarian brought the horizontal man level with his waist. Then a rolling motion snapped the man up high over his head.

201

"I just fixed that window," Arumn Gardpeck said dryly, helplessly, seeing the barbarian's aim.

The man flew through it to bounce across Half Moon Street.

"Then fix it again," Wulfgar replied, casting a glare over Arumn that the barkeep did not dare to question.

Arumn just shook his head and went back to wiping his bar, reminding himself that, by keeping such complete order in the place Wulfgar was attracting customers—many of them. Folk now came looking for a safe haven in which to waste a night, and then there were those interested in the awesome displays of power. These came both as challengers to the mighty barbarian or, more often, merely as spectators. Never had the Cutlass seen so many patrons, and never had Arumn Gardpeck's purse been so full.

But how much more full it would be, he knew, if he didn't have to keep fixing the place.

"Shouldn't've done that," a man near the bar remarked to Arumn. "That's Rossie Doone, he throwed, a soldier."

"Not wearing any uniform," Arumn remarked.

"Came in unofficial," the man explained. "Wanted to see this Wulfgar thug."

"He saw him," Arumn replied in the same resigned and dry tones.

"And he'll be seein' him again," the man promised. "Only next time with friends."

Arumn sighed and shook his head, not out of any fear for Wulfgar, but because of the expenses he anticipated if a whole crew of soldiers came in to fight the barbarian.

Wulfgar spent that night—half the night—in Delly Curtie's room again, taking a bottle with him from the bar, then grabbing another one on his way outside. He went down to the docks and sat on the edge of a long wharf, watching the sparkles grow on the water as the sun rose behind him.

* * * * *

Josi Puddles saw them first, entering the Cutlass the very next night, a half-dozen grim-faced men including the one the patron had identified as Rossie Doone. They moved to the far side of the room, evicting several patrons from tables, then pulling three of the benches together so they could all sit side by side with their backs to the wall.

"Full moon tonight," Josi remarked.

Arumn knew what that meant. Every time the moon was full the crowd was a bit rowdier. And what a crowd had come in this evening, every sort of rogue and thug Arumn could imagine.

"Been the talk of the street all the day," Josi said quietly.

"The moon?" Arumn asked.

"Not the moon," Josi replied. "Wulfgar and that Rossie fellow. All have been talking of a coming brawl."

"Six against one," Arumn remarked.

"Poor soldiers," Josi said with a snicker.

Arumn nodded to the side then, to Wulfgar, who, sitting with a foaming mug in hand, seemed well aware of the group that had come in. The look on the barbarian's face, so calm and yet so cold, sent a shiver along Arumn's spine. It was going to be a long night.

*   *   *   *   *

On the other side of the room, in a corner opposite where sat the six soldiers, another man, quiet and unassuming, also noted the tension and the prospective combatants with more than a passing interest. The man's name was well known on the streets of Luskan, though his face was not. He was a shadow stalker by trade, a man cloaked in secrecy, but a man whose reputation brought trembles to the hardiest of thugs.

Morik the Rogue had been hearing quite a bit about Arumn Gardpeck's new strong-arm; too much, in fact. Story after story had come to him about the man's incredible feats of strength. About how he had been hit squarely in the face with a heavy club and had shaken it away seemingly without care. About how he lifted two men high into the air, smashed their heads together, then simultaneously tossed them through opposite walls of the tavern. About how he had thrown one man out into the street, then rushed out and blocked a team of two horses with his bare chest to stop the wagon from running down the prone drunk. . . .

Morik had been living among the street people long enough to understand the exaggerated nonsense in most of these tales. Each storyteller tried to outdo the previous one. But he couldn't deny the impressive stature of this man Wulfgar. Nor could he deny the many wounds showing about the head of Rossie Doone, a soldier Morik knew well and whom he had always respected as a solid fighter.

Of course Morik, his ears so attuned to the streets and alleyways, had heard of Rossie's intention to return with his friends and settle the score. Of course Morik had also heard of another's intention to put this newcomer squarely in his place. And so Morik had come in to watch, and nothing more, to measure this huge northerner, to see if he had the strength, the skills, and the temperament to survive and become a true threat.

Never taking his gaze off Wulfgar, the quiet man sipped his wine and waited.

*   *   *   *   *

As soon as he saw Delly moving near to the six men, Wulfgar drained his beer in a single swallow and tightened his grip on the table. He saw it coming, and how predictable it was, as one of Rossie Doone's sidekicks reached out and grabbed Delly's bottom as she moved past.

Wulfgar came up in a rush, storming in right before the offender, and right beside Delly.

"Oh, but 'tis nothing," the woman said, pooh-poohing Wulfgar away. He grabbed her by the shoulders, lifted her, and turned, depositing her behind him. He turned back, glaring at the offender, then at Rossie Doone, the true perpetrator.

Rossie remained seated, laughing still, seeming completely relaxed with three burly fighters on his right, two more on his left.

"A bit of fun," Wulfgar stated. "A cloth to cover your wounds, deepest of all the wound to your pride."

Rossie stopped laughing and stared hard at the man.

"We have not yet fixed the window," Wulfgar said. "Do you prefer to leave by that route once more?"

The man next to Rossie bristled, but Rossie held him back. "In truth, northman, I prefer to stay," he answered. "In my own eyes it's yourself who should be leaving."

Wulfgar didn't blink. "I ask you a second time, and a last time, to leave of your own accord," he said.

The man farthest from Rossie, down to Wulfgar's left, stood up and stretched languidly. "Think I'll get me a bit o' drink," he said calmly to the man seated beside him, and then, as if going to the bar, he took a step Wulfgar's way.

The barbarian, already a seasoned veteran of barroom brawls, saw it coming. He understood that the man would grab at him to hold and slow him so that Rossie and the others could pummel him. He kept his apparent focus directly on Rossie and waited. Then, as the man came within two steps, as his hands started coming up to grab at Wulfgar, the barbarian spun suddenly, stepping inside the other's reach. The barbarian snapped his back muscles, launching his forehead into the man's face, crushing his nose and sending him staggering backward.

Wulfgar turned back fast, fist flying, and caught Rossie across the jaw as he started to rise, slamming the man back against the wall. Hardly slowing, Wulfgar grabbed the stunned Rossie by the shoulders and yanked him hard to the side, flipping him to the left to deflect the coming rush of the two men remaining there. Then around went the barbarian again, growling, fists flying, to swap heavy punches with the two men leaping at him from that direction.

A knee came up for his groin, but Wulfgar recognized the move and reacted fast. He turned his leg in to catch the blow with his thigh, then reached down under the bent leg. The attacker instinctively grabbed at Wulfgar, catching shoulder and hair, trying to use him for balance. But the powerful barbarian, simply too strong, drove on, heaving him up and over his shoulder, turning as he went to again deflect the attack from the two men coming in at his back.

The movement cost Wulfgar several punches from the man who had been standing next to the latest human missile. Wulfgar accepted them stoically, hardly seeming to care. He came back hard, legs pumping, to drive the puncher into the wall, wrestling him around.

The desperate soldier grabbed on with all his strength, and the man's friends fast approached from behind. A roar, a wriggle, and a stunning punch extracted Wulfgar from the man's grasp. He skittered back away from the wall and the pursuers, instinctively ducking a punch as he went and grabbing a table by the leg.

Wulfgar spun back, facing the group, and halted the swinging momentum of the table so fully that the item snapped apart. The bulk of the table flew into the chest of the closest man, leaving Wulfgar standing with a wooden table leg in hand, a club he wasted no time in putting to good use. The barbarian smacked it below the table at the exposed legs of the man he had hit with the missile, cracking the side of the soldier's knee once and then again. The man howled in pain and shoved the table back out at Wulfgar, but he accepted the missile strike with merely a shrug, concentrating instead on turning the club in line and jabbing the man in the eye with its narrow end.

A half turn and full swing caught another across the side of the head, splitting the club apart and dropping the attacker like a sack of ground meal. Wulfgar ran right over him as he fell—the barbarian understood that mobility was his only defense against so many. He barreled into the next man in line, carrying him halfway across the room to slam into a wall, a journey that ended with a wild flurry of fists from both. Wulfgar took a dozen blows and gave a like number, but his were by far the heavier, and the dazed and defeated man crumbled to the floor—or would have, had not Wulfgar grabbed him as he slumped. The barbarian turned about fast and let his latest human missile fly, spinning him in low across the ankles of the closest pursuer, who tripped headlong, both arms reaching out to grab the barbarian. Wulfgar, still in his turn, using the momentum of that spin, dived forward, punch leading, stretching right between those arms. His force combined with the momentum of the stumbling man, and he felt his fist sink deep into the man's face, snapping his head back violently.

That man, too, went down hard.

Wulfgar stood straight, facing Rossie and his one standing ally, who had blood rolling freely from his nose. Another man holding his torn eye tried to stand beside them, but his broken knee wouldn't support his weight. He stumbled away to the side to slam into a wall and sink there into a sitting position.

In the first truly coordinated attack since the chaos had begun, Rossie and his companion came in slow and then leaped together atop Wulfgar, thinking to bear him down. But though the two were both large men, Wulfgar didn't fall, didn't stumble in the least. The barbarian caught them as they soared in and held his footing. His thrashing had them both holding on for dear life. Rossie slipped away, and Wulfgar managed to get both arms on the other, dragging the clutching man horizontally across in front of his face. The man's arms flailed about Wulfgar's head, but the angle of attack was all wrong, and the blows proved ineffectual.

Wulfgar roared again and bit the man's stomach hard, then started a full-out, blind run across the tavern floor. Gauging the distance, Wulfgar dipped his head at the last moment to put his powerful neck muscles in proper alignment, then rammed full force into the wall. He bounced back, holding the man with just one arm hooked under his shoulder, and kept it there long enough to allow the man to come down on his feet.

The man stood, against the wall, watching in confusion as Wulfgar ran back a few steps, and then his eyes widened indeed when the huge barbarian turned about, roared, and charged, dipping his shoulder as he came.

The man put his arms up, but that hardly mattered, for Wulfgar shoulder-drove him against the planking—right into the planking, which cracked apart. Louder than the splitting wood came the sound of a groan and a sigh from resigned Arumn Gardpeck.

Wulfgar bounced back again but leaned in fast, slamming left and right repeatedly, each thunderous blow driving the man deeper into the wall. The poor man, crumbled and bloody, splinters deep in his back, his nose already broken and half his body feeling the same way, held up a feeble arm to show that he had had enough.

Wulfgar smashed him again, a vicious left hook that came in over the upraised arm and shattered his jaw, throwing him into oblivion. He would have fallen except that the broken wall held him fast in place.

Wulfgar didn't even notice, for he had turned around to face Rossie, the lone enemy still showing any ability to fight. One of the others, the man Wulfgar had traded blows with against the wall, crawled about on hands and knees, seeming as if he didn't even know where he was. Another, the side of his head split wide by the vicious club swing, kept trying to stand and kept falling over, while a third still sat against the wall, clutching his torn eye and broken knee. The fourth of Rossie's companions, the one Wulfgar had hit with the single, devastating punch, lay very still with no sign of consciousness.

"Gather your friends and be gone," a tired Wulfgar offered to Rossie. "And do not return."

In answer, the outraged man reached down to his boot and drew out a long knife. "But I want to play," Rossie said wickedly, approaching a step.

"Wulfgar!" came Delly's cry from across the way, from behind the bar, and both Wulfgar and Rossie turned to see the woman throwing Aegis-fang out toward her friend, though she couldn't get the heavy warhammer half the distance.

That hardly mattered, though, for Wulfgar reached for it with his arm and with his mind, telepathically calling to the hammer.

The hammer vanished, then reappeared in the barbarian's waiting grasp. "So do I," Wulfgar said to an astonished and horrified Rossie. To accentuate his point, he swung Aegis-fang, one armed, out behind him. The swing hit and split a beam, which drew another profound groan from Arumn.

Rossie, his eager expression long gone, glanced about and backed away liked a trapped animal. He wanted to back out, to find some way to flee—that much was apparent to everybody in the room.

And then the outside door banged open, turning all heads—those that weren't broken open—Rossie Doone's and Wulfgar's included, and in strode the largest human, if he was indeed a human, that Wulfgar had ever seen. He was a giant man, taller than Wulfgar by a foot at least, and almost as wide, weighing perhaps twice the barbarian's three hundred pounds. Even more impressive was the fact that very little of the giant's bulk jiggled as he stormed in. He was all muscle, and gristle, and bone.

He stopped inside the suddenly hushed tavern, his huge head turning slowly to scan the room. His gaze finally settled on Wulfgar. He brought his arms out slowly from under the front folds of his cloak to reveal that he held a heavy length of chain in one hand and a spiked club in the other.

"Ye too tired for me, Wulfgar the dead?" Tree Block Breaker asked, spittle flying with each word. He finished with a growl, then brought his arm across powerfully, slamming the length of chain across the top of the nearest table and splitting the thing neatly down the middle. The three patrons sitting at that particular table didn't scamper away. They didn't dare to move at all.

A smile widened across Wulfgar's face. He flipped Aegis-fang into the air, a single spin, to catch it again by the handle.

Arumn Gardpeck groaned all the louder; this would be an expensive night.

Rossie Doone and those of his friends who could still move scrambled across the room, out of harm's way, leaving the path between Wulfgar and Tree Block Breaker clear.

In the shadows across the room, Morik the Rogue took another sip of wine. This was the fight he had come to see.

"Well, ye give me no answer," Tree Block Breaker said, whipping his chain across again. This time it did not connect solidly but whipped about one angled leg of the fallen table. Then, after slapping the leg of one sitting man, its tip got a hold on the man's chair. With a great roar, Tree Block yanked the chain back, sending table and chair flying across the room and dropping the unfortunate patron on his bum.

"Tavern etiquette and my employer require that I give you the opportunity to leave quietly," Wulfgar calmly replied, reciting Arumn's creed.

On came Tree Block Breaker, a great, roaring monster, a giant gone wild. His chain flailed back and forth before him, his club raised high to strike.

Wulfgar realized that he could have taken the giant out with a well-aimed throw of Aegis-fang before Tree Block had gone two steps, but he let the creature come on, relishing the challenge. To everyone's surprise he dropped Aegis-fang to the floor as Tree Block closed. When the chain swished for his head, he dropped into a sudden squat but held his arm vertically above him.

The chain hooked around, and Wulfgar reached over it and grabbed on, giving a great tug that only increased Tree Block's charge. The huge man swung with his club, but he was too close and still coming. Wulfgar went down low, driving his shoulder against the man's legs. Tree Block's momentum carried his bulk across the bent barbarian's back.

Amazingly, stunningly, Wulfgar stood up straight, bringing Tree Block up above him. Then, to the astonished gasps of all watching, he bent at the knees quickly and jerked back up straight. Pushing with all his strength, he lifted Tree Block into the air above his head.

Before the huge man could wriggle about and bring his club to bear, Wulfgar ran back the way Tree Block had charged, and with a great roar of his own, threw the man right through the door, taking it and the jamb out completely and depositing the huge man in a jumble of kindling outside the Cutlass. His arm still enwrapped by the chain, Wulfgar gave a huge tug that sent Tree Block spinning about in the pile of wood before he surrendered the chain altogether.

The stubborn giant thrashed about, finally extricating himself from the wood heap. He stood roaring, his face and neck cut in a dozen places, his club whirling about wildly.

"Turn and leave," Wulfgar warned. The barbarian reached behind him and with a thought brought Aegis-fang back to his hand.

If Tree Block even heard the warning, he showed no indication. He smacked his club against the ground and came forward in a rush, snarling.

And then he was dead. Just like that, caught by surprise as the barbarian's arm came forward, as the mighty warhammer twirled out, too fast for his attempted deflection with the club, too powerfully for Tree Block's massive chest to absorb the hit.

He stumbled backward and went down with more a whisper than a bang and lay very still.

Tree Block Breaker was the first man Wulfgar had killed in his tenure at Arumn Gardpeck's bar, the first man killed in the Cutlass in many, many months. All the tavern, Delly and Josi, Rossie Doone and his thugs, seemed to stop in pure amazement. The place went perfectly silent.

Wulfgar, Aegis-fang returned to his grasp, calmly turned about and walked over to the bar, paying no heed to the dangerous Rossie Doone. He placed Aegis-fang on the bar before Arumn, indicating that the barkeep should replace it on the shelves behind the counter, then casually remarked, "You should fix the door, Arumn, and quickly, else someone walks in and steals your stock."

And then, as if nothing had happened, Wulfgar walked back across the room, seemingly oblivious to the silence and the open-mouthed stares that followed his every stride.

Arumn Gardpeck shook his head and lifted the warhammer, then stopped as a shadowy figure came up opposite him.

"A fine warrior you have there, Master Gardpeck," the man said. Arumn recognized the voice, and the hairs on the back of his neck stood up.

"And Half Moon Street is a better place without that bully Tree Block running about," Morik went on. "I'll not lament his demise."

"I have never asked for any quarrel," Arumn said. "Not with Tree Block and not with you."

"Nor will you find one," Morik assured the innkeeper as Wulfgar, noting the conversation, came up beside the man—as did Josi Puddles and Delly, though they kept a more respectful distance from the dangerous rogue.

"Well fought, Wulfgar, son of Beornegar," Morik said. He slid a glass of drink along the bar before Wulfgar, who looked down at it, then back at Morik suspiciously. After all, how could Morik know his full name, one he had not used since his entry into Luskan, one that he had purposely left far, far behind.

Delly slipped in between the two, calling for Arumn to fetch her a couple of drinks for other patrons, and while the two stood staring at each other, she slyly swapped the drink Morik had placed with one from her tray. Then she moved out of the way, rolling back behind Wulfgar, wanting the security of his massive form between her and the dangerous man.

"Nor will you find one," Morik said again to Arumn. He tapped his forehead in salute and walked away, out of the Cutlass.

Wulfgar eyed him curiously, recognizing the balanced gait of a warrior, then moved to follow, pausing only long enough to lift and drain the glass.

"Morik the Rogue," Josi Puddles remarked to Arumn and Delly, moving opposite the barkeep. Both he and Arumn noted that Delly was holding the glass Morik had offered to Wulfgar.

"And likely this'd kill a fair-sized minotaur," she said, reaching over to dump the contents into a basin.

Despite Morik's assurances, Arumn Gardpeck did not disagree. Wulfgar had solidified his reputation a hundred times over this night, first by absolutely humbling Rossie Doone and his crowd—there would be

no more trouble from them—and then by downing—and oh, so easily—
the toughest fighter Half Moon Street had known in years.

But with such fame came danger, all three knew. To be in the eyes of
Morik the Rogue was to be in the sights of his deadly weapons. Perhaps
the man would keep his promise and let things lay low for a time, but
eventually Wulfgar's reputation would grow to become a distraction, and
then, perhaps, a threat.

Wulfgar seemed oblivious to it all. He finished his night's work with
hardly another word, not even to Rossie Doone and his companions, who
chose to stay—mostly because several of them needed quite a bit of potent
drink to dull the pain of their wounds—but quietly so. And then, as was
his growing custom, he took two bottles of potent liquor, took Delly by the
arm, and retired to her room for half the night.

When that half a night had passed he, the remaining bottle in hand,
went to the docks to watch the reflection of the sunrise.

To bask in the present, care nothing about the future, and forget the
past.

Chapter 18

Of Imps and Priests and a Great Quest

"Your name and reputation have preceded you," Captain Vaines explained to Drizzt as he led the drow and his companions to the boarding plank. Before them loomed the broken skyline of Baldur's Gate, the great port city halfway between Waterdeep and Calimport. Many structures lined the impressive dock areas, from low warehouses to taller buildings set with armaments and lookout positions, giving the region an uneven, jagged feel.

"My man found little trouble in gaining you passage on a river runner," Vaines went on.

"Discerning folk who'd take a drow," Bruenor said dryly.

"Less so if they'd take a dwarf," Drizzt replied without the slightest hesitation.

"Captained and crewed by dwarves," Vaines explained. That brought a groan from Drizzt and a chuckle from Bruenor. "Captain Bumpo Thunderpuncher and his brother, Donat, and their two cousins thrice removed on their mother's side."

"Ye know them well," Catti-brie remarked.

"All who meet Bumpo meet his crew, and admittedly they are a hard foursome to forget," Vaines said. "My man had little trouble in gaining your passage, as I said, for the dwarves know well the tale of Bruenor

Battlehammer and the reclamation of Mithral Hall. And of his companions, including the dark elf."

"Bet ye'd never see the day when ye'd become a hero to a bunch o' dwarves," Bruenor remarked to Drizzt.

"Bet I'd never see the day when I'd want to," the ranger replied.

The group came to the rail then, and Vaines moved aside, holding his arm out toward the plank. "Farewell, and may your journey return you safely to your home," he said. "If I am in port or nearby when you return to Baldur's Gate, perhaps we will sail together again."

"Perhaps," Regis politely replied, but he, like all the others, understood that, if they did get to Cadderly and get rid of the Crystal Shard, they meant to ask for Cadderly's help in bringing them magically to Luskan. They had approximately another two weeks of travel before them if they moved swiftly, but Cadderly could wind walk all the way back to Luskan in a matter of minutes. So said Drizzt and Catti-brie, who had taken such a walk with the powerful priest before. Then they could get on with the pressing business of finding Wulfgar.

They entered Baldur's Gate without incident, and though Drizzt felt many stares following him, they were not ominous glares but looks of curiosity. The drow couldn't help contrast this experience with his other visit to the city, when he'd gone in pursuit of Regis who had been whisked away to Calimport by Artemis Entreri. On that occasion, Drizzt, with Wulfgar beside him, had entered the city under the disguise of a magical mask that had allowed him to appear as a surface elf.

"Not much like the last time ye came through?" Catti-brie, who knew well the tale of the first visit asked, seeing Drizzt's gaze.

"Always I wished to walk freely in the cities of the Sword Coast," Drizzt replied. "It appears that our work with Captain Deudermont has granted me that privilege. Reputation has freed me from some of the pains of my heritage."

"Ye thinking that's a good thing?" the so perceptive woman asked, for she had noted clearly the slight wince at the corner of Drizzt's eye when he made the claim.

"I do not know," Drizzt admitted. "I like that I can walk freely now in most places without persecution."

"But it pains ye to think that ye had to earn the right," Catti-brie finished perfectly. "Ye look at me, a human, and know that I had to earn no such thing. And at Bruenor and Regis, dwarf and halfling, and know that they can walk anywhere without earnin' a thing."

"I do not begrudge any of you that," Drizzt replied. "But see their gazes?" He looked around at the many people walking the streets of Baldur's Gate, almost every one turning to regard the drow curiously, some with admiration in their eyes, some with disbelief.

"So even though ye're walking free, ye're not walking free," the woman observed, and her nod told Drizzt that she understood then. Given the choice between facing the hatred of prejudice or the similarly ignorant looks of those viewing him as a curiosity piece, the latter seemed the better by far. But both were traps, both prisons, jailing Drizzt within the confines of the preceding reputation of a drow elf, of any drow elf, and thus limiting Drizzt to his heritage.

"Bah, they're just a stupid lot," Bruenor interrupted.

"Those who know you, know better," Regis added.

Drizzt took it all in stride, all with a smile. Long ago he had abandoned any futile hopes of truly fitting in among the surface-dwellers—his kinfolk's well-earned reputation for treachery and catastrophe would always prevent that—and had learned instead to focus his energy on those closest to him, on those who had learned to see him beyond his physical trappings. And now here he was with three of his most trusted and beloved friends, walking freely, easily booking passage, and presenting no problems to them other than those created by the relic they had to carry. That was truly what Drizzt Do'Urden had desired from the time he had come to know Catti-brie and Bruenor and Regis, and with them beside him how could the stares, be they of hatred or of ignorant curiosity, bother him?

No, his smile was sincere; if Wulfgar was beside them, then all the world would be right for the drow, the king's treasure at the end of his long and difficult road.

* * * * *

Rai'gy rubbed his black hands together as the smallish creature began to form in the center of the magical circle he had drawn. He didn't know Gromph Baenre by anything more than reputation, but despite Jarlaxle's insistence that the archmage would be trustworthy on this issue, the mere fact that Gromph was drow and of the ruling house of Menzoberranzan worried Rai'gy profoundly. The name Gromph had given him was supposedly of a minor denizen, easily controlled, but Rai'gy couldn't know for certain until the creature appeared before him.

A bit of treachery from Gromph could have had him opening a gate to a major demon, to Demogorgon himself, and the impromptu magical circle Rai'gy had drawn here in the sewers of Calimport would hardly prove sufficient protection.

The wizard-priest relaxed a bit as the creature took shape—the shape, as Gromph had promised, of an imp. Even without the magical circle, a wizard-priest as powerful as Rai'gy would have little trouble in handling a mere imp.

"Who is it that calls my name?" asked the imp in the guttural language of the Abyss, obviously more than a little perturbed and, both Rai'gy and Jarlaxle noted, a bit trepidatious—and even more so when he noted that his summoners were drow elves. "You should not bother

Druzil. No, no, for he serves a great master," Druzil went on, speaking fluently in the drow tongue.

"Silence!" Rai'gy commanded, and the little imp was compelled to obey. The wizard-priest looked to Jarlaxle.

"Why do you protest?" Jarlaxle asked Druzil. "Is it not the desire of your kind to find access to this world?"

Druzil tilted his head and narrowed his eyes, a pensive yet still apprehensive pose.

"Ah, yes," the mercenary leader went on. "But of late, you have been summoned not by friends, but by enemies, so I have been told. By Cadderly of Caradoon."

Druzil bared his pointy teeth and hissed at the mention of the priest. That brought a smile to the faces of both dark elves. Gromph Baenre, it seemed, had not steered them wrong.

"We would like to pain Cadderly," Jarlaxle explained with a wicked grin. "Would Druzil like to help?"

"Tell me how," the imp eagerly replied.

"We need to know everything about the human," Jarlaxle explained. "His appearance and demeanor, his history and present place. We were told that Druzil, above all others in the Abyss, knows the man."

"Hates the man," the imp corrected, and he seemed eager indeed. But suddenly he backed off, staring suspiciously at the two. "I tell you, and then you dismiss me," he remarked.

Jarlaxle looked to Rai'gy, for they had anticipated such a reaction. The wizard-priest stood up, walked to the side in the tiny room, and pulled aside a screen, revealing a small kettle, bubbling and boiling.

"I am without a familiar," Rai'gy explained. "An imp would serve me well."

Druzil's coal black eyes flared with red fires. "Then we can pain Cadderly and so many other humans together," the imp reasoned.

"Does Druzil agree?" Jarlaxle asked.

"Does Druzil have a choice?" the imp retorted sarcastically.

"As to serving Rai'gy, yes," the drow replied, and the imp was obviously surprised, as was Rai'gy. "As to revealing all that you know about Cadderly, no. It is too important, and if we must torment you for a hundred years, we shall."

"Then Cadderly would be dead," Druzil said dryly.

"The torment would remain pleasurable to me," Jarlaxle was quick to respond, and Druzil knew enough about dark elves to understand that this was no idle threat.

"Druzil wishes to pain Cadderly," the imp admitted, dark eyes sparkling.

"Then tell us," Jarlaxle said. "Everything."

Later on that day, while Druzil and Rai'gy worked the magic spells that would bind them as master and familiar, Jarlaxle sat alone in the room he had taken in the sub-basement of House Basadoni. He had indeed learned much from the imp, most important of all that he had no desire to bring his band anywhere near the one named Cadderly Bonaduce. This was to Druzil's ultimate dismay. The leader of the Spirit Soaring, armed with magic far beyond even Rai'gy and Kimmuriel, might prove too great a foe. Even worse, Cadderly was apparently rebuilding an order of priests, surrounding himself with young and strong acolytes, enthusiastic idealists.

"The worst kind," Jarlaxle said as Entreri entered the room. "Idealists," he explained to the assassin's perplexed expression. "Above all else, I hate idealists."

"They are blind fools," Entreri agreed.

"They are unpredictable fanatics," Jarlaxle explained. "Blind to danger and blind to fear as long as they think their path is according to the tenets of their particular god-figure."

"And the leader of this other guild is an idealist?" a confused Entreri asked, for he thought he had been summoned to discuss his upcoming meeting with the remaining guilds of Calimport, to stop a war before it ever began.

"No, no, it is another matter," Jarlaxle explained, waving his hand dismissively. "One that concerns my activities in Menzoberranzan and not here in Calimport. Let it not trouble you, for you have business more important by far."

And Jarlaxle, too, put it out of his mind then, focusing on the more immediate problem. He had been surprised by Druzil's accounting of Cadderly, never imagining that this human would present such a problem. Though he held firm to his determination to keep his minions away from Cadderly, he was not dismayed, for he understood that Drizzt and his friends were still a long way from the great library known as the Spirit Soaring.

It was a place Jarlaxle had no intention of ever allowing them to see.

* * * * *

"Yes, a pleasure meetin' ye! Oh, a pleasure, King Bruenor, and to yer kin, me blessin's," Bumpo Thunderpuncher, a rotund and short little dwarf with a fiery orange beard and a huge and flat nose that was pushed over to one side of his ruddy face, said to Bruenor for perhaps the tenth time since *Bottom Feeder* had put out of Baldur's Gate. The dwarven vessel was a square-bottomed, shallow twenty-footer with two banks of oars—though only one was normally in use—and a long aft pole for steering and for pushing off the bottom. Bumpo and his equally rotund and bumbling brother Donat had fallen all over themselves at the sight of the Eighth King of Mithral Hall. Bruenor had seemed honestly surprised that his name had grown to such proportions, even among his own race.

215

Now, though, that surprise was turning to mere annoyance, as Bumpo and Donat and their two oar-pulling cousins, Yipper and Quipper Fishsquisher, continued to rain compliments, promises of fealty, and general slobber all over him.

Sitting back from the dwarves, Drizzt and Catti-brie smiled. The ranger alternated his looks between Catti-brie—how he loved to gaze upon her when she wasn't looking—and the tumult of the dwarves. Then Regis—who was lying on his belly at the prow, head hanging over the front of the boat, his hands drawing pictures in the water—and back behind them to the diminishing skyline of Baldur's Gate.

Again he thought about his passage through the city, as easy a time of it as the drow had ever known, including those occasions when he had worn the magical mask. He had earned this peace; they all had. Once this mission was completed and the crystal shard was safely in the hands of Cadderly, and once they had recovered Wulfgar and helped him through his darkness, then perhaps they could journey the wide world again, for no better reason than to see what lay over the next horizon and with no troubles beyond the fawning of bumbling dwarves.

Truly Drizzt wore a contented smile, finding hope again, for Wulfgar and for them all. He could never have dreamed that he would ever find such a life on that day decades before when he had walked out of Menzoberranzan.

It occurred to him then that his father, Zaknafein, who had died to give him this chance, was watching him at that moment from another plane, a goodly place for one as deserving as Zak.

Watching him and smiling.

216

Part 4

Kingdoms

Whether a king's palace, a warrior's bastion, a wizard's tower, an encampment for nomadic barbarians, a farmhouse with stone-lined or hedge-lined fields, or even a tiny and unremarkable room up the back staircase of a ramshackle inn, we each of us spend great energy in carving out our own little kingdoms. From the grandest castle to the smallest nook, from the arrogance of nobility to the unpretentious desires of the lowliest peasant, there is a basic need within the majority of us for ownership, or at least for stewardship. We want to—need to—find our realm, our place in a world often too confusing and too overwhelming, our sense of order in one little corner of a world that oft looms too big and too uncontrollable.

And so we carve and line, fence and lock, then protect our space fiercely with sword or pitchfork.

The hope is that this will be the end of that road we chose to walk, the peaceful and secure rewards for a life of trials. Yet, it never comes to that, for peace is not a place, whether lined by hedges or by high walls. The greatest king with the largest army in the most invulnerable fortress is not necessarily a man at peace. Far from it, for the irony of it all is that the acquisition of such material wealth can work against any hope of true serenity. But beyond any physical securities there lies yet another form of

219

*t, one that neither the king nor the peasant will escape. Even that
 .t king, even the simplest beggar will, at times, be full of the unspeak-
.le anger we all sometimes feel. And I do not mean a rage so great that
it cannot be verbalized but rather a frustration so elusive and permeat-
ing that one can find no words for it. It is the quiet source of irrational
outbursts against friends and family, the perpetrator of temper. True
freedom from it cannot be found in any place outside one's own mind and
soul.*

*Bruenor carved out his kingdom in Mithral Hall, yet found no peace
there. He preferred to return to Icewind Dale, a place he had named home
not out of desire for wealth, nor out of any inherited kingdom, but because
there, in the frozen northland, Bruenor had come to know his greatest
measure of inner peace. There he surrounded himself with friends, myself
among them, and though he will not admit this—I am not certain he even
recognizes it—his return to Icewind Dale was, in fact, precipitated by his
desire to return to that emotional place and time when he and I, Regis,
Catti-brie, and yes, even Wulfgar, were together. Bruenor went back in
search of a memory.*

*I suspect that Wulfgar now has found a place along or at the end of his
chosen road, a niche, be it a tavern in Luskan or Waterdeep, a borrowed
barn in a farming village, or even a cave in the Spine of the World. Because
what Wulfgar does not now have is a clear picture of where he emotionally
wishes to be, a safe haven to which he can escape. If he finds it again, if he
can get past the turmoil of his most jarring memories, then likely he, too,
will return to Icewind Dale in search of his soul's true home.*

*In Menzoberranzan I witnessed many of the little kingdoms we fool-
ishly cherish, houses strong and powerful and barricaded from enemies in
a futile attempt at security. And when I walked out of Menzoberranzan into
the wild Underdark, I, too, sought to carve out my niche. I spent time in
a cave talking only to Guenhwyvar and sharing space with mushroomlike
creatures that I hardly understood and who hardly understood me. I ventured to Blingdenstone, city of the deep gnomes, and could have made that
my home, perhaps, except that staying there, so close to the city of drow,
would have surely brought ruin upon those folk.*

*And so I came to the surface and found a home with Montolio deBrouchee
in his wondrous mountain grove, perhaps the first place I ever came to
know any real measure of inner peace. And yet I came to learn that the
grove was not my home, for when Montolio died I found to my surprise that
I could not remain there.*

*Eventually I found my place and found that the place was within me,
not about me. It happened when I came to Icewind Dale, when I met Catti-
brie and Regis and Bruenor. Only then did I learn to defeat the unspeakable anger within. Only there did I learn true peace and serenity.*

*Now I take that calm with me, whether my friends accompany me or
not. Mine is a kingdom of the heart and soul, defended by the security of*

honest love and friendship and the warmth of memories. Better than any land-based kingdom, stronger than any castle wall, and most importantly of all, portable.

I can only hope and pray that Wulfgar will eventually walk out of his darkness and come to this same emotional place.

—Drizzt Do'Urden

Chapter 19

Concerning Wulfgar

Delly pulled her coat tighter about her, more trying to hide her gender than to fend off any chill breezes. She moved quickly along the street, skipping fast to try and keep up with the shadowy figure turning corners ahead of her, a man one of the other patrons of the Cutlass had assured her was indeed Morik the Rogue, no doubt come on another spying mission.

She turned into an alleyway, and there he was. He was standing right before her, waiting for her, dagger in hand.

Delly skidded to a stop, hands up in a desperate plea for her life. "Please Mister Morik!" she cried. "I'm just wantin' to talk to ye."

"Morik?" the man echoed, and his hood slipped back revealing a dark-skinned face—too dark for the man Delly sought.

"Oh, but I'm begging yer pardon, good sir," Delly stammered, backing away. "I was thinking ye were someone else." The man started to respond, but Delly hardly heard him, for she turned about and sprinted back toward the Cutlass.

When she got safely away, she calmed and slowed enough to consider the situation. Ever since the fight with Tree Block Breaker, she and many other patrons had seen Morik the Rogue in every shadow, had heard him skulking about every corner. Or had they all, in their fears, just thought they had seen the dangerous man? Frustrated by that thought, knowing that there was indeed more than a little truth to her reasoning, Delly gave a great sigh and let her coat droop open.

"Selling your wares, then, Delly Curtie?" came a question from the side.

Delly's eyes widened as she turned to regard the shadowy figure against the wall, the figure belonging to a voice she recognized. She felt the lump grow in her throat. She had been looking for Morik, but now that he had found her on his terms she felt foolish indeed. She glanced down the street, back toward the Cutlass, wondering if she could make it there before a dagger found her back.

"You have been asking about me and looking for me," Morik casually remarked.

"I've been doing no such—"

"I was one of those whom you asked," Morik interrupted dryly. His voice changed pitch and accent completely as he added, "So be tellin' me, missy, why ye're wantin' to be seein' that nasty little knife-thrower."

That set Delly back on her heels, remembering well her encounter with an old woman who had said those very words in that very voice. And even if she hadn't recognized the phrasing or the voice, she wouldn't for a moment doubt the man who was well-known as Luskan's master of disguise. She had seen Morik on several occasions, intimately, many months before. Every time he had appeared differently to her, not just in physical features but in demeanor and attitude as well, walking differently, talking differently, even making love differently. Rumors circulating through Luskan for years had claimed that Morik was, in fact, several different men, and while Delly thought them exaggerated, she realized just then that if they turned out to be correct, she wouldn't be surprised.

"So you have found me," Morik said firmly.

Delly paused, not sure how to proceed. Only Morik's obvious agitation and impatience prompted her to blurt out, "I'm wanting ye to leave Wulfgar alone. He gave Tree Block what Tree Block asked for and wouldn't've gone after the man if the man didn't go after him."

"Why would I care for Tree Block Breaker?" Morik asked, still using a tone that seemed to say that he had hardly given it a thought. "An irritating thug, if ever I knew one. Half Moon Street seems a better place without him."

"Well, then ye're not for avenging that one," Delly reasoned. "But word's out that ye're none too fond o' Wulfgar and looking to prove—"

"I have nothing to prove," Morik interrupted.

"And what of Wulfgar then?" Delly asked.

Morik shrugged noncommittally. "You speak as if you love the man, Delly Curtie."

Delly blushed fiercely. "I'm speaking for Arumn Gardpeck, as well," she insisted. "Wulfgar's been good for the Cutlass, and as far as we're knowing, he's been not a bit o' trouble outside the place."

"Ah, but it seems as if you do love him, Delly, and more than a bit," Morik said with a laugh. "And here I thought that Delly Curtie loved every man equally."

Delly blushed again, even more fiercely.

"Of course, if you do love him, then I, out of obligation to all other suitors, would have to see him dead," Morik reasoned. "I would consider that a duty to my fellows of Luskan, you see, for a treasure such as Delly Curtie is not to be hoarded by any one man."

"I'm not loving him," Delly said firmly. "But I'm asking ye, for meself and for Arumn, not to kill him."

"Not in love with him?" Morik asked slyly.

Delly shook her head.

"Prove it," Morik said, reaching out to pull the tie string on the neck of Delly's dress.

The woman teetered for just a moment, unsure. And then—for Wulfgar only, for she did not wish to do this—she nodded her agreement.

Later on, Morik the Rogue lay alone in his rented bed, Delly long gone—to Wulfgar's bed, he figured. He took a deep draw on his pipe, savoring the intoxicating aroma of the exotic and potent pipeweed.

He considered his good fortune this night, for he hadn't been with Delly Curtie in more than a year and had forgotten how marvelous she could be.

Especially when it didn't cost him anything, and on this nigh, it most certainly had not. Morik had indeed been watching Wulfgar but had no intention of killing the man. The fate of Tree Block Breaker had shown him well how dangerous a proposition that attempt could prove.

He did plan to have a long talk with Arumn Gardpeck, though, one that Delly would surely make easier now. There was no need to kill the barbarian, as long as Arumn kept the huge man in his place.

*   *   *   *   *

Delly fumbled with her dress and cloak, all in a fit after her encounter with Morik, as she stumbled through the upstairs rooms of the inn. She turned a corner in the hallway and was surprised indeed to see the street looming in front of her, right in front of her, and before she could even stop herself, she was outside. And then the world was spinning all about.

When she at last re-oriented herself, she glanced back behind her, seeing the open street under the moonlight, and the inn where she had left Morik many yards away. She didn't understand, for hadn't she been walking inside just a moment ago? And in an upstairs hallway? Delly merely shrugged. For this woman, not understanding something was not so uncommon an occurrence. She shook her head, figured that Morik had really set her thoughts to spinning that night, and headed back for the Cutlass.

On the other side of the dimensional door that had transported the woman out of the inn, Kimmuriel Oblodra almost laughed aloud at the bumbling spectacle. Glad of his camouflaging *piwafwi* cloak, for Jarlaxle had insisted that he leave no traces of his ever being in Luskan, and Jarlaxle considered murdered humans as traces, the drow turned the corner in the hallway and lined up his next spatial leap.

He winced at the notion, reminding himself that he had to handle this one delicately; he and Rai'gy had done some fine spying on Morik the Rogue, and Kimmuriel knew the man to be dangerous, for a human, at least. He brought up his kinetic barrier, focused all his thoughts on it, then enacted the dimensional path down the corridor and beyond Morik's door.

There lay the man on his bed, bathed in the soft glow of his pipe and the embers from the hearth across the room. Morik sat up immediately, obviously sensing the disturbance, and Kimmuriel went through the portal, focusing his thoughts more strongly on the kinetic barrier. If the disorientation of the spatial walk defeated his concentration, he would likely be dead before his thoughts ever unscrambled.

Indeed, the drow felt Morik come into him hard, felt the jab of a dagger against his belly. But the kinetic barrier held, and he absorbed the blow. As he found again his conscious focus and took two more hits, he pushed back against the man and wriggled out to the side, standing facing Morik and laughing at him.

"You can not hurt me," he said haltingly, his command of the common tongue less than perfect, even with the magics Rai'gy had bestowed upon him.

Morik's eyes widened considerably as he recognized the truth of the intruder, as his mind came to grips with the fact that a drow elf had come into his room. He glanced about, apparently seeking an escape route.

"I come to talk, Morik," Kimmuriel explained, not wanting to have to chase this one all across Luskan. "Not to hurt you."

Morik hardly seemed to relax at the assurance of a dark elf.

"I bring gifts," Kimmuriel went on, and he tossed a small box onto the bed, its contents jingling. "Belaern, and pipeweed from the great cavern of Yoganith. Very good. You must answer questions."

"Questions about what?" the still nervous thief asked, remaining in his defensive crouch, one hand turning his dagger over repeatedly. "Who are you?"

"My master is . . ." Kimmuriel paused, searching for the right word. "Generous," he decided. "And my master is merciless. You deal with us."

He stopped there and held up his hand to halt any reply before Morik could respond. Kimmuriel felt the energy tingling within him, and holding it had become a drain he could ill afford. He focused on a small chair, sending his thoughts into it, animating it and having it walk right past him.

He touched it as it crossed before him, releasing all the energy of Morik's hits, shattering the wooden chair completely.

Morik eyed him skeptically, without comprehension. "A warning?" he asked.

Kimmuriel only smiled.

"You did not like my chair?"

"My master wishes to hire you," Kimmuriel explained. "He needs eyes in Luskan."

"Eyes and a sword?" Morik asked, his own eyes narrowing.

"Eyes and no more," Kimmuriel came back. "You tell me of the one called Wulfgar now, and then you will watch him closely and tell me about him when occasions have me return to you."

"Wulfgar?" Morik muttered under his breath, fast growing tired of the name.

"Wulfgar," answered Kimmuriel, who shouldn't have been able to hear, but of course, with his keen drow ears, certainly did. "You watch him."

"I would rather kill him," Morik remarked. "If he is trouble—" He stopped abruptly as murderous intent flashed across Kimmuriel's dark eyes.

"Not that," the drow explained. "Kyorlin . . . watch him. Quietly. I return with more belaern for more answers." He motioned to the box on the bed and repeated the drow word, "Belaern," with great emphasis.

Before Morik could ask anything else the room darkened utterly, a blackness so complete that the man couldn't see his hand if he had waved it an inch before his eyes. Fearing an attack, he went lower and skittered forward, dagger slashing.

But the dark elf was long gone, was back through his dimensional door into the hallway, then through that onto the street, then back through Rai'gy's teleportation gate, walking all that way back to Calimport before the globe of darkness even dissipated in Morik's room. Rai'gy and Jarlaxle, both of whom had watched the exchange, nodded their approval.

Jarlaxle's grasp on the surface world widened.

* * * * *

Morik came out from under his bed tentatively when the embers of the hearth at last reappeared. What a strange night it had been! he thought. First with Delly, though that was not so unexpected, since she obviously loved Wulfgar and knew that Morik could easily kill him.

But now . . . a drow elf! Coming to Morik to talk about Wulfgar! Was everything on Luskan's street suddenly about Wulfgar? Who was this man, and why did he attract such amazing attention?

Morik looked at the blasted chair—an impressive feat—then, frustrated, threw his dagger across the room so that it sank deep into the opposite wall. Then he went to the bed.

"Belaern," he said quietly, wondering what that might mean. Hadn't the dark elf said something about pipeweed?

He gingerly inspected the unremarkable box, looking for any traps. Finding none and reasoning that the dark elf could have used a more straightforward method of killing him if that had been the drow's intent, he set the box solidly on a night table and gently pulled its latch back and opened the lid.

Gems and gold stared back at him, and packets of a dark weed.

"Belaern," Morik said again, his smile gleaming as did the treasure before him. So he was to watch Wulfgar, something he had planned to do anyway, and he would be rewarded handsomely for his efforts.

He thought of Delly Curtie; he looked at the contents of the opened box and the rumpled sheets.

Not a bad night.

* * * * *

Life at the Cutlass remained quiet and peaceful for several days, with no one coming in to challenge Wulfgar after the demise of the legendary Tree Block Breaker. But when the peace finally broke, it did so in grand fashion. A new ship put in to Luskan harbor with a crew too long on the water and looking for a good row.

And they found one in the form of Wulfgar, in a tavern they nearly pulled down around them.

Finally, after many minutes of brawling, Wulfgar lifted the last squirming sailor over his head and tossed the man out through the hole in the wall created by the four previous men the barbarian had thrown out. Another stubborn sea dog tried to rush back in through the hole, and Wulfgar hit him in the face with a bottle.

Then the big man wiped a bloody forearm across his bloody face, took up another bottle—this one full—and staggered to the nearest intact table. Falling into a chair and taking a deep swig, Wulfgar grimaced as he drank, as the alcohol washed over his torn lip.

At the bar, Josi and Arumn sat exhausted and also beaten. Wulfgar had taken the brunt of it, though; these two had minor cuts and bruises only.

"He's hurt pretty bad," Josi remarked, motioning to the big man—to his leg in particular, for Wulfgar's pants were soaked in blood. One of the sailors had struck him hard with a plank. The board had split apart and torn fabric and skin, leaving many large slivers deeply embedded in the barbarian's leg.

Even as Arumn and Josi regarded him, Delly moved beside him, falling to her knees and wrapping a clean cloth about the leg. She pushed hard on the deep slivers and made Wulfgar growl in agony. He took another deep drink of the pain-killing liquor.

"Delly will see to him again," Arumn remarked. "That's become her lot in life."

"A busy lot, then," Josi agreed, his tone solemn. "I'm thinking that the last crew Wulfgar dumped, Rossie Doone and his thugs, probably pointed this bunch in our direction. There'll always be another to challenge the boy."

"And one day he will find his better. As did Tree Block Breaker," Arumn said quietly. "He'll not die comfortably in bed, I fear."

"Nor will he outlive either of us," Josi added, watching as Delly, supporting the barbarian, led him out of the room.

Just then another pair of rowdy sailors came rushing through the broken wall, running straight for the staggering Wulfgar's back. Just before they got to him, the huge barbarian found a surge of energy. He pushed Delly safely away, then spun, fist flying between the reaching arms of one man to slam him in the face. He dropped as though his legs had turned to liquid beneath him.

The other sailor barreled into Wulfgar, but the big man didn't move an inch, just grunted and accepted the man's left and right combination.

But then Wulfgar had him, grabbing tight under his arms and squeezing hard, lifting the man right from the floor. When the sailor tried to punch and kick at him, the barbarian shook him so violently that the man bit the tip right off his tongue.

Then he was flying, Wulfgar taking two running steps and launching him for the hole in the wall. Wulfgar's aim wasn't true, though, and the man crashed against the wall a foot or so to the left.

"I'll push him out for ye," Josi Puddles called from the bar.

Wulfgar nodded, accepted Delly's arm again, and ambled away.

"But he will take his share down with him, now won't he?" Arumn Gardpeck remarked with a chuckle.

Chapter 20

Dangling a Locket

"My dear Domo," Sharlotta Vespers purred, moving over seductively to put her long fingers on the wererat leader's shoulders. "Can you not see the mutual gain to our alliance?"

"I see Basadonis moving into my sewers," Domo Quillilo replied with a snarl. He was in human form now, but still carried characteristics—such as the way he twitched his nose—that seemed more fitting to a rat. "Where is the old wretch?"

Artemis Entreri started to respond, but Sharlotta shot him a plaintive look, begging him to follow her lead. The assassin sat back in his chair, more than content to let Sharlotta handle the likes of Domo.

"The old wretch," the woman began, imitating Domo's less-than-complimentary tone, "is even now securing a partnership with an even greater ally, one whom Domo would not wish to cross."

The wererat's eyes narrowed dangerously; he was not accustomed to being threatened. "Who?" he asked. "Those smelly kobolds we found running through our sewers?"

"Kobolds?" Sharlotta echoed with a laugh. "Hardly them. No, they are just fodder, the leading edge of our new ally's forces."

The wererat leader pulled away from the woman, rose out of his chair, and strode across the room. He knew that a fight had occurred in the sewers and subbasement of the Basadoni House. He knew that it concerned many kobolds and the Basadoni soldiers and also, so his spies had told him, some other creatures. These were unseen but obviously powerful, with cunning magics and tricks. He also knew, simply from the fact that Sharlotta still lived, that the Basadonis, some of them at least, had survived. Domo suspected that a coup had occurred with these two, Sharlotta and Entreri, masterminding it. They claimed that old man Basadoni was still alive, though Domo wasn't sure he believed that, but had admitted that Kadran Gordeon, a friend of Domo's, had been killed. Unfortunately, so said Sharlotta, but Domo understood that luck, good or bad, had nothing to do with it.

"Why does he speak for the old man?" the wererat asked Sharlotta, nodding toward Entreri, and with more than a bit of distaste in his tone. Domo held no love for Entreri. Few wererats did since Entreri had murdered one of the more legendary of their clan in Calimport, a conniving and wicked fellow named Rassiter.

"Because I choose to," Entreri cut in sharply before Sharlotta could intervene. The woman cast a sour look the assassin's way, then mellowed her visage as she turned back to Domo. "Artemis Entreri is well skilled in the ways of Calimport," she explained. "A proper emissary."

"I am to trust him?" Domo asked incredulously.

"You are to trust that the deal we offer you and yours is the best one you shall find in all the city," Sharlotta replied.

"You are to trust that if you do not take the deal," Entreri added, "you are thus declaring war against us. Not a pleasant prospect, I assure you."

Domo's rodent's eyes narrowed again as he considered the assassin, but he was respectful enough, and wise enough, not to push Artemis Entreri any farther.

"We will talk again, Sharlotta," he said. "You, me, and old man Basadoni." With that, the wererat took his leave with two Basadoni guards flanking him as soon as he exited the room and escorting him back to the subbasement where he could then find his way back into his sewer lair.

He was hardly gone before a secret door opened on the wall behind Sharlotta and Entreri, and Jarlaxle strode into the room.

"Leave us," the drow mercenary instructed Sharlotta, his tone showing that he wasn't overly pleased with the results.

Sharlotta gave another sour look Entreri's way and started out of the room.

"You performed quite admirably," Jarlaxle said to her, and she nodded.

"But I failed," Entreri said as soon as the door closed behind the woman. "A pity."

"These meetings mean everything to us," Jarlaxle said to him. "If we can secure our power and assure the other guilds that they are in no danger, I will have completed my first order of business."

"And then trade can begin between Calimport and Menzoberranzan," Entreri said dramatically, sarcastically, sweeping his arms out wide. "All to the gain of Menzoberranzan."

"All to the profit of Bregan D'aerthe," Jarlaxle corrected.

"And for that, I am to care?" Entreri bluntly asked.

Jarlaxle paused for a long moment to consider the man's posture and tone. "There are those among my group who fear that you do not have the will to carry this through," he said, and though the mercenary leader had allowed no hint of a threatening tone into his voice, Entreri understood the practices of the dark elves well enough to recognize the dire implications.

"Have you no heart for this?" the mercenary leader asked. "Why, you are on the verge of becoming the most influential pasha ever to rule the streets of Calimport. Kings will bow before you and pay you homage and treasures."

"And I will yawn in their ugly faces," Entreri replied.

"Yes, it all bores you," Jarlaxle remarked. "Even the fighting. You have lost your goals and desires, thrown them away. Why? Is it fear? Or is it simply that you believe there is nothing left to attain?"

Entreri shifted uncomfortably. Of course, he had known for a long time exactly the thing about which Jarlaxle was now speaking, but to hear another verbalize the emptiness within him struck him profoundly.

"Are you a coward?" Jarlaxle asked.

Entreri laughed at the absurdity of the remark, even considered leaping from his chair in a full attack upon the drow. He understood Jarlaxle's techniques and knew that he would likely be dead before he ever reached the taunting mercenary, but still he seriously considered the move. Then Jarlaxle hit him with a preemptive strike that put him back on his heels.

"Or is it that you have witnessed Menzoberranzan?" he asked.

That was indeed a huge part of it, Entreri knew, and his expression showed Jarlaxle clearly that he had struck a nerve.

"Humbled?" the drow asked. "Did you find the sights of Menzoberranzan humbling?"

"Daunting," Entreri corrected, his voice full of force and venom. "To see such stupidity on so grand a scale."

"Ah, and you know it to be a stupidity that mirrors your own existence," Jarlaxle remarked. "All that Artemis Entreri strove to achieve he found played out before him on a grand scale in the city of drow."

Still sitting, Entreri wrung his hands and bit his lip, edging closer, closer, to an attack.

"Is your life, then, a lie?" an unperturbed Jarlaxle went on, and then he sent a verbal dagger flying for Entreri's heart. "That is what Drizzt Do'Urden claimed to you, is it not?"

For just an instant, a flash of seething rage crossed Entreri's stoic face, and Jarlaxle laughed loudly. "At last, a sign of life from you!" he said. "A sign of desire, even if that desire was to tear out my heart." He gave a great sigh and lowered his voice. "Many of my companions do not think you worth the trouble," he admitted. "But I know better, Artemis Entreri. We are friends, you and I, and more alike than either of us wish to admit. You have greatness before you, if only I can show you the way."

"You speak foolishness," Entreri said evenly.

"That way lies through Drizzt Do'Urden," Jarlaxle continued without hesitation. "That is the hole in your heart. You must fight him again on terms of your choosing, because your pride will not allow you to go on with any other facet of your life until that business is settled."

"I have fought him too many times already," Entreri retorted, his anger rising. "Never do I wish to see that one again."

"So you may profess to believe," Jarlaxle said. "But you lie, to me and to yourself. Twice have you and Drizzt Do'Urden battled fairly, and twice has Entreri been sent running."

"In these very sewers he was mine!" the assassin insisted. "And would have been, had not his friends come to his aid."

"And on the cliff overlooking Mithral Hall it was he who proved the stronger."

"No!" Entreri insisted, losing his calm edge for just a moment. "No. I had him beaten."

"So you honestly believe, and thus you are trapped by the pain of the memories," Jarlaxle reasoned. "You told me of that fight in detail, and I did watch some of it from afar. We both know that either of you could have won that duel. And that is your turmoil. If Drizzt had cleanly beaten you and yet you had managed to survive, you could have gone on with your life. And if you had beaten him, whether he had lived or not, you would think no more about him. It is the not knowing that so gnaws at you, my friend. The pain of recognizing that there is one challenge that has not been decided, one challenge blocking all other aspirations you might find, be they a desire for greater power or merely for hedonistic pleasure, both easily within your reach."

Entreri sat back, seeming more intrigued than angry then.

"And that, too, I can give to you," Jarlaxle explained. "That which you desire most of all, if you'll only admit what is in your heart. I can continue my plans for Calimport without you now; Sharlotta is a fine front, and I am too firmly entrenched to be uprooted. Yet I do not desire such an arrangement. For my ventures to the surface, I want Artemis Entreri leading Bregan D'aerthe, the real Artemis Entreri and not this shell of your former self, too absorbed by this futile and empty challenge with the rogue Drizzt to concentrate on those skills that elevate you above all others."

"Skills," Entreri echoed skeptically and turned away.

But Jarlaxle knew he had gotten to the man, knew that he had dangled a treat before Entreri's eyes that the assassin could not resist.

"There is one meeting remaining, the most important of the lot," Jarlaxle explained. "My drow associates and I will watch you closely when you speak with the leaders of the Rakers, Pasha Wroning's emissaries, Quentin Bodeau, and Dwahvel Tiggerwillies. Perform your duties well, and I will deliver Drizzt Do'Urden to you."

"They will demand to see Pasha Basadoni," Entreri reasoned, and the mere fact that he was giving any thought at all to the coming meeting told Jarlaxle that his bait had been taken.

"Have you not the mask of disguise?" Jarlaxle asked.

Entreri halted for a moment, not understanding, but then he realized what Jarlaxle was speaking of: a magical mask he had taken from Cattibrie in Menzoberranzan. The mask he had used to impersonate Gromph Baenre, the archmage of the drow city, to sneak right into Gromph's quarters to secure the valuable Spider Mask that had allowed him to get into House Baenre in search of Drizzt. "I do not have it," he said brusquely, obviously not wanting to elaborate.

"A pity," said Jarlaxle. "It would make things much simpler. But not to worry, for it will all be arranged," the drow promised, and with a sweeping bow he left the room, left Artemis Entreri sitting there, wondering.

"Drizzt Do'Urden," the assassin said, and there was no venom in his voice now, just an emotionless resignation. Indeed, Jarlaxle had tempted him, had shown him a different side of his inner turmoil that he had not considered—not honestly, at least. After the escape from Menzoberranzan, the last time he had set eyes upon Drizzt, Entreri had told himself with more than a little convictio, that he was through with the rogue drow, that he hoped never to see wretched Drizzt Do'Urden again.

But was that the truth?

Jarlaxle had spoken correctly when he had insisted that the issue as to who was the better swordsman had not been decided between the two. They had fought against each other in two razor-close battles and other minor skirmishes, and had fought together on two separate occasions, in Menzoberranzan and in the lower tunnels of Mithral Hall before Bruenor's clan had reclaimed the place. All those encounters had shown them was that with regard to fighting styles and prowess they were practically mirrors of each other.

In the sewers the fight had been even until Entreri spat dirty water in Drizzt's face, gaining the upper hand. But then that wretched Cattibrie with her deadly bow had arrived, chasing the assassin away. The fight on the ledge had been Entreri's, he believed, until the drow used an unfair advantage, using his innate magics to drop a globe of darkness over them both. Even then, Entreri had maintained a winning edge until his own eagerness had caused him to forget his enemy.

What was the truth between them, then? Who would win?

The assassin gave a great sigh and rested his chin in his palm, wondering, wondering. From a pocket inside his cloak he took out a small locket, one that Jarlaxle had taken from Catti-brie and that Entreri had recovered from the mercenary leader's own desk in Menzoberranzan, a locket that could lead him to Drizzt' Do'Urden.

Many times over the past few years Artemis Entreri had stared at this locket, wondering over the whereabouts of the rogue, wondering what Drizzt might be doing, wondering what enemies he had recently battled.

Many times the assassin had stared at the locket and wondered, but never before had he seriously considered using it.

* * * * *

A noticeable spring enhanced Jarlaxle's always fluid step as he went from Entreri. The mercenary leader silently congratulated himself for the foresight of spending so much energy in hunting Drizzt Do'Urden and for his cunning in planting so powerful a seed within Entreri.

"But that is the thing," he said to Rai'gy and Kimmuriel when he found them in Rai'gy's room, Jarlaxle finishing aloud his silent pondering. "Foresight, always."

The two looked at him quizzically.

Jarlaxle dismissed those looks with a laugh. "And where are we with our scouting?" the mercenary leader asked, and he was pleased to see that Druzil was still with the mage; Rai'gy's intentions to make the imp his familiar seemed to be well on course.

The other two dark elves looked to each other, and it was their turn to laugh. Rai'gy began a quiet chant, moving his arms in slow and specified motions. Gradually he increased the speed of his waving, and he began turning about, his flowing robes flying behind him. A gray smoke arose about him, obscuring him and making it seem as if he were moving and twirling faster and faster.

And then it stopped, and Rai'gy was gone. Standing in his place was a human dressed in a tan tunic and trousers, a light blue silken cape, and a curious—curiously like Jarlaxle's own—wide-brimmed hat. The hat was blue and banded in red, plumed on the right side, and with a porcelain and gold pendant depicting a candle burning above an open eye set in its center.

"Greetings, Jarlaxle, I am Cadderly Bonaduce of Caradoon," the impostor said, bowing low.

Jarlaxle didn't miss the fact that this supposed human spoke fluently in the tongue of the drow, a language rarely heard on the surface.

"The imitation is perfect," the imp Druzil rasped. "So much does he look like the wretch Cadderly that I want to stick him with my poisoned tail!" Druzil finished with a flap of his little leathery wings that sent him up into a short flight, clapping his clawed hands and feet as he went.

236

"I doubt that Cadderly Bonaduce of Caradoon speaks drow," Jarlaxle said dryly.

"A simple spell will correct that," Rai'gy assured his leader, and indeed Jarlaxle knew of such a spell, had often employed it in his travels and meetings with varied races. But that spell had its limitations, Jarlaxle knew.

"I will look as Cadderly looks and speak as Cadderly speaks," Rai'gy went on, smiling at his cleverness.

"Will you?" Jarlaxle asked in all seriousness. "Or will our perceptive adversary hear you transpose a subject and verb, more akin to the manner of our language, and will that clue him that all is not as it seems?"

"I will be careful," Rai'gy promised, his tone showing that he did not appreciate anyone doubting his prowess.

"Careful may not prove to be enough," Jarlaxle replied. "As magnificent as your work has been we can take no chances here."

"If we are to go to Drizzt, as you said, then how?" Rai'gy asked.

"We shall need a professional impersonator," Jarlaxle said, drawing a groan from both his drow companions.

"What does he mean?" Druzil asked nervously.

Jarlaxle looked to Kimmuriel. "Baeltimazifas is with the illithids," he instructed. "You can go to them."

"Baeltimazifas," Rai'gy said with obvious disgust, for he knew the creature and hated it profoundly, as did most. "The illithids control the creature and set his fees exorbitantly high."

"It will be expensive," added Kimmuriel, who had the most experience in dealing with the strange illithids, the mind flayers.

"The gain is worth the price," Jarlaxle assured them both.

"And the possibility of treachery?" Rai'gy asked. "Those kinds, both Baeltimazifas and the illithids, have never been known to follow through with bargains nor to fear the drow or any other race."

"Then we will be the first and best at treachery," Jarlaxle insisted, nodding, smiling, and seeming completely unafraid. "And what of this Wulfgar who was left behind?"

"In Luskan," Kimmuriel replied. "He is of no consequence. A minor player and nothing more, unconnected to the rogue at this time."

Jarlaxle assumed a pensive posture, putting all the pieces together. "Minor in fact but not in tale," he decided. "If you went to Drizzt in the guise of Cadderly would you have enough remaining power—clerical powers and not wizardly—to magically bring them all to Luskan?"

"Not I and not Cadderly," Rai'gy replied. "They are too many for any clerical transport spell. I could take one or two, but not four. Nor could Cadderly, unless he is possessed of powers I do not understand."

Again Jarlaxle paused, thinking, thinking. "Not Luskan, then," he remarked, more thinking aloud than talking to his companions. "Baldur's

Gate, or even a village near that city, will suit our needs." It all fell into place for the cunning mercenary leader then, the lure that would help separate Drizzt and friends from the crystal shard. "Yes, this could be rather enjoyable."

"And profitable?" Kimmuriel asked.

Jarlaxle laughed. "I cannot have one without the other."

Chapter 21
Timely Wounds

"We always put in here," Bumpo Thunderpuncher explained as *Bottom Feeder* bumped hard against a fallen tree overhanging the river. The jarring shock nearly sent Regis and Bruenor tumbling off the side of the boat. "Don't like carrying too many supplies all at once," the rotund dwarf explained. "Me brother and cousins eat 'em to dangnabbit fast!"

Drizzt nodded—they did indeed need some food, mostly because of the gluttonous dwarves—and glanced warily at the trees clustered about the river. Several times over the previous two days the friends had noted movements shadowing their journey, and once Regis had seen the pursuers clearly enough to identify them as a band of goblins. By the dogged pursuit, and any pursuit longer than a few hours would be considered dogged by goblin standards, it seemed as if Crenshinibon was calling out yet again.

"How long to resupply and get back out?" the drow asked.

"Oh, not more'n an hour," Bumpo replied.

"Half that time," Bruenor bade him. "And me and me halfling friend'll help." He nodded to Drizzt and Catti-brie then, and they took the signal; Bruenor hadn't included them because he knew they had to go out and do a bit of scouting.

It didn't take the seasoned pair of hunters long to find goblin sign, the tracks of at least a score of the wicked little creatures. And not far away. The goblins had apparently veered from the river at this point, and when Drizzt and Catti-brie moved to higher ground, looking east to see more of the silvery snake that was the river bending about up ahead, the two understood the goblins' reasoning. *Bottom Feeder* had been going generally north for the past hour, for the river hooked at this juncture, but the boat would soon turn back east, then south, then back to the east once more. Crossing the fairly open ground moving directly to the east, the goblin band would get to the banks in the east far ahead of the dwarves' boat.

"Ah, they're knowing the river then," Bumpo said when Drizzt and Catti-brie returned to report their findings. "They'll be beatin' us to the spot, and the river's narrower there, not wide enough for us to avoid a fight."

Bruenor turned a serious gaze upon Drizzt. "How many're ye figuring, elf?" he asked.

"A score," Drizzt replied. "Perhaps as many as thirty."

"Let's be picking our place for fighting, then," Bruenor said. "If we're to fight, then let it be on ground of our own choosing."

Everyone around noted the lack of dismay in Bruenor's tone.

"They'll be seein' the boat a long way off," Bumpo explained. "If we're to keep it here, tied up, they might be catching on."

Drizzt was shaking his head before the dwarf ever finished. "*Bottom Feeder* will go along as planned," he explained, "but without we three." He indicated Bruenor and Catti-brie, then moved near to Regis, unstrapping his belt so that he could slide off the pouch that held the Crystal Shard. "This remains on the boat," he explained to the halfling. "Above all else, keep it safe."

"So they will come after the boat, and you three will come after them," Regis reasoned, and Drizzt nodded.

"Be quick, if you please," the halfling added.

"What're ye grumbling over, Rumblebelly?" Bruenor asked with a chuckle. "Ye just loaded a ton o' food on the boat, and knowing ye the way I do I'm figuring there won't be much left for me when we get back aboard!"

Regis looked down doubtfully at the pouch, but his face did brighten as he turned to regard the supply-laden boat.

They parted company then, Bumpo, his crew, and Regis pushed off from the impromptu tree landing back into the swift currents. Before they had gone far Drizzt, on the riverbank, took out his onyx figurine, set it down, and called for his panther companion. Then he and his three companions set off, running straight to the east, following the same course as the goblin troupe.

Guenhwyvar took the point position, blending into the brush, barely seeming to stir the grasses and bushes as she passed. Drizzt came along

240

next, working as liaison between the cat and the other two, who brought up the rear, Bruenor with his axe comfortably across his shoulder and Catti-brie with Taulmaril in hand, arrow notched and ready.

* * * * *

"Well, if we're to be fightin', then this'll be the place," Donat said a short while later as *Bottom Feeder* rounded a bend in the river, crossing into a region of narrower banks and swifter current and with many tree limbs overhanging the water.

Regis took one look at the area and groaned, not liking the prospects at all. Goblins could be anywhere, he realized, taking a good measure of the many bushes and hillocks. He took little comfort in the apparent giddiness of the four dwarves, for he had been around dwarves long enough to know that they were always happy before a fight, no matter the prospects.

And even more disconcerting to the halfling came a voice within his head, a tempting, teasing voice, reminding him that with a word he could construct a crystalline tower—a tower that a thousand goblins couldn't breach—if Regis just took control of the crystal shard. The goblins wouldn't even try to take the tower, Regis knew, for Crenshinibon would work with him to control the little wretches.

They could not resist.

* * * * *

Drizzt, looking back with his back against a tree some distance ahead of Bruenor and Catti-brie, motioned for the woman to hold her shot. He, too, had seen the goblin on the branch above, a goblin intent on the river ahead and taking no note of the approaching friends. No need to tell the whole troupe that danger was about, the ranger decided, and Catti-brie's thunderous bow would certainly raise the general alarm.

So up the tree went the drow ranger, one scimitar in hand. With amazing stealth and equal agility, he made a branch level with the goblin. Then, balancing perfectly without using his free hand, he closed suddenly in five quick steps. The drow clamped his empty hand around the creature's side, through bow and bowstring and over the surprised goblin's mouth, and drove his scimitar into the creature's back, hooking the blade upward as he went to slice smoothly through heart and lung. He held the goblin for a few seconds, letting it descend into the complete blackness of death, then carefully set it down over the branch, laying the crude bow atop it.

Drizzt looked all around for Guenhwyvar, but the panther was nowhere to be seen. He had instructed the cat to hold back until the main fighting started and trusted that Guenhwyvar would do as told.

That fight fast approached, Drizzt knew, for the goblins were all about, huddled in bushes and in trees near to the riverbank. He didn't like the prospects for a quick victory here; the region was too jumbled, with too many physical barriers and too many hiding holes. He would have liked the luxury of spending an hour or more locating all the goblins.

But then *Bottom Feeder* came into sight, rounding a bend not so far away.

Drizzt looked back to his waiting friends, motioning strongly for them to come on fast.

A roar from Bruenor and a sizzling arrow from Taulmaril led the way, Catti-brie's missile cutting by the base of Drizzt's tree, diving through some underbrush and taking a goblin in the hip, dropping it squirming to the ground.

Three other goblins emerged from that same brush, running out and screaming wildly.

Those screams fast diminished as the drow, now holding both his deadly blades, leaped down atop them. He struck hard as he crashed in, stabbing one to the side, and felling the one under him by tucking the hilt of his second blade tight against his torso and using his momentum to drive it halfway through the unfortunate creature.

And he nearly collided in midair with another soaring, dark form. Guenhwyvar, leaping strong, crossed by the descending drow and crashed into yet another bush atop a shadowy goblin form.

The one goblin of the three to escape Drizzt's initial leap staggered to the side against the trunk of the same tree from which Drizzt had jumped and turned about, spear raised to throw.

It heard the cursing howl and tried to turn its angle to the newest foe, but Bruenor came in too quick, moving within the sharpened tip of the long weapon and transferring his momentum into his overhead axe with a skidding stop, every muscle in his body snapping forward.

"Damn!" the dwarf grumbled, realizing that it might take him some time to extricate the embedded weapon from the split skull.

Even as the dwarf tugged and twisted, Catti-brie came running by, dropping to one knee and letting fly another arrow. This one blasted a goblin from a tree. She dropped her bow and in one fluid motion drew out Khazid'hea, her powerfully enchanted sword. The blade glowing fiercely, she ran on.

Still Bruenor tugged.

Drizzt, both the other two goblins quite dead, leaped up and ran on, disappearing through a small cluster of trees.

Up ahead, Guenhwyvar ran up the side of a tree, and the terrified goblins on the lowest branches both threw their spears errantly and tried to leap to the ground. One made it; the other got caught in midair by a swiping panther claw and was pulled, squirming wildly, back up to its death.

"Damn," Bruenor said again, tugging and tugging, missing all the fun. "I gotta hit the stinkin' things softer!"

* * * * *

He couldn't raise the crystal tower on the boat, of course, but right over the side, even in the river. Yes, the bottom levels of the structure might be under the water, but Crenshinibon would still show him a way in.

"They got spears!" Bumpo Thunderpuncher cried. "To the wall! To the wall!" On cue, the dwarf captain and his three kinsfolk dived down to the deck and rolled up against the blocking side wall closest to the goblin-infested shore. Donat, who got there first, quickly broke open a wooden locker, each dwarf taking up a crossbow and huddling tight against the shielding planking while loading.

All of the movement finally caught Regis's eye, and he shook away his visions of a crystal tower, hardly believing that he could have even considered raising the thing, and looked, quite startled, at the dwarves. He looked up as the boat drifted beneath an overhanging limb and saw a goblin there, its arm poised to throw.

The four dwarves rolled in unison to their backs, lining up their crossbows and letting fly. Each bolt hit its mark, driving into the goblin and jerking it up and over so that it tumbled into the river behind the floating craft.

But not before it had thrown the spear and thrown it well.

Regis yelped and tried to dodge, but too late. He felt the spear dive into the back of his shoulder. The halfling heard, with sickening clarity, the tip of it prodding right through him to knock against the deck. He was down, facedown, and he heard himself howling, though his voice came from no conscious act.

Then he felt the uneven edges of the decking planks as the dwarves pulled him to the side, and he heard, as if from a great distance, Donat crying, "They killed him! They killed him to death!"

And then he was alone, and so cold, and he heard the splashing of water as swimming goblins made the edge of the boat.

* * * * *

Down from a high branch came the panther, graceful and beautiful, a soaring black arrow. She went past one goblin, one paw kicking out swiftly enough to rake out the oblivious creature's throat, and then crashed upon another pair, bearing one down under her great weight and ripping the life from it in an instant, then skipping on to the next before it could rise and flee.

The goblin rolled to its back, flailed its arms wildly to try to fend off the great cat. But Guenhwyvar was too strong and too fast and soon got her maw clamped about the creature's throat.

Not far to the side, Drizzt and Catti-brie, independently in pursuit of goblins, discovered each other in a small clearing and found that they had become ringed by goblins, who, seeing a sudden advantage, leaped out of the brush and encircled the pair.

"A bit o' good luck, I'd say," Catti-brie remarked with a wink to her friend, and they fell together defensively, back-to-back.

The goblins tried to coordinate their attacks, calling to each other, opposite ones coming in at the same time, while those beside them waited to see if the first attack might leave the two humans vulnerable.

They simply didn't understand.

Drizzt and Catti-brie rolled about each other's back, thus changing their angles of attack, the drow going after those goblins that had come in at Catti-brie and vice versa. Out Drizzt came, scimitars flashing in circling motions, hooking inside spear shafts and turning them harmlessly aside. A subtle shift in wrist angle, a quick step forward, and both goblins staggered backward, guts torn.

Across the way Catti-brie went down low under the high thrust of one spear and sent Khazid'hea slashing across, the wickedly edged blade taking the goblin's leg off cleanly at the knee. A goblin to the side tried to adjust its spear angle down at the woman, but she caught the weapon shaft with her free hand and turned it aside, using it as leverage to propel her up and out, a single thrust taking the creature in the chest.

"Straight on!" Drizzt yelled, rushing by and hooking Catti-brie under the shoulder, helping her to her feet and pushing her along in his charge, their momentum shattering the line of the frightened creatures.

Those behind didn't dare follow that charge, except for one, and thus Drizzt knew that Crenshinibon had crazed this one.

In the span of three heartbeats it lay dead.

* * * * *

Still behind the main fighting, Bruenor heard the commotion, and that made him madder than ever. Twisting and pulling, tugging with all his strength, the dwarf nearly toppled as his axe came free—almost free, he realized with revulsion, for instead of pulling the heavy blade from the creature's skull he had torn the dead goblin's head right off.

"Well, that's pretty," he said with disgust, and then he had no more time to complain as a pair of goblins crashed out of the brush near to him. He hit the closest hard, a roundabout throw that slammed its kin's head right into its belly and sent it staggering backward.

Weaponless, Bruenor took a hit from the second goblin, a club smash across his shoulders that stung but hardly slowed him. He leaped in close, moving right before the goblin, and snapped his forehead into the creature's face, sending it reeling and taking its club from its weakened grasp as it staggered.

Before the goblin could retrieve its bearings, that club smashed down hard once, twice, thrice, and left the thing twitching helplessly on the ground.

Bruenor spun about and launched the club into the legs of the first goblin as it tried to charge at his back, tripping the creature and sending it headlong to the ground. Bruenor quickstepped over it, back to the brush to retrieve his axe.

"Enough playin'!" the dwarf roared. Finesse aside, he slammed his axe against the nearest tree trunk, shattering away the remnants of the head.

Up and spinning, the goblin took one look at the ferocious dwarf and his axe, took one look at the decapitated remains of Bruenor's first kill, and turned and ran.

"No ye don't!" the dwarf howled, and he let fly an overhead throw that sent his axe spinning hard into the goblin's back, dropping it facedown into the dirt.

Bruenor ran by, thinking to pull the axe free in full stride, heading to rejoin his companions.

It was stuck again, this time hooked on the dying goblin's spine.

"Orc-brained, troll-smellin', bug-eater!" Bruenor cursed.

* * * * *

Donat worked hard over Regis, trying to hold the spear shaft steady so the embedded weapon wouldn't do any more damage, while his three kinfolk rushed about frantically, working furiously themselves to keep *Bottom Feeder* free of goblins. One creature nearly made the deck, but Bumpo smashed his crossbow across its face, shattering the weapon and the goblin's jaw.

The dwarf howled in glee, lifted the stunned creature above his head and threw it into two others that were trying to come over the side, dropping all three back into the water.

His two cousins proved equally effective and equally damaging to expensive crossbows, but the boat stayed clear of goblins, soon outdistancing those giving stubborn pursuit in the swift current.

That allowed Bumpo to take up Donat's crossbow, the only one still working, and pluck a few in the water.

Most of the creatures did make the other bank but had seen enough of the fight—too much, actually—and simply ran off into the underbrush.

* * * * *

Bruenor planted his heavy boots on the back of the still-groaning goblin, spat in both his hands, took up his axe handle, and gave a great tug, ripping the head and half the goblin's backbone free.

The dwarf went over in a backward roll to wind up sitting in the dirt.

"Oh, even prettier," he remarked, noting the torn creature and the length of spine lying across his extended legs. He shook his head and hopped to his feet, running fast to join his friends, but by the time he arrived the battle had ended. Drizzt and Catti-brie stood amidst several dead creatures, and Guenhwyvar circled about, searching for any others.

But those held in Crenshinibon's mental grasp were already dead, and those still of free will were long gone.

"Tell the stupid crystal shard to call in thicker-skinned creatures," Bruenor grumbled. He gave Drizzt a sidelong glance as they headed for the riverbank. "Ye're sure we got to get rid of that thing?"

Drizzt only smiled and ran along. One goblin did come out of the river on this side, but Guenhwyvar buried it before the friends ever got close.

Up ahead, Bumpo maneuvered *Bottom Feeder* into a small side pool out of the main current. The three friends laughed all the way, replaying the battle and talking lightheartedly about how good it was to be back on the road.

Their expressions changed abruptly when they saw Regis lying on the deck, pale and very still.

*   *   *   *   *

From a dark room in the subbasement of House Basadoni, Jarlaxle and his wizard-priest assistant watched it all.

"This could not be any easier," the mercenary leader remarked with a laugh. He turned to Rai'gy. "Find yourself a human persona in the guise of a priest much like Cadderly and in the same ceremonial dress. Not his hat, though," the mercenary added after a short pause. "That might constitute rank, I believe, or prove more a matter of Cadderly's personal taste."

"But Kimmuriel has gone for Baeltimazifas," Rai'gy protested.

"And you shall accompany the doppleganger to Drizzt and his companions," Jarlaxle explained, "as a student of Cadderly Bonaduce's Spirit Soaring library. Prepare spells of powerful healing."

Rai'gy's eyes widened with surprise. "I am to pray to Lady Lolth for spells with which to heal a halfling?" he asked incredulously. "And you believe that she will grant me such spells, given that intent?"

Jarlaxle, supremely confident, nodded. "She will, because bestowing such spells shall further the cause of her drow," he explained, and he smiled widely, knowing that the outcome of the battle had just made his life a lot easier and much more interesting.

Chapter 22

Saving Grace

Aegis gasped and groaned in agony, squirming just a bit, which only made things worse for the poor halfling. Every movement made the spear shaft quiver, sending waves of burning pain through his body.

Bruenor brushed aside any soft emotions and blinked away any tears, realizing that he would be doing his grievously injured friend no favors by showing any sympathy at all. "Do it quick," he said to Drizzt. The dwarf knelt down over Regis, setting himself firmly, pressing the halfling by the shoulders and putting one knee on his back to hold him perfectly still.

Drizzt wasn't sure how to proceed. The spear was barbed, that much he recognized, but to push it all the way through and out the other side seemed too brutal a technique for Regis to possibly survive. Yet, how could Drizzt cut the spear quickly enough and smoothly enough so that Regis did not have to endure such unbearable agony? Even a minor shift in the long shaft had the halfling groaning in pain. What might the jarring of the shaft being hacked by a scimitar do to him?

"Take it in both yer hands," Catti-brie instructed. "One hand on the wound, t'other on the spear, right above where ye want the thing broken."

Drizzt looked at her and saw that she had Taulmaril in hand again, an arrow readied. He looked from the bow to the spear and understood her intent. While he doubted the potential of such a technique, he simply had no other answers. He gripped the spear shaft tightly just above the entry wound, then again two handsbreadths up. He looked to Bruenor, who secured his hold on Regis even more—drawing another whimper from the poor halfling—and nodded grimly.

Drizzt then nodded to Catti-brie who bent low, lining up her shot and the angle of the arrow after it passed through, so that it would not hit one of her friends. If she was not perfect, she realized, or even if she simply was not lucky, the arrow might deflect badly, and then they'd have another seriously wounded companion lying on the deck beside Regis. With that thought in mind Catti-brie relaxed her bowstring a bit, but then Regis whimpered again, and she understood that her poor little friend was fast running out of time.

She drew back, took perfect aim, and left fly, the blinding, lightning-streaking arrow sizzling right through the shaft cleanly, and soaring into, and through the opposite deck wall and off across the river.

Drizzt, stunned by the sudden flash even though he had expected the shot, held in place for just a moment. After allowing his senses to catch up with the scene he handed the broken piece of the shaft to Bumpo.

"Lift him gently," the drow instructed Bruenor, who did so, raising the halfling's injured shoulder slowly from the deck.

Then, with a plaintive and helpless look to all about, the drow grasped the remaining piece of shaft firmly and began to push.

Regis howled and screamed and wriggled too much for sympathetic Drizzt to continue. At a loss, he let go of the shaft and held his hands out helplessly to Bruenor.

"The ruby pendant," Catti-brie remarked suddenly, dropping to her knees beside her friends. "We'll get him thinking of better things." She moved quickly as Bruenor lifted the groaning Regis a bit higher, reaching into the front of the halfling's shirt and pulling forth the dazzling ruby pendant.

"Watch it close," Catti-brie said to Regis several times. She held the gemstone, spinning alluringly at the end of its chain before the halfling's half-closed eyes. Regis's head started to droop, but Catti-brie grabbed him by the chin and forced him steady.

"Ye remember the party after we rescued ye from Pook?" she asked calmly, forcing a wide smile across her face.

Gradually she brought him into her words with more coaxing, more reminding of that enjoyable affair, one in which Regis had become quite intoxicated. And intoxicated was what the halfling seemed to be now. He was groaning no more, his gaze locked on the spinning gemstone.

"Ah, but didn't ye have the fun of it in the pillowed room?" the woman said, speaking of the harem in Pook's house. "We thought ye'd never come forth!" As she spoke, she looked to Drizzt and nodded. The drow took up the remaining piece of embedded shaft once more and, with a look to Bruenor to make certain that the dwarf had Regis properly secured and braced, he slowly began to push.

Regis winced as the rest of the wide-bladed head tore through the front of his shoulder but offered no real resistance and no screaming. Drizzt soon had the spear fully extracted.

It came out with a gush of blood, and both Drizzt and Bruenor had to work fast and furiously to stem the flow. Even then, as they lay Regis gently on his back, they saw his arm discoloring.

"He's bleeding inside," Bruenor said through gritted teeth. "We'll be taking the arm off if we can't fix it!"

Drizzt didn't respond, just went back to work on his small friend, moving aside the bandages and trying to reach his nimble fingers right into the wound to pinch the blood flow.

Catti-brie kept up her soothing talk, doing a marvelous job of distracting the halfling, concentrating so fully on the task before her that she managed to minimize her nervous glances Drizzt's way.

Had Regis seen the drow's face the spell of the ruby pendant might have shattered. For Drizzt understood the trouble here and understood that his little friend was in real danger. He couldn't stop the flow. Bruenor's drastic measure of amputating the arm might be necessary, and even that, Drizzt understood, would likely kill the halfling.

"Ye got it?" Bruenor asked again and again. "Ye got it?"

Drizzt grimaced, looking pointedly at Bruenor's already bloodstained axe blade, and went at his work more determinedly. Finally, he relaxed his grip on the vein just a bit, easing, easing, breathing a bit easier as he lessened the pressure and felt no more blood spurting from the tear.

"I'm taking the damned arm!" Bruenor declared, misinterpreting Drizzt's resigned look.

The drow held up his hand and shook his head. "It is stemmed," he announced.

"But for how long?" Catti-brie asked, genuinely concerned.

Again Drizzt shook his head helplessly.

"We should be going," Bumpo Thunderpuncher remarked, seeing that the commotion about Regis had subsided. "Them goblins might not be far."

"Not yet," Drizzt insisted. "We cannot move him until we're sure the wound will not reopen."

Bumpo gave a concerned look to his brother. Then both of them glanced nervously at their thrice-removed cousins.

But Drizzt was right, of course, and Regis could not be immediately moved. All three friends stayed close to him; Catti-brie kept the ruby pendant in hand, should its calming hypnosis prove necessary. For the time being, though, Regis knew nothing at all, nothing beyond the relieving blackness of unconsciousness.

* * * * *

"You are nervous," Kimmuriel Oblodra remarked, obviously taking great pleasure in seeing the normally unshakable Jarlaxle pacing the floor.

Jarlaxle stopped and stared at the psionicist incredulously. "Nonsense," he insisted. "Baeltimazifas performed his impersonation of Pasha Basadoni perfectly."

It was true enough. At the important meeting that same morning, the doppleganger had impersonated Pasha Basadoni perfectly, no small feat considering that the man was dead and Baeltimazifas could not probe his mind for the subtle details. Of course, his role in the meeting was minor—hindered, so Sharlotta had explained to the other guildmasters, by the fact that he was very old and not in good health. Pasha Wroning had been convinced by the doppelganger's performance. With the powerful Wroning satisfied, Domo Quillilo of the wererats and the younger and more nervous leaders of the Rakers could hardly protest. Calm had returned to Calimport's streets, and all, as far as the others were concerned, was as it had been.

"He told the other guildmasters that which they desired to hear," Kimmuriel said.

"And so we shall do the same with Drizzt and his friends," Jarlaxle assured the psionicist.

"Ah, but you know that the target this time is more dangerous," said the ever-observant Kimmuriel. "More alert, and more . . . drow."

Jarlaxle stopped and stared hard at the Oblodran, then laughed aloud, admitting his edginess. "Ever has it proven interesting where Drizzt Do'Urden is concerned," he explained. "This one has again and again outrun, outsmarted, or merely out-lucked the most powerful enemies one can imagine. And look at him," he added, motioning to the magical reflective pool Rai'gy had left in place. "Still he survives, nay, thrives. Matron Baenre herself wanted to make a trophy of that one's head, and she, not he, has passed from this world."

"We do not desire his death," Kimmuriel reminded. "Though that, too, might prove quite profitable."

Jarlaxle shook his head fiercely. "Never that," he said determinedly.

Kimmuriel spent a long while studying the mercenary leader. "Could it be that you have come to like this outcast?" he asked. "That is the way of Jarlaxle, is it not?"

Jarlaxle laughed again. " 'Respect' would be a better word."

"He would never join Bregan D'aerthe," the psionicist reminded.

"Not knowingly," the opportunistic mercenary replied. "Not knowingly."

Kimmuriel didn't press the point but rather motioned to the reflective pool excitedly. "Pray that Baeltimazifas lives up to his fees," he said.

Jarlaxle, who had witnessed the catastrophe of many futile attempts against the likes of Drizzt I●'Urden, certainly was praying.

Artemis Entreri entered the room then, as Jarlaxle had bade him. He took one look at the two dark elves, then moved cautiously to the side of the reflecting pool—and his eyes widened when he saw the image displayed within, the image of his greatest adversary.

"Why are you so surprised?" Jarlaxle asked. "I told you I can deliver to you that which you most desire."

Entreri worked hard to keep his breathing steady, not wanting the mercenary to draw too much enjoyment from his obvious excitement. He recognized the truth of it all now, that Jarlaxle—damned Jarlaxle!—had been right. There in the pool stood the source of Entreri's apathy, the symbol that his life had been a lie. There stood the one challenge yet facing the master assassin, the one remaining uneasiness that so prevented him from enjoying his present life.

Right there, Drizzt Do'Urden. Entreri looked back at Jarlaxle and nodded.

The mercenary, hardly surprised, merely smiled.

* * * * *

Regis squirmed and groaned, resisting Catti-brie's attempts with the pendant this time, for as the emergency had dictated, she had not begun the charming process until after Drizzt's fingers were already working furiously inside the halfling's torn shoulder.

Bruenor, his axe right beside him, did well to hold the halfling steady, but Drizzt kept growling and shaking his head in frustration. The wound had reopened, and badly, and this time the nimble-fingered drow could not possibly close it.

"Take the damned arm!" Drizzt finally cried in ultimate frustration, falling back, his own arm soaked in blood. The four dwarves behind him gave a unified groan, but Bruenor, always steady and reliable, understood the truth and moved methodically for his axe.

Catti-brie continued to talk to Regis, but he was no longer listening to her or to anything, his consciousness long flown.

Bruenor leveled the axe, lining up the stroke. Catti-brie, having no logical arguments, understanding that they had to stem the bleeding even if that meant cutting off the arm and cauterizing the wound with fire, hesitantly extended the torn arm.

"Take it," Drizzt instructed, and the four dwarves groaned again.

Bruenor spat in his hands and took up the axe, but doubt crossed his face as he looked down at his poor little friend.

"Take it!" Drizzt demanded.

Bruenor lifted the axe and brought it down again slowly, lining up the hit.

"Take it!" Catti-brie said.

"Do not!" came a voice from the side, and all the friends turned to see two men walking toward them.

"Cadderly!" Catti-brie cried, and so it seemed to be. So surprised and pleased was she, and was Drizzt, that neither noticed that the man seemed older than the last time they had seen him, though they knew the priest was not aging, but was rather growing more youthful as his health returned. The great effort of raising the magical Spirit Soaring library from the rubble had taken its toll on the young man.

Cadderly nodded to his companion, who rushed over to Regis. "Good it is that beside you we arrived," the other priest said, a curious comment and in a dialect that none of the others had heard before.

They didn't question him about it, though, not with their friend Cadderly standing beside him, and certainly not while he bent over and began a quiet chant over the prone halfling.

"My associate, Arrabel, will see to the wound," Cadderly explained. "Truly I am surprised to see you out here so far from home."

"Coming to see yerself," Bruenor explained.

"Well, turn about," Baeltimazifas, in the guise of Cadderly, said dramatically, exactly as Jarlaxle had instructed. "I will welcome you indeed in a grand manner, when you arrive at the Spirit Soaring, but your road now is in the other direction, for you've a friend in dire need."

"Wulfgar," Catti-brie breathed, and the others were surely thinking the same.

Cadderly nodded. "He tried to follow your course, it would seem, and has come into a small hamlet east of Baldur's Gate. The downstream currents will take you there quickly."

"What hamlet?" Bumpo asked.

The doppleganger shrugged, having no name. "Four buildings behind a bluff and trees. I know not its name."

"That'd be Yogerville," Donat insisted, and Bumpo nodded his agreement.

"Get ye there in a day," the dwarf captain told Drizzt.

The drow looked questioningly to Cadderly.

"It would take me a day to pray for such a spell of transport," the phony priest explained. "And even then I could take but one of you along."

Regis groaned then, drawing the attention of all, and to the companions' amazement and absolute joy the halfling sat up, looking much better already, and even managed to flex the fingers at the end of his torn arm.

Beside him, Rai'gy, in the uncomfortable mantle of a human, smiled and silently thanked Lady Lolth for being so very understanding.

"He can travel, and immediately," the doppleganger explained. "Now be off. Your friend is in dire need. It would seem that his temper has angered the farmers, and they have him prisoner and plan to hang him.

You have time to save him, for they'll not act until their leader returns, but be off at once."

Drizzt nodded, then reached down and took his pouch from Regis's belt. "Will you join us?" he asked, and even then, eager Catti-brie, Bruenor, Regis, and the dwarves began readying the boat for departure. Drizzt and Cadderly's associate moved out of the craft to join the priest.

"No," the doppleganger replied, perfectly mimicking Cadderly's voice, according to the imp who had supplied the strange, creature with most of the details and insights. "You'll not need me, and I have other urgent matters to attend."

Drizzt nodded and handed the pouch over. "Take care with it," he explained. "It has the ability to call in would-be allies."

"I will be back in the Spirit Soaring in a matter of minutes," the doppleganger replied.

Drizzt paused at that curious comment—hadn't Cadderly just proclaimed that he needed a day to memorize a spell of transport?

"Word of recall," Rai'gy, picking up the uneasiness, put in quickly. "Get us home to the Spirit Soaring will the spell, but not to any other place."

"Come on, elf!" Bruenor cried. "Me boy's waiting."

"Go," Cadderly bade Drizzt, taking the pouch and in the same movement, putting his hand on Drizzt's shoulder and turning him back to the boat, pushing him gently along. "Go at once. You've not a moment to spare."

Silent alarms continued to ring out in Drizzt's head, but he had no time then to stop and consider them. *Bottom Feeder* was already sliding back out into the river, the four crew working to turn her about. With a nimble leap Drizzt joined them, then turned back to see Cadderly waving and smiling, his associate already in the throes of spellcasting. Before the craft had gone very far the friends watched the pair dissipate into the wind.

"Why didn't the durned fool just take one of us to me boy now?" Bruenor asked.

"Why not, indeed?" Drizzt replied, staring back at the empty spot and wondering.

Wondering.

Bright and early the next morning, *Bottom Feeder* put in against the bank a couple hundred yards short of Yogerville and the four friends, including Regis, who was feeling much better, leaped ashore.

They had all agreed that the dwarves would remain with the boat, and also, on the suggestion of Drizzt, had decided that Bruenor, Regis, and Catti-brie would go in to speak with the townsfolk alone while the ranger circumvented the hamlet, getting a full lay of the region.

The three were greeted by friendly farm folk, by wide smiles, and then, when asked about Wulfgar, by expressions of confusion.

"Ye thinking that we'd forget one of that description?" one old woman asked with a cackle.

The three friends looked at each other with confusion.

"Donat picked the wrong town," Bruenor said with a great sigh.

* * * * *

Drizzt harbored troubling thoughts. A magical spell had obviously brought Cadderly to him and his companions, but if Wulfgar was in such dire need, why hadn't the cleric just gone to him first instead? He could explain it, of course, considering that Regis was in more dire peril, but why hadn't Cadderly gone to one, while his associate went to the other? Again, logical explanations were there. Perhaps the priests had only one spell that could bring them to one place and had been forced to choose. Yet there was something else nagging at Drizzt, and he simply could not place it.

But then he understood his inner turmoil. How had Cadderly even known to look for Wulfgar, a man he had never met and had only heard about briefly?

"Just good fortune," he told himself, trying logically to trace Cadderly's process, one that had obviously brought him onto Drizzt's trail, and there he had discovered Wulfgar, not so far behind. Luck alone had informed the priest of whom this great man might be.

Still, there seemed holes in that logic, but ones that Drizzt hoped might be filled in by Wulfgar when at last they managed to rescue him. With all that in mind Drizzt made his way around the back side of the hamlet, moving behind the blocking ridge south of the town, out of sight of his friends and their surprising exchange with the townsfolk, who honestly had no idea who Wulfgar might be.

But Drizzt could have guessed as much anyway when he came around that ridgeline, to see a crystalline tower, an image of Crenshinibon, sparkling in the morning light.

Chapter 23

The Last Challenge

Drizzt stood transfixed as a line appeared on the unblemished side of the crystalline tower, widening, widening, until it became an open doorway.

And inside the door, beckoning to Drizzt, stood a drow elf wearing a great plumed hat that Drizzt surely recognized. For some reason he could not immediately discern, Drizzt was not as surprised as he should have been.

"Well met again, Drizzt Do'Urden," Jarlaxle said, using the common surface tongue. "Please do come in and speak with me."

Drizzt put one hand to a scimitar hilt, the other to the pouch holding Guenhwyvar—though he had only recently sent the panther back to her astral home and knew she would be weary if recalled. He tensed his leg muscles and measured the distance to Jarlaxle, recognizing that he, with the enchanted ankle bracers he wore, could cover the ground in the blink of an eye, perhaps even get a solid strike in against the mercenary.

But then he would be dead, he knew, for if Jarlaxle was here, then so was Bregan D'aerthe, all about him, weapons trained upon him.

"Please," Jarlaxle said again. "We have business we must discuss to the benefit of us both and to our friends."

255

That last reference, coupled with the fact that Drizzt had come back this way on the word of an impostor—who was obviously working for the mercenary leader or was, perhaps the mercenary leader—that Wulfgar was in some danger, made Drizzt relax his grip on his weapon.

"I guarantee that neither I nor my associates shall strike against you," Jarlaxle assured him. "And furthermore the friends who accompanied you to this village will walk away unharmed as long as they take no action against me."

Drizzt held a fair understanding of the mysterious mercenary, enough to trust Jarlaxle's word, at least. Jarlaxle had held all the cards in previous meetings, times when the mercenary could have easily killed Drizzt, and Catti-brie as well. And yet he had not, despite the fact that bringing the head of Drizzt Do'Urden back to Menzoberranzan at that time might have proven quite profitable. With a look back to the direction of the town, blocked from view by the high ridge, Drizzt moved to the door.

Many memories came to Drizzt as he followed Jarlaxle into the structure, the magical door sliding closed behind them. Though this ground level was not as the ranger remembered it, he could not help but recall the first time he entered a manifestation of Crenshinibon, when he had gone after the wizard Akar Kessell back in Icewind Dale. It was not a pleasant memory to be sure, but a somewhat comforting one, for within those recollections came to Drizzt an understanding of how he could defeat this tower, of how he could sever its power and send it crumbling down.

Looking back at Jarlaxle, though, as the mercenary settled comfortably into a lavish chair beside a huge upright mirror, Drizzt understood he wouldn't likely get any such chance.

Jarlaxle motioned to a chair opposite him, and again Drizzt moved to comply. The mercenary was as dangerous as any creature Drizzt had ever know, but he was not reckless and not vicious.

One thing Drizzt did notice, though, as he moved for the seat: his feet seemed just a bit heavier to him, as though the dweomer of his bracers had diminished.

"I have followed your movements for many days," Jarlaxle explained. "A friend of mine requires your services, you see."

"Services?" Drizzt asked suspiciously.

Jarlaxle only smiled and continued. "It became important for me to bring the two of you together again."

"And important for you to steal the crystal shard," Drizzt reasoned.

"Not so," the mercenary honestly answered. "Not so. Crenshinibon was not known to me when this began. Acquiring it was merely a pleasant extra in seeking that which I most needed: you."

"What of Cadderly?" Drizzt asked with some concern. He still was not certain whether it really had been Cadderly who had come to Regis's aid. Had Jarlaxle subsequently garnered Crenshinibon from the priest? Or had the entire episode with Cadderly been merely a clever ruse?

"Cadderly remains quite comfortable in the Spirit Soaring, oblivious to your quest," Jarlaxle explained. "Much to the dismay of my wizard friend's new familiar, who holds a particular hatred for Cadderly."

"Promise me that Cadderly is safe," Drizzt said in all seriousness.

Jarlaxle nodded. "Indeed, and you are quite welcome for our actions to save your halfling friend."

That caught Drizzt off guard, but he had to admit that it was true enough. Had not Jarlaxle's cronies come in the guise of Cadderly and enacted great healing upon Regis, the halfling likely would have died, or at the very least would have lost an arm.

"Of course, for the minor price of a spellcasting you gained much of our confidence," Drizzt did remark, reminding Jarlaxle that he understood the mercenary rarely did anything that did not bring some benefit to him.

"Not so minor a spellcasting," Jarlaxle bantered. "And we could have faked it all, providing only the illusion of healing, a spell that would have temporarily healed the halfling's wounds, only to have them reopen later on to his ultimate demise.

"But I assure you that we did not," he quickly added, seeing Drizzt's eyes narrow dangerously. "No, your friend is nearly fully healed."

"Then I do thank you," Drizzt replied. "Of course, you understand that I must take Crenshinibon back from you?"

"I do not doubt that you are brave enough to try," Jarlaxle admitted. "But I do understand that you are not stupid enough to try."

"Not now, perhaps."

"Then why ever?" the mercenary asked. "What care is it to Drizzt Do'Urden if Crenshinibon works its wicked magic upon the dark elves of Menzoberranzan?"

Again, the mercenary had put Drizzt somewhat off his guard. What care, indeed? "But does Jarlaxle remain in Menzoberranzan?" he asked. "It would seem not."

That brought a laugh from the mercenary. "Jarlaxle goes where Jarlaxle needs to go," he answered. "But think long and hard on your choice before coming for the crystal shard, Drizzt Do'Urden. Are there truly any hands in all the world better suited to wield the artifact than mine?"

Drizzt did not reply but was indeed considering the words carefully.

"Enough of that," Jarlaxle said, coming forward in his chair, suddenly more intent. "I have brought you here that you might meet an old acquaintance, one you have battled beside and battled against. It seems as if he has some unfinished business with Drizzt Do'Urden, and that uncertainty is costing me precious time with him."

Drizzt stared hard at the mercenary, having no idea what Jarlaxle might be talking about—for just a moment. Then he remembered the last time he had seen the mercenary, right before Drizzt and Artemis Entreri had parted ways. His expression showed his disappointment clearly as he came to suspect the truth of it all.

* * * * *

"Ye picked the wrong durned town," Bruenor said to Bumpo and Donat when he and the other two returned to *Bottom Feeder*.

The two dwarven brothers looked curiously at each other, Donat scratching his head.

"Had to be this one," Bumpo insisted. "By yer friend's description, I mean."

"The townsfolk might have been lying to us," Regis put in.

"They're good at it, then," said Catti-brie. "Every one o' them."

"Well, I know a way to find out for certain," the halfling said, a mischievous twinkle in his eye. When Bruenor and Catti-brie, recognizing that tone in his voice, turned to regard him, they found him dangling his hypnotic ruby pendant.

"Back we go," Bruenor said, starting away from the boat once more. He paused and looked back at the four dwarves. "Ye're sure, are ye?" he asked.

All four heads began wagging enthusiastically.

Just before the threesome arrived back among the cluster of houses, a small boy ran out to meet them. "Did you find your friend?" he asked.

"Why no, we haven't," Catti-brie replied, holding back both Bruenor and Regis with a wave of her hand. "Have ye seen him?"

"He might be in the tower," the youngster offered.

"What tower?" Bruenor asked gruffly before Catti-brie could reply.

"Over there," the young boy answered, unruffled by the dwarf's stern tone. "Out back." He pointed to the ridge that rose up behind the small village, and as the friends followed that line they noted several villagers ascending the ridge. About halfway up the villagers began gasping in astonishment, some pointing, others falling to the ground, and still others running back the way they had come.

The three friends began running, too, to the ridge and up. Then they too skidded to abrupt stops, staring incredulously at the tower image of Crenshinibon.

"Cadderly?" Regis asked incredulously.

"I'm not thinkin' so," said Catti-brie. Crouching low, she led them on cautiously.

* * * * *

"Artemis Entreri wishes this contest between you two at last resolved," Jarlaxle confirmed.

"And why would I go along?" Drizzt asked, coming right out of his chair. "I have no desire ever to see the likes of Artemis Entreri again, let alone do battle with the wretch. If his inability to fight with me brings him discomfort, then all the better, I say!"

Drizzt's uncharacteristic outburst made it quite obvious to Jarlaxle just how much he despised Entreri and just how sincere he was in his claim to never want to go against the man again.

"Never do you disappoint me," Jarlaxle said with a chuckle. "Your lack of hubris is commendable, my friend. I applaud you for it and do wish, in all sincerity, that I could grant you your desire and send you and your friends on your way. But that I cannot do, I fear, and I assure you that you must settle your relationship with Entreri. For your friends, if not for yourself."

Drizzt chewed on that threat for a long moment. While he did, Jarlaxle waved his hand in front of the mirror beside his chair, which clouded over immediately. As Drizzt watched the fog swirled away, leaving a clear image of Catti-brie, Bruenor, and Regis making their way up to the base of the tower. Catti-brie was in the lead, moving in a staggered manner, trying to utilize the little cover available.

"I could kill them with a thought," the mercenary assured Drizzt.

"But why would you?" Drizzt asked. "You gave me your word."

"And so I shall keep it," Jarlaxle replied. "As long as you cooperate."

Drizzt paused, digesting the information. "What of Wulfgar?" he asked suddenly, thinking that Jarlaxle must have some information regarding the man since he'd used Wulfgar's name to lure Drizzt and his friends to this place.

Now it was Jarlaxle's turn to pause and think, but just for a moment. "He is alive and well from what I can discern," the mercenary admitted. "I have not spoken with him, but looked in on him long enough to find out how his present situation might benefit me."

"Where?" Drizzt asked.

Jarlaxle smiled widely. "There will be time for such talk later," he said, looking back over his shoulder to the one staircase ascending from the room.

"You will find that your magics will not work in here," the mercenary went on, and Drizzt understood then why his feet seemed heavier. "None of them, not your scimitars, the bracers you took from Dantrag Baenre when you killed him, nor even your innate drow powers."

"Yet a new and wondrous aspect of the crystal shard," Drizzt remarked sarcastically.

"No," Jarlaxle admitted, smiling. "More the help of a friend. It was necessary to defeat all magic, you see, because this last meeting between you and Artemis Entreri must be on perfectly equal footing, with no possible unfair advantages to be gained by either party."

"Yet your mirror worked," Drizzt reasoned, as much trying to buy himself some time as out of any curiosity. "Is that not magic?"

"It is yet another piece of the tower, nothing I brought in, and all the tower is impervious to my associate's attempts to defeat the magic," Jarlaxle explained. "What a marvelous gift you gave to me—or to my

259

associate—in handing over Crenshinibon. It has told me so much about itself . . . how to raise the towers and how to manipulate them to fit my needs"

"You know that I cannot allow you to keep it," Drizzt said again.

"And you know well that I would never have invited you here if I thought there was anything at all you could do to take Crenshinibon away from me," Jarlaxle said with a laugh. He ended the sentence by looking again at the mirror to his side.

Drizzt followed that gaze to the mirror, to see his friends moving about the base of the tower then, searching for a door—a door that Drizzt knew they would not find unless Jarlaxle willed it to be so. Catti-brie did find something of interest, though: Drizzt's tracks.

"He's in there!" she cried.

"Please be Cadderly," both dark elves heard Regis remark nervously. That brought a chuckle from Jarlaxle.

"Go to Entreri," the mercenary said more seriously, waving his hand so that the mirror clouded over again, the image dissipating. "Go and satisfy his curiosity, and then you and your friends will go your way, and I will go mine."

Drizzt spent a long while staring at the mercenary. Jarlaxle didn't press him for many moments, just locked stares with him. In that moment they came to a silent understanding.

"Whatever the outcome?" Drizzt asked again, just to be sure.

"Your friends walk away unharmed," Jarlaxle assured him. "With you, or with your body."

Drizzt turned his gaze back to the staircase. He could hardly believe that Artemis Entreri, his nemesis for so long, awaited him just up those steps. His words to Jarlaxle had been sincere and heartfelt; he never wanted to see the man again, let alone fight with him. That was Entreri's emotional pain, not Drizzt's. Even now, with the fight so close and obviously so necessary, the drow ranger did not look forward to his climb up those stairs. It wasn't that he was afraid of the assassin. Not at all. While Drizzt respected Entreri's fighting prowess, he didn't fear the challenge.

He rose from his chair and started for the stairs, silently recounting all the good he might accomplish in this fight. In addition to satisfying Jarlaxle, Drizzt might well be ridding the world of a scourge.

Drizzt stopped and turned about. "This counts as one of my friends," he said, producing the onyx figurine from his pouch.

"Ah, yes, Guenhwyvar," Jarlaxle said, his face brightening.

"I will not see Guenhwyvar in Entreri's hands," Drizzt said. "Nor in yours. Whatever the outcome, she is to be returned to me or to Catti-brie."

"A pity," Jarlaxle remarked with a laugh. "I had thought you might forget to include the magnificent panther in your conditions. How much I would love a companion such as Guenhwyvar."

Drizzt stood up straighter, lavender eyes narrowing.

"You would never trust me with such a treasure," Jarlaxle said. "Nor could I blame you. I do indeed have a weakness for things magical!" The mercenary was laughing, but Drizzt was not.

"Give it to them yourself," Jarlaxle offered, motioning for the door. "Just toss the figurine at the wall, above where you entered. Watch the results for yourself," he added, motioning to the mirror, which cleared again of fog and produced an image of Drizzt's friends.

The ranger looked back to the door to see a small opening appear right above it. He rushed over. "Be gone from this place!" he cried, hoping his friends would hear, and tossed the onyx figurine through the portal. Thinking suddenly that the whole episode might be just one of Jarlaxle's tricks, he swung about and scrambled to watch in the mirror.

To his relief he saw the trio, Catti-brie calling for him and Regis picking up the panther from the ground. The halfling wasted no time in setting the thing down and calling to Guenhwyvar, and the cat soon appeared beside Drizzt's friends, growling out to the trapped drow even as the other three called for him.

"You know they'll not leave," Jarlaxle said dryly. "But go on and be done with this. You have my word that your friends, all four, will not be harmed."

Drizzt hesitated just one more time, glancing back at the mercenary who still sat comfortably in his chair as though Drizzt presented no threat to him whatsoever. For a moment Drizzt considered calling that bluff, drawing his weapons enchanted or not, and rushing over to cut the mercenary down. But he could not, of course, not when the safety of his friends hung in the balance.

Jarlaxle, so smug in his chair, knew that implicitly.

Drizzt took a deep breath, trying to throw away all the confusion of this last day, the craziness that had handed the mighty artifact over to Jarlaxle and brought Drizzt to this place, to fight Artemis Entreri, no less.

He took a second deep breath, stretched out his fingers and arms, and started up the stairs.

*　*　*　*　*

Artemis Entreri paced the room nervously, studying the many contours, staircases, and elevated planks. No simple circular, empty chamber for Jarlaxle. The mercenary had constructed this, the second floor of the tower, with many ups and downs, places where strategy could play in to the upcoming fight. At the center of the room was a staircase of four steps, rising to a landing large enough for only one man. The back side mirrored the front, another four steps back down to the floor level. More steps completely bordered the room, five up to the wall, where another

261

landing ran all the way around. From these, on Entreri's left, went a plank, perhaps a foot wide, connecting the fourth step to the top landing of the center case.

Yet another obstacle, a two-sided ramp, loomed near the back wall beside where Entreri paced. Two others, low, circular platforms, were set about the room by the door across the way, the door through which Drizzt Do'Urden would enter.

But how to make all of these props work for him? Entreri pondered, and he realized that his thoughts mattered little, for Drizzt was too unpredictable a foe, was too quick and quick thinking for Entreri to lay out a plan of attack. No, he would have to improvise every step and roll of the way, to counter and anticipate, and fight in measured thrusts.

He drew out his weapons then, dagger and sword. At first he had considered coming in with two swords to offset Drizzt's twin scimitars. In the end he decided to go with the style he knew best, and with the weapon, though its magic would not work in here, that he loved best.

Back and forth he paced, stretching his muscles, arms, and neck. He talked quietly to himself, reminding himself of all that he had to do, warning himself to never, not for a single instant, underestimate his enemy. And then he stopped suddenly, and considered his own movements, his own thoughts.

He was indeed nervous, anxious and, for the first time since he had left Menzoberranzan, excited. A slight sound turned him around.

Drizzt Do'Urden stood on the landing.

Without a word the drow ranger entered, then flinched not at all as the door slid closed behind him.

"I have waited for this for many years," Entreri said.

"Then you are a bigger fool than I supposed," Drizzt replied.

Entreri exploded into motion, rushing up the back side of the center stairs, brandishing dagger and sword as he came over the lip, as if he expected Drizzt to meet him there, battling for the high ground.

The ranger hadn't moved, hadn't even drawn his weapons.

"And a bigger fool still if you believe that I will fight you this day," Drizzt said.

Entreri's eyes widened. After a long pause he came down the front stairs slowly, sword leading, dagger ready, moving to within a couple of steps of Drizzt.

Who still did not draw his weapons.

"Ready your scimitars," Entreri instructed.

"Why? That we might play as entertainment for Jarlaxle and his band?" Drizzt replied.

"Draw them!" Entreri growled. "Else I'll run you through."

"Will you?" Drizzt calmly asked, and he slowly drew out his blades. As Entreri came on another measured step, the ranger dropped those scimitars to the ground.

Entreri's jaw dropped nearly as far.

"Have you learned nothing in all the years?" Drizzt asked. "How many times must we play this out? Must all of our lives be dedicated to revenge upon whichever of us won the last battle?"

"Pick them up!" Entreri shouted, rushing in so that his sword tip came in at Drizzt's breastbone.

"And then we shall fight," Drizzt said nonchalantly. "And one of us will win, but perhaps the other will survive. And then, of course, we will have to do this all over again, because you believe that you have something to prove."

"Pick them up," Entreri said through gritted teeth, prodding his sword just a bit. Had that blade still been carrying the weight of its magic, the prod surely would have slid it through Drizzt's ribs. "This is the last challenge, for one of us will die this day. Here it is, laid out for us by Jarlaxle, as fair a fight as we might ever find."

Drizzt didn't move.

"I will run you through," Entreri promised.

Drizzt only smiled. "I think not, Artemis Entreri. I know you better than you believe, and surely better than you are comfortable with. You would take no pleasure in killing me in such a manner and would hate yourself for the rest of your life for doing so, for stealing from yourself the only chance you might ever have to know the truth. Because that is what this is about, is it not? The truth, your truth, the moment when you hope to either validate your miserable existence or put an end to it."

Entreri growled loudly and came forward, but he did not, could not, press his arm forward and impale the drow. "Damn you!" he cried, spinning away, growling and slashing, back around the stairs, cursing with every step. "Damn you!"

Behind him Drizzt nodded, bent, and retrieved his scimitars. "Entreri," he called, and the change in his tone told the assassin that something was suddenly very different.

Entreri, on the other side of the room now, turned about to see Drizzt standing ready, blades in hand, to see the vision he so desperately craved.

"You passed my test," Drizzt explained. "Now I'll take yours."

* * * * *

"Are we to watch or just wait to see who shall walk out victorious?" Rai'gy asked as he and Kimmuriel walked out from a small chamber off to the side of the first floor's main room.

"This show will be worth the watching," Jarlaxle assured the pair. He motioned to the stairs. "We will ascend to the landing, and I will make the door translucent."

"An amazing artifact," Kimmuriel said, shaking his head. In only a day of communing with the crystal shard Jarlaxle had learned so very much. He had learned how to shape and design the tower reflection of the shard, to make doors appear and seemingly vanish, to create walls, transparent or opaque, and to use the tower as one great scrying device, as he was now. Both Kimmuriel and Rai'gy noted this as they came around to see the image of Catti-brie, Regis, Bruenor, and the great cat showing in the mirror.

"We shall watch, and they should as well," Jarlaxle said. He closed his eyes, and all three drow heard a scraping sound along the outside of Crenshinibon. "There," Jarlaxle announced a moment later. "Now we may go."

*　　*　　*　　*　　*　　*

Catti-brie, Bruenor, and Regis stood dumbfounded as the crystalline tower seemed to snake to life, one edge rolling out wide, releasing a hidden fold. Then, amazingly, a stairway appeared, circling down along the tower from a height of about twenty feet.

The three hesitated, looking to each other for answers, but Guenhwyvar waited not at all, bounding up the stairs, roaring with every mighty leap.

*　　*　　*　　*　　*　　*

They stared at each other for some time, looks of respect more than hatred, for they had come past hatred, these two, losing a good deal of their enmity by the sheer exertions of their running battle.

So now they stared from opposite sides of the thirty-foot diameter room, across the central stairs, each waiting for the other to make the first move, or rather, for the other to show that he was about to move.

They broke as one, both charging for the center stairs, both seeking the higher ground. Even without the aid of the magical bracers Drizzt gained a step advantage, perhaps because though he was twice the assassin's actual age, he was much younger in terms of a drow lifetime than Entreri was for a human.

Always the improviser, Entreri took one step on the staircase, then dived to the side, headlong in a roll that brought him harmlessly past Drizzt's swishing blades. He went right under the raised plank, using it as a barrier against the scimitars.

Drizzt turned completely around, falling into a ready crouch at the top of the stairs and preventing Entreri from coming back in.

But Entreri knew that the ranger would protect his high-ground position, and so the assassin never slowed, coming out of his roll back to his feet and running to the side of the room, up the five steps, then moving along that higher ground to the end of the raised plank. When Drizzt did not pursue, neither by following Entreri's course nor rushing across the

264

plank, Entreri hopped down to that narrow walkway and moved halfway along it toward the center stair.

Drizzt held his ground on the wider platform of the staircase apex.

"Come along," Entreri bade him, indicating the walkway. "Even footing."

*　*　*　*　*

They feared climbing that stair, for how vulnerable they would all be perched on the side of Crenshinibon, but when Guenhwyvar, at the landing and looking into the tower, roared louder and began clawing at the wall they could not resist. Again Catti-brie arrived first to find a translucent wall at the top of the stairs, a window into the room where Drizzt and Entreri faced off.

She banged on the unyielding glass. So did Bruenor when he arrived, with the back of his axe, but to no avail, for they could not even scratch the thing. If Drizzt and Entreri heard them, or even saw them, neither showed it.

*　*　*　*　*

"You should have made the room smaller," Rai'gy remarked dryly when he, Jarlaxle, and Kimmuriel arrived at their landing, similarly watching the action—or lack thereof—within.

"Ah, but the play's the thing," Jarlaxle replied. He pointed across the way then, to Catti-brie and the others. "We can see the combatants and Drizzt's friends across the way, and those friends can see us," he explained, and even as he did so the three drow saw Catti-brie pointing their way, screaming something that they could not hear but could well imagine. "But Drizzt and Entreri can see only each other."

"Quite a tower," Rai'gy had to admit.

*　*　*　*　*

Drizzt wanted to hold the secure position, but Entreri showed patience now, and the ranger knew that if he did not go out, this fight that he desperately wanted to be done with could take a long, long time. He hopped onto the narrow walkway easily and came out toward Entreri slowly, inch by inch, setting each foot firmly before taking the next small step.

He snapped into sudden motion as he neared, a quick-step thrust of his right blade. Entreri's dagger, his left-hand weapon, wove inside the thrust perfectly and pushed the scimitar out wide. In the same fluid movement the assassin turned his shoulder and moved ahead, sword tip leading.

Drizzt's second scimitar was halfway into the parry before the thrust ever began, turning a complete circle in the air, then ascending inside the angle of the thrust on the second pass, deflecting the rushing sword, rolling right over it and around as his first blade did the same with the dagger. Into the dance fully he went, his curving blades accentuating the spinning circular motions, cutting over and around, reversing the direction of one, then both, then one again. Spinning, seeking opening, thrusting ahead, slashing down.

And Entreri matched every movement, his actions in straighter lines, straight to the side or above or straight ahead, picking off the blades, forcing Drizzt to parry. The metal screamed continuously, hit after hit after hit.

But then Drizzt's left hand came in cleanly and cleanly swished through the air, for the assassin did not try to parry but dived into a forward roll instead, his sword knocking one scimitar at bay, his movement causing the other to miss, and his dagger, leading the ascent out of the roll, aimed for Drizzt's heart with no chance for the ranger to bring his remaining scimitar in to block.

So up went Drizzt, up and out, a great leap to the left side, tucking and turning to avoid the strike, landing on the floor in a roll that brought him back to his feet. He took two running steps away as he spun about, knowing that Entreri, slight advantage gained, would surely pursue. He came around just in time to meet a furious attack from dagger and sword.

Again the metal rang out repeatedly in protest, and Drizzt was forced back by the sheer momentum of Entreri's charge. He accepted that retreat, though, quickstepping all the way to maintain perfect balance, his hands working in a blur.

* * * * *

At the interior landing the three drow, who had lived all their lives around expert swordsmen and had witnessed many, many battles, watched every subtle movement with mounting amazement.

"Did you arrange this for Entreri's benefit or ours?" Rai'gy remarked, his tone surely different, surely without hint of sarcasm.

"Both," Jarlaxle admitted. As he spoke, Drizzt darted past Entreri up the center stairs and did not stop, but rather leaped off, turning in midair as he went, then landing in a rush back to the side toward the plank. Entreri took a shorter route instead of a direct pursuit, leaping up to the plank ahead of Drizzt, stealing the advantage the dark elf had hoped to achieve.

As much the improviser as his opponent, Drizzt dived down low, skittering under the plank even as Entreri got his footing, and slashing back up and over his head, an amazingly agile move that would have

266

hamstrung the assassin had Entreri not anticipated just that and continued on his way, leaping off the plank back to the floor and turning around.

Still, Drizzt had scored a hit, tearing the back of Entreri's trousers and a line across the back of his calf.

"First blood to Drizzt," Kimmuriel observed. He looked to Jarlaxle, who was smiling and looking across the way. Following the mercenary's gaze Rai'gy saw that Drizzt's friends, including even the panther, were similarly entranced, watching the battle with open-mouthed admiration.

And so it was well-earned, Kimmuriel silently agreed, turning his full attention back to the dance, brutal and beautiful all at once.

* * * * *

Now they came in at floor level, rushing together in a blur of swords and flying capes, their routines neither attack nor defense, but somewhere in between. Blade scraped along blade, throwing sparks, the metal shrieking in protest.

Drizzt's left blade swished across at neck level. Entreri dropped suddenly below it into a squat from which he seemed to gain momentum, coming back up with a double thrust of sword and dagger. But Drizzt didn't stop his turn with the miss. The dark elf went right around, a complete circuit, coming back with a right-handed, backhand down-and-over parry. The inside hook of his curving blade caught both the assassin's blades and turned them aside. Then Drizzt altered the angle of his left before it swished overhead, the blade screaming down for Entreri's head.

But the assassin, his hands even closer together because of Drizzt's block, switched blades easily, then extracted the dagger by bringing his right arm in suddenly, pumping it back out, dagger tip rising as scimitar descended.

Then they both howled in pain, Drizzt leaping back with a deep puncture in his wrist, Entreri falling back with a gash along the length of his forearm.

But only for a second, only for the time it took each to realize that he could continue, that he would not drop a weapon. Both Drizzt's scimitars started out wide, closing like the jaws of a wolf as he and Entreri came together. The assassin, though his blades had the inside track, found himself a split second behind and had to double block, throwing his own blades, and the scimitars they caught, out wide and coming forward with the momentum. He hesitated just an instant to see if he could possibly bring one of his blades back in.

Drizzt hadn't hesitated at all, though, dipping his forehead just ahead of Entreri's similar movement, so that when they came smacking together, head to head, Entreri got the brunt of it.

But the assassin, dazed, punched out straight with his right hand, knuckles and dagger crosspiece slamming into Drizzt's face.

They fell apart again, one of Entreri's eyes fast swelling, Drizzt's cheek and nose bleeding.

The assassin pressed the attack fiercely then, before his eye closed and gave Drizzt a huge advantage. He went in hard, stabbing his sword down low.

Drizzt's scimitar crossed down over it, and he pivoted perfectly, launching a kick that got Entreri in the face.

The kick hardly slowed him, for the assassin had anticipated that exact move indeed, he had counted on it. He ducked as the foot came in, a grazing blow, but one that nonetheless stung his already injured eye. Skittering forward he launched his dagger in a roundabout manner, the edge coming in at the back of Drizzt's knee.

Drizzt could have struck with his second blade, hoping to get it past the already engaged sword, but if he tried and Entreri somehow managed to parry, he knew that the fight would be all but over, that the dagger would tear the back out of his leg.

He knew all of that, instinctively, without thinking at all, so instead he just kicked his one supporting leg forward, falling backward over the dagger. Drizzt was scraped but not skewered. He meant to go all the way around in the roll and come right back up to his feet, but before he even really started he saw that the growling Entreri was fast pursuing and would catch him defenseless halfway around.

So he stopped and set himself on his back as the assassin came in.

On both sides of the room, dark elves and Drizzt's friends alike gasped, thinking the contest at its end. But Drizzt fought on, scimitars whirling, smacking, and stabbing to somehow, impossibly, hold Entreri at bay. And then the ranger managed to tuck one foot under him and come up in a wild rush, fighting ferociously, hitting each of Entreri's blades and hitting them hard, driving, driving to gain an equal footing.

Now they were in it, face to face, blades working too quickly for the onlookers to even discern individual moves, but rather to watch the general flow of the battle. A gash appeared here on one combatant, a gash appeared there on the other, but neither warrior found the opportunity to bring any cut to completion. They were superficial nicks, torn clothes and skin. It went on and on, up one side of the staircase and down the other, and any misgivings that Drizzt might have had about this fight had long flown, and any doubts Entreri had ever had about desiring to battle Drizzt Do'Urden again had been fully erased. They fought with passion and fury, their blades striking so rapidly that the ring came as constant.

They were out on the plank then, but they didn't know it. They came down together, each knocking the other from his perch, on opposite sides, then went under the plank together, battling in a crouch. They moved past each other, coming up on either side, then leaping back atop the narrow walkway in perfect balance to begin anew.

On and on it went, and the seconds became minutes, and sweat mixed with blood and stung open wounds. One of Drizzt's sleeves got sliced so badly that it interfered with his movements, and he had to launch an explosive flurry to drive Entreri back long enough so he could flip his blade in the air and pull the remnants of the sleeve from his arm, then catch his blade as it descended, just in time to react to the assassin's charge. A moment later Entreri lost his cape as Drizzt's scimitar came in for his throat, cutting the garment's drawstring and tearing a gash under Entreri's chin as it rose.

Both labored for breath; neither would back off.

But for all the nicks and blood, for all the sweat and bruises, one injury alone stood out, for Entreri's vision on his right side was indeed blurring. The assassin switched weapon hands, dagger back in left and the longer, better blocking sword back in his right.

Drizzt understood. He launched a feint, a right, left, right combination that Entreri easily picked off, but the attacks had not been designed to score any definitive hit anyway, just to allow Drizzt to put his feet in line.

To the side of the room cunning Jarlaxle saw it and understood that the fight was about to end.

Now Drizzt came in again with a left, but he stepped into the blow and launched his scimitar from far out to the side, from a place where Entreri's closed eye could hardly make out the movement. The assassin did instinctively parry with the sword and counter with the dagger, but Drizzt rolled his scimitar right over the intended parry, then snapped it back out, slashing Entreri's wrist and launching the sword away. At the same time, the ranger dropped his blade from his right hand and caught Entreri's stabbing dagger arm at the wrist. Stepping in and rolling his wrist and turning his weapon hand, Drizzt twisted Entreri's dagger arm back under itself, holding it out wide while before the assassin's free hand could hold Drizzt's arm back the dark elf's scimitar tip came in at Entreri's throat.

All movement stopped suddenly. The assassin, with one arm twisted out wide and the other behind Drizzt's scimitar arm, was helpless to stop the ranger's momentum if Drizzt decided to plunge the blade through Entreri's throat.

Growling and trembling, as close to the very edge of control as he had ever been, Drizzt held the blade back. "So what have we proven?" he demanded, voice full of venom, his lavender orbs locked in a wicked stare with Entreri's dark eyes. "Because my head connected in a favorable place with yours, limiting your vision, I am the better fighter?"

"Finish it!" Entreri snarled back.

Drizzt growled again and twisted Entreri's dagger arm more, bending the assassin's wrist so that the dagger fell to the floor. "For all those you have killed, and all those you surely will, I should kill you," Drizzt said, but he knew even as he said the words, and Entreri did, too, that he could not press home his blade, not now. In that awful moment Drizzt lamented not going through with the move in the first instant, before he had found the time to consider his actions.

But now he could not, so with a sudden explosion of motion he let go of Entreri's arm and drove his open palm hard into the assassin's face, disengaging them and knocking Entreri staggering backward.

"Damn you, Jarlaxle, have you had your pleasure?" Drizzt cried, turning about to see the mercenary and his companions, for Jarlaxle had opened the door.

Drizzt came forward determinedly, as if he meant to run right over Jarlaxle, but a noise behind him stopped him, for Entreri came on, yelling.

Yelling. The significance of that was lost on Drizzt in that moment as he spun about, right to left, his free right arm brushing out and across, lifting Entreri's leading arm, which held again that awful dagger. And around came Drizzt's left arm, scimitar leading, in a stab as Entreri crashed in, a stab that should have plunged the weapon into the assassin's chest to its hilt.

The two came together and Drizzt's eyes widened indeed, for somehow, somehow, Entreri's very skin had repelled the blow.

But Artemis Entreri, his body tingling with the energy of the absorbed hit, with the psionics Kimmuriel had suddenly given back to him, surely understood, and in a purely reactive move, without any conscious thought—for if the tormented man had considered it he would have loosed the energy back into himself—Entreri reached out and clasped Drizzt's chest and gave him back his blow with equal force.

His hand sank into Drizzt's chest even as Drizzt, blood bubbling from the wound, fell to the ground.

*   *   *   *   *

Out on the landing time seemed to freeze, stuck fast in that awful, awful moment. Guenhwyvar roared and leaped into the translucent wall, but merely bounced away. Outraged, roaring wildly, the cat went back at the wall, claws screeching against the unyielding pane.

Bruenor, too, went into a fighting frenzy, hacking futilely with his axe while Regis stood dumbfounded, saying, "No, it cannot be," over and over.

And there stood Catti-brie, wavering back and forth, her jaw drooping open, her eyes locked on that horrible sight. She suffered through every agonizing second as Entreri's empowered hand melted into Drizzt's chest, as the lifeblood of her dearest friend, of the ranger she had come to love so dearly, spurted from him. She watched the strength leave his legs, the buckling knees, and the sinking, sinking as Entreri guided him to the floor, and the sinking, sinking, of her own heart, an emptiness she had felt before, when she had seen Wulfgar fall with the yochlol.

And even worse it seemed for her this time.

* * * * *

"What have I done?" the assassin wailed, falling to his knees beside the drow. He turned an evil glare over Jarlaxle. "What have you done?"

"I gave you your fight and showed you the truth," Jarlaxle calmly replied. "Of yourself and your skills. But I am not finished with you. I came to you for my own purposes, not your own. Having done this for you, I demand that you perform for me."

"No! No!" the assassin cried, reaching down furiously to try to stem the spurting blood. "Not like this!"

Jarlaxle looked to Kimmuriel and nodded. The psionicist gripped Entreri with a mental hold, a telekinetic force that lifted Entreri from Drizzt and dragged him behind Kimmuriel as the psionicist headed out of the room, back down the stairs.

Entreri thrashed and cursed, aiming his outrage at Jarlaxle but eyeing Drizzt, who lay very still on the floor. Indeed he had been granted his fight and, indeed, as he should have foreseen, it had proven nothing. He had lost—or would have, had not Kimmuriel intervened—yet he was the one who had lived.

Why, then, was he so angry? Why did he want at that moment, to put his dagger across Jarlaxle's slender throat?

Kimmuriel hauled him away.

"He fought beautifully," Rai'gy remarked to Jarlaxle, indicating Drizzt, the blood flowing much lighter now, a pool of it all about his prone and very still form. "I understand now why Dantrag Baenre is dead."

Jarlaxle nodded and smiled. "I have never seen Drizzt Do'Urden's equal," he admitted, "unless it is Artemis Entreri. Do you understand now why I chose that one."

"He is drow in everything but skin color," Rai'gy said with a laugh.

An explosion rocked the tower.

"Catti-brie and her marvelous bow," Jarlaxle explained, looking to the landing where only Guenhwyvar remained, roaring and clawing futilely at the unyielding glass. "They saw, of course, every bit of it. I should go and speak with them before they bring the place down around us."

With a thought to the crystal shard, Jarlaxle turned that wall in front of Guenhwyvar opaque once more.

Then he nodded to the still form of Drizzt Do'Urden and walked out of the room.

Epilogue

"He is sulking," Kimmuriel remarked, joining Jarlaxle sometime later in the main chamber of the lower floor. "But at least he has stopped swearing to cut off your head."

Jarlaxle, who had just witnessed one of the most enjoyable days of his long life, laughed yet again. "He will come to his senses and will at last be free of the shadow of Drizzt Do'Urden. For that Artemis Entreri will thank me openly." He paused and considered his own words. "Or at least," the mercenary corrected, "he will . . . silently thank me."

"He tried to die," Kimmuriel stated flatly. "When he went at Drizzt's back with the dagger he led the way with a shout that alerted the outcast. He tried to die and we, and I, at your bidding, stopped that."

"Artemis Entreri will no doubt find other opportunities for stupidity if he holds that course," the mercenary leader replied with a shrug. "And we will not need him forever."

Drizzt Do'Urden came down the stairs then in tattered clothing, stretching his sore arm, but otherwise seeming not too badly injured.

"Rai'gy will have to pray to Lady Lolth for a hundred years to regain her favor after using one of her bestowed healing spells upon your dying

273

form," Jarlaxle remarked with a laugh. He nodded to Kimmuriel, who bowed and left the room.

"May she take him to her side for those prayers," Drizzt replied dryly. His witty demeanor did not hold, though, could not hold, in the face of all that he had just come through. He eyed Jarlaxle with all seriousness. "Why did you save me?"

"Future favors?" Jarlaxle asked more than stated.

"Forget it."

Yet again Jarlaxle found himself laughing. "I envy you, Drizzt Do'Urden," he replied honestly. "Pride played no part in your fight, did it?"

Drizzt shrugged, not quite understanding.

"No, you were free of that self-defeating emotion," Jarlaxle remarked. "You did not need to prove yourself Artemis Entreri's better. Indeed, I do envy you, to have found such inner peace and confidence."

"You still have not answered my question."

"A measure of respect, I suppose," Jarlaxle answered with a shrug. "Perhaps I did not believe that you deserved death after your worthy performance."

"Would I have deserved death if my performance did not measure up to your standards, then?" Drizzt asked. "Why does Jarlaxle decide?"

Jarlaxle wanted to laugh again but held it to a smile in deference to Drizzt. "Or perhaps I allowed my cleric to save you as a favor to your dead father," he said, and that put Drizzt on his heels, catching him completely by surprise.

"Of course I knew Zaknafein," Jarlaxle explained. "He and I were friends, if I can be said to have any friends. We were not so different, he and I."

Drizzt screwed up his face with obvious doubts.

"We both survived," Jarlaxle explained. "We both found a way to thrive in a hostile land, in a place we despised but could not find the courage to leave."

"But you have left now," Drizzt said.

"Have I?" came the reply. "No, by building my empire in Menzoberranzan I have inextricably tied myself to the place. I will die there, I am sure, and probably by the hands of one of my own soldiers—perhaps even Artemis Entreri."

Somehow Drizzt doubted the claim, suspecting that Jarlaxle would die of old age centuries hence.

"I respected him greatly," the mercenary went on, his tone steady and serious. "Your father, I mean, and I believe it was mutual."

Drizzt considered the words carefully and found that he couldn't disagree with Jarlaxle's claims. For all Jarlaxle's capacity for cruelty, there was indeed a code of honor about the mercenary leader. Jarlaxle had proven that when he had held Catti-brie captive and had not taken advantage of her, though he had even professed to her that he wanted to.

He had proven it by allowing Drizzt, Catti-brie, and Entreri to walk out of the Underdark after their escape from House Baenre, though surely he could have captured or killed them and such an act would have brought him great favor of the ruling house.

And now, by not letting Drizzt die in such a manner, he had proven it again.

"He'll not bother you ever again," Jarlaxle remarked, drawing Drizzt from his contemplation.

"So I dared to hope once before."

"But now it is settled," the mercenary leader explained. "Artemis Entreri has his answer, and though it is not what he had hoped it will suffice."

Drizzt considered it for a moment then nodded, hoping Jarlaxle, who seemed to understand so very much about everyone, was right yet again.

"Your friends await you in the village," Jarlaxle explained. "And it was no easy task getting them to go there and wait. I feared that I would taste the axe of Bruenor Battlehammer, and given the fate of Matron Baenre, that I did not wish at all."

"But you persuaded them without injuring any of them," Drizzt said.

"I gave you my word, and that word I honor . . . sometimes."

Now Drizzt, despite himself, couldn't hold back a grin. "Perhaps, then, I owe you yet again."

"Future favors?"

"Forget it."

"Surrender the panther then," Jarlaxle teased. "How I would love to have Guenhwyvar at my side!"

Drizzt understood that the mercenary was just teasing, that his promise concerning the panther, too, would hold. "Already you will have to look over your shoulder as I come for the crystal shard," the ranger replied. "If you take the cat, I will not only have to retrieve her but will have to kill you, as well."

Those words surely raised the eyebrows of Rai'gy as he came onto the top of the stairs, but the two were merely bantering. Drizzt would not come for Crenshinibon, and Jarlaxle would not take the panther.

Their business was completed.

Drizzt left the crystalline tower then to rejoin his friends, all together and waiting for him in the village, unharmed as Jarlaxle had promised.

After many tears and many hugs they left the village. But they did not go straight to the waiting *Bottom Feeder* but rather, back up the ridge.

The crystalline tower was gone. Jarlaxle and the other drow were gone. Entreri was gone.

"Good enough for them, if they bring the foul artifact back to yer old home and it brings all the ceiling down atop 'em!" Bruenor snorted. "Good enough for them!"

"And now we need not go to Cadderly," Catti-brie said. "Where then?"

"Wulfgar?" Regis reminded.

Drizzt paused a moment to consider Jarlaxle's words—trustworthy words—about their missing friend. He shook his head. It wasn't time for that road just yet. "We have the whole world open before us," he said. "And any direction will prove as good as another."

"And now we don't have the damned crystal shard bringing monsters in on us at every turn," Catti-brie noted.

"Won't be as much fun then," said Bruenor.

And off they went to catch the sunset . . . or the sunrise.

* * * * *

Back in Calimport Artemis Entreri, possibly the most powerful man on the streets, mulled over the titanic events of the last days, the amazing twists and turns his life's road had shown him.

Drizzt Do'Urden was dead, he believed, and by his hand, though he had not proven the stronger.

Or hadn't he? For wasn't it Entreri, and not Drizzt, who had befriended the more powerful allies?

Or did it even matter?

For the first time in many months a sincere smile found its way onto Artemis Entreri's face as he walked easily down Avenue Paradise, assured that none would dare move against him. He found the halfling door guards at the Copper Ante more than happy to see and admit him, and he found his way into Dondon's room without the slightest hindrance, without even questioning stares.

He emerged a short while later to find an angry Dwahvel waiting for him.

"You did it, didn't you?" she accused.

"It had to be done," was all Entreri bothered to reply, wiping his bloodstained dagger on the cloak of one of the guards flanking Dwahvel, as if daring them to make a move against him. They did not, of course, and Entreri moved unhindered to the outside door.

"Our arrangement is still in force?" he heard a plaintive Dwahvel call from behind. With a grin that nearly took in his ears, the ruler of House Basadoni left the inn.

* * * * *

Wulfgar left Delly Curtie that night, as he did every night, bottle in hand. He went down to the wharves where his newest drinking buddy, a man of some repute, waited for him.

"Wulfgar, my friend," Morik the Rogue said happily, taking the bottle and a deep, deep swallow of the burning liquid. "Is there anything that we two cannot accomplish together?"

Wulfgar considered the words with a dull smile. Indeed, they were the kings of Half Moon Street, the two men who rated deferential nods from everyone they passed, the two men in all of Luskan's belly who could part a crowd merely by walking through it.

Wulfgar took the bottle from Morik and, though it was more than half full, drained it in one swallow.

He just had to.

THE
SPINE OF THE
WORLD

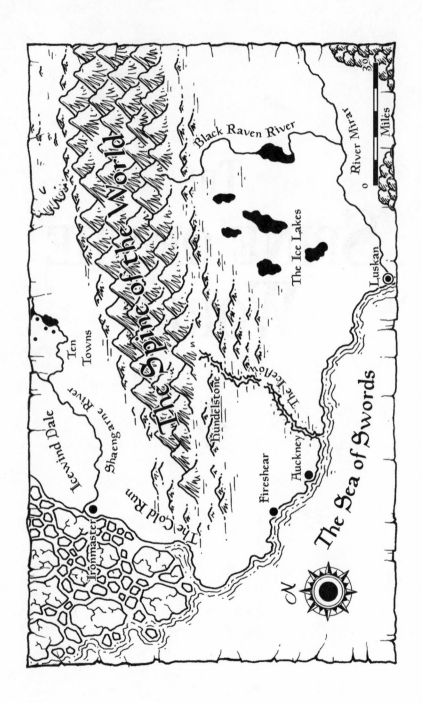

Prologue

The smaller man, known by many names in Luskan but most commonly Tas Morik the Rogue, held the bottle up in the air and gave it a shake, for it was a dirty thing and he wanted to measure the dark line of liquid against the orange light of sunset.

"Down to one," he said, and he brought his arm back in as if to take that final swig.

The huge man sitting on the end of the wharf beside him snatched the bottle away, moving with agility exceptional in a man of his tremendous size. Instinctively, Morik moved to grab the bottle back, but the large man held his muscular arm up to fend off the grabbing hands and drained the bottle in a single hearty swig.

"Bah, Wulfgar, but you're always getting the last one of late," Morik complained, giving Wulfgar a halfhearted swat across the shoulder.

"Earned it," Wulfgar argued.

Morik eyed him skeptically for just a moment, then remembered their last contest wherein Wulfgar had, indeed, earned the right to the last swig of the next bottle.

"Lucky throw," Morik mumbled. He knew better, though, and had long ago ceased to be amazed by Wulfgar's warrior prowess.

"One that I'll make again," Wulfgar proclaimed, pulling himself to his feet and hoisting Aegis-fang, his wondrous warhammer. He staggered as he slapped the weapon across his open palm, and a sly smile spread across Morik's swarthy face. He, too, climbed to his feet, taking up the empty bottle, swinging it easily by the neck.

"Will you, now?" the rogue asked.

"You throw it high enough, or take a loss," the blond barbarian explained, lifting his arm and pointing the end of the warhammer out to the open sea.

"A five-count before it hits the water." Morik eyed his barbarian friend icily as he recited the terms of the little gambling game they had created many days ago. Morik had won the first few contests, but by the fourth day Wulfgar had learned to properly lead the descending bottle, his hammer scattering tiny shards of glass across the bay. Of late, Morik had a chance of winning the bet only when Wulfgar indulged too much in the bottle.

"Never will it hit," Wulfgar muttered as Morik reached back to throw.

The little man paused, and once again he eyed the big man with some measure of contempt. Back and forth swayed the arm. Suddenly Morik jerked as if to throw.

"What?" Surprised, Wulfgar realized the feint, realized that Morik had not sailed the bottle into the air. Even as Wulfgar turned his gaze upon Morik, the little man spun in a complete circuit and let the bottle fly high and far.

Right into the line of the descending sun.

Wulfgar hadn't followed it from the beginning of its flight, so he could only squint into the glare, but he caught sight of it at last. With a roar he let fly his mighty warhammer, the magical and brilliantly crafted weapon spinning out low over the bay.

Morik squealed in glee, thinking he had outfoxed the big man, for the bottle was low in the sky by the time Wulfgar threw and fully twenty strides out from the wharf. No one could skim a warhammer so far and so fast as to hit that, Morik believed, especially not a man who had just drained more than half the contents of the target!

The bottle nearly clipped a wave when Aegis-fang took it, exploding it into a thousand tiny pieces.

"It touched water!" Morik yelled.

"My win," Wulfgar said firmly, his tone offering no debate.

Morik could only grumble in reply, for he knew that the big man was right; the warhammer got the bottle in time.

"Seeming a mighty waste of a good hammer fer just a bottle," came a voice behind the duo. The pair turned as one to see two men, swords drawn, standing but a few feet away.

"Now, Mister Morik the Rogue," remarked one of them, a tall and lean fellow with a kerchief tied about his head, a patch over one eye, and a rusty, curving blade weaving in the air before him. "I'm knowin' ye got yerself a good haul from a gem merchant a week back, and I'm thinkin' that ye'd be wise to share a bit o' the booty with me and me friend."

Morik glanced up at Wulfgar, his wry grin and the twinkle in his dark eyes telling the barbarian that he didn't mean to share a thing, except perhaps the blade of his fine dagger.

"And if ye still had yer hammer, ye might be arguin' the point," laughed the other thug, as tall as his friend, but much wider and far dirtier. He prodded his sword toward Wulfgar. The barbarian staggered backward, nearly falling off the end of the wharf—or at least, pretending to.

"I'm thinking that you should have found the gem merchant before me," Morik replied calmly. "Assuming there was a gem merchant, my friend, because I assure you that I have no idea what you are talking about."

The slender thug growled and thrust his sword ahead. "Now, Morik!" he started to yell, but before the words even left his mouth, Morik had leaped ahead, spinning inside the angle of the curving sword blade, rolling about, putting his back against the man's forearm and pushing out. He ducked right under the startled man's arm, lifting it high with his right hand, while his left hand flashed, a silver sparkle in the last light of day, Morik's dagger stabbing into the stunned man's armpit.

Meanwhile, the other thug, thinking he had an easy, unarmed target, waded in. His bloodshot eyes widened when Wulfgar brought his right arm from behind his hip, revealing that the mighty warhammer had magically returned to his grip. The thug skidded to a stop and glanced in panic at his companion. But by now Morik had the newly unarmed man turned about and in full flight with Morik running right behind him, taunting him and laughing hysterically as he repeatedly stabbed the man in the buttocks.

"Whoa!" the remaining thug cried, trying to turn.

"I can hit a falling bottle," Wulfgar reminded him. The man stopped abruptly and turned back slowly to face the huge barbarian.

"We don't want no trouble," the thug explained, slowly laying his sword down on the boarding of the wharf. "No trouble at all, good sir," he said, bowing repeatedly.

Wulfgar dropped Aegis-fang to the decking, and the thug stopped bobbing, staring hard at the weapon.

"Pick up your sword, if you choose," the barbarian offered.

The thug looked up at him incredulously. Then, seeing the barbarian without a weapon—except, of course, for those formidable fists—the man scooped up his sword.

Wulfgar had him before his first swing. The powerful warrior snapped out his hand to catch the man's sword arm at the wrist. With a sudden and ferocious jerk, Wulfgar brought that arm straight up, then hit the thug in the chest with a stunning right cross that blasted away his breath and his strength. The sword fell to the wharf.

Wulfgar jerked the arm again, lifting the man right from his feet and popping his shoulder out of joint. The barbarian let go, allowing the thug to fall heavily back to his feet, then hit him with a vicious left hook across the jaw. The only thing that stopped the man from flipping headlong over the side of the wharf was Wulfgar's right hand, catching him by the front of his shirt. With frightening strength, Wulfgar easily lifted the thug from the deck, holding him fully a foot off the planking.

The man tried to grab at Wulfgar and break the hold, but Wulfgar shook him so violently that he nearly bit off his tongue, and every limb on the man seemed made of rubber.

"This one's not got much of a purse," Morik called. Wulfgar looked past his victim to see that his companion had gone right around the fleeing thug, herding him back toward the end of the dock. The thug was limping badly now and whining for mercy, which only made Morik stick him again in the buttocks, drawing more yelps.

"Please, friend," stammered the man Wulfgar held aloft.

"Shut up!" the barbarian roared, bringing his arm down forcefully, bending his head and snapping his powerful neck muscles so that his forehead collided hard with the thug's face.

A primal rage boiled within the barbarian, an anger that went beyond this incident, beyond the attempted mugging. No longer was he standing on a dock in Luskan. Now he was back in the Abyss, in Errtu's lair, a tormented prisoner of the wicked demon. Now this man was one of the great demon's minions, the pincer-armed Glabrezu, or worse, the tempting succubus. Wulfgar was back there fully, seeing the gray smoke, smelling the foul stench, feeling the sting of whips and fires, the pincers on his throat, the cold kiss of the demoness.

So clear it came to him! So vivid! The waking nightmare returned, holding him in a grip of the sheerest rage, stifling his mercy or compassion, throwing him into the pits of torment, emotional and physical torture. He felt the itching and burning of those little centipedes that Errtu used, burrowing under his skin and crawling inside him, their venomous pincers lighting a thousand fires within. They were on him and in him, all over him, their little legs tickling and exciting his nerves so that he would feel the exquisite agony of their burning venom all the more.

Tormented again, indeed, but suddenly and unexpectedly, Wulfgar found that he was no longer helpless.

Up into the air went the thug, Wulfgar effortlessly hoisting him overhead, though the man weighed well over two hundred pounds. With a primal roar, a scream torn from his churning gut, the barbarian spun him about toward the open sea.

"I cannot swim!" the man shrieked. Arms and legs flailing pitifully, he hit the water fully fifteen feet from the wharf, where he splashed and bobbed, crying out for help. Wulfgar turned away. If he heard the man at all, he showed no indication.

Morik eyed the barbarian with some surprise. "He can't swim," Morik remarked as Wulfgar approached.

"Good time to learn, then," the barbarian muttered coldly, his thoughts still whirling down the smoky corridors of Errtu's vast dungeon. He kept brushing his hands along his arms and legs as he spoke, slapping away the imagined centipedes.

Morik shrugged. He looked down to the man who was squirming and crying on the planks at his feet. "Can you swim?"

The thug glanced up timidly at the little rogue and gave a slight, hopeful nod.

"Then go to your friend," Morik instructed. The man started to slowly crawl away.

"I fear his friend will be dead before he gets to his side," Morik remarked to Wulfgar. The barbarian didn't seem to hear him.

"Oh, do help the wretch," Morik sighed, grabbing Wulfgar by the arm and forcing that vacant gaze to focus. "For me. I would hate to start a night with a death on our hands."

With a sigh of his own, Wulfgar reached out his mighty hands. The thug on his knees suddenly found himself rising from the decking, one hand holding the back of his breeches, another clamped about his collar. Wulfgar took three running strides and hurled the man long and high. The flying thug cleared his splashing companion, landing nearby with a tremendous belly smack.

Wulfgar didn't see him land. Having lost all interest in the scene, he turned about and, after mentally recalling Aegis-fang to his grasp, stormed past Morik, who bowed in deference to his dangerous and powerful friend.

Morik caught up to Wulfgar as the barbarian exited the wharf. "They are still scrambling in the water," the rogue remarked. "The fat one, he keeps foolishly grabbing his friend, pulling them both underwater. Perhaps they will both drown."

Wulfgar didn't seem to care, and that was an honest reflection of his heart, Morik knew. The rogue gave one last look back at the harbor, then merely shrugged. The two thugs had brought it on themselves, after all.

Wulfgar, son of Beornegar, was not one to be toyed with.

So Morik, too, put them out of his mind—not that he was ever really concerned—and focused instead on his companion. His surprising companion, who had learned to fight at the training of a drow elf, of all things!

Morik winced, though, of course, Wulfgar was too distracted to catch it. The rogue thought of another drow, a visitor who had come unexpectedly to him not so long ago, bidding him to keep a watchful eye on Wulfgar and paying him in advance for his services (and not-so-subtly explaining that if Morik failed in the "requested" task, the dark elf's master would not be pleased). Morik hadn't heard from the dark elves again, to his relief, but still he kept to his end of the agreement to watch over Wulfgar.

No, that wasn't it, the rogue had to admit, at least to himself. He had started his relationship with Wulfgar for purely personal gain, partly out of fear of the drow, partly out of fear of Wulfgar and a desire to learn more about this man who had so obviously become his rival on the street. That had been in the beginning. He no longer feared Wulfgar, though he did sometimes fear *for* the deeply troubled, haunted man. Morik hardly ever thought about the drow elves, who had not come around in weeks and weeks. Surprisingly, Morik had come to like Wulfgar, had come to enjoy the man's company despite the many times when surliness dominated the barbarian's demeanor.

He almost told Wulfgar about the visit from the drow elves then, out of some basic desire to warn this man who had become his friend. Almost. . . . but the practical side of Morik, the cautious pragmatism that allowed him to stay alive in such a hostile environment as Luskan's streets, reminded him that to do so would do no one good. If the dark elves came for Wulfgar, whether Wulfgar expected them or not, the barbarian would be defeated. These were drow elves, after all, wielders of mighty magic and the finest of blades, elves who could walk uninvited into Morik's bedroom and rouse him from his slumber. Even Wulfgar had to sleep. If those dark elves, after they were finished with poor Wulfgar, ever learned that Morik had betrayed them . . .

A shudder coursed along Morik's spine, and he forcefully shook the unsettling thoughts away, turning his attention back to his large friend. Oddly, Morik saw a kindred spirit here, a man who could be (and indeed had been) a noble and mighty warrior, a leader among men, but who, for one reason or another, had fallen from grace.

Such was the way Morik viewed his own situation, though in truth, he had been on a course to his present position since his early childhood. Still, if only his mother hadn't died in childbirth, if only his father hadn't abandoned him to the streets . . .

Looking at Wulfgar now, Morik couldn't help but think of the man he himself might have become, of the man Wulfgar had been. Circumstance had damned them both, to Morik's thinking, and so he held no illusions about their relationship now. The truth of his bond to Wulfgar—the real reason he stayed so close to him—despite all his sensibilities (the barbarian was being watched by dark elves, after all!), was that he regarded the barbarian as he might a younger brother.

That, and the fact that Wulfgar's friendship brought him more respect among the rabble. For Morik, there always had to be a practical reason.

The day neared its end, the night its beginning, the time of Morik and Wulfgar, the time of Luskan's street life.

286

Part 1

The Present

In my homeland of Menzoberranzan, where demons play and drow revel at the horrible demise of rivals, there remains a state of necessary alertness and wariness. A drow off-guard is a drow murdered in Menzoberranzan, and thus few are the times when dark elves engage in exotic weeds or drinks that dull the senses.

Few, but there are exceptions. At the final ceremony of Melee-Magthere, the school of fighters that I attended, graduated students engage in an orgy of mind-blurring herbs and sensual pleasures with the females of Arach-Tinilith, a moment of the purest hedonism, a party of the purest pleasures without regard to future implications.

I rejected that orgy, though I knew not why at the time. It assaulted my sense of morality, I believed (and still do), and cheapened so many things that I hold precious. Now, in retrospect, I have come to understand another truth about myself that forced rejection of that orgy. Aside from the moral implications, and there were many, the mere notion of the mind-blurring herbs frightened and repulsed me. I knew that all along, of course—as soon as I felt the intoxication at that ceremony, I instinctively rebelled against it—but it wasn't until very recently that I came to understand the truth of that rejection, the real reason why such influences have no place in my life.

289

These herbs attack the body in various ways, of course, from slow-ing reflexes to destroying coordination altogether, but more importantly, they attack the spirit in two different ways. First, they blur the past, eras-ing memories pleasant and unpleasant, and second, they eliminate any thoughts of the future. Intoxicants lock the imbiber in the present, the here and now, without regard for the future, without consideration of the past. That is the trap, a defeatist perspective that allows for attempted satia-tion of physical pleasures wantonly, recklessly. An intoxicated person will attempt even foolhardy dares because that inner guidance, even to the point of survival instinct itself, can be so impaired. How many young warriors foolishly throw themselves against greater enemies, only to be slain? How many young women find themselves with child, conceived with lovers they would not even consider as future husbands?

That is the trap, the defeatist perspective, that I cannot tolerate. I live my life with hope, always hope, that the future will be better than the present, but only as long as I work to make it so. Thus, with that toil, comes the satisfaction in life, the sense of accomplishment we all truly need for real joy. How could I remain honest to that hope if I allowed myself a moment of weakness that could well destroy all I have worked to achieve and all I hope to achieve? How might I have reacted to so many unexpected crises if, at the time of occurrence, I was influenced by a mind-altering substance, one that impaired my judgment or altered my perspective?

Also, the dangers of where such substances might lead cannot be underestimated. Had I allowed myself to be carried away with the mood of the graduation ceremony of Melee-Magthere, had I allowed myself the sen-sual pleasures offered by the priestesses, how cheapened might any honest encounter of love have been?

Greatly, to my way of thinking. Sensual pleasures are, or should be, the culmination of physical desires combined with an intellectual and emo-tional decision, a giving of oneself, body and spirit, in a bond of trust and respect. In such a manner as that graduation ceremony, no such sharing could have occurred; it would have been a giving of body only, and more so than that, a taking of another's offered wares. There would have been no higher joining, no spiritual experience, and thus, no true joy.

I cannot live in such a hopeless basking as that, for that is what it is: a pitiful basking in the lower, base levels of existence brought on, I believe, by the lack of hope for a higher level of existence.

And so I reject all but the most moderate use of such intoxicants, and while I'll not openly judge those who so indulge, I will pity them their empty souls.

What is it that drives a person to such depths? Pain, I believe, and memories too wretched to be openly faced and handled. Intoxicants can, indeed, blur the pains of the past at the expense of the future. But it is not an even trade.

With that in mind, I fear for Wulfgar, my lost friend. Where will he find escape from the torments of his enslavement?

— Drizzt Do'Urden

Chapter 1

Into Port

"I do so hate this place," remarked Robillard, the robed wizard. He was speaking to Captain Deudermont of *Sea Sprite* as the three-masted schooner rounded a long jettie and came in sight of the harbor of the northern port of Luskan.

Deudermont, a tall and stately man, mannered as a lord and with a calm, pensive demeanor, merely nodded at his wizard's proclamation. He had heard it all before, and many times. He looked to the city skyline and noted the distinctive structure of the Hosttower of the Arcane, the famed wizards' guild of Luskan. That, Deudermont knew, was the source of Robillard's sneering attitude concerning this port, though the wizard had been sketchy in his explanations, making a few offhand remarks about the "idiots" running the Hosttower and their inability to discern a true wizardly master from a conniving trickster. Deudermont suspected that Robillard had once been denied admission to the guild.

"Why Luskan?" the ship's wizard complained. "Would not Waterdeep have better suited our needs? No harbor along the entire Sword Coast can compare with Waterdeep's repair facilities."

"Luskan was closer," Deudermont reminded him.

"A couple of days, no more," Robillard retorted.

"If a storm found us in those couple of days, the damaged hull might have split apart, and all our bodies would have been food for the crabs and the fishes," said the captain. "It seemed a foolish gamble for the sake of one man's pride."

Robillard started to respond but caught the meaning of the captain's last statement before he could embarrass himself further. A great frown shadowed his face. "The pirates would have had us had I not timed the blast perfectly," the wizard muttered after he took a few moments to calm down.

Deudermont conceded the point. Indeed, Robillard's work in the last pirate hunt had been nothing short of spectacular. Several years before, *Sea Sprite*—the new, bigger, faster, and stronger *Sea Sprite*—had been commissioned by the lords of Waterdeep as a pirate hunter. No vessel had ever been as successful at the task, so much so that when the lookout spotted a pair of pirateers sailing the northern waters off the Sword Coast, so near to Luskan, where *Sea Sprite* often prowled, Deudermont could hardly believe it. The schooner's reputation alone had kept those waters clear for many months.

These pirates had come looking for vengeance, not easy merchant ship prey, and they were well prepared for the fight, each of them armed with a small catapult, a fair contingent of archers, and a pair of wizards. Even so, they found themselves outmaneuvered by the skilled Deudermont and his experienced crew, and out-magicked by the mighty Robillard, who had been wielding his powerful dweomers in vessel-to-vessel warfare for well over a decade. One of Robillard's illusions had given the appearance that *Sea Sprite* was dead in the water, her mainmast down across her deck, with dozens of dead men at the rails. Like hungry wolves, the pirates had circled, closer and closer, then had come in, one to port and one to starboard, to finish off the wounded ship.

In truth, *Sea Sprite* hadn't been badly damaged at all, with Robillard countering the offensive magic of the enemy wizards. The small pirate catapults had little effect against the proud schooner's armored sides.

Deudermont's archers, brilliant bowmen all, had struck hard at the closing vessels, and the schooner went from battle sail to full sail with precision and efficiency, the prow of the ship verily leaping from the water as she scooted out between the surprised pirateers.

Robillard dropped a veil of silence upon the pirate ships, preventing their wizards from casting any defensive spells, then plopped three fireballs—*Boom! Boom! Boom!*—in rapid succession, one atop each ship and one in between. Then came the conventional barrage from ballista and catapult, *Sea Sprite*'s gunners soaring lengths of chain to further destroy sails and rigging and balls of pitch to heighten the flames.

De-masted and drifting, fully ablaze, the two pirateers soon went down. So great was the conflagration that Deudermont and his crew managed to pluck only a few survivors from the cold ocean waters.

Sea Sprite hadn't escaped unscathed, though. She was under the power of but one full sail now. Even more dangerous, she had a fair-sized crack just above the waterline. Deudermont had to keep nearly a third of his crew at work bailing, which was why he had steered for the nearest port—Luskan.

Deudermont considered it a fine choice, indeed. He preferred Luskan to the much larger port of Waterdeep, for while his financing had come from the southern city and he could find dinner at the house of any lord in town, Luskan was more hospitable to his common crew members, men without the standing, the manners, or the pretensions to dine at the table of nobility. Luskan, like Waterdeep, had its defined classes, but the bottom rungs on Luskan's social ladder were still a few above the bottom of Waterdeep's.

Calls of greeting came to them from every wharf as they neared the city, for *Sea Sprite* was well known here and well respected. The honest fishermen and merchant sailors of Luskan, of all the northern reaches of the Sword Coast, had long ago come to appreciate the work of Captain Deudermont and his swift schooner.

"A fine choice, I'd say," the captain remarked.

"Better food, better women, and better entertainment in Waterdeep," Robillard replied.

"But no finer wizards," Deudermont couldn't resist saying. "Surely the Hosttower is among the most respected of mage guilds in all the Realms."

Robillard groaned and muttered a few curses, pointedly walking away.

Deudermont didn't turn to watch him go, but he couldn't miss the distinctive stomping of the wizard's hard-soled boots.

* * * * *

"Just a short ride, then," the woman cooed, twirling her dirty blonde hair in one hand and striking a pouting posture. "A quick one to take me jitters off before a night at the tables."

The huge barbarian ran his tongue across his teeth, for his mouth felt as if it were full of fabric, and dirty cloth at that. After a night's work in the tavern of the Cutlass, he had returned to the wharves with Morik for a night of harder drinking. As usual, the pair had stayed there until after dawn, then Wulfgar had crawled back to the Cutlass, his home and place of employment, and straight to his bed.

But this woman, Delly Curtie, a barmaid in the tavern and Wulfgar's lover for the past few months, had come looking for him. Once, he had viewed her as a pleasurable distraction, the icing on his whisky cake, and even as a caring friend. Delly had nurtured Wulfgar through his first difficult days in Luskan. She had seen to his needs, emotional and physical, without question, without judgment, without asking anything in return. But of late the relationship had begun to shift, and not even subtly. Now that he had settled more comfortably into his new life, a life devoted almost entirely to fending the remembered pain of his years with Errtu, Wulfgar had come to see a different picture of Delly Curtie.

Emotionally, she was a child, a needful little girl. Wulfgar, who was well into his twenties, was several years older than she. Now, suddenly, he had become the adult in their relationship, and Delly's needs had begun to overshadow his own.

"Oh, but ye've got ten minutes for me, me Wulfgar," she said, moving closer and rubbing her hand across his cheek.

Wulfgar grabbed her wrist and gently but firmly moved her hand away. "A long night," he replied. "And I had hoped for more rest before beginning my duties for Arumn."

"But I've got a tingling—"

"More rest," Wulfgar repeated, emphasizing each word.

Delly pulled away from him, her seductive pouting pose becoming suddenly cold and indifferent. "Good enough for ye, then," she said coarsely. "Ye think ye're the only man wanting to share me bed?"

Wulfgar didn't justify the rant with an answer. The only answer he could have given was to tell her he really didn't care, that all of this—his drinking, his fighting—was a manner of hiding and nothing more. In truth, Wulfgar did like and respect Delly and considered her a friend—or would have if he honestly believed that he could be a friend. He didn't mean to hurt her.

Delly stood in Wulfgar's room, trembling and unsure. Suddenly, feeling very naked in her slight shift, she gathered her arms in front of her and ran out into the hall and to her own room, slamming the door hard.

Wulfgar closed his eyes and shook his head. He chuckled helplessly and sadly when he heard Delly's door open again, followed by running footsteps heading down the hall toward the outside door. That one, too, slammed, and Wulfgar understood that all the ruckus had been for his benefit Delly wanted him to hear that she was, indeed, going out to find comfort in another's arms.

She was a complicated one, the barbarian understood, carrying more emotional turmoil than even he, if that were possible. He wondered how it had ever gone this far between them. Their relationship had been so simple at the start, so straightforward: two people in need of each other. Recently, though, it had become more complex, the needs having grown into emotional crutches. Delly needed Wulfgar to take care of her, to shelter her, to tell her she was beautiful, but Wulfgar knew he couldn't even take care of himself, let alone another. Delly needed Wulfgar to love her, and yet the barbarian had no love to give. For Wulfgar there was only pain and hatred, only memories of the demon Errtu and the prison of the Abyss, wherein he had been tortured for six long years.

Wulfgar sighed and rubbed the sleep from his eyes, then reached for a bottle, only to find it empty. With a frustrated snarl, he threw it across the room, where it shattered against a wall. He envisioned, for just a moment, that it had smashed against Delly Curtie's face. The image startled Wulfgar, but it didn't surprise him. He vaguely wondered if Delly hadn't brought him to this point on purpose; perhaps this woman was no innocent child, but a conniving huntress. When she had first come to him, offering comfort, had she intended to take advantage of his emotional weakness to pull him into a trap? To get him to marry her, perhaps? To rescue him that he might one day rescue her from the miserable existence she had carved out for herself as a tavern wench?

Wulfgar realized that his knuckles had gone white from clenching his hands so very hard, and he pointedly opened them and took several deep, steadying breaths. Another sigh, another rub of his tongue over dirty teeth, and the man stood and stretched his huge, nearly seven-foot, frame. He discovered, as he did nearly every afternoon when he went through this ritual, that he had even more aches in his huge muscles and bones this day. Wulfgar glanced over at his large arms, and though they were still thicker and more muscular than that of nearly any man alive, he couldn't help but notice a slackness in those muscles, as if his skin was starting to hang a bit too loosely on his massive frame.

How different his life was now than it had been those mornings years ago in Icewind Dale, when he had worked the long day with Bruenor, his adoptive dwarven father, hammering and lifting huge stones, or when he had gone out hunting for game or giants with Drizzt, his warrior friend, running all the day, fighting all the day. The hours had been even more strenuous then, more filled with physical burden, but that burden had been just physical and not emotional. In that time and in that place, he felt no aches.

The blackness in his heart, the sorest ache, was the source of it all.

He tried to think back to those lost years, working and fighting beside Bruenor and Drizzt, or when he had spent the day running along the wind-blown slopes of Kelvin's Cairn, the lone mountain in Icewind Dale, chasing Catti-brie. . . .

The mere thought of the woman stopped him cold and left him empty, and in that void, images of Errtu and the demon's minions inevitably filtered in. Once, one of those minions, the horrid succubus, had assumed the form of Catti-brie, a perfect image, and Errtu had convinced Wulfgar that he had managed to snare the woman, that she had been taken to suffer the same eternal torment as Wulfgar, *because* of Wulfgar.

Errtu had taken the succubus, Catti-brie, right before Wulfgar's horrified eyes and had torn the woman apart limb from limb, devouring her in an orgy of blood and gore.

Gasping for his breath, Wulfgar fought back to his thoughts of Catti-brie, of the real Catti-brie. He had loved her. She was, perhaps, the only

297

woman he had ever loved, but she was lost to him now forever, he believed. Though he might travel to Ten-Towns in Icewind Dale and find her again, the bond between them had been severed, cut by the sharp scars of Errtu and by Wulfgar's own reactions to those scars.

The long shadows coming in through the window told him that the day neared its end and that his work as Arumn Gardpeck's bouncer would soon begin. The weary man hadn't lied to Delly when he had declared that he needed more rest, though, and so he collapsed back onto his bed and fell into a deep sleep.

Night had settled thickly about Luskan by the time Wulfgar staggered into the crowded common room of the Cutlass.

"Late again, as if we're to be surprised by that," a thin, beady-eyed man named Josi Puddles, a regular at the tavern and a good friend of Arumn Gardpeck, remarked to the barkeep when they both noticed Wulfgar's entrance. "That one's workin' less and drinkin' ye dry."

Arumn Gardpeck, a kind but stern and always practical man, wanted to give his typical response, that Josi should just shut his mouth, but he couldn't refute Josi's claim. It pained Arumn to watch Wulfgar's descent. He had befriended the barbarian those months before, when Wulfgar had first come to Luskan. Initially, Arumn had shown interest in the man only because of Wulfgar's obvious physical prowess—a mighty warrior like Wulfgar could indeed be a boon to business for a tavern in the tough dock section of the feisty city. After his very first conversation with the man, Arumn had understood that his feelings for Wulfgar went deeper than any business opportunity. He truly liked the man.

Always, Josi was there to remind Arumn of the potential pitfalls, to remind Arumn that, sooner or later, mighty bouncers made meals for rats in gutters.

"Ye thinkin' the sun just dropped in the water?" Josi asked Wulfgar as the big man shuffled by, yawning.

Wulfgar stopped, and turned slowly and deliberately to glare at the little man.

"Half the night's gone," Josi said, his tone changing abruptly from accusational to conversational, "but I was watchin' the place for ye. Thought I might have to break up a couple o' fights, too."

Wulfgar eyed the little man skeptically. "You couldn't break up a pane of thin glass with a heavy cudgel," he remarked, ending with another profound yawn.

Josi, ever the coward, took the insult with a bobbing head and a self-deprecating grin.

"We *do* have an agreement about yer time o' work," Arumn said seriously.

"And an understanding of your true needs," Wulfgar reminded the man. "By your own words, my real responsibility comes later in the night, for trouble rarely begins early. You named sundown as my time of duty but explained that I'd not truly be needed until much later."

"Fair enough," Arumn replied with a nod that brought a groan from Josi. He was anxious to see the big man—the big man whom he believed had replaced him as Arumn's closest friend—severely disciplined.

"The situation's changed," Arumn went on. "Ye've made a reputation and more than a few enemies. Every night, ye wander in late, and yer . . . our enemies take note. I fear that one night soon ye'll stagger in here past the crest o' night to find us all murdered."

Wulfgar put an incredulous expression on his face and turned away with a dismissive wave of his hand.

"Wulfgar," Arumn called after him forcefully.

The barbarian turned about, scowling.

"Three bottles missing last night," Arumn said calmly, quietly, a note of concern evident in his tone.

"You promised me all the drink I desired," Wulfgar answered.

"For yerself," Arumn insisted. "Not for yer sculking little friend."

All about widened their eyes at that remark, for not many of Luskan's tavernkeepers would speak so boldly concerning the dangerous Morik the Rogue.

Wulfgar lowered his gaze and chuckled, shaking his head. "Good Arumn," he began, "would you prefer to be the one to tell Morik he is not welcome to your drink?"

Arumn narrowed his eyes, and Wulfgar returned the glare for just a moment.

Delly Curtie entered the room just then, her eyes red and still lined with tears. Wulfgar looked at her and felt a pang of guilt, but it was not something he would admit publicly. He turned and went about his duties, moving to threaten a drunk who was getting a bit too loud.

"He's playing her like he'd pick a lute," Josi Puddles remarked to Arumn.

Arumn blew a frustrated sigh. He had become quite fond of Wulfgar, but the big man's increasingly offensive behavior was beginning to wear that fondness thin. Delly had been as a daughter to Arumn for a couple of years. If Wulfgar was playing her without regard for her emotions, he and Arumn were surely heading for a confrontation.

Arumn turned his attention from Delly to Wulfgar just in time to see the big man lift the loudmouth by the throat, carry him to the door, and none too gently heave him out into the street.

"Man didn't do nothing," Josi Puddles complained. "He keeps with that act, and you'll not have single customer."

Arumn merely sighed.

* * * * *

A trio of men in the opposite corner of the bar also studied the huge barbarian's movements with more than a passing interest. "Cannot be,"

299

one of them, a skinny, bearded fellow, muttered. "The world's a wider place than that."

"I'm telling ye it is," the middle one replied. "Ye wasn't aboard *Sea Sprite* back in them days. I'd not forget that one, not Wulfgar. Sailed with him all the way from Waterdeep to Memnon, I did, then back again, and we fought our share o' pirates along the way."

"Looks like a good one to have along for a pirate fight," remarked Waillan Micanty, the third of the group.

"So 'tis true!" said the second. "Not as good as his companion, though. Ye're knowin' that one. A dark-skinned fellow, small and pretty lookin', but fiercer than a wounded sahuagin, and quicker with a blade—or a pair o' the things—than any I ever seen."

"Drizzt Do'Urden?" asked the skinny one. "That big one traveled with the drow elf?"

"Yep," said the second, now commanding their fullest attention. He was smiling widely, both at being the center of it all and in remembering the exciting voyage he had taken with Wulfgar, Drizzt, and the drow's panther companion.

"What about Catti-brie?" asked Waillan, who, like all of Deudermont's crew, had developed a huge crush on the beautiful and capable woman soon after she and Drizzt had joined their crew a couple of years before. Drizzt, Catti-brie, and Guenhwyvar had sailed aboard *Sea Sprite* for many months, and how much easier scuttling pirates had been with that trio along!

"Catti-brie joined us south o' Baldur's Gate," the storyteller explained. "She came in with a dwarf, King Bruenor of Mithral Hall, on a flying chariot that was all aflame. Never seen anything like it, I tell ye, for that wild dwarf put the thing right across the sails o' one o' the pirate ships we was fighting. Took the whole danged ship down, he did, and was still full o' spit and battle spirit when we pulled him from the water!"

"Bah, but ye're lyin'," the skinny sailor started to protest.

"No, I heard the story," Waillan Micanty put in. "Heard it from the captain himself, and from Drizzt and Catti-brie."

That quieted the skinny man. All of them just sat and studied Wulfgar's movements a bit longer.

"Ye're sure that's him?" the first asked. "That's the Wulfgar fellow?"

Even as he asked the question, Wulfgar brought Aegis-fang off of his back and placed it against a wall.

"Oh, by me own eyes, that's him," the second answered. "I'd not be forgettin' him or that hammer o' his. He can split a mast with the thing, I tell ye, and put it in a pirate's eye, left or right, at a hunnerd long strides."

Across the room, Wulfgar had a short argument with a patron. With one mighty hand the barbarian reached out and grabbed the man's throat and easily, so very easily, hoisted him from his seat and into the air. Wulfgar strode calmly across the inn to the door and tossed the drunk into the street.

"Strongest man I ever seen," the second sailor remarked, and his two companions weren't about to disagree. They drained their drinks and watched a bit longer before leaving the Cutlass for home, where they found themselves running anxiously to inform their captain of who they'd seen.

*   *   *   *   *

Captain Deudermont rubbed his fingers pensively across his neatly trimmed beard, trying to digest the tale Waillan Micanty had just related to him. He was trying very hard, for it made no sense to him. When Drizzt and Catti-brie had sailed with him during those wonderful early years of chasing pirates along the Sword Coast, they had told him a sad tale of Wulfgar's demise. The story had had a profound effect on Deudermont, who had befriended the huge barbarian on that journey to Memnon years before.

Wulfgar was dead, so Drizzt and Catti-brie had claimed, and so Deudermont had believed. Yet here was one of Duedermont's trusted crewmen claiming that the barbarian was very much alive and well and working in the Cutlass, a tavern Deudermont had frequented.

The image brought Deudermont back to his first meeting with the barbarian and Drizzt in the Mermaid's Arms tavern in Waterdeep. Wulfgar had avoided a fight with a notorious brawler by the name of Bungo. What great things the barbarian and his companions had subsequently accomplished, from rescuing their little halfling friend from the clutches of a notorious pasha in Calimport to the reclamation of Mithral Hall for Clan Battlehammer. The thought of Wulfgar working as a brawler in a seedy tavern in Luskan seemed preposterous.

Especially since, according to Drizzt and Catti-brie, Wulfgar was dead.

Deudermont thought of his last voyage with the duo when *Sea Sprite* had put onto a remote island far out at sea. A blind seer had accosted Drizzt with a riddle about one he thought he had lost. The last time Deudermont had seen Drizzt and Catti-brie was at their parting, on an inland lake, no less, where *Sea Sprite* had been inadvertently transported.

So might Wulfgar be alive? Captain Deudermont had seen too much to dismiss the possibility out of hand.

Still, it seemed likely to the captain that his crewmen had been mistaken. They had little experience with northern barbarians, all of whom seemed huge and blond and strong. One might look like another to them. The Cutlass had taken on a barbarian warrior as a bouncer, but it was not Wulfgar.

301

He thought no more of it, having many duties and engagements to attend at the more upscale homes and establishments in the city. Three days later, however, when dining at the table of one of Luskan's noble families, the conversation turned to the death of one of the city's most reknowned bullies.

"We're a lot better off without Tree Block Breaker," one of the guests insisted. "The purest form of trouble ever to enter our city."

"Just a thug and nothing more," another replied, "and not so tough."

"Bah, but he could take down a running horse by stepping in front of the thing," the first insisted. "I saw him do so!"

"But he couldn't take down Arumn Gardpeck's new boy," the other put in. "When he tried to fight that fellow, our Tree Block Breaker flew out of the Cutlass and brought the frame of a door with him."

Deudermont's ears perked up.

"Yeah, that one," the first agreed. "Too strong for any man, from the stories I am hearing, and that warhammer! Most beautiful weapon I've ever seen."

The mention of the hammer nearly made Deudermont choke on his food, for he remembered well the power of Aegis-fang. "What is his name?" the captain inquired.

"Who's name?"

"Arumn Gardpeck's new boy."

The two men looked at each other and shrugged. "Wolf-something, I believe," the first said.

When he left the noble's house, a couple of hours later, Captain Deudermont found himself wandering not back to *Sea Sprite*, but along infamous Half-Moon Street, the toughest section of Luskan, the home of the Cutlass. He went in without hesitation, pulling up a chair at the first empty table. Duedermont spotted the big man before he even sat down. It was, without doubt, Wulfgar, son of Beornegar. The captain hadn't known Wulfgar very well and hadn't seen him in years, but there could be no question about it. The sheer size, the aura of strength, and the piercing blue eyes of the man gave him away. Oh, he was more haggard-looking now, with an unkempt beard and dirty clothes, but he was Wulfgar.

The big man met Duedermont's stare momentarily, but there was no recognition in the barbarian's eyes when he turned away. Deudermont became even more certain when he saw the magnificent warhammer, Aegis-fang, strapped across Wulfgar's broad back.

"Ye drinking or looking for a fight?"

Deudermont turned about to see a young woman standing beside his table, tray in hand.

"Well?"

"Looking for a fight?" the captain repeated dully, not understanding.

"The way ye're staring at him," the young woman responded, motioning toward Wulfgar. "Many's the ones who come in here looking for a fight. Many's the ones who get carried away from here. But good enough for ye if ye're wanting to fight him, and good enough for him if ye leave him dead in the street."

"I seek no fight," Deudermont assured her. "But, do tell me, what is his name?"

The woman snorted and shook her head, frustrated for some reason Deudermont could not fathom. "Wulfgar," she answered. "And better for us all if he never came in here." Without asking again if he wanted a drink, she merely walked away.

Deudermont paid her no further heed, staring again at the big man. How had Wulfgar wound up here? Why wasn't he dead? And where were Drizzt, and Catti-brie?

He sat patiently, watching the lay of the place as the hours passed, until dawn neared and all the patrons, save he and one skinny fellow at the bar, had drifted out.

"Time for leaving," the barkeep called to him. When Duerdermont made no move to respond or rise from his chair, the man's bouncer made his way over to the table.

Looming huge, Wulfgar glared down upon the seated captain. "You can walk out, or you can fly out," he explained gruffly. "The choice is yours to make."

"You have traveled far from your fight with pirates south of Baldur's Gate," the captain replied. "Though I question your direction."

Wulfgar cocked his head and studied the man more closely. A flicker of recognition, just a flicker, crossed his bearded face.

"Have you forgotten our voyage south?" Deudermont prompted him. "The fight with pirate Pinochet and the flaming chariot?"

Wulfgar's eyes widened. "What do you know of these things?"

"Know of them?" Deudermont echoed incredulously. "Why, Wulfgar, you sailed on my vessel to Memnon and back. Your friends, Drizzt and Catti-brie, sailed with me again not too long ago, though surely they thought you dead!"

The big man fell back as if he had been slapped across the face. A jumbled mixture of emotions flashed across his clear blue eyes, everything from nostalgia to loathing. He spent a long moment trying to recover from the shock.

"You are mistaken, good man," he replied at last to Deudermont's surprise. "About my name and about my past. It is time for you to leave."

"But Wulfgar," Deudermont started to protest. He jumped in surprise to find another man, small and dark and ominous, standing right behind him, though he had heard not a footfall of approach. Wulfgar looked to the little man, then motioned to Arumn. The barkeep, after a moment's hesitation, reached behind the bar and produced a bottle, tossing it across the way where sure-fingered Morik caught it easily.

303

"Walk or fly?" Wulfgar asked Deudermont again. The sheer emptiness of his tone, not icy cold, but purely indifferent, struck Deudermont profoundly, told him that the man would make good on the promise to launch him out of the tavern without hesitation if he didn't move immediately.

"*Sea Sprite* is in port for another week at the least," Deudermont explained, rising and heading for the door. "You are welcomed there as a guest or to join the crew, for I have not forgotten," he finished firmly, the promise ringing in his wake as he slipped from the inn.

"Who was that?" Morik asked Wulfgar after Deudermont had disappeared into the dark Luskan night.

"A fool," was all that the big man would answer. He went to the bar and pointedly pulled another bottle from the shelf. Turning his gaze from Arumn to Delly, the surly barbarian left with Morik.

*   *   *   *   *

Captain Duedermont had a long walk ahead of him to the dock. The sights and sounds of Luskan's nightlife washed over him—loud, slurred voices through open tavern windows, barking dogs, clandestine whispers in dark corners—but Duedermont scarcely heard them, engrossed as he was in his own thoughts.

So Wulfgar *was* alive, and yet in worse condition than the captain could ever have imagined the heroic man. His offer to the barbarian to join the crew of *Sea Sprite* had been genuine, but he knew from the barbarian's demeanor that Wulfgar would never take him up on it.

What was Deudermont to do?

He wanted to help Wulfgar, but Deudermont was experienced enough in the ways of trouble to understand that you couldn't help a man who didn't want help.

"If you plan to leave a dinner engagement, kindly inform us of your whereabouts," came a reproachful greeting as the captain approached his ship. He looked up to see both Robillard and Waillan Micanty staring down at him from the rail.

"You shouldn't be out alone," Waillan Micanty scolded, but Deudermont merely waved away the notion.

Robillard frowned his concern. "How many enemies have we made these last years?" the wizard demanded in all seriousness. "How many would pay sacks of gold for a mere chance at your head?"

"That's why I employ a wizard to watch over me," Deudermont replied calmly, setting foot up the plank.

Robillard snorted at the absurdity of the remark. "How am I to watch over you if I don't even know where you are?"

Duedermont stopped in his tracks, and a wide smile creased his face as he gazed up at his wizard. "If you can't locate me magically, what faith should I hold that you could find those who wish me harm?"

"But it is true, Captain," Waillan interjected while Robillard flushed darkly. "Many would love to meet up with you unguarded in the streets."

"Am I to bottle up the whole crew, then?" Deudermont asked. "None shall leave, for fear of reprisals by friends of the pirates?"

"Few would leave *Sea Sprite* alone," Waillan argued.

"Fewer still would be known enough to pirates to be targets!" Robillard spouted. "Our enemies would not attack a minor and easily replaced crewman, for to do so would incur the wrath of Deudermont and the lords of Waterdeep, but the price might be worth paying for the chance to eliminate the captain of *Sea Sprite*." The wizard blew a deep sigh and eyed the captain pointedly. "You should not be out alone," he finished firmly.

"I had to check on an old friend," Deudermont explained.

"Wulfgar, by name?" asked the perceptive wizard.

"So I thought," replied Deudermont sourly as he continued up the plank and by the two men, going to his quarters without another word.

* * * * *

It was too small and nasty a place to even have a name, a gathering hole for the worst of Luskan's wretches. They were sailors mostly, wanted by lords or angry families for heinous crimes. Their fears that walking openly down a street in whatever port their ship entered would get them arrested or murdered were justified. So they came to holes like this, back rooms in shanties conveniently stocked near to the docks.

Morik the Rogue knew these places well, for he'd got his start on the streets working as lookout for one of the most dangerous of these establishments when he was but a young boy. He didn't go into such holes often anymore. Among the more civilized establishments, he was highly respected and regarded, and feared, and that was probably the emotion Morik most enjoyed. In here, though, he was just another thug, a little thief in a nest of assassins.

He couldn't resist entering a hole this night, though, not with the captain of the famed *Sea Sprite* showing up to have a conversation with his new friend, Wulfgar.

"How tall?" asked Creeps Sharky, one of the two thugs at Morik's table. Creeps was a grizzled old sea dog with uneven clumps of dirty beard on his ruddy cheeks and one eye missing. "Cheap Creeps," the patrons often called him, for the man was quick with his rusty old dagger and slow with his purse. So tight was Creeps with his booty that he wouldn't even buy a proper patch for his missing eye. The dark edge of the empty socket stared out at Morik from beneath the lowest folds of the bandana Creeps had tied about his head.

"Head and a half taller than me," Morik answered. "Maybe two."

Creeps glanced to his pirate companion, an exotic specimen, indeed. The man had a thick topknot of black hair and tattoos all about his face,

305

neck, and practically every other patch of exposed flesh—and since all he wore was a kilt of tiger skin, there was more than a little flesh exposed. Just following Creeps's glance to the other sent a shudder along Morik's spine, for while he didn't know the specifics of Creeps's companion, he had certainly heard the rumors about the "man," Tee-a-nicknick. This pirate was only half human, the other half being qullan, some rare and ferocious warrior race.

"*Sea Sprite*'s in port," Creeps remarked to Morik. The rogue nodded, for he had seen the three-masted schooner on his way to this drinking hole.

"He wore a beard just about the jawline," Morik added, trying to give as complete a description as he could.

"He sit straight?" the tattooed pirate asked.

Morik looked at Tee-a-nicknick as if he did not understand.

"Did he sit straight in his chair?" Creeps clarified, assuming a pose of perfect posture. "Lookin' like he had a plank shoved up his arse all the way to his throat?"

Morik smiled and nodded. "Straight and tall."

Again the two pirates shared a glance.

"Soundin' like Deudermont," Creeps put in. "The dog. I'd give a purse o' gold to put me knife across that one's throat. Put many o' me friends to the bottom, he has, and cost all o' us prettily."

The tattooed pirate showed his agreement by hoisting a bulging purse of coins onto the table. Morik realized then that every other conversation in the hole had come to an abrupt halt and that all eyes were upon him and his two rakish companions.

"Aye, Morik, but ye're likin' the sight," Creeps remarked, indicating the purse. "Well, it's yer own to have, and ten more like it, I'm guessin'." Creeps jumped up suddenly, sending his chair skidding back across the floor. "What're ye sayin', lads?" he cried. "Who's got a gold coin or ten for the head o' Deudermont o' *Sea Sprite*?"

A great cheer went up throughout the rathole, with many curses spoken against Deudermont and his pirate-killing crew.

Morik hardly heard them, so focused was he on the purse of gold. Deudermont had come to see Wulfgar. Every man in the place, and a hundred more like them, no doubt, would pitch in a few more coins. Deudermont knew Wulfgar well and trusted him. A thousand gold pieces. Ten thousand? Morik and Wulfgar could get to Deudermont, and easily. Morik's greedy, thieving mind reeled at the possibilities.

Chapter 2

Enchantment

She came skipping down the lane, so much like a little girl, and yet so obviously a young woman. Shiny black hair bounced around her shoulders, and her green eyes flashed as brightly as the beaming smile upon her fair face.

She had just spoken to *him,* to Jaka Sculi, with his soulful blue eyes and his curly brown hair, one strand hanging across the bridge of his nose. And just speaking to him made her skip where she might have walked, made her forget the mud that crept in through the holes in her old shoes or the tasteless food she would find in her wooden bowl at her parents' table that night. None of that mattered, not the bugs, not the dirty water, nothing. She had spoken to Jaka, and that alone made her warm and tingly and scared and alive all at the same time.

It went as one of life's little unrealized ironies that the same spirit freed by her encounter with the brooding Jaka inspired the eyes of another to settle upon her happy form.

Lord Feringal Auck had found his heart fluttering at the sight of many different women over his twenty-four years, mostly merchant's daughters whose fathers were looking for another safe haven northwest of Luskan. The village was near to the most traveled pass through the

307

Spine of the World where they might resupply and rest on the perilous journey to and from Ten-Towns in Icewind Dale.

Never before had Feringal Auck found his breathing so hard to steady that he was practically gasping for air as he hung from the window of his decorated carriage.

"Feri, the pines have begun sending their yellow dust throughout the winds," came the voice of Priscilla, Feringal's older sister. She, alone, called him Feri, to his everlasting irritation. "Do get inside the coach! The sneezing dust is thick about us. You know how terrible—"

The woman paused and studied her brother more intently, particularly the way he was gawking. "Feri?" she asked, sliding over in her seat, close beside him and grabbing his elbow and giving it a shake. "Feri?"

"Who is she?" the lord of Auckney asked, not even hearing his sister. "Who is that angelic creature, the avatar of the goddess of beauty, the image of man's purest desires, the embodiment of temptation?"

Priscilla shoved her brother aside and thrust her head out the carriage window. "What, that peasant girl?" she asked incredulously, a clear note of contempt sounding in her tone.

"I must know," Lord Feringal sang more than said. The side of his face sank against the edge of the carriage window, and his unblinking gaze locked on the skipping young woman. She slipped from his sight as the carriage sped around a bend in the curving road.

"Feri!" Priscilla scolded. She moved as if to slap her younger brother but held up short of the mark.

The lord of Auckney shook away his love-inspired lethargy long enough to eye his sister directly, even dangerously. "I shall know who she is," he insisted.

Priscilla Auck settled back in her seat and said no more, though she was truly taken aback by her younger brother's uncharacteristic show of emotion. Feringal had always been a gentle, quiet soul easily manipulated by his shrewish sister, fifteen years his senior. Now nearing her fortieth birthday, Priscilla had never married. In truth, she had never had any interest in a man beyond fulfilling her physical needs. Their mother had died giving birth to Feringal, their father passed on five years later, which left Priscilla, along with her father's counselor, Temigast, the stewardship of the fiefdom until Feringal grew old enough to rule. Priscilla had always enjoyed that arrangement, for even when Feringal had come of age, and even now, nearly a decade after that, her voice was substantial in the rulership of Auckney. She had never desired to bring another into the family, so she had assumed the same of Feri.

Scowling, Pricilla glanced back one last time in the general direction of the young lass, though they were far out of sight now. Their carriage rambled along the little stone bridge that arched into the sheltered bay toward the tiny isle where Castle Auck stood.

Like Auckney itself, a village of two hundred people that rarely showed up on any maps, the castle was of modest design. There were a dozen rooms for the family, and for Temigast, of course, and another five for the half-dozen servants and ten soldiers who served at the place. A pair of low and squat towers anchored the castle, barely topping fifteen feet, for the wind always blew strongly in Auckney. A common joke was, if the wind ever stopped blowing, all the villagers would fall over forward, so used were they to leaning as they walked.

"I should get out of the castle more often," Lord Feringal insisted as he and his sister moved through the foyer and into a sitting room, where old Steward Temigast sat painting another of his endless seascapes.

"To the village proper, you mean?" Priscilla said with obvious sarcasm. "Or to the outlying peat farms? Either way, it is all mud and stone and dirty."

"And in that mud, a jewel might shine all the brighter," the love-struck lord insisted with a deep sigh.

The steward cocked an eyebrow at the odd exchange and looked up from his painting. Temigast had lived in Waterdeep for most of his younger days, coming to Auckney as a middle-aged man some thirty years before. Worldly compared to the isolated Auckney citizens (including the ruling family), Temigast had had little trouble in endearing himself to the feudal lord, Tristan Auck, and in rising to the post of principal counselor, then steward. That worldliness served Temigast well now, for he recognized the motivation for Feringal's sigh and understood its implications.

"She was just a girl," Priscilla complained. "A child, and a dirty one at that." She looked to Temigast for support, seeing that he was intent upon their conversation. "Feringal is smitten, I fear," she explained. "And with a peasant. The lord of Auckney desires a dirty, smelly peasant girl."

"Indeed," replied Temigast, feigning horror. By his estimation, by the estimation of anyone who was not from Auckney, the "lord of Auckney" was barely above a peasant himself. There *was* history here: The castle had stood for more than six hundred years, built by the Dorgenasts who had ruled for the first two centuries. Then, through marriage, it had been assumed by the Aucks.

But what, really, were they ruling? Auckney was on the very fringe of the trade routes, south of the westernmost spur of the Spine of the World. Most merchant caravans traveling between Ten-Towns and Luskan avoided the place all together, many taking the more direct pass through the mountains many miles to the east. Even those who dared not brave the wilds of that unguarded pass crossed east of Auckney, through another pass that harbored the town of Hundelstone, which had six times the population of Auckney and many more valuable supplies and craftsmen.

Though a coastal village, Auckney was too far north for any shipping trade. Occasionally a ship—often a fisherman caught in a gale out of

Fireshear to the south—would drift into the small harbor around Auckney, usually in need of repair. Some of those fishermen stayed on in the fiefdom, but the population here had remained fairly constant since the founding by the roguish Lord Dorgenast and his followers, refugees from a minor and failed power play among the secondary ruling families in Waterdeep. Now nearing two hundred, the population was as large as it had ever been (mostly because of an influx of gnomes from Hundelstone), and on many occasions it was less than half of that. Most of the villagers were related, usually in more ways than one, except, of course, for the Aucks, who usually took their brides or husbands from outside stock.

"Can't you find a suitable wife from among the well-bred families of Luskan?" Priscilla asked. "Or in a favorable deal with a wealthy merchant? We could well use a large dowery, after all."

"Wife?" Temigast said with a chuckle. "Aren't we being a bit premature?"

"Not at all," Lord Feringal insisted evenly. "I love her. I know that I do."

"Fool!" Priscilla wailed, but Temigast patted her shoulder to calm her, chuckling all the while.

"Of course you do, my lord," the steward said, "but the marriage of a nobleman is rarely about love, I fear. It is about station and alliance and wealth," Temigast gently explained.

Feringal's eyes widened. "I love her!" the young lord insisted.

"Then take her as a mistress," Temigast suggested reasonably. "A plaything. Surely a man of your great station is deserving of at least one of those."

Hardly able to speak past the welling lump in his throat, Feringal ground his heel into the stone floor and stormed off to his private room.

* * * * *

"Did you kiss him?" Tori, the younger of the Ganderlay sisters, asked, giggling at the thought of it. Tori was only eleven, and just beginning to realize the differences between boys and girls, an education fast accelerating since Meralda, her older sister by six years, had taken a fancy to Jaka Sculi, with his delicate features and long eyelashes and brooding blue eyes.

"No, I surely did not," Meralda replied, brushing back her long black hair from her olive-skinned face, the face of beauty, the face that had unknowingly captured the heart of the lord of Auckney.

"But you wanted to," Tori teased, bursting into laughter, and Meralda joined her, as sure an admission as she could give.

"Oh, but I did," the older sister said.

"And you wanted to touch him," her young sister teased on. "Oh, to hug him and kiss him! Dear, sweet Jaka." Tori ended by making sloppy kissing noises and wrapping her arms about her chest, hands grabbing her shoulders as she turned about so that it looked as if someone was hugging her.

"You stop that!" Meralda said, slapping her sister across the back playfully.

"But you didn't even kiss him," Tori complained. "Why not, if you wanted to? Did he not want the same?"

"To make him want it all the more," the older girl explained. "To make him think about me all the time. To make him dream about me."

"But if you're wanting it—"

"I'm wanting more than that," Meralda explained, "and if I make him wait, I can make him beg. If I make him beg, I can get all that I want from him and more."

"What more?" Tori asked, obviously confused.

"To be his wife," Meralda stated without reservation.

Tori nearly swooned. She grabbed her straw pillow and whacked her sister over the head with it. "Oh, you'll never!" she cried. Too loudly.

The curtain to their bedroom pulled back, and their father, Dohni Ganderlay, a ruddy man with strong muscles from working the peat fields and skin browned from both sun and dirt, poked his head in.

"You should be long asleep," Dohni scolded.

The girls dived down as one, scooting under the coarse, straw-lined ticking and pulling it tight to their chins, giggling all the while.

"Now, I'll be having none of that silliness!" Dohni yelled, and he came at them hard, falling over them like a great hunting beast, a wrestling tussle that ended in a hug shared between the two girls and their beloved father.

"Now, get your rest, you two," Dohni said quietly a moment later. "Your ma's a bit under the stone, and your laughter is keeping her awake." He kissed them both and left. The girls, respectful of their father and concerned about their mother, who had indeed been feeling even worse than usual, settled down to their own private thoughts.

Meralda's admission was strange and frightening to Tori. But while she was uncertain about her sister getting married and moving out of the house, she was also very excited at the prospect of growing into a young woman like her sister.

Lying next to her sister, Meralda's mind raced with anticipation. She had kissed a boy before, several boys actually, but it had always been out of curiosity or on a dare from her friends. This was the first time she really wanted to kiss someone. And how she did want to kiss Jaka Sculi! To kiss him and to run her fingers through his curly brown hair and gently down his soft, hairless cheek, and to have his hands caressing her thick hair, her face . . .

Meralda fell asleep to warm dreams.

* * * * *

In a much more comfortable bed in a room far less drafty not so many doors away, Lord Feringal nestled into his soft feather pillows. He longed to escape to dreams of holding the girl from the village, where he could throw off his suffocating station, where he could do as he pleased without interference from his sister or old Temigast.

He wanted to escape too much, perhaps, for Feringal found no rest in his huge, soft bed, and soon he had twisted and turned the feather ticking into knots about his legs. It was fortunate for him that he was hugging one of the pillows, for it was the only thing that broke his fall when he rolled right off the edge and onto the hard floor.

Feringal finally extricated himself from the bedding tangle, then paced about his room, scratching his head, his nerves more on edge than they'd ever been. What had this enchantress done to him?

"A cup of warm goat's milk," he muttered aloud, thinking that would calm him and afford him some sleep. Feringal slipped from his room and started along the narrow staircase. Halfway down he heard voices from below.

He paused, recognizing Priscilla's nasal tone, then a burst of laughter from his sister as well as from old, wheezing Temigast. Something struck Feringal as out of place, some sixth sense told him that he was the butt of that joke. He crept down more quietly, coming under the level of the first floor ceiling and ducking close in the shadows against the stone bannister.

There sat Priscilla upon the divan, knitting, with old Temigast in a straight-backed chair across from her, a decanter of whisky in hand.

"Oh, but I love her," Priscilla wailed, stopping her knitting to sweep one hand across her brow dramatically. "I cannot live without her!"

"Got along well enough for all these years," Temigast remarked, playing along.

"But I am tired, good steward," Priscilla replied, obviously mocking her brother. "What great effort is lovemaking alone!"

Temigast coughed in his drink, and Priscilla exploded with laughter.

Feringal could take no more. He swept down the stairs, full of anger. "Enough! Enough I say!" he roared. Startled, the two turned to him and bit their lips, though Priscilla could not hold back one last bubble of laughter.

Lord Feringal glowered at her, his fists clenched at his sides, as close to rage as either of them had ever seen the gentle-natured man. "How dare you?" he asked through gritted teeth and trembling lips. "To mock me so!"

"A bit of a jest, my lord," Temigast explained weakly to defuse the situation, "nothing more."

Feringal ignored the steward's explanation and turned his ire on his sister. "What do you know of love?" he screamed at Priscilla. "You have never had a lustful thought in your miserable life. You couldn't even imagine what it would be like to lay with a man, could you, dear sister?"

"You know less than you think," Priscilla shot back, tossing aside her knitting and starting to rise. Only Temigast's hand, grabbing hard at her knee, kept her in place. She calmed considerably at that, but the old man's expression was a clear reminder to watch her words carefully, to keep a certain secret between them.

"My dear Lord Feringal," the steward began quietly, "there is nothing wrong with your desires. Quite the contrary; I should consider them a healthy sign, if a bit late in coming. I don't doubt that your heart aches for this peasant girl, but I assure you there's nothing wrong with taking her as your mistress. Certainly there is precedent for such an act among the previous lords of Auckney, and of most kingdoms, I would say."

Feringal gave a long and profound sigh and shook his head as Temigast rambled on. "I love her," he insisted again. "Can't you understand that?"

"You don't even know her," Priscilla dared to interject. "She farms peat, no doubt, with dirty fingers."

Feringal took a threatening step toward her, but Temigast, agile and quick for his age, moved between them and gently nudged the young man back into a chair. "I believe you, Feringal. You love her, and you wish to rescue her."

That caught Feringal by surprise. "Rescue?" he echoed blankly.

"Of course," reasoned Temigast. "You are the lord, the great man of Auckney, and you alone have the power to elevate this peasant girl from her station of misery."

Feringal held his perplexed pose for just a moment then said, "Yes, yes," with an exuberant nod of his head.

"I have seen it before," Temigast said, shaking his head. "It is a common disease among young lords, this need to save some peasant or another. It will pass, Lord Feringal, and rest assured that you may enjoy all the company you need of the girl."

"You cheapen my feelings," Feringal accused.

"I speak the truth," Temigast was quick to reply.

"No!" insisted Feringal. "What would you know of my feelings, old man? You could never have loved a woman to suggest such a thing. You can't know what burns within me."

That statement seemed to hit a nerve with the old steward, but for whatever reason Temigast quieted, and his lips got very thin. He moved back to his chair and settled uncomfortably, staring blankly at Feringal.

The young lord, more full of the fires of life than he had ever been, would not buckle to that imposing stare. "I'll not take her as a mistress," he said determinedly. "Never that. She is the woman I shall love forever, the woman I shall take as my wife, the lady of Castle Auck."

"Feri!" Priscilla screeched.

The young lord, determined not to buckle as usual to the desires of his overbearing sister, turned and stormed off, back to the sanctuary of his room. He took care not to run, as he usually did in confrontations with his shrewish sister, but rather, afforded himself a bit of dignity, a stern and regal air. He was a man now, he understood.

"He has gone mad," Priscilla said to Temigast when they heard Feringal's door close. "He saw this girl but once from afar."

If Temigast even heard her, he made no indication. Stubborn Priscilla slipped down from the divan to her knees and moved up before the seated man. "He saw her but once," she said again, forcing Temigast's attention.

"Sometimes that's all it takes," the steward quietly replied.

Priscilla quieted and stared hard at the old man whose bed she had secretly shared since the earliest days of her womanhood. For all their physical intimacy, though, Temigast had never shared his inner self with Priscilla except for one occasion, and only briefly, when he had spoken of his life in Waterdeep before venturing to Auckney. He had stopped the conversation quickly, but only after mentioning a woman's name. Priscilla had always wondered if that woman had meant more to Temigast than he let on. Now, she recognized that he had fallen under the spell of some memory, coaxed by her brother's proclamations of undying love.

The woman turned away from him, jealous anger burning within her, but, as always, she was fast to let it go, to remember her lot and her pleasures in life. Temigast's own past might have softened his resolve against Feringal running after this peasant girl, but Priscilla wasn't so ready to accept her brother's impetuous decision. She had been comfortable with the arrangement in Castle Auck for many years, and the last thing she wanted now was to have some peasant girl, and perhaps her smelly peasant family, moving in with them.

*　*　*　*　*

Temigast retired soon after, refusing Priscilla's invitation to share her bed. The old man's thoughts slipped far back across the decades to a woman he had once known, a woman who had so stolen his heart and who, by dying so very young, had left a bitterness and cynicism locked within him to this very day.

Temigast hadn't recognized the depth of those feelings until he realized his own doubt and dismissal of Lord Feringal's obvious feelings. What an old wretch he believed himself at that moment.

He sat in a chair by the narrow window overlooking Auckney Harbor. The moon had long ago set, leaving the cold waters dark and showing dull whitecaps under the starry sky. Temigast, like Priscilla, had never seen his young charge so animated and agitated, so full of fire and full of life. Feringal always had a dull humor about him, a sense of perpetual lethargy, but there had been nothing lethargic in the manner in which

314

the young man had stormed down the stairs to proclaim his love for the peasant girl, nothing lethargic in the way in which Feringal had accosted his bullying older sister.

That image brought a smile to Temigast's face. Perhaps Castle Auck needed such fire now; perhaps it was time to shake the place and all the fiefdom about it. Maybe a bit of spirit from the lord of Auckney would elevate the often overlooked village to the status of its more notable neighbors, Hundelstone and Fireshear. Never before had the lord of Auckney married one of the peasants of the village. There were simply too few people in that pool, most from families who had been in the village for centuries, and the possibility of bringing so many of the serfs into the ruling family, however distantly, was a definite argument against letting Feringal have his way.

But the sheer energy the young lord had shown seemed as much an argument in favor of the union at that moment, and so he decided he would look into this matter very carefully, would find out who this peasant girl might be and see if something could be arranged.

Chapter 3
Final Straw

"He knew you," Morik dared to say after he had rejoined Wulfgar very late that same night following his venture to the seedy drinking hole. By the time the rogue had caught up to his friend on the docks the big man had drained almost all of the second bottle. "And you knew him."

"He thought he knew me," Wulfgar corrected, slurring each word.

He was hardly able to sit without wobbling, obviously more drunk than usual for so early an hour. He and Morik had split up outside the Cutlass, with Wulfgar taking the two bottles. Instead of going straight to the docks the barbarian had wandered the streets and soon found himself in the more exclusive section of Luskan, the area of respectable folk and merchants. No city guards had come to chase him off, for in that area of town stood the Prisoner's Carnival, a public platform where outlaws were openly punished. A thief was up on the stage this night, asked repeatedly by the torturer if he admitted his crime. When he did not, the torturer took out a pair of heavy shears and snipped off his little finger. The thief's answer to the repeated question brought howls of approval from the scores of people watching the daily spectacle.

Of course, admitting to the crime was no easy way out for the poor man. He lost his whole hand, one finger at a time, the mob cheering and hooting with glee.

But not Wulfgar. No, the sight had proven too much for the barbarian, had catapulted him back in time, back to Errtu's Abyss and the helpless agony. What tortures he had known there! He had been cut and whipped and beaten within an inch of his life, only to be restored by the healing magic of one of Errtu's foul minions. He'd had his fingers bitten off and put back again.

The sight of the unfortunate thief brought all that back to him vividly now.

The anvil. Yes, that was the worst of all, the most agonizing physical torture Errtu had devised for him, reserved for those moments when the great demon was in such a fit of rage that he could not take the time to devise a more subtle, more crushing, mental torture.

The anvil. Cold it was, like a block of ice, so cold that it seemed like fire to Wulfgar's thighs when Errtu's mighty minions pulled him across it, forced him to straddle it, naked and stretched out on his back.

Errtu would come to him then, slowly, menacingly, would walk right up before him, and in a single, sudden movement, smash a small mallet set with tiny needles down into Wulfgar's opened eyes, exploding them and washing waves of nausea and agony through the barbarian.

And, of course, Errtu's minions would heal him, would make him whole again that their fun might be repeated.

Even now, long fled from Errtu's abyssal home, Wulfgar often awoke, curled like a baby, clutching his eyes, feeling the agony. Wulfgar knew of only one escape from the pain. Thus, he had taken his bottles and run away, and only by swallowing the fiery liquid had he blurred that memory.

"*Thought* he knew you?" Morik asked doubtfully.

Wulfgar stared at him blankly.

"The man in the Cutlass," Morik explained.

"He was mistaken," Wulfgar slurred.

Morik flashed him a skeptical look.

"He knew who I once was," the big man admitted. "Not who I am."

"Deudermont," Morik reasoned.

Now it was Wulfgar's turn to look surprised. Morik knew most of the folk of Luskan, of course—the rogue survived through information—but it surprised Wulfgar that he knew of an obscure sailor (which is what Wulfgar thought Deudermont to be) merely visiting the port.

"Captain Deudermont of the *Sea Sprite*," Morik explained. "Much known and much feared by the pirates of the Sword Coast. He knew you, and you knew him."

"I sailed with him once . . . a lifetime ago," Wulfgar admitted.

"I have many friends, profiteers of the sea, who would pay hand-somely to see that one eliminated," Morik remarked, bending low over the seated Wulfgar. "Perhaps we could use your familiarity with this man to some advantage."

Even as the words left Morik's mouth, Wulfgar came up fast and hard, his hand going about Morik's throat. Staggering on unsteady legs, Wulfgar still had the strength in just that one arm to lift the rogue from the ground. A fast few strides, as much a fall as a run, brought them hard against the wall of a warehouse where Wulfgar pinned Morik the Rogue, whose feet dangled several inches above the ground.

Morik's hand went into a deep pocket, closing on a nasty knife, one that he knew he could put into the drunken Wulfgar's heart in an instant. He held his thrust, though, for Wulfgar did not press in any longer, did not try to injure him. Besides, there remained those nagging memories of drow elves holding an interest in Wulfgar. How would Morik explain killing the man to them? What would happen to the rogue if he didn't manage to finish the job?

"If ever you ask that of me again, I will—" Wulfgar left the threat unfinished, dropping Morik. He spun back to the sea, nearly overbalancing and tumbling from the pier in his drunken rush.

Morik rubbed a hand across his bruised throat, momentarily stunned by the explosive outburst. When he thought about it, though, he merely nodded. He had touched on a painful wound, one opened by the unexpected appearance of Wulfgar's old companion, Deudermont. It was the classic struggle of past and present, Morik knew, for he had seen it tear men apart time and again as they went about their descent to the bottom of a bottle. The feelings brought on by the sight of the captain, the man with whom he had once sailed, were too raw for Wulfgar. The barbarian couldn't put his present state in accord with what he had once been. Morik smiled and let it go, recognizing clearly that the emotional fight, past against present, was far from finished for his large friend.

Perhaps the present would win out, and Wulfgar would listen to Morik's potentially profitable proposition concerning Deudermont. Or, if not, maybe Morik would act independently and use Wulfgar's familiarity with the man to his own gain without Wulfgar's knowledge.

Morik forgave Wulfgar for attacking him. This time. . . .

"Would you like to sail with him again, then?" Morik asked, deliberately lightening his tone.

Wulfgar plopped to a sitting position, then stared incredulously through blurry eyes at the rogue.

"We must keep our purses full," Morik reminded him. "You do seem to be growing bored with Arumn and the Cutlass. Perhaps a few months at sea—"

Wulfgar waved him to silence, then turned about and spat into the sea. A moment later, he bent low over the dock and vomited.

Morik looked upon him with a mixture of pity, disgust, and anger. Yes, the rogue knew then and there he would get to Deudermont, whether

Wulfgar went along with the plan or not. The rogue would use his friend to find a weakness in the infamous captain of *Sea Sprite*. A pang of guilt hit Morik as he came to that realization. Wulfgar was his friend, after all, but this was the street, and a wise man would not pass up so obvious an opportunity to grab a pot of gold.

* * * * *

"You stink Morik get done it?" the tattooed pirate, Tee-a-nicknick, asked first thing when he awoke in an alley.

Next to him among the trash, Creeps Sharky looked over curiously, then deciphered the words. "Think, my friend, not stink," he corrected.

"You stink him done it?"

Propped on one elbow, Creeps snorted and looked away, his one-eyed gaze drifting about the fetid alley.

With no answer apparently forthcoming, Tee-a-nicknick swatted Creeps Sharky hard across the back of his head.

"What're you about?" the other pirate complained, trying to turn around but merely falling face down on the ground, then slowly rolling to his back to glare at his exotic half-qullan companion.

"Morik done it?" Tee-a-nicknick asked. "Kill Deudermont?"

Creeps coughed up a ball of phlegm and managed, with great effort, to move to a sitting position. "Bah," he snorted doubtfully. "Morik's a sneaky one, to be sure, but he's out of his pond with Deudermont. More likely the captain'll be taking that one down."

"Ten thousand," Tee-a-nicknick said with great lament, for he and Creeps, in circulating the notion that Deudermont might be taken down before *Sea Sprite* ever left Luskan, had secured promises of nearly ten thousand gold pieces in bounty money, funds they knew the offering pirates would gladly pay for the completed deed. Creeps and Tee-a-nicknick had already decided that should Morik finish the task, they would pay him seven of the ten, keeping three for themselves.

"I been thinking that maybe Morik'll set up Deudermont well enough," Creeps went on. "Might be that the little rat'll play a part without knowing he's playing it. If Deudermont's liking Morik's friend, then Deudermont might be letting down his guard a bit too much."

"You stink we do it?" Tee-a-nicknick asked, sounding intrigued.

Creeps eyed his friend. He chuckled at the half-qullan's continuing struggles with the language, though Tee-a-nicknick had been sailing with humans for most of his life, ever since he had been plucked from an island as a youth. His own people, the savage eight-foot-tall qullans were intolerant of mixed blood and had abandoned him as inferior.

Tee-a-nicknick gave a quick blow, ending in a smile, and Creeps Sharky didn't miss the reference. No pirate in any sea could handle a certain weapon, a long hollow tube that the tattooed pirate called a blowgun, better than Tee-a-nicknick. Creeps had seen his friend shoot a fly from the rail from across a wide ship's deck. Tee-a-nicknick also had a substantial understanding of poisons, a legacy of his life with the exotic qullans, Creeps believed, to tip the cat's claws he sometimes used as blow-gun missiles. Poisons human clerics could not understand and counter.

One well-placed shot could make Creeps and Tee-a-nicknick wealthy men indeed, perhaps even wealthy enough to secure their own ship.

"You got a particularly nasty poison for Mister Deudermont?" Creeps asked.

The tattooed half-qullan smiled. "You stink we do it," he stated.

*   *   *   *   *

Arumn Gardpeck sighed when he saw the damage done to the door leading to the guest wing of the Cutlass. The hinges had been twisted so that the door no longer stood straight within its jamb. Now it tilted and wouldn't even close properly.

"A foul mood again," observed Josi Puddles, standing behind the tavernkeeper. "A foul mood today, a foul mood tomorrow. Always a foul mood for that one."

Arumn ignored the man and moved along the hallway to the door of Delly Curtie's room. He put his ear against the wood and heard soft sobbing from within.

"Pushed her out again," Josi spat. "Ah, the dog."

Arumn glared at the little man, though his thoughts weren't far different. Josi's whining didn't shake the tavernkeeper in the least. He recognized that the man had developed a particular sore spot against Wulfgar, one based mostly on jealousy, the emotion that always seemed to rule Josi's actions. The sobs of Delly Curtie cut deeply into troubled Arumn, who had come to think of the girl as his own daughter. At first, he had been thrilled by the budding relationship between Delly and Wulfgar, despite the protests of Josi, who had been enamored of the girl for years. Now those protests seemed to hold a bit of truth in them, for Wulfgar's actions toward Delly of late had brought a bitter taste to Arumn's mouth.

"He's costin' ye more than he's bringin' in," Josi went on, skipping to keep up with Arumn as the big man made his way determinedly toward Wulfgar's door at the end of the hall, "breakin' so much, and an honest fellow won't come into the Cutlass anymore. Too afraid to get his head busted."

Arumn stopped at the door and turned pointedly on Josi. "Shut yer mouth," he instructed plainly and firmly. He turned back and lifted his hand as if to knock, but he changed his mind and pushed right through the door. Wulfgar lay sprawled on the bed, still in his clothes and smelling of liquor.

"Always the drink," Arumn lamented. The sadness in his voice was indeed genuine, for despite all his anger at Wulfgar, Arumn couldn't dismiss his own responsibility in this situation. He had introduced the troubled barbarian to the bottle, but he hadn't recognized the depth of the big man's despair. The barkeep understood it now, the sheer desperation in Wulfgar to escape the agony of his recent past.

"What're ye thinking to do?" Josi asked.

Arumn ignored him and moved to the bed to give Wulfgar a rough shake. After a second, then a third shake the barbarian lifted his head and turned it to face Arumn, though his eyes were hardly open.

"Ye're done here," Arumn said plainly and calmly, shaking Wulfgar again. "I cannot let ye do this to me place and me friends no more. Ye gather all yer things tonight and be on yer way, wherever that road might take ye, for I'm not wanting to see ye in the common room. I'll put a bag o' coins inside yer door to help ye get set up somewhere else. I'm owin' ye that much, at least."

Wulfgar didn't respond.

"Ye hearin' me?" Arumn asked.

Wulfgar nodded and grumbled for Arumn to go away, a request heightened by a wave of the barbarian's arm, which, as sluggish as Wulfgar was, still easily and effectively pushed Arumn back from the bed.

Another sigh, another shake of his head, and Arumn left. Josi Puddles spent a long moment studying the huge man on the bed and the room around him and particularly the magnificent warhammer resting against the wall in the far corner.

* * * * *

"I owe it to him," Captain Deudermont said to Robillard, the two standing at the rail of the docked, nearly repaired *Sea Sprite*.

"Because he once sailed with you?" the wizard asked skeptically.

"More than sailed."

"He performed a service for your vessel, true enough," Robillard reasoned, "but did you not reciprocate? You took him and his friends all the way to Memnon and back."

Deudermont bowed his head in contemplation, then looked up at the wizard. "I owe it to him not out of any financial or business arrangement," he explained, "but because we became friends."

"You hardly knew him."

"But I know Drizzt Do'Urden and Catti-brie," Deudermont argued. "How many years did they sail with me? Do you deny our friendship?"

"But—"

"How can you so quickly deny my responsibility?" Deudermont asked.

"He is neither Drizzt nor Catti-brie," Robillard replied.

"No, but he is a dear friend of both and a man in great need."

"Who doesn't want your help," finished the wizard.

Deudermont bowed his head again, considering the words. They seemed true enough. Wulfgar had, indeed, denied his offers of help. Given the barbarian's state, the captain had to admit, privately, that chances were slim he could say or do anything to bring the big man from his downward spiral.

"I must try," he said a moment later, not bothering to look up.

Robillard didn't bother to argue the point. The wizard understood, from the captain's determined tone, that it was not his place to do so. He had been hired to protect Deudermont, and so he would do just that. Still, by his estimation, the sooner *Sea Sprite* was out of Luskan and far, far from this Wulfgar fellow, the better off they would all be.

* * * * *

He was conscious of the sound of his breathing, gasping actually, for he was as scared as he had ever been. One slip, one inadvertent noise, would wake the giant, and he doubted any of the feeble explanations he'd concocted would save him then.

Something greater than fear prodded Josi Puddles along. More than anything, he had come to hate this man. Wulfgar had taken Delly from him—from his fantasies, at least. Wulfgar had enamored himself of Arumn, replacing Josi at the tavernkeeper's side. Wulfgar could bring complete ruin to the Cutlass, the only home Josi Puddles had ever known.

Josi didn't believe that the huge, wrathful barbarian would take Arumn's orders to leave without a fight, and Josi had seen enough of the brawling man to understand just how devastating that fight might become. Josi also understood that if it came to blows in the Cutlass, he would likely prove a prime target for Wulfgar's wrath.

He cracked open the door. Wulfgar lay on the bed in almost exactly the same position as he had been when Josi and Arumn had come there two hours earlier.

Aegis-fang leaned against the wall in the far corner. Josi shuddered at the sight, imagining the mighty warhammer spinning his way.

The little man crept into the room and paused to consider the small bag of coins Arumn had left to the side of the door beside Wulfgar's bed. Drawing out a large knife, he put his fingertip to the barbarian's back, just under the shoulder-blade, feeling for a heartbeat, then replaced his fingertip with the tip of the knife. All he had to do was lean on it hard, he told himself. All he had to do was drive the knife through Wulfgar's heart, and his troubles would be at their end. The Cutlass would survive as it had before this demon had come to Luskan, and Delly Curtie would be his for the taking.

He leaned over the blade. Wulfgar stirred, but just barely, the big man very far from consciousness.

What if he missed the mark? Josi thought with sudden panic. What if his thrust only wounded the big man? The image of a roaring Wulfgar leaping from the bed to corner a would-be assassin sapped the strength from Josi's knees, and he nearly fell over the sleeping barbarian. The little man skittered back from the bed and turned for the door, trying not to cry out in fright.

He composed himself and remembered his fears for the expected scene of that night, when Wulfgar would come down to confront Arumn, when the barbarian and that terrible warhammer would take down the Cutlass and everyone in the place.

Before he could even consider the action, Josi rushed across the room and, with great effort, hoisted the heavy hammer, cradling it like a baby. He ran out of the room and out the inn's back door.

*   *   *   *   *

"Ye shouldn't've brought 'em," Arumn scolded Josi Puddles again. Even as he finished, the door separating the common room from the private quarters swung open and a haggard-looking Wulfgar walked in.

"A foul mood," Josi remarked, as if that was vindication against Arumn's scolding. Josi had invited a few friends to the Cutlass that night, a thick-limbed rogue named Reef and his equally tough friends, including one thin man with soft hands—not a fighter, to be sure—whom Arumn believed he had seen before but in flowing robes and not breeches and a tunic. Reef had a score to settle against Wulfgar, for on the first day the barbarian arrived in the Cutlass Reef and a couple of his friends were working as Arumn's bouncers. When they tried to forcefully remove Wulfgar from the tavern, the barbarian had slapped Reef across the room.

Arumn's glare did not diminish. He was somewhat surprised to see Wulfgar in the tavern, but still he wanted to handle this with words alone. A fight with an outraged Wulfgar could cost the proprietor greatly.

The crowd in the common room went into a collective hush as Wulfgar made his way across the floor. Staring suspiciously at Arumn, the big man plopped a bag of coins on the bar.

"It's all I can give to ye," Arumn remarked, recognizing the bag as the one he had left for Wulfgar.

"Who asked for it?" Wulfgar replied, sounding as if he had no idea what was going on.

"It's what I told ye," Arumn started, then stopped and patted his hands in the air as if trying to calm Wulfgar down, though in truth, the mighty barbarian didn't seem the least bit agitated.

"Ye're not to stay here anymore," Arumn explained. "I can't be having it."

Wulfgar didn't respond other than to glare intensely at the tavernkeeper.

"Now, I'm wanting no trouble," Arumn explained, again patting his hands in the air.

Wulfgar wouldn't have given him any, though the big man was surely in a foul mood. He noticed a movement from Josi Puddles, obviously a signal, and half a dozen powerful men, including a couple Wulfgar recognized as Arumn's old crew, formed a semicircle around the huge man.

"No trouble!" Arumn said more forcefully, aiming his remark more at Josi's hunting pack than at Wulfgar.

"Aegis-fang," Wulfgar muttered.

A few seats down the bar, Josi stiffened and prayed that he had placed the hammer safely out of Wulfgar's magical calling range.

A moment passed; the warhammer did not materialize in Wulfgar's hand.

"It's in yer room," Arumn offered.

With a sudden, vicious movement, Wulfgar slapped the bag of coins away, sending them clattering across the floor. "Are you thinking that to be ample payment?"

"More than I owe ye," Arumn dared to argue.

"A few coins for Aegis-fang?" Wulfgar asked incredulously.

"Not for the warhammer," Arumn stuttered, sensing that the situation was deteriorating very fast. "That's in yer room."

"If it were in my room, then I would have seen it," Wulfgar replied, leaning forward threateningly. Josi's hunting pack closed in just a bit, two of them taking out small clubs, a third wrapping a chain about his fist. "Even if I did not see it, it would have come to my call from there," Wulfgar reasoned, and he called again, yelling this time, "Aegis-fang!"

Nothing.

"Where is my hammer?" Wulfgar demanded of Arumn.

"Just leave, Wulfgar," the tavernkeeper pleaded. "Just be gone. If we find yer hammer, we'll get it brought to ye, but go now."

Wulfgar saw it coming, so he baited it in. He reached across the bar for Arumn's throat, then pulled up short and snapped his arm back, catching the attacker coming in at his right flank, Reef, square in the face with a flying elbow. Reef staggered and wobbled, until Wulfgar pumped his arm and slammed him again, sending him flying away.

Purely on instinct, the barbarian spun back and threw his left arm up defensively. Just in time as one of Reef's cronies came in hard, swinging a short, thick club that smashed Wulfgar hard on the forearm.

All semblance of strategy and posturing disappeared in the blink of an eye, as all five of the thugs charged at Wulfgar. The barbarian began kicking and swinging his mighty fists, yelling out for Aegis-fang repeatedly and futilely. He even snapped his head forward viciously several times, connecting solidly with an attacker's nose, then again, catching another man on the side of the head and sending him staggering away.

Delly Curtie screamed, and Arumn cried "No!" repeatedly.

But Wulfgar couldn't hear them. Even if he could, he could not have taken a moment to heed the command. He had to buy some time and some room, for he was taking three hits for every one he was delivering in these close quarters. Though his punches and kicks were heavier by far, Reef's friends were no novices to brawling.

The rest of the Cutlass's patrons stared at the row in amusement and confusion, for they knew that Wulfgar worked for Arumn. The only ones moving were skidding safely out of range of the whirling ball of brawlers. One man in the far corner stood up, waving his arms wildly and spinning in circles.

"They're attacking the Cutlass crew!" the man cried. "To arms, patrons and friends! Defend Arumn and Wulfgar! Surely these thugs will destroy our tavern!"

"By the gods," Arumn Gardpeck muttered, for he knew the speaker, knew that Morik the Rogue had just condemned his precious establishment to devastation. With a shake of his head and a frustrated groan, the helpless Arumn ducked down behind the bar.

As if on cue, the entire Cutlass exploded into a huge brawl. Men and women, howling and taking no time to sort out allegiance, were just punching at the nearest potential victim.

Still at the bar, Wulfgar had to leave his right flank exposed, taking a brutal slug across the jaw, for he was focusing on the left, where the man with the club came at him yet again. He got his hands up to deflect the first strike and the second, then stepped toward the man, accepting a smack across the ribs, but catching the attacker by the forearm. Holding tightly Wulfgar shoved the man away, then yanked him powerfully back in, ducking and snapping his free hand into the staggering man's crotch. The man went high into the air, Wulfgar pressing him up to the limit of his reach and turning a quick circle, seeking a target.

The man flew away, hitting another, both of them falling into poor Reef and sending the big man sprawling once again.

Yet another attacker came hard at Wulfgar, arm cocked to punch. The barbarian steeled his gaze and his jaw, ready to trade hit for hit, but this ruffian had a chain wrapped around his fist. A flash of burning pain exploded on Wulfgar's face, and the taste of blood came thick in his mouth. Out pumped the dazed Wulfgar's arm, his fist just clipping the attacker's shoulder.

Another man dipped his shoulder in full charge, slamming Wulfgar's side, but the braced barbarian didn't budge. A second chain-wrapped punch came at his face—he saw the links gleaming red with his own blood—but he managed to duck the brunt of this one, though he still got a fair-sized gash across his cheek.

The other man, who had bounced off him harmlessly, leaped onto Wulfgar's side with a heavy flying tackle, but Wulfgar, with a defiant roar, held fast his footing. He twisted and wriggled his left arm up under the clinging man's shoulder and grabbed him by the hair on the back of his head.

Ahead strode the barbarian, roaring, punching again and again with his free right hand, while tugging with his left to keep the clinging man in check. The chain-fisted ruffian backed defensively, using his left arm to deflect the blows. He saw an opening he couldn't resist and came forward hard to land another solid blow on Wulfgar, clipping the barbarian's collar bone. The ruffian should have continued retreating, though, for Wulfgar had his footing and his balance now, enough to put all his weight behind one great hooking right.

The chain-fisted ruffian's blocking arm barely deflected the heavy blow. Wulfgar's fist smashed through the defenses and came crashing down against the side of the ruffian's face, spinning him in a downward spiral to the floor.

* * * * *

Morik sat at his table in the far corner, every now and then dodging a flying bottle or body, unperturbed as he sipped his drink. Despite his calm facade, the rogue was worried for his friend and for the Cutlass, for he could not believe the brutality of the row this night. It seemed as if all of Luskan's thugs had risen up in this one great opportunity to brawl in a tavern that had been relatively fight-free since Wulfgar had arrived, scaring off or quickly beating up any potential ruffians.

Morik winced as the chain slammed into Wulfgar's face, splattering blood. The rogue considered going to his friend's aid, but he quickly dismissed the notion. Morik was a clever information gatherer, a thief who survived through his wiles and his weapons, neither of which would help him in a common tavern brawl.

So he sat at his table, watching the tumult around him. Nearly everyone in the common room was into it now. One man came by, dragging a woman by her long, dark hair, heading for the door. He had hardly gone past Morik, though, when another man smashed a chair over his head, dropping him to the floor.

When that rescuer turned to the woman, she promptly smashed a bottle across the smile on his face, then turned and ran back to the melee, leaping atop one man and bearing him down, her fingernails raking his face.

Morik studied the woman more intently, marking well her features and thinking that her feisty spirit might prove quite enjoyable in some future private engagement.

Seeing movement from his right, Morik moved fast to slide his chair back and lift both his mug and bottle as two men came sailing across his table, smashing it and taking away the pieces with their brawl.

Morik merely shrugged, crossed his legs, leaned against the wall, and took another sip.

* * * * *

Wulfgar found a temporary reprieve after dropping the chain-fisted man, but another quickly took his place, pressing in harder, hanging on Wulfgar's side. He finally gave up trying to wrestle away the powerful barbarian's arm. Instead he latched onto Wulfgar's face with two clawing hands and tried to pull the barbarian's head toward him, biting at his ear.

Yelping with pain, roaring with outrage, Wulfgar yanked hard on the man's hair, jerking his head and a small piece of Wulfgar's ear away. Wulfgar brought his right hand under the man's left arm, rolled it over and out, twisting the arm until breaking the hold on Wulfgar's shirt. He grabbed hard to the inside of the man's biceps. A twist turned Wulfgar square to the bar, and he drove both his arms down toward it hard, slamming the man's head against the wood so forcefully that the planking cracked. Wulfgar pulled the man back up. Hardly noticing that all struggling had abruptly ceased, Wulfgar slammed him facedown into the wood again. With a great shrug followed by a greater roar, Wulfgar sent the unconscious thug flying away. He spun about, preparing for the next round of attacks.

Wulfgar's blood-streaked eyes focused briefly. He couldn't believe the tumult. It seemed as if all the world had gone mad. Tables and bodies flew. Practically everyone in the place, near to a hundred patrons this night, was into the brawl. Across the way Wulfgar spotted Morik where he sat quietly leaning against the far wall, shifting his legs now and then to avoid whatever flew past them. Morik noticed him and lifted his glass cordially.

Wulfgar ducked and braced. A man, chopping a heavy board down at Wulfgar's head, went rolling over the barbarian's back.

Wulfgar spotted Delly then, rushing across the room, ducking for cover where she could and calling out for him. She was halfway across the inn from him when a flying chair cracked across the side of her head, dropping her straight down.

Wulfgar started for her, but another man came at the distracted barbarian hard and low, crunching him across the knees. The barbarian fought to hold his balance, staggered once, then another man leaped onto his back. The man below him grabbed an ankle in a two-armed hug and rolled around, twisting Wulfgar's leg. A third man rammed him full speed, and over they all went, falling down in a jumble of flailing arms and kicking legs.

Wulfgar rolled atop the last attacker, slamming his forearm down across the man's face and using that as leverage to try to rise, but a heavy boot stomped on his back. He went down hard, his breath blasted away. The unseen attacker above him tried to stomp him again, but Wulfgar kept the presence of mind to roll aside, and the attacker wound up stepping on his own comrade's exposed belly.

The abrupt shift only reminded Wulfgar that he still had a man hanging tough onto his ankle. The barbarian kicked at him with his free leg, but he had no leverage, lying on his back as he was, and so he went into a jerking, thrashing frenzy, trying desperately to pull free.

The man held on stubbornly, mostly because he was too scared to let go. Wulfgar took a different tact, drawing his leg up and taking the man along for the slide, then kicking straight out again, bringing his trapped foot somewhat below his opponent's grasp. At the same time, the barbarian snapped his other leg around the back of the man and managed to hook his ankles together.

A second thug jumped atop the barbarian, grabbing one arm and bringing it down under his weight while a third did likewise to the other arm. Wulfgar fought them savagely, twisting his arms. When that didn't work, he simply growled and pushed straight up, locking his arms in right angles at the elbows and drawing them up and together above his massive chest. At the same time, Wulfgar squeezed with his powerful legs. The man fought frantically against the vice and tried to cry out, but the only sound that came from him was the loud snap as his shoulder popped out of its socket.

Feeling the struggling ended down below, Wulfgar wriggled his legs free and kicked and kicked until the groaning man rolled away. The barbarian turned his attention to the two above who were punching and scratching him. With strength that mocked mortal men, Wulfgar extended his arms, lifting both the ruffians up to arms' length, then pulling them up above his head suddenly, at the same time rolling his legs up with a jerk. The momentum sent Wulfgar right over backward, and he managed to push off with his hands as he came around, landing unsteadily on his feet, facing the two prone and scrambling men.

Instinct alone spun the barbarian around to meet the latest charge, his fist flying. He caught the attacker, the chain-fisted man, square in the chest. It was a tremendous collision, but Wulfgar hadn't turned fast enough to get any defense in place against the man's flying fist, which hit him square in the face at the same time. The two shuddered to a stop, and the chain-fisted man fell over into Wulfgar's arms. The barbarian brushed him aside to land heavily, facedown, far, far from consciousness.

The blow had hurt Wulfgar badly, he knew, for his vision spun and blurred, and he had to keep reminding himself where he was. He got an arm up suddenly, but only partially deflected a flying chair, one leg spinning about to poke him hard in the forehead, which only heightened his dizziness. The fight around him was slowing now, for more men were down and groaning than still standing and punching, but Wulfgar needed another reprieve, a temporary one at least. He took the only route apparent to him, rushing to the bar and rolling over it, landing on his feet behind the barricade.

He landed face-to-face with Arumn Gardpeck. "Oh, but ye've done a wonderful thing this night, now haven't ye?" Arumn spat at him. "A fight every night for Wulfgar, or it's not a fun one."

Wulfgar grabbed the man by the front of his tunic. He pulled him up roughly from his crouch behind the bar, lifted him with ease, and slammed him hard against the back wall above the bottle shelving, destroying more than a bit of expensive stock in the process.

"Be glad your face is not at the end of my fist," the unrepentant barbarian growled.

"Or more, be glad ye've not toyed with me own emotions the way ye've burned poor Delly," Arumn growled right back.

His words hurt Wulfgar profoundly, for he had no answers to Arumn's accusation, could not rightly argue that he had no blame where Delly Curtie was involved. Wulfgar gave Arumn a little jerk, then set him down and took a step back, glaring at the tavernkeeper unblinkingly. He noticed a movement to the side, and he glanced over to see a huge, disembodied fist hovering in the air above the bar.

Wulfgar was hit on the side of the head, harder than he ever remembered being struck. He reeled, grabbing another shelf of potent whisky and pulling it down, then staggered and spun, grabbing the bar for support.

Across from him, Josi Puddles spat in his face. Before Wulfgar could respond, he noted the magical floating hand coming at him hard from the side. He was hit again, and his legs went weak. He was hit yet again, lifted right from his feet and slammed hard into the back wall. All the world was spinning, and he felt as if he were sinking into the floor.

He was half-carried, half-dragged, out from behind the bar and across the floor, all the fighting coming to an abrupt end at the sight of mighty Wulfgar finally defeated.

"Finish it outside," Reef said, kicking open the door. Even as the man turned for the street, he found a dagger point at his throat.

"It's already finished," Morik casually explained, though he betrayed his calm by glancing back inside toward the thin wizard who was packing up his things, apparently unconcerned by any of this. Reef had hired him as a bit of insurance. Since the wizard apparently held no personal stake in the brawl, the rogue calmed a bit and muttered under his breath, "I hate wizards." He turned his attention back to Reef and dug the knife in a bit more.

Reef looked to his companion, holding Wulfgar's other arm, and together they unceremoniously threw the barbarian into the mud.

Wulfgar climbed back to his feet, sheer willpower alone forcing him back into a state of readiness. He turned back toward the closed door, but Morik was there, grabbing his arm.

"Don't," the rogue commanded. "They don't want you in there. What will you prove?"

Wulfgar started to argue, but he looked Morik in the eye and saw no room for debate. He knew the rogue was right. He knew that he had no home.

Chapter 4
A Lady's Life

"Ganderlay," Temigast announced as he entered the room to join Priscilla and Feringal. Both looked at the steward curiously, not understanding. "The woman you saw, my Lord Feringal," Temigast explained. "Her family name is Ganderlay."

"I know of no Ganderlays in Auckney," Priscilla argued.

"There are few families in the village whose names are familiar to you, my dear lady," Temigast replied, his tone somewhat dry, "but this woman is indeed a Ganderlay. She lives with her family on the south slope of Maerlon Mountain," he explained, referring to a fairly populated region of Auckney some two miles from the castle on a step-carved mountainside facing the harbor.

"Girl," Priscilla corrected condescendingly. "She's nowhere near to being a woman."

Feringal didn't even seem to hear the comment, too excited by the steward's news. "Are you certain?" he asked Temigast, jumping up and striding determinedly to stand right before the man. "Can it be?"

"The gir—the woman, was walking the road at the same time your coach rolled through," the steward confirmed. "She matches the description given by several people who know her and saw her on the road at the time. They all mentioned her striking long, black hair, which matches your own description of her, my lord. I am certain she is the eldest daughter of one Dohni Ganderlay."

"I'll go to her," Feringal announced, pacing back and forth eagerly, tapping one finger to his teeth, then turning fast, and then again, as if he didn't know where to go or what to do. "I will call the coach."

"My Lord Feringal," Temigast said quietly in a commanding tone that seemed to steady the eager young man. "That would be most inappropriate."

Feringal stared at him wide-eyed. "But why?"

"Because she is a peasant and not worthy of . . ." Priscilla began, but her voice trailed off for it was obvious that no one was listening to her.

"One does not go unannounced to the house of a proper lady," Temigast explained. "The way must be prepared by your steward and her father."

"But I am the lord of Auckney," Feringal protested. "I can—"

"You can do as you like if you desire her as a plaything," Temigast was quick to interrupt, drawing a frown from both Feringal and Priscilla, "but if you desire her as a wife proper, then arrange things properly. There is a way, my Lord Feringal, a manner in which we are all expected to act. To go against the etiquette in this matter could prove most disastrous, I assure you."

"I don't understand."

"Of course you don't," Temigast said, "but I do, fortunately for us all. Now go and bathe. If the young Ganderlay doe stood downwind of you she would run away." With that he turned Lord Feringal toward the door and gave him a solid push to start him on his way.

"You have betrayed me!" Priscilla wailed when her brother was gone.

Temigast snorted at the ridiculous assertion.

"I'll not have her in this house," the woman said determinedly.

"Have you not come to realize that there's nothing short of murder you can do to stop it?" Temigast replied in all seriousness. "The murder of your brother, I mean, not of the girl, for that would only invite Feringal's wrath upon you."

"But you have aided him in this foolish pursuit."

"I have provided only what he could have learned on his own by asking questions of any peasant, including three women who work in this very house, one of whom was on the road yesterday."

"If the fool even noticed them," Priscilla argued.

"He would have discovered the girl's name," insisted Temigast, "and he might have embarrassed us all in the process of his undignified hunt." The steward chuckled and moved very close to Priscilla, draping one arm across her shoulders. "I understand your concerns, dear Priscilla," he said, "and I don't entirely disagree with you. I, too, would have preferred your brother to fall in love with some wealthy merchant girl from another place, rather than with a peasant of Auckney—or for him to forget the concept of love altogether and merely give in to his lust when and where it suited him without taking a wife. Perhaps it will yet come to that."

"Less likely, now that you have so aided him," Priscilla said sharply.

"Not so," Temigast explained with a wide smile, one that caught Priscilla's attention, for her expression changed to intrigue. "All I have done is heightened your brother's trust in me and my judgments. Perhaps he will hold fast to his notion of loving this girl, of marrying her, but I will watch him every step, I promise. I'll not allow him to bring shame to family Auck, nor will I allow the girl and her family to take from us what they do not deserve. We cannot defeat his will in this, I assure you, and your indignation will only strengthen Feringal's resolve."

Priscilla snorted doubtfully.

"Can't you hear his anger when you berate him about this?" Temigast demanded, and she winced at his words. "If we distance ourselves from your brother now, I warn you, the Ganderlay girl's hold over him—over Auckney—will only heighten."

Priscilla didn't snort, didn't shake her head, didn't show any sign of disagreement. She just stared at Temigast long and hard. He kissed her on the cheek and moved away, thinking that he should summon the castle coach at once and be on with his duties as emissary of Lord Feringal.

*　*　*　*　*

Jaka Sculi looked up from the field of mud along with all the other workers, human and gnome, as the decorated coach made its way along the dirt lane. It came to a stop in front of Dohni Ganderlay's small house. An old man climbed out of the carriage door and ambled toward the house. Jaka's eyes narrowed slightly. Remembering suddenly that others might be watching him, he resumed his typically distant air. He was Jaka Sculi, after all, the fantasy lover of every young lady in Auckney, especially the woman who lived in the house where the lord's carriage had stopped. The notion that beautiful Meralda desired him was no small thing to the young man—though, of course, he couldn't let anyone else believe he cared.

"Dohni!" one of the other field workers, a crooked little gnome with a long and pointy nose, called. "Dohni Ganderlay, you've got guests!"

"Or mighten be they've figured you for the scoundrel you are!" another gnome cried out, and they all had a good laugh.

Except for Jaka, of course. Jaka wouldn't let them see him laugh.

Dohni Ganderlay walked over the ridge behind the peat field. He looked to those who yelled for some explanation, but they merely nodded their chins in the direction of his house. Dohni followed that movement, spotted the coach, and broke into a frantic run.

Jaka Sculi watched him run all the way home.

"You figuring to do some digging, boy?" came a question beside Jaka. When he turned to regard the toothless old man, the fool ran a hand through Jaka's curly brown hair.

The young man shook his head with disgust, noting the black peat encasing the old digger's fingers. He shook his head again and brushed his hair robustly, then slapped the man's hand away when it reached up to give another rub.

"Hee hee hee," the old man giggled. "Seems your little girlie's got a caller," he snickered.

"And an old one at that," remarked another, also more than willing to join in the play at Jaka's expense.

"But I'm thinking I might give the girl a try meself," the dirty old duffer at Jaka's side remarked. That drew a frown from Jaka, and so the old man only laughed all the harder at finally evoking some response from the boy.

Jaka turned his head slowly about, surveying the field and the workers, the few houses scattered on the mountainside, Castle Auck far in the distance, and the dark, cold waters beyond that. Those waters had brought him, his mother, and his uncle to this forlorn place only four years before. Jaka didn't know why they had come to Auckney—he had been quite content with his life in Luskan—except that it had something to do with his father, who used to beat his mother mercilessly. He suspected that they were running, either from the man or from the executioner. It seemed to be a typical tactic for the Sculi family, for they had done the same thing when Jaka was a toddler, fleeing from their ancestral home in the Blade Kingdoms all the way to Luskan. Certainly his father, a vicious man whom Jaka hardly knew, would search them out and kill his mother and her brother for running away. Or perhaps Jaka's father was already dead, left in his own blood by Rempini, Jaka's uncle.

Either way, it didn't matter to Jaka. All that he knew was that he was in this place, a dreadful, windy, cold, and barren fiefdom. Until recently, the only good thing about it all, in his view, was that the perpetual melancholy of the place enhanced his poetic nature. Even though he fancied himself quite the romantic hero, Jaka had passed his seventeenth birthday now, and had many times considered tagging along with one of the few merchants who happened through, going out into the wide world, back to Luskan perhaps, or even better, all the way to mighty Waterdeep. He planned to make his fortune there someday, somehow, and perhaps get all the way back to the Blade Kingdoms.

But those plans had been put on hold, for yet another positive aspect of Auckney had revealed itself to the young man. Jaka could not deny the attraction he felt to a certain young Ganderlay girl.

Of course, he couldn't let her or anyone else know that, not until he was certain that she would give herself over to him fully.

* * * * *

Hurrying past the coach, Dohni Ganderlay recognized the driver, a gray-bearded gnome he knew as Liam Woodgate. Liam smiled and nodded at him, which relaxed Dohni considerably, though he still kept his swift pace through the door. At his small kitchen table sat the steward of Castle Auck. Across from him was Dohni's ill wife, Biaste, whose beaming expression the peat farmer hadn't seen in a long, long time.

"Master Ganderlay," Temigast said politely. "I am Temigast, steward of Castle Auck, emissary of Lord Feringal."

"I know that," Dohni said warily. Never taking his eyes from the old man, Dohni Ganderlay made his way around the table, avoiding one of the two remaining chairs to stand behind his wife, dropping his hands on her shoulders.

"I was just explaining to your wife that my lord, and yours, requests the presence of your eldest daughter at the castle for dinner this evening," the steward said.

The startling news hit Dohni Ganderlay as solidly as any club ever could, but he held his balance and his expression, letting it sink in. He looked behind the words into Temigast's old, gray eyes.

"Of course, I have suitable clothing for Miss Meralda in the coach, should you agree," Temigast finished with a comforting smile.

Proud Dohni Ganderlay saw behind that smiling facade, behind the polite and respectful tone. He saw the condescension there and recognized the confidence within Temigast. Of course they could not refuse, Temigast believed, for they were but dirty peasants. The lord of Auckney had come a'calling, and the Ganderlays would welcome that call eagerly, hungrily.

"Where is Meralda?" the man asked his wife.

"She and Tori've gone to trading," the woman explained. Dohni couldn't ignore the weak trembling in her voice. "To get a few eggs for supper."

"Meralda can eat at a banquet this night, and perhaps for many nights," Temigast remarked.

Dohni saw it so clearly again, the wretched condescension that reminded him of his lot in life, of the fate of his children, all his friends, and their children as well.

"Then she will come?" Temigast prompted after a long and uncomfortable silence.

"That'll be Meralda's to choose," Dohni Ganderlay replied more sharply than he had intended.

"Ah," said the steward, nodding and smiling, always smiling. He rose from his chair and motioned for Biaste to remain seated. "Of course, of course, but do come and retrieve the gown, Master Ganderlay. Should you decide to send the young lady, it will be better and easier if she had it here."

337

"And if she doesn't want to go?"

Temigast arched a brow, suggesting he thought the notion that she might refuse absurd. "Then I will have my coachman return tomorrow to retrieve the gown, of course," he said.

Dohni looked down at his ill wife, at the plaintive expression on her too-delicate features.

"Master Ganderlay?" Temigast asked, motioning for the door. Dohni patted Biaste on the shoulders and walked beside the steward out to the coach. The gnome driver was waiting for them, gown in hand, and his arms uplifted to keep the delicate fabric from dragging in the dusty road.

"You would do well to urge your daughter to attend," Temigast advised, handing over the gown, which only made Dohni Ganderlay steel his features all the more.

"Your wife is sick," Temigast reasoned. "No doubt a meager existence in a drafty house will not do her well with the cold winter approaching."

"You speak as if we've a choice in the matter," Dohni replied.

"Lord Feringal is a man of great means," Temigast explained. "He has easy access to amazing herbs, warm beds, and powerful clerics. It would be a pity for your wife to suffer needlessly." The steward patted the gown. "We shall dine just after sundown," he explained. "I will have the coach pass by your home at dusk." With that, Temigast stepped into the coach and closed the door. The driver wasted no time in putting whip to horses to speed them away.

Dohni Ganderlay stood for a long while in the cloud of dust left by the departing coach, gown in hand, staring at the empty air before him. He wanted to scream out that if Lord Feringal was such a connected and beneficent lord, then he should willingly use his means for the welfare of his flock. People like Biaste Ganderlay should be able to get the aid they needed without selling their daughters. What Temigast had just offered him was akin to selling his daughter for the benefit of the family. Selling his daughter!

And yet, for all his pride, Dohni Ganderlay could not deny the opportunity that lay before him.

* * * * *

"It was the lord's coach," Jaka Sculi insisted to Meralda when he intercepted her on her way home later that same day. "At your own front door," he added with his exotic accent, a dialect thick with sighs and dramatic huffs.

Tori Ganderlay giggled. Meralda punched her in the shoulder and motioned for her to be on her way. "But I want to know," she whined.

"You'll be knowing the taste of dirt," Meralda promised her. She started for her sister but stopped abruptly and composed herself, remembering her audience. Meralda turned back to Jaka after painting a sweet smile on her face, still managing to glare at Tori out of the corner of her eye.

Tori started skipping down the road. "But I wanted to see you kiss him," she squealed happily as she ran on.

"Are you sure about the coach?" Meralda asked Jaka, trying very hard to leave Tori's embarrassing remarks behind.

The young man merely sighed with dramatic exasperation.

"But what business has Lord Feringal with my folks?" the young woman asked.

Jaka hung his head to the side, hands in pockets, and shrugged.

"Well, I should be going, then," Meralda said, and she took a step, but Jaka shifted to block her way. "What're you about?"

Jaka looked at her with those light blue eyes, running a hand through his mop of curly hair, his face tilted up at her.

Meralda felt as if she would choke for the lump that welled in her throat, or that her heart would beat so forcefully that it would pound right out of her chest.

"What're you about?" she asked again, much more quietly and without any real conviction.

Jaka moved toward her. She remembered her own advice to Tori, about how one had to make a boy beg. She reminded herself that she should not be doing this, not yet. She told herself that pointedly, and yet she was not retreating at all. He came closer, and as she felt the heat of his breath she, too, moved forward. Jaka just let his lips brush hers, then backed away, appearing suddenly shy.

"What?" Meralda asked again, this time with obvious eagerness.

Jaka sighed, and the woman came forward again, moving to kiss him, her whole body trembling, telling, begging him to kiss her back. He did, long and soft, then he moved away.

"I'll be waiting for you after supper," he said, and he turned with a shrug and started slowly away.

Meralda could hardly catch her breath, for that kiss had been everything she had dreamed it would be and more. She felt warm in her belly and weak in her knees and tingly all over. Never mind that Jaka, with one simple hesitation, had done to her exactly what she had told Tori a woman must do to a man. Meralda couldn't even think of that at the time, too entranced was she by the reality of what had just happened and by the promise of what might happen next.

She took the same path down the road Tori had taken, and her skipping was no less full of the girlish joy, as if Jaka's kiss had freed her of the bonds of temperance and dignity that came with being a woman.

Meralda entered her house all smiles. Her eyes widened when she saw her sick mother standing by the table, as happy as she had seen the woman in weeks. Biaste held a beautiful gown, rich emerald green with glittering gems sewn into its seams.

"Oh, but you'll be the prettiest Auckney's ever seen when you put this on," Biaste Ganderlay said, and beside her, Tori exploded in giggles.

Meralda stared at the gown wide-eyed, then turned to regard her father who was standing at the side of the room, smiling as well. Meralda recognized that his expression was somewhat more strained than Biaste's.

"But Ma, we've not the money," Meralda reasoned, though she was truly enchanted by the gown. She moved up to stroke the soft material, thinking how much Jaka would love to see her in it.

"A gift, and nothing to buy," Biaste explained, and Tori giggled all the more.

Meralda's expression turned to one of curiosity, and she looked to her father again for some explanation, but, surprisingly, he turned away.

"What's it about, Ma?" the young woman asked.

"You've a suitor, my girl," Biaste said happily, pulling the gown out so that she could hug her daughter. "Oh, but you've got a lord hisself wanting to court you!"

Always considerate of her mother's feelings, especially now that the woman was ill, Meralda was glad that Biaste's head was on Meralda's shoulder, so her mother couldn't see the stunned and unhappy expression that crossed her daughter's face. Tori did see it, but the girl only looked up at Meralda and pursed her lips repeatedly in a mockery of a kiss. Meralda looked to her father, who now faced her but only nodded solemnly.

Biaste pulled her back to arms' length. "Oh, my little girl," she said. "When did you get so beautiful? To think that you've caught the heart of Lord Feringal."

Lord Feringal. Meralda could hardly catch her breath, and not for any joy. She hardly knew the lord of Castle Auck, though she had seen him on many occasions from afar, usually picking his fingernails and looking bored at the celebratory gatherings held in the town square.

"He's sweet on you, girl," Biaste went on, "and in it thick, by the words of his steward."

Meralda managed a smile for her mother's sake.

"They'll be coming for you soon," Biaste explained. "So be quick to get a bath. Then," she added, pausing to bring one hand up to her mouth, "then we'll put you in this gown, and oh, how all the men who see you will fall before your feet."

Meralda moved methodically, taking the gown and turning for her room with Tori on her heels. It all seemed a dream to the young woman, and not a pleasant one. Her father walked past her to her mother. She heard them strike up a conversation, though the words seemed all garbled to her, and the only thing she truly heard was Biaste's exclamation, "A lord for my girl!"

* * * * *

Auckney was not a large place, and though its houses weren't cluttered together, the folk were certainly within shouting distance of each other. It didn't take long for word of the arrangement between Lord Feringal and Meralda Ganderlay to spread.

Jaka Sculi learned the truth about the visit of Lord Feringal's steward before he finished eating that same evening, before the sun touched the western horizon.

"To think one of his station will dip low enough to touch the likes of a peasant," Jaka's ever-pessimistic mother remarked, her voice still thick with the heavy peasant accent of their long-lost homeland in the Blade Kingdoms. "Ah, to the ruin of all the world!"

"Evil tiding," Jaka's uncle agreed, a grizzled old man who appeared to have seen too much of the world.

Jaka, too, thought this a terrible turn of events, but for a very different reason—at least he thought his anger had come from a different source, for he wasn't certain of the reason his mother and uncle were so upset by the news, and his expression clearly revealed that confusion.

"We've each our station," his uncle explained. "Clear lines, and not ones to be crossed."

"Lord Feringal brings dishonor to his family," said his mother.

"Meralda is a wonderful woman," Jaka argued before he could catch and hold the words secret.

"She's a peasant, as we all be," his mother was quick to explain. "We've our place, and Lord Feringal's got his. Oh, them folk will rejoice at the news, do not doubt, thinking to draw some of their own hope at Meralda's good fortunes, but they're not knowing the truth of it."

"What truth?"

"He'll use her to no good ends," foretold his mother. "He'll make himself the fool and the girl a tramp."

"And in the end, she'll be broken or dead, and Lord Feringal will have lost all favor with his peers," added his uncle. "Evil tiding."

"Why do you believe that she will succumb?" the young man asked, working hard to keep the desperation out of his tone.

His mother and uncle merely laughed at that question. Jaka understood their meaning all too clearly. Feringal was the lord of Auckney. How could Meralda refuse him?

It was more than poor, sensitive Jaka could take. He banged the table hard with his fist and slid his chair back. Rising fast to his feet, he matched the surprised stares of his mother and uncle with a glower of utter rage. With that Jaka turned on his heel and rushed out, slamming the door behind him.

Before he knew it he was running, his thoughts whirling. Jaka soon came to high ground, a small tumble of rocks just above the muddy field he had been working earlier that same day, a place affording him a splendid view of the sunset, as well as Meralda's house. In the distant south-

341

west he saw the castle, and he pictured the magnificent coach making its deliberate way up the road to it with Meralda inside.

Jaka felt as if a heavy weight were pressing on his chest, as if all the limitations of his miserable existence had suddenly become tangible walls, closing, closing. For the last few years Jaka had gone to great lengths to acquire just the correct persona, the correct pose and the correct attitude, to turn the heart of any young lady. Now here came this foolish nobleman, this prettily painted and perfumed fop with no claim to reputation other than the station to which he had been born, to take all that Jaka had cultivated right out from under him.

Jaka, of course, didn't see things with quite that measure of clarity. To him it seemed a plain enough truth: a grave injustice played against him simply because of the station, or lack thereof, of his birth. Because these pitiful peasants of Auckney didn't know the truth of him, the greatness that lay within him hidden by the dirt of farm fields and peat bogs.

The distraught young man ran his hands through his brown locks and heaved a great sigh.

* * * * *

"You best get it all cleaned, because you're not knowing what Lord Feringal will be seeing," Tori teased, and she ran a rough cloth across Meralda's back as her sister sat like a cat curled up in the steaming hot bath.

Meralda turned at the words and splashed water in Tori's face. The younger girl's giggles halted abruptly when she noted the grim expression on Meralda's face.

"I'm knowing what Lord Feringal will be seeing, all right," Meralda assured her sister. "If he's wanting his dress back, he'll have to be coming back to the house to get it."

"You'd refuse him?"

"I won't even kiss him," Meralda insisted, and she lifted a dripping fist into the air. "If he tries to kiss me, I'll—"

"You'll play the part of a lady," came the voice of her father. Both girls looked to the curtain to see the man enter the room. "Leave," he instructed Tori. The girl knew that tone well enough to obey without question.

Dohni Ganderlay stayed at the door a moment longer to make sure that too-curious Tori had, indeed, scooted far away, then he moved to the side of the tub and handed Meralda a soft cloth to dry herself. They lived in a small house where modesty was pointless, so Meralda was not the least bit embarrassed as she stepped from her bath, though she draped the cloth about her before she sat on a nearby stool.

"You're not happy about the turn of events," Dohni observed.

Meralda's lips grew thin, and she leaned over to splash a nervous hand in the cold bath water.

"You don't like Lord Feringal?"

"I don't know him," the young woman retorted, "and he's not knowing me. Not at all!"

"But he's wanting to," Dohni argued. "You should take that as the highest compliment."

"And taking a compliment means giving in to the one complimenting?" Meralda asked with biting sarcasm. "I've no choice in the matter? Lord Feringal's wanting you, so off you go?"

Her nervous splashing of water turned angry, and she accidently sent a small wave washing over Dohni Ganderlay. The young woman understood that it was not the wetness, but the attitude, that provoked his unexpectedly violent reaction. He caught her wrist in his strong hand and tugged it back, turning Meralda toward him.

"No," he answered bluntly. "You've no choice. Feringal is the lord of Auckney, a man of great means, a man who can lift us from the dirt."

"Maybe I'd rather be dirty," Meralda started to say, but Dohni Ganderlay cut her short.

"A man who can heal your mother."

He could not have stunned her more with the effect of those seven words than if he had curled his great fist into a tight ball and punched Meralda hard in the face. She stared at her father incredulously, at the desperate, almost wild, expression on his normally stoic face, and she was afraid, truly afraid.

"You've no choice," he said again, his voice a forced monotone. "Your ma's got the wilting and won't likely see the next turn of spring. You'll go to Lord Feringal and play the part of a lady. You'll laugh at his wit, and you'll praise his greatness. This you'll do for your ma," he finished simply, his voice full of defeat. As he turned away and rose Meralda caught a glint of moisture rimming his eye, and she understood.

Knowing how truly horrible this was for her father did help the young woman prepare for the night, helped greatly to cope with this seemingly cruel twist that fate had thrown before her.

* * * * *

The sun was down, and the sky was turning dark blue. The coach passed below him on the way to Meralda's meager house. She stepped from the door, and even from this great distance Jaka could see how beautiful she appeared, like some shining jewel that mocked the darkness of twilight.

His jewel. The just reward for the beauty that was within him, not a bought present for the spoiled lord of Auckney.

He pictured Lord Feringal holding his hand out of the coach, touching her and fondling her as she stepped inside to join him. The image made him want to scream out at the injustice of it all. The coach rolled back

343

down the road toward the distant castle with Meralda inside, just as he had envisioned earlier. Jaka could not have felt more robbed if Lord Feringal had reached into his pockets and taken his last coin.

He sat wallowing on the peat-dusted hill for a long, long while, running his hands through his hair repeatedly and cursing the inequities of this miserable life. So self-involved was he that he was taken completely by surprise by the sudden sound of a young girl's voice.

"I knew you'd be about."

Jaka opened his dreamy, moist eyes to see Tori Ganderlay staring at him.

"I knew it," the girl teased.

"What do you know?"

"You heard about my sister's dinner and had to see for yourself," Tori reasoned. "And you're still waiting and watching."

"Your sister?" Jaka repeated dumbly. "I come here every night," he explained.

Tori turned from him to gaze down at the houses, at her own house, the firelight shining bright through the window. "Hoping to see Meralda naked through the window?" she asked with a giggle.

"I come out alone in the dark to get away from the fires and the light," Jaka replied firmly. "To get away from pestering people who cannot understand."

"Understand what?"

"The truth," the young man answered cryptically, hoping he sounded profound.

"The truth of what?"

"The truth of life," Jaka replied.

Tori looked at him long and hard, her face twisting as she tried to decipher his words. She looked back to her house. "Bah, I'm thinking you're just wanting to see Meralda naked," she said again, then skipped happily back down the path.

Wouldn't she have fun with Meralda at his expense, Jaka thought. He heaved another of his great sighs, then turned and walked away to the even darker fields higher up the mountainside.

"Fie this life!" he cried out, lifting his arms to the rising full moon. "Fie, fie, and fly from me now, trappings mortal! What cruel fate to live and to see the undeserving gather the spoils from me. When justice lies in spiked pit. When worth's measure is heredity. Oh, Lord Feringal feeds at Meralda's neck. Fie this life, and fly from me!"

He ended his impromptu verse by falling to his knees and clutching at his teary face, and there he wallowed for a long, long while.

Anger replaced self-pity, and Jaka came up with a new line to finish his verse. "When justice lies in spiked pit," he recited, his voice quivering with rage. "When worth's measure is heredity." Now a smile crept onto his undeniably handsome features. "Wretched Feringal feeds at Meralda's neck, but he'll not have her virginity!"

Jaka climbed unsteadily to his feet and looked up again at the full moon. "I swear to it," he said with a growl, then muttered dramatically, "Fie this life," one last time and started for home.

* * * * *

Meralda took the evening in stoic stride, answering questions politely and taking care to avoid the direct gaze of an obviously unhappy Lady Priscilla Auck. She found that she liked Steward Temigast quite a bit, mostly because the old man kept the conversation moving by telling many entertaining stories of his past and of the previous lord of the castle, Feringal's father. Temigast even set up a signal system with Meralda to help her understand which piece of silverware she should use for the various courses of food.

Though she remained unimpressed with the young lord of Auckney, who sat directly opposite her and stared unceasingly, the young woman couldn't deny her wonder at the delicious feast the servants laid out before her. Did they eat like this every day in Castle Auck—squab and fish, potatoes and sea greens—delicacies Meralda had never tasted before?

At Lord Feringal's insistence, after dinner the group retired to the drawing room, a comfortable, windowless square chamber at the center of the castle's ground floor. Thick walls kept out the chill ocean wind, and a massive hearth, burning with a fire as large as a village bonfire added to the coziness of the place.

"Perhaps you would like more food," Priscilla offered, but there was nothing generous about her tone. "I can have a serving woman bring it in."

"Oh, no, my lady," Meralda replied. "I couldn't eat another morsel."

"Indeed," said Priscilla, "but you did overindulge at dinner proper, now didn't you?" she asked, a sweet and phoney smile painted on her ugly face. It occurred to Meralda that Lord Feringal was almost charming compared to his sister. Almost.

A servant entered then, bearing a tray of snifters filled with a brownish liquid Meralda didn't recognize. She took her glass, too afraid to refuse, and on Temigast's toast and motion, she raised it up and took a healthy swallow. The young woman nearly choked from the burning sensation that followed the liquid down her throat.

"We don't take such volumes of brandy here," Priscilla remarked dryly. "That is a peasant trait."

Meralda felt like crawling under the thick rug. Crinkling his nose at her, Lord Feringal didn't help much.

"More a trait for one who is not familiar with the potent drink," Temigast interjected, coming to Meralda's aid. "Tiny sips, my dear. You will learn, though you may never acquire a taste for this unique liquor. I haven't yet myself."

Meralda smiled and nodded a silent thank you to the old man, which relieved the tension again, and not for the last time. Feeling a bit light in the head, Meralda faded out of the conversation, oblivious to Priscilla's double-edged remarks and Lord Feringal's stares. Her mind drifted off, and she was beside Jaka Sculi—in a moonlit field, perhaps, or this very room. How wonderful this place would be, with its thick carpet, huge fire, and this warming drink if she had the companionship of her dear Jaka instead of the wretched Auck siblings.

Temigast's voice penetrated her fog, reminding Lord Feringal that they had promised to return the young lady by a certain hour, and that the hour was fast approaching.

"A few moments alone, then," Feringal replied.

Meralda tried not to panic.

"Hardly a proper request," Priscilla put in. She looked at Meralda and snickered. "Of course, what could possibly be the harm?"

Feringal's sister left, as did Temigast, the old steward patting Meralda comfortingly on the shoulder as he slipped past to the door.

"I trust you will act as a gentleman, my lord," he said to Feringal, "as your station demands. There are few women in all the wide world as beautiful as Lady Meralda." He gave the young woman a smile. "I will order the coach to the front door."

The old man was her ally, Meralda recognized, a very welcome ally.

"It was a wonderful meal, was it not?" Lord Feringal asked, moving quickly to take a seat on the chair beside Meralda's.

"Oh, yes, my lord," she replied, lowering her gaze.

"No, no," Feringal scolded. "You must call me Lord Feringal, not 'my lord.'"

"Yes, my—Lord Feringal." Meralda tried to keep her gaze averted, but the man was too close, too imposing. She looked up at him, and to his credit, he did take his stare from her breasts and looked into her eyes.

"I saw you on the road," he explained. "I had to know you. I had to see you again. Never has there been any woman as beautiful."

"Oh, my—Lord Feringal," she said, and she did look away again, for he was moving even closer, far too close, by Meralda's estimate.

"I had to see you," he said again, his voice barely a whisper, but he was close enough that Meralda heard it clearly and felt his breath hot on her ear.

Meralda fought hard to swallow her panic as the back of Feringal's hand brushed gently down her cheek. He cupped her chin then and turned her head to face him. He kissed her softly at first, then, despite the fact that she was hardly returning the kiss, more urgently, even rising out of his chair to lean into her. As he pressed and kissed, Meralda thought of Jaka and of her sick mother and tolerated it, even when his hand covered the soft fabric over her breast.

"Your pardon, Lord Feringal," came Temigast's voice from the door. Flushing, the young man broke away and stood up to face the steward.

"The coach is waiting," Temigast explained. "It is time for Lady Meralda to return to her home." Meralda nearly ran from the room.

"I will call for you again," Lord Feringal said after her. "And soon, to be sure."

By the time the coach had moved over the bridge that separated Castle Auck from the mainland, Meralda had managed to slow her heartbeat somewhat. She understood her duty to her family, to her sick mother, but she felt as if she would faint, or vomit. Wouldn't the wretch Priscilla have a grand time with that, if she found that the peasant had thrown up in the gilded coach.

A mile later, still feeling sick and aching to be out of all these trappings, Meralda leaned out the coach's window.

"Stop! Oh, please stop!" she yelled to the driver. The carriage shuddered to a halt, but even before it had completely stopped the young woman threw open the door and scrambled out.

"My lady, I am to take you to your home," Liam Woodgate said, leaping down to Meralda's side.

"And so you have," the woman replied. "Close enough."

"But you've a long dark lane before you," the gnome protested. "Steward Temigast'll have my heart in his hand if—"

"He'll never know," Meralda promised. "Don't fear for me. I walk this lane every night and know every bush and rock and person in every house between here and my own."

"But . . ." the gnome began to argue, but Meralda pushed past him, shot him a confident smile, and skipped away into the darkness.

The coach shadowed her for a short while, then, apparently convinced the woman was indeed familiar enough with this area to be safe, Liam turned it around and sped away.

The night was chill, but not too cold. Meralda veered from the road, moving to the dark fields higher up. She hoped to find Jaka there, waiting for her as they had arranged, but the place was empty. Alone in the dark, Meralda felt as if she were the only person in all the world. Anxious to forget tonight, to forget Lord Feringal and his wretched sister, she stripped off her gown, needing to be out of the fancy thing. Tonight she had dined as nobility, and other than the food and perhaps the warm drink, she had not been impressed. Not in the least.

Wearing only her plain undergarments, the young woman moved about the moonlit field, walking at first, but as thoughts of Jaka Sculi erased the too recent image of Lord Feringal, her step lightened to a skip, then a dance. Meralda reached up to catch a shooting star, spinning to follow its tail, then falling to her rump in the soft grass and mud, laughing all the while and thinking of Jaka.

She didn't know that she was in almost exactly the same spot where Jaka had been earlier that night. The place where Jaka had spat his protests at an unhearing god, where he'd cried out against the injustice of

347

it all, where he'd called for his life to flee, and where he'd vowed to steal Meralda's virginity for no better reason than to ensure that Lord Feringal did not get it.

Chapter 5

Inside a Tight Frame

"Where'd you put the durned thing?" a frustrated Arumn Gardpeck asked Josi Puddles the next afternoon. "I know ye took it, so don't be lying to me."

"Be glad that I took it," an unrepentant Josi countered, wagging his finger in Arumn's face. "Wulfgar would've torn the whole place apart to kindling with that warhammer in his hands."

"Bah, you're a fool, Josi Puddles," Arumn replied. "He'd a left without a fight."

"So ye're saying," Josi retorted. "Ye're always saying such, always taking up the man's cause, though he's been naught but trouble to yerself and to all who been loyal to ye. What good's Wulfgar done for ye, Arumn Gardpeck? What good ever?"

Arumn narrowed his eyes and stared hard at the man.

"And every fight he stopped was one he started," Josi added. "Bah, he's gone, and good enough for him, and good enough for all of us."

"Where'd ye put the warhammer?" Arumn pressed again.

Josi threw up his hands and spun away, but Arumn wouldn't let him go that easily. He grabbed the little man by the shoulder and whipped him about violently. "I asked ye twice already," he said grimly. "Don't ye make me ask again."

349

"It's gone," Josi replied. "Just gone, and far enough so that Wulfgar couldn't call to the thing."

"Gone?" Arumn echoed. His expression grew sly, for he understood Josi better than to think the man had simply thrown so wondrous a weapon into the ocean. "And how much did ye get for it?"

Josi stuttered a protest, waved his hand and stammered again, which only confirmed Arumn's suspicions. "Ye go get it back, Josi Puddles," the tavernkeeper instructed.

Josi's eyes widened. "Cannot—" he started to say, but Arumn grabbed him by the shoulder and the seat of his pants and ushered him along toward the door.

"Go get it back," Arumn said again, no room for debate in his stern tone, "and don't come back to me until ye got the hammer in hand."

"But I cannot," Josi protested. "Not with that crew."

"Then ye're not welcome here anymore," Arumn said, shoving Josi hard through the door and out into the street. "Not at all, Josi Puddles. Ye come back with the hammer, or ye don't come back!" He slammed the door, leaving a stunned Josi out in the street.

The skinny man's eyes darted around, as if he expected some thugs to step out and rob him. He had good cause for concern. Arumn's Cutlass was Josi's primary affiliation and, in a sense, his source of protection on the streets. Few bothered with Josi, mostly because he wasn't worth bothering with, but mainly because troubling Josi would shut down all routes to the Cutlass, a favorite place.

Josi had made more than few enemies on the street, and once word spread that he and Arumn had fallen out. . . .

He had to get back in Arumn's favor, but when he considered the necessary task before him, his knees went weak. He had sold Aegis-fang cheaply to a nasty pirate in a wretched drinking hole, a place he visited as rarely as possible. Josi's eyes continued to dart all around, surveying Half-Moon Street and the alleys that would take him to the private and secret drinking hole by the docks. Sheela Kree would not be there yet, he knew. She would be at her ship, *Leaping Lady*. The name referred to the image of Sheela Kree leaping from her ship to that of her unfortunate victims, bloody saber in hand. Josi shuddered at the thought of meeting her on the very deck where she was known to have tortured dozens of innocent people to horrible deaths. No, he decided, he would wait to meet with her at the drinking hole, a place a bit more public.

The little man fished through his pockets. He still had all the gold Sheela had paid him for Aegis-fang and a couple of his own coins as well.

He hardly thought it enough, but with Arumn's friendship at stake, he had to try.

* * * * *

"It's wonderful to be with ye," Delly Curtie said, running her hand over Wulfgar's huge, bare shoulder, which drew a wince from the big man. That shoulder, like every other part of his body, had not escaped the battering at the Cutlass.

Wulfgar muttered something unintelligible and rose from the bed, and while Delly's hands continued to caress him, he continued to ignore the touch.

"Are ye sure ye're wantin' to leave already?" the woman asked in a seductive manner.

Wulfgar turned to regard her, stretching languidly on the rumpled bed.

"Yeah, I'm sure," he grumbled as he pulled on his clothes and headed for the door.

Delly started to call out after him but bit back her begging. She started to scold him but bit that back, too, understanding the futility of it and knowing that her own harsh words wouldn't cover her hurt. Not this time. She had gone to Wulfgar the previous night, as soon as Arumn closed his doors, which was not long after the fight had scuttled the Cutlass. Delly knew where to find the now homeless man, for Morik kept a room nearby.

How thrilled she had been when Wulfgar had taken her in, despite Morik's protests. She had let her guard back down again, for Delly had spent the night in Wulfgar's arms, fantasizing about escaping her miserable life with the heroic man. They could run away from Luskan, perhaps, and back to wild Icewind Dale, where she might raise his children as his proper wife.

Of course, the morning—or rather, the early afternoon—had shown her the truth of those fantasies in the form of a grumbling rejection.

She lay on the bed now, feeling empty and alone, helpless and hopeless. Though things between her and Wulfgar had been hurtful of late, the mere fact that the man was still around had allowed her to hold onto her dreams. If Wulfgar wouldn't be around anymore, Delly would be without any chance of escape.

"Did you expect anything different?" came a question from Morik, as if the rogue were reading her mind.

Delly gave him a sad, sour look.

"You must know by now what to expect from that one," Morik reasoned, moving to sit on the bed. Delly started to pull the covers up but remembered that it was just Morik, and he knew well enough what she looked like.

"He will never give you that which you truly desire," Morik added. "Too many burdens clouding his mind, too many remembered agonies. If he opened up to you as you hope, he'd likely kill you by mistake."

Delly looked at him as if she didn't understand. Hardly surprised, Morik merely smiled and said again, "He'll not give you that which you truly desire."

"And will Morik then?" Delly asked with open sarcasm.

The rogue laughed at the thought. "Hardly," he admitted, "but at least I tell you that openly. Except for my word, I am no honest man and want no honest woman. My life is my own, and I don't wish to be bothered with a child or a wife."

"Sounds lonely."

"Sounds free," Morik corrected with a laugh. "Ah, Delly," he said, reaching up to run a hand through her hair. "You would find life so much more enjoyable if you basked in present joys without fearing for future ones."

Delly Curtie leaned back against the headboard, considering the words and showing no practical response against them.

Morik took that as a cue and climbed into the bed beside her.

* * * * *

"I'll give you this part, me squeaky little friend, for your offered coins," the rowdy Sheela Kree said, tapping the flat of Aegis-fang's head. She exploded into a violent movement that brought the warhammer arching over her head to smash down on the center of the table separating her from Josi Puddles.

Suddenly, Josi realized with great alarm that there was only empty air between him and the vicious pirate, for the table had collapsed to splinters across the floor.

Sheela Kree smiled wickedly and lifted Aegis-fang. With a squeak Josi sprinted for and through the door, out into the wet, salty night air. He heard the explosion behind him, the hurled hammer connecting solidly against the jamb, heard the howls of laughter from the many cutthroats within.

Josi didn't look back. In fact, by the time he stopped running he was leaning against the wall of the Cutlass, wondering how in the Nine Hells he was going to explain the situation to Arumn.

He was still gasping to regain a steady breath when he spotted Delly moving fast down the road, her shawl pulled tight around her. She would not normally be returning to the Cutlass so late, for the place was already brimming with patrons, unless she were on an errand from Arumn. Her hands were empty, except for the folds of the shawl, so Josi had little trouble figuring out where she had gone, or at least who she had gone to visit.

As she neared, the little man heard her sobs, which only confirmed that Delly had gone to see Wulfgar and that the barbarian had ripped her heart open a bit wider.

"Are ye all right?" the man asked, moving out to intercept the woman. Delly jumped in surprise, unaware that Josi had been standing there. "What pains ye?" Josi asked softly, moving closer, lifting his hands

352

to pat Delly's shoulders and thinking that he might use this moment of pain and vulnerability to his own gain, to finally bed the woman about whom he had fantasized for years.

Delly, despite her sobs and downcast expression, abruptly pulled away from him. The look she returned was not one of lust, not even of friendship.

"He hurt ye, Delly," Josi remarked quietly and comfortingly. "He hurt ye, and I can help ye feel better."

Delly scoffed openly. "Ye're the one who set it all up, aren't ye now, Josi Puddles?" she accused. "What a happy sot ye are for chasing Wulfgar away."

Before Josi could begin to answer, the woman brushed past him and disappeared into the Cutlass, a place where Josi could not follow. He stood out in the empty street, in the dark of night, with no place to go and no friends to speak of. He blamed Wulfgar for all of it.

Josi Puddles spent that night wandering the alleyways and drinking holes of the toughest parts of Luskan. He spoke not a word to anyone through the dark hours, but instead, listened carefully, always on the alert in these dangerous parts. To his surprise he heard something important and not threatening. It was an interesting story concerning Morik the Rogue and his large barbarian friend, and a hefty contract to eliminate a certain ship's captain.

Chapter 6

Altruism

"Well, Lord Dohni, I'll bow until my face blackens in the mud," one old peasant geezer said to Dohni Ganderlay in the field the next morning. All the men and gnomes who had gathered about Dohni broke into mocking laughter.

"Should I be tithing you direct now?" asked another. "A bit of this and a bit of that, the feed for the pig and the pig himself?"

"Just the back half of the pig," said the first. "You get to keep the front."

"You keep the part what eats the grain, but not the plump part that holds it for the meal," said a pointy-nosed gnome. "Don't that sound like a nobleman's thinking!"

They broke into peals of laughter again. Dohni Ganderlay tried hard, but unsuccessfully, to join in. He understood their mirth, of course. These peasants had little chance of lifting themselves up from the mud they tilled, but now, suddenly and unexpectedly, it appeared as if fortunes might have changed for the Ganderlay family, as if one of their own might climb that impossible ladder.

Dohni could have accepted their teasing, could have joined in whole-heartedly with the laughter, even adding a few witticisms of his own, except for one uncomfortable fact, one truth that nagged at him all the sleepless night and all that morning: Meralda hadn't wanted to go. If his girl had expressed some feelings, positive feelings, for Lord Feringal, then Dohni would be one of the happiest men in all the northland. He knew the truth of it, and he could not get past his own guilt. Because of it, the teasing bit hard at him that rainy morning in the muddy field, striking at raw nerves his friends couldn't begin to understand.

"So when are you and your family taking residence in the castle, Lord Dohni?" another man asked, moving right in front of Dohni and dipping an awkward bow.

Purely on instinct, before he could even consider the move, Dohni shoved the man's shoulder, sending him sprawling to the mud. He came up laughing, as were all the others.

"Oh, but ain't he acting the part of a nobleman already!" the first old geezer cried. "Down to the mud with us all, or Lord Dohni's to stomp us flat!"

On cue, all the peasant workers fell to their knees in the mud and began genuflecting before Dohni.

Biting back his rage, reminding himself that these were his friends and that they just didn't understand, Dohni Ganderlay shuffled through their ranks and walked away, fists clenched so tightly that his knuckles were white, teeth gnashing until his jaw hurt, and a stream of mumbled curses spewing forth from his mouth.

*　*　*　*　*

"Didn't I feel the fool," Meralda said honestly to Tori, the two girls in their room in the small stone house. Their mother had gone out for the first time in more than two weeks, so eager was she to run and tell her neighbor friends about her daughter's evening with Lord Feringal.

"But you were so beautiful in the gown," Tori argued.

Meralda managed a weak but grateful smile for her sister.

"He couldn't have stopped looking at you, I'm sure," Tori added. From her expression, the young girl seemed to be lost in a dreamland of romantic fantasies.

"Nor could his sister, Lady Priscilla, stop mudding me," Meralda replied, using the peasant term for insults.

"Well, she's a fat cow," Tori snapped back, "and your own beauty only reminded her of it."

The two girls had a giggle at that, but Meralda's proved short-lived, her frown returning.

"How can you not be smiling?" Tori asked. "He's the lord of Auckney and can give you all that anyone would ever want."

"Can he now?" Meralda came back sarcastically. "Can he give me my freedom? Can he give me my Jaka?"

"Can he give you a kiss?" Tori asked impishly.

"I couldn't stop him on the kiss," Meralda replied, "but he'll get no more, don't you doubt. I'm giving me heart to Jaka and not to any pretty-smelling lord."

Her declaration lost its steam, her voice trailing away to a whisper, as the curtain pulled aside and a raging Dohni Ganderlay stormed into the room. "Leave us," he commanded Tori. When she hesitated, putting a concerned look over her sister, he roared even louder, "Be gone, little pig feeder!"

Tori scrambled from the room and turned to regard her father, but his glare kept her moving out of the house altogether.

Dohni Ganderlay dropped that awful scowl over Meralda, and she didn't know what to make of it, for it was no look she was accustomed to seeing stamped on her father's face.

"Da," she began tentatively.

"You let him kiss you?" Dohni Ganderlay retorted, his voice trembling. "And he wanted more?"

"I couldn't stop him," Meralda insisted. "He came at me fast."

"But you wanted to stop him."

"Of course I did!"

The words were barely out of her mouth when Dohni Ganderlay's big, calloused hand came across Meralda's face.

"And you're wanting to give your heart and all your womanly charms to that peasant boy instead, aren't you?" the man roared.

"But, Da—"

Another smack knocked Meralda from the bed, to land on the floor. Dohni Ganderlay, all his frustration pouring out, fell over her, his big, hard hands slapping at her, beating her about the head and shoulders, while he cried out that she was "trampin' " and "whorin' " without a thought for her ma, without a care for the folks who fed and clothed her.

She tried to protest, tried to explain that she loved Jaka and not Lord Feringal, that she hadn't done anything wrong, but her father wasn't hearing anything. He just kept raining blows and curses on her, one after another, until she lay flat on the floor, arms crossed over her head in a futile attempt to protect herself.

The beating stopped as suddenly as it had begun. After a moment, Meralda dared to lift her bruised face from the floor and slowly turn about to regard her father. Dohni Ganderlay sat on the bed, head in his hands, weeping openly. Meralda had never seen him this way before. She came up to him slowly, calmly, whispering to him that it was all right. A sudden anger replaced his tears, and he grabbed the girl by the hair and pulled her up straight.

"Now you hear me, girl," he said through clamped teeth, "and hear me good. It's not yours to choose. Not at all. You'll give Lord Feringal all that he's wanting and more, and with a happy smile on your face. Your ma's close to dying, foolish girl, and Lord Feringal alone can save her. I'll not have her die, not for your selfishness." He gave her a rough shake and let her go. She stared at him as if he were some stranger, and that, perhaps, was the most painful thing of all to frustrated Dohni Ganderlay.

"Or better," he said calmly, "I'll see Jaka Sculi dead, his body on the rocks for the gulls and terns to pick at."

"Da . . ." the young woman protested, her voice barely a whisper, and a quivering whisper at that.

"Stay away from him," Dohni Ganderlay commanded. "You're going to Lord Feringal, and not a word of arguing."

Meralda didn't move, not even to wipe the tears that had begun flowing from her delicate green eyes.

"Get yourself cleaned up," Dohni Ganderlay instructed. "Your ma'll be home soon, and she's not to see you like that. This is all her hopes and dreams, girl, and if you take them from her, she'll surely go into the cold ground."

With that, Dohni rose from the bed and started for Meralda as if to hug her, but when he put his hands near to her, she tensed in a manner the man had never experienced before. He walked past her, his shoulders slumping in true defeat.

He left her alone in the house, then, walking deliberately to the northwest slope of the mountain, the rocky side where no men farmed, where he could be alone with his thoughts. And his horrors.

* * * * *

"What're you to do?" Tori asked Meralda after the younger girl rushed back into the house as soon as their father had walked out of sight. Meralda, busy wiping the last remnants of blood from the side of her lip, didn't answer.

"You should run away with Jaka," Tori said suddenly, her face brightening as if she had just found the perfect solution to all the problems of the world. Meralda looked at her doubtfully.

"Oh, but it'd be the peak of love," the young girl beamed. "Running away from Lord Feringal. I can't believe how our da beat you."

Meralda looked back in the silver mirror at her bruises, so poignant a reminder of the awful explosion. Unlike Tori, she could believe it, every bit of it. She was no child anymore, and she had recognized the agony on her father's face even as he had slapped at her. He was afraid, so very afraid, for her mother and for all of them.

She came then to understand her duty. Meralda recognized that duty to her family was paramount and not because of threats but because of her love for her mother, father, and pesky little sister. Only then, staring into the mirror at her bruised face, did Meralda Ganderlay come to understand the responsibility that had been dropped upon her delicate shoulders, the opportunity that had been afforded her family.

Still, when she thought of Lord Feringal's lips against hers and his hand on her breast, she couldn't help but shudder.

* * * * *

Dohni Ganderlay was hardly aware of the sun dipping behind the distant water, or of the gnats that had found him sitting motionless and were feasting on his bare arms and neck. The discomfort hardly mattered. How could he have hit his beloved little girl? Where had the rage come from? How could he be angry with her, she who had done nothing wrong, who had not disobeyed him?

He replayed those awful moments again and again in his mind, saw Meralda, his beautiful, wonderful Meralda, falling to the floor to hide from him, to cover herself against his vicious blows. In his mind, Dohni Ganderlay understood that he was not angry with her, that his frustration and rage were against Lord Feringal. His anger came from his meager place in the world, a place that had left his family peasants, that had allowed his wife to sicken and would allow her to die, but for the possible intervention of Lord Feringal.

Dohni Ganderlay knew all of that, but in his heart he knew only that for his own selfish reasons he had sent his beloved daughter into the arms and bed of a man she did not love. Dohni Ganderlay knew himself to be a coward at that moment, mostly because he could not summon the courage to throw himself from the mountain spur, to break apart on the jagged rocks far below.

Part 2

Walking Down
A Dark Road

I have lived in many societies, from Menzoberranzan of the drow, to Blingdenstone of the deep gnomes, to Ten-Towns ruled as the most common human settlements, to the barbarian tribes and their own curious ways, to Mithral Hall of the Clan Battlehammer dwarves. I have lived aboard ship, another type of society altogether. All of these places have different customs and mores, all of them have varied government structures, social forces, churches and societies.

Which is the superior system? You would hear many arguments concerning this, mostly based on prosperity, or god-given right, or simple destiny. For the drow, it is simply a religious matter—they structure their society to the desires of the chaotic Spider Queen, then wage war constantly to change the particulars of that structure, though not the structure itself. For the deep gnomes, it is a matter of paying homage and due respect to the elders of their race, accepting the wisdom of those who have lived for so many years. In the human settlement of Ten-Towns, leadership comes from popularity, while the barbarians choose their chieftains purely on physical prowess. For the dwarves, rulership is a matter of bloodline. Bruenor became king because his father was king, and his father's father before him, and his father's father's father before him.

I measure the superiority of any society in a different manner, based completely on individual freedom. Of all the places I have lived, I favor Mithral Hall, but that, I understand, is a matter of Bruenor's wisdom in allowing his flock their freedom, and not because of the dwarven political structure. Bruenor is not an active king. He serves as spokesman for the clan in matters politic, as commander in matters martial, and as mediator in disputes among his subjects, but only when so asked. Bruenor remains fiercely independent and grants that joy to those of Clan Battlehammer.

I have heard of many queens and kings, matron mothers and clerics, who justify rulership and absolve themselves of any ills by claiming that the commoners who serve them are in need of guidance. This might be true in many long-standing societies, but if it is, that is only because so many generations of conditioning have stolen something essential from the heart and soul of the subjects, because many generations of subordination have robbed the common folk of confidence in determining their own way. All of the governing systems share the trait of stealing freedom from the individual, of forcing certain conditions upon the lives of each citizen in the name of "community."

That concept, "community," is one that I hold dear, and surely, the individuals within any such grouping must sacrifice and accept certain displeasures in the name of the common good to make any community thrive. How much stronger might that community be if those sacrifices came from the heart of each citizen and not from the edicts of the elders or matron mothers or kings and queens?

Freedom is the key to it all. The freedom to stay or to leave, to work in harmony with others or to choose a more individual course. The freedom to help in the larger issues or to abstain. The freedom to build a good life or to live in squalor. The freedom to try anything, or merely to do nothing.

Few would dispute the desire for freedom; everyone I have ever met desires free will, or thinks he does. How curious then, that so many refuse to accept the inverse cost of freedom: responsibility.

An ideal community would work well because the individual members would accept their responsibility toward the welfare of each other and to the community as a whole, not because they are commanded to do so, but because they understand and accept the benefits to such choices. For there are, indeed, consequences to every choice we make, to everything we do or choose not to do. Those consequences are not so obvious, I fear. The selfish man might think himself gaining, but in times when that person most needs his friends, they likely will not be there, and in the end, in the legacy the selfish person leaves behind, he will not be remembered fondly if at all. The selfish person's greed might bring material luxuries, but cannot bring the true joys, the intangible pleasures of love.

So it is with the hateful person, the slothful person, the envious person, the thief and the thug, the drunkard and the gossip. Freedom allows each

364

the right to choose the life before him, but freedom demands that the person accept the responsibility for those choices, good and bad.

I have often heard tales of those who believed they were about to die replaying the events of their lives, even long past occurrences buried deep within their memories. In the end, I believe, in those last moments of this existence, before the mysteries of what may come next, we are given the blessing, or curse, to review our choices, to see them bared before our consciousness, without the confusion of the trappings of day-to-day living, without blurring justifications or the potential for empty promises to make amends.

How many priests, I wonder, would include this most naked moment in their descriptions of heaven and hell?

—Drizzt Do'Urden

Chapter 7

Letting Go of an Old Friend

The big man was only a stride away. Josi Puddles saw him coming too late. Squeamish Josi hunched against the wall, trying to cover up, but Wulfgar had him in an instant, lifting him with one hand, batting away his feeble attempts to slap with the other.

Then, *slam,* Josi went hard against the wall.

"I want it back," the barbarian said calmly. To poor Josi, the measure of serenity in Wulfgar's voice and his expression was perhaps the most frightening thing of all.

"Wh-what're ye lookin' t-to find?" the little man stuttered in reply.

Still with just one arm, Wulfgar pulled Josi out from the wall and slammed him back against it. "You know what I mean," he said, "and I know you took it."

Josi shrugged and shook his head, and that bought him another slam against the wall.

"You took Aegis-fang," Wulfgar clarified, now bringing his scowl right up to Josi's face, "and if you do not return it to me, I will break you apart and assemble your bones to make my next weapon."

"I . . . I . . . I *borrowed* it . . ." Josi started to say, his rambling interrupted

367

by yet another slam. "I thought ye'd kill Arumn!" the little man cried. "I thought ye'd kill us all."

Wulfgar calmed a bit at those curious words. "Kill Arumn?" he echoed incredulously.

"When he kicked ye out," Josi explained. "I knew he was kickin' ye out. He told me as much while ye slept. I thought ye'd kill him in yer rage."

"So you took my warhammer?"

"I did," Josi admitted, "but I meant to get it back. I tried to get it back."

"Where is it?" Wulfgar demanded.

"I gave it to a friend," Josi replied. "He gave it to a sailor woman to hold, to keep it out of the reach of yer call. I tried to get it back, but the sailor woman won't give it up. She tried to squish me head, she did!"

"Who?" Wulfgar asked.

"Sheela Kree of *Leapin' Lady*," Josi blurted. "She got it, and she's meanin' to keep it."

Wulfgar paused for a long moment, digesting the information, measuring its truth. He looked up at Josi again, and his scowl returned tenfold. "I am not fond of thieves," he said. He jostled Josi about, and when the little man tried to resist, even slapping Wulfgar, the barbarian brought him out from the wall and slammed him hard, once, then again.

"We stone thieves in my homeland," Wulfgar growled as he smashed Josi so hard against the wall the building shook.

"And in Luskan we shackle ruffians," came a voice to the side. Wulfgar and Josi turned their heads to see Arumn Gardpeck exit the establishment, along with several other men. Those others hung far back, though, obviously wanting nothing to do with Wulfgar, while Arumn, club in hand, approached cautiously. "Put him down," the tavernkeeper said.

Wulfgar slammed Josi one more time, then brought him down to his feet, but shook him roughly and did not let go. "He stole my warhammer, and I mean to get it back," the barbarian said determinedly.

Arumn glared at Josi.

"I tried," Josi wailed, "but Sheela Kree—yeah, that's her. She got it and won't give it over."

Wulfgar gave him another shake, rattling the teeth in his mouth. "She has it because you gave it to her," he reminded Josi.

"But he tried to retrieve it," Arumn said. "He's done all he can. Now, are ye meanin' to bust him up for that? Is that to make ye feel better, Wulfgar the brute? For suren it won't help to get yer hammer back."

Wulfgar glared at Arumn, then let the look fall over poor Josi. "It would, indeed, make me feel better," he admitted, and Josi seemed to shrink down, trembling visibly.

"Then ye'll have to beat me, as well," Arumn said. "Josi's me friend, as I thought yerself to be, and I'll be fighting for him."

Wulfgar scoffed at the notion. With a mere flick of his powerful arm, he sent Josi sprawling at Arumn's feet.

"He told ye where to find yer hammer," Arumn said.

Wulfgar took the cue and started away, but he glanced back to see Arumn helping Josi from the ground, then putting his arm around the trembling man's shoulders, leading him into the Cutlass.

That last image, a scene of true friendship, bothered the barbarian profoundly. He had known friendship like that, had once been blessed with friends who would come to his aid even when the odds seemed impossible. Images of Drizzt and Bruenor, of Regis and Guenhwyvar, and mostly of Catti-brie flitted across his thoughts.

But it was all a lie, a darker part of Wulfgar's deepest thoughts reminded him. The barbarian closed his eyes and swayed, near to falling over. There were places where no friends could follow, horrors that no amount of friendship could alleviate. It was all a lie, friendship, all a facade concocted by that so very human and ultimately childish need for security, to wrap oneself in false hopes. He knew it, because he had seen the futility, had seen the truth, and it was a dark truth indeed.

Hardly conscious of the action, Wulfgar ran to the door of the Cutlass and shoved it open so forcefully that the slam drew the attention of every one in the place. A single stride brought the barbarian up to Arumn and Josi, where he casually swatted aside Arumn's club, then slapped Josi across the face, launching him several feet to land sprawling on the floor.

Arumn came right back at him, swinging the club, but Wulfgar caught it in one hand, yanked it away from the tavernkeeper, then pushed Arumn back. He brought the club out in front of him, one hand on either end, and with a growl and a great flex of his huge neck and shoulders, he snapped the hard wood in half.

"Why're ye doin' this?" Arumn asked him.

Wulfgar had no answers, didn't even bother to look for them. In his swirling thoughts he had scored a victory here, a minor one, over Errtu and the demons. Here he had denied the lie of friendship, and by doing so, had denied Errtu one weapon, that most poignant weapon, to use against him. He tossed the splintered wood to the floor and stalked out of the Cutlass, knowing that none of his tormentors would dare follow.

He was still growling, still muttering curses, at Errtu, at Arumn, at Josi Puddles, when he arrived at the docks. He stalked up and down the long pier, his heavy boots clunking against the wood.

"Ere, what're you about?" one old woman asked him.

"The *Leaping Lady*?" Wulfgar asked. "Where is it?"

"That Kree's boat?" the woman asked, more to herself than to Wulfgar. "Oh, she's out. Out and running, not to doubt, fearing that one." As she finished, she pointed to the dark silhouette of a sleek vessel tied on the other side of the long wharf.

Wulfgar, curious, moved closer, noting the three sails, the last one triangular, a design he had never seen before. When he crossed the boardwalk, he remembered the tales Drizzt and Catti-brie had told to him, and he understood. *Sea Sprite.*

Wulfgar stood up very straight, the name sobering him from his jumbled thoughts. His eyes trailed up the planking, from the name to the deck rail, and there stood a sailor, staring back at him.

"Wulfgar," Waillan Micanty hailed. "Well met!"

The barbarian turned on his heel and stomped away.

* * * * *

"Perhaps he was reaching out to us," Captain Deudermont reasoned.

"It seems more likely that he was merely lost," a skeptical Robillard replied. "By Micanty's description, the barbarian's reaction upon seeing *Sea Sprite* seemed more one of surprise."

"We can't be certain." Deudermont insisted, starting for the cabin door.

"We don't have to be certain," Robillard retorted, and he grabbed the captain by the arm to stop him. Deudermont did stop and turned to glare at the wizard's hand, then into the man's unyielding eyes.

"He is not your child," Robillard reminded the captain. "He's barely an acquaintance, and you bear him no responsibility."

"Drizzt and Catti-brie are my friends," Deudermont replied. "They're *our* friends, and Wulfgar is their friend. Are we to ignore that fact simply for convenience?"

The frustrated wizard let go of the captain's arm. "For safety, Captain," he corrected, "not convenience."

"I will go to him."

"You already tried and were summarily rejected," the wizard bluntly reminded him.

"Yet he came to us last night, perhaps rethinking that rejection."

"Or lost on the docks."

Deudermont nodded, conceding the possibility. "We'll never know if I don't return to Wulfgar and ask," he reasoned, and started for the door.

"Send another," Robillard said suddenly, the thought just popping into his mind. "Send Mister Micanty, perhaps. Or I shall go."

"Wulfgar knows neither you nor Micanty."

"Certainly there are crewmen aboard who were with Wulfgar on that voyage long ago," the stubborn wizard persisted. "Men who know him."

Deudermont shook his head, his jaw set determinedly. "There is but one man aboard *Sea Sprite* who can reach out to Wulfgar," he said. "I'll go back to him, then again, if necessary, before we put out to sea."

Robillard started to respond but finally recognized the futility of it all and threw up his hands in defeat. "The streets of Luskan's dockside are no haven for your friends, Captain," he reminded. "Beware that every shadow might hold danger."

"I always am and always have been," Deudermont said with a grin, a grin that widened as Robillard walked up to him and put several enchantments upon him, spells to stop blows or defeat missiles, and even one to diffuse certain magical attacks.

"Take care of the duration," the wizard warned.

Deudermont nodded, thankful for his friend's precautions, then turned back to the door.

Robillard slumped into a chair as soon as the man had gone. He considered his crystal ball and the energy it would take for him to operate it. "Unnecessary work," he said with an exasperated sigh. "For the captain and for me. A useless effort for an undeserving gutter rat."

It was going to be a long night.

* * * * *

"And do you need it so badly?" Morik dared to ask. Given Wulfgar's foul mood, he knew that he was indeed taking a great risk in even posing the question.

Wulfgar didn't bother to answer the absurd question, but the look he gave Morik told the little thief well enough. "It must be a wondrous weapon, then," Morik said, abruptly shifting the subject to excuse his obviously sacrilegious thinking. Of course Morik had known all along how magnificent a weapon Aegis-fang truly was, how perfect the craftsmanship and how well it fit Wulfgar's strong hands. In the pragmatic thief's mind, even that didn't justify an excursion onto the open sea in pursuit of Sheela Kree's cutthroat band.

Perhaps the emotions went deeper, Morik wondered. Perhaps Wulfgar held a sentimental attachment to the warhammer. His adoptive father had crafted it for him, after all. Perhaps Aegis-fang was the one remaining piece of his former life, the one reminder of who he had been. It was a question Morik didn't dare ask aloud, for even if Wulfgar agreed with him the proud barbarian would never admit it, though he might launch Morik through the air for even asking.

"Can you make the arrangements?" an impatient Wulfgar asked again. He wanted Morik to charter a ship fast enough and with a captain knowledgeable enough to catch Sheela Kree, to shadow her into another harbor perhaps, or merely to get close enough so that Wulfgar could take a small boat in the dark of night and quietly board the privateer. He didn't expect any help in retrieving the warhammer once delivered to Kree. He didn't think he'd need any.

"What of your captain friend?" Morik replied.

371

Wulfgar looked at him incredulously.

"Deudermont's *Sea Sprite* is the most reputable pirate chaser on the Sword Coast," Morik stated bluntly. "If there is a boat in Luskan that can catch Sheela Kree, it's *Sea Sprite*, and from the way Captain Deudermont greeted you, I'll wager he would take on the task."

Wulfgar had no direct answer to Morik's claims other than to say, "Arrange for a different boat."

Morik eyed him for a long while, then nodded. "I will try," he promised.

"Now," Wulfgar instructed. "Before the *Leaping Lady* gets too far out."

"We have a job," Morik reminded him. Running a bit low on funds, the pair had agreed to help an innkeeper unload a ship's hold of slaughtered cattle that night.

"I'll unload the meat," Wulfgar offered, and those words sounded like music to Morik, who never really liked honest work. The little thief had no idea where to begin chartering a boat that could catch Sheela Kree, but he much preferred searching for that answer, and perhaps finding a few pockets to pick along the way, to getting soggy and smelly under tons of salted meat.

* * * * *

Robillard stared into the crystal ball, watching Deudermont as the captain made his way along one wide and well-lit boulevard, heavily patrolled by city guards. Most of them stopped to greet the captain and offer praise. Robillard understood their intent though he couldn't hear their words through the crystal ball, which granted images only and no sound.

A knock on the door broke the wizard's concentration and sent the image in his crystal ball into a swirl of foggy grayness. He could have retrieved the scene immediately but figured that Deudermont was in no danger at that time, especially with the multitude of defensive spells the wizard had cast over the man. Still, always preferring his privacy, he called out a gruff, "Be gone!" then moved to pour himself a strong drink.

Another knock sounded, this one more insistent. "Ye must see this, Master Robillard," came a call, a voice Robillard recognized. With a grunt of protest and drink in hand, Robillard opened the door to find a crewman standing there, glancing back over his shoulder to the rail by the boarding plank.

Waillan Micanty and another seaman stood there, looking down at the docks, apparently speaking to someone.

"We've a guest," the crewman at Robillard's door remarked, and the wizard immediately thought it must be Wulfgar. Not sure if that was a good thing or bad, Robillard started across the deck, pausing only to turn back and shut his door in the face of the overly curious crewman.

"You're not to come up until Master Robillard says so," Micanty called down, and there came a plea for quiet from below in response.

Robillard moved to Micanty's side. The wizard looked down to see a pitiful figure huddled under a blanket, a tell-tale sign, for the night surely wasn't cold.

"Wants to speak to Captain Deudermont," Waillan Micanty explained.

"Indeed," Robillard replied. To the man on the wharf he said, "Are we to let every vagabond who wanders in come aboard to speak with Captain Deudermont?"

"Ye don't understand," the man below answered, lowering his voice and glancing nervously about as if expecting a murderer to descend upon him at any moment. "I got news ye're needin' to hear. But not here," he went on, glancing about yet again. "Not where any can hear."

"Let him up," Robillard instructed Micanty. When the crewman looked at him skeptically, the wizard returned the stare with an expression that reminded Micanty of who he was. It also demonstrated that Robillard thought it absurd to worry that this pitiful little man might cause mischief in the face of Robillard's wizardly power.

"I will see him in my quarters," the wizard instructed as he walked away.

A few moments later, Waillan Micanty led the shivering little man through Robillard's cabin door. Several other curious crewmen poked their heads into the room, but Micanty, without waiting for Robillard's permission, moved over and closed them out.

"Ye're Deudermont?" the little man asked.

"I am not," the wizard admitted, "but rest assured that I am the closest you will ever get to him."

"Got to see Deudermont," the little man explained.

"What is your name?" the wizard asked.

The little man shook his head. "Just got to tell Deudermont," he said. "But it don't come from me, if ye understand."

Never a patient man, Robillard certainly did not understand. He flicked his finger and sent a bolt of energy into the little man that jolted him backward. "Your name?" he asked again, and when the man hesitated, he hit him with another jolt. "There are many more waiting, I assure you," Robillard said.

The little man turned for the door but got hit in the face with a tremendous magical gust of wind that nearly knocked him over and sent him spinning to again face the wizard.

"Your name?" Robillard asked calmly.

"Josi Puddles," Josi blurted before he could think to create an alias.

Robillard pondered the name for a moment, putting his finger to his chin. He leaned back in his chair and struck a pensive pose. "Do tell me your news, Mister Puddles."

"For Captain Deudermont," an obviously overwhelmed Josi replied. "They're looking to kill 'im. Lots o' money for his head."

"Who?"

"A big man," Josi replied. "Big man named Wulfgar and his friend Morik the Rogue."

Robillard did well to hide his surprise. "And how do you know this?" he asked.

"All on the street know," Josi answered. "Lookin' to kill Deudermont for ten thousand pieces o' gold, so they're sayin'."

"What else?" Robillard demanded, his voice taking on a threatening edge.

Josi shrugged, little eyes darting.

"Why have you come?" Robillard pressed.

"I was thinkin' ye should know," Josi answered. "I know I'd want to be knowin' if people o' Wulfgar's and Morik's reputation was hunting me."

Robillard nodded, then chuckled. "You came to a ship—a pirate hunter—infamous among the most dangerous folk along the docks, to warn a man you have never met, knowing full well that to do so could put you in mortal danger. Your pardon, Mister Puddles, but I sense an inconsistency here."

"I thinked ye should know," Josi said again, lowering his eyes. "That's all."

"I think not," Robillard said calmly. Josi looked back at him, his expression fearful. "How much do you desire?"

Josi's expression turned curious.

"A wiser man would have bargained before offering the information," Robillard explained, "but we are not ungrateful. Will fifty gold pieces suffice?"

"W-well, yes," Josi stuttered, then he said, "Well, no. Not really, I mean. I was thinkin' a hunnerd."

"You are a powerful bargainer, Mister Puddles," Robillard said, and he nodded at Micanty to calm the increasingly agitated sailor. "Your information may well prove valuable, if you aren't lying, of course."

"No, sir, never that!"

"Then a hundred gold it is," Robillard said. "Return tomorrow to speak with Captain Deudermont, and you shall be paid."

Josi glanced all around. "I'm not comin' back, if ye please, Master Robillard," he said.

Robillard chuckled again. "Of course," he replied as he reached into a neck purse. He produced a key and tossed it to Waillan Micanty.

"See to it," he told the man. "You will find the sum in the left locker, bottom. Pay him in pieces of ten. Then escort Mister Puddles from our good ship and send a pair of crewmen along to get him safely off the docks."

Micanty could hardly believe what he was hearing, but he wasn't about to argue with the dangerous wizard. He took Josi Puddles by the arm and left the room.

When he returned a short while later, he found Robillard leaning over his crystal ball, studying the image intently.

"You believe him," Micanty stated. "Enough to pay him without any proof."

"A hundred copper pieces is not so great a sum," Robillard replied.

"Copper?" Micanty replied. "It was gold by my own eyes."

"So it seemed," the wizard explained, "but it was copper, I assure you, and coins that I can trace easily to find our Mister Puddles—to punish him if necessary, or to properly reward him if his information proves true."

"He did not come to us searching for any reward," the observant Micanty remarked. "Nor is he any friend of Captain Deudermont, surely. No, it seems to me that our friend Puddles isn't overly fond of Wulfgar or this Morik fellow."

Robillard glanced in his crystal ball again, then leaned back in his chair, thinking.

"Have you found the captain?" Micanty dared to ask.

"I have," the wizard answered. "Come, see this."

When Micanty got near to Robillard, he saw the scene in the crystal ball shift from Luskan's streets to a ship somwhere out on the open ocean. "The captain?" he said with concern.

"No, no," Robillard replied. "Wulfgar, perhaps, or at least his magical warhammer. I know of the weapon. It was described to me in depth. Thinking that it would show me Wulfgar, my magical search took me to this boat, *Leaping Lady* by name."

"Pirate?"

"Likely," the wizard answered. "If Wulfgar is indeed on her, we shall likely meet up with the man again. Though, if he is, our friend Puddles's story seems a bit unlikely."

"Can you call to the captain?" Micanty asked, still concerned. "Bring him home?"

"He'd not listen," Robillard said with a smirk. "Some things our stubborn Captain Deudermont must learn for himself. I will watch him closely. Go and secure the ship. Double the guard, triple it even, and tell every man to watch the shadows closely. If there are, indeed, some determined to assassinate Captain Deudermont, they might believe him to be here."

Robillard was alone again, and he turned to the crystal ball, returning the image to Captain Deudermont. He sighed in disappointment. He expected as much, but he was still sad to discover that the captain had again traveled to the rougher section of town. As Robillard focused in on him again, Deudermont passed under the sign for Half-Moon Street.

* * * * *

Had Robillard been able to better scan the wide area, he might have noticed two figures slipping into an alley paralleling the avenue Deudermont had just entered.

Creeps Sharky and Tee-a-nicknick rushed along, then cut down an alley, emerging onto Half-Moon Street right beside the Cutlass. They dashed inside, for Sharky was convinced that was where Deudermont was headed. The pair took the table in the corner to the right of the door, evicting the two patrons sitting there with threatening growls. They sat back, ordering drinks from Delly Curtie. Their smug smiles grew wider when Captain Deudermont walked through the door, making his way to the bar.

"He no stay long witout Wufgar here," Tee-a-nicknick remarked.

Creeps considered that, deciphered the words first, then the thought behind them and nodded. He had a fair idea of where Wulfgar and Morik might be. A comrade had spotted them along the dock area earlier that night. "Keep a watch on him," Creeps instructed. He held up a pouch he had prepared earlier, then started to leave.

"Too easy," Tee-a-nicknick remarked, reiterating his complaints about the plan Creeps had former earlier that day.

"Aye, but that's the beauty of it, my friend," said Creeps. "Morik's too cocky and too curious to cast it away. No, he'll have it, he will, and it'll bring him runnin' to us all the faster."

Creeps went out into the night and scanned the street. He had little trouble locating one of the many street children who lurked in the area, serving as lookouts or couriers.

" 'Ere boy," he called to one. The waif, a lad of no more than ten winters, eyed him suspiciously but did not approach. "Got a job for ye," Creeps explained, holding up the bag.

The boy made his way tentatively toward the dangerous-looking pirate.

"Take this," Creeps instructed, handing the little bag over. "And don't look in it!" he commanded when the boy started to loosen the top to peek inside.

Creeps had a change of mind immediately, realizing that the waif might then think there was something special in the bag—gold or magic—and might just run off with it. He pulled it back from the boy and tugged it open, revealing its contents: a few small claws, like those from a cat, a small vial filled with a clear liquid, and a seemingly unremarkable piece of stone.

"There, ye seen it, and so ye're knowin' it's nothing worth stealin'," Creeps said.

"I'm not for stealin'," the boy argued.

"Course ye're not," said Creeps with a knowing chuckle. "Ye're a good boy, now ain't ye? Well, ye know o' one called Wulfgar? A big fellow with yellow hair who used to beat up people for Arumn at the Cutlass?"

The boy nodded.

"And ye know his friend?"

"Morik the Rogue," the boy recited. "Everybody's knowin' Morik."

"Good enough for ye," said Creeps. "They're down at the docks, or between here and there, by my guess. I want ye to find 'em and give this to Morik. Tell him and Wulfgar that a Captain Deudermont's lookin' to meet them outside the Cutlass. Somethin' about a big hammer. Can ye do that?"

The boy smirked as if the question were ridiculous.

"And will ye do it?" Creeps asked. He reached into a pocket and produced a silver piece. Creeps started to hand it over, then changed his mind, and his hand went in again, coming back out with several of the glittering silver coins. "Ye get yer little friends lookin' all over Luskan," he instructed, handing the coins to the wide-eyed waif. "There'll be more for ye, don't ye doubt, if ye bring Wulfgar and Morik to the Cutlass."

Before Creeps could say another word, the boy snatched the coins, turned, and disappeared into the alleyway.

Creeps was smilling when he rejoined Tee-a-nicknick a few moments later, confident that the lad and the extensive network of street urchins he would tap would complete the task in short order.

"He just wait," Tee-a-nicknick explained, motioning to Deudermont, who stood leaning on the bar, sipping a glass of wine.

"A patient man," said Creeps, flashing that green-and-yellow toothy smile. "If he knew how much time he got left to live, he might be a bit more urgent, he might." He motioned to Tee-a-nicknick to exit the Cutlass. They soon found a low rooftop close enough to afford them a fine view of the tavern's front door.

Tee-a-nicknick pulled a long hollow tube out of the back of his shirt, then took a cat's claw, tied with a small clutch of feathers, from his pocket. Kneeling low and moving very carefully, the tattooed half-qullan savage turned his right hand palm up, then, taking the cat's claw in his left hand, squeezed a secret packet on the bracelet about his right wrist. Slowly, slowly, the tattooed man increased the pressure until the packet popped open and a drop of molasseslike syrup oozed out. He caught most of it on the tip of the cat's claw, then stuffed the dart into the end of his blowgun.

"Tee-a-nicknick patient man, too," he said with a wicked grin.

Chapter 8

Warm Feelings

"Oh, look at you!" Biaste Ganderlay exclaimed when she moved to help Meralda put on the new gown Lord Feringal had sent for their dinner that night. Only then, only after Meralda had taken off the bunched-collar shift she had been wearing all the day, did her mother see the extent of her bruises, distinct purple blotches all about her neck and shoulders, bigger marks than the two showing on her face. "You can't be going to see Lord Feringal looking so," Biaste wailed. "What'll he think of you?"

"Then I'll not go," an unenthusiastic Meralda answered, but that only made Biaste fuss more urgently. Meralda's answer brought a frown to Biaste's gray and weary face, poignantly reminding Meralda of her mother's sickness, and of the only possible way to heal her.

The girl lowered her eyes and kept her gaze down as Biaste went to the cupboards, fumbling with boxes and jars. She found beeswax and lavender, comfrey root and oil, then she scurried outside and collected some light clay to put in the mixture. She was back in Meralda's room shortly, holding a mortar she used to crunch the herbs and oil and clay together vigorously with her pestle.

"I'll tell him it was an accident," Meralda offered as Biaste moved to begin applying the masking and comforting salve. "If he fell down the stone stairs at Castle Auck, surely he'd have such bruises as to make these seem like nothing."

"Is that how this happened to you?" Biaste asked, though Meralda had already insisted that she hurt herself by absentmindedly running into a tree.

A twinge of panic hit the girl, for she did not want to reveal the truth, did not want to tell her mother that her loving, adoring father had beaten her. "What're you saying?" she asked defensively. "Do you think I'm daft enough to run into a tree on purpose, Ma?"

"Now, of course I don't," said Biaste, managing a smile. Meralda did, too, glad that her deflection had worked. Biaste took the scrap of flannel she was using to wipe the bruises and swatted Meralda playfully across the head. "It don't look so bad. Lord Feringal will not even see."

"Lord Feringal's looking at me more carefully than you think," Meralda replied, which brought a great laugh from Biaste and she wrapped her daughter in a hug. It seemed to Meralda that her mother was a bit stronger today.

"Steward Temigast said you'll be walking in the gardens tonight," said Biaste. "Oh, and the moon'll be big in the sky. My girl, could I even have dared hope for such a thing for you?"

Meralda answered with another smile, for she feared that if she opened her mouth all of her anger at this injustice would pour out and knock her mother back into bed.

Biaste took Meralda by the hand, and led her to the main room of the cottage where the table was already set for dinner. Tori was sitting, shifting impatiently. Dohni Ganderlay came in the front door at that moment and looked directly at the two women.

"She ran into a tree," Biaste remarked. "Can you believe the girl's foolishness? Running into a tree when Lord Feringal's a-calling!" She laughed again, and Meralda did, too, though she never blinked as she stared at her father.

Dohni and Tori shared an uncomfortable glance, and the moment passed. The Ganderlay family sat down together for a quiet evening meal. At least it would have been quiet, had it not been for the bubbling exuberance of an obviously thrilled Biaste Ganderlay.

Soon after, long before the sun even touched the rim of the western horizon, the Ganderlays stood outside their house, watching Meralda climb into the gilded coach. Biaste was so excited she ran out into the middle of the dirt lane to wave good-bye. That effort seemed to drain her of all her strength, though, for she nearly swooned and would have stumbled had not Dohni Ganderlay been there to catch and support her.

"Now get yourself to bed," he instructed. Dohni tenderly handed his wife over to Tori, who helped her into the house.

Dohni waited outside, watching the diminishing coach and the dusty road. The man was torn in heart and soul. He didn't regret the lesson he had given to Meralda—the girl needed to put her priorities straight—but hitting Meralda hurt Dohni Ganderlay as much as it had hurt the girl.

"Why'd Ma nearly fall down, Da?" Tori asked a moment later, the sound of the girl's voice catching the distracted Dohni by surprise. "She was so strong and smiling and all."

"She gave too much of herself," Dohni explained, not overly concerned. He knew the truth of Biaste's condition, "the wilting" as it was commonly called, and understood that it would take more than high spirits to heal her. Good spirits would bolster her temporarily, but the sickness would have its way with her in the end. It would take the efforts of Lord Feringal's connections to truly bring healing.

He looked down at Tori then and saw the honest fear there. "She's just needing rest," he explained, draping an arm across the young girl's shoulder

"Meralda told Ma she ran into a tree," Tori dared to say, drawing a frown from Dohni.

"So she did," Dohni agreed softly, sadly. "Why's she resisting?" he asked his youngest daughter impulsively. "She's got the lord himself fretting over her. A brighter world than ever she could've hoped to find."

Tori looked away, which told Dohni that the younger girl knew more than she was letting on. He moved in front of Tori, and when she tried to continue to look away, he caught her by the chin and forced her to eye him directly. "What do ye know?"

Tori didn't respond.

"Tell me girl," Dohni demanded, giving Tori a rough shake. "What's in your sister's mind?"

"She loves another," Tori said reluctantly.

"Jaka Sculi," he reasoned aloud. Dohni Ganderlay relaxed his grip, but his eyes narrowed. He had suspected as much, had figured that Meralda's feelings for Jaka Sculi might go deeper, or at least that Meralda thought they went deeper. Dohni knew Jaka well enough to understand that the boy was more facade than depth. Still, Dohni was not blind to the fact that nearly all of the village girls were taken with that moody young lad.

"She'll kill me if she thinks I told you," Tori pleaded, but she was cut short by another rough shake. The look on her father's face was one she had never seen before, but she was sure it was the same one Meralda had witnessed earlier that day.

"Do you think it's all a game?" Dohni scolded.

Tori burst into tears, and Dohni let her go. "Keep your mouth shut to your ma and your sister," he instructed.

"What're you going to do?"

"I'll do what needs doing and without answering to my girls!" Dohni shot back. He turned Tori about and shoved her toward the house. The young girl was more than willing to leave, sprinting through the front door without looking back.

381

Dohni stared down the empty road toward the castle where his oldest daughter, his beautiful Meralda, was off bartering her heart and body for the sake of her family. He wanted to run to Castle Auck and throttle Lord Feringal at that moment, but he dismissed the notion, reminding himself that there was another eager young man who needed his attention.

*　*　*　*　*

Down the rocky beach from Castle Auck, Jaka Sculi watched the fancy carriage ramble along the bridge and into Lord Feringal's castle. He knew who was in the coach even before watching Meralda disappear into the young lord's domain. His blood boiled at the sight and brought a great sickness to his stomach.

"Damn you!" he snarled, shaking his fist at the castle. "Damn, damn, damn! I should, I shall, find a sword and cut your heart, as you have cut mine, evil Feringal! The joy of seeing your flowing blood staining the ground beneath you, of whispering in your dying ear that I, and not you, won out in the end.

"But fie, I cannot!" the young man wailed, and he rolled back on the wet rock and slapped his arm across his forehead.

"But wait," he cried, sitting up straight and turning his arm over so that he felt his forehead with his fingers. "A fever upon me. A fever brought by Meralda. Wicked enchantress! A fever brought by Meralda and by Feringal, who deigns to take that which is rightfully mine. Deny him, Meralda!" he called loudly, and he broke down, kicking his foot against the stone and gnashing his teeth. He regained control quickly, reminding himself that only his wiles would allow him to beat Lord Feringal, that only his cleverness would allow him to overcome his enemy's unjust advantage, one given by birth and not quality of character. So Jaka began his plotting, thinking of how he might turn the mortal sickness he felt festering within his broken heart to some advantage over the stubborn girl's willpower.

*　*　*　*　*

Meralda couldn't deny the beautiful aromas and sights of the small garden on the southern side of Castle Auck. Tall roses, white and pink, mingled with lady's mantle and lavender to form the main garden, creating a myriad of shapes and colors that drew Meralda's eye upward and back down again. Pansies filled in the lower level, and bachelor's buttons peeked out from hiding among the taller plants like secret prizes for the cunning examiner. Even in the perpetually dismal fog of Auckney, and perhaps in some large part because of it, the garden shone brightly, speaking of birth and renewal, of springtime and life itself.

Enchanted as she was, Meralda couldn't help but wish that her escort this waning afternoon was not Lord Feringal, but her Jaka. Wouldn't she love to take him and kiss him here amidst the flowery scents and sights, amidst the hum of happy bees?

"Priscilla tends the place, mostly," Lord Feringal remarked, walking politely a step behind Meralda as she made her way along the garden wall.

The news caught Meralda somewhat by surprise and made her rethink her first impression of the lady of Castle Auck. Anyone who could so carefully and lovingly tend a garden to this level of beauty must have some redeeming qualities. "And do you not come out here at all?" the woman asked, turning back to regard the young lord.

Feringal shrugged and smiled sheepishly, as if embarrassed to admit that he rarely ventured into the place.

"Do you not think it beautiful, then?" Meralda asked.

Lord Feringal rushed up to the woman and took her hand in his. "Surely it is not more beautiful than you," he blurted.

Bolder by far than she had been on their first meeting, Meralda pulled her hand away. "The garden," she insisted. "The flowers—all their shapes and smells. Don't you find it beautiful?"

"Of course," Lord Feringal answered immediately, obediently, Meralda realized.

"Well, look at it!" Meralda cried at him. "Don't just be staring at me. Look at the flowers, at the bounty of your sister's fine work. See how they live together? How one flower makes room for another, all bunching, but not blocking the sun?"

Lord Feringal did turn his gaze from Meralda to regard the myriad flowers, and a strange expression of revelation came over his face.

"You do see," Meralda remarked after a long, long silence. Lord Feringal continued to study the color surrounding them.

He turned back to Meralda, a look of wonder in his eyes. "I have lived here all my life," he said. "And in those years—no, decades—this garden has been here, yet never before have I seen it. It took you to show me the beauty." He came nearer to Meralda and took her hand in his, then leaned in gently and kissed her, though not urgently and demandingly as he had done their previous meeting. He was gentle and appreciative. "Thank you," he said as he pulled back from her.

Meralda managed a weak smile in reply. "Well, you should be thanking your sister," she said. "A load of work to get it this way."

"I shall," Lord Feringal replied unconvincingly.

Meralda smiled knowingly and turned her attention back to the garden, thinking again how grand it would be to walk through the place with Jaka at her side. The amorous young lord was beside her again, so close, his hands upon her, and she could not maintain the fantasy. Instead, she focused on the flowers, thinking that if she could

383

just lose herself in their beauty, just stare at them until the sun went down, and even after, in the soft glow of the moon, she might survive this night.

To his credit, Lord Feringal allowed her a long, long while to simply stand quietly and stare. The sun disappeared and the moon came up, and though it was full in the sky, the garden lost some of its luster and enchantment except for the continuing aroma, mixing sweetly with the salty air.

"Won't you look at me all the night?" Feringal asked, gently turning her about.

"I was just thinking," Meralda replied.

"Tell me your thoughts," he eagerly prompted.

The woman shrugged. "Silly ones, only," she replied.

Lord Feringal's face brightened with a wide smile. "I'll wager you were thinking it would be grand to walk among these flowers every day," he ventured. "To come to this place whenever you desired, by sun or by moon, in winter even, to stare at the cold waters and the bergs as they build in the north?"

Meralda was wiser than to openly deny the guess or to add to it that she would only think of such things if another man, her Jaka, was beside her instead of Lord Feringal.

"Because you can have all of that," Feringal said excitedly. "You can, you know. All of it and more."

"You hardly know me," the girl exclaimed, near to panic and hardly believing what she was hearing.

"Oh, but I do, my Meralda," Feringal declared, and he fell to one knee, holding her hand in one of his and stroking it gently with the other. "I do know you, for I have looked for you all my life."

"You're speaking foolishness," Meralda muttered, but Feringal pressed on.

"I wondered if ever I would find the woman who could so steal my heart," he said, and he seemed to Meralda to be talking as much to himself as to her. "Others have been paraded before me, of course. Many merchants would desire to create a safe haven in Auckney by bartering their daughters as my wife, but none gave me pause." He rose dramatically, moving to the sea wall.

"None," he repeated. Feringal turned back, his eyes boring into hers. "Until I saw the vision of Meralda. With my heart, I know that there is no other woman in all the world I would have as a wife."

Meralda stammered over that one, stunned by the man's forwardness, by the sheer speed at which he was trying to move this courtship. Even as she stood trying to think of something to reply, he enveloped her, kissing her again and again, not gently, pressing his lips hard against hers, his hands running over her back.

"I must have you," he said, nearly pulling her off-balance.

384

Meralda brought her arm up between them, slamming her palm hard into Lord Feringal's face and driving him back a step. She pulled away, but he pressed in again.

"Please, Meralda!" he cried. "My blood boils within me!"

"You're saying you want me for a wife, but you're treating me like a harlot!" she cried. "No man takes a wife he's already bedded," Meralda pleaded.

Lord Feringal skidded to a stop. "But why?" asked the naive young man. "It is love, after all, and so it is right, I say. My blood boils, and my heart pounds in my chest for want of you."

Meralda looked about desperately for escape and found one from an unexpected source.

"Your pardon, my lord," came a voice from the door, and the pair turned to see Steward Temigast stepping from the castle. "I heard the cry and feared that one of you might have slipped over the rail."

"Well, you see that is not the case, so be gone with you," an exasperated Feringal replied, waving his hand dismissively, and turning back to Meralda.

Steward Temigast stared at her frightened, white face for a long while, a look of sympathy upon his own. "My lord," he ventured calmly. "If you are, indeed, serious about marrying this woman, then you must treat her like a lady. The hour grows long," he announced. "The Ganderlay family will be expecting the return of their child. I will summon the carriage."

"Not yet," Lord Feringal replied immediately, before Temigast could even turn around. "Please," he said more quietly and calmly to Temigast, but mostly to Meralda. "A short while longer?"

Temigast looked to Meralda, who reluctantly nodded her assent. "I will return for you soon," Temigast said, and he went back into the castle.

"I'll have no more of your foolery," Meralda warned her eager suitor, taking confidence in his sheepish plea.

"It is difficult for me, Meralda," he tried sincerely to explain. "More than you can understand. I think about you day and night. I grow impatient for the day when we shall be wed, the day when you shall give yourself to me fully."

Meralda had no reply, but she had to work hard to keep any expression of anger from appearing on her fair face. She thought of her mother then, remembered a conversation she had overheard between her father and a woman friend of the family, when the woman bemoaned that Biaste likely would not live out the winter if they could find no better shelter or no cleric or skilled healer to tend her.

"I'll not wait long, I assure you," Lord Feringal went on. "I will tell Priscilla to make the arrangements this very night."

"I haven't even said I would marry you," Meralda squealed a weak protest.

"But you will marry me, of course," Feringal said confidently. "All the village will be in attendance, a faire that will stay in hearts and memories for all the lives of all who witness it. On that day, Meralda, it will be you whom they rejoice in most of all," he said, coming over and taking her hand again, but gently and respectfully this time. "Years—no, decades—from now, the village women will still remark on the beauty of Lord Feringal's bride."

Meralda couldn't deny she was touched by the man's sincerity and somewhat thrilled by the prospect of having as great a day as Feringal spoke of, a wedding that would be the talk of Auckney for years and years to come. What woman would not desire such a thing?

Yet, Meralda also could not deny that while the glorious wedding was appealing, her heart longed for another. She was beginning to notice another side of Lord Feringal now, a decent and caring nature, perhaps, buried beneath the trappings of his sheltered upbringing. Despite that, Meralda could not forget, even for one moment, that Lord Feringal, simply was not her Jaka.

Steward Temigast returned and announced that the coach was ready, and Meralda went straight to him, but she was still not quick enough to dodge the young man's last attempt to steal a kiss.

It hardly mattered. Meralda was beginning to see things clearly now, and she understood her responsibility to her family and would put that responsibility above all else. Still, it was a long and miserable ride across the bridge and down the road, the young woman's head swirling with so many conflicting thoughts and emotions.

Once again she bade the gnomish driver to let her out some distance from her home. Pulling off the uncomfortable shoes Temigast had sent along with the dress, Meralda walked barefoot down the lane under the moon. Too confused by the events—to think that she was to be married!—Meralda was barely conscious of her surroundings and wasn't even hoping, as she had after her first meeting, that Jaka would find her on the road. She was taken completely by surprise when the young man appeared before her.

"What did he do to you?" Jaka asked before Meralda could even say his name.

"Do?" she echoed.

"What did you do?" Jaka demanded. "You were there for a long time."

"We walked in the garden," the woman answered.

"Just walked?" Jaka's voice took on a frightful edge at that moment, one that set Meralda back on her heels.

"What're you thinking?" she dared ask.

Jaka gave a great sigh and spun away. "I am not thinking, and that is the problem," he wailed. "What enchantment have you cast upon me, Meralda? Oh, the bewitching! I know miserable Feringal must feel the same," he added, spinning back on her. "What man could not?"

386

A great smile erupted on the young woman's face, but it didn't hold, not at all. Why was Jaka acting so peculiar, so lovestruck all of a sudden? she wondered. Why hadn't he behaved this way before?

"Did he have you?" Jaka asked, coming very close. "Did you let him?"

The questions hit Meralda like a wet towel across the face. "How can you be asking me such a thing?" she protested.

Jaka fell to his knees before her, taking both her hands and pressing them against his cheek. "Because I shall die to think of you with him," he explained.

Meralda felt weak in her knees and sick to her stomach. She was too young and too inexperienced, she realized, and could not fathom any of this, not the marriage, not Lord Feringal's polite and almost animalistic polarities, and not Jaka's sudden conversion to lovesick suitor.

"I . . ." she started. "We did nothing. Oh, he stole a kiss, but I didn't kiss him back."

Jaka looked at her, and the smile upon his face was somehow unnerving to Meralda. He came closer then, moving his lips to brush against hers and lighting fires everywhere in her body, it seemed. She felt his hands roaming her body, and she did not fear them—at least not in the same manner in which she had feared her noble suitor. No, this time it was an exciting thing, but still she pushed the man back from her.

"Do you deny the love that we feel for each other?" a wounded Jaka asked.

"But it's not about how we're feeling," Meralda tried to explain.

"Of course it is," the young man said quietly, and he came forward again. "That is all that matters."

He kissed her gently again, and Meralda found that she believed him. The only thing in all the world that mattered at that moment was how she and Jaka felt for each other. She returned the kiss, falling deeper and deeper, tumbling away to an abyss of joy.

Then he was gone from her, too abruptly. Meralda popped open her eyes to see Jaka tumbling to the ground, a raging Dohni Ganderlay standing before her.

"Are you a fool then?" the man asked, and he lifted his arm as if to strike Meralda. A look of pain crossed his rugged face then, and he quickly put his arm down, but up it came again, grabbing Meralda roughly by the shoulder and spinning her toward the house. Dohni shoved her along, then turned on Jaka, who put his hands up defensively in front of his face and darted about, trying to escape.

"Don't hit him, Da!" the young woman cried, and that plea alone stopped Dohni.

"Stay far from my girl," Dohni warned Jaka.

"I love—" Jaka started to reply.

"They'll find yer body washing on the beach," Dohni said.

387

When Meralda cried out again, the imposing man turned on her viciously. "Home!" he commanded. Meralda ran off at full speed, not even bothering to retrieve the shoe she had dropped when Dohni had shoved her.

Donny turned on Jaka, his eyes, red from anger and nights of restless sleep, as menacing as any sight the young man had ever witnessed. Jaka turned on his heel and ran away. He started to, anyway, for before he had gone three steps Dohni hit him with a flying tackle across the back of his knees, dropping him face down on the ground.

"Meralda begged you not to hit me!" the terrified young man pleaded.

Dohni climbed atop him, roughly pulling the young man over. "Meralda's not knowing what's best for Meralda," Dohni answered with a growl and a punch that jerked Jaka's head to the side.

The young man began to cry and to flail his arms wildly, trying to fend off Dohni. The blows got through, though, one after another, swelling Jaka's pretty eyes and fattening both his lips, knocking one tooth out of his perfect smile and bringing blue bruises to his normally rosy cheeks. Jaka finally had the sense to bring his arms down across his battered face, but Dohni, his rage not yet played out, only aimed his blows lower, pounding, pounding Jaka about the chest. Every time Jaka dropped one arm down lower to block there, Dohni cunningly slipped a punch in about his face again.

Finally, Dohni leaped off the man, grabbed him by the front of the shirt, and hoisted him to his feet with a sudden, vicious jerk. Jaka held his palms out in front of him in a sign of surrender. That cowardly act only made Dohni slug him one more time, a brutal hook across the jaw that sent the young man flying to the ground again. Dohni pulled him upright, and he cocked his arm once more. Jaka's whimper made Dohni think of Meralda, of the inevitable look upon her face when he walked in, his knuckles all bloody. He grabbed Jaka in both hands and whipped him around, sending him running on his way.

"Get yourself gone!" the man growled at Jaka. "And don't be sniffing about my girl again!"

Jaka gave a great wail and stumbled off into the darkness.

Chapter 9

The Barrel's Bottom

Robillard scratched his chin when he saw the pair, Wulfgar and Morik, moving down the alley toward the front door of the Cutlass. Deudermont was still inside, a fact that did not sit well with the divining wizard, given all the activity he had seen outside the tavern's door. Robillard had watched a seedy character come out and pay off a street urchin. The wizard understood the uses of such children. That same character, an unusual figure indeed, had exited the Cutlass again and moved off into the shadows.

Wulfgar appeared with a small, swarthy man. Robillard was not surprised when the same street urchin peeked out from an alley some distance away, no doubt waiting for his opportunity to return to his chosen place of business.

Robillard realized the truth after putting the facts together and adding a heavy dose of justifiable suspicion. He turned to the door and chanted a simple spell, grabbing at the air and using it to blast open the portal. "Mister Micanty!" he called, amplifying his voice with yet another spell.

"Go out with a pair of crewmen and alert the town guard," Robillard demanded. "To the Cutlass on Half-Moon Street with all speed."

With a growl the wizard reversed his first spell and slammed the door shut again, then fell back intently into the images within the crystal ball, focusing on the front door of the Cutlass. He moved inside to find Deudermont leaning calmly against the bar.

A few uneventful minutes passed; Robillard shifted his gaze back outside just long enough to note Wulfgar and his small friend lurking in the shadows, as if waiting for something.

Even as the wizard's roving magical eye moved back through the tavern's door, he found Deudermont approaching the exit.

"Hurry, Micanty," Robillard mouthed quietly, but he knew that the town guard, well-drilled as they were, wouldn't likely arrive in time and that he would have to take some action. The wizard plotted his course quickly: a dimensional door to the other end of the docks, and a second to the alley that ran beside the Cutlass. One final look into the crystal ball showed Deudermont walking out and Wulfgar and the other man moving toward him. Robillard let go his mental connection with the ball and brought up the first dimensional door.

* * * * *

Creeps Sharky and Tee-a-nicknick crouched in the shadows on the rooftop. The tattooed man brought the blowgun up to his lips the second Deudermont exited the tavern.

"Not yet," Creeps instructed, grabbing the barrel and pulling the weapon low. "Let him talk to Wulfgar and Morik, and get near to my stone that'll kill any magical protections he might be wearin'. And let others see 'em together, afore and when Deudermont falls dead."

The wretched pirate licked his lips in anticipation. "They gets the blame, we gets the booty," he said.

* * * * *

"Wulfgar," Captain Deudermont greeted him when the barbarian and his sidekick shifted out of the shadows and steadily approached. "My men said you came to *Sea Sprite*."

"Not from any desire," Wulfgar muttered, drawing an elbow from Morik.

"You said you want your warhammer back," the little man quietly reminded him.

What Morik was really thinking, though, was that this might be the perfect time for him to learn more about Deudermont, about the man's protections and, more importantly, his weaknesses. The street urchin had found the barbarian and the rogue down by the docks, handing over the small bag and its curious contents and explaining that Captain Deudermont desired their presence in front of the Cutlass on Half-Moon Street.

Again, Morik had spoken to Wulfgar about the potential gain here, but he backed off immediately as soon as he recognized that dangerous scowl. If Wulfgar would not go along with the assassination, then Morik meant to find a way to do it on his own. He had nothing against Deudermont, of course, and wasn't usually a murderer, but the payoff was just too great to ignore. Good enough for Wulfgar, Morik figured, when he was living in luxury, the finest rooms, the finest food, the finest booze, and the finest whores.

Wulfgar nodded and strode right up to stand before Deudermont, though he did not bother accepting the man's offered hand. "What do you know?" he asked.

"Only that you came to the docks and looked up at Waillan Micanty," Deudermont replied. "I assumed that you wished to speak with me."

"All that I want from you is information concerning Aegis-fang," he said sourly.

"Your hammer?" Deudermont asked, and he looked curiously at Wulfgar, as if only then noticing that the barbarian was not wearing the weapon.

"The boy said you had information," Morik clarified.

"Boy?" the confused captain asked.

"The boy who gave me this," Morik explained, holding up the bag.

Deudermont moved to take it but stopped, seeing Robillard rushing out of the alley to the side.

"Hold!" the wizard cried.

Deudermont felt a sharp sting on the side of his neck. He reached up instinctively with his hand to grab at it, but before his fingers closed around the cat's claw, a great darkness overcame him, buckling his knees. Wulfgar leaped ahead to grab him.

Robillard yelled and reached out magically for Wulfgar, extending a wand and blasting the huge barbarian square in the chest with a glob of sticky goo that knocked him back against the Cutlass and held him there. Morik turned and ran.

"Captain! Captain!" Robillard cried, and he let fly another glob for Morik, but the agile thief was too quick and managed to dodge aside as he skittered down another alley. He had to reverse direction almost immediately, for entering the other end came a pair of city guard, brandishing flaming torches and gleaming swords. He did keep his wits about him enough to toss the satchel the boy had given him into a cubby at the side of the alley before he turned away.

All of Half-Moon Street seemed to erupt in a frenzy then, with guardsmen and crewmen of *Sea Sprite* exiting from every conceivable angle.

Against the wall of the Cutlass, Wulfgar struggled mightily to draw breath. His mind whirled back to the grayness of the Abyss, back to some of the many similar magics demon Errtu had put on him to hold him so, helpless in the face of diabolical minions. That vision lent him rage, and that rage lent him strength. The frantic barbarian got his balance and pulled hard, tearing planking from the side of the building.

Robillard, howling with frustration and fear as he knelt over the scarcely breathing Deudermont, hit Wulfgar with another glob, pasting him to the wall again.

"They've killed him," the wizard yelled to the guardsmen. "Catch the little rat!"

* * * * *

"We go," Tee-a-nicknick said as soon as Deudermont's legs buckled.

"Hit him again," Creeps begged.

The tattooed man shook his head. "One enough. We go."

Even as he and Creeps started to move, the guards descended upon Half-Moon Street and all the other avenues around the area. Creeps led his friend to the shadows by a dormer on the building, where they deposited the blowgun and poison. They moved to another dormer across the way and sat down with their backs against the wall. Creeps took out a bottle, and the pair started drinking, pretending to be oblivious, happy drunks.

Within a few minutes, a trio of guardsmen came over the lip of the roof and approached them. After a cursory inspection and a cry from below revealing that one of the assassins had been captured and the other was running loose through the streets, the guards turned away in disgust.

* * * * *

Morik spun and darted one way, then another, but the noose was closing around him. He found a shadow in the nook of a building and thought he might wait the pursuit out, when he began glowing with magical light.

"Wizards," the rogue muttered. "I hate wizards!"

Off he ran to a building and started to climb, but he was caught by the legs and hauled down, then beaten and kicked until he stopped squirming.

"I did nothing!" he protested, spitting blood with every word as they hauled him roughly to his feet.

"Shut your mouth!" one guard demanded, jamming the hilt of his sword into Morik's gut, doubling the rogue over in pain. He half-walked and was half-dragged back to where Robillard worked feverishly over Deudermont.

"Run for a healer," the wizard instructed, and a guard and a pair of crewmen took off.

"What poison?" the wizard demanded of Morik.

Morik shrugged as if he did not understand.

"The bag," said Robillard. "You held a bag."

"I have no—" Morik started to say, but he lost the words as the guard beside him slammed him hard in the belly yet again.

"Retrace his steps," Robillard instructed the other guards. "He carried a small satchel. I want it found."

"What of him?" one of the guards asked, motioning to the mound of flesh that was Wulfgar. "Surely he can't breath under that."

"Cut his face free, then," Robillard hissed. "He should not die as easily as that."

"Captain!" Waillan Micanty cried upon seeing Deudermont. He ran to kneel beside his fallen captain. Robillard put a comforting hand on the man's shoulder, turning a violent glare on Morik.

"I am innocent," the little thief declared, but even as he did a cry came from the alley. A moment later a guardsman ran out with the satchel in hand.

Robillard pulled open the bag, first lifting the stone from it and sensing immediately what it might be. He had lived through the Time of Troubles after all, and he knew all about dead magic regions and how stones from such places might dispel any magic near them. If his guess was right, it would explain how Morik and Wulfgar had so easily penetrated the wards he'd placed on the captain.

Next Robillard lifted a cat's claw from the bag. He led Morik's gaze and the stares of all the others from that curious item to Deudermont's neck, then produced another, similar claw, the one he had pulled from the captain's wound.

"Indeed," Robillard said dryly, eyebrows raised.

"I hate wizards," Morik muttered under his breath.

A sputter from Wulfgar turned them all around. The big man was coughing out pieces of the sticky substance. He started roaring in rage almost immediately and began tugging with such ferocity that all the Cutlass shook from the thrashing.

Robillard noted then that Arumn Gardpeck and several others had exited the place and stood staring incredulously at the scene before them. The tavernkeeper walked over to consider Wulfgar, then shook his head.

"What have ye done?" he asked.

"No good, as usual," remarked Josi Puddles.

Robillard walked over to them. "You know this man?" he asked Arumn, jerking his head toward Wulfgar.

"He's worked for me since he came to Luskan last spring," Arumn explained. "Until—" the tavernkeeper hesitated and stared at the big man yet again, shaking his head.

"Until?" Robillard prompted.

"Until he got too angry with all the world," Josi Puddles was happy to put in.

"You will be summoned to speak against him before the magistrates," Robillard explained. "Both of you."

Arumn nodded dutifully, but Josi's head bobbed eagerly. Perhaps too eagerly, Robillard observed, but he had to privately admit his gratitude to the little wretch.

A host of priests came running soon after, their numbers and haste alone a testament to the great reputation of the pirate-hunting Captain Deudermont. In mere minutes, the stricken man was born away on a litter.

On a nearby rooftop, Creeps Sharky smiled as he handed the empty bottle to Tee-a-nicknick.

* * * * *

Luskan's gaol consisted of a series of caves beside the harbor, winding and muddy, with hard and jagged stone walls. Perpetually stoked fires kept the place brutally hot and steamy. Thick veils of moisture erupted wherever the hot air collided with the cold, encroaching waters of the Sword Coast. There were a few cells, reserved for political prisoners mostly, threats to the ruling families and merchants who might grow stronger if they were made martyrs. Most of the prisoners, though, didn't last long enough to be afforded cells, soon to be victims of the macabre and brutally efficient Prisoner's Carnival.

This revolving group's cell consisted of a pair of shackles set high enough on the wall to keep them on the tips of their toes, dangling agonizingly by their arms. Compounding that torture were the mindless gaolers, huge and ugly thugs, half-ogres mostly, walking slowly and methodically through the complex with glowing pokers in their hands.

"This is all a huge mistake, you understand," Morik complained to the most recent gaoler to move in his and Wulfgar's direction.

The huge brute gave a slow chuckle that sounded like stones grating together and casually jabbed the orange end of a poker at Morik's belly. The nimble thief leaped sidelong, pulling hard with his chained arm but still taking a painful burn on the side. The ogre gaoler just kept on walking, approaching Wulfgar, and chuckling slowly.

"And what've yerself?" the brute said, moving his smelly breath close to the barbarian. "Yerself as well, eh? Ne'er did nothin' deservin' such imprisonin'?"

Wulfgar, his face blank, stared straight ahead. He barely winced when the powerful brute slugged him in the gut or when that awful poker slapped against his armpit, sending wispy smoke from his skin.

"Strong one," the brute said and chuckled again. "More fun's all." He brought the poker up level with Wulfgar's face and began moving it slowly in toward the big man's eye.

"Oh, but ye'll howl," he said.

394

"But we have not yet been tried!" Morik complained.

"Ye're thinkin' that matters?" the gaoler replied, pausing long enough only to turn a toothy grin on Morik. "Ye're all guilty for the fun of it, if not the truth."

That struck Wulfgar as a profound statement. Such was justice. He looked at the gaoler as if acknowledging the ugly creature for the first time, seeing simple wisdom there, a viewpoint come from observation. From the mouths of idiots, he thought.

The poker moved in, but Wulfgar set the gaoler with such a calm and devastating stare, a look borne of the barbarian's supreme confidence that this man—that all these foolish mortal men—could do nothing to him to rival the agonies he had suffered at the clawed hands of the demon Errtu.

The gaoler apparently got that message, or a similar one, for he hesitated, even backed the poker up so he could more clearly view Wulfgar's set expression.

"Ye think ye can hold it?" the brutal torturer asked Wulfgar. "Ye think ye can keep yer face all stuck like that when I pokes yer eye?" And on he came again.

Wulfgar gave a growl that came from somewhere very, very deep within, a feral, primal sound that stole the words from Morik's mouth as the little thief was about to protest. A growl that came from his torment in the pits of the Abyss.

The barbarian swelled his chest mightily, gathered his strength, and drove one shoulder forward with such ferocity and speed that the shackle anchor exploded from the wall, sending the stunned gaoler skittering back.

"Oh, but I'll kill ye for that!" the half-ogre cried, and he came ahead brandishing the poker like a club.

Wulfgar was ready for him. The barbarian coiled about, almost turning to face the wall, then swung his free arm wide, the chain and block of metal and stone fixed to its other end swishing across to clip the glowing poker and tear it from the gaoler's hand. Again the brute skittered back, and this time Wulfgar turned back on the wall fully, running his legs right up it so that he had his feet planted firmly, one on either side of the remaining shackle.

"Knock all the walls down!" Morik cheered.

The gaoler turned and ran.

Another growl came from Wulfgar, and he pulled with all his strength, every muscle in his powerful body straining. This anchor was more secure than the last, the stone wall more solid about it, but so great was Wulfgar's pull that a link in the heavy chain began to separate.

"Pull on!" Morik cried.

Wulfgar did, and he was sailing out from the wall, spinning into a back somersault. He tumbled down, unhurt, but then it hit him, a wave of anguish more powerful than any torture the sadistic gaoler might bring. In his mind he was no longer in the dungeon of Luskan but back in the Abyss, and though no shackles now held him he knew there could be no escape, no victory over his too-powerful captors. How many times had Errtu played this trick on him, making him think he was free only to snare him and drag him back to the stench and filth, only to beat him, then heal him, and beat him some more?

"Wulfgar?" Morik begged repeatedly, pulling at his own shackles, though with no results at all. "Wulfgar!"

The barbarian couldn't hear him, couldn't even see him, so lost was he in the swirling fog of his own thoughts. Wulfgar curled up on the floor, trembling like a babe when the gaoler returned with a dozen comrades.

A short while later, the beaten Wulfgar was hanging again from the wall, this time in shackles meant for a giant, thick and solid chains that had his feet dangling several feet from the floor and his arms stretched out straight to the side. As an extra precaution a block of sharpened spikes had been set behind the barbarian so if he pulled hard he would impale himself rather than tug the chains from their anchors. He was in a different chamber now, far removed from Morik. He was all alone with his memories of the Abyss, with no place to hide, no bottle to take him away.

* * * * *

"It should be working," the old woman grumbled. "Right herbs fer de poison."

Three priests walked back and forth in the room, one muttering prayers, another going from one side of Captain Deudermont to the other, listening for breath, for a heartbeat, checking for a pulse, while the third just kept rubbing his hand over his tightly cropped hair.

"But it is not working," Robillard argued, and he looked to the priests for some help.

"I don't understand," said Camerbunne, the ranking cleric among the trio. "It resists our spells and even a powerful herbal antidote."

"And wit some o' de poison in hand, it should be workin'," said the old woman.

"If that is indeed some of the poison," Robillard remarked.

"You yourself took it from the little one called Morik," Camerbunne explained.

"That does not necessarily mean . . ." Robillard started to reply. He let the thought hang in the air. The expressions on the faces of his four companions told him well enough that they had caught on. "What do we do, then?" the wizard asked.

"I can'no be promisin' anything," the old woman claimed, throwing up her hands dramatically. "Wit none o' de poison, me herbs'll do what dey will."

She moved to the side of the room, where they had placed a small table to act as her workbench, and began fiddling with different vials and jars and bottles. Robillard looked to Camerbunne. The man returned a defeated expression. The clerics had worked tirelessly over Deudermont in the day he had been in their care, casting spells that should have neutralized the vicious poison flowing through him. Those spells had provided temporary relief only, slowing the poison and allowing the captain to breath more easily and lowering his fever a bit, at least. Deudermont had not opened his eyes since the attack. Soon after, the captain's breathing went back to raspy, and he began bleeding again from his gums and his eyes. Robillard was no healer, but he had seen enough death to understand that if they did not come up with something soon, his beloved Captain Deudermont would fade away.

"Evil poison," Camerbunne remarked.

"It is an herb, no doubt," Robillard said. "Neither evil nor malicious. It just is what it is."

Camerbunne shook his head. "There is a touch of magic about it, do not doubt, good wizard," he declared. "Our spells will defeat any natural poison. No, this one has been specially prepared by a master and with the help of dark magic."

"Then what can we do?" the wizard asked.

"We can keep casting our spells over him to try and offer as much comfort as possible and hope that the poison works its way out of him," Camerbunne explained. "We can hope that old Gretchen finds the right mixture of herbs."

"Easier it'd be if I had a bit o' the poison," old Gretchen complained.

"And we can pray," Camerbunne finished.

The last statement brought a frown to the atheistic Robillard. He was a man of logic and specified rules and did not indulge in prayer.

"I will go to Morik the Rogue and learn more of the poison," Robillard said with a snarl.

"He has been tortured already," Camerbunne assured the wizard. "I doubt that he knows anything at all. It is merely something he purchased on the street, no doubt."

"Tortured?" Robillard replied skeptically. "A thumbscrew, a rack? No, that is not torture. That is a sadistic game and nothing more. The art of torture becomes ever more exquisite when magic is applied." He started for the door, but Camerbunne caught him by the arm.

"Morik will not know," he said again, staring soberly into the outraged wizard's hollowed eyes. "Stay with us. Stay with your captain. He may not survive the night, and if he does come out of the sleep before he dies, it would be better if he found a friend waiting for him."

Robillard had no argument against that heavy-handed comment, so he sighed and moved back to his chair, plopping down.

A short while later, a city guardsman knocked and entered the room, the routine call from the magistrate.

"Tell Jerem Boll and old Jharkheld that the charge against Wulfgar and Morik will likely be heinous murder," Camerbunne quietly explained.

Robillard heard the priest, and the words sank his heart even lower. It didn't matter much to Wulfgar and Morik what charge was placed against them. Either way, whether it was heinous murder or intended murder, they would be executed, though with the former the process would take much longer, to the pleasure of the crowd at the Prisoner's Carnival.

Watching them die would be of little satisfaction to Robillard, though, if his beloved captain did not survive. He put his head in his hands, considering again that he should go to Morik and punish the man with spell after spell until he broke down and revealed the type of poison that had been used.

Camerbunne was right, Robillard knew, for he understood city thieves like Morik the Rogue. Certainly Morik hadn't brewed the poison but had merely gotten some of it from a well-paid source.

The wizard lifted his head from his hands, a look of revelation on his haggard face. He remembered the two men who had been in the Cutlass before Wulfgar and Morik had arrived, the two men who had gone to the boy who had subsequently run off to find Wulfgar and Morik, the grimy sailor and his exotic, tattooed companion. He remembered *Leaping Lady,* sailing out fast from Luskan's harbor. Had Wulfgar and Morik traded the barbarian's marvelous warhammer for the poison to kill Deudermont?

Robillard sprang up from his chair, not certain of where to begin, but thinking now that he was on to something important. Someone, either the pair who had signaled Deudermont's arrival, the street urchin they had paid to go get Wulfgar and Morik, or someone on *Leaping Lady,* knew the secrets of the poison.

Robillard took another look at his poor, bedraggled captain, so obviously near to death. He stormed out of the room, determined to get some answers.

Chapter 10

Passage

Meralda walked tentatively into the kitchen the next morning, conscious of the stare her father leveled her way. She looked to her mother as well, seeking some indication that her father had told the woman about her indiscretion with Jaka the previous night. But Biaste was beaming, oblivious.

"Oh, the garden!" Biaste cried, all smiles. "Tell me about the garden. Is it as pretty as Gurdy Harkins says?"

Meralda glanced at her father. Relieved to find him smiling as well, she took her seat and moved it right beside Biaste's chair. "Prettier," she said, her grin wide. "All the colors, even in the late sun! And under the moon, though it's not shining so bright, the smells catch and hold you."

"That's not all that caught my fancy," Meralda said, forcing a cheerful voice as she launched into the news they were all waiting to hear. "Lord Feringal has asked me to marry him."

Biaste squealed with glee. Tori let out a cry of surprise, and a good portion of her mouthful of food, as well. Dohni Ganderlay slammed his hands upon the table happily.

Biaste, who could hardly get out of bed the week before, rushed about, readying herself, insisting that she had to go out at once and tell all of her

399

friends, particularly Gurdy Harkins, who was always acting so superior because she sometimes sewed dresses for Lady Priscilla.

"Why'd you come in last night so flustered and crying?" Tori asked Meralda as soon as the two were alone in their room.

"Just mind what concerns you," Meralda answered.

"You'll be living in the castle and traveling to Hundelstone and Fireshear, and even to Luskan and all the wondrous places," pressed Tori, insisting, "but you were crying. I heard you."

Eyes moistening again, Meralda glared at the girl then went back to her chores.

"It's Jaka," Tori reasoned, a grin spreading across her face. "You're still thinking about him."

Meralda paused in fluffing her pillow, moved it close to her for a moment—a gesture that revealed to Tori her guess was true—then spun suddenly and launched the pillow into Tori's face, following it with a tackle that brought her sister down on the small bed.

"Say I'm the queen!" the older girl demanded.

"You just might be," stubborn Tori shot back, which made Meralda tickle her all the more. Soon Tori could take it no more and called out "Queen! Queen!" repeatedly.

"But you are sad about Jaka," Tori said soberly a few moments later, when Meralda had gone back to fixing the bedclothes.

"I saw him last night," Meralda admitted. "On my way home. He's gone sick thinking about me and Lord Feringal."

Tori gasped and swayed, then leaned closer, hanging on every word.

"He kissed me, too."

"Better than Lord Feringal?"

Meralda sighed and nodded, closing her eyes as she lost herself in the memory of that one brief, tender moment with Jaka.

"Oh, Meralda, what're you to do?" Tori asked.

"Jaka wants me to run away with him," she answered.

Tori moaned and hugged her pillow. "And will you?"

Meralda stood straighter then and flashed the young girl a brave smile. "My place is with Lord Feringal," she explained.

"But Jaka—"

"Jaka can't do nothing for Ma, and nothing for the rest of you," Meralda went on. "You can give your heart to whomever you want, but you give your life to the one who's best for you and for the ones you love."

Tori started to protest again, but Dohni Ganderlay entered the room. "You got work," he reminded them, and he put a look over Meralda that told the young woman that he had, indeed, overheard the conversation. He even gave a slight nod of approval before exiting the room.

Meralda walked through that day in a fog, trying to align her heart with acceptance of her responsibility. She wanted to do what was right for her family, she really did, but she could not ignore the pull of her heart, the desire to learn the ways of love in the arms of a man she truly loved.

Out in the fields higher on the carved steps of the mountain, Dohni Ganderlay was no less torn. He saw Jaka Sculi that morning, and the two didn't exchange more than a quick glance—one-eyed for Jaka, whose left orb was swollen shut. As much as Dohni wanted to throttle the young man for jeopardizing his family, he could not deny his own memories of young love, memories that made him feel guilty looking at the beaten Jaka. Something more insistent than responsibility had pulled Jaka and Meralda together the previous night, and Dohni reminded himself pointedly not to hold a grudge, either against his daughter or against Jaka, whose only crime, as far as Dohni knew, was to love Meralda.

* * * * *

The house was quiet and perfectly still in the darkness just after dusk, which only amplified the noise made by every one of Meralda's movements. The family had retired early after a long day of work and the excitement of Meralda receiving yet another invitation to the castle, three days hence, accompanied by the most beautiful green silk gown the Ganderlay women had ever seen. Meralda tried to put the gown on quietly and slowly, but the material ruffled and crackled.

"What're you doing?" came a sleepy whisper from Tori.

"Shh!" Meralda replied, moving right beside the girl's bed and kneeling so that Tori could hear her whispered reply. "Go back to sleep and keep your mouth shut," she instructed.

"You're going to Jaka," Tori exclaimed, and Meralda slapped her hand over the girl's mouth.

"No such thing," Meralda protested. "I'm just trying it out."

"No you're not!" said Tori, coming fully awake and sitting up. "You're going to see Jaka. Tell me true, or I'll yell for Da."

"Promise me that you'll not say," Meralda said, sitting on the bed beside her sister. Tori's head bobbed excitedly. "I'm hoping to find Jaka out there in the dark," Meralda explained. "He goes out every night to watch the moon and the stars."

"And you're running away to be married?"

Meralda gave a sad chuckle. "No, not that," she replied. "I'm giving my life to Lord Feringal for the good of Ma and Da and yourself," she explained. "And not with regrets," she added quickly, seeing her sister about to protest. "No, he'll give me a good life at the castle, of that I'm sure. He's not a bad man, though he has much to learn. But I'm taking tonight for my own heart. One night with Jaka to say good-bye." Meralda patted Tori's arm as she stood to leave. "Now, go back to sleep."

"Only if you promise to tell me everything tomorrow," Tori replied. "Promise, or I'll tell."

"You won't tell," Meralda said with confidence, for she understood that Tori was as enchanted by the romance of it all as she was. More, perhaps, for the young girl didn't understand the lifelong implications of these decisions as much as Meralda did.

"Go to sleep," Meralda said softly again as she kissed Tori on the forehead. Straightening the dress with a nervous glance toward the curtain door of the room, Meralda headed for the small window and out into the night.

*   *   *   *   *

Dohni Ganderlay watched his eldest daughter disappear into the darkness, knowing full well her intent. A huge part of him wanted to follow her, to catch her with Jaka and kill the troublesome boy once and for all, but Dohni also held faith that his daughter would return, that she would do what was right for the family as she had said to her sister that morning.

It tore at his heart, to be sure, for he understood the allure and insistence of young love. He decided to give her this one night, without question and without judgment.

*   *   *   *   *

Meralda walked through the dark in fear. Not of any monsters that might leap out at her—no, this was her home and the young woman had never been afraid of such things—but of the reaction of her parents, particularly her father, if they discovered her missing.

Soon enough, though, the woman left her house behind and fell into the allure of the sparkling starry sky. She came to a field and began spinning and dancing, enjoying the touch of the wet grass on her bare feet, feeling as if she were stretching up to the heavens above to join with those magical points of light. She sang softly to herself, a quiet tune that sounded spiritual and surely fit her feelings out here, alone, at peace, and as one with the stars.

She hardly thought of Lord Feringal, of her parents, of her responsibility, even of her beloved Jaka. She wasn't thinking at all, was just existing in the glory of the night and the dance.

"Why are you here?" came a question from behind her, Jaka's lisping voice.

The magic vanished, and Meralda slowly turned around to face the young man. He stood, hands in pockets, head down, curly brown hair flopping over his brow so that she couldn't even see his eyes. Suddenly another fear gripped the young woman, the fear of what she anticipated would happen this night with this man.

"Did Lord Feringal let you out?" Jaka asked sarcastically.

"I'm no puppet of his," Meralda replied.

"Are you not to be his wife?" Jaka demanded. He looked up and stared hard at the woman, taking some satisfaction in the moisture that glistened in her eyes. "That's what the villagers are saying," he went on, then he changed his voice. "Meralda Ganderlay," he cackled, sounding like an old gnome woman. "Oh, but what a lucky one, she is! To think that Lord Feringal himself'd come a-calling for her."

"Stop it," Meralda begged softly.

Jaka only went on more forcefully, his voice shifting timbre. "And what's he thinking, that fool, Feringal?" he said, now in the gruff tones of a village man. "He'll bring disgrace to us all, marrying so low as that. And what, with a hunnerd pretty and rich merchant girls begging for his hand. Ah, the fool!"

Meralda turned away and suddenly felt more silly than beautiful in her green gown. She also felt a hand on her shoulder, and Jaka was there, behind her.

"You have to know," he said softly. "Half of them think Lord Feringal a fool, and the other half are too blind by the false hopes of it all, like they're reliving their own courtships through you, wishing that their own miserable lives could be more like yours."

"What're you thinking?" Meralda said firmly, turning about to face the man, and starting as she did to see more clearly the bruises on his face, his fat lip and closed eye. She composed herself at once, though, understanding well enough where Jaka had found that beating.

"I think that Lord Feringal believes himself to be above you," Jaka answered bluntly.

"And so he is."

"No!" The retort came out sharply, making Meralda jump back in surprise. "No, he is not your better," Jaka went on quietly, and he lifted his hand to gently stroke Meralda's wet cheek. "Rather, you are too good for him, but he will not view things that way. Nay, he will use you at his whim, then cast you aside."

Meralda wanted to argue, but she wasn't sure the young man was wrong. It didn't matter, though, for whatever Lord Feringal had in mind for her, the things he could do for her family remained paramount.

"Why did you come out here?" Jaka asked again, and it seemed to Meralda as if he only then noticed her gown, for he ran the material of one puffy sleeve through his thumb and index finger, feeling its quality.

"I came out for a night for Meralda," the young woman explained. "For a night when my desires would outweigh me responsibility. One night . . ."

She stopped when Jaka put a finger over her lips, holding it there for a long while. "Desires?" he asked slyly. "And do you include me among them? Did you come out here, all finely dressed, just to see me?"

Meralda nodded slowly and before she had even finished, Jaka was against her, pressing his lips to hers, kissing her hungrily, passionately. She felt as if she were floating, and then she realized that Jaka was

403

guiding her down to the soft grass, holding the kiss all the way. His hands continued to move about her, and she didn't stop them, didn't even stiffen when they brushed her in private places. No, this was her night, the night she would become a woman with the man of her choosing, the man of her desires and not her responsibilities.

Jaka reached down and pulled the gown halfway up her legs and wasted no time in putting his own legs between hers.

"Slower, please," Meralda said softly, taking his face in both her hands and holding him very close to her, so that he had to look in her eyes. "I want it to be perfect," she explained.

"Meralda," the young man breathed, seeming desperate. "I cannot wait another minute."

"You don't have to," the young woman assured him, and she pulled him close and kissed him gently.

Soon after, the pair lay side by side, naked on the wet grass, the chill ocean air tickling their bodies as they stared up at the starry canopy. Meralda felt different, giddy and lightheaded almost, and somehow spiritual, as if she had just gone through something magical, some rite of passage. A thousand thoughts swirled in her mind. How could she go back to Lord Feringal after this wondrous lovemaking with Jaka? How could she turn her back on these feelings of pure joy and warmth? She felt wonderful at that moment, and she wanted the moment to last and last for the rest of her life. The rest of her life with Jaka.

But it would not, the woman knew. It would be gone with the break of dawn, never to return. She'd had her one moment. A lump caught in her throat.

For Jaka Sculi, the moment was a bit different, though certainly no less satisfying. He had taken Meralda's virginity, had beaten the lord of Auckney himself to that special place. He, a lowly peasant in Lord Feringal's eyes, had taken something from Feringal that could never be replaced, something more valuable than all the gold and gems in Castle Auck.

Jaka liked that feeling, but he feared, as did Meralda, that this afterglow would not last. "Will you marry him?" he asked suddenly.

Beautiful in the moonlight, Meralda turned a sleepy eye his way. "Let's not be talking about such things tonight," the woman implored him. "Nothing about Lord Feringal or anyone else."

"I must know, Meralda," Jaka said firmly, sitting up to stare down at her. "Tell me."

Meralda gave the young man the most plaintive look he had ever seen. "He can do for my ma and da," she tried to explain. "You must understand that the choice is not mine to make," an increasingly desperate Meralda finished lamely.

"Understand?" Jaka echoed incredulously, leaping to his feet and walking away. "Understand! How can I after what we just did? Oh, why did you come to me if you planned to marry Lord Feringal?"

Meralda caught up to him and grabbed him by the shoulders. "I came out for one night where I might choose," she explained. "I came out because I love you and wish with all my heart that things could be different."

"We had just one brief moment," Jaka whined, turning back to face her.

Meralda came up on her tiptoes and kissed him gently. "We've more time," she explained, an offer Jaka couldn't resist. A short while later, Jaka was lying on the grass again, while Meralda stood beside him, pulling on her clothes.

"Deny him," Jaka said unexpectedly, and the young woman stopped and stared down at him. "Deny Lord Feringal," Jaka said again, as casually as if it were the most simple decision. "Forget him and run away with me. To Luskan, or even all the way to Waterdeep."

Meralda sighed and shook her head. "I'm begging you not to ask it of me," she started to say, but Jaka would not relent.

"Think of the life we might find together," he said. "Running through the streets of Waterdeep, magical Waterdeep! Running and laughing and making love. Raising a family together—how beautiful our children shall be."

"Stop it!" Meralda snapped so forcefully that she stole the words from Jaka's mouth. "You know I want to, and you also know I can't." Meralda sighed again profoundly. It was the toughest thing she had ever done in her entire life, but she bent to kiss Jaka's angry mouth one last time, then started toward home.

Jaka lay on the field for a long while, his mind racing. He had achieved his conquest, and it had been as sweet as he had expected. Still, it would not hold. Lord Feringal would marry Meralda, would beat him in the end. The thought of it made him sick. He stared up at the moon, now shaded behind lines of swift-moving clouds. "Fie this life," he grumbled.

There had to be something he could do to beat Lord Feringal, something to pull Meralda back to him.

A confident smile spread over Jaka's undeniably handsome face. He remembered the sounds Meralda had made, the way her body had moved in harmony with his own.

He wouldn't lose.

Chapter 11

All Hands Joined

"You will tell me of the poison," said Prelate Vohltin, an associate of Camerbunne. He was sitting in a comfortable chair in the middle of the brutally hot room, his frame outlined by the glow of the huge, blazing hearth behind him.

"Never good," Morik replied, drawing another twist of the thumbscrew from the bulky, sadistic, one-eyed (and he didn't even bother to wear an eyepatch) gaoler. This one had more orcish blood than human. "Poison, I mean," the rogue clarified, his voice going tight as waves of agony shot up his arm.

"It was not the same as the poison in the vial," Vohltin explained, and he nodded to the gaoler, who walked around the back of Morik. The rogue tried to follow the half-orc's movements, but both his arms were pulled outright, shackled tight at the wrists. One hand was in a press, the other in a framework box of strange design, its panels holding the hand open, fingers extended so that the gaoler could "play" with them one at a time.

The prelate shrugged, held his hands up, and when Morik didn't immediately reply a cat-o'-nine-tails switched across the rogue's naked back, leaving deep lines that hurt all the more for the sweat.

407

"You had the poison," Vohltin logically asserted, "and the insidious weapons, but it was not the same poison in the vial we recovered. A clever ruse, I suspect, to throw us off the correct path in trying to heal Captain Deudermont's wounds."

"A ruse indeed," Morik said dryly. The gaoler hit him again with the whip and raised his arm for a third strike. However, Vohltin raised his arm to hold the brutal thug at bay.

"You admit it?" Vohltin asked.

"All of it," Morik replied. "A ruse perpetrated by someone else, delivering to me and Wulfgar what you consider the evidence against us, then striking out at Deudermont when he came over to speak—"

"Enough!" said an obviously frustrated Vohltin, for he and all of the other interrogators had heard the same nonsense over and over from both Morik and Wulfgar. The prelate rose and turned to leave, shaking his head. Morik knew what that meant.

"I can tell you other things," the rogue pleaded, but Vohltin just lifted his arm and waved his hand dismissively.

Morik started to speak out again, but he lost his words and his breath as the gaoler slugged him hard in the kidney. Morik yelped and jumped, which only made the pain in his hand and thumb all the more exquisite. Still, despite all self-control, he jumped again when the gaoler struck him another blow, for the thug was wearing a metal strip across his knuckles, inlaid with several small pins.

Morik thought of his drow visitors that night long ago in the small apartment he kept near the Cutlass. Did they know what was happening? Would they come and rescue Wulfgar, and if they did, would they rescue Morik as well? He had almost told Wulfgar about them in those first hours when they had been chained in the same room, hesitating only because he feared that Wulfgar, so obviously lost in agonizing memories, wouldn't even hear him and that somebody else might.

Wouldn't it be wonderful if the magistrates could pin on him, as well a charge that he was an associate of dark elves? Not that it mattered. Another punch slammed in, then the gaoler went for the whip again to cut a few new lines on his back.

If those drow didn't come, his fate, Morik knew, was sealed in a most painful way.

*　*　*　*　*

Robillard had only been gone for a few minutes, but when he returned to Deudermont's room he found half a dozen priests working furiously on the captain. Camerbunne stood back, directing the group.

"He is on fire inside," the priest explained, and even from this distance Robillard could see the truth of that statement from the color of the feverish Deudermont and the great streaks of sweat that trailed down his face. Robillard noticed, too, that the room was growing colder, and he realized that a pair of the six working on Deudermont were casting spells, not to heal, but to create cold.

"I have spells that will do the same," Robillard offered. "Powerful spells on scrolls back at *Sea Sprite*. Perhaps my captain would be better served if your priests were able to focus on healing."

"Run," Camerbunne said, and Robillard did him one better, using a series of dimensional doors to get back to *Sea Sprite* in a matter of moments. The wizard fished through his many components and scroll tubes, magical items and finely crafted pieces he meant to enchant when he found the time, at last coming upon a scroll with a trio of spells for creating ice, along with the necessary components. Cursing himself for not being better prepared and vowing that he would devote all his magical energies the next day to memorizing such spells, Robillard gated back to the chamber in the chapel. The priests were still working frenetically, and the old herb woman was there as well, rubbing a creamy, white salve all over Deudermont's wet chest.

Robillard prepared the components—a vial of ice troll blood, a bit of fur from the great white bear—and unrolled the scroll, flattening it on a small table. He tore his gaze from the dying Deudermont, focusing on the task at hand, and with the discipline only a wizard might know he methodically went to work, chanting softly and waggling his fingers and hands. He poured the cold ice troll blood on his thumb and index finger, then clasped the fur between them and blew onto it, once, twice, thrice, then cast the fur to the floor along a bare wall at the side of the room. A tap-tapping began there, hail bouncing off the floor, louder as the chunks came larger and larger, until, within a matter of seconds, Captain Deudermont was laid upon a new bed, a block of ice.

"This is the critical hour," Camerbunne explained. "His fever is too great, and I fear he may die of it. Blood as thin as water pours from his orifices. I have more priests waiting to step in when this group has exhausted their healing spells, and I have sent several to other chapels, even of rival gods, begging aid." Camerbunne smiled at the wizard's surprised expression. "They will come," he assured Robillard. "All of them."

Robillard was not a religious man, mainly because in his days of trying to find a god that fit his heart, he found himself distressed at the constant bickering and rivalries of the many varied churches. So he understood the compliment Camerbunne had just paid to the captain. What a great reputation Deudermont had built among the honest folk of the northern Sword Coast that all would put aside rivalries and animosity to join in for his sake.

They did come as Camerbunne promised, priests of nearly every persuasion in Luskan, flocking in six at a time to expend their healing energies over the battered captain.

Deudermont's fever broke around midnight. He opened a weary eye to find Robillard asleep next to him. The wizard's head was craddled on his folded arms on the captain's small bed, next to Deudermont's side.

"How many days?" the weak captain asked, for he recognized that something was very wrong here, very strange, as if he had just awakened from a long and terrible nightmare. Also, though he was wrapped in a sheet, he knew that he was on no normal bed, for it was too hard and his backside was wet.

Robillard jumped up at the sound, eyes wide. He put his hand to Deudermont's forehead, and his smile widened considerably when he felt that the man was cool to the touch.

"Camerbunne!" he called, drawing a curious look from the confused captain.

It was the most beautiful sight Robillard had ever seen.

* * * * *

"Three circuits," came the nasally voice of Jharkheld the Magistrate, a thin old wretch who took far too much pleasure in his tasks for Morik's liking.

Every day the man walked through the dungeon caverns, pointing out those whose time had come for Prisoner's Carnival and declaring, based on the severity of their crime, or, perhaps, merely from his own mood, the preparation period for each. A "circuit," according to the gaoler who regularly beat Morik, was the time it took for a slow walk around the plaza where the Prisoner's Carnival was held, roughly about ten minutes. So the man Jharkheld had just labeled for three circuits would be brought up to carnival and tortured by various nonmortal means for about half an hour before Jharkheld even began the public hearing. It was done to rouse the crowd, Morik understood, and the old wretch Jharkheld liked the hearty cheers.

"So you have come to beat me again," Morik said when the brutish gaoler walked into the natural stone chamber where the rogue was chained to the wall. "Have you brought the holy man with you? Or the magistrate, perhaps? Is he to join us to order me up to the carnival?"

"No beatin' today, Morik the Rogue," the gaoler said. "They're not wantin' anything more from ye. Captain Deudermont's not needin' ye anymore."

"He died?" Morik asked, and he couldn't mask a bit of concern in his tone. If Deudermont had died, the charge against Wulfgar and Morik would be heinous murder, and Morik had been around Luskan long enough to witness more than a few executions of people so charged, executions by torture that lasted the better part of a day, at least.

"Nah," the gaoler said with obvious sadness in his tone. "Nah, we're not so lucky. Deudermont's livin' and all the better, so it looks like yerself and Wulfgar'll get killed quick and easy."

"Oh, joy," said Morik.

The brute paused for a moment and looked around, then waded in close to Morik and hit him a series of wicked blows about the stomach and chest.

"I'm thinkin' that Magistrate Jharkheld'll be callin' ye up to carnival soon enough," the gaoler explained. "Wanted to get in a few partin's, is all."

"My thanks," the ever-sarcastic rogue replied, and that got him a left hook across the jaw that knocked out a tooth and filled his mouth with warm blood.

*   *   *   *   *

Deudermont's strength was fast returning, so much so that the priests had a very difficult task in keeping the man in his bed. Still they prayed over him, offering spells of healing, and the old herbalist woman came in with pots of tea and another soothing salve.

"It could not have been Wulfgar," Deudermont protested to Robillard, who had told him the entire story since the near tragedy in front of the Cutlass.

"Wulfgar and Morik," Robillard said firmly. "I watched it, Captain, and a good thing for you that I was watching!"

"It makes no sense to me," Deudermont replied. "I know Wulfgar."

"Knew," Robillard corrected.

"But he is a friend of Drizzt and Catti-brie, and we both know that those two would have nothing to do with an assassin—nothing good, at least."

"*Was* a friend," Robillard stubbornly corrected. "Now Wulfgar makes friends the likes of Morik the Rogue, a notorious street thug, and another pair, I believe, worse by far."

"Another pair?" Deudermont asked, and even as he did, Waillan Micanty and another crewman from *Sea Sprite* entered the room. They went to the captain first, bowed and saluted, both smiling widely, for Deudermont seemed even better than he had earlier in the day when all the crew had come running to Robillard's joyous call.

"Have you found them?" the wizard asked impatiently.

"I believe we have," a smug-looking Waillan replied. "Hiding in the hold of a boat just two berths down from *Sea Sprite*."

"They haven't come out much of late," the other crewman offered, "but we talked to some men at the Cutlass who thought they knew the pair and claimed that the one-eyed sailor was dropping gold coins without regard."

Robillard nodded knowingly. So it was a contracted attack, and those two were a part of the plan.

"With your permission, Captain," the wizard said, "I should like to take *Sea Sprite* out of dock."

411

Deudermont looked at him curiously, for the captain had no idea what this talk might be about.

"I sent Mister Micanty on a search for two other accomplices in the attack against you," Robillard explained. "It appears that we may have located them."

"But Mister Micanty just said they were in port," Deudermont reasoned.

"They're aboard *Bowlegged Lady,* as paying passengers. When I put *Sea Sprite* behind them, all weapons to bear, they will likely turn the pair over without a fight," Robillard reasoned, his eyes aglow.

Now Deudermont managed a chuckle. "I only wish that I could go with you," he said. The three took that as their cue and turned immediately for the door.

"What of Magistrate Jharkheld?" Deudermont asked quickly before they could skitter away.

"I bade him to hold on the justice for the pair," Robillard replied, "as you requested. We shall need them to confirm that these newest two were in on the attack, as well."

Deudermont nodded and waved the trio away, falling into his own thoughts. He still didn't believe that Wulfgar could be involved, though he had no idea how he might prove it. In Luskan, as in most of the cities of Faerûn, even the appearance of criminal activity could get a man hanged, or drawn and quartered, or whatever unpleasant manner of death the presiding magistrate could think up.

* * * * *

"An honest trader, I be, and ye got no proof otherways," Captain Pinnickers of *Bowlegged Lady* declared, leaning over the taffrail and calling out protests against the appearance of the imposing *Sea Sprite,* catapult and ballista and ranks of archers trained on his decks.

"As I have already told you, Captain Pinnickers, we have come not for your ship, nor for you, but for a pair you harbor," Robillard answered with all due respect.

"Bah! Go away with ye, or I'll be callin' out the city guard!" the tough, old sea dog declared.

"No difficult task," Robillard replied smugly, and he motioned to the wharves beside *Bowlegged Lady.* Captain Pinnickers turned to see a hundred city soldiers or more lining the dock, grim-faced and armed for battle.

"You have nowhere to run or hide," Robillard explained. "I ask your permission one more time as a courtesy to you. For your own sake, allow me and my crew to board your ship and find the pair we seek."

"My ship!" Pinnicker said, poking a finger into his chest.

"Or I shall order my gunners to have at it," Robillard explained, standing tall and imposing at *Sea Sprite's* rail, all pretense of politeness flown. "I shall join in with spells of destruction you cannot even begin to imagine. Then we will search the wreckage for the pair ourselves."

Pinnicker seemed to shrink back just a bit, but he held fast his grim and determined visage.

"I offer you the choice one last time," Robillard said, his mock politeness returning.

"Fine choice," Pinnicker grumbled. He gave a helpless little wave, indicating that Robillard and the others should cross to his deck.

They found Creeps Sharky and Tee-a-nicknick in short order, with Robillard easily identifying them. They also found an interesting item on a beam near the tattooed man-creature: a hollow tube.

"Blowgun," Waillan Micanty explained, presenting it to Robillard.

"Indeed," said the wizard, examining the exotic weapon and quickly confirming its use from the design. "What might someone shoot from it?"

"Something small with an end shaped to fill the tube," Micanty explained. He took the weapon back, pursed his lips, and blew through the tube. "It wouldn't work well if too much wind escaped around the dart."

"Small, you say. Like a cat's claw?" Robillard asked, eyeing the captured pair. "With a pliable, feathered end?"

Following Robillard's gaze at the miserable prisoners, Waillan Micanty nodded grimly.

*   *   *   *   *

Wulfgar was lost somewhere far beyond pain, hanging limply from his shackled wrists, both bloody and torn. The muscles on the back of his neck and shoulders had long ago knotted, and even if he had been released and dropped to the floor, only gravity would have changed his posture.

The pain had pushed too far and too hard and had released Wulfgar from his present prison. Unfortunately for the big man, that escape had only taken him to another prison, a darker place by far, with torments beyond anything these mortal men could inflict upon him. Tempting, naked, and wickedly beautiful succubi flew about him. The great pincer-armed glabrezu came at him repeatedly, snapping, snapping, nipping pieces of his body away. All the while he heard the demonic laughter of Errtu the conqueror. Errtu the great balor who hated Drizzt Do'Urden above all other mortals and played out that anger continually upon Wulfgar.

"Wulfgar?" The call came from far away, not a throaty, demonic voice like Errtu's, but gentle and soft.

Wulfgar knew the trap, the false hopes, the feigned friendship. Errtu had played this one on him countless times, finding him in his moments of despair, lifting him from the emotional valleys, then dropping him even deeper into the pit of black hopelessness.

413

"I have spoken with Morik," the voice went on, but Wulfgar was no longer listening.

"He claims innocence," Captain Deudermont stubbornly continued, despite Robillard's huffing doubts at his side. "Yet the dog Sharky has implicated you both."

Trying to ignore the words, Wulfgar let out a low growl, certain that it was Errtu come again to torment him.

"Wulfgar?" Deudermont asked.

"It is useless," Robillard said flatly.

"Give me something, my friend," Deudermont went on, leaning heavily on a cane for support, for his strength had far from returned. "Some word that you are innocent so that I might tell Magistrate Jharkheld to release you."

No response came back other than the continued growl.

"Just tell me the truth," Deudermont prodded. "I don't believe that you were involved, but I must hear it from you if I am to demand a proper trial."

"He can't answer you, Captain," Robillard said, "because there is no truth to tell that will exonerate him."

"You heard Morik," Deudermont replied, for the two had just come from Morik's cell, where the little thief had vehemently proclaimed his and Wulfgar's innocence. He explained that Creeps Sharky had offered quite a treasure for Deudermont's head, but that he and Wulfgar had flatly refused.

"I heard a desperate man weave a desperate tale," Robillard replied.

"We could find a priest to interrogate him," Deudermont said. "Many of them have spells to detect such lies."

"Not allowed by Luskan law," Robillard replied. "Too many priests bring their own agendas to the interrogation. The magistrate handles his questioning in his own rather successful manner."

"He tortures them until they admit guilt, whether or not the admission is true," Deudermont supplied.

Robillard shrugged. "He gets results."

"He fills his carnival."

"How many of those in the carnival do you believe to be innocent, Captain?" Robillard asked bluntly. "Even those innocent of the particular crime for which they are being punished have no doubt committed many other atrocities."

"That is a rather cynical view of justice, my friend," Deudermont said.

"That is reality," Robillard answered.

Deudermont sighed and looked back to Wulfgar, hanging and growling, not proclaiming his innocence, not proclaiming anything at all. Deudermont called to the man again, even moved over and tapped him on the side. "You must give me a reason to believe Morik," he said.

414

Wulfgar felt the gentle touch of a succubus luring him into emotional hell. With a roar, he swung his hips and kicked out, just grazing the surprised captain, but clipping him hard enough to send him staggering backward to the floor.

Robillard sent a ball of sticky goo from his wand, aiming low to pin Wulfgar's legs against the wall. The big man thrashed wildly, but with his wrists firmly chained and his legs stuck fast to the wall, the movement did little but reinvigorate the agony in his shoulders.

Robillard was before him, hissing and sneering, whispering some chant. The wizard reached up, grabbed Wulfgar's groin, and sent a shock of electricity surging into the big man that brought a howl of pain.

"No!" said Deudermont, struggling to his feet. "No more."

Robillard gave a sharp twist and spun away, his face contorted with outrage. "Do you need more proof, Captain?" he demanded.

Deudermont wanted to offer a retort but found none. "Let us leave this place," he said.

"Better that we had never come," Robillard muttered.

Wulfgar was alone again, hanging easier until Robillard's wand material dissipated, for the goo supported his weight. Soon enough, though, he was hanging by just the shackles again, his muscles bunching in renewed pain. He fell away, deeper and darker than ever before.

He wanted a bottle to crawl into, needed the burning liquid to release his mind from the torments.

Chapter 12

To Her Family True

"Merchant Banci to speak with you," Steward Temigast announced as he stepped into the garden. Lord Feringal and Meralda had been standing quiet, enjoying the smells and the pretty sights, the flowers and the glowing orange sunset over the dark waters.

"Bring him out," the young man replied, happy to show off his newest trophy.

"Better that you come to him," Temigast said. "Banci is a nervous one, and he's in a rush. He'll not be much company to dear Meralda. I suspect he will ruin the mood of the garden."

"Well, we cannot allow that," Lord Feringal conceded. With a smile to Meralda and a pat of her hand, he started toward Temigast.

Feringal walked past the steward, and Temigast offered Meralda a wink to let her know he had just saved her from a long tenure of tedium. The young woman was far from insulted at being excluded. Also, the ease with which Feringal had agreed to go along surprised her.

Now she was free to enjoy the fabulous gardens alone, free to touch the flowers and take in their silky texture, to bask in their aromas without the constant pressure of having an adoring man following her every movement with his eyes and hands. She savored the moment and vowed

417

that after she was lady of the castle she would spend many such moments out in this garden alone.

But she was not alone. She spun around to find Priscilla watching her.

"It is *my* garden, after all," the woman said coldly, moving to water a row of bright blue bachelor buttons.

"So Steward Temigast told me," Meralda replied.

Priscilla didn't respond, didn't even look up from her watering.

"It surprised me to learn of it," Meralda went on, her eyes narrowing. "It's so beautiful, after all."

That brought Priscilla's eyes up in a flash. The woman was very aware of insults. Scowling mightily, she strode toward Meralda. For a moment the younger woman thought Priscilla might try to strike her, or douse her, perhaps, with the bucket of water.

"My, aren't you the pretty one?" Priscilla remarked. "And only a pretty one like you could make so beautiful a garden, of course."

"Pretty inside," Meralda replied, not backing down an inch. She recognized that her posture had, indeed, caught the imposing Priscilla off guard. "And yes, I'm knowing enough about flowers to understand that the way you talk to them and the way you're touching them is what makes them grow. Begging your pardon, Lady Priscilla, but you're not for showing me any side of yourself that's favoring to flowers."

"Begging my pardon?" Priscilla echoed. She stood straight, her eyes wide, stunned by the peasant woman's bluntness. She stammered over a couple of replies before Meralda cut her off.

"By my own eyes, it's the most beautiful garden in all of Auckney," she said, breaking eye contact with Priscilla to take in the view of the flowers, emphasizing her words with a wondrous look of approval. "I thought you hateful and all."

She turned back to face the woman directly, but Meralda was not scowling. Priscilla's frown, too, had somewhat abated. "Now I'm knowing better, for anyone who could make a garden so delightful is hiding delights of her own." She ended with a disarming grin that even Priscilla could not easily dismiss.

"I have been working on this garden for years," the older woman explained. "Planting and tending, finding flowers to come to color every week of every summer."

"And the work's showing," Meralda sincerely congratulated her. "I'll wager there's not a garden to match it in Luskan or even Waterdeep."

Meralda couldn't suppress a bit of a smile to see Priscilla blushing. She'd found the woman's weak spot.

"It is a pretty garden," the woman said, "but Waterdeep has gardens the size of Castle Auck."

"Bigger then, but sure to be no more beautiful," the unrelenting Meralda remarked.

Priscilla stammered again, so obviously off guard from the unexpected flattery from this peasant girl. "Thank you," she managed to blurt out, and her chubby face lit up with as wide a smile as Meralda could ever have imagined. "Would you like to see something special?"

Meralda was at first wary, for she certainly had a hard time trusting Priscilla, but she decided to take a chance. Priscilla grabbed her by the hand and tugged her back into the castle, through a couple of small rooms, down a hidden stairway, and to a small open-air courtyard that seemed more like a hole in the castle design, an empty space barely wide enough for the two of them to stand side by side. Meralda laughed aloud at the sight, for while the walls were naught but cracked and weathered gray stone, there, in the middle of the courtyard, stood a row of poppies, most the usual deep red, but several a delicate pink variety that Meralda didn't recognize.

"I work with the plants in here," Priscilla explained, guiding Meralda to the pots. She knelt before the red poppies first, stroking the stem with one hand while pushing down the petals to reveal the dark core of the flower with the other. "See how rough the stem is?" she asked. Meralda nodded as she reached out to touch the solid plant.

Priscilla abruptly stood and guided Meralda to the other pots containing lighter colored poppies. Again she revealed the core of the flower, this time showing it to be white, not dark. When Meralda touched the stem of this plant she found it to be much more delicate.

"For years I have been using lighter and lighter plants," Priscilla explained. "Until I achieved this, a poppy so very different from its original stock."

"Priscilla poppies!" Meralda exclaimed. She was delighted to see surly Priscilla Auck actually break into a laugh.

"But you've earned the name," Meralda went on. "You should be taking them to the merchants when they come in on their trek between Hundelstone and Luskan. Wouldn't the ladies of Luskan pay a high price for so delicate a poppy?"

"The merchants who come to Auckney are interested only in trading for practical things," Priscilla replied. "Tools and weapons, food and drink, always drink, and perhaps a bit of Ten-Towns scrimshaw. Lord Feri has quite a collection of that."

"I'd love to see it."

Priscilla gave her a rather strange look then. "You will, I suppose," she said somewhat dryly, as if only remembering then that this was no ordinary peasant servant but the woman who would soon be the lady of Auckney.

"But you should be selling your flowers," Meralda continued encouragingly. "Take them to Luskan, perhaps, to the open air markets I've heard are so very wonderful."

The smile returned to Priscilla's face, at least a bit. "Yes, well, we shall see," she replied, a haughty undercurrent returning to her tone. "Of course, only village peasants hawk their wares."

Meralda wasn't too put off. She had made more progress with Priscilla in this one day than she ever expected to make in a lifetime.

"Ah, there you are." Steward Temigast stood in the doorway to the castle. As usual, his timing couldn't have been better. "Pray forgive us, dear Meralda, but Lord Feringal will be caught in a meeting all the night, I fear, for Banci can be a demon in bartering, and he has actually brought a few pieces that have caught Lord Feringal's eye. He bade me to inquire if you would like to visit tomorrow during the day."

Meralda looked to Priscilla, hoping for some clue, but the woman was tending her flowers again as if Meralda and Temigast weren't even there.

"Tell him that surely I will," Meralda replied.

"I pray that you are not too angry with us," said Temigast. Meralda laughed at the absurd notion. "Very well, then. Perhaps you should be right away, for the coach is waiting and I fear a storm will come up tonight," Temigast said as he moved aside.

"Your Priscilla poppies are as beautiful a flower as I've ever seen," Meralda said to the woman who would soon be kin. Priscilla caught her by the pleat of her dress, and when she turned back, startled, she grew even more surprised, for Priscilla held a small pink poppy out to her.

The two shared a smile, and Meralda swept past Temigast into the castle proper. The steward hesitated in following, though, turning his attention to Lady Priscilla. "A friend?" he asked.

"Hardly," came the cold reply. "Perhaps if she has her own flower, she will leave mine in peace."

Temigast chuckled, drawing an icy stare from Priscilla. "A friend, a *lady* friend, might not be so bad a thing as you seem to believe," the steward remarked. He turned and hastened to catch up to Meralda, leaving Priscilla kneeling in her private garden with some very curious and unexpected thoughts.

*　*　*　*　*

Many budding ideas rode with Meralda on the way back to her house from Castle Auck. She had handled Priscilla well, she thought, and even dared to hope that she and the woman might become real friends one day.

Even as that notion crossed her mind, it brought a burst of laughter from the young woman's lips. In truth, she couldn't imagine ever having a close friendship with Priscilla, who would always, always, consider herself Meralda's superior.

But Meralda knew better now, and not because of that day's interaction with the woman but rather, because of the previous night's interaction with Jaka Sculi. How much better Meralda understood the world now, or at least her corner of it. She had used the previous night as a

420

turning point. It had taken that one moment of control, by Meralda and for Meralda, to accept the wider and less appealing responsibility that had been thrown her way. Yes, she would play Lord Feringal now, bringing him on her heel to the wedding chapel of Castle Auck. She, and more importantly, her family, would get from him what they required. While such gains would come at a cost to Meralda, it was a cost that this new woman, no more a girl, would pay willingly and with some measure of control.

She was glad she hadn't seen much of Lord Feringal tonight, though. No doubt he would have tried to force himself on her, and Meralda doubted she could have maintained the self-control necessary to not laugh at him.

Smiling, satisfied, the young woman stared out the coach's window as the twisting road rolled by. She saw him, and suddenly her smile disappeared. Jaka Sculi stood atop a rocky bluff, a lone figure staring down at the place where the driver normally let Meralda out.

Meralda leaned out the coach window opposite Jaka so she would not be seen by him. "Good driver, please take me all the way to my door this night."

"Oh, but I hoped you'd ask me that this particular ride, Miss Meralda," Liam Woodgate replied. "Seems one of my horses is having a bit of a problem with a shoe. Might your father have a straight bar and a hammer?"

"Of course he does," Meralda replied. "Take me to my house, and I'm sure that me da'll help you fix that shoe."

"Good enough, then!" the driver replied. He gave the reins a bit of a snap that sent the horses trotting along more swiftly.

Meralda fell back in her seat and stared out the window at the silhouette of a slender man she knew to be Jaka from his forlorn posture. In her mind she could see his expression clearly. She almost reconsidered her course and told the driver to let her out. Maybe she should go to Jaka again and make love under the stars one more time, be free for yet another night. Perhaps she should run away with him and live her life for her sake and no one else's.

No, she couldn't do that to her mother, or her father, or Tori. Meralda was a daughter her parents could depend upon to do the right thing. The right thing, Meralda knew, was to put her affections for Jaka Sculi far behind her.

The coach pulled up before the Ganderlay house. Liam Woodgate, a nimble fellow, hopped down and pulled open Meralda's door before she could reach for the latch.

"You're not needing to do that," the young woman stated as the gnome helped her out of the carriage.

"But you're to be the lady of Auckney," the cheery old fellow replied with a smile and a wink. "Can't be having you treated like a peasant, now can we?"

421

"It's not so bad," Meralda replied, adding, "being a peasant, I mean." Liam laughed heartily. "Gets you out of the castle at night."

"And gets you back in, whenever you're wanting," Liam replied. "Steward Temigast says I'm at your disposal, Miss Meralda. I'm to take you and your family, if you so please, wherever you're wanting to go."

Meralda smiled widely and nodded her thanks. She noticed then that her grim-faced father had opened the door and was standing just within the house.

"Da!" Meralda called. "Might you help my friend . . ." The woman paused and looked to the driver. "Why, I'm not even knowing your proper name," she remarked.

"Most noble ladies don't take the time to ask," he replied, and both he and Meralda laughed again. "Besides, we all look alike to you big folks." He winked mischeviously, then bowed low. "Liam Woodgate, at your service."

Dohni Ganderlay walked over. "A short stay at the castle this night," he remarked suspiciously.

"Lord Feringal got busy with a merchant," Meralda replied. "I'm to return on the morrow. Liam here's having a bit of trouble with a horse-shoe. Might you help him?"

Dohni looked past the driver to the team and nodded. " 'Course," he answered. "Get yourself inside, girl," he instructed Meralda. "Your ma's taken ill again."

Meralda bolted for the house. She found her mother in bed, hot with fever again, her eyes sunken deep into her face. Tori was kneeling beside the bed, a mug of water in one hand, a wet towel in the other.

"She got the weeps soon after you left," Tori explained, a nasty affliction that had been plaguing Biaste off and on for several months.

Looking at her mother, Meralda wanted to fall down and cry. How frail the woman appeared, how unpredictable her health. It was as if Biaste Ganderlay had been walking a fine line on the edge of her own grave day after day. Good spirits alone had sustained the woman these last days, since Lord Feringal had come calling, Meralda knew. Desperately, the young woman grasped at the only medication she had available.

"Oh, Ma," she said, feigning exasperation. "Aren't you picking a fine time to fall ill again?"

"Meralda," Biaste Ganderlay breathed, and even that seemed a labor to her.

"We'll just have to get you better and be quick about it," Meralda said sternly.

"Meralda!" Tori complained.

"I told you about Lady Priscilla's garden," Meralda went on, ignoring her sister's protest. "Get better, and be quick, because tomorrow you're to join me at the castle. We'll walk the garden together."

"And me?" Tori pleaded. Meralda turned to regard her and noticed that she had another audience member. Dohni Ganderlay stood at the door, leaning on the jamb, a surprised expression on his strong but weary face.

"Yeah, Tori, you can join us," Meralda said, trying hard to ignore her father, "but you must promise that you'll behave."

"Oh, Ma, please get better quickly!" Tori implored Biaste, clutching the woman's hand firmly. It did seem as if the sickly woman showed a little bit more life at that moment.

"Go, Tori," Meralda instructed. "Run to the coach driver—Liam's his name—and tell him that we three'll be needing a ride to the castle at midday tomorrow. We can't have Ma walking all the way."

Tori ran off as instructed, and Meralda bent low over her mother. "Get well," she whispered, kissing the woman on the forehead. Biaste smiled and nodded her intent to try.

Meralda walked out of the room under the scrutinizing gaze of Dohni Ganderlay. She heard the man pull the curtain closed to her parents' room, then follow her to the middle of the common room.

"Will he let you bring them both?" Dohni asked, softly so that Biaste would not hear.

She shrugged. "I'm to be his wife, and that's his idea. He'd be a fool to not grant me this one favor."

Dohni Ganderlay's face melted into a grateful smile as he fell into his daughter, hugging her closely. Though she couldn't see his face, Meralda knew that he was crying.

She returned that hug tenfold, burying her face in her father's strong shoulder, a not so subtle reminder to her that, though she was being the brave soldier for the good of her family, she was still, in many ways, a scared little girl.

How warm it felt to her, a reassurance that she was doing the right thing, when her father kissed her on top of her head.

*   *   *   *   *

Up on the hill a short distance away, Jaka Sculi watched Dohni Ganderlay help the coachman fix the horseshoe, the two of them talking and chuckling as if they were old friends. Considering the treatment Dohni Ganderlay had given him the previous night, the sight nearly leveled poor, jealous Jaka. Didn't Dohni understand that Lord Feringal wanted the same things for which Dohni had chastised him? Couldn't the man see that Jaka's intentions were better than Lord Feringal's, that he was more akin to Meralda's class and background and would therefore be a better choice for her?

Dohni went back into the house then, and Meralda's sister soon emerged, jumping for joy as she rushed over to speak with the coachman.

"Have I no allies?" Jaka asked quietly, chewing on his bottom lip petulantly. "Are they all against me, blinded by the unearned wealth and prestige of Feringal Auck? Damn you, Meralda! How could you betray me so?" he cried, heedless if his wail carried down to Tori and the driver.

He couldn't look at them anymore. Jaka clenched his fists and smacked them hard against his eyes, falling on his back to the hard ground. "What justice is this life?" he cried. "O fie, to have been born a pauper, I, when the mantle of a king would better suit! What justice allows that fool Feringal to claim the prize? What universal order so decrees that the purse is stronger than the loins? O fie this life! And damn Meralda!"

He lay there, muttering curses and mewling like a trapped cat, long after Liam Woodgate had repaired the shoe, shared a drink with Dohni Ganderlay, and departed. Long after Meralda's mother had fallen into a comfortable sleep at last, long after Meralda had confided to Tori all that had happened with Jaka, with Feringal, and with Priscilla and Temigast. Long after the storm Temigast had predicted arrived with all its fury, pelting the prone Jaka with drenching rain and buffeting him with cold ocean winds.

He still lay upon the hill when the clouds were swept away, making room for a brilliant sunrise, when the workers made their way to the fields. One worker, the only dwarf among the group, moved over to the young man and nudged him with the toe of one boot.

"You dead or dead drunk?" the gnarly creature asked.

Jaka rolled away from him, stifling the groan that came from the stiffness in his every muscle and joint. Too wounded in pride to respond, too angry to face anyone, the young man scrambled up to his feet and ran off.

"Strange bird, that one," the dwarf remarked, and those around him nodded.

Much later that morning, when his clothes had dried and with the chill of the night's wind and rain still deep under his skin, Jaka returned to the fields for his workday, suffering the berating of the field boss and the teasing of the other workers. He fought hard to tend to his work properly but it was a struggle, for his thoughts remained jumbled, his spirit sagged, and his skin felt clammy under the relentless sun.

It only got worse for him when he saw Lord Feringal's coach roll by on the road below, first heading toward Meralda's house, then back again, loaded with more than one passenger.

They were all against him.

*   *   *   *   *

Meralda enjoyed that day at Castle Auck more than any of her previous visits, though Lord Feringal did little to hide his disappointment that he would not have Meralda to himself. Priscilla boiled at the thought of three peasants in her wondrous garden.

Still, Feringal got over it soon enough, and Priscilla, with some coughing reminders from Steward Temigast, remained outwardly polite. All that mattered to Meralda was to see her mother smiling and holding her frail face up to the sunlight, basking in the warmth and the sweet scents. The scene only strengthened Meralda's resolve and gave her hope for the future.

They didn't remain at the castle for long, just an hour in the garden, a light lunch, then another short stroll around the flowers. At Meralda's bidding, an apology of sorts to Lord Feringal for the unexpected additions, the young lord rode in the coach back to the Ganderlay house, leaving a sour Priscilla and Temigast at the castle door.

"Peasants," Priscilla muttered. "I should batter that brother of mine about the head for bringing such folk to Castle Auck."

Temigast chuckled at the woman's predictability. "They are uncultured, indeed," the steward admitted. "Not unpleasant, though."

"Mud-eaters," said Priscilla.

"Perhaps you view this situation from an errant perspective," Temigast said, turning a wry smile on the woman.

"There is but one way to view peasants," Priscilla retorted. "One must look down upon them."

"But the Ganderlays are to be peasants no more," Temigast couldn't resist reminding her.

Priscilla scoffed doubtfully.

"Perhaps you should view this as a challenge," suggested Temigast. He paused until Priscilla turned a curious eye upon him. "Like coaxing a delicate flower from a bulb."

"Ganderlays? Delicate?" Priscilla remarked incredulously.

"Perhaps they could be with the help of Lady Priscilla Auck," said Temigast. "What a grand accomplishment it would be for Priscilla to enlighten them so, a feat that would make her brother brag to every merchant who passed through, an amazing accomplishment that would no doubt reach the ears of Luskan society. A plume in Priscilla's bonnet."

Priscilla snorted again, her expression unconvinced, but she said no more, not even her usual muttered insults. As she walked away, her expression changed to one of thoughtful curiosity, in the midst of some planning, perhaps.

Temigast recognized that she had taken his bait, or nibbled it, at least. The old steward shook his head. It never ceased to amaze him how most nobles considered themselves so much better than the people they ruled, even though that rule was always no more than an accident of birth.

Chapter 13

Prisoner's Carnival

It was an hour of beatings and taunting, of eager peasants throwing rotten food and spitting in their faces.

It was an hour that Wulfgar didn't even register. The man was so far removed from the spectacle of Prisoner's Carnival, so well hidden within a private emotional place, a place created through the mental discipline that had allowed him to survive the torments of Errtu, that he didn't even see the twisted, perverted faces of the peasants or hear the magistrate's assistant stirring up the mob for the real show when Jharkheld joined them on the huge stage. The barbarian was bound, as were the other three, with his hands behind his back and secured to a strong wooden post. Weights were chained about his ankles and another one around his neck, heavy enough to bow the head of powerful Wulfgar.

He had recognized the crowd with crystalline clarity. The drooling peasants, screaming for blood and torture, the excited, almost elated, ogre guards working the crowd, and the unfortunate prisoners. He'd seen them for what they were, and his mind had transformed them into something else, something demonic, the twisted, leering faces of Errtu's minions, slobbering over him with their acidic drool, nipping at him with their sharpened fangs and horrid breath. He smelled the fog of Errtu's

427

home again, the sulphuric Abyss burning his nostrils and his throat, adding an extra sting to all of his many, many wounds. He felt the itching of the centipedes and spiders crawling over and inside his skin. Always on the edge of death. Always wishing for it.

As those torments had continued, day after week after month, Wulfgar had found his escape in a tiny corner of his consciousness. Locked inside, he was oblivious to his surroundings. Here at the carnival he went to that place.

One by one the prisoners were taken from the posts and paraded about, sometimes close enough to be abused by the peasants, other times led to instruments of torture. Those included cross ties for whipping; a block and tackle designed to hoist victims into the air by a pole lashed under their arms locked behind their back; ankle stocks to hang prisoners upside down in buckets of filthy water, or, in the case of unfortunate Creeps Sharky, a bucket of urine. Creeps cried through most of it, while Tee-a-nicknick and Wulfgar stoically accepted whatever punishment the magistrate's assistant could dish out without a sound other than the occasional, unavoidable gasp of air being blasted from their lungs. Morik took it all in stride, protesting his innocence and throwing witty comments about, which only got him beaten all the worse.

Magistrate Jharkheld appeared, entering to howls and cheers, wearing a thick black robe and cap, and carrying a silver scroll tube. He moved to the center of the stage, standing between the prisoners to eye them deliberately one by one.

Jharkheld stepped out front. With a dramatic flourish he presented the scroll tube, the damning documents, bringing eager shouts and cheers. Each movement distinct, with an appropriate response mounting to a crescendo, Jharkheld popped the cap from the tube's end and removed the documents. Unrolling them, the magistrate showed the documents to the crowd one at a time, reading each prisoner's name.

The magistrate surely seemed akin to Errtu, the carnival barker, ordering the torments. Even his voice sounded to the barbarian like that of the balor: grating, guttural, inhuman.

"I shall tell to you a tale," Jharkheld began, "of treachery and deceit, of friendship abused and murder attempted for profit. That man!" he said powerfully, pointing to Creeps Sharky, "that man told it to me in full, and the sheer horror of it has stolen my sleep every night since." The magistrate went on to detail the crime as Sharky had presented it. All of it had been Morik's idea, according to the wretch. Morik and Wulfgar had lured Deudermont into the open so that Tee-a-nicknick could sting him with a poisoned dart. Morik was supposed to sting the honorable captain, too, using a different variety of poison to ensure that the priests could not save the man, but the city guard had arrived too quickly for that second assault. Throughout the planning, Creeps Sharky had tried to talk them out of it, but he'd said nothing to anyone else out of fear of Wulfgar. The big man had threatened to tear his head from his shoulders and kick it down every street in Luskan.

Enough of those gathered in the crowd had fallen victim to Wulfgar's enforcer tactics at the Cutlass to find that last part credible.

"You four are charged with conspiracy and intent to heinously murder goodman Captain Deudermont, a visitor in excellent standing to our fair city," Jharkheld said when he completed the story and let the howls and jeers from the crowd die away. "You four are charged with the infliction of serious harm to the same. In the interest of justice and fairness, we will hear your answers to these charges."

He walked over to Creeps Sharky. "Did I relate the tale as you told it to me?" he asked.

"You did sir, you did," Creeps Sharky eagerly replied. "They done it, all of it!"

Many in the crowd yelled out their doubts about that, while others merely laughed at the man, so pitiful did he sound.

"Mister Sharky," Jharkheld went on, "do you admit your guilt to the first charge?"

"Innocent!" Sharky protested, sounding confident that his cooperation had allowed him to escape the worst of the carnival, but the jeers of the crowd all but drowned out his voice.

"Do you admit your guilt to the second charge against you?"

"Innocent!" the man said defiantly, and he gave a gap-toothed smile to the magistrate.

"Guilty!" cried an old woman. "Guilty he is, and deserving to die horrible for trying to blame the others!"

A hundred cries arose agreeing with the woman, but Creeps Sharky held fast his smile and apparent confidence. Jharkheld walked out to the front of the platform and patted his hands in the air, trying to calm the crowd. When at last they quieted he said, "The tale of Creeps Sharky has allowed us to convict the others. Thus, we have promised leniency to the man for his cooperation." That brought a rumble of boos and derisive whistles. "For his honesty and for the fact that he, by his own words—undisputed by the others—was not directly involved."

"I'll dispute it!" Morik cried, and the crowd howled. Jharkheld merely motioned to one of the guards, and Morik got the butt of a club slammed into his belly.

More boos erupted throughout the crowd, but Jharkheld denied the calls and a smile widened on the face of clever Creeps Sharky.

"We promised him leniency," Jharkheld said, throwing up his hands as if there was nothing he could do about it. "Thus, we shall kill him quickly."

That stole the smile from the face of Creeps Sharky and turned the chorus of boos into roars of agreement.

Sputtering protests, his legs failing him, Creeps Sharky was dragged to a block and forced to kneel before it.

"Innocent I am!" he cried, but his protest ended abruptly as one of the guards forced him over the block, slamming his face against the wood. A huge executioner holding a monstrous axe stepped up to the block.

"The blow won't fall clean if you struggle," a guard advised him.

Creeps Sharky lifted his head. "But ye promised me!"

The guards slammed him back down on the block. "Quit yer wiggling!" one of them ordered. The terrified Creeps jerked free and fell to the platform, rolling desperately. There was pandemonium as the guards grabbed at him. He kicked wildly, the crowd howled and laughed, and cries of "Hang him!" "Keel haul!" and other horrible suggestions for execution echoed from every corner of the square.

* * * * *

"Lovely gathering," Captain Deudermont said sarcastically to Robillard. They stood with several other members of *Sea Sprite* among the leaping and shouting folk.

"Justice," the wizard stated firmly.

"I wonder," the captain said pensively. "Is it justice, or entertainment? There is a fine line, my friend, and considering this almost daily spectacle, it's one I believe the authorities in Luskan long ago crossed."

"You were the one who wanted to come here," Robillard reminded him.

"It is my duty to be here in witness," Deudermont answered.

"I meant here in Luskan," Robillard clarified. "You wanted to come to this city, Captain. I preferred Waterdeep."

Deudermont fixed his wizard friend with a stern stare, but he had no rebuttal to offer.

* * * * *

"Stop yer wiggling!" the guard yelled at Creeps, but the dirty man fought all the harder, kicking and squealing desperately. He managed to evade their grasps for some time to the delight of the onlookers who were thoroughly enjoying the spectacle. Creeps's frantic movements brought his gaze in line with Jharkheld. The magistrate fixed him with a glare so intense and punishing that Creeps stopped moving.

"Draw and quarter him," Jharkheld said slowly and deliberately.

The gathering reached a new level of joyous howling.

Creeps had witnessed that ultimate form of execution only twice in his years, and that was enough to steal the blood from his face, to send him into a fit of trembling, to make him, right there in front of a thousand onlookers, wet himself.

"Ye promised," he mouthed, barely able to draw breath, but loud enough for the magistrate to hear and come over to him.

"I did promise leniency," Jharkheld said quietly, "and so I will honor my word to you, but only if you cooperate. The choice is yours to make."

Those in the crowd close enough to hear groaned their protests, but Jharkheld ignored them.

"I have four horses in waiting," Jharkheld warned.

Creeps started crying.

"Take him to the block," the magistrate instructed the guards. This time Creeps made no move against them, offered no resistance at all as they dragged him back, forced him into a kneeling position, and pushed his head down.

"Ye promised," Creeps softly cried his last words, but the cold magistrate only smiled and nodded. Not to Creeps, but to the large man standing beside him.

The huge axe swept down, the crowd gasped as one, then broke into howls. The head of Creeps Sharky tumbled to the platform and rolled a short distance. One of the guards rushed to it and held it up, turning it to face the headless body. Legend had it that with a perfect, swift cut and a quick guard the beheaded man might still be conscious for a split second, long enough to see his own body, his face contorted into an expression of the purest, most exquisite horror.

Not this time, though, for Creeps Sharky wore the same sad expression.

* * * * *

"Beautiful," Morik muttered sarcastically at the other end of the platform. "Yet, it's a better fate by far than the rest of us will find this day."

Flanking him on either side, neither Wulfgar nor Tee-a-nicknick offered a reply.

"Just beautiful," the doomed rogue said again. Morik was not unaccustomed to finding himself in rather desperate situations, but this was the first time he ever felt himself totally without options. He shot Tee-a-nicknick a look of utter contempt then turned his attention to Wulfgar. The big man seemed so impassive and distanced from the mayhem around them that Morik envied him his oblivion.

The rogue heard Jharkheld's continuing banter as he worked up the crowd. He apologized for the rather unentertaining execution of Creeps Sharky, explaining the occasional need for such mercy. Else, why would anyone ever confess?

Morik drowned out the magistrate's blather and willed his mind to a place where he was safe and happy. He thought of Wulfgar, of how, against all odds, they had become friends. Once they had been rivals, the new barbarian rising in reputation on Half-Moon Street, particularly

431

after he had killed the brute, Tree Block Breaker. The only remaining operator with a reputation to protect, Morik had considered eliminating Wulfgar, though murder had never really been the rogue's preferred method.

Then there had come the strangest of encounters. A dark elf—a damned drow!—had come to Morik in his rented room, had just walked in without warning, and had bade Morik to keep a close watch over Wulfgar but not to hurt the man. The dark elf had paid Morik well. Realizing that gold coins were better payment than the sharpened edge of drow weapons, the rogue had gone along with the plan, watching Wulfgar more and more closely as the days slipped past. They'd even becoming drinking partners, spending late nights, often until dawn, together at the docks.

Morik had never heard from that dark elf again. If the order had come from for him to eliminate Wulfgar, he doubted he would have accepted the contract. He realized now that if he heard the dark elves were coming to kill the barbarian, Morik would have stood by Wulfgar.

Well, the rogue admitted more realistically, he might not have stood beside Wulfgar, but he would have warned the barbarian, then run far, far away.

Now there was nowhere to run. Morik wondered briefly again if those dark elves would show up to save this human in whom they had taken such an interest. Perhaps a legion of drow warriors would storm Prisoner's Carnival, their fine blades slicing apart the macabre onlookers as they worked their way to the platform.

The fantasy could not hold, for Morik knew they would not be coming for Wulfgar. Not this time.

"I am truly sorry, my friend," he apologized to Wulfgar, for Morik could not dismiss the notion that this situation was largely his fault.

Wulfgar didn't reply. Morik understood that the big man had not even heard his words, that his friend was already gone from this place, fallen deep within himself.

Perhaps that was the best course to take. Looking at the sneering mob, hearing Jharkheld's continuing speech, watching the headless body of Creeps Sharky being dragged across the platform, Morik wished that he, too, could so distance himself.

* * * * *

The magistrate again told the tale of Creeps Sharky, of how these other three had conspired to murder that most excellent man, Captain Deudermont. Jharkheld made his way over to Wulfgar. He looked at the doomed man, shook his head, then turned back to the mob, prompting a response.

There came a torrent of jeers and curses.

432

"You are the worst of them all!" Jharkheld yelled in the barbarian's face. "He was your friend, and you betrayed him!"

"Keel haul 'im on Deudermont's own ship!" came one anonymous demand.

"Draw and quarter and feed 'im to the fishes!" yelled another.

Jharkheld turned to the crowd and lifted his hand, demanding silence, and after a bristling moment they obeyed. "This one," the magistrate said, "I believe we shall save for last."

That brought another chorus of howls.

"And what a day we shall have," said Jharkheld, the showman barker. "Three remaining, and all of them refusing to confess!"

"Justice," Morik whispered under his breath.

Wulfgar stared straight ahead, unblinkingly, and only thoughts of poor Morik held him from laughing in Jharkheld's ugly old face. Did the magistrate really believe that he could do anything to Wulfgar worse than the torments of Errtu? Could Jharkheld produce Catti-brie on the stage and ravish her, then dismember her in front of Wulfgar, as Errtu had done so many times? Could he bring in an illusionary Bruenor and bite through the dwarf's skull, then use the remaining portion of the dwarf's head as a bowl for brain stew? Could he inflict more physical pain upon Wulfgar than the demon who had practiced such torturing arts for millennia? At the end of it all, could Jharkheld bring Wulfgar back from the edge of death time and again so that it would begin anew?

Wulfgar realized something profound and actually brightened. This was where Jharkheld and his stage paled against the Abyss. He would die here. At last he would be free.

* * * * *

Jharkheld ran from the barbarian, skidding to a stop before Morik and grabbing the man's slender face in his strong hand, turning Morik roughly to face him. "Do you admit your guilt?" he screamed.

Morik almost did it, almost screamed out that he had indeed conspired to kill Deudermont. Yes, he thought, a quick plan formulating in his mind. He would admit to the conspiracy, but with the tattooed pirate only, trying to somehow save his innocent friend.

His hesitation cost him the chance at that time, for Jharkheld gave a disgusted snort and snapped a backhanded blow across Morik's face, clipping the underside of the rogue's nose, a stinging technique that brought waves of pain shifting behind Morik's eyes. By the time the man blinked away his surprise and pain, Jharkheld had moved on, looming before Tee-a-nicknick.

"Tee-a-nicknick," the magistrate said slowly, emphasizing every syllable, his method reminding the gathering of how strange, how foreign, this half-man was. "Tell me, Tee-a-nicknick, what role did you play?"

The tattooed half-qullan pirate stared straight ahead, did not blink, and did not speak.

Jharkheld snapped his fingers in the air, and his assistant ran out from the side of the platform, handing Jharkheld a wooden tube.

Jharkheld publicly inspected the item, showing it to the crowd. "With this seemingly innocent pole, our painted friend here can blow forth a dart as surely as an archer can launch an arrow," he explained. "And on that dart, the claw of a small cat, for instance, our painted friend can coat some of the most exquisite poisons. Concoctions that can make blood leak from your eyes, bring a fever so hot as to turn your skin the color of fire, or fill your nose and throat with enough phlegm to make every breath a forced and wretched-tasting labor are but a sampling of his vile repetoire."

The crowd played on every word, growing more disgusted and angry. Master of the show, Jharkheld measured their response and played to them, waiting for the right moment.

"Do you admit your guilt?" Jharkheld yelled suddenly in Tee-a-nicknick's face.

The tattooed pirate stared straight ahead, did not blink, and did not speak. Had he been full-blooded qullan, he might have cast a confusion spell at that moment, sending the magistrate stumbling away, baffled and forgetful, but Tee-a-nicknick was not pure blooded and had none of the innate magical abilities of his race. He did have qullan concentration, though, a manner, much like Wulfgar's, of removing himself from the present scene before him.

"You shall admit all," Jharkheld promised, wagging his finger angrily in the man's face, unaware of the pirate's heritage and discipline, "but it will be too late."

The crowd went into a frenzy as the guards pulled the pirate free of his binding post and dragged him from one instrument of torture to another. After about half an hour of beating and whipping, pouring salt water over the wounds, even taking one of Tee-a-nicknick's eyes with a hot poker, the pirate still showed no signs of speaking. No confession, no pleading or begging, hardly even a scream.

Frustrated beyond endurance, Jharkheld went to Morik just to keep things moving. He didn't even ask the man to confess. In fact he slapped Morik viciously and repeatedly every time the man tried to say a word. Soon they had Morik on the rack, the torturer giving the wheel a slight, almost imperceptible (except to the agonized Morik) turn every few minutes.

Meanwhile, Tee-a-nicknick continued to bear the brunt of the torment. When Jharkheld went to him again, the pirate couldn't stand, so the guards pulled him to his feet and held him.

"Ready to tell me the truth?" Jharkheld asked.

Tee-a-nicknick spat in his face.

"Bring the horses!" the magistrate shrieked, trembling with rage. The crowd went wild. It wasn't often that the magistrate went to the trouble of a drawing and quartering. Those who had witnessed it boasted it was the greatest show of all.

Four white horses, each trailing a sturdy rope, were ridden into the square. The crowd was pushed back by the city guard as the horses approached the platform. Magistrate Jharkheld guided his men through the precise movements of the show. Soon Tee-a-nicknick was securely strapped in place, wrists and ankles bound one to each horse.

On the magistrate's signal, the riders nudged their powerful beasts, one toward each point on the compass. The tattooed pirate instinctively bunched up his muscles, fighting back, but resistance was useless. Tee-a-nicknick was stretched to the limits of his physical coil. He grunted and gasped, and the riders and their well-trained mounts kept him at the very limits. A moment later, there came the loud popping of a shoulder snapping out of joint; soon after one of Tee-a-nicknick's knees exploded.

Jharkheld motioned for the riders to hold steady, and he walked over to the man, a knife in one hand and a whip in the other. He showed the gleaming blade to the groaning Tee-a-nicknick, rolling it over and over before the man's eyes. "I can end the agony," the magistrate promised. "Confess your guilt, and I will kill you swiftly."

The tattooed half-qullan grunted and looked away. On Jharkheld's wave, the riders stepped their horses out a bit more.

The man's pelvis shattered, and how he howled at last! How the crowd yelled in appreciation as the skin started to rip!

"Confess!" Jharkheld yelled.

"I stick him!" Tee-a-nicknick cried. Before the crowd could even groan its disappointment Jharkheld yelled, "Too late!" and cracked his whip.

The horses jumped away, tearing Tee-a-nicknick's legs from his torso. Then the two horses bound to the man's wrists had him out straight, his face twisted in the horror of searing agony and impending death for just an instant before quartering that portion as well.

Some gasped, some vomited, and most cheered wildly.

* * * * *

"Justice," Robillard said to the growling, disgusted Deudermont. "Such displays make murder an unpopular profession."

Deudermont snorted. "It merely feeds the basest of human emotions," he argued.

"I don't disagree," Robillard replied. "I don't make the laws, but unlike your barbarian friend, I abide by them. Are we any more sympathetic to pirates we catch out on the high seas?"

435

"We do as we must," Deudermont argued. "We do not torture them to sate our twisted hunger."

"But we take satisfaction in sinking them," Robillard countered. "We don't cry for their deaths, and often, when we are in pursuit of a companion privateer, we do not stop to pull them from the sharks. Even when we do take them as prisoners, we subsequently drop them at the nearest port, often Luskan, for justice such as this."

Deudermont had run out of arguments, so he just stared ahead. Still, to the civilized and cultured captain's thinking, this display in no way resembled justice.

*　*　*　*　*

Jharkheld went back to work on Morik and Wulfgar before the many attendants had even cleared the blood and grime from the square in front of the platform.

"You see how long it took him to admit the truth?" the magistrate said to Morik. "Too late, and so he suffered to the end. Will you be as much a fool?"

Morik, whose limbs were beginning to pull past the breaking point, started to reply, started to confess, but Jharkheld put a finger over the man's lips. "Now is not the time," he explained.

Morik started to speak again, so Jharkheld had him tightly gagged, a dirty rag stuffed into his mouth, another tied about his head to secure it.

The magistrate moved around the back of the rack and produced a small wooden box, the rat box it was called. The crowd howled its pleasure. Recognizing the horrible instrument, Morik's eyes popped wide and he struggled futilely against the unyielding bonds. He hated rats, had been terrified of them all of his life.

His worst nightmare was coming true.

Jharkheld came to the front of the platform again and held the box high, turning it slowly so that the crowd could see its ingenious design. The front was a metal mesh cage, the other three walls and the ceiling solid wood. The bottom was wooden as well, but it had a sliding panel that left an exit hole. A rat would be pushed into the box, then the box would be put on Morik's bared belly and the bottom door removed. Then the box would be lit on fire.

The rat would escape through the only means possible—through Morik.

A gloved man came out holding the rat and quickly got the boxed creature in place atop Morik's bared belly. He didn't light it then, but rather, let the animal walk about, its feet tapping on flesh, every now and then nipping. Morik struggled futilely.

Jharkheld went to Wulfgar. Given the level of excitement and enjoyment running through the mob, the magistrate wondered how he would top it all, wondered what he might do to this stoic behemoth that would bring more spectacle than the previous two executions.

"Like what we're doing to your friend Morik?" the magistrate asked.

Wulfgar, who had seen the bowels of Errtu's domain, who had been chewed by creatures that would terrify an army of rats, did not reply.

* * * * *

"They hold you in the highest regard," Robillard remarked to Deudermont. "Rarely has Luskan seen so extravagant a multiple execution."

The words echoed in Captain Deudermont's mind, particularly the first sentence. To think that his standing in Luskan had brought this about. No, it had provided sadistic Jharkheld with an excuse for such treatment of fellow human beings, even guilty ones. Deudermont remained unconvinced that either Wulfgar or Morik had been involved. The realization that this was all done in his honor disgusted Deudermont profoundly.

"Mister Micanty!" he ordered, quickly scribbling a note he handed to the man.

"No!" Robillard insisted, understanding what Deudermont had in mind and knowing how greatly such an action would cost *Sea Sprite,* both with the authorities and the mob. "He deserves death!"

"Who are you to judge?" Deudermont asked.

"Not I!" the wizard protested. "Them," he explained, sweeping his arm out to the crowd.

Deudermont scoffed at the absurd notion.

"Captain, we'll be forced to leave Luskan, and we'll not be welcomed back soon," Robillard pointed out.

"They will forget as soon as the next prisoners are paraded out for their enjoyment, likely on the morrow's dawn." He gave a wry, humorless smile. "Besides, you don't like Luskan anyway."

Robillard groaned, sighed, and threw up his hands in defeat as Deudermont, too civilized a man, gave the note to Micanty and bade him to rush it to the magistrate.

* * * * *

"Light the box!" Jharkheld called from the stage after the guards had brought Wulfgar around so that the barbarian could witness Morik's horror.

Wulfgar could not distance himself from the sight of setting the rat cage on fire. The frightened creature scurried about, and then began to burrow.

The scene of such pain inflicted on a friend entered into Wulfgar's private domain, clawed through his wall of denial, even as the rat bit through Morik's skin. The barbarian loosed a growl so threatening, so preternaturally feral, that it turned the eyes of those near him from the spectacle of Morik's horror. Huge muscles bunched and flexed, and Wulfgar snapped his torso out to the side, launching the man holding him there away. The barbarian lashed out with one leg, swinging the iron ball and chain so that it wrapped the legs of the other man holding him. A sharp tug sent the guard to the ground.

Wulfgar pulled and pulled as others slammed against him, as clubs battered him, as Jharkheld, angered by the distraction, yelled for Morik's gag to be removed. Somehow, incredibly, powerful Wulfgar pulled his arms free and lurched for the rack.

Guard after guard slammed into him. He threw them aside as if they were children, but so many rushed the barbarian that he couldn't beat a path to Morik, who was screaming in agony now.

"Get it off me!" cried Morik.

Suddenly Wulfgar was facedown. Jharkheld got close enough to snap his whip across the man's back with a loud *crack!*

"Admit your guilt!" the frenzied magistrate demanded as he beat Wulfgar viciously.

Wulfgar growled and struggled. Another guard tumbled away, and another got his nose splattered all over his face by a heavy slug.

"*Get it off me!*" Morik cried again.

The crowd loved it. Jharkheld felt certain he'd reached a new level of showmanship.

"Stop!" came a cry from the audience that managed to penetrate the general howls and hoots. "Enough!"

The excitement died away fast as the crowd turned and recognized the speaker as Captain Deudermont of *Sea Sprite*. Deudermont looked haggard and leaned heavily on a cane.

Magistrate Jharkheld's trepidation only heightened as Waillan Micanty pushed past the guards to climb onto the stage. He rushed to Jharkheld's side and presented him with Deudermont's note.

The magistrate pulled it open and read it. Surprised, stunned even, he grew angrier by the word. Jharkheld looked up at Deudermont, causally motioned for one of the guards to gag the screaming Morik again, and for the others to pull the battered Wulfgar up to his feet.

Unconcerned for himself and with no comprehension of what was happening beyond the torture of Morik, Wulfgar bolted from their grasp. He staggered and tripped over the swinging balls and chains but managed to dive close enough to reach out and slap the burning box and rat from Morik's belly.

He was beaten again and hauled before Jharkheld.

"It will only get worse for Morik now," the sadistic magistrate promised quietly, and he turned to Deudermont, a look of outrage clear on his face. "Captain Deudermont!" he called. "As the victim and a recognized nobleman, you have the authority to pen such a note, but are you *sure?* At this late hour?"

Deudermont came forward, ignoring the grumbles and protests, even threats, and stood tall in the midst of the bloodthirsty crowd. "The evidence against Creeps Sharky and the tattooed pirate was solid," he explained, "but plausible, too, is Morik's tale of being set up with Wulfgar to take the blame, while the other two took only the reward."

"But," Jharkheld argued, pointing his finger into the air, "plausible, too, is the tale that Creeps Sharky told, one of conspiracy that makes them all guilty."

The crowd, confused but suspecting that their fun might soon be at an end, seemed to like Magistrate Jharkheld's explanation better.

"And plausible, too, is the tale of Josi Puddles, one that further implicates both Morik the Rogue and Wulfgar," Jharkheld went on. "Might I remind you, Captain, that the barbarian hasn't even denied the claims of Creeps Sharky!"

Deudermont looked then to Wulfgar, who continued his infuriating, expressionless stance.

"Captain Deudermont, do you declare the innocence of this man?" Jharkheld asked, pointing to Wulfgar and speaking slowly and loudly enough for all to hear.

"That is not within my rights," Deudermont replied over the shouts of protest from the bloodthirsty peasants. "I cannot determine guilt or innocence but can only offer that which you have before you."

Magistrate Jharkheld stared at the hastily penned note again, then held it up for the crowd to see. "A letter of pardon for Wulfgar," he explained.

The crowd hushed as one for just an instant, then began jostling and shouting curses. Both Deudermont and Jharkheld feared that a riot would ensue.

"This is folly," Jharkheld snarled.

"I am a visitor in excellent standing, by your own words, Magistrate Jharkheld," Deudermont replied calmly. "By that standing I ask the city to pardon Wulfgar, and by that standing I expect you to honor that request or face the questioning of your superiors."

There it was, stated flatly, plainly, and without any wriggle room at all. Jharkheld was bound, Deudermont and the magistrate knew, for the captain was, indeed, well within his rights to offer such a pardon. Such letters were not uncommon, usually given at great expense to the family of the pardoned man, but never before in such a dramatic fashion as this. Not at the Prisoner's Carnival, at the very moment of Jharkheld's greatest show!

"Death to Wulfgar!" someone in the crowd yelled, and others joined in, while Jharkheld and Deudermont looked to Wulfgar in that critical time.

439

Their expressions meant nothing to the man, who still thought that death would be a relief, perhaps the greatest escape possible from his haunting memories. When Wulfgar looked to Morik, the man stretched near to breaking, his stomach all bloody and the guards bringing forth another rat, he realized it wasn't an option, not if the rogue's loyalty to him meant anything at all.

"I had nothing to do with the attack," Wulfgar flatly declared. "Believe me if you will, kill me if you don't. It matters not to me."

"There you have it, Magistrate Jharkheld," Deudermont said. "Release him, if you please. Honor my pardon as a visitor in excellent standing to Luskan."

Jharkheld held Deudermont's stare for a long time. The old man was obviously disapproving, but he nodded to the guards, and Wulfgar was immediately released from their grasp. Tentatively, and only after further prompting from Jharkheld, one of the men brought a key down to Wulfgar's ankles, releasing the ball and chain shackles.

"Get him out of here," an angry Jharkheld instructed, but the big man resisted the guards' attempts to pull him from the stage.

"Morik is innocent," Wulfgar declared.

"What?" Jharkheld exclaimed. "Drag him away!"

Wulfgar, stronger than the guards could ever imagine, held his ground. "I proclaim the innocence of Morik the Rogue!" he cried. "He did nothing, and if you continue here, you do so only for your own evil pleasures and not in the name of justice!"

"How much you two sound alike," an obviously disgusted Robillard whispered to Deudermont, coming up behind the captain.

"Magistrate Jharkheld!" the captain called above the cries of the crowd.

Jharkheld eyed him directly, knowing what was to come. The captain merely nodded. Scowling, the magistrate snapped up his parchments, waved angrily to his guards, and stormed off the stage. The frenzied crowd started pressing forward, but the city guard held them back.

Smiling widely, sticking his tongue out at those peasants who tried to spit at him, Morik was half dragged, half carried from the stage behind Wulfgar.

* * * * *

Morik spent most of the walk through the magistrate offices talking soothingly to Wulfgar. The rogue could tell from the big man's expression that Wulfgar was locked into those awful memories again. Morik feared that he would tear down the walls and kill half the magistrate's assistants. The rogue's stomach was still bloody, and his arms and legs ached more profoundly than anything he had ever felt. He had no desire to go back to Prisoner's Carnival.

Morik thought they would be brought before Jharkheld. That prospect, given Wulfgar's volatile mood, scared him more than a little. To his relief, the escorting guards avoided Jharkheld's office and turned into a small, nondescript room. A nervous little man sat behind a tremendous desk littered with mounds of papers.

One of the guards presented Deudermont's note to the man. He took a quick look at it and snorted, for he had already heard of the disappointing show at Prisoner's Carnival. The little man quickly scribbled his initials across the note, confirming that it had been reviewed and accepted.

"You are not innocent," he said, handing the note to Wulfgar, "and thus are not declared innocent."

"We were told that we would be free to go," Morik argued.

"Indeed," said the bureaucrat. "Not really free to go, but rather compelled to go. You were spared because Captain Deudermont apparently had not the heart for your execution, but understand that in the eyes of Luskan you are guilty of the crime charged. Thus, you are banished for life. Straightaway to the gate with you, and if you are ever caught in our city again, you'll face Prisoner's Carnival one last time. Even Captain Deudermont will not be able to intervene on your behalf. Do you understand?"

"Not a difficult task," Morik replied.

The wormy bureaucrat glared at him, to which Morik only shrugged.

"Get them out of here," the man commanded. One guard grabbed Morik by the arm, the other reached for Wulfgar, but a shrug and a look from the barbarian had him thinking better of it. Still, Wulfgar went along without argument, and soon the pair were out in the sunshine, unshackled and feeling free for the first time in many days.

To their surprise, though, the guards did not leave them there, escorting them all the way to the city's eastern gate.

"Get out, and don't come back," one of them said as the gates slammed closed behind them.

"Why would I want to return to your wretched city?" Morik cried, making several lewd and insulting gestures at those soldiers staring down from the wall.

One lifted a crossbow and leveled it Morik's way. "Looky," he said. "The little rat's already trying to sneak back in."

Morik knew that it was time to leave, and in a hurry. He turned and started to do just that, then looked back to see the soldier, a wary look upon the man's grizzled face, quickly lower the bow. When Morik looked back, he understood, for Captain Deudermont and his wizard sidekick were fast approaching.

For a moment, it occurred to Morik that Deudermont might have saved them from Jharkheld only because he desired to exact a punishment of his own. That fear was short-lived, for the man strode right up to Wulfgar, staring hard but making no threatening moves. Wulfgar met his stare, neither blinking nor flinching.

"Did you speak truly?" Deudermont asked.

Wulfgar snorted, and it was obvious it was all the response the captain would get.

"What has happened to Wulfgar, son of Beornegar?" Deudermont said quietly. Wulfgar turned to go, but the captain rushed around to stand before him. "You owe me this, at least," he said.

"I owe you nothing," Wulfgar replied.

Deudermont considered the response for just a moment, and Morik recognized that the seaman was trying to see things from Wulfgar's point of view.

"Agreed," the captain said, and Robillard huffed in displeasure. "You claimed your innocence. In that case, you owe nothing to me, for I did nothing but what was right. Hear me out of past friendship."

Wulfgar eyed him coldly but made no immediate move to walk away.

"I don't know what has caused your fall, my friend, what has led you away from companions like Drizzt Do'Urden and Catti-brie, and your adoptive father, Bruenor, who took you in and taught you the ways of the world," the captain said. "I only pray that those three and the halfling are safe and well."

Deudermont paused, but Wulfgar said nothing.

"There is no lasting relief in a bottle, my friend," the captain said, "and no heroism in defending a tavern from its customary patrons. Why would you surrender the world you knew for this?"

Having heard enough, Wulfgar started to walk away. When the captain stepped in front of him again, the big man just pushed on by without slowing, with Morik scrambling to keep up.

"I offer you passage," Deudermont unexpectedly (even to Deudermont) called after him.

"Captain!" Robillard protested, but Deudermont brushed him away and scrambled after Wulfgar and Morik.

"Come with me to *Sea Sprite,*" Deudermont said. "Together we shall hunt pirates and secure the Sword Coast for honest sailors. You will find your true self out there, I promise!"

"I would hear only your definition of me," Wulfgar clarified, spinning back and hushing Morik, who seemed quite enthralled by the offer, "and that's one I don't care to hear." Wulfgar turned and started away.

Jaw hanging open, Morik watched him go. By the time he turned back, Deudermont had likewise retreated into the city. Robillard, though, held his ground and his sour expression.

"Might I?" Morik started to ask, walking toward the wizard.

"Be gone and be fast about it, rogue," Robillard warned. "Else you will become a stain on the ground, awaiting the next rain to wash you away."

Clever Morik, the ultimate survivor, who hated wizards, didn't have to be told twice.

Part 3

A Wild Land Made Wilder

The course of events in my life have often made me examine the nature of good and evil. I have witnessed the purest forms of both repeatedly, particularly evil. The totality of my early life was spent living among it, a wickedness so thick in the air that it choked me and forced me away.

Only recently, as my reputation has begun to gain me some acceptance among the human populations—a tolerance, at least, if not a welcome— have I come to witness a more complex version of what I observed in Menzoberranzan, a shade of gray varying in lightness and darkness. So many humans, it seems, a vast majority, have within their makeup a dark side, a hunger for the macabre, and the ability to dispassionately dismiss the agony of another in the pursuit of the self.

Nowhere is this more evident than in the Prisoner's Carnival at Luskan and other such pretenses of justice. Prisoners, sometimes guilty, sometimes not—it hardly matters—are paraded before the blood-hungry mob, then beaten, tortured, and finally executed in grand fashion. The presiding magistrate works very hard to exact the most exquisite screams of the purest agony; his job is to twist the expressions of those prisoners into the epitome of terror, the ultimate horror reflected in their eyes.

445

Once, when in Luskan with Captain Deudermont of the Sea Sprite, *I ventured to the carnival to witness the "trials" of several pirates we had fished from the sea after sinking their ship. Witnessing the spectacle of a thousand people crammed around a grand stage, yelling and squealing with delight as these miserable pirates were literally cut into pieces, almost made me walk away from Deudermont's ship, almost made me forego a life as a pirate hunter and retreat to the solitude of the forest or the mountains.*

Of course, Catti-brie was there to remind me of the truth of it, to point out that these same pirates often exacted equal tortures upon innocent prisoners. While she admitted that such a truth did not justify the Prisoner's Carnival—Catti-brie was so horrified by the mere thought of the place that she would not go anywhere near it—she argued that such treatment of pirates was preferable to allowing them free run of the high seas.

But why? Why any of it?

The question has bothered me for all these years, and in seeking its answer I have come to explore yet another facet of these incredibly complex creatures called humans. Why would common, otherwise decent folk, descend to such a level as the spectacle of Prisoner's Carnival? Why would some of the Sea Sprite's *own crew, men and women I knew to be honorable and decent, take pleasure in viewing such a macabre display of torture?*

The answer, perhaps (if there is a more complicated answer than the nature of evil itself), lies in an examination of the attitudes of other races. Among the goodly races, humans alone "celebrate" the executions and torments of prisoners. Halfling societies would have no part of such a display—halfling prisoners have been known to die of overeating. Nor would dwarves, as aggressive as they can be. In dwarven society, prisoners are dealt with efficiently and tidily, without spectacle and out of public view. A murderer among dwarves would be dealt a single blow to the neck. Never did I see any elves at Prisoner's Carnival, except on one occasion when a pair ventured by, then quickly left, obviously disgusted. My understanding is that in gnome society there are no executions, just a lifetime of imprisonment in an elaborate cell.

So why humans? What is it about the emotional construct of the human being that brings about such a spectacle as Prisoner's Carnival? Evil? I think that too simple an answer.

Dark elves relish torture—how well I know!—and their actions are, indeed, based on sadism and evil, and an insatiable desire to satisfy the demonic hunger of the spider queen, but with humans, as with everything about humans, the answer becomes a bit more complex. Surely there is a measure of sadism involved, particularly on the part of the presiding magistrate and his torturer assistants, but for the common folk, the powerless paupers cheering in the audience, I believe their joy stems from three sources.

446

First, peasants in Faerûn are a powerless lot, subjected to the whims of unscrupulous lords and landowners, and with the ever-present threat of some invasion or another by goblins, giants, or fellow humans, stomping flat the lives they have carved. Prisoner's Carnival affords these unfortunate folk a taste of power, the power over life and death. At long last they feel some sense of control over their own lives.

Second, humans are not long-lived like elves and dwarves; even halflings will usually outlast them. Peasants face the possibility of death daily. A mother fortunate enough to survive two or three birthings will likely witness the death of at least one of her children. Living so intimately with death obviously breeds a curiosity and fear, even terror. At Prisoner's Carnival these folk witness death at its most horrible, the worst that death can give, and take solace in the fact that their own deaths, unless they become the accused brought before the magistrates, will not likely be nearly as terrible. I have witnessed your worst, grim Death, and I fear you not.

The third explanation for the appeal of Prisoner's Carnival lies in the necessity of justice and punishment in order to maintain order in a society. This was the side of the debate held up by Robillard the wizard upon my return to the Sea Sprite *after witnessing the horror. While he took no pleasure in viewing the carnival and rarely attended, Robillard defended it as vigorously as I might expect from the magistrate himself. The public humiliation of these men, the public display of their agony, would keep other folk on an honest course, he believed. Thus, the cheers of the peasant mob were no more than a rousing affirmation of their belief in the law and order of their society.*

It is a difficult argument to defeat, particularly concerning the effectiveness of such displays in dissuading future criminals, but is it truly justice?

Armed with Robillard's arguments, I went to some minor magistrates in Luskan on the pretense of deciding better protocol for the Sea Sprite *to hand over captured pirates, but in truth to get them talking about Prisoner's Carnival. It became obvious to me, and very quickly, that the carnival itself had little to do with justice. Many innocent men and women had found their way to the stage in Luskan, forced into false confession by sheer brutality, then punished publicly for those crimes. The magistrates knew this and readily admitted it by citing their relief that at least the prisoners we brought to them were assuredly guilty!*

For that reason alone I can never come to terms with the Prisoner's Carnival. One measure of any society is the way it deals with those who have walked away from the course of community and decency, and an indecent treatment of these criminals decreases the standards of morality to the level of the tortured.

Yet the practice continues to thrive in many cities in Faerûn and in many, many rural communities, where justice, as a matter of survival, must be even more harsh and definitive.

447

Perhaps there is a fourth explanation for the carnival. Perhaps the crowds gather around eagerly merely for the excitement of the show. Perhaps there is no underlying cause or explanation other than the fun of it. I do not like to consider this a possibility, for if humans on as large a scale are capable of eliminating empathy and sympathy so completely as to actually enjoy the spectacle of watching another suffer horribly, then that, I fear, is the truest definition of evil.

After all of the hours of investigation, debate, and interrogation, and many, many hours of contemplation on the nature of these humans among whom I live, I am left without simple answers to travesties such as the Prisoner's Carnival.

I am hardly surprised. Rarely do I find a simple answer to anything concerning humans. That, perhaps, is the reason I find little tedium in my day-to-day travels and encounters. That, perhaps, is the reason I have come to love them.

—Drizzt Do'Urden

Chapter 14
Stolen Seed

Wulfgar stood outside of Luskan, staring back at the city where he had been wrongly accused, tortured, and publicly humiliated. Despite all of that, the barbarian held no anger toward the folk of the town, even toward the vicious magistrate. If he happened upon Jharkheld, he would likely twist the man's head off, but out of a need for closure on that particular incident and not out of hatred. Wulfgar was past hatred, had been for a long time. As it was when Tree Block Breaker had come hunting him at the Cutlass, and he had killed the man. As it was when he happened upon the Sky Ponies, a barbarian tribe akin to his own. He had taken vengeance upon their wicked shaman, an oath of revenge he had sworn years before. It was not for hatred, not even for unbridled rage, but simply Wulfgar's need to try to push forward in a life where the past was too horrible to contemplate.

Wulfgar had come to realize that he wasn't moving forward, and that point seemed obvious to him now as he stared back at the city. He was going in circles, small circles, that left him in the same place over and over, a place made tolerable only through use of the bottle, only by blurring the past into oblivion and putting the future out of mind.

Wulfgar spat on the ground, trying for the first time since he had come to Luskan months before to figure out how he had entered this downward spiral. He thought of the open range to the north, his home-land of Icewind Dale, where he had shared such excitement and joy with his friends. He thought of Bruenor, who had beaten him in battle when he was but a boy, but had shown him such mercy. The dwarf had taken him in as his own, then brought Drizzt to train him in the true ways of the warrior. What a friend Drizzt had been, leading him on grand adventures, standing by him in any fight, no matter the odds. He'd lost Drizzt.

He thought again of Bruenor, who had given Wulfgar his greatest achievement in craftsmanship, the wondrous Aegis-fang. The symbol of Bruenor's love for him. And now he'd lost not only Bruenor, but Aegis-fang as well.

He thought of Catti-brie, perhaps the most special of all to him, the woman who had stolen his heart, the woman he admired and respected above all. Perhaps they could not be lovers, or husband and wife. Perhaps she would never bear his children, but she was his friend, honest and true. When he thought of their last encounter he came to understand the truth of that friendship. Catti-brie would have given anything to help him, would have shared with him her most intimate moments and feelings, but Wulfgar understood that her heart was truly for another.

The fact didn't bring anger or jealousy to the barbarian. He felt only respect, for despite her feelings, Catti-brie would have given all to help him. Now Cattie-brie was lost to him, too.

Wulfgar spat again. He didn't deserve them, not Bruenor, Drizzt, nor Catti-brie. Not even Regis, who, despite his diminutive size and lack of fighting prowess, would leap in front of Wulfgar in time of crisis, would shield the barbarian, as much as he could, from harm. How could he have thrown all that away?

His attention shifted abruptly back to the present as a wagon rolled out of Luskan's western gate. Despite his foul mood, Wulfgar could not hold back a smile as the wagon approached. The driver, a plump elderly woman, came into view.

Morik. The two had been banished only days before, but they had hung about the city's perimeter. The rogue explained that he was going to have to secure some supplies if he was to survive on the open road, so he'd reentered the city alone. Judging from the way the pair of horses labored, judging from the fact that Morik had a wagon and horses at all, Wulfgar knew his sneaky little friend had succeeded.

The rogue turned the wagon off the wide road and onto a small trail that wove into the forest where Wulfgar waited. He came right up to the bottom of the bluff where Wulfgar sat, then stood up and bowed.

"Not so difficult a thing," he announced.

"The guards didn't notice you?" Wulfgar asked.

Morik snorted, as if the notion were preposterous. "They were the same guards as when we were escorted out," he explained, his tone full of pride.

450

Their experience at the hands of Luskan's authorities had reminded Wulfgar that he and Morik were just big players in a small pond, insignificant when measured against the larger pond that was the backdrop of the huge city—but what a large player Morik was in their small corner! "I even lost a bag of food at the gate," Morik went on. "One of the guards ran to catch up to me so that he could replace it on the wagon."

Wulfgar moved down the bluff to the side of the wagon and pulled aside the canvas that covered the load. There were bags of food at the back, along with rope and material for shelter, but most prominent to Wulfgar's sensibilities were the cases of bottles, full bottles of potent liquor.

"I thought you would be pleased," Morik remarked, moving beside the big man as he stared at the haul. "Leaving the city doesn't have to mean leaving our pleasures behind. I was thinking of dragging Delly Curtie along as well."

Wulfgar snapped an angry glare at Morik. The mention of the woman in such a lewd manner profoundly offended him.

"Come," Morik said, clearing his throat and obviously changing the subject. "Let us find a quiet place where we may quench our thirst." The rogue pulled off his disguise slowly, wincing at the pain that still permeated his joints and his ripped stomach. Those wounds, particularly in his knees, would be slow to heal. He paused again a moment later, holding up the wig to admire his handiwork, then climbed onto the driving bench, taking the reins in hand.

"The horses are not so fine," Wulfgar noted. The team seemed an old, haggard pair.

"I needed the gold to buy the drink," Morik explained.

Wulfgar glanced back at the load, thinking that Morik should have spent the funds on a better team of horses, thinking that his days in the bottle had come to an end. He started up the bluff again, but Morik stopped him with a call.

"There are bandits on the road," the rogue announced, "or so I was informed in town. Bandits on the road north of the forest, and all the way to the pass through the Spine of the World."

"You fear bandits?" Wulfgar asked, surprised.

"Only ones who've never heard of me," Morik explained, and Wulfgar understood the deeper implications. In Luskan, Morik's reputation served him well by keeping most thugs at bay.

"Better that we are prepared for trouble," the rogue finished. Morik reached under the driver's bench and produced a huge axe. "Look," he said with a grin, obviously quite proud of himself as he pointed to the axe head. "It's still stained with Creeps Sharky's blood."

The headsman's own axe! Wulfgar started to ask Morik how in the Nine Hells he'd managed to get his hands on that weapon but decided he simply didn't want to know.

"Come along," Morik instructed, patting the bench beside him. The rogue pulled a bottle from the closest case. "Let's ride and drink and plot our defense."

Wulfgar stared long and hard at that bottle before climbing onto the bench. Morik offered him the bottle, but he declined with gritted teeth. Shrugging, the rogue took a healthy swallow and offered it again. Again Wulfgar declined.That brought a puzzled look to Morik's face, but it fast turned into a smile as he decided that Wulfgar's refusal would leave more for him.

"We needn't live like savages just because we're on the road," Morik stated.

The irony of that statement from a man guzzling so potent a drink was not lost on Wulfgar. The barbarian managed to resist the bottle throughout the afternoon, and Morik happily drained it. Keeping the wagon at a swift pace, Morik tossed the empty bottle against a rock as they passed, then howled with delight when it shattered into a thousand pieces.

"You make a lot of noise for one trying to avoid highwaymen," Wulfgar grumbled.

"Avoid?" Morik asked with a snap of his fingers. "Hardly that. Highwaymen often have well-equipped campsites where we might find some comfort."

"Such well-equipped campsites must belong to successful highwaymen," Wulfgar reasoned, "and successful highwaymen are likely very good at what they do."

"As was Tree Block Breaker, my friend," Morik reminded. When Wulfgar still didn't seem convinced, he added, "Perhaps they will accept our offer to join with them."

"I think not," said Wulfgar.

Morik shrugged, then nodded. "Then we must chase them off," he said matter-of-factly.

"We'll not even find them," Wulfgar muttered.

"Oh?" Morik asked, and he turned the wagon down a side trail so suddenly that it went up on two wheels and Wulfgar nearly tumbled off.

"What?" the barbarian groweled as they bounced along. He just barely ducked a low branch, then got a nasty scratch as another whipped against his arm. "Morik!"

"Quiet, my large friend," the rogue said. "There's a river up ahead with but one bridge across it, a bridge bandits would no doubt guard well." They burst out of the brush, bouncing to the banks of the river. Morik slowed the tired horses to a walk, and they started across a rickety bridge. To the rogue's dismay they crossed safely with no bandits in sight.

"Novices," a disappointed Morik grumbled, vowing to go a few miles, then turn back and cross the bridge again." Morik abruptly stopped the wagon. A large and ugly man stepped onto the road up ahead, pointing a sword their way.

"How interesting that such a pair as yourselves should be walking in my woods without my permission," the thug remarked, bringing the sword back and dropping it across his shoulder.

"Your woods?" Morik asked. "Why, good sir, I had thought this forest open for travel." Under his breath to Wulfgar, he added, "Half-orc."

"Idiot," Wulfgar replied so that only Morik could hear. "You, I mean, and not the thief. To look for this trouble. . . ."

"I thought it would appeal to your heroic side," the rogue replied. "Besides, this highwayman has a camp filled with comforts, no doubt."

"What're you talking about?' the thug demanded.

"Why, you, good sir," Morik promptly replied. "My friend here was just saying that he thought you might be a thief and that you do not own this forest at all."

The bandit's eyes widened, and he stuttered over several responses unsuccessfully. He wound up spitting on the ground. "I'm saying it's my wood!" he declared, poking his chest. "Togo's wood!"

"And the cost of passage through, good Togo?" Morik asked.

"Five gold!" the thug cried and after a pause, he added, "Each of you!"

"Give it to him," Wulfgar muttered.

Morik chuckled, then an arrow zipped past, barely an inch in front of his face. Surprised that this band was so well organized, the rogue abruptly changed his mind and started reaching for his purse.

However, Wulfgar had changed his mind as well, enraged that someone had nearly killed him. Before Morik could agree on the price, the barbarian leaped from the wagon and rushed at Togo barehanded, then suddenly changed his mind and direction. A pair of arrows cut across his initial path. He turned for the monstrous archer he'd spotted perched high in a tree a dozen feet back from the road. Wulfgar crashed through the first line of brush and slammed hard into a fallen log. Hardly slowing, he lifted the log and threw it into the face of another crouching human, then continued his charge.

He made it to the base of the tree just as an arrow thunked into the ground beside him, a near miss Wulfgar ignored. Leaping to a low branch, he caught hold and hauled himself upward with tremendous strength and agility, nearly running up it. Bashing back small branches, scrambling over others, he came level with the archer. The creature, a gnoll bigger than Wulfgar, was desperately trying to set another arrow.

"Keep it!" the cowardly gnoll yelled, throwing the bow at Wulfgar and stepping off the branch, preferring the twenty-foot drop to Wulfgar's rage.

Escape wasn't that easy for the gnoll. Wulfgar thrust out a hand and caught the falling creature by the collar. Despite all the wriggling and punching, the awkward position and the gnoll's weight, Wulfgar had no trouble hauling it up.

Then he heard Morik's cry for help.

* * * * *

Standing on the driver's bench, the rogue worked furiously with his slender sword to fend off the attacks from both Togo and another human swordsman who had come out from the brush. Worse, he heard a third approaching from behind, and worse still, arrows regularly cut the air nearby.

"I'll pay!" he cried, but the monstrous thugs only laughed.

Out of the corner of his eye Morik spotted an archer taking aim. He leaped backward as the missile came on, dodging both it and the thrust from the surprisingly deft swordsman in front of him. The move cost him, though, for he tumbled over the back of the bench, crashing into a case of bottles, shattering them. Morik leaped up and shrieked his outrage, smashing his sword impotently across the chair back.

On came Togo, gaining the bench position, but angry Morik matched his movements, coming ahead powerfully without regard for the other swordsman or archers. Togo retracted his arm for a swing, but Morik, quick with the blade, stabbed first, scoring a hit on Togo's hand that cost the thug his grip. Even as Togo's sword clanged against the wooden bench Morik closed in, turning his sword out to fend off the attacks from Togo's partner. He produced a dagger from his belt, a blade he promptly and repeatedly drove into Togo's belly. The half-orc tried desperately to fend off the attacks, using his bare hands, but Morik was too quick and too clever, stabbing around them even as his sword worked circles about Togo's partner's blade.

Togo fell back from the bench to the ground. He managed only a single running step before he collapsed, clutching his torn guts.

Morik heard the third attacker coming in around the side of the wagon. He heard a terrified scream from above, then another from the approaching enemy. The rogue glanced that way just in time to see Wulfgar's captured gnoll archer flying down from on high, arms flailing, screaming all the way. The humanoid missile hit the third thug, a small human woman, squarely, smashing both hard against the wagon in a heap. Groaning, the woman began trying to crawl away; the archer lay very still.

Morik pressed the attack on the remaining swordsman, as much to get down from the open driver's bench as to continue the fight. The swordsman, though, apparently had little heart remaining in the battle with his friends falling all around him. He parried Morik's thrust, backing all the while as the man leaped down to the road.

On Morik came, his sword working the thug's blade over and under. He thrust ahead and retracted quickly when the swordsman blocked, then came forward after a subtle roll of his slender sword that disengaged the thug's blade. Staggering, the man retreated, blood running from one shoulder. He started to turn and flee, but Morik kept pace, forcing him to work defensively.

Morik heard another cry of alarm behind him, followed by the crack of breaking branches. He smiled with the knowledge that Wulfgar continued to clear out the archers.

"Please, mister," Morik's prey grunted as more and more of the rogue's attacks slipped through with stinging results and it became clear that Morik was the superior swordsman. "We was just needing your money."

"Then you wouldn't have harmed me and my friend after you took our coin?" Morik asked cynically.

The man shook his head vigorously, and Morik used the distraction to slip through yet again, drawing a line of red on the man's cheek. Morik's prey fell to his knees with a yelp and tossed his sword to the ground, begging for mercy.

"I am known as a merciful sort," Morik said with mock sympathy, hearing Wulfgar approaching fast, "but my friend, I fear, is not."

Wulfgar stormed by and grabbed the kneeling man by the throat, hoisting him into the air and running him back into a tree. With one arm—the other tucked defensively with a broken arrow shaft protruding from his shoulder—Wulfgar held the highwayman by the throat off the ground, choking the life out of him.

"I could stop him," Morik explained, walking over and putting his hand on his huge friend's bulging forearm. Only then did he notice Wulfgar's serious wound. "You must lead us to your camp."

"No camp!" the man gasped. Wulfgar pressed and twisted.

"I will! I will!" the thug squealed, his voice going away as Wulfgar tightened his grip, choking all sounds and all air. His face locked in an expression of the purest rage, the barbarian pressed on.

"Let him go," Morik said.

No answer. The man in Wulfgar's grasp wriggled and slapped but could neither break the hold nor draw breath.

"Wulfgar!" Morik called, and he grabbed at the big man's arm with both hands, tugging fiercely. "Snap out of it, man!"

Wulfgar wasn't hearing any of it, didn't even seem to notice the rogue.

"You will thank me for this," Morik vowed, though he was not so sure as he balled up his fist and smashed Wulfgar on the side of the head.

Wulfgar did let go of the thug, who slumped unconscious at the base of the tree, but only to backhand Morik, a blow that sent the rogue staggering backward, with Wulfgar coming in pursuit. Morik lifted his sword, ready to plunge it through the big man's heart if necessary, but at the last moment Wulfgar stopped, blinking repeatedly, as if he had just come awake. Morik recognized that Wulfgar had returned from wherever he had gone to this time and place.

"He'll take us to the camp now," the rogue said.

Wulfgar nodded dumbly, his gaze still foggy. He looked dispassionately at the broken arrow shaft poking from his wounded shoulder. The barbarian blanched, looked to Morik in puzzlement, then collapsed face down in the dirt.

* * * * *

Wulfgar awoke in the back of the wagon on the edge of a field lined by towering pines. He lifted his head with some effort and nearly panicked. A woman walking past was one of the thugs from the road. What happened? Had they lost? Before full panic set in, though, he heard Morik's lighthearted voice, and he forced himself up higher, wincing with pain as he put some weight on his injured arm. Wulfgar looked at that shoulder curiously; the arrow shaft was gone, the wound cleaned and dressed.

Morik sat a short distance away, chatting amiably and sharing a bottle with another of the gnollish highwaymen as if they were old friends. Wulfgar slid to the end of the wagon and rolled his legs over, climbing unsteadily to his feet. The world swam before his eyes, black spots crossing his field of vision. The feeling passed quickly, though, and Wulfgar gingerly but deliberately made his way over to Morik.

"Ah, you're awake. A drink, my friend?" the rogue asked, holding out the bottle.

Frowning, Wulfgar shook his head.

"Come now, ye gots to be drinkin'," the dog-faced gnoll sitting next to Morik slurred. He spooned a glob of thick stew into his mouth, half of it falling to the ground or down the front of his tunic.

Wulfgar glared at Morik's wretched new comrade.

"Rest easy, my friend," Morik said, recognizing that dangerous look. "Mickers here is a friend, a loyal one now that Togo is dead."

"Send him away," Wulfgar said, and the gnoll dropped his jaw in surprise.

Morik came up fast, moving to Wulfgar's side and taking him by the good arm. "They are allies," he explained. "All of them. They were loyal to Togo, and now they are loyal to me. And to you."

"Send them away," Wulfgar repeated fiercely.

"We're out on the road," Morik argued. "We need eyes, scouts to survey potential territory and swords to help us hold it fast."

"No," Wulfgar said flatly.

"You don't understand the dangers, my friend," Morik said reasonably, hoping to pacify his large friend.

"Send them away!" Wulfgar yelled suddenly. Seeing he'd make no progress with Morik, he stormed up to Mickers. "Be gone from here and from this forest!"

Mickers looked past the big man. Morik gave a resigned shrug.

456

Mickers stood up. "I'll stay with him," he said, pointing to the rogue.

Wulfgar slapped the stew bowl from the gnoll's hand and grabbed the front of his shirt, pulling him up to his tiptoes. "One last chance to leave of your own accord," the big man growled as he shoved Mickers back several steps.

"Mister Morik?" Mickers complained.

"Oh, be gone," Morik said unhappily.

"And the rest of us, too?" asked another one of the humans of the bandit band, standing amidst a tumble of rocks on the edge of the field. He held a strung bow.

"Them or me, Morik," Wulfgar said, his tone leaving no room for debate. The barbarian and the rogue both glanced back to the archer to see that the man had put an arrow to his bowstring.

Wulfgar's eyes flared with simmering rage, and he started toward the archer. "One shot," he called steadily. "You will get one shot at me. Will you hit the mark?"

The archer lifted his bow.

"I don't think you will," Wulfgar said, smiling. "No, you will miss because you know."

"Know what?" the archer dared ask.

"Know that even if your arrow strikes me, it will not kill me," Wulfgar replied, and he continued his deliberate stalk. "Not right away, not before I get my hands around your throat."

The man drew his bowstring back, but Wulfgar only smiled more confidently and continued forward. The archer glanced around nervously, looking for support, but there was none to be found. Realizing he had taken on too great a foe, the man eased his string, turned, and ran off.

Wulfgar turned back. Mickers, too, had sprinted away.

"Now we'll have to watch out for them," Morik observed glumly when Wulfgar returned to him. "You cost us allies."

"I'll not ally myself with murdering thieves!" Wulfgar said simply.

Morik jumped back from him. "What am I, if not a thief?"

Wulfgar's expression softened. "Well, perhaps just one," he corrected with a chuckle.

Morik laughed uneasily. "Here, my big and not so smart friend," he said, reaching for another bottle. "A drink to the two of us. Highwaymen!"

"Will we find the same fate as our predecessors?" Wulfgar wondered aloud.

"Our predecessors were not so smart," Morik explained. "I knew where to find them because they were too predictable. A good highwayman strikes and runs on to the next target area. A good highwayman seems like ten separate bands, always one step ahead of the city guards, ahead of those who ride into the cities with information enough to find and defeat him."

457

"You sound as if you know the life well."

"I have done it from time to time," Morik admitted. "Just because we're on the wild road doesn't mean we must live like savages," the rogue repeated what was fast becoming his mantra. He held the bottle out toward Wulfgar.

It took all the willpower he could muster for Wulfgar to refuse that drink. His shoulder ached, and he was still agitated about the thugs. Retreat into a swirl of semiconsciousness was very inviting at that moment.

But he did refuse by walking away from a stunned Morik. Moving to the other end of the field, he scrambled up a tree, settled into a comfortable niche, and sat back to survey the outlying lands.

His gaze was drawn repeatedly to the mountains in the north, the Spine of the World, the barrier between him and that other world of Icewind Dale, that life he might have known and might still know. He thought of his friends again, mostly of Catti-brie. The barbarian fell asleep to dreams of her close in his arms, kissing him gently, a respite from the pains of the world.

Suddenly Catti-brie backed away, and as Wulfgar watched, small ivory horns sprouted from her forehead and great bat wings extended behind her. A succubus, a demon of the Abyss, tricking him again in the hell of Errtu's torments, assuming the guise of comfort to seduce him.

Wulfgar's eyes popped open wide, his breath coming in labored gasps. He tried to dismiss the horrible images, but they wouldn't let him go. Not this time. So poignant and distinct were they that the barbarian wondered if all of this, his last months of life, had been but a ruse by Errtu to bring him hope again so that the demon might stomp it. He saw the succubus, the horrid creature that had seduced him . . .

"No!" Wulfgar growled, for it was too ugly a memory, too horrible for him to confront it yet again.

I stole your seed, the succubus said to his mind, and he could not deny it. They had done it to him several times in the years of his torment, had taken his seed and spawned alu-demons, Wulfgar's children. It was the first time Wulfgar had been able to consciously recall the memory since his return to the surface, the first time the horror of seeing his demonic offspring had forced itself through the mental barriers he had erected.

He saw them now, saw Errtu bring to him one such child, a crying infant, its mother succubus standing behind the demon. He saw Errtu present the infant high in the air, and then, right before Wulfgar's eyes, right before its howling mother's eyes, the great demon bit the child's head off. A spray of blood showered Wulfgar, who was unable to draw breath, unable to comprehend that Errtu had found a way to get at him yet again, the worst way of all.

Wulfgar half scrambled and half tumbled out of the tree, landing hard on his injured shoulder, reopening the wound. Ignoring the pain, he sprinted across the field and found Morik resting beside the wagon. Wulfgar went right to the crates and frantically tore one open.

His children! The offspring of his stolen seed!

The potent liquid burned all the way down, the heat of it spreading, spreading, dulling Wulfgar's senses, blurring the horrid images.

Chapter 15

A Child No More

"You must give love time to blossom, my lord," Temigast whispered to Lord Feringal. He'd ushered the young lord to the far side of the garden, away from Meralda, who was staring out over the sea wall. The steward had discovered the amorous young man pressuring Meralda to marry him the very next week. The flustered woman was making polite excuse after polite excuse, with stubborn Feringal defeating each one.

"Time to blossom?" Feringal echoed incredulously. "I am going mad with desire. I can think of nothing but Meralda!"

He said the last loudly, and both men glanced to see a frowning Meralda looking back at them.

"As it should be," Steward Temigast whispered. "Let us discover if the feeling holds strong over the course of time. The duration of such feelings is the true meaning of love, my lord."

"You doubt me still?" a horrified Lord Feringal replied.

"No, my lord, not I," Temigast explained, "but the villagers must see your union to a woman of Meralda's station as true love and not infatuation. You must consider her reputation."

That last statement gave Lord Feringal pause. He glanced back at the

461

woman, then at Temigast, obviously confused. "If she is married to me, then what harm could come to her reputation?"

"If the marriage is quickly brought, then the peasants will assume she used her womanly tricks to bewitch you," Temigast explained. "Better for her, by far, if you spend the weeks showing your honest and respectful love for her. Many will resent her in any case, my lord, out of jealousy. Now you must protect her, and the best way to do that is to take your time with the engagement."

"How much time?" the eager young lord asked.

"The spring equinox," Temigast offered, bringing another horrified look from Feringal. "It is only proper."

"I shall die," wailed Feringal.

Temigast frowned at the overwrought lord. "We can arrange a meeting with another woman if your needs become too great."

Lord Feringal shook his head vigorously. "I cannot think of passion with another woman."

Smiling warmly, Temigast patted the young man on the shoulder. "That is the correct answer for a man who is truly in love," he said. "Perhaps we can arrange the wedding for the turn of the year."

Lord Feringal's face brightened, then he frowned again. "Five months," he grumbled.

"But think of the pleasure when the time has passed."

"I think of nothing else," said a glum Feringal.

"What were you speaking of?" Meralda asked when Feringal joined her by the wall after Temigast excused himself from the garden.

"The wedding, of course," the lord replied. "Steward Temigast believes we must wait until the turn of the year. He believes love to be a growing, blossoming thing," said Feringal, his voice tinged with doubt.

"And so it is," Meralda agreed with relief and gratitude to Temigast.

Feringal grabbed her suddenly and pulled her close. "I cannot believe that my love for you could grow any stronger," he explained. He kissed her, and Meralda returned it, and glad she was that he didn't try to take it any further than that, as had been his usual tactics.

Instead, Lord Feringal pushed her back to arms' length. "Temigast has warned me to show my respect for you," he admitted. "To show the villagers that our love is a real and lasting thing. And so I shall by waiting. Besides, that will give Priscilla the time she needs to prepare the event. She has promised a wedding such as Auckney—as the whole of the North—has never before seen."

Meralda's smile was genuine indeed. She was glad for the delay, glad for the time she needed to put her feelings for Lord Feringal and Jaka in the proper order, to come to terms with her decision and her responsibility. Meralda was certain she could go through with this, and not as a suffering woman. She could marry Lord Feringal and act as lady of Auckney for the sake of her mother and her family. Perhaps it would not be such a terrible thing.

The woman looked with a glimmer of affection at Feringal, who stood watching the dark waves. Impulsively she put an arm around the man's waist and rested her head on his shoulder and was rewarded with a chaste but grateful smile from her husband-to-be. He said nothing, didn't even try to take the touch further. Meralda had to admit it was . . . pleasant.

*   *   *   *   *

"Oh, tell me everything!" Tori whispered, scrambling to Meralda's bed when the older girl at last returned home that night. "Did he touch you?"

"We talked and watched the waves," Meralda replied noncommittally.

"Do you love him yet?"

Meralda stared at her sister. Did she love Lord Feringal? No, she could say for certain she did not, at least not in the heated manner in which she longed for Jaka, but perhaps that was all right. Perhaps she would come to love the generous lord of Auckney. Certainly Lord Feringal wasn't an ugly man—far from it. As their relationship grew, as they began to move beyond the tortured man's desperate groping, Meralda was starting to see his many good qualities, qualities she could indeed grow to love.

"Don't you still love Jaka?" Tori asked.

Meralda's contented smile dissipated at once with the painful reminder. She didn't answer, and for once Tori had the sense to let it drop as Meralda turned over, curled in upon herself, and tried hard not to cry.

It was a night of torrid dreams that left her tangled in her blankets. Still, Meralda's mood was better that next morning, and it improved even more when she entered the common room to hear her mother talking with Mam Gardener, one of their nosier neighbors (the little gnome had a beak that could shame a vulture), happily telling the visitor about her stroll in the castle garden.

"Mam Gardener brought us some eggs," Biaste Ganderlay explained, pointing to a skillet of scrambled egs. "Help yourself, as I'm not wanting to get back up."

Meralda smiled at the generous gnome, then moved to the pan. Unexplicably, the young woman felt her stomach lurch at the sight and the smell and had to rush from the house to throw up beside the small bush outside the door.

Mam Gardener was there beside her in an instant. "Are you all right, girl?" she asked.

Meralda, more surprised than sick, stood back up. "The rich food at the castle," she explained. "They're feeding me too good, I fear."

Mam Gardener howled with laughter. "Oh, but you'll be getting used to that!" she said. "All fat and plump you'll get, living easy and eating well."

Meralda returned her smile and went back into the house.

"You still got to eat," Mam Gardener said, guiding her toward the eggs.

Even the thought of the eggs made Meralda's stomach turn again. "I'm thinking that I need to go and lay down," she explained, pulling away to head back to her room.

She heard the older ladies discussing her plight, with Mam telling Biaste about the rich food. Biaste, no stranger to illness, hoped that to be all it was.

Privately, Meralda wasn't so sure. Only then did she consider the timeline since her encounter with Jaka three weeks before. It was true she'd not had her monthly, but she hadn't thought much about it, for she'd never been regular in that manner anyway. . . .

The young woman clutched at her belly, both overwhelmed with joy and fear.

She was sick again the next morning, and the next after that, but she was able to hide her condition by going nowhere near the smell or sight of eggs. She felt well after throwing up in the morning and was not troubled with it after that, and so it became clear to her that she was, indeed, with child.

In her fantasies, the thought of having Jaka Sculi's babe was not terrible. She could picture herself married to the young rogue, living in a castle, walking in the gardens beside him, but the reality of her situation was far more terrifying.

She had betrayed the lord of Auckney, and worse, she had betrayed her family. Stealing that one night for herself, she had likely condemned her mother to death and branded herself a whore in the eyes of all the village.

Would it even get that far? she wondered. Perhaps when her father learned the truth he would kill her—he'd beaten her for far less. Or perhaps Lord Feringal would have her paraded through the streets so that the villagers might taunt her and throw rotten fruit and spit upon her. Or perhaps in a fit of rage Lord Feringal would cut the baby from her womb and send soldiers out to murder Jaka.

What of the baby? What might the nobles of Auckney do to a child who was the result of the cuckolding of their lord? Meralda had heard stories of such instances in other kingdoms, tales of potential threats to the throne, tales of murdered infants.

All the possibilities whirled in Meralda's mind one night as she lay in her bed, all the terrible possibilities, events too wicked for her to truly imagine, and too terrifying for her to honestly face. She rose and dressed quietly, then went in to see her mother, sleeping comfortably, curled up in her father's arms.

Meralda silently mouthed a heartsick apology to them both, then stole out of the house. It was a wet and windy night. To the woman's dismay, she didn't find Jaka in his usual spot in the fields above the houses, so she went to his house. Trying not to wake his kin, Meralda tossed pebbles against the curtain screening his glassless window.

The curtain was abruptly yanked to the side, and Jaka's handsome face poked through the opening.

"It's me, Meralda," she whispered, and the young man's face brightened in surprise. He held his hand out to her, and when she clenched it, he pulled it close to his face through the opening, his smile wide enough to take in his ears.

"I must talk with you," Meralda explained. "Please come outside."

"It's warmer in here," Jaka replied in his usual sly, lewd tone.

Knowing it unwise but shivering in the chill night air, Meralda motioned to the front door and scurried to it. Jaka was there in a moment, stripped bare to the waist and holding a single candle. He put his finger over his pursed lips and took Meralda by the arm, walking her quietly through the curtained doorway that led to his bedchamber. Before the young woman could begin to explain, Jaka was against her, kissing her, pulling her down beside him.

"Stop!" she hissed, pulling away. "We must talk."

"Later," Jaka said, his hands roaming.

Meralda rolled off the side of the bed and took a step away. "Now," she said. " 'Tis important."

Jaka sat up on the edge of the bed, grinning still but making no move to pursue her.

"I'm running too late," Meralda explained bluntly.

Jaka's face screwed up as though he didn't understand.

"I am with child," the woman blurted softly. "Your child."

The effect of her words would have been no less dramatic if she had smashed Jaka across the face with a cudgel. "How?" he stammered after a long, trembling pause. "It was only once."

"I'm guessing that we did it right, then," the woman returned dryly.

"But—" Jaka started, shaking his head. "Lord Feringal? What are we to do?" He paused again, then turned a sharp eye upon Meralda. "Have you and he—?"

"Only yourself," Meralda firmly replied. "Only that once in all my life."

"What are we to do?" Jaka repeated, pacing nervously. Meralda had never seen him so agitated.

"I was thinking that I had to marry Lord Feringal," Meralda explained, moving over and taking hold of the man to steady him. "For the sake of my family, if not my own, but now things are changed," she said, looking Jaka in the eyes. "I cannot bring another man's child into Castle Auck, after all."

"Then what?" asked Jaka, still appearing on the very edge of desperation.

"You said you wanted me," Meralda said softly, hopefully. "So, with what's in my belly you've got me, and all my heart."

"Lord Feringal will kill me."

"We'll not stay, then," Meralda replied. "You said we'd travel the Sword Coast to Luskan and to Waterdeep, and so we shall, and so I must."

The thought didn't seem to sit very well with Jaka. He said "But . . ." and shook his head repeatedly. Finally, Meralda gave him a shake to steady him and pushed herself up against him.

"Truly, this is for the better," she said. "You're my love, as I'm your own, and now fate has intervened to put us together."

"It's crazy," Jaka replied, pulling back from her. "We can't run away. We have no money. We have nothing. We shall die on the road before we ever get near Luskan."

"Nothing?" Meralda echoed incredulously, starting to realize that this was more than shock speaking. "We've each other. We've our love, and our child coming."

"You think that's enough?" Jaka asked in the same incredulous tone. "What life are we to find under such circumstances as this? Paupers forever, eating mud and raising our child in mud?"

"What choice have we?"

"We?" Jaka bit back the word as soon as it left his mouth, realizing too late that it had not been wise to say aloud.

Meralda fought back tears. "Are you saying that you lied to get me to lay down with you? Are you saying that you do not love me?"

"That's not what I'm saying," Jaka reassured her, coming over to put a hand on her shoulder, "but what chance shall we have to survive? You don't really believe that love is enough, do you? We shall have no food, no money, and three to feed. And how will it be when you get all fat and ugly, and we have not even our lovemaking to bring us joy?"

The woman blanched and fell back from his reach. He came for her, but she slapped him away. "You said you loved me," she said.

"I did," Jaka replied. "I do."

She shook her head slowly, eyes narrowing in a moment of clarity. "You lusted for me but never loved me." Her voice quivered, but the woman was determined to hold strong her course. "You fool. You're not even knowing the difference." With that she turned and ran out of the house. Jaka didn't make a move to go after her.

Meralda cried all through the night on the rainy hillside and didn't return home until early in the morning. The truth was there before her now, whatever might happen next. What a fool she felt for giving herself to Jaka Sculi. For the rest of her life, when she would look back on the moment she became a woman, the moment she left her innocent life as a girl behind her, it would not be the night she lost her virginity. No, it would be this night, when she first realized she had given her most secret self to a selfish, uncaring, shallow man. No, not a man—a boy. What a fool she had been.

Chapter 16

Home Sweet Home

They sat huddled under the wagon as the rain pelted down around them. Rivulets of water streamed in, and the ground became muddy even in their sheltered little place.

"This is not the life I envisioned," a glum Morik remarked. "How the mighty have fallen."

Wulfgar smirked at his friend and shook his head. He was not as concerned with physical comforts as Morik, for the rain hardly bothered him. He had grown up in Icewind Dale, after all, a climate more harsh by far than anything the foothills on this side of the Spine of the World could offer.

"Now I've ruined my best breeches," Morik grumbled, turning around and slapping the mud from his pants.

"The farmers would have offered us shelter," Wulfgar reminded him. Earlier that day, the pair had passed clusters of farmhouses, and Wulfgar had mentioned several times that the folk within would likely offer them food and a warm place to stay.

"Then the farmers would know of us," Morik said by way of explanation, the same answer he had given each time Wulfgar had brought up the possibility. "If or when we have someone looking for us, our trail would be easier to follow."

A bolt of lightning split a tree a hundred yards away, bringing a startled cry from Morik.

"You act as though you expect half the militias of the region to be chasing us before long," Wulfgar replied.

"I have made many enemies," Morik admitted, "as have you, my friend, including one of the leading magistrates of Luskan."

Wulfgar shrugged; he hardly cared.

"We'll make more, I assure you," Morik went on.

"Because of the life you have chosen for us."

The rogue cocked an eyebrow. "Are we to live as farmers, tilling dirt?"

"Would that be so terrible?"

Morik snorted, and Wulfgar only chuckled again helplessly.

"We need a base," Morik announced suddenly as another rivulet found its way to his bottom. "A house . . . or a cave."

"There are many caves in the mountains," Wulfgar offered. The look on Morik's face, both hopeful and fearful, told him he needn't speak the thought: mountain caves were almost always occupied.

The sun was up the next morning, shining bright in a blue sky, but that did little to change Morik's complaining mood. He grumbled and slapped at the dirt, then stripped off his clothes and washed them when the pair came across a clear mountain stream.

Wulfgar, too, washed his clothes and his dirty body. The icy water felt good against his injured shoulder. Lying on a sunny rock waiting for their clothes to dry, Wulfgar spotted some smoke drifting lazily into the air.

"More houses," the barbarian remarked. "Friendly folk to those who come as friends, no doubt."

"You never stop," Morik replied dryly, and he reached behind the rock and pulled out a bottle of wine he had cooling in the water. He took a drink and offered it to Wulfgar, who hesitated, then accepted.

Soon after, their clothes still wet, and both a bit lightheaded, the pair started off along the mountain trails. They couldn't take their wagon, so they stashed it under some brush and let the horses graze nearby, with Morik noting the irony of how easy it would be for someone to rob them.

"Then we would just have to steal them back," Wulfgar replied, and Morik started to laugh, missing the barbarian's sarcasm.

He stopped abruptly, though, noting the suddenly serious expression on his large friend's face. Following Wulfgar's gaze to the trail ahead, Morik began to understand, for he spotted a broken sapling, recently snapped just above the trunk. Wulfgar went to the spot and bent low, studying the ground around the sapling.

"What do you think broke the tree?" Morik asked from behind him.

Wulfgar motioned for the rogue to join him, then pointed out the heel print of a large, large boot.

"Giants?" Morik asked, and Wulfgar looked at him curiously. Already Wulfgar recognized the signs of Morik becoming unhinged, as the rogue had over the rat in the cage at Prisoner's Carnival.

"You don't like giants, either?" Wulfgar asked.

Morik shrugged. "I have never seen one," he admitted, "but who truly likes them?"

Wulfgar stared at him incredulously. Morik was a seasoned veteran, skilled as a thief and warrior. A significant portion of Wulfgar's own training had come at the expense of giants. To think one as skilled as Morik had never even seen one surprised the barbarian.

"I saw an ogre once," Morik said. "Of course, our gaoler friends had more than a bit of ogre blood in them."

"Bigger," Wulfgar said bluntly. "Giants are much bigger."

Morik blanched. "Let us return the way we came."

"If there are giants about, they'll very likely have a lair," Wulfgar explained. "Giants would not suffer rain and hot sun when there are comfortable caves in the region. Besides, they prefer their meals cooked, and they try not to advertise their presence with campfires under the open sky."

"Their meals," Morik echoed. "Are barbarians and thieves on their menu of cooked meals?"

"A delicacy," Wulfgar said earnestly, nodding.

"Let us go and speak with the farmers," said Morik, turning around.

"Coward," Wulfgar remarked quietly. The word had Morik spinning back to face him. "The trail is easy enough to follow," Wulfgar explained. "We don't even know how many there are. Never would I have expected Morik the Rogue to run from a fight."

"Morik the rogue fights with this," Morik countered, poking his finger against his temple.

"A giant would eat that."

"Then Morik the Rogue runs with his feet," the thief said.

"A giant would catch you," Wulfgar assured him. "Or it would throw a rock at you and squash you from afar."

"Pleasant choices," said Morik cynically. "Let us go and speak with the farmers."

Wulfgar settled back on his heels, studying his friend and making no move to follow. He couldn't help but contrast Morik to Drizzt at that moment. The rogue was turning to leave, while the drow would, and often had, eagerly rushed headlong into such adventure as a giant lair. Wulfgar recalled the time he and Drizzt had dispatched an entire lair of verbeeg, a long and brutal fight but one that Drizzt had entered laughing. Wulfgar thought of the last fight he had waged beside his ebon-skinned friend, against another band of giants. That time they'd chased them into the mountains after learning that the brutes had set their eyes on the road to Ten-Towns.

It seemed to Wulfgar that Morik and Drizzt were similar in so many way, but in the most important ways they were nothing alike. It was a contrast that continually nagged at Wulfgar, a reminder of the startling differences in his life now, the difference between that world north of the Spine of the World and this world south of it.

"There may only be a couple of giants," Wulfgar suggested. "They rarely gather in large numbers."

Morik pulled out his slender sword and his dagger. "A hundred hits to fell one?" he asked. "Two hundred? And all the time I spend sticking the behemoth two hundred times, I'll be comforted by the thought that one strike from the giant will crush me flat."

Wulfgar's grin widened. "That's the fun of it," he offered. The barbarian hoisted the headman's axe over one shoulder and started after the giant, having little trouble in discerning the trail.

Crouching on the backside of a wide boulder by mid-afternoon, Wulfgar and Morik had the giants and their lair in sight. Even Morik had to admit that the location was perfect: an out-of-the-way cave nestled among rocky crests, yet less than half a day's march to one of two primary mountain passes, the easternmost of the pair, separating Icewind Dale from the southlands.

They watched for a long while and noted only a pair of giants, then a third appeared. Even so, Wulfgar was not impressed.

"Hill giants," he remarked disparagingly, "and only a trio. I have battled a single mountain giant who could fell all three."

"Well, let us see if we can find that mountain giant and prompt him to come and evict this group," said Morik.

"That mountain giant is dead," Wulfgar replied. "As these three shall soon be." He took up the huge axe in hand and glanced about, finally deciding on a roundabout trail that would bring him to the lair.

"I have no idea of how to fight them," Morik whispered.

"Watch and learn," Wulfgar replied, and off he went.

Morik didn't know whether he should follow or not, so he stayed put on the rock, noting his friend's progress, watching the trio of giants disappear into the cave. Wulfgar crept up to that dark entrance soon after, slipping to the edge and peering in. Glancing back Morik's way, he went spinning into the gloom.

"You don't even know if there are others inside," Morik muttered to himself, shaking his head. He wondered if coming out here with Wulfgar had been a wise idea after all. The rogue could get back into Luskan easily, he knew, with a new identity as far as the authorities were concerned, but with the same old position of respect on the streets. Of course, there remained the not-so-little matter of the dark elves who had come calling.

Still, given the size of those giants, Morik was thinking that he just might have to return to Luskan. Alone.

472

* * * * *

The initial passageway inside the cave was not very high or open, at least for giants. Wulfgar took comfort in the knowledge that his adversaries would have to stoop very low, perhaps even crawl, to get under one overhanging boulder. Pursuit would not be swift if Wulfgar were forced to retreat.

The tunnel widened and heightened considerably beyond that curving walk of about fifty feet. After that it opened into a wide, high chamber where a tremendous bonfire reflected enough orange light down the tunnel so that Wulfgar was not walking in darkness.

He noted that the walls were broken and uneven, a place of shadows. There was one particularly promising perch about ten feet off the ground. Wulfgar crept along a bit farther, hoping to catch a glimpse of the entire giant clan within. He wanted to make sure that there were only three and that they didn't have any of the dangerous pets giants often harbored, like cave bears or huge wolves. The barbarian had to backtrack, though, before he even got near the chamber entrance, for he heard one of the giants approaching, belching with every booming step. Wulfgar went up the wall to the perch and melted back into the shadows to watch.

Out came the giant, rubbing its belly and belching yet again. It stooped and bent in preparation for the tight stretch of corridor ahead. Caution dictated that Wulfgar hold his attack, that he scout further and discern the exact strength of his enemy, but Wulfgar wasn't feeling cautious.

Down he came with a great roar and a tremendous overhead chop of the headsman's axe, his pure strength adding to the momentum of the drop.

The startled giant managed a slight dodge, enough so that the axe didn't sheer through its neck. Despite its great size, Wulfgar's power would have decapitated the behemoth. Still, the axe drove through the giant's shoulderblade, tearing skin and muscle and crushing bone, knocking the giant into a howling, agonized stagger that left it crouched on one knee.

But in the process, Wulfgar's weapon snapped at mid-shaft. Ever one to improvise, the barbarian hit the ground in a roll, came right back to his feet, and rushed in on the wounded, kneeling giant, stabbing it hard in the throat with the pointed, broken end of the shaft. As the gurgling behemoth reached for him with huge, trembling hands, Wulfgar tore the shaft free, tightened his grip on the end, and smashed the giant across the face.

He left the giant there on one knee, knowing that its friends would soon come out. Looking for a defensible position, he noticed then that the action of his attack, or perhaps the landing on the floor, had re-opened his shoulder wound, his tunic already growing wet with fresh blood.

473

Wulfgar didn't have time to think about it. He made it back to his high perch as the other two entered the area below him. He found his next weapon in the form of a huge rock. With a stifled grunt, Wulfgar brought it up overhead and waited.

The last giant in line, the smallest of the three, heard that grunt and looked up just as Wulfgar brought the rock smashing down—and how that giant howled!

Wulfgar scooped his club and leaped down, once again using his momentum to heighten the strike as he smashed this one across the face. The barbarian hit the floor and pivoted back at the behemoth, rushing past its legs to smash at its kneecaps. Altering his grip, he stabbed hard at the tender hamstrings on the back of the giant's legs, just as Bruenor had taught him.

Still holding its smashed face and howling in pain, the giant tumbled to the ground behind Wulfgar, where it fell in the way of the last of the group, the only one who had not yet felt the sting of Wulfgar's weapons.

*　*　*　*　*

Outside the cave, Morik winced as he heard the cries and the groans, the howls and the unmistakable sound of boulder against bone.

Curious despite himself, the rogue moved up closer to the entrance, trying to get a look inside, though he feared and honestly believed that his friend was already dead.

"You should be well on your way to Luskan," Morik scolded himself under his breath. "A warm bed for Morik tonight."

*　*　*　*　*

He'd hit them as hard as he could both times, yet he hadn't killed a single one of the trio, probably hadn't even knocked one of them out of the fight for long. Here he was, exposed and running into the main chamber without even knowing if the place had another exit.

But memories of Errtu weren't with the barbarian now. He was temporarily free of that emotional bondage, on the very edge of present desperation, and he loved it.

For once luck was with him. Inside the lair proper Wulfgar found the spoils of the giants' last raid, including the remains of a trio of dwarves, one of whom had carried a small, though solid hammer and another with several hand axes set along a bandolier.

Roaring, the giant rushed in, and Wulfgar let fly one, two, three, with the hand axes, scoring two gouging hits. Still the brute came on, and it was only a single running stride away when a desperate Wulfgar, thinking he was about to get squished into the wall, spun the hammer right into its thigh.

Wulfgar dived desperately, for the staggering giant couldn't begin to halt its momentum. It slammed headlong into the stone wall, dropping more than a bit of dust and pebbles from the cave ceiling. Somehow Wulfgar managed to avoid the crunch, but he had left his new weapons behind and couldn't possibly get to them in time as the giant Wulfgar had smashed with the rock came limping into the chamber.

Wulfgar went for the snapped axe shaft instead. Scooping it up, he dived aside in another roll as the behemoth stomped down with a heavy boot. Wulfgar was already in motion, charging for those vulnerable knees, smashing one repeatedly, then spinning about the trunklike leg, out of the giant's grasp. Turning his weapon point out as he pivoted, he stabbed again at the back of the bloodied leg. The giant lying against the wall kicked out, clipping Wulfgar's wounded shoulder and launching the man away to slam hard against the far wall.

Wulfgar was in his warrior rage now. He came out of the slam with a bellow, charging right back at the limping behemoth too fast for it to recognize the movement. His relentless club went at the knees again, and though the giant slapped at him, Wulfgar took hope in finally hearing the bone crunch apart. Down went the behemoth, clutching its broken knee, the sheer volume of its cries shaking the entire cave. Shaking off the dull ache of that slap, Wulfgar taunted it with laughter.

The one against the wall tried to rise, but Wulfgar was there in an instant, standing on its back, his club battering it about the back of the head. He scored several thunderous hits and had the behemoth flat down and trying to cover. Wulfgar dared hope he might finally finish one off.

Then the huge hand of the other giant tightened about his leg.

* * * * *

Morik could hardly believe his movements, felt as if his own feet were betraying him, as he crept right up to the cave entrance and peered inside.

He saw the first of the giant group, standing bent over at the waist under the overhanging rock, one arm extended against the wall to lend support as it coughed up the last remnants of blood from its mouth.

Before his own good sense could overrule him, Morik was on the move, silently creeping into the gloom of the cave along the wall. He got by the giant with hardly a whisper of sound, his small noises easily covered by the giant's hacking and wheezing, then climbed to a ledge several feet from the ground.

The sounds of battle rang out from the inner chamber, and he could only hope that Wulfgar was doing well, both for his friend's sake and because he realized that if the other giants came out now he would be in a difficult position indeed.

The rogue held his nerve, and waited, poised, dagger in hand, lining up his strike. He considered the attack from the perspective of those backstabs he knew from his experiences fighting men, but he looked at his puny dagger doubtfully.

The giant began to turn around. Morik was out of time. Knowing he had to be perfect, figuring that this was going to hurt more than a little, and wondering why in the Nine Hells he had come in here after foolish Wulfgar, Morik went with his instinct and leaped for the giant's torn throat.

His dagger flashed. The giant howled and leaped up—and slammed its head on the overhanging boulder. Groaning, it tried to straighten, flailing its arms, and Morik flew aside, his breath blasted away. Half-tumbling, half-running, and surely screaming, Morik exited the cave with the gasping, grasping giant right behind.

He felt the giant closing, step by step. At the last instant Morik dived aside and the behemoth stumbled past, one hand clutching its throat, wheezing horribly, its face blue, eyes bulging.

Morik sprinted back the other way, but the giant didn't pursue. The huge creature was down on its knees now, gasping for air.

"Going home to Luskan," Morik mumbled over and over, but he kept moving for the cave entrance as he spoke.

* * * * *

Wulfgar spun and stabbed with all his strength, then drove ahead ferociously, twisting and pulling at the giant's leg. The giant was on one knee, its broken leg held out straight as it struggled to maintain some balance. The other meaty hand came at Wulfgar, but he slipped under it and pulled on furiously, breaking free and leaping to the giant's shoulder.

He scrambled behind the behemoth's head and wrapped his hands back around, lining up the point of his axe shaft with the creature's eye. Wulfgar locked his hands around that splintered pole and pushed hard. The giant's hands grabbed at him to stop his progress, but he growled and pulled on.

The terrified giant tried to wriggle away, pulled with its huge hands with all its strength, bunched muscle that would stop nearly any human cold.

But Wulfgar had the angle and was possessed of a strength beyond that of nearly any human. He saw the other giant climbing back to its feet, but reminded himself to take the fight one at a time. Wulfgar felt the tip of his axe shaft sink into the giant's eye. It went into a frenzy, even climbing back to its feet, but Wulfgar held on. Driving, driving.

The giant ran blindly for the wall and turned around, going in hard, trying to crush the man. Wulfgar growled away the pain and pressed on with all his strength until the spear slipped in deeper to the behemoth's brain.

The other giant came in then. Wulfgar fell away, scrambling across the chamber, using the spasms of the dying giant to cover his retreat. The butt end of Wulfgar's impromptu spear remained visible within the folds of the dying brute's closed eyelid. Wulfgar scarcely had time to notice as he dived headlong across the way to retrieve the hammer and one of the bloody hand axes.

The giant threw its dead companion aside and strode forward, then staggered back with a hand axe embedded deep into its forehead.

Wulfgar continued to press in with a mighty overhead chop that slammed the hammer hard into the behemoth's chest. He hit it again, and a third time, then went down under the flailing fists and struck a brutal blow against the giant's knee. Wulfgar skittered past and ran behind the brute to the wall, leaping upward two full strides, then springing off with yet another wicked, downward smash as the turning giant came around.

The hammer's head cracked through the giant's skull. The behemoth dropped straight down and lay very still on the floor.

Morik entered the chamber at that moment and gaped at the battered Wulfgar. The barbarian's shoulder was soaked with blood, his leg bruised from ankle to thigh, and his knees and hands were skinned raw.

"You see?" Wulfgar said with a triumphant grin. "No trouble at all. Now we have a home."

Morik looked past his friend to the gruesome remains of the half-eaten dwarves and the two dead giants oozing blood throughout the chamber. "Such as it is," he answered dryly.

*   *   *   *   *

They spent the better part of the next three days cleaning out their cave, burying the dwarves, chopping up and disposing of the giants, and retrieving their supplies. They even managed to get the horses and the wagon up to the place along a roundabout route, though they simply let the horses run free after the great effort, figuring that they would never be very useful as a pulling team.

A full pack on his back, Morik took Wulfgar out along the trails. The pair finally came to a spot overlooking a wide pass, the one true trail through this region of the Spine of the World. It was the same trail that Wulfgar and his former friends had used whenever they'd ventured out of Icewind Dale. There was another pass to the west that ran through Hundelstone, but this was the most direct route, though more dangerous by far.

"Many caravans will roll through this place before winter," Morik explained. "They'll be heading north with varied goods and south with scrimshaw knucklehead carvings."

477

More familiar with the routine than Morik would ever understand, Wulfgar merely nodded.

"We should hit them both ways," the rogue suggested. "Secure our provisions from those coming from the south and our future monies from those coming from the north."

Wulfgar sat down on a slab and stared north along the pass, beyond it to Icewind Dale. He was reminded again of the sharp contrast between his past and his present. How ironic it would be if his former friends were the ones to track down the highwaymen.

He pictured Bruenor, roaring as he charged up the rocky slope, agile Drizzt skipping past him, scimitars in hand. Guenhwyvar would already be above them, Wulfgar knew, cutting off any retreat. Morik would likely flee, and Catti-brie would cut him down with a single, blazing arrow.

"You look a thousand miles away. What's on your mind?" Morik inquired. As usual, he was holding an open bottle he'd already begun sampling.

"I'm thinking I need a drink," Wulfgar replied, taking the bottle and lifting it to his lips. Burning all the way down, the huge swallow helped calm him somewhat, but he still couldn't reconcile himself to his present position. Perhaps his friends would come after him, as he, Drizzt and Guenhwyvar, and the others following, had gone after the giant band they suspected to be highwaymen in Icewind Dale.

Wulfgar took another long drink. He didn't like the prospects if they came after him.

Chapter 17

Coercion

"I cannot wait until the spring, I fear," Meralda said coyly to Feringal after dinner one night at Auckney Castle. At Meralda's request the pair was walking the seashore this evening, instead of their customary stroll in the garden.

The young lord stopped in his tracks, eyes wider than Meralda had ever seen them. "The waves," he said, drawing closer to Meralda. "I fear I did not hear you correctly."

"I said that I cannot wait for the spring," Meralda repeated. "For the wedding, I mean."

A grin spread from ear to ear across Feringal's face, and he seemed as if he were about to dance a jig. He took her hand gently, brought it up to his lips, and kissed it. "I would wait until the end of time, if you so commanded," he said solemnly. To her great surprise—and wasn't this man always full of surprises?—Meralda found that she believed him. He had never betrayed her.

As thrilled as Meralda was, however, she had pressing problems. "No, my lord, you'll not be waiting long," she replied, pulling her hand from his and stroking his cheek. "Suren I'm glad that you'd wait for me, but I can no longer wait for the spring for my own desires." She moved in close and kissed him, and felt him melting against her.

Feringal pulled away from her for the first time. "You know we cannot," he said, though it obviously pained him. "I have given my word to Temigast. Propriety, my love. Propriety."

"Then make it proper, and soon," Meralda replied, stroking the man's cheek gently. She thought that Feringal might collapse under her tender touch, so she moved in close again and added breathlessly, "I simply can't wait."

Feringal lost his thin resolve and wrapped her in his arms, burying her in a kiss.

Meralda didn't want this, but she knew what she had to do. She feared too much time had passed already. The young woman started to pull the man down to the sand with her, setting her mind firmly that she would seduce him and be done with it, but there came a call from the castle wall: Priscilla's shrill voice.

"Feri!"

"I detest it when she calls me that!" With great effort, the young lord jumped back from Meralda and cursed his sister under his breath. "Can I never escape her?"

"Feri, is that you?" Priscilla called again.

"Yes, Priscilla," the man replied with barely concealed irritation.

"Do come back to the castle," the woman beckoned. "It grows dark, and Temigast says there are reports of thieves about. He wants you within the walls."

Brokenhearted Feringal looked to Meralda and shook his head. "We must go," he said.

"I can't wait for spring," the woman said determinedly.

"And you shan't," Lord Feringal replied, "but we shall do it properly, in accordance with etiquette. I will move the wedding day forward to the winter solstice."

"Too long," Meralda replied.

"The autumn equinox then."

Meralda considered the timeline. The autumn equinox was six weeks away, and she was already more than a month pregnant. Her expression revealed her dismay.

"I cannot possibly move it up more than that," Lord Feringal explained. "As you know, Priscilla is doing the planning, and she will already howl with anger when she hears that I wish to move it up at all. Temigast desires that we wait until the turn of the year, at least, but I will convince him otherwise."

He was talking more to himself than to Meralda, and so she let him ramble, falling within her own thoughts as the pair made their way back to the castle. She knew that the man's fears of his sister's rage were, if anything, an underestimation. Priscilla would fight their plans for a change of date. Meralda was certain the woman was hoping the whole thing would fall apart.

It *would* fall apart before the wedding if anyone suspected she was carrying another man's child.

"You should know better than to go out without guards in the night," Priscilla scolded as soon as the pair entered the foyer. "There are thieves about."

She glared at Meralda, and the woman knew the truth of Priscilla's ire. Feringal's sister didn't fear thieves on her brother's account. Rather, she was afraid of what might happen between Feringal and Meralda, of what had nearly happened between them on the beach.

"Thieves?" Feringal replied with a chuckle. "There are no thieves in Auckney. We have had no trouble here in many years, not since before I became lord."

"Then we are overdue," Priscilla replied dryly. "Would you have it that the first attack in Auckney in years happen upon the lord and his future wife? Have you no sense of responsibility toward the woman you say you love?"

That set Feringal back on his heels. Priscilla always seemed able to do that with just a few words. She made a mental note to remedy that situation as soon as she had a bit of power behind her.

" 'Twas my own fault," Meralda interrupted, moving between the siblings. "I'm often walking the night, my favorite time."

"You are no longer a common peasant," Priscilla scolded bluntly. "You must understand the responsibility that will accompany your ascent into the family."

"Yes, Lady Priscilla," Meralda replied, dipping a polite curtsey, head bowed.

"If you wish to walk at night, do so in the garden," Priscilla added, her tone a bit less harsh.

Meralda, head still bowed so that Priscilla could not see her face, smiled knowingly. She was beginning to figure out how to get to the woman. Priscilla liked a feisty target, not an agreeable, humble one.

Priscilla turned to leave with a frustrated huff.

"We have news," Lord Feringal said suddenly, stopping the woman short. Meralda's head shot up, her face flush with surprise and more than a little anger. She wanted to choke her intended's words back at that moment; this wasn't the time for the announcement.

"We have decided that we cannot wait until the spring to marry," the oblivious Feringal went on. "The wedding shall be on the day of the autumn equinox."

As expected, Priscilla's face turned bright red. It was obviously taking all of the woman's willpower to keep her from shaking. "Indeed," she said through clenched teeth. "And have you shared your news with Steward Temigast?"

"You're the first," Lord Feringal replied. "Out of courtesy, and since you are the one making the wedding preparations."

481

"Indeed," Priscilla said again with ice in her voice. "Do go tell him, Feri," she bade. "He is in the library. I will see that Meralda is escorted home."

That brought Lord Feringal rushing back to Meralda. "Not so long now, my love," he said. Gently kissing her knuckles, he strode away eagerly to find the steward.

"What did you do to him out there?" Priscilla snapped at Meralda as soon as her brother was gone.

Meralda pursed her lips. "Do?"

"You, uh, worked your charms upon him, didn't you?"

Meralda laughed out loud at Priscilla's efforts to avoid coarse language, a response the imposing Priscilla certainly did not expect. "Perhaps I should have," she replied. "Put a calming on the beast, we call it, but no, I didn't. I love him, you know, but my ma didn't raise a slut. Your brother's to marry me, and so we'll wait. Until the autumn equinox, by his own words."

Priscilla narrowed her eyes threateningly.

"You hate me for it," Meralda accused her bluntly. Priscilla was not prepared for that. Her eyes widened, and she fell back a step. "You hate me for taking your brother and disrupting the life you had set out for yourself, but I'm finding that to be a bit selfish, if I might be saying so. Your brother loves me and I him, and so we're to marry, with or without your blessings."

"How dare you—"

"I dare tell the truth," cut in Meralda, surprised at her own forwardness but knowing she could not back down. "My ma won't live the winter in our freezing house, and I'll not let her die. Not for the sake of what's proper, and not for your own troubles. I know you're doing the planning, and so I'm grateful to you, but do it faster."

"That is what this is all about, then?" Priscilla asked, thinking she had found a weakness here. "Your mother?"

" 'Tis about your brother," Meralda replied, standing straight, shoulders squared. "About Feringal and not about Priscilla, and that's what's got you so bound up."

Priscilla was so overwrought and surprised that she couldn't even force an argument out of her mouth. Flustered, she turned and fled, leaving Meralda alone in the foyer.

The young woman spent a long moment considering her own words, hardly able to believe that she had stood her ground with Priscilla. She considered her next move and thought it prudent to be leaving. She'd spotted Liam with the coach out front when she and Feringal had returned, so she went to him and bade him to take her home.

* * * * *

He watched the coach travel down the road from the castle, as he did every time Meralda returned from another of her meetings with the lord of Auckney.

Jaka Sculi didn't know what to make of his own feelings. He kept thinking back to the moment when Meralda had told him about the child, about his child. He had rebuffed her, allowing his guard to slip so that his honest feelings showed clearly on his face. Now this was his punishment, watching her come back down the road from Castle Auck, from *him*.

What might Jaka have done differently? He surely didn't want the life Meralda had offered. Never that! The thought of marrying the woman, of her growing fat and ugly with a crying baby about, horrified him, but perhaps not as much as the thought of Lord Feringal having her.

That was it, Jaka understood now, though the rationalization did little to change what he felt in his heart. He couldn't bear the notion of Meralda lying down for the man, of Lord Feringal raising Jaka's child as if it were his own. It felt as if the man were stealing from him outright, as every lord in every town did to the peasants in more subtle ways. Yes, they always took from the peasants, from honest folk like Jaka. They lived in comfort, surrounded by luxury, while honest folk like Jaka broke their fingernails in the dirt and ate rotten food. They took the women of their choice, offering nothing of character, only wealth against which peasants like Jaka could not compete. Feringal took his woman, and now he would take Jaka's child.

Trembling with rage, Jaka impulsively ran down to the road waving his arms, bidding the coach to stop.

"Be gone!" Liam Woodgate called down from above, not slowing one bit.

"I must speak with Meralda," Jaka cried. "It is about her ma."

That made Liam slow the coach enough so that he could glance down and get Meralda's thoughts. The young woman poked her head out the coach window to learn the source of the commotion. Spotting an obviously agitated Jaka, she blanched but did not retreat.

"He wants me to stop so he can speak with you. Something about your ma," the coachman explained.

Meralda eyed Jaka warily. "I'll speak with him," she agreed. "You can stop and let me out here, Liam."

"Still a mile to your home," the gnome driver observed, none too happy about the disturbance. "I could be taking you both there," he offered.

Meralda thanked him and waved him away. "A mile I'll walk easy," she answered and was out the door before the coach had even stopped rolling, leaving her alone on the dark road with Jaka.

"You're a fool to be out here," Meralda scolded as soon as Liam had turned the coach around and rambled off. "What are you about?"

"I had no choice," Jaka replied, moving to hug her. She pushed him away.

483

"You know what I'm carrying," the woman went on, "and so will Lord Feringal soon enough. If he puts you together with my child he'll kill us both."

"I'm not afraid of him," Jaka said, pressing toward her. "I know only how I feel, Meralda. I had no choice but to come to you tonight."

"You've made your feelings clear enough," the woman replied coldly.

"What a fool I was," Jaka protested. "You must understand what a shock the news was, but I'm over that. Forgive me, Meralda. I cannot live without your charity."

Meralda closed her eyes, her body swaying as she tried to digest it all. "What're you about, Jaka Sculi?" she asked again quietly. "Where's your heart?"

"With you," he answered softly, coming closer.

"And?" she prompted, opening her eyes to stare hard at him. He didn't seem to understand. "Have you forgotten the little one already then?" she asked.

"No," he blurted, catching on. "I'll love the child, too, of course."

Meralda found that she did not believe him, and her expression told him so.

"Meralda," he said, taking her hands and shaking his head. "I can't bear the thought of Lord Feringal raising my—our child as his own."

Wrong answer. All of Meralda's sensibilities, her eyes still wide open from her previous encounter with this boy, screamed the truth at her. It wasn't about his love for the child, or even his love for her. No, she realized, Jaka didn't have the capacity for such emotions. He was here now, pleading his love, because he couldn't stand the thought of being bested by Lord Feringal.

Meralda took a deep and steadying breath. Here was the man she thought she had loved saying all the things she'd once longed to hear. The two of them would be halfway to Luskan by now if Jaka had taken this course when she'd come to him. Meralda Ganderlay was a wiser woman now, a woman thinking of her own well-being and the welfare of her child. Jaka would never give them a good life. In her heart she knew he'd come to resent her and the child soon enough, when the trap of poverty held them in its inescapable grip. This was a competition, not love. Meralda deserved better.

"Be gone," she said to Jaka. "Far away, and don't you come back."

The man stood as if thunderstruck. "But—"

"There are no answers you can give that I'll believe," the woman went on. "There's no life for us that would keep you happy."

"You're wrong."

"No, I'm not, and you know it, too," Meralda said. "We had a moment, and I'll hold it dear for all of my life. Another moment revealed the truth of it all. You've no room in your life for me or the babe. You never will."

What she really wanted to tell him was to go away and grow up, but he didn't need to hear that from her.

"You expect me to stand around quietly and watch Lord Feringal—"

Clapping her hands to her ears, Meralda cut him off. "Every word you speak takes away from my good memories. You've made your heart plain to me."

"I was a fool," Jaka pleaded.

"And so you still are," Meralda said coldly. She turned and walked away.

Jaka called after her, his cries piercing her as surely as an arrow, but she held her course and didn't look back, reminding herself every step of the truth of this man, this boy. She broke into a run and didn't stop until she reached her home.

A single candle burned in the common room. To her relief, her parents and Tori were all asleep, a merciful bit of news for her because she didn't want to talk to anyone at that time. She had resolved her feelings about Jaka at last, could accept the pain of the loss. She tried hard to remember the night of passion and not the disappointments that had followed, but those disappointments, the revelations about who this boy truly was, were the thing of harsh reality, not the dreamy fantasies of young lovers. She really did want him to just go away.

Meralda knew that she had another more pressing problem. The autumn equinox was too far away, but she understood that she would never convince Lord Feringal, let alone Priscilla and Temigast, to move the wedding up closer than that.

Perhaps she wouldn't have to, she thought as an idea came to her. The fifedom would forgive them if they were married in the fall and it was somehow revealed that they had been making love beforehand. Auckney was filled with "seven month babies."

Lying in her dark room, Meralda nodded her head, knowing what she had to do. She would seduce Feringal again, and very soon. She knew his desires and knew, too, that she could blow them into flame with a simple kiss or brush of her hand.

Meralda's smile dissipated almost immediately. She hated herself for even thinking such a thing. If she did soon seduce Feringal he would think the child his own, the worst of all lies, for Feringal and for the child.

She hated the plan and herself for devising it, but then, in the other chamber, her mother coughed. Meralda knew what she had to do.

Chapter 18

The Heart for It

"Our first customers," Morik announced. He and Wulfgar stood on a high ridge overlooking the pass into Icewind Dale. A pair of wagons rolled down the trail, headed for the break in the mountains, their pace steady but not frantic.

"Travelers or merchants?" Wulfgar asked, unconvinced.

"Merchants, and with wealth aboard," the rogue replied. "Their pace reveals them, and their lack of flanking guardsmen invites our presence."

It seemed foolish to Wulfgar that merchants would make such a dangerous trek as this without a heavy escort of soldiers, but he didn't doubt Morik's words. On his own last journey from the dale beside his former friends, they had come upon a single merchant wagon, riding alone and vulnerable.

"Surprised?" Morik asked, noting his expression.

"Idiots always surprise me," Wulfgar replied.

"They cannot afford the guards," Morik explained. "Few who make the run to Icewind Dale can, and those who can usually take the safer, western pass. These are minor merchants, you see, trading pittances. Mostly they rely on good fortune, either in finding able warriors looking for a ride or an open trail to get them through."

"This seems too easy."

"It is easy!" Morik replied enthusiastically. "You understand, of course, that we are doing this caravan a favor." Wulfgar didn't appear convinced of that.

"Think of it," prompted the rogue. "Had we not killed the giants, these merchants would likely have found boulders raining down on them," Morik explained. "Not only would they be stripped of their wealth, but their skin would be stripped from their bones in a giant's cooking pot." He grinned. "So do not fret, my large friend," he went on. "All we want is their money, fair payment for the work we have done for them."

Strangely, it made a bit of sense to Wulfgar. In that respect, the work to which Morik referred was no different than Wulfgar had been doing for many years with Drizzt and the others, the work of bringing justice to a wild land. The difference was that never before had he asked for payment, as Morik was obviously thinking to do now.

"Our easiest course would be to show them our power without engaging," the rogue explained. "Demand a tithe in payment for our efforts, some supplies and a perhaps a bit of gold, then let them go on their way. With only two wagons, though, and no other guards evident, we might be able to just knock them off completely, a fine haul, if done right, with no witnesses." His smile as he explained that latter course disappeared when he noted Wulfgar's frown.

"A tithe then, no more," Morik compromised. "Rightful payment for our work on the road."

Even that sat badly with the barbarian, but he nodded his head in agreement.

* * * * *

He picked a section of trail littered with rocks where the wagons would have to slow considerably or risk losing a wheel or a horse. A single tree on the left side of the trail provided Wulfgar with the prop he would need to carry out his part of the attack, if it came to that.

Morik waited in clear view along the trail as the pair of wagons came bouncing along.

"Greetings!" he called, moving to the center of the trail, his arms held high. Morik shrank back just a bit, seeing the man on the bench seat beside the driver lifting a rather large crossbow his way. Still, he couldn't back up too much, for he had to get the wagon to stop on the appropriate mark.

"Out o' the road, or I'll shoot ye dead!" the crossbowman yelled.

In response, Morik reached down and lifted a huge head, the head of a slain giant, into the air. "That would be ill-advised," he replied, "both morally and physically."

The wagon bounced to a stop, forcing the one behind it to stop as well.

Morik used his foot, nearly straining his knee in the process, to move a second severed giant head out from behind a rock. "I am happy to inform you that the trail ahead is now clear."

"Then get outta me way," the driver of the first wagon replied, "or he'll shoot ye down, and I'll run ye into ruts."

Morik chuckled and moved aside the pack he had lain on the trail, revealing the third giant head. Despite their bravado, he saw that those witnessing the spectacle of the heads were more than a little impressed—and afraid. Any man who could defeat three giants was not one to take lightly.

"My friends and I have worked hard all the week to clear the trail," Morik explained.

"Friends?"

"You think I did this alone?" Morik said with a laugh. "You flatter me. No, I had the help of many friends." Morik cast his gaze about the rocky outcroppings of the pass as if acknowledging his countless "friends." "You must forgive them, for they are shy."

"Ride on!" came a cry from inside the wagon, and the two men on the bench seat looked at each other.

"Yer friends hide like thieves," the driver yelled at Morik. "Clear the way!"

"Thieves?" Morik echoed incredulously. "You would be dead already, squashed flat under a giant's boulder, were it not for us."

The wagon door creaked open and an older man leaned out, standing with one foot inside and the other on the running board. "You're demanding payment for your actions," he remarked, obviously knowing this routine all too well (as did most merchants of the northern stretches of Faerûn).

"Demand is such a nasty word," Morik replied.

"Nasty as your game, little thief," the merchant replied.

Morik narrowed his eyes threateningly and glanced pointedly down at the three giant heads.

"Very well, then," the merchant conceded. "What is the price of your heroism?"

"We need supplies that we might maintain our vigil and keep the pass safe," Morik explained reasonably. "And a bit of gold, perhaps, as a reward for our efforts." It was the merchant's turn to scowl. "To pay the widows of those who did not survive our raid on the giant clan," Morik improvised.

"I'd hardly call three a clan," the merchant replied dryly, "but I'll not diminish your efforts. I offer you and your hiding friends a fine meal, and if you agree to accompany us to Luskan as guards, I will pay each of you a gold piece a day," the merchant added, proud of his largesse and obviously pleased with himself for having turned the situation to his advantage.

489

Morik's eyes narrowed at the weak offer. "We have no desire to return to Luskan at this time."

"Then take your meal and be happy with that," came the curt response.

"Idiot," Morik remarked under his breath. Aloud he countered the merchant's offer. "We will accept no less than fifty gold pieces and enough food for three fine meals for seven men."

The merchant laughed. "You will accept our willingness to let you walk away with your life," he said. He snapped his fingers, and a pair of men leaped from the second wagon, swords drawn. The driver of that wagon drew his as well.

"Now be gone!" he finished, and he disappeared back into the coach. "Run him down," he cried to his driver.

"Idiots!" Morik screamed, the cue for Wulfgar.

The driver hesitated, and that cost him. Holding the end of a strong rope, Wulfgar leaped from his concealment along the lefthand rock wall and swooped in a pendulum arc with a bloodcurdling howl. The crossbow-man spun and fired but missed badly. Wulfgar barreled in at full speed, letting go of the rope and swinging his mighty arms out wide to sweep both crossbowman and driver from the bench, landing atop them in a pile on the far side. An elbow to the face laid the driver low. Reversing his swing, Wulfgar slammed the crossbowman on the jaw, surely breaking it as blood gushed forth.

The three swordsmen from the trailing wagon came on, two to the left of the first wagon, the third going to the right. Morik went right, a long and slender sword in one hand, a dagger in the other, intercepting the man before he could get to Wulfgar.

The man came at the rogue in a straightforward manner. Morik put his sword out beside the thrusting blade but rolled it about, disengaging. He stepped ahead, looping his dagger over the man's sword and pulling it harmlessly aside while he countered with a thrust of his own sword, heading for the man's throat. He had him dead, or would have, except that Morik's arm was stopped as surely as if he were trying to poke his sword through solid stone.

"What are you doing?" he demanded of Wulfgar as the barbarian stepped up and slugged the guard, nearly losing his ear to the thrashing sword and dagger. The man got his free hand up to block, but Wulfgar's heavy punch went right through the defense, planting his fist and the man's own forearm into his face and launching him away. But it was a short-lived victory.

Though staggered by Wulfgar's elbow, the driver was up again with blade in hand. Worse still, the other two swordsmen had found strong positions, one atop the bench, the other in front of the wagon. If that weren't bad enough, the merchant burst from the door, a wand in hand.

"Now *we* are the idiots!" Morik yelled to Wulfgar, cursing and spinning out from the attack of the swordsman on the bench. From the man's one thrust-and-cut routine, Morik could tell that this one was no novice to battle.

Wulfgar went for the merchant. Suddenly he was flying backward, his hair dancing on end, his heart palpitating wildly.

"So that's what the wand does," Morik remarked after the flash. "I hate wizards."

He went at the swordsman on the ground, who defeated his initial attempt at a quick kill with a circular parry that almost had the rogue overbalancing. "Do hurry back!" Morik called to Wulfgar, then he ducked and thrust his sword up frantically as the swordsman from the bench leaped atop the horse team and stabbed at his head.

The driver came at Wulfgar, as did the man he had just slugged, and the barbarian worked fast to get the hammer off his back. He started to meet the driver's charge but stopped fast and reversed his grip and direction, spinning the hammer the merchant's way instead, having no desire to absorb another lightning bolt.

The hammer hit the mark perfectly, not on the merchant, but against the coach door, slamming it on the man's extended arm just as he was about to loose yet another blast. Fire he did, though, a sizzling bolt that just missed the other man rushing Wulfgar.

"All charge!" Morik called, looking back to the rocky cliff on the left. The bluff turned his opponents' heads for just an instant. When they turned back, they found the rogue in full flight, and Morik was a fast runner indeed when his life was on the line.

The driver came in hesitantly, respectful of Wulfgar's strength. The other man, though, charged right in, until the barbarian turned toward him with a leap and a great bellow. Wulfgar reversed direction almost immediately, going back for the driver, catching the man by surprise with his uncanny agility. He accepted a stinging cut along the arm in exchange for grabbing the man's weapon hand. Pulling him close with a great tug, Wulfgar bent low, clamped his free hand on the man's belt, and hoisted the flailing fool high over his head. A turn and a throw sent the driver hard into his charging companion.

Wulfgar paused, to note Morik skittering by in full flight. A reasonable choice, given the course of the battle, but the barbarian's blood was up, and he turned back to the wagons and the two swordsmen, just in time to get hammered by another lightning stroke. With his long legs, Wulfgar passed Morik within fifty yards up the rocky climb.

Another bolt slammed in near to the pair, splintering rocks. A crossbow quarrel followed soon after, accompanied by taunts and threats, but there came no pursuit, and soon the pair were running up high along the cliffs. When they dared to stop and catch their breath, Wulfgar looked down at the two scars on his tunic, shaking his head.

491

"We would have won if you had gone straight for the merchant after your sweep of the driver and crossbowman as planned," Morik scolded.

"And you would have cut out that man's throat," charged Wulfgar.

Morik scowled. "What of it? If you've not the heart for this life, then why are we out here?"

"Because you chose to deal with murderers in Luskan," Wulfgar reminded him, and they shared icy stares. Morik put his hand on his blade, thinking that the big man might attack him.

Wulfgar thought about doing just that.

They walked back to the cave separately. Morik beat him there and started in. Wulfgar changed his mind and stayed outside, moving to a small stream nearby where he could better tend his wounds. He found that his chest wasn't badly scarred, just the hair burned away from what was a minor lightning strike. However, his shoulder wound had reopened rather seriously. Only then, with his heavy tunic off, did the barbarian understand how much blood he had lost.

Morik found him out there several hours later, passed out on a flat rock. He roused the barbarian with a nudge. "We did not fare well," the rogue remarked, holding up a pair of bottles, "but we are alive, and that is cause for celebration."

"We need cause?" Wulfgar replied, not smiling, and he turned away.

"First attacks are always disastrous," Morik explained reasonably. "We must become accustomed to each other's fighting style, is all."

Wulfgar considered the words in light of his own experience, in light of the first true battle he and Drizzt had seen together. True, at one point, he had almost clobbered the drow with a low throw of Aegis-fang, but from the start there had been a symbiosis with Drizzt, a joining of heart that had brought them to a joining of battle routines. Could he say the same with Morik? Would he ever be able to?

Wulfgar looked back at the rogue, who was smiling and holding out the bottles of potent liquor. Yes, he would come to terms with Morik. They would become of like heart and soul. Perhaps that was what bothered Wulfgar most of all.

"The past no longer exists, and the future does not yet exist," Morik reasoned. "So live in the present and enjoy it, my friend. Enjoy every moment."

Wulfgar considered the words, a common mantra for many of those living day-to-day on the streets. He took the bottle.

Chapter 19

The Chance

"We've not much time! What am I to wear?" Biaste Ganderlay wailed when Meralda told her the wedding had been moved up to the autumn equinox.

"If we're to wear anything more than we have, Lord Feringal will be bringing it by," Dohni Ganderlay said, patting the woman's shoulder. He gave Meralda a look of pride, and mostly of appreciation, and she knew that he understood the sacrifice she was making here.

How would that expression change, she wondered, if her father learned of the baby in her belly?

She managed a weak smile in reply despite her thoughts and went into her room to dress for the day. Liam Woodgate had arrived earlier to inform Meralda that Lord Feringal had arranged for her to meet late that same day with the seamstress who lived on the far western edge of Auckney, some two hours' ride.

"No borrowed gowns for the great day." Liam had proclaimed. "If you don't mind my saying so, Biaste, your daughter will truly be the most beautiful bride Auckney's ever known."

How Biaste's face had glowed and her eyes sparkled! Strangely, that also pained Meralda, for though she knew that she was doing right by her family, she could not forgive herself for her stupidity with Jaka. Now she had to seduce Lord Feringal, and soon, perhaps that very night. With the wedding moved up, she could only hope that others, mostly Priscilla and Temigast, would forgive her for conceiving a child before the official ceremony. Worst of all, Meralda would have to take the truth of the child with her to her grave.

What a wretched creature she believed herself to be at that moment. Madam Prinkle, a seamstress renowned throughout the lands, would no doubt make her a most beautiful gown with gems and rich, colorful fabrics, but she doubted she would be wearing the glowing face to go with it.

Meralda got cleaned up and dressed, ate a small meal, and was all smiles when Liam Woodgate returned for her, guiding her into the coach. She sat with her elbow propped on the sill, staring at the countryside rolling by. Men and gnomes worked in the high fields, but she neither looked for nor spotted Jaka Sculi among them. The houses grew sparse, until only the occasional cottage dotted the rocky landscape. The carriage went through a small wood, where Liam stopped briefly to rest and water the horses.

Soon they were off again, leaving the small woods and traveling into rocky terrain again. On Meralda's right was the sea. Sheer rock cliffs rose on the north side of the path, some reaching down so close to the water's edge that Meralda wondered how Liam would get the coach through.

She wondered, too, how any woman could live out here alone. Meralda resolved to ask Liam about it later. Now she spied an outpost, a stone keep flying Lord Feringal's flag. Only then did she begin to appreciate the power of the lord of Auckney. The slow-moving coach had only traveled about ten miles, but it seemed as if they had gone halfway around the world. For some reason she couldn't understand, the sight of Feringal's banner in this remote region made Meralda feel better, as if powerful Lord Feringal Auck would protect her.

Her smile was short lived as she remembered he would only protect her if she lied.

The woman sank back into her seat, sighed, and felt her still-flat belly, as if expecting the baby to kick right then and there.

* * * * *

"The flag is flying, so there are soldiers within," Wulfgar reasoned.

"Within they shall stay," Morik answered. "The soldiers rarely leave the shelter of their stones, even when summoned. Their lookout, if they have one, is more concerned with those attacking the keep and not with anything down on the road. Besides, there can't be more than a dozen of them this far out from any real supply towns. I doubt there are even half that number."

494

Wulfgar thought to remind Morik that far fewer men had routed them just a couple of days before, but he kept quiet.

After the disaster in the pass, Morik had suggested they go out from the region, in case the merchant alerted Luskan guards, true to his belief that a good highwayman never stays long in one place, particularly after a failed attack. Initially, Morik wanted to go north into Icewind Dale, but Wulfgar had flatly refused.

"West, then," the rogue had offered. "There's a small fiefdom squeezed between the mountains and the sea southwest of the Hundelstone pass. Few go there, for it's not on most maps, but the merchants of the northern roads know of it, and sometimes they travel there on their way to and from Ten-Towns. Perhaps we will even meet up with our friend and his lightning wand again."

The possibility didn't thrill Wulfgar, but his refusal to go back into Icewind Dale had really left them only two options. They'd be deeper into the unaccommodating Spine of the World if they went east to the realm of goblins and giants and other nasty, unprofitable monsters. That left south and west, and given their relationship with the authorities of Luskan in the south, west seemed a logical choice.

It appeared as if that choice would prove to be a good one, for the pair watched as a lone wagon, an ornate carriage such as a nobleman might ride, rambled down the road.

"It could be a wizard," Wulfgar reasoned, painfully recalling the lightning bolts he'd suffered.

"I know of no wizards of any repute in this region," Morik replied.

"You haven't been in this region for years," Wulfgar reminded him. "Who would dare travel in such an elaborate carriage alone?" he wondered aloud.

"Why not?" Morik countered. "This area south of the mountains sees little trouble, and there are outposts along the way, after all," he added, waving his hand at the distant stone keep. "The people here are not trapped in their homes by threats of goblins."

Wulfgar nodded, but it seemed too easy. He figured that the coach driver must be a veteran fighter, at least. It was likely there would be others inside, and perhaps they held nasty wands or other powerful magical items. One look at Morik, though, told the barbarian that he'd not dissuade his friend. Morik was still smarting from the disaster in the pass. He needed a successful hit.

The road below made a great bend around a mountain spur. Morik and Wulfgar took a more direct route, coming back to the road far ahead of the coach, out of sight of the stone outpost. Wulfgar immediately began laying out his rope, looking for some place he might tie it off. He found one slender tree, but it didn't look promising.

"Just jump in," Morik reasoned, pointing to an overhang. The rogue rushed down to the road, taking out a whip as he went, for the coach appeared, rambling around the southern bend.

"Clear the way!" came Liam Woodgate's call a moment later.

"I must speak with you, good sir!" Morik cried, holding his ground in the middle of the narrow trail. The gnome slowed the coach and brought it to a halt a safe distance from the rogue—and too far, Morik noted, for Wulfgar to make the leap.

"By order of Lord Feringal of Auckney, clear the way," Liam stated.

"I am in need of assistance, sir," Morik explained, watching out of the corner of his eye as Wulfgar scrambled into position. Morik took a step ahead then, but Liam warned him back.

"Keep your distance, friend," the gnome said. "I've an errand for my lord, and don't doubt that I'll run you down if you don't move aside."

Morik chuckled. "I think not," he said.

Something in Morik's tone, or perhaps just a movement along the high rocks caught the corner of Liam's eye. Suddenly the gnome understood the imminent danger and spurred his team forward.

Wulfgar leaped out at that moment, but he hit the side of the carriage behind the driver, his momentum and the angle of the rocky trail putting the thing up on two wheels. Inside the coach a woman screamed.

Purely on instinct, Morik brought forth his whip and gave a great *crack* right in front of the horses. The beasts cut left against the lean, and before the driver could control them, before Wulfgar could brace himself, before the passenger inside could even cry out again, the coach fell over on its side, throwing both the driver and Wulfgar.

Dazed, Wulfgar forced himself to his feet, expecting to be battling the driver or someone else climbing from the coach, but the driver was down among some rocks, groaning, and no sounds came from within the coach. Morik rushed to calm the horses, then leaped atop the coach, scrambling to the door and pulling it open. Another scream came from within.

Wulfgar went to the driver and gently lifted the gnome's head. He set it back down, secure that this one was out of the fight but hoping he wasn't mortally wounded.

"You must see this," Morik called to Wulfgar. He reached into the coach, offering his hand to a beautiful young woman, who promptly backed away. "Come out, or I promise I will join you in there," Morik warned, but still the frightened woman curled away from him.

"Now that is the way true highwaymen score their pleasures," Morik announced to Wulfgar as the big man walked over to join him. "And speaking of pleasures. . . ." he added, then dropped into the coach.

The woman screamed and flailed at him, but she was no match for the skilled rogue. Soon he had her pinned against the coach's ceiling, which was now a wall, her arms held in place, his knee blocking her from kicking his groin, his lips close to hers. "A kiss for the winner?"

Morik rose suddenly, caught by the collar and hoisted easily out of the coach by a fuming Wulfgar. "You cross a line," Wulfgar replied, dropping the rogue on the ground.

"She is fairly caught," Morik argued, not understanding his friend's problem. "We have our way, and we let her go. What's the harm?"

Wulfgar glared at him. "Go tend the driver's wounds," he said. "Then find what treasures you may about the wagon."

"The girl—"

"—does not count as a treasure," Wulfgar growled at him.

Morik threw his hands up in defeat and moved to check on the fallen gnome.

Wulfgar reached into the coach, much as Morik had done, offering his huge paw to the frightened young woman. "Come out," he bade her. "I promise you won't be harmed."

Stunned and sore, the woman dodged his hand.

"We can't turn your wagon upright with you in it," Wulfgar explained reasonably. "Don't you wish to be on your way?"

"I want you to be on your way," the woman snarled.

"And leave you here alone?"

"Better alone than with thieves," Meralda shot back.

"It would be better for your driver if you got out. He'll die if we leave him lying on the rocks," Wulfgar was trying very hard to comfort the woman, or at least frighten her into action. "Come. I'll not hurt you. Rob you, yes, but not hurt you."

She timidly lifted her hand. Wulfgar took hold and easily hoisted her out of the coach. Setting her down, he stared at her for a long moment. Despite a newly forming bruise on the side of her face she was truly a beautiful young woman. He could understand Morik's desire, but he had no intention of forcing himself on any woman, no matter how beautiful, and he certainly wasn't going to let Morik do so.

The two thieves spent a few moments going through the coach, finding, to Morik's delight, a purse of gold. Wulfgar searched about for a log to use as a lever.

"You don't intend to upright the carriage, do you?" Morik asked incredulously.

"Yes, I do," Wulfgar replied.

"You can't do that," the rogue argued. "She'll drive right up to the stone keep and have a host of soldiers pursuing us within the hour."

Wulfgar wasn't listening. He found some large rocks and placed them near the roof of the fallen carriage. With a great tug, he brought the thing off the ground. Seeing no help forthcoming from Morik, he braced himself and managed to free one hand to slide a rock into place under the rim.

The horses snorted and tugged, and Wulfgar almost lost the whole thing right there. "At least go and calm them," he instructed Morik. The rogue made no move. Wulfgar looked to the woman, who ran to the team and steadied them.

"I can't do this alone," Wulfgar called again to Morik, his tone growing more angry.

Blowing out a great, long-suffering sigh, the rogue ambled over. Studying the situation briefly, he trotted off to where Wulfgar had left the rope, which he looped about the tree then brought one end back to tie off the upper rim of the coach. Morik passed by the woman, who jumped back from him, but he scarcely noticed.

Next, Morik took the horses by their bridle and pulled them around, dragging the coach carefully and slowly so that its wheels were equidistant from the tree. "You lift, and I will set the rope to hold it," he instructed Wulfgar. "Then brace yourself and lift it higher, and soon we will have it upright."

Morik was a clever one, Wulfgar had to admit. As soon as the rogue was back in place at the rope and the woman had a hold of the team again, Wulfgar bent low and gave a great heave, and up the carriage went.

Morik quickly took up the slack, tightening the rope about the tree, allowing Wulfgar to reset his position. A moment later, the barbarian gave another heave, and again Morik held the coach in place at its highest point. The third pull by Wulfgar brought it over bouncing onto its four wheels.

The horses nickered nervously and stamped the ground, tossing their heads in protest so forcefully that the woman couldn't hold on. Wulfgar was beside her instantly, though, grabbing the bridles and pulling hard, steadying the beasts. Then, using the same rope, he tied them off to the tree and went to the fallen driver.

"What's his name?" he asked of the woman. Seeing her hesitation he said, "We can't do anything worse to you than we have already, just by knowing your name. I feel strange helping him but not knowing what to call him."

The woman's expression lightened as she saw the sense of his remark. "His name's Liam." Apparently having found some courage, she came over and crouched next to her driver, concern replacing fear on her face. "Is he going to be all right?"

"Don't know yet."

Poor Liam seemed far from consciousness, but he was alive, and upon closer inspection his injuries didn't appear too serious. Wulfgar lifted him gently and brought him to the coach, laying him on the bench seat inside. The barbarian went back to the woman, taking her arm and pulling her along behind him.

"You said you wouldn't hurt me," she protested and tried to fight back. She would have had an easier time holding back the two horses.

Morik's smile grew wide when Wulfgar dragged her by. "A change of heart?" the rogue asked.

"She's coming with us for a while," Wulfgar explained.

"No!" the young woman protested. Balling up her fist, she leaped up and smacked Wulfgar hard across the back of his head.

He stopped and turned to her, his expression amused and a little impressed at her spunk. "Yes," he answered, pinning her arm as she tried to hit him again. "You'll come with us for just a mile," he explained. "Then I'll let you loose to return to the coach and the driver, and you may go wherever you please."

"You won't hurt me?"

"Not I," Wulfgar answered. He glowered at Morik. "Nor him."

Realizing she had little choice in the matter, the young woman went along without further argument. True to his word, Wulfgar released her a mile or so from the coach. Then he and Morik and their purse of gold melted into the mountains.

* * * * *

Meralda ran the whole way back to poor Liam. Her side was aching by the time she found the old gnome. He was awake but hardly able to climb out of the coach, let alone drive it.

"Stay inside," the woman bade him. "I'll turn the team around and get us back to Castle Auck."

Liam protested, but Meralda just shut the door and went to work. Soon she had them moving back west along the road, a bumpy and jostling ride, for she was not experienced in handling horses and the road was not an easy one. Along the way, the miles and the hours rolling out behind her, an idea came to the woman, a seemingly simple solution to all her troubles.

It was long after sunset when they pulled back into Auckney proper at the gates of Castle Auck. Lord Feringal and Priscilla came out to greet them, and their jaws dropped when they saw the bedraggled woman and the battered coachman within.

"Thieves on the road," Meralda explained. Priscilla climbed to her side, uncharacteristically concerned. In a voice barely above a whisper, Meralda added, "He hurt me." With that, she broke into sobs in Priscilla's arms.

* * * * *

The wind moaned about him, a sad voice that sang to Wulfgar about what had been and what could never be again, a lost time, a lost innocence, and friends he sorely missed yet could not seek out.

Once more he sat on the high bluff at the northern end of the pass through the Spine of the World, overlooking Icewind Dale, staring out to the northeast. He saw a sparkle out there. It might have been a trick of the light, or maybe it was the slanted rays of late afternoon sunlight reflecting off of Maer Dualdon, the largest of the three lakes of the Ten-Towns region. Also, he thought he saw Kelvin's Cairn, the lone mountain north of the range.

499

It was probably just his imagination, he told himself again or a trick of the light, for the mountain was a long way from him. To Wulfgar, it seemed like a million miles.

"They have camped outside the southern end of the pass," Morik announced, moving to join the big man. "There are not so many. It should be a clean take."

Wulfgar nodded. After the success along the shore road to the west, the pair had returned to the south, the region between Luskan and the pass, and had even bought some goods from one passing merchant with their ill-found gold. Then they had come back to the pass and had hit another caravan. This time it went smoothly, with the merchant handing over a tithe and no blood spilled. Morik had spotted their third group of victims, a caravan of three wagons heading north out of Luskan, bound for Icewind Dale.

"Always you are looking north," the rogue remarked, sitting next to Wulfgar, "and yet you will not venture there. Have you enemies in Ten-Towns?"

"I have friends who would stop us if they knew what we were about," Wulfgar explained.

"Who would *try* to stop us?" cocky Morik replied.

Wulfgar looked him right in the eye. "They *would* stop us," he insisted, his grave expression offering no room for argument. He let that look linger on Morik for a moment, then turned back to the dale, the wistfulness returning as well to his sky-blue eyes.

"What life did you leave behind there?" Morik asked.

Wulfgar turned back, surprised. He and Morik didn't often talk about their respective pasts, at least not unless they were drinking.

"Will you tell me?" Morik pressed. "I see so much in your face. Pain, regret, and what else?"

Wulfgar chuckled at that observation. "What did I leave behind?" he echoed. After a moment's pause, he answered, "Everything."

"That sounds foolish."

"I could be a king," Wulfgar went on, staring out at the dale again as if speaking to himself. Perhaps he was. "Chieftain of the combined tribes of Icewind Dale, with a strong voice on the council of Ten-Towns. My father—" He looked at Morik and laughed. "You would not like my father, Morik. Or at least, he would not like you."

"A proud barbarian?"

"A surly dwarf," Wulfgar countered. "He's my adoptive father," he clarified as Morik sputtered over that one. "The Eighth King of Mithral Hall and leader of a clan of dwarves mining in the valley before Kelvin's Cairn in Icewind Dale."

"Your father is a dwarven king?" Wulfgar nodded. "And you are out on the road beside me, sleeping on the ground?" Again the nod. "Truly you are a bigger fool than I had believed."

Wulfgar just stared out at the tundra, hearing the sad song of the wind. He couldn't disagree with Morik's assessment, but neither did he have the power to change things. He heard Morik reaching for his pack, then heard the familiar clink of bottles.

Part 4

Birth

We think we understand those around us. The people we have come to know reveal patterns of behavior, and as our expectations of that behavior are fulfilled time and again we begin to believe that we know the person's heart and soul.

I consider that to be an arrogant perception, for one cannot truly understand the heart and soul of another, one cannot truly appreciate the perceptions another might hold toward similar or recounted experiences. We all search for truth, particularly within our own sphere of existence, the home we have carved and those friends with whom we choose to share it. But truth, I fear, is not always evident where individuals, so complex and changing, are concerned.

If ever I believe that the foundations of my world are rooted in stone, I think of Jarlaxle and I am humbled. I have always recognized that there is more to the mercenary than a simple quest for personal gain—he let me and Catti-brie walk away from Menzoberranzan, after all, and at a time when our heads would have brought him a fine price, indeed. When Catti-brie was his prisoner and completely under his power, he did not take advantage of her, though he has admitted, through actions if not words, that he thinks her quite attractive. So always have I seen a level of character beneath the cold mercenary clothing, but despite that knowledge my last encounter with Jarlaxle has shown me that he is far more complex, and certainly more compassionate, than ever I could have guessed. Beyond that, he called himself a friend of Zaknafein, and though I initially recoiled at such a notion, now I consider it to be not only believable, but likely.

Do I now understand the truth of Jarlaxle? And is it the same truth that those around him, within Bregan D'aerthe, perceive? Certainly not, and though I believe my current assessment to be correct, I'll not be as arrogant as to claim certainty, nor do I even begin to believe that I know more of him than my surface reasoning.

What about Wulfgar, then? Which Wulfgar is the true Wulfgar? Is he the proud and honorable man Bruenor raised, the man who fought beside me against Biggrin and in so many subsequent battles? The man who saved the barbarian tribes from certain extermination and the folk of Ten-Towns from future disasters by uniting the groups diplomatically? The man who ran across Faerûn for the sake of his imprisoned friend? The man who helped Bruenor reclaim his lost kingdom?

Or is Wulfgar the man who harmed Catti-brie, the haunted man who seems destined, in the end, to fail utterly?

He is both, I believe, a compilation of his experiences, feelings, and perceptions, as are we all. It is the second of that composite trio, feelings, brought on by experiences beyond his ability to cope, that control Wulfgar now. The raw emotion of those feelings alter his perceptions to the negative. Given that reality, who is Wulfgar now, and more importantly, if he survives this troubled time, who will he become?

How I long to know. How I wish that I could walk beside him on this perilous journey, could speak with him and influence him, perhaps. That I could remind him of who he was, or at least, who we perceived him to be.

But I cannot, for it is the heart and soul of Wulfgar, ultimately, and not his particular daily actions, that will surface in the end. And I, and anyone else, could no more influence that heart and soul as I could influence the sun itself.

Curiously, it is in the daily rising of that celestial body that I take my comfort now when thinking about Wulfgar. Why watch the dawn? Why then, why that particular time, instead of any other hour of daylight?

Because at dawn the sun is more brilliant by far. Because at dawn, we see the resurgence after the darkness. There is my hope, for as with the sun, so it can be true of people. Those who fall can climb back up, then brighter will they shine in the eyes of those around them.

I watch the dawn and think of the man I thought I knew, and pray that my perceptions were correct.

— Drizzt Do'Urden

Chapter 20

The Last Great Act
Of Selfishness

He kicked at the ground, splashing mud, then jammed his toe hard against an unyielding buried rock that showed only one-hundredth of its actual size. Jaka didn't even feel the pain, for the tear in his heart—no, not in his heart, but in his pride—was worse by far. A thousand times worse.

The wedding would take place at the turn of the season, the end of this very week. Lord Feringal would have Meralda, would have Jaka's own child.

"What justice, this?" he cried. Reaching down to pick up the rock he learned the truth of its buried size. Jaka grabbed another and came back up throwing, narrowly missing a pair of older farmers leaning on their hoes.

The pair, including the old long-nosed dwarf, came storming over, spitting curses, but Jaka was too distracted by his own problems, not understanding that he had just made another problem, and didn't even notice them.

Until, that is, he spun around to find them standing right behind him. The surly dwarf leaped up and launched a balled fist right into Jaka's face, laying him low.

"Damn stupid boy," the dwarf grumbled, then turned to walk away.

507

Humiliated and hardly thinking, Jaka kicked at his ankles, tripping him up.

In an instant, the slender young man was hauled to his feet by the other farmer. "Are you looking to die then?" the man asked, giving him a good shake.

"Perhaps I am," Jaka came back with a great, dramatic sigh. "Yes, all joy has flown from this coil."

"Boy's daft," the farmer holding Jaka said to his companion. The dwarf was coming back over, fists clenched, jaw set firm under his thick beard. As he finished, the man whipped Jaka around and shoved him backward toward the other farmer. The dwarf didn't catch Jaka but instead shoved him back the other way, high up on the back so that the young man went face down in the dirt. The dwarf stepped on the small of Jaka's back, pressing down with his hard-soled boots.

"You watch where you're throwing stones," he said, grinding down suddenly and for just an instant, blowing the breath out of Jaka.

"The boy's daft," the other farmer said as he and his companion walked away.

Jaka lay on the ground and cried.

* * * * *

"All that good food at the castle," remarked Madam Prinkle, an old, gray woman with a smiling face. The woman's skin, hanging in wrinkled folds, seemed too loose for her bones. She grabbed Meralda's waist and gave a pinch. "If you change your size every week, how's my dress ever to fit you? Why, girl, you're three fingers bigger."

Meralda blushed and looked away, not wanting to meet the stare of Priscilla, who was standing off to the side, watching and listening intently.

"Truly I've been hungry lately," Meralda replied. "Been eating everything I can get into my mouth. A bit on the jitters, I am." She looked anxiously at Priscilla, who had been working hard with her to help her lose her peasant accent.

Priscilla nodded, but hardly seemed convinced.

"Well, you best find a different way for calming," Madam Prinkle replied, "or you'll split the dress apart walking to Lord Feringal's side." She laughed riotously then, one big, bobbing ball of too-loose skin. Meralda and Priscilla both laughed self-consciously as well, though neither seemed the least bit amused.

"Can you alter it correctly?" Priscilla asked.

"Oh, not to fear," replied Madam Prinkle. "I'll have the girl all beautiful for her day." She began to gather up her thread and sewing tools. Priscilla moved to help her while Meralda quickly removed the dress, gathered up her own things, and rushed out of the room.

508

Away from the other two, the woman put her hand on her undeniably larger belly. It was over two and a half months now since her encounter with Jaka in the starlit field, and though she doubted that the baby was large enough to be pushing her belly out so, she certainly had been eating volumes of late. Perhaps it was nerves, perhaps it was because she was nourishing two, but whatever the cause, she would have to be careful for the rest of the week so as not to draw more attention to herself.

"She will have the dress back to us on the morrow," Priscilla said behind her, and the young woman nearly jumped out of her boots. "Is something wrong, Meralda?" the woman asked, moving beside her and dropping a hand on her shoulder.

"Would you not be scared if you were marrying a lord?"

Priscilla arched a finely plucked brow. "I would not be frightened, because I would not be in such a situation," she replied.

"But if ye—you, were?" Meralda pressed. "If you were born a peasant, and the lord—"

"Preposterous," the woman interrupted. "If I had been born a peasant, I would not be who I am, and so your whole question makes little sense."

Meralda stared at her, obviously confused.

"I am not a peasant because I've not the soul nor blood of a peasant," Priscilla explained. "You people think it an accident that you were born of your family, and we of nobility born of ours, but that is not the case, my dear. Station comes from within, not without."

"So you're better, then?" Meralda asked bluntly.

Priscilla smiled. "Not better, dear," she answered condescendingly. "Different. We each have our place."

"And mine's not with your brother," the younger woman posited.

"I do not approve of mixing blood," Priscilla stated, and the two stared at each other for a long and uncomfortable while.

Then you should marry him yourself, Meralda thought, but bit back.

"However, I shall honor my brother's choice," Priscilla went on in that same denigrating tone. "It is his own life to ruin as he pleases. I will do what I may do to bring you as close to his level as possible. I do like you, my dear," she added, reaching out to pat Meralda's shoulder.

You'd let me clean your commode then, Meralda silently fumed. She wanted to speak back against Priscilla's reasoning, truly she did, but she wasn't feeling particularly brave at that moment. No, given the child, Jaka's child, growing within her womb, she was vulnerable now, and feeling no match for the likes of vicious Priscilla Auck.

* * * * *

It was late in the morning when Meralda awoke. She could tell from the height of the sun beaming through her window. Worried, she scrambled out of bed. Why hadn't her father awakened her earlier for chores? Where was her mother?

She pushed through the curtain into the common room and calmed immediately, for there sat her family, gathered about the table. Her mother's chair was pulled back, and the woman sat facing the ceiling. A curious man, dressed in what seemed to be religious garments, chanted softly and patted her forehead with sweet-smelling oil.

"Da?" she started to ask, but the man held his hand up to quiet her, motioning her to move near him.

"Watcher Beribold," he explained. "From the Temple of Helm in Luskan. Lord Feringal sent him to get your ma up and strong for the wedding."

Meralda's mouth dropped open. "You can heal her then?"

"A difficult disease," Watcher Beribold replied. "Your mother is strong to have fought on with such resilience." Meralda started to press him, but he answered her with a reassuring smile. "Your mother will be on the mend and free of the wilting before I and High Watcher Risten depart Auckney," he promised.

Tori squealed, and Meralda's heart leaped with joy. She felt her father's strong arm go around her waist, pulling her in close. She could hardly believe the good news. She had known that Lord Feringal would heal her mother, but never had she imagined that the man would see to it before the wedding. Her mother's illness was like a huge sword Feringal had hanging over her head, and yet he was removing it.

She considered the faith Lord Feringal was showing in her to send a healer unbidden to her family door. Jaka would never have relinquished such an obvious advantage. Not for her, not for anyone. Yet here was Feringal—and the man was no fool—holding enough faith in Meralda to take the sword away.

The realization brought a smile to Meralda's face. For so long, she had considered the courtship with Feringal to be a sacrifice for her family, but now, suddenly, she was recognizing the truth of it all. He was a good man, a handsome man, a man of means who loved her honestly. The only reason she'd been unable to return his feeling was because of her unhealthy infatuation with a selfish boy. Strange, but she, too, had been cured of her affliction by the arrival of Feringal's healer.

The young woman went back into her room to dress for the day. She could hardly wait for her next visit with Lord Feringal, for she suspected—no, she knew—that she would see the man a bit differently now.

She was with him that very afternoon for what would be their last meeting before the wedding. Feringal, excited about the arrangements and the guest list, said nothing at all about the healer's visit to Meralda's house.

"You sent your healer to my house today," she blurted, unable to contain the thoughts any longer. "Before the wedding. With my ma sick and you alone the power to heal her, you could have made me your slave."

Feringal looked as if he simply couldn't digest her meaning. "Why would I desire such a thing?"

That honest and innocent question confirmed that which she had already known. A smile wreathed her beautiful face, and she leaped up impulsively to plant a huge kiss on Feringal's cheek. "Thank you for healing my ma, for healing my family."

Her thanks filled his heart and face with joy. When she tried to kiss him again on the cheek, he turned so that his lips met hers. She returned it tenfold, confident that her life with this kind and wonderful man would be more than tolerable. Far more.

Pondering the scene on the ride back to her home, Meralda's emotions took a downward swing as her thoughts shifted back to the baby and the lie she would have to tell for the rest of her days. How much more awful her actions seemed now! Meralda believed she was guilty of nothing more than poor judgment, but the reality would make it much more than that, would elevate her errant longing for one night of love to the status of treason.

And so it was with fear and hope and joy combined that Meralda stepped into the garden early the next morning to where every one of Auckney's nobles and important witnesses, her own family, Lord Feringal's sister and Steward Temigast included, stood smiling and staring at her. There was Liam Woodgate dressed in his finery, holding the door and beaming from ear to ear, and at the opposite end of the garden from her stood High Watcher Kalorc Risten, a more senior priest of Helm, Feringal's chosen god, in his shining armor and plumed, open-faced helmet.

What a day and what a setting for such an event! Priscilla had replaced her summer flowers with autumn-blooming mums, kaphts, and marigolds, and though they weren't as brilliant as the previous batch, the woman had supplemented their hues with bright banners. It had rained before the dawn, but the clouds had flown, leaving a clean smell in the air. Puddles atop the low wall and droplets on petals caught the morning sunlight in a sparkling display. Even the wind off the ocean smelled clean this day.

Meralda's mood brightened. About to be married, she couldn't be vulnerable any longer. She was not afraid of anything more than tripping over her own feet as she made her way to the ceremonial stand, a small podium bedecked on top by a war gauntlet and with a tapestry depicting a blue eye set on its front. That confidence was only bolstered when Meralda looked upon the shining face of her mother, for Kalorc Risten's young assistant had, indeed, worked a miracle upon the woman. Meralda had feared that her mother would not be healthy enough to attend the ceremony, but now her face was aglow, her eyes sparkling with health she had not enjoyed in years.

Beaming herself, all fears about her secret put away, the young woman began her walk to the podium. She didn't trip. Far from it. Those watching thought Meralda seemed to float along the garden path, the perfect bride, and if she was a bit thicker in the middle, they all believed it a sign that the young woman was at last eating well.

Standing beside the prefect, Meralda turned to watch Lord Feringal's entrance. He stepped out in his full Auckney Castle Guard Commander's uniform, a shining suit of mail crossed in gold brocade, a plumed helmet on his head, and a great sword belted to his hip. Many in the crowd gasped, women tittered, and Meralda thought again that her union with the man might not be such a bad thing. How handsome Feringal seemed to her, even more so now because she knew the truth of his gentle heart. His dashing soldiery outfit was little more than show, but he did cut a grand and impressive figure.

All smiles, Feringal joined her beside the High Watcher. The clergyman began the ceremony, solemnly appointing all gathered as witnesses to the sacred joining. Meralda focused her gaze not on Lord Feringal but on her family. She scarcely heard Kalorc Risten as he preached through the ceremony. At one point she was given a chalice of wine to sip, then to hand to Lord Feringal.

The birds were singing around them, the flowers were spectacular, the couple handsome and happy—it was the wedding that all the women of Auckney envied. Everyone not in attendance at the ceremony was invited to greet the couple afterward outside the castle's front gate. To those of lesser fortune, the spectacle evoked vicarious pleasure. Except from one person.

"*Meralda!*"

The cry cut the morning air and sent a flock of gulls rushing out from the cliffs east of the castle. All eyes turned toward the voice from high on a cliff. There stood a lone figure, the unmistakable, saggy-shouldered silhouette of Jaka Sculi.

"Meralda!" the foolish young man cried again, as if the name had been torn from his heart.

Meralda looked to her parents, to her fretting father, then to the face of her soon-to-be husband.

"Who is that?" Lord Feringal asked in obvious agitation.

Meralda sputtered and shook her head, her expression one of honest disgust. "A fool," she finally managed to say.

"You cannot marry Lord Feringal! Run away with me, I beg you, Meralda!" Jaka took a step precariously close to edge of the cliff.

Lord Feringal, and everyone else, it seemed, stared hard at Meralda.

"A childhood friendship," she explained hastily. "A fool, I tell you, a little boy, and nothing to be concerned with." Seeing that her words were having little effect, she put her hand on Feringal's forearm and moved very close. "I'm here to marry you because we found a love I never dreamed possible," she said, trying desperately to reassure him.

"*Meralda!*" Jaka wailed.

Lord Feringal scowled up at the cliff. "Someone shut the fool up," he demanded. He looked to High Watcher Risten. "Drop a globe of silence on his foolish head."

"Too far," Risten replied, shaking his head, though in truth, he hadn't even prepared such a spell.

At the other end of the garden, Steward Temigast feared where this interruption could lead, so he hustled guards off to silence the loud-mouthed young man.

Like Temigast, Meralda was truly afraid, wondering how stupid Jaka would prove to be. Would the idiot say something that could cost Meralda the wedding, that might cost them both their reputations and perhaps their very lives?

"Run away with me, Meralda," Jaka yelled. "I am your true love."

"Who is that bastard?" Lord Feringal demanded again, past agitated.

"A field worker who thinks he is in love with me," she whispered while the crowd watched the couple. Meralda recognized the danger here, the volatile fires simmering in Feringal's eyes. She looked at him directly and stated flatly, without room for debate, "If you and I were not to be married, if we hadn't found love together, I'd still have nothing to do with that fool."

Lord Feringal stared at her a while longer, but he couldn't stay angry after hearing Meralda's honest assessment.

"Shall I continue, my lord?" High Watcher Risten asked.

Lord Feringal held up his hand. "When the fool is dragged away," he replied.

"Meralda! If you do not come out to me, I shall throw myself to the rocks below!" Jaka yelled suddenly, and he stepped forward to the rim of the cliff.

Several people in the garden gasped, but not Meralda. She stood eyeing Jaka coldly, so angry that she cared little if the fool went through with his threat, because she was certain he wouldn't. He hadn't the courage to kill himself. He wanted only to torture and humilate her publicly to show up Lord Feringal. This was petty revenge, not love.

"Hold!" cried a guard, fast approaching Jaka on the cliff.

The young man spun around at the call, but as he did so his foot slipped out from under him, dropping him to his belly. He clawed with his hands but slid farther out so that he was hanging in air from the chest down, a hundred-foot drop to jagged rocks below him.

The guard lunged for him, but he was too late.

"Meralda!" came Jaka's last cry, a desperate, wailing howl as he dropped from sight.

Stunned as she was by the sudden, dramatic turn, Meralda was torn between disbelieving grief for Jaka and awareness that Feringal's scrutinizing gaze was upon her, watching and measuring her every reaction. She immediately understood that any failure on her part now would be held against her when the truth of her condition became evident.

"By the gods!" she gasped, slapping her hand over her mouth. "Oh, the poor fool!" She turned to Lord Feringal and shook her head, seeming very much at a loss.

And surely she was, her heart a jumble of hatred, horror, and remembered passion. She hated Jaka—how she hated him—for his reaction to the knowledge that she was pregnant, and hated him even more for his stupidity on this day. Still, she could not deny those remembered feelings, the way the mere sight of Jaka had put such a spring in her skip just a few short months before. Meralda knew that Jaka's last cry would haunt her for the rest of her life.

She hid all of that and reacted as those around her did to the gruesome sight—with shock and horror.

They postponed the wedding. Three days later they would complete the ceremony on a gray and thickly overcast morning. It seemed fitting.

* * * * *

Meralda felt the hesitance in her husband's movements for the rest of the day during the grand celebration that was open to all of Auckney. She tried to approach Feringal about it, but he would not reveal himself. Meralda understood he was afraid. And why wouldn't Feringal be afraid? Jaka had died crying out to Feringal's wife-to-be.

But still, as the wine flowed and the merriment continued, Lord Feringal managed more than a few smiles. How those smiles widened when Meralda whispered into his ear that she could hardly wait for their first night together, the consummation of their love.

In truth, the young woman was excited by the prospect, if not a bit fearful. He would recognize, of course, that her virginity wasn't intact, but that was not such an uncommon thing among women living in the harsh farming environment, working hard, often riding horses, and could be explained away. She wondered if perhaps it might be better to reveal the truth of her condition and the lie she had concocted to explain it.

No, she decided, even as she and her husband ascended the staircase to their private quarters. No, the man had been through enough turmoil in the last few days. This would be a night for his pleasure, not his pain.

She would see to that.

* * * * *

It was a grand first week of marriage, full of love and smiles, and those of Biaste Ganderlay touched Meralda most of all. Her family had not come to live with her at Castle Auck. She wouldn't dare suggest such a thing to Priscilla, not yet, but High Watcher Risten had worked tirelessly with Meralda's mother and had declared the woman completely cured. Meralda could see the truth of it painted clearly on Biaste's beaming face.

She could see, too, that though still shaken by Jaka's act upon the cliff, Feringal would get by the event. The man loved her, of that she was sure, and he fawned over her constantly.

Meralda had come to terms with her own feelings for Jaka. She was sorry for what had happened, but she carried no guilt for the man's death. Jaka had done it to himself, and for himself and surely not for her. Meralda understood now that Jaka had done everything for himself. There would always be a tiny place in her heart for the young man, for the fantasies that would never be, but it was more than compensated for by the knowledge that her family would be better off than any of them could ever have hoped. Eventually, she'd move Biaste and Dohni into the castle or a proper estate of their own, and she'd help Tori find a suitable husband, a wealthy merchant perhaps, when the girl was ready.

There remained only one problem. Meralda feared that Priscilla was catching on to her condition, for the woman, though outwardly pleasant, had cast her a few unmistakable glances. Suspicious glances, like those of Steward Temigast. They knew of her condition or suspected it. In any case they would all know soon enough, which brought a measure of desperation creeping into Meralda's otherwise perfect existence.

Meralda had even thought of going to High Watcher Risten to see if there was some magic that might rid her of the child. She had dismissed that thought almost immediately, however, and not for any fears that Risten would betray her. While she wanted no part of Jaka Sculi, she couldn't bring herself to destroy the life that was growing within her.

By the end of the first week of her marriage, Meralda had determined the only course open to her, and by end of the second week she had mustered the courage to initiate her plan. She asked the cook to prepare eggs for breakfast and waited at the table with Feringal, Priscilla, and Temigast. Better to get it over with all of them at once.

Even before the cook came out with the eggs the smell of the food drifted in to Meralda and brought that usual queasy feeling to her. She bent over and clutched at her belly.

"Meralda?" Feringal asked with concern.

"Are you all right, child?" Temigast added.

Meralda looked across the table to Priscilla and saw suspicion there.

She came up fast with a wail and began crying immediately. It was not hard for Meralda to bring forth those tears.

"No, I am not all right!" she cried.

"What is it, dearest?" Lord Feringal asked, leaping up and running to her side.

"On the road," Meralda explained between sobs, "to Madam Prinkle's . . ."

"When you were attacked?" Steward Temigast supplied gently.

"The man, the big one," Meralda wailed. "He ravished me!"

Lord Feringal fell back as if struck.

"Why did you not tell us?" Temigast demanded after a hesitation that seemed to hit all three of them. Indeed, the cook, entering with Meralda's breakfast plate, dropped it to the floor in shock.

"I feared to tell you," Meralda wailed, looking to her husband. "I feared you'd hate me."

"Never!" Feringal insisted, but he was obviously shaken to the core, and he made no move to come back to his wife's side.

"And you're telling us now because . . . ?" Priscilla's tone and Temigast's wounded expression revealed to the young woman that they both knew the answer.

"Because I'm with child, I fear," Meralda blurted. Overwhelmed by her own words and the smell of those damned eggs, she leaned to the side and vomited. Meralda heard Feringal's cry of despair through her own coughs, and it truly hurt the woman to wound him so.

Then there came only silence.

Meralda, finished with the sickness, feared to sit up straight, feared to face the three. She didn't know what they would do, though she had heard of a village woman who had become pregnant through rape. That woman had not been held to blame.

A comforting hand gripped her shoulder and eased her out of the chair. Priscilla hugged Meralda close and whispered softly into her ear that it would be all right.

"What am I to do?" Lord Feringal stuttered, hardly able to speak through the bile in his throat. His tone made Meralda think that he might banish her from the castle, from his life, then and there.

Steward Temigast moved to support the young man. "This is not without precedence, my lord," the old man explained. "Even in your own kingdom." All three stared at the steward.

"There is no betrayal here, of course," Temigast went on. "Except that Meralda did not immediately tell us. For that, you may punish her as you see fit, though I pray you will be generous toward the frightened girl."

Feringal looked at Meralda hard, but he nodded just a bit.

"As for the child," Temigast went on, "it must be announced openly and soon. It will be made clear and binding that this child will not be heir to your throne."

"I will slay the babe as it is born!" Lord Feringal said with a growl. Meralda wailed, as did Priscilla, to Meralda's absolute surprise.

"My lord," said Steward Temigast. Feringal punched his fists against the sides of his legs in utter frustration. Meralda noted his every movement then, and recognized that his claim of murder was pure bluster.

Steward Temigast just shook his head and walked over to pat Lord Feringal's shoulder. "Better to give the babe to another," he said. "Let it be gone from your sight and from your lives."

Feringal stared questioningly at his wife.

"I'm not wanting it," Meralda answered that look with an honest answer. "I'm not wanting to think at all of that night, er, time." She bit her lip as she finished, hoping that her slip of the tongue had not been detected.

To her relief and continued surprise it was Priscilla who stayed close to her, who escorted her to her room. Even when they were out of earshot of Temigast and Lord Feringal, the older woman's gentle demeanor did not waver in the least.

"I cannot guess your pain," Priscilla said.

"I'm sorry I didn't tell you sooner."

Priscilla patted her cheek. "It must have been too painful," she offered, "but you did nothing wrong. My brother was still your first lover, the first man to whom you gave yourself willingly, and a husband can ask no more than that."

Meralda swallowed the guilt she felt, swallowed it and pushed it aside with the justification that Feringal was, indeed, her first true lover, the first man she'd lain with who had honest feelings for her.

"Perhaps we will come to some agreement when the child is born," Priscilla said unexpectedly.

Meralda looked at her strangely, not quite catching on.

"I was thinking that perhaps it would be better if I found another place to live," Priscilla explained. "Or took a wing of the castle for myself, perhaps, and made it my own."

Meralda squinted in puzzlement, then it hit her. She was so shocked that her previous peasant dialect came rushing back. "Ye're thinking o' taking the babe for yerself," she blurted.

"Perhaps, if we could agree," Priscilla said hesitantly.

Meralda had no idea of how to respond but suspected she wouldn't know until after the child was born. Would she be able to have the baby anywhere near her? Or would she find that she could not part with an infant that was hers, after all?

No, she decided, not that. She would not, could not, keep the child, however she might feel after its birth.

"We plan too far ahead," Priscilla remarked as if reading Meralda's mind. "For now we must make sure you eat well. You are my brother's wife now and will give him heirs to the throne of Auckney. We must keep you healthy until then."

Meralda could hardly believe the words, the genuine concern. She had never expected this level of success with her plan, which only made her feel even more guilty about it all.

And so it went for several days, with Meralda believing that things were on a steady course. There were a few rough spots, particularly in the bedroom, where she had to constantly assuage her husband's pride, insisting that the barbarian who had savaged her had given her no pleasure at all. She even went to the extent of claiming that she was

517

practically unconscious throughout the ordeal and wasn't even sure it had happened until she came to realize that she was with child.

Then one day, Meralda encountered an unexpected problem with her plan.

"Highwaymen do not travel far," she heard Lord Feringal tell Temigast as she joined the two in the drawing room.

"Certainly the scoundrels are nowhere near Auckney," the steward replied.

"Close enough," Feringal insisted. "The merchant Galway has a powerful wizard for hire."

"Even wizards must know what to look for," Temigast remarked.

"I don't remember his face," Meralda blurted, hurrying to join them.

"But Liam Woodgate does," said Feringal, wearing the smug smile of one who intended to find his revenge.

Meralda worked very hard to not appear distressed.

Chapter 21

The Bane Of Any Thief

The little creature scrambled over the rocks, descending the steep slope as if death itself were chasing it. With an outraged Wulfgar close behind, roaring in pain from his reopened shoulder wound, the goblin would've had better odds against death.

The trail ended at a fifteen-foot drop, but the goblin's run didn't end there as it leaped with hardly a thought. Landing with a thump and a rather sorry attempt at a roll, it got back up, bloody but still moving.

Wulfgar didn't follow; he couldn't afford to take himself so far from the cave entrance where Morik was still battling. The barbarian skidded to a stop and searched about for a rock. Snatching one up, he heaved it at the fleeing goblin. He missed, the goblin too far away, but satisfied that it wouldn't return, Wulfgar turned and sprinted back to the cave.

Long before he arrived there, though, he saw that the battle had ended. Morik was perched on a rock at the base of a jagged spur of stones, huffing and puffing. "The little rats run fast," Morik remarked.

Wulfgar nodded and fell into a sitting position on the ground. They had gone out to scout the pass earlier. Upon returning, they'd found a dozen goblins determined to take the cave home as their own. Twelve against two—the goblins hadn't had a chance.

Only one of the goblins was dead, one Wulfgar had caught first by the throat and squeezed. The others had been sent running to the four winds, and both men knew that none of the cowardly creatures would return for a long, long time.

"I did get its purse, if not its heart," Morik remarked holding up a little leather bag. He blew into his empty hand for luck (and also because the mountain wind whistled chilly this day) then emptied the bag, his eyes wide. Wulfgar, too, leaned in eagerly. A pair of silver pieces, several copper, and three shiny stones—not gemstones, just stones—tumbled out.

"Our luck that we did not encounter a merchant on the path," Wulfgar muttered sarcastically, "for this is a richer haul by far."

Morik flung the meager treasure to the ground. "We still have plenty of gold from the raid on the coach in the west," he remarked.

"So nice to hear you admit it," came an unexpected voice from above. The pair looked up the rocky spur to see a man in flowing blue robes and holding a tall oaken staff staring down at them. "I would hate to believe I'd found the wrong thieves, after all."

"A wizard," Morik muttered with disgust, tensing. "I hate wizards."

The robed man lifted his staff and began chanting. Wulfgar moved quicker, skidding down to scoop a fair-sized stone, then coming up fast and launching it. His aim proved perfect. The rock crashed against the wizard's chest, though it harmlessly bounced away. If the man even noticed it, he showed no sign.

"I hate wizards!" Morik yelled again, diving out of the way. Wulfgar started to move, but he was too late, for the lightning bolt firing from the staff clipped him and sent him flying.

Up came Wulfgar, rolling and cursing, a rock in each hand. "How many hits can you take?" he cried to the wizard, letting fly one that narrowly missed. The second one went spinning into the obviously amused wizard's blocking arm and bounced away as surely as if it had hit solid stone.

"Does everybody in all of Faerûn have access to a wizard?" Morik cried, picking his trail from cover to cover as he tried to ascend the spur. Morik believed he could get away from, outwit, or outfight (particularly with Wulfgar beside him) any bounty hunter or warrior lord in the area. However, wizards were an entirely different manner, as he had learned so many painful times before, most recently in his capture on the streets of Luskan.

"How many can you take?" Wulfgar yelled again, hurling another stone that also missed its mark.

"One!" the wizard replied. "I can take but one."

"Then hit him!" Morik yelled to Wulfgar, misunderstanding. The wizard was not talking about taking hits on his magical stoneskin, but about taking prisoners. Even as Morik cried out, the robed man pointed at Wulfgar with his free hand. A black tendril shot from his extended

520

fingers, snaking down the spur at tremendous speed to wrap around Wulfgar, binding him fast to the mage.

"I'll not leave the other unscathed!" the wizard cried to no one present. He clenched his fist, his ring sparkled, and he stamped his staff on the stone. A blinding light, a puff of smoke, and Wulfgar and the mage were gone amid a thunderous rumble along the spur.

"Wizards," Morik spat with utter contempt, just before the spur, with Morik halfway up it, collapsed.

* * * * *

He was in the audience hall of a castle. The incessant black tendril continued to wrap him stubbornly in its grip, looping his torso several times, trying to pin his powerful arms. Wulfgar punched at it, but it was a pliable thing, and it merely bent under the blows, absorbing all the energy. He grabbed at the tendril, tried to twist and tear it, but even as his hands worked one area, the long end of the tendril, released from the wizard's hand, looped his legs and tripped him up, bringing him crashing to the hard floor. Wulfgar rolled and squirmed and wriggled to no avail. He was caught.

The barbarian used his arms to keep the thing from wrapping his neck, and when he was at last sure that it could not harm him, he turned his attention more fully to the area around him. There stood the wizard before a pair of chairs, wherein sat a man in his mid-twenties and a younger, undeniably beautiful woman—a woman Wulfgar recognized all too well.

Beside them stood an old man, and in a chair to the side sat a plump woman of perhaps forty winters. Wulfgar also noted that several soldiers lined the room, grim-faced and well-armed.

"As I promised," the wizard said, bowing before the man on the throne. "Now, if you please, there is the small matter of my payment."

"You will find the gold awaiting you in the quarters I provided," the man replied. "I never doubted you, good sir. Your merchant mentor Galway recommended you most highly."

The wizard bowed again. "Are my services further required?" he asked.

"How long will it last?" the man asked, indicating the tendril holding Wulfgar.

"A long time," the wizard promised. "Long enough for you to question and condemn him, certainly, then to drag him down to your dungeon or kill him where he lies."

"Then you may go. Will you dine with us this night?"

"I fear that I have pressing business at the Hosttower," the wizard replied. "Well met, Lord Feringal." He bowed again and walked out, chuckling as he passed the prone barbarian.

To everyone's surprise, Wulfgar growled and grabbed the tendril in both hands and tore it apart. He had just managed to gain his feet, many voices screaming about him, when a dozen soldiers descended, pounding him with mailed fists and heavy clubs. Still fighting against the tendril, Wulfgar managed to free his hand for one punch, sending a soldier flying, and to grab another by the neck and slam him facedown on the floor. Wulfgar went down, dazed and battered. As the wizard magically dispelled the remnants of the tendril, the barbarian's arms were brought behind him and looped with heavy chains.

"If it were just me and you, wizard, would you have anything left with which to stop me?" the stubborn barbarian growled.

"I would have killed you out in the mountains," snapped the mage, obviously embarrassed by the failure of his magic.

Wulfgar launched a ball of spit that struck the man in the face. "How many can you take?" he asked.

The enraged wizard began waggling his fingers, but before he could get far Wulfgar plowed through the ring of soldiers and shoulder-slammed the man, sending him flying away. The barbarian was subdued again almost immediately, but the shaken wizard climbed up from the floor and skittered out of the room.

"Impressive display," Lord Feringal said sarcastically, scowling. "Am I to applaud you before I castrate you?"

That got Wulfgar's attention. He started to respond, but a guard slugged him to keep him quiet.

Lord Feringal looked to the young woman seated beside him. "Is this the man?" he asked, venom in every word.

Wulfgar stared hard at the woman, at the woman he had stopped Morik from harming on the road, at the woman he had released unscathed. He saw something there in her rich, green eyes, some emotion he could not quite fathom. Sorrow, perhaps? Certainly not anger.

"I . . . don't think so," the woman said and looked away.

Lord Feringal's eyes widened, indeed. The old man standing beside him gasped openly, as did the other woman.

"Look again, Meralda," Feringal commanded sharply. "Is it him?"

No answer, and Wulfgar could clearly see the pain in the woman's eyes.

"Answer me!" the lord of Auckney demanded.

"No!" the woman cried, refusing to meet any gaze.

"Fetch Liam," Lord Feringal yelled. Behind Wulfgar, a soldier rushed out of the room, returning a moment later with an old gnome.

"Oh, be sure it is," the gnome said, coming around to stare Wulfgar right in the eye. "You thinking I won't know you?" he asked. "You got me good, with your little rat friend distracting my eyes and you swinging down. I know you, thieving dog, for I seen you afore you hit me!" He turned to Lord Feringal. "Aye," he said. "He's the one."

Feringal eyed the woman beside him for a long, long time. "You are certain?" he asked Liam, his eyes still on the woman.

"I've not been bested often, my lord," Liam replied. "You've named me as the finest fighter in Auckney, which's why you entrusted me with your lady. I failed you, and I'm not taking that lightly. He's the one, I say, and oh, but what I'd pay you to let me fight him fairly."

He turned back and glared into Wulfgar's eyes. Wulfgar matched that stare, and though he had no doubt he could snap this gnome in half with hardly an effort, he said nothing. Wulfgar couldn't escape the fact that he had wronged the diminutive fellow.

"Have you anything to say for yourself?" Lord Feringal asked Wulfgar. Before the barbarian could begin to reply, the young lord rushed forward, brushing Liam aside to stand very close. "I have a dungeon for you," he whispered harshly. "A dark place, filled with the waste and bones of the previous occupants. Filled with rats and biting spiders. Yes, fool, I have a place for you to rot until I decide the time has come to kill you most horribly."

Wulfgar knew the procedure well by this point in his life and merely heaved a heavy sigh. He was promptly dragged away.

* * * * *

In the corner of the audience hall, Steward Temigast watched it all very carefully, shifting his gaze from Wulfgar to Meralda and back again. He noted Priscilla, sitting quietly, no doubt taking it all in, as well.

He noted the venom on Priscilla's face as she regarded Meralda. She was thinking that the woman had enjoyed being ravished by the barbarian, Temigast realized. She was thinking that, perhaps, it hadn't really been a rape.

Given the size of the man, Temigast couldn't agree with that assessment.

* * * * *

The cell was everything Lord Feringal had promised, a wretched, dark and damp place filled with the awful stench of death. Wulfgar couldn't see a thing, not his own hand if he held it an inch in front of his face. He scrabbled around in the mud and worse, pushing past sharp bones in a futile attempt to find some piece of dry ground upon which he might sit. And all the while he slapped at the spiders and other crawling things that scurried in to learn what new meal had been delivered to them.

To most, this dungeon would have seemed worse than Luskan's prison tunnels, mostly because of its purest sense of emptiness and solitude, but Wulfgar feared neither rats nor spiders. His terrors ran much deeper than that. Here in the dark he found he was somewhat able to fend off those horrors.

And so the day passed. Sometime during the next one, the barbarian awoke to torchlight and the sound of a guard slipping a plate of rotten food through the small slit in the half-barred, half-metal hatch that sealed the filthy burrow cell from the wet tunnels beyond. Wulfgar started to eat but spat it out, thinking he might be better off trying to catch and skin a rat.

That second day a turmoil of emotions found the barbarian. Mostly he was angry at all the world. Perhaps he deserved punishment for his highwayman activities—he could accept responsibility for that—but this went beyond justice concerning his actions on the road with Lord Feringal's coach.

Also, Wulfgar was angry at himself. Perhaps Morik had been right all along. Perhaps he did not have the heart for this life. A true highwayman would have let the gnome die or at least finished him quickly. A true highwayman would have taken his pleasures with the woman, then dragged her along either to be sold as a slave or kept as a slave of his own.

Wulfgar laughed aloud. Yes, indeed, Morik had been right. Wulfgar hadn't the heart for any of it. Now here he was, the wretch of wretches, a failure at the lowest level of civilized society, a fool too incompetent to even be a proper highwayman.

He spent the next hour not in his cell, but back in the Spine of the World, that great dividing line between who he once was and what he had become, that physical barrier that seemed such an appropriate symbol of the mental barrier within him, the wall he had thrown up like an emotional mountain range to hold back the painful memories of Errtu.

In his mind's eye he was there now, sitting on the Spine of the World, staring out over Icewind Dale and the life he once knew, then turning around to face south and the miserable existence he now suffered. He kept his eyes closed, though he wouldn't have seen much in the dark anyway, ignored the many crawling things assaulting him, and got more than a few painful spider bites for his inattentiveness.

Sometime later that day, a noise brought him from his trance. He opened his eyes to see the flickers of another torch in the tunnel beyond his door.

"Living still?" came a question from the voice of an old man.

Wulfgar shifted to his knees and crawled to the door, blinking repeatedly as his eyes adjusted to the light. After a few moments he recognized the man holding the torch as the advisor Wulfgar had seen in the audience hall, a man who physically reminded him of Magistrate Jharkheld of Luskan.

Wulfgar snorted and squeezed one hand through the bars. "Burn it with your torch," he offered. "Take your perverted pleasures where you will find them."

"Angry that you were caught, I suppose," the man called Temigast replied.

"Twice imprisoned wrongly," Wulfgar replied.

"Are not all prisoners imprisoned wrongly by their own recounting?" the steward asked.

"The woman said that it wasn't me."

"The woman suffered greatly," Temigast countered. "Perhaps she cannot face the truth."

"Or perhaps she spoke correctly."

"No," Temigast said immediately, shaking his head. "Liam remembered you clearly and would not be mistaken." Wulfgar snorted again. "You deny that you were the thief who knocked over the carriage?" Temigast asked bluntly.

Wulfgar stared at him unblinking, but his expression spoke clearly that he did not deny the words.

"That alone would cost you your hands and imprison you for as many years as Lord Feringal decided was just," Temigast explained. "Or that alone could cost you your life."

"Your driver, Liam, was injured," Wulfgar replied, his voice a growl. "Accidentally. I could have let him die on the road. The girl was not harmed in any way."

"Why would she say differently?" Temigast asked calmly.

"Did she?" Wulfgar came back, and he tilted his head, beginning to catch on, beginning to understand why the young lord had been so completely outraged. At first he had thought mere pride to be the source—the man had failed to properly protect his wife, after all—but now, in retrospect, Wulfgar began to suspect there had been something even deeper there, some primal outrage. He remembered Lord Feringal's first words to him, a threat of castration.

"I pray that Lord Feringal has a most unpleasant death prepared for you, barbarian," Temigast remarked. "You cannot know the agony you have brought to him, to Lady Meralda, or to the folk of Auckney. You are a scoundrel and a dog, and justice will be served when you die, whether in public execution or down here alone in the filth."

"You came down here just to deliver this news?" Wulfgar asked sarcastically. Temigast struck him in the hand with the lit torch, forcing Wulfgar to quickly retract his arm.

With that the old man turned and stormed away, leaving Wulfgar alone in the dark and with some very curious notions swirling about in his head.

*   *   *   *   *

Despite his final outburst and genuine anger, Temigast didn't walk away with his mind made up about anything. He had gone to see the barbarian because of Meralda's reaction to the man in the audience hall, because he had to learn the truth. Now that truth, seemed fuzzier by far. Why wouldn't Meralda identify Wulfgar if she had, indeed, recognized him? How could she not? The man was remarkable, after all, being near to seven feet in height and with shoulders as broad as a young giant's.

Priscilla was wrong, Temigast knew, for he recognized that she was thinking that Meralda had enjoyed the rape. "Ridiculous," the steward muttered, verbalizing his thoughts that he might make some sense of them. "Purely and utterly ridiculous.

"But would Meralda protect her rapist?" he asked himself quietly.

The answer hit him as clearly as the image of an idiotic young man slipping off a cliff.

Chapter 22
Good Lord Brandeburg

"I hate wizards," Morik muttered, crawling out of the rubble of the slide, a dozen cuts and bruises decorating his body. "Not really a fair fight. I must learn this spellcasting business!"

The rogue spent a long while surveying the area, but of course, Wulfgar was nowhere to be found. The wizard's choice in taking Wulfgar seemed a bit odd to Morik. Likely the man thought Wulfgar the more dangerous of the two foes, probably the leader. But it had been Morik, and surely not Wulfgar, who had made an attempt at the lady in the carriage. Wulfgar was the one who had insisted that they let her go, and quickly enough to save the wounded driver. Obviously, the wizard had not come well informed.

Now where was Morik to turn? He went back to the cave first, tending his wounds and collecting the supplies he would need for the road. He didn't want to stay here, not with an angry band of goblins nearby and Wulfgar gone from his side. But where to go?

The choice seemed obvious after but a moment's serious thought— back to Luskan. Morik had always known he would venture back to the streets he knew so well. He'd concoct a new identity as far as most were concerned, but he'd remain very much the same intimidating rogue to those whose alliance he needed. The snag in his plans thus far had been Wulfgar. Morik couldn't walk into Luskan with the huge barbarian beside him and hope to maintain secrecy for any length of time.

Of course, there was also the not-so-little matter of dark elves.

Even that potential problem didn't hold up, though, for Morik had done his best to remain with Wulfgar, as he had been instructed. Now Wulfgar was gone, and the way was left open. Morik took the first steps out of the Spine of the World, heading back for the place he knew so well.

But something very strange happened just then to Morik's sensibilities. The rogue found himself taking two steps westward for every one south. It was no trick of the wizard but a spell cast by his own conscience, a spell of memory that whispered the demands Wulfgar had placed on Captain Deudermont at Prisoner's Carnival that Morik, too, must be set free. Bound by friendship for the first time in his miserable life, Morik the Rogue was soon trotting along the road, sorting out his plan.

He camped on the side of a mountain that night and spotted the campfire of a group of circled wagons. He wasn't far from the main northern pass. The wagons had come from Ten-Towns, no doubt, and were on the road to the south, thus wouldn't go anywhere near to the fiefdom in the west. It was unlikely these merchants had even heard of the place.

"Greetings!" Morik called to the lone sentry later that night.

"Stand fast!" the man called back. Behind him, the others scrambled.

"I am no enemy," Morik explained. "I'm a wayward adventurer separated from my group, wounded a bit, but more angry than hurt."

After a short discussion, which Morik could not hear, another voice announced that he could approach, but it warned that a dozen archers were trained on his heart and he would be wise to keep his palms showing empty.

Wanting no part of a fight, Morik did just that, walking through twin lines of armed men into the firelight to stand before two middle-aged merchants, one a great bear of a man, the other leaner, but still quite sturdy.

"I am Lord Brandeburg of Waterdeep," Morik began, "returning to Ten-Towns, to Maer Dualdon, where I hope to find some remaining sport fishing for knucklehead. Fun business that!"

"You are a long way from anywhere, Lord Brandeburg," the heavier merchant replied.

"Late in the year to be out on Maer Dualdon," the other replied, suspicious.

"Yet that is where I am going, if I find my playful, wandering friends," Morik replied with a laugh. "Perchance have you seen them? A dwarf, Bruenor Battlehammer by name, his human daughter Catti-brie—oh, but the sun itself bows before her beauty!—a rather fat halfling, and . . ."

Morik hesitated and appeared somewhat nervous suddenly, though the smiles of recognition on the faces of the merchants were exactly what he had hoped to see.

"And a dark elf," the heavy man finished for him. "Go ahead and speak openly of Drizzt Do'Urden, Lord Brandeburg. Well known, he is, and no enemy of any merchant crossing into the dale."

Morik sighed with feigned relief and silently thanked Wulfgar for telling him so much of his former friends during their drinking binges over the last few days.

"Well met, I say to you," the heavy man continued. "I am Petters, and my associate Goodman Dawinkle." On a motion from Petters, the guards behind Morik relaxed, and the trio settled into seats around the fire, where Morik was handed a bowl of thick stew.

"Back to Icewind Dale, you say?" Dawinkle asked. "How have you lost that group? No trouble, I pray."

"More a game," Morik answered. "I joined them many miles to the south, and perhaps in my ignorance I got a little forward with Catti-brie." Both merchants scowled darkly

"Nothing serious, I assure you," Morik quickly added. "I was unaware that her heart was for another, an absent friend, nor did I realize that grumbling Bruenor was her father. I merely requested a social exchange, but that, I fear was enough to make Bruenor wish to pay me back."

The merchants and guards laughed now. They had heard of surly and overprotective Bruenor Battlehammer, as had anyone who spent time in Icewind Dale.

"I fear that I bragged of some tracking, some ranger skills," Morik continued, "and so Bruenor decided to test me. They took my horse, my fine clothes, and disappeared from the road—so well into the brush, led by Drizzt, that one not understanding the dark elf's skills would think they had magical aid." The merchants bobbed their heads, laughing still.

"So now I must find them, though I know they are already nearing Icewind Dale." He chuckled at himself. "I'm sure they'll laugh when I arrive on foot, wearing soiled and tattered clothing."

"You look as if you've had a fight," Dawinkle remarked, noticing the signs of the landslide and the goblin battle.

"A row with a few goblins and a single ogre, nothing serious," the rogue replied nonchallantly. The men raised their eyebrows, but not in doubt—never that for someone who had traveled with those powerful companions. Morik's charm and skill was such that he understood how to weave tales beneath tales beneath tales, that the basic premise became quickly accepted as fact.

"You are welcome to spend the night, good sir," merchant Petters offered, "or as many nights as you choose. We are returning to Luskan, though, the opposite direction from your intended path."

"I will accept the bed this night," Morik replied, "and perhaps . . ." He let the words hang in the air, bringing his fingers to his lips in a pensive pose.

Both Petters and Dawinkle leaned forward in anticipation.

"Would you know where I might purchase a horse, a fine riding horse?" Morik asked. "Perhaps a fine set of clothing as well. My friends have left the easy road, and so I might still beat them to Ten-Towns. What wondrous expressions I might paint on their faces when they enter Lonelywood to find me waiting and looking grand, indeed."

The men about him howled.

"Why, *we* have both, horse and clothing," Petters roared, sliding over to slap Morik on the shoulder, which made him wince because he had been battered there by rocks. "A fine price we shall offer to Lord Brandeburg!"

They ate, they exchanged stories, and they laughed. By the time he finished with the group, Morik had procured their strongest riding horse and a wondrous set of clothing, two-toned green of the finest material with gold brocade, for a mere pittance, a fraction of the cost in any shop in Luskan.

He stayed with them through the night but left at first light, riding north and singing a song of adventure. When the caravan was out of sight he turned to the west and charged on, thinking that he should further alter his appearance before he, Lord Brandeburg of Waterdeep, arrived in the small fiefdom.

He hoped the wizard wouldn't be around. Morik hated wizards.

*　*　*　*　*

Errtu found him. There, in the darkness of his dungeon cell, Wulfgar could not escape the haunting memories, the emotional agony, twisted into his very being by the years of torment at the clawed hands of Errtu and his demonic minions.

The demon found him once again and held him, taunted him with alluring mistresses to tempt and destroy him, to destroy, too, the fruit of his seed.

He saw it all again so vividly, the demon standing before him, the babe—Wulfgar's child—in its powerful arms. He had been revulsed at the thought that he had sired such a creature, an alu-demon, but he remembered, too, his recognition of that child—innocent child?—as his own.

Errtu had opened wide his drooling maw, showing those awful canine teeth. The demon's face moved lower, pointed teeth hovering an inch above the head of Wulfgar's child, jaws wide enough to fit the babe's head inside. Errtu moved lower . . .

Wulfgar felt the succubi fingers tickling his body, and he woke with a start. He screamed, kicked, and batted, slapping away several spiders but taking bites from more. The barbarian scrambled to his feet and ran full out in the pitch darkness of his cell, nearly knocking himself unconscious as he barreled into the unyielding door.

He fell back to the dirt floor, sobbing, face buried in his hands, full of anger and frustration. Then he understood what had so startled him from his nightmare-filled sleep, for he heard footsteps out in the corridor. When he looked up he saw the flickers of a torch approaching his door.

Wulfgar moved back and sat up straight, trying to regain some measure of his dignity. He recalled that doomed men were often granted one last request. His would be a bottle of potent drink, a fiery liquid that would burn those memories from his mind for the last time.

The light appeared right outside his cell, and Lord Feringal's face stared in at him. "Are you prepared to admit your crime, dog?" he asked.

Wulfgar stared at him for a long, long moment.

"Very well, then," the unshaken lord continued. "You have been identified by my trusted driver, so by law I need only tell you your crime and punishment."

Still no response.

"For the robbery on the road, I shall take your hands," Lord Feringal explained matter-of-factly. "One at a time and slowly. For your worse crime—" He hesitated, and it seemed to Wulfgar, even in that meager light, as if the man was suddenly pained.

"My lord," prompted old Temigast behind him.

"For your worse crime," Lord Feringal began again, his voice was stronger, "for the ravishing of Lady Meralda you shall be publicly castrated, then chained for public spectacle for one day. And then, dog Wulfgar, you shall be burned at the stake."

Wulfgar's face screwed up incredulously at the reading of the last crime. He had saved the woman from such a fate! He wanted to yell that in Lord Feringal's face, to scream at the man and tear the door from its fitting. He wanted to do all of that, and yet, he did nothing, just sat there quietly, accepting the injustice.

Or was it injustice? Wulfgar asked himself. Did he not deserve such a fate? Did it even matter?

That was it, Wulfgar decided. It mattered to him not at all. He would find freedom in death. Let Lord Feringal kill him and be done with it, doing them both a favor. The woman had falsely accused him, and he could not understand why, but . . . no matter.

"Have you nothing to say?" Lord Feringal demanded.

"Will you grant a final request?"

The young man trembled visibly at the absurd notion. "I would give you *nothing!*" he screamed. "Nothing more than a night, hungry and wretched, to consider your horrid fate."

"My lord," Temigast said again to calm him. "Guard, lead Lord Feringal back to his chambers." The young man scowled one last time at

Wulfgar through the opening in the door, then let himself be led away.

Temigast stayed, though, taking one of the torches and waving the remaining guards away. He stood at the cell door for a long while, staring at Wulfgar.

"Go away, old man," the barbarian said.

"You did not deny the last charge," Temigast said, "though you protested your innocence to me."

Wulfgar shrugged, but said nothing and did not meet the man's gaze. "What would be the point of repeating myself? You've already condemned me."

"You did not deny the rape," Temigast stated again.

Wulfgar's head swung up to return Temigast's stare. "Nor did you speak up for me," he replied.

Temigast looked at him as if slapped. "Nor shall I."

"So you would let an innocent man die."

Temigast snorted aloud. "Innocent?" he declared. "You are a thief and a dog, and I'll do nothing against Lady Meralda, nor against Lord Feringal, for your miserable sake."

Wulfgar laughed at him, at the ridiculousness of it all.

"But I offer you this," Temigast went on. "Say not a word against Lady Meralda, and I will ensure that your death will be quick. That is the best I can offer."

Wulfgar stopped laughing and stared hard at the complicated steward.

"Or else," Temigast warned, "I promise to drag the spectacle of your torture out for the length of a day and more, shall make you beg for your death a thousand thousand times before setting you free of the agony."

"Of the agony?" Wulfgar echoed hollowly. "Old man, you know nothing of agony."

"We shall see," Temigast growled, and he turned away, leaving Wulfgar along in the dark . . . until Errtu returned to him, as the demon always did.

*   *   *   *   *

Morik rode as fast as his horse would take him, for as long as the poor beast would last. He crossed along the same road where he and Wulfgar had encountered the carriage, past the same spot where Wulfgar had overturned the thing.

He came into Auckney late one afternoon to the stares of many peasants. "Pray tell me the name of your lord, good sir," he called to one, accentuating his request with a tossed gold piece.

"Lord Feringal Auck," the man supplied quickly. "He lives with his new bride in Castle Auck, there," he finished, pointing a gnarly finger toward the coast.

532

"Many thanks!" Morik bowed his head, tossed another couple of silver coins, then kicked his horse's flanks, trotting down the last few hundred yards of road to the small bridge leading to Castle Auck. He found the gate open with a pair of bored-looking guards standing to either side.

"I am Lord Brandeburg of Waterdeep," he said to them, bringing his steed to a stop. "Pray announce me to your lord, for I've a long road behind me and a longer one ahead."

With that, the rogue dismounted and brushed off his fine pantaloons, going so far as to draw his slender sword from his belt, wiping clean the blade as he brought it forth, then launching into a sudden, dazzling display of swordsmanship before replacing it on his hip. He had impressed them, he realized, as one ran off for the castle and the other moved to tend his horse.

Within the span of a few minutes, Morik, Lord Brandeburg, stood before Lord Feringal in the audience hall of Castle Auck. He dipped a low bow and introduced himself as a traveler who had lost his companions to a band of giants in the Spine of the World. He could see from Feringal's eyes that the minor nobleman was thrilled and proud to be visited by a lord of the great city of Waterdeep and would drop his guard in his efforts to please.

"I believe that one or two of my friends escaped," Morik finished his tale, "though on my word not a giant can say the same."

"How far away was this?" asked Lord Feringal. The man seemed somewhat distracted, but Morik's tale obviously alarmed him.

"Many miles, my lord," Morik supplied, "and no threat to your quiet kingdom. As I said, the giants are all dead." He looked around and smiled. "A pity it would be for such monsters to descend on such a quiet and safe place as this."

Lord Feringal took the bait. "Not so quiet, and not so safe," he growled through clenched teeth.

"Danger, here?" he said incredulously. "Pirates, perhaps?" Morik appeared surprised and looked to the old steward standing beside the throne. The man shook his head imperceptibly, which Morik took to mean he should not press the issue, but that was exactly the point.

"Highwaymen," Lord Feringal snarled.

Morik started to respond but held his tongue, and his breath, as a woman whom Morik surely recognized entered the room.

"My wife," Lord Feringal introduced her distractedly. "Lady Meralda Auck."

Morik bowed low, took her hand in his, and lifted it to his lips, pointedly staring her right in the eyes as he did. To his ultimate relief, and pride at his own clever disguise, he detected no flicker of recognition there.

"A most beautiful wife," Morik stated. "You have my envy, Lord Feringal."

That brought a smile at last to Feringal's face, but it quickly turned into a frown. "My wife was in the coach attacked by these highwaymen."

Morik gasped. "I would find them, Lord Feringal," he said. "Find them and slay them on the road. Or bring them back to you, if you would prefer."

Lord Feringal waved his hands, quieting the man. "I have the one I desire," he said. "The other was buried under a rockslide."

Morik's lips pursed at the painful thought. "A fitting fate," he said.

"More fitting is the fate I have planned for the captured barbarian," Feringal grimly replied. "A most horrible death, I assure you. You may witness it if you will stay in Auckney for the night."

"Of course, I shall," Morik said. "What have you planned for the scoundrel?"

"First, castration," Lord Feringal explained. "The barbarian will be killed properly two mornings hence."

Morik assumed a pensive pose. "A barbarian, you say?"

"A huge northerner, yes," Feringal replied.

"Strong of arm?"

"As strong as any man I have ever seen," the lord of Auckney replied. "It took a powerful wizard to bring him to justice, and even that man would have fallen to him had not my guards surrounded him and beat him down."

Morik almost choked over the mention of the wizard, but he held his calm.

"Killing a highwayman is surely an appropriate ending," Morik said, "but perhaps you would be better served in another manner." He waited, watching carefully as Lord Feringal eyed him closely.

"Perhaps I might purchase the man," Morik explained. "I am a man of no small means, I assure you, and could surely use a strong slave at my side as I begin the search for my missing companions."

"Not a chance," Feringal replied rather sharply.

"But if he is familiar with these parts . . ." Morik started to reason.

"He is going to die horribly for the harm he brought to my wife," Lord Feringal retorted.

"Ah, yes, my lord," Morik said. "The incident has distressed her."

"The incident has left her with child!" Feringal yelled, grabbing the arms of his chair so forcefully that his knuckles whitened.

"My lord!" the steward cried at the unwise announcement, and Meralda gasped. Morik was glad for their shock, as it covered his own.

Lord Feringal calmed quickly, forcing himself back into his seat and mumbling an apology to Meralda. "Lord Brandeburg, I beg your forgiveness," he said. "You understand my anger."

"I will castrate the dog for you," Morik replied, drawing forth his sword. "I assure you that I am skilled at such arts."

That broke the tension in the room somewhat. Even Lord Feringal managed a smile. "We will take care of the unpleasantries," he replied, "but I would, indeed, enjoy your company at the execution of sentence. Will you stay as my guest for the two days?"

Morik bowed very low. "I am at your service, my lord."

Soon after, Morik was brought to an inn just beyond the castle bridge. He wasn't thrilled to learn that Lord Feringal kept guests outside the castle walls. That would make it all the harder for him to get near Wulfgar. He did learn from the escort, though, that Wulfgar was being kept in a dungeon beneath the castle.

Morik had to get to his friend, and fast, for, given the false accusations placed against Wulfgar, Lord Feringal would surely and horribly kill the man. A daring rescue had never been a part of Morik's plan. Many thieves were sold to adventuring lords, and so he had hoped Lord Feringal would part with this one for a handsome sum—and the lord's own gold, at that—but rapists, particularly men who ravished noblewomen, found only one, horrible fate.

Morik stared out the window of his small room, looking to Castle Auck and the dark waters beyond. He would try to find some way to get to Wulfgar, but he feared he would be returning to Luskan alone.

Chapter 23

The Second Attempted Justice

"Here's your last meal, dog," said one of the two guards standing outside Wulfgar's cell. The man spat on the food and slipped the tray in through the slot.

Wulfgar ignored them and made no move for the food. He could hardly believe that he had escaped execution in Luskan, only to be killed in some nondescript fiefdom. It struck him, then, that perhaps he had earned this. No, he hadn't harmed the woman, of course, but his actions of the last months, since he had left Drizzt and the others in Icewind Dale—since he had slapped Catti-brie across the face—were not those of a man undeserving of such a grim fate. Hadn't Wulfgar and Drizzt killed monsters for the same crimes that Wulfgar had committed? Had the pair not gone into the Spine of the World in pursuit of a giant band that had been scouting out the trail, obviously planning to waylay merchant wagons? What mercy had they shown the giants? What mercy, then, did Wulfgar deserve?

Still, it bothered the big man more than a little, shook what little confidence he had left in justice and humanity, that both in Luskan and in Auckney he had been convicted of crimes for which he was innocent. It made no sense to him. If they wanted to kill him so badly, why not just

537

do it for those crimes he had committed? There were plenty of those from which to chose.

He caught the last snatches of the guards' conversation as they walked away down the tunnel. "A wretched child it'll be, coming from such loins as that."

"It'll tear Lady Meralda apart, with its da so big!"

That gave Wulfgar pause. He sat in the dark for a long while, his mouth hanging open. Now it began to make a little more sense to him as he put the pieces of the puzzle together. He knew from the guards' previous conversations that Lord Feringal and Lady Meralda were only recently married, and now she was with child, but not by Lord Feringal.

Wulfgar nearly laughed aloud at the absurdity of it all. He had become a convenient excuse for an adulterous noblewoman, a balm against Lord Feringal's cuckolding.

"What luck," he muttered, but he understood that more than bad luck had caused his current predicament. A series of bad choices on his part had landed him here in the dark with the spiders and the stench and the visits of the demon.

Yes, he deserved this, he believed. Not for the crimes accused, but for those committed.

*   *   *   *   *

She couldn't sleep, couldn't even begin to close her eyes. Feringal had left her early and returned to his own room, for she had claimed discomfort and begged him to give her a reprieve from his constant amorous advances. It wasn't that she minded the man's attention. In fact, her lovemaking with Feringal was certainly pleasant, and were it not for the child and the thought of the poor man in the dungeon, it would go far beyond pleasant.

Meralda had come to know that her change of heart concerning Feringal was well founded, that he was a gentle and decent man. She had little trouble looking at Feringal in a fresh way, recognizing his handsome features and his charm, though that was somewhat buried by his years under the influences of his shrewish sister. Meralda could unearth that charm, she knew, could bring out the best in Feringal and live in bliss with the good man.

However, the woman found that she could not tolerate herself. How her foolishness had come back to haunt her in the form of the baby in her womb, in the simmering anger within her husband. Perhaps the most bitter blow of all to Meralda was the forthcoming execution of an innocent man, a man who had saved her from the very crime for which he was to be horribly killed.

After Wulfgar had been dragged away, Meralda tried to rationalize the sentence, reminding herself that the man was, indeed, a highwayman, going so far as to tell herself that the barbarian had victimized others, perhaps even raped other women.

But those arguments hadn't held water, for Meralda knew better. Though he had robbed her carriage, she'd gotten a fair glimpse into the man's character. Her lie had caused this. Her lie would bring the brutal execution to a man undeserving.

Meralda lay late into the night, thinking herself the most horrible person in all the world. She hardly realized that she was moving sometime later, padding barefoot along the castle's cold stone floor with the guiding light of a single candle. She went to Temigast's room, pausing at the door to hear the reassuring sounds of the old man's snoring, and in she crept. As the steward, Temigast kept the keys to every door in the castle on a large wrought iron ring.

Meralda found the ring on a hook above the steward's dresser, and she took it quietly, glancing nervously at Temigast with every little noise. Somehow she got out of the room without waking the man, then skittered across the audience hall, past the servant's quarters, and into the kitchen. There she found the trap door leading to the levels below, bolted and barred so strongly that no man, not even a giant, could hope to open it. Unless he had the keys.

Meralda fumbled with them, trying each until she had finally thrown every lock and shifted every bar aside. She paused, collecting herself, trying to form a more complete plan. She heard the guards then, laughing in a side room, and paced over to peer inside. They were playing bones.

Meralda went to the larder door, a hatch really, that led to the outside wall of the castle. There wasn't much room among the rocks out there, especially if the tide was in, which it was, but it would have to do. Unlocking it as well, the woman went to the trap door and gently pulled it open. Slipping down to the dirty tunnels, she walked barefoot in the slop, hiking her dressing gown up so that it would carry no revealing stains.

Wulfgar awoke to sounds of a key in the lock of his cell door, and a thin, flickering light outside in the corridor. Having lost all track of time in the dark, he thought the morning of his torture had arrived. How surprised he was to find Lady Meralda staring in at him though the bars of his locked cell.

"Can you forgive me?" she whispered, glancing over her shoulder nervously.

Wulfgar just gaped at her.

"I didn't know he'd come after you," the woman explained. "I thought he'd let it go, and I'd be—"

"Safe," he finished for her. "You thought that your child would be safe." Now it was Meralda's turn for an incredulous stare. "Why have you come?" Wulfgar asked.

"You could've killed us," she replied. "Me and Liam on the road, I mean. Or done as they said you done."

"As *you* said I did," Wulfgar reminded.

"You could've let your friend have his way on the road, could've let Liam die," Meralda went on. "I'm owing you this much at least." To Wulfgar's astonishment she turned the key in the lock. "Up the ladder and to the left, then through the larder," she explained. "The way's clear." She lit another candle and left it for him, then turned and ran off.

Wulfgar gave her a lead, not wanting to catch up to her, for he didn't want her implicated if he were caught. Outside his cell, he pulled a metal sconce from the wall and used it to batter the lock as quietly as he could to make it look as though he had broken out of his own accord. Then he moved down the corridors to the ladder and up into the kitchen.

He, too, heard the guards arguing and rolling bones in a nearby room, so he couldn't similarly destroy the locks and bars up here. He relocked and barred the trap door. Let them think he'd found some magical assistance. Going straight through the larder, as Meralda had bade him, Wulfgar squeezed through the small door, a tight fit indeed, and found a precarious perch on wet rocks outside at the base of the castle. The stones were worn and smooth. Wulfgar couldn't hope to scale it, nor was there any apparent way around the corner, for the tide was crashing in.

Wulfgar leaped into the cold water.

* * * * *

Hiding in the kitchen, Meralda nodded as Wulfgar heightened her ruse by securing the trap door. She similarly locked the larder, washed all signs of her subterranean adventure from her feet, and padded quietly back to return the keys to Steward Temigast's room without further incident.

Meralda was back in her bed soon after, the terrible demons of guilt—some of them, at least—banished at last.

* * * * *

The breeze off the water was chill, but Morik was still sweating under the heavy folds of his latest disguise as an old washerwoman. He stood behind a stone wall near the entrance to the short bridge leading to Castle Auck.

"Why did they put the thing on an island?" the rogue muttered disgustedly, but of course, his own current troubles answered the question. A lone guard leaned on the wall above the huge castle gate. The man was very likely half asleep, but Morik could see no way to get near to him. The bridge was well lit, torches burning all the night long from what he had heard, and it offered no cover whatsoever. He would have to swim to the castle.

Morik looked at the dark waters doubtfully. He wouldn't have much of a disguise left after crossing through that, if he even made it. Morik wasn't a strong swimmer and didn't know the sea or what monsters might lurk beneath the dark waves.

Morik realized then and there that his time with Wulfgar was at its end. He would go to the place of torture in the morning, he decided, but probably only to say farewell, for it was unlikely he could rescue the man there without jeopardizing himself.

No, he decided, he wouldn't even attend. "What good might it bring?" he muttered. It could even bring disaster for Morik if the wizard who had caught Wulfgar was there and recognized him. "Better that I remember Wulfgar from our times of freedom.

"Farewell, my big friend," Morik said aloud sadly. "I go now back to Luskan—"

Morik paused as the water churned at the base of the wall. A large, dark form began crawling from the surf. The rogue's hand went to his sword.

"Morik?" Wulfgar asked, his teeth chattering from the icy water. "What are you doing here?"

"I could ask the same of you!" the rogue cried, delighted and astounded all at once. "I, of course, came to rescue you," the cocky rogue added, bending to take Wulfgar's arm and help pull the man up beside him. "This will require a lot of explaining, but come, let us be fast on our way."

Wulfgar wasn't about to argue.

* * * * *

"I shall have every guard in this place executed!" Lord Feringal fumed when he learned of the escape the next morning, the morning he was planning to exact his revenge upon the barbarian.

The guard shrank back, fearing Lord Feringal would attack him then and there, and indeed, it seemed as if the young man would charge him from his chair. Meralda grabbed him by the arm, settling him. "Calm, my lord," she said.

"Calm?" Lord Feringal balked. "Who failed me?" he yelled at the guard. "Who shall pay in Wulfgar's stead?"

"None," Meralda answered before the stammering guard could begin to reply. Feringal looked at her incredulously. "Anyone you harm will be because of me," the woman explained. "I'll have no blood on my hands. You'd only be making things worse."

The young lord calmed somewhat and sat back, staring at his wife, at the woman he wanted, above all else, to protect. After a moment's thought, a moment of looking into that beautiful, innocent face, Feringal nodded his agreement. "Search all the lands," he instructed the guard, "and the castle again from dungeon to parapet. Return him to me alive."

541

Beads of sweat on his forehead, the guard bowed and ran out of the room.

"Fear not, my love," Lord Feringal said to Meralda. "I shall recall the wizard and begin the search anew. The barbarian shall not escape."

"Please, my lord," Meralda begged. "Don't summon the wizard again, or any other." That raised a few eyebrows, including Priscilla's and Temigast's. "I'm wanting it all done," she explained. "It's done, I say, and on the road behind me. I'm not wanting to look back ever again. Let the man go and die in the mountains, and let us look ahead to our own life, to when you might be siring children of our own."

Feringal continued to stare, unblinking. Slowly, very slowly, his head nodded, and Meralda relaxed back in her chair.

* * * * *

Steward Temigast watched it all with growing certainty. He knew, without doubt, that Meralda was the one who had freed the barbarian. The wise old man, suspicious since seeing the woman's reaction when Wulfgar had first been dragged before her, had little trouble in understanding why. He resolved to say nothing, for it was not his place to inflict unnecessary pain on his lord. In any event, the child would be put out of the way and in no line of ascension.

But Temigast was far from easy with it all, especially after he looked at Priscilla and saw her wearing an expression that might have been his own. She was always suspicious, that one, and Temigast feared she was harboring his same doubts about the child's heritage. Though Temigast felt it not his place to inflict unnecessary pain, Priscilla Auck seemed to revel in just that sort of thing. The road to which Meralda had referred was far from clear in either direction.

Chapter 24

Winter's Pause

"This is our chance," Wulfgar explained to Morik. The pair were crouched behind a shielding wall of stone on a mountainside above one of the many small villages on the southern side of the Spine of the World.

Morik looked at his friend and shook his head, giving a less-than-enthusiastic sigh. Not only had Wulfgar refrained from the bottle in the three weeks since their return from Auckney, but had forbidden either of them to engage in any more highwayman activities. The season was getting late, turning toward winter, which meant a nearly constant stream of caravans as the last merchants returned from Icewind Dale. The seasonal occupants of the northern stretches left then as well, the men and women who went to Ten-Towns to fish for the summers then rolled their wagons back to Luskan when the season ended.

Wulfgar had made it clear to Morik that their thieving days were over. So here they were, overlooking a small, incredibly boring village they'd learned was expecting some sort of orc or goblin attack.

"They will not attack from below," Wulfgar remarked, pointing to a wide field east of the village on the same height as the higher buildings. "From there," Wulfgar explained.

"That's where they've constructed their wall and best defenses," Morik replied, as if that should settle it all. They believed that the coming band of monsters numbered less than a score, and while there weren't more than half that number in the town, Morik didn't see any real problems here.

"More may come down from above," Wulfgar reasoned. "The villagers might be sorely pressed if attacked from two sides."

"You're looking for an excuse," Morik accused. Wulfgar stared at him curiously. "An excuse to get into the fight," the rogue clarified, which brought a smile to Wulfgar's face. "Unless it's against merchants," Morik glumly added.

Wulfgar held his calm and contented expression. "I wish to battle deserving opponents," he said.

"I know many peasants who would argue that merchants are more deserving than goblinkind," Morik replied.

Wulfgar shook his head, in no mood and with no time to sit and ponder the philosophical points. They saw the movement beyond the village, the approach of monsters Wulfgar knew, of creatures the barbarian could cut down without remorse or regard. A score of orcs charged wildly across the field, rushing past the ineffective arrow volleys from the villagers.

"Go and be done with it," Morik said, starting to rise.

Wulfgar, a student of such attacks, held him down and turned his gaze up the slopes to where a huge boulder soared down, smashing the side of one building.

"There's a giant above," Wulfgar whispered, already starting his circle up the mountain. "Perhaps more."

"So that is where we shall go," Morik grumbled with resignation, though he obviously doubted the wisdom of such a course.

Another rock soared down, then a third. The giant was lifting a fourth when Wulfgar and Morik turned a bend in the trail and slipped between a pair of boulders, spotting the behemoth from behind.

Wulfgar's hand axe bit into the giant's arm, and it dropped the boulder onto its own head. The giant bellowed and spun about to where Morik stood shrugging, slender sword in hand. Bellowing, the giant came at him in one long stride. Morik yelped and turned to flee back through the boulders. The giant came on in swift pursuit, but as it reached the narrow pass Wulfgar leaped atop one of the boulders and brought his ordinary hammer in hard against the side of the behemoth's head, sending it staggering. By the time the dazed giant managed to look to the boulder Wulfgar was already gone. Back on the ground, the barbarian rushed at the giant's side to smash its kneecap hard, then dashed back into the boulders.

The giant ran in pursuit, clutching its bruised head, then its aching knee, then looking at the axe deep into its forearm. It changed direction suddenly, having had enough of this fight, and ran up the mountainside instead, back into the wilds of the Spine of the World.

Morik stepped from the boulders and offered his hand to Wulfgar. "A job well done," he congratulated him.

Wulfgar ignored the hand. "A job just begun," he corrected, sprinting down the mountainside toward the village and the battle being waged at the eastern barricade.

"You do love the fighting," Morik commented dryly after his friend. Sighing, he loped behind.

Below, the battle at the barricade was practically at a standoff, with no orcs yet breaching the shielding wall, but few had taken any solid hits, either. That changed abruptly when Wulfgar came down from on high, running full out across the field, howling at the top of his lungs. Leaping, soaring, arms outstretched, he crashed into four of the creatures, bearing them all to the ground. A frenzy of clubbing and stabbing, punching and kicking ensued. More orcs moved to join the fight but in the end, bloody, battered, but smiling widely, Wulfgar was the only one to emerge alive.

Rallied by his amazing assault and by the appearance of Morik, who had struck down another orc on his way down the slope, the villagers poured into the remaining raiding party. The routed creatures, the dozen who still could run, fled back the way they had come.

By the time Morik got near Wulfgar, the barbarian was surrounded by villagers, patting him, cheering him, promising eternal friendship, offering him a place to live for the coming winter.

"You see," Wulfgar said to Morik with a happy smile. "Easier than any work at the pass."

Wiping off his blade, the rogue eyed his friend skeptically. The fight had been easy, even more so than an optimistic Wulfgar had predicted. Morik, too, was quickly surrounded by appreciative villagers, including a couple of young and attractive women. A quiet winter of relaxation in front of a blazing hearth might not be so bad a thing. Perhaps he would hold off on his plans to return to Luskan after all.

* * * * *

Meralda's first three months of married life had been wonderful. Not blissful, but wonderful, as she watched her mother grow strong and healthy for the first time in years. Even life at the castle was not as bad as she had feared. Priscilla was there, of course, never more than casually friendly and often glowering, but she'd made no move against Meralda. How could she with her brother so obviously enamored of his wife?

She, too, had grown to love her husband. That combined with the sight of her healthy mother had made it a lovely autumn for the young woman, a time of things new, a time of comfort, a time of hope.

But as winter deepened about Auckney, ghosts of the past began to creep into the castle.

Jaka's child growing large and kicking reminded Meralda in no uncertain terms of her terrible lie. She found herself thinking more and more about Jaka Sculi, of her own moments of foolishness regarding him, and there had been many. She pondered the last moments of Jaka's life when he had cried out her name, had risked his entire existence for her. At the time, Meralda had convinced herself that it was out of jealousy for Lord Feringal and not love. Now, with Jaka's child kicking in her womb and the inevitable haze brought by the passage of time, she wasn't so sure. Perhaps Jaka had loved her in the end. Perhaps the tingling they'd felt on their night of passion had also planted the seeds of deeper emotions that had only needed time to find their way through the harsh reality of a peasant's existence.

More likely her mood was just the result of winter's gloom playing on her thoughts, and on her new husband's as well. It didn't help that their lovemaking decreased dramatically as Meralda's belly increased in size. He came to her one morning when the snow was deep about the castle and the wind howled through the cracks in the stone. Even as he began kissing her, he stopped and stared hard at her, then he'd asked her an unthinkable question.

What had it been like with the barbarian?

If he had kicked her in the head, it would not have hurt so much, yet Meralda was not angry at her husband, could surely understand his doubts and fears given her distant mood and the tangible evidence that she had been with another man.

The woman told herself repeatedly that once the child was born and taken away, she and Feringal would settle into a normal existence. In that time when the obvious pressures were gone, they would come to love each other deeply. She could only hope that it all would not disintegrate in the months she had left carrying the child.

Of course, as the tension grew between Feringal and Meralda, so too did the scowls Priscilla shot Meralda's way. Power wrought of having Lord Feringal wrapped around her little finger had given Meralda the upper hand in the constant silent war Priscilla waged against her. Growing thick with another man's child, she found that power waning.

She didn't understand it, though, considering Priscilla's initial response to learning that she had been raped. Priscilla had even mentioned taking the child as her own, to raise away from the castle, as was often done in such situations.

"You are uncommonly large for so early in the pregnancy," Priscilla remarked to her on the same winter day that Feringal had asked her about Wulfgar. It occurred to Meralda that the shrewish woman had obviously sensed the palpable tension between the couple. Priscilla's voice was uncommonly thick with suspicion and venom, which told Meralda that her sister-in-law was keeping close track of the passage of time. There would be trouble, indeed, when Meralda delivered a healthy, full-term baby only seven months after the incident on the road. Yes, Priscilla would have questions.

Meralda deflected the conversation by sharing her fears about the barbarian's size, that perhaps the child would tear her apart. That had silenced Priscilla briefly, but Meralda knew the truce wouldn't last and the questions would return.

Indeed, as winter waned and Meralda's belly swelled, the whispers began throughout Auckney. Whispers about the child's due date. Whispers about the incident on the road. Whispers about the tragic death of Jaka Sculi. No fool, Meralda saw people counting on their fingers, saw the tension in her mother's face, though the woman wouldn't openly ask for the truth.

When the inevitable happened, predictably, Priscilla proved the source of it.

"You will birth the child in the month of Ches," the woman said rather sharply as she and Meralda dined with Steward Temigast one cold afternoon. The equinox was fast approaching, but winter hadn't released its grip on the land yet, a howling blizzard whipping the snow deep around the castle walls. Meralda looked at her skeptically.

"Mid-Ches," Priscilla remarked. "Or perhaps late in the month, or even early in the Month of the Storms."

"Do you sense a problem with the pregnancy?" Steward Temigast intervened.

Once again Meralda recognized that the man was her ally. He too knew, or at least he suspected as much as Priscilla, yet he'd shown no hostility toward Meralda. She'd begun to regard Temigast as a father figure, but the comparison seemed even more appropriate when she thought back to the morning after her night with Jaka, when Dohni Ganderlay had suspected the truth but had forgiven it in light of the larger sacrifice, the larger good.

"I sense a problem, all right," Priscilla replied brittly, somehow managing to convey through her tone that she meant no problem with the physical aspects of the pregnancy. Priscilla looked at Meralda and huffed, then threw down her napkin and rushed away, heading right up the stairs.

"What's she about?" Meralda asked Temigast, her eyes fearful. Before he could respond, she had her answer, when shouts rang out from upstairs. Neither of them could make out any distinct words, but it was obvious Priscilla had gone to speak with her brother.

"What should I do—" Meralda started to say, but Temigast hushed her.

"Eat, my lady," he said calmly. "You must remain strong, for you've trials ahead." Meralda understood the double meaning in those words.

"I'm certain you'll come through them as long as you keep your wits about you," the old steward added with a comforting wink. "When it is all past, you will find the life you desire."

Meralda wanted to run over and bury her head on the man's shoulder, or to run out of the castle altogether, down the road to the warm and comfortable house Lord Feringal had given to her family and bury her face on her father's shoulder. Instead, she took a deep breath to steady herself, then did as Temigast suggested and ate her meal.

* * * * *

The snow came early and deep that year. Morik would have preferred Luskan, but he'd come to see Wulfgar's point in bringing them to this village refuge. There was plenty of work to do, particularly after snowfalls when the grounds had to be cleared and defensible berms built, but Morik managed to avoid most of it by feigning an injury from the battle that had brought them here.

Wulfgar, though, went at the work with relish, using it to keep his body so occupied he hadn't time to think or dream. Still, Errtu found him in that village as he had in every place Wulfgar went, every place he would ever go. Now, instead of hiding in a bottle from the demon, the barbarian met those memories head-on, replayed the events, however horrible, and forced himself to admit that it had happened, all of it, and that he had faced moments of weakness and failure. Many times Wulfgar sat alone in the dark corner of the room he had been given, trembling, wet with cold sweat, and with tears he could hold back no longer. Many times he wanted to run to Morik's inexhaustible supply of potent liquor, but he did not.

He growled and he cried out, and yet he held fast his resolve to accept the past for what it was and to somehow move beyond it. Wulfgar didn't know where he had found the strength and determination, but he suspected it had laid dormant within him, summoned when he'd witnessed the courage Meralda had displayed to free him. She'd had so much more to lose than he, and yet she had rejuvenated his faith in the world. He knew now that his fight with Errtu would continue until he had honestly won, that he could hide in a bottle, but not forever.

They fought another battle around the turn of the year, a minor skirmish with another band of orcs. The villagers had seen the attack coming and had prepared the battlefield, pouring melted snow over the field of approach. When the orcs arrived they came skidding in on sheets of ice that left them floundering in the open while archers picked them off.

The unexpected appearance of a group of Luskan soldiers who had lost their way on patrol did more to distress Wulfgar and Morik and shatter their idyllic existence than that battle. Wulfgar was certain at least one of the soldiers recognized the pair from Prisoner's Carnival, but either the soldiers said nothing to the villagers or the villagers simply didn't care,. The pair heard no tremors of unrest after the soldiers departed.

In the end, it was the quietest winter Wulfgar and Morik had ever known, a needed respite. The season turned to spring, though the snow remained thick, and the pair began to lay their future plans.

"No more highwaymen," Wulfgar reminded Morik one quiet night halfway through the month of Ches.

"No," the rogue agreed. "I don't miss the life."

"What, then, for Morik?"

"Back to Luskan, I'm afraid," the rogue said. "My home. Ever my home."

"And your disguise will keep you safe?" Wulfgar asked with genuine concern.

Morik smiled. "The folk have short memories, my friend," he explained, silently adding that he hoped that drow had short memories, as well, for returning to Luskan meant abandoning his mission to watch over Wulfgar. "Since we were . . . exported they have no doubt sated their bloodthirst on a hundred unfortunates at Prisoner's Carnival. My disguise will protect me from the authorities, and my true identity will again grant me the respect needed on the streets."

Wulfgar nodded, not doubting Morik in the least. Out here in the wilds the rogue was not nearly as impressive as on the streets of Luskan, where few could match his wiles.

"And what for Wulfgar?" Morik asked, surprised by the honest concern on his own voice. "Icewind Dale?" Morik asked. "Friends of old?"

The barbarian shook his head, for he simply didn't know the road ahead of him. He would have dismissed that possibility with hardly a thought, but he considered it now. Was he ready to return to the side of the companions of the hall, as he, Drizzt, Bruenor, Catti-brie, Guenhwyvar and Regis had once been called? Had he escaped the demon and the demon bottle? Had he come to terms with Errtu and the truth of his imprisonment?

"No," he answered, and left it at that, wondering if he would ever again meet the gazes of his former friends.

Morik nodded, though a bit dismayed for his own reasons. He didn't want Wulfgar to return to Luskan with him. Disguising the huge man would be difficult enough, but it was more than that. Morik didn't want Wulfgar to be caught by the dark elves.

* * * * *

"She is playing you for a fool, and all of Auckney knows it, Feri!" Priscilla screamed at her brother

"Don't call me that!" he snapped, pushing past her, looking for distraction from the subject. "You know I hate it."

Priscilla would not let it go. "Can you deny the stage of her pregnancy?" she pressed. "She will give birth within two weeks."

"The barbarian was a large man," Feringal growled. "The child will be large, and that is what is deceiving you."

"The child will be average," Priscilla retorted, "as you shall learn within the month." Her brother started to walk away. "I'll wager he'll be a pretty thing with the curly brown hair of his father." That brought Feringal spinning about, glaring at her. "His dead father," the woman finished, not backing down an inch.

Lord Feringal crossed the few feet separating them in one stride and slapped his sister hard across the face. Horrified by his own actions, he fell back, holding his face in his hands.

"My poor cuckolded brother," Priscilla replied to that slap, glaring at him above the hand she had brought to her bruise. "You will learn." With that, she stalked from the room.

Lord Feringal stood there, motionless for a long, long time, trying hard to steady his breathing.

*   *   *   *   *

Three days after their discussion, the weather had warmed enough to bring about a thaw, allowing Morik and Wulfgar to depart the village. The villagers were unhappy to see them go, especially because the thaw signaled the time of renewed monster attacks. The pair, particularly impatient Morik, would hear none of their pleas.

"Perhaps I will return to you," Wulfgar remarked, and he was thinking that he might indeed, once he and Morik had gone their own ways outside of Luskan. Where else might the barbarian go, after all?

The road out of the foothills was slow and so muddy and treacherous that the pair often had to walk, leading their horses carefully. Once the mountains gave way to the flatter plain just north of Luskan they found the going relatively easy.

"You still have the wagon and the supplies we left at the cave," Morik remarked.

Wulfgar realized the rogue was beginning to feel a pang of guilt about leaving him. "The cave did not remain empty throughout the winter I'm sure," the barbarian remarked. "Not so many supplies left, I would guess."

"Then take the belongings of the present occupants," Morik replied with a wink. "Giants, perhaps, nothing for Wulfgar to fear." That brought a smile to both their faces, but they didn't hold.

"You should have stayed in the village," Morik reasoned. "You can't go back to Luskan with me, so the village seems as good a place as any while you decide your course."

They'd come to a fork in the road. One path headed south to Luskan, the other to the west. When Morik turned to regard Wulfgar, he found the man staring out that second course, back toward the small fiefdom where he had been imprisoned, where Morik (to hear Morik tell it) had rescued him from a torturous death.

"Plotting revenge?" the rogue asked.

Wulfgar looked at him curiously, then caught on. "Hardly," he replied. "I am wondering the fate of the lady of the castle."

"The one who wrongly accused you of raping her?" Morik asked.

Wulfgar shrugged, as if not wanting to concede that point. "She was with child," he explained, "and very much afraid."

"You believe she cuckolded her husband?" Morik asked.

Wulfgar wrinkled his lips and nodded.

"So she offered your head to protect her reputation," Morik said derisively. "Typical noble lady."

Wulfgar didn't reply, but he wasn't seeing things quite that way. The barbarian understood that she had never intended for him to be caught, but rather, that he should remain a distant and mysterious solution to her personal problems. It was understandable, if not honorable.

"She must have had the babe by now," he mumbled to himself. "I wonder how she faired when they saw it and realized the child couldn't be mine."

Morik recognized Wulfgar's tone, and it worried him. "I'll not have to wonder your fate if you go back to determine hers," Morik dryly remarked. "You couldn't get into that town without being recognized."

Wulfgar nodded, not disagreeing, but he was smiling all the while, a look that was not lost on Morik. "But you could," he said.

Morik spent a long while studying his friend. "If my road was not Luskan," he replied.

"A road of your own making, and with no appointments needing prompt attention," said Wulfgar.

"Winter is not yet gone. We took a chance in coming down from the foothills. Another storm might descend at any time, burying us deep." Morik continued to protest, but Wulfgar could tell by the rogue's tone that he was considering it.

"The storms are not so bad south of the mountains."

Morik scoffed.

"This last favor?" Wulfgar asked.

"Why do you care?" Morik argued. "The woman nearly had you killed, and in a manner horrible enough to have satisfied the crowd at Prisoner's Carnival."

Wulfgar shrugged, not honestly sure of that answer himself, but he wasn't about to back down. "A last act of friendship between us two," he prodded, "that we might properly part in the hopes of seeing each other again."

Morik scoffed again. "One last fight with me at your side is all you're after," he said half humorously. "Admit it, you're nothing as a fighter without me!" Even Wulfgar had to laugh at Morik's irony, but he followed it up with a plaintive expression.

"Oh, lead on," Morik grumbled, conceding as Wulfgar knew he would. "I will play the part of Lord Brandeburg yet again. I only hope that Brandeburg was not connected with your escape and that our common departure times were seen by Feringal as pure coincidence."

"If captured, I will honestly tell Lord Feringal that you played no part in my escape," Wulfgar said, a crooked smile showing under his thick winter beard.

"You have no idea how the promise comforts me," Morik said wryly as he pushed his friend ahead of him toward the west, toward trouble in Auckney.

Chapter 25
Epiphany

Two days later, Morik's predicted snowstorm did come on, but its fury was somewhat tempered by the late season, leaving the road passable. The two riders plodded along, taking care to stay on the trail. They made good time, despite the foul weather, with Wulfgar driving them hard. Soon they came to a region of scattered farmhouses and stone cottages. Now the storm proved to be their ally, for few curious faces showed in the heavily curtained windows, and through the snow, wrapped in thick skins, the pair were hardly recognizable.

Soon after, Wulfgar waited in a sheltered overhang along the foothills, while Morik, Lord Brandeburg of Waterdeep, rode down into the village. The day turned late, the storm continued, but Morik didn't return. Wulfgar left his shelter to move to a vantage point that would afford him a view of Castle Auck. He wondered if Morik had been discovered. If so, should he rush down to find some way to aid his friend?

Wulfgar gave a chuckle. It was more likely that Morik had stayed on at the castle for a fine meal and was warming himself before the hearth at that very moment. The barbarian retreated again to his shelter to brush down his horse, telling himself to be patient.

Finally Morik did return, wearing a grim expression indeed. "I was not met with friendly hugs," he explained.

"Your disguise did not hold?"

"It's not that," said the rogue. "They thought me Lord Brandeburg, but just as I feared they considered it a bit odd that I disappeared at the same time you did."

Wulfgar nodded. They had discussed that very possibility. "Why did they let you leave if they were suspicious?"

"I convinced them it was but a coincidence," he reported, "else why would I return to Auckney? Of course, I had to share a large meal to persuade them."

"Of course," Wulfgar agreed archly, his tone dry. "What of Lady Meralda and her child? Did you see her?" the barbarian prompted.

Morik pulled the saddle from his horse and began brushing his own beast down, as if preparing again for the road. "It is time for us to be gone," he replied flatly. "Far from here."

"What news?" Wulfgar pressed, now truly concerned.

"We have no allies here, and no acquaintances even, in any mood to entertain visitors," Morik replied. "Better for all that Wulfgar, Morik, and Lord Brandeburg, put this wretched little pretend fiefdom far behind their horses' tails."

Wulfgar leaned over and grabbed the rogue's shoulder, roughly turning him from his work on the horse. "The Lady Meralda?" he demanded.

"She birthed a child late last night," Morik admitted reluctantly. Wulfgar's eyes grew wide with trepidation. "Both survived," Morik quickly added, "for now." Pulling away, the rogue went back to his work with renewed vigor.

Feeling Wulfgar's eyes on him expectantly, Morik sighed and turned back. "Look, she told them that you had ravished her," he reminded his friend. "It seems likely that she was covering an affair," Morik reasoned. "She lied, condemning you, to hide her own betrayal of the young lord." Again, the knowing nod, for this was no news to Wulfgar.

Morik looked at him hard, surprised that he was not shaken somewhat by the blunt expression of all that had occurred, surprised that he was showing no anger at all despite the fact that, because of the woman, he had been beaten and nearly brutally executed.

"Well, now there is doubt concerning the heritage of the child," Morik explained. "The birth was too soon, considering our encounter with the girl on the road, and there are those within the village and castle who do not believe her tale."

Wulfgar gave a profound sigh. "I suspected as much would happen."

"I heard some talk of a young man who fell to his death on the day of the wedding between Lord Feringal and Meralda, a man who died crying out for her."

"Lord Feringal believes he's the one who cuckolded him?" Wulfgar asked.

"Not specifically," Morik replied. "Since the child was surely conceived before the wedding—even if it had been your child, that would have been so—but he knows, of course, that his wife once lay with another, and now he may be thinking that it was of her own volition and not something forced upon her on a wild road."

"A ravished woman is without blame," Wulfgar put in, for it all made sense.

"While a cheating woman. . . ." Morik added ominously.

Wulfgar gave another sigh and walked out of the shelter, staring again at the castle. "What will happen to her?" he called back to Morik.

"The marriage will be declared invalid, surely," Morik answered, having lived in human cities long enough to understand such things.

"And the Lady Meralda will be sent from the castle," the barbarian said hopefully.

"If she's fortunate, she'll be banished from Feringal Auck's domain with neither money nor title," Morik replied.

"And if she's *un*fortunate?" Wulfgar asked.

Morik winced. "Noblemen's wives have been put to death for such offenses," the worldly rogue replied.

"What of the child?" an increasingly agitated Wulfgar demanded. The images of his own horrible past experiences began edging in at the corners of his consciousness.

"If fortunate, banished," Morik replied, "though I fear such an action will take more good fortune than the banishment of the woman. It is very complicated. The child is a threat to Auck's domain, but also to his pride."

"They would kill a child, a helpless babe?" Wulfgar asked, his teeth clenched tightly as those awful memories began to creep ever closer.

"The rage of a betrayed lord cannot be underestimated," Morik answered grimly. "Lord Feringal cannot show weakness, else risk the loss of the respect of his people and the loss of his lands. Complicated and unpleasant business, all. Now let us be gone from this place."

Wulfgar was indeed gone, storming out from under the overhang and stalking down the trails. Morik was quick to catch him.

"What will you do?" the rogue demanded, recognizing Wulfgar's resolve.

"I don't know, but I've got to do something," Wulfgar said, increasing his pace with the level of his agitation while Morik struggled to keep up. As they entered the village, the storm again proved an ally, for no peasants were about. Wulfgar's eyes were set on the bridge leading to Castle Auck.

* * * * *

"Give the child away, as you planned," Steward Temigast suggested to the pacing Lord Feringal.

"It is different now," the young man stammered, slapping his fists helplessly at his sides. He glanced over at Priscilla. His sister was sitting comfortably, her smug smile a reminder that she'd warned him against marrying a peasant in the first place.

"We don't know that anything has changed," Temigast said, always the voice of reason.

Priscilla snorted. "Can you not count?" she asked.

"The child could be early," Temigast protested.

"As well-formed a babe as ever I've seen," said Priscilla. "She was not early, Temigast, and you know it." Priscilla looked straight at her brother, reiterating the talk that had been buzzing about Castle Auck all day. "The child was conceived mid-summer," she said, "before the supposed attack on the road."

"How can I know for sure?" Lord Feringal wailed. His hands tore at the sides of his pants, an accurate reflection of the rending going on inside his mind.

"How can you not know?" Priscilla shot back. "You've been made a fool to the mirth of all the village. Will you compound that now with weakness?"

"You still love her," Steward Temigast cut in.

"Do I?" Lord Feringal said, so obviously torn and confused. "I don't know anymore."

"Send her away, then," the steward offered. "Banish her with the child."

"That would make the villagers laugh all the harder," Priscilla observed sourly. "Do you want the child to return in a score of years and take your kingdom from you? How many times have we heard of such tales?"

Temigast glared at the woman. Such things had occurred, but they were far from common.

"What am I to do, then?" Lord Feringal demanded of his sister.

"A trial of treason for the whore," Priscilla answered matter-of-factly, "and a swift and just removal of the result of her infidelity."

"Removal?" Feringal echoed skeptically.

"She wants you to kill the child," Temigast explained archly.

"Throw it to the waves," Priscilla supplied feverishly, coming right out of her chair. "If you show no weakness now, the folk will still respect you."

"They will hate you more if you murder an innocent child," Temigast said angrily, more to Priscilla than Lord Feringal.

"Innocent?" Priscilla balked as if the notion were preposterous.

"Let them hate you," she said to Lord Feringal, moving her face to within an inch of his. "Better that than to laugh at you. Would you suffer the bastard to live? A reminder, then, of he who lay with Meralda before you?"

"Shut your mouth!" Lord Feringal demanded, pushing her back.

Priscilla didn't back down. "Oh, but how she purred in the arms of Jaka Sculi," she said, and her brother was trembling so much that he couldn't even speak through his grinding teeth. "I'll wager she arched that pretty back of hers for him," Priscilla finished lewdly.

Feral, sputtering sounds escaped the young lord. He grabbed his sister by the shoulders with both hands and flung her aside. She was smiling the whole time, satisfied, for the enraged lord shoved past Temigast and ran for the stairs. The stairs that led to Meralda and her bastard child.

* * * * *

"It's guarded, you know," Morik reminded him, yelling though his voice sounded thin in the howling wind.

Wulfgar wouldn't have heeded the warning anyway. His eyes were set on Castle Auck, and his line to the bridge didn't waver. He pictured the mounds of snow as the Spine of the World, as that barrier between the man he had been and the victim he had become. Now, his mind free at last of all influence of potent liquor, his strength of will granting him armor against those awful images of his imprisonment, Wulfgar saw the choices clearly before him. He could turn back to the life he had found or he could press on, could cross that emotional barrier, could fight and claw his way back to the man he once was.

The barbarian growled and pressed on against the storm. He even picked up speed as he reached the bridge, a fast walk, a trot, then a full run as he picked his course, veering to the right, where the snow had drifted along the railing and the castle's front wall. Up the drift Wulfgar went, crunching into snow past his knees, but growling and plowing on, maintaining his momentum. He leaped from the top of the drift, reaching with an outstretched arm to hook his hammer's head atop the wall. Wulfgar heard a startled call from above as it caught loudly against the stone, but he hardly slowed, great muscles cording and tugging, propelling him upward, where he rolled around, slipping right over the crenelated barrier. He landed nimbly on his feet on the parapet within, right between two dumbfounded guards, neither of them holding a weapon as they tried to keep their hands warm.

Morik rushed up the same path as Wulfgar, using agile moves to scale the wall nearly as fast as his friend had done with brute strength. Still, by the time he got to the parapet Wulfgar was already down in the courtyard, storming for the main keep. Both guards were down, too, lying on the ground and groaning, one holding his jaw, the other curled up and clutching his belly.

"Secure the door!" one of the guards managed to cry out.

The main door cracked open then, a man peeking out. Seeing Wulfgar bearing in, he tried to close it fast. Wulfgar got there just before it slammed, pushing back with all his strength. He heard the man calling frantically for help, felt the greater push as another guard joined the first, both leaning heavily.

"I'm coming, too," Morik called, "though only the gods know why!"

His thoughts far away, in a dark and smoky place where his child's last terrified cry rent the air, Wulfgar didn't hear his friend, didn't need him. Bellowing, he shoved with all his strength until the door flew in, tossing the two guards like children against the back wall of the foyer.

"Where is she?" Wulfgar demanded, and even as he spoke the foyer's other door swung open. Liam Woodgate appeared, rushing in with sword in hand.

"Now you pay, dog!" the coachman cried, coming in fast and hard, stabbing, a feint. Pulling the blade back in, he sent it into a sudden twirl, then feigned a sidelong slice, turning it over again and coming straight in with a deadly thrust.

Liam was good, the best fighter in all of Auckney, and he knew it. That's why it was difficult to understand how Wulfgar's hammer came out so fast to hook over Liam's blade and take it safely wide of the mark. How could the huge barbarian turn so nimbly on his feet to get within reach of Liam's sword? How was he able to come around perfectly, sending his thick arm spiking up under Liam's sword arm? Liam knew his own skill, and so it was even harder for him to understand how his clever attack had been turned against him so completely. Liam knew only that his face was suddenly pressed against the stone wall, his arms pulled tight behind his back, and the snarling barbarian's breath was on his neck.

"Lady Meralda and the child," Wulfgar asked. "Where are they?"

"I'd die afore I'd tell you!" Liam declared. Wulfgar pressed in. The poor old gnome thought he surely *would* die, but Liam held his determined tongue and growled against the pain.

Wulfgar spun him around and slammed him once, then slammed him again when he managed somehow to hold his feet, launching him over to the floor. Liam nearly tripped up Morik, who skipped right on by through the other door and into the castle proper.

Wulfgar was right behind him. They heard voices, and Morik led the way, crashing through a set of double doors and into a comfortable sitting room.

"Lord Brandeburg?" Lady Priscilla asked.

She squealed in fright and fell back in her chair as Wulfgar followed the rogue into the room. "Where is Lady Meralda and the child?" he roared.

"Haven't you caused enough harm?" Steward Temigast demanded, moving to stand boldly before the huge man.

Wulfgar looked him right in the eye. "Too much," he admitted, "but none here."

That set Temigast back on his heels.

"Where are they?" Wulfgar demanded, rushing up to Priscilla.

"Thieves! Murderers!" Priscilla cried, swooning.

Wulfgar locked stares with Temigast. To Wulfgar's surprise, the old steward nodded and motioned toward the staircase.

Even as he did, Priscilla Auck ran full-out up the staircase.

* * * * *

"Do you have any idea what you've done to me?" Feringal asked Meralda, standing by the edge of her bed, the infant girl lying warm beside her. "To us? To Auckney?"

"I beg you to try to understand, my lord," the woman pleaded.

Feringal winced, pounding his fists into his eyes. His visage steeled, and he reached down and plucked the babe from her side. Meralda started up toward him, but she hadn't the strength and fell back on the bed. "What're you about?"

Feringal strode over to the window and pulled the curtain aside. "My sister says I should toss it to the waves upon the rocks," he said through teeth locked in a tight grimace, "to rid myself of the evidence of your betrayal."

"Please, Feringal, do not—" Meralda began.

"It's what they're all saying, you know," Feringal said as if she hadn't spoken. He blinked his eyes and wiped his nose with his sleeve. "The child of Jaka Sculi."

"My lord!" she cried, her red-rimmed eyes fearful.

"How could you?" Feringal yelled, then looked from the baby in his hands to the open window. Meralda started to cry.

"The cuckold, and now the murderer," Feringal muttered to himself as he moved closer to the window. "You have damned me, Meralda!" he cursed. Holding out his arms, he moved the crying baby to the opening, then he looked down at the innocent little girl and pulled her back close, his tears mixing with the baby's. "Damned me, I say!" he cried, and the breath came in labored, forced gasps.

Suddenly the door to the room flew open, and Lady Priscilla burst in. She slammed it shut and secured the bolt behind her. Surveying the scene quickly, she ran to her brother, her voice shrill. "Give it to me!"

Lord Feringal rolled his shoulder between the child and Priscilla's grasping hands.

"Give it to me!" the woman shrieked again, and a tussle for the baby ensued.

* * * * *

Wulfgar went in fast pursuit, taking the curving staircase four steps at a stride. He came to a long hallway lined with rich tapestries where he ran into yet another bumbling castle guard. The barbarian slapped the prone man's sword away, caught him by the throat, and lifted him into the air.

Morik skittered past him, going from door to door, ear cocked, then he stopped abruptly at one. "They're in here," he announced. He grabbed the handle only to find it locked.

"The key?" Wulfgar demanded, giving the guard a shake.

The man grabbed the barbarian's iron arm. "No key," he gasped breathlessly. Wulfgar looked about to strangle him, but the thief intervened.

"Don't bother, I'll pick the lock," he said, going fast to his belt pouch.

"Don't bother, I have a key," Wulfgar cried. Morik looked up to see the barbarian bearing down on him, the guard still dangling at the end of one arm. Seeing his intent, Morik skittered out of the way as Wulfgar hurled the hapless man through the wooden door. "A key," the barbarian explained.

"Well thrown," Morik commented.

"I have had practice," explained Wulfgar, thundering past the dazed guard to leap into the room.

Meralda sat up on the bed, sobbing, while Lord Feringal and his sister stood by the open window, the babe in Feringal's arms. He was leaning toward the opening as if he meant to throw the child out. Both siblings and Meralda turned stunned expressions Wulfgar's way, and their eyes widened even more when Morik crashed in behind the barbarian.

"Lord Brandeburg!" Feringal cried.

Lady Priscilla shouted at her brother, "Do it now, before they ruin every—"

"The child is mine!" Wulfgar declared. Priscilla bit off the end of her sentence in surprise. Feringal froze as if turned to stone.

"What?" the young lord gasped.

"What?" Lady Priscilla gasped.

"What?" gasped Morik, at the same time.

"What?" gasped Meralda, quietly, and she coughed quickly to cover her surprise.

"The child is mine," Wulfgar repeated firmly, "and if you throw her out the window, then you shall follow so quickly that you'll pass her by and your broken body will pad her fall."

"You are so eloquent in emergencies," Morik remarked. To Lord Feringal, he added, "The window is small, yes, but I'll wager that my big friend can squeeze you through it. And your plump sister, as well."

"You can't be the father," Lord Feringal declared, trembling so violently that it seemed as if his legs would just buckle beneath him. He looked to Priscilla for an answer, to his sister who was always hovering above him with all of the answers. "What trick is this?"

"Give it to me!" Priscilla demanded. Taking advantage of her brother's paralyzing confusion, she moved quickly and tore the child from Feringal's grasp. Meralda cried out, the baby cried, and Wulfgar started forward, knowing that he could never get there in time, knowing that the innocent was surely doomed.

Even as Priscilla turned for the window, her brother leaped before her and slugged her in the face. Stunned, she staggered back a step. Feringal snatched the child from her arms and shoved her again, sending his sister stumbling to the floor.

Wulfgar eyed the man for a long and telling moment, understanding then beyond any doubt that despite his obvious anger and revulsion, Feringal would not hurt the child. The barbarian strode across the room, secure in his observations, confident that the young man would take no action against the babe.

"The child is mine," the barbarian said with a growl, reaching over to gently pull the wailing baby from Feringal's weakening grasp. "I meant to wait another month before returning," he explained, turning to face Meralda. "But it's good you delivered early. A child of mine come to full term would likely have killed you in birthing."

"Wulfgar!" Morik cried suddenly.

Lord Feringal, apparently recovering some of his nerve and most of his rage, produced a dagger from his belt and came in hard at the barbarian. Morik needn't have worried, though, for Wulfgar heard the movement. Lifting the babe high with one arm to keep her from harm's way, he spun and slapped the dagger aside with his free hand. As Feringal came in close, Wulfgar brought his knee up hard into the man's groin. Down Lord Feringal went, curling into a mewling heap on the floor.

"I think my large friend can make it so that you never have children of your own," Morik remarked with a wink to Meralda.

Meralda didn't even hear the words, staring dumbfounded at Wulfgar, at the child he had proclaimed as his own.

"For my actions on the road, I truly apologize, Lady Meralda," the barbarian said, and he was playing to a full audience now, as Liam Woodgate, Steward Temigast and the remaining half dozen castle guards appeared at the door, staring in wide-eyed disbelief. On the floor before Wulfgar, Lady Priscilla looked up at him, confusion and unbridled anger simmering in her eyes.

"It was the bottle and your beauty that took me," Wulfgar explained. He turned his attention to the child, his smile wide as he lifted the infant girl into the air for his sparkling blue eyes to behold. "But I'll not apologize for the result of that crime," he said. "Never that."

"I will kill you," Lord Feringal growled, struggling to his knees.

Wulfgar reached down with one hand and grabbed him by the collar. Helping him up with a powerful jerk, he spun the lord around into a choke hold. "You will forget me, and the child," Wulfgar whispered into his ear. "Else the combined tribes of Icewind Dale will sack you and your wretched little village."

Wulfgar pushed the young lord, spinning him into Morik's waiting grasp. Staring at Liam and the other dangerous guards, the rogue wasted no time in putting a sharp dagger to the man's throat.

"Secure us supplies for the road," Wulfgar instructed. "We need wrappings and food for the babe." Everyone in the room, save Wulfgar and the baby, wore incredulous expressions. "Do it!" the barbarian roared. Frowning, Morik pushed toward the door with Lord Feringal, waving a scrambling Priscilla out ahead of him.

"Fetch!" the rogue instructed Liam and Priscilla. He glanced back and saw Wulfgar moving toward Meralda then, so he pushed out even further, backing them all away.

"What made you do such a thing?" Meralda asked when she was alone with Wulfgar and the child.

"Your problem was not hard to discern," Wulfgar explained.

"I falsely accused you."

"Understandably so," Wulfgar replied. "You were trapped and scared, but in the end you risked everything to free me from prison. I could not let that deed go unpaid."

Meralda shook her head, too overwhelmed to even begin to sort this out. So many thoughts and emotions whirled in her mind. She had seen the look of despair on Feringal's face, had thought he would, indeed, drop the baby to the rocks. Yet, in the end he hadn't been able to do it, hadn't let his sister do it. She did love this man—how could she not? And yet, she could hardly deny her unexpected feelings for her child, though she knew that never, ever, could she keep her.

"I am taking the babe far from here," Wulfgar said determinedly, as if he had read her mind. "You are welcome to come with us."

Meralda laughed softly, without humor, because she knew she would be crying soon enough. "I can't," she explained, her voice a whisper. "I've a duty to my husband, if he'll still have me, and to my family. My folks would be branded if I went with you."

"Duty? Is that the only reason you're staying?" Wulfgar asked her, apparently sensing something more.

"I love him, you know," Meralda replied, tears streaming down her beautiful face. "I know what you must think of me, but truly, the babe was made before I ever—"

Wulfgar held up his hand. "You owe me no explanation," he said, "for I am hardly in a position to judge you or anyone else. I came to understand your . . . problem, and so I returned to repay your generosity, that is all." He looked to the door through which Morik held Lord Feringal. "He does love you," he said. "His eyes and the depth of his pain showed that clearly."

"You think I'm right in staying?"

Wulfgar shrugged, again refusing to offer any judgments.

"I can't leave him," Meralda said, and she reached up and tenderly stroked the child's face, "but I cannot keep her, either. Feringal would never accept her," she admitted, her tone empty and hollow, for she realized her time with her daughter was nearing its end. "But perhaps he'd give her over to another family in Auckney now that he's thinking I didn't betray him," she suggested faintly.

"A reminder to him of his pain, and to you of your lie," Wulfgar said softly, not accusing the woman, but surely reminding her of the truth. "And within the reach of his shrewish sister."

Meralda lowered her gaze and accepted the bitter truth. The baby was not safe in Auckney.

"Who better to raise her than me?" Wulfgar asked suddenly, resolve in his voice. He looked down at the little girl, and his mouth turned up into a warm smile.

"You'd do that?"

Wulfgar nodded. "Happily."

"You'd keep her safe?" Meralda pressed. "Tell her of her ma?"

Wulfgar nodded. "I don't know where my road now leads," he explained, "but I suspect I'll not venture too far from here. Perhaps someday I will return, or at least she will, to glimpse her ma."

Meralda was shaking with sobs, her face gleaming with tears. Wulfgar glanced to the doorway to make sure that he was not being watched, then bent down and kissed her on the cheek. "I think it best," he said quietly. "Do you agree?"

After she studied the man for a moment, this man who had risked everything to save her and her child though they had done nothing to deserve his heroism, Meralda nodded.

The tears continued to flow freely. Wulfgar could appreciate the pain she was feeling, the depth of her sacrifice. He leaned in, allowing Meralda to stroke and kiss her baby girl one last time, but when she moved to take her away, Wulfgar pulled back. Meralda's smile of understanding was bittersweet.

"Fairwell, little one," she said through her sobs and looked away. Wulfgar bowed to Meralda one last time, then, with the baby cradled in his big arms, he turned and left the room.

He found Morik in the hallway, barking commands for plenty of food and clothing—and gold, for they'd need gold to properly situate the child in warm and comfortable inns. Barbarian, baby, and thief, made their way through the castle, and no one made a move to stop them. It seemed as if Lord Feringal had cleared their path, wanting the two thieves and the bastard child out of his castle and out of his life as swiftly as possible.

Priscilla, however, was a different issue. They ran into her on the first floor, where she came up to Wulfgar and tried to take the baby, glaring at him defiantly all the while. The barbarian held her at bay, his expression making it clear that he would break her in half if she tried to harm the child. Priscilla huffed her disgust, threw a thick wool wrap at him, and with a final growl of protest, turned on her heel.

"Stupid cow," Morik muttered under his breath.

Chuckling, Wulfgar tenderly wrapped the baby in the warm blanket, finally silencing her crying. Outside, the daylight was fast on the wane, but the storm had faded, the last clouds breaking apart and rushing across the sky on swift winds. The gate was lowered. Across the bridge they saw Steward Temigast waiting for them with a pair of horses, Lord Feringal at his side.

Feringal stood staring at Wulfgar and the baby for a long moment. "If you ever come back . . ." he started to say.

"Why would I?" the barbarian interrupted. "I have my child now, and she will grow up to be a queen in Icewind Dale. Entertain no thoughts of coming after me, Lord Feringal, to the ruin of all your world."

"Why would I?" Feringal returned in the same grim tone, facing up to Wulfgar boldly. "I have my wife, my beautiful wife. My innocent wife, who gives herself to me willingly. I do not have to force myself upon her."

That last statement, a recapture of some measure of manly pride, told Wulfgar that Feringal had forgiven Meralda, or that he soon enough would. Wulfgar's desperate, unconsidered and purely improvised plan had somehow, miraculously, worked. He bit back any semblance of a chuckle at the ridiculousness of it all, let Feringal have his needed moment. He didn't even blink as the lord of Auckney composed himself, squared his shoulders, and walked back across the bridge through the lowered gate to his home and his wife.

Steward Temigast handed the reins to the pair. "She isn't yours," the steward said unexpectedly. Starting to pull himself and the babe up into the saddle, Wulfgar pretended not to hear him.

"Fear not, for I'll not tell, nor will Meralda, whose life you have truly saved this day," the steward went on. "You are a fine man, Wulfgar, son of Beornegar, of the Tribe of the Elk of Icewind Dale." Wulfgar blinked in amazement, both at the compliment and at the simple fact that the man knew so much of him.

"The wizard who caught you told him," Morik reasoned. "I hate wizards."

"There will be no pursuit," said Temigast. "On my word."

And that word held true, for Morik and Wulfgar rode without incident back to the overhang, where they retrieved their own horses, then continued down the east road and out of Auckney for good.

"What is it?" Wulfgar asked Morik later that night, seeing the rogue's amused expression. They were huddled about a blazing fire, keeping the child warm. Morik smiled and held up a pair of bottles, one with warm goat's milk for the child, the other with their favored potent drink. Wulfgar took the one with the goat's milk.

"I will never understand you, my friend," Morik remarked.

Wulfgar smiled, but did not respond. Morik could never truly know of Wulfgar's past, of the good times with Drizzt and the others, and of the very worst times with Errtu and the offspring of his stolen seed.

"There are easier ways to make gold," Morik remarked, and that brought Wulfgar's steely gaze over him. "You mean to sell the child, of course," Morik reasoned.

Wulfgar scoffed.

"A fine price," Morik argued, taking a healthy swig from the bottle.

"Not fine enough," said Wulfgar, turning back to the babe. The little girl wriggled and cooed.

"You cannot plan to keep her!" Morik argued. "What place has she with us? With you, wherever you plan to go? Have you lost all sensibility?"

Scowling, Wulfgar spun on him, slapped the bottle from his hands, then shoved him back to the ground, as determined an answer as Morik the Rogue had ever heard.

"She's not even yours!" Morik reminded him.

The rogue could not have been more wrong.

Epilogue

Morik looked at Wulfgar's disguise one more time and sighed help-lessly. There was only so much one could do to change the appearance of a nearly seven-foot-tall, three hundred pound, blond-haired barbarian.

Wulfgar was clean shaven again for the first time since his return from the Abyss. Morik had taught him to walk in a way that would some-what lessen his height, with shoulders drooped but arms crooked so that they did not hang to his knees. Also, Morik had procured a large brown robe such as a priest might wear, with a bunched collar that allowed Wulfgar to scrunch down his neck without being obvious about it.

Still, the rogue was not entirely happy with the disguise, not when so much was riding on it. "You should wait out here," he offered, for perhaps the tenth time since Wulfgar had told him his wishes.

"No," Wulfgar said evenly. "They would not come at your word alone. This is something I must do."

"Get us both killed?" the rogue asked sarcastically.

"Lead on," Wulfgar said, ignoring him. When Morik tried to argue, the barbarian slapped a hand over the smaller man's mouth and turned him around to face the distant city gate.

With one last sigh and a shake of his head, Morik led the way back into Luskan. To the great relief of both of them, for Wulfgar surely did not wish to be discovered while carrying the baby, they were not recognized, were not detained at all, but merely strode into the city where the spring festival was on in full.

They had come in late in the day by design. Wulfgar went straight to Half-Moon Street, arriving at the Cutlass as one of the evening's first patrons. He moved to the bar, right beside Josi Puddles.

"What're ye drinking?" Arumn Gardpeck asked, but the question caught in his throat and his eyes went wide as he looked more carefully at the big man. "Wulfgar," he gasped.

Behind the barbarian a tray dropped, and Wulfgar turned to see Delly Curtie standing there, stunned. Josi Puddles gave a squeal and leaned away.

"Well met, Arumn," Wulfgar said to the tavernkeeper. "I drink only water."

"What're ye doing here?" the tavernkeeper gasped, suspicious and more than a little fearful.

Josi hopped off his stool and started for the door, but Wulfgar caught him by the arm and held him in place. "I came to apologize," the barbarian offered. "To you, and to you," he added, turning to Josi.

"Ye tried to kill me," Josi sputtered.

"I was blind with anger, and likely drink," Wulfgar replied.

"He took yer hammer," Arumn reminded.

"Out of rightful fear that I would use it against you," the barbarian answered. "He acted as a friend, which is much more than I can say for Wulfgar."

Arumn shook his head, hardly believing any of this. Wulfgar released Josi, but the man made no move to continue for the door, just stood there, dumbfounded.

"You took me in, gave me food, a paying job, and friendship when I needed it most," Wulfgar continued to Arumn alone. "I wronged you, terribly so, and can only hope that you will find it in your heart to forgive me."

"Are ye looking to live here again?" Arumn asked.

Wulfgar smiled sadly and shook his head. "I risk my life by even entering the city," he replied. "I'll be gone within the hour, but I had to come, to apologize to you two, and mostly," he turned about, facing Delly, "to you."

Delly Curtie blanched as Wulfgar approached, as if she didn't know how to react to the man's words, to the mere sight of him again.

"I am most humbly sorry for any pain that I ever caused you, Delly," he said. "You were as true a friend as any man could ever have desired."

"More than a friend," Wulfgar quickly added, seeing her frown.

Delly eyed the bundle in his arms. "Ye've a little one," the woman said, her voice thick with emotion.

568

"Mine by chance and not by heritage," Wulfgar replied. He handed the little girl over to her. Delly took her, smiling tenderly, playing with the child's fingers and bringing a smile to that innocent little face.

"I wish ye might be stayin' again," Arumn offered, and he sounded sincere, though Josi's eyes widened in doubt at the mere mention.

"I cannot," Wulfgar replied. Smiling at Delly, he leaned over and took the babe back, then kissed Delly on the forehead. "I pray you find all the happiness you deserve, Delly Curtie," he said, and with a look and a nod at Arumn and Josi, he started for the door.

Delly, too, looked hard at Arumn, so much her father. The man understood and nodded once again. She caught up to Wulfgar before he reached the exit.

"Take me with ye," she said, her eyes sparkling with hope—something few had seen from the woman in a long, long time.

Wulfgar looked puzzled. "I did not return to rescue you," he explained.

"Rescue?" Delly echoed incredulously. "I'm not needin' yer rescue, thank ye very much, but you're needin' help with the little one, I can see. I'm good with tykes—spent most o' me young life raisin' me brothers and sisters—and I've grown more than a bit bored with me life here."

"I don't know where my road shall lead," Wulfgar argued.

"Safe enough, I'm guessing," Delly replied. "Since ye've the little one to care for, I mean."

"Waterdeep, perhaps," said Wulfgar.

"A place I've always wanted to see," she said, her smile growing with every word, for it seemed obvious that Wulfgar was becoming more than a little intrigued by her offer.

The barbarian looked curiously to Arumn, and the tavernkeeper nodded his head yet again. Even from that distance Wulfgar could see a bit of moisture rimming the man's eyes.

He gave the child back to Delly, bade her wait there, and moved back to the bar with Arumn and Josi. "I'll not hurt her ever again," Wulfgar promised Arumn.

"If ye do, I'll hunt ye down and kill ye," Josi growled.

Wulfgar and Arumn looked at the man, Arumn doubtfully, but Wulfgar working hard to keep his expression serious. "I know that, Josi Puddles," he replied without sarcasm, "and your wrath is something I would truly fear."

When he got past his own surprise, Josi puffed up his little chest with pride. Wulfgar and Arumn exchanged stares.

"No drinking?" Arumn asked.

Wulfgar shook his head. "I needed the bottle to hide in," he answered honestly, "but I have learned it to be worse than what haunts me."

"And if ye get bored with the girl?"

"I didn't come here for Delly Curtie," Wulfgar replied. "Only to apologize. I didn't think she would accept my apology so completely, but glad

569

I am that she did. We'll find a good road to travel, and I'll protect her as best I can, from myself most of all."

"See that ye do," Arumn replied. "I'll expect ye back."

Wulfgar shook Arumn's hand, patted Josi on the shoulder, and moved to take Delly's arm, leading her out of the Cutlass. Together they walked away from a significant part of their lives.

*　*　*　*　*

Lord Feringal and Meralda walked along the garden, hand in hand, enjoying the springtime fragrance and beauty. Wulfgar's ploy had worked. Feringal and all the fiefdom believed Meralda the wronged party again, freeing her from blame and the young lord from ridicule.

Truly the woman felt pain at the loss of her child, but it, like her marriage, seemed well on the mend. She kept telling herself over and over that the babe was with a good and strong man, a better father than Jaka could ever have been. Many were the times Meralda cried for the lost child, but always she repeated her logical litany and remembered that her life, given her mistakes and station by birth, was better by far than she could ever have imagined. Her mother and father were healthy, and Tori visited her every day, bobbing happily among the flowers and proving more of a thorn to Priscilla than Meralda had ever been.

Now the couple was simply enjoying the splendor of spring, the woman adjusting to her new life. Feringal snapped his fingers suddenly and pulled away. Meralda regarded him curiously.

"I have forgotten something," her husband replied. Feringal motioned for her to wait, then ran back into the castle, nearly running down Priscilla, who was coming out the garden door.

Of course, Priscilla still didn't believe any of Wulfgar's tale. She scowled at Meralda, but the younger woman just turned away and moved to the wall, staring out over the waves.

"Watching for your next lover to arrive?" Priscilla muttered under her breath as she moved by. She often launched verbal jabs Meralda's way, and Meralda often just let them slide down her shoulders.

Not this time, though. Meralda stepped in front of her sister-in-law, hands on her hips. "You've never felt an honest emotion in your miserable life, Priscilla Auck, which is why you're so bitter." she said. "Judge me not."

Priscilla's eyes widened with shock and she trembled, unused to being spoken to in such a forward manner. "You ask—"

"I'm not asking you, I'm telling you," Meralda said curtly.

Priscilla stood up and grimaced, then slapped Meralda across the face.

Feeling the sting, Meralda slapped her back harder. "Judge me not, or I'll whisper the truth of your wretchedness into your brother's ear," Meralda warned, so calm and calculating that her words alone made

Priscilla's face burn hot. "You can't doubt that I have his ear," Meralda finished. "Have you thought of what a life in the village among the peasants might be like for you?"

Even as she finished her husband bounded back out, a huge bouquet of flowers in his hand, flowers for his dear Meralda. Priscilla took one look at her fawning brother, gave a great cry, and ran into the castle.

Feringal watched her go, confused, but so little did he care what Priscilla thought or felt these days that he didn't even bother to ask Meralda about it.

Meralda, too, watched the wretched woman depart. Her smile was wrought from more than delight at her husband's thoughtful present. Much more.

* * * * *

Morik said his farewells to Wulfgar and to Delly, then began at once to reestablish himself on Luskan's streets. He took a room at an inn on Half-Moon Street but spent little time there, for he was out working hard, telling the truth of his identity to those who needed to know, establishing a reputation as a completely different man, Burglar Brandeburg, to those who did not.

By the end of the week many nodded in deference as he passed them on the streets. By the end of the month, the rogue no longer feared retribution from the authorities. He was home again, and soon things would be as they had been before Wulfgar had ever come to Luskan.

He was leaving his room one night with just that in mind when he stepped out of his bedroom door into the inn's upper hallway. Instead he found himself sliding through a dizzying tunnel, coming to rest in a crystalline room whose circular walls gave the appearance of one level in a tower.

Dazed, Morik started to reach for his dagger, but he saw the ebon-skinned forms and changed his mind, wise enough not to resist the dark elves.

"You know me, Morik," said Kimmuriel Oblodra, moving close to the man.

Morik did, indeed, recognize the drow as the messenger who had come to him a year before, bidding him to keep a watch over Wulfgar.

"I give you my friend, Rai-gy," Kimmuriel said politely, indicating the other dark elf in the room, one wearing a sinister expression.

"Did we not ask you to watch over the one named Wulfgar?" Kimmuriel asked.

Morik stuttered, not knowing what to say.

"And have you not failed us?" Kimmuriel went on.

"But . . . but that was a year ago," Morik protested. "I have heard nothing since."

"Now you are in hiding, in disguise, knowing your crime against us," said Kimmuriel.

"My supposed crimes are of another matter," Morik stuttered, feeling as if the very walls were tightening around him. "I hide from the Luskan authorities, not from you."

"From them you hide?" said the other drow. "Help you, I can!" He strode over to Morik and lifted his hands. Sheets of flame erupted from his fingertips, burning Morik's face and lighting his hair on fire. The rogue howled and fell to the floor, slapping at his singed skin.

"Now you appear different," Kimmuriel remarked, and both dark elves chuckled wickedly. They dragged him up the tower stairs into another room, where a bald-headed drow holding a great plumed purple hat sat comfortably in a chair.

"My apologies, Morik," he said. "My lieutenants are an excitable lot."

"I was with Wulfgar for months," Morik claimed, obviously on the edge of hysteria. "Circumstance forced us apart and forced him from Luskan. I can find him for you—"

"No need," said the drow in the chair, holding up his hand to calm the groveling man. "I am Jarlaxle, of Menzoberranzan, and I forgive you in full."

Morik rubbed one hand over what was left of his hair, as if to say that he wished Jarlaxle had been so beneficent earlier.

"I had planned for Wulfgar to be my primary trading partner in Luskan, my representative here." Jarlaxle explained. "Now, with him gone, I ask you to assume the role."

Morik blinked, and his heart skipped a beat.

"We will make you wealthy and powerful beyond your dreams," the mercenary leader explained, and Morik believed him. "You'll not need to hide from the authorities. Indeed, many will invite you to their homes almost daily, for they will desperately want to remain in good standing with you. If there are any you wish . . . eliminated, that, too, can be easily arranged."

Morik licked what was left of his lips.

"Does this sound like a position Morik the Rogue would be interested in pursuing?" Jarlaxle asked, and Morik returned the dark elf's sly look tenfold.

"I warn you," Jarlaxle said, coming forward in his chair, his dark eyes flashing, "if you ever fail me, my friend Rai-gy will willingly alter your appearance yet again."

"And again," the wizard happily added.

"I hate wizards," Morik muttered under his breath.

*   *   *   *   *

Wulfgar and Delly looked down on Waterdeep, the City of Splendors. The most wondrous and powerful city on the Sword Coast, it was a place of great dreams and greater power.

572

"Where are ye thinkin' we'll be staying?" the happy woman asked, gently rocking the child.

Wulfgar shook his head. "I have coins," he replied, "but I don't know how long we'll remain in Waterdeep."

"Ye're not thinkin' to make our lives here?"

The barbarian shrugged, for he hadn't given it much thought. He had come to Waterdeep with another purpose. He hoped to find Captain Deudermont and *Sea Sprite* in port, or hoped that they would come in soon, as they often did.

"Have you ever been to sea?" he asked the woman, his best friend and partner now, with a wide smile.

It was time for him to get Aegis-fang back.

SERVANT OF THE SHARD

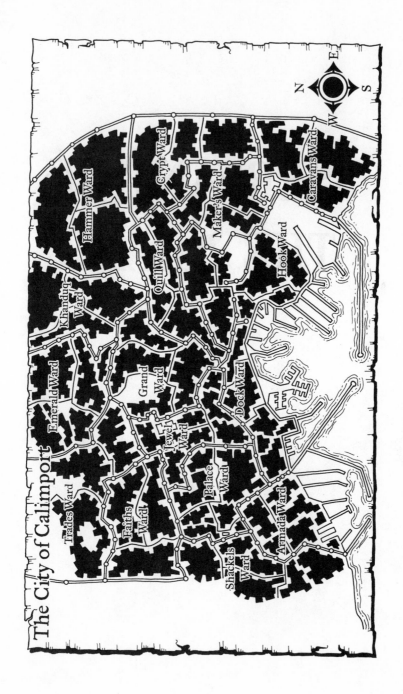

The City of Calimport

N E W S

Hammer Ward

Grypt Ward

Maker's Ward

Caravans Ward

Quill Ward

Hook Ward

Khandhq Ward

Emerald Ward

Grand Ward

Dock Ward

Jewel Ward

Trades Ward

Faiths Ward

Palace Ward

Shackels Ward

Armada Ward

Prologue

He glided through the noonday sunshine's oppressive heat, moving as if always cloaked in shadows, though the place had few, and as if even the ever-present dust could not touch him. The open market was crowded—it was always crowded—with yelling merchants and customers bargaining for every copper piece. Thieves were positioning themselves in all the best and busiest places, where they might cut a purse string without ever being noticed, or if they were discovered, where they could melt away into a swirling crowd of bright colors and flowing robes.

Artemis Entreri noted the thieves clearly. He could tell with a glance who was there to shop and who was there to steal, and he didn't avoid the latter group. He purposely set his course to bring him right by every thief he could find, and he'd pushed back one side of his dark cloak, revealing his ample purse—

—revealing, too, the jewel-decorated dagger that kept his purse and his person perfectly safe. The dagger was his trademark weapon, one of the most feared blades on all of Calimport's dangerous streets.

Entreri enjoyed the respect the young thieves offered him, and more than that, he demanded it. He had spent years earning his reputation as the finest assassin in Calimport, but he was getting older. He was losing,

577

perhaps, that fine edge of brilliance. Thus, he came out brazenly—more so than he ever would have in his younger days—daring them, any of them, to make a try for him.

He crossed the busy avenue, heading for a small outdoor tavern that had many round tables set under a great awning. The place was bustling, but Entreri immediately spotted his contact, the flamboyant Sha'lazzi Ozoule with his trademark bright yellow turban. Entreri moved straight for the table. Sha'lazzi wasn't sitting alone, though it was obvious to Entreri that the three men seated with him were not friends of his, were not known to him at all. The others held a private conversation, chattering and chuckling, while Sha'lazzi leaned back, glancing all around.

Entreri walked up to the table. Sha'lazzi gave a nervous and embarrassed shrug as the assassin looked questioningly at the three uninvited guests.

"You did not tell them that this table was reserved for our luncheon?" Entreri calmly asked.

The three men stopped their conversation and looked up at him curiously.

"I tried to explain . . ." Sha'lazzi started, wiping the sweat from his dark-skinned brow.

Entreri held up his hand to silence the man and fixed his imposing gaze on the three trespassers. "We have business," he said.

"And we have food and drink," one of them replied.

Entreri didn't reply, other than to stare hard at the man, to let his gaze lock with the other's.

The other two made a couple of remarks, but Entreri ignored them completely and just kept staring hard at the first challenger. On and on it went, and Entreri kept his focus, even tightened it, his gaze boring into the man, showing him the strength of will he now faced, the perfect determination and control.

"What is this about?" one of the others demanded, standing up right beside Entreri.

Sha'lazzi muttered the quick beginning of a common prayer.

"I asked you," the man pushed, and he reached out to shove Entreri's shoulder.

Up snapped the assassin's hand, catching the approaching hand by the thumb and spinning it over, then driving it down, locking the man in a painful hold.

All the while Entreri didn't blink, didn't glance away at all, just kept visually holding the first one, who was sitting directly across from him, in that awful glare.

The man standing at Entreri's side gave a little grunt as the assassin applied pressure, then brought his free hand to his belt, to the curved dagger he had secured there.

Sha'lazzi muttered another line of the prayer.

The man across the table, held fast by Entreri's deadly stare, motioned for his friend to hold calm and to keep his hand away from the blade.

Entreri nodded to him, then motioned for him to take his friends and be gone. He released the man at his side, who clutched at his sore thumb, eyeing Entreri threateningly. He didn't come at Entreri again, nor did either of his friends make any move, except to pick up their plates and sidle away. They hadn't recognized Entreri, yet he had shown them the truth of who he was without ever drawing his blade.

"I meant to do the same thing," Sha'lazzi remarked with a chuckle as the three departed and Entreri settled into the seat opposite him.

Entreri just stared at him, noting how out-of-sorts this one always appeared. Sha'lazzi had a huge head and a big round face, and that put on a body so skinny as to appear emaciated. Furthermore, that big round face was always, always smiling, with huge, square white teeth glimmering in contrast to his dark skin and black eyes.

Sha'lazzi cleared his throat again. "Surprised I am that you came out for this meeting," he said. "You have made many enemies in your rise with the Basadoni Guild. Do you not fear treachery, O powerful one?" he finished sarcastically and again with a chuckle.

Entreri only continued to stare. Indeed he had feared treachery, but he needed to speak with Sha'lazzi. Kimmuriel Oblodra, the drow psionicist working for Jarlaxle, had scoured Sha'lazzi's thoughts completely and had come to the conclusion that there was no conspiracy afoot.

Of course, considering the source of the information—a dark elf who held no love for Entreri—the assassin hadn't been completely comforted by the report.

"It can be a prison to the powerful, you understand," Sha'lazzi rambled on. "A prison to *be* powerful, you see? So many pashas dare not leave their homes without an entourage of a hundred guards."

"I am not a pasha."

"No, indeed, but Basadoni belongs to you and to Sharlotta," Sha'lazzi returned, referring to Sharlotta Vespers. The woman had used her wiles to become Pasha Basadoni's second and had survived the drow takeover to serve as figurehead of the guild. And the guild had suddenly become more powerful than anyone could imagine. "Everyone knows this." Sha'lazzi gave another of his annoying chuckles. "I always understood that you were good, my friend, but never this good!"

Entreri smiled back, but in truth his amusement came from a fantasy of sticking his dagger into Sha'lazzi's skinny throat, for no better reason than the fact that he simply couldn't stand this parasite.

Entreri had to admit that he needed Sha'lazzi, though—and that was exactly how the notorious informant managed to stay alive. Sha'lazzi had made a living, indeed an art, out of telling anybody anything he wanted to know—for a price—and so good was he at his craft, so connected to every pulse beat of Calimport's ruling families and street thugs alike, that he had made himself too valuable to the often-warring guilds to be murdered.

"So tell me of the power behind the throne of Basadoni," Sha'lazzi remarked, grinning widely. "For surely there is more, yes?"

Entreri worked hard to keep himself stone-faced, knowing that a responding grin would give too much away—and how he wanted to grin at Sha'lazzi's honest ignorance of the truth of the new Basadonis. Sha'lazzi would never know that a dark elf army had set up shop in Calimport, using the Basadoni Guild as its front.

"I thought we had agreed to discuss Dallabad Oasis?" Entreri asked in reply.

Sha'lazzi sighed and shrugged. "Many interesting things to speak of," he said. "Dallabad is not one of them, I fear."

"In your opinion."

"Nothing has changed there in twenty years," Sha'lazzi replied. "There is nothing there that I know that you do not, and have not, for nearly as many years."

"Kohrin Soulez still retains Charon's Claw?" Entreri asked.

Sha'lazzi nodded. "Of course," he said with a chuckle. "Still and forever. It has served him for four decades, and when Soulez is dead, one of his thirty sons will take it, no doubt, unless the indelicate Ahdania Soulez gets to it first. An ambitious one is the daughter of Kohrin Soulez! If you came to ask me if he will part with it, then you already know the answer. We should indeed speak of more interesting things, such as the Basadoni Guild."

Entreri's hard stare returned in a heartbeat.

"Why would old Soulez sell it now?" Sha'lazzi asked with a dramatic wave of his skinny arms—arms that looked so incongruous when lifted beside that huge head. "What is this, my friend, the third time you have tried to purchase that fine sword? Yes, yes! First, when you were a pup with a few hundred gold pieces—a gift of Basadoni, eh?—in your ragged pouch."

Entreri winced at that despite himself, despite his knowledge that Sha'lazzi, for all of his other faults, was the best in Calimport at reading gestures and expressions and deriving the truth behind them. Still, the memory, combined with more recent events, evoked the response from his heart. Pasha Basadoni had indeed given him the extra coin that long-ago day, an offering to his most promising lieutenant for no good reason but simply as a gift. When he thought about it, Entreri realized that Basadoni was perhaps the only man who had ever given him a gift without expecting something in return.

And Entreri had killed Basadoni, only a few months ago.

"Yes, yes," Sha'lazzi said, more to himself than to Entreri, "then you asked about the sword again soon after Pasha Pook's demise. Ah, but he fell hard, that one!"

Entreri just stared at the man. Sha'lazzi, apparently just then beginning to catch on that he might be pushing the dangerous assassin too far, cleared his throat, embarrassed.

"Then I told you that it was impossible," Sha'lazzi remarked. "Of course it is impossible."

"I have more coin now," Entreri said quietly.

"There is not enough coin in all of the world!" Sha'lazzi wailed.

Entreri didn't blink. "Do you know how much coin is in all the world, Sha'lazzi?" he asked calmly—too calmly. "Do you know how much coin is in the coffers of House Basadoni?"

"House Entreri, you mean," the man corrected.

Entreri didn't deny it, and Sha'lazzi's eyes widened. There it was, as clearly spelled out as the informant could ever have expected to hear it. Rumors had said that old Basadoni was dead, and that Sharlotta Vespers and the other acting guildmasters were no more than puppets for the one who clearly pulled the strings: Artemis Entreri.

"Charon's Claw," Sha'lazzi mused, a smile widening upon his face. "So, the power behind the throne is Entreri, and the power behind Entreri is . . . well, a mage, I would guess, since you so badly want that particular sword. A mage, yes, and one who is getting a bit dangerous, eh?"

"Keep guessing," said Entreri.

"And perhaps I will get it correct?"

"If you do, I will have to kill you," the assassin said, still in that awful, calm tone. "Speak with Sheik Soulez. Find his price."

"He has no price," Sha'lazzi insisted.

Entreri came forward quicker than any cat after a mouse. One hand slapped down on Sha'lazzi's shoulder, the other caught hold of that deadly jeweled dagger, and Entreri's face came within an inch of Sha'lazzi's.

"That would be most unfortunate," Entreri said. "For you."

The assassin pushed the informant back in his seat, then stood up straight and glanced around as if some inner hunger had just awakened within him and he was now seeking some prey with which to sate it. He looked back at Sha'lazzi only briefly, then walked out from under the awning, back into the tumult of the market area.

As he calmed down and considered the meeting, Entreri silently berated himself. His frustration was beginning to wear at the edges of perfection. He could not have been more obvious about the roots of his problem than to so eagerly ask about purchasing Charon's Claw. Above all else, that weapon and gauntlet combination had been designed to battle wizards.

And psionicists, perhaps?

For those were Entreri's tormentors, Rai-guy and Kimmuriel—Jarlaxle's Bregan D'aerthe lieutenants—one a wizard and one a psionicist. Entreri hated them both, and profoundly, but more importantly he knew that they hated him. To make things worse Entreri understood that his only armor against the dangerous pair was Jarlaxle himself. While to his surprise he had cautiously come to trust the mercenary dark elf, he doubted Jarlaxle's protection would hold forever.

Accidents did happen, after all.

Entreri needed protection, but he had to go about things with his customary patience and intelligence, twisting the trail beyond anyone's ability to follow, fighting the way he had perfected so many years before on Calimport's tough streets, using many subtle layers of information and misinformation and blending the two together so completely that neither his friends nor his foes could ever truly unravel them. When only he knew the truth, then he, and only he, would be in control.

In that sobering light, he took the less than perfect meeting with perceptive Sha'lazzi as a distinct warning, a reminder that he could survive his time with the dark elves only if he kept an absolute level of personal control. Indeed, Sha'lazzi had come close to figuring out his current plight, had gotten half of it, at least, correct. The pie-faced man would obviously offer that information to any who'd pay well enough for it. On Calimport's streets these days many were scrambling to figure out the enigma of the sudden and vicious rise of the Basadoni Guild.

Sha'lazzi had figured out half of it, and so all the usual suspects would be considered: a powerful arch-mage or various wizards' guilds.

Despite his dour mood, Entreri chuckled when he pictured Sha'lazzi's expression should the man ever learn the other half of that secret behind Basadoni's throne, that the dark elves had come to Calimport in force!

Of course, his threat to the man had not been an idle one. Should Sha'lazzi ever make such a connection, Entreri, or any one of a thousand of Jarlaxle's agents, would surely kill him.

* * * * *

Sha'lazzi Ozoule sat at the little round table for a long, long time, replaying Entreri's every word and every gesture. He knew that his assumption concerning a wizard holding the true power behind the Basadoni rise was correct, but that was not really news. Given the expediency of the rise, and the level of devastation that had been enacted upon rival houses, common sense dictated that a wizard, or more likely many wizards, were involved.

What caught Sha'lazzi as a revelation, though, was Entreri's visceral reaction.

Artemis Entreri, the master of control, the shadow of death itself, had never before shown him such an inner turmoil—even fear, perhaps?—as that. When before had Artemis Entreri ever touched someone in threat? No, he had always looked at him with that awful gaze, let him know in no uncertain terms that he was walking the path to ultimate doom. If the offender persisted, there was no further threat, no grabbing or beating.

There was only quick death.

The uncharacteristic reaction surely intrigued Sha'lazzi. How he wanted to know what had so rattled Artemis Entreri as to facilitate such behavior—but at the same time, the assassin's demeanor also served as a clear and frightening warning. Sha'lazzi knew well that anything that could so unnerve Artemis Entreri could easily, so easily, destroy Sha'lazzi Ozoule.

It was an interesting situation, and one that scared Sha'lazzi profoundly.

Part 1

Sticking To The Web

I live in a world where there truly exists the embodiment of evil. I speak not of wicked men, nor of goblins—often of evil weal—nor even of my own people, the dark elves, wickeder still than the goblins. These are creatures—all of them—capable of great cruelty, but they are not, even in the very worst of cases, the true embodiment of evil. No, that title belongs to others, to the demons and devils often summoned by priests and mages. These creatures of the lower planes are the purest of evil, untainted vileness running unchecked. They are without possibility of redemption, without hope of accomplishing anything in their unfortunately nearly eternal existence that even borders on goodness.

I have wondered if these creatures could exist without the darkness that lies within the hearts of the reasoning races. Are they a source of evil, as are many wicked men or drow, or are they the result, a physical manifestation of the rot that permeates the hearts of far too many?

The latter, I believe. It is not coincidental that demons and devils cannot walk the material plane of existence without being brought here by the actions of one of the reasoning beings. They are no more than a tool, I know, an instrument to carry out the wicked deeds in service to the truer source of that evil.

What then of Crenshinibon? It is an item, an artifact—albeit a sentient one—but it does not exist in the same state of intelligence as does a reasoning being. For the Crystal Shard cannot grow, cannot change, cannot mend its ways. The only errors it can learn to correct are those of errant attempts at manipulation, as it seeks to better grab at the hearts of those around it. It cannot even consider, or reconsider, the end it desperately tries to achieve—no, its purpose is forever singular.

Is it truly evil, then?

No.

I would have thought differently not too long ago, even when I carried the dangerous artifact and came better to understand it. Only recently, upon reading a long and detailed message sent to me from High Priest Cadderly Bonaduce of the Spirit Soaring, have I come to see the truth of the Crystal Shard, have I come to understand that the item itself is an anomaly, a mistake, and that its never-ending hunger for power and glory, at whatever cost, is merely a perversion of the intent of its second maker, the eighth spirit that found its way into the very essence of the artifact.

The Crystal Shard was created originally by seven liches, so Cadderly has learned, who designed to fashion an item of the very greatest power. As a further insult to the races these undead kings intended to conquer, they made the artifact a draw against the sun itself, the giver of life. The liches were consumed at the completion of their joining magic. Despite what some sages believe, Cadderly insists that the conscious aspects of those vile creatures were not drawn into the power of the item, but were, rather, obliterated by its sunlike properties. Thus, their intended insult turned against them and left them as no more than ashes and absorbed pieces of their shattered spirits.

That much of the earliest history of the Crystal Shard is known by many, including the demons that so desperately crave the item. The second story, though, the one Cadderly uncovered, tells a more complicated tale, and shows the truth of Crenshinibon, the ultimate failure of the artifact as a perversion of goodly intentions.

Crenshinibon first came to the material world centuries ago in the far-off land of Zakhara. At the time, it was merely a wizard's tool, though a great and powerful one, an artifact that could throw fireballs and create great blazing walls of light so intense they could burn flesh from bone. Little was known of Crenshinibon's dark past until it fell to the hands of a sultan. This great leader, whose name has been lost to the ages, learned the truth of the Crystal Shard, and with the help of his many court wizards, decided that the work of the liches was incomplete. Thus came the "second creation" of Crenshinibon, the heightening of its power and its limited consciousness.

This sultan had no dreams of domination, only of peaceful existence with his many warlike neighbors. Thus, using the newest power of the artifact, he envisioned, then created, a line of crystalline towers. The towers stretched from his capital across the empty desert to his kingdom's second city, an oft-raided frontier city, in intervals equating to a single day's travel. He strung as many as a hundred of the crystalline towers, and nearly completed the mighty defensive line.

But alas, the sultan overreached the powers of Crenshinibon, and though he believed that the creation of each tower strengthened the artifact, he was, in fact, pulling the Crystal Shard and its manifestations too thin. Soon after, a great sandstorm came up, sweeping across the desert. It was a natural disaster that served as a prelude to an invasion by a neighboring sheikdom. So thin were the walls of those crystalline towers that they shattered under the force of the glass, taking with them the sultan's dream of security.

The hordes overran the kingdom and murdered the sultan's family while he helplessly looked on. Their merciless sheik would not kill the sultan, though—he wanted the painful memories to burn at the man—but Crenshinibon took the sultan, took a piece of his spirit, at least.

Little more of those early days is known, even to Cadderly, who counts demigods among his sources, but the young high priest of Deneir is convinced that this "second creation" of Crenshinibon is the one that remains key to the present hunger of the artifact. If only Crenshinibon could have held its highest level of power. If only the crystalline towers had remained strong. The hordes would have been turned away, and the sultan's family, his dear wife and beautiful children, would not have been murdered.

Now the artifact, imbued with the twisted aspects of seven dead liches and with the wounded and tormented spirit of the sultan, continues its desperate quest to attain and maintain its greatest level of power, whatever the cost.

There are many implications to the story. Cadderly hinted in his note to me, though he drew no definitive conclusions, that the creation of the crystalline towers actually served as the catalyst for the invasion, with the leaders of the neighboring sheikdom fearful that their borderlands would soon be overrun. Is the Crystal Shard, then, a great lesson to us? Does it show clearly the folly of overblown ambition, even though that particular ambition was rooted in good intentions? The sultan wanted strength for the defense of his peaceable kingdom, and yet he reached for too much power.

That was what consumed him, his family, and his kingdom.

What of Jarlaxle, then, who now holds the Crystal Shard? Should I go after him and try to take back the artifact, then deliver it to Cadderly for destruction? Surely the world would be a better place without this mighty and dangerous artifact.

Then again, there will always be another tool for those of evil weal, another embodiment of their evil, be it a demon, a devil, or a monstrous creation similar to Crenshinibon.

No, the embodiments are not the problem, for they cannot exist and prosper without the evil that is within the hearts of reasoning beings.

Beware, Jarlaxle. Beware.

—Drizzt Do'Urden

Chapter 1
When He Looked Inside

Dwahvel Tiggerwillies tiptoed into the small, dimly lit room in the back of the lower end of her establishment, the Copper Ante. Dwahvel, that most competent of halfling females—good with her wiles, good with her daggers, and better with her wits—wasn't used to walking so gingerly in this place, though it was as secure a house as could be found in all of Calimport. This was Artemis Entreri, after all, and no place in all the world could truly be considered safe when the deadly assassin was about.

He was pacing when she entered, taking no obvious note of her arrival at all. Dwahvel looked at him curiously. She knew that Entreri had been on edge lately and was one of the very few outside of House Basadoni who knew the truth behind that edge. The dark elves had come and infiltrated Calimport's streets, and Entreri was serving as a front man for their operations. If Dwahvel held any preconceived notions of how terrible the drow truly could be, one look at Entreri surely confirmed those suspicions. He had never been a nervous one—Dwahvel wasn't sure that he was now—and had never been a man Dwahvel would have expected to find at odds with himself.

Even more curious, Entreri had invited her into his confidence. It just wasn't his way. Still, Dwahvel suspected no trap. This was, she knew,

591

exactly as it seemed, as surprising as that might be. Entreri was speaking to himself as much as to her, as a way of clarifying his thoughts, and for some reason that Dwahvel didn't yet understand, he was letting her listen in.

She considered herself complimented in the highest way and also realized the potential danger that came along with that compliment. That unsettling thought in mind, the halfling guildmistress quietly settled into a chair and listened carefully, looking for clues and insights. Her first, and most surprising, came when she happened to glance at a chair set against the back wall of the room. Resting on it was a half-empty bottle of Moonshae whiskey.

"I see them at every corner on every street in the belly of this cursed city," Entreri was saying. "Braggarts wearing their scars and weapons like badges of honor, men and women so concerned about reputation that they have lost sight of what it is they truly wish to accomplish. They play for the status and the accolades, and with no better purpose."

His speech was not overly slurred, yet it was obvious to Dwahvel that Entreri had indeed tasted some of the whiskey.

"Since when does Artemis Entreri bother himself with the likes of street thieves?" Dwahvel asked.

Entreri stopped pacing and glanced at her, his face passive. "I see them and mark them carefully, because I am well aware that my own reputation precedes me. Because of that reputation, many on the street would love to sink a dagger into my heart," the assassin replied and began to pace again. "How great a reputation that killer might then find. They know that I am older now, and they think me slower—and in truth, their reasoning is sound. I cannot move as quickly as I did a decade ago."

Dwahvel's eyes narrowed at the surprising admission.

"But as the body ages and movements dull, the mind grows sharper," Entreri went on. "I, too, am concerned with reputation, but not as I used to be. It was my goal in life to be the absolute best at that which I do, at out-fighting and out-thinking my enemies. I desired to become the perfect warrior, and it took a dark elf whom I despise to show me the error of my ways. My unintended journey to Menzoberranzan as a 'guest' of Jarlaxle humbled me in my fanatical striving to be the best and showed me the futility of a world full of that who I most wanted to become. In Menzoberranzan, I saw reflections of myself at every turn, warriors who had become so callous to all around them, so enwrapped in the goal, that they could not begin to appreciate the process of attaining it."

"They are drow," Dwahvel said. "We cannot understand their true motivations."

"Their city is a beautiful place, my little friend," Entreri replied, "with power beyond anything you can imagine. Yet, for all for that, Menzoberranzan is a hollow and empty place, bereft of passion unless that passion is hate. I came back from that city of twenty thousand assassins changed indeed, questioning the very foundations of my existence. What is the point of it, after all?"

Dwahvel interlocked the fingers of her plump little hands and brought them up to her lips, studying the man intently. Was Entreri announcing his retirement? she wondered. Was he denying the life he had known, the glories to which he had climbed? She blew a quiet sigh, shook her head, and said, "We all answer that question for ourselves, don't we? The point is gold or respect or property or power . . ."

"Indeed," he said coldly. "I walk now with a better understanding of who I am and what challenges before me are truly important. I know not yet where I hope to go, what challenges are left before me, but I do understand now that the important thing is to enjoy the process of getting there.

"Do I care that my reputation remains strong?" Entreri asked suddenly, even as Dwahvel started to ask him if he had any idea at all of where his road might lead—important information, given the power of the Basadoni Guild. "Do I wish to continue to be upheld as the pinnacle of success among assassins within Calimport?

"Yes, to both, but not for the same reasons that those fools swagger about the street corners, not for the same reasons that many of them will make a try for me, only to wind up dead in the gutter. No, I care about reputation because it allows me to be so much more effective in that which I choose to do. I care for celebrity, but only because in that mantle my foes fear me more, fear me beyond rational thinking and beyond the bounds of proper caution. They are afraid, even as they come after me, but instead of a healthy respect, their fear is almost paralyzing, making them continuously second-guess their own every move. I can use that fear against them. With a simple bluff or feint, I can make the doubt lead them into a completely erroneous position. Because I can feign vulnerability and use perceived advantages against the careless, on those occasions when I am truly vulnerable the cautious will not aggressively strike."

He paused and nodded, and Dwahvel saw that his thoughts were indeed sorting out. "An enviable position, to be sure," she offered.

"Let the fools come after me, one after another, an endless line of eager assassins," Entreri said, and he nodded again. "With each kill, I grow wiser, and with added wisdom, I grow stronger."

He slapped his hat, that curious small-brimmed black bolero, against his thigh, spun it up his arm with a flick of his wrist so that it rolled right over his shoulder to settle on his head, complementing the fine haircut he had just received. Only then did Dwahvel notice that the man had trimmed his thick goatee as well, leaving only a fine mustache and a small patch of hair below his lower lip, running down to his chin and going to both sides like an inverted T.

Entreri looked at the halfling, gave a sly wink, and strode from the room.

What did it all mean? Dwahvel wondered. Surely she was glad to see that the man had cleaned up his look, for she had recognized his uncharacteristic slovenliness as a sure signal that he was losing control, and worse, losing his heart.

She sat there for a long time, bouncing her clasped hands absently against her puckered lower lip, wondering why she had been invited to such a spectacle, wondering why Artemis Entreri had felt the need to open up to her, to anyone—even to himself. The man had found some epiphany, Dwahvel realized, and she suddenly realized that she had, too.

Artemis Entreri was her friend.

Chapter 2

Life in the Dark Lane

"Faster! Faster, I say!" Jarlaxle howled. His arm flashed repeatedly, and a seemingly endless stream of daggers spewed forth at the dodging and rolling assassin.

Entreri worked his jeweled dagger and his sword—a drow-fashioned blade that he was not particularly enamored of—furiously, with in and out vertical rolls to catch the missiles and flip them aside. All the while he kept his feet moving, skittering about, looking for an opening in Jarlaxle's superb defensive posture—a stance made all the more powerful by the constant stream of spinning daggers.

"An opening!" the drow mercenary cried, letting fly one, two, three more daggers.

Entreri sent his sword back the other way but knew that his opponent's assessment was correct. He dived into a roll instead, tucking his head and his arms in tight to cover any vital areas.

"Oh, well done!" Jarlaxle congratulated as Entreri came to his feet after taking only a single hit, and that a dagger sticking into the trailing fold of his cloak instead of his skin.

Entreri felt the dagger swing in against the back of his leg as he stood up. Fearing that it might trip him, he tossed his own dagger into the air, then quickly pulled the cloak from his shoulders, and in the same fluid movement, started to toss it aside.

An idea came to him, though, and he didn't discard the cloak but rather caught his deadly dagger and set it between his teeth. He stalked a semicircle about the drow, waving his cloak, a drow *piwafwi*, slowly about as a shield against the missiles.

Jarlaxle smiled at him. "Improvisation," he said with obvious admiration. "The mark of a true warrior." Even as he finished, though, the drow's arm starting moving yet again. A quartet of daggers soared at the assassin.

Entreri bobbed and spun a complete circuit, but tossed his cloak as he did and caught it as he came back around. One dagger skidded across the floor, another passed over Entreri's head, narrowly missing, and the other two got caught in the fabric, along with the previous one.

Entreri continued to wave the cloak, but it wasn't flowing wide anymore, weighted as it was by the three daggers.

"Not so good a shield, perhaps," Jarlaxle commented.

"You talk better than you fight," Entreri countered. "A bad combination."

"I talk because I so enjoy the fight, my quick friend," Jarlaxle replied.

His arm went back again, but Entreri was already moving. The human held his arm out wide to keep the cloak from tripping him, and dived into a roll right toward the mercenary, closing the gap between them in the blink of an eye.

Jarlaxle did let fly one dagger. It skipped off Entreri's back, but the drow mercenary caught the next one sliding out of his magical bracer into his hand and snapped his wrist, speaking a command word. The dagger responded at once, elongating into a sword. As Entreri came over, his sword predictably angled up to gut Jarlaxle, the drow had the parry in place.

Entreri stayed low and skittered forward instead, swinging his cloak in a roundabout manner to wrap it behind Jarlaxle's legs. The mercenary quick-stepped and almost got out of the way, but one of the daggers hooked his boot and he fell over backward. Jarlaxle was as agile as any drow, but so too was Entreri. The human came up over the drow, sword thrusting.

Jarlaxle parried fast, his blade slapping against Entreri's. To the drow's surprise, the assassin's sword went flying away. Jarlaxle understood soon enough, though, for Entreri's now free hand came forward, clasping Jarlaxle's forearm and holding the drow's weapon out wide.

And there loomed the assassin's other hand, holding again that deadly jeweled dagger.

Entreri had the opening and had the strike, and Jarlaxle couldn't block it or begin to move away from it. A wave of such despair, an overwhelming barrage of complete and utter hopelessness, washed over

Entreri. He felt as if someone had just entered his brain and began scattering all of his thoughts, starting and stopping all of his reflexes. In the inevitable pause, Jarlaxle brought his other arm forward, launching a dagger that smacked Entreri in the gut and bounced away.

The barrage of discordant, paralyzing emotions continued to blast away in Entreri's mind, and he stumbled back. He hardly felt the motion and was somewhat confused a moment later, as the fuzziness began to clear, to find that he was on the other side of the small room sitting against the wall and facing a smiling Jarlaxle.

Entreri closed his eyes and at last forced the confusing jumble of thoughts completely away. He assumed that Rai-guy, the drow wizard who had imbued both Entreri and Jarlaxle with stoneskin spells that they could spar with all of their hearts without fear of injuring each other, had intervened. When he glanced that way, he saw that the wizard was nowhere to be seen. He turned back to Jarlaxle, guessing then that the mercenary had used yet another in his seemingly endless bag of tricks. Perhaps he had used his newest magical acquisition, the powerful Crenshinibon, to overwhelm Entreri's concentration.

"Perhaps you *are* slowing down, my friend," Jarlaxle remarked. "What a pity that would be. It is good that you defeated your avowed enemy when you did, for Drizzt Do'Urden has many centuries of youthful speed left in him."

Entreri scoffed at the words, though in truth, the thought gnawed at him. He had lived his entire life on the very edge of perfection and preparedness. Even now, in the middle years of his life, he was confident that he could defeat almost any foe—with pure skill or by out-thinking any enemy, by properly preparing any battlefield—but Entreri didn't want to slow down. He didn't want to lose that edge of fighting brilliance that had so marked his life.

He wanted to deny Jarlaxle's words, but he could not, for he knew in his heart that he had truly lost that fight with Drizzt, that if Kimmuriel Oblodra had not intervened with his psionic powers, then Drizzt would have been declared the victor.

"You did not outmatch me with speed," the assassin started to argue, shaking his head.

Jarlaxle came forward, his glowing eyes narrowing dangerously—a threatening expression, a look of rage, that the assassin rarely saw upon the handsome face of the always-in-control dark elf mercenary leader.

"I have *this!*" Jarlaxle announced, pulling wide his cloak and showing Entreri the tip of the artifact, Crenshinibon, the Crystal Shard, tucked neatly into one pocket. "Never forget that. Without it, I could likely still defeat you, though you are good, my friend—better than any human I have ever known. But with this in my possession . . . you are but a mere mortal. Joined in Crenshinibon, I can destroy you with but a thought. Never forget that."

Entreri lowered his gaze, digesting the words and the tone, sharpening that image of the uncharacteristic expression on Jarlaxle's always smiling face. *Joined in Crenshinibon? . . . but a mere mortal?* What in the Nine Hells did that mean? *Never forget that,* Jarlaxle had said, and indeed, this was a lesson that Artemis Entreri would not soon dismiss.

When he looked back up again, Entreri saw Jarlaxle wearing his typical expression, that sly, slightly amused look that conferred to all who saw it that this cunning drow knew more than he did, knew more than he possibly could.

Seeing Jarlaxle relaxed again also reminded Entreri of the novelty of these sparring events. The mercenary leader would not spar with any other. Rai-guy was stunned when Jarlaxle had told him that he meant to battle Entreri on a regular basis.

Entreri understood the logic behind that thinking. Jarlaxle survived, in part, by remaining mysterious, even to those around him. No one could ever really get a good look at the mercenary leader. He kept allies and opponents alike off-balance and wondering, always wondering, and yet, here he was, revealing so much to Artemis Entreri.

"Those daggers," Entreri said, coming back at ease and putting on his own sly expression. "They were merely illusions."

"In your mind, perhaps," the dark elf replied in his typically cryptic manner.

"They were," the assassin pressed. "You could not possibly carry so many, nor could any magic create them that quickly."

"As you say," Jarlaxle replied. "Though you heard the clang as your own weapons connected with them and felt the weight as they punctured your cloak."

"I *thought* I heard the clang," Entreri corrected, wondering if he had at last found a chink in the mercenary's never-ending guessing game.

"Is that not the same thing?" Jarlaxle replied with a laugh, but it seemed to Entreri as if there was a darker side to that chuckle.

Entreri lifted that cloak, to see several of the daggers—solid metal daggers—still sticking in its fabric folds, and to find several more holes in the cloth. "Some were illusions, then," he argued unconvincingly.

Jarlaxle merely shrugged, never willing to give anything away.

With an exasperated sigh, Entreri started out of the room.

"Do keep ever present in your thoughts, my friend, that an illusion can kill you if you believe in it," Jarlaxle called after him.

Entreri paused and glanced back, his expression grim. He wasn't used to being so openly warned or threatened, but he knew that with this one particular companion, the threats were never, ever idle.

"And the real thing can kill you whether you believe in it or not," Entreri replied, and he turned back for the door.

The assassin departed with a shake of his head, frustrated and yet intrigued. That was always the way with Jarlaxle, Entreri mused, and what surprised him even more was that he found that aspect of the clever drow mercenary particularly compelling.

* * * * *

That is the one, Kimmuriel Oblodra signaled to his two companions, Rai-guy and Berg'inyon Baenre, the most recent addition to the surface army of Bregan D'aerthe.

The favored son of the most powerful house in Menzoberranzan, Berg'inyon had grown up with all the drow world open before him—to the level that a drow male in Menzoberranzan could achieve, at least—but his mother, the powerful Matron Baenre, had led a disastrous assault on a dwarven kingdom, ending in her death and throwing all the great drow city into utter chaos. In that time of ultimate confusion and apprehension, Berg'inyon had thrown his hand in with Jarlaxle and the ever elusive mercenary band of Bregan D'aerthe. Among the finest of fighters in all the city, and with familial connections to still-mighty House Baenre, Berg'inyon was welcomed openly and quickly promoted, elevated to the status of high lieutenant. Thus, he was not here now serving Rai-guy and Kimmuriel, but as their peer, taken out on a sort of training mission.

He considered the human Kimmuriel had targeted, a shapely woman posing in the dress of a common street whore.

You have read her thoughts? Rai-guy signaled back, his fingers weaving an intricate pattern, perfectly complementing the various expressions and contortions of his handsome and angular drow features.

Raker spy, Kimmuriel silently assured his companion. *The coordinator of their group. All pass her by, reporting their finds.*

Berg'inyon shifted nervously from foot to foot, uncomfortable around the revelations of the strange and strangely powerful Kimmuriel. He hoped that Kimmuriel wasn't reading his thoughts at that moment, for he was wondering how Jarlaxle could ever feel safe with this one about. Kimmuriel could walk into someone's mind, it seemed, as easily as Berg'inyon could walk through an open doorway. He chuckled then but disguised it as a cough, when he considered that clever Jarlaxle likely had that doorway somehow trapped. Berg'inyon decided that he'd have to learn the technique, if there was one, to keep Kimmuriel at bay.

Do we know where the others might be? Berg'inyon's hands silently asked.

Would the show be complete if we did not? came Rai-guy's responding gestures. The wizard smiled widely, and soon all three of the dark elves wore sly, hungry expressions.

Kimmuriel closed his eyes and steadied himself with long, slow breaths.

Rai-guy took the cue, pulling an eyelash encased in a bit of gum arabic out of one of his several belt pouches. He turned to Berg'inyon and began waggling his fingers. The drow warrior flinched reflexively—as most sane people would do when a drow wizard began casting in their direction.

The first spell went off, and Berg'inyon, rendered invisible, faded from view. Rai-guy went right back to work, now aiming a spell designed mentally to grab at the target, to hold the spy fast.

The woman flinched and seemed to hold for a second, but shook out of it and glanced around nervously, now obviously on her guard.

Rai-guy growled and went at the spell again. Invisible Berg'inyon stared at him with an almost mocking smile—yes, there were advantages to being invisible! Rai-guy continually demeaned humans, called them every drow name for offal and carrion. On the one hand, he was obviously surprised that this one had resisted the hold spell—no easy mental task—but on the other, Berg'inyon noted, the blustery wizard had prepared more than one of the spells. One, without any resistance, should have been enough.

This time, the woman took one step, and held fast in her walking pose.

Go! Kimmuriel's fingers waved. Even as he gestured, the powers of his mind opened the doorway between the three drow and the woman. Suddenly she was there, though she was still on the street, but only a couple of strides away. Berg'inyon leaped out and grabbed the woman, tugging her hard into the extra-dimensional space, and Kimmuriel shut the door.

It had happened so fast that to any watching on the street, it would have seemed as if the woman had simply disappeared.

The psionicist raised his delicate black hand up to the victim's forehead, melding with her mentally. He could feel the horror in there, for though her physical body had been locked in Rai-guy's stasis, her mind was working and she knew indeed that she now stood before dark elves.

Kimmuriel took just a moment to bask in that terror, thoroughly enjoying the spectacle. Then he imparted psionic energies to her. He built around her an armor of absorbing kinetic energy, using a technique he had perfected in Entreri's battle with Drizzt Do'Urden.

When it was done, he nodded.

Berg'inyon became visible again almost immediately, as his fine drow sword slashed across the woman's throat, the offensive strike dispelling the defensive magic of Rai'guy's invisibility spell. The drow warrior went into a fast dance, slashing and thrusting with both of his fine swords, stabbing hard, even chopping once with both blades, a heavy drop down onto the woman's head.

But no blood spewed forth, no groans of pain came from the woman, for Kimmuriel's armor accepted each blow, catching and holding the tremendous energy offered by the drow warrior's brutal dance.

It went on and on for several minutes, until Rai-guy warned that the spell of holding was nearing its end. Berg'inyon backed away, and Kimmuriel closed his eyes again as Rai-guy began yet another casting.

Both onlookers, Kimmuriel and Berg'inyon, smiled wickedly as Rai-guy produced a tiny ball of bat guano that held a sulfuric aroma and shoved it, along with his finger into the woman's mouth, releasing his spell. A flash of fiery light appeared in the back of the woman's mouth, disappearing as it slid down her throat.

The sidewalk was there again, very close, as Kimmuriel opened a second dimension portal to the same spot on the street, and Rai-guy roughly shoved the woman back out.

Kimmuriel shut the door, and they watched, amused.

The hold spell released first, and the woman staggered. She tried to call out, but coughed roughly from the burn in her throat. A strange expression came over her, one of absolute horror.

She feels the energy contained in the kinetic barrier, Kimmuriel explained. *I hold it no longer—only her own will prevents its release.*

How long? a concerned Rai-guy asked, but Kimmuriel only smiled and motioned for them to watch and enjoy.

The woman broke into a run. The three drow noted other people moving about her, some closing cautiously—other spies, likely—and others seeming merely curious. Still others grew alarmed and tried to stay away from her.

All the while, she tried to scream out, but just kept hacking from the continuing burn in her throat. Her eyes were wide, so horrifyingly and satisfyingly wide! She could feel the tremendous energies within her, begging release, and she had no idea how she might accomplish that.

She couldn't hold the kinetic barrier, and her initial realization of the problem transformed from horror into confusion. All of Berg'inyon's terrible beating came out then, so suddenly. All of the slashes and the stabs, the great chop and the twisting heart thrust, burst over the helpless woman. To those watching, it seemed almost as if she simply fell apart, gallons of blood erupting about her face, head, and chest.

She went down almost immediately, but before anyone could even begin to react, could run away or charge to her aid, Rai-guy's last spell, a delayed fireball, went off, immolating the already dead woman and many of those around her.

Outside the blast, wide-eyed stares came at the charred corpse from comrade and ignorant onlooker alike, expressions of the sheerest terror that surely pleased the three merciless dark elves.

A fine display. Worthy indeed.

For Berg'inyon, the spectacle served a second purpose, a clear reminder to him to take care around these fellow lieutenants himself. Even taking into consideration the high drow standards for torture and murder, these two were particularly adept, true masters of the craft.

601

Chapter 3

A Humbling Encounter

He had his old room back. He even had his name back. The memories of the authorities in Luskan were not as long as they claimed.

The previous year, Morik the Rogue had been accused of attempting to murder the honorable Captain Deudermont of the good ship *Sea Sprite,* a famous pirate hunter. Since in Luskan accusation and conviction were pretty much the same thing, Morik had faced the prospect of a horrible death in the public spectacle of Prisoner's Carnival. He had actually been in the process of realizing that ultimate torture when Captain Deudermont, horrified by the gruesome scene, had offered a pardon.

Pardoned or not, Morik had been forever banned from Luskan on pain of death. He had returned anyway, of course, the following year. At first he'd taken on an assumed identity, but gradually he had regained his old trappings, his true mannerisms, his connections on the streets, his apartment, and, finally, his name and the reputation it carried. The authorities knew it too, but having plenty of other thugs to torture to death, they didn't seem to care.

Morik could look back on that awful day at Prisoner's Carnival with a sense of humor now. He thought it perfectly ironic that he had been

603

tortured for a crime that he hadn't even committed when there were so many crimes of which he could be rightly convicted.

It was all a memory now, the memory of a whirlwind of intrigue and danger by the name of Wulfgar. He was Morik the Rogue once more, and all was as it had once been . . . almost.

For now there was another element, an intriguing and also terrifying element, that had come into Morik's life. He walked up to the door of his room cautiously, glancing all about the narrow hallway, studying the shadows. When he was confident that he was alone, he walked up tight to the door, shielding it from any magically prying eyes, and began the process of undoing nearly a dozen deadly traps, top to bottom along both sides of the jamb. That done, he took out a ring of keys and undid the locks—one, two, three—then he clicked open the door. He disarmed yet another trap—this one explosive—then entered, closing and securing the door and resetting all the traps. The complete process took him more than ten minutes, yet he performed this ritual every time he came home. The dark elves had come into Morik's life, unannounced and uninvited. While they had promised him the treasure of a king if he performed their tasks, they had also promised him and had shown him the flip side of that golden coin as well.

Morik checked the small pedestal at the side of the door next. He nodded, satisfied to see that the orb was still in place in the wide vase. The vessel was coated with contact poison and maintained a sensitive pressure release trap. He had paid dearly for that particular orb—an enormous amount of gold that would take him a year of hard thievery to retrieve—but in Morik's fearful eyes, the item was well worth the price. It was enchanted with a powerful anti-magic dweomer that would prevent dimensional doors from opening in his room, that would prevent wizards from strolling in on the other side of a teleportation spell.

Never again did Morik the Rogue wish to be awakened by a dark elf standing at the side of his bed, looming over him.

All of his locks were in place, his orb rested in its protected vessel, and yet some subtle signal, an intangible breeze, a tickling on the hairs at the back of his neck, told Morik that something was out of place. He glanced all around, from shadow to shadow, to the drapes that still hung over the window he had long ago bricked up. He looked to his bed, to the tightly tucked sheets, with no blankets hanging below the edge. Bending just a bit, Morik saw right through the bottom of the bed. There was no one hiding under there.

The drapes, then, he thought, and he moved in that general direction but took a circuitous route so that he wouldn't force any action from the intruder. A sudden shift and quick-step brought him there, dagger revealed, and he pulled the drapes aside and struck hard, catching only air.

Morik laughed in relief and at his own paranoia. How different his world had become since the arrival of the dark elves. Always now he was

604

on the edge of his nerves. He had seen the drow a total of only five times, including their initial encounter way back when Wulfgar was new to the city and they, for some reason that Morik still did not completely understand, wanted him to keep an eye on the huge barbarian.

He was always on his edge, always wary, but he reminded himself of the potential gains his alliance with the drow would bring. Part of the reason that he was Morik the Rogue again, from what he had been able to deduce, had to do with a visit to a particular authority by one of Jarlaxle's henchmen.

He gave a sigh of relief and let the drapes swing back, then froze in surprise and fear as a hand clamped over his mouth and the fine edge of a dagger came tight against his throat.

"You have the jewels?" a voice whispered in his ear, a voice showing incredible strength and calm despite its quiet tone. The hand slipped off of his mouth and up to his forehead, forcing his head back just enough to remind him of how vulnerable and open his throat was.

Morik didn't answer, his mind racing through many possibilities—the least likely of which seeming to be his potential escape, for that hand holding him revealed frightening strength and the hand holding the dagger at his throat was too, too steady. Whoever his attacker might be, Morik understood immediately that he was overmatched.

"I ask one more time; then I end my frustration," came the whisper.

"You are not drow," Morik replied, as much to buy some time as to ensure that this man—and he knew that it was a man and certainly no dark elf—would not act rashly.

"Perhaps I am, though under the guise of a wizard's spell," the assailant replied. "But that could not be—or could it?—since no magic will work in this room." As he finished, he roughly pushed Morik away, then grabbed his shoulder to spin the frightened rogue around as he fell back.

Morik didn't recognize the man, though he still understood that he was in imminent danger. He glanced down at his own dagger, and it seemed a pitiful thing indeed against the magnificent, jewel-handled blade his opponent carried—almost a reflection of the relative strengths of their wielders, Morik recognized with a wince.

Morik the Rogue was as good a thief as roamed the streets of Luskan, a city full of thieves. His reputation, though bloated by bluff, had been well-earned across the bowels of the city. This man before him, older than Morik by a decade, perhaps, and standing so calm and so balanced . . .

This man had gotten into his apartment and had remained there unobserved despite Morik's attempted scrutiny. Morik noted then that the bed sheets were rumpled—but hadn't he just looked at them, to see them perfectly smooth?

"You are not drow," Morik dared to say again.

"Not all of Jarlaxle's agents are dark elves, are they, Morik the Rogue?" the man replied.

Morik nodded and slipped his dagger into its sheath at his belt, a move designed to alleviate the tension, something that Morik desperately wanted to do.

"The jewels?" the man asked.

Morik could not hide the panic from his face.

"You should have purchased them from Telsburgher," the man remarked. "The way was clear and the assignment was not difficult."

"The way would have been clear," Morik corrected, "but for a minor magistrate who holds old grudges."

The intruder continued to stare, showing neither intrigue nor anger, telling Morik nothing at all about whether or not he was even interested in any excuses.

"Telsburgher is ready to sell them to me," Morik quickly added, "at the agreed price. His hesitation is only a matter of his fear that there will be retribution from Magistrate Jharkheld. The evil man holds an old grudge. He knows that I am back in town and wishes to drag me back to his Prisoner's Carnival, but he cannot, by word of his superiors, I am told. Thank Jarlaxle for me."

"You thank Jarlaxle by performing as instructed," the man replied, and Morik nervously shifted from foot to foot. "He helps you to fill his purse, not to fill his heart with good feelings."

Morik nodded. "I fear to go after Jharkheld," he explained. "How high might I strike without incurring the wrath of the greater powers of Luskan, thus ultimately wounding Jarlaxle's purse?"

"Jharkheld is not a concern," the man answered with a tone so assured that Morik found that he believed every word. "Complete the transaction."

"But . . ." Morik started to reply.

"This night," came the answer, and the man turned away and started for the door.

His hands worked in amazing circles right before Morik's eyes as trap after trap after lock fell open. It had taken Morik several minutes to get through that door, and that with an intricate knowledge of every trap—which he had set—and with the keys for the three supposedly difficult locks, and yet, within the span of two minutes, the door now swung open wide.

The man glanced back and tossed something to the floor at Morik's feet.

A wire.

"The one on your bottom trap had stretched beyond usefulness," the man explained. "I repaired it for you."

He went out then and closed the door, and Morik heard the clicks and sliding panels as all the locks and traps were efficiently reset.

Morik went to his bed cautiously and pulled the bed sheets aside. A hole had been cut into his mattress, perfectly sized to hold the intruder.

Morik gave a helpless laugh, his respect for Jarlaxle's band multiplying. He didn't even have to go over to his trapped vase to know that the orb now within it was a fake and that the real one had just walked out his door.

*   *   *   *   *

Entreri blinked as he walked out into the late afternoon Luskan sun. He dropped a hand into his pocket, to feel the enchanted device he had just taken from Morik. This small orb had frustrated Rai-guy. It defeated his magic when he'd tried to visit Morik himself, as it was likely doing now. That thought alone pleased Entreri greatly. It had taken Bregan D'aerthe nearly a tenday to discern the source of Morik's sudden distance, how the man had made his room inaccessible to the prying eyes of the wizards. Thus, Entreri had been sent. He held no illusions that his trip had to do with his thieving prowess, but rather, it was simply because the dark elves weren't certain of how resistant Morik might be and simply hadn't wished to risk any of their brethren in the exploration. Certainly Jarlaxle wouldn't have been pleased to learn that Rai-guy and Kimmuriel had forced Entreri to go, but the pair knew that Entreri wouldn't go to Jarlaxle with the information.

So Entreri had played message boy for the two formidable, hated dark elves.

His instructions upon taking the orb and finishing his business with Morik had been explicit and precise. He was to place the orb aside and use the magical signal whistle Rai-guy had given him to call to the dark elves in faraway Calimport, but he wasn't in any hurry.

He knew that he should have killed Morik, both for the man's impertinence in trying to shield himself and for failing to produce the required jewels. Rai-guy and Kimmuriel would demand such punishment, of course. Now he'd have to justify his actions, to protect Morik somewhat.

He knew Luskan fairly well, having been through the city several times, including an extended visit only a few days before, when he, along with several other drow agents, had learned the truth of Morik's magic-blocking device. Wandering the streets, he soon heard the shouts and cheers of the vicious Prisoner's Carnival. He entered the back of the open square just as some poor fool was having his intestines pulled out like a great length of rope. Entreri hardly noticed the spectacle, concentrating instead on the sharp-featured, diminutive, robed figure presiding over the torture.

The man screamed at the writhing victim, telling him to surrender his associates, there and then, before it was too late. "Secure a chance for a more pleasant afterlife!" the magistrate screeched, his voice as sharp as his angry, angular features. "Now! Before you die!"

607

The man only wailed. It seemed to Entreri as if he was far beyond any point of even comprehending the magistrate's words.

He died soon enough and the show was over. The people began filtering out of the square, most nodding their heads and smiling, speaking excitedly of Jharkheld's fine show this day.

That was all Entreri needed to hear.

He moved shadow to shadow, following the magistrate down the short walk from the back of the square to the tower that housed the quarters of the officials of Prisoner's Carnival as well as the dungeons holding those who would soon face the public tortures.

He mused at his own good fortune in carrying Morik's orb, for it gave him some measure of protection from any wizard hired to further secure the tower. That left only sentries and mechanical traps in his way.

Artemis Entreri feared neither.

He went into the tower as the sun disappeared in the west.

* * * * *

"They have too many allies," Rai-guy insisted.

"They would be gone without a trace," Jarlaxle replied with a wide smile. "Simply gone."

Rai-guy groaned and shook his head, and Kimmuriel, across the room and sitting comfortably in a plush chair, one leg thrown over the cushioning arm, looked up at the ceiling and rolled his eyes.

"You continue to doubt me?" Jarlaxle asked, his tone light and innocent, not threatening. "Consider all that we have already accomplished here in Calimport and across the surface. We have agents in several major cities, including Waterdeep."

"We are *exploring* agents in other cities," Rai-guy corrected. "We have but one currently working, the little rogue in Luskan." He paused and glanced over at his psionicist counterpart and smiled. "Perhaps."

Kimmuriel chuckled as he considered their second agent now working in Luskan, the one Jarlaxle did not know had left Calimport.

"The others are preliminary," Rai-guy went on. "Some are promising, others not so, but none are worthy of the title of agent at this time."

"Soon, then," said Jarlaxle, coming forward in his own comfortable chair. "Soon! They will become profitable partners or we will find others—not so difficult a thing to do among the greedy humans. The situation here in Calimport . . . look around you. Can you doubt our wisdom in coming here? The gems and jewels are flowing fast, a direct line to a drow population eager to expand their possessions beyond the limited wealth of Menzoberranzan."

"Fortunate are we if the houses of Ched Nasad determine that we are undercutting their economy," Rai-guy, who hailed from that other drow city, remarked sarcastically.

Jarlaxle scoffed at the notion.

"I cannot deny the profitability of Calimport," the wizard lieutenant went on, "yet when we first planned our journey to the surface, we all agreed that it would show immediate and strong returns. As we all agreed it would likely be a short tenure, and that, after the initial profits, we would do well to reconsider our position and perhaps retreat to our own land, leaving only the best of the trading connections and agents in place."

"So we should reconsider, and so I have," said Jarlaxle. "It seems obvious to me that we underestimated the potential of our surface operations. Expand! Expand, I say."

Again came the disheartened expressions. Kimmuriel was still staring at the ceiling, as if in abject denial of what Jarlaxle was proposing.

"The Rakers desire that we limit our trade to this one section," Jarlaxle reminded, "yet many of the craftsmen of the more exotic goods—merchandise that would likely prove most attractive in Menzoberranzan—are outside of that region."

"Then we cut a deal with the Rakers, let them in on the take for this new and profitable market to which they have no access," said Rai-guy, a perfectly reasonable suggestion in light of the history of Bregan D'aerthe, a mercenary and opportunistic band that always tried to use the words "mutually beneficial" as their business credo.

"They are pimples," Jarlaxle replied, extending his thumb and index finger in the air before him and pressing them together as if he was squeezing away an unwanted blemish. "They will simply disappear."

"Not as easy a task as you seem to believe," came a feminine voice from the doorway, and the three glanced over to see Sharlotta Vespers gliding into the room, dressed in a long gown slit high enough to reveal one very shapely leg. "The Rakers pride themselves on spreading their organizational lines far and wide. You could destroy all of their houses and all of their known agents, even all of the people dealing with all of their agents, and still leave many witnesses."

"Who would do what?" Jarlaxle asked, but he was still smiling, even patting his chair for Sharlotta to go over and sit with him, which she did, curling about him familiarly.

The sight of it made Rai-guy glance again at Kimmuriel. Both knew that Jarlaxle was bedding the human woman, the most powerful remnant—along with Entreri—of the old Basadoni Guild, and neither of them liked the idea. Sharlotta was a sly one, as humans go, almost sly enough to be accepted among the society of drow. She had even mastered the language of the drow and was now working on the intricate hand signals of the dark elven silent code. Rai-guy found her perfectly repulsive, and Kimmuriel, though seeing her as exotic, did not like the idea of having her whispering dangerous suggestions into Jarlaxle's ear.

In this particular matter, though, it seemed to both of them that Sharlotta was on their side, so they didn't try to interrupt her as they usually did.

"Witnesses who would tell every remaining guild," Sharlotta explained, "and who would inform the greater powers of Calimshan. The destruction of the Rakers Guild would imply that a truly great power had secretly come to Calimport."

"One has," Jarlaxle said with a grin.

"One whose greatest strength lies in remaining secret," Sharlotta replied.

Jarlaxle pushed her from his lap, right off the chair, so that she had to move quickly to get her shapely legs under her in time to prevent falling unceremoniously on her rump.

The mercenary leader then rose as well, pushing right past Sharlotta as if her opinion mattered not at all, and moving closer to his more important lieutenants. "I once envisioned Bregan D'aerthe's role on the surface as that of importer and exporter," he explained. "This we have easily achieved. Now I see the truth of the human dominated societies, and that is a truth of weakness. We can go further—we *must* go further."

"Conquest?" Rai-guy asked sourly, sarcastically.

"Not as Baenre attempted with Mithral Hall," Jarlaxle eagerly explained. "More a matter of absorption." Again came that wicked smile. "For those who will play."

"And those who will not simply disappear?" Rai-guy asked, but his sarcasm seemed lost on Jarlaxle, who only smiled all the wider.

"Did you not execute a Raker spy only the other day?" Jarlaxle asked.

"There is a profound difference in defending our privacy and trying to expand our borders," the wizard replied.

"Semantics," Jarlaxle said with a laugh. "Simply semantics."

Behind him, Sharlotta Vespers bit her lip and shook her head, fearing that her newfound benefactors might be about to make a tremendous and very dangerous blunder.

*　　*　　*　　*　　*

From an alley not so far away, Entreri listened to the shouts and confusion coming from the tower. When he had entered, he'd gone downstairs first, to find a particularly unpleasant prisoner to free. Once he had ushered the man to relative safety, to the open tunnels at the back of the dungeons, he had gone upstairs to the first floor, then up again, moving quietly and deliberately along the shadowy, torch-lit corridors.

Finding Jharkheld's room proved easy enough.

The door hadn't even been locked.

Had he not just witnessed the magistrate's work at Prisoner's Carnival, Artemis Entreri might have reasoned with him concerning Morik.

Now the way was clear for Morik to complete his task and proffer the jewels.

Entreri wondered if the escaped prisoner, the obvious murderer of poor Jharkheld, had been found in the maze of tunnels yet. What misery the man would face. A wry grin found its way onto Entreri's face, for he hardly felt any guilt about using the wretch for his own gain. The idiot should have known better, after all. Why would someone come in unannounced and at obvious great personal risk to save him? Why hadn't he even questioned Entreri while the assassin was releasing him from the shackles? Why, if he was smart enough to deserve his life, hadn't he tried to capture Entreri in his place, to put this unasked-for and unknown savior up in the shackles in his stead, to face the executioner? So many prisoners came through these dungeons that the gaolers likely wouldn't even have been aware of the change.

So, his fate was the thug's own to accept, and in Entreri's thinking, of his own doing. Of course, the thug would claim that someone else had helped him to escape, had set it all up to make it look like it was his doing.

Prisoner's Carnival hardly cared for such excuses.

Nor did Artemis Entreri.

He dismissed all thoughts of those problems, glanced around to ensure that he was alone, and placed the magic dispelling orb along the side of the alley. He walked across the way and blew his whistle. He wondered then how this might work. Magic would be needed, after all, to get him back to Calimport, but how might that work if he had to take the orb along? Wouldn't the orb's dweomer simply dispel the attempted teleportation?

A blue screen of light appeared beside him. It was a magical doorway, he knew, and not one of Rai-guy's, but rather the doing of Kimmuriel Oblodra. So that was it, he mused. Perhaps the orb wouldn't work against psionics.

Or perhaps it would, and that thought unsettled the normally unshakable Entreri profoundly as he moved to collect the item. What would happen if the orb somehow did affect Kimmuriel's dimension warp? Might he wind up in the wrong place—even in another plane of existence, perhaps?

Entreri shook that thought away as well. Life was risky when dealing with drow, magical orbs or not. He took care to pocket the orb slyly, so that any prying eyes would have a difficult time making out the movement in the dark alley, then strode quickly up to the portal, and with a single deep breath, stepped through.

He came out dizzy, fighting hard to hold his balance, in the guild hall's private sorcery chambers back in Calimport, hundreds and hundreds of miles away.

There stood Kimmuriel and Rai-guy, staring at him hard.

611

"The jewels?" Rai-guy asked in the drow language, which Entreri understood, though not well.

"Soon," the assassin replied in his shaky command of Deep Drow. "There was a problem."

Both dark elves lifted their white eyebrows in surprise.

"*Was*," Entreri emphasized. "Morik will have the jewels presently."

"Then Morik lives," Kimmuriel remarked pointedly. "What of his attempts to hide from us?"

"More the attempts of local magistrates to seal him off from any outside influences," Entreri lied. "One local magistrate," he quickly corrected, seeing their faces sour. "The issue has been remedied."

Neither drow seemed pleased, but neither openly complained.

"And this local magistrate had magically sealed off Morik's room from outside, prying eyes?" Rai-guy asked.

"And all other magic," Entreri answered. "It has been corrected."

"With the orb?" Kimmuriel added.

"Morik proffered the orb," Rai-guy remarked, narrowing his eyes.

"He apparently did not know what he was buying," Entreri said calmly, not getting alarmed, for he recognized that his ploys had worked.

Rai-guy and Kimmuriel would hold their suspicions that it had been Morik's work, and not that of any minor official, of course. They would suspect that Entreri had bent the truth to suit his own needs, but the assassin knew that he hadn't given them anything overt enough for them to act upon—at least, not without raising the ire of Jarlaxle.

Again, the realization that his security was almost wholly based on the mercenary leader did not sit well with Entreri. He didn't like being dependent, equating the word with weakness.

He had to turn the situation around.

"You have the orb," Rai-guy remarked, holding out his slender, deceivingly delicate hand.

"Better for me than for you," the assassin dared to reply, and that declaration set the two dark elves back on their heels.

Even as he finished speaking, though, Entreri felt the tingling in his pocket. He dropped a hand to the orb, and his sensitive fingers felt a subtle vibration coming from deep within the enchanted item. Entreri's gaze focused on Kimmuriel. The drow was standing with his eyes closed, deep in concentration.

Then he understood. The orb's enchantment would do nothing against any of Kimmuriel's formidable mind powers, and Entreri had seen this psionic trick before. Kimmuriel was reaching into the latent energy within the orb and was exciting that energy to explosive levels.

Entreri toyed with the idea of waiting until the last moment then throwing the orb into Kimmuriel's face. How he would enjoy the sight of that wretched drow caught in one of his own tricks!

612

With a wave of his hand, Kimmuriel opened a dimensional portal, from the room to the nearly deserted dusty street outside. It was a portal large enough for the orb, but that would not allow Entreri to step through.

Entreri felt the energy building, building . . . the vibrations were not so subtle any longer. Still he held back, staring at Kimmuriel—just staring and waiting, letting the drow know that he was not afraid.

In truth this was no contest of wills. Entreri had a mounting explosion in his pocket, and Kimmuriel was far enough away so that he would feel little effect from it other than the splattering of Entreri's blood. Again the assassin considered throwing the orb into Kimmuriel's face, but again he realized the futility of such a course.

Kimmuriel would simply stop exciting the latent energy within the orb, would shut off the explosion as completely as dipping a torch into water snuffed out its flame. Entreri would have given Rai-guy and Kimmuriel all the justification they needed to utterly destroy him. Jarlaxle might be angry, but he couldn't and wouldn't deny them their right to defend themselves.

Artemis Entreri wasn't ready for such a fight.

Not yet.

He tossed the orb out through the open door and watched, a split second later, as it exploded into dust.

The magical door went away.

"You play dangerous games," Rai-guy remarked.

"Your drow friend is the one who brought on the explosion," Entreri casually replied.

"I speak not of that," the wizard retorted. "There is a common saying among your people that it is foolhardy to send a child to do a man's work. We have a similar saying, that it is foolhardy to send a human to do a drow's work."

Entreri stared at him hard, having no response. This whole situation was starting to feel like those days when he had been trapped down in Menzoberranzan, when he had known that, in a city of twenty thousand dark elves, no matter how good he got, no matter how perfect his craft, he would never be considered any higher in society's rankings than twenty thousand and one.

Rai-guy and Kimmuriel tossed out a few phrases between themselves, insults mostly, some crude, some subtle, all aimed at Entreri.

He took them, every one, and said nothing, because he could say nothing. He kept thinking of Dallabad Oasis and a particular sword and gauntlet combination.

He accepted their demeaning words, because he had to.

For now.

Chapter 4

Many Roads to Many Places

Entreri stood in the shadows of the doorway, listening with great curiosity to the soliloquy taking place in the room. He could only make out small pieces of the oration. The speaker, Jarlaxle, was talking quickly and excitedly in the drow tongue. Entreri, in addition to his limited Deep Drow vocabulary, couldn't hear every word from this distance.

"They will not stay ahead of us, because we move too quickly," the mercenary leader remarked. Entreri heard and was able to translate every word of that line, for it seemed as if Jarlaxle was cheering someone on. "Yes, street by street they will fall. Who can stand against us joined?"

"Us *joined?*" the assassin silently echoed, repeating the drow word over and over to make sure that he was translating it properly. *Us?* Jarlaxle could not be speaking of his alliance with Entreri, or even with the remnants of the Basadoni Guild. Compared to the strength of Bregan D'aerthe, these were minor additions. Had Jarlaxle made some new deal, then, without Entreri's knowledge? A deal with some pasha, perhaps, or an even greater power?

The assassin bent in closer, listening particularly for any names of demons or devils—or of illithids, perhaps. He shuddered at the thought of any of the three. Demons were too unpredictable and too savage to serve any alliance. They would do whatever served their specific needs at any particular moment, without regard for the greater benefit to the alliance. Devils were more predictable—were *too* predictable. In their hierarchical view of the world, they inevitably sat on top of the pile.

Still, compared to the third notion that had come to him, that of the illithids, Entreri was almost hoping to hear Jarlaxle utter the name of a mighty demon. Entreri had been forced to deal with illithids during his stay in Menzoberranzan—the mind flayers were an unavoidable side of life in the drow city—and he had no desire to ever, ever, see one of the squishy-headed, wretched creatures again.

He listened a bit longer, and Jarlaxle seemed to calm down and to settle more comfortably into his seat. The mercenary leader was still talking, just muttering to himself about the impending downfall of the Rakers, when Entreri strode into the room.

"Alone?" the assassin asked innocently. "I thought I heard voices."

He noted with some relief that Jarlaxle wasn't wearing his magical, protective eye patch this day, which made it unlikely that the drow had just encountered, or soon planned to encounter, any illithids. The eye patch protected against mind magic, and none in all the world were more proficient at such things as the dreaded mind flayers.

"Sorting things out," Jarlaxle explained, and his ease with the common tongue of the surface world seemed no less fluent than that of his native language. "There is so much afoot."

"Danger, mostly," Entreri replied.

"For some," said Jarlaxle with a chuckle.

Entreri looked at him doubtfully.

"Surely you do not believe that the Rakers can match our power?" the mercenary leader asked incredulously.

"Not in open battle," Entreri answered, "but that is how it has been with them for many years. They cannot match many, blade to blade, and yet they have ever found a way to survive."

"Because they are fortunate."

"Because they are intricately tied to greater powers," Entreri corrected. "A man need not be physically powerful if he is guarded by a giant."

"Unless the giant has more tightly befriended a rival," Jarlaxle interjected. "And giants are known to be unreliable."

"You have arranged this with the greater lords of Calimport?" Entreri asked, unconvinced. "With whom, and why was I not involved in such a negotiation?"

Jarlaxle shrugged, offering not a clue.

"Impossible," Entreri decided. "Even if you threatened one or more of them, the Rakers are too long-standing, too entrenched in the power web of all Calimshan, for such treachery against them to prosper. They have allies to protect them against other allies. There is no way that even

Jarlaxle and Bregan D'aerthe could have cleared the opposition to such a sudden and destabilizing shift in the power structure of the region as the decimation of the Rakers."

"Perhaps I have allied with the most powerful being ever to come to Calimport," Jarlaxle said dramatically, and typically, cryptically.

Entreri narrowed his dark eyes and stared at the outrageous drow, looking for clues, any clues, as to what this uncharacteristic behavior might herald. Jarlaxle was often cryptic, always mysterious, and ever ready to grab at an opportunity that would bring him greater power or profits, and yet, something seemed out of place here. To Entreri's thinking, the impending assault on the Rakers was a blunder, which was something the legendary Jarlaxle never did. It seemed obvious, then, that the cunning drow had indeed made some powerful connection or ally, or was possessed of some deeper understanding of the situation. This Entreri doubted since he, not Jarlaxle, was the best connected person on Calimport's streets.

Even given one of those possibilities, though, something just didn't seem quite right to Entreri. Jarlaxle was cocky and arrogant—of course he was!—but never before had he seemed this self-assured, especially in a situation as potentially explosive as this.

The situation seemed only more explosive if Entreri looked beyond the inevitability of the downfall of the Rakers. He knew well the murderous power of the dark elves and held no doubt that Bregan D'aerthe would slaughter the competing guild, but there were so many implications to that victory—too many, certainly, for Jarlaxle to be so comfortable.

"Has your role in this been determined?" Jarlaxle asked.

"No role," Entreri answered, and his tone left no doubt that he was pleased by that fact. "Rai-guy and Kimmuriel have all but cast me aside."

Jarlaxle laughed aloud, for the truth behind that statement—that Entreri had been willingly cast aside—was all too obvious.

Entreri stared at him and didn't crack a smile. Jarlaxle had to know the dangers he had just walked into, a potentially catastrophic situation that could send him and Bregan D'aerthe fleeing back to the dark hole of Menzoberranzan. Perhaps that was it, the assassin mused. Perhaps Jarlaxle longed for home and was slyly facilitating the move. The mere thought of that made Entreri wince. Better that Jarlaxle kill him outright than drag him back there.

Perhaps Entreri would be set up as an agent, as was Morik in Luskan. No, the assassin decided, that would not suffice. Calimport was more dangerous than Luskan, and if the power of Bregan D'aerthe was forced away, he would not take such a risk. Too many powerful enemies would be left behind.

"It will begin soon, if it has not already," Jarlaxle remarked. "Thus, it will be over soon."

Sooner than you believe, Entreri thought, but he kept silent. He was a man who survived through careful calculation, by weighing scrupulously the consequences of every step and every word. He knew Jarlaxle to be a kindred spirit, but he could not reconcile that with the action that was being undertaken this very night, which, in searching it from any angle, seemed a tremendous and unnecessary gamble.

What did Jarlaxle know that he did not?

* * * * *

No one ever looked more out of place anywhere than did Sharlotta Vespers as she descended the rung ladder into one of Calimport's sewers. She was wearing her trademark long gown, her hair neatly coiffed as always, her exotic face painted delicately to emphasize her brown, almond-shaped eyes. Still, she was quite at home there, and anyone who knew her would not have been surprised to find her there.

Especially if they considered her warlord escorts.

"What word from above?" Rai-guy asked her, speaking quickly and in the drow tongue. The wizard, despite his misgivings about Sharlotta, was impressed by how quickly she had absorbed the language.

"There is tension," Sharlotta replied. "The doors of many guilds are locked fast this night. Even the Copper Ante is accepting no patrons—an unprecedented event. The streets know that something is afoot."

Rai-guy flashed a sour look at Kimmuriel. The two had just agreed that their plans depended mostly on stealth and surprise, that all of the elements of the Basadoni Guild and Bregan D'aerthe would have to reach their objectives nearly simultaneously to ensure that few witnesses remained.

How much this seemed like Menzoberranzan! In the drow city, one house going after another—a not-uncommon event—would measure success not only by the result of the actual fighting, but by the lack of credible witnesses left to produce evidence of the treachery. Even if every drow in the great city knew without doubt which house had precipitated the battle, no action would ever be taken unless the evidence demanding it was overwhelming.

But this was not Menzoberranzan, Rai-guy reminded himself. Up here, suspicion would invite investigation. In the drow city, suspicion without undeniable evidence only invited quiet praise.

"Our warriors are in place," Kimmuriel remarked. "The drow are beneath the guild houses, with force enough to batter through, and the Basadoni soldiers have surrounded the main three buildings. It will be swift, for they cannot anticipate the attack from below."

Rai-guy kept his gaze upon Sharlotta as his associate detailed the situation, and he did not miss a slight arch of one of her eyebrows. Had

Bregan D'aerthe been betrayed? Were the Rakers setting up defenses against the assault from below?

"The agents have been isolated?" the drow wizard pressed to Sharlotta, referring to the first round of the invasion: the fight with—or rather, the assassinations of—Raker spies in the streets.

"The agents are not to be found," Sharlotta replied matter-of-factly, a surprising tone given the enormity of the implications.

Again Rai-guy glanced at Kimmuriel.

"All is in place," the psionicist reminded.

"Keego's swarm cramps the tunnels," Rai-guy replied, his words an archaic drow proverb referring to a long-ago battle in which an overwhelming swarm of goblins led by the crafty, rebellious slave, Keego, had been utterly destroyed by a small and sparsely populated city of dark elves. The drow had gone out from their homes to catch the larger force in the tight tunnels beyond the relatively open drow city. Simply translated, given the current situation, Rai-guy's words followed up Kimmuriel's remark. All was in place to fight the wrong battle.

Sharlotta looked at the wizard curiously, and he understood her confusion, for the soldiers of Bregan D'aerthe waiting in the tunnels beneath the Rakers' houses hardly constituted a "swarm."

Of course, Rai-guy hardly cared whether Sharlotta understood or not.

"Have we traced the course of the missing agents?" Rai-guy asked Sharlotta. "Do we know where they have fled?"

"Back to the houses, likely," the woman replied. "Few are on the streets this night."

Again, the less-than-subtle hint that too much had been revealed. Had Sharlotta herself betrayed them? Rai-guy fought the urge to interrogate her on the spot, using drow torture techniques that would quickly and efficiently break down any human. If he did so, he knew, he would have to answer to Jarlaxle, and Rai-guy was not ready for that fight . . . yet.

If he called it all off at that critical moment—if all the fighters, Basadoni and dark elf, returned to the guild house with their weapons unstained by Raker blood—Jarlaxle would not be pleased. The drow was determined to see this conquest through despite the protests of all of his lieutenants.

Rai-guy closed his eyes and logically sifted through the situation, trying to find some safer common ground. There was one Raker house far removed from the others, and likely only lightly manned. While destroying it would do little to weaken the structure and effectiveness of the opposition guild, perhaps such a conquest would quiet Jarlaxle's expected rampage.

"Recall the Basadoni soldiers," the wizard ordered. "Have their retreat be a visible one—instruct some to enter the Copper Ante or other establishments."

"The Copper Ante's doors are closed," Sharlotta reminded him.

"Then open them," Rai-guy instructed. "Tell Dwahvel Tiggerwillies that there is no need for her and her diminutive clan to cower this night. Let our soldiers be seen about the streets—not as a unified fighting force, but in smaller groups."

"What of Bregan D'aerthe?" Kimmuriel asked with some concern. Not as much concern, Rai-guy noted, as he would have expected, given that he had just countermanded Jarlaxle's explicit orders.

"Reposition Berg'inyon and all of our magic-users to the eighth position," Rai-guy replied, referring to the sewer hold beneath the exposed Raker house.

Kimmuriel arched his white eyebrows at that. They knew the maximum resistance they could expect from that lone outpost, and it hardly seemed as if Berg'inyon and more magic-users would be needed to win out easily in that locale.

"It must be executed as completely and carefully as if we were attacking House Baenre itself," Rai-guy demanded, and Kimmuriel's eyebrows went even higher. "Redefine the plans and reposition all necessary drow forces to execute the attack."

"We could summon our kobold slaves alone to finish this task," Kimmuriel replied derisively.

"No kobolds and no humans," Rai-guy explained, emphasizing every word. "This is work for drow alone."

Kimmuriel seemed to catch on to Rai-guy's thinking then, for a wry smile showed on his face. He glanced at Sharlotta, nodded back at Rai-guy, and closed his eyes. He used his psionic energies to reach out to Berg'inyon and the other Bregan D'aerthe field commanders.

Rai-guy let his gaze settle fully on Sharlotta. To her credit, her expression and posture did not reveal her thoughts. Still, Rai-guy felt certain she was wondering if he had come to suspect her or some other Raker informant.

"You said that our power would prove overwhelming," Sharlotta remarked.

"For today's battle, perhaps," Rai-guy replied. "The wise thief does not steal the egg if his action will awaken the dragon."

Sharlotta continued to stare at him, continued to wonder, he knew. He enjoyed the realization that this too-clever human woman, guilty or not, was suddenly worried. She turned for the ladder again and took a step up.

"Where are you going?" Rai-guy asked.

"To recall the Basadoni soldiers," she replied, as if the explanation should have been obvious.

Rai-guy shook his head and motioned for her to step down. "Kimmuriel will relay the commands," he said.

Sharlotta hesitated—Rai-guy enjoyed the moment of confusion and concern—but she did step back down to the tunnel floor.

* * * * *

Berg'inyon could not believe the change in plans—what was the point of this entire offensive if the bulk of the Rakers' Guild escaped the onslaught? He had grown up in Menzoberranzan, and in that matriarchal society, males learned how to take orders without question. So it was now for Berg'inyon.

He had been trained in the finest battle tactics of the greatest house of Menzoberranzan and had at his disposal a seemingly overwhelming force for the task at hand, the destruction of a small, exposed Raker house—an outpost sitting on unfriendly streets. Despite his trepidation at the change in plans, his private questioning of the purpose of this mission, Berg'inyon Baenre wore an eager smile.

The scouts, the stealthiest of the stealthy drow, returned. Only minutes before, they had been inserted into the house above through wizard-made tunnels.

Drow fingers flashed, the silent hand gesture code.

While Berg'inyon's confidence mounted, so did his confusion over why this target alone had been selected. There were only a score of humans in the small house above, and none of them seemed to be magic-users. According to the drow scouts' assessment they were street thugs—men who survived by keeping to favorable shadows.

Under the keen eyes of a dark elf, there were no favorable shadows.

While Berg'inyon and his army had a strong idea of what they would encounter in the house above them, the humans could not understand the monumental doom that lay below them.

You have outlined to the group commanders all routes of retreat? Berg'inyon's fingers and facial gestures asked. He made it clear from the fact that he signaled retreat with his left hand that he was referring to any possible avenues their enemies might take to run away.

The wizards are positioned accordingly, one scout silently replied.

The lead hunters have been given their courses, another added.

Berg'inyon nodded, flashed the signal for commencing the operation, then moved to join his assault group. His would be the last group to enter the building, but they were the ones who would cut the fastest path to the very top.

There were two wizards in Berg'inyon's group. One stood with his eyes closed, ready to convey the signal. The other positioned himself accordingly, his eyes and hands pointed up at the ceiling, a pinch of seeds from the Underdark selussi fungus in one hand.

It is time, came a magical whisper, one that seeped through the walls and to the ears of all the drow.

The magic-user eyeing the ceiling began his spellcasting, weaving his hands as if tracing joining semicircles with each, thumbs touching, little fingers touching, back and forth, back and forth, chanting quietly all the while.

He finished with a chant that sounded more like a hiss, and reached his outstretched fingers to the ceiling.

That part of the stone ceiling began to ripple, as if the wizard had stabbed his fingers into clear water. The wizard held the pose for many seconds. The rippling increased until the stone became an indistinct blur.

The stone above the wizard disappeared—was just gone. In its place was an upward reaching corridor that cut through several feet of stone to end at the ground floor of the Raker house.

One unfortunate Raker had been caught by surprise, his heels right over the edge of the suddenly appearing hole. His arms worked great circles as he tried to maintain his balance. The drow warriors shifted into position under the hole and leaped. Enacting their innate drow levitation abilities, they floated up, up.

The first dark elf floating up beside the falling Raker grabbed him by the collar and yanked him backward, tumbling him into the hole. The human managed to land in a controlled manner, feet first, then buckling his legs and tumbling to the side to absorb the shock. He came up with equal grace, drawing a dagger.

His face blanched when he saw the truth about him: dark elves—drow!—were floating up into his guild house. Another drow, handsome and strong, holding the finest-edged blade the Raker could ever have imagined, faced him.

Maybe he tried to reason with the dark elf, offering his surrender, but while his mouth worked in a logical, hide-saving manner, his body, paralyzed by stark terror, did not. He still held his knife out before him as he spoke, and since Berg'inyon did not understand well the language of the surface dwellers, he had no way of understanding the Raker's intent.

Nor was the drow about to pause to figure it out. His fine sword stabbed forward and slashed down, taking the dagger and the hand that held it. A quick retraction re-gathered his balance and power, and out went the sword again. Straight and sure, it tore through flesh and sliced rib, biting hard at the foolish man's heart.

The man fell, quite dead, and still wearing that curious, stunned expression.

Berg'inyon didn't pause long enough to wipe his blade. He crouched, sprang straight up, and levitated fast into the house. His encounter had delayed him no more than a span of a few heartbeats, and yet, the floor of the room and the corridor beyond the open door was already littered with human corpses.

Berg'inyon's team exited the room soon after, before the wizard's initial passwall spell had even expired. Not a drow had been more than slightly injured and not a human remained alive. The Raker house held no treasure when they were done—not even the few coins several of the guildsmen had secretly tucked under loose floorboards—and even the furniture was gone. Magical fires had consumed every foot of flooring and all of the partitioning walls. From the outside, the house seemed quiet and secure. Inside, it was no more than a charred and empty husk.

Bregan D'aerthe had spoken.

* * * * *

"I accept no accolades," Berg'inyon Baenre remarked when he met up with Rai-guy, Kimmuriel, and Sharlotta. It was a common drow saying, with clear implications that the vanquished opponent was not worthy enough for the victor to take any pride in having defeated him.

Kimmuriel gave a wry smile. "The house was effectively purged," he said. "None escaped. You performed as was required. There is no glory in that, but there is acceptance."

As he had done all day, Rai-guy continued his scrutiny of Sharlotta Vespers. Was the human woman even comprehending the sincerity of Kimmuriel's words, and if so, did that allow her any insight into the true power that had come to Calimport? For any guild to so completely annihilate one of another's houses was no small feat—unless the attacking guild happened to be comprised of drow warriors who understood the complexities of inter-house warfare better than any race in all the world. Did Sharlotta recognize this? And if she did, would she be foolish enough to try to use it to her advantage?

Her expression now was mostly stone-faced, but with just a trace of intrigue, a hint to Rai-guy that the answer would be yes, to both questions. The drow wizard smiled at that, a confirmation that Sharlotta Vespers was walking onto very dangerous ground. *Quiensin ful biezz coppon quangolth cree, a drow,* went the old saying in Menzoberranzan, and elsewhere in the drow world. Doomed are those who believe they understand the designs of the drow.

"What did Jarlaxle learn to change his course so?" Berg'inyon asked.

"Jarlaxle has learned nothing of yet," Rai-guy replied. "He chose to remain behind. The operation was mine to wage."

Berg'inyon started to redirect his question to Rai-guy then, but he stopped in midsentence and merely offered a bow to the appointed leader.

"Perhaps later you will explain to me the source of your decision, that I will better understand our enemies," he said respectfully.

Rai-guy gave a slight nod.

"There is the matter of explaining to Jarlaxle," Sharlotta remarked, in her surprising command of the drow tongue. "He will not accept your course with a mere bow."

Rai-guy's gaze darted over at Berg'inyon as she finished, quickly enough to catch the moment of anger flash through his red-glowing eyes. Sharlotta's observations were correct, of course, but coming from a

623

non-drow, an *iblith*—which was also the drow word for excrement—they intrinsically cast an insulting reflection upon Berg'inyon, who had so accepted the offered explanation. It was a minor mistake, but a few more quips like that against the young Baenre, Rai-guy knew, and there would remain too little of Sharlotta Vespers for anyone ever to make a proper identification of the pieces.

"We must tell Jarlaxle," the drow wizard put in, moving the conversation forward. "To us out here, the course change was obviously required, but he has secluded himself, too much so perhaps, to view things that way."

Kimmuriel and Berg'inyon both looked at him curiously—why would he speak so plainly in front of Sharlotta, after all?—but Rai-guy gave them a quick and quiet signal to follow along.

"We could implicate Domo and the wererats," Kimmuriel put in, obviously catching on. "Though I fear that we will then have to waste our time in slaughtering them." He looked to Sharlotta. "Much of this will fall to you."

"The Basadoni soldiers were the first to leave the fight," Rai-guy added. "And they will be the ones to return without blood on their blades." Now all three gazes fell upon Sharlotta.

The woman held her outward calm quite well. "Domo and the wererats, then," she agreed, thinking things through, obviously, as she went. "We will implicate them without faulting them. Yes, that is the way. Perhaps they did not know of our plans and coincidentally hired on with Pasha Da'Daclan to guard the sewers. As we did not wish to reveal ourselves fully to the coward Domo, we held to the unguarded regions, mostly around the eighth position."

The three drow exchanged looks, and nodded for her to continue.

"Yes," Sharlotta went on, gathering momentum and confidence. "I can turn this into an advantage with Pasha Da'Daclan as well. He felt the press of impending doom, no doubt, and that fear will only heighten when word of the utterly destroyed outer house reaches him. Perhaps he will come to believe that Domo is much more powerful than any of us believed, and that he was in league with the Basadonis, and that only House Basadoni's former dealings with the Rakers cut short the assault."

"But will that not implicate House Basadoni clearly in the one executed attack?" asked Kimmuriel, playing the role of Rai-guy's mouthpiece, drawing Sharlotta in even deeper.

"Not that we played a role, but only that we allowed it to happen," Sharlotta reasoned. "A turn of our heads in response to their increased spying efforts against our guild. Yes, and if this is conveyed properly, it will only serve to make Domo seem even more powerful. If we make the Rakers believe that they were on the edge of complete disaster, they will behave more reasonably, and Jarlaxle will find his victory." She smiled as she finished, and the three dark elves returned the look.

"Begin," Rai-guy offered, waving his hand toward the ladder leading out of their sewer quarters.

Sharlotta smiled again, the ignorant fool, and left them.

"Her deception against Pasha Da'Daclan will necessarily extend, to some level, to Jarlaxle," Kimmuriel remarked, clearly envisioning the web Sharlotta was foolishly weaving about herself.

"You have come to fear that something is not right with Jarlaxle," Berg'inyon bluntly remarked, for it was obvious that these two would not normally act so independently of their leader.

"His views have changed," Kimmuriel responded.

"You did not wish to come to the surface," Berg'inyon said with a wry smile that seemed to question the motives of his companions' reasoning.

"No, and glad will we be to see the heat of Narbondel again," Rai-guy agreed, speaking of the great glowing clock of Menzoberranzan, a pillar that revealed its measurements with heat to the dark elves, who viewed the Underdark world in the infrared spectrum of light. "You have not been up here long enough to appreciate the ridiculousness of this place. Your heart will call you home soon enough."

"Already," Berg'inyon replied. "I have no taste for this world, nor do I like the sight or smell of any I have seen up here, Sharlotta Vespers least of all."

"Her and the fool Entreri," said Rai-guy. "Yet Jarlaxle favors them both."

"His tenure in Bregan D'aerthe may be nearing its end," said Kimmuriel, and both Berg'inyon and Rai-guy opened their eyes wide at such a bold proclamation.

In truth, though, both were harboring the exact same sentiments. Jarlaxle had reached far in merely bringing them to the surface. Perhaps he'd reached too far for the rogue band to continue to hold much favor among their former associates, including most of the great houses back in Menzoberranzan. It was a gamble, and one that might indeed pay off, especially as the flow of exotic and desirable goods increased to the city.

The plan, however, had been for a short stay, only long enough to establish a few agents to properly facilitate the flow of trade. Jarlaxle had stepped in more deeply then, conquering House Basadoni and renewing his ties with the dangerous Entreri. Then, seemingly for his own amusement, Jarlaxle had gone after the most hated rogue, Drizzt Do'Urden. After completing his business with the outcast and stealing the mighty artifact Crenshinibon, he had let Drizzt walk away, had even forced Rai-guy to use a Lolth-bestowed spell of healing to save the miserable renegade's life.

And now this, a more overt grab for not profit but power, and in a place where none of Bregan D'aerthe other than Jarlaxle wished to remain.

Jarlaxle had taken small steps along this course, but he had put a long and winding road behind him. He brought all of Bregan D'aerthe further and further from their continuing mission, from the allure that had brought most of the members, Rai-guy, Kimmuriel, and Berg'inyon among them, into the organization in the first place.

"What of Sharlotta Vespers?" Kimmuriel asked.

"Jarlaxle will eliminate that problem for us," Rai-guy replied.

"Jarlaxle favors her," Berg'inyon reminded.

"She just entered into a deception against him," Rai-guy replied with all confidence. "We know this, and she knows that we know, though she has not yet considered the potentially devastating implications. She will follow our commands from this point forward."

The drow wizard smiled as he considered his own words. He always enjoyed seeing an *iblith* fall into the web of drow society, learning piece by piece that the sticky strands were layered many levels deep.

* * * * *

"I know of your hunger, for I share in it," Jarlaxle remarked. "This is not as I had envisioned, but perhaps it was not yet time."

Perhaps you place too much faith in your lieutenants, the voice in his head replied.

"No, they saw something that we, in our hunger, did not," Jarlaxle reasoned. "They are troublesome, often annoying, and not to be trusted when their personal gain is at odds with their given mission, but that was not the case here. I must examine this more carefully. Perhaps there are better avenues toward our desired goal."

The voice started to respond, but the drow mercenary cut short the dialogue, shutting it out.

The abruptness of that dismissal reminded Crenshinibon that its respect for the dark elf was well-placed. This Jarlaxle was as strong of will and as difficult to beguile as any wielder the ancient sentient artifact had ever known, even counting the great demon lords who had often joined with Crenshinibon through the centuries.

In truth, the only wielder the artifact had ever known who could so readily and completely shut out its call had been the immediate predecessor to Jarlaxle, another drow, Drizzt Do'Urden. That one's mental barrier had been constructed of morals. Crenshinibon would have been no better off in the hands of a goodly priest or a paladin, fools all and blind to the need to attain the greatest levels of power.

All that only made Jarlaxle's continued resistance even more impressive, for the artifact understood that this one held no such conscience-based mores. There was no intrinsic understanding within Jarlaxle that Crenshinibon was some evil creation and thus to be avoided out of hand. No, to Crenshinibon's reasoning, Jarlaxle viewed everyone and everything he encountered as tools, as vehicles to carry him along his desired road.

The artifact could build forks along that road, and perhaps even sharper turns as Jarlaxle wandered farther and farther from the path, but there would be no abrupt change in direction at this time.

Crenshinibon, the Crystal Shard, did not even consider seeking a new wielder, as it had often done when confronting obstacles in the past. While it sensed resistance in Jarlaxle, that resistance did not implicate danger or even inactivity. To the sentient artifact, Jarlaxle was powerful and intriguing, and full of the promise of the greatest levels of power Crenshinibon had ever known.

The fact that this drow was not a simple instrument of chaos and destruction, as were so many of the demon lords, or an easily duped human—perhaps the most redundant thought the artifact had ever considered—only made him more interesting.

They had a long way to go together, Crenshinibon believed.

The artifact would find its greatest level of power. The world would suffer greatly.

Chapter 5

The First Threads on a Grand Tapestry

Others have tried, and some have even come close," said Dwahvel Tiggerwillies, the halfling entrepreneur and leader of the only real halfling guild in all the city, a collection of pickpockets and informants who regularly congregated at Dwahvel's Copper Ante. "Some have even supposedly gotten their hands on the cursed thing."

"Cursed?" Entreri asked, resting back comfortably in his chair—a pose Artemis Entreri rarely assumed.

So unusual was the posture, that it jogged Entreri's own thoughts about this place. It was no accident that this was the only room in all the city in which Artemis Entreri had ever partaken of liquor—and even that only in moderate amounts. He had been coming here often of late—ever since he had killed his former associate, the pitiful Dondon Tiggerwillies, in the room next door. Dwahvel was Dondon's cousin, and she knew of the murder but knew, too, that Entreri had, in some respects, done the wretch a favor. Whatever ill will Dwahvel harbored over that incident couldn't hold anyway, not when her pragmatism surfaced.

Entreri knew that and knew that he was welcomed here by Dwahvel and all of her associates. Also, he knew that the Copper Ante was likely the most secure house in all of the city. No, its defenses were not formidable—

Jarlaxle could flatten the place with a small fraction of the power he had brought to Calimport—but its safeguards against prying eyes were as fine as those of a wizards' guild. That was the area, as opposed to physical defenses, where Dwahvel utilized most of her resources. Also, the Copper Ante was known as a place to purchase information, so others had a reason to keep it secure. In many ways, Dwahvel and her comrades survived as Sha'lazzi Ozoule survived, by proving of use to all potential enemies.

Entreri didn't like the comparison. Sha'lazzi was a street profiteer, loyal to no one other than Sha'lazzi. He was no more than a middleman, collecting information with his purse and not his wits, and auctioning it away to the highest bidder. He did no work other than that of salesman, and in that regard, the man was very good. He was not a contributor, just a leech, and Entreri suspected that Sha'lazzi would one day be found murdered in an alley, and that no one would care.

Dwahvel Tiggerwillies might find a similar fate, Entreri realized, but if she did, her murderer would find many out to avenge her.

Perhaps Artemis Entreri would be among them.

"Cursed," Dwahvel decided after some consideration.

"To those who feel its bite."

"To those who feel it at all," Dwahvel insisted.

Entreri shifted to the side and tilted his head, studying his surprising little friend.

"Kohrin Soulez is trapped by his possession of it," Dwahvel explained. "He builds a fortress about himself because he knows the value of the sword."

"He has many treasures," Entreri reasoned, but he knew that Dwahvel was right on this matter, at least as far as Kohrin Soulez was concerned.

"That one treasure alone invites the ire of wizards," Dwahvel predictably responded, "and the ire of those who rely upon wizards for their security."

Entreri nodded, not disagreeing, but neither was he persuaded by Dwahvel's arguments. Charon's Claw might indeed be a curse for Kohrin Soulez, but if that was so it was because Soulez had entrenched himself in a place where such a weapon would be seen as a constant lure and a constant threat. Once he got his hands on the powerful sword, Artemis Entreri had no intention of staying anywhere near to Calimport. Soulez's chains would be his escape.

"The sword is an old artifact," Dwahvel remarked, drawing Entreri's attention more fully. "Everyone who has ever claimed it has died with it in his hands."

She thought her warning dramatic, no doubt, but the words had little effect on Entreri. "Everyone dies, Dwahvel," the assassin replied without hesitation, his response fueled by the living hell that had come to him in Calimport. "It is how one lives that matters."

Dwahvel looked at him curiously, and Entreri wondered if he had, perhaps, revealed too much, or tempted Dwahvel too much to go and learn even more about the reality of the power backing Entreri and the Basadoni Guild. If the cunning halfling ever learned too much of the truth, and Jarlaxle or his lieutenants learned of her knowledge, then none of her magical wards, none of her associates—even Artemis Entreri—and none of her perceived usefulness would save her from Jarlaxle's merciless soldiers. The Copper Ante would be gutted, and Entreri would find himself without a place in which to relax.

Dwahvel continued to stare at him, her expression a mixture of professional curiosity and personal—what was it?—compassion?

"What is it that so unhinges Artemis Entreri?" she started to ask, but even as the words came forth, so too came the assassin, his jeweled dagger flashing out of his belt as he leaped out of the chair and across the expanse, too quickly for Dwahvel's guards to even register the movement, too quickly for Dwahvel to even realize what was happening.

He was simply there, hovering over her, her hairy head pulled back, his dagger just nicking her throat.

But she felt it—how she felt the bite of that vicious, life-stealing dagger. Entreri had opened a tiny wound, yet through it Dwahvel could feel her very life-force being torn out of her body.

"If such a question as that ever echoes outside of these walls," the assassin promised, his breath hot on her face, "you will regret that I did not finish this strike."

He backed away then, and Dwahvel quickly threw up one hand, fingers flapping back and forth, the signal to her crossbowmen to hold their shots. With her other hand, she rubbed her neck, pinching at the tiny wound.

"You are certain that Kohrin Soulez still has it?" Entreri asked, more to change the subject and put things back on a professional level than to gather any real information.

"He had it, and he is still alive," the obviously shaken Dwahvel answered. "That seems proof enough."

Entreri nodded and assumed his previous posture, though the relaxed position did not fit the dangerous light that now shone in his eyes.

"You still wish to leave the city by secure routes?" Dwahvel asked.

Entreri gave a slight nod.

"We will need to utilize Domo and the were—" the halfling guildmaster started to say, but Entreri cut her short.

"No."

"He has the fastest—"

"No."

Dwahvel started to argue yet again. Fulfilling Entreri's request that she get him out of Calimport without anyone knowing it would prove no easy feat, even with Domo's help. Entreri was publicly and intricately

631

tied to the Basadoni Guild, and that guild had drawn the watchful eyes of every power in Calimport. She stopped short, and this time Entreri hadn't interrupted her with a word but rather with a look, that all-too-dangerous look that Artemis Entreri had perfected decades before. It was the look that told his target that the time was fast approaching for final prayers.

"It will take some more time, then," Dwahvel remarked. "Not long, I assure you. An hour perhaps."

"No one is to know of this other than Dwahvel," Entreri instructed quietly, so that the crossbowmen in the shadows of the room's corners couldn't hear. "Not even your most trusted lieutenants."

The halfling blew a long, resigned sigh. "Two hours, then," she said.

Entreri watched her go. He knew that she couldn't possibly accede to his wishes to get him out of Calimport without anyone at all knowing of the journey—the streets were too well monitored—but it was a strong reminder to the halfling guildmaster that if anyone started talking about it too openly, Entreri would hold her personally responsible.

The assassin chuckled at the thought, for he couldn't imagine himself killing Dwahvel. He liked and respected the halfling, both for her courage and her skills.

He did need this departure to remain secret, though. If some of the others, particularly Rai-guy or Kimmuriel, found out that he had gone out, they would investigate and soon, no doubt, discern his destination. He didn't want the two dangerous drow studying Kohrin Soulez.

Dwahvel returned soon after, well within the two hours she had pessimistically predicted, and handed Entreri a rough map of this section of the city, with a route sketched on it.

"There will be someone waiting for you at the end of Crescent Avenue," she explained. "Right before the bakery."

"Detailing the second stretch your halflings have determined to be clear for travel," the assassin reasoned.

Dwahvel nodded. "My kin and other associates."

"And, of course, they will watch the movements as each map is collected," Entreri indicated.

Dwahvel shrugged. "You are a master of disguises, are you not?"

Entreri didn't answer. He set out immediately, exiting the Copper Ante and turning down a dark ally, emerging on the other side looking as though he had gained fifty pounds and walking with a pronounced limp.

He was out of Calimport within the hour, running along the northwestern road. By dawn, he was on a dune, looking down upon the Dallabad Oasis. He considered Kohrin Soulez long and hard, recalling everything he knew about the old man.

"Old," he said aloud with a sigh, for in truth, Soulez was in his early fifties, less than fifteen years older than Artemis Entreri.

The assassin turned his thoughts to the palace-fortress itself, trying to recall vivid details about the place. From this angle, all Entreri could make out were a few palm trees, a small pond, a single large boulder, a handful of tents including one larger pavilion, and behind them all, seeming to blend in with the desert sands, a brown, square-walled fortress. A handful of robed sentries walked around the fortress walls, seeming quite bored. The fortress of Dallabad did not appear very formidable—certainly nothing against the likes of Artemis Entreri—but the assassin knew better.

He had visited Soulez and Dallabad on several occasions when he had been working for Pasha Basadoni, and again more recently, when he had been in the service of Pasha Pook. He knew of the circular building within those square wall with its corridors winding in tighter and tighter circles toward the great treasury rooms of Kohrin Soulez, culminating in the private quarters of the oasis master himself.

Entreri considered Dwahvel's last description of the man and his place in the context of those memories and chuckled as he recognized the truth of her observations. Kohrin Soulez was indeed a prisoner.

Still, that prison worked well in both directions, and there was no way that Entreri could easily slip in and take that which he desired. The palace was a fortress, and a fortress full of soldiers specifically trained to thwart any attempts by the too-common thieves of the region.

The assassin thought that Dwahvel was wrong on one point, though. Kohrin himself, and not Charon's Claw, was the source of that prison. The man was so fearful of losing his prized weapon that he allowed it to dominate and consume him. His own fear of losing the sword had paralyzed him from taking any chances with it. When had Soulez last left Dallabad? the assassin wondered. When had he last visited the open market or chatted with his old associates on Calimport's streets?

No, people made their own prisons, Entreri knew, and knew well, for hadn't he, in fact, done the same thing in his obsession with Drizzt Do'Urden? Hadn't he been consumed by a foolish need to do battle with an insignificant dark elf who really had nothing to do with him?

Confident that he would never again make such an error, Artemis Entreri looked down upon Dallabad and smiled widely. Yes, Kohrin Soulez had done well to design his fortress against any would-be thieves skulking in from shadow to shadow or under cover of the darkness of night, but how would those many sentries fare when an army of dark elves descended upon them?

* * * * *

"You were with him when he learned of the retreat," Sharlotta Vespers asked Entreri the next night, soon after the assassin had quietly returned to Calimport. "How did Jarlaxle accept the news?"

633

"With typical nonchalance," Entreri answered honestly. "Jarlaxle has led Bregan D'aerthe for centuries. He is not one to betray that which is in his heart."

"Even to Artemis Entreri, who can read a man's eyes and tell him what he had for dinner the night before?" Sharlotta asked, grinning.

That smirk couldn't hold against the deadly calm expression that came over Entreri's face. "You do not begin to understand these new allies who have come to join with us," he said in all seriousness.

"To conquer us, you mean," Sharlotta replied, the first time since the takeover that Entreri had heard her even hint ill will against the dark elves. He wasn't surprised—who wouldn't quickly come to hate the wretched drow? On the other hand, Entreri had always known Sharlotta as someone who accepted whatever allies she could find, as long as they brought to her the power she so desperately craved.

"If they so choose," Entreri replied without missing a beat and in a most serious tone. "Underestimate any facet of the dark elves, from their fighting abilities to whether or not they betray themselves with expressions, and you will wind up dead, Sharlotta."

The woman started to respond but did not, fighting hard to keep an uncharacteristic hopelessness off of her expression. He knew she was beginning to feel the same way he had during his journey to Menzoberranzan, the same way that he was beginning to feel once more, particularly whenever Rai-guy and Kimmuriel were around. There was something humbling about even being near these handsome, angular creatures. The drow always knew more than they should and always revealed less than they knew. Their mystery was only heightened by the undeniable power behind their often subtle threats. And always there was that damned condescension toward anyone who was not drow. In the current situation, where Bregan D'aerthe could obviously easily overwhelm the remnants of House Basadoni, Artemis Entreri included, that condescension took on even uglier tones. It was a poignant and incessant reminder of who was the master and who was the slave.

He recognized that same feeling in Sharlotta, growing with every passing moment, and he almost used that to enlist her aid in his secret scheme to take Dallabad and its greatest prize.

Almost—then Entreri considered the course and was shocked that his feelings toward Rai-guy and Kimmuriel had almost brought forth such a blunder as that. For all his life, with only very rare exceptions, Artemis Entreri had worked alone, had used his wits to ensnare unintentional and unwitting allies. Cohorts inevitably knew too much for Entreri ever to be comfortable with them. The one exception he now made, out of simple necessity, was Dwahvel Tiggerwillies, and she, he was quite sure, would never double-cross him, not even under the questioning of the dark elves. That had always been the beauty of Dwahvel and her halfling comrades.

Sharlotta, however, was a completely different sort, Entreri now pointedly reminded himself. If he tried to enlist Sharlotta in his plan to go after Kohrin Soulez, he'd have to watch her closely forever after. She'd likely take the information from him and run to Jarlaxle, or even to Rai-guy and Kimmuriel, using Entreri's soon-to-be-lifeless body as a ladder with which to elevate herself.

Besides, Entreri did not need to bring up Dallabad to Sharlotta, for he had already made arrangements toward that end. Dwahvel would entice Sharlotta toward Dallabad with a few well-placed lies, and Sharlotta, who was predictable indeed when one played upon her sense of personal gain, would take the information to Jarlaxle, only strengthening Entre-ri's personal suggestions that Dallabad would prove a meaningful and profitable conquest.

"I never thought I would miss Pasha Basadoni," Sharlotta remarked off-handedly, the most telling statement the woman had yet made.

"You hated Basadoni," Entreri reminded.

Sharlotta didn't deny that, but neither did she change her stance.

"You did not fear him as much as you fear the drow, and rightly so," Entreri remarked. "Basadoni was loyal, thus predictable. These dark elves are neither. They are too dangerous."

"Kimmuriel told me that you lived among them in Menzoberranzan," Sharlotta mentioned. "How did you survive?"

"I survived because they were too busy to bother with killing me," Entreri honestly replied. "I was *dobluth* to them, a non-drow outcast, and not worth the trouble. Also, it seems to me now that Jarlaxle might have been using me to further his understanding of the humans of Calimport."

That brought a chuckle to Sharlotta's thick lips. "I would hardly con-sider Artemis Entreri the typical human of Calimport," she said. "And if Jarlaxle had believed that all men were possessed of your abilities, I doubt he would have dared come to the city, even if all of Menzoberranzan marched behind him."

Entreri gave a slight bow, taking the compliment in polite stride, though he never had use for flattery. To Entreri's way of thinking, one was good enough or one wasn't, and no amount of self-serving chatter could change that.

"And that is our goal now, for both our sakes," Entreri went on. "We must keep the drow busy, which would seem not so difficult a task given Jarlaxle's sudden desire rapidly to expand his surface empire. We are safer if House Basadoni is at war."

"But not within the city," Sharlotta replied. "The authorities are starting to take note of our movements and will not stand idly by much longer. We are safer if the drow are engaged in battle, but not if that battle extends beyond house-to-house."

Entreri nodded, glad that Dwahvel's little suggestions to Sharlotta that other eyes might be pointing their way had brought the clever woman to these conclusions so quickly. Indeed, if House Basadoni reached too far and too fast, the true power of the house would likely be discovered. Once the realm of Calimshan came to that revelation, their response against Jarlaxle's band would be complete and overwhelming. Earlier on, Entreri had entertained just such a scenario, but he had come to dismiss it. He doubted that he, or any other *iblith* of House Basadoni, would survive a Bregan D'aerthe retreat.

That ultimate chaos, then, had been relegated to the status of a backup plan.

"But you are correct," Sharlotta went on. "We must keep them busy—their military arm, at least."

Entreri smiled and easily held back the temptation to enlist her then and there against Kohrin Soulez. Dwahvel would take care of that, and soon, and Sharlotta would never even figure out that she had been used for the gain of Artemis Entreri.

Or perhaps the clever woman would come to see the truth.

Perhaps, then, Entreri would have to kill her.

To Artemis Entreri, who had suffered the double-dealing of Sharlotta Vespers for many years, it was not an unpleasant thought.

Chapter 6

Mutual Benefit

Artemis Entreri surely recognized the voice but hardly the tone. In all the months he had spent with Jarlaxle, both here and in the Underdark, he had never known the mercenary leader to raise his voice in anger.

Jarlaxle was shouting now, and to Entreri's pleasure as much as his curiosity, he was shouting at Rai-guy and Kimmuriel.

"It will symbolize our *ascension*," Jarlaxle roared.

"It will allow our enemies a focal point," Kimmuriel countered.

"They will not see it as anything more than a new guild house," Jarlaxle came back.

"Such structures are not uncommon," came Rai-guy's response, in calmer, more controlled tones.

Entreri entered the room then, to find the three standing and facing each other. A fourth drow, Berg'inyon Baenre, sat back comfortably against one wall.

"They will not know that drow were behind the construction of the tower," Rai-guy went on, after a quick and dismissive glance at the human, "but they will recognize that a new power has come to the Basadoni Guild."

"They know that already," Jarlaxle reasoned.

"They suspect it, as they suspect that old Basadoni is dead," Rai-guy retorted. "Let us not confirm their suspicions. Let us not do their reconnaissance for them."

Jarlaxle narrowed his one visible eye—the magical eye patch was over his left this day—and turned his gaze sharply at Entreri. "You know the city better than any of us," he said. "What say you? I plan to construct a tower, a crystalline image of Crenshinibon similar to the one in which you destroyed Drizzt Do'Urden. My associates here fear that such an act will prompt dangerous responses from other guilds and perhaps even the greater authorities of Calimshan."

"From the wizards' guild, at least," Entreri put in calmly. "A dangerous group."

Jarlaxle backed off a step in apparent surprise that Entreri had not readily gone along with him. "Guilds construct new houses all the time," the mercenary leader argued. "Some more lavish than anything I plan to create with Crenshinibon."

"But they do so by openly hiring out the proper craftsmen—and wizards, if magic is necessary," Entreri explained.

He was thinking fast on his feet here, totally surprised by Jarlaxle's dangerous designs. He didn't want to side with Rai-guy and Kimmuriel completely, though, because he knew that such an alliance would never serve him. Still, the notion of constructing an image of Crenshinibon right in the middle of Calimport seemed foolhardy at the very least.

"There you have it," Rai-guy cut in with a chortle. "Even your lackey does not believe it to be a wise or even feasible option."

"Speak your words from your own mouth, Rai-guy," Entreri promptly remarked. He almost expected the volatile wizard to make a move on him then and there, given the look of absolute hatred Rai-guy shot his way.

"A tower in Calimport would invite trouble," Entreri said to Jarlaxle, "though it is not impossible. We could, perhaps, hire a wizard of the prominent guild as a front for our real construction. Even that would be more easily accomplished if we set our sights on the outskirts of the city, out in the desert, perhaps, where the tower can better bask in the brilliant sunlight."

"The point is to erect a symbol of our strength," Jarlaxle put in. "I hardly wish to impress the little lizards and vipers that will view our tower in the empty desert."

"Bregan D'aerthe has always been better served by hiding its strength," Kimmuriel dared to interject. "Are we to change so successful a policy here in a world full of potential enemies? Time and again you seem to forget who we are, Jarlaxle, and *where* we are."

"We can mask the true nature of the tower's construction for a handsome price," Entreri reasoned. "And perhaps I can discern a location that will serve your purposes," he said to Jarlaxle, then turned to Kimmuriel and Rai-guy, "and alleviate your well-founded fears."

"You do that," Rai-guy remarked. "Show some worth and prove me wrong."

Entreri took the left-handed compliment with a quiet chuckle. He already had the perfect location in mind, yet another prompt to push Jarlaxle and Bregan D'aerthe against Kohrin Soulez and Dallabad Oasis.

"Have we heard any response from the Rakers?" Jarlaxle asked, walking to the side of the room and taking his seat.

"Sharlotta Vespers is meeting with Pasha Da'Daclan this very hour," Entreri replied.

"Will he not likely kill her in retribution?" Kimmuriel asked.

"No loss for us," Rai-guy quipped sarcastically.

"Pasha Da'Daclan is too intrigued to—" Entreri began.

"Impressed, you mean," corrected Rai-guy.

"He is too *intrigued*," Entreri said firmly, "to act so rashly as that. He harbors no anger at the loss of a minor outpost, no doubt, and is more interested in weighing our true strength and intentions. Perhaps he will kill her, mostly to learn if such an act might illicit a response."

"If he does, perhaps we will utterly destroy him and all of his guild," Jarlaxle said, and that raised a few eyebrows.

Entreri was less surprised. The assassin was beginning to suspect that there was some method behind Jarlaxle's seeming madness. Typically, Jarlaxle would have been the type to find a way for his relationship to be mutually beneficial with a man as entrenched in the power structures as Pasha Da'Daclan of the Rakers. The mercenary dark elf didn't often waste time, energy, and valuable soldiers in destruction—no more than was necessary for him to gain the needed foothold. At this time, the foothold in Calimport was fairly secure, and yet Jarlaxle's hunger seemed only to be growing.

Entreri didn't understand it, but he wasn't too worried, figuring that he could find some way to use it to his own advantage.

"Before we take any action against Da'Daclan, we must weaken his outer support," the assassin remarked.

"Outer support?" The question came from both Jarlaxle and Rai-guy.

"Pasha Da'Daclan's arms have a long reach," Entreri explained. "I suspect that he has created some outer ring of security, perhaps even beyond Calimport's borders."

From the look on the faces of the dark elves, Entreri realized that he had just successfully laid the groundwork, and that nothing more needed to be said at that time. In truth, he knew Pasha Da'Daclan better than to believe that the old man would harm Sharlotta Vespers. Such overt revenge simply wasn't Da'Daclan's way. No, he would invite the continued dialogue with Sharlotta, because for the Basadonis to have moved so brazenly against him as to destroy one of his outer houses, they would, by his reasoning, have to have some new and powerful weapons or allies. Pasha Da'Daclan wanted to know if the attack had been precipitated by the mere cocksureness of the new leaders of the guild—if Basadoni was indeed dead, as the common rumors implied—or by well-placed confidence. The fact that Sharlotta herself, who in the event of Basadoni's death would certainly have been elevated to the very highest levels within the organization, had come out to him hinted, at least, at the second explanation for the attack. In that instance, Pasha Da'Daclan wasn't about to invite complete disaster.

So Sharlotta would leave Da'Daclan's house very much alive, and she would hearken to Dwahvel Tiggerwillies's previous call. When she returned to Jarlaxle late that night, the mercenary would hear confirmation that Da'Daclan had an ally outside the city, an ally, Entreri would later explain, whose location would be the perfect setting for a new and impressive tower.

Yes, this was all going along quite well, in the assassin's estimation.

* * * * *

"Silence Kohrin Soulez, and Pasha Da'Daclan has no voice outside of Calimport," Sharlotta Vespers explained to Jarlaxle that same evening.

"He needs no voice outside the city," Jarlaxle returned. "Given the information that you and my other lieutenants have provided, there is too much backing for the human right here within Calimport for us wisely to consider any course of true conquest."

"But Pasha Da'Daclan does not understand that," Sharlotta replied without hesitation.

It was obvious to Jarlaxle that the woman had thought this through quite extensively. She had returned from her meeting with Da'Daclan, and later meetings with her street informants, quite excited and animated. She hadn't really accomplished anything conclusive with Da'Daclan, but she had sensed that the man was on the defensive. He was truly worried about the state of complete destruction that had befallen his outer, minor house. Da'Daclan didn't understand Basadoni's new level of power, nor the state of control within the Basadoni Guild, and that too made him nervous.

Jarlaxle rested his angular chin in his delicate black hand. "He believes Pasha Basadoni to be dead?" he asked for the third time, and for the third time, Sharlotta answered, "Yes."

"Should that not imply a new weakness, then, within the guild?" the mercenary leader reasoned.

"Perhaps in your world," Sharlotta replied, "where the drow houses are ruled by Matron Mothers who serve Lolth directly. Here the loss of a leader implies nothing more than instability, and that, more than anything else, frightens rivals. The guilds do not normally wage war because to do so would be detrimental to all sides. This is something the old pashas have learned through years, even decades, of experience. It's something they have passed down to their children, or other selected followers, for generations."

Of course it all made sense to Jarlaxle, but he held his somewhat perplexed look, prompting her to continue. In truth, Jarlaxle was learning more about Sharlotta than about anything to do with the social workings of Calimport's underground guilds.

"As a result of our attack, Pasha Da'Daclan believes the rumors that speak of old Basadoni's death," the woman continued. "To Da'Daclan's thinking, if Basadoni is dead—or has at least lost control of the guild—then we are more dangerous by far." Sharlotta flashed her wicked and ironic smile.

"So with every outer strand we cut—first the minor house and now this Dallabad Oasis—we lessen Da'Daclan's sense of security," Jarlaxle reasoned.

"And make it easier for me to force a stronger treaty with the Rakers," Sharlotta explained. "Perhaps Da'Daclan will even give over to us the entire block about the destroyed minor house to appease us. His base of operations is gone from that area anyway."

"Not so big a prize," Jarlaxle remarked.

"Ah yes, but how much more respect will the other guilds offer to Basadoni when they learn that Pasha Da'Daclan turned over some of his ground to us after we so wronged him?" Sharlotta purred. Her continuing roll of intrigue, her building of level upon level of gain, heightened Jarlaxle's respect for her.

"Dallabad Oasis?" he asked.

"A prize in and of itself," Sharlotta was quick to answer, "even without the gains it will afford us in our game with Pasha Da'Daclan."

Jarlaxle thought it over for a bit, nodded, and, with a sly look at Sharlotta, nodded toward the bed. Thoughts of great gain had ever been an aphrodisiac for Jarlaxle.

* * * * *

Jarlaxle paced his room later that night, having dismissed Sharlotta that he could consider in private the information she had brought to him. According to the woman—who had been so ill-briefed by Dwahvel—Dallabad Oasis was working as a relay point for Pasha Da'Daclan, the exit for information to Da'Daclan's more powerful allies far from Calimport. Run by some insignificant functionary named Soulez, Dallabad was an independent fortress. It was not an official part of the Rakers or any other guild from the city. Soulez apparently accepted payment to serve as information-relay, and also, Sharlotta had explained, sometimes collected tolls along the northwestern trails.

Jarlaxle continued to pace, digesting the information, playing it in conjunction with the earlier suggestions of Artemis Entreri. He felt the telepathic intrusion of his newest ally then, but he merely adjusted his magical eye patch to ward off the call.

There had to be some connection here, some truth within the truth, some planned relationship between Dallabad's tenuous position and the mere convenience of this all. Hadn't Entreri earlier suggested that Jarlaxle conquer some place outside of Calimport where he could more safely set up a crystalline tower?

And now this: a perfect location practically handed over to him for conquest, a place so conveniently positioned for Bregan D'aerthe to make a double gain.

The mental intrusions continued. It was a strong call, the strongest Jarlaxle had ever felt through his eye patch.

He wants something, Crenshinibon said in the mercenary leader's head.

Jarlaxle started to dismiss the shard, thinking that his own reasoning could bring him to a clearer picture of this whole situation, but Crenshinibon's next statement leaped past the conclusions he was slowly forming.

Artemis Entreri has deeper designs here, the shard insisted. *An old grudge, perhaps, or some treasure within the obvious prize.*

"Not a grudge," Jarlaxle said aloud, removing the protective eye patch so that he and the shard could better communicate. "If Entreri harbored such feelings as that, then he would see to this Soulez creature personally. Ever has he prided himself on working alone."

You believe the sudden imposition of Dallabad Oasis, a place never before mentioned, into both the equation of the Rakers and our need to construct a tower to be a mere fortunate coincidence? the shard asked, and before Jarlaxle could even respond, Crenshinibon made its assessment clear. *Artemis Entreri harbors some ulterior motive for an assault against Dallabad Oasis. There can be no doubt. Likely, he knew that our informants would bring to us the suggestion that conquering Dallabad would frighten Pasha Da'Daclan and considerably strengthen our bargaining power with him.*

"More likely, Artemis Entreri arranged for our informants to come to that very conclusion," Jarlaxle reasoned, ending with a chuckle.

Perhaps he views this as a way toward our destruction, the shard imparted. *That he can break free of us and rule on his own.*

Jarlaxle was shaking his head before the full reasoning even entered his mind. "If Artemis Entreri wished to be free of us, he would find some excuse to depart the city."

And run as faraway as Morik the Rogue, perhaps? came the ironic thought.

It was true enough, Jarlaxle had to admit. Bregan D'aerthe had already proven that its arms on the surface world were long indeed, long enough, perhaps, to catch a runaway deserter. Still, Jarlaxle highly doubted the shard's last reasoning. First of all, Artemis Entreri was wise enough to understand that Bregan D'aerthe would not go blindly against Dallabad or any other foe. Also, to Jarlaxle's thinking, such a ploy to bring about Bregan D'aerthe's downfall on the surface would be far too risky—and would it not be more easily accomplished merely by telling the greater authorities of Calimshan that a band of dark elves had come to Calimport?

He offered all of the reasoning to Crenshinibon, building common ground with the artifact that the most likely scenario here involved the shard's second line of reasoning, that of a secret treasure within the oasis.

The drow mercenary closed his eyes and absorbed the Crystal Shard's feelings on these plausible and growing suspicions and laughed again when he learned that he and the artifact had both come to accept the conclusion and were of like mind concerning it. Both were more amused and impressed than angry. Whatever Entreri's personal motives, and whether or not the information connecting Dallabad to Pasha Da'Daclan held any truth or not, the oasis would be a worthy and seemingly safe acquisition.

More so to the artifact than to the dark elf, for Crenshinibon had made it quite clear to Jarlaxle that it needed to construct an image of itself, a tower to collect the brilliant sunlight.

A step closer to its ever-present, final goal.

Chapter 7

Turning Advantage Into Disaster

Kohrin Soulez held his arm up before him, focusing his thoughts on the black, red-laced gauntlet that he wore on his right hand. Those laces seemed to pulse now, an all-too-familiar feeling for the secretive and secluded man.

Someone was trying to look in on him and his fortress at Dallabad Oasis.

Soulez forced his concentration deeper into the magical glove. He had recently been approached by a mediator from Calimport inquiring about a possible sale of his beloved sword, Charon's Claw. Soulez, of course, had balked at the absurd notion. He held this item more dear to his heart than he had any of his numerous wives, even above his many, many children. The offer had been serious, promising wealth beyond imagination for the single item.

Soulez had gained enough understanding of Calimport's guildsmen and had been in possession of Charon's Claw long enough to know what a serious offer, obviously refused and without room for bargaining, might bring, and so he was not surprised to find that prying eyes were seeking him out now. Since further investigation had whispered that the would-be purchaser might be Artemis Entreri and the Basadoni Guild, Soulez had been watching carefully for those eyes in particular.

They would look for weakness but would find none, and thus, he believed, they would merely go away.

As Soulez fell deeper into the energies of the gauntlet, he came to recognize a new element, dangerous only because it hinted that the would-be thief this time might not be so easily dissuaded. These were not the magical energies of a wizard he felt, nor the prayers of a divining priest. No, this energy was different than the expected, but certainly nothing beyond the understanding of Soulez and the gauntlet.

"Psionics," he said aloud, looking past the gauntlet to his lieutenants, who were standing at attention about his throne room.

Three of them were his own children. The fourth was a great military commander from Memnon, and the fifth was a renowned, and now retired, thief from Calimport. Conveniently, Soulez thought, a former member of the Basadoni Guild.

"Artemis Entreri and the Basadonis," Soulez told them, "if it is them, have apparently found access to a psionicist."

The five lieutenants muttered among themselves about the implications of that.

"Perhaps that has been Artemis Entreri's edge for all these years," the youngest of them, Kohrin Soulez's daughter, Ahdahnia, remarked.

"Entreri?" laughed Preelio, the old thief. "Strong of mind? Certainly. Psionics? Bah! He never needed them, so fine was he with the blade."

"But whoever seeks my treasure has access to the mind powers," said Soulez. "They believe that they have found an edge, a weakness of mine and of my treasure's, that they can exploit. That only makes them more dangerous, of course. We can expect an attack."

All five of the lieutenants stiffened at that proclamation, but none seemed overly concerned. There was no grand conspiracy against Dallabad among the guilds of Calimport. Kohrin Soulez had paid dearly to certify that information right away. The five knew that no one guild, or even two or three of the guilds banded together, could muster the power to overthrow Dallabad—not while Soulez carried the sword and the gauntlet and could render any wizards all but ineffective.

"No soldiers will break through our walls," Ahdahnia remarked with a confident smirk. "No thieves will slide through the shadows to the inner structures."

"Unless through some devilish mind power," Preelio put in, looking to the elder Soulez.

Kohrin Soulez only laughed. "They *believe* they have found a weakness," he reiterated. "I can stop them with this—" he held up the glove— "and of course, I have other means." He let the thought hang in the air, his smile bringing grins to the faces of all in attendance. There was a sixth lieutenant, after all, one little seen and little bothered, one used primarily as an instrument of interrogation and torture, one who preferred to spend as little time with the humans as possible.

"Secure the physical defenses," Soulez instructed them. "I will see to the powers of the mind."

He waved them away and sat back, focusing again on his mighty black gauntlet, on the red stitching that ran through it like veins of blood. Yes, he could feel the meager prying, and while he wished that the jealous folk would simply leave him to his business in peace, he believed that he would enjoy this little bit of excitement.

He knew that Yharaskrik certainly would.

* * * * *

Far below Kohrin Soulez's throne room, in deep tunnels that few of Soulez's soldiers even knew existed, Yharaskrik was already well aware that someone or something using psionic energies had breached the oasis. Yharaskrik was a mind flayer, an illithid, a humanoid creature with a bulbous head that resembled a huge brain, with several tentacles protruding from the part of his face where a nose, mouth, and chin should have been. Illithids were horrible to behold, and could be quite formidable physically, but their real powers lay in the realm of the mind, in psionic energies that dwarfed the powers of human practitioners, even of drow practitioners. Illithids could simply overwhelm an opponent with stunning blasts of mental energies, and either enslave the unfortunate victim, his mind held in a fugue state, or move in for a feast, attaching their horrid tentacles to the helpless victim and burrowing in to suck out brain matter.

Yharaskrik had been working with Kohrin Soulez for many years. Soulez considered the creature as much an indentured servant as a minion. He believed he had cut a fair deal with the creature after Soulez had apparently rendered Yharaskrik helpless in a short battle, capturing the illithid's mind blast within the magical netting of his gauntlet and thus leaving Yharaskrik open to a devastating counterstrike with the deadly sword. In truth, had Soulez gone for that strike, Yharaskrik would have melted away into the stone, using energies not directed against Soulez and thus beyond the reach of the gauntlet.

Soulez had not pressed the attack, though, as Yharaskrik's communal brain had calculated. The opportunistic man had struck a deal instead, offering the illithid its life and a comfortable place to do its meditation—or whatever else it was that illithids did—in exchange for certain services whenever they were needed, primarily to aid in the defense of Dallabad Oasis.

In all these years, Kohrin Soulez had never once harbored any suspicions that coming to Dallabad in such a capacity had been Yharaskrik's duty all along, that the illithid had been chosen among its strange kin to seek out and study the black and red gauntlet, as mind flayers were often sent to learn of anything that could so block their devastating energies. In truth, Yharaskrik had learned little of use concerning the gauntlet

647

over the years, but the creature was never anxious about that. Brilliant illithids were among the most patient of all the creatures in the multiverse, savoring the process more than the goal. Yharaskrik was quite content in its tunnel home.

Some psionic force had tickled the illithid's sensibility, and Yharaskrik felt enough of the stream of energy to know that it was no other illithid psionically prying about Dallabad Oasis.

The mind flayer, as confident in his superiority as all of his kind, was more intrigued than concerned. He was actually a bit perturbed that the fool Soulez had captured that psychic call with his gauntlet, but now the call had returned, redirected. Yharaskrik had called back, bringing his roving mind eye down, down, to the deep caverns.

The illithid did not try to hide its surprise when it discerned the source of that energy, nor did the creature on the other end, a drow, even begin to mask his own stunned reaction.

Haszakkin! the drow's thoughts instinctively screamed, their word for illithid—a word that conveyed a measure of respect the drow rarely gave to any creature that was not drow.

Dyon G'ennivalz? Yharaskrik asked, the name of a drow city the illithid had known well in its younger days.

Menzoberranzan, came the psionic reply.

House Oblodra, the brilliant creature imparted, for that atypical drow house was well known among all the mind flayer communities of Faerûn's Underdark.

No more, came Kimmuriel's response.

Yharaskrik sensed anger there, and understood it well as Kimmuriel relayed the memories of the downfall of his arrogant family. There had been, during the Time of Troubles, a period when magic, but not psionics, had ceased to function. In that too-brief time, the leaders of House Oblodra had challenged the greater houses of Menzoberranzan, including mighty Matron Baenre herself. The energies shifted with the shifting of the gods, and psionics had become temporarily impotent, while the powers of conventional magic had returned. Matron Baenre's response to the threats of House Oblodra had wiped the structure and all of the family—except for Kimmuriel, who had wisely used his ties with Jarlaxle and Bregan D'aerthe to make a hasty retreat—from the city, dropping it into the chasm called the Clawrift.

You seek the conquest of Dallabad Oasis? Yharaskrik asked, fully expecting an answer, for creatures communicating through psionics often held their own loyalties to each other even above those of their kindred.

Dallabad will be ours before the night has passed, Kimmuriel honestly replied.

The connection abruptly ended, and Yharaskrik understood the hasty retreat as Kohrin Soulez sauntered into the dark chamber, his right hand clad in the cursed gauntlet that so interfered with psionic energy.

The illithid bowed before his supposed master.

"We have been scouted," Soulez said, getting right to the point, his tension obvious as he stood before the horrid mind flayer.

"Mind's eye," the illithid agreed in its physical, watery voice. "I sensed it."

"Powerful?" Soulez asked.

Yharaskrik gave a quiet gurgle, the illithid equivalent of a resigned shrug, showing his lack of respect for any psionicist that was not illithid. It was an honest appraisal, even though the psionicist in question was drow and not human, and tied to a drow house that was well known among Yharaskrik's people. Still, though the mind flayer was not overly concerned about any battle he might see against the drow psionicist, Yharaskrik knew the dark elves well enough to understand that the Oblodran psionicist would likely be the least of Kohrin Soulez's problems.

"Power is always a relative concept," the illithid answered cryptically.

* * * * *

Kohrin Soulez felt the tingling of magical energy as he ascended the long spiral staircase that took him back to the ground level of his palace in Dallabad. The guildmaster broke into a run, scrambling, muscles working to their limits and his old bones feeling no pain. He thought that the attack must already be underway.

He calmed somewhat, slowing and huffing and puffing to catch his breath. He came up into the guild house to find many of his soldiers milling about, talking excitedly, but seeming more curious than terrified.

"Is it yours, Father?" asked Ahdahnia, her dark eyes gleaming.

Kohrin Soulez stared at her curiously, and taking the cue, Ahdahnia led him to an outer room with an east-facing window.

There it stood, right in the middle of Dallabad Oasis, *within* the outer walls of Kohrin Soulez's fortress.

A crystalline tower, gleaming in the bright sunlight, an image of Crenshinibon, the calling card of doom.

Kohrin Soulez's right hand throbbed with tingling energy as he looked at the magical structure. His gauntlet could capture magical energy and even turn it back against the initiator. It had never failed him, but in just looking at this spectacular tower the guildmaster suddenly recognized that he and his toys were puny things indeed. He knew without even going out and trying that he could not hope to drag the magical energies from that tower, that if he tried, it would consume him and his gauntlet. He shuddered as he pictured a physical manifestation of that absorption, an image of Kohrin Soulez frozen as a gargoyle on the top rim of that magnificent tower.

"Is it yours, Father?" Ahdahnia asked again.

649

The eagerness left her voice and the sparkle left her eyes as Kohrin turned to her, his face bloodless.

* * * * *

Outside of Dallabad fortress's wall, under the shelter of a copse of palm trees and surrounded by globes of magical darkness, Jarlaxle called to the tower. Its outer wall elongated, and sent forth a tendril, a stairway tunnel that breached the darkness globes and reached to the mercenary's feet. Secure that his soldiers were all in place, Jarlaxle ascended the stairs into the tower proper. With a thought to the Crystal Shard, he retracted the tunnel, effectively sealing himself in.

From that high vantage point in the middle of the fortress courtyard, Jarlaxle watched the unfolding drama around him.

Could you dim the light? he telepathically asked the tower.

Light is strength, Crenshinibon answered.

For you, perhaps, the mercenary replied. *For me, it is uncomfortable.*

Jarlaxle felt a sensation akin to a chuckle from the Crystal Shard, but the artifact did comply and thicken its eastern wall, considerably dulling the light in the room. It also provided a floating chair for Jarlaxle, so that he could drift about the perimeter of the room, studying the battle that would soon unfold.

Notice that Artemis Entreri will partake of the attack, the Crystal Shard remarked, and it sent the chair floating to the northern side of the room. Jarlaxle took the cue and focused hard down below, outside the fortress wall, to the tents and trees and boulders. Finally, with helpful guidance from the artifact, the drow spotted the figure lurking about the shadows.

He did not do so when we planned the attack on Pasha Da'Daclan, Crenshinibon added. Of course, the Crystal Shard knew that Jarlaxle was considering the same thing. The implications continued to follow the line that Entreri had some secret agenda here, some private gain that was either outside of the domain of Bregan D'aerthe, or held some consequence within the second level of the band's hierarchy.

Either way, both Jarlaxle and Crenshinibon thought it more amusing than in any way threatening.

The floating chair drifted back across the small circular room, putting Jarlaxle in line with the first diversionary attack, a series of darkness globes at the top of the outer wall. The soldiers there went into a panic, running and crying out to reform a defensive line away from the magic, but even as they moved back—in fairly good order, Jarlaxle noted—the real attack began, bubbling up from the ground within the fortress courtyard.

Rai-guy had crossed the courtyard, ten difficult feet at a time, casting a series of passwall spells out of a wand. Now, from a natural tunnel that he had fortunately located below the fortress, the drow wizard enacted the last of those passwalls, vanishing a section of stone and dirt.

Immediately the soldiers of Bregan D'aerthe arose, floating with drow levitation into the courtyard, enacting darkness globes above them to confuse their enemies and to lessen the blinding impact of the hated sun.

"We should have attacked at night," Jarlaxle said aloud.

Daytime is when my power is at its peak, Crenshinibon responded immediately, and Jarlaxle felt the rest of the thought keenly. Crenshinibon was none-too-subtly reminding him that it was more powerful than all of Bregan D'aerthe combined.

That expression of confidence was more than a little disconcerting to the mercenary leader, for reasons that he hadn't yet begun to untangle.

* * * * *

Rai-guy stood in the hole, issuing orders to those dark elves running and leaping into levitation, floating up and eager for battle. The wizard was particularly animated this day. His blood was up, as always during a conquest, but he was not pleased at all that Jarlaxle had decided to launch the attack at dawn, a seemingly foolish trade-off of putting his soldiers, used to a world of blackness, at a disadvantage, for the simple gain of constructing a crystalline tower vantage point. The appearance of the tower was an amazing thing, without doubt, one that showed the power of the invaders clearly to those defending inside. Rai-guy did not diminish the value of striking such terror, but every time he saw one of his soldiers squint painfully as he rose up out of the hole into the daylight, the wizard considered his leader's continuing surprising behavior and gritted his teeth in frustration.

Also, the mere fact that they were using dark elves openly against the fortress seemed more than a bit of a gamble. Could they not have accomplished this conquest, as they had planned to do with Pasha Da'Daclan, by striking openly with human, perhaps even kobold soldiers, while the dark elves infiltrated more quietly? What would be left of Dallabad after the conquest now, after all? Almost all remaining alive within—and there would be many, since the dark elves led every assault with their trademark sleep-poisoned hand crossbow darts—would have to be executed anyway, lest they communicate the truth of their conquerors.

Rai-guy reminded himself of his place in the guild and knew it would take a monumental error on the part of Jarlaxle, one that cost the lives of many of Bregan D'aerthe, for him to rally enough support truly to overthrow Jarlaxle. Perhaps this would be that mistake.

The wizard heard a change in the timbre of the shouts from above. He glanced up, taking note that the sunlight seemed brighter, that the globes of magical darkness had gone away. The magically created shaft, too, suddenly disappeared, capturing a pair of levitating soldiers within

651

it as the stone and dirt rematerialized. It lasted only a moment, as if something suddenly reached out and grabbed away the magic that was trying to dispel Rai-guy's vertical passwall dweomers. That moment was long enough to destroy utterly the two unfortunate drow soldiers.

The wizard cursed at Jarlaxle, but under his breath.

He reminded himself to keep safe and to see, in the end, if this attack, even if a complete failure, might not prove personally beneficial.

* * * * *

Kohrin Soulez fell back. His sensibilities were stung, both by the realization that these were dark elves that had come to secluded Dallabad, and by the magical counterattack that had overwhelmed his gauntlet. He had come out from the main house to rally his soldiers, the blood-red blade of Charon's Claw bared and waving, leaving streaks of ashy blackness in the air. Soulez had run to the area of obvious invasion, where globes of darkness and screams of pain and terror heralded the fighting.

Dispelling those globes was no major task for the gauntlet, nor was closing the hole in the ground through which the enemy continued to arrive, but Soulez had nearly been overwhelmed by a wave of energy that countered the countering energy he was exerting himself. It was a blast of magical power so raw and pure that he could not hope to contain it. He knew it had come from the tower.

The tower!

The dark elves!

His doom was at hand!

He fell back into the main house, ordering his soldiers to fight to the last. As he ran along the more deserted corridors leading to his private chambers, his dear Ahdahnia right behind him, he called out to Yharaskrik to come and whisk him away.

There was no answer.

"He has heard me," Soulez assured his daughter anyway. "We need only escape long enough for Yharaskrik to come to us. Then we will run out to inform the lords of Calimport that the dark elves have come."

"The traps and locks along the hallways will keep our enemies at bay," Ahdahnia replied.

Despite the surprising nature of their enemies, the woman actually believed the claim. These long corridors weaving along the somewhat circular main house of Dallabad were lined with heavy, metal-banded doors of stone and wood layers that could defeat most intrusions, wizardly or physical. Also, the sheer number of traps in place between the outer walls and Kohrin Soulez's inner sanctuary would deter and daunt the most seasoned of thieves.

* * * * *

But not the most clever.

Artemis Entreri had worked his way unnoticed to the base of the fortress's northern wall. It was no small feat—an impossible one under normal circumstances, for there was an open field surrounding the fortress, running nearly a hundred feet to the trees and tents and boulders, and several of the small ponds that marked the place—but this was not a normal circumstance. With a tower materializing *inside* the fortress, most of the guards were scurrying about, trying to find some answers as to whether it was an invading enemy or some secret project of Kohrin Soulez's. Even those guards on the walls couldn't help but stare in awe at that amazing sight.

Entreri dug himself in. His borrowed black cloak—a camouflaging drow *piwafwi* that wouldn't last long in the sun—offered him some protection should any of the guards lean over the twenty foot wall and look down at him.

The assassin waited until the sounds of fighting erupted from within.

To untrained eyes, the wall of Kohrin Soulez's fortress would have seemed a sheer thing indeed, all of polished white marble joints forming an attractive contrast to the brownish sandstone and gray granite. To Entreri, though, it seemed more of a stairway than a wall, with many seam-steps and finger-holds.

He was up near the top in a matter of seconds. The assassin lifted himself up just enough to glance over at the two guards anxiously reloading their crossbows. They were looking in the direction of the courtyard where the battle raged.

Over the wall without a sound went the *piwafwi*-cloaked assassin. He came down from the wall only a few moments later, dressed as one of Kohrin Soulez's guards.

Entreri joined in with some others running frantically around to the front courtyard, but he broke away from them as he came in sight of the fighting. He melted back against the wall and toward the open, main door, where he spotted Kohrin Soulez. The guildmaster was battling drow magic and waving that wondrous sword. Entreri kept several steps ahead of the man as he was forced to fall back. The assassin entered the main building before Soulez and his daughter.

Entreri ran, silent and unseen, along those corridors, through the open doors, past the unset traps, ahead of the two fleeing nobles and those soldiers trailing their leader to secure the corridor behind him. The assassin reached the main door of Soulez's private chambers with enough time to spare to recognize that the alarms and traps on this portal were indeed in place and to do something about them.

Thus, when Ahdahnia Soulez pushed open that magnificent, gold-leafed door, leading her father into his seemingly secure chamber, Artemis Entreri was already there, standing quietly ready behind a floor-to-ceiling tapestry.

*   *   *   *   *

The three Dallabad soldiers—well-trained, well-armed, and well-armored with shining chain and small bucklers—faced off against the three dark elves along the western wall of the fortress. The men, frightened as they were, kept the presence of mind to form a triangular defense, using the wall behind them to secure their backs.

The dark elves fanned out and came at them in unison. Their amazing drow swords—two for each warrior—worked circular attack routines so quickly that the paired weapons seemed to blur the line between where one sword stopped and the other began.

The humans, to their credit, held strong their position, offered parries and blocks wherever necessary, and suppressed any urge to scream out in terror and charge blindly—as some of their nearby comrades were doing to disastrous results. Gradually, talking quickly between them to analyze each of their enemy's movements, the trio began to decipher the deceptive and brilliant drow sword dance, enough so, at least, to offer one or two counters of their own.

Back and forth it went, the humans wisely holding their position, not following any of the individually retreating dark elves and thus weakening their own defenses. Blade rang against blade, and the magical swords Kohrin Soulez had provided his best-trained soldiers matched up well enough against the drow weapons.

The dark elves exchanged words the humans did not understand. Then the three drow attacked in unison, all six swords up high in a blurring dance. Human swords and shields came up to meet the challenge and the resulting clang of metal against metal rang out like a single note.

That note soon changed, diminished, and all three of the human soldiers came to recognize, but not completely to comprehend, that their attackers had each dropped one sword.

Shields and swords up high to meet the continuing challenge, they only understood their exposure below the level of the fight when they heard the clicks of three small crossbows and felt the sting as small darts burrowed into their bellies.

The dark elves backed off a step. Tonakin Ta'salz, the central soldier, called out to his companions that he was hit, but that he was all right. The soldier to Tonakin's left started to say the same, but his words were slurred and groggy. Tonakin glanced over just in time to see him tumble facedown in the dirt. To his right, there came no response at all.

Tonakin was alone. He took a deep breath and skittered back against the wall as the three dark elves retrieved their dropped swords. One of them said something to him that he did not understand, but while the words escaped him, the expression on the drow's face did not.

He should have fallen down asleep, the drow was telling him. Tonakin agreed wholeheartedly as the three came in suddenly, six swords slashing in brutal and perfectly coordinated attacks.

To his credit, Tonakin Ta'salz actually managed to block two of them.

* * * * *

And so it went throughout the courtyard and all along the wall of the fortress. Jarlaxle's mercenaries, using mostly physical weapons but with more than a little magic thrown in, overwhelmed the soldiers of Dallabad. The mercenary leader had instructed his killers to spare as many as possible, using sleep darts and accepting surrender. He noted, though, that more than a few were not waiting long enough to find out if any opponents who had resisted the sleep poison might offer a surrender.

The dark elf leader merely shrugged at that, hardly concerned. This was open battle, the kind that he and his mercenaries didn't see often enough. If too many of Kohrin Soulez's soldiers were killed for the oasis fortress to properly function, then Jarlaxle and Crenshinibon would simply find replacements. In any case, with Soulez chased back into his house by the sheer power of the Crystal Shard, the assault had already reached its second stage.

It was going along beautifully. The courtyard and wall were already secured, and the house had been breached at several points. Now Kimmuriel and Rai-guy at last came onto the scene.

Kimmuriel had several of the captives who were still awake dragged before him, forcing them to lead the way into the house. He would use his overpowering will to read their thoughts as they walked him and the drow through the trapped maze to the prize that was Soulez.

Jarlaxle rested back in the crystalline tower. A part of him wanted to go down and join in the fun, but he decided instead to remain and share the moment with his most powerful companion, the Crystal Shard. He even allowed the artifact to thin the eastern wall once more, allowing more sunlight into the room.

* * * * *

"Where is he?" Kohrin Soulez fumed, stomping about the room. "Yharaskrik!"

"Perhaps he cannot get through," Ahdahnia reasoned. She moved nearer to the tapestry as she spoke.

Entreri knew he could step out and take her down, then go for his prize. He held the urge, intrigued and wary.

"Perhaps the same force from the tower—" Ahdahnia went on.

"No!" Kohrin Soulez interrupted. "Yharaskrik is beyond such things. His people see things—everything—differently."

655

Even as he finished, Ahdahnia gasped and skittered back across Entreri's field of view. Her eyes went wide as she looked back in the direction of her father, who had walked out of Entreri's very limited line of sight.

Confident that the woman was too entranced by whatever it was that she was watching, Entreri slipped down low to one knee and dared peek out around the tapestry.

He saw an illithid step out of the psionic dimensional doorway and into the room to stand before Kohrin.

A mind flayer!

The assassin fell back behind the tapestry, his thoughts whirling. Very few things in all the world could rattle Artemis Entreri, who had survived life on the streets from a tender young age and had risen to the very top of his profession, who had survived Menzoberranzan and many, many encounters with dark elves. One of those few things was a mind flayer. Entreri had seen a few in the dark elf city, and he abhorred them more than any other creature he had ever met. It wasn't their appearance that so upset the assassin, though they were brutally ugly by any but illithid standards. No, it was their very demeanor, their different view of the world, as Kohrin had just alluded to.

Throughout his life, Artemis Entreri had gained the upper hand because he understood his enemies better than they understood him. He had found the dark elves a bit more of a challenge, based on the fact that the drow were too experienced—were simply too good at conspiring and plotting for him to gain any real comprehension . . . any that he could hold confidence in, at least.

With illithids, though he had only dealt with them briefly, the disadvantage was even more fundamental and impossible to overcome. There was no way Artemis Entreri could understand that particular enemy because there was no way he could bring himself to any point where he could view the world as an illithid might.

No way.

So Entreri tried to make himself very small. He listened to every word, every inflection, every intake of breath, very carefully.

"Why did you not come earlier to my call?" Kohrin Soulez demanded.

"They are dark elves," Yharaskrik responded in that bubbling, watery voice that sounded to Entreri like a very old man with too much phlegm in his throat. "They are within the building."

"You should have come earlier!" Ahdahnia cried. "We could have beaten—" Her voice left her with a gasp. She stumbled backward and seemed about to fall. Entreri knew the mind flayer had just hit her with some scrambling burst of mental energy.

"What do I do?" Kohrin Soulez wailed.

"There is nothing you can do," answered Yharaskrik. "You cannot hope to survive."

"P-par-parlay with them, F-father!" cried the recovering Ahdahnia. "Give them what they want—else you cannot hope to survive."

"They will take what they want," Yharaskrik assured her, and turned back to Kohrin Soulez. "You have nothing to offer. There is no hope."

"Father?" Ahdahnia asked, her voice suddenly weak, almost pitiful.

"You attack them!" Kohrin Soulez demanded, holding his deadly sword out toward the illithid. "Overwhelm them!"

Yharaskrik made a sound that Entreri, who had mustered enough willpower to peek back around the tapestry, recognized to be an expression of mirth. It wasn't a laugh, actually, but more like a clear, gasping cough.

Kohrin Soulez, too, apparently understood the meaning of the reply, for his face grew very red.

"They are drow. Do you now understand that?" the illithid asked. "There is no hope."

Kohrin Soulez started to respond, to demand again that Yharaskrik take the offensive, but as if he had suddenly come to figure it all out, he paused and stared at his octopus-headed companion. "You knew," he accused. "When the psionicist entered Dallabad, he conveyed . . ."

"The psionicist was drow," the illithid confirmed.

"*Traitor!*" Kohrin Soulez cried.

"There is no betrayal. There was never friendship, or even alliance," the illithid remarked logically.

"But you *knew!*"

Yharaskrik didn't bother to reply.

"Father?" Ahdahnia asked again, and she was trembling visibly.

Kohrin Soulez's breath came in labored gasps. He brought his left hand up to his face and wiped away sweat and tears. "What am I to do?" he asked, speaking to himself. "What will . . ."

Yharaskrik began that coughing laughter again, and this time, it sounded clearly to Entreri that the creature was mocking pitiful Soulez.

Kohrin Soulez composed himself suddenly and glared at the creature. "This amuses you?" he asked.

"I take pleasure in the ironies of the lesser species," Yharaskrik responded. "How much your whines sound as those of the many you have killed. How many have begged for their lives futilely before Kohrin Soulez, as he will now futilely beg for his at the feet of a greater adversary than he can possibly comprehend?"

"But an adversary that you know well!" Kohrin cried.

"I prefer the drow to your pitiful kind," Yharaskrik freely admitted. "They never beg for mercy that they know will not come. Unlike humans, they accept the failings of individual-minded creatures. There is no greater joining among them, as there is none among you, but they understand and accept that fallibility." The illithid gave a slight bow. "That is all the respect I now offer to you, in the hour of your death," Yharaskrik

657

explained. "I would throw energy your way, that you might capture it and redirect it against the dark elves—and they are close now, I assure you—but I choose not to."

Artemis Entreri recognized clearly the change that came over Kohrin Soulez then, the shift from despair to nothing-to-lose anger that he had seen so many times during his decades on the tough streets.

"But I wear the gauntlet!" Kohrin Soulez said powerfully, and he moved the magnificent sword out toward Yharaskrik. "I will at least get the pleasure of first witnessing your end!"

But even as he made the declaration, Yharaskrik seemed to melt into the stone at his feet and was gone.

"Damn him!" Kohrin Soulez screamed. "Damn you—" His tirade cut short as a pounding came on the door.

"Your wand!" the guildmaster cried to his daughter, turning to face her, in the direction of the floor-to-ceiling tapestry that decorated his private chamber.

Ahdahnia just stood there, wide-eyed, making no move to reach for the wand at her belt. Her expression changing not at all, she crumpled to the floor.

There stood Artemis Entreri.

Kohrin Soulez's eyes widened as he watched her descent, but as if he hardly cared for the fall of Ahdahnia other than its implications for his own safety, his gaze focused clearly on Entreri.

"It would have been so much easier if you had merely sold the blade to me," the assassin remarked.

"I knew this was your doing, Entreri," Soulez growled back at him, advancing a step, the blood-red blade gleaming at the ready.

"I offer you one more chance to sell it," Entreri said, and Soulez stopped short, his expression one of pure incredulity. "For the price of her life," the assassin added, pointing down at Ahdahnia with his jeweled dagger. "Your own life is yours to bargain for, but you'll have to make that bargain with others."

Another bang sounded out in the corridor, followed by the sounds of some fighting.

"They are close, Kohrin Soulez," Entreri remarked, "close and over-whelming."

"You brought dark elves to Calimport," Soulez growled back at him.

"They came of their own accord," Entreri replied. "I was merely wise enough not to try to oppose them. So I make my offer, but only this one last time. I can save Ahdahnia—she is not dead but merely asleep." To accentuate his point, he held up a small crossbow quarrel of unusual design, a drow bolt that had been tipped with sleeping poison. "Give me the sword and gauntlet—now—and she lives. Then you can bargain for your own life. The sword will do you little good against the dark elves, for they need no magic to destroy you."

"But if I am to bargain for my life, then why not do so with the sword in hand?" Kohrin Soulez asked.

In response, Entreri glanced down at the sleeping form of Ahdahnia. "I am to trust that you will keep your word?" Soulez answered.

Entreri didn't answer, other than to fix the man with a cold stare.

There came a sharp rap on the heavy door. As if incited by that sound of imminent danger, Kohrin Soulez leaped forward, slashing hard.

Entreri could have killed Ahdahnia and still dodged, but he did not. He slipped back behind the tapestry and went down low, scrambling along its length. He heard the tearing behind him as Soulez slashed and stabbed. Charon's Claw easily sliced the heavy material, even took chunks out of the wall behind it.

Entreri came out the other side to find Soulez already moving in his direction, the man wearing an expression that seemed half crazed, even jubilant.

"How valuable will the drow elves view me when they enter to find Artemis Entreri dead?" he squealed, and he launched a thrust, feint and slash for the assassin's shoulder.

Entreri had his own sword out then, in his right hand, his dagger still in his left, and he snapped it up, driving the slash aside. Soulez was good, very good, and he had the formidable weapon back in close defensively before the assassin could begin to advance with his dagger.

Respect kept Artemis Entreri back from the man, and more importantly, from that devastating weapon. He knew enough about Charon's Claw to understand that a simple nick from it, even one on his hand that he might suffer in a successful parry, would fester and grow and would likely kill him.

Confident that he'd find the right opening, the deadly assassin stalked the man slowly, slowly.

Soulez attacked again with a low thrust that Entreri hopped back from, and a thrust high that the assassin ducked. Entreri slapped at the red blade with his sword and thrust at his opponent's center mass. It was a brilliantly quick routine that would have left almost any opponent at least shallowly stabbed.

He never got near to hitting Entreri. Then he had to scramble and throw out a cut to the side to keep the assassin, who had somehow quick-stepped to his right while slapping hard at the third thrust, at bay.

Kohrin Soulez growled in frustration as they came up square again, facing each other from a distance of about ten feet, with Entreri continuing that composed stalk. Now Soulez also moved, angling to intercept.

He was dragging his back foot behind him, Entreri noted, keeping ready to change direction, trying to cut off the room and any possible escape routes.

"You so desperately desire Charon's Claw," Soulez said with a chuckle, "but do you even begin to understand the true beauty of the weapon? Can you even guess at its power and its tricks, assassin?"

Entreri continued to back and pace—back to the left, then back to the right—allowing Soulez to shrink down the battlefield. The assassin was growing impatient, and also, the sounds on the door indicated that the resistance in the hallway had come to an end. The door was magnificent and strong, but it would not hold out long, and Entreri wanted this finished before Rai-guy and the dark elves arrived.

"You think I am an old man," Soulez remarked, and he came forward in a short rush, thrusting.

Entreri picked it off and this time came forward with a counter of his own, rolling his sword under Soulez's blade and sliding it out. The assassin turned and stepped ahead, dagger rushing forward, but he had to disengage from the powerful sword too soon. The angle of the parry was forcing the enchanted blade dangerously close to Entreri's exposed hand, and without the block, he had to skitter into a quick retreat as Soulez slashed across.

"I am an old man," Soulez continued, sounding undaunted, "but I draw strength from the sword. I am your fighting equal, Artemis Entreri, and with this sword you are surely doomed."

He came on again, but Entreri retreated easily, sliding back toward the wall opposite the door. He knew he was running out of room, but to him that only meant that Kohrin Soulez was running out of room, too, and out of time.

"Ah, yes, run back, little rabbit," Soulez taunted. "I know you, Artemis Entreri. I know you. Behold!" As he finished, he began waving the sword before him, and Entreri had to blink, for the blade began trailing blackness.

No, not trailing, the assassin realized to his surprise, but emitting blackness. It was thick ash that held in place in the air in great sweeping opaque fans, altering the battlefield to Kohrin Soulez's designs.

"I know you!" Soulez cried and came forward, sweeping, sweeping more ash screens into the air.

"Yes, you know me," Entreri answered calmly, and Soulez slowed. The timbre of Entreri's voice had reminded him of the power of this particular opponent. "You see me at night, Kohrin Soulez, in your dreams. When you look into the darkest shadows of those nightmares, do you see those eyes looking back at you?"

As he finished, he came forward a step, tossing his sword slightly into the air before him, and at just the right angle so that the approaching sword was the only thing Kohrin Soulez could see.

The room's door exploded into a thousand tiny little pieces.

Soulez hardly noticed, coming forward to meet the attack, slapping the apparently thrusting sword on top, then below and to the side. So beautifully angled was Entreri's toss that the man's own quick parry strikes, one countering the spin of the other, gave Soulez the illusion that Entreri was still holding the other end of the blade.

He leaped ahead, through the opaque fans of the sword's conjured ash, and struck hard for where he knew the assassin had to be.

Soulez stiffened, feeling the sting in his back. Entreri's dagger cut into his flesh.

"Do you see those eyes looking back at you from the shadows of your nightmares, Kohrin Soulez?" Entreri asked again. "Those are my eyes."

Soulez felt the dagger pulling at his life-force. Entreri hadn't driven it home yet, but he didn't have to. The man was beaten, and he knew it. Soulez dropped Charon's Claw to the floor and let his arm slip down to his side.

"You are a devil," he growled at the assassin.

"I?" Entreri answered innocently. "Was it not Kohrin Soulez who would have sacrificed his daughter for the sake of a mere weapon?"

As he finished, he was fast to reach down with his free hand and yank the black gauntlet from Soulez's right hand. To Soulez's surprise, the glove fell to the floor right beside the sword.

From the open doorway across the room came the sound of a voice, melodic yet sharp, and speaking in a language that rolled but was oft-broken with harsh and sharp consonant sounds.

Entreri backed away from the man. Soulez turned around to see the ash lines drifting down to the floor, showing him several dark elves standing in the room.

* * * * *

Kohrin Soulez took a deep, steadying breath. He had dealt with worse than drow, he silently reminded himself. He had parlayed with an illithid and had survived meetings with the most notorious guildmasters of Calimport. Soulez focused on Entreri then, seeing the man engaged in conversation with the apparent leader of the dark elves, seeing the man drifting farther and farther from him.

There, right beside him, lay his precious sword, his greatest possession—an artifact he would indeed protect even at the cost of his own daughter's life.

Entreri moved a bit farther from him. None of the drow were advancing or seemed to pay Soulez any heed at all.

Charon's Claw, so conveniently close, seemed to be calling to him.

Gathering all his energy, tensing his muscles and calculating the most fluid course open to him, Kohrin Soulez dived down low, scooped the black, red-stitched gauntlet onto his right hand, and before he could even register that it didn't seem to fit him the same way, scooped up the powerful, enchanted sword.

He turned toward Entreri with a growl. "Tell them that I will speak with their leader . . ." he started to say, but his words quickly became a jumble, his tone going low and his pace slowing, as if something was pulling at his vocal chords.

Kohrin Soulez's face contorted weirdly, his features seeming to elongate in the direction of the sword.

All conversation in the room stopped. All eyes turned to stare incredulously at Soulez.

"T-to the Nine . . . Nine Hells with y-you, Entreri!" the man stammered, each word punctuated by a croaking groan.

"What is he doing?" Rai-guy demanded of Entreri.

The assassin didn't answer, just watched in amusement as Kohrin Soulez continued to struggle against the power of Charon's Claw. His face elongated again and wisps of smoke began wafting up from his body. He tried to cry out, but only an indecipherable gurgle came forth. The smoke increased, and Soulez began to tremble violently, all the while trying to scream out.

Nothing more than smoke poured from his mouth.

It all seemed to stop then, and Soulez stood staring at Entreri and gasping.

* * * * *

The man lived just long enough to put on the most horrified and stunned expression Artemis Entreri had ever seen. It was an expression that pleased Entreri greatly. There was something too familiar in the way in which Soulez had abandoned his daughter.

Kohrin Soulez erupted in a sudden, sizzling burst. The skin burned off his head, leaving no more than a whitened skull and wide, horrified eyes.

Charon's Claw hit the hard floor again, making more of a dull thump than any metallic ring. The skull-headed corpse of Kohrin Soulez crumpled in place.

"Explain," Rai-guy demanded.

Entreri walked over and, wearing a gauntlet that appeared identical to the one Kohrin Soulez had but not a match for the other since it was shaped for the same hand, reached down and calmly gathered up his newest prize.

"Pray I do not go to the Nine Hells, as you surely will, Kohrin Soulez," the deadly assassin said to the corpse. "For if I see you there, I will continue to torment you throughout eternity."

"Explain!" Rai-guy demanded more forcefully.

"Explain?" Entreri echoed, turning to face the angry drow wizard. He gave a shrug, as if the answer seemed obvious. "I was prepared, and he was a fool."

Rai-guy glared at him ominously, and Entreri only smiled back, hoping his amused expression would tempt the wizard to action.

He held Charon's Claw now, and he wore the gauntlet that could catch and redirect magic.

The world had just changed in ways that the wretched Rai-guy couldn't begin to understand.

Chapter 8

The Simple Reason

"The tower will remain. Jarlaxle has declared it," said Kimmuriel. "The fortress weathered our attack well enough to keep Dallabad operating smoothly, and without anyone outside of the oasis even knowing that an assault had taken place."

"Operating," Rai-guy echoed, spitting the distasteful word out. He stared at Entreri, who walked beside him into the crystal tower. Rai-guy's look made it quite clear that he considered the events of this day the assassin's doing and planned on holding Entreri personally responsible if anything went wrong. "Is Bregan D'aerthe to become the overseers of a great toll booth, then?"

"Dallabad will prove more valuable to Bregan D'aerthe than you assume," Entreri replied in his stilted use of the drow language. "We can keep the place separate from House Basadoni as far as all others are concerned. The allies we place out here will watch the road and gather news long before those in Calimport are aware. We can run many of our ventures from out here, farther from the prying eyes of Pasha Da'Daclan and his henchmen."

"And who are these trusted allies who will operate Dallabad as a front for Bregan D'aerthe?" Rai-guy demanded. "I had thought of sending Domo."

"Domo and his filthy kind will not leave the offal of the sewers," Shar-lotta Vespers put in.

"Too good a hole for them," Entreri muttered.

"Jarlaxle has hinted that perhaps the survivors of Dallabad will suf-fice," Kimmuriel explained. "Few were killed."

"Allied with a conquered guild," Rai-guy remarked with a sigh, shak-ing his head. "A guild whose fall we brought about."

"A very different situation from allying with a fallen house of Menzo-berranzan," Entreri declared, seeing the error in the dark elf's apparent internal analogy. Rai-guy was viewing things through the dark glass of Menzoberranzan, was considering the generational feuds and grudges that members of the various houses, the various families, held for each other.

"We shall see," the drow wizard replied, and he motioned for Entreri to hang back with him as Kimmuriel, Berg'inyon, and Sharlotta started up the staircase to the second level of the magical crystalline tower.

"I know that you desired Dallabad for personal reasons," Rai-guy said when the two were alone. "Perhaps it was an act of vengeance, or that you might wear that very gauntlet upon your hand and carry that same sword you now have sheathed on your hip. Either way, do not believe you've done anything here I don't understand, human."

"Dallabad is a valuable asset," Entreri replied, not backing away an inch. "Jarlaxle has a place where he can safely construct and maintain the crystalline tower. There was gain here to be had by all."

"Even to Artemis Entreri," Rai-guy remarked.

In answer, the assassin drew forth Charon's Claw, presenting it hori-zontally to Rai-guy for inspection, letting the drow wizard see the beauty of the item. The sword had a slender, razor-edged, gleaming red blade, its length inscribed with designs of cloaked figures and tall scythes, accen-tuated by a black blood trough running along its center. Entreri opened his hand enough for the wizard to see the skull-bobbed pommel, with a hilt that appeared like whitened vertebrae. Running from it toward the crosspiece, the hilt was carved to resemble a backbone and rib-cage, and the crosspiece itself resembled a pelvic skeleton, with legs spread out wide and bent back toward the head, so that the wielder's hand fit neatly within the "bony" boundaries. All of the pommel, hilt and crosspiece was white, like bleached bones—perfectly white, except for the eye sockets of the skull pommel, which seemed like black pits at one moment and flared with red fires the next.

"I am pleased with the prize I earned," Entreri admitted.

Rai-guy stared hard at the sword, but his gaze inevitably kept drift-ing toward the other, less-obvious treasure: the black, red-stitched gauntlet on Entreri's hand.

"Such weapons can be more of a curse than a blessing, human," the wizard remarked. "They are possessed of arrogance, and too often does that foolish pride spill over into the mind of the wielder, to disastrous result."

The two locked stares, with Entreri's expression melting into a wry grin. "Which end would you most like to feel?" he asked, presenting the deadly sword closer to Rai-guy, matching the wizard's obvious threat with one of his own.

Rai-guy narrowed his dark eyes, and walked away.

Entreri held his grin as he watched the wizard move up the stairs, but in truth, Rai-guy's warning had struck a true chord to him. Indeed, Charon's Claw was strong of will—Entreri could feel that clearly—and if he was not careful with the blade always, it could surely lead him to disaster or destroy him as it had utterly slaughtered Kohrin Soulez.

Entreri glanced down at his own posture, reminding himself—a humble self-warning—not to touch any part of the sword with his unprotected hand.

Even Artemis Entreri could not deny a bit of caution against the horrific death he had witnessed when Charon's Claw had burned the skin from the head of Kohrin Soulez.

*　*　*　*　*

"Crenshinibon easily dominates the majority of the survivors," Jarlaxle announced to his principal advisors a short while later in an audience chamber he had crafted of the second level the magical tower. "To those outside of Dallabad Oasis, the events of this day will seem like nothing more than a coup within the Soulez family, followed by a strong alliance to the Basadoni Guild."

"Ahdahnia Soulez agreed to remain?" Rai-guy asked.

"She was willing to assume the mantle of Dallabad even before Crenshinibon invaded her thoughts," Jarlaxle explained.

"Loyalty," Entreri remarked under his breath.

Even as the assassin was offering the sarcastic jibe, Rai-guy admitted, "I am beginning to like the young woman more already."

"But can we trust her?" Kimmuriel asked.

"Do you trust me?" Sharlotta Vespers interjected. "It would seem a similar situation."

"Except that her guildmaster was also her father," Kimmuriel reminded.

"There is nothing to fear from Ahdahnia Soulez or any of the others who will remain at Dallabad," Jarlaxle put in, forcefully, thus ending the philosophical debate. "Those who survived and will continue to do so belong to Crenshinibon now, and Crenshinibon belongs to me."

Entreri didn't miss the doubting look that flashed briefly across Rai-guy's face at the moment of Jarlaxle's final proclamation, and in truth, he, too, wondered if the mercenary leader wasn't a bit confused as to who owned whom.

667

"Kohrin Soulez's soldiers will not betray us," Jarlaxle went on with all confidence. "Nor will they even remember the events of this day, but rather, they will accept the story we tell them to put forth as truth, if that is what we choose. Dallabad Oasis belongs to Bregan D'aerthe now as surely as if we had installed an army of dark elves here to facilitate the operations."

"And you trust the woman Ahdahnia to lead, though we just murdered her father?" Kimmuriel said more than asked.

"Her father was killed by his obsession with that sword; so she told me herself," Jarlaxle replied, and as he spoke, all gazes turned to regard the weapon hanging easily at Entreri's belt. Rai-guy, in particular, kept his dangerous glare upon Entreri, as if silently reiterating the warnings of their last conversation.

The wizard meant those warnings to be a threat to Entreri, a reminder to the assassin that he, Rai-guy, would be watching Entreri's every move much more closely now, a reminder that he believed that the assassin had, in effect, used Bregan D'aerthe for the sake of his personal gain—a very dangerous practice.

* * * * *

"You do not like this," Kimmuriel remarked to Rai-guy when the two were back in Calimport.

Jarlaxle had remained behind at Dallabad Oasis, securing the remnants of Kohrin Soulez's forces and explaining the slight shift in direction that Ahdahnia Soulez should now undertake.

"How could I?" Rai-guy responded. "Every day, it seems that our purpose in coming to the surface has expanded. I had thought that we would be back in Menzoberranzan by this time, yet our footpads have tightened on the stone."

"On the sand," Kimmuriel corrected, in a tone that showed he, too, was not overly pleased by the continuing expansion of Bregan D'aerthe's surface ventures.

Originally, Jarlaxle had shared plans to come to the surface and establish a base of contacts, humans mostly, who would serve as profiteering front men for the trading transactions of the mercenary drow band. Though he had never specified the details, Jarlaxle's original explanation had made the two believe that their time on the surface would be quite limited.

But now they had expanded, had even constructed a physical structure, with more apparently planned, and had added a second base to the Basadoni conquest. Worse than that, both dark elves were thinking, though not openly saying, perhaps there was something even more behind Jarlaxle's continuing shift of attitude. Perhaps the mercenary leader had erred in taking a certain relic from the renegade Do'Urden.

"Jarlaxle seems to have taken a liking to the surface," Kimmuriel went on. "We all knew that he had tired somewhat of the continuing struggles within our homeland, but perhaps we underestimated the extent of that weariness."

"Perhaps," Rai-guy replied. "Or perhaps our friend merely needs to be reminded that this is not our place."

Kimmuriel stared at him hard, his expression clearly asking how one might "remind" the great Jarlaxle of anything.

"Start at the edges," Rai-guy answered, echoing one of Jarlaxle's favorite sayings, and favorite tactics for Bregan D'aerthe. Whenever the mercenary band went into infiltration or conquest mode, they started gnawing at the edges of their opponent—circling the perimeter and chewing, chewing—as they continued their ever-tightening ring. "Has Morik yet delivered the jewels?"

* * * * *

There it lay before him, in all its wicked splendor.

Artemis Entreri stared long and hard at Charon's Claw, the fingers on both of his unprotected hands rubbing in against his moist palms. Part of him wanted to reach out and grasp the sword, to effect now the battle that he knew would soon enough be fought between his own will-power and that of the sentient weapon. If he won that battle, the sword would truly be his, but if he lost. . . .

He recalled, and vividly, the last horrible moments of Kohrin Soulez's miserable life.

It was exactly that life, though, that so propelled Entreri in this seemingly suicidal direction. He would not be as Soulez had been. He would not allow himself to be a prisoner to the sword, a man trapped in a box of his own making. No, he would be the master, or he would be dead.

But still, that horrific death. . . .

Entreri started to reach for the sword, steeling his willpower against the expected onslaught.

He heard movement in the hallway outside his room.

He had the glove on in a moment and scooped up the sword in his right hand, moving it to its sheath on his hip in one fluid movement even as the door to his private chambers—if any chambers for a human among Bregan D'aerthe could be considered private—swung open.

"Come," instructed Kimmuriel Oblodra, and he turned and started away.

Entreri didn't move, and as soon as the drow realized it, he turned back. Kimmuriel had a quizzical look upon his handsome, angular face. That look of curiosity soon turned to one of menace, though, as he considered the standing, but hardly moving assassin.

"You have a most excellent weapon now," Kimmuriel remarked. "One to greatly complement your nasty dagger. Fear not. Neither Rai-guy nor

669

I have underestimated the value of that gauntlet you seem to keep forever upon your right hand. We know its powers, Artemis Entreri, and we know how to defeat it."

Entreri continued to stare, unblinking, at the drow psionicist. A bluff? Or had resourceful Kimmuriel and Rai-guy indeed found some way around the magic-negating gauntlet? A wry smile found its way onto Entreri's face, a look bolstered by the assassin's complete confidence that whatever secret Kimmuriel might now be hinting of would do the drow little good in their immediate situation. Entreri knew, and his look made Kimmuriel aware as well, that he could cross the room then and there, easily defeat any of Kimmuriel's psionically created defenses with the gauntlet, and run him through with the mighty sword.

If the drow, so cool and so powerful, was bothered or worried at all, he did a fine job of masking it.

But so did Entreri.

"There is work to be done in Luskan," Kimmuriel remarked at length. "Our friend Morik still has not delivered the required jewels."

"I am to go and serve as messenger again?" Entreri asked sarcastically.

"No message for Morik this time," Kimmuriel said coldly. "He has failed us."

The finality of that statement struck Entreri profoundly, but he managed to hide his surprise until Kimmuriel had turned around and started away once more. The assassin understood clearly, of course, that Kimmuriel had, in effect, just told him to got to Luskan and murder Morik. The request did not seem so odd, given that Morik apparently was not living up to Bregan D'aerthe's expectations. Still, it seemed out of place to Entreri that Jarlaxle would so willingly and easily cut his only thread to a market as promising as Luskan without even asking for some explanation from the tricky little rogue. Jarlaxle had been acting strange, to be sure, but was he as confused as that?

It occurred to Entreri even as he started after Kimmuriel that perhaps this assassination had nothing to do with Jarlaxle.

His feelings, and fears, were only strengthened when he entered the small room. He came in not far behind Kimmuriel but found Rai-guy, and Rai-guy alone, waiting for him.

"Morik has failed us yet again," the wizard stated immediately. "There can be no further chances for him. He knows too much of us, and with such an obvious lack of loyalty, well, what are we to do? Go to Luskan and eliminate him. A simple task. We care not for the jewels. If he has them, spend them as you will. Just bring me Morik's heart." As he finished, he stepped aside, clearing the way to a magical portal he had woven, the blurry image inside showing Entreri the alleyway beside Morik's building.

"You will need to remove the gauntlet before you stride through," Kimmuriel remarked, slyly enough for Entreri to wonder if perhaps this whole set-up was but a ruse to force him into an unguarded position. Of course, the resourceful assassin had considered that very thing on the walk over, so he only chuckled at Kimmuriel, walked up to the portal, and stepped right through.

He was in Luskan now, and he looked back to see the magical portal closing behind him. Kimmuriel and Rai-guy were looking at him with expressions that showed everything from confusion to anger to intrigue.

Entreri held up his gloved hand in a mocking wave as the pair faded out of sight. He knew they were wondering how he could exercise such control over the magic-dispelling gauntlet. They were trying to get a feel for its power and its limitations, something that even Entreri had not yet figured out. He certainly didn't mean to offer any clues to his quiet adversaries, thus he had changed from the real magical gauntlet to the decoy that had so fooled Soulez.

When the portal closed he started out of the alleyway, changing once again to the real gauntlet and dropping the fake one into a small sack concealed under the folds of his cloak at the back of his belt.

He went to Morik's room first and found that the little thief had not added any further security traps or tricks. That surprised Entreri, for if Morik was again disappointing his merciless leaders he should have been expecting company. Furthermore, the thief obviously had not fled the small apartment.

Not content to sit and wait, Entreri went back out onto Luskan's streets, making his way from tavern to tavern, from corner to corner. A few beggars approached him, but he sent them away with a glare. One pickpocket actually went for the purse he had secured to his belt on the right side. Entreri left him sitting in the gutter, his wrist shattered by a simple twist of the assassin's hand.

Sometime later, and thinking that it was about time for him to return to Morik's abode, the assassin came into an establishment on Half-Moon Street known as the Cutlass. The place was nearly empty, with a portly barkeep rubbing away at the dirty bar and a skinny little man sitting across from him, chattering away. Another figure among the few patrons remaining in the place caught Entreri's attention.

The man was sitting comfortably and quietly at the far left end of the bar with his back against the wall and the hood of his weathered cloak pulled over his head. He appeared to be sleeping, judging from his rhythmic breathing, the hunch of his shoulders, and the loll of his head, but Entreri caught a few tell-tale signs—like the fact that the rolling head kept angling to give the supposedly sleeping man a fine view of all around him—that told him otherwise.

The assassin didn't miss the slight tensing of the shoulders when that angle revealed his presence to the supposedly sleeping man.

Entreri strode up to the bar, right beside the nervous, skinny little man, who said, "Arumn's done serving for the night."

Entreri glanced over, his dark eyes taking a full measure of this one. "My gold is not good enough for you?" he asked the barkeep, turning back slowly to consider the portly man behind the bar.

Entreri noted that the barkeep took a long, good measure of him. He saw respect coming into Arumn's eyes. He wasn't surprised. This barkeep, like so many others, survived primarily by understanding his clientele. Entreri was doing little to hide the truth of his skills in his graceful, solid movements. The man pretending to sleep at the bar said nothing, and neither did the nervous one.

"Ho, Josi's just puffing out his chest, is all," the barkeep, Arumn, remarked, "though I had planned on closing her up early. Not many looking for drink this night."

Satisfied with that, Entreri glanced to the left, to the compact form of the man pretending to be asleep. "Two honey meads," he said, dropping a couple of shining gold coins on the bar, ten times the cost of the drinks.

The assassin continued to watch the "sleeper," hardly paying any heed at all to Arumn or nervous little Josi, who was constantly shifting at his other side. Josi even asked Entreri his name, but the assassin ignored him. He just continued to stare, taking a measure, studying every movement and playing them against what he already knew of Morik.

He turned back when he heard the clink of glass on the bar. He scooped up one drink in his gloved right hand, bringing the dark liquid to his lips, while he grasped the second glass in his left hand, and instead of lifting it, just sent it sliding fast down the bar, angled slightly for the outer lip, perfectly set to dump onto the supposedly-sleeping man's lap.

The barkeep cried out in surprise. Josi Puddles jumped to his feet, and even started toward Entreri, who simply ignored him.

The assassin's smile widened when Morik, and it was indeed Morik, reached up at the last moment and caught the mead-filled missile, bringing his hand back and wide to absorb the shock of the catch and to make sure that any liquid that did splash over did not spill on him.

Entreri slid off the barstool, took up his glass of mead and motioned for Morik to go with him outside. He had barely taken a step, though, when he sensed a movement toward his arm. He turned back to see Josi Puddles reaching for him.

"No, ye don't!" the skinny man remarked. "Ye ain't leavin' with Arumn's glasses."

Entreri watched the hand coming toward him and lifted his gaze to look Josi Puddles straight in the eye, to let the man know, with just a look and just that awful, calm and deadly demeanor, that if he so much as brushed Entreri's arm with his hand, he would surely pay for it with his life.

"No, ye . . ." Josi started to say again, but his voice failed him and his hand stopped moving. He knew. Defeated, the skinny man sank back against the bar.

"The gold should more than pay for the glasses," Entreri remarked to the barkeep, and Arumn, too, seemed quite unnerved.

The assassin headed for the door, taking some pleasure in hearing the barkeep quietly scolding Josi for being so stupid.

The street was quiet outside, and dark, and Entreri could sense the uneasiness in Morik. He could see it in the man's cautious stance and in the way his eyes darted about.

"I have the jewels," Morik was quick to announce. He started in the direction of his apartment, and Entreri followed.

The assassin thought it interesting that Morik presented him with the jewels—and the size of the pouch made Entreri believe that the thief had certainly met his master's expectations—as soon as they entered the darkened room. If Morik had them, why hadn't he simply given them over on time? Certainly Morik, no fool, understood the volatile and extremely dangerous nature of his partners.

"I wondered when I would be called upon," Morik said, obviously trying to appear completely calm. "I have had them since the day after you left but have gotten no word from Rai-guy or Kimmuriel."

Entreri nodded, but showed no surprise—and in truth, when he thought about it, the assassin wasn't really surprised at all. These were drow, after all. They killed when convenient, killed when they felt like it. Perhaps they had sent Entreri here to slay Morik in the hopes that Morik would prove the stronger. Perhaps it didn't matter to them either way. They would merely enjoy the spectacle of it.

Or perhaps Rai-guy and Kimmuriel were anxious to clip away at the entrenchment that Jarlaxle was obviously setting up for Bregan D'aerthe. Kill Morik and any others like him, sever all ties, and go home. He lifted his black gauntlet into the air, seeking any magical emanations. He detected some upon Morik and some other minor dweomers in and around the room, but nothing that seemed to him to be any kind of scrying spell. It wasn't that he could have done anything about any spells or psionics divining the area, anyway. Entreri had come to understand already that the gauntlet could only grab at spells directed at him specifically. In truth, the thing was really quite limited. He might catch one of Rai-guy's lightning bolts and hurl it back at the wizard, but if Rai-guy filled the room with a fireball. . . .

"What are you doing?" Morik asked the distracted assassin.

"Get out of here," Entreri instructed. "Out of this building and out of the city altogether, for a short while at least."

The obviously puzzled Morik just stared at him.

"Did you not hear me?"

"That order comes from Jarlaxle?" Morik asked, seeming quite confused. "Does he fear that I have been discovered, that he, by association, has been somehow implicated?"

"I tell you to begone, Morik," Entreri answered. "I, and not Jarlaxle, nor, certainly, Rai-guy or Kimmuriel."

"Do I threaten you?" asked Morik. "Am I somehow impeding your ascension within the guild?"

"Are you that much a fool?" Entreri replied.

"I have been promised a king's treasure!" Morik protested. "The only reason I agreed—"

"Was because you had no choice," Entreri interrupted. "I know that to be true, Morik. Perhaps that lack of choice is the only thing that saves you now."

Morik was shaking his head, obviously upset and unconvinced. "Luskan is my home," he started to say.

Charon's Claw came out in a red and black flash. Entreri swiped down beside Morik, left and right, then slashed across right above the man's head. The sword left a trail of black ash with all three swipes so that Entreri had Morik practically boxed in by the opaque walls. So quickly had he struck, the dazed and dazzled rogue hadn't even had a chance to draw his weapon.

"I was not sent to collect the jewels or even to scold and warn you, fool," Entreri said coldly—so very, very coldly. "I was sent to kill you."

"But . . ."

"You have no idea the level of evil with which you have allied yourself," the assassin went on. "Flee this place—this building *and* this city. Run for all your life, fool Morik. They will not look for you if they cannot find you easily—you are not worth their trouble. So run away, beyond their vision and take hope that you are free of them."

Morik stood there, encapsulated by the walls of black ash that still magically hung in the air, his jaw hanging open in complete astonishment. He looked left and right, just a bit, and swallowed hard, making it clear to Entreri that he had just then come to realize how overmatched he truly was. Despite the assassin's previous visit, easily getting through all of Morik's traps, it had taken this display of brutal swordsmanship to show Morik the deadly truth of Artemis Entreri.

"Why would they . . . ?" Morik dared to ask. "I am an ally, eyes for Bregan D'aerthe in the northland. Jarlaxle himself instructed me to . . ." He stopped at the sound of Entreri's laughter.

"You are *iblith*," Entreri explained. "Offal. Not of the drow. That alone makes you no more than a plaything to them. They *will* kill you—I am to kill you here and now by their very words."

"Yet you defy them," Morik said, and it wasn't clear from his tone if he had come around yet truly to believe Entreri or not.

"You are thinking that this is some test of your loyalty," Entreri correctly guessed, shaking his head with every word. "The drow do not test loyalty, Morik, because they expect none. With them, there is only the predictability of actions based in simple fear."

"Yet you are showing yourself disloyal by letting me go," Morik remarked. "We are not friends, with no debt and little contact between us. Why do you tell me this?"

674

Entreri leaned back and considered that question more deeply than Morik could have expected, allowing the thief's recognition of illogic to resonate in his thoughts. For surely Entreri's actions here made little logical sense. He could have been done with his business and back on his way to Calimport, without any real threat to him. By contrast, and by all logical reasoning, there would be little gain for Entreri in letting Morik walk away.

Why this time? the assassin asked himself. He had killed so many, and often in situations similar to this, often at the behest of a guild-master seeking to punish an impudent or threatening underling. He had followed orders to kill people whose offense had never been made known to him, people, perhaps, similar to Morik, who had truly committed no offense at all.

No, Artemis Entreri couldn't quite bring himself to accept that last thought. His killings, every one, had been committed against people associated with the underworld, or against misinformed do-gooders who had somehow become entangled in the wrong mess, impeding the assassin's progress. Even Drizzt Do'Urden, that paladin in drow skin, had named himself as Entreri's enemy by preventing the assassin from retrieving Regis the halfling and the magical ruby pendant the little fool had stolen from Pasha Pook. It had taken years, but to Entreri, killing Drizzt Do'Urden had been the justified culmination of the drow's unwanted and immoral interference. In Entreri's mind and in his heart, those who had died at his hands had played the great game, had tossed aside their innocence in pursuit of power or material gain.

In Entreri's mind, everyone he had killed had indeed deserved it, because he was a killer among killers, a survivor in a brutal game that would not allow it to be any other way.

"Why?" Morik asked again, drawing Entreri from his contemplation.

The assassin stared at the rogue for a moment, and offered a quick and simple answer to a question too complex for him to sort out properly, an answer that rang of more truth than Artemis Entreri even realized.

"Because I hate drow more than I hate humans."

675

Part 2

Which the Tool?
Which the Master?

Entreri again teamed with Jarlaxle?

What an odd pairing that seems, and to some (and initially to me, as well) a vision of the most unsettling nightmare imaginable. There is no one in all the world, I believe, more crafty and ingenious than Jarlaxle of Bregan D'aerthe, the consummate opportunist, a wily leader who can craft a kingdom out of the dung of rothé. Jarlaxle, who thrived in the matriarchal society of Menzoberranzan as completely as any Matron Mother.

Jarlaxle of mystery, who knew my father, who claims a past friendship with Zaknafein.

How could a drow who befriended Zaknafein ally with Artemis Entreri? At quick glance, the notion seems incongruous, even preposterous. And yet, I do believe Jarlaxle's claims of the former and know the latter to be true—for the second time.

Professionally, I see no mystery in the union. Entreri has ever preferred a position of the shadows, serving as the weapon of a high-paying master—no, not master. I doubt that Artemis Entreri has ever known a master. Rather, even in the service of the guilds, he worked as a sword for hire. Certainly such a skilled mercenary could find a place within Bregan D'aerthe, especially since they've come to the surface and likely need

679

humans to front and cover their true identity. For Jarlaxle, therefore, the alliance with Entreri is certainly a convenient thing.

But there is something else, something more, between them. I know this from the way Jarlaxle spoke of the man, and from the simple fact that the mercenary leader went so far out of his way to arrange the last fight between me and Entreri. It was for the sake of Entreri's state of mind, no less, and certainly as no favor to me, and as no mere source of entertainment for Jarlaxle. He cares for Entreri as a friend might, even as he values the assassin's multitude of skills.

There lies the incongruity.

For though Entreri and Jarlaxle have complementary professional skills, they do not seem well matched in temperament or in moral standards—two essentials, it would seem, for any successful friendship.

Or perhaps not.

Jarlaxle's heart is far more generous than that of Artemis Entreri. The mercenary can be brutal, of course, but not randomly so. Practicality guides his moves, for his eye is ever on the potential gain, but even in that light of efficient pragmatism, Jarlaxle's heart often overrules his lust for profit. Many times has he allowed my escape, for example, when bringing my head to Matron Malice or Matron Baenre would have brought him great gain. Is Artemis Entreri similarly possessed of such generosity?

Not at all.

In fact, I suspect that if Entreri knew that Jarlaxle had saved me from my apparent death in the tower, he would have first tried to kill me and turned his anger upon Jarlaxle. Such a battle might well yet occur, and if it does, I believe that Artemis Entreri will learn that he is badly overmatched. Not by Jarlaxle individually, though the mercenary leader is crafty and reputedly a fine warrior in his own right, but by the pragmatic Jarlaxle's many, many deadly allies.

Therein lies the essence of the mercenary leader's interest in, and control of, Artemis Entreri. Jarlaxle sees the man's value and does not fear him, because what Jarlaxle has perfected, and what Entreri is sorely lacking in, is the ability to build an interdependent organization. Entreri won't attempt to kill Jarlaxle because Entreri will need Jarlaxle.

Jarlaxle will make certain of that. He weaves his web all around him. It is a network that is always mutually beneficial, a network in which all security—against Bregan D'aerthe's many dangerous rivals—inevitably depends upon the controlling and calming influence that is Jarlaxle. He is the ultimate consensus builder, the purest of diplomats, while Entreri is a loner, a man who must dominate all around him.

Jarlaxle coerces. Entreri controls.

But with Jarlaxle, Entreri will never find any level of control. The mercenary leader is too entrenched and too intelligent for that.

And yet, I believe that their alliance will hold, and their friendship will grow. Certainly there will be conflicts and perhaps very dangerous ones for both parties. Perhaps Entreri has already learned the truth of my departure and has killed Jarlaxle or died trying. But the longer the alliance holds, the stronger it will become, the more entrenched in friendship.

I say this because I believe that, in the end, Jarlaxle's philosophy will win out. Artemis Entreri is the one of this duo who is limited by fault. His desire for absolute control is fueled by his inability to trust. While that desire has led him to become as fine a fighter as I have ever known, it has also led him to an existence that even he is beginning to recognize as empty.

Professionally, Jarlaxle offers Artemis Entreri security, a base for his efforts, while Entreri gives Jarlaxle and all of Bregan D'aerthe a clear connection to the surface world.

But personally, Jarlaxle offers even more to Entreri, offers him a chance to finally break out of the role that he has assumed as a solitary creature. I remember Entreri upon our departure from Menzoberranzan, where we were both imprisoned, each in his own way. He was with Bregan D'aerthe then as well, but down in that city, Artemis Entreri looked into a dark and empty mirror that he did not like. Why, then, is he now returned to Jarlaxle's side?

It is a testament to the charm that is Jarlaxle, the intuitive understanding that that most clever of dark elves holds for creating desire and alliance. The mere fact that Entreri is apparently with Jarlaxle once again tells me that the mercenary leader is already winning the inevitable clash between their basic philosophies, their temperament and moral standards. Though Entreri does not yet understand it, I am sure, Jarlaxle will strengthen him more by example than by alliance.

Perhaps with Jarlaxle's help, Artemis Entreri will find his way out of his current empty existence.

Or perhaps Jarlaxle will eventually kill him.

Either way, the world will be a better place, I think.

—Drizzt Do'Urden

Chapter 9

Control and Cooperation

The Copper Ante was fairly busy this evening, with halflings mostly crowding around tables, rolling bones or playing other games of chance and all whispering about the recent events in and around the city. Every one of them spoke quietly, though, for among the few humans in the tavern that night were two rather striking figures, operatives central to the recent tumultuous events.

Sharlotta Vespers was very aware of the many stares directed her way, and she knew that many of these halflings were secret allies of her companion this night. She had almost refused Entreri's invitation for her to come and meet with him privately here, in the house of Dwahvel Tiggerwillies, but she recognized the value of the place. The Copper Ante was beyond the prying eyes of Rai-guy and Kimmuriel, a condition necessary, so Entreri had said, for any meeting.

"I can't believe you openly walk Calimport's streets with that sword," Sharlotta remarked quietly.

"It is rather distinctive," Entreri admitted, but there wasn't the slightest hint of alarm in his voice.

"It's a well-known blade," Sharlotta answered. "Anyone who knew of Kohrin Soulez and Dallabad knows he would never willingly part with

683

it, yet here you are, showing it to all who would glance your way. One might think that a clear connection between the downfall of Dallabad and House Basadoni."

"How so?" Entreri asked, and he took pleasure indeed at the look of sheer exasperation that washed over Sharlotta.

"Kohrin is dead and Artemis Entreri is wearing his sword," Sharlotta remarked dryly.

"He is dead, and thus the sword is no longer of any use to him," Entreri flippantly remarked. "On the streets, it is understood that he was killed in a coup by his very own daughter, who, by all rumors, had no desire to be captured by Charon's Claw as was Kohrin."

"Thus it falls to the hands of Artemis Entreri?" Sharlotta asked incredulously.

"It has been hinted that Kohrin's refusal to sell at the offered price— an absurd amount of gold—was the very catalyst for the coup," Entreri went on, leaning back comfortably in his chair. "When Ahdahnia learned that he refused the transaction. . . ."

"Impossible," Sharlotta breathed, shaking her head. "Do you really expect that tale to be believed?"

Entreri smiled wryly. "The words of Sha'lazzi Ozoule are often believed," he remarked. "Inquiries to purchase the sword were made through Sha'lazzi only days before the coup at Dallabad."

That set Sharlotta back in her chair as she tried hard to digest and sort through all of the information. On the streets, it was indeed being said that Kohrin had been killed in a coup—Jarlaxle's domination of the remaining Dallabad forces through use of the Crystal Shard had provided consistency in all of the reports coming out of the oasis. As long as Crenshinibon's dominance held out, there was no evidence at all to reveal the truth of the assault on Dallabad. If Entreri had spoken truly—and Sharlotta had no reason to think that he had not—the refusal by Kohrin to sell Charon's Claw would be linked not to any theft or any attack by House Basadoni, but rather as one of the catalysts for the coup.

Sharlotta stared hard at Entreri, her expression a mixture of anger and admiration. He had covered every possible aspect of his procurement of the coveted sword beforehand. Sharlotta, given her understanding of Entreri's relationship with the dangerous Rai-guy and Kimmuriel, held no doubts that Entreri had helped guide the dark elves to Dallabad specifically with the intent of collecting that very sword.

"You weave a web with many layers," the woman remarked.

"I have been around dark elves for far too long," Entreri casually replied.

"But you walk the very edge of disaster," said Sharlotta. "Many of the guilds had already linked the downfall of Dallabad with House Basadoni, and now you openly parade about with Charon's Claw. The other rumors are plausible, of course, but your actions do little to distance us from the assassination of Kohrin Soulez."

"Where stands Pasha Da'Daclan or Pasha Wroning?" Entreri asked, feigning concern.

"Da'Daclan is cautious and making no overt moves," Sharlotta replied. Entreri held his grin private at her earnest tones, for she had obviously taken his bait. "He is far from pleased with the situation, though, and the strong inferences concerning Dallabad."

"As they all will be," Entreri reasoned. "Unless Jarlaxle grows too bold with his construction of crystalline towers."

Again he spoke with dramatically serious tones, more to measure Sharlotta's reaction than to convey any information the woman didn't already know. He did note a slight tremor in her lip. Frustration? Fear? Disgust? Entreri knew that Rai-guy and Kimmuriel were not happy with Jarlaxle, and that the two independent-minded lieutenants, perhaps, were thinking that the influences of the sentient and dominating Crystal Shard might be causing some serious problems. They had sent him after Morik to weaken the guild's presence on the surface, obviously, but why, then, was Sharlotta still alive? Had she thrown in with the two potential usurpers to Bregan D'aerthe's dark throne?

"The deed is completed now and cannot be undone," Entreri remarked. "Indeed I did desire Charon's Claw—what warrior would not?—but with Sha'lazzi Ozoule spreading his tales of a generous offer to buy being refused by Kohrin, and with Ahdahnia Soulez speaking openly of her disdain for her father's choices, particularly concerning the sword, it all plays to the advantage of Bregan D'aerthe and our work here. Jarlaxle needed a haven to construct the tower, and we gave him one. Bregan D'aerthe now has eyes beyond the city, where we might watch all mounting threats that are outside of our immediate jurisdiction. Everyone wins."

"And Entreri gets the sword," Sharlotta remarked.

"Everyone wins," the assassin said again.

"Until we step too far, and too boldly, and all the world unites against us," said Sharlotta.

"Jarlaxle has lived on such a precipice for centuries," Entreri replied. "He has not stumbled over yet."

Sharlotta started to respond but held her words at the last moment. Entreri knew them anyway, words taken from her by the quick give and take of the conversation, the mounting excitement and momentum bringing a rare unguarded moment. She was about to remark that never in all those centuries had Jarlaxle possessed Crenshinibon, the clear inference being that never in those centuries had Crenshinibon possessed Jarlaxle.

"Say nothing of our concerns to Rai-guy and Kimmuriel," Entreri bade her. "They are fearful enough, and frightened creatures, even drow, can make serious errors. You and I will watch from afar—perhaps there is a way out of this if it comes to an internal war."

Sharlotta nodded, and rightly took Entreri's tone as a dismissal. She rose, nodded again, and moved out of the room.

Entreri didn't believe that nod for a moment. He knew the woman would likely go running right to Rai-guy and Kimmuriel, attempting to bend this conversation her way. But that was the point of it all, was it not? Entreri had just forced Sharlotta's hand, forced her to show her true alliances in this ever-widening web of intrigue. Certainly his last claim, that there might be a way out for the two of them, would ring hollow to Sharlotta, who knew him well, and knew well that he would never bother to take her along with him on any escape from Bregan D'aerthe. He'd put a dagger in her back as surely as he had killed any previous supposed partners, from Tallan Belmer to Rassiter the wererat. Sharlotta knew that, and Entreri knew she knew it.

It did occur to the assassin that perhaps Sharlotta, Rai-guy, and Kimmuriel were correct in their apparent assessment that Crenshinibon was having unfavorable influences on Jarlaxle, that the artifact was leading the cunning mercenary in a direction that could spell doom for Bregan D'aerthe's surface ambitions. That hardly mattered to Entreri, of course, who wasn't sure the retreat of the dark elves back to Menzoberranzan would be such a bad thing. What was more important, to Entreri's thinking, were the dynamics of his relationship with the principles of the mercenary band. Rai-guy and Kimmuriel were notorious racists and hated him as they hated anyone who was not drow—more, even, because Entreri's skill and survival instincts threatened them profoundly. Without Jarlaxle's protection, it wasn't hard for Artemis Entreri to envision his fate. While he felt somewhat bolstered by his acquisition of Charon's Claw, the bane of wizards, he hardly thought it evened the odds in any battle he might find with the duo of the drow wizard-cleric and psionicist. If those two wound up in command of Bregan D'aerthe, with over a hundred drow warriors at their immediate disposal . . .

Entreri didn't like the odds at all.

He knew, without doubt, that Jarlaxle's fall would almost immediately precede his own.

*   *   *   *   *

Kimmuriel walked along the tunnels beneath Dallabad with some measure of trepidation. This was a *haszakkin*, after all, an illithid—unpredictable and deadly. Still, the drow had come alone, had deceived Rai-guy that he might do so.

There were some things that psionicists alone could understand and appreciate.

Around a sudden bend in the tunnel, Kimmuriel came upon the bulbous-headed creature, sitting calmly on a rock against the back end of the alcove. Yharaskrik's eyes were closed, but he was awake, Kimmuriel knew, for he could feel the mental energy beaming out from the creature.

I chose well in siding with Bregan D'aerthe, it would seem, the illithid telepathically remarked. *There was never any doubt.*

The drow are stronger than the humans, Kimmuriel agreed, using the illithid's telepathic link to impart his exact thoughts.

Stronger than these *humans,* Yharaskrik corrected.

Kimmuriel bowed, figuring to let the matter drop there, but Yharaskrik had more to discuss.

Stronger than Kohrin Soulez, the illithid went on. *Crippled, he was, by his obsession with a particular magical item.*

That brought some understanding to Kimmuriel, some logical connection between the mind flayer and the pitiful gang of Dallabad Oasis. Why would a creature as great as Yharaskrik waste its time with such inferior beings, after all?

You were sent to observe the powerful sword and the gauntlet, he reasoned.

We wish to understand that which can sometimes defeat our attacks, Yharaskrik freely admitted. *Yet neither item is without limitations. Neither is as powerful as Kohrin Soulez believed, or your attack would never have succeeded.*

We have discerned as much, Kimmuriel agreed.

My time with Kohrin Soulez was nearing its end, said Yharaskrik, a clear inference that the illithid—creatures known as among the most meticulous of all in the multiverse—believed that it had learned every secret of the sword and gauntlet.

The human, Artemis Entreri, confiscated both the gauntlet and Charon's Claw, the drow psionicist explained.

That was his intent, of course, the illithid replied. *He fears you and wisely so. You are strong in will, Kimmuriel of House Oblodra.*

The drow bowed again.

Respect the sword named Charon's Claw, and even more so the gauntlet the human now wears on his hand. With these, he can turn your powers back against you if you are not careful.

Kimmuriel imparted his assurances that Artemis Entreri and his dangerous new weapon would be closely watched. *Are your days of watching the paired items now ended?* he asked as he finished.

Perhaps, Yharaskrik answered.

Or perhaps Bregan D'aerthe could find a place suited to your special talents, Kimmuriel offered. He didn't think it would be hard to persuade Jarlaxle of such an arrangement. Dark elves often allied with illithids in the Underdark.

Yharaskrik's pause was telling to the perceptive and intelligent drow. "You have a better offer?" Kimmuriel asked aloud, and with a chuckle.

Better it would be if I remained to the side of events, unknown to Bregan D'aerthe other than to Kimmuriel Oblodra, Yharaskrik answered in all seriousness.

The response at first confused Kimmuriel and made him think that the illithid feared that Bregan D'aerthe would side with Entreri and Charon's Claw if any such conflict arose between Yharaskrik and Entreri, but before he could begin to offer his assurances against that, the illithid imparted a clear image to him, one of a crystalline tower shining in the sun above the palm trees of Dallabad Oasis.

"The towers?" Kimmuriel asked aloud. "They are just manifestations of Crenshinibon."

Crenshinibon. The word came to Kimmuriel with a sense of urgency and great importance.

It is an artifact, the drow telepathically explained. *A new toy for Jarlaxle's collection.*

Not so, came Yharaskrik's response. *Much more than that, I fear, as should you.*

Kimmuriel narrowed his red-glowing eyes, focusing carefully on Yharaskrik's thoughts, which he expected might confirm the fears he and Rai-guy had long been discussing.

Weave into the thoughts of Jarlaxle, I cannot, the illithid went on. *He wears a protective item.*

The eye patch, Kimmuriel silently replied. *It denies entrance to his mind by wizard, priest, or psionicist.*

But such a simple tool cannot defeat the encroachment of Crenshinibon, Yharaskrik explained.

How do you know of the artifact?

Crenshinibon is no mystery to my people, for it is an ancient item indeed, and one that has crossed the trails of the illithids on many occasions, Yharaskrik admitted. *Indeed, Crenshinibon, the Crystal Shard, despises us, for we alone are quite beyond its tempting reach. We alone as a great race are possessed of the mental discipline necessary to prevent the Crystal Shard from its greatest desires of absolute control. You, too, Kimmuriel, can step beyond the orb of Crenshinibon's influence and easily.*

The drow took a long moment to contemplate the implications of that claim, but naturally, he quickly came to the conclusion that Yharaskrik was relating that psionics alone might fend the intrusions of the Crystal Shard, since Jarlaxle's potent eye patch was based in wizardly magic and not the potent powers of the mind.

Crenshinibon's primary attack is upon the ego, the illithid explained. *It collects slaves with promises of greatness and riches.*

Not unlike the drow, Kimmuriel related, thinking of the tactics Bregan D'aerthe had used on Morik.

Yharaskrik laughed a gurgling, bubbly sound. *The more ambitious the wielder, the easier he will be controlled.*

But what if the wielder is ambitious yet ultimately cautious? Kimmuriel asked, for never had he known Jarlaxle to allow his ambition to overrule good judgment—never before, at least, for only recently had he, Rai-guy, and others come to question the wisdom of the mercenary leader's decisions.

Some lessers can deny the call, the illithid admitted, and it was obvious to Kimmuriel that Yharaskrik considered anyone who was not illithid or who was not at least a psionicist a lesser. *Crenshinibon has little sway over paladins and goodly priests, over righteous kings and noble peasants, but one who desires more—and who of the lesser races, drow included, does not?—and who is not above deception and destruction to further his ends, will inevitably sink into Crenshinibon's grasp.*

It made perfect sense to Kimmuriel, of course, and explained why Drizzt Do'Urden and his "heroic" friends had seemingly put the artifact away. It also explained Jarlaxle's recent behavior, confirming Kimmuriel's suspicions that Bregan D'aerthe was indeed being led astray.

I would not normally refuse an offer of Bregan D'aerthe, Yharaskrik imparted a moment later, after Kimmuriel had digested the information. *You and your reputable kin would be amusing at the least—and likely enlightening and profitable as well—but I fear that all of Bregan D'aerthe will soon fall under the domination of Crenshinibon.*

And why would Yharaskrik fear such a thing, if Crenshinibon becomes leader in order to take us in the same ambitious direction that we have always pursued? Kimmuriel asked, and he feared that he already knew the answer.

I trust not the drow, Yharaskrik admitted, *but I understand enough of your desires and methods to recognize that we need not be enemies among the cattle humans. I trust you not, but I fear you not, because you would find no gain in facilitating my demise. Indeed, you understand that I am connected to the one community that is my people, and that if you killed me you would be making many powerful enemies.*

Kimmuriel bowed, acknowledging the truth of the illithid's observations.

Crenshinibon, however, Yharaskrik went on, *acts not with such rationality. It is all-devouring, a scourge upon the world, controlling all that it can and consuming that which it cannot. It is the bane of devils, yet the love of demons, a denier of laws for the sake of the destruction wrought by chaos. Your Lady Lolth would idolize such an artifact and truly enjoy the chaos of its workings—except of course that Crenshinibon, unlike her drow agents, works not for any ends, but merely to devour. Crenshinibon will bring great power to Bregan D'aerthe—witness the new willing slaves it has made for you, among them the very daughter of the man you overthrew. In the end, Crenshinibon will abandon you, will bring upon you foes too great to fend. This is the history*

689

of the Crystal Shard, repeated time and again through the centuries. It is unbridled hunger without discipline, doomed to bloat and die.

Kimmuriel unintentionally winced at the thoughts, for he could see that very path being woven right before the still-secretive doorstep of Bregan D'aerthe.

All-devouring, Yharaskrik said again. *Controlling all that it can and consuming that which it cannot.*

And you are among that which it cannot, Kimmuriel reasoned.

"As are you," Yharaskrik said in its watery voice. "Tower of Iron Will and Mind Blank," the illithid recited, two typical and readily available mental defense modes that psionicists often used in their battles with each other.

Kimmuriel growled, understanding well the trap that the illithid had just laid for him, the alliance of necessity that Yharaskrik, obviously fearing that Kimmuriel might betray him to Jarlaxle and the Crystal Shard, had just forced upon him. He knew those defensive mental postures, of course, and if the Crystal Shard came after him, seeking control, now that he knew the two defenses would prevent the intrusions, he would inevitably and automatically summon them up. For, like any psionicist, like any reasoning being, Kimmuriel's ego and id would never allow such controlling possession.

He stared long and hard at the illithid, hating the creature, and yet sympathizing with Yharaskrik's fears of Crenshinibon. Or, perhaps, it occurred to him that Yharaskrik had just saved him. Crenshinibon would have come after him, to dominate if not to destroy, and if Kimmuriel had discovered the correct ways to block the intrusion in time, then he would have suddenly become an enemy in an unfavorable position, as opposed to now, when he, and not Crenshinibon, properly understood the situation at hand.

"You will shadow us?" he asked the illithid, hoping the answer would be yes.

He felt a wave of thoughts roll through him, ambiguous and lacking any specifics, but indicating clearly that Yharaskrik meant to keep a watchful eye on the dangerous Crystal Shard.

They were allies, then, out of necessity.

* * * * *

"I do not like her," came the high-pitched, excited voice of Dwahvel Tiggerwillies. The halfling shuffled over to take Sharlotta's vacated seat at Entreri's table.

"Is it her height and beauty that so offend you?" Entreri sarcastically replied.

Dwahvel shot him a perfectly incredulous look. "Her dishonesty," the halfling explained.

690

That answer raised Entreri's eyebrow. Wasn't everyone on the streets of Calimport, Entreri and Dwahvel included, basically a manipulator? If a claim of dishonesty was a reason not to like someone in Calimport, then the judgmental person would find herself quite alone.

"There is a difference," Dwahvel explained, intercepting a nearby waiter with a wave of her hand and taking a drink from his laden tray.

"So it comes back to that height and beauty problem, then," Entreri chided with a smile.

His own words did indeed amuse him, but what caught his fancy even more was the realization that he could, and often did, talk to Dwahvel in such a manner. In all of his life, Artemis Entreri had known very few people with whom he could have a casual conversation, but he found himself so at ease with Dwahvel that he had even considered hiring a wizard to determine if she was using some charming magic on him. In fact, then and there, Entreri clenched his gloved fist, concentrating briefly on the item to see if he could determine any magical emanations coming from Dwahvel, aimed at him.

There was nothing, only honest friendship, which to Artemis Entreri was a magic more foreign indeed.

"I have often been jealous of human women," Dwahvel answered sarcastically, doing well to keep a perfectly straight face. "They are often tall enough to attract even ogres, after all."

Entreri chuckled, an expression from him so rare that he actually surprised himself in hearing it.

"There is a difference between Sharlotta and many others, yourself included," Dwahvel went on. "We all play the game—that is how we survive, after all—and we all deceive and plot, twisting truths and lies alike to reach our own desired ends. The confusion for some, Sharlotta included, lies in those ends. I understand you. I know your desires, your goals, and know that I impede those goals at my peril. But I trust as well that, as long as I do not impede those goals, I'll not find the wrong end of either of your fine blades."

"So thought Dondon," Entreri put in, referring to Dondon Tiggerwillies, Dwahvel's cousin and once Entreri's closest friend in the city. Entreri had murdered the pitiful Dondon soon after his return from his final battle with Drizzt Do'Urden.

"Your actions against Dondon did not surprise him, I assure you," Dwahvel remarked. "He was a good enough friend to you to have killed you if he had ever found you in the same situation as you found him. You did him a favor."

Entreri shrugged, hardly sure of that, not even sure of his own motivations in killing Dondon. Had he done so to free Dondon from his own gluttonous ends, from the chains that kept him locked in a room and in a state of constant incapacity? Or had he killed Dondon simply because he was angry at the failed creature, simply because he could not stand to look at the miserable thing he had become any longer?

691

"Sharlotta is not trustworthy because you cannot understand her true goals and motivations," Dwahvel continued. "She desires power, yes, as do many, but with her, one can never understand where she might be thinking that she can find that power. There is no loyalty there, even to those who maintain consistency of character and action. No, that one will take the better deal at the expense of any and all."

Entreri nodded, not disagreeing in the least. He had never liked Sharlotta, and like Dwahvel, he had never even begun to trust her. There were no scruples or codes within Sharlotta Vespers, only blatant manipulation.

"She crosses the line every time," Dwahvel remarked. "I have never been fond of women who use their bodies to get that which they desire. I've got my own charms, you know, and yet I have never had to stoop to such a level."

The lighthearted ending brought another smile to Entreri's face, and he knew that Dwahvel was only half joking. She did indeed have her charms: a pleasant appearance and fine, flattering dress, as sharp a wit as was to be found, and a keen sense of her surroundings.

"How are you getting on with your new companion?" Dwahvel asked.

Entreri looked at her curiously—she did have a way of bouncing about a conversation.

"The sword," Dwahvel clarified, feigning exasperation. "You have it now, or it has you."

"*I* have *it*," Entreri assured her, dropping his hand to the bony hilt.

Dwahvel eyed him suspiciously.

"I have not yet fought my battle with Charon's Claw," Entreri admitted to her, hardly believing that he was doing so, "but I do not think it so powerful a weapon that I need fear it."

"As Jarlaxle believes with Crenshinibon?" Dwahvel asked, and again, Entreri's eyebrow lifted high.

"He constructed a crystalline tower," the ever-observant halfling argued. "That is one of the most basic desires of the Crystal Shard, if the old sages are to be believed."

Entreri started to ask her how she could possibly know of any of that, of the shard and the tower at Dallabad and of any connection, but he didn't bother. Of course Dwahvel knew. She always knew—that was one of her charms. Entreri had dropped enough hints in their many discussions for her to figure it all out, and she did have an incredible number of other sources as well. If Dwahvel Tiggerwillies learned that Jarlaxle carried an artifact known as Crenshinibon, then there would be little doubt that she would go to the sages and pay good coin to learn every little-known detail about the powerful item.

"He thinks he controls it," Dwahvel said.

"Do not underestimate Jarlaxle," Entreri replied. "Many have. They all are dead."

"Do not underestimate the Crystal Shard," Dwahvel returned without hesitation. "Many have. They all are dead."

"A wonderful combination then," Entreri said matter-of-factly. He dropped his chin in his hand, stroking his smooth cheek and bringing his finger to a pinch at the small tuft of hair that remained on his chin, considering the conversation and the implications. "Jarlaxle can handle the artifact," he decided.

Dwahvel shrugged noncommitally.

"Even more than that," Entreri went on, "Jarlaxle will welcome the union if Crenshinibon proves his equal. That is the difference between him and me," he explained, and though he was speaking to Dwahvel, he was, in fact, really talking to himself, sorting out his many feelings on this complicated issue. "He will allow Crenshinibon to be his partner, if that is necessary, and will find ways to make their goals one and the same."

"But Artemis Entreri has no partners," Dwahvel reasoned.

Entreri considered the words carefully, and even glanced down at the powerful sword he now wore, a sword possessed of sentience and influence, a sword whose spirit he surely meant to break and dominate. "No," he agreed. "I have no partners, and I want none. The sword is mine and will serve me. Nothing less."

"Or?"

"Or it will find its way into the acid mouth of a black dragon," Entreri strongly assured the halfling, growling with every word, and Dwahvel wasn't about to argue with those words spoken in that tone.

"Who is the stronger then," Dwahvel dared to ask, "Jarlaxle the partner or Entreri the loner?"

"I am," Entreri assured her without the slightest hesitation. "Jarlaxle might seem so for now, but inevitably he will find a traitor among his partners who will bring him down."

"You never could stand the thought of taking orders," Dwahvel said with a laugh. "That is why the shape of the world so bothers you!"

"To take an order implies that you must trust the giver of such," Entreri retorted, and the tone of his banter showed that he was taking no offense. In fact, there was an eagerness in his voice rarely heard, a true testament to those many charms of Dwahvel Tiggerwillies. "That, my dear little Dwahvel, is why the shape of the world so bothers me. I learned at a very young age that I cannot trust in or count on anyone but myself. To do so invites deceit and despair and opens a vulnerability that can be exploited. To do so is a weakness."

Now it was Dwahvel's turn to sit back a bit and digest the words. "But you have come to trust in me, it would seem," she said, "merely by speaking with me such. Have I brought out a weakness in you, my friend?"

Entreri smiled again, a crooked smile that didn't really tell Dwahvel whether he was amused or merely warning her not to push this observation too far.

"Perhaps it is merely that I know you and your band well enough to hold no fear of you," the cocky assassin remarked, rising from his seat and stretching. "Or maybe it is merely that you have not yet been foolish enough to try to give me an order."

Still that grin remained, but Dwahvel, too, was smiling, and sincerely. She saw it in Entreri's eyes now, that little hint of appreciation. Perhaps their talks were a bit of weakness to Entreri's jaded way of thinking. The truth of it, whether he wanted to admit it or not, was that he did indeed trust her, perhaps more deeply than he had ever trusted anyone in all of his life. At least, more deeply than he had since that first person—and Dwahvel figured that it had to have been a parent or a close family friend—had so deeply betrayed and wounded him.

Entreri headed for the door, that casual, easy walk of his, perfect in balance and as graceful as any court dancer. Many heads turned to watch him go—so many were always concerned with the whereabouts of deadly Artemis Entreri.

Not so for Dwahvel, though. She had come to understand this relationship, this friendship of theirs, not long after Dondon's death. She knew that if she ever crossed Artemis Entreri, he would surely kill her, but she knew, too, where those lines of danger lay.

Dwahvel's smile was indeed genuine and comfortable and confident as she watched her dangerous friend leave the Copper Ante that night.

Chapter 10
Not as Clever as They Think

"My master, he says that I am to pay you, yes?" the slobbering little brown-skinned man said to one of the fortress guards. "Kohrin Soulez is Dallabad, yes? My master, he says I pay Kohrin Soulez for water and shade, yes?"

The Dallabad soldier looked to his amused companion, and both of them regarded the little man, who continued bobbing his head stupidly.

"You see that tower?" the first asked, drawing the little man's gaze with his own toward the crystalline structure gleaming brilliantly over Dallabad. "That is Ahdahnia's tower. Ahdahnia Soulez, who now rules Dallabad."

The little man looked up at the tower with obvious awe. "Ah-dahn-ee-a," he said carefully, slowly, as if committing it to memory. "Soulez, yes? Like Kohrin."

"The daughter of Kohrin Soulez," the guard explained. "Go and tell your master that Ahdahnia Soulez now rules Dallabad. You pay her, through me."

The little man's head bobbed frantically. "Yes, yes," he agreed, handing over the modest purse, "and my master will meet with her, yes?"

The guard shrugged. "If I get around to asking her, perhaps," he said, and he held his hand out, and the little man looked at it curiously.

"If I find the time to bother to tell her," the guard said pointedly.

"I pay you to tell her?" the little man asked, and the other guard snorted loudly, shaking his head at the little man's continuing stupidity.

"You pay me, I tell her," the guard said plainly. "You do not pay me, and your master does not meet with her."

"But if I pay you, we . . . he, meets with her?"

"If she so chooses," the guard explained. "I will tell her. I can promise no more than that."

The little man's head continued to bob, but his stare drifted off to the side, as if he was considering the options laid out before him. "I pay," he agreed, and handed over another, smaller, purse.

The guard snatched it away and bounced it in his hand, checking the weight, and shook his head and scowled, indicating clearly that it was not enough.

"All I have!" the little man protested.

"Then get more," ordered the guard.

The little man hopped all about, seeming unsure and very concerned. He reached for the second purse, but the guard pulled it back and scowled at him. A bit more shuffling and hopping, and the little man gave a shriek and ran off.

"You think they will attack?" the other guard asked, and it was obvious from his tone that he wasn't feeling very concerned about the possibility.

The group of six wagons had pulled into Dallabad that morning, seeking reprieve from the blistering sun. The drivers were twenty strong, and not one of them seemed overly threatening, and not one of them even looked remotely like any wizard. Any attack that group made against Dallabad's fortress would likely bring only a few moments of enjoyment to the soldiers now serving Ahdahnia Soulez.

"I think that our little friend has already forgotten his purse," the first soldier replied. "Or at least, he has forgotten the truth of how he lost it."

The second merely laughed. Not much had changed at the oasis since the downfall of Kohrin Soulez. They were still the same pirating band of toll collectors. Of course the guard would tell Ahdahnia of the wagon leader's desire to meet with her—that was how Ahdahnia collected her information, after all. As for his extortion of some of the stupid little wretch's funds, that would fade away into meaninglessness very quickly.

Yes, little had really changed.

* * * * *

"So it is true that Kohrin is dead," remarked Lipke, the coordinator of the scouting party, the leader of the "trading caravan."

He glanced out the slit in his tent door to see the gleaming tower, the source of great unease throughout Calimshan. While it was no great event that Kohrin Soulez had at last been killed, nor that his daughter had apparently taken over Dallabad Oasis, rumors tying this event to another not-so-minor power shift among a prominent guild in Calimport had put the many warlords of the region on guard.

"It is also true that his daughter has apparently taken his place," Trulbul replied, pulling the padding from the back collar of his shirt, the "hump" that gave him the slobbering, stooped-over appearance. "Curse her name for turning on her father."

"Unless she had no choice in the matter," offered Rolmanet, the third of the inner circle. "Artemis Entreri has been seen in Calimport with Charon's Claw. Perhaps Ahdahnia sold it to him, as some rumors say. Perhaps she bartered it for the magic that would construct that tower, as say others. Or perhaps the foul assassin took it from the body of Kohrin Soulez."

"It has to be Basadoni," Lipke reasoned. "I know Ahdahnia, and she would not have so viciously turned against her father, not over the sale of a sword. There is no shortage of gold in Dallabad."

"But why would the Basadoni Guild leave her in command of Dallabad?" asked Trulbul. "Or more particularly, how would they leave her in command, if she holds any loyalty to her father? Those guards were not Basadoni soldiers," he added. "I am sure of it. Their skin shows the weathering of the open desert, as with all the Dallabad militia, and not the grime of Calimport's streets. Kohrin Soulez treated his guild well—even the least of his soldiers and attendants always had gold for the gambling tents when we passed through here. Would so many so quickly abandon their loyalties to the man?"

The three looked at each other for a moment and burst into laughter. Loyalty had never been the strong suit of any of Calimshan's guilds and gangs.

"Your point is well taken," Trulbul admitted, "yet it still does not seem right to me. Somehow there is more to this than a simple coup."

"I do not believe that either of us disagrees with you," Lipke replied. "Artemis Entreri carries Kohrin's mighty sword, yet if it is a simple matter that Ahdahnia Soulez decided that the time had come to secure Dallabad Oasis for herself, would she so quickly part with such a powerful defensive item? Is this not the time when she will likely be most open to reprisals?"

"Unless she hired Entreri to kill her father, with payment to be Charon's Claw," Rolmanet reasoned. He was nodding as he improvised the words, thinking that he had stumbled onto something very plausible, something that would explain much.

"If that is so, then this is the most expensive assassination Calimshan has known in centuries," Lipke remarked.

697

"But if not that, then what?" a frustrated Rolmanet asked.

"Basadoni," Trulbul said definitively. "It has to be Basadoni. They extended their grasp within the city, and now they have struck out again, hoping it to be away from prying eyes. We must confirm this."

The others were nodding, reluctantly it seemed.

* * * * *

Jarlaxle, Kimmuriel, and Rai-guy sat in comfortable chairs in the second level of the crystalline tower. An enchanted mirror, a collaboration between the magic of Rai-guy and Crenshinibon, conveyed the entire conversation between the three scouts, as it had followed the supposedly stupid little hunched man from the moment he had handed his purses over to the guard outside the fortress.

"This is not acceptable," Rai-guy dared to remark, turning to face Jarlaxle. "We are grasping too far and too fast, inviting prying eyes."

Kimmuriel sent his thoughts to his wizardly friend. *Not here. Not within the tower replica of Crenshinibon.* Even as he sent the message, he felt the energies of the shard tugging at him, prying around the outside of his mental defenses. With Yharaskrik's warnings echoing in his mind, and surely not wanting to alert Crenshinibon to the truth of his nature at that time, Kimmuriel abruptly ceased all psionic activity.

"What do you plan to do with them?" Rai-guy asked more calmly. He glanced at Kimmuriel, relaying to his friend that he had gotten the message and would heed the wise thoughts well.

"Destroy them," Kimmuriel reasoned.

"Incorporate them," Jarlaxle corrected. "There are a score in their party, and they are obviously connected to other guilds. What fine spies they will become."

"Too dangerous," Rai-guy remarked.

"Those who submit to the will of Crenshinibon will serve us," Jarlaxle replied with utmost calm. "Those who do not will be executed."

Rai-guy didn't seem convinced. He started to reply, but Kimmuriel put his hand on his friend's forearm and motioned for him to let it go.

"You will deal with them?" Kimmuriel asked Jarlaxle. "Or would you prefer that we send in soldiers to capture them and drag them before the Crystal Shard for judgment?"

"The artifact can reach their minds from the tower," Jarlaxle replied. "Those who submit will willingly slay those who do not."

"And if those who do not are the greater?" Rai-guy had to ask, but again, Kimmuriel motioned for him to be quiet, and this time, the psionicist rose and bade the wizard to follow him away.

"With the changes in Dallabad's hierarchy and the tower so evident, we will have to remain fully on our guard for some time to come," Kimmuriel did say to Jarlaxle.

The mercenary leader nodded. "Crenshinibon is ever wary," he explained.

Kimmuriel smiled in reply, but in truth, Jarlaxle's assurances were only making him more nervous, were only confirming to him that Yharaskrik's information concerning the devastating Crystal Shard was, apparently, quite accurate.

The two left their leader alone then with his newest partner, the sentient artifact.

*   *   *   *   *

Rolmanet and Trulbul blinked repeatedly as they exited their tent into the stinging daylight. All about them, the other members of their band worked methodically, if less than enthusiastically, brushing the horses and camels and filling the waterskins for the remaining journey to Calimport.

Others should have been out scouting the perimeter of the oasis and doing guard counts on Dallabad fortress, but Rolmanet soon realized that all seventeen of the remaining force was about. He also noticed that many kept glancing his way, wearing curious expressions.

One man in particular caught Rolmanet's eye. "Did he not already fill those skins?" Rolmanet quietly asked his companion. "And should he not be at the east wall, counting sentries?" As he finished, he turned to Trulbul, and his last words faded away as he considered his companion, the man standing quietly, staring up at the crystalline tower with a wistful look in his dark eyes.

"Trulbul?" Rolmanet asked, starting toward the man but, sensing that something was amiss, changing his mind and stepping away instead.

An expression of complete serenity came over Trulbul's face. "Can you not hear it?" he asked, glancing over to regard Rolmanet. "The music . . ."

"Music?" Rolmanet glanced at the man curiously, and snapped his gaze back to regard the tower and listened carefully.

"Beautiful music," Trulbul said rather loudly, and several others nearby nodded their agreement.

Rolmanet fought hard to steady his breathing and at least appear calm. He did hear the music then, a subtle note conveying a message of peace and prosperity, promising gain and power and . . . demanding. Demanding fealty.

"I am staying at Dallabad," Lipke announced suddenly, coming out of the tent. "There is more opportunity here than with Pasha Broucalle."

Rolmanet's eyes widened in spite of himself, and he had to fight very hard to keep from glancing all around in alarm or from simply running away. He was gasping now as it all came clear to him: a wizard's spell, he believed, charming enemies into friends.

"Beautiful music," another man off to the side agreed.

"Do you hear it?" Trulbul asked Rolmanet.

Rolmanet fought very hard to steady himself, to paint a serene expression upon his face, before turning back to stare at his friend.

"No, he does not," Lipke said from afar before Rolmanet had even completed the turn. "He does not see the opportunity before us. He will betray us!"

"It is a spell!" Rolmanet cried loudly, drawing his curved sword. "A wizard's enchantment to ensnare us in his grip. Fight back! Deny it, my friends!"

Lipke was at him, slashing hard with his sword, a blow that skilled Rolmanet deftly parried. Before he could counter, Trulbul was there beside Lipke, following the first man's slash with a deadly thrust at Rolmanet's heart.

"Can you not understand?" Rolmanet cried frantically, and only luck allowed him to deflect that second attack.

He glanced about as he retreated steadily, seeking allies and taking care for more enemies. He noted another fight over by the water, where several men had fallen over another, knocking him to the ground and kicking and beating him mercilessly. All the while, they screamed at the man that he could not hear the music, that he would betray them in this, their hour of greatest glory.

Another man, obviously resisting the tempting call, rushed away to the side, and the group took up the chase, leaving the beaten man face-down in the water.

A third fight erupted on the other side.

Rolmanet turned to his two opponents, the two men who had been his best friends for several years now. "It is a lie, a trick!" he insisted. "Can you not understand?"

Lipke came at him hard with a cunning low thrust, followed by an upward slash, a twisting hand-over maneuver, and yet another upward slash that forced Rolmanet to lean backward, barely keeping his balance. On came Lipke, another straight-ahead charge and thrust, with Rolmanet quite vulnerable.

Trulbul's blade slashed across, intercepting Lipke's killing blow.

"Wait!" Trulbul cried to the astonished man. "Rolmanet speaks the truth! Look more deeply at the promise, I beg!"

Lipke was fully into the coercion of the Crystal Shard. He did pause, only long enough to allow Trulbul to believe that he was indeed reflecting on the seeming inconsistency here. As Trulbul nodded, grinned, and lowered his blade, Lipke hit him with a slashing cut that opened wide his throat.

He turned back to see Rolmanet in full flight, running to the horses tethered beside the water.

"Stop him! Stop him!" Lipke cried, giving chase. Several others came in as well, trying to cut off any escape routes as Rolmanet scrambled onto his horse and turned the beast around, hooves churning the sand. The man was a fine rider, and he picked his path carefully, and they could not hope to stop him.

He thundered out of Dallabad, not even pausing to try to help the other resister, who had been cut off, forced to turn, and would soon be caught and overwhelmed. No, Rolmanet's path was straight and fast, a dead gallop down the sandy road toward distant Calimport.

* * * * *

Jarlaxle's thoughts, and those of Crenshinibon, angled the magical mirror to follow the retreat of the lone escapee.

The mercenary leader could feel the power building within the crystalline tower. It was a quiet humming noise as the structure gathered in the sunlight, focusing it more directly through a series of prisms and mirrors to the very tip of the pointed tower. He understood what Crenshinibon meant to do, of course. Given the implications of allowing someone to escape, it seemed a logical course.

Do not kill him, Jarlaxle instructed anyway, and he wasn't sure why he issued the command. *There is little he can tell his superiors that they do not already know. The spies have no idea of the truth behind Dallabad's overthrow, and will only assume that a wizard . . .* He felt the energy continuing to build, with no conversation, argument or otherwise, coming back at him from the artifact.

Jarlaxle looked into the mirror at the fleeing, terrified man. The more he thought about it, the more he realized that he was right, that there was no real reason to kill this one. In fact, allowing him to return to his masters with news of such a complete failure might actually serve Bregan D'aerthe. Likely these were no minor spies sent on such an important mission as this, and the manner in which the band was purely overwhelmed would impress—perhaps enough so that the other pashas would come to Dallabad openly to seek truce and parlay.

Jarlaxle filtered all of that through his thoughts to the Crystal Shard, reiterating his command to halt, for the good of the band, and secretly, because he simply didn't want to kill a man if he did not have to,

He felt the energy building, building, now straining release.

"Enough!" he said aloud. "Do not!"

"What is it, my leader?" came Rai-guy's voice, the wizard and his sidekick psionicist rushing back into the room.

They entered to see Jarlaxle standing, obviously angry, staring at the mirror.

Then how that mirror brightened! There was a flash as striking, and as painful to sensitive drow eyes, as the sun itself. A searing beam of pure heat energy shot out of the tower's tip, shooting down across the sands to catch the rider and his horse, enveloping them in a white-yellow shroud.

It was over in an instant, leaving the charred bones of Rolmanet and his horse lying on the empty desert sands.

Jarlaxle closed his eyes and clenched his teeth, suppressing his urge to scream out.

"Impressive display," Kimmuriel said.

"Fifteen have come over to us, and it would seem the other five are dead," Rai-guy remarked. "The victory is complete."

Jarlaxle wasn't so sure of that, but he composed himself and turned a calm look upon his lieutenants. "Crenshinibon will discern those who are most easily and completely dominated," he informed the wary pair. "They will be sent back to their guild—or guilds, if this was a collaboration—with a proper explanation for the defeat. The others will be interrogated—and they will willingly submit to all of our questions—so that we might learn everything about this enemy that came prying into our affairs."

Rai-guy and Kimmuriel exchanged a glance that Jarlaxle did not miss, a clear indication that they had seen him distressed when they had entered. What they might discern from that, the mercenary leader did not know, but he wasn't overly pleased at that moment.

"Entreri is back in Calimport?" he asked.

"At House Basadoni," Kimmuriel answered.

"As we should all be," Jarlaxle decided. "We will ask our questions of our newest arrivals and give them over to Ahdahnia. Leave Berg'inyon and a small contingent behind to watch over the operation here."

The two glanced at each other again but offered no other response. They bowed and left the room.

Jarlaxle stared into the mirror at the blackened bones of the man and horse.

It had to be done, came the whisper of Crenshinibon into his mind. *His escape would have brought more curious eyes, better prepared. We are not yet ready for that.*

Jarlaxle recognized the lie for what it was. Crenshinibon feared no prying, curious eyes, feared no army at all. The Crystal Shard, in its purest of arrogance, believed that it would simply convert the majority of any attacking force, turning them back on any who did not submit to its will. How many could it control? Jarlaxle wondered. Hundreds? Thousands? Millions?

Images of domination, not merely of the streets of Calimport, not merely of the city itself, but of the entire realm, flittered through his thoughts as Crenshinibon "heard" the silent questions and tried to answer.

Jarlaxle shifted his eye patch and focused on it, lessening the connection with the artifact, and tightened his willpower to try to keep his thoughts as much to himself as possible. No, he knew, Crenshinibon had not killed the fleeing man for fear of any retribution. Nor had it struck out with such overwhelming fury against that lone rider because it did not agree with the merits of Jarlaxle's arguments against doing so.

No, the Crystal Shard had killed the man precisely because Jarlaxle had ordered it not to do so, because the mercenary leader had crossed over the line of the concept of partner and had tried to assume control.

That Crenshinibon would not allow.

If the artifact could so easily disallow such a thing, could it also step back over the line the other way?

The rather disturbing notion did not bring much solace to Jarlaxle, who had spent the majority of his life serving as no man's, nor Matron Mother's, slave.

* * * * *

"We have new allies under our domination, and thus we are stronger," Rai-guy remarked sarcastically when he was alone with Kimmuriel and Berg'inyon.

"Our numbers grow," Berg'inyon agreed, "but so too mounts the danger of discovery."

"And of treachery," Kimmuriel added. "Witness that one of the spies, under the influence of Jarlaxle's artifact, turned against us when the fighting started. The domination is not complete, nor is it unbreakable. With every unwitting soldier we add in such a manner, we run the risk of an uprising from within. While it is unlikely that any would so escape the domination and subsequently cause any real damage to us—they are merely humans, after all—we cannot dismiss the likelihood that one will break free and escape us, delivering the truth of the new Basadoni Guild and of Dallabad to some of the guilds."

"We already have agreed upon the consequences of Bregan D'aerthe being discovered for what it truly is," Rai-guy added ominously. "This group came to Dallabad looking specifically for the answers behind the facade, and the longer we stretch that facade, the more likely that we will be discovered. We are forfeiting our anonymity in this foolish quest for expansion."

The other two remained very silent for a long while. Then Kimmuriel quietly asked, "Are you going to explain this to Jarlaxle?"

"Should we be addressing this problem to Jarlaxle," Rai-guy countered, his voice dripping with sarcasm, "or to the true leader of Bregan D'aerthe?"

That bold proclamation gave the other two even more pause. There it was, set out very clearly, the notion that Jarlaxle had lost control of the band to a sentient artifact.

"Perhaps it is time for us to reconsider our course," Kimmuriel said somberly.

Both he and Rai-guy had served under Jarlaxle for a long, long time, and both understood the tremendous weight of the implications of Kimmuriel's remark. Wresting Bregan D'aerthe from Jarlaxle would be something akin to stealing House Baenre away from Matron Baenre during the centuries of her iron-fisted rule. In many ways, Jarlaxle, so cunning, so layered in defenses and so full of understanding of everything around him, might prove an even more formidable foe.

Now the course seemed obvious to the three, a coup that had been building since the first expansive steps of House Basadoni.

"I have a source who can offer us more information on the Crystal Shard," Kimmuriel remarked. "Perhaps there is a way to destroy it or at least temporarily to cripple its formidable powers so that we can get to Jarlaxle."

Rai-guy looked to Berg'inyon and both nodded grimly.

* * * * *

Artemis Entreri was beginning to understand just how much trouble was brewing for Jarlaxle and therefore for him. He heard about the incident at Dallabad soon after the majority of the dark elves returned to House Basadoni, and knew from the looks and the tone of their voices that several of Jarlaxle's prominent underlings weren't exactly thrilled by the recent events.

Neither was Entreri. He knew that Rai-guy's and Kimmuriel's complaints were quite valid, knew that Jarlaxle's expansionist policies were leading Bregan D'aerthe down a very dangerous road indeed. When the truth about House Basadoni's change and the takeover of Dallabad eventually leaked out—and Entreri was now harboring few doubts that it would—all the guilds and all the lords and every power in the region would unite against Bregan D'aerthe. Jarlaxle was cunning, and the band of mercenaries was indeed powerful—even more so with the Crystal Shard in their possession—but Entreri held no doubts that they would be summarily destroyed, every one.

No, the assassin realized, it wouldn't likely come to that. The groundwork had been clearly laid before them all, and Entreri held little doubt that Kimmuriel and Rai-guy would move against Jarlaxle and soon. Their scowls were growing deeper by the day, their words a bit bolder.

That understanding raised a perplexing question to Entreri. Was the Crystal Shard actually spurring the coup, as Lady Lolth often did among the houses in Menzoberranzan? Was the artifact reasoning that perhaps either of the more volatile magic-using lieutenants might be a more suitable wielder? Or was the coup being inspired by the actions of Jarlaxle under the prodding, if not the outright influence, of Crenshinibon?

Either way, Entreri knew that he was becoming quite vulnerable, even with his new magical acquisitions. However he played through the scenario, Jarlaxle alone remained the keystone to his survival.

The assassin turned down a familiar avenue, moving inconspicuously among the many street rabble out this evening, keeping to the shadows and keeping to himself. He had to find some way to get Jarlaxle back in command and on strong footing. He needed for Jarlaxle to be in control of Bregan D'aerthe—not only of their actions but of their hearts as well. Only then could he fend a coup—a coup that could only mean disaster for Entreri.

Yes, he had to secure Jarlaxle's position. Then he had to find a way to get himself far, far away from the dark elves and their dangerous intrigue.

The sentries at the Copper Ante were hardly surprised to see him and even informed him that Dwahvel was expecting him and waiting for him in the back room.

She had already heard of the most recent events at Dallabad, he realized, and he shook his head, reminding himself that he should not be surprised, and also reminding himself that it was just her amazing ability for the acquisition of knowledge that had brought him to Dwahvel this evening.

"It was House Broucalle of Memnon," Dwahvel informed him as soon as he entered and sat on the plush pillows set upon the floor opposite the halfling.

"They were quick to move," Entreri replied.

"The crystalline tower is akin to a huge beacon set out on the wasteland of the desert," Dwahvel replied. "Why do your compatriots, with their obvious need for secrecy, so call attention to themselves?"

Entreri didn't answer verbally, but the expression on his face told Dwahvel much of his fears.

"They err," Dwahvel concurred with those fears. "They have House Basadoni, a superb front for their exotic trading business. Why reach further and invite a war that they cannot hope to win?"

Still Entreri did not answer.

"Or was that the whole purpose for the band of drow to come to the surface?" Dwahvel asked with sincere concern. "Were you, too, perhaps, misinformed about the nature of this band, led to believe that they were here for profit—mutual profit, potentially—when in fact they are but an advanced war party, setting the stage for complete disaster for Calimport and all Calimshan?"

Entreri shook his head. "I know Jarlaxle well," he replied. "He came here for profit—mutual profit for those who work along with him. That is his way. I do not think he would ever serve in anything as potentially disastrous as a war party. Jarlaxle is not a warlord, in any capacity. He is an opportunist and nothing more. He cares little for glory and much for comfort."

"And yet he invites disaster by erecting such an obvious, and obviously inviting, monument as that remarkable tower," Dwahvel answered.

She tilted her plump head, studying Entreri's concerned expression carefully. "What is it?" she asked.

"How great is your knowledge of Crenshinibon?" the assassin asked. "The Crystal Shard?"

Dwahvel scrunched up her face, deep in thought for just a moment, and shook her head. "Cursory," she admitted. "I know of its tower images but little more."

"It is an artifact of exceeding power," Entreri explained. "I am not so certain that the sentient item's goals and Jarlaxle's are one and the same."

"Many artifacts have a will of their own," Dwahvel stated dryly. "That is rarely a good thing."

"Learn all that you can about it," Entreri bade her, "and quickly, before that which you fear inadvertently befalls Calimport." He paused and considered the best course for Dwahvel to take in light of fairly recent events. "Try to find out how Drizzt came to possess it, and where—"

"What in the Nine Hells is a Drizzt?" Dwahvel asked.

Entreri started to explain but just stopped and laughed, remembering how very wide the world truly was. "Another dark elf," he answered, "a dead one."

"Ah, yes," said Dwahvel. "Your rival. The one you call 'Do'Urden.' "

"Forget him, as have I," Entreri instructed. "He is only relevant here because it was from him that Jarlaxle's minions acquired the Crystal Shard. They impersonated a priest of some renown and power, a cleric named Cadderly, I believe, who resides somewhere in or around the Snowflake Mountains."

"A long journey," the halfling remarked.

"A worthwhile one," Entreri replied. "And we both know that distance is irrelevant to a wizard possessing the proper spells."

"This will cost you greatly."

With just a twitch of his honed leg muscles, a movement that would have been difficult for a skilled fighter half his age, Entreri rose up tall and fearsome before Dwahvel, then leaned over and patted her on the shoulder—with his gloved right hand.

She got the message.

Chapter 11

Groundwork

It is what you desired all along, Kimmuriel said to Yharaskrik.

The illithid feigned surprise at the drow psionicist's blunt proposition. Yharaskrik had explaining to Kimmuriel how he might fend the intrusions of the Crystal Shard. The illithid desired that the situation be brought to this very point all along.

Who will possess it? Yharaskrik silently asked. *Kimmuriel or Rai-guy?*

Rai-guy, the drow answered. *He and Crenshinibon will perfectly complement one another—by Crenshinibon's own impartations to him from afar.*

So you both believe, the illithid responded. *Perhaps, though, Crenshinibon sees you as a threat—a likely and logical assumption—and is merely goading you into this so that you and your comrades might be thoroughly destroyed.*

I have not dismissed that possibility, Kimmuriel returned, seeming quite at ease. *That is why I have come to Yharaskrik.*

The illithid paused for a long while, digesting the information. *The Crystal Shard is no minor item,* the creature explained. *To ask of me—*

A temporary reprieve, Kimmuriel interrupted. *I do not wish to pit Yharaskrik against Crenshinibon, for I understand that the artifact would*

707

overwhelm you. He imparted those thoughts without fear of insulting the mind flayer. Kimmuriel understood that the perfectly logical illithids were not possessed of ego beyond reason. Certainly they believed their race to be superior to most others, to humans, of course, and even to drow, but within that healthy confidence there lay an element of reason that prevented them from taking insult to statements made of perfect logic. Yharaskrik knew that the artifact could overwhelm any creature short of a god.

There is, perhaps, a way, the illithid replied, and Kimmuriel's smile widened. *A Tower of Iron Will's sphere of influence could encompass Crenshinibon and defeat its mental intrusions, and its commands to any towers it has constructed near the battlefield. Temporarily,* the creature added emphatically. *I hold no illusions that any psionic force short of that conducted by a legion of my fellow illithids could begin to permanently weaken the powers of the great Crystal Shard.*

"Long enough for the downfall of Jarlaxle," Kimmuriel agreed aloud. "That is all that I require." He bowed and took his leave then, and his last words echoed in his mind as he stepped through the dimensional doorway that would bring him back to Calimport and the private quarters he shared with Rai-guy.

The downfall of Jarlaxle! Kimmuriel could hardly believe that he was a party to this conspiracy. Hadn't it been Jarlaxle, after all, who had offered him refuge from his own Matron Mother and vicious female siblings of House Oblodra, and who had then taken him in and sheltered him from the rest of the city when Matron Baenre had declared that House Oblodra must be completely eradicated? Aside from any loyalty he held for the mercenary leader, there remained the practical matter of the problem of decapitating Bregan D'aerthe. Jarlaxle above all others had facilitated the rise of the mercenary band, had brought them to prominence more than a century before, and no one in all the band, not even self-confident Rai-guy, doubted for a moment how important Jarlaxle was politically for the survival of Bregan D'aerthe.

All those thoughts stayed with Kimmuriel as he made his way back to Rai-guy's side, to find the drow thick into the plotting of the attacks they would use to bring Jarlaxle down.

"Your new friend can give us that which we require?" the eager wizard-cleric asked as soon as Kimmuriel arrived.

"Likely," Kimmuriel replied.

"Neutralize the Crystal Shard, and the attack will be complete," Rai-guy said.

"Do not underestimate Jarlaxle," Kimmuriel warned. "He has the Crystal Shard now and so we must first eliminate that powerful item, but even without it, Jarlaxle has spent many years solidifying his hold on Bregan D'aerthe. I would not have gone against him before the acquisition of the artifact."

"But it is just that acquisition that has weakened him," Rai-guy explained. "Even the common soldiers fear this course we have taken."

"I have heard some remark that they cannot believe our rise in power," Kimmuriel argued. "Some have proclaimed that we will dominate the surface world, that Jarlaxle will take Bregan D'aerthe to prominence among the weakling humans, and return in glory to conquer Menzoberranzan."

Rai-guy laughed aloud at the proclamation. "The artifact is powerful, I do not doubt, but it is limited. Did not the mind flayer tell you that Crenshinibon sought to reach its limit of control?"

"Whether or not the fantasy conquest can occur is irrelevant to our present situation," Kimmuriel replied. "What matters is whether or not the soldiers of Bregan D'aerthe believe in it."

Rai-guy didn't have an argument for that line of reasoning, but still, he wasn't overly concerned. "Though Berg'inyon is with us, the drow will be limited in their role in the battle," he explained. "We have humans at our disposal now and thousands of kobolds."

"Many of the humans were brought into our fold by Crenshinibon," Kimmuriel reminded. "The Crystal Shard will have little difficulty in dominating the kobolds, if Yharaskrik cannot completely neutralize it."

"And we have the wererats," Rai-guy went on, unfazed. "Shapechangers are better suited to resisting mental intrusions. Their internal strife denies any outside influences."

"You have enlisted Domo?"

Rai-guy shook his head. "Domo is difficult," he admitted, "but I have enlisted several of his wererat lieutenants. They will fall to our cause if Domo is eliminated. To that end, I have had Sharlotta Vespers inform Jarlaxle that the wererat leader has been speaking out of turn, revealing too much about Bregan D'aerthe, to Pasha Da'Daclan, and we believe to the leader of the guild that came to investigate Dallabad."

Kimmuriel nodded, but his expression remained concerned. Jarlaxle was a tough opponent in games of the mind—he might see the ruse for what it was, and use Domo to turn the wererats back to his side.

"His actions now will be telling," Rai-guy admitted. "Crenshinibon, no doubt, will want to believe Sharlotta's tale, but Jarlaxle will desire to proceed more cautiously before acting against Domo."

"You believe that the wererat leader will be dead this very day," Kimmuriel reasoned after a moment.

Rai-guy smiled. "The Crystal Shard has become Jarlaxle's strength and thus his weakness," he said with a wicked grin.

* * * * *

"First the gauntlet and now this," Dwahvel Tiggerwillies said with a profound sigh. "Ah, Entreri, what shall I ever do for extra coin when you are no more?"

709

Entreri didn't appreciate the humor. "Be quick about it," he instructed.

"Sharlotta's actions have made you very nervous," Dwahvel remarked, for she had observed the woman busily working the streets during the last few hours, with many of her meetings with known operatives of the wererat guild.

Entreri just nodded, not wanting to share the latest news with Dwahvel—just in case. Things were moving fast now, he knew, too fast. Rai-guy and Kimmuriel were laying the groundwork for their assault, but at least Jarlaxle had apparently caught on to some of the budding problems. The mercenary leader had summoned Entreri just a few moments before, telling the man that he had to go and meet with a particularly wretched wererat by the name of Domo. If Domo was in on the conspiracy, Entreri suspected that Rai-guy and Kimmuriel would soon have a hole to fill in their ranks.

"I will return within two hours," Entreri explained. "Have it ready."

"We have no proper material to make such an item as you requested," Dwahvel complained.

"Color and consistency alone," Entreri replied. "The material does not need to be exact."

Dwahvel shrugged.

Entreri went out into Calimport's night, moving swiftly, his cloak pulled tight around his shoulders. Not far from the Copper Ante, he turned down an alley. Then after a quick check to ensure that he was not being followed, he slipped down an open sewer hole into the tunnels below the city.

A few moments later, he stood before Jarlaxle in the appointed chamber.

"Sharlotta has informed me that Domo has been whispering secrets about us," Jarlaxle remarked.

"The wererat is on the way?"

Jarlaxle nodded. "And likely with many allies. You are prepared for the fight?"

Entreri wore the first honest grin he had known in several days. Prepared for a fight with wererats? How could he not be? Still he could not dismiss the source of Jarlaxle's information. He realized that Sharlotta was working both ends of the table here, that she was in tight with Rai-guy and Kimmuriel but was in no overt way severing her ties to Jarlaxle. He doubted that Sharlotta and her drow allies had set this up as the ultimate battle for control of Bregan D'aerthe. Such intricate planning would take longer, and the sewers of Calimport would not be a good location for a fight that would grow so very obvious.

Still . . .

"Perhaps you should have stayed at Dallabad for a while," Entreri remarked, "within the crystalline tower, overseeing the new operation."

"Domo hardly frightens me," Jarlaxle replied.

Entreri stared at him hard. Could he really be so oblivious to the apparent underpinnings of a coup within Bregan D'aerthe? If so, did that enhance the possibility that the Crystal Shard was indeed prompting the disloyal actions of Rai-guy and Kimmuriel? Or did it mean, perhaps, that Entreri was being too cautious here, was seeing demons and uprisings where there were none?

The assassin took a deep breath and shook his head, clearing his thoughts.

"Sharlotta could be mistaken," the assassin did say. "She would have reasons of her own to wish to be rid of troublesome Domo."

"We will know soon enough," Jarlaxle replied, nodding in the direction of a tunnel, where the wererat leader, in the form of a huge humanoid rat, was approaching, along with three other ratmen.

"My dear Domo," Jarlaxle greeted, and the wererat leader bowed.

"It is good that you came to us," Domo replied. "I do not enjoy any journeys to the surface at this time, not even to the cellars of House Basadoni. There is too much excitement, I fear."

Entreri narrowed his eyes and considered the wretched lycanthrope, thinking that answer curious, at least, but trying hard not to interpret it one way or the other.

"Do the agents of the other guilds similarly come down to meet with you?" Jarlaxle asked, a question that surely set Domo back on his heels.

Entreri stared hard at the drow now, catching on that Crenshinibon was instructing Jarlaxle to put Domo on his guard, to get him thinking of any potentially treasonous actions that they might be more easily read. Still, it seemed to him that Jarlaxle was moving too quickly here, that a little small talk and diplomacy might have garnered the necessary indicators without resorting to any crude mental intrusions by the sentient artifact.

"On those rare occasions when I must meet with agents of other guilds, they often do come to me," Domo answered, trying to remain calm, though he betrayed his sudden edge to Entreri when he shifted his weight from one foot to the other. The assassin calmly dropped his hands to his belt, hooking his wrists over the pommels of his two formidable weapons, a posture that seemed more relaxed and comfortable, but also one that had him in touch with his weapons, ready to draw and strike.

"And have you met with any recently?" Jarlaxle asked.

Domo winced, and winced again, and Entreri caught on to the truth of it. The artifact was trying to scour his thoughts then and there.

The three wererats behind the leader glanced at each other and shifted nervously.

Domo's face contorted, began to form into his human guise, and went back almost immediately to the trapping of the wererat. A low, feral growl escaped his throat.

"What is it?" one of the wererats behind him asked.

711

Entreri could see the frustration mounting on Jarlaxle's face. He glanced back to Domo curiously, wondering if he had perhaps underestimated the ugly creature.

* * * * *

Jarlaxle and Crenshinibon simply could not get a fix on the wererat's thoughts, for the Crystal Shard's intrusion had brought about the lycanthropic internal strife, and that wall of red pain and rage had now denied any access.

Jarlaxle, growing increasingly frustrated, stared at the wererat hard.

He betrayed us, Crenshinibon decided suddenly.

Jarlaxle's thoughts filled with doubt and confusion, for he had not seen any such revelation.

A moment of weakness, came Crenshinibon's call. *A flash of the truth within that wall of angry torment. He betrayed us . . . twice.*

Jarlaxle turned to Entreri, a subtle signal, but one that the eager assassin, who hated wererats profoundly, was quick to catch and amplify.

Domo and his associates caught it, too, and their swords came flashing out of their scabbards. By the time they'd drawn their weapons, Entreri was on the charge. Charon's Claw waved in the air before him, painting a wall of black ash that Entreri could use to segment the battleground and prevent his enemies from coordinating their movements.

He spun to the left, around the ash wall, ducking as he turned so that he came around under the swing of Domo's long and slender blade. Up went the assassin's sword, taking Domo's far and wide. Entreri, still in a crouch, scrambled forward, his dagger leading.

Domo's closest companion came on hard, though, forcing Entreri to skitter back and slash down with his sword to deflect the attack. He went into a roll, over backward, and planted his right hand, pushing hard to launch him back to his feet, working those feet quickly as he landed to put him in nearly the same position as when he had started. The foolish wererat followed, leaving Domo and its two companions on the other side of the ash wall.

Behind Entreri, Jarlaxle's hand pumped once, twice, thrice, and daggers sailed past Entreri, barely missing his head, plunging through the ash wall, blasting holes in the drifting curtain.

On the other side came a groan, and Entreri realized that Domo's companions were down to two.

A moment later, down to one, for the assassin met the wererat's charge full on, his sword coming up in a rotating fashion, taking the thrusting blade aside. Entreri continued forward, and so did the wererat, thinking to bite at the man.

How quickly it regretted that choice when Entreri's dagger blade filled its mouth.

A sudden second thrust yanked the creature's head back, and the assassin disengaged and quickly turned. He saw yet another of the beasts coming fast through the ash wall and heard the footsteps of a retreating Domo.

Down he went into a shoulder roll, under the ash wall, catching the ankles of the charging wererat and sending it flying over him to fall face-down right before Jarlaxle.

Entreri didn't even slow, rolling forward and back to his feet and running off full speed in pursuit of the fleeing wererat. Entreri was no stranger to the darkness, even the complete blackness of the tunnels. Indeed, he had done some of his best work down there, but recognizing the disadvantage he faced against infravision-using wererats, he held his powerful sword before him and commanded it to bring forth light—hoping that it, like many magical swords, could produce some sort of glow.

That magical glow surprised him, for it was a light of blackish hue and nothing like Entreri had ever seen before, giving all the corridor a surrealistic appearance. He glanced down at the sword, trying to see how blatant a light source it appeared, but he saw no definitive glow and hoped that meant that he might use a bit of stealth, at least, despite the fact that he was the source of the light.

He came to a fork and skidded to a stop, turning his head and focusing his senses.

The slight echo of a footfall came from the left, so on he ran.

* * * * *

Jarlaxle finished the prone wererat in short order, pumping his arm repeatedly and hitting the squirming creature with dagger after dagger. He put a hand in his pocket, on the Crystal Shard, as he ran through the gap in the ash wall, trying to catch up with his companion.

Guide me, he instructed the artifact.

Up, came the unexpected reply. *They have returned to the streets.*

Jarlaxle skidded to a stop, puzzled.

Up! came the more emphatic silent cry. *To the streets.*

The mercenary leader rushed back the other way, down the corridor to the ladder that would take him back up through the sewer grate and into the alley outside the neighborhood of the Copper Ante.

Guide me, he instructed the shard again.

We are too exposed, the artifact returned. *Keep to the shadows and move back to House Basadoni—Artemis Entreri and Domo lie in that direction.*

* * * * *

713

Entreri rounded a bend in the corridor, slowing cautiously. There, standing before him, was Domo and two more wererats, all holding swords. Entreri started forward, thinking himself seen, and figuring to attack before the three could organize their defenses. He stopped abruptly, though, when the ratman to Domo's left whispered.

"I smell him. He is near."

"Too near," agreed the other lesser creature, squinting, the tell-tale red glow of infravision evident in its eyes.

Why did they even need that infravision? Entreri wondered. He could see them clearly in the black light of Charon's Claw, as clearly as if they were all standing in a dimly lit room. He knew that he should go straight in and attack, but his curiosity was piqued now and so he stepped out from the wall, in clear view, in plain sight.

"His smell is thick," Domo agreed. All three were glancing about nervously, their swords waving. "Where are the others?"

"They have not come but should have been here," the one to his left answered. "I fear we are betrayed."

"Damn the drow to the Nine Hells, then," Domo said.

Entreri could hardly believe they could not see him—yet another wondrous effect of the marvelous sword. He wondered if perhaps they could see him had they been focusing their eyes in the normal spectrum of light, but that, he realized, had to be a question for another day. Concentrating now on moving perfectly silently, he slid one foot, and then the other, ahead of him, moving to Domo's right.

"Perhaps we should have listened more carefully to the dark elf wizard," the one to the left went on, his voice a whisper.

"To go against Jarlaxle?" Domo asked incredulously. "That is doom. Nothing more."

"But . . ." the other started to argue, but Domo began whispering harshly, sticking his finger in the other's face.

Entreri used their distraction to get right up behind the third of the group, his dagger tip coming against the wererat's spine. The creature stiffened as Entreri whispered into its ear. "Run," he said.

The ratman sped off down the corridor, and Domo stopped his arguing long enough to chase his fleeing soldier a few steps, calling threats out after him.

"Run," said Entreri, who had shifted across the way to the side of the remaining lesser wererat.

This one, though, didn't run, but let out a shriek and spun, its sword slashing across at chest level.

Entreri ducked below the blade easily and came up with a stab that brought his deadly jeweled dagger under the wererat's ribs and up into its diaphragm. The creature howled again, but then spasmed and convulsed violently.

"What is it?" Domo asked, spinning about. "What?"

714

The wererat fell to the floor, twitching still as it died. Entreri stood there, in the open, dagger in hand. He called up a glow from his smaller blade.

Domo jumped back, bringing his sword out in front of him. "Dancing blade?" he asked quietly. "Is this you, wizard drow?"

"Dancing blade?" Entreri repeated quietly, looking down at his glowing dagger. It made no sense to him. He looked back to Domo, to see the glow leave the wererat's eyes as he shifted from ratman, to nearly human form. Likewise his vision shifted from the infrared to the normal viewing spectrum.

He nearly jumped out of his boots again, as the specter of Artemis Entreri came clear to him. "What trick is that?" the wererat gasped.

Entreri wasn't even sure how to answer. He had no idea what Charon's Claw was doing with its black light. Did it block infravision completely but apparently hold a strange illuminating effect that was clearly visible in the normal spectrum? Did it act like a black campfire then, even though Entreri felt no heat coming from the blade? Infravision could be severely limited by strong heat sources.

It was indeed intriguing—one of so many riddles that seemed to be presenting themselves before Artemis Entreri—but again, it was a riddle to be solved another day.

"So you are without allies," he said to Domo. "It is you and I alone."

"Why does Jarlaxle fear me?" Domo asked as Entreri advanced a step.

The assassin stopped. "Fear you? Or loathe you? They are not the same thing, you know."

"I am his ally!" Domo protested. "I stood beside him, even against the advances of his lessers."

"So you said to him," Entreri remarked, glancing down at the still-twitching, still-groaning form. "What do you know? Speak it clearly and quickly, and perhaps you will walk out of here."

Domo's rodent eyes narrowed angrily. "As Rassiter walked away from your last meeting?" he asked, referring to one of his greatest predecessors in the wererat guild, a powerful leader who had served Pasha Pook along with Entreri, and whom Entreri had subsequently murdered—a deed never forgotten by the wererats of Calimport.

"I ask you one last time," Entreri said calmly.

He caught a slight movement to the side and knew that the first wererat had returned, waiting in the shadows to leap out at him. He was hardly surprised and hardly afraid.

Domo gave a wide, toothy smile. "Jarlaxle and his companions are not as unified a force as you believe," he teased.

Entreri advanced another step. "You must do better than that," he said, but before the words even left his mouth, Domo howled and leaped at him, stabbing with his slender sword.

Entreri barely moved Charon's Claw, just angled the blade to intercept Domo's and slide it off to the side.

The wererat retracted the strike at once, thrust again, and again. Each time Entreri, with barely any motion at all, positioned his parry perfectly and to a razor-thin angle, with Domo's sword stabbing past him, missing by barely an inch.

Again the wererat retracted and this time came across with a great slash.

But he had stepped too far back, and Entreri had to lean only slightly backward for the blade to swish harmlessly past before him.

The expected charge came from Domo's companion in the shadows to the side, and Domo played his part in the routine perfectly, rushing ahead with a powerful thrust.

Domo didn't understand the beauty, the efficiency, of Artemis Entreri. Again Charon's Claw caught and turned the attack, but this time, Entreri rolled his hand right over, and under the outside of Domo's blade. He pulled in his gut as he threw Domo's blade up high, and brought forth another wall of ash, blackening the air between him and the wererat. Following his own momentum, Entreri went into a complete spin, around to the right. As he came back square with Domo he brought his right arm swishing down, the sword trailing ash, while his left crossed his body over the down-swing, launching his jeweled dagger right into the gut of the charging wererat.

Charon's Claw did a complete circuit in the air between the combatants, forming a wide, circular wall. Domo came ahead right through it with yet another stubborn thrust, but Entreri wasn't there. He dived to the side into a roll and came up and around with a powerful slash at the legs of the wererat still struggling with the dagger in its belly. To the assassin's surprise and delight, the mighty sword sheared through not only the wererat's closest knee, but through the other as well. The creature tumbled to the stone, howling in agony, its life-blood pouring out freely.

Entreri hardly slowed, spinning about and coming up powerfully, slapping Domo's sword out wide yet again, and snapping Charon's Claw down and across to pick off a dagger neatly thrown by the wererat leader.

Domo's expression changed quickly then, his last trick obviously played. Now it was Entreri's turn to take the offensive, and he did so with a powerful thrust high, thrust center, thrust low routine that had Domo inevitably skittering backward, fighting hard merely to keep his balance.

Entreri, leaping ahead, didn't make it any easier on the overmatched creature. His sword worked furiously, sometimes throwing ash, sometimes not, and all with a precision designed to limit Domo's vision and options. Soon he had the wererat nearly to the back wall, and a glance from Domo told Entreri that he wasn't thrilled about the prospect of getting cornered.

Entreri took the cue to slash and slash again, bringing up a wall of ash perpendicular to the floor then perpendicular to the first, an L-shaped design that blocked Domo's vision of Entreri and his vision of the area to his immediate right.

With a growl, the wererat went right with a desperate thrust, thinking that Entreri would use the ash wall to try to work around him. He hit only air. Then he felt the assassin's presence at his back, for the man, anticipating the anticipation, had simply gone around the other way.

Domo threw his sword to the ground. "I will tell you everything," he cried. "I will—"

"You already did," Entreri assured him and the wererat stiffened as Charon's Claw sliced through his backbone and drove on to the hilt, coming out the front just below Domo's ribs.

"It . . . hurts," Domo gasped.

"It is supposed to," Entreri replied, and he gave the sword a sudden jerk, and Domo gasped, and he died.

Entreri tore his blade free and rushed to retrieve his dagger. His thoughts were whirling now, as Domo's confirmation of some kind of an uprising within Bregan D'aerthe incited a plethora of questions. Domo had not been Jarlaxle's deceiver, nor was he in on the plotting against the mercenary leader—of that much, at least, Entreri was pretty sure. Yet it was Jarlaxle who had prompted this attack on Domo.

Or was it?

Wondering just how much the Crystal Shard was playing Jarlaxle's best interests against Jarlaxle, Artemis Entreri scrambled out of Calimport's sewers.

* * * * *

"Beautiful," Rai-guy remarked to Kimmuriel, the two of them using a mirror of scrying to witness Artemis Entreri's return to House Basadoni. The wizard broke the connection almost immediately after, though, for the look upon the cunning assassin's face told him that Entreri might be sensing the scrying. "He unwittingly does our bidding. The wererats will stand against Jarlaxle now."

"Alas for Domo," Kimmuriel said, laughing. He stopped abruptly, though, and assumed a more serious demeanor. "But what of Entreri? He is formidable—even more so with that gauntlet and sword—and is too wise to believe that he would be better served in joining our cause. Perhaps we should eliminate him before turning our eyes toward Jarlaxle."

Rai-guy thought it over for just a moment, and nodded his agreement. "It must come from a lesser," he said. "From Sharlotta and her minions, perhaps, as they will be little involved in the greater coup."

"Jarlaxle would not be pleased if he came to understand that we were going against Entreri," Kimmuriel agreed. "Sharlotta, then, and not as a straightforward command. I will plant the thought in her that Entreri is trying to eliminate her."

"If she came to believe that, she would likely simply run away," Rai-guy remarked.

"She is too full of pride for that," Kimmuriel came back. "I will also make it clear to her, subtly and through other sources, that Entreri is not in the favor of many of Bregan D'aerthe, that even Jarlaxle has grown tired of his independence. If she believes that Entreri stands alone in some vendetta or rivalry against her, and that she can utilize the veritable army at her disposal to destroy him, then she will not run but will strike and strike hard." He gave another laugh. "Though unlike you, Rai-guy, I am not so certain that Sharlotta and all of House Basadoni will be able to get the job done."

"They will keep him occupied and out of our way, at least," Rai-guy replied. "Once we have finished with Jarlaxle . . ."

"Entreri will likely be far gone," Kimmuriel observed, "running as Morik has run. Perhaps we should see to Morik, if for no other reason than to hold him up as an example to Artemis Entreri."

Rai-guy shook his head, apparently recognizing that he and Kimmuriel had far more pressing problems than the disposition of a minor deserter in a faraway and insignificant city. "Artemis Entreri cannot run far enough away," he said determinedly. "He is far too great a nuisance for me ever to forget him or forgive him."

Kimmuriel thought that statement might be a bit extravagant, but in essence, he agreed with the sentiment. Perhaps Entreri's greatest crime was his own ability, the drow psionicist mused. Perhaps his rise above the standards of humans alone was the insult that so sparked hatred in Rai-guy and in Kimmuriel. The psionicist, and the wizard as well, were wise enough to appreciate that truth.

But that didn't make things any easier for Artemis Entreri.

Chapter 12

When All is a Lie

"Layer after layer!" Entreri raged. He pounded his fist on the small table in the back room of the Copper Ante. It was still the one place in Calimport where he could feel reasonably secure from the ever-prying eyes of Rai-guy and Kimmuriel—and how often he had felt those eyes watching him of late! "So many layers that they roll back onto each other in a never-ending loop!"

Dwahvel Tiggerwillies leaned back in her chair and studied the man curiously. In all the years she had known Artemis Entreri, she had never seen him so animated or so angry—and when Artemis Entreri was angry, those anywhere in the vicinity of the assassin did well to take extreme care. Even more surprising to the halfling was the fact that Entreri was so angry so soon after killing the hated Domo. Usually killing a wererat put him in a better mood for a day at least. Dwahvel could understand his frustration, though. The man was dealing with dark elves, and though Dwahvel had little real knowledge of the intricacies of drow culture, she had witnessed enough to understand that the dark elves were the masters of intrigue and deception.

"Too many layers," Entreri said more calmly, his rage played out. He turned to Dwahvel and shook his head. "I am lost within the web within the web. I hardly know what is real anymore."

719

"You are still alive," Dwahvel offered. "I would guess, then, that you are doing something right."

"I fear that I erred greatly in killing Domo," Entreri admitted, shaking his head. "I have never been fond of wererats, but this time, perhaps, I should have let him live, if only to provide some opposition to the growing conspiracy against Jarlaxle."

"You do not even know if Domo and his wretched, lying companions were speaking truthfully when they uttered words about the drow conspiracy," Dwahvel reminded. "They may have been doing that as misinformation that you would take back to Jarlaxle, thus bringing about a rift in Bregan D'aerthe. Or Domo might have been sputtering for the sake of saving his own head. He knows your relationship with Jarlaxle and understands that you are better off as long as Jarlaxle is in command."

Entreri just stared at her. Domo knew all of that? Of course he did, the assassin told himself. As much as he hated the wererat, he could not dismiss the creature's cunning in controlling that most difficult of guilds.

"It is irrelevant anyway," Dwahvel went on. "We both know that the ratmen will be minor players at best in any internal struggles of Bregan D'aerthe. If Rai-guy and Kimmuriel start a coup, Domo and his kin would do little to dissuade them."

Entreri shook his head again, thoroughly frustrated by it all. Alone he believed that he could outfight or out-think any drow, but they were not alone, were never alone. Because of that harmony of movement within the band's cliques, Entreri could not be certain of the truth of anything. The addition of the Crystal Shard was merely compounding matters, blurring the truth about the source of the coup—if there was a coup—and making the assassin honestly wonder if Jarlaxle was in charge or was merely a slave to the sentient artifact. As much as Entreri knew that Jarlaxle would protect him, he understood that the Crystal Shard would want him dead.

"You dismiss all that you once learned," Dwahvel remarked, her voice soothing and calm. "The drow play no games beyond those that Pasha Pook once played—or Pasha Basadoni, or any of the others, or all of the others together. Their dance is the same as has been going on in Calimport for centuries."

"But the drow are better dancers."

Dwahvel smiled and nodded, conceding the point. "But is not the solution the same?" she asked. "When all is a facade. . . ." She let the words hang out in the air, one of the basic truths of the streets, and one that Artemis Entreri surely knew as well as anyone. "When all is a facade . . . ?" she said again, prompting him.

Entreri forced himself to calm down, forced himself to dismiss the overblown respect, even fear, he had been developing toward the dark elves, particularly toward Rai-guy and Kimmuriel. "In such situations, when layer is put upon layer," he recited, a basic lesson for all bright prospects within the guild structures, "when all is a facade, wound within webs of deception, the truth is what you make of it."

Dwahvel nodded. "You will know which path is real, because that is the path you will make real," she agreed. "Nothing pains a liar more than when an opponent turns one of his lies into truth."

Entreri nodded his agreement, and indeed he felt better. He knew that he would, which was why he had slipped out of House Basadoni after sensing that he was being watched and had gone straight to the Copper Ante.

"Do you believe Domo?" the halfling asked.

Entreri considered it for a moment, and nodded. "The hourglass has been turned, and the sand is flowing," he stated. "Have you the information I requested?"

Dwahvel reached under the low dust ruffle of the chair in which she was sitting and pulled out a portfolio full of parchments. "Cadderly," she said, handing them over.

"What of the other item?"

Again the halfling's hand went down low, this time producing a small sack identical to the one Jarlaxle now carried on his belt, and, Entreri knew without even looking, containing a block of crystal similar in appearance to Crenshinibon.

Entreri took it with some trepidation, for it was, to him, the final and irreversible acknowledgment that he was indeed about to embark upon a very dangerous course, perhaps the most dangerous road he had ever walked in all his life.

"There is no magic about it," Dwahvel assured him, noting his concerned expression. "Just a mystical aura I ordered included so that it would replicate the artifact to any cursory magical inspection."

Entreri nodded and hooked the pouch on his belt, behind his hip so that it would be completely concealed by his cloak.

"We could just get you out of the city," Dwahvel offered. "It would have been far cheaper to hire a wizard to teleport you far, far away."

Entreri chuckled at the thought. It was one that had crossed his mind a thousand times since Bregan D'aerthe had come to Calimport, but one that he had always dismissed. How far could he run? Not farther than Rai-guy and Kimmuriel could follow, he understood.

"Stay close to him," Dwahvel warned. "When it happens, you will have to be the quicker."

Entreri nodded and started to rise, but paused and stared hard at Dwahvel. She honestly cared how he managed in this conflict, he realized, and the truth of that—that Dwahvel's concern for him had little to do with her own personal gain—struck him profoundly. It showed him something he'd not known often in his miserable existence—a friend.

721

He didn't leave the Copper Ante right away but went into an adjoining room and began ruffling through the reams of information that Dwahvel had collected on the priest, Cadderly. Would this man be the answer to Jarlaxle's dilemma and thus Entreri's own?

* * * * *

Frustration more than anything else guided Jarlaxle's movements as he made his swift way back to Dallabad, using a variety of magical items to facilitate his silent and unseen passage, but not—pointedly not—calling upon the Crystal Shard for any assistance.

This was it, the drow leader realized, the true test of his newest partnership. It had struck Jarlaxle that perhaps the Crystal Shard had been gaining too much the upper hand in their relationship, and so he had decided to set the matter straight.

He meant to take down the crystalline tower.

Crenshinibon knew it, too. Jarlaxle could feel the artifact's unhappy pulsing in his pouch, and he wondered if the powerful item might force a desperate showdown of willpower, one in which there could emerge only one victor.

Jarlaxle was ready for that. He was always willing to share in responsibility and decision-making, as long as it eventually led to the achievement of his own goals. Lately, though, he'd come to sense, the Crystal Shard seemed to be altering those very goals. It seemed to be bending him more and more in directions not of his choosing.

Soon after the sun had set, a very dark Calimshan evening, Jarlaxle stood before the crystalline tower, staring hard at it. He strengthened his resolve and mentally bolstered himself for the struggle that he knew would inevitably ensue. With a final glance around to make certain that no one was nearby, he reached into his pouch and took out the sentient artifact.

No! Crenshinibon screamed in his thoughts, the shard obviously knowing exactly what it was the dark elf meant to do. *I forbid this. The towers are a manifestation of my—of our strength and indeed heighten that strength. To destroy one is forbidden!*

Forbidden? Jarlaxle echoed skeptically.

It is not in the best interests of—

I decide what is in my best interests, Jarlaxle strongly interrupted. *And now it is in my interest to tear down this tower.* He focused all his mental energies into a singular and powerful command to the Crystal Shard.

And so it began, a titanic, if silent, struggle of willpower. Jarlaxle, with his centuries of accumulated knowledge and perfected cunning, was pitted squarely against the ages-old dweomer that was the Crystal Shard. Within seconds of the battle, Jarlaxle felt his will bend backward, as if the artifact meant to break his mind completely. It seemed to him as if every fear he had ever harbored in every dark corner of his imagination had become real, stalking inexorably toward his thoughts, his memories, his very identity.

How naked he felt! How open to the darts and slings of the mighty Crystal Shard!

Jarlaxle composed himself and worked very hard to separate the images, to single out each horrid manifestation and isolate it from the others. Then, focusing as much as he possibly could on that one vividly imagined horror, he counterattacked, using feelings of empowerment and strength, calling upon all of those many, many experiences he had weathered to become this leader of Bregan D'aerthe, this male dark elf who had for so long thrived in the matriarchal hell that was Menzoberranzan.

One after another the nightmares fell before him. As his internal struggles began to subside, Jarlaxle sent his willpower out of his inner mind, out to the artifact, issuing that singular, powerful command:

Tear down the crystalline tower!

Now came the coercion, the images of glory, of armies falling before fields of crystalline towers, of kings coming to him on their knees, bearing the treasures of their kingdoms, of the Matron Mothers of Menzoberranzan anointing him as permanent ruler of their council, speaking of him in terms previously reserved for Lady Lolth herself.

This second manipulation was, in many ways, even more difficult for Jarlaxle to control and defeat. He could not deny the allure of the images. More importantly, he could not deny the possibilities for Bregan D'aerthe and for him, given the added might that was the Crystal Shard.

He felt his resolve slipping away, a compromise reached that would allow Crenshinibon and Jarlaxle both to find all they desired.

He was ready to release the artifact from his command, to admit the ridiculousness of tearing down the tower, to give in and reform their undeniably profitable alliance.

But he remembered.

This was no partnership, for the Crystal Shard was no partner, no real, controllable, replaceable and predictable partner. No, Jarlaxle reminded himself. It was an artifact, an enchanted item, and though sentient it was a created intelligence, a method of reasoning based upon a set and predetermined goal. In this case, apparently, its goal was the acquisition of as many followers and as much power as its magic would allow.

While Jarlaxle could sympathize, even agree with that goal, he reminded himself pointedly and determinedly that he would have to be the one in command. He fought back against the temptations, denied the Crystal Shard its manipulations as he had beaten back its brute force attack in the beginning of the struggle.

He felt it, as tangible as a snapping rope, a click in his mind that gave him his answer.

Jarlaxle was the master. His were the decisions that would guide Bregan D'aerthe and command the Crystal Shard.

He knew then, without the slightest bit of doubt, that the tower was his to destroy, and so he led the shard again to that command. This time, Jarlaxle felt no anger, no denial, no recriminations, only sadness.

The beaten artifact began to hum with the energies needed to deconstruct its large magical replica.

Jarlaxle opened his eyes and smiled with satisfaction. The fight had been everything he had feared it would be, but in the end, he knew without doubt he had triumphed. He felt the tingling as the essence of the crystalline tower began to weaken. Its binding energy would be stolen away. Then the material bound together by Crenshinibon's magic would dissipate to the winds. The way he commanded it—and he knew that Crenshinibon could comply—there would be no explosions, no crashing walls, just fading away.

Jarlaxle nodded, as satisfied as with any victory he had ever known in his long life of struggles.

He pictured Dallabad without the tower and wondered what new spies would then show up to determine where the tower had gone, why it had been there in the first place, and if Ahdahnia was, therefore, still in charge.

"Stop!" he commanded the artifact. "The tower remains, by *my* word."

The humming stopped immediately and the Crystal Shard, seeming very humbled, went quiet in Jarlaxle's thoughts.

Jarlaxle smiled even wider. Yes, he would keep the tower, and he decided in the morning he would construct a second one beside the first. The twin towers of Dallabad. Jarlaxle's twin towers.

At least two.

For now the mercenary leader did not fear those towers, nor the source that had inspired him to erect the first one. No, he had won the day and could use the mighty Crystal Shard to bring him to new heights of power.

And Jarlaxle knew it would never threaten him again.

* * * * *

Artemis Entreri paced the small room he had rented in a nondescript inn far from House Basadoni and any of the other street guilds. On a small table to the side of the bed was his black, red-stitched gauntlet, with Charon's Claw lying right beside it, the red blade gleaming in the candlelight.

Entreri was not certain of this at all. He wondered what the innkeeper might think if he came in later to find Entreri's skull-headed corpse smoldering on the floor.

It was a very real possibility, the assassin reminded himself. Every time he used Charon's Claw, it showed him a new twist, a new trick, and he understood sentient magic well enough to understand that the more powers such a sword possessed, the greater its willpower. Entreri had already seen the result of a defeat in a willpower battle with this particularly nasty sword. He could picture the horrible end of Kohrin Soulez as vividly as if it had happened that very morning, the man's facial skin rolling up from his bones as it melted away.

But he had to do this and now. He would soon be going against the Crystal Shard, and woe to him if, at that time, he was still waging any kind of mental battle against his own sword. With just that fear in mind, he had even contemplated selling the sword or hiding it away somewhere, but as he considered his other likely enemies, Rai-guy and Kimmuriel, he realized that he had to keep it.

He had to keep it, and he had to dominate it completely. There could be no other way.

Entreri walked toward the table, rubbing his hands together, then bringing them up to his lips, and blowing into them.

He turned around before he reached the sword, thinking, thinking, seeking some alternative. He wondered again if he could sell the vicious blade or hand it over to Dwahvel to lock in a deep hole until after the dark elves had left Calimport and he could, perhaps, return.

That last thought, of being chased from the city by Jarlaxle's wretched lieutenants, fired a sudden anger in the assassin, and he strode determinedly over to the table. Before he could again consider the potential implications, he growled and reached over, snapping up Charon's Claw in his bare hand.

He felt the immediate tug—not a physical tug, but something deeper, something going to the essence of Artemis Entreri, the spirit of the man. The sword was hungry—how he could feel that hunger! It wanted to consume him, to obliterate his very essence simply because he was bold enough, or foolish enough, to grasp it without that protective gauntlet.

Oh, how it wanted him!

He felt a twitching in his cheek, an excitement upon his skin, and wondered if he would combust. Entreri forced that notion away and concentrated again on winning the mental battle.

The sentient sword pulled and pulled, relentlessly, and Entreri could hear something akin to laughter in his head, a supreme confidence that reminded him that Charon's Claw would not tire, but he surely would. Another thought came, the realization that he could not even let go of the weapon if he chose to, that he had locked in this combat and there could be no turning back, no surrender.

That was the ploy of the devilish sword, to impart a sense of complete hopelessness on the part of anyone challenging it, to tell the challenger, in no uncertain terms, that the fight would be to the bitter and disastrous end. For so many before Entreri, such a message had resulted in a breaking of the spirit that the sword had used as a springboard to complete its victory.

But with Entreri, the ploy only brought forth greater feelings of rage, a red wall of determined and focused anger and denial.

"You are mine!" the assassin growled through gritted teeth. "You are a possession, a thing, a piece of beaten metal!" He lifted the gleaming red blade before him and commanded it to bring forth its black light.

It did not comply. The sword kept attacking Entreri as it had attacked Kohrin Soulez, trying to defeat him mentally that it might burn away his skin, trying to consume him as it had so many before him.

"You are mine," he said again, his voice calm now, for while the sword had not relented its attack, Entreri's confidence that he could fend that attack began to rise.

He felt a sudden sting within him, a burning sensation as Charon's Claw threw all of its energy into him. Rather than deny it he welcomed that energy and took it from the sword. It mounted to a vibrating crescendo and broke apart.

The black light appeared in the small room, and Entreri's smile gleamed widely within it. The light was confirmation that Entreri had overwhelmed Charon's Claw, that the sword was indeed his now. He lowered the blade, taking several deep breaths to steady himself, trying not to consider the fact that he had just come back from the very precipice of obliteration.

That did not matter anymore. He had beaten the sword, had broken the sword's spirit, and it belonged to him now as surely as did the jeweled dagger he wore on his other hip. Certainly he would ever after have to take some measure of care that Charon's Claw would try to break free of him, but that was, at most, a cursory inconvenience.

"You are mine," he said again, calmly, and he commanded the sword to dismiss the black light.

The room was again bathed in only candlelight. Charon's Claw, the sword of Artemis Entreri, offered no arguments.

* * * * *

Jarlaxle *thought* he knew. Jarlaxle *thought* that he had won the day.

Because Crenshinibon made him think that. Because Crenshinibon wanted the battle between the mercenary leader and his upstart lieutenants to be an honest one, so that it could then determine which would be the better wielder.

The Crystal Shard still favored Rai-guy, because it knew that drow to be more ambitious and more willing, even eager, to kill.

But the possibilities here with Jarlaxle did not escape the artifact. Turning him within the layers of deception had been no easy thing, but indeed, Crenshinibon had taken Jarlaxle exactly to that spot where it had desired he go.

At dawn the very next morning, a second crystalline tower was erected at Dallabad Oasis.

Chapter 13

Flipping the Hourglass

"You understand your role in every contingency?" Entreri asked Dwahvel at their next meeting, an impromptu affair conducted in the alley beside the Copper Ante, an area equally protected from divining wizards by Dwahvel's potent anti-spying resources.

"In every contingency that you have outlined," the halfling replied with a warning smirk.

"Then you understand every contingency," Entreri answered without hesitation. He returned her grin with one of complete confidence.

"You have thought *every* possibility through?" the halfling asked doubtfully. "These are dark elves, the masters of manipulation and intrigue, the makers of the layers of their own reality and of the rules within that layered reality."

"And they are not in their homeland and do not understand the nuances of Calimport," Entreri assured her. "They view the whole world as an extension of Menzoberranzan, an extension in temperament, and more importantly, in how they measure the reactions of those around them. I am *iblith*, thus inferior, and thus, they will not expect the turn their version of reality is about to take."

"The time has come?" Dwahvel asked, still doubtfully. "Or are you bringing the critical moment upon us?"

"I have never been a patient man," Entreri admitted, and his wicked grin did not dissipate with the admission but intensified.

"Every contingency," Dwahvel remarked, "thus every layer of the reality you intend to create. Beware, my competent friend, that you do not get lost somewhere in the mixture of your realities."

Entreri started to scowl but held back the negative thoughts, recognizing that Dwahvel was offering him sensible advice here, that he was playing a most dangerous game with the most dangerous foes he had ever known. Even in the best of circumstances, Artemis Entreri realized that his success, and therefore his very life, would hang on the movements of a split second and would be forfeited by the slightest turn of bad luck. This culminating scenario was not the precision strike of the trained assassin but the desperate move of a cornered man.

Still, when he looked at his halfling friend, Entreri's confidence and resolve were bolstered. He knew that Dwahvel would not disappoint him in this, that she would hold up her end of the reality-making process.

"If you succeed, I'll not see you again," the halfling remarked. "And if you fail, I'll likely not be able to find your blasted and torn corpse."

Entreri took the blunt words for the offering of affection that he knew they truly were. His smile was wide and genuine—so rare a thing for the assassin.

"You will see me again," he told Dwahvel. "The drow will grow weary of Calimport and will recede back to their sunless holes where they truly belong. Perhaps it will happen in months, perhaps in years, but they will eventually go. That is their nature. Rai-guy and Kimmuriel understand that there is no long-term benefit for them or for Bregan D'aerthe in expanding any trading business on the surface. Discovery would mean all-out war. That is the main focus of their ire with Jarlaxle, after all. So they will go, but you will remain, and I will return."

"Even if the drow do not kill you now, am I to believe that your road will be any less dangerous once you're gone?" the halfling asked with a snort that ended in a grin. "Is there any such road for Artemis Entreri? Not likely, I say. Indeed, with your new weapon and that defensive gauntlet, you will likely take on the assassinations of prominent wizards as your chosen profession. And, of course, eventually one of those wizards will understand the truth of your new toys and their limitations, and he will leave you a charred and smoking husk." She chuckled and shook her head. "Yes, go after Khelben, Vangerdahast, or Elminster himself. At least your death will be painlessly quick."

"I did say I was not a patient man," Entreri agreed.

To his surprise, and to the halfling's as well, Dwahvel then rushed up to him and leaped upon him, wrapping him in a hug. She broke free quickly and backed away, composing herself.

"For luck and nothing more," she said. "Of course I prefer your victory to that of the dark elves."

"If only the dark elves," Entreri said, needing to keep this conversation lighthearted.

He knew what awaited him. It would be a brutal test of his skills—of all of his skills—and of his nerve. He walked the very edge of disaster. Again, he reminded himself that he could indeed count on the reliability of one Dwahvel Tiggerwillies, that most competent of halflings. He looked at her hard then and understood that she was going to play along with his last remark, was not going to give him the satisfaction of disagreeing, of admitting that she considered him a friend.

Artemis Entreri would have been disappointed in her if she had.

"Beware that you do not catch yourself within the very layers of lies that you have perpetrated," Dwahvel said after the assassin as he started away, already beginning to blend seamlessly into the shadows.

Entreri took those words to heart. The potential combinations of the possible events was indeed staggering. Improvisation alone might keep him alive in this critical time, and Entreri had survived the entirety of his life on the very edge of disaster. He had been forced to rely on his wits, on complete improvisation, dozens of times, scores of times, and had somehow managed to survive. In his mind, he held contingency plans to counter every foreseeable event. While he kept confidence in himself and in those he had placed strategically around him, he did not for one moment dismiss the fact that if one eventuality materialized that he had not counted on, if one wrong turn appeared before him and he could not find a way around that bend, he would die.

And, given the demeanor of Rai-guy, he would die horribly.

* * * * *

The street was busy, as were most of the avenues in Calimport, but the most remarkable person on it seemed the most unremarkable. Artemis Entreri, wearing the guise of a beggar, kept to the shadows, not moving suspiciously from one to another, but blending invisibly against the backdrop of the bustling street.

His movements were not without purpose. He kept his prey in sight at every moment.

Sharlotta Vespers attempted no such anonymity as she moved along the thoroughfare. She was the recognized figurehead of House Basadoni, walking bidden into the domain of dangerous Pasha Da'Daclan. Many suspicious, even hateful eyes cast more than the occasional glance her way, but none would move against her. She had requested the meeting with Da'Daclan, on orders from Rai-guy, and had been accepted under his protection. Thus, she walked now with the guise of complete confidence, bordering on bravado.

She didn't seem to realize that one of those watching her, shadowing her, was not under any orders from Pasha Da'Daclan.

Entreri knew this area well, for he had worked for the Rakers on several occasions in the past. Sharlotta's demeanor told him without doubt that she was coming for a formal parlay. Soon enough, as she passed one potential meeting area after another, he was able to deduce exactly where that meeting would take place. What he did not know, however, was how important this meeting might be to Rai-guy and Kimmuriel.

"Are you watching her every step with your strange mind powers, Kimmuriel?" he asked quietly

His mind worked through the contingency plans he had to keep available should that be the case. He didn't believe that the two drow, busy with planning of their own, no doubt, would be monitoring Sharlotta's every move, but it was certainly possible. If that came to pass, Entreri realized that he would know it, in no uncertain terms, very soon. He could only hope that he'd be ready and able to properly adjust his course.

He moved more quickly then, outpacing the woman by taking the side alleys, even climbing to one roof, and scrambling across to another and to another.

Soon after, he reached the house bordering the alley he believed Sharlotta would turn down, a suspicion only heightened by the fact that a sentry was in position on that very roof, overlooking the alley on the far side.

As silent as death, Entreri moved into position behind the sentry, with the man's attention obviously focused on the alleyway and completely oblivious to him. Working carefully, for he knew that others would be about, Entreri spent some amount of time casing the entire area, locating the two sentries on the rooftops across the way and one other on this side of the alley, on the adjoining roof of a building immediately behind the one Entreri now stood upon.

He watched those three more than the man directly in front of him, measured their every movement, their every turn of the head. Most of all, he gauged their focus. Finally, when he was certain that they were not attentive, the assassin struck, yanking his victim back behind a dormer.

A moment later, all four of Pasha Da'Daclan's sentries seemed in place once more, all of them honestly intent on the alleyway below as Sharlotta Vespers, a pair of Da'Daclan's guards at her back, turned into the alleyway.

Entreri's thoughts whirled. Five enemy soldiers, and a supposed comrade who seemed more of an enemy than the others. He didn't delude himself into thinking that these five were alone. Da'Daclan's stooges probably included a significant portion of the scores of people milling about on the main avenue.

Entreri went anyway, rolling over the edge of the roof of the two-story building, catching hold with his hand, stretching to his limit, and dropping agilely to the surprised Sharlotta's side.

"A trap," he whispered harshly, and he turned to face the two soldiers following her and held up his hand for them to halt. "Kimmuriel has a dimensional portal in place for our escape on the roof."

Sharlotta's facial expression went from surprise to anger to calm so quickly, each one buried in her practiced manner, that only Entreri caught the range of expressions. He knew that he had her befuddled, that his mention of Kimmuriel had given credence to his outlandish claim that this was a trap.

"I will take her from here," Entreri said to the guards. He heard movement farther along and across the alley, as two of the other three sentries, including the one on the same side of the alley as Entreri, came down to see what was going on.

"Who are you?" one of the soldiers following Sharlotta asked skeptically, his hand going inside his common traveling cloak to the hilt of a finely crafted sword.

"Go," Entreri whispered to Sharlotta.

The woman hesitated, so Entreri prompted her retreat in no uncertain terms. Out came the jeweled dagger and Charon's Claw, the assassin throwing back his cloak, revealing himself in all his splendor. He leaped forward, slashing with his sword and thrusting with his dagger at the second soldier.

Out came the swords in response. One picked off the swipe of Charon's Claw, but with the man inevitably retreating as he parried. That had been Entreri's primary goal. The second soldier, though, had less fortune. As his sword came forth to parry, Entreri gave a subtle twist of his wrist and looped his dagger over the blade, then thrust it home into the man's belly.

With others closing fast, the assassin couldn't follow through with the kill, but he did hold the strike long enough to bring forth the dagger's life-stealing energies to let the man know the purest horror he could ever imagine. The soldier wasn't really badly wounded, but he fell away to the ground, clutching his belly and howling in terror.

The assassin broke back, turning away from the wall where Sharlotta Vespers was scrambling to gain the roof.

The one who had fallen back from the sword slash came at Entreri from the left. Another came from the right, and two rushed across the alleyway, coming straight in. Entreri started right, sword leading, then turned back fast to the left. Even as the four began to compensate for the change—a change that was not completely unexpected—the assassin turned back fast to the right, charging in hard just as that soldier had begun to accelerate in pursuit.

The soldier found himself in a flurry of slashing and stabbing. He worked his own blades, a sword and dirk, quite well. The soldier was no novice to battle, but this was Artemis Entreri. Whenever the man moved to parry, Entreri altered the angle. His fury kept the ring of metal in the air for a long few seconds, but the dagger slipped through, gashing the

733

soldier's right arm. As that limb drooped, Entreri went into a spin, Charon's Claw coming around fast to pick off a thrust from the man coming in at his back, then continuing through, over the wounded man's lowered defense, slashing him hard across the chest.

Also on that maneuver, Entreri's devilish sword trailed out the black ash wall. The line was horizontal, not vertical, so that ash did not impede the vision of his adversaries, but still the mere sight of it hanging there in midair gave them enough pause for Entreri to dispatch the man who had come in on his right. Then the assassin went into a wild flurry, sword waving and bringing up an opaque wall.

The remaining three soldiers settled back behind it, confused and trying to put some coordination into their movements. When at last they mustered the nerve to charge through the ash wall, they discovered that the assassin was nowhere to be found.

Entreri watched them from the rooftop, shaking his head at their ineptness, and also at the little values offered by this wondrous sword—a weapon to which he was growing more fond with each battle.

"Where is it?" Sharlotta called to him from across the way.

Entreri looked at her quizzically.

"The doorway?" Sharlotta asked. "Where is it?"

"Perhaps Da'Daclan has interfered," Entreri replied, trying to hide his satisfaction that apparently Rai-guy and Kimmuriel were not closely monitoring Sharlotta's movements. "Or perhaps they decided to leave us," he added, figuring that if he could throw a bit of doubt into Sharlotta Vespers' view of the world and her dark-elven compatriots, then so be it.

Sharlotta merely scowled at that disturbing thought.

Noise from behind told them that the soldiers in the alleyway weren't giving up and reminded them that they were on hostile territory here. Entreri ran past Sharlotta, motioning for her to follow, then made the leap across the next alleyway to another building, then to a third, then down and out the back end of an alley, and finally, down into the sewers— a place that Entreri wasn't thrilled about entering at that time, given his recent assassination of Domo. He didn't remain underground for long, coming up in the more familiar territory beyond Da'Daclan's territory and closer to the Basadoni guild house.

Still leading, Entreri made his way along at a swift pace until he reached the alleyway beside the Copper Ante, where he abruptly stopped.

Seeming more angry than grateful, obviously doubting the sincerity of the escape and the very need for it, Sharlotta continued past, hardly glancing his way.

Until the assassin's sword came out and settled in front of her neck. "I think not," he remarked.

Sharlotta glanced sidelong at him, and he motioned for her to head down the alley beside Dwahvel's establishment.

"What is this?" the woman asked.

"Your only chance at continuing to draw breath," Entreri replied. When she still didn't move, he grabbed her by the arm, and with frightening strength yanked her in front of him heading down the alley. He pointedly reminded her to keep going, prodding her with his sword.

They came to a tiny room, having entered through a secret alley entrance. The room held a single chair, into which Entreri none-too-gently shoved Sharlotta.

"Have you lost what little sense you once possessed?" the woman asked.

"Am I the one bargaining secret deals with dark elves?" Entreri replied, and the look Sharlotta gave him in the instant before she found her control told him volumes about the truth of his suspicions.

"We have both been dealing as need be," the woman indignantly answered.

"Dealing? Or double-dealing? There is a difference, even with dark elves."

"You speak the part of a fool," snapped Sharlotta.

"Yet you are the one closer to death," Entreri reminded, and he came in very close, now with his jeweled dagger in hand, and a look on his face that told Sharlotta that he was certainly not bluffing here. Sharlotta knew well the life-stealing powers of that horrible dagger. "Why were you going to meet with Pasha Da'Daclan?" Entreri asked bluntly.

"The change at Dallabad has raised suspicions," the woman answered, an honest and obvious—if obviously incomplete—response.

"No suspicions that trouble Jarlaxle, apparently," Entreri reasoned.

"But some that could turn to serious trouble," Sharlotta went on, and Entreri knew that she was improvising here. "I was to meet with Pasha Da'Daclan to assure him the situation on the streets, and elsewhere, will calm to normal."

"That any expansion by House Basadoni is at its end?" Entreri asked doubtfully. "Would you not be lying, though, and would that not invite even greater wrath when the next conquest falls before Jarlaxle?"

"The next?"

"Have you come to believe that our suddenly ambitious leader means to stop?" Entreri asked.

Sharlotta spent a long while mulling that one over. "I have been told that House Basadoni will begin pulling back, to all appearances, at least," she said. "As long as we encounter no further outside influences."

"Like the spies at Dallabad," Entreri agreed.

Sharlotta nodded—a bit too eagerly, Entreri thought.

"Then Jarlaxle's hunger is at last sated, and we can get back to a quieter and safer routine," the assassin remarked.

Sharlotta did not respond.

Entreri's lips curled up into a smile. He knew the truth of it, of course, that Sharlotta had just blatantly lied to him. He would never have put it past Jarlaxle to have played such opposing games with his underlings in days past, leading Entreri in one direction and Sharlotta in another, but he knew that the mercenary leader was in the throes of Crenshinibon's hunger now, and given the information supplied by Dwahvel, he understood the truth of that. It was a truth very different from the lie Sharlotta had just outlined.

Sharlotta, by going to Da'Daclan and claiming that Jarlaxle had been behind the meeting, which meant that Rai-guy and Kimmuriel certainly had been, confirmed to Entreri that time was indeed running short.

He stepped back and paused, digesting all of the information, trying to reason when and where the actual in-fighting might occur. He noted, too, that Sharlotta was watching him very carefully.

Sharlotta moved with the grace and speed of a hunting cat, rolling off the chair to one knee, drawing and throwing a dagger at Entreri's heart, and bolting for the room's other, less remarkable doorway.

Entreri caught the dagger in midflight, turned it over in his hand and hurled it into that door with a thump, to stick, quivering, before Sharlotta's widening eyes.

He grabbed her and turned her roughly around, hitting her with a heavy punch across the face.

She drew out another dagger—or tried to. Entreri caught her wrist even as it came out of its concealed sheath, turning a quick spin under the arm and tugging so violently that all of Sharlotta's strength left her hand and the dagger fell harmlessly to the floor. Entreri tugged again, and let go. He leaped around in front of the woman, slapping her twice across the face, and grabbed her hard by the shoulders. He ran her backward, to crash back into the chair.

"Do you not even understand those with whom you play these foolish games?" he growled in her face. "They will use you to their advantage, and discard you. In their eyes you are *iblith,* a word that means "not drow," a word that also means offal. Those two, Rai-guy and Kimmuriel, are the greatest racists among Jarlaxle's lieutenants. You will find no gain beside them, Sharlotta the Fool, only horrible death."

"And what of Jarlaxle?" she cried out in response.

It was just the sort of instinctive, emotional explosion the assassin had been counting on. There it was, as clear as it could be, an admission that Sharlotta had fallen into league with two would-be kings of Bregan D'aerthe. He moved back from her, just a bit, leaving her ruffled in the chair.

"I offer you one chance," he said to her. "Not out of any favorable feelings I might hold toward you, because there are none, but because you have something I need."

Sharlotta straightened her shirt and tunic and tried to regain some of her dignity.

"Tell me everything," Entreri said bluntly. "All of this coup—when, where, and how. I know more than you believe, so try none of your foolish games with me."

Sharlotta smirked at him doubtfully. "You know nothing," she replied. "If you did, you'd know you've come to play the role of the idiot."

Even as the last word left her mouth, Entreri was there, back against her, one hand roughly grabbing her hair and yanking her head back, the other, holding his awful dagger point in at her exposed throat. "Last chance," he said, so very calmly. "And do remember that I do not like you, dearest Sharlotta."

The woman swallowed hard, her eyes locked onto Entreri's deadly gaze.

Entreri's reputation heightened the threat reflected in his eyes to the point where Sharlotta, with nothing to lose and no reason for loyalty to the dark elves, spilled all she knew of the entire plan, even the method Rai-guy and Kimmuriel planned to use to incapacitate the Crystal Shard—some kind of mind magic transformed into a lantern.

None of it came as any surprise to Entreri, of course. Still, hearing the words spoken openly did bring a shock to him, a reminder of how precarious his position truly had become. He quietly muttered his litany of creating his own reality within the strands of the layered web and reminded himself repeatedly that he was every bit the player as were his two opponents.

He moved away from Sharlotta to the inner door. He pulled free the stuck dagger and banged hard three times on the door. It opened a few moments later and a very surprised looking Dwahvel Tiggerwillies bounded into the room.

"Why have you come?" she started to ask of Entreri, but she stopped, her gaze caught by the ruffled Sharlotta. Again she turned to Entreri, this time her expression one of surprise and anger. "What have you done?" the halfling demanded of the assassin. "I'll play no part in any of the rivalries within House Basadoni!"

"You will do as you are instructed," the assassin replied coldly. "You will keep Sharlotta here as your comfortable but solitary guest until I return to permit her release."

"Permit?" Dwahvel asked doubtfully, turning from Entreri to Sharlotta. "What insanity have you brought upon me, fool?"

"The next insult will cost you your tongue," Entreri said coldly, perfectly playing the role. "You will do as I've instructed. Nothing more, nothing less. When this is finished, even Sharlotta will thank you for keeping her safe in times when none of us truly are."

Dwahvel stared hard at Sharlotta as Entreri spoke, making silent contact. The human woman gave the slightest nod of her head.

Dwahvel turned back to the assassin. "Out," she ordered.

Entreri looked to the alleyway door, so perfectly fitted that it was barely an outline on the wall.

"Not that way . . . it opens only in," Dwahvel said sourly, and she pointed to the conventional door. "That way." She moved up to him and pushed him along, out of the room, turning to close and lock the door behind them.

"It has come this far already?" Dwahvel asked when the two were safely down the corridor.

Entreri nodded grimly.

"But you are still on course for your plan?" Dwahvel asked. "Despite this unexpected turn?"

Entreri's smile reminded the halfling that nothing would be, or could be, unexpected.

Dwahvel nodded. "Logical improvisation," she remarked.

"You know your role," Entreri replied.

"And I thought I played it quite well," Dwahvel said with a smile.

"Too well," Entreri said to her as they reached another doorway farther along the wall up the alleyway. "I was not joking when I said I would take your tongue."

With that, he went out into the alley, leaving a shaken Dwahvel behind. After a moment, though, the halfling merely chuckled, doubting that Entreri would ever take her tongue, whatever insults she might throw his way.

Doubting, but not sure—never sure. That was the way of Artemis Entreri.

* * * * *

Entreri was out of the city before dawn, riding hard for Dallabad Oasis on a horse he'd borrowed without the owner's permission. He knew the road well. It was often congested with beggars and highwaymen. That knowledge didn't stop the assassin, though, didn't slow his swift ride one bit. When the sun rose over his left shoulder he only increased his pace, knowing that he had to get to Dallabad on time.

He'd told Dwahvel that Jarlaxle was back at the crystalline tower, where the assassin now had to go with all haste. Entreri knew the halfling would be prompt about her end of the plan. Once she released Sharlotta. . . .

Entreri put his head down and drove on in the growing morning sunlight. He was still miles away, but he could see the sharp focus at the top of the tower . . . no, towers, he realized, for he saw not one, but two pillars rising in the distance to meet the morning light.

He didn't know what that meant, of course, but he didn't worry about it. Jarlaxle was there, according to his many sources—informants independent of, and beyond the reach of Rai-guy and Kimmuriel and their many lackeys.

He sensed the scrying soon after and knew he was being watched. That only made the desperate assassin put his head down and drive the stolen horse on at greater speeds, determined to beat the brutal, self-imposed timetable.

* * * * *

"He goes to Jarlaxle with great haste, and we know not where Sharlotta Vespers has gone," Kimmuriel remarked to Rai-guy.

The two of them, along with Berg'inyon Baenre, watched the assassin's hard ride out from Calimport.

"Sharlotta may remain with Pasha Da'Daclan," Rai-guy replied. "We cannot know for certain."

"Then we should learn," said an obviously frustrated and nervous Kimmuriel.

Rai-guy looked at him. "Easy, my friend," he said. "Artemis Entreri is no threat to us but merely a nuisance. Better that all of the vermin gather together."

"A more complete and swift victory," Berg'inyon agreed.

Kimmuriel thought about it and held up a small square lantern, three sides shielded, the fourth open. Yharaskrik had given it to him with the assurance that, when Kimmuriel lit the candle and allowed its glow to fall over Crenshinibon, the powers of the Crystal Shard would be stunted. The effects would be temporary, the illithid had warned. Even confident Yharaskrik held no illusions that anything would hold the powerful artifact at bay for long.

But it wouldn't take long, Kimmuriel and the others knew, even if Artemis Entreri was at Jarlaxle's side. With the artifact shut down, Jarlaxle's fall would be swift and complete, as would the fall of all of those, Entreri included, who stood beside him.

This day would be sweet indeed—or rather, this night. Rai-guy and Kimmuriel had planned to strike at night, when the powers of the Crystal Shard were at their weakest.

* * * * *

"He is a fool, but one, I believe, acting on honest fears," Dwahvel Tiggerwillies said to Sharlotta when she joined the woman in the small room. "Find a bit of sympathy for him, I beg."

Sharlotta, the prisoner, looked at the halfling incredulously.

"Oh, he's gone now," said Dwahvel, "and so should you be."

"I thought I was your prisoner," the woman asked.

Dwahvel chuckled. "Forever and ever?" she asked with obvious sarcasm. "Artemis Entreri is afraid, and so you should be too. I know little about dark elves, I admit, but—"

739

"Dark elves?" Sharlotta echoed, feigning surprise and ignorance. "What has any of this to do with dark elves?"

Dwahvel laughed again. "The word is out," she said, "about Dallabad and House Basadoni. The power behind the throne is well-known around the streets."

Sharlotta started to mumble something about Entreri, but Dwahvel cut her short. "Entreri told me nothing," she explained. "Do you think I would need to deal with one as powerful as Entreri for such common information? I am many things, but I do not number fool among them."

The woman settled back in her chair, staring hard at the halfling. "You believe you know more than you really know," she said. "That is a dangerous mistake."

"I know only that I want no part of any of this," Dwahvel returned. "No part of House Basadoni or of Dallabad Oasis. No part of the feud between Sharlotta Vespers and Artemis Entreri."

"It would seem that you are already a part of that feud," the woman replied, her sparkling dark eyes narrowing.

Dwahvel shook her head. "I did and do as I had to do, nothing more," she said.

"Then I am free to leave?"

Dwahvel nodded and stood aside, leaving the path to the door open. "I came back here as soon as I was certain Entreri was long gone. Forgive me, Sharlotta, but I would not make of you an ally if doing so made Entreri an enemy."

Sharlotta continued to stare hard at the surprising halfling, but she couldn't argue with the logic of that statement. "Where has he gone?" she asked.

"Out of Calimport, my sources relay," Dwahvel answered. "To Dallabad, perhaps? Or long past the oasis—all the way along the road and out of Calimshan. I believe I might take that very route, were I Artemis Entreri."

Sharlotta didn't reply, but silently she agreed wholeheartedly. She was still confused by the recent events, but she recognized clearly that Entreri's supposed "rescue" of her was no more than a kidnapping of his own, so he could squeeze information out of her. And she had offered much, she understood to her apprehension. She had told him more than she should have, more than Rai-guy and Kimmuriel would likely find acceptable.

She left the Copper Ante trying to sort it all out. What she did know was that the dark elves would find her and likely soon. The woman nodded, recognizing the only real course left open before her, and started off with all speed for House Basadoni. She would tell Rai-guy and Kimmuriel of Entreri's treachery.

* * * * *

Entreri looked at the sun hanging low in the eastern sky and took a deep, steadying breath. The time had passed. Dwahvel had released Sharlotta, as arranged. The woman, no doubt, had run right to Rai-guy and Kimmuriel, thus setting into motion momentous events.

If the two dark elves were even still in Calimport.

If Sharlotta had not figured out the ruse within the kidnapping, and had gone off the other way, running for cover.

If the dark elves hadn't long ago found Sharlotta in the Copper Ante and leveled the place, in which case, Dallabad and the Crystal Shard might already be in Rai-guy's dangerous hands.

If, in learning of the discovery, Rai-guy and Kimmuriel hadn't just turned around and run back to Menzoberranzan.

If Jarlaxle still remained at Dallabad.

That last notion worried Entreri profoundly. The unpredictable Jarlaxle was, perhaps, the most volatile on a long list of unknowns. If Jarlaxle had left Dallabad, what trouble might he bring to every aspect of this plan? Would Kimmuriel and Rai-guy catch up to him unawares and slay him easily?

The assassin shook all of the doubts away. He wasn't used to feelings of self-doubt, even inadequacy. Perhaps that was why he so hated the dark elves. In Menzoberranzan, the ultimately capable Artemis Entreri had felt tiny indeed.

Reality is what you make of it, he reminded himself. He was the one weaving the layers of intrigue and deception here, so he—not Rai-guy and Kimmuriel, not Sharlotta, not even Jarlaxle and the Crystal Shard—was the one in command.

He looked at the sun again, and glanced to the side, to the imposing structures of the twin crystalline towers set among the palms of Dallabad, reminding himself that this time he, and no one else, had turned over that hourglass.

Reminding himself pointedly that the sand was running, that time was growing short, he kicked his horse's flanks and leaped away, galloping hard to the oasis.

Chapter 14

When the Sand Ran Out

Entreri kept the notion that he had come to steal the Crystal Shard foremost in his mind. All he thought of was that he'd come to take it as his own, whatever the cost to Jarlaxle, though he made certain that he kept a bit of compassion evident whenever he thought of the mercenary leader. Entreri replayed that singular thought and purpose over and over again, suspecting that the artifact, in this place of its greatest power, would scan those thoughts.

Jarlaxle was waiting for him on the second floor of the tower in a round room sparsely adorned with two chairs and a small desk. The mercenary leader stood across the way, directly opposite the doorway through which Entreri entered. Jarlaxle put himself as far, Entreri noted, as he could be from the approaching assassin.

"Greetings," Entreri said.

Jarlaxle, curiously wearing no eye patch this day, tipped his broad-brimmed hat and asked, "Why have you come?"

Entreri looked at him as if surprised by the question, but turned the not-so-secret notion in his head to one appearing as an ironic twist: Why have I come indeed!

Jarlaxle's uncharacteristic scowl told the assassin that the Crystal

743

Shard had heard those thoughts and had communicated them instantly to its wielder. No doubt, the artifact was now telling Jarlaxle to dispose of Entreri, a suggestion the mercenary leader was obviously resisting.

"Your course is that of the fool," Jarlaxle remarked, struggling with the words as his internal battle heightened. "There is nothing here for you."

Entreri settled back on his heels, assuming a pensive posture. "Then perhaps I should leave," he said.

Jarlaxle didn't blink.

Hardly expecting one as cunning as Jarlaxle to be caught off guard, Entreri exploded into motion anyway, a forward dive and roll that brought him up in a run straight at his opponent.

Jarlaxle grabbed his belt pouch—he didn't even have to take the artifact out—and extended his other hand toward the assassin. Out shot a line of pure white energy.

Entreri caught it with his red-stitched gauntlet, took the energy in, and held it there. He held some of it, anyway, for it was too great a power to be completely held at bay. The assassin felt the pain, the intense agony, though he understood that only a small fraction of the shard's attack had gotten through.

How powerful was that item? he wondered, awestruck and thinking that he might be in serious trouble.

Afraid that the energy would melt the gauntlet or otherwise consume it, Entreri turned the magic right back out. He didn't throw it at Jarlaxle, for he hardly wanted to kill the drow. Entreri loosed it on the wall to the dark elf's side. It exploded in a blistering, blinding, thunderous blow that left both man and dark elf staggering to the side.

Entreri kept his course straight, dodging and parrying with his blade as Jarlaxle's arm pumped, sending forth a stream of daggers. The assassin blocked one, got nicked by a second, and squirmed about two more. He then came on fast, thinking to tackle the lighter dark elf.

He missed cleanly, slamming the wall behind Jarlaxle.

The drow was wearing a displacement cloak, or perhaps it was that ornamental hat, Entreri mused, but only briefly, for he understood that he was vulnerable and came right around, bringing Charon's Claw in a broad, ash-making sweep that cut the view between the opponents.

Hardly slowing, Entreri crashed straight through that visual barrier, his straightforwardness confusing Jarlaxle long enough for him to get by—and properly gauge his attack angle this time—close enough to work his own form of magic.

With skills beyond those of nearly any man alive, Entreri sheathed Charon's Claw, drew forth his dagger in his gloved hand, and pulled out his replica pouch with his other. He spun past Jarlaxle, deftly cutting the scrambling drow's belt pouch and catching it in the same gloved hand, while dropping the false pouch at the mercenary's feet.

Jarlaxle hit him with a series of sharp blows then, with what felt like an iron maul. Entreri went rolling away, glancing back just in time to pick off another dagger, then to catch the next in his side. Groaning and doubled over in pain, Entreri scrambled away from his adversary, who held, he now saw, a small warhammer.

"Do you think I need the Crystal Shard to destroy you?" Jarlaxle confidently asked, stooping over to retrieve the pouch. He held up the warhammer then and whispered something. It shrank into a tiny replica that Jarlaxle tucked up under the band of his great hat.

Entreri hardly heard him and hardly saw the move. The pain, though the dagger hadn't gone in dangerously far, was searing. Even worse, a new song was beginning to play in his head, a demand that he surrender himself to the power of the artifact he now possessed.

"I have a hundred ways to kill you, my former friend," Jarlaxle remarked. "Perhaps Crenshinibon will prove the most efficient in this, and in truth, I have little desire to torture you."

Jarlaxle clasped the pouch then, and a curious expression crossed his face.

Still, Entreri could hardly register any of Jarlaxle's words or movements. The artifact assailed him powerfully, reaching into his mind and showing such overwhelming images of complete despair that the mighty assassin nearly fell to his knees sobbing.

Jarlaxle shrugged and rubbed the moisture from his hand on his cloak, and produced yet another of his endless stream of daggers from his enchanted bracer. He brought it back, lining up the killing throw on the seemingly defenseless man.

"Please tell me why I must do this," the drow asked. "Was it the Crystal Shard calling out to you? Your own overblown ambitions, perhaps?"

The images of despair assailed him, a sense of hopelessness more profound than anything Entreri had ever known.

One thought managed to sort itself out in the battered mind of Artemis Entreri: Why didn't the Crystal Shard summon forth its energy and consume him then and there?

Because it cannot! Entreri's willpower answered. Because I am now the wielder, something that the Crystal Shard does not enjoy at all!

"Tell me!" Jarlaxle demanded.

Entreri summoned up all his mental strength, every ounce of discipline he had spent decades grooming, and told the artifact to cease, simply commanded it to shut down all connection to him. The sentient artifact resisted, but only for a moment. Entreri's wall was built of pure discipline and pure anger, and the Crystal Shard was closed off as completely as it had been during those days when Drizzt Do'Urden had carried it. The denial that Drizzt, a goodly ranger, had brought upon the artifact had been wrought of simple morality, while Entreri's was wrought of simple strength of will, but to the same effect. The shard was shut down.

And not an instant too soon, Entreri realized as he blinked open his eyes and saw a stream of daggers coming at him. He dodged and parried with his own dagger, hardly picking anything off cleanly, but deflecting the missiles so that they did not, at least, catch him squarely. One hit him in the face, high on his cheekbone and just under his eye, but he had altered the spin enough so that it slammed in pommel first and not point first. Another grazed his upper arm, cutting a long slash.

"I could have killed you with the return bolt!" Entreri managed to cry out.

Jarlaxle's arm pumped again, this dagger going low and clipping the dancing assassin's foot. The words did register, though, and the mercenary leader paused, his arm cocked, another dagger in hand, ready to throw. He stared at Entreri curiously.

"I could have struck you dead with your own attack," Entreri growled out through teeth gritted in pain.

"You feared you would destroy the shard," Jarlaxle reasoned.

"The shard's energy cannot destroy the shard!" Entreri snapped back.

"You came in here to kill me," Jarlaxle declared.

"No!"

"To take the Crystal Shard, whatever the cost!" Jarlaxle countered.

Entreri, leaning heavily back against the wall now, his legs growing weak from pain, mustered all his determination and looked the drow in the eye—though he did so with only one eye, for his other had already swollen tightly closed. "I came in here," he said slowly, accentuating every word, "making you believe, through the artifact, that such was my intent."

Jarlaxle's face screwed up in one of his very rare expressions of confusion, and his dagger arm began to slip lower. "What are you about?" he asked, his anger seemingly displaced now by honest curiosity.

"They are coming for you," Entreri vaguely explained. "You have to be prepared."

"They?"

"Rai-guy and Kimmuriel," the assassin explained. "They have decided that your reign over Bregan D'aerthe is at its end. You have exposed the band to too many mighty enemies."

Jarlaxle's expression shifted several times, through a spectrum of emotions, confusion to anger. He looked down at the pouch he held in his hand.

"The artifact has deceived you," Entreri said, managing to straighten a bit as the pain at last began to wane. He reached down and, with trembling fingers, pulled the dagger out of his side and dropped it to the floor. "It pushes you past the point of reason," he went on. "And at the same time, it resents your ability to . . ."

He paused as Jarlaxle opened the pouch and reached in to touch the shard—the imitation item. Before he could begin again, Entreri noted a shimmering in the air, a bluish glow across the room. Then, suddenly, he was looking out as if through a window, at the grounds of Dallabad Oasis.

Through that portal stepped Rai-guy and Kimmuriel, along with Berg'inyon Baenre and another pair of Bregan D'aerthe soldiers.

Entreri forced himself to straighten, growled away the pain, knowing that he had to be at his best here or he would be lost indeed. He noted, then, even as Rai-guy brought forth a curious-looking lantern, that Kimmuriel had not dismissed his dimensional portal.

They were expecting the tower to fall, perhaps, or Kimmuriel was keeping open his escape route.

"You come unbidden," Jarlaxle remarked to them, and he pulled forth the shard from his pouch. "I will summon you when you are needed." The mercenary leader stood tall and imposing, his gaze locked onto Rai-guy. His expression was one of absolute competence, Entreri thought, one of command.

Rai-guy held forth the lantern, its glow bathing Jarlaxle and the shard in quiet light.

That was it, Entreri realized. That was the item to neutralize the Crystal Shard, the tip in the balance of the fight. The intruders had made one tactical error, the assassin knew, one Entreri had counted on. Their focus was the Crystal Shard, as well as it should have been, along with the assumption that Jarlaxle's toy would be the dominant artifact.

You see how they would deny you, Entreri telepathically imparted to the artifact, tucked securely into his belt. *Yet these are the ones you call to lead you to deserved glory?*

He felt the artifact's moment of confusion, felt its reply that Rai-guy would disable it only thereby to possess it, and that . . .

In that instant of confusion, Artemis Entreri exploded into motion, sending a telepathic roar into Crenshinibon, demanding that the tower be brought crumbling down. At the same time he leaped at Jarlaxle and drew forth Charon's Claw.

Indeed, caught so off its guard, the shard nearly obeyed. A violent shudder ran through the tower. It caused no real damage, but was enough of a shake to put Berg'inyon and the other two warriors, who were moving to intercept Entreri, off their balance and to interrupt Rai-guy's attempt to cast a spell.

Entreri altered direction, rushing at the closest drow warrior, batting the sword of the off-balance dark elf aside and stabbing him hard. The dark elf fell away, and the assassin brought his sword through a series of vertical sweeps, filling the air with black ash, filling the room with confusion.

He dived toward Jarlaxle into a sidelong roll. Jarlaxle stood transfixed, staring at the shard he held in his hand as if he had been betrayed.

"Forget it," the assassin cried, yanking Jarlaxle aside just as a hand crossbow dart—poisoned, of course—whistled past. "To the door," he whispered to Jarlaxle, shoving him forward. "Fight for your life!"

With a growl, Jarlaxle put the shard in his pouch and went into action beside the slashing, fighting assassin. His arm flashed repeatedly, sending a stream of daggers at Rai-guy, where they were defeated, predictably, by a stoneskin enchantment. Another barrage was sent at Kimmuriel, who merely absorbed their power into his kinetic barrier.

"Just give it to them!" Entreri cried unexpectedly. He crashed against Jarlaxle's side, taking the pouch back and tossing it to Rai-guy and Kimmuriel, or rather past the two, to the far edge of the room beyond Kimmuriel's magic door. Rai-guy turned immediately, trying to keep the mighty artifact in the glow of his lantern, and Kimmuriel scrambled for it. Entreri saw his one desperate chance.

He grabbed the surprised Jarlaxle roughly and pulled him along, charging for Kimmuriel's magical portal.

Berg'inyon met the charge head on, his two swords working furiously to find a hole in Entreri's defenses. The assassin, a rival of Drizzt Do'Urden, was no stranger to the two-handed style. He neatly parried while working around the skilled drow warrior.

Jarlaxle ducked fast under a swing by the other soldier, pulled the great feather from his magnificent hat, put it to his lips, and blew hard. The air before him filled with feathers.

The soldier cried out, slapping the things away. He hit one that did not so easily move and realized to his horror that he was now facing a ten-foot-tall, monstrous birdlike creature—a diatryma.

Entreri, too, added to the confusion by waving his sword wildly, filling the air with ash. He always kept his focus, though, kept moving around the slashing blades and toward the dimensional portal. He could easily get through it alone, he knew, and he had the real Crystal Shard, but for some reason he didn't quite understand, and didn't bother even to think about, he turned back and grabbed Jarlaxle again, pulling him behind.

The delay brought him some more pain. Rai-guy managed to fire off a volley of magic missiles that stung the assassin profoundly. Those the wizard had launched Jarlaxle's way, Entreri noted sourly, were absorbed by the broach on the band in his hat. Did this one ever run out of tricks?

"Kill them!" Entreri heard Kimmuriel yell, and he felt Berg'inyon's deadly sword coming in fast at his back.

Entreri found himself rolling, disoriented, out onto the sand of Dallabad, out the other side of Kimmuriel's magical portal. He kept his wits about him enough to keep scrambling, grabbing the similarly disoriented Jarlaxle and pulling him along.

"They have the shard!" the mercenary protested.

"Let them keep it!" Entreri cried back.

748

Behind him, on the other side of the portal, he heard Rai-guy's howling laughter. Yes, the drow wizard thought he now possessed the Crystal Shard, the assassin realized. He'd soon try to put it to use, no doubt calling forth a beam of energy as Jarlaxle had done to the fleeing spy. Perhaps that was why no pursuit came out of the portal.

As he ran, Entreri dropped his hand once more to the real Crystal Shard. He sensed that the artifact was enraged, shaken, and understood that it had not been pleased when Entreri had gone near to Jarlaxle, thus bringing it within the glow of Rai-guy's nullifying light.

"Dispel the magical doorway," he commanded the item. "Trap them and crush them."

Glancing back he saw that Kimmuriel's doorway, half of it within the province of Crenshinibon's absolute domain, was gone.

"The tower," Entreri instructed. "Bring it tumbling down and together we will construct a line of them across Faerûn!"

The promise, spoken so full of energy and enthusiasm, offering the artifact the very same thing it always offered its wielders, was seized upon immediately.

Entreri and Jarlaxle heard the ground rumbling beneath their feet.

They ran on, across the way to a campground beside the small pond of Dallabad. They heard cries from behind them, from soldiers of the fortress, and the cries of astonishment before them from traders who had come to the oasis.

Those cries only multiplied when the traders saw the truth of the two approaching, saw a dark elf coming at them!

Entreri and Jarlaxle had no time to engage the frightened, confused group. They ran straight for the horses that were tethered to a nearby wagon and pulled them free. In a few seconds, with a chorus of angry shouts and curses behind them, the duo charged out of Dallabad, riding hard, though Jarlaxle looked more than a little uncomfortable atop a horse in bright daylight.

Entreri was a fine rider, and he easily paced the dark elf, despite his posture, which was bent over and to the side in an attempt to keep his blood from flowing freely.

"They have the Crystal Shard!" Jarlaxle cried angrily. "How far can we run?"

"Their own magic defeated the artifact," Entreri lied. "It cannot help them now in their pursuit."

Behind them the first tower crashed down, and the second toppled atop the first in a thunderous explosion, all the binding energies gone, and all the magic fast dissipating to the wind.

Entreri held no illusions that Rai-guy and Kimmuriel, or their henchmen, had been caught in that catastrophe. They were too quick and too cunning. He could only hope that the wreckage had diverted them long enough for he and Jarlaxle to get far enough away. He didn't know the extent of his wounds, but he knew that they hurt badly, and that he felt very weak. The last thing he needed then was another fight with the wizard and psionicist or with a swordsman as skilled as Berg'inyon Baenre.

Fortunately, no pursuit became evident as the minutes turned to an hour, and both horses and riders had to slow to a stop, fully exhausted. In his head, Entreri heard the chanting promises of Crenshinibon, whispering to him to construct another tower then and there for shelter and rest.

He almost did it and wondered for a moment why he was even thinking of disagreeing with the Crystal Shard, whose methods seemed to lead to the very same goals that he now held himself.

With a smile of comprehension that seemed more a grimace to the pained assassin, Entreri dismissed the notion. Crenshinibon was clever indeed, sneaking always around the edges of opposition.

Besides, Artemis Entreri had not run away from Dallabad Oasis into the open desert unprepared. He slipped down from his horse, to find that he could hardly stand. Still, he managed to slip his backpack off his shoulders and drop it to the ground before him, then drop to one knee and pull at the strings.

Jarlaxle was soon beside him, helping him to open the pack.

"A potion," Entreri explained, swallowing hard, his breath becoming labored.

Jarlaxle fiddled around in the pack, producing a small vial with a bluish-white liquid within. "Healing?" he asked.

Entreri nodded and motioned for it.

Jarlaxle pulled it back. "You have much to explain," he said. "You attacked me, and you gave them the Crystal Shard."

Entreri, his brow thick with sweat, motioned again for the potion. He put his hand to his side and brought it back up, wet with blood. "A fine throw," he said to the dark elf.

"I do not pretend to understand you, Artemis Entreri," said Jarlaxle, handing over the potion. "Perhaps that is why I do so enjoy your company."

Entreri swallowed the liquid in one gulp, and fell back to a sitting position, closing his eyes and letting the soothing concoction go to work mending some of his wounds. He wished he had about five more of the things, but this one would have to suffice—and would, he believed, keep him alive and start him on the mend.

Jarlaxle watched him for a few moments, and turned his attention to a more immediate problem, glancing up at the stinging, blistering sun. "This sunlight will make for our deaths," he remarked.

In answer, Entreri shifted over and stuck his hand into his backpack, soon producing a small scale model of a brown tent. He brought it in close, whispered a few words, and tossed it off to the side. A few seconds later, the model expanded, growing to full-size and beyond.

"Enough!" Entreri said when it was big enough to comfortably hold him, the dark elf, and both of their horses.

"Not so hard to find on the open desert," Jarlaxle remarked.

"Harder than you believe," Entreri, still gasping with every word, assured him. "Once we're inside, it will recede into a pocket dimension of its own making."

Jarlaxle smiled. "You never told me you possessed such a useful desert tool," he said.

"Because I did not, until last night."

"Thus, you knew that it would come to this, with us out running in the open desert," the mercenary leader reasoned, thinking himself sly.

Far from arguing the point, Entreri merely shrugged as Jarlaxle helped him to his feet. "I hoped it would come to this," the assassin said.

Jarlaxle looked at him curiously, but didn't press the issue. Not then. He looked back in the direction of distant Dallabad, obviously wondering what had become of his former lieutenants, wondering how all of this had so suddenly come about. It was not often that the cunning Jarlaxle was confused.

* * * * *

"We have that which we desired," Kimmuriel reminded his outraged companion. "Bregan D'aerthe is ours to lead—back to the Underdark and Menzoberranzan where we belong."

"It is not the Crystal Shard!" Rai-guy protested, throwing the imitation piece to the floor.

Kimmuriel looked at him curiously. "Was our purpose to procure the item?"

"Jarlaxle still has it," Rai-guy growled back at him. "How long do you believe he will allow us our position of leadership? He should be dead, and the artifact should be mine."

Kimmuriel's sly expression did not change at the wizard's curious choice of words—words, he understood, inspired by Crenshinibon itself and the desire to hold Rai-guy as its slave. Yes, Yharaskrik had done well in teaching the drow psionicist the nuances of the powerful and dangerous artifact. Kimmuriel did agree, though, that their position was tenuous, given that mighty Jarlaxle was still alive.

Kimmuriel had never really wanted Jarlaxle as an enemy—not out of friendship to the older drow but out of simple fear. Perhaps Jarlaxle was already on his way back to Menzoberranzan, where he would rally the remaining members of Bregan D'aerthe, far more than half the band, against Rai-guy and Kimmuriel and those who might follow them back to the drow city. Perhaps Jarlaxle would call upon Gromph Baenre, the archmage of Menzoberranzan himself, to test his wizardly skills against those of Rai-guy.

It was not a pleasant thought, but Kimmuriel understood clearly that Rai-guy's frustration was far more involved with the wizard's other complaint, that the Crystal Shard and not Jarlaxle had gotten away.

"We have to find them," Rai-guy said a moment later. "I want Jarlaxle dead. How else might I ever know a reprieve?"

"You are now the leader of a mercenary band of males housed in Menzoberranzan," Kimmuriel replied. "You will find no reprieve, no break from the constant dangers and matron games. This is the trapping of power, my companion."

Rai-guy's returning expression was not one of friendship. He was angry, perhaps more so than Kimmuriel had ever seen him. He wanted the artifact desperately. So did Yharaskrik, Kimmuriel knew. Should they find a way to catch up to Jarlaxle and Crenshinibon, he had every intention of making certain that the illithid got it. Let Yharaskrik and his mighty mind flayer kin take control of Crenshinibon, study it, and destroy it. Better that than having it in Rai-guy's hands back in Menzoberranzan—if it would even agree to go to Menzoberranzan, for Yharaskrik had told Kimmuriel that the artifact drew much of its power from the sunlight. How much more on his guard might Kimmuriel have to remain with Crenshinibon as an ally? The artifact would never accept him, would never accept the fact that he, with his mental disciplines, could deny it entrance and control of his mind.

He was tempted to work against Rai-guy now, to foil the search for Jarlaxle however he might, but he understood clearly that Jarlaxle, with or without the Crystal Shard, was far too powerful an adversary to be allowed to run free.

A knock on the door drew him from his contemplation. It opened, and Berg'inyon Baenre entered, followed by several drow soldiers dragging a chained and beaten Sharlotta Vespers behind them. More drow soldiers followed, escorting a bulky and imposing ratman.

Kimmuriel motioned for Sharlotta's group to move aside, that he could face the ratman directly.

"Gord Abrix at your service, good Kimmuriel Oblodra," the ratman said, bowing low.

Kimmuriel stared at him hard. "You lead the wererats of Calimport now?" he asked in his halting command of the common tongue.

Gord nodded. "The wererats in the service of House Basadoni," he said. "In the service of—"

"That is all you need to know, and all that you would ever be wise to speak," Rai-guy growled at him and the wererat, as imposing as he was, inevitably shrank back from the dark elves.

"Get him out of here," Kimmuriel commanded the drow escorts, in his own language. "Tell him we will call when we have decided the new course for the wererats."

Gord Abrix managed one last bow before being herded out of the room.

"And what of you?" Kimmuriel asked Sharlotta, and the mere fact that he could speak to her in his own language reminded him of this woman's resourcefulness and thus her potential usefulness.

"What have I done to deserve such treatment?" Sharlotta, stubborn to the end, replied.

"Why do you believe you had to do anything?" Kimmuriel calmly replied.

Sharlotta started to respond, but quickly realized that there was really nothing she could say against the simple logic of that question.

"We sent you to meet with Pasha Da'Daclan, a necessary engagement, yet you did not," Rai-guy reminded her.

"I was tricked by Entreri and captured," the woman protested.

"Failure is failure," Rai-guy said. "Failure brings punishment—or worse."

"But I escaped and warned you of Entreri's run to Jarlaxle's side," Sharlotta argued.

"Escaped?" Rai-guy asked incredulously. "By your own words, the halfling was too afraid to keep you and so she let you go."

Those words rang uncomfortably in Kimmuriel's thoughts. Had that, too, been a part of Entreri's plan? Because had not Kimmuriel and Rai-guy arrived at the crystalline tower in Dallabad at precisely the wrong moment for the coup? With the Crystal Shard hidden away somewhere and an imitation playing decoy to their greatest efforts? A curious thought, and one the drow psionicist figured he might just take up with that halfling, Dwahvel Tiggerwillies, at a later time.

"I came straight to you," Sharlotta said plainly and forcefully, speaking then like someone who had at last come to understand that she had absolutely nothing left to lose.

"Failure is failure," Rai-guy reiterated, just as forcefully.

"But we are not unmerciful," Kimmuriel added immediately. "I even believe in the possibility of redemption. Artemis Entreri put you in this unfortunate position, so you say, so find him and kill him. Bring me his head, or I shall take your own."

Sharlotta held up her hands helplessly. "Where to begin?" she asked. "What resources—"

"All the resources and every soldier of House Basadoni and of Dallabad, and the complete cooperation of that rat creature and its minions," Kimmuriel replied.

Sharlotta's expression remained skeptical, but there flashed a twinkle in her eyes that Kimmuriel did not miss. She was outraged at Artemis Entreri for all of this, at least as much as were Rai-guy and Kimmuriel. Yes, she was cunning and a worthy adversary. Her efforts to find and destroy Entreri would certainly aid Kimmuriel and Rai-guy's efforts to neutralize Jarlaxle and the dangerous Crystal Shard.

"When do I begin?" Sharlotta asked.

"Why are you still here?" Kimmuriel asked.

The woman took the cue and began scrambling to her feet. The drow guards took the cue, too, and rushed to help her up, quickly unlocking her chains.

Chapter 15

Dear Dwahvel

"Ah, my friend, how you have deceived me," Jarlaxle whispered to Entreri, whose wounds had far from healed, leaving him in a weakened, almost helpless state. As Entreri had floated into semiconsciousness, Jarlaxle, possessed of the magic to heal him fully, had instead taken the time to consider all that had happened.

He was in the process of trying to figure out if Entreri had saved him or damned him when he heard an all-too familiar call.

Jarlaxle's gaze fell over Entreri and a great smile widened on his black-skinned face. Crenshinibon! The man had Crenshinibon! Jarlaxle replayed the events in his mind and quickly figured that Entreri had done more than simply cut the pouch loose from Jarlaxle's belt in that first, unexpected attack. No, the clever—so clever!—human had switched Jarlaxle's pouch for an imitation pouch, complete with an imitation Crystal Shard.

"My sneaky companion," the mercenary remarked, though he wasn't sure if Entreri could hear him or not. "It is good to know that once again, I have not underestimated you!" As he finished, the mercenary leader went for Entreri's belt pouch, smiling all the while.

The assassin's hand snapped up and grabbed Jarlaxle by the arm.

Jarlaxle had a dagger in his free hand in the blink of an eye, prepared to stab it through the nearly helpless man's heart, but he noted that Entreri wasn't pressing the attack any further. The assassin wasn't reaching for his dagger or any other weapon, but rather, was staring at Jarlaxle plaintively. In his head, Jarlaxle could hear the Crystal Shard calling to him, beckoning him to finish this man off and take back the artifact that was rightfully his.

He almost did it, despite the fact that Crenshinibon's call wasn't nearly as powerful and melodious as it had been when he had been in possession of the artifact.

"Do not," Entreri whispered to him. "You cannot control it."

Jarlaxle pulled back, staring hard at the man. "But you can?"

"That is why it is calling to you," Entreri replied, his breath even more labored than it had been earlier, and blood flowing again from the wound in his side. "The Crystal Shard has no hold over me."

"And why is that?" Jarlaxle asked doubtfully. "Has Artemis Entreri taken up the moral code of Drizzt Do'Urden?"

Entreri started to chuckle, but grimaced instead, the pain nearly unbearable. "Drizzt and I are not so different in many ways," he explained. "In discipline, at least."

"And discipline alone will keep the Crystal Shard from controlling you?" Jarlaxle asked, his tone still one of abject disbelief. "So, you are saying that I am not as disciplined as either of—"

"No!" Entreri growled, and he nearly came up to a sitting position as he tightened his side against a wave of pain.

"No," he said more calmly a moment later, easing back and breathing hard. "Drizzt's code denied the artifact, as does my own—not a code of morality, but one of independence."

Jarlaxle fell back a bit, his expression going from doubtful to curious. "Why did you take it?"

Entreri looked at him and started to respond but wound up just grimacing. Jarlaxle reached under the folds of his cloak and produced a small orb, which he held out to Entreri as he began to chant.

The assassin felt better almost immediately, felt his wound closing and his breathing easier to control. Jarlaxle chanted for a few seconds, each one making Entreri feel that much better, but long before the healing had been completely facilitated, the mercenary stopped.

"Answer my question," he demanded.

"They were coming to kill you," Entreri replied.

"Obviously," said Jarlaxle. "Could you not have merely warned me?"

"It would not have been enough," Entreri insisted. "There were too many against you, and they knew that your primary weapon would be the artifact. Thus, they neutralized it, temporarily."

Jarlaxle's first instinct was to demand the Crystal Shard again, that he could go back and repay Rai-guy and Kimmuriel for their treachery.

He held the thought, though, and let Entreri go on.

"They were right in wanting to take it from you," the assassin finished boldly.

Jarlaxle glared at him but just for a moment.

"Step back from it," Entreri advised. "Shut out its call and consider the actions of Jarlaxle over the last few tendays. You could not remain on the surface unless your true identity remained secret, yet you brought forth crystalline towers! Bregan D'aerthe, for all of its power, and with all of the power of Crenshinibon behind it, could not rule the world—not even the city of Calimport—yet look at what you tried to do."

Jarlaxle started to respond several times, but each of his arguments died in his throat before he could begin to offer them. The assassin was right, he knew. He had erred, and badly.

"We cannot go back and try to explain this to the usurpers," the mercenary remarked.

Entreri shook his head. "It was the Crystal Shard that inspired the coup against you," he explained, and Jarlaxle fell back as if slapped. "You were too cunning, but Crenshinibon figured that ambitious Rai-guy would easily fall to its chaotic plans."

"You say that to placate me," Jarlaxle accused.

"I say that because it is the truth, nothing more," Entreri replied. Then he had to pause and grimace as a spasm of pain came over him. "And, if you take the time to consider it, you know that it is. Crenshinibon kept you moving in its preferred direction but not without interference."

"The Crystal Shard did not control me, or it did. You cannot have it both ways."

"It did manipulate you. How can you doubt that?" Entreri replied. "But not to the level that it knew it could manipulate Rai-guy."

"I went to Dallabad to destroy the crystal tower, something the artifact surely did not desire," Jarlaxle argued, "and yet, I could have done it! All interference from the shard was denied."

He continued, or tried to, but Entreri easily cut him short. "You *could* have done it?" the assassin asked incredulously.

Jarlaxle stammered to reply. "Of course."

"But you did not?"

"I saw no reason to drop the tower as soon as I knew that I could . . ." Jarlaxle started to explain, but when he actually heard the words coming out of his mouth, it hit him, and hard. He had been duped. He, the master of intrigue, had been fooled into believing that he was in control.

"Leave it with me," Entreri said to him. "The Crystal Shard tries to manipulate me, constantly, but it has nothing to offer me that I truly desire, and thus, it has no power over me."

"It will wear at you," Jarlaxle told him. "It will find every weakness and exploit them."

Entreri nodded. "Its time is running short," he remarked.

Jarlaxle looked at him curiously.

"I would not have spent the energy and the time pulling you away from those wretches if I did not have a plan," the assassin remarked.

"Tell me."

"In time," the assassin promised. "Now I beg of you not to take the Crystal Shard, and I beg of you, too, to allow me to rest."

He settled back and closed his eyes, knowing full well that the only defense he would have if Jarlaxle came at him was the Crystal Shard. He knew that if he used the artifact, it would likely find many, many ways to weaken his defenses and the effect might be that he would abandon his mission and simply let the artifact become his guide.

His guide to destruction, he knew, and perhaps to a fate worse than death.

When Entreri looked at Jarlaxle, he was somewhat comforted, for he saw again that clever and opportunistic demeanor, that visage of one who thought things through carefully before taking any definitive and potentially rash actions. Given all that Entreri had just explained to the mercenary drow, the retrieval of Crenshinibon would have to fall into that very category. No, he trusted that Jarlaxle would not move against him. The mercenary drow would let things play out a bit longer before making any move to alter a situation he obviously didn't fully comprehend.

With that thought in mind, Entreri fell fast asleep.

Even as he was drifting off, he felt the healing magic of Jarlaxle's orb falling over him again.

*   *   *   *   *

The halfling was surprised to see her fingers trembling as she carefully unrolled the note.

"Why Artemis, I did not even know you could write," Dwahvel said with a snicker, for the lines on the parchment were beautifully constructed, if a bit spare and efficient for Dwahvel's flamboyant flair. "My dear Dwahvel," she read aloud, and she paused and considered the words, not certain how she should take that greeting. Was it a formal and proper heading, or a sign of true friendship?

It occurred to the halfling then how little she really understood what went on inside of the heart of Artemis Entreri. The assassin had always claimed that his only desire was to be the very best, but if that was true why didn't he put the Crystal Shard to devastating use soon after acquiring it? And Dwahvel knew that he had it. Her contacts at Dallabad had described in detail the tumbling of the crystalline towers, and the flight of a human, Entreri, and a dark elf, whom Dwahvel had to believe must be Jarlaxle.

All indications were that Entreri's plan had succeeded. Even without her eyewitness accounts and despite the well-earned reputations of his adversaries, Dwahvel had never doubted the man.

The halfling moved to her doorway and made certain it was locked. Then she took a seat at her small night table and placed the parchment flat upon it, holding down the ends with paperweights fashioned of huge jewels, and read on, deciding to hold her analysis for the second read through.

My dear Dwahvel,

And so the time has come for us to part ways, and I do so with more than a small measure of regret. I will miss our talks, my little friend. Rarely have I known one I could trust enough to so speak what was truly on my mind. I will do so now, one final time, not in any hopes that you will advise me of my way, but only so that I might more clearly come to understand my own feelings on these matters . . . but that was always the beauty of our talks, was it not?

Now that I consider those discussions, I recognize that you rarely offered any advice. In fact, you rarely spoke at all but simply listened. As I listened to my own words, and in hearing them, in explaining my thoughts and feelings to another, I came to sort them through. Was it your expressions, a simple nod, an arched eyebrow, that led me purposefully down different roads of reasoning?

I know not.

I know not—that has apparently become the litany of my existence, Dwahvel. I feel as if the foundation upon which I have built my beliefs and actions is not a solid thing, but one as shifting as the sands of the desert. When I was younger, I knew all the answers to all the questions. I existed in a world of surety and certainty. Now that I am older, now that I have seen four decades of life, the only thing I know for certain is that I know nothing for certain.

It was so much easier to be a young man of twenty, so much easier to walk the world with a purpose grounded in—

Grounded in hatred, I suppose, and in the need to be the very best at my dark craft. That was my purpose, to be the greatest warrior in all of the world, to etch my name into the histories of Faerûn. So many people believed that I wished to achieve that out of simple pride, that I wanted people to tremble at the mere mention of my name for the sake of my vanity.

They were partially right, I suppose. We are all vain, whatever arguments we might make against the definition. For me, though, the desire to further my reputation was not as important as the desire—no, not the desire, but the need—truly to be the very best at my craft. I welcomed the increase in reputation, not for the sake of my pride, but because I knew that having such fear weaving through the emotional armor of my opponents gave me even more of an advantage.

A trembling hand does not thrust the blade true.

I still aspire to the pinnacle, fear not, but only because it offers me some purpose in a life that increasingly brings me no joy.

759

It seems a strange twist to me that I learned of the barren nature of my world only when I defeated the one person who tried in so many ways to show that very thing to me. Drizzt Do'Urden—how I still hate him!—perceived my life as an empty thing, a hollow trapping with no true benefit and no true happiness. I never really disagreed with his assessment, I merely believed that it did not matter. His reason for living was ever based upon his friends and community, while mine was more a life of the self. Either way, it seems to me as if it is just a play, and a pointless one, an act for the pleasure of the viewing gods, a walk that takes us up hills we perceive as huge, but that are really just little mounds, and through valleys that appear so very deep, but are really nothing at all that truly matters. All the pettiness of life itself is my complaint, I fear.

Or perhaps it was not Drizzt who showed me the shifting sands beneath my feet. Perhaps it was Dwahvel, who gave to me something I've rarely known and never known well.

A friend? I am still not certain that I understand the concept, but if I ever bother to attempt to sort through it, I will use our time together as a model.

Thus, this is perhaps a letter of apology. I should not have forced Sharlotta Vespers upon you, though I trust that you tortured her to death as I instructed and buried her far, far away.

How many times you asked me my plans, and always I merely laughed, but you should know, dear Dwahvel, that my intent is to steal a great and powerful artifact before other interested parties get their hands upon it. It is a desperate attempt, I know, but I cannot help myself, for the artifact calls to me, demands of me that I take it from its current, less-than-able wielder.

So I will have it, because I am indeed the best at my craft, and I will be gone, far, far from this place, perhaps never to return.

Farewell, Dwahvel Tiggerwillies, in whatever venture you attempt. You owe me nothing, I assure you, and yet I feel as if I am in your debt. The road before me is long and fraught with peril, but I have my goal in sight. If I attain it, nothing will truly bring me any harm.

Farewell!

—AE

Dwahvel Tiggerwillies pushed aside the parchment and wiped a tear from her eye, and laughed at the absurdity of it all. If anyone had told her months before that she would regret the day Artemis Entreri walked out of her life, she would have laughed at him and called him a fool.

But here it was, a letter as intimate as any of the discussions Dwahvel had shared with Entreri. She found that she missed those discussions already, or perhaps she lamented that there would be no such future talks with the man. None in the near future, at least.

Entreri would also miss those talks by his own words. That struck Dwahvel profoundly. To think that she had so engaged this man—this killer who had secretly ruled Calimport's streets off and on for more than twenty years. Had anyone ever become so close to Artemis Entreri?

None who were still alive, Dwahvel knew.

She reread the ending of the letter, the obvious lies concerning Entreri's intentions. He had taken care not to mention anything that would tell the remaining dark elves that Dwahvel knew anything about them or the stolen artifact, or anything about his proffering of the Crystal Shard. His lie about his instructions concerning Sharlotta certainly added even more security to Dwahvel, buying her, should the need arise, some compassion from the woman and her secret backers.

That thought sent a shudder along Dwahvel's spine. She really didn't want to depend on the compassion of dark elves!

It would not come to that, she realized. Even if the trail led to her and her establishment, she could willingly and eagerly show Sharlotta the letter and Sharlotta would then see her as a valuable asset.

Yes, Artemis Entreri had taken great pains to cover Dwahvel's efforts in the conspiracy, and that, more than any of the kind words he had written to her, revealed to her the depth of their friendship.

"Run far, my friend, and hide in deep holes," she whispered.

She gently rerolled the parchment and placed it in one of the drawers of her crafted bureau. The sound of that closing drawer resonated hard against Dwahvel's heart.

She would indeed miss Artemis Entreri.

Part 3

Now What?

There is a simple beauty in the absolute ugliness of demons. There is no ambiguity there, no hesitation, no misconception, about how one must deal with such creatures.

You do not parlay with demons. You do not hear their lies. You cast them out, destroy them, rid the world of them—even if the temptation is present to utilize their powers to save what you perceive to be a little corner of goodness.

This is a difficult concept for many to grasp and has been the downfall of many wizards and priests who have errantly summoned demons and allowed the creatures to move beyond their initial purpose—the answering of a question, perhaps—because they were tempted by the power offered by the creature. Many of these doomed spellcasters thought they would be doing good by forcing the demons to their side, by bolstering their cause, their army, with demonic soldiers. What ill, they supposed, if the end result proved to the greater good? Would not a goodly king be well advised to add "controlled" demons to his cause if goblins threatened his lands?

I think not, because if the preservation of goodness relies upon the use of such obvious and irredeemable evil to defeat evil, then there is nothing, truly, worth saving.

The sole use of demons, then, is to bring them forth only in times when they must betray the cause of evil, and only in a setting so controlled that there is no hope of their escape. Cadderly has done this within the secure summoning chamber of the Spirit Soaring, as have, I am sure, countless priests and wizards. Such a summoning is not without peril, though, even if the circle of protection is perfectly formed, for there is always a temptation that goes with the manipulation of powers such as a balor or a nalfeshnie.

Within that temptation must always lie the realization of irredeemable evil. Irredeemable. Without hope. That concept, redemption, must be the crucial determinant in any such dealings. Temper your blade when redemption is possible, hold it when redemption is at hand, and strike hard and without remorse when your opponent is beyond any hope of redemption.

Where on that scale does Artemis Entreri lie, I wonder? Is the man truly beyond help and hope?

Yes, to the former, I believe, and no to the latter. There is no help for Artemis Entreri because the man would never accept any. His greatest flaw is his pride—not the boasting pride of so many lesser warriors, but the pride of absolute independence and unbending self-reliance. I could tell him his errors, as could anyone who has come to know him in any way, but he would not hear my words.

Yet perhaps there may be hope of some redemption for the man. I know not the source of his anger, though it must have been great. And yet I will not allow that the source, however difficult and terrible it might have been, in any way excuses the man from his actions. The blood on Entreri's sword and trademark dagger is his own to wear.

He does not wear it well, I believe. It burns at his skin as might the breath of a black dragon and gnaws at all that is within him. I saw that during our last encounter, a quiet and dull ache at the side of his dark eyes. I had him beaten, could have killed him, and I believe that in many ways he hoped I would finish the task and be done with it, and end his mostly self-imposed suffering.

That ache is what held my blade, that hope within me that somewhere deep inside Artemis Entreri there is the understanding that his path needs to change, that the road he currently walks is one of emptiness and ultimate despair. Many thoughts coursed my mind as I stood there, weapons in hand, with him defenseless before me. How could I strike when I saw that pain in his eyes and knew that such pain might well be the precursor to redemption? And yet how could I not, when I was well aware that letting Artemis Entreri walk out of that crystalline tower might spell the doom of others?

Truly it was a dilemma, a crisis of conscience and of balance. I found my answer in that critical moment in the memory of my father, Zaknafein. To Entreri's thinking, I know, he and Zaknafein are not so different, and there are indeed similarities. Both existed in an environment hostile and to their respective perceptions evil. Neither, to their perceptions, did either go out of his way to kill anyone who did not deserve it. Are the warriors and assassins who fight for the wretched pashas of Calimport any better than the soldiers of the drow houses? Thus, in many ways, the actions of Zaknafein and those of Artemis Entreri are quite similar. Both existed in a world of intrigue, danger, and evil. Both survived their imprisonment through ruthless means. If Entreri views his world, his prison, as full of wretchedness as Zaknafein viewed Menzoberranzan, then is not Entreri as entitled to his manner as was Zaknafein, the weapons master who killed many, many dark elves in his tenure as patron of House Do'Urden?

It is a comparison I realized when first I went to Calimport, in pursuit of Entreri, who had taken Regis as prisoner (and even that act had justification, I must admit), and a comparison that truly troubled me. How close are they, given their abilities with the blade and their apparent willingness to kill? Was it, then, some inner feelings for Zaknafein that stayed my blade when I could have cut Entreri down?

No, I say, and I must believe, for Zaknafein was far more discerning in whom he would kill or would not kill. I know the truth of Zaknafein's heart. I know that Zaknafein was possessed of the ability to love, and the reality of Artemis Entreri simply cannot hold up against that.

Not in his present incarnation, at least, but is there hope that the man will find a light beneath the murderous form of the assassin?

Perhaps, and I would be glad indeed to hear that the man so embraced that light. In truth, though, I doubt that anyone or anything will ever be able to pull that lost flame of compassion through the thick and seemingly impenetrable armor of dispassion that Artemis Entreri now wears.

—Drizzt Do'Urden

Chapter 16

A Dark Note on a Sunny Day

Danica sat on a ledge of an imposing mountain beside the field that housed the magnificent Spirit Soaring, a cathedral of towering spires and flying buttresses, of great and ornate windows of multicolored glass. Acres of grounds were striped by well-maintained hedgerows, many of them shaped into the likeness of animals, and one wrapping around and around itself in a huge maze.

The cathedral was the work of Danica's husband, Cadderly, a mighty priest of Deneir, the god of knowledge. This structure had been Cadderly's most obvious legacy, but his greatest one, to Danica's reasoning, were the twin children romping around the entrance to the maze and their younger sibling, sleeping within the cathedral. The twins had gone running into the hedgerow maze, much to the dismay of the dwarf Pikel Bouldershoulder. Pikel, a practitioner of the druidic ways—magic that his surly brother Ivan still denied—had created the maze and the other amazing gardens.

Pikel had gone running into the maze behind the children screaming, "*Eeek!*" and other such Pikelisms, and pulling at his green-dyed hair and beard. His maze wasn't quite ready for visitors yet, and the roots hadn't properly set.

Of course, as soon as Pikel had gone running in, the twins had sneaked right back out and were now playing quietly in front of the maze entrance. Danica didn't know how far along the confusing corridors the green-bearded dwarf had gone, but she had heard his voice fast receding and figured that he'd be lost in the maze, for the third time that day, soon enough.

A wind gust came whipping across the mountain wall, blowing Danica's thick mop of strawberry blond hair into her face. She blew some strands out of her mouth and tossed her head to the side, just in time to see Cadderly walking toward her.

What a fine figure he cut in his tan-white tunic and trousers, his light blue silken cape and his trademark blue, wide-brimmed, and plumed hat. Cadderly had aged greatly while constructing the Spirit Soaring, to the point where he and Danica honestly believed he would expire. Much to Danica's dismay Cadderly had expected to die and had accepted that as the sacrifice necessary for the construction of the monumental library. Soon after he had completed the construction of the main building—the details, like the ornate designs of the many doors and the golden leaf work around the beautiful archways, might never be completed—the aging process had reversed, and the man had grown younger almost as fast as he'd aged. Now he seemed a man in his late twenties with a spring in his step, and a twinkle in his eye every time he glanced Danica's way. Danica had even worried that this process would continue, and that soon she'd find herself raising four children instead of three.

He eventually grew no younger, though, stopping at the point where Cadderly seemed every bit the vivacious and healthy young man he had been before all the trouble had started within the Edificant Library, the structure that had stood on this ground before the advent of the chaos curse and the destruction of the old order of Deneir. The willingness to sacrifice everything for the new cathedral and the new order had sufficed in the eyes of Deneir, and thus, Cadderly Bonaduce had been given back his life, a life so enriched by the addition of his wife and their children.

"I had a visitor this morning," Cadderly said to her when he moved beside her. He cast a glance at the twins and smiled all the wider when he heard another frantic call from the lost Pikel.

Danica marveled at how her husband's gray eyes seemed to smile as well. "A man from Carradoon," she replied, nodding. "I saw him enter."

"Bearing word from Drizzt Do'Urden," Cadderly explained, and Danica turned to face him directly, suddenly very interested. She and Cadderly had met the unusual dark elf the previous year and had taken him back to the northland using one of Cadderly's wind-walking spells.

Danica spent a moment studying Cadderly, considering the intense expression upon his normally calm face. "He has retrieved the Crystal Shard," she reasoned, for when last she and Cadderly had been with

770

Drizzt and his human companion, Catti-brie, they had spoken of just that. Drizzt promised that he would retrieve the ancient, evil artifact and bring it to Cadderly to be destroyed.

"He did," Cadderly said.

He handed a roll of parchment sheets to Danica. She took them and unrolled them. A smile crossed her face when she learned of the fate of Drizzt's lost friend, Wulfgar, freed from his prison at the clutches of the demon Errtu. By the time she got to the second page, though, Danica's mouth drooped open, for the note went on to describe the subsequent theft of the Crystal Shard by a rogue dark elf named Jarlaxle, who had sent one of his drow soldiers to Drizzt in the guise of Cadderly.

Danica paused and looked up, and Cadderly took back the parchments. "Drizzt believes the artifact has likely gone underground, back to the dark elf city of Menzoberranzan, where Jarlaxle makes his home," he explained.

"Well, good enough for Menzoberranzan, then," Danica said in all seriousness.

She and Cadderly had discussed the powers of the sentient shard at length, and she understood it to be a tool of destruction—destruction of the wielder's enemies, of the wielder's allies, and ultimately of the wielder himself. There had never been, and to Cadderly's reasoning, could never be, a different outcome where Crenshinibon was concerned. To possess the Crystal Shard was, ultimately, a terminal disease, and woe to all those nearby.

Cadderly was shaking his head before Danica ever finished the sentiment. "The Crystal Shard is an artifact of sunlight, which is perhaps, in the measure of symbolism, its greatest perversion."

"But the drow are creatures of their dark holes," Danica reasoned. "Let them take it and be gone. Perhaps in the Underdark, the Crystal Shard's power will be lessened, even destroyed."

Again Cadderly was shaking his head. "Who is the stronger?" he asked. "The artifact or the wielder?"

"It sounds as if this particular dark elf was quite cunning," Danica replied. "To have fooled Drizzt Do'Urden is no easy feat, I would guess."

Cadderly shrugged and grinned. "I doubt that Crenshinibon, once it finds its way into the new wielder's heart—which it surely will unless this Jarlaxle is akin in heart to Drizzt Do'Urden—will allow him to retreat to the depths," he explained. "It is not necessarily a question of who is the stronger. The subtlety of the artifact is its ability to manipulate its wielder into agreement, not dominate him."

"And the heart of a dark elf would be easily manipulated," Danica reasoned.

"A typical dark elf, yes," Cadderly agreed.

A few moments of quiet passed as each considered the words and the new information.

"What are we to do, then?" Danica asked at length. "If you believe that the Crystal Shard will not allow a retreat to the sunless Underdark, then are we to allow it to wreak havoc on the surface world? Do we even know where it might be?"

Still deep in thought, Cadderly did not answer right away. The question of what to do, of what their responsibilities might be in this situation, went to the very core of the philosophical trappings of power. Was it Cadderly's place, because of his clerical power, to hunt down the new wielder of the Crystal Shard, this dark elf thief, and take the item by force, bringing it to its destruction? If that was the case, then what of every other injustice in the world? What of the pirates on the Sea of Fallen Stars? Was Cadderly to charter a boat and go out hunting them? What of the Red Wizards of Thay, that notorious band? Was it Cadderly's duty to seek them out and do battle with each and every one? Then there were the Zhentarim, the Iron Throne, the Shadow Thieves. . . .

"Do you remember when we met here with Drizzt Do'Urden and Catti-brie?" Danica asked, and it seemed to Cadderly that the woman was reading his mind. "Drizzt was distressed when we realized that our summoning of the demon Errtu had released the great beast from its banishment—a banishment handed out to it by Drizzt years before. What did you tell Drizzt about that to calm him?"

"The releasing of Errtu was no major problem," Cadderly admitted again. "There would always be a demon available to a sorcerer with evil designs. If not Errtu, then another."

"Errtu was just one of a number of agents of chaos," Danica reasoned, "as the Crystal Shard is just another element of chaos. Any havoc it brings would merely replace the myriad other tools of chaos in wreaking exactly that, correct?"

Cadderly smiled at her, staring intently into the seemingly limitless depths of her almond-shaped brown eyes. How he loved this woman. She was so much his partner in every aspect of his life. Intelligent and possessed of the greatest discipline Cadderly had ever known, Danica always helped him through any difficult questions and choices, just by listening and offering suggestions.

"It is the heart that begets evil, not the instruments of destruction," he completed the thought for her.

"Is the Crystal Shard the tool or the heart?" Danica asked.

"That is the question, is it not?" Cadderly replied. "Is the artifact akin to a summoned monster, an instrument of destruction for one whose heart was already tainted? Or is it a manipulator, a creator of evil where there would otherwise be none?" He held out his arms, having no real answer for that. "In either case, I believe I will contact some extraplanar sources and see if I can locate the artifact and this dark elf, Jarlaxle. I wish to know the use to which he has put the Crystal Shard, or perhaps even more troubling, the use to which the Crystal Shard plans to put him."

Danica started to ask what he might be talking about, but she figured it out before she could utter the words, and her lips grew very thin. Might the Crystal Shard, rather than let this Jarlaxle creature take it to the lightless Underdark, use him to spearhead an invasion by an army of drow? Might the Crystal Shard use the position and race of its new wielder to create havoc beyond anything it had ever known before? Even worse for them personally, if Jarlaxle had stolen the artifact by using an imitation of Cadderly, then Jarlaxle certainly knew of Cadderly. If Jarlaxle knew, the Crystal Shard knew—and knew, too, that Cadderly might have information about how to destroy it. A flash of worry crossed Danica's face, one that Cadderly could not miss, and she instinctively turned to regard her children.

"I will try to discover where he might be with the artifact, and what trouble they together might already be causing," Cadderly explained, not reading Danica's expression very well and wondering, perhaps, if she was doubting him.

"You do that," the more-than-convinced woman said in all seriousness. "Right away."

A squeal from inside the maze turned them both in that direction.

"Pikel," the woman explained.

Cadderly smiled. "Lost again?"

"Again?" Danica asked. "Or still?"

They heard some rumbling off to the side and saw Pikel's more traditional brother, Ivan Bouldershoulder, rolling toward the maze grumbling with every step. "Doo-dad," the yellow-bearded dwarf said sarcastically, referring to Pikel's pronunciation of his calling. "Yeah, Doo-dad," Ivan grumbled. "Can't even find his way out of a hedgerow."

"And you will help him?" Cadderly called to the dwarf.

Ivan turned curiously, noting the pair, it seemed, for the first time. "Been helpin' him all me life," he snorted.

Both Cadderly and Danica nodded and allowed Ivan his fantasy. They knew well enough, if Ivan did not, that his helping Pikel more often caused problems for both of the dwarves. Sure enough, within the span of a few minutes, Ivan's calls about being lost echoed no less than Pikel's. Cadderly and Danica, and the twins sitting outside the devious maze, thoroughly enjoyed the entertainment.

* * * * *

A few hours later, after preparing the proper sequence of spells and after checking on the magical circle of protection the young-again priest always used when dealing with even the most minor of the creatures of the lower planes, Cadderly sat in a cross-legged position on the floor of his summoning chamber, chanting the incantation that would bring a minor demon, an imp, to him.

A short while later, the tiny, bat-winged, horned creature materialized in the protection circle. It hopped all about, confused and angry, finally focusing on Cadderly. It spent some time studying the man, no doubt trying to get some clues to his demeanor. Imps were often summoned to the material plane, sometimes for information, other times to serve as familiars for wizards of evil weal.

"Deneir?" the imp asked in a coughing, raspy voice that Cadderly thought seemed both typical and fitting to its smoky natural environment. "You wear the clothing of a priest of Deneir."

The creature was staring at the red band on his hat, Cadderly knew, on which was set a porcelain-and-gold pendant depicting a candle burning above an eye, the symbol of Deneir.

Cadderly nodded.

"*Ahck!*" the imp said and spat upon the ground.

"Hoping for a wizard in search of a familiar?" Cadderly asked slyly.

"Hoping for anything other than you, priest of Deneir," the imp replied.

"Accept that which has been given to you," Cadderly said. "A glimpse of the material plane is better than none, after all, and a reprieve from your hellish existence."

"What do you want, priest of Deneir?"

"Information," Cadderly replied, but even as he said it, he realized that his questions would be difficult indeed, perhaps too much so for so minor a demon. "All that I require of you is that you give to me the name of a greater demonic source, that I might bring it forth."

The imp looked at him curiously, tilting its head as a dog might, and licking its thin lips with a pointed tongue.

"Nothing greater than a nalfeshnie," Cadderly quickly clarified, seeing the impish smile growing and wanting to limit the power of whatever being he next summoned. A nalfeshnie was no minor demon, but was certainly within Cadderly's power to control, at least long enough for him to get what he needed.

"Oh, I has a name for you, priest of Deneir . . ." the imp started to say, but it jerked spasmodically as Cadderly began to chant a spell of torment. The imp fell to the floor, writhing and spitting curses.

"The name?" Cadderly asked. "And I warn you, if you deceive me and try to trick me into summoning a greater creature, I will dismiss it promptly and find you again. This torment is nothing compared to that which I will exact upon you!"

He said the words with conviction and with strength, though in truth, it pained the gentle man to be doing even this level of torture, even upon a wretched imp. He reminded himself of the importance of his quest and bolstered his resolve.

"Mizferac!" the imp screamed out. "A glabrezu, and a stupid one!"

Cadderly released the imp from his spell of torment, and the creature gave a beat of its wings and righted itself, staring at him coldly. "I did your bidding, evil priest of Deneir. Let me go!"

"Be gone, then," said Cadderly, and even as the little beast began fading from view, offering a few obscene gestures, Cadderly had to toss in, "I will tell Mizferac what you said concerning its intelligence."

He did indeed enjoy that last expression of panic on the face of the little imp.

Cadderly brought Mizferac in later that same day and found the towering pincer-armed glabrezu to be the embodiment of all that he hated about demons. It was a nasty, vicious, conniving, and wretchedly self-serving creature that tried to get as much gain as it could out of every word. Cadderly kept their meeting short and to the point. The demon was to inquire of other extra-planar creatures about the whereabouts of a dark elf named Jarlaxle, who was likely on the surface of Faerûn. Furthermore, Cadderly put a powerful geas on the demon, preventing it from actually walking the material world, but retreating only back to the Abyss and using sources to discern the information.

"That will take longer," Mizferac said.

"I will call on you daily," Cadderly replied, putting as much anger without adding any passion whatsoever as he could into his timbre. "Each passing day I will grow more impatient, and your torment will increase."

"You make a terrible enemy in Mizferac, Cadderly Bonaduce, Priest of Deneir," the glabrezu replied, obviously trying to shake him with its knowledge of his name.

Cadderly, who heard the mighty song of Deneir as clearly as if it was a chord within his own heart, merely smiled at the threat. "If ever you find yourself free of your bonds and able to walk the surface of Toril, do come and find me, Mizferac the fool. It will please me greatly to reduce your physical form to ash and banish your spirit from this world for a hundred years."

The demon growled, and Cadderly dismissed it, simply and with just a wave of his hand and an utterance of a single word. He had heard every threat a demon could give and many times. After the trials the young priest had known in his life, from facing a red dragon to doing battle with his own father, to warring against the chaos curse, to, most of all, offering his very life up as sacrifice to his god, there was little any creature, demonic or not, could say to him that would frighten him.

He recalled the glabrezu every day for the next tenday, until finally the fiend brought him some news of the Crystal Shard and the drow, Jarlaxle, along with the surprising information that Jarlaxle no longer possessed the artifact, but traveled in the company of a human, Artemis Entreri, who did.

Cadderly knew that name well from the stories that Drizzt and Catti-brie had told him in their short stay at the Spirit Soaring. The man was an assassin, a brutal killer. According to the demon, Entreri, along with the Crystal Shard and the dark elf Jarlaxle, was on his way to the Snow-flake Mountains.

Cadderly rubbed his chin as the glabrezu passed along the informa-tion—information that he knew to be true, for he had enacted a spell to make certain the demon had not lied to him.

"I have done as you demanded," the glabrezu growled, clicking its pincer-ended appendages anxiously. "I am released from your bonds, Cadderly Bonaduce."

"Then begone, that I do not have to look upon your ugly face any longer," the young priest replied.

The demon narrowed its huge eyes threateningly and clicked its pin-cers. "I will not forget this," it promised.

"I would be disappointed if you did," Cadderly replied casually.

"I was told that you have young children, fool," Mizferac remarked, fading from view.

"Mizferac, *ehugu-winance!*" Cadderly cried, catching the departing demon before it had dissipated back to the swirling smoke of the Abyss. Holding it in place by the sheer strength of his enchantment, Cadderly twisted the demon's physical form painfully by the might of his spell.

"Do I smell fear, human?" Mizferac asked defiantly.

Cadderly smiled wryly. "I doubt that, since a hundred years will pass before you are able to walk the material plane again." The threat, spoken openly, freed Mizferac of the summoning binding—and yet, the beast was not freed, for Cadderly had enacted another spell, one of exaction.

Mizferac created magical darkness to fill the room. Cadderly fell into his own chanting, his voice trembling with feigned terror.

"I can smell you, foolish mortal," Mizferac remarked, and Cadderly heard the voice from the side, though he guessed correctly that Mizferac was using ventriloquism to throw him off guard. The young priest was fully into the flow of Deneir's song now, hearing every beautiful note and accessing the magic quickly and completely. First he detected evil, easily locating the great negative force of the glabrezu—then another mighty negative force as the demon gated in a companion.

Cadderly held his nerve and continued casting.

"I will kill the children first, fool," Mizferac promised, and it began speaking to its new companion in the guttural tongue of the Abyss—one that Cadderly, through the use of another spell that he had enacted before he had ever brought Mizferac to him this day, understood perfectly. The glabrezu told its fellow demon to keep the foolish priest occupied while it went to hunt the children.

"I will bring them before you for sacrifice," Mizferac started to prom-ise, but the end of the sentence came out as garbled screams as Cadderly's spell went off, creating a series of spinning, slicing blades all around the two demons. The priest then brought forth a globe of light to counter Mizferac's darkness. The spectacle of Mizferac and its companion, a lesser demon that looked like a giant gnat, getting sliced and chopped was revealed.

Mizferac roared and uttered a guttural word—one designed to teleport him away, Cadderly assumed. It failed. The young priest, so strong in the flow of Deneir's song, was the quicker. He brought forth a prayer that dispelled the demon's magic before Mizferac could get away.

A spell of binding followed immediately, locking Mizferac firmly in place, while the magical blades continued their spinning devastation.

"I will never forget this!" Mizferac roared, words edged with outrage and agony.

"Good, then you will know better than ever to return," Cadderly growled back.

He brought forth a second blade barrier. The two demons were torn apart, their material forms ripped into dozens of bloody pieces, thus banishing them from the material plane for a hundred years. Satisfied with that, Cadderly left his summoning chamber covered in demon blood. He'd have to find a suitable spell from Deneir to clean up his clothes.

As for the Crystal Shard, he had his answers—and it seemed to him a good thing that he had bothered to check, since a dangerous assassin, an equally dangerous dark elf, and the even more dangerous Crystal Shard were apparently on their way to see him.

He had to talk to Danica, to prepare all the Spirit Soaring and the order of Deneir, for the potential battle.

Chapter 17

A Call for Help

"There is something enjoyable about these beasts, I must admit," Jarlaxle noted when he and Entreri pulled up beside a mountain pass.

The assassin quickly dismounted and ran to the ledge to view the trail below—and to view the band of orcs he suspected were still stubbornly in pursuit. The pair had left the desert behind, at long last, entering a region of broken hills and rocky trails.

"Though if I had one of my lizards from Menzoberranzan, I could simply run away to the top of the hill and over the other side," the drow went on. He took off his great plumed hat and rubbed a hand over his bald head. The sun was strong this day, but the dark elf seemed to be handling it quite well—certainly better than Entreri would have expected of any drow under this blistering sun. Again the assassin had to wonder if Jarlaxle might have a bit of magic about him to protect his sensitive eyes. "Useful beasts, the lizards of Menzoberranzan," Jarlaxle remarked. "I should have brought some to the surface with me."

Entreri gave him a smirk and a shake of his head. "It will be hard enough getting into half the towns with a drow beside me," he remarked. "How much more welcoming might they be if I rode in on a lizard?"

779

He looked back down the mountainside, and sure enough, the orc band was still pacing them, though the wretched creatures were obviously exhausted. Still, they followed as if compelled beyond their control.

It wasn't hard for Artemis Entreri to figure out exactly what might be so compelling them.

"Why can you not just take out your magical tent, that we can melt away from them?" Jarlaxle asked for the third time.

"The magic is limited," Entreri answered yet again.

He glanced back at Jarlaxle as he replied, surprised that the cunning drow would keep asking the same question. Was Jarlaxle, perhaps, trying to garner some information about the tent? Or even worse, was the Crystal Shard reaching out to the drow, subtly asking him to goad Entreri in that direction? If they did take out the tent and disappear, after all, they would have to reappear in the same place. That being true, had the Crystal Shard figured out how to send its telepathic call across the planes of existence? Perhaps the next time Entreri and Jarlaxle used the plane-shifting tent, they would return to the material plane to find an orc army, inspired by Crenshinibon, waiting for them.

"The horses grow weary," Jarlaxle noted.

"They can outrun orcs," Entreri replied.

"If we let them run free, perhaps."

"They're just orcs," Entreri muttered, though he could hardly believe how persistent this group remained.

He turned back to Jarlaxle, no longer doubting the drow's claim. The horses were indeed tired—they had been riding a long day before even realizing the orcs were following their trail. They had ridden the beasts practically into the desert sands in an effort to get out of that barren, wide-open region as quickly as possible.

Perhaps it was time to stop running.

"There are only about a score of them," Entreri remarked, watching their movements as they crawled over the lower slopes.

"Twenty against two," Jarlaxle reminded. "Let us go and hide in your tent, that the horses can rest, and come out and begin the chase anew."

"We can defeat them and drive them away," Entreri insisted, "if we choose and prepare the battlefield."

It surprised the assassin that Jarlaxle didn't look very eager about that possibility. "They're only orcs," Entreri said again.

"Are they?" Jarlaxle asked.

Entreri started to respond but paused long enough to consider the meaning behind the dark elf's words. Was this pursuit a chance encounter? Or was there something more to this seemingly nondescript band of monsters?

"You believe that Kimmuriel and Rai-guy are secretly guiding this band," Entreri stated more than asked.

Jarlaxle shrugged. "Those two have always favored using monsters as fodder," he explained. "They let the orcs—or kobolds, or whatever other creature is available—rush in to weary their opponents while they prepare the killing blow. It is nothing new in their tactics. They used such a ruse to take House Basadoni, forcing the kobolds to lead the charge and take the bulk of the casualties."

"It could be," Entreri agreed with a nod. "Or it could be a conspiracy of another sort, one with its roots in our midst."

It took Jarlaxle a few moments to sort that out. "Do you believe that I have urged the orcs on?" he asked.

In response, Entreri patted the pouch that held the Crystal Shard. "Perhaps Crenshinibon has come to believe that it needs to be rescued from our clutches," he said.

"The shard would prefer an orcish wielder to either you or me?" Jarlaxle asked doubtfully.

"I am not its wielder, nor will I ever be," Entreri answered sharply. "Nor will you, else you would have taken it from me our first night on the road from Dallabad, when I was too weak with my wounds to resist. I know this truth, so do you, and so does Crenshinibon. It understands that we are beyond its reach now, and it fears us, or fears me, at least, because it recognizes what is in my heart."

He spoke the words with perfect calm and perfect coldness, and it wasn't hard for Jarlaxle to figure out what he might be talking about. "You mean to destroy it," the drow remarked, and his tone made the sentence seem like an accusation.

"And I know how to do it," Entreri bluntly admitted. "Or at least, I know someone who knows how to do it."

The expressions that crossed Jarlaxle's handsome face ranged from incredulity to sheer anger to something less obvious, something buried deep. The assassin knew that he had taken a chance in proclaiming his intent so openly with the drow who had been fully duped by the Crystal Shard and who was still not completely convinced, despite Entreri's many reminders, that giving up the artifact had been a good thing to do. Was Jarlaxle's unreadable expression a signal to him that the Crystal Shard had indeed gotten to the drow leader once again and was even then working through, and with, Jarlaxle to find a way to get rid of Entreri's bothersome interference?

"You will never find the strength of heart to destroy it," Jarlaxle remarked.

Now it was Entreri's turn to wear a confused expression.

"Even if you discover a method, and I doubt that there is one, when the moment comes, Artemis Entreri will never find the heart to be rid of so powerful and potentially gainful an item as Crenshinibon," Jarlaxle proclaimed slyly. A grin widened across the dark elf's face. "I know you, Artemis Entreri," he said, grinning still, "and I know that you'll not throw away such power and promise, such beauty as Crenshinibon!"

781

Entreri looked at him hard. "Without the slightest hesitation," he said coldly. "And so would you, had you not fallen under its spell. I see that enchantment for what it is, a trap of temporary gain through reckless action that can only lead to complete and utter ruin. You disappoint me, Jarlaxle. I had thought you smarter than this."

Jarlaxle's expression, too, turned cold. A flash of anger lit his dark eyes. For just a moment, Entreri thought his first fight of the day was upon him, thought the dark elf would attack him. Jarlaxle closed his eyes, his body swaying as he focused his thoughts and his concentration.

"Fight the urge," the assassin found himself whispering under his breath. Entreri the consummate loner, the man who, for all his life, had counted on no one but himself, was surely surprised to hear himself now.

"Do we continue to run, or do we fight them?" Jarlaxle asked a moment later. "If these creatures are being guided by Rai-guy and Kimmuriel, we will learn of it soon enough—likely when we are fully engaged in battle. The odds of ten-to-one, of even twenty-to-one, against orcs on a mountain battlefield of our choosing does not frighten me in the least, but in truth, I do not wish to face my former lieutenants, even two-against-two. With his combination of wizardly and clerical powers, Rai-guy has variables enough to strike fear into the heart of Gromph Baenre, and there is nothing predictable, or even understandable, about many of Kimmuriel Oblodra's tactics. In all the years he has served me, I have not begun to sort the riddle that is Kimmuriel. I know only that he is extremely effective."

"Keep talking," Entreri muttered, looking back down at the orcs, who were much closer now, and at all the potential battlefield areas. "You are making me wish that I had left you and the Crystal Shard behind."

He caught a slight shift in Jarlaxle's expression as he said that, a subtle hint that perhaps the mercenary leader had been wondering all along why Entreri had bothered with both the theft and the rescue. If Entreri meant to destroy the Crystal Shard anyway, after all, why not just run away and leave it and the feud between Jarlaxle and his dangerous lieutenants behind?

"We will discuss that," Jarlaxle replied.

"Another time," Entreri said, trotting along the ledge to the right. "We have much to do, and our orc friends are in a hurry."

"Headlong into doom," Jarlaxle remarked quietly. He slid off of his horse and moved to follow Entreri.

Soon after, the pair had set up in a location on the northeastern side of the range, the steepest ascent. Jarlaxle worried that perhaps some of the orcs would come up from the other paths, the same ones they had taken, stealing from them the advantage of the higher ground, but Entreri was convinced that the artifact was calling out to the creatures insistently, and that they would alter their course to follow the most direct line to

Crenshinibon. That line would take them up several high bluffs on this side of the hills, and along narrow and easily defensible trails.

Sure enough, within a few minutes of attaining their new perch, Entreri and Jarlaxle spotted the obedient and eager orc band, scrambling over stony outcroppings below them.

Jarlaxle began his customary chatting, but Entreri wasn't listening. He turned his thoughts inward, listening for the Crystal Shard, knowing that it was calling out to the orcs. He paid close heed to its subtle emanations, knowing them all too well from his time in possession of the item, for though he had denied the Crystal Shard, had made it as clear as possible that the artifact could offer him nothing, it had not relented its tempting call.

He heard that call now, drifting out over the mountain passes, reaching out to the orcs and begging them to come and find the treasure.

Halt the call, Entreri silently commanded the artifact. *These crea-tures are not worthy to serve either you or me as slaves.*

He sensed it then, a moment of confusion from the artifact, a moment of fleeting hope—there, Entreri knew without the slightest of doubts, Crenshinibon did desire him as a wielder!—followed by . . . questions. Entreri seized the moment to interject his own thoughts into the stream of the telepathic call. He offered no words, for he didn't even speak Orcish, and doubted that the creatures would understand any of the human tongues he did speak, but merely imparted images of orc slaves, serving the master dark elf. He figured Jarlaxle would be a more impos-ing figure to orcs than he. Entreri showed them one orc being eaten by drow, another being beaten and torn apart with savage glee.

"What are you doing, my friend?" he heard Jarlaxle's insistent call, in a loud voice that told him his drow companion had likely asked that same question several times already.

"Putting a little doubt into the minds of our ugly little camp-follow-ers," Entreri replied. "Joining Crenshinibon's call to them in the hopes that they will hardly sort out one lie from the other."

Jarlaxle wore a perplexed expression indeed, and Entreri understood all the questions that were likely behind it, for he was harboring many of the same doubts. One lie from another indeed. Or were the promises of Crenshinibon truly lies? the assassin had to ask himself. Even beyond that fundamental confusion, the assassin understood that Jarlaxle would, and had to, fear Entreri's motivations. Was Entreri, perhaps, shading his words to Jarlaxle in a way that would make the mercenary drow come to agree with Entreri's assessment that he, and not the dark elf, should carry the Crystal Shard?

"Ignore whatever doubts Crenshinibon is now giving to you," Entreri said matter-of-factly, reading the dark elf's expression perfectly.

"Even if you speak the truth, I fear that you play a dangerous game with an artifact that is far beyond your understanding," Jarlaxle retorted after another introspective pause.

"I know what it is," Entreri assured him, "and I know that it understands the truth of our relationship. That is why the Crystal Shard so desperately wants to be free of me—and is thus calling to you once more."

Jarlaxle looked at him hard, and for just a moment, Entreri thought the drow might move against him.

"Do not disappoint me," the assassin said simply.

Jarlaxle blinked, took off his hat, and rubbed the sweat from his bald head again.

"There!" Entreri said, pointing down to the lower slopes, to where a fight had broken out between different factions among the orcs. Few of the ugly brutes seemed to be trying to make peace, as was the way with chaotic orcs. The slightest spark could ignite warfare within a tribe of the beasts that would continue at the cost of many lives until one side was simply wiped out. Entreri, with his imparted images of torture and slavery and images of a drow master, had done more than flick a little spark. "It would seem that some of them heeded my call over that of the artifact."

"And I had thought this day would bring some excitement," Jarlaxle remarked. "Shall we join them before they kill each other? To aid whichever side is losing, of course."

"And with our aid, that side will soon be winning," Entreri reasoned, and Jarlaxle's quick response came as no surprise.

"Of course," said the drow, "we are then honor-bound to join in with the side that is losing. It could be a complicated afternoon."

Entreri smiled as he worked his way around the ledge of the current perch, looking for a quick way down to the orcs.

By the time the pair got close to the fighting, they realized that their estimates of a score of orcs had been badly mistaken. There were at least fifty of the beasts, all running around in a frenzy now, whacking at each other with abandon, using clubs, branches, sharpened sticks, and a few crafted weapons.

Jarlaxle tipped his hat to the assassin, motioned for Entreri to go left, and went right, blending into the shadows so perfectly that Entreri had to blink to make sure they were not deceiving him. He knew that Jarlaxle, like all dark elves, was stealthy. Likewise he knew that while Jarlaxle's cloak was not the standard drow *piwafwi*, it did have many magical qualities. It surprised him that anyone, short of using a wizard's invisibility spell, could find a way so to completely hide that great plumed hat.

Entreri shook it off and ran to the left, finding an easy path of shadows through the sparse trees, boulders, and rocky ridges. He approached the first group of orcs—four of the beasts squared up in battle, three against one. Moving silently, the assassin worked his way around the back of the trio, thinking to even up the odds with a sudden strike. He knew he was making no noise, knew he was hiding perfectly from tree to tree to rock to ridge. He had performed attacks like this for nearly three decades, had perfected the stealthy strike to an unprecedented level—and these were only orcs, simple, stupid brutes.

How surprised Entreri was, then, when two of the fighting trio howled and leaped around, charging right for him. The orc they had been fighting, with complete disregard to the battle at hand, similarly charged at the assassin. The remaining orc opponent promptly cut it down as it ran past.

Hard-pressed, Entreri worked his sword left and right, parrying the thrusts of the two makeshift spears and shearing the tip off one in the process. He was back on his heels, in a position of terrible balance. Had he been fighting an opponent of true skill he surely would have been killed, but these were only orcs. Their weapons were poorly crafted and their tactics were utterly predictable. He had defeated their first thrusts, their only chance, and yet, still they came on, headlong, with abandon.

Charon's Claw waved before them, filling the air with an opaque wall of ash. They plunged right through—of course they did!—but Entreri had already skittered to the left, and he spun back behind the charge of the closest orc, plunging his dagger deep into the creature's side. He didn't retract the blade immediately, though he had broken free. He could have made an easy kill of the second stumbling orc. No, he used the dagger to draw out the life-force from the already dying creature, taking that life-force into his own body to speed the healing of his own previous wounds.

By the time he let the limp creature drop to the ground, the second orc was at him, stabbing wildly. Entreri caught the spear with the crosspiece of his dagger and easily turned it up high, over his shoulder, and ducked and stepped ahead, shearing across with a great sweep of Charon's Claw. The orc instinctively tried to block with its arm, but the sword cut right through the limb, and drove hard into the orc's side, splintering ribs and tearing a great hole in its lung, all the way to its heart.

Entreri could hardly believe that the third of the group was still charging at him after seeing how easily and completely he had destroyed its two companions. He casually planted his left foot against the chest of the drooping, dead creature impaled on his sword, and waited for the exact moment. When that moment came, he turned the dead orc and kicked it free, dropping it in the path of its charging, howling companion.

The orc tripped, diving headlong past Entreri. The assassin stabbed up hard with the dagger, catching the orc under the chin and driving the blade up into its head. He bent as the heavy orc continued its facedown dive, ending with him holding the creature's head from the ground and the orc twitching spasmodically as it died.

A twist and yank tore the dagger free, and Entreri paused only long enough to wipe both his blades on the dead beast's back before running off in pursuit of other prey.

His stride was more tempered this time, though, for his failure in approaching the trio from behind bothered him greatly. He believed he understood what had happened—the Crystal Shard had called out a warning to the group—but the thought that carrying the cursed item left him without his favored mode of attack and his greatest ability to defend himself was more than a little unsettling.

He charged across the side of the rock facing, picking shadows where he could find them but worrying little about cover. He understood that with the Crystal Shard on his belt, he was likely as obvious as he would be sitting beside a blazing campfire on a dark night. He came past one small area of brush onto the lower edge of sloping, bare stone. Cursing the open ground but hardly slowing, Entreri started across.

He saw the charge of another orc out of the corner of his eye, the creature rushing headlong at him, one arm back and ready to launch a spear his way.

The orc was barely five strides away when it threw, but Entreri didn't even have to parry the errant missile, just letting it fly harmlessly past. He did react to it, though, with dramatic movement, and that only spurred on the eager orc attacker.

It leaped at the seemingly vulnerable man, a flying tackle aimed for Entreri's waist. Two quick steps took the assassin out of harm's way, and he swished his sword down onto the orc's back as it flew past, cracking the powerful weapon right through the creature's backbone. The orc skidded down hard on its face, its upper torso and arms squirming wildly, but its legs making no movement of their own.

Entreri didn't even bother finishing the wretched creature. He just ran on. He had a direction sorted for his run, for he heard the unmistakable laughter of a drow who seemed to be having too much fun.

He found Jarlaxle standing atop a boulder amidst the largest tumult of battling orcs, spurring one side on with excited words that Entreri could not understand, while systematically cutting down their opponents with dagger after thrown dagger.

Entreri stopped in the shadow of a tree and watched the spectacle.

Sure enough, Jarlaxle soon changed sides, calling out to the other orcs, and launching that endless stream of daggers at members of the side he had just been urging on.

The numbers dwindled, obviously so, and eventually, even the stupid orcs caught on to the deadly ruse. As one, they turned on Jarlaxle.

The drow only laughed at them all the harder as a dozen spears came his way—every one of them missing the mark badly due to the displacement magic in the drow's cloak and the bad aim of the orcs. The drow countered, throwing one dagger after another. Jarlaxle spun around on his high perch, always seeking the closest orc, and always hitting home with a nearly perfect throw.

Out of the shadows came Entreri, a whirlwind of fury, dagger working efficiently, but sword waving wildly, building walls of floating ash as the assassin sliced up the battlefield to suit his designs. Inevitably, Entreri worked his way into a situation that put him one-on-one against an orc. Just as inevitably, that creature was down and dying within the span of a few thrusts and stabs.

Entreri and Jarlaxle walked slowly back up the mountain slope soon after, with the drow complaining at the meager take of silver pieces they had found on the orcs. Entreri was hardly listening, was more concerned with the call that had brought the creatures to them in the first place—the plea, the scream, for help from Crenshinibon. These were just a ragtag band of orcs, but what more powerful creatures might the Crystal Shard find to come to its call next?

"The call of the shard is strong," he admitted to Jarlaxle.

"It has existed for centuries," the drow answered. "It knows well how to preserve itself."

"That existence is soon to end," Entreri said grimly.

"Why?" Jarlaxle asked with perfect innocence.

The tone more than the word stopped Entreri cold in his tracks and made him turn around to regard his surprising companion.

"Do we have to go through this all over again?" the assassin asked.

"My friend, I know why you believe the Crystal Shard to be unacceptable for either of us to wield, but why does that translate into the need to destroy it?" Jarlaxle asked. He paused and glanced around, and motioned for Entreri to follow and led the assassin to the edge of a fairly deep ravine, a remote valley. "Why not just throw it away then?" he asked. "Toss it from this cliff and let it land where it may?"

Entreri stared out at the remote vale and almost considered taking Jarlaxle's advice. Almost, but a very real truth rang clear in his mind. "Because it would find its way back to the hands of our adversaries soon enough," he replied. "The Crystal Shard saw great potential in Rai-guy,"

Jarlaxle nodded. "Sensible," he said. "Ever was that one too ambitious for his own good. Why do you care, though? Let Rai-guy have it and have all of Calimport, if the artifact can deliver the city to him. What does it matter to Artemis Entreri, who is gone from that place, and who will not return anytime soon in any event? Likely, my former lieutenant will be too preoccupied with the potential gains he might find with the artifact in his hands even to worry about our whereabouts. Perhaps freeing ourselves of the burden of the artifact will indeed save us from the pursuit we now fear at our backs."

Entreri spent a long moment musing over that reasoning, but one fact kept nagging at him. "The Crystal Shard knows I wish to see it destroyed," he replied. "It knows that in my heart I hate it and will find some way to be rid of the thing. Rai-guy knows the threat that is Jarlaxle. As long as you live, he can never be certain of his position within Bregan D'aerthe.

What would happen if Jarlaxle reappeared in Menzoberranzan, reaching out to old comrades against the fools who tried to steal the throne of Bregan D'aerthe?"

Jarlaxle offered no response, but the twinkle in his dark eyes told Entreri that his drow companion would like nothing more than to play out that very scenario.

"He wants you dead," Entreri said bluntly. "He needs you dead, and with the Crystal Shard at his disposal, that might not prove to be an overly difficult task."

The twinkle in Jarlaxle's dark eyes remained, but after a moment's thought, he just shrugged and said, "Lead on."

Entreri did just that, back to their horses and back to the trails that would take them to the northeast, to the Snowflake Mountains and the Spirit Soaring. Entreri was quite pleased with the way he had handled Jarlaxle, quite pleased in the strength of his argument for destroying the Crystal Shard.

But it was all just so much dung, he knew, all a justification for that which was in his heart. Yes, he was determined to destroy the Crystal Shard, and would see the artifact obliterated, but it was not for any fear of retribution or of pursuit. Entreri wanted Crenshinibon destroyed simply because the mere existence of the dominating artifact revolted him. The Crystal Shard, in trying to coerce him, had insulted him profoundly. He didn't hold any notion that the wretched world would be a better place without the artifact, and hardly cared whether it would be or not, but he did believe that he would more greatly enjoy his existence in the world knowing that one less wretched and perverted item such as the Crystal Shard remained in existence.

Of course, as Entreri harbored these thoughts, Crenshinibon realized them as well. The Crystal Shard could only seethe, could only hope that it might find someone weaker of heart and stronger of arm to slay Artemis Entreri and free it from his grasp.

Chapter 18
Respectable Opponents

"It was Entreri," Sharlotta Vespers said with a sly grin as she examined the orc corpse on the side of the mountain a couple days later. "The precision of the cuts . . . and see, a dagger thrust here, a sword slash there."

"Many fight with sword and dirk," the wererat, Gord Abrix, replied. The wretch, wearing his human form at that time, moved his hands out wide as he spoke, revealing his own sword and dagger hanging on his belt.

"But few strike so well," Sharlotta argued.

"And these others," Berg'inyon Baenre agreed in his stilted command of the common tongue. He swung his arm about to encompass the many orcs lying dead around the base of a large boulder. "Wounds consistent with a dagger throw—and so many of them. Only one warrior that I know of carries such a supply as that."

"You are counting wounds, not daggers!" Gord Abrix argued.

"They are one and the same in a fight this frantic," Berg'inyon reasoned. "These are throws, not stabs, for there is no tearing about the sides of the cuts, just a single fast puncture. And I think it unlikely that anyone would throw a few daggers at one opponent, somehow run down and pull them free, then throw them at another."

"Where are these daggers, then, drow?" the wererat leader asked doubtfully.

"Jarlaxle's missiles are magical in nature and disappear," Berg'inyon answered coldly. "His supply is nearly endless. This is the work of Jarlaxle, I know—and not his best work, I warn both of you."

Sharlotta and Gord Abrix exchanged nervous glances, though the wererat leader still held that doubting expression.

"Have you not yet learned the proper respect for the drow?" Berg'inyon asked him pointedly and threateningly.

Gord Abrix went back on his heels and held his empty hands up before him.

Sharlotta eyed him closely. Gord Abrix wanted a fight, she knew, even with this dark elf standing before him. Sharlotta hadn't really seen Berg'inyon Baenre in action, but she had seen his lessers, dark elves who had spoken of this young Baenre with the utmost respect. Even those lessers would have had little trouble in slaughtering the prideful Gord Abrix. Yes, Sharlotta realized then and there, her own self-preservation would depend upon her getting as far away from Gord Abrix and his sewer dwellers as possible, for there was no respect here, only abject hatred for Artemis Entreri and a genuine dislike for the dark elves. No doubt, Gord Abrix would lead his companions, wererat and otherwise, into absolute devastation.

Sharlotta Vespers, the survivor, wanted no part of that.

"The bodies are cold, the blood dried, but they have not been cleanly picked," Berg'inyon observed.

"A couple of days, no more," Sharlotta added, and she looked to Gord Abrix, as did Berg'inyon.

The wererat nodded and smiled wickedly. "I will have them," he declared. He walked off to confer with his wererat companions, who had been standing off to the side of the battleground.

"He will have a straight passageway to the realm of death," Berg'inyon quietly remarked to Sharlotta when the two were alone.

Sharlotta looked at the drow curiously. She agreed, of course, but she had to wonder why, if the dark elves knew this, they were allowing Gord Abrix to hold so critical a role in this all-important pursuit.

"Gord Abrix thinks he will get them," she replied, "both of them, yet you do not seem so confident."

Berg'inyon chuckled at the remark—one he obviously believed absurd. "No doubt, Entreri is a deadly opponent," he said.

"More so than you understand," Sharlotta, who knew the assassin's exploits well, was quick to add.

"And yet he is still, by any measure, the easier of the prey," Berg'inyon assured her. "Jarlaxle has survived for centuries with his intelligence and skill. He thrives in a land more violent than Calimport could ever know. He ascends to the highest levels of power in a warring city that prevents the ascent of males. Our wretched companion Gord Abrix cannot understand the truth of Jarlaxle, nor can you, so I tell you this now—out of the respect I have gained for you in these short tendays—beware that one."

Sharlotta paused and stared long and hard at the surprising drow warrior. Offering her respect? The notion pleased her and made her fearful all at once, for Sharlotta had already learned to try to look beneath every word uttered by her dark elf comrades. Perhaps Berg'inyon had just paid her a high and generous compliment. Perhaps he was setting her up for disaster.

Sharlotta glanced down at the ground, biting her lower lip as she fell into her thoughts, sorting it all out. Perhaps Berg'inyon was setting her up, she reasoned again, as Rai-guy and Kimmuriel had set up Gord Abrix. As she thought of the mighty Jarlaxle and the item he possessed, she came to realize, of course, that there was no way Rai-guy could believe Gord Abrix and his ragged wererat band could possibly bring down the great Entreri and the great Jarlaxle. If that came to pass, then Gord Abrix would have the Crystal Shard in his possession, and what trouble might he bring about before Rai-guy and Kimmuriel could take it away from him? No, Rai-guy and Kimmuriel did not believe that the wererat leader would get anywhere near the Crystal Shard, and furthermore, they didn't want him anywhere near it.

Sharlotta looked back up at Berg'inyon to see him smiling slyly, as if he had just followed her reasoning as clearly as if she had spoken it aloud. "The drow always use a lesser race to lead the way into battle," the dark elf warrior said. "We never truly know, of course, what surprises our enemies might have in store."

"Fodder," Sharlotta remarked.

Berg'inyon's expression was perfectly blank, was absent of any sense of compassion at all, giving Sharlotta all the confirmation she needed.

A shudder coursed up Sharlotta's spine as she considered the sheer coldness of that look, dispassionate and inhuman, a less-than-subtle reminder to her that these dark elves were indeed very different, and much, much more dangerous. Artemis Entreri was, perhaps, the closest creature she had ever met in temperament to the drow, but it seemed to her that, in terms of sheer evil, even he paled in comparison. These long-lived dark elves had perfected the craft of efficient heartlessness to a level beyond human comprehension, let alone human mimicry. She turned to regard Gord Abrix and his eager wererats, and made a silent vow then to stay as far away from the doomed creatures as possible.

* * * * *

The demon writhed on the floor in agony, its skin smoking, its blood boiling.

791

Cadderly did not pity the creature, though it pained him to have to lower himself to this level. He did not enjoy torture—even the torture of a demon, as deserving a creature as ever existed. He did not enjoy dealing with the denizens of the lower planes at all, but he had to for the sake of the Spirit Soaring, for the sake of his wife and children.

The Crystal Shard was coming to him, was coming for him, he knew, and his impending battle with the vile artifact might prove to be as important as his war had been against *Tuanta Quiro Miancay,* the dreaded Chaos Curse. It was as important as his construction of the Spirit Soaring, for what lasting effect might the remarkable cathedral hold if Crenshinibon reduced it to rubble?

"You know the answer," Cadderly said as calmly as he could. "Tell me, and I will release you."

"You are a fool, priest of Deneir!" the demon growled, its guttural words broken apart as spasm after spasm wracked its physical form. "Do you know the enemy you make in Mizferac?"

Cadderly sighed. "And so it continues," he said, as if he were speaking to himself, though well aware that Mizferac would hear his words and understand the painful implications of them with crystalline clarity.

"Release me!" the glabrezu demanded.

"Yokk tu Mizferac be-enck do-tu", Cadderly recited, and the demon howled and jerked wildly about the floor within the perfectly designed protective circle.

"This will take as long as you wish," Cadderly said coldly to the demon. "I have no mercy for your kind, I assure you."

"We . . . want . . . no . . . mercy," Mizferac growled. Then a great spasm wracked the beast, and it jerked wildly, rolling about and shrieking curses in its profane, demonic language.

Cadderly just quietly recited more of the exaction spell, bolstering his resolve with the continual reminder that his children might soon be in mortal danger.

* * * * *

"Ye wasn't lost! Ye was playing!" Ivan Bouldershoulder roared at his green-bearded brother.

"Doo-dad maze!" Pikel argued vehemently.

The normally docile dwarf's tone took his brother somewhat by surprise. "Ye getting talkative since ye becomed a doo-dad, ain't ye?" he asked.

"Oo oi!" Pikel shrieked, punching his fist in the air.

"Well, ye shouldn't be playin' in yer maze when Cadderly's at such dark business," Ivan scolded.

"Doo-dad maze," Pikel whispered under his breath, and he lowered his gaze.

"Yeah, whatever ye might be callin' it," grumbled Ivan, who had never been overly fond of his brother's woodland calling and considered it quite an unnatural thing for a dwarf. "He might be needin' us, ye fool." Ivan held up his great axe as he spoke, flexing the bulging muscles on his short but powerful arm.

Pikel responded with one of his patented grins and held up a wooden cudgel.

"Great weapon for fighting demons," Ivan muttered.

"Sha-la—" Pikel started.

"Yeah, I'm knowin' the name," Ivan cut in. "Sha-la-la. I'm thinking that a demon might be callin' it kind-lind-ling."

Pikel's grin drooped into a severe frown.

The door to the summoning chamber pulled open and a very weary Cadderly emerged—or tried to. He tripped over something and sprawled facedown to the floor.

"Oops," said Pikel.

"Me brother put one o' his magic trips on the doorway," Ivan explained, helping the priest back to his feet. "We was worryin' that a demon might be walkin' out."

"So of course, Pikel would trip the thing to the floor and bash it with his club," Cadderly said dryly, pulling himself back to his feet.

"Sha-la-la!" Pikel squealed gleefully, completely missing the sarcasm in the young cleric's tone.

"Ain't one coming, is there?" Ivan asked, looking past Cadderly.

"The glabrezu, Mizferac, has been dismissed to its own foul plane," Cadderly assured the dwarves. "I brought it forth again, thus rescinding the hundred year banishment I had just exacted upon it, to answer a specific question, and with that done, I had—and have, I hope—no further need of it."

"Ye should've kept him about just so me and me brother could bash him a few times," said Ivan.

"Sha-la-la!'" Pikel agreed.

"Save your strength, for I fear we will need it," Cadderly explained. "I have learned the secret to destroying the Crystal Shard, or at least, I have learned of the creature that might complete the task."

"Demon?" Ivan asked.

"Doo-dad?" Pikel added hopefully.

Cadderly, shaking his head, started to reply to Ivan, but paused to put a perfectly puzzled expression over the green-bearded dwarf. Embarrassed, Pikel merely shrugged and said, "Ooo."

"No demon," he said to the other dwarf at length. "A creature of this world."

"Giant?"

"Think bigger."

Ivan started to speak again, but paused, taking in Cadderly's sour expression and studying it in light of all that they had been through together.

"Let me guess one more time," the dwarf said.

Cadderly didn't answer.

"Dragon," Ivan said.

"Ooo," said Pikel.

Cadderly didn't answer.

"Red dragon," Ivan clarified.

"Ooo," said Pikel.

Cadderly didn't answer.

"Big red dragon," said the dwarf. "*Huge* red dragon! Old as the mountains."

"Ooo," said Pikel, three more times.

Cadderly merely sighed.

"Old Fyren's dead," Ivan said, and there was indeed a slight tremor in the tough dwarf's voice, for that fight with the great red dragon had nearly been the end of them all.

"Fyrentennimar was not the last of its kind, nor the greatest, I assure you," Cadderly replied evenly.

"Ye're thinking that we got to take the thing to another of the beasts?" Ivan asked incredulously. "To one bigger than old Fyren?"

"So I am told," explained Cadderly. "A red dragon, ancient and huge."

Ivan shook his head, and snapped a glare over Pikel, who said, "Ooo," once again.

Ivan couldn't help but chuckle. They had met up with mighty Fyrentennimar on their way to find the mountain fortress that housed the minions of Cadderly's own wicked father. Through Cadderly's powerful magic, the dragon had been "tamed" into flying Cadderly and the others across the Snowflake Mountains. A battle deeper in those mountains had broken the spell though, and old Fyren had turned on its temporary masters with a vengeance. Somehow, Cadderly had managed to hold onto enough magical strength to weaken the beast enough for Vander, a giant friend, to lop off its head, but Ivan knew, and so did the others, that the win had been as much a feat of luck as of skill.

"Drizzt Do'Urden told ye about another of the reds, didn't he?" Ivan remarked.

"I know where we can find one," Cadderly replied grimly.

Danica walked in, then, her smile wide—until she noted the expressions on the faces of the other three.

"Poof!" said Pikel and he walked out of the room, muttering squeaky little sounds.

A puzzled Danica watched him go. Then she turned to his brother.

"He's a doo-dad," Ivan explained, "and fearin' no natural creature. There ain't nothin' less natural than a red dragon, I'm guessing, so he's not too happy right now." Ivan snorted and walked out behind his brother.

"Red dragon?" Danica asked Cadderly.

"Poof," the priest replied.

Chapter 19

Because He Never Had To

Entreri frowned when he glanced from the not-too-distant village to his ridiculously plumed drow companion. The hat alone, with its wide brim and huge diatryma feather that always grew back after Jarlaxle used it to summon a real giant bird, would invite suspicion and likely open disdain, from the farmers of the village. Then there was the fact that the wearer was a dark elf. . . .

"You really should consider a disguise," Entreri said dryly, and shook his head, wishing he still had a particular magic item, a mask that could transform the wearer's appearance. Drizzt Do'Urden had once used the thing to get from the northlands around Waterdeep all the way to Calimport disguised as a surface elf.

"I have considered a disguise," the drow replied, and to Entreri's—temporary—relief, he pulled the hat from his head. A good start, it seemed.

Jarlaxle merely brushed the thing off and plopped it right back in place. "You wear one, as well," the drow protested to Entreri's scowl, pointing to the small-brimmed black hat Entreri now wore. The hat was called a bolero, named after the drow wizard who had given it its tidy shape and had imbued it, and several others of the same make, with certain magical properties.

"Not the hat!" the frustrated Entreri replied, and he rubbed a hand across his face. "These are simple farmers, likely with very definite feelings about dark elves—and likely, those feelings are not favorable."

"For most dark elves, I would agree with them," said Jarlaxle, and he ended there, and merely kept riding on his way toward the village, as if Entreri had said nothing to him at all.

"Hence, the disguise," the assassin called after him.

"Indeed," said Jarlaxle, and he kept on riding.

Entreri kicked his heels into his horse's flanks, spurring the mount into a quick canter to bring him up beside the elusive drow. "I mean that you should consider wearing one," Entreri said plainly.

"But I am," the drow replied. "And you, Artemis Entreri, above all others, should recognize me! I am Drizzt Do'Urden, your most hated rival."

"What?" the assassin asked incredulously.

"Drizzt Do'Urden, the perfect disguise for me," Jarlaxle casually replied. "Does not Drizzt walk openly from town to town, neither hiding nor denying his heritage, even in those places where he is not well-known?"

"*Does* he?" Entreri asked slyly.

"*Did* he not?" Jarlaxle quickly replied, correcting the tense, for of course, as far as Artemis Entreri knew, Drizzt Do'Urden was dead.

Entreri stared hard at the drow.

"Well, did he not?" Jarlaxle asked plainly. "And it was Drizzt's nerve, I say, in parading about so openly, that prevented townsfolk from organizing against him and slaying him. Because he remained so obvious, it became obvious that he had nothing to hide. Thus, I use the same technique and even the same name. I am Drizzt Do'Urden, hero of Icewind Dale, friend of King Bruenor Battlehammer of Mithral Hall, and no enemy of these simple farmers. Rather, I might be of use to them, should danger threaten."

"Of course," Entreri replied. "Unless one of them crosses you, in which case you will destroy the entire town."

"There is always that," Jarlaxle admitted, but he didn't slow his mount, and he and Entreri were getting close to the village now, close enough to be seen for what they were—or at least, for what they were pretending to be.

There were no guards about, and the pair rode in undisturbed, their horses' hooves clattering on cobblestone roads. They pulled up before one two-story building, on which hung a shingle painted with a foamy mug of mead and naming the place as

Gent eman Briar's Good y
P ace of Si ing

in lettering old and weathered.

"Si ing," Jarlaxle read, scratching his head, and he gave a great and dramatic sigh. "This is a gathering hall for those of melancholy?"

"Not sighing," Entreri replied. He looked at Jarlaxle, snorted, and rolled off the side of his horse. "Sitting, or perhaps sipping. Not sighing."

"Sitting, then, or sipping," Jarlaxle announced, looping his right leg over his horse, and rolling over backward off the mount into a somersault to land gracefully on his feet. "Or perhaps a bit of both! Ha!" He ended with a great gleaming smile.

Entreri stared at him hard yet again, and just shook his head, thinking that perhaps he would have been better off leaving this one with Raiguy and Kimmuriel.

A dozen patrons were inside the place, ten men and a pair of women, along with a grizzled old barkeep whose snarl seemed to be eternally etched upon his stubbly face, a locked expression amidst the leathery wrinkles and acne scars. One by one, the thirteen took note of the pair entering, and inevitably, each nodded or merely glanced away, and shot a stunned expression back at the duo, particularly at the dark elf, and sent a hand to the hilt of the nearest weapon. One man even leaped up from his chair, sending it skidding out behind him.

Entreri and Jarlaxle merely tipped their hats and moved to the bar, making no threatening movements and keeping their expressions perfectly friendly.

"What're ye about?" the barkeep barked at them. "Who're ye, and what's yer business?"

"Travelers," Entreri answered, "weary of the road and seeking a bit of respite."

"Well, ye'll not be finding it here, ye won't!" the barkeep growled. "Get yer hats back on yer ugly heads and get yer arses out me door!"

Entreri looked to Jarlaxle, who seemed perfectly unperturbed. "I do believe we will stay a bit," the drow stated. "I do understand your hesitance, good sir . . . good Eman Briar," he added, remembering the sign.

"Eman?" the barkeep echoed in obvious confusion.

"Eman Briar, so says your placard," Jarlaxle answered innocently.

"Eh?" the puzzled man asked, then his old yellow eyes lit up as he caught on. "*Gentle*man Briar," he insisted. "The L's all rotted away. *Gentleman* Briar."

"Your pardon, good sir," the charming and disarming Jarlaxle said with a bow. He gave a great sigh and threw a wink at Entreri's predictable scowl. "We have come in to sigh, sit, and sip, a bit of all three. We want no trouble and bring none, I assure you. Have you not heard of me? Drizzt Do'Urden of Icewind Dale, who reclaimed Mithral Hall for dwarven King Bruenor Battlehammer?"

"Never heard o' no Drizzit Dudden," Briar replied. "Now get ye outta me place afore me friends and me haul ye out!" His voice rose as he spoke, and several of the gathered men did, as well, moving together and readying their weapons.

Jarlaxle glanced around at the lot of them, smiling, seeming perfectly amused. Entreri, too, was quite entertained by it all, but he didn't bother looking around, just leaned back on his barstool, watching his friend and trying to see how Jarlaxle might wriggle out of this one. Of course, the ragged band of farmers hardly bothered the skilled assassin, especially since he was sitting next to the dangerous Jarlaxle. If they had to leave the town in ruin, so be it.

Thus, Entreri did not even search the ever-present silent call of the imprisoned Crystal Shard. If the artifact wanted these simple fools to take it from Entreri, then let them try!

"Did I not just tell you that I reclaimed a dwarven kingdom?" Jarlaxle asked. "And mostly without help. Hear me well, Gent Eman Briar. If you and your friends here try to expel me, your kin will be planting more than crops this season."

It wasn't so much what he said as it was the manner in which he said it, so casual, so confident, so perfectly assured that this group could not begin to frighten him. The men approaching slowed to a halt, all of them glancing to the others for some sign of leadership.

"Truly, I desire no trouble," Jarlaxle said calmly. "I have dedicated my life to erasing the prejudices—rightful conceptions, in many instances— that so many hold for my people. I am not merely a weary traveler, but a warrior for the causes of common men. If goblins attacked your fair town, I would fight beside you until they were driven away, or until my heart beat its last!" His voice continued a dramatic climb. "If a great dragon swooped down upon your village, I would brave its fiery breath, draw forth my weapons and leap to the parapets. . . ."

"I think they understand your point," Entreri said to him, grabbing him by the arm and easing him back to his seat.

Gentleman Briar snorted. "Ye're not even carryin' no weapon, drow," he observed.

"A thousand dead men have said the same thing," Entreri replied in all seriousness. Jarlaxle tipped his hat to the assassin. "But enough banter," Entreri added, hopping from his seat and pulling back his cloak to reveal his two fabulous weapons, the jeweled dagger and the magnificent Charon's Claw with its distinctive bony hilt. "If you mean to fight us, then do so now, that I can finish this business and still find a good meal, a better drink, and a warm bed before the fall of night. If not, then go back to your tables, I beg, and leave us in peace, else I'll forget my delusional paladin friend's desire to become the hero of the land."

Again, the patrons glanced nervously at each other, and some grumbled under their breaths.

"Gentleman Briar, they await your signal," Entreri remarked. "Choose well which signal that will be, or else find a way to mix blood with your drink, for you shall have gallons of it pooling about your tavern."

Briar waved his hand, sending his patrons retreating to their respective tables, and gave a great snort and snarl.

"Good!" Jarlaxle remarked, slapping his leg. "My reputation is saved from the rash actions of my impetuous friend. Now, if you would be so kind as to fetch me a fine and delicate drink, Gentleman Briar," he instructed, pulling forth his purse, which was bulging with coins.

"I'm servin' no damned drow in me tavern," Briar insisted, crossing his thin but muscled arms over his chest.

"Then I will gladly serve myself," Jarlaxle answered without hesitation, and he politely tipped his great plumed hat. "Of course, that will mean fewer coins for you."

Briar stared at him hard.

Jarlaxle ignored him and stared instead at the fairly wide selection of bottles on the shelves behind the bar. He tapped a delicate finger against his lip, scrutinizing the colors, and the words of the few that were actually marked.

"Suggestions?" he asked Entreri.

"Something to drink," the assassin replied.

Jarlaxle pointed to one bottle, uttered a simple magical command, and snapped his finger back, and the bottle flew from the shelf to his waiting grasp. Two more points and commands had a pair of glasses sitting upon the bar before the companions.

Jarlaxle reached for the bottle. The stunned and angry Briar snapped his hand out to grab the dark elf's arm.

He never got close.

Faster than Briar could possibly react, faster than he could think to react, Entreri snapped his hand on the barkeep's reaching arm, slamming it down to the bar and holding it fast. In the same fluid motion, the assassin's other hand came, holding the jeweled dagger, and Entreri plunged it hard into the wooden shelf right between Gentleman Briar's fingers. The blood drained from the man's ruddy face.

"If you persist, there will be little left of your tavern," Entreri promised in the coldest, most threatening voice Gentleman Briar had ever heard. "Enough to build a proper box to bury you in, perhaps."

"Doubtful," said Jarlaxle.

The drow was perfectly at ease, hardly paying attention, seeming as though he had expected Entreri's intervention all along. He poured the two drinks and eased himself back, sniffing, and sipping his liquor.

Entreri let the man go, glanced around to make sure that none of the others were moving, and slid his dagger back into its sheath on his belt.

"Good sir," Jarlaxle said. "I tell you one more time that we have no argument with you, nor do we wish one. Our road behind us has been long and dry, and the road before us will no doubt prove equally harsh.

Thus we have entered your fair tavern in this fair village. Why would you think to deny us?"

"The better question is, why would you wish to be killed?" Entreri put in.

Gentleman Briar looked from one to the other and threw up his hands in defeat. "To the Nine Hells with both of ye," he growled, spinning away.

Entreri looked to Jarlaxle, who merely shrugged and said, "I have already been there. Hardly worth a return visit." He took up his glass and the bottle and walked away. Entreri, with his own glass, followed him across the room to the one free table in the small place.

Of course, the two tables near that one soon became empty as well, when the patrons took up their glasses and other items and scurried away from the dark elf.

"It will always be like this," Entreri said to his companion a short while later.

"It had not been so for Drizzt Do'Urden of late, so my spies indicated," the drow answered. "His reputation, in those lands where he was known, outshone the color of his skin in the eyes of even the small-minded men. So, soon, will my own."

"A reputation for heroic deeds?" Entreri asked with a doubting laugh. "Are you to become a hero for the land, then?"

"That, or a reputation for leaving burned-out villages behind me," Jarlaxle replied. "Either way, I care little."

That brought a smile to Entreri's face, and he dared to hope then that he and his companion would get along famously.

*　*　*　*　*

Kimmuriel and Rai-guy stared at the mirror enchanted for divining, watching the procession of nearly a score of ratmen, all in their human guise, trotting into the village.

"It is already tense," Kimmuriel observed. "If Gord Abrix plays correctly, the townsfolk will join with him against Entreri and Jarlaxle. Thirty-to-two. Fine odds."

Rai-guy gave a derisive snort. "Strong enough odds, perhaps, so that Jarlaxle and Entreri will be a bit weary before we go in to finish the task," he said.

Kimmuriel looked to his friend but, thinking about it, merely shrugged and grinned. He wasn't about to mourn the loss of Gord Abrix and a bunch of flea-infested wererats.

"If they do get in and get lucky," Kimmuriel remarked, "we must be quick. The Crystal Shard is in there."

"Crenshinibon is not calling to Gord Abrix and his fools," Rai-guy replied, his dark eyes gleaming with anticipation. "It is calling to me, even now. It knows we are close and knows how much greater it will be when I am the wielder."

Kimmuriel said nothing, but studied his friend intently, suspecting that if Rai-guy achieved his goal, he and Crenshinibon would likely soon be at odds with Kimmuriel.

*   *   *   *   *

"How many does the tiny village hold?" Jarlaxle asked when the tavern doors opened and a group of men walked in.

Entreri started to answer flippantly, but held the thought and scrutinized the new group a bit more closely. "Not that many," he answered, shaking his head.

Jarlaxle followed the assassin's lead, studying the movements of the new arrivals, studying their weapons—swords mostly, and more ornate than anything the villagers were carrying.

Entreri's head snapped to the side as he noted other forms moving about the two small windows. He knew then, beyond any doubt.

These are not villagers, Jarlaxle silently agreed, using the intricate sign language of the dark elves, but moving his fingers much more slowly than normal in deference to Entreri's rudimentary understanding of the form.

"Ratmen," the assassin whispered in reply.

"You hear the shard calling to them?"

"I smell them," Entreri corrected. He paused a moment to consider whether the Crystal Shard might indeed be calling out to the group, a beacon for his enemies, but he just dismissed the thought, for it hardly mattered.

"Sewage on their shoes," Jarlaxle noted.

"Vermin in their blood," the assassin spat. He got up from his seat and took a step out from the table. "Let us begone," he said to Jarlaxle, loudly enough for the closest of the dozen ratmen who had entered the tavern to hear.

Entreri took a step toward the door, and a second, aware that all eyes were upon him and his flamboyant companion, who was just then rising from his seat. Entreri took a third step, then . . . he leaped to the side, driving his dagger into the heart of the closest ratman before it could begin to draw its sword.

"Murderers!" someone yelled, but Entreri hardly heard, leaping forward and drawing forth Charon's Claw.

Metal rang out loudly as he brutally parried the swinging sword of the next closest wererat, hitting the blade so hard that he sent it flying out wide. A quick reversal sent Entreri's sword slashing out to catch the ratman across the face, and it fell back, clutching its torn eyes.

Entreri had no time to pursue, for all the place was in motion then.

803

A trio of ratmen, swords slashing the air before them, were closing fast. He waved Charon's Claw, creating a wall of ash, and leaped to the side, rolling under a table. The ratmen reacted, turning to pursue, but by the time they had their bearings, Entreri came up hard, bringing the table with him, launching it into their faces. Now he cut down low, taking a pair out at the knees, the fine blade cleanly severing one leg and nearly a second.

Ratmen bore down on him, but a rain of daggers came whipping past the assassin, driving them back.

Entreri waved his sword wildly, making a long and wavy vision-blocking wall. He managed a glance back at his companion to see Jarlaxle's arm furiously pumping, sending dagger after dagger soaring at an enemy. One group of ratmen, though, hoisted a table, as had Entreri, and used it as a shield. Several daggers thumped into it, catching fast. Bolstered by the impromptu shield, the group charged hard at the drow.

Too occupied suddenly with more enemies of his own, including a couple of townsfolk, Entreri turned his attention back to his own situation. He brought his sword up parallel to the floor, intercepting the blade of one villager and lifting it high. Entreri started to tilt the blade point up, the expected parry, which would bring the man's sword out wide. As the farmer pushed back against the block, Entreri fooled him by bringing up the hilt instead, turning the blade down and forcing the man's sword across his body. Faster than the man could react with any backhand move, Entreri snapped his hand, his weapon's skull-capped pommel, into the man's face, laying him low.

Back across came Charon's Claw, a mighty cut to intercept the sword of another, a ratman, and to slide through the parry and take the tip from another farmer's pitchfork. The assassin followed powerfully, stepping into his two foes, his sword working hard and furiously against the ratman's blade, driving it back, back, and to the side, forcing openings.

The jeweled dagger worked fast as well, with Entreri making circular motions over the broken pitchfork shaft, turning it one way and another and keeping the inexperienced farmer stumbling forward and off his balance. He would have been an easy kill, but Entreri had other ideas.

"Do you not understand the nature of your new allies?" he cried at the man, and as he spoke, he worked his sword even harder, slapping the blade against the wererat's sword to bat it slightly out of angle, and slapping the flat of the blade against the wererat's head. He didn't want to kill the creature, just to tempt the anger out of it. Again and again, the assassin's sword slapped at the wererat, bruising, taunting, stinging.

Entreri noted the creature's twitch and knew what was coming.

He drove the wererat back with a sudden but shortened stab, and went fully at the farmer, looping his dagger over and around the pitchfork, forcing it down at an angle. He went in one step toward the farmer, drove the wooden shaft down farther, forcing the man at an awkward angle that had him leaning on the assassin. Entreri broke away suddenly.

The farmer stumbled forward helplessly and Entreri had him in a lock, looping his sword arm around the man and turning him as he came on so that he was then facing the twitching, changing wererat.

The man gave a slight gasp, thinking his life was at its end, but caught fully in Entreri's grasp, a dagger at his back but not plunging in, he calmed enough to take in the spectacle.

His scream at the horrid transformation, as the wererat's face broke apart, twisted and wrenched, reforming into the head of a giant rodent, rent the air and brought all attention to the sight.

Entreri shoved the farmer toward the wrenching, changing ratman. To his satisfaction, he saw the farmer drive the broken pitchfork shaft through the beast's gut.

Entreri spun away with many more enemies still to fight. The farmers were standing perplexed, not knowing which side to take. The assassin knew enough about the shape-changers to understand that he had started a chain reaction here, that the enraged and excited wererats would look upon their transformed kin and likewise revert to their more primal form.

He took a moment to glance Jarlaxle's way then and saw the drow up in the air, levitating and turning circles, daggers flying from his pumping arm. Following their paths, Entreri saw one wererat, and another, stumble backward under the assault. A farmer grabbed at his calf, a blade deeply embedded there.

Jarlaxle purposely hadn't killed the human, Entreri noted, though he surely could have.

Entreri winced suddenly as a barrage of missiles soared back up at Jarlaxle, but the drow anticipated it and let go his levitation, dropping lightly and gracefully to the floor. He drew out two daggers as a host of opponents rushed in at him, grabbing them from hidden scabbards on his belt and not his enchanted bracer in a cross-armed maneuver. As he brought his arms back to their respective sides, Jarlaxle snapped his wrists and muttered something under his breath. The daggers elongated into fine, gleaming swords.

The drow planted his feet wide and exploded into motion, his arms pumping, his swords cutting fast circles, over and under, at his sides, chopping the air with popping, whipping sounds. He brought one across his chest, then the next, spinning them wildly, then went up high with one, turning his hand to put the blade over his head and parallel with the floor.

Entreri's expression soured. He had expected better of his drow companion. He had seen this fighting style many times, particularly among the pirates who frequented the seas off Calimport. It was called "swashbuckling," a deceptive, and deceptively easy, fighting technique that was more show than substance. The swashbuckler relied on the hesitance and fear of his opponents to afford him opportunities for better strikes. While often effective against weaker opponents, Entreri found the style ridiculous against any of true talent. He had killed several swashbucklers in his day—two in one fight when they had inadvertently tied each other up with their whirling blades—and had never found them to be particularly challenging.

The group of wererats coming in at Jarlaxle at that moment apparently didn't have much respect for the technique either. They quickly rushed around the drow, forming a box, and came in at him alternately, forcing him to turn, turn, and turn some more.

Jarlaxle was more than up to the task, keeping his spinning swords in perfect harmony as he countered every testing thrust or charge.

"They will tire him," Entreri whispered under his breath as he worked away from his newest opponents. He was trying to pick a path that would bring him to his drow friend that he might get Jarlaxle out of his predicament. He glanced back at the drow then, hoping he might get there in time, but honestly wondering if the disappointing Jarlaxle was still worth the trouble.

He gasped, first in confusion, and then in admiration.

Jarlaxle did a sudden back flip, twisting as he somersaulted so that he landed facing the opponent who had been at his back. The wererat stumbled away, hit twice by shortened stabs—shortened because Jarlaxle had other targets in mind.

The drow rolled around, falling into a crouch, and exploded out of it with a devastating double thrust at the wererat opposite. The creature leaped back, throwing its hips behind it and slapping its blade down in a desperate parry.

Before he could even think about it, Entreri cried out, thinking his friend doomed, for one sword-wielding wererat charged from Jarlaxle's direct left, another from behind and to the right, leaving the drow no room to skitter away.

* * * * *

"They reveal themselves," Kimmuriel said with a laugh. He, Rai-guy, and Berg'inyon watched the action through a dimensional portal that in effect put them in the thick of the fighting.

Berg'inyon thought the spectacle of the changing wererats equally amusing. He leaped forward, then, catching one farmer who was inadvertently stumbling through the portal, stabbing the man once in the side, and shoving him back through and to the tavern floor.

More forms rushed by, more cries came in at them, with Kimmuriel and Berg'inyon watching attentively and Rai-guy behind them, his eyes closed as he prepared his spells—a process that was taking the drow wizard longer because of the continuing, eager call of the imprisoned Crystal Shard.

Gord Abrix flashed by the door.

"Catch him!" Kimmuriel cried, and the agile Berg'inyon leaped through the doorway, grabbed Gord Abrix in a debilitating lock, and dived back through with the wererat in tow. He kept Gord Abrix held firmly out of the way, the wererat crying protests at Kimmuriel.

But the drow psionicist wasn't listening, for he was focused fully on his wizard companion. His timing in closing the door had to be perfect.

* * * * *

Jarlaxle didn't even try to get out of there, and Entreri realized, he had expected the attacks all along, had baited them.

Down low, his left leg far in front of his right, both arms and blades fully extended before him, Jarlaxle somehow managed to reverse his grip, and in a sudden and perfectly balanced momentum shift, the drow came back up straight. His left arm and blade stabbed out to the left. The sword in his right hand was flipped over in his hand so that when Jarlaxle turned his fist down, the tip was facing behind him, cocking straight back.

Both charging wererats halted suddenly, their chests ripped open by the perfect stabs.

Jarlaxle retracted the blades, put them back into their respective spins, and turned left, the whirling blades drawing lines of bright blood all over the wounded wererat there, and completing the turn, slashing the wererat behind him repeatedly and finishing with a powerful crossing backhand maneuver that took the creature's head from its shoulders.

Thus disintegrating Entreri's ideas about the weakness of the swashbuckling technique.

The drow rushed past into the path of the first wererat he had struck, his spinning swords intercepting his opponent's, and bringing it into the spin with them. In a moment, all three blades were in the air, turning circles, and only two of them, Jarlaxle's, were still being held. The third was kept aloft by the slapping and sliding of the other two.

Jarlaxle hooked the hilt of that sword with the blade of one of his own, angled it out to the side and launched it into the chest of another attacker, knocking him back and to the floor.

He went ahead suddenly and brutally, blades whirling with perfect precision, to take the wererat's arm, then drop the other arm limply to its side with a well-placed blow to the collarbone, then slash its face, then its throat.

Up came Jarlaxle's foot, planting against the staggered wererat's chest, and he kicked out, knocking the creature to its back and running over it.

Entreri had meant to get to Jarlaxle's side, but instead, the drow came rushing up to Entreri's side, uttering a command under his breath that retracted one of his swords to dagger size. He quickly slid the weapon back to its sheath, and with his free hand grabbed Entreri by the shoulder and pulled him along.

The puzzled assassin glanced at his companion. More wererats were piling into the tavern, through the windows, through the door, but those remaining farmers were falling back now, moving into purely defensive positions. Though more than a dozen wererats remained, Entreri did not believe that he and this amazingly skilled drow warrior would have any trouble at all tearing them apart.

Furthermore and even more puzzling, Jarlaxle had their run angled for the closest wall. While putting a solid barrier at their backs might be effective in some cases against so many opponents, Entreri thought this ridiculous, given Jarlaxle's flamboyant, room-requiring style.

Jarlaxle let go of Entreri then and reached up to the top of his huge hat.

From somewhere unseen in the strange hat, he brought forth a black disk made of some fabric Entreri did not know and sent it spinning at the wall. It elongated as it went, turning flat side to the wooden wall, then it hit . . . and stuck.

And it was no longer a disk of fabric, but rather a hole—a real hole—in the wall.

Jarlaxle pushed Entreri through, dived through right behind him, and paused only long enough to pull the magical hole out behind him, leaving the wall solid once more.

"Run!" the dark elf cried, sprinting away, with Entreri right on his heels.

Before Entreri could even ask what the drow knew that he did not, the building exploded into a huge and consuming fireball that took the tavern, took all of those wererats still scrambling about the entrances and exits, and took the horses, including Entreri's and Jarlaxle's, tethered anywhere near to the place.

The pair went flying to the ground but got right back up, running full speed out of the village and back into the shadows of the surrounding hills and woodlands.

They didn't even speak for many, many minutes, just ran on, until Jarlaxle finally pulled up behind one bluff and fell against the grassy hill, huffing and puffing.

"I had grown fond of my mount," he said. "A pity."

"I did not see the spellcaster," Entreri remarked.

"He was not in the room," Jarlaxle explained, "not physically, at least."

"Then how did you sense him?" Entreri started to ask, but he paused and considered the logic that had led Jarlaxle to his saving conclusion.

"Because Kimmuriel and Rai-guy would never take the chance that Gord Abrix and his cronies would get the Crystal Shard," he reasoned. "Nor would they ever expect the wretched wererats ever to be able to take the thing from us in the first place."

"I have already explained to you that it is a common tactic for the two," Jarlaxle reminded. "They send their fodder in to engage their enemies, and Kimmuriel opens a window through which Rai-guy throws his potent magic."

Entreri looked back in the direction of the village, at the plume of black smoke drifting into the air. "Well thought," he congratulated. "You saved us both."

"Well, you at least," Jarlaxle replied, and Entreri looked back at him curiously, to see the drow waggling the fingers of one hand against his cheek, showing off a reddish-gold ring that Entreri had not noticed before.

"It was just a fireball," Jarlaxle said with a grin.

Entreri nodded and returned that grin, wondering if there was anything, anything at all, that Jarlaxle was not prepared for.

Chapter 20

Balancing Prudence and Desire

Lord Abrix gasped and fell over as the small globe of fire soared past him, through the doorway, and into the tavern. As soon as it went through, Kimmuriel dropped the dimensional door. Gord Abrix had seen fireballs cast before and could well imagine the devastation back in the tavern. He knew he had just lost nearly a score of his loyal wererat soldiers.

He came up unsteadily, glancing around at his three dark elf companions, unsure, as he always seemed to be with this group, of what they might do next.

"You and your soldiers performed admirably," Rai-guy remarked.

"You killed them," Gord Abrix dared to say, though certainly not in any accusatory tone.

"A necessary sacrifice," Rai-guy replied. "You did not believe that they would have any chance of defeating Artemis Entreri and Jarlaxle, did you?"

"Then why send them?" the frustrated wererat leader started to ask, but his voice died away as the question left his mouth, the reasoning dissipated by his own internal reminders of who these creatures truly were. Gord Abrix and his henchmen had been sent in for just the diversion they provided, to occupy Entreri and Jarlaxle while Rai-guy and Kimmuriel prepared their little finish.

Kimmuriel opened the dimensional door then, showing the devastated tavern, charred bodies laying all about and not a creature stirring. The drow's lip curled up in a wicked smile as he surveyed the grisly scene, and a shudder coursed Gord Abrix's spine as he realized the fate he had only barely escaped.

Berg'inyon Baenre went through the door, into what remained of the tavern room, which was more outdoors than indoors now, and returned a moment later.

"A couple of wererats still stir but barely," the drow warrior informed his companions.

"What of our friends?" Rai-guy asked.

Berg'inyon shrugged. "I saw neither Jarlaxle nor Entreri," he explained. "They could be among the wreckage or could be burned beyond immediate recognition."

Rai-guy considered it for a moment, and motioned for Berg'inyon and Gord Abrix to go back to the tavern and snoop around.

"What of my soldiers?" the wererat asked.

"If they can be saved, pull them back through," Rai-guy replied. "Lady Lolth will grant me the power to healing them . . . should I choose to do so."

Gord Abrix started for the dimensional doorway, and paused and glanced back curiously at the obscure and dangerous drow, not sure how to sort through the wizard-cleric's words.

"Do you believe our prey are still in there?" Kimmuriel asked Rai-guy, using the drow tongue to exclude the wererat leader.

Berg'inyon answered from the doorway. "They are not," he said with confidence, though it was obvious he hadn't found the time yet to scour the ruins. "It would take more than a diversion and a simple wizard's spell to bring down that pair."

Rai-guy's eyes narrowed at the affront to his spellcasting, but in truth, he couldn't really disagree with the assessment. He had been hoping he could catch his prey easily and tidily, but he knew better in his heart, knew that Jarlaxle would prove a difficult and cagey quarry.

"Search quickly," Kimmuriel ordered.

Berg'inyon and Gord Abrix ran off, poking through the smoldering ruins.

"They are not in there," Rai-guy said to his psionicist friend a moment later.

"You agree with Berg'inyon's reasoning?" Kimmuriel asked.

"I hear the call of the Crystal Shard," Rai-guy explained with a snarl, for he did indeed hear the renewed call of the artifact, the prisoner of stubborn Artemis Entreri. "That call comes not from the tavern."

"Then where?" Kimmuriel asked.

Rai-guy could only shake his head in frustration. Where indeed. He heard the pleas, but there was no location attached to them, just an insistent call.

"Bring our henchmen back to us," the wizard instructed, and Kimmuriel went through the doorway, returning a moment later with Berg'inyon, Gord Abrix, and a pair of horribly burned, but still very much alive, wererats.

"Help them," Gord Abrix pleaded, dragging his torched friends to Rai-guy. "This is Poweeno, a close advisor and friend."

Rai-guy closed his eyes and began to chant, and opened his eyes and held his hand out toward the prone and squirming Poweeno. He finished his spell by waggling his fingers and uttering another line of arcane words, and a sharp spark crackled from his fingertips, jolting the unfortunate wererat. The creature cried out and jerked spasmodically, howling in agony as smoking blood and gore began to ooze from its layers of horrible wounds.

A few moments later, Poweeno lay very still, quite dead.

"What . . . what have you done?" Gord Abrix demanded of Rai-guy, the wizard already into spellcasting once more.

When Rai-guy didn't answer, Gord Abrix made a move toward him, or at least tried to. He found his feet stuck to the floor, as if he was standing in some powerful glue. He glanced about, his gaze settling on Kimmuriel. He recognized from the drow's satisfied expression that it was indeed the psionicist holding him fast in place.

"You failed me," Rai-guy explained opening his eyes and holding one hand out toward the other wounded wererat.

"You just said we performed admirably," Gord Abrix protested.

"That was before I knew that Jarlaxle and Artemis Entreri had escaped," Rai-guy explained.

He finished his spell, releasing a tremendous bolt of lightning into the other wounded wererat. The creature flipped over weirdly, then rolling into a fetal position, fast following its companion to the grave.

Gord Abrix howled and drew forth his sword, but Berg'inyon was there, smashing the blade away with his own, fine drow weapon. The warrior looked to his two drow companions. On a nod from Rai-guy, he slashed Gord Abrix across the throat.

The wererat, his feet still stuck fast, sank to the floor, staring helplessly and pleadingly at Rai-guy.

"I do not accept failure," the drow wizard said coldly.

* * * * *

"King Elbereth has sent the word out wide to our scouts," the elf Shayleigh assured Ivan and Pikel when the two dwarven emissaries arrived in Shilmista Forest to the west of the Snowflake Mountains.

813

Cadderly had sent the dwarves straight out to their elf friends, confident that anyone approaching would surely be noticed by King Elbereth's wide network of scouts.

Pikel gave a sound then, which seemed to Ivan to be more one of trepidation than one of hope, though Shayleigh had just given them the assurances they had come here to get.

Or had she?

Ivan Bouldershoulder studied the elf maiden carefully. With her violet eyes and thick golden hair hanging far below her shoulders, she was undeniably beautiful, even to the thinking of a dwarf whose tastes usually ran to shorter, thicker, and more heavily bearded females. There was something else about Shayleigh's posture and attitude, though, about the subtle undertone of her melodious voice.

"Ye're not to kill 'em, ye know," Ivan remarked bluntly.

Shayleigh's posture did not change very much. "You yourself have named them as ultimately dangerous," she replied, "an assassin and a drow."

Ivan noted that the ominous flavor of her voice increased when she named the dark elf, as if the creature's mere race offended her more than the profession of his traveling companion.

"Cadderly's needin' to talk to 'em," Ivan grumbled.

"Can he not speak to the dead?"

"Ooo," said Pikel and he hopped away suddenly, disappearing briefly into the underbrush, and reemerging with one hand behind his back. He hopped up to stand before Shayleigh, a disarming grin on his face. "Drizzit," he reminded, and he pulled his hand around, revealing a delicate flower he had just picked for her.

Shayleigh could hardly hold her stern demeanor against that emotional assault. She smiled and took the wildflower, bringing it to her nose that she could smell its beautiful fragrance. "There is often a flower among the weeds," she said, catching on to Pikel's meaning. "As there may be a druid among a clan of dwarves. That does not mean there are others."

"Hope," said Pikel.

Shayleigh gave a helpless chuckle.

"Ye get yer heart in the right place," Ivan warned, "so says Cadderly, else the Crystal Shard'll find yer heart and twist it to its own needs. It's a big bit o' hope he's puttin' on ye, elf."

Shayleigh's sincere smile was all the assurance he needed.

* * * * *

"Brother Chaunticleer has outlined a grand scheme for keeping the children busy," Danica said to Cadderly. "I will be ready to leave as soon as the artifact arrives."

Cadderly's expression hardly seemed to support that notion.

"You did not think I would let you go visit an ancient dragon without me beside you, did you?" Danica asked, sincerely wounded.

Cadderly blew a sigh.

"We've met one before and would have had no trouble at all with it if we had not brought it along with us across the mountains," the woman reminded.

"This time may be more difficult," Cadderly explained. "I will be expending energy merely in controlling the Crystal Shard at the same time I am dealing with the beast. Worse, the artifact will also be speaking to the dragon, I am sure. What better wielder for an instrument of chaos and destruction than a mighty red dragon?"

"How strong is your magic?" Danica asked.

"Not that strong, I fear," Cadderly replied.

"All the more reason that I, and Ivan and Pikel, must be with you," Danica remarked.

"Without the aid of Deneir, do you give any of us a chance of battling such a wyrm?" the priest asked sincerely.

"If Deneir is not with you, you will need us to drag you out of there and quickly," the woman said with a wide smile. "Is that not what your friends are supposed to do?"

Cadderly started to respond, but he really couldn't say much against the look of determination, and of something even more than that—of serenity—stamped across Danica's fair face. Of course she meant to go with him, and he knew he couldn't possibly prevent that unless he left magically and with great deception. Of course, Ivan and Pikel would travel with him as well, though he had to wince when he considered the would-be druid, Pikel, facing a red dragon. They did not want to disturb the great beast any more than to borrow its fiery breath for a single burst of fire. Pikel, so dedicated to the natural, might not be so willing to walk away from a dragon, which was perhaps the greatest perversion of nature in all the world.

Danica cupped her hand under Cadderly's chin then and tilted his head back up so that he was eyeing her directly as she moved very close to him.

"We will finish this and to our satisfaction," she said, and she kissed him gently on the lips. "We have battled worse, my love."

Cadderly didn't begin to deny her words, or her presence, or her determination to go along on this important and dangerous journey. He brought her closer and kissed her again and again.

* * * * *

"We are too busy elsewhere," Sharlotta Vespers tried to explain to Kimmuriel and Rai-guy. The pair were not pleased to learn that Dallabad had somehow been infiltrated by spies of great warlords from Memnon.

The dark elves exchanged concerned looks. Sharlotta had insisted repeatedly that every spy had been caught and killed, but what if she were wrong? What if even one spy had escaped to tell the warlords in Memnon the truth about the change at Dallabad? Or what if other spies had now discerned the real power behind the overthrow of House Basadoni?

"Every danger that Jarlaxle has sown may soon come to harvest," Kimmuriel said to his companion in the drow tongue.

While Sharlotta understood the words well enough, she surely didn't catch the subtleties of the common drow saying, one that referred to revenge taken on a drow house for crimes against another house. Kimmuriel's words were a stern warning, a reminder that Jarlaxle's involvement with Crenshinibon may have left them all vulnerable, no matter what remedial steps they now took.

Rai-guy nodded and stroked his chin, whispering something under his breath that the others could not catch. He stepped forward suddenly to stand right before Sharlotta, bringing his hands up in front of him, thumb-to-thumb. He uttered another word, and a gout of flame burst forth, engulfing the surprised woman's head. She slapped at the fire and screamed, running around the room, and dived to the floor, rolling.

"Make sure that all others who know too much are similarly uninformed," Rai-guy said coldly, as Sharlotta finally died on the floor at his feet.

Kimmuriel nodded, his expression grim, though a hint of an eager grin did turn up the edges of his thin lips.

"I will open the portal back to Menzoberranzan," the wizard explained. "I hold no love for this place and know now, as do you, that our potential gains here do not outweigh the risk to Bregan D'aerthe. I do not even consider it a pity that Jarlaxle foolishly overstepped the bounds of rational caution."

"Better that he did," Kimmuriel agreed. "That we can be on our way to the caverns where we truly belong." He glanced down at Sharlotta, her head blackened and smoking, and smiled once more. He bowed to his companion, his friend of like mind, and left the room, eager to begin the debriefing of others.

Rai-guy also left the room, though through another door, one that led him to the staircase to the basement of House Basadoni, where he could relax more privately in secure chambers. His words of retreat to Kimmuriel followed his every step.

Logical words. Words of survival in a place grown too dangerous.

But still . . . there remained a call in his head, an insistent intrusion, a plea for help.

A promise of greatness beyond his comprehension.

Rai-guy settled into a comfortable chair in his private room, reminding himself continually that a return to Menzoberranzan was the correct move for Bregan D'aerthe, that the risk of remaining on the surface, even in pursuit of the powerful artifact, was too great for the potential gains.

Soon after, the exhausted drow fell into a sort of reverie, as close to true sleep as a dark elf might know.

And in that "sleep," the call of Crenshinibon came again to Rai-guy, a plea for help, for rescue, and a promise of great gain in return.

That predictable call was soon magnified a hundred times over, with even greater promises of glory and power, with images not of magnificent crystalline towers on the deserts of Calimshan, but of a tower of the purest opal set in the center of Menzoberranzan, a black structure gleaming with inner heat and energy.

Rai-guy's reminders of prudence could not hold against that image, against the parade of Matron Mothers, the hated Triel Baenre among them, coming to the tower to pay homage to him.

The dark elf's eyes popped open wide. He collected his thoughts and sprang from the chair, moving quickly to locate Kimmuriel, to alter the psionisict's instructions. Yes, he would open the gate back to Menzoberranzan, and yes, much of Bregan D'aerthe would return to their home.

But Rai-guy and Kimmuriel were not finished here just yet. They would remain with a strike force until the Crystal Shard had found a proper wielder, a dark elf wizard-cleric who would bring to the artifact its greatest level of power, and who would take from it the same.

* * * * *

In a dark chamber far under Dallabad Oasis, Yharaskrik silently congratulated himself on altering the promises of the Crystal Shard more greatly to entice Rai-guy. Kimmuriel had informed Yharaskrik of the change in Bregan D'aerthe's plans, but though Yharaskrik had outwardly accepted that change, the illithid was not willing to let the artifact go running off unchecked just yet. Through great concentration and mind control, Yharaskrik had been able to catch the subtle notes of the artifact's quiet call, but the illithid had not been able to begin to backtrack that call to the source.

Yharaskrik needed Bregan D'aerthe a bit longer, though the illithid recognized that once the drow band had fulfilled its purpose in locating the Crystal Shard, he and Rai-guy would likely be on opposite sides of the inevitable battle.

Let that be as it may, Yharaskrik realized. Kimmuriel Oblodra, a fellow psionicist who understood the deeper truths about Crenshinibon's shortcomings, would surely stand on his side of the battlefield.

Chapter 21

The Mask of a God

"Why would you live in a desert, when such beauty is so near?" Jarlaxle asked Entreri.

The pair had moved quickly in the days after the disaster at Gentleman Briar's tavern, with Entreri even enlisting one wizard they found in an out-of-the-way tower magically to transport them many miles closer to their goal of the Spirit Soaring and the priest, Cadderly.

It didn't hurt, of course, that Jarlaxle seemed to have an inexhaustible supply of gold coins.

Now the Snowflake Mountains were in clear sight, towering before them. Summer was on the wane, and the wind blew chill, but Entreri could hardly argue Jarlaxle's assessment of the landscape. It surprised the assassin that a drow would find beauty in such a surface environment. They looked down on a canopy of great and ancient trees that filled a long, wide vale nestled right up against the Snowflake's westernmost slopes. Even Entreri, who seemed to spend most of his time denying beauty, could not deny the majesty of the mountains themselves, tall and jagged, capped with bright snow gleaming brilliantly in the daylight.

"Calimport is where I make my living," Entreri answered after a while.

Jarlaxle snorted at the thought. "With your skills, you could make your home anywhere in the world," he said. "In Waterdeep or in Luskan, in Icewind Dale or even here. Few would deny the value of a powerful warrior in cities large and villages small. None would evict Artemis Entreri—unless, of course, they knew the man as I know him."

That brought a narrow-eyed gaze from the assassin, but it was all in jest, both knew—or perhaps it wasn't. Even in that case, there was too much truth to Jarlaxle's statement for Entreri rationally to take offense.

"We must swing around the mountains to the south to get to Carradoon, and the trails leading us to the Spirit Soaring," Entreri explained. "A few days should have us standing before Cadderly, if we make all haste."

"All haste, then," said Jarlaxle. "Let us be rid of the artifact, and . . ." He paused and looked curiously at Entreri.

Then what?

That question hung palpably in the air between them, though it had not been spoken. Ever since they had fled the crystalline tower in Dallabad, the pair had run with purpose and direction—to the Spirit Soaring to be rid of the dangerous artifact—but what, indeed, awaited them after that? Was Jarlaxle to return to Calimport to resume his command of Bregan D'aerthe? both wondered. Entreri knew at once as he pondered the possibility that he would not follow his dark elf companion in that case. Even if Jarlaxle could somehow overcome the seeds of change sown by Rai-guy and Kimmuriel, Entreri had no desire to be with the drow band again. He had no desire to measure his every step in light of the knowledge that the vast majority of his supposed allies would prefer it if he were dead.

Where would they go? Together or apart? Both were contemplating that question when a voice, strong yet melodic, resonant with power, drifted across the field to them.

"Halt and yield!" it said.

Entreri and Jarlaxle glanced over as one to see a solitary figure, a female elf, beautiful and graceful. She was approaching them openly, a finely crafted sword at her side.

"Yield?" Jarlaxle muttered. "Must everyone expect us to yield? And halt? Why, we were not even moving!"

Entreri was hardly listening, was focusing his senses on the trees around them. The elf maiden's gait told him much, and he confirmed his suspicions almost immediately, spotting one, and another, elf archer among the boughs, bows trained upon him and his companion.

"She is not alone," the assassin whispered to Jarlaxle, though he tried to keep the smile on his face as he spoke, an inviting expression for the approaching warrior.

"Elves rarely are," Jarlaxle replied quietly. "Particularly when they are confronting drow."

Entreri couldn't hold his smile, facing that simple truth. He expected the arrows to begin raining down upon them at any moment.

"Greetings!" Jarlaxle called loudly. He swept off his hat, making a point to show his heritage openly.

Entreri noted that the elf maiden did wince and slow briefly at the revelation, for even from her distance—and she was still thirty strides away—Jarlaxle, without the visually overwhelming hat, was obviously drow.

She came a bit closer, her expression holding perfectly calm and steady, revealing nothing. It occurred to Entreri then that this was no chance meeting. He took a moment to listen for the silent call of Crenshinibon, to try to determine if the Crystal Shard had brought in more opponents to free it from Entreri's grasp.

He sensed nothing unusual, no contact at all between the artifact and this elf.

"There are a hundred warriors about you," the elf maiden said, stopping some twenty paces from the pair. "They would like nothing better than to pierce your tiny drow heart with their arrows, but we have not come here for that—unless you so desire it."

"Preposterous!" Jarlaxle said, quite animatedly. "Why would I desire such a thing, fair elf? I am Drizzt Do'Urden of Icewind Dale, a ranger, and of heart not unlike your own, I am sure!"

The elf's lips grew very thin.

"She does not know of you, my friend," Entreri offered.

"Shayleigh of Shilmista Forest knows of Drizzt Do'Urden," Shayleigh assured them both. "And she knows of Jarlaxle of Bregan D'aerthe, and of Artemis Entreri, most vile of assassins."

That made the pair blink more than a few times. "Must be the Crystal Shard telling her," Jarlaxle whispered to his companion.

Entreri didn't deny that, but neither did he believe it. He closed his eyes, trying to sense some connection between the artifact and the elf maiden again, and again he found nothing. Nothing at all.

But how else could she know?

"And you are Shayleigh of Shilmista?" Jarlaxle asked politely. "Or were you, perchance, speaking of another?"

"I am Shayleigh," the elf announced. "I, and my friends gathered in the trees all around you, were sent out here to find you, Jarlaxle of Bregan D'aerthe. You carry an item of great importance to us."

"Not I," the drow said, feigning confusion and glad that he could further mask that confusion by speaking truthful words.

"The Crystal Shard is in the possession of Jarlaxle and Artemis Entreri," Shayleigh stated definitively. "I care not which of you carries it, only that you have it."

"They will strike fast," Jarlaxle whispered to Entreri. "The shard coaxes them in. No parlay here, I fear."

821

Entreri didn't get that feeling, not at all. The Crystal Shard was not calling to Shayleigh, nor to any of the other elves. If it had been, that call had undoubtedly been completely denied.

The assassin saw Jarlaxle making some subtle motions then—the movements of a spell, he figured—and he put a hand on the dark elf's arm, holding him still.

"We do indeed possess the item you claim," Entreri said to Shayleigh, stepping up ahead of Jarlaxle. He was playing a hunch here, and nothing more. "We are bringing it to Cadderly of the Spirit Soaring."

"For what purpose?" Shayleigh asked.

"That he may rid the world of it," Entreri answered boldly. "You say that you know of Drizzt Do'Urden. If that is true, and if you know Cadderly of the Spirit Soaring as well—which I believe you do—then you likely know that Drizzt was bringing this very artifact to Cadderly."

"Until it was stolen from him by a dark elf posing as Cadderly," Shayleigh said determinedly and in a leading tone. In truth, that was about as much as Cadderly had told her about how this particular pair had come to acquire the artifact.

"There are reasons for things that a casual observer might not understand," Jarlaxle interjected. "Be satisfied with the knowledge that we have the Crystal Shard and are delivering it, rightfully so, to Cadderly of the Spirit Soaring, that he might rid the world of the menace that is Crenshinibon."

Shayleigh motioned to the trees, and her companions walked out from the shadows. There were dozens of grim-faced elves, warriors all, armed with crafted bows and wearing fine weapons and gleaming, supple armor.

"I was instructed to deliver you to the Spirit Soaring," Shayleigh explained. "It was not clear whether or not you had to be alive. Walk swiftly and silently, make no movements that indicate any hostility, and perhaps you will live to see the great doors of the cathedral, though I assure you that I hope you do not."

She turned then and started away. The elves began to close in on the dark elf and his assassin companion, with their bows still in hand and arrows aimed for the kill.

"This is going better than I expected," Jarlaxle said dryly.

"You are an eternal optimist, then," Entreri replied in the same tone. He searched all around for some weakness in the ring of elves, but he saw only swift, inescapable death stamped on every fair face.

Jarlaxle saw it, too, even more clearly. "We are caught," he remarked.

"And if they know all the details of our encounter with Drizzt Do'Urden. . . ." Entreri said ominously, letting the words hang in the air.

Jarlaxle held his wry smile until Entreri had turned away, hoping that he wouldn't be forced to reveal the truth of that encounter to his companion. He didn't want to tell Entreri that Drizzt was still alive.

While Jarlaxle believed Entreri had gone beyond that destructive obsession with Drizzt, if he was wrong and Entreri learned the truth, he would likely be fighting for his life against the skilled warrior.

Jarlaxle glanced around at the many grim-faced elves and decided he already had enough problems.

*   *   *   *   *

As the meeting at the Spirit Soaring wore on, Cadderly fired back a testy remark concerning the feelings between the drow and the surface elves when Jarlaxle implied that he and his companion really couldn't trust anyone who brought them in under a guard of a score of angry elves.

"But you have already said that this is not about us," Jarlaxle reasoned. He glanced over at Entreri, but the assassin wasn't offering any support, wasn't offering anything at all.

Entreri hadn't spoken a word since they'd arrived, and neither had Cadderly's second at the meeting, a confident woman named Danica. Indeed, she and Entreri seemed cut of similar stuff—and neither of them seemed to like that fact. They had been staring, glowering at each other for nearly the entire time, as if there was some hidden agenda between them, some personal feud.

"True enough," Cadderly finally admitted. "In another situation, I would have many questions to ask of you, Jarlaxle of Menzoberranzan, and most of them far from complimentary toward your apparent actions."

"A trial?" the dark elf asked with a snort. "Is that your place, then, Magistrate Cadderly?"

The yellow-bearded dwarf behind the priest, obviously the more serious of the two dwarves, grumbled and shifted uncomfortably. His green-bearded brother just held his stupid, naive smile. To Jarlaxle's way of thinking, where he was always searching for layers under lies, that smile marked the green-bearded dwarf as the more dangerous of the two.

Cadderly eyed Jarlaxle without blinking. "We must all answer for our actions," he said.

"But to whom?" the drow countered. "Do you even begin to believe that you can understand the life I have lived, judgmental priest? How might you fare in the darkness of Menzoberranzan, I wonder?"

He meant to continue, but both Entreri and Danica broke their silence then, saying in unison, "Enough of this!"

"Ooo," mumbled the green-bearded dwarf, for the room went perfectly silent. Entreri and Danica were as surprised as the others at the coordination of their remarks. They stared hard at each other, seeming on the verge of battle.

"Let us conclude this," Cadderly said. "Give over the Crystal Shard and go on your way. Let your past haunt your own consciences then, and I will be concerned only with that which you do in the future. If you remain near to the Spirit Soaring, then know that your actions are indeed my province, and know that I will be watching."

"I tremble at the thought," Entreri said, before Jarlaxle could utter a similar, though less blunt, reply. "Unfortunately, for all of us, our time together has only just begun. I need you to destroy the wretched artifact, and you need me because I carry it."

"Give it over," Danica said, eyeing the man coldly.

Entreri smirked at her. "No."

"I am sworn to destroy it," Cadderly argued.

"I have heard such words before," Entreri replied. "Thus far, I am the only one who has been able to ignore the temptation of the artifact, and therefore, it remains with me until it is destroyed." He felt an inner twinge at that, a combination of a plea, a threat, and the purest rage he had ever known, all emanating from the imprisoned Crystal Shard.

Danica scoffed as if his claim was purely preposterous, but Cadderly held her in check.

"There is no need for such heroics from you," the priest assured Entreri. "You do not need to do this."

"I do," Entreri replied, though when he looked to Jarlaxle, it seemed to him as if his drow companion was siding with Cadderly.

Entreri could certainly see that point of view. Powerful enemies pursued them, and the Crystal Shard itself was not likely to be destroyed without a terrific battle. Still, Entreri knew in his heart that he had to see this through. He hated the artifact profoundly. He needed to see this controlling, awful item be utterly obliterated. He didn't know why he felt so strongly, but he did, plain and simple, and he wasn't giving over the artifact not to Cadderly or to Danica, not to Rai-guy and Kimmuriel, not to anyone while he still had breath in his body.

"I will finish this," Cadderly remarked.

"So you say," the assassin answered sarcastically and without hesitation.

"I am a priest of Deneir," Cadderly started to protest.

"I name supposedly goodly priests among the least trustworthy of all creatures," Entreri interrupted coldly. "They are on my scale just below troglodytes and green slime, the greatest hypocrites and liars in all the world."

"Please, my friend, do not temper your feelings," Jarlaxle said dryly.

"I would have thought that such a distinction would belong to assassins, murderers, and thieves," Danica remarked, her tone and expression making her hatred for Artemis Entreri quite evident.

"Dear girl, Artemis Entreri is no thief," Jarlaxle said with a grin, hoping to diffuse some of the mounting tension before it exploded—and he and his companion found themselves squared off against the formidable array within this room and without, where scores of priests and a group of elves were no doubt discussing the arrival of the two less-than-exemplary characters with more than a passing concern.

Cadderly put a hand on Danica's arm, calming her, and took a deep breath and started to reason it all out again.

Again Entreri cut him short. "However you wish to parse your words, the simple truth is that I possess the Crystal Shard, and that I, above all others who have tried, have shown the control necessary to hold its call in check.

"If you wish to take the artifact from me," Entreri continued, "then try, but know that I'll not give it over easily—and that I will even utilize the powers of the artifact against you. I wish it destroyed—you wish it destroyed, so you say. Thus, we do it together."

Cadderly paused for a long while, glanced over at Danica a couple of times, and to Jarlaxle, and neither offered him any answers. With a shrug, the priest looked back at Entreri.

"As you wish," he agreed. "The artifact must be engulfed in magical darkness and breathed upon by an ancient and huge red dragon."

Jarlaxle nodded, but then stopped, his dark eyes going wide. "Give it to him," he said to his companion.

Artemis Entreri, though he had no desire to face a red dragon of any size or age, feared more the consequence of Crenshinibon's becoming free to wield its power once more. He knew how to destroy it now—they all did—and the Crystal Shard would never suffer them to live, unless that life was as its servant.

That possibility Artemis Entreri loathed most of all.

* * * * *

Jarlaxle thought to mention that Drizzt Do'Urden had shown equal control, but he held the thought silent, not wanting to bring up the drow ranger in any context. Given Cadderly's understanding of the situation, it seemed obvious to Jarlaxle that the priest knew the truth of his encounter with Drizzt, and Jarlaxle did not want Entreri to discover that his nemesis was still alive—not now, at least, with so many other pressing issues before him.

Jarlaxle considered blurting it all out, on a sudden thought that speaking the truth plainly would heighten Entreri's willingness to be done with all of this, to give over the shard that he and Jarlaxle could pursue a more important matter—that of finding the drow ranger.

Jarlaxle held it back, and smiled, recognizing the source of the inspiration as a subtle telepathic ruse by the imprisoned artifact.

"Clever," he whispered, and merely smiled as all eyes turned to regard him.

* * * * *

Soon after, while Cadderly and his friends made preparations for the journey to the lair of some dragon Cadderly knew of, Entreri and Jarlaxle walked the grounds outside of the magnificent Spirit Soaring, well aware, of course, that many watchful eyes were upon their every move.

"It is undeniably beautiful, do you not agree?" Jarlaxle asked, looking back at the soaring cathedral, with its tall spires, flying buttresses, and great, colored windows.

"The mask of a god," Entreri replied sourly.

"The mask or the face?" asked the always-surprising Jarlaxle.

Entreri stared hard at his companion, and back at the towering cathedral. "The mask," he said, "or perhaps the illusion, concocted by those who seek to elevate themselves above all others and have not the skills to do so."

Jarlaxle looked at him curiously.

"A man inferior with the blade or with his thoughts can still so elevate himself," Entreri explained curtly, "if he can impart the belief that some god or other speaks through him. It is the greatest deception in all the world, and one embraced by kings and lords, while minor lying thieves on the streets of Calimport and other cities lose their tongues for so attempting to coax the purses of others."

That struck Jarlaxle as the most poignant and revealing insight he had yet pried from the mouth of the elusive Artemis Entreri, a great clue as to who this man truly was.

Up to that point, Jarlaxle had been trying to figure out a way that he could wait behind while Entreri, Cadderly, and whomever Cadderly chose to bring along went to face the dragon and destroy the artifact.

Now, because of this seemingly unrelated glimpse into the heart of Artemis Entreri, Jarlaxle realized he had to go along.

Chapter 22

In The Eye of the Beholder

The great beast lay at rest, but even in slumber did the dragon seem a terrible and wrathful thing. It curled catlike, its long tail running up past its head, its huge, scaly back rising like a giant wave and sinking in a great exhalation that sent plumes of gray smoke from its nostrils and injected a vibrating rumble throughout the stone of the cavern floor. There was no light in the rocky chamber, save the glow of the dragon itself, a reddish-gold hue—a hot light, as if the beast were too full of energy and savage fires to hold it all in with mere scales.

On the other end of the scrying mirror, the six unlikely companions—Cadderly, Danica, Ivan, Pikel, Entreri, and Jarlaxle—watched the dragon with a mixture of awe and dread.

"We could use Shayleigh and her archers," Danica remarked, but of course, that was not possible, since the elves had absolutely refused to work alongside the dark elf for any purpose whatsoever and had returned to their forest home in Shilmista.

"We could use King Elbereth's entire army," Cadderly added.

"Ooo," said Pikel, who seemed truly mesmerized by the beast, a great wyrm at least as large and horrific as old Fyrentennimar.

"There is the dragon," Cadderly said, turning to Entreri. "Are you certain you still wish to accompany me?" His question ended weakly, though, given the eager glow in Artemis Entreri's eyes.

The assassin reached into his pouch and brought forth the Crystal Shard.

"Witness your doom," he whispered to the artifact. He felt the shard reaching out desperately and powerfully—Cadderly felt those sensations as well. It called to Jarlaxle first, and indeed, the opportunistic drow did begin physically to reach for it, but he resisted.

"Put it away," Danica whispered harshly, looking from the green-glowing shard to the shifting beast. "It will awaken the dragon!"

"My dear, do you expect to coax the fiery breath from a dragon that remains asleep?" Jarlaxle reminded her, but Danica turned an angry glare at him.

Entreri, hearing the Crystal Shard's call clearly and recognizing its attempt, understood that the woman spoke wisely, though, for while they would indeed have to wake the beast, they would be far better served if it did not know why. The assassin looked at the artifact and gave a confident, cocky grin, and dropped it back into his pouch and nodded for Cadderly to disenchant the scrying mirror.

"When do we go?" the assassin asked Cadderly, and his tone made it perfectly clear that he wasn't shaken in the least by the sight of the monstrous dragon, made it clear that he was eager to be done with the destruction of the vile artifact.

"I have to prepare the proper spells," Cadderly replied. "It will not be long."

The priest motioned for Danica and his other friends to escort their two undesirable companions away then, though he only dropped the image from the scrying mirror temporarily. As soon as he was alone, he called up the dragon cave again, after placing another spell upon himself that allowed him to see in the dark. He sent the roving eye of the scrying mirror all around the large, intricate lair.

There were many great cracks in the floor, he noted, and when he followed one down, he came to recognize that a maze of tunnels and chambers lay beneath the sleeping wyrm. Furthermore, Cadderly wasn't convinced that the dragon's cave was very secure structurally. Not at all.

He'd have to keep that well in mind while choosing the spells he would bring with him to the home of this great beast known as Hephaestus.

* * * * *

Rai-guy, deep in concentration, his eyes closed, allowed the calls of Crenshinibon to invade his thoughts fully. He caught only flashes of anger and despair, the pleas for help, the promises of ultimate glory.

He saw some other images, as well, particularly one of a great curled red dragon, and he heard a word, a name echoing in his head: Hephaestus.

Rai-guy knew he had to act quickly. He settled back in his private chamber beneath House Basadoni and prayed with all his heart to his Lady Lolth, telling her of the Crystal Shard, and of the glorious chaos the artifact might allow him to bring to the world.

For hours, Rai-guy stayed alone, praying, sending away any who knocked at his door—Berg'inyon and Kimmuriel among them—with a gruff and definitive retort.

Then, when he believed he'd caught the attention of his dark Spider Queen, or at least the ear of one of her minions, the wizard fell into powerful spellcasting, opening an extra-planar gate.

As always with such a spell, Rai-guy had to take care that no unwanted or overly powerful planar denizens walked through that gate. His suspicions were correct, though, and indeed, the creature that came through the portal was one of the yochlol. These were the handmaidens of Lolth, beasts that more resembled half-melted candles with longer appendages than the Spider Queen herself.

Rai-guy held his breath, wondering suddenly and fearfully if he had erred in letting on about the artifact. Might Lolth desire the artifact herself and instruct Rai-guy to deliver it to her?

"You have called for help from the Lady," the yochlol said, its voice watery and guttural all at once, a dual-toned and horrible sound.

"I wish to return to Menzoberranzan," Rai-guy admitted, "and yet I cannot at this time. An instrument of chaos is about to be destroyed . . ."

"Lady Lolth knows of the artifact, Crenshinibon, Rai-guy of House Teyachumet," the yochlol replied, and the title the creature bestowed upon him surprised the drow wizard-cleric.

He had indeed been a son of House Teyachumet—but that house of Ched Nasad had been obliterated more than a century before. A subtle reminder, the drow realized, that the memory of Lolth and her minions was long indeed.

And a warning, perhaps, that he should take great care about how he planned to put the mighty artifact to use in the city of Lolth's greatest priestesses.

Rai-guy saw his dreams of domination over Menzoberranzan melt then and there.

"Where will you retrieve this item?" the handmaiden asked.

Rai-guy stammered a reply, his thoughts elsewhere for the moment. "Hephaestus's lair . . . a red dragon," he said. "I know not where . . ."

"Your answer will be given," the handmaiden promised.

It turned around and walked through Rai-guy's gate, and the portal closed immediately, though the drow wizard had done nothing to dispel it.

Had Lolth herself been watching the exchange? Rai-guy had to wonder and to fear. Again he understood the futility of his dreams of conquest over Menzoberranzan. The Crystal Shard was powerful indeed, perhaps powerful enough for Rai-guy to manipulate or otherwise unseat enough of the Matron Mothers for him to achieve a position of tremendous power, but something about the way the yochlol had spoken his full name told him he should be careful indeed. Lady Lolth would not permit such a change in the balance of Menzoberranzan's power structure.

For just a brief moment, Rai-guy considered abandoning his quest to retrieve the Crystal Shard, considered taking his remaining allies and his gains and retreating to Menzoberranzan as the coleader, along with his friend, Kimmuriel, of Bregan D'aerthe.

A brief moment it was, for the call of the Crystal Shard came rushing back to him then, whispering its promises of power and glory, showing Rai-guy that the surface was not so forbidding a place as he believed. With Crenshinibon, the dark elf could carry on Jarlaxle's designs, but in more appropriate regions—a mountainous area teeming with goblins, perhaps—and build a magnificent and undyingly loyal legion of minions, of slaves.

The drow wizard rubbed his slender black fingers together, waiting anxiously for the answer the yochlol had promised him.

* * * * *

"You cannot deny the beauty," Jarlaxle remarked, he and Entreri again sitting outside of the cathedral, relaxing before their journey. Both were well aware that many wary gazes were focused upon them from many vantage points.

"Its very purpose denies that beauty," Entreri replied, his tone showing that he had little desire to replay this conversation yet again.

Jarlaxle studied the man closely, as if hoping that physical scrutiny alone would unlock this apparently dark episode in Artemis Entreri's past. The drow wasn't surprised by Entreri's dislike of "hypocritical" priests. In many ways, Jarlaxle agreed with him. The dark elf had been alive for a long, long time, and had often ventured out of Menzoberranzan—and had known the movements of practically every visitor to that dark city—and he had seen enough of the many varied religious sects of Toril to understand the hypocritical nature of many so-called priests. There was something far deeper than that looming here within Artemis Entreri, though, something visceral. It had to be an event in Entreri's past, a deeply disturbing episode involving a priest. Perhaps he had been wrongly accused of some crime and tortured by a priest, who often served as jailers for the smaller communities of the surface. Perhaps he had known love once, and that woman had been stolen from him or had been murdered by a priest.

Whatever it was, Jarlaxle could clearly see the hatred in Entreri's dark eyes as the man looked upon the magnificent—and it was magnificent, by any standards—Spirit Soaring. Even for Jarlaxle, a creature of the Underdark, the place lived up to its name, for when he gazed upon those soaring towers, his very soul was lifted, his spirit enlightened and elevated.

Not so for his companion, obviously, and yet another mystery of Artemis Entreri for Jarlaxle to unravel. He did indeed find this man interesting.

"Where will you go after the artifact is destroyed?" Entreri asked unexpectedly.

Jarlaxle had to pause, both fully to digest the question and to consider his answer—for in truth, he really had no answer. "*If* we destroy it, you mean," he corrected. "Have you ever dealt with the likes of a red dragon, my friend?"

"Cadderly has, as I'm sure have you," Entreri replied.

"Only once, and I truly have little desire ever to speak with such a beast again," Jarlaxle said. "One cannot reason with a red dragon beyond a certain level, because they are not creatures with any definitive goals for personal gain. They see, they destroy, and take what is left over. A simple existence, really, and one that makes them all the more dangerous."

"Then let it see the Crystal Shard and destroy it," Entreri remarked, and he felt a twinge then as Crenshinibon cried out.

"Why?" Jarlaxle asked suddenly, and Entreri recognized that his ever-opportunistic friend had heard that silent call.

"Why?" the assassin echoed, turning to regard Jarlaxle fully.

"Perhaps we are being premature in our planning," Jarlaxle explained. "We know how to destroy the Crystal Shard now—likely that will be enough for us to use against the artifact to bend it continually to our will."

Entreri started to laugh.

"There is truth in what I say, and a gain to be had in following my reasoning," Jarlaxle insisted. "Crenshinibon began to manipulate me, no doubt, but now that we have determined that you, and not the artifact, are truly the master of your relationship, why must we rush ahead to destroy it? Why not determine first if you might control the item enough for our own gain?"

"Because if you know, beyond doubt, that you can destroy it, and the Crystal Shard knows that, as well, there may well be no need to destroy it," Entreri played along.

"Exactly!" said the now-excited dark elf.

"Because if you know you can destroy the crystalline tower, then there is no possible way that you will wind up with two crystalline towers," Entreri replied sarcastically, and the eager grin disappeared from Jarlaxle's black-skinned face in the blink of an astonished eye.

831

"It did it again," the drow remarked dryly.

"Same bait on the hook, and the Jarlaxle fish chomps even harder," Entreri replied.

"The cathedral is beautiful, I say," Jarlaxle remarked, looking away and pointedly changing the subject.

Entreri laughed again.

* * * * *

Delay him, then, Yharaskrik imparted to Kimmuriel when the drow told the illithid the plan to intercept Jarlaxle, Entreri, and the priest Cadderly and his friends at the lair of Hephaestus the red dragon.

Rai-guy will not be deterred in any way short of open battle, Kimmuriel explained. *He will have the Crystal Shard at all costs.*

Because the Crystal Shard so instructs him, Yharaskrik replied.

Yet it seems as if he has freed himself, partially at least, from its grasp, Kimmuriel argued. *He dismissed many of the drow soldiers back to our warren in Menzoberranzan and has systematically relinquished our holdings here on the surface.*

True enough, the illithid admitted, *but you are fooling yourself if you believe that the Crystal Shard will allow Rai-guy to take it to the lightless depths of the Underdark. It is a relic that derives its power from the light of the sun.*

Rai-guy believes that a few crystalline towers on the surface will allow the artifact to channel that sunlight power back to Menzoberranzan, Kimmuriel explained, for indeed, the drow wizard had told him of that very possibility—a possibility that Crenshinibon itself had imparted to Rai-guy.

Rai-guy has come to see many possibilities, Yharaskrik's thoughts imparted, and there was a measure of doubt, translated into sarcasm, in the illithid's response. *The source of those varied and marvelous possibilities is always the same.*

It was a point on which Kimmuriel Oblodra, who now found himself caught in the middle of five dangerous adversaries—Rai-guy, Yharaskrik, Jarlaxle, Artemis Entreri, and the Crystal Shard itself—did not wish to dwell. There was little he could do to alter the approaching events. He would not go against Rai-guy, out of respect for the wizard-cleric's prowess and intelligence, and also because of his deep relationship with the drow. Of his potential enemies, Kimmuriel feared Yharaskrik least of all. With Rai-guy at his side, he knew the illithid could not win. Kimmuriel could neutralize Yharaskrik's mental weaponry long enough for Rai-guy to obliterate the creature.

While he held respect for the manipulative powers of the Crystal Shard and knew that the mighty artifact would not be pleased with any psionicist, Kimmuriel was honestly beginning to believe that the artifact was indeed a fine match for Rai-guy, a joining that would be of mutual benefit. Jarlaxle hadn't been able to control the artifact, but Jarlaxle had not been properly forewarned about its manipulative powers. Kimmuriel doubted that Rai-guy would make that same mistake.

Still, the psionicist believed that all would be simpler and cleaner if the Crystal Shard were indeed destroyed, but he wasn't about to go against Rai-guy to ensure that event.

He looked at the illithid and realized that he already had gone against his friend, to some extent, merely by informing this bulbous-headed creature, who was certainly an enemy of Rai-guy, that Rai-guy meant to enter an alliance with the Crystal Shard.

Kimmuriel bowed to Yharaskrik out of respect, and floated away on psionic winds, back to House Basadoni and his private chambers. Not far down the hall, he knew, Rai-guy was awaiting his answer from the yochlol and plotting his strike against Jarlaxle and the fallen leader's newfound companions.

Kimmuriel had no idea where he was going to fit into all of this.

Chapter 23

The Face of Disaster

Artemis Entreri eyed the priest of Deneir with obvious mistrust as Cadderly walked up before him and began a slow chant. Cadderly had already cast prepared defensive spells upon himself, Danica, Ivan, and Pikel, but it occurred to Entreri that the priest might use this opportunity to get rid of him. What better way to destroy Entreri than to have him face the breath of a dragon errantly thinking he had proper magical defenses against such a firestorm?

The assassin glanced over at Jarlaxle, who had refused Cadderly's aid, claiming he had his own methods. The dark elf nodded to him and waggled his fingers, silently assuring Entreri that Cadderly had indeed placed the antifire enchantment upon him.

When he was done, Cadderly stepped back and inspected the group. "I still believe that I can do this better alone," he remarked, drawing a scowl from both Danica and Entreri.

"If it was as simple as erecting a fire barrier and tossing out the artifact for the dragon to breathe upon, I would agree," Jarlaxle replied. "You may need to goad the beast to breathe, I fear. Wyrms are not quick to use their most powerful weapon."

"When it sees us all, it will more likely loose its breath," Danica reasoned.

"Poof!" agreed Pikel.

"Contingencies, my dear Cadderly," said Jarlaxle. "We must allow for every contingency, must prepare for every eventuality and turn in the game. With an ancient and intelligent wyrm, no variable is unlikely."

Their conversation ended as they both noted Pikel hopping about his brother, sprinkling some powder over the protesting and slapping Ivan, while singing a whimsical song. He finished with a wide smile, and hopped up and whispered into Ivan's ear.

"Says he got a spell of his own to add," the yellow-bearded dwarf remarked. "Put one on meself and on himself, and's wondering which o' ye others'll be wantin' one."

"What type of spell?"

"Another fire protection," Ivan explained. "Says doo-dads can do that."

That brought a laugh to Jarlaxle—not because he didn't believe the dwarf's every word, but because he found the entire spectacle of a dwarven druid quite charming. He bowed to Pikel and accepted the dwarf's next spellcasting. The others followed suit.

"We will be as quick as possible," Cadderly explained, moving them all to the large window at the back of the room on a high floor in one of the Spirit Soaring's towering spires. "Our goal is to destroy the item and nothing more. We are not to battle the beast, not to raise its ire, and," he looked at Entreri and Jarlaxle as he finished, "surely not to attempt to steal anything from mighty Hephaestus.

"Remember," the priest added, "the enchantments upon you may diminish one blast of Hephaestus's fire, perhaps two, but not much more than that."

"One will be enough," Entreri replied.

"Too much," muttered Jarlaxle.

"Does everyone know his or her role and position when we enter the dragon's main chamber?" Danica asked, ignoring the grumbling drow.

No questions came back at her. Taking that as an affirmative answer, Cadderly began casting yet again, a wind-walking spell that soon carried them out of the cathedral and across the miles to the south and east to the caverns of mighty Hephaestus. The priest didn't magically walk them in the front door, but rather soared along deeper chambers, the under-structure of the cavern complex, coming into a large antechamber to the dragon's main lair.

When he broke the spell, depositing their material forms in the cavern, they could hear the great sighing sound of the sleeping wyrm, the huge intake and smoky exhalation.

Jarlaxle put a finger to pursed lips and inched ahead, as silent as could be. He disappeared around an outcropping of stone, and came right back in, actually clutching the wall to steady himself. He looked at the others and nodded grimly, though there could be no doubt he had seen the beast simply from the expression on his normally confident face.

Cadderly and Entreri led the way, Danica and Jarlaxle followed, with the Bouldershoulder brothers behind. The tunnel behind the outcropping wound only for a short distance, and opened up widely into a huge cavern, its floor crisscrossed by many cracks and crevices.

The companions hardly noticed the physical features of that room, though, for there before them, looming like a mountain of doom, lay Hephaestus, its red-gold scales gleaming from its own inner heat. The beast was huge, even curled as it was, its size alone mocking them and making every one of them want to fall to his knees and pay homage.

That was one of the traps in dealing with dragons, that awe-inspiring aura of sheer power, that emanation of helplessness to all who would look upon their horrible splendor.

These were not novice warriors, though, trying to make a quick stab at great fame. These were seasoned veterans, every one. Each, with the exception of Artemis Entreri, had faced a beast such as Hephaestus before. Despite his inexperience in this particular arena, nothing in all the world—not a dragon, not an arch-devil, not a demon lord—could take the heart from Artemis Entreri.

The wyrm's eye, seeming more like that of a cat than a lizard, with a green iris and a slitted pupil that quickly widened to adjust to the dim light, popped open as soon as the group entered. Hephaestus watched their every movement.

"Did you think to catch me sleeping?" the dragon said quietly, which still made its voice sound like an avalanche to the companions.

Cadderly called out a cueing word to his companions, and snapped his fingers, bringing forth a magical light that filled all the chamber.

Up snapped Hephaestus's great horned head, the pupils of its eyes fast thinning. It turned as it rose, to face the impertinent priest directly.

To the side, Entreri eased the Crystal Shard out of his pouch, ready to throw it before the beast as soon as Hephaestus seemed about to loose its fiery breath. Jarlaxle, too, was ready, for his job in this was to use his innate dark elf powers to bring forth a globe of darkness over the artifact as the flames consumed it.

"*Thieves!*" the dragon roared. Its voice shook the chamber and sent shudders through the floor—a poignant reminder to Cadderly of the instability of this place. "You have come to steal the treasure of Hephaestus. You have prepared your proper spells and wear items of magic that you consider powerful, but are you truly prepared? Can any mere mortal truly be prepared to face the awful splendor that is Hephaestus?"

Cadderly tuned out the words and fell into the song of Deneir, seeking some powerful spell, some type of mighty magical chaos, perhaps, as he had once used against Fyrentennimar, that he could trick the beast and be done with this. His best spells against the previous dragon had been of reverse aging, lessening the beast with mighty spellcasting, but he could not use those this time, for so doing would diminish the dragon's breath as well, and defeat their very purpose in being there. He had other magic at his disposal, though, and the Song of Deneir rang triumphantly in his head. Along with that song, though, the priest heard the calls of Cren-shinibon, discordant notes in the melody and surely a distraction.

"Something is amiss," Jarlaxle whispered to Entreri. "The beast expected us and anticipates our movements. It should have risen with attacks, not words."

Entreri glanced at him, and back at Hephaestus, the great head swaying back and forth, back and forth. He glanced down at the Crystal Shard, wondering if it had betrayed them to the beast.

* * * * *

Indeed, Crenshinibon was sending forth its plea at that time, to the beast and against Cadderly's spellcasting, but it had not been the Crystal Shard that had warned Hephaestus of intruders. No, that distinction fell to a certain dark elf wizard-cleric, hiding in a tunnel across the way along with a handful of drow companions. Right before Cadderly and the others had wind-walked into the lair, Rai-guy had sent a magical whisper to Hephaestus, a warning of intruders and a suggestion that these thieves had come with magic designed to use the creature's own breath against it.

Now Rai-guy waited for the appearance of the Crystal Shard, for the moment when he and his companions, including Kimmuriel, could strike hard and begone, their prize in hand.

* * * * *

"Thieves we are, and we'll have your treasure!" shouted Jarlaxle. He used a language that none of the others, save Hephaestus, understood, a tongue of the red dragons, and one that the great wyrms believed that few others could begin to master. Jarlaxle, using a whistle that he kept on a chain around his neck, spoke it with perfect inflection. Hephaestus's head snapped down in line with him, the wyrm's eyes going wide.

Entreri dived aside in a roll, coming right back to his feet.

"What did you say?" the assassin asked.

Jarlaxle's fingers worked furiously. *He thinks that I am another red dragon.*

There seemed a long, long moment of absolute quiet, of a gigantic hush before a more gigantic storm. Then everything exploded into motion, beginning with Cadderly's leap forward, his arm extended, finger pointing accusingly at the beast.

"Hephaestus!" the priest roared at the appropriate moment of spellcasting. "Burn me if you can!"

838

It was more than a dare, more than a challenge, and more than a threat. It was a magical compulsion, launched through a powerful spell. Though forewarned by some vague suggestions against the action, Hephaestus sucked in its tremendous breath, the force of the intake drawing Cadderly's curly brown locks forward onto his face.

Entreri dived ahead and pulled forth Crenshinibon, tossing it to the floor before the priest. Jarlaxle, even as Hephaestus tilted back its head, came forward with the great exhalation and produced his globe of darkness.

No! Crenshinibon screamed in Entreri's head, so powerful and angry a call that the assassin grabbed at his ears and stumbled aside, dazed.

The artifact's call was abruptly cut off.

Hephaestus's head came forward, a great line of fire roaring down, mocking Jarlaxle's globe, mocking Cadderly and all his spells.

* * * * *

Even as the globe of darkness came up over the Crystal Shard, Rai-guy grabbed at it with a spell of telekinesis, a sudden and powerful burst of snatching power that sent the item flying fast across the way, past Hephaestus, who was seemingly oblivious to it, and down the corridor to the hiding wizard-cleric's waiting hand.

Rai-guy's red-glowing eyes narrowed as he turned to regard Kimmuriel, for it had been Kimmuriel's task to so snatch the item—a task the psionicist had apparently neglected.

I was not fast enough, the psionicist's fingers waggled at his companion.

But Rai-guy knew better, and so did Crenshinibon, for the powers of the mind were among the quickest of magic to enact. Still staring hard at his companion, Rai-guy began spellcasting once more, aiming for the great chamber.

* * * * *

On and on went the fiery maelstrom, and in the middle of it stood Cadderly, his arms out wide, praying to Deneir to see him through.

Danica, Ivan, and Pikel stared at him intently, praying as well, but Jarlaxle was more concerned with his darkness, and Entreri was looking more to Jarlaxle.

"I hear not the continuing call of Crenshinibon!" Entreri cried hopefully above the fiery roar.

Jarlaxle was shaking his head. "The darkness should have been consumed by the artifact's destruction," he cried back, sensing that something was terribly, terribly wrong.

The fires ended, leaving a seething Hephaestus still staring at the unharmed priest of Deneir. The dragon's eyes narrowed to threatening slits.

Jarlaxle dispelled his darkness globe, and there remained no sign of Crenshinibon among the bubbling, molten stone.

"We done it!" Ivan cried.

"Home!" Pikel pleaded.

"No," insisted Jarlaxle.

Before he could explain, a low humming sound filled the chamber, a noise the dark elf had heard before and one that didn't strike him as overly pleasant at that dangerous moment.

"A magical dispel!" the dark elf warned. "Our enchantments are threatened!"

This left them, they all realized, in a room with an outraged, ancient, huge red dragon without many of their protections in place.

"What d' we do?" Ivan growled, slapping the handle of his battle axe across his open palm.

"Wee!" Pikel answered.

"Wee?" the perplexed yellow-bearded dwarf echoed, his face screwed up as he stared at his green-haired brother.

"Wee!" Pikel said again, and to accentuate his point, he grabbed Ivan by the collar and ran him a short distance to the side, to the edge of a crevice, and leaped off, taking Ivan on the dive with him.

Hephaestus's great wings beat the air, lifting the huge wyrm's front half high above the floor. Its hind legs clawed at the floor, digging deep gullies in the stone.

"Run away!" Cadderly cried, agreeing wholeheartedly with Pikel's choice. "All of you!"

Danica rushed forward, as did Jarlaxle, the woman rolling into a ready crouch before the wyrm. Hephaestus wasted not a second in snapping its great maw down at her. She scrambled aside, coming up from her roll in a crouch again, taunting the beast.

Cadderly couldn't watch it, reminding himself that he simply had to trust in her. She was buying him precious moments, he knew, that he might launch another magical attack or defensive spell, perhaps, at Hephaestus. He fell into the song of Deneir again and heard its notes more clearly this time, as he sorted through an array of spells to launch.

He heard a scream, Danica's scream, and he looked up to see Hephaestus's fiery breath drive down upon her, striking the stone floor and spraying up in an inverted fan of fires.

Cadderly, too, cried out, and reached desperately into the song of Deneir for the first spell he could find that would alter that horrible scene, the first enchantment he could think of to stop it.

He brought forth an earthquake.

Even as it started—a violent shudder and rumbling, like waves on a pond, lifting and rolling the floor—Jarlaxle drew the dragon's attention his way by hitting the beast with a stream of stinging daggers.

Entreri, too, moved—and surprised himself by going ahead instead of back, toward the spot where Hephaestus had just breathed.

There, too, there was only bubbling stone.

Cadderly called out for Danica, desperately, but his voice fell away as the floor collapsed beneath him.

* * * * *

"Let us begone, and quickly," Kimmuriel remarked, "before the great wyrm recognizes that there were more than those six intruders in its lair this day."

He and the other drow had already moved some distance down the tunnel, away from the main chamber. Leaving altogether seemed a prudent suggestion, one that had Berg'inyon Baenre and the other five drow soldiers nodding eagerly, but one that, for some reason, did not seem acceptable to the stern Rai-guy.

"No," he said firmly. "They must all die, here and now."

"As the dragon will likely kill them," Berg'inyon agreed, but Rai-guy was shaking his head, indicating that such a probability simply wasn't good enough for him.

Rai-guy and Crenshinibon were already fully into their bonding by then. The Crystal Shard demanded that Cadderly and the others, these infidels who understood the secret to its destruction, be killed immediately. It demanded that nothing concerning the group be left to chance. Besides, it telepathically coaxed Rai-guy, would not a red dragon be an enormous asset to add to Bregan D'aerthe?

"Find them and kill them, every one!" Rai-guy demanded emphatically.

Berg'inyon considered the command, and broke his soldiers into two groups and ran off with one group, the other heading a different direction. Kimmuriel spent a longer time staring hard at Rai-guy, seeming less than pleased. He, too, disappeared eventually, seemed simply to fall through the floor.

Leaving Rai-guy alone with his newest and most beloved ally.

* * * * *

In an alcove off to the side of the tunnel where Rai-guy stood, Yharaskrik's less-than-corporeal form slid through the stone and materialized, the illithid's Crenshinibon-defeating lantern in its hand.

Chapter 24

Chaos

With skills honed to absolute perfection, Danica had avoided the flames by a short distance, close enough so that her skin was bright red on the left side of her face. No magic would aid Danica now, she knew, only her thousands and thousands of hours of difficult training, those many years she had spent perfecting her style of fighting and, more importantly, dodging. Danica had no intention of battling the great wyrm, of striking out in any offensive manner against a beast she doubted she could even hurt, let alone slay. All her abilities, all her energy and concentration, was solely on the defensive now, her posture a balanced crouch that would allow her to skitter out to either side, ahead, or back.

Hephaestus's fang-filled jaws snapped down at her with a tremendous clapping noise, but the dragon hit only air as the monk dived out to the right. A claw followed, a swipe that surely would have cut Danica into pieces, except that she altered the momentum of her roll to go straight back in a sudden retreat.

Then came the breath, another burst of fire that seemed to go on and on forever.

Danica had to dive and roll a couple of times to put out the flames on the back side of her clothing. Sensing that Hephaestus had noted her escape and would adjust the line of fiery breath, she cut a fast corner around a jag in the wall, throwing herself flat against the stone behind the protective rock.

She noted two figures then. Artemis Entreri was running her way, but leaping short of her position into a wide crevice that had opened with Cadderly's earthquake. The strange dark elf, Jarlaxle, skittered behind the dragon, and to Danica's astonishment, launched a spell Hephaestus's way. A sudden arc of lightning caught the dragon's attention and gave Danica a moment of freedom. She didn't waste it.

Danica ran flat out, leaping even as the spinning Hephaestus swept its great tail around to squash her. She disappeared into the same crevice as had Artemis Entreri.

She knew as soon as she crossed the lip of the crack that she was in trouble—but still far less trouble, she supposed, than she would have found back in the dragon's lair. The descent twisted and turned, lined with broken and often sharp-edged, stone. Again Danica's training came into play, her hands and legs working furiously to buffer the blows and slow her descent. Some distance down, the crack opened into a chamber, and Danica had nothing to hold onto for the last twenty feet of her drop. Still, she coordinated her movements so that she landed feet first, but with her legs turned slightly, propelling her into a sidelong somersault. She tumbled over and over again, her roll absorbing the momentum of the fall.

She came up to her feet a few moments later, and there before her, leaning on a wall looking bruised but hardly battered, stood Artemis Entreri. He was staring at her intently and held a lit torch in his hand but tossed it aside as soon as Danica took note of him.

"I had thought you consumed by the first of Hephaestus's fires," the assassin remarked, coming away from the wall and drawing both sword and dagger, the smaller blade glowing with a white, fiery light.

"One cannot always get what one most wants," the woman answered coldly.

"You have hated me since the moment you saw me," the assassin remarked, ending with a chuckle to show that he hardly cared.

"Long before that, Artemis Entreri," Danica replied coldly, and she advanced a step, eyeing the assassin's weapons intently.

"We know not what enemies we will find down here," Entreri explained, but he knew even as he said the words, as he looked upon Danica's mask of hatred, that no explanation would suffice, that anything short of his surrender to her would invite her wrath. Artemis Entreri had little desire to battle the woman, to do any unnecessary fighting down here, but neither would he shy from any fight.

"Indeed," was all that Danica answered. She continued coming forward.

This had been coming for some time, both knew, and despite the fact that they were both separated from their respective companions, despite the fact that an angry dragon was barely fifty feet above their heads, and all of it in a cavern that seemed on the verge of complete collapse, Danica saw this encounter as more than an opportunity but a necessity.

For all his logic and common sense, Artemis Entreri really wasn't disappointed by her feelings.

* * * * *

As soon as Hephaestus began its stunningly fast spin, Jarlaxle had to question the wisdom of his distracting lightning bolt. Still, the drow had reacted as any ally would, taking the beast's attention so that both Entreri and the woman might escape.

In truth, after the initial shock of seeing an outraged red dragon turning at him, Jarlaxle wasn't overly worried. Despite the powerful dispel that had saturated the room—too powerful a spell for any dragon to cast, the mercenary leader recognized—Jarlaxle remained confident that he possessed enough tricks to get away from this one.

Hephaestus's great jaws snapped down at the drow, who was standing perfectly still and seemed an easy target. The magic of Jarlaxle's cloak forced the wyrm to miss, and Hephaestus roared all the louder when its head slammed into a solid wall.

Next, predictably, came the fiery breath, but even as Hephaestus began its great exhale, Jarlaxle waggled a ringed finger, opening a dimension door that brought him behind the dragon. He could have simply skittered away then, but he wanted to hold the beast at bay a little bit longer. Out came a wand, one of several the drow carried, and it spewed a gob of greenish semiliquid at the very tip of Hephaestus's twitching tail.

"Now you are caught!" Jarlaxle proclaimed loudly as the fiery breath at last ceased.

Hephaestus spun around again, and indeed, the wyrm's tail looped about, its end stuck fast by the temporary but incredibly effective goo.

Jarlaxle let fly another wad from the wand, this one smacking the dragon in the face.

Of course, then Jarlaxle remembered why he had never wanted to face such a beast as this again, for Hephaestus went into a terrific frenzy, issuing growls through its clamped mouth that resonated through the very stones of the cavern. It thrashed about so wildly its tail tore the stone from the floor.

With a tip of his wide-brimmed hat, the mercenary drow called upon his magical ring again, one of the last portal-enacting enchantments it could offer, and disappeared back behind the wyrm, a bit further along the wall than he had been before his first dimension door. There was another exit from the room back there, one that Jarlaxle suspected would bring him to some old friends.

845

Some old friends who likely had the Crystal Shard, he knew, for certainly it had not been destroyed by Hephaestus's first breath, certainly it had been magically stolen away right before the powerful magic-defeating spell had filled the room.

The last thing Jarlaxle wanted was for Rai-guy and Kimmuriel to get their hands on the Crystal Shard and, undoubtedly, come looking for him once more.

He was out of the cavern a moment later, the thunderous sounds of Hephaestus's thrashing thankfully left behind. He reached up into his marvelous hat and brought forth a piece of black cloth in the shape of a small bat. He whispered a few magical words and tossed it into the air. The cloth swatch transformed into a living, breathing creature, a servant of its creator that fluttered back to Jarlaxle's shoulder. The drow whispered some instructions into its ear and tossed it up before him again, and his little scout flew off into the gloom.

* * * * *

"We will take Hephaestus as our own," Rai-guy whispered to the Crystal Shard, the drow considering all the great gains that might be made this day. Logically, the dark elf knew he should be well on his way out of the place, for could Kimmuriel and the others really defeat Jarlaxle and the powerful companions he had brought to the dragon's lair?

Rai-guy smiled, hardly afraid, for how could he be fearful with Crenshinibon in his possession? Soon, very soon, he knew, he would be allied with a great wyrm. He turned and started down the wide tunnel toward the main chamber of Hephaestus's lair.

He noticed some movement off to the side, in an alcove, and Crenshinibon screamed a warning in his head.

Yharaskrik stepped out, not ten paces away. The tentacles around the illithid's mouth were waving menacingly.

"Kimmuriel's friend, no doubt," the dark elf remarked, "who betrayed Kohrin Soulez."

Betrayal implies alliance, Yharaskrik telepathically answered. *There was no betrayal.*

"If you were to venture here with us, then why not do so openly?" the drow asked.

I came for you, not with you, the ever-confident illithid answered.

Rai-guy understood well what was going on, for the Crystal Shard was making its abject hatred of the creature quite apparent in his thoughts.

"The drow and your race have been allied many times in the past," Rai-guy remarked, "and rarely have we found reason to do battle. So it should be now."

The wizard wasn't trying to talk the illithid out of any rash actions out of fear—far from it. He was thinking he might have, perhaps, made another powerful connection here, one that could be exploited.

The screaming in his mind, Crenshinibon's absolute hatred of the mind flayer, made that alliance seem less likely.

And even less likely a moment later, when Yharaskrik lit the magical lantern and aimed its glow Crenshinibon's way. The protests in the drow wizard's mind faded far, far away.

The artifact will be brought back before the dragon, came Yharaskrik's telepathic call. It was a psionically enhanced command, and one that had Rai-guy involuntarily taking a step toward the main chamber once more.

The cunning dark elf had survived more than a century in the hostile territory of his own homeland, and he was no novice to any type of battle. He fought back against the compelling suggestion and rooted his feet to the floor, turning back to regard the octopus-headed creature, his red-glowing eyes narrowing threateningly.

"Release the Crystal Shard and perhaps we will let you live," Rai-guy said.

It must be destroyed! Yharaskrik screamed into his mind. *It is an item of no gain, of loss to all, even to itself.* As the creature finished, it held the lantern up even higher and advanced a step, its tentacles wriggling out, reaching for Rai-guy hungrily though the drow was still too far away for any physical attack, but not out of range for psionic attacks, the drow found out a split second later, even as he began casting his own spell.

A blast of stunning and confusing energy washed over him, reached into him, and scrambled his mind. He felt himself falling over backward, watched almost helplessly as his line of vision rolled up the wall, and to the high ceiling.

He called for Crenshinibon, but it was too far away, lost in the swirl of the magical lantern's glow. He thought of the illithid, of those horrid tentacles burrowing under his skin, reaching for his brain.

Rai-guy steadied himself and fought desperately, finally regaining his balance and glancing back to see Yharaskrik very close—too close, those tentacles almost touching him.

He nearly exploded into the motion of yet another spellcasting, but he recognized that he had to be more subtle here, that he had to make the creature believe he was defeated. That was the secret of battling illithids, as many drow had been trained. Play upon their arrogance. Yharaskrik, like all of its kind, would hardly be able to comprehend that an inferior creature like a drow had somehow resisted its psionic attacks.

Rai-guy worked a simple spell, with subtle movements, and all the while feigning helplessness.

It must be done! the illithid screamed in his thoughts. The tentacles moved toward Rai-guy's face, and Yharaskrik's hand reached for the Crystal Shard.

Rai-guy released his spell. It was not a devastating blast, not a rumble of some great explosion, not a bolt of lightning nor a gout of fire. A simple gust of wind came from the drow's hand, a sharp and surprising burst that snapped Yharaskrik's tentacles back across its ugly face, that blew the creature's robes back behind it and forced it to retreat a step.

That blew out the lantern.

Yharaskrik glanced down, thought to summon some psionic energy to relight the lantern, and looked up and thought to strike Rai-guy with another psionic blast of scrambling energy, fearing some second spellcasting.

As quickly as the illithid could begin to do either of those things, a wave of crushing emotions washed over it, a Crenshinibon-imparted flood of despair and hopelessness, and, paradoxically of hope, with subtle promises that all could be put right, with greater glory gained for all.

Yharaskrik's psionic defenses came up almost immediately, dulling the Crystal Shard's demanding call.

A jolt of energy, the shocking grasp of Rai-guy, caught the illithid on the chest, lifted it from the ground, and sent it sprawling backward to the floor.

"Fool!" Rai-guy growled. "Do you think I need Crenshinibon to destroy the likes of you?"

Indeed, when Yharaskrik looked back at the drow wizard, thinking to attack mentally, he stared at the end of a small black wand. The illithid let go the blast anyway, and indeed it staggered Rai-guy backward, but the drow had already enacted the power of the wand. It was a wand similar to the one Jarlaxle had used to pin down Hephaestus's tail and momentarily clamp the dragon's mouth shut.

It took Rai-guy a long moment to fight through this burst of scrambling energy, but when he did stand straight again, he laughed aloud at the spectacle of the illithid splayed out on the floor, held in place by a viscid green glob.

The mental domination from Crenshinibon began on the creature anew, wearing at its resolve. Rai-guy walked to tower over Yharaskrik, to look the helpless mind flayer in the bulbous eye, letting it know in no uncertain terms that this fight was at its end.

* * * * *

She had no apparent weapon, but Entreri knew better than to ask for her surrender, knew well enough what this skilled warrior was capable of. He had battled fighting monks before, though not often, and had always found them full of surprises. He could see the honed muscles of Danica's legs twitching eagerly, the woman wanting badly to come at him.

"Why do you hate me so?" the assassin asked with a wry grin, halting his advance a mere three strides from Danica. "Or is it, perhaps, that you simply fear me and are afraid to show it? For you should fear me, you understand."

Danica stared at him hard. She did indeed hate this man, and had heard much about him from Drizzt Do'Urden, and even more—and even more damning—testimony from Catti-brie. Everything about him assaulted her sensibilities. To Danica, finding Artemis Entreri in the company of dark elves seemed more an indictment of the dark elves.

"But perhaps we would do better to settle our differences when we are far, far from this place," Entreri offered. "Though our fight is inevitable in your eyes, is it not?"

"Logic would so dictate to both," Danica replied. As she finished the sentence, she came forward in a rush, slid down to the floor beneath Entreri's extending blade, and swept him from his feet. "But neither of us is a slave to wise thinking, are we, foul assassin?"

Entreri accepted the trip without resistance, indeed, even helped the flow of Danica's leg along by tumbling backward, throwing himself into a roll, and lifting his feet up high to get them over her swinging leg. He didn't quite get all the way back to his feet before reversing momentum, planting his toes, and throwing himself forward in a sudden, devastating rush.

Danica, still prone, angled herself to put her feet in line with the charging Entreri, then rolled back suddenly and with perfect timing to get one foot against the assassin's inner thigh as he fell over her, his sword reaching for her gut. With precision born of desperation, Danica rolled back up onto her shoulders, every muscle in her torso and legs working in perfect coordination to drive Entreri away, to keep that awful sword back.

He went up and over, flying past Danica and dipping his head at the last moment to go into a forward roll. He came back to his feet with a spin, facing the monk, who was up and charging, and stopping cold in her tracks as she faced again the deadly sword and its dagger companion.

Entreri felt the adrenaline coursing through his body, the rush of a true challenge. As much as he realized the foolishness of it all, he was enjoying this.

So was the woman.

The sound of a voice came from the side, the melodious call of a dark elf. "Do slay each other and save us the trouble," Berg'inyon Baenre explained, entering the small area along with a pair of dark elf companions. All three of them carried twin swords that gleamed with powerful enchantments.

* * * * *

Coughing and bleeding from a dozen scrapes, Cadderly pulled himself out of the rockslide and stumbled across a small corridor. He fished in a pouch to bring forth his light tube, a cylindrical object with a continual light spell cast into it, the enchantment focused into an adjustable beam out one end. He had to find Danica. He had to see her again. That last image of her, the dragon's fiery breath falling over her, had him dizzy with fear.

What would his life be without Danica? What would he say to the children? Everything about the life of Cadderly Bonaduce was wrapped inextricably around that wonderful and capable woman.

Yes, capable, he pointedly told himself again and again, as he staggered along in the dusty corridor, pausing only once to cast a minor spell of healing upon a particularly deep cut on one shoulder. He bent over and coughed again, and spat out some dirt that had gotten into his throat.

He shook his head, muttered again that he had to find her, and stood straight, pointing his light ahead—pointing his light so that it reflected off of the black skin of a drow.

That beam stung Kimmuriel Oblodra's sensitive eyes, but he was not caught unawares by it.

It all fell into place quickly for the intelligent priest. He had learned much of Jarlaxle in speaking with the drow and his assassin companion and had deduced much more with information gleaned from denizens of the lower planes. He was indeed surprised to see another dark elf—who could not be?—but he was far from overwhelmed.

The drow and Cadderly stood ten paces apart, staring at each other, sizing each other up. Kimmuriel reached for the priest's mind with psionic energy—enough energy to crush the willpower of a normal man.

But Cadderly Bonaduce was no normal human. The manner in which he accessed his god, the flowing song of Deneir, was somewhat akin to the powers of psionics. It was a method of the purest mental discipline.

Cadderly could not lash out with his mind, as Kimmuriel had just done, but he could surely defend against such an attack, and furthermore, he surely recognized the attack for what it was.

He thought of the Crystal Shard then, of all he knew about it, of its mannerisms and its powers.

The drow psionicist waved a hand, breaking the mental connection, and drew out a gleaming sword. He enacted another psionic power, one that would physically enhance him for the coming fight.

Cadderly did no similar preparations. He just stood staring at Kimmuriel and grinning knowingly. He cast one simple spell of translation.

The drow regarded him curiously, inviting an explanation.

"You wish Crenshinibon destroyed as much as I," the priest remarked, his magic translating the words as they came out of his mouth. "You are a psionicist, the bane of the Crystal Shard, its most hated enemy."

Kimmuriel paused and stared hard, with his physical and his mental eye. "What do you know, foolish human?" he asked.

"The Crystal Shard will not suffer you to live for long," Cadderly said, "and you know it."

"You believe I would help a human against Rai-guy?" Kimmuriel asked incredulously.

Cadderly didn't know who this Rai-guy might be, but Kimmuriel's question made it obvious that he was a dark elf of some power and importance.

"Save yourself, then, and leave," Cadderly offered, and he said it with such calm and confidence that Kimmuriel narrowed his eyes and regarded him even more closely.

Again came the psionic intrusions. This time Cadderly let the drow in somewhat, guided his probing mind's eye to the song of Deneir, let him see the truth of the power of the harmonious flow, let him see the truth of his doom should he persist in this battle.

The psionic connection again went away, and Kimmuriel stood up straight, staring hard at Cadderly.

"I am not normally this generous, dark elf," Cadderly said, "but I have greater problems before me. You hold no love for Crenshinibon and wish it destroyed perhaps more passionately than do I. If it is not, if your companion, this Rai-guy you spoke of, is allowed to possess it, it will be the end of you. So help me if you will in destroying the Crystal Shard. If you and your kin intend to return to your lightless home, I will in no way interfere."

Kimmuriel held his impassive pose for a short while, and smiled and shook his head. "You will find Rai-guy a formidable foe," he promised, "especially with Crenshinibon in his possession."

Before Cadderly could begin to respond, Kimmuriel waved his hand and became something less than corporeal. That transparent form turned and simply walked through the stone wall.

Cadderly waited a long moment and breathed a huge sigh of relief. How he had improvised there and bluffed. The spells he had prepared this day were for dealing with dragons, not dark elves, and the power of that one was substantial indeed. He had felt that keenly with the psionic intrusions.

Now he had a name, Rai-guy, and now his fears about the truth of Hephaestus's breathing had been confirmed. Cadderly, like Jarlaxle, understood enough about the mighty relic to know that if the breath had destroyed Crenshinibon, everyone in the area would have known it in no uncertain terms. Now Cadderly could guess easily enough where and how the Crystal Shard had gone. Knowing that there were other dark elves about, compounding the problem of one very angry red dragon, didn't make him feel any better about the prospects for his three missing friends.

He started away as fast as he dared, and fell again into the song of Deneir, praying for guidance to Danica's side.

* * * * *

851

"Always I seem doomed to protect those I most despise," Entreri whispered to Danica, motioning with his hand for the woman to shift over to the side.

The dark elves broke ranks. One moved to square off against Danica, and Berg'inyon and one other headed for the assassin. Berg'inyon waved his companion aside.

"Kill the woman, and quickly," he said in the drow tongue. "I wish to try this one alone."

Entreri glanced over at Danica and held up two fingers, pointing to the two that would go for her, and pointing to her. The woman gave a quick nod, and a great deal passed between them in that instant. She would try to keep the two dark elves busy, but both understood that Entreri would have to be done with the third quickly.

"I have often wondered how I would fare against Drizzt Do'Urden," Berg'inyon said to the assassin. "Now that I will apparently never get the chance, I will settle for you, Drizzt's equal by all accounts."

Entreri bowed. "It is good to know that I serve some value for you, cowardly son of House Baenre," he said.

He knew as he came back up that Berg'inyon wouldn't hesitate in the face of those words. Still, the sheer ferocity of the drow's attack nearly had Entreri beaten before the fight ever really began. He leaped back, staying up on his heels, skittering away as the two swords came in hard, side by side down low, then low again, then high, then at his belly. He jumped back once, twice, thrice, then managed to bat his sword across those of Berg'inyon on the fourth double-thrust, hoping to drive the blades down low. This was no farmer he faced, and no orc or wererat, but a skilled, veteran drow warrior. Berg'inyon kept his left-handed sword pressing up against the assassin's blade, but dropped his right into a quick circle, then came up and over hard.

The jeweled dagger hooked it and turned it aside at the last second. Entreri rolled his other hand over, the tip of his own sword going toward Berg'inyon. He didn't follow through with the thrust, though, but continued the roll, bringing his blade down and around under the drow's, and stabbing straight ahead.

Berg'inyon quickly turned his left-hand blade across his body and down, disengaged his right from the dagger and brought it across over the left, further driving Entreri's sword down. In the same fluid motion, the skilled drow rolled his right-hand blade up and over his crossing left, the blade going forward at the assassin's head, a brilliant move that Berg'inyon knew would be the end of Artemis Entreri.

* * * * *

Across the way, Danica fared no better. Her fight was a mixture of pure chaos and lightning fast, almost violent movement. The woman crouched and dropped, sprang up hard, and rushed side to side, avoiding slash after slash of drow blades. These two were nowhere near as good as the one across the way battling her companion, but they were dark elves after all, and even the weakest of drow warriors was skilled by surface standards. Furthermore, they knew each other well and complemented each other's movements with deadly precision, preventing Danica from getting any real counterattacks. Every time one came ahead in a rush that seemed to offer the woman some hope of rolling past his double-thrusting blades, or even skittering in under them and kicking at a knee, the companion drow beat her to the potential attack zone, two gleaming swords holding her at bay.

With those long blades and precise movements, they were working her to exhaustion. She had to react, to overreact even, to every thrust and slash. She had to leap away from a blade sent across by a mere flick of a drow wrist.

She looked over at Entreri and the other drow, their blades ringing in a wild song and with the dark elf seeming, if anything, to be gaining an advantage. She knew she had to try something dangerous, even desperate.

Danica came ahead in a rush, and cut left suddenly, bursting out to the side though she had only three strides to the wall. Seeing her apparently caught, the closest dark elf cut fast in pursuit, stabbing at . . . nothing.

Danica ran right up the wall, turning over as she went and kicking out into a backward somersault that brought her down and to the side of the pursuing dark elf. She fell low as she landed and spun around viciously, one leg extended to kick out the dark elf's legs.

She would have had him, but there was his companion, swords extended, blade driving deeply into Danica's thigh. She howled and scrambled back, kicking futilely at the pursuing dark elves.

A globe of darkness fell over her. She slammed her back against the stone and had nowhere left to go.

* * * * *

He ran along, with the less-than-corporeal Kimmuriel Oblodra following close behind.

"You seek an exit?" the drow psionicist asked with a voice that seemed impossibly thin.

"I seek my friends," Cadderly replied.

"They are out of the mountain, likely," Kimmuriel remarked, and that slowed the priest considerably.

For indeed, would not Danica and the dwarves search for a way out of the mountain—and there were many easy exits from the lower tunnels, Cadderly knew from his searching of the place before this journey.

Dozens of corridors crisscrossed down there, but a quiet pause and a lifted and wetted finger would show the drafts of air. Certainly Ivan and Pikel would have little trouble in finding their way out of the underground maze, but what of Danica?

"Something comes this way," Kimmuriel warned, and Cadderly turned to see the drow shrink back against the wall, and stand perfectly still, seeming simply to disappear.

Cadderly knew the drow wouldn't aid him in any fight and would likely even join in if the approaching footsteps were those of Kimmuriel's dark elf companions.

They were not, Cadderly knew almost as soon as that worry cropped up, for these were not the steps of any stealthy creature.

"Ye stupid doo-dad!" came the roar of a familiar voice. "Droppin' me in a hole, and one full o' rocks!"

"Ooo oi!" Pikel replied as they came bounding around the bend in the tunnel, right into the path of Cadderly's light beam.

Ivan shrieked and started to charge, but Pikel grabbed him and pulled him down, whispering into his ear.

"Hey, ye're right," the yellow-bearded dwarf admitted. "Damned drows don't use light."

Cadderly came up beside them. "Where is Danica?"

Any relief the two dwarves had felt at the sight of their friend disappeared immediately.

"Help me find her!" Cadderly said to the dwarves and to Kimmuriel, as he spun around.

Kimmuriel Oblodra, apparently fearing that Cadderly and his companions would not be safe traveling company, was already long gone.

* * * * *

His smile, a wicked grin indeed, widened as one of his blades came up over the other, for he knew that Entreri had nothing left with which to parry. Out went Berg'inyon's killing stab.

But the assassin was not there!

Berg'inyon's thoughts whirled frantically. Where had he gone? How were his weapons still in place with the previous parries? He knew Entreri could not have moved far, and yet, he was not there.

The angle of the sudden disengage clued Berg'inyon in to the truth, told the drow that in the same moment Berg'inyon had executed the roll, Entreri had also come forward, but down low, using Berg'inyon's own blade as the visual block.

The dark elf silently congratulated the cunning human, this man rumored to be the equal of Drizzt Do'Urden, even as he felt the jeweled dagger sliding into his back, reaching for his heart.

"You should have kept one of your lackeys with you," Entreri whispered in the drow's ear, easing the dying Berg'inyon Baenre to the floor. "He could have died beside you."

The assassin pulled free his dagger and turned around to consider the woman. He saw her get slashed, saw her skitter away, saw the globe fall over her.

Entreri winced as the two dark elves—too far away for him to offer any timely assistance—rolled out in opposite directions, flanking the woman and rushing into that darkness, swords before them.

* * * * *

Just a split second before the darkness fell, the dark elf standing before Danica to the right began to execute a roll farther that way, spinning a circle to bring him around quickly and with momentum, the only clue for Danica.

The other one, she guessed, was moving to her left, but both were surely coming in at a tight enough angle to prevent her from rushing straight ahead between them. Those three options: left, right, and ahead, were unavailable, as was moving back, for the stone of the wall was solid indeed.

She sensed their movements, not specifically, but enough to realize that they were coming in fast for the kill.

One option presented itself. One alone.

Danica leaped straight up, tucking her legs under her, so full of desperation that she hardly felt the burn of the wound in her thigh.

She couldn't see the double-thrust low attack of the drow to her right, nor the double-thrust high attack from the one on the left, but she felt the disturbance below her as she cleared both sets of blades. She came up high in a tuck, and kicked out to both sides with a sudden and devastating spreading snap of her legs.

She connected on both sides, driving a foot into the forehead of the drow on her right, and another into the throat of the drow on her left. She pressed through to complete extension, sending both dark elves flying away. She landed in perfect balance and burst ahead three running steps. A forward dive brought her rolling out of the darkness. She came up and around—to see the dark elf now on her left, and the one she had kicked on the forehead, still staggering backward out of the darkness globe and into the waiting grasp of Artemis Entreri.

The drow jerked suddenly, violently, and Entreri's fine sword exploded through his chest. The assassin held it there for a moment, let Charon's Claw work its demonic power, and the dark elf's face began to smolder, burn, and roll back from his skull.

Danica looked away, focusing on the darkness, waiting for the other dark elf to come rushing out. Blood was pouring from her wounded leg, and her strength was fast receding.

She was too lightheaded a moment later to hear the final gurgling of the drow dying in the darkness globe, its throat too crushed to bring in anymore air, but even if she had heard that reassuring sound, it would have done little to bolster her hopes.

She could not hold her footing, she knew, or her consciousness.

Artemis Entreri, surely no ally, was still very much alive, and very, very close.

* * * * *

Yharaskrik was overwhelmed. The combination of Rai-guy's magic and the continuing mental attack of the Crystal Shard had the illithid completely overmatched. Yharaskrik couldn't even focus its mental energies enough at that moment to melt away through the stone, away from the imprisoning goo.

"Surrender!" the drow wizard-cleric demanded. "You cannot escape us. We will take your word that you will promise fealty to us," the drow explained, oblivious to the shadowy form that darted out behind him to retrieve an item. "Crenshinibon will know if you lie, but if you speak of honest fealty, you will be rewarded!"

Indeed, as the dark elf proclaimed those words, Crenshinibon echoed them deep in Yharaskrik's mind. The thought of servitude to Crenshinibon, one of the most hated artifacts for all of the mind flayers, surely repulsed the bulbous-headed creature, but so, too, did the thought of obliteration. That was precisely what Yharaskrik faced. The illithid could not win, could not escape. Crenshinibon would melt its mind even as Rai-guy blasted its body.

I yield, the illithid telepathically communicated to both of its attackers.

Rai-guy relented his magic and considered Crenshinibon. The artifact informed him that Yharaskrik had truthfully surrendered.

"Wisely done," the drow said to the illithid. "What a waste your death would be when you might bolster my army, when you might serve me as liaison to your powerful people."

"My people hate Crenshinibon and will not hear those calls," Yharaskrik said in its watery voice.

"But you understand differently," said the drow. He spoke a quick spell, dissolving the goo around the illithid. "You see the value of it now."

"A value above that of death, yes," Yharaskrik admitted, climbing back to its feet.

"Well, well, my traitorous lieutenant," came a voice from the side. Both Rai-guy and Yharaskrik turned to see Jarlaxle perched a bit higher on the wall, tucked into an alcove.

Rai-guy growled and called upon Crenshinibon mentally to crush his former master. Even as he started that silent call, up came the magical lantern. Its glow fell over the artifact, defeating its powers.

Rai-guy growled again. "You need do more than defeat the artifact!" he roared and swept his arm out toward Yharaskrik. "Have you met my new friend?"

"Indeed, and formidable," Jarlaxle admitted, tipping his wide-brimmed hat in deference to the powerful illithid. "Have you met mine?" As he finished, his gaze aimed to the side, further along the wide tunnel.

Rai-guy swallowed hard, knowing the truth before he even turned that way. He began waving his arms wildly, trying to bring up some defensive magic.

Using his innate drow abilities, Jarlaxle dropped a globe of darkness over the wizard and the mind flayer, a split second before Hephaestus's fiery breath fell over them, immolating them in a terrible blast of devastation.

Jarlaxle leaned back and shielded his eyes from the glow of the fire, the reddish-orange line that so disappeared into the blackness.

Then there came a sudden sizzling noise, and the darkness was no more. The tunnel reverted to its normal blackness, lightened somewhat by the glow of the dragon. That light intensified a hundred times over, a thousand times over, into a brilliant glow, as if the sun itself had fallen upon them.

Crenshinibon, Jarlaxle realized. The dragon's breath had done its work, and the binding energy of the artifact had been breached. In the moment before the glare became too great, Jarlaxle saw the surprised look on the reptilian face of the great wyrm, saw the charred corpse of his former lieutenant, and saw a weird image of Yharaskrik, for the illithid had begun to melt into the stone when Hephaestus had breathed. The retreat had done little good, since Hephaestus's breath had bubbled the stone.

It was soon too bright for the eyes of the drow. "Well fired . . . er, breathed," he said to Hephaestus.

Jarlaxle spun around, slipped through a crack at the back of the alcove, and sprinted away not a moment too soon. Hephaestus's terrible breath came forth yet again, melting the stone in the alcove, chasing Jarlaxle down the tunnel, and singeing the seat of his trousers.

He ran and ran in the still-brightening light. Crenshinibon's releasing power filled every crack in every stone. Soon Jarlaxle knew he was near the outside wall, and so he utilized his magical hole again, throwing it against the wall and crawling through into the twilight of the outside beyond.

That area, too, brightened immediately and considerably, seeming as if the sun had risen. The light poured through Jarlaxle's magical hole. With a snap of his wrist, the drow took the magic item away, closing the portal and dimming the area to natural light again—except for the myriad beams shooting out of the glowing mountain in other places.

857

"Danica!" came Cadderly's frantic call behind him. "Where is Danica?"

Jarlaxle turned to see the priest and the two bumbling dwarves—an odd pair of brothers if ever the drow had seen one—running toward him.

"She went down the hole after Artemis Entreri," Jarlaxle said in a comforting tone. "A fine and resourceful ally."

"Boom!" said Pikel Bouldershoulder.

"What's the light about?" Ivan added.

Jarlaxle looked back to the mountain and shrugged. "It would seem that your formula for defeating the Crystal Shard was correct after all," the drow said to Cadderly.

He turned with a smile, but that look was not reflected on the face of the priest. He was staring back at the mountain with horror, wondering and worrying about his dear wife.

Chapter 25

The Light at the End of the Tunnel

Hephaestus was an intelligent dragon, smart enough to master many powerful spells, to speak the tongues of a dozen races, to defeat all of the many, many foes who had come against it. The dragon had lived for centuries, gaining wisdom as dragons do, and in that depth of wisdom, Hephaestus recognized that it should not be staring at the brilliance of the Crystal Shard's released energy.

But the dragon could not turn away from the brilliance, from the sheerest and brightest, the purest power it had ever seen.

The wyrm marveled as a skeletal shadow rolled out of the brilliantly glowing object, then another, and a third, and so on, until the specters of seven long-consumed liches danced about the destroyed Crystal Shard, as they had danced around the object during its dark creation.

Then, one by one, they dissipated into nothingness.

The dragon stared incredulously, feeling the honest emotions as clearly as if it were empathically bound to the next form that flowed out of the artifact, the shadow of a man, hunched and broken with sadness. The stolen soul of the long-dead sheik sat on the floor, staring at the stone forlornly, an aura so devastated flowing out from the shadow that Hephaestus the Merciless felt a twinge in its cold heart.

That last specter, too, thinned to nothingness, and, finally, the light of the Crystal Shard dimmed.

Only then did Hephaestus recognize the depth of its mistake. Only then did the ancient red dragon realize that it was now totally blind, its eyes utterly destroyed by the pureness of the power released.

The dragon roared—how it roared! The greatest scream of anger, of rage, that ever-angry Hephaestus had ever issued. In that roar, too, was a measure of fear, of regret, of the realization that the wyrm could not dare go forth from its lair to pursue the intruders who had brought this cursed item before it, could not go out from the confines to the open world where it would need its eyes as well as those other keen senses to truly thrive, indeed to survive.

Hephaestus's olfactory senses told the wyrm that it had at least destroyed the drow and the illithid that had been standing in the corridor a few moments before. Taking that satisfaction in the realization that it was likely the only satisfaction Hephaestus could hope to find this day, the wyrm retreated to the large chamber secretly and magically concealed behind its main sleeping hall, the chamber where there was only one possible entrance, and the one where the dragon kept its piled hoard of gold, gems, jewels, and trinkets.

There the outraged but defeated wyrm curled up again, desiring sleep, peaceful slumber among its hoarded riches, hoping that the passing years would cure its burned eyes. It would dream, yes it would, of consuming those intruders, and it would set its great intelligent mind to work at solving the problem of blindness if the slumber did not bring the desired cure.

*　*　*　*　*

Cadderly nearly leaped for joy when the form came rushing out of the tunnels, but when he recognized the running man for who he was, Artemis Entreri, and noted that the woman slung across his shoulders was hardly moving and was covered in blood, his heart sank fast.

"What'd ye do to her?" Ivan roared, starting forward, but he found that he was moving slowly, as if in a dream. He looked to Pikel and found that his brother, too, was moving with unnatural sluggishness.

"Be at ease," Jarlaxle said to them. "Danica's wounds are not of Entreri's doing."

"How can ye know?" Ivan demanded.

"He would have left her dead in the darkness," the drow reasoned, and the simple logic of it did indeed calm the volatile brothers a bit.

Cadderly, though, ran on. As he was beyond the parameters of Jarlaxle's spell when it was cast, he was not slowed in the least. He rushed up to Entreri, who, upon seeing his approach, had stopped and turned one shoulder down, moving Danica to a standing, or at least leaning, position.

"Drow blade," the assassin said as soon as Cadderly got close enough to see the wound—and the feeble attempt at tying it off the assassin had made.

The priest went to work at once, falling into the song of Deneir, bringing forth all the healing energies he could find. Indeed, he discovered to his absolute relief that his love's wounds were not so critical, that she would certainly mend and quickly enough.

By the time he finished, the Bouldershoulders and Jarlaxle had arrived. Cadderly looked up at the dwarves and smiled and nodded, and turned a puzzled expression on the assassin.

"Her actions saved me in the tunnels," Entreri said sourly. "I do not enjoy being in anyone's debt." That said, he walked away, not once looking back.

* * * * *

Cadderly and his companions, including Danica, caught up to Entreri and Jarlaxle later on that day, after it became apparent, to everyone's relief, that Hephaestus would not be coming out of its lair in pursuit.

"We are returning to the Spirit Soaring with the same spell that brought us here," the priest announced. "It would be impolite, at least, if I did not offer you magical transport for the journey back."

Jarlaxle looked at him curiously.

"No tricks," Cadderly assured the cagey drow. "I hold no trials over either of you, for your actions have been no less than honorable since you came to my domain. I do warn you both, however, that I will tolerate no—"

"Why would we wish to return with you?" Artemis Entreri cut him short. "What in your hole of falsehood is for our gain?"

Cadderly started to respond—in many directions all at once. He wanted to yell at the man, to coerce the man, to convert the man, to destroy the man—anything he could do against that sudden wall of negativism. In the end, he said not a word, for indeed, what at the Spirit Soaring would be for the benefit of these two?

Much, he supposed, if they desired to mend their souls and their ways. Entreri's actions with Danica did hint that there might indeed be a possibility of that in the future. On a whim, the priest entered Deneir's song and brought forth a minor spell, one that revealed the general weal of those he surveyed.

A quick look at Entreri and Jarlaxle was all he needed to confirm that the Spirit Soaring, Carradoon, Shilmista Forest, and all the region about that section of the Snowflake Mountains would be better off if these two went in the opposite direction.

"Farewell, then," he said with a tip of his hat. "At least you found the opportunity to do one noble act in your wretched existence, Artemis Entreri." He walked by the pair, Ivan and Pikel in tow.

Danica took her time, though, eyeing Entreri with every step. "I am not ungrateful for what you did when my wound overcame me," she admitted, "but neither would I shy from finishing that which we started in the tunnels below Hephaestus's lair."

Entreri started to say, "To what end?" but changed his mind before the first word had escaped his lips. He merely shrugged, smiled, and let the woman pass.

"A new rival for Entreri?" Jarlaxle remarked when the four had gone. "A replacement for Drizzt, perhaps?"

"Hardly," Entreri replied.

"She is not worthy, then?"

The assassin only shrugged, not caring enough to try to determine whether she was or not.

Jarlaxle's laugh brought him from his contemplation.

"Growth," the drow remarked.

"I warn you that I'll tolerate little of your judgments," Entreri replied.

Jarlaxle laughed all the harder. "Then you plan to remain with me."

Entreri looked at him hard, stealing the mirth, considering a question that he could not immediately answer.

"Very well, then," Jarlaxle said lightheartedly, as if he took the silence as confirmation. "But I warn you, if you cross me, I will have to kill you."

"That will be difficult to do from beyond the grave," Entreri promised.

Jarlaxle laughed once more. "When I was young," he began, "a friend of mine, a weapon master whose ultimate frustration was that he believed I was the better fighter—though in truth, the one time I bested him was more good fortune than superior skill—remarked to me that at last he had found one who would grow to be at least my equal, and perhaps my superior, a child, really, who showed more promise as a warrior than any before.

"That weapon master's name was Zaknafein—you may have heard of him," Jarlaxle went on.

Entreri shook his head.

"The young warrior he spoke of was none other than Drizzt Do'Urden," Jarlaxle explained with a grin.

Entreri tried hard to show no emotion, but his inner feelings at the surprise betrayed him a tiny bit, and certainly enough for Jarlaxle to note it. "And did the prophecy of Zaknafein come true?" Entreri asked.

"If it did, does that hold any revelation for Artemis Entreri?" Jarlaxle asked slyly. "For would discovering the relative strength of Drizzt and Jarlaxle tell Entreri anything pertinent? How does Artemis Entreri believe he measures up against Drizzt Do'Urden?" Then the critical question: "Does Entreri believe he truly defeated Drizzt?"

Entreri looked at Jarlaxle long and hard, but as he stared, his expression inevitably softened. "Does it matter?" he answered, and that indeed was the answer that Jarlaxle most wanted to hear from his new, and, to his way of thinking, long-term companion.

"We are not yet done here," Jarlaxle announced then, changing the subject abruptly. "There is one group lingering about, fearful and angry. Their leader has decided that he cannot leave yet, not with things as they stand."

Entreri didn't ask, but just followed Jarlaxle as the dark elf made his way around the outcroppings of mountain stone. The assassin fell back a few steps when he saw the group Jarlaxle had spoken of: four dark elves led by a dangerous psionicist. Entreri put his hands immediately to the hilt of his deadly dagger and sword. A short distance away, Jarlaxle and Kimmuriel spoke in the drow tongue, but Entreri could make out most of their words.

"Do we battle now?" Kimmuriel Oblodra asked when Jarlaxle neared.

"Rai-guy is dead, the Crystal Shard destroyed," Jarlaxle replied. "What would be the purpose?"

Entreri noted that Kimmuriel did not wince at either proclamation.

"Ah, but I guess that you have tasted the sweetness of power, yes?" Jarlaxle asked with a chuckle. "You are seated at the head of Bregan D'aerthe now, it would seem, and you suppose all by yourself. You have little desire to relinquish your garnered position?"

Kimmuriel started to shake his head—it was obvious to Entreri that he was about to try to make peace here with Jarlaxle—but the surprising Jarlaxle cut short Kimmuriel's response. "Very well then!" Jarlaxle said dramatically. "I have little desire for yet another fight, Kimmuriel, and I accept and understand that my actions of late have likely earned me too many enemies within the ranks of Bregan D'aerthe for my return as leader."

"You are surrendering?" Kimmuriel asked doubtfully, and he seemed even more on his guard then, as did the foot-soldiers standing behind him.

"Hardly," Jarlaxle replied with another chuckle. "And I warn you, if you continue to do battle with me, or even to pursue me and track my whereabouts, I will indeed challenge you for the position you have rightly earned."

Entreri listened intently, shaking his head, certain that he must be getting some of the words, at least, very wrong.

Kimmuriel started to respond, but stuttered over a few words, and just gave up with a great sigh.

"Do well with Bregan D'aerthe," Jarlaxle warned. "I will rejoin you one day and will demand of you that we share the leadership. I expect to find a band of mercenaries as strong as the one I now willingly leave behind." He looked to the other three. "Serve him with honor."

"Any reunion between us will not be in Calimport," Kimmuriel assured him, "nor anywhere else on the cursed surface. I am bound for home, Jarlaxle, back to the caverns that are our true domain."

Jarlaxle nodded, as did the three foot-soldiers.

"And you?" Kimmuriel asked.

The former mercenary leader only shrugged and smiled again. "I cannot know where I most wish to be because I have not seen all that there is."

Again, Kimmuriel could only stare at his former leader curiously. In the end, he merely nodded and, with a snap of his fingers and a thought, opened a dimensional portal through which he and his three minions passed.

"Why?" Entreri asked, moving up beside his unexpected companion.

"Why?" Jarlaxle echoed.

"You could have returned with them," the assassin clarified, "though I'd have never gone with you. You chose not to go, not to resume control of your band. Why would you give that up to remain out here, to remain beside me?"

Jarlaxle thought it over for a few moments. Then, using words that Entreri himself had used before, he said with a laugh, "Perhaps I hate drow more than I hate humans."

In that instant, Artemis Entreri could have been blown over by a gentle breeze. He didn't even want to know how Jarlaxle had known to say that.

Epilogue

For days, Entreri and Jarlaxle wandered the region, at last happening upon a town where the folk had heard of Drizzt Do'Urden and seemed, at least, to accept the imposter Jarlaxle's presence.

In the nondescript and ramshackle little common house that served as a tavern, Artemis Entreri discovered a posting that he found, in light of his present situation, somewhat promising.

"Bounty hunters?" Jarlaxle asked with surprise when Entreri presented the posting to him. The drow was sitting in a corner, sipping wine and with his back to the corner. "A call by the forces of justice for bounty hunters?"

"A call by someone," Entreri corrected, sliding into a chair across the table. "Whether it begets justice or not seems of little consequence."

Jarlaxle looked at him with a wry grin. "Does it?" he said, seeming less than convinced. "And what gain did you derive, then, from carrying Danica from the tunnels?"

"The gain of keeping a powerful priest from becoming an enemy," the pragmatic Entreri answered coldly.

"Or perhaps there was more," said Jarlaxle. "Perhaps Artemis Entreri had not the heart to let the woman die alone in the darkness."

Entreri shrugged as if it did not matter.

"How many of Artemis Entreri's victims would be surprised?" Jarlaxle asked, pressing the point.

"How many of Artemis Entreri's victims deserved better than they found?" the assassin retorted.

There it was, Jarlaxle knew, the justification for a life lived in the shadows. To a degree, the drow, who had survived among shadows darker than anything Entreri had ever known, couldn't rightfully disagree. Perhaps, in that context, there was more to the measure of Artemis Entreri. Still, the transformation of this killer to the side of justice seemed a curious and odd occurrence.

"Artemis the Compassionate?" he had to ask.

Entreri sat perfectly still for a moment, digesting the words. "Perhaps," he said with a nod. "And perhaps if you keep saying foolish things, I will show you some compassion and kill you quickly. Then again, perhaps not."

Jarlaxle enjoyed a great laugh at that, at the absurdity of it all, of the newfound life that loomed before him. He understood Entreri well enough to take the man's threats seriously, but in truth, the dark elf trusted Entreri the way he would trust one of his own brothers.

However, Jarlaxle Baenre, the third son of Matron Baenre, once sacrificed to Lady Lolth by his mother and his siblings, knew better than to trust his own brother.

SEA OF

SWORDS

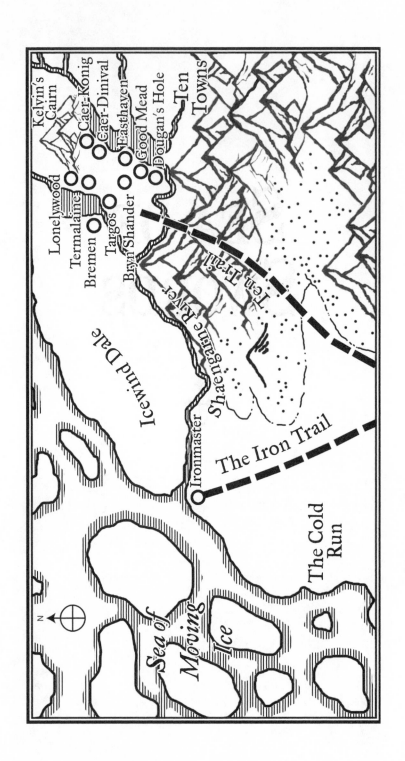

Prologue

He worked his scimitars in smooth, sure circular motions, bringing them through delicate and deceiving arcs. When the opportunity presented itself he stepped ahead and slashed down at a seemingly exposed shoulder with one blade. But the elf, bald head shining in the sunlight, was faster. The elf dropped a foot back and raised a long sword in a solid parry, then came forward in a straight rush, stabbing with a dirk, then stepping ahead again to thrust with the sword.

He danced in perfect harmony with the elf's fluid movements, twirling his twin scimitars defensively, each rolling down and over to ring against the thrusting sword. The elf stabbed again, mid-torso, then a third time, aiming low.

Over and down went the scimitars, the classic, double-block-low. Then up those twin weapons came as the agile, hairless elf tried to kick through the block.

The elf's kick was no more than a feint, and as the scimitars came up, the elf fell into a crouch and let fly the dagger. It sailed in before he could get the scimitars down low enough to block, before he could set his feet and dodge aside.

A perfect throw for disembowelment, the devilish dagger caught him in the belly.

* * * * *

"It's Deudermont, to be sure," the crewman called, tone growing frantic. "He's caught sight of us again!"

"Bah, but he's no way to know who we are," another reminded.

"Just put us around the reef and past the jetties," Sheila Kree instructed her pilot.

Tall and thick, with arms rock-hard from years of hard labor and green eyes that showed resentment for those years, the red-headed woman stared angrily at the pursuit. The three-masted schooner forced a turn from what would certainly have proven to be a most profitable pillaging of a lightly-armed merchant ship.

"Bring us a fog to block their watchin'," the nasty pirate added, yelling at Bellany, *Bloody Keel*'s resident sorceress.

"A fog," the sorceress huffed, shaking her head so that her raven-black hair bounced all about her shoulders.

The pirate, who more often spoke with her sword than with her tongue, simply did not understand. Bellany shrugged and began casting her strongest spell, a fireball. As she finished, she aimed the blast not at the distant, pursuing ship—which was long out of range, and which, if it was *Sea Sprite*, would have had no trouble repelling such an attack anyway—but at the water behind *Bloody Keel*.

The surf sizzled and sputtered in protest as the flames licked at it, bringing a thick steam up behind the fast-sailing ship. Sheila Kree smiled and nodded her approval. Her pilot, a heavyset woman with a big dimpled face and a yellow smile, knew the waters around the western tip of the Spine of the World better than anyone alive. She could navigate there on the darkest of nights, using no more than the sound of the currents splashing over the reefs. Deudermont's ship wouldn't dare follow them through the dangerous waters ahead. Soon enough *Bloody Keel* would sail out beyond the third jetty, around the rocky bend, and into open waters if she chose, or turn even closer inland to a series of reefs and rocks—a place Sheila and her companions had come to call home.

"He's no way to know 'twas us," the crewman said again.

Sheila Kree nodded, and hoped the man was right—believed he probably was, for while *Sea Sprite,* a three-masted schooner, had such a unique signature of sails, *Bloody Keel* appeared to be just another small, unremarkable caravel. Like any other wise pirate along the Sword Coast, though, Sheila Kree had no desire to tangle with Deudermont's legendary *Sea Sprite* or his skilled and dangerous crew, whoever he thought she was.

And she'd heard rumors that Deudermont was looking for her, though why the famous pirate-hunter might be singling her out, she could only guess. Reflexively, the powerful woman reached back over her shoulder to feel the mark she'd had branded upon herself, the symbol of her new-found power and ambition. As with all the women serving in Kree's new sea and land group, Sheila wore the mark of the mighty warhammer she'd purchased from a fool in Luskan, the mark of Aegis-fang.

Was that, then, the source of Deudermont's sudden interest? Sheila Kree had learned a bit of the warhammer's history, had learned that its previous owner, a drunken brute named Wulfgar, was a known friend of Captain Deudermont. That was a connection, but the pirate woman couldn't be certain. Hadn't Wulfgar been tried in Luskan for attempting to murder Deudermont after all?

Sheila Kree shrugged it all away a short while later, as *Bloody Keel* worked dangerously through the myriad of rocks and reefs to the secret, sheltered Golden Cove. Despite the expert piloting, *Bloody Keel* connected more than once on a jagged shelf, and by the time they entered the bay, the caravel was listing to port.

No matter, though, for in this pirate cove, surrounded by towering walls of jagged rock, Sheila and her crew had the means to repair the ship. They took *Bloody Keel* into a large cave, the bottom of a system of tunnels and caverns that climbed through this easternmost point of the Spine of the World, natural tunnels now smoky from torches lining the walls, and rocky caverns made comfortable by the plunder of what was fast becoming the most successful pirate band anywhere along the northern reaches of the Sword Coast.

The small-framed, black-haired sorceress gave a sigh. She likely knew that with her magic she'd be doing most of the work on these latest repairs.

"Damn that Deudermont!" Bellany remarked.

"Damn our own cowardice, ye mean," one smelly sea dog remarked as he walked by.

Sheila Kree stepped in front of the grumbling man, sneered at him, and decked him with a right cross to the jaw.

"I didn't think he even saw us," the prone man protested, looking up at the red-haired pirate with an expression of sheer terror.

If one of the female crew of *Bloody Keel* crossed Sheila, they'd likely get a beating, but if one of the men stepped too far over the vicious pirate's line, he'd likely find out how the ship got its name. Keel-hauling was one of Sheila Kree's favorite games, after all.

Sheila Kree let the dog crawl away, her thoughts more focused on the latest appearance of Deudermont. She had to admit it was possible that *Sea Sprite* hadn't really even seen them, and likely, if Deudermont and his crew had spotted the distant sails of *Bloody Keel*, they didn't know the ship's true identity.

871

But Sheila Kree would remain cautious where Captain Deudermont was concerned. If the captain and his skilled crew were indeed determined to find her, then let it be here, at Golden Cove, the rocky fortress Sheila Kree and her crew shared with a formidable clan of ogres.

* * * * *

The dagger struck him squarely—

—and bounced harmlessly to the floor.

"Drizzt Do'Urden would never have fallen for such a feint!" Le'lorinel, the bald-headed elf, grumbled in a high and melodic voice. His eyes, blue flecked with gold, shone with dangerous intensity from behind the black mask that Le'lorinel always wore. With a snap of the wrist, the sword went back into its scabbard. "If he did, he would have been quick enough a'foot to avoid the throw, or quick enough a'hand to get a scimitar back down for a block," the elf finished with a huff.

"I am not Drizzt Do'Urden," the half-elf, Tunevec, said simply. He moved to the side of the roof and leaned heavily against a crenellation, trying to catch his breath.

"Mahskevic enchanted you with magical haste to compensate," the elf replied, retrieving the dagger and adjusting his sleeveless light brown tunic.

Tunevec snorted at his opponent. "You do not even know how Drizzt Do'Urden fights," he reminded. "Truly! Have you ever seen him in battle? Have you ever watched the movements—impossible movements, I say!— that you so readily attribute to him?"

If Le'lorinel was impressed by the reasoning, it did not show. "The tales of his fighting style and prowess are common in the northland."

"Common, and likely exaggerated," Tunevec reminded.

Le'lorinel's bald head was shaking before Tunevec finished the statement, for the elf had many times detailed the prowess of Drizzt to his half-elf sparring partner.

"I pay you well for your participation in these training sessions," Le'lorinel said. "You would do well to consider every word I have told you about Drizzt Do'Urden to be the truth and to emulate his fighting style to the best of your meager abilities."

Tunevec, who was naked to the waist, toweled off his thin and muscular frame. He held the towel out to Le'lorinel, who just looked at him with contempt, which was usual after such a failure. The elf walked past, right to the trapdoor that led down to the top floor of the tower.

"Your enchantment of stoneskin is likely used up," the elf said with obvious disgust.

Alone on the roof, Tunevec gave a helpless chuckle and shook his head. He moved to retrieve his shirt but noted a shimmering in the air before he ever got there. The half-elf paused, watching as old Mahskevic the wizard materialized into view.

"Did you please him this day?" the gray-bearded old man asked in a voice that seemed pulled out of his tight throat. Mahskevic's somewhat mocking smile, full of yellow teeth, showed that he already knew the answer.

"Le'lorinel is obsessed with that one," Tunevec answered. "More so than I would ever have believed possible."

Mahskevic merely shrugged, as if that hardly mattered. "He has labored for me for more than five years, both to earn the use of my spells and to pay you well," the wizard reminded. "We searched for many months to even find you, one who seemed promising in being able to emulate the movements of this strange dark elf, Drizzt Do'Urden."

"Why waste the time, then?" the frustrated half-elf retorted. "Why do you not accompany Le'lorinel to find this wretched drow and be done with him once and for all. Far easier that would seem than this endless sparring."

Mahskevic chuckled, as if to tell Tunevec clearly that he was underestimating this rather unusual drow, whose exploits, as Le'lorinel and Mahskevic had uncovered them, were indeed remarkable. "Drizzt is known to be the friend of a dwarf named Bruenor Battlehammer," the wizard explained. "Do you know the name?"

Tunevec, putting on his gray shirt, looked to the old human and shook his head.

"King of Mithral Hall," Mahskevic explained. "Or at least, he was. I have little desire to turn a clan of wild dwarves against me—bane of all wizards, dwarves. Making an enemy of Bruenor Battlehammer does not seem to me to be an opportunity for advancement of wealth or health.

"Beyond that, I have no grudge against this Drizzt Do'Urden," Mahskevic added. "Why would I seek to destroy him?"

"Because Le'lorinel is your friend."

"Le'lorinel," Mahskevic echoed, again with that chuckle. "I am fond of him, I admit, and in trying to hold my responsibilities of friendship, I often try to convince him that his course is self-destructive folly, and nothing more."

"He will hear none of that, I am sure," said Tunevec.

"None," agreed Mahskevic. "A stubborn one is Le'lorinel Tel'e'brenequiette."

"If that is even his name," snorted Tunevec, who was in a rather foul mood, especially concerning his sparring partner. " 'I to you as you to me,' " he translated, for indeed Le'lorinel's name was nothing more than a variation on a fairly common Elvish saying.

"The philosophy of respect and friendship, is it not?" asked the old wizard.

"And of revenge," Tunevec replied grimly.

* * * * *

Down on the tower's middle floor, alone in a small, private room, Le'lorinel pulled off the mask and slumped to sit on the bed, stewing in frustration and hatred for Drizzt Do'Urden.

"How many years will it take?" the elf asked, and finished with a small laugh, while fiddling with an onyx ring. "Centuries? It does not matter!"

Le'lorinel pulled off the ring and held it up before glittering eyes. It had taken two years of hard work to earn this item from Mahskevic. It was a magical ring, designed to hold enchantments. This one held four, the four spells Le'lorinel believed it would take to kill Drizzt Do'Urden.

Of course, Le'lorinel knew that to use these spells in the manner planned would likely result in the deaths of both combatants.

It did not matter.

As long as Drizzt Do'Urden died, Le'lorinel could enter the netherworld contented.

Part 1

Hints Of Darkness

It is good to be home. It is good to hear the wind of Icewind Dale, to feel its invigorating bite, like some reminder that I am alive.

That seems such a self-evident thing—that I, that we, are alive—and yet, too often, I fear, we easily forget the importance of that simple fact. It is so easy to forget that you are truly alive, or at least, to appreciate that you are truly alive, that every sunrise is yours to view and every sunset is yours to enjoy.

And all those hours in between, and all those hours after dusk, are yours to make of what you will.

It is easy to miss the possibility that every person who crosses your path can become an event and a memory, good or bad, to fill in the hours with experience instead of tedium, to break the monotony of the passing moments. Those wasted moments, those hours of sameness, of routine, are the enemy, I say, are little stretches of death within the moments of life.

Yes, it is good to be home, in the wild land of Icewind Dale, where monsters roam aplenty and rogues threaten the roads at every turn. I am more alive and more content than in many years. For too long, I struggled with the legacy of my dark past. For too long, I struggled with the reality of my longevity, that I would likely die long after Bruenor, Wulfgar, and Regis.

And Catti-brie.

What a fool I am to rue the end of her days without enjoying the days that she, that we, now have! What a fool I am to let the present slip into the past, while lamenting a potential—and only potential—future!

We are all dying, every moment that passes of every day. That is the inescapable truth of this existence. It is a truth that can paralyze us with fear, or one that can energize us with impatience, with the desire to explore and experience, with the hope—nay, the iron will!—to find a memory in every action. To be alive, under sunshine or under starlight, in weather fair or stormy. To dance every step, be they through gardens of bright flowers or through deep snows.

The young know this truth so many of the old, or even middle-aged, have forgotten. Such is the source of the anger, the jealousy, that so many exhibit toward the young. So many times have I heard the common lament, "If only I could go back to that age, knowing what I now know!" Those words amuse me profoundly, for in truth, the lament should be, "If only I could reclaim the lust and the joy I knew then!"

That is the meaning of life, I have come at last to understand, and in that understanding, I have indeed found that lust and that joy. A life of twenty years where that lust and joy, where that truth is understood might be more full than a life of centuries with head bowed and shoulders slumped.

I remember my first battle beside Wulfgar, when I led him in, against tremendous odds and mighty giants, with a huge grin and a lust for life. How strange that as I gained more to lose, I allowed that lust to diminish!

It took me this long, through some bitter losses, to recognize the folly of that reasoning. It took me this long, returned to Icewind Dale after unwittingly surrendering the Crystal Shard to Jarlaxle and completing at last (and forever, I pray) my relationship with Artemis Entreri, to wake up to the life that is mine, to appreciate the beauty around me, to seek out and not shy away from the excitement that is there to be lived.

There remain worries and fears, of course. Wulfgar is gone from us—I know not where—and I fear for his head, his heart, and his body. But I have accepted that his path was his own to choose, and that he, for the sake of all three—head, heart, and body—had to step away from us. I pray that our paths will cross again, that he will find his way home. I pray that some news of him will come to us, either calming our fears or setting us into action to recover him.

But I can be patient and convince myself of the best. For to brood upon my fears for him, I am defeating the entire purpose of my own life.

That I will not do.

There is too much beauty.

There are too many monsters and too many rogues.

There is too much fun.

—Drizzt Do'Urden

Chapter 1

Back to Back

His long white hair rolled down Catti-brie's shoulder, tickling the front of her bare arm, and her own thick auburn hair cascaded down Drizzt's arm and chest.

The two sat back to back on the banks of Maer Dualdon, the largest lake in Icewind Dale, staring up at the hazy summer sky. Lazy white clouds drifted slowly overhead, their white fluffy lines sometimes cut in sharp contrast as one of many huge schinlook vultures coasted underneath. It was the clouds, not the many birds that were out this day, that held the attention of the couple.

"A knucklehead trout on the gaff," Catti-brie said of one unusual cloud formation, a curving oblong before a trailing, thin line of white.

"How do you see that?" the dark elf protested with a laugh.

Catti-brie turned her head to regard her black-skinned, violet-eyed companion. "How do ye not?" she asked. "It's as plain as the white line o' yer own eyebrows."

Drizzt laughed again, but not so much at what the woman was saying, but rather, at how she was saying it. She was living with Bruenor's clan again in the dwarven mines just outside of Ten-Towns, and the mannerisms and accent of the rough-and-tumble dwarves were obviously again wearing off on her.

Drizzt turned his head a bit toward the woman, as well, his right eye barely a couple of inches from Catti-brie's. He saw the sparkle there—it was unmistakable—a look of contentment and happiness only now returning in the months since Wulfgar had left them, a look that seemed, in fact, even more intense than ever before.

Drizzt laughed and looked back up at the sky. "Your fish got away," he announced, for the wind had blown the thin line away from the larger shape.

"It is a fish," Catti-brie insisted petulantly—or at least, the woman made it sound as if she was being petulant.

Smiling, Drizzt didn't pursue the argument.

* * * * *

"Ye durn fool little one!" Bruenor Battlehammer grumbled and growled, spittle flying as his frustration increased. The dwarf stopped and stamped his hard boot ferociously on the ground, then smacked his one-horned helmet onto his head, his thick orange hair flying wildly from beneath the brim of the battered helm. "I'm here thinkin' I got a friend on the council, and there ye go, letting Kemp o' Targos go and spout the price without even a fight!"

Regis the halfling, thinner than he had been in years and favoring one arm from a ghastly wound he'd received on his last adventure with his friends, just shrugged and replied, "Kemp of Targos speaks only of the price of the ore for the fishermen."

"And the fishermen buy a considerable portion of the ore!" Bruenor roared. "Why'd I put ye back on the council, Rumblebelly, if ye ain't to be making me life any easier?"

Regis gave a little smile at the tirade. He thought to remind Bruenor that the dwarf hadn't put him back on the council, that the folk of Lonelywood, needing a new representative since the last one had wound up in the belly of a yeti, had begged him to go, but he wisely kept the notion to himself.

"Fishermen," the dwarf said, and he spat on the ground in front of Regis's hairy, unshod feet.

Again, the halfling merely smiled and sidestepped the mark. He knew Bruenor was more bellow than bite, and knew, too, that the dwarf would let this matter drop soon enough—as soon as the next crisis rolled down the road. Ever had Bruenor Battlehammer been an excitable one.

The dwarf was still grumbling when the pair rounded a bend in the path to come in full view of Drizzt and Catti-brie, still sitting on the mossy bank, lost in their cloud-dreams and just enjoying each other's company. Regis sucked in his breath, thinking Bruenor might explode at the sight of his beloved adopted daughter in so intimate a position with Drizzt—or with anyone, for that matter—but Bruenor just shook his hairy head and stormed off the other way.

"Durned fool elf," he was saying when Regis caught up to him. "Will ye just kiss the girl and be done with it?"

Regis's smile nearly took in his ears. "How do you know that he has not?" he remarked, for no better reason than to see the dwarf's cheeks turn as fiery red as his hair and beard.

And of course, Regis was quick to skitter far out of Bruenor's deadly grasp.

The dwarf just put his head down, muttering curses and stomping along. Regis could hardly believe that boots could make such thunder on a soft, mossy dirt path.

*   *   *   *   *

The clamor in Brynn Shander's Council Hall was less of a surprise to Regis. He tried—he really did—to stay attentive to the proceedings, as Elderman Cassius, the highest-ranking leader in all of Ten-Towns, led the discussion through mostly procedural matters. Always before had the ten towns been ruled independently, or through a council comprised of one representative of each town, but so great had Cassius's service been to the region that he was no longer the representative of any single community, even that of Brynn Shander, the largest town by far and Cassius's home. Of course, that didn't sit well with Kemp of Targos, leader of the second city of Ten-Towns. He and Cassius had often been at odds, and with the elevation of Cassius and the appointment of a new councilor from Brynn Shander, Kemp felt outnumbered.

But Cassius had continued to rise above it all, and over the last few months even stubborn Kemp had grudgingly come to admit that the man was acting in a generally fair and impartial manner.

To the councilor from Lonelywood, though, the level of peace and community within the council hall in Brynn Shander only added to the tedium. The halfling loved a good debate and a good argument, especially when he was not a principal but could, rather, snipe in from the edges, fanning the emotions and the intensity.

Alas for the good old days!

Regis tried to stay awake—he really did—when the discussion became a matter of apportioning sections of the Maer Dualdon deepwaters to specific fishing vessels, to keep the lines untangled and keep the tempers out on the lake from flaring.

That rhetoric had been going on in Ten-Towns for decades, and Regis knew no rules would ever keep the boats apart out there on the cold waters of the large lake. Where the knucklehead were found, so the boats would go, whatever the rules. Knucklehead trout, perfect for scrimshaw and good eating besides, were the staple of the towns' economy, the lure that brought so many ruffians to Ten-Towns in search of fortune.

The rules established in this room so far from the banks of the three great lakes of Icewind Dale were no more than tools councilors could use to bolster subsequent tirades, when the rules had all been ignored.

By the time the halfling councilor from Lonelywood woke up, the discussion had shifted (thankfully) to more concrete matters, one that concerned Regis directly. In fact, the halfling only realized a moment later, the catalyst for opening his eyes had been Cassius's call to him.

"Pardon me for disturbing your sleep," the Elderman of Ten-Towns quietly said to Regis.

"I-I have been, um, working many days and nights in preparation for, uh, coming here," the halfling stammered, embarrassed. "And Brynn Shander is a long walk."

Cassius, smiling, held his hand up to quiet Regis before the halfling embarrassed himself even more. Regis didn't need to make excuses to this group, in any case. They understood his shortcomings and his value—a value that depended upon, to no small extent, the powerful friends he kept.

"Can you take care of this issue for us, then?" Kemp of Targos, who among the councilors was the least enamored of Regis, asked gruffly.

"Issue?" Regis asked.

Kemp put his head down and cursed quietly.

"The issue of the highwaymen," Cassius explained. "Since this newly sighted band is across the Shaengarne and south of Bremen, we know it would be a long ride for your friends, but we would certainly appreciate the effort if once again you and your companions could secure the roads into the region."

Regis sat back, crossed his hands over his still ample (if not as obviously as before) belly, and assumed a rather elevated expression. So that was it, he mused. Another opportunity for him and his friends to serve as heroes to the folk of Ten-Towns. This was where Regis was fully in his element, even though he had to admit he was usually only a minor player in the heroics of his more powerful friends. But in the council sessions, these were the moments when Regis could shine, when he could stand as tall as powerful Kemp. He considered the task Cassius had put to him. Bremen was the westernmost of the towns, across the Shaengarne River, which would be low now that it was late summer.

"I expect we can be there within the tenday, securing the road," Regis said after the appropriate pause.

He knew his friends would agree, after all. How many times in the last couple of months had they gone after monsters and highwaymen? It was a role Drizzt and Catti-brie, in particular, relished, and one that Bruenor, despite his constant complaining over it, did not truly mind at all.

As he sat there, thinking it over, Regis realized that he, too, wasn't upset to learn that he and his friends would have to be out on the adventurous road again. Something had happened to the halfling's sensibilities on the last long road, when he'd felt the piercing agony of a goblin spear through his shoulder—when he'd nearly died. Regis hadn't recognized the change back then. At that time, all the wounded halfling wanted was to be back in his comfortable little home in Lonelywood, carving knucklehead bones into beautiful scrimshaw and fishing absently from the banks of Maer Dualdon. Upon arriving at the comfy Lonelywood home, though, Regis had discovered a greater thrill than expected in showing off his scar.

So, yes, when Drizzt and the others headed out to defeat this newest threat, Regis would happily go along to play whatever role he might.

* * * * *

The end of the first tenday on the road south of Bremen seemed to be shaping up as another dreary day. Gnats and mosquitoes buzzed the air in ravenous swarms. The mud, freed of the nine-month lock of the Icewind Dale cold season, grabbed hard at the wheels of the small wagon and at Drizzt's worn boots as the drow shadowed the movements of his companions.

Catti-brie drove the one-horse wagon. She wore a long, dirty woolen dress, shoulder to toe, with her hair tied up tight. Regis, wearing the guise of a young boy, sat beside her, his face all ruddy from hours and hours under the summer sun.

Most uncomfortable of all was Bruenor, though, and by his own design. He had constructed a riding box for himself, to keep him well-hidden, nailing it underneath the center portion of the wagon. In there he rode, day after day.

Drizzt picked his path carefully about the mud-pocked landscape, spending his days walking, always on the alert. There were far greater dangers out in the open tundra of Icewind Dale than the highwayman band the group had come to catch. While most of the tundra yetis were likely farther to the south now, following the caribou herd to the foot-hills of the Spine of the World, some might still be around. Giants and goblins often came down from the distant mountains in this season, seeking easy prey and easy riches. And on many occasions, crossing areas of rocks and bogs, Drizzt had to quick-step past the deadly, gray-furred snakes, some measuring twenty feet or more and with a poison-ous bite that could fell a giant.

With all of that on his mind, the drow still had to keep the wagon in sight out of one corner of his eye, and keep his gaze scanning all about, in every direction. He had to see the highwaymen before they saw him if this was to be an easy catch.

Easier, anyway, the drow mused. They had a fairly good description of the band, and it didn't seem overwhelming in numbers or in skill. Drizzt reminded himself almost constantly, though, not to let preconceptions garner overconfidence. A single lucky bow shot could reduce his band to three.

So the bugs were swarming despite the wind, the sun was stinging his eyes, every mud puddle before him might conceal a gray-furred snake ready to make of him a meal or a tundra yeti hiding low in waiting, and a band of dangerous bandits was reputedly in the area, threatening him and his friends.

Drizzt Do'Urden was in a splendid mood!

He quick-stepped across a small stream, then slid to a stop, noting a line of curious puddles, foot-sized and spaced appropriately for a man walking swiftly. The drow went to the closest and knelt to inspect it. Tracks didn't last long out there, he knew, so this one was fresh. Drizzt's finger went under water to the second knuckle before his fingertip hit the ground beneath—again, the depth consistent with these being the tracks of an adult man.

The drow stood, hands going to the hilts of his scimitars under the folds of his camouflaging cloak. Twinkle waited on his right hip, Icing-death on his left, ready to flash out and cut down any threats.

Drizzt squinted his violet eyes, lifting one hand to further shield them from the sunlight. The tracks went out toward the road, to a place where the wagon would soon cross.

There lay the man, muddy and lying flat out on the ground, in wait.

Drizzt didn't head toward him but stayed low and circled back, meaning to cross over the road behind the rolling wagon to look for similar ambush spots on the other side. He pulled the cowl of his gray cloak lower, making sure it concealed his white hair, then came up into a full run, his black fingers rubbing against his palms with every eager stride.

* * * * *

Regis gave a yawn and a stretch, then leaned over against Catti-brie, nestling against her side and closing his big brown eyes.

"A fine time to be napping," the woman whispered.

"A fine time to be making any observers think that I'm napping," Regis corrected. "Did you see them back there, off to the side?"

"Aye," said Catti-brie. "A dirty pair."

As she spoke, the woman dropped one hand from the reins and slid it under the front lip of the wagon seat. Regis watched her fingers close on the item, and he knew she was taking comfort that Taulmaril the Heartseeker, her devastating bow, was in place and ready for her.

In truth, the halfling took more than a little comfort from that fact as well.

Regis reached one hand over the back of the driver's bench and slapped it absently, but hard, against the wooden planking inside the wagon bed, the signal to Bruenor to be alert and ready.

"Here we go," Catti-brie whispered to him a moment later.

Regis kept his eyes closed, kept his hand tap-tapping, at a quicker pace now. He did peek out of his left eye just a bit, to see a trio of scruffy-looking rogues walking down the road.

Catti-brie brought the wagon to a halt. "Oh, good sirs!" she cried. "Can ye be helpin' me and me boy, if ye please? My man done got hisself killed back at the mountain pass, and I'm thinking we're a bit o' the lost. Been days going back and forth, and not knowing which way's best for the Ten-Towns."

"Very clever," Regis whispered, covering his words by smacking his lips and shifting in his seat, seeming very much asleep.

Indeed, the halfling was impressed by the way Catti-brie had covered their movements, back and forth along the road, over the last few days. If the band had been watching, they'd be less suspicious now.

"But I don't know what I'm to do!" Catti-brie pleaded, her voice taking on a shrill, fearful edge. "Me and me boy here, all alone and lost!"

"We'll be helping ye," said the skinny man in the center, red-headed and with a beard that reached nearly to his belt.

"But fer a price," explained the rogue to his left, the largest of the three, holding a huge battle-axe across his shoulders.

"A price?" Catti-brie asked.

"The price of your wagon," said the third, seeming the most refined of the group, in accent and in appearance. He wore a colorful vest and tunic, yellow on red, and had a fine-looking rapier set in his belt on his left hip.

Regis and Catti-brie exchanged glances, hardly surprised.

Behind them they heard a bump, and Regis bit his lip, hoping Bruenor wouldn't crash out and ruin everything. Their plans had been carefully laid, their initial movements choreographed to the last step.

Another bump came from behind, but the halfling had already draped his arm over the bench and banged his fist on the backboard of the seat to cover the sound.

He looked to Catti-brie, at the intensity of her blue eyes, and knew it would be his turn to move very, very soon.

* * * * *

He'll be the most formidable, Catti-brie told herself, looking to the rogue on the right, the most refined of the trio. She did glance to the other end of their line, though, at the huge man. She didn't doubt for a moment that he could cut her in two with that monstrous axe of his.

885

"And a bit o' the womanflesh," the rogue on the left remarked, showing an eager, gap-toothed smile. The man in the middle smiled evilly, as well, but the one on the right glanced at the other two with disdain.

"Bah, but she's lost her husband, so she's said!" the burly one argued. "She could be using a good ride, I'd be guessing."

The image of Khazid-hea, her razor-sharp sword, prodding the buffoon's groin, crossed Catti-brie's mind, but she did well to hide her smile.

"Your wagon will, perhaps, suffice," the refined highwayman explained, and Catti-brie noted that he hadn't ruled out a few games with her completely.

Yes, she understood this one well enough. He'd try to take with his charms what the burly one would grab with his muscles. It would be more fun for him if she played along, after all.

"And all that's in it, of course," the refined highwayman went on. "A pity we must accept this donation of your goods, but I fear that we, too, must survive out here, patrolling the roads."

"Is that what ye're doing, then?" Catti-brie asked. "I'd've marked ye out as a bunch o' worthless thieves, meself."

That opened their eyes!

"Two to the right and three to the left," Catti-brie whispered to Regis. "The dogs in front are mine."

"Of course they are," Regis replied, and Catti-brie glanced over at him in surprise.

That surprise lasted only a moment, though, only the time it took for Catti-brie to remind herself that Regis understood her so very well, and had likely followed her emotions through the discussion with the highwayman as clearly as she had recognized them herself.

She turned back to the halfling, smiling wryly, and gave a slight motion, then turned back to the highwaymen.

"Ye've no call or right to be taking anything," she said to the thieves, putting just enough of a tremor in her voice to make them think her bold front was just that, a front hiding sheer terror.

Regis yawned and stretched, then popped wide his eyes, feigning surprise and terror. He gave a yelp and leaped off the right side of the wagon, running out into the mud.

Catti-brie took the cue, standing tall, and in a single tug pulling off her phony woolen dress, tossing it aside and revealing herself as the warrior she was. Out came Khazid-hea, the deadly Cutter, and the woman reached under the lip of the wagon seat, pulling forth her bow. She leaped ahead, one stride along the hitch and to the ground beside the horse, pulling the beast forward in a sudden rush, using its bulk to separate the big man from his two partners.

* * * * *

The three thugs to the left hand side of the wagon saw the movement and leaped up from the mud, drawing swords and howling as they charged forward.

A lithe and quick-moving form rose up from a crouch behind a small banking to the side of them, silent as a ghost, and seeming almost to float, so quick were its feet moving, across the sloppy ground.

Shining twin scimitars came out from under the folds of a gray cloak; a white smile and violet eyes greeting the charging trio.

" 'Ere, get him!" one thug cried and all three went at the drow. Their movements, two stabbing thrusts and a wild slash, were uncoordinated and awkward.

Drizzt's right arm went straight out to the side, presenting Icingdeath at a perfect angle to deflect the sidelong slash way up high, while his left hand worked over and in, driving the concave side of Twinkle down across both stabbing blades. Down came Icingdeath as Twinkle retracted, to slam against the extended swords, and down and across came Twinkle, to hit them both again. A subtle dip and duck backward had the drow's head clear of the outraged thug's backhand slash, and Drizzt snapped Icingdeath up quickly enough to stick the man in the hand as the sword whistled past.

The thug howled and let go, his sword flying free.

But not far, for the drow was already in motion with his left hand. He brought Twinkle across to hook the blade as it spun free. What followed was a dance that mesmerized the three thugs. A swift movement of the twin scimitars had the sword spinning in the air, over, under, and about, with the drow playing a song, it seemed, on the weapon's sides.

Drizzt finished with an over and about movement of Icingdeath that perfectly presented the sword back to its original owner.

"Surely you can do better than that," the smiling drow offered as the hilt of the sword landed perfectly in the hand of the stunned thug.

The man screamed and dropped his weapon to the ground, turning around and running off.

"It's the Drizzit!" another of them shouted, similarly following.

The third, though, out of fear or anger or stupidity, came on instead. His sword worked furiously, forward in a thrust then back, then forward higher and in a roundabout turn back down.

Or at least, it started down.

Up came the drow's scimitars, hitting it alternately, twice each. Then over went Twinkle, forcing the sword low, and the drow went into a furious attack, his blades smashing hard, side to side against the overmatched thug's sword, hitting it so fast and with such fury that the song sounded as one long note.

The man surely felt his arm going numb, but he tried to take advantage of his opponent's furious movements by rushing forward suddenly, an obvious attempt to get in close and tie up the drow's lightning-fast hands.

He found himself without his weapon, though he did not know how. The thug lunged forward, arms wide to capture his foe in a bear hug, to catch only air.

He must have felt a painful sting between his legs as the drow, somehow behind him, slapped the back side of a scimitar up between his legs, bringing him up to tip-toe.

Drizzt retracted the scimitar quickly, and the man had to leap up, then stumble forward, nearly falling.

Then Drizzt had a foot on the thug's back, between his shoulderblades, and the dark elf stomped him facedown into the muck.

"You would do well to stay right there until I ask you to get up," Drizzt said. After a look at the wagons to ensure that his friends were all right, the drow headed off at a leisurely pace to follow the trail of the fleeing duo.

*   *   *   *   *

Regis did a fine impression of a frightened child as he scrambled across the muck, arms waving frantically, and yelling, "Help! Help!" all the way.

The two men Catti-brie had warned him of stood up to block his path. He gave a cry and scrambled out to the side, stumbling and falling to his knees.

"Oh, don't ye kill me, please misters!" Regis wailed pitifully as the two stalked in, wicked grins on their faces, nasty weapons in their hand.

"Oh, please!" said Regis. "Here, I'll give ye me dad's necklace, I will!"

Regis reached under the front of his shirt, pulled forth a ruby pendant, and held it up by a short length of chain, just enough to send it swaying and spinning.

The thugs approached, their grins melting into expressions of curiosity as they regarded the spinning gemstones, the thousand, thousand sparkles and the tantalizing way it seemed to catch and hold the light.

*   *   *   *   *

Catti-brie let go of the trotting horse, dropped her bow and quiver to the side of the road, and skipped out to the side to avoid the passing wagon and to square up against the large rogue and his huge axe.

He came at her aggressively and clumsily, sweeping the axe across in front of him, then back across, then up and over with a tremendous downward chop.

Nimble Catti-brie had little trouble avoiding the three swipes. The miss on the third, the axe diving into the soft ground, left her the perfect opportunity to score a quick kill and move on. She heard the more refined rogue's voice urging the horse on and saw the wagon rumble past, the other two highwaymen sitting on the driver's bench.

They were Bruenor's problem now.

She decided to take her time. She hadn't appreciated this one's lewd remarks.

*   *   *   *   *

"Durn latch!" Bruenor grumbled, for the catch on his makeshift compartment, too full of mud from the wheels, would not budge.

The wagon was moving faster now, exaggerating each bump, bouncing the dwarf about wildly.

Finally, Bruenor managed to get one foot under him, then the other, steadying himself in a tight, tight crouch. He gave a roar that would make a red dragon proud, and snapped up with all his might, blasting his head right through the floorboards of the wagon.

"Ye think ye might be slowin' it down?" he asked the finely dressed highwayman driver and the red-headed thug sitting beside him. Both turned back, their expressions quite entertaining.

That is, until the red-headed thug drew out a dagger and spun about, leaping over the seat in a wild dive at Bruenor, who only then realized he wasn't in a very good defensive posture there, with his arms pinned to his sides by splintered boards.

*   *   *   *   *

One of the rogues seemed quite content to stand there stupidly watching the spinning gemstone. The other, though, watched for only a few moments, then stood up straight and shook his head roughly, his lips flapping.

" 'Ere now, ye little trickster!" he bellowed.

Regis hopped to his feet and snapped the ruby pendant up into his plump little hand.

"Don't let him hurt me!" he cried to the entranced man as the other came forward, reaching for Regis's throat with both hands.

Regis was quicker than he looked, though, and he skittered backward. Still, the taller man had the advantage and would easily catch up to him.

Except that the other rogue, who knew beyond any doubt that this little guy here was a friend, a dear friend, slammed against his companion's side and drove him down to the ground. In a moment, the two rolled and thrashed, trading punches and oaths.

"Ye're a fool, and he's a trickster!" the enemy yelled and put his fist in the other one's eye.

"Ye're a brute, and he's a friendly little fellow!" the other countered, and countered, too, with a punch to the nose.

889

Regis gave a sigh and turned about to regard the battle scene. He had played out his role perfectly, as he had in all the recent exploits of the Companions of the Hall. But still, he thought of how Drizzt would have handled these two, scimitars flashing brilliantly in the sunlight, and he wished he could do that.

He thought of how Catti-brie would have handled them, a combination, no doubt, of a quick and deadly slice of Cutter, followed by a well-aimed, devastating lightning arrow from that marvelous bow of hers. And again, the halfling wished he could do it like that.

He thought of how Bruenor would have handled the thugs, taking a smash in the face and handing out one, catching a smash on the side that might have felled a giant, but rolling along until the pair had been squashed into the muck, and he wished he could do it like that.

"Nah," Regis said. He rubbed his shoulder out of sympathy for Bruenor. Each had their own way, he decided, and he turned his attention to the combatants rolling about the muck before him.

His new pet was losing.

Regis took out his own weapon, a little mace Bruenor had crafted for him, and, as the pair rolled about, gave a couple of well-placed *bonks* to get things moving in the right direction.

Soon his pet had the upper hand, and Regis was well on his way to success.

To each his own.

* * * * *

She came ahead with a thrust, and the thug tore his axe free and set it into a blocking position before him, snapping it this way and that to intercept, or at least deflect, the stabbing sword.

Catti-brie strode forward powerfully, presenting herself too far forward, she knew, at least in the eyes of the thug.

For she knew that this one would underestimate her. His remarks when first he'd seen her told her pretty much the way this one viewed women.

Taking the bait, the thug shoved out with his axe, turning it head-out toward the woman and trying to slam her with it.

A planted foot and a turn brought her right by the awkward weapon, and while she could have pierced the man's chest with Khazid-hea, she used her foot instead, kicking him hard in the crotch.

She skittered back, and the man, with a groan, set himself again.

Catti-brie waited, allowing him to take the offensive again. Predictably, he worked his way around to launch another of those mighty—and useless—horizontal slashes. This time Catti-brie backed away only enough so the flying blade barely missed her. She turned as she came forward past the man's extended reach, pivoting on her left foot and back-kicking with her right, again slamming the man in the crotch.

She didn't really know why, but she just felt like doing that.

Again, the woman was out of harm's way before the thug could begin to react, before he had even recovered from the sickening pain that was likely rolling up from his loins.

He did manage to straighten, barely, and he brought his axe up high and roared, rushing forward—the attack of a desperate opponent. Khazid-hea's hungry tip dived in at the man's belly, stopping him short. A flick of Catti-brie's wrist sent the deadly blade snapping down, and a quick step had the woman right up against the man, face to face.

"Bet it hurts," she whispered, and up came her knee, hard.

Catti-brie jumped back then leaped forward in a spin, her sword cutting across inside the angle of the downward-chopping axe, the fine blade shearing through the axe handle as easily as if it was made of candle wax. Catti-brie rushed back out again, but not before one last, well-placed kick.

The thug, his eyes fully crossed, his face locked in a grimace of absolute pain, tried to pursue, but the down cut of Khazid-hea had taken off his belt and all other supporting ties of his pants, dropping them to the man's ankles.

One shortened step, and another, and the man tripped up and tumbled headlong into the muck. Mud-covered, waves of pain obviously rolling through his body, he scrambled to his knees and swiped at the woman as she stalked in. Only then did he seem to realize he was holding no more than half an axe handle. The swing fell way short and brought the man too far out to the left. Catti-brie stepped in behind it, braced her foot on the brute's right shoulder, and pushed him back down in the muck.

He got up to his knees again, blinded by mud and swinging wildly.

She was behind him.

She kicked him to the muck again.

"Stay down," the woman warned.

Sputtering curses, mud, and brown water, the stubborn, stunned ruffian rose again.

"Stay down," Catti-brie said, knowing he would focus in on her voice.

He threw one leg out to the side for balance and shifted around, launching a desperate swing.

Catti-brie hopped over both the club and the leg, landing before the man and shifting her momentum into one more great kick to the crotch.

This time, as the man curled in the fetal position in the muck, making little mewling sounds and clutching at his groin, the woman knew he wouldn't be getting back up.

With a look over at Regis and a wide grin, Catti-brie started back for her bow.

* * * * *

Desperation drove Bruenor's arm and leg forward, hand pushing and knee coming up to support it. A plank cracked apart, coming up as a shield against the charging dagger, and Bruenor somehow managed to free his hand enough to angle the plank to knock the dagger free of the red-haired man's hand.

Or, the dwarf realized, maybe the thug had just decided to let it go.

The man's fist came around the board and slugged him good in the face. There came a following left, and another right, and Bruenor had no way to defend, so he didn't. He just let the man pound on him while he wriggled and forced both of his hands free, and finally he managed to come forward while offering some defense. He caught the man's slugging left by the wrist with his right and launched his own left that seemed as if it would tear the thug's head right off.

But the ruffian managed to catch that arm, as Bruenor had caught his, and so the two found a stand-off, struggling in the back of the rolling and bouncing wagon.

"C'mere, Kenda!" the red-headed man cried. "Oh, we got him!" He looked back to Bruenor, his ugly face barely an inch from the dwarf's. "What're ye gonna do now, dwarfie?"

"Anyone ever tell ye that ye spit when ye talk?" the disgusted Bruenor asked.

In response, the man grinned stupidly and snorted and hocked, filling his mouth with a great wad to launch at the dwarf.

Bruenor's entire body tightened, and like a singular giant muscle, like the body of a great serpent, perhaps, the dwarf struck. He smashed his forehead into the ugly rogue's face, snapping the man's head back so that he was staring up at the sky, so that, when he spit—and somehow, he still managed to do that—the wad went straight up and fell back upon him.

Bruenor tugged his hand free, let go of the man's arm, and clamped one hand on the rogue's throat, the other grabbing him by the belt. Up he went, over the dwarf's head, and flying off the side of the speeding wagon.

Bruenor saw the composure on the face of the remaining ruffian as the man set down the reins and calmly turned and drew out his fine rapier. Calmly, too, went Bruenor, pulling himself fully from the compartment and reaching back in to pick up his many-notched axe.

The dwarf slapped the axe over his right shoulder, assuming a casual stance, feet wide apart to brace him against the bouncing.

"Ye'd be smart to just put it down and stop the stupid wagon," he said to his opponent, the man waving his rapier out before him.

"It is you who should surrender," the highwayman remarked, "foolish dwarf!" As he finished, he lunged forward, and Bruenor, with enough experience to understand the full measure of his reach and balance, didn't blink.

The dwarf had underestimated just a bit, though, and the rapier tip did jab in against his mithral chest-piece, finding enough of a seam to poke the dwarf hard.

"Ouch," Bruenor said, seeming less than impressed.

The highwayman retracted, ready to spring again. "Your clumsy weapon is no match for my speed and agility!" he proclaimed, and he started forward. "Hah!"

A flick of Bruenor's strong wrist sent his axe flying forward, a single spin before embedding in the thrusting highwayman's chest, blasting him backward to fall against the back of the driver's seat.

"That so?" the dwarf asked. He stomped one foot on the highwayman's breast and yanked his weapon free.

* * * * *

Catti-brie lowered her bow, seeing that Bruenor had the wagon under control. She had the rapier-wielding highwayman in her sights and would have shot him dead if necessary.

Not that she believed for a moment that Bruenor Battlehammer would need her help against the likes of those two.

She turned to regard Regis, approaching from the right. Behind him came his obedient pet, carrying the captive across his shoulders.

"Ye got some bandages for the one Bruenor dropped?" Catti-brie asked, though she wasn't very confident that the man was even alive.

Regis started to nod, but then shouted, "Left!" with alarm.

Catti-brie spun, Taulmaril coming up, and noted the target. The man Drizzt had dropped to the mud was starting to rise.

She put an arrow that streaked and sparked like a bolt of lightning into the ground right beneath his rising head. The man froze in place, and seemed to be whimpering.

"Ye would do well to lie back down," Catti-brie called from the road.

He did.

* * * * *

More than two hours later, the two escaping rogues crashed through the brush, the one break through the ring of boulders that concealed their encampment. Still stumbling, still frantic, they pushed past the horses and moved around the stolen wagon, to find Jule Pepper, their leader, the strategist of the outfit and also the cook, stirring a huge caldron.

"Nothing today?" the tall black-haired woman asked, her brown eyes scrutinizing them. Her tone and her posture revealed the truth, though neither of the rogues were smart enough to catch on. Jule understood that something had happened, and likely, nothing good.

"The Drizzit," one of the rogues spurted, gasping for breath with every word. "The Drizzit and 'is friends got us."

"Drizzt?" Jules asked.

"Drizzit Dudden, the damned drow elf," said the other. "We was takin' a wagon—just a woman and her kid—and there he was, behind the three of us. Poor Walken got him in the fight, head up."

"Poor Walken," the other said.

Jule closed her eyes and shook her head, seeing something that the others apparently had not. "And this woman," she asked, "she merely surrendered the wagon?"

"She was puttin' up a fight when we runned off," said the first of the dirty pair. "We didn't get to see much."

"She?" Jule asked. "You mean Catti-brie? The daughter of Bruenor Battlehammer? You were baited, you fools!"

The pair looked at each other in confusion. "And we're payin' with the loss of a few, don't ye doubt," one finally said, mustering the courage to look back at the imposing woman. "Could'a been worse."

"Could it?" Jule asked doubtfully. "Tell me, then, did this dark elf's panther companion make an appearance?"

Again the two looked at each other.

As if in response, a low growl reverberated through the encampment, resonating as if it was coming from the ground itself, running into the bodies of the three rogues. The horses at the side of the camp neighed and stomped and tossed their heads nervously.

"I would guess that it did," Jule answered her own question, and she gave a great sigh.

A movement to the side, a flash of flying blackness, caught their attention, turning all three heads to regard the new arrival. It was a huge black cat, ten feet long at least, and with muscled shoulders as high as a tall man's chest.

"Drow elf's cat?" one of the dirty rogues asked.

"They say her name is Guenhwyvar," Jule confirmed.

The other rogue was already backing away, staring at the cat all the while. He bumped into a wagon then edged around it, moving right before the nervous and sweating horses.

"And so you ran right back to me," Jule said to the other with obvious contempt. "You could not understand that the drow *allowed* you to escape?"

"No, he was busy!" the remaining rogue protested.

Jule just shook her head. She wasn't really surprised it had ended like this, after all. She supposed that she deserved it for taking up with a band of fools.

Guenhwyvar roared and sprang into the middle of the camp, landing right between the pair. Jule, wiser than to even think of giving a fight against the mighty beast, just threw up her hands. She was about to instruct her companions to do the same when she heard one of them hit the ground. He'd fainted dead away.

The remaining dirty rogue didn't even see Guenhwyvar's spring. He spun around and rushed through the break in the boulder ring, crashing through the brush, thinking to leave his friends behind to fight while he made his escape, as he had done back on the road. He came through, squinting against the slapping branches, and did notice a dark form standing to the side and did notice a pair of intense violet eyes regarding him—just an instant before the hilt of a scimitar rushed up and slammed him in the face, laying him low.

Chapter 2

Conflicted

The wind and salty spray felt good on his face, his long blond hair trailing out behind him, his crystal blue eyes squinting against the glare. Wulfgar's features remained strong, but boyish, despite the ruddiness of his skin from tendays at sea. To the more discerning observer, though, there loomed in Wulfgar's eyes a resonance that denied the youthful appearance, a sadness wrought of bitter experience.

That melancholy was not with him now, though, for up there, on the prow of *Sea Sprite*, Wulfgar, son of Beornegar, felt the same rush of adrenaline he'd known all those years growing up in Icewind Dale, all those years learning the ways of his people, and all those years fighting beside Drizzt. The exhilaration could not be denied; this was the way of the warrior, the proud and tingling anticipation before the onset of battle.

And battle would soon be joined, the barbarian did not doubt. Far ahead, across the sparkling waters, Wulfgar saw the sails of the running pirate.

Was this *Bloody Keel*, Sheila Kree's boat? Was his warhammer, mighty Aegis-fang, the gift of his adoptive father, in the hands of a pirate aboard that ship?

Wulfgar winced as he considered the question, at the myriad of feelings that the mere thought of once again possessing Aegis-fang brought up inside him. He'd left Delly Curtie and Colson, the baby girl they'd taken in as their own daughter, back in Waterdeep. They were staying at Captain Deudermont's beautiful home while he had come out with *Sea Sprite* for the express purpose of regaining the warhammer. Yet, the thought of Aegis-fang, of what he might do once he had the weapon back in his grasp, was, at that time, still beyond Wulfgar's swirling sensibilities. What did the warhammer mean, really?

That warhammer, a gift from Bruenor, had been meant as a symbol of the dwarf's love for him, of the dwarf's recognition that Wulfgar had risen above his stoic and brutal upbringing to become a better warrior, and more importantly, a better man. But had Wulfgar, really? Was he deserving of the warhammer, of Bruenor's love? Certainly the events since his return from the Abyss would argue against that. Over the past months Wulfgar hadn't done many things of which he was proud and had an entire list of accomplishments, beginning with his slapping Catti-brie's face, that he would rather forget.

And so this pursuit of Aegis-fang had come to him as a welcome relief, a distraction that kept him busy, and positively employed for a good cause, while he continued to sort things out. But if Aegis-fang was on that boat ahead, or the next one in line, and Wulfgar retrieved it, where would it lead? Was his place still waiting for him in Icewind Dale among his former friends? Would he return to a life of adventure and wild battles, living on the edge of disaster with Drizzt and the others?

Wulfgar's thoughts returned to Delly and the child. Given the new reality of his life, given those two, how could he return to that previous life? What did such a reversion mean regarding his responsibilities to his new family?

The barbarian gave a laugh, recognizing that it was far more than responsibilities hindering him, though he didn't often admit it, even to himself. When he had first taken the child from Auckney, a minor kingdom nestled in the eastern reaches of the Spine of the World, it had been out of responsibility, it had been because the person he truly was (or wanted to be again!) demanded of him that he not let the child suffer the sins of the mother or the cowardice and stupidity of the father.

It had been responsibility that had taken him back to the Cutlass tavern in Luskan, a debt owed to his former friends, Arumn, Delly, and even Josi Puddles, whom he had surely let down with his drunken antics. Asking Delly to come along with him and the child had been yet another impulse wrought of responsibility—he had seen the opportunity to make some amends for his wretched treatment of the poor woman, and so he had offered her a new road to explore. In truth, Wulfgar hadn't given the decision to ask Delly along much thought at all, and even after her surprising acceptance, the barbarian had not understood how profoundly her choice would come to affect his life. Because now . . . now his relationship with Delly and their adopted child had become something more. This child he had taken out of generosity—and, in truth, because Wulfgar had instinctively recognized that he needed the generosity more than the child ever would—had become to him his daughter, his own child. In every way. Much as he had long ago become the child of Bruenor Battlehammer. Never before had Wulfgar held even a hint of the level of vulnerability the new title, father, had brought to him. Never had he imagined that anyone could truly hurt him, in any real way. Now all he had to do was look into Colson's blue eyes, so much like her real mother's, and Wulfgar knew his entire world could be destroyed about him.

Similarly, with Delly Curtie, the barbarian had come to understand that he'd taken on more than he'd bargained for. This woman he'd invited to join him, again in the spirit of generosity and as a denial of the thug he'd become, was now something much more important than a mere traveling companion. In the months since their departure from Luskan, Wulfgar had come to see Delly Curtie in a completely different light, had come to see the depth of her spirit and the wisdom that had been buried beneath the sarcastic and gruff exterior she'd been forced to assume in order to survive in her miserable existence.

Delly had told him of the few glorious moments she had known—and none of those had been in the arms of one of her many lovers. She told him of the many hours she'd spent along the quiet wharves of Luskan before having to force herself to begin her nights at the Cutlass. There she'd sit and watch the sun sinking into the distant ocean, seeming to set all the water ablaze.

Delly loved the dusk—the quiet hour, she called it—when the daytime folk of Luskan returned home to their families and the nighttime crowd had not yet awakened to the bustle of their adventurous but ultimately empty nights. In the months he'd known Delly at the Cutlass, in the nights they'd spent in each others' arms, Wulfgar had never begun to imagine that there was so much more to her, that she was possessed of hopes and dreams, and that she held such a deep understanding of the people around her. When men bedded her, they often thought her an easy target, tossing a few words of compliment to get their prize.

What Wulfgar came to understand about Delly was that none of those words, none of that game, had ever really meant anything to her. Her one measure of power on the streets was her body, and so she used it to gain favor, to gain knowledge, to gain security, in a place lacking in all three. How strange it seemed to Wulfgar to recognize that while all the men had believed they were taking advantage of Delly's ignorance, she was, in fact, taking advantage of their weakness in the face of lust.

Yes, Delly Curtie could play the "using" game as well as any, and that was why this blossoming relationship seemed so amazing to him. Because Delly wasn't using him at all, he knew, and he wasn't using her.

For the first time in all their history together, the two had merely been sharing each others' company, honestly and without pretense, without an agenda.

And Wulfgar would be a liar indeed if he couldn't admit that he was enjoying it.

A liar Wulfgar would be indeed, and a coward besides, if he couldn't admit that he'd fallen in love with Delly Curtie. Thus, the couple had married. Not formally, but in heart and soul, and Wulfgar knew that this woman, this unlikely companion, had completed him in ways he had never known possible.

"Killer banner up!" came a call from the crow's nest, meaning that this was indeed a pirate vessel ahead of *Sea Sprite,* for in her arrogance, she was flying a recognized pirate pennant.

With nothing but open water ahead, the ship had no chance of escape. No vessel on the Sword Coast could outrun *Sea Sprite*, especially with the powerful wizard Robillard sitting atop the back of the flying bridge, summoning gusts of wind repeatedly into the schooner's mainsail.

Wulfgar took a deep breath, and another, but found little in them to help steady his nerves.

I am a warrior! he reminded himself, but that other truth, that he was a husband and a father, would not be so easily put down.

How strange this change in heart seemed to him. Just a few months before, he had been the terror of Luskan, throwing himself into fights with abandon, reckless to the point of self-destructive. But that was when he had nothing to lose, when he believed that death would take away the pain. Now, it was something even greater than those things he had to lose, it was the realization that if he perished out here, Delly and Colson would suffer.

And for what? the barbarian had to ask himself. For a warhammer, a symbol of a past he wasn't even sure he wanted to recapture?

Wulfgar grabbed tight to the line running back to the foremast, clenching it so tightly his knuckles whitened from the press, and again took in a deep and steadying breath, letting it out as a feral growl. Wulfgar shook the thoughts away, recognizing them as anathema to the heart of a true warrior. Charge in bravely, that was his mantra, his code, and indeed, that was the way a true warrior survived. Overwhelm your enemies, and quickly, and you will likely walk away. Hesitation only provided opportunity for the enemy to shoot you down with arrows and spears.

Hesitation, cowardice, would destroy him.

* * * * *

Sea Sprite gained quickly on the vessel, and soon it could be seen clearly as a two-masted caravel. How fast that pirate insignia pennant came down when the ship recognized its pursuer!

900

Sea Sprite's rear catapult and forward ballista both let fly, neither scoring a hit of any consequence, and the pirate responded with a catapult shot of its own, a meager thing that fell far short of the approaching hunter.

"A second volley?" Captain Deudermont asked his ship's wizard. The captain was a tall and straight-backed man with a perfectly trimmed goatee that was still more brown than gray.

"To coax?" Robillard replied. "Nay, if they've a wizard, he is too cagey to be baited, else he would have shown himself already. Move into true range and let fly, and so will I."

Deudermont nodded and lifted his spyglass to his eye to better see the pirate—and he could make out the individuals on the deck now, scrambling every which way.

Sea Sprite closed with every passing second, her sails gathering up the wind greedily, her prow cutting walls of water high into the air.

Deudermont looked behind, to his gunners manning the catapult on the poop deck. One used a spyglass much like the captain's own, lining up the vessel with a marked stick set before him. He lowered the glass to see the captain and nodded.

"Let fly for mainsail," Deudermont said to the crewman beside him, and the cry went out, gaining momentum and volume, and both catapult and ballista let fly again. This time, a ball of burning pitch clipped the sails and rigging of the pirate, who was bending hard into a desperate turn, and the ballista bolt, trailing chains, tore through a sail.

A moment later came a brilliant flash, a streak of lightning from Robillard that smacked the pirate's hull at the water line, splintering wood.

"Going defensive!" came Robillard's cry, and he enacted a semi-translucent globe about him and rushed to the prow, shoving past Wulfgar, who was moving amidships.

A responding lightning bolt did come from the pirate, not nearly as searing and bright as Robillard's. *Sea Sprite*'s wizard, considered among the very finest of sea-fighting mages in all Faerûn, had his shields in place to minimize the damage to no more than a black scar on the side of *Sea Sprite*'s prow, one of many badges of honor the proud pirate hunter had earned in her years of service.

The pirate continued its evasive turn, but *Sea Sprite*, more nimble by far, cut right inside her angle, closing even more rapidly.

Deudermont smiled as he considered Robillard, the wizard rubbing his fingers together eagerly, ready to drop a series of spells to counter any defenses, followed by a devastating fireball that would consume rigging and sails, leaving the pirate dead in the water.

The pirates would likely surrender soon after.

* * * * *

901

A row of archers lined *Sea Sprite*'s side rail, with several standing forward, as obvious targets. Robillard had placed enchantments on these few, making them impervious to unenchanted arrows, and so they were the brave ones inviting the shots.

"Volley as we pass!" the group leader commanded, and every man and woman began checking their draw and their arrows, finding ones that would fly straight and true.

Behind them, Wulfgar paced nervously, anxiously. He wanted this to be done—a perfectly reasonable and rational desire—and yet he cursed himself for those feelings.

"A pop to steady yer hands?" one greasy crewman said to him, holding forth a small bottle of rum, which the boarding party had been passing around.

Wulfgar stared at the bottle long and hard. For months he had hidden inside one of those seemingly transparent things. For months he had bottled up his fears and his horrible memories, a futile attempt to escape the truth of his life and his past.

He shook his head and went back to pacing.

A moment later came the sound of twenty bowstrings humming, the cries of many pirates, and of a couple from *Sea Sprite*'s crew, hit by the exchange.

Wulfgar knew he should be moving into position with the rest of the boarding party, and yet he found he could not. His legs would not walk past conjured images of Delly and Colson. How could he be doing this? How could he be out here, chasing a warhammer, while they waited back in Waterdeep?

The questions sounded loudly and horribly in Wulfgar's mind. All he had once been screamed back at him. He heard the name of Tempus, the barbarian god of war, pounding in his head, telling him to deny his fears, telling him to remember who he was.

With a roar that sent those men closest to him scurrying in fear, Wulfgar, son of Beornegar, charged for the rail, and though no boarding party had been called and though Robillard was even then preparing his fiery blast and though the two ships were still a dozen feet apart, with *Sea Sprite* fast passing, the furious barbarian leaped atop that rail and sprang forward.

Cries of protest sounded behind him, cries of surprise and fear sounded before him.

But the only cry Wulfgar heard was his own. "Tempus!" he bellowed, denying his fears and his hesitance.

"Tempus!"

* * * * *

Captain Deudermont rushed to Robillard and grabbed the skinny wizard, pinning his arms to his side and interrupting his spellcasting.

"The fool!" Robillard shouted as soon as he opened his eyes, to see what had prompted the captain's interference.

Not that the wizard was surprised, for Wulfgar had been a thorn in Robillard's side ever since he'd joined up with the crew. Unlike his old companions, Drizzt and Catti-brie, this barbarian simply did not seem to understand the subtleties of wizardly combat. And, to Robillard's thinking, wizardly combat was all-important, certainly far above the follies of meager warriors.

Robillard pulled free of Deudermont. "I will be throwing the fireball soon enough," he insisted. "When Wulfgar is dead!"

Deudermont was hardly listening. He called out to his crew to bring *Sea Sprite* about and called to his archers to find angles for their shots that they might lend aid to the one-man boarding party.

* * * * *

Wulfgar clipped the rail as he went aboard the pirate ship, tripping forward onto the deck. On came pirate swordsmen, rolling like water to cover him—but he was up and roaring, a long length of chain held in each hand.

The closest pirate slashed with a sword and scored a hit against the barbarian's shoulder, though Wulfgar quickly got his forearm up and pressed out, stopping the blade from doing more than a surface cut. The barbarian pumped out a right cross as he parried, hitting the man hard in the chest, lifting him from his feet and throwing him across the deck, where he lay broken on his back.

Chains snapping and smashing, roaring to his god, the barbarian went into a rampage, scattering pirates before him. They had never seen anything like this before, a nearly seven-foot-tall wild man, and so most fled before his thunderous charge.

Out went one length of chain, entwining a pair of legs, and Wulfgar gave a mighty jerk that sent the poor pirate flying to the deck. Out went the second length of chain, rolling about the shoulder of a man to Wulfgar's left, going completely around him to snap up and smack him in the chest. Wulfgar's tug took a considerable amount of skin from that one, and sent him into a fast-descending spin.

"Run away!" came the cries before him. "Oh, but a demon he is!"

Both his chains were entangled quickly enough, so Wulfgar dropped them and pulled a pair of small clubs from his belt. He leaped forward and cut fast to the side, catching one pirate, obviously the leader of the deck crew and the most heavily armored of the bunch, against the rail.

The pirate slashed with a fine sword, but Wulfgar jumped back out of reach, then reversed stride with another roar.

Up came a large, fine shield, and that should have been enough, but never before had this warrior faced the primal fury of Wulfgar.

The barbarian's first smash against the shield numbed the pirate's arm. Wulfgar's second blow bent in the top of the shield and drove the blocking arm low. His third strike took the defense away all together, and his fourth, following so quickly his opponent hadn't even found the opportunity to bring his sword back in, smacked the pirate on the side of his helmet and staggered him to the side.

Wulfgar bore in, raining a series of blows that left huge dents in the fine armor and that sent the pirate stumbling to the deck. He had barely hit the planking though, before Wulfgar grabbed him by the ankle and jerked him back up, feet first.

A twist and a single stride had the mighty barbarian standing at the rail, the armored pirate hanging in midair over the side. Wulfgar held him there, with hardly any effort, it seemed, and with only one arm. The barbarian eyed the rest of the crew dangerously. Not a man approached, and not an archer lifted a bow against him.

From the flying bridge, though, there did indeed come a challenge, and Wulfgar turned to see the pirate wizard, staring at him while in the throes of spellcasting.

A flick of Wulfgar's wrist sent his remaining club spinning at the man, and the wizard had to dodge aside, interrupting his own spell.

But now Wulfgar was unarmed, and the pirate crew seemed recovered from the initial shock of his overwhelming charge. The pirate captain appeared, promising a horde of treasure to the one who brought the barbarian giant down. The wizard was back into casting.

The sea scum approached, murder in their eyes.

And they stopped and stood straighter, and some dropped their weapons, as *Sea Sprite* glided alongside their ship right behind the barbarian, archers ready, boarding party ready.

Robillard let fly another lightning bolt that smashed the distracted pirate wizard, driving him right over the far rail of the ship and into the cold sea.

One pirate called for a charge, but was stopped short as a pair of arrows thudded into his chest.

Sea Sprite's crew was too well trained, too disciplined, too experienced. The fight was over before it had even really begun.

"You can probably bring him back over the rail," Deudermont said to Wulfgar a short while later, with the barbarian still standing there, holding the armored pirate upside-down above the short expanse of water between the ships, though Wulfgar was now using two hands, at least.

"Yes, do!" the embarrassed pirate demanded, lifting the cage visor of his expensive helm. "I am the Earl of Taskadale Manor! I demand—"

"You are a pirate," Deudermont said to him, simply.

"A bit of adventure and nothing more," the man replied haughtily. "Now please have your ogre friend put me down!"

904

Before the captain could say a word, Wulfgar went into a half spin and sent the earl flying across the deck, to smack the mainmast with a great clang and roll right around it, crumbling down in a noisy lump.

"Earl of Taskadale, whatever that might be," Deudermont remarked.

"Not impressed," Wulfgar replied, and he started away, to the plank that would take him back to *Sea Sprite*.

A fuming Robillard was waiting for him on the other side.

"Who instructed you to board?" the furious wizard demanded. "They could have been taken with a single spell!"

"Then cast your spell, wizard," Wulfgar grumbled at him, striding right past, having no time to explain his emotions and impulses to another when he hadn't even sorted them out for himself.

"Do not think that next time I shan't!" Robillard yelled at him, but Wulfgar just went on his way. "And pity Wulfgar when burning pieces of sail rain down upon his head, lighting his hair and curling his skin! Pity Wulfgar when—"

"Rest easy," Deudermont remarked, coming up behind the wizard. "The pirate is taken and not a crewman lost."

"As it would have been," Robillard insisted, "with less chance. Their magical defenses were down, their sails exposed. I had—"

"Enough, my friend," Deudermont interrupted.

"That one, Wulfgar, is a fool," Robillard replied. "A barbarian indeed! A savage to his heart and soul, and with no better understanding of tactics and advantage than an orc might hold."

Deudermont, who had sailed with Wulfgar before and who knew well the dark elf who had trained this warrior, knew better. But he said nothing, just let the always-grumpy Robillard play out his frustration with a string of curses and protests.

In truth, Captain Deudermont was beginning to rethink the decision to allow Wulfgar to join *Sea Sprite*'s crew, though he certainly believed he owed that much to the man, out of friendship and respect. Wulfgar's apparent redemption had struck well the heart of Captain Deudermont, for he had seen the man at his lowest point, on trial before the vicious magistrates of Luskan for attempting to assassinate Deudermont.

The captain hadn't believed the charge then—that was the only reason Wulfgar was still alive—though he had recognized that something terrible had happened to the noble warrior, that some unspeakable event had dropped Wulfgar to the bottom of the lowest gutter. Deudermont had been pleased indeed when Wulfgar had arrived at the dock in Waterdeep, asking to come aboard and join the crew, asking Deudermont to help him in retrieving the mighty warhammer that Bruenor Battlehammer had crafted for him.

Now it was clear to the captain, though, that the scars of Wulfgar's pain had not yet fully healed. His charge back there had been reckless and foolish and could have endangered the entire crew. That, Captain

Deudermont could not tolerate. He would have to speak with Wulfgar, and sternly.

More than that, the captain decided then and there that he would make finding Sheila Kree and her elusive ship a priority, would get Wulfgar back Aegis-fang, and would put him back ashore in Waterdeep.

To the benefit of all.

Chapter 3

Bells and Whistles

Great gargoyles leered down from twenty feet; a gigantic stone statue of a humanoid lizard warrior—a golem of some sorts, perhaps, but more likely just a carving—guarded the door, which was set between its wide-spread legs. Just inside that dark opening, a myriad of magical lights danced and floated about, some throwing sparks in a threatening manner.

Le'lorinel was hardly impressed by any of it. The elf knew the schools of magic used by this one, studies that involved illusion and divination, and feared neither. No, E'kressa the Seer's guards and wards did not impress the seasoned warrior. They were more show than substance. Le'lorinel didn't even draw a sword and even removed a shining silver helmet when crossing through that darkened opening and into a circular corridor.

"E'kressa diknomin tue?" the elf asked, using the tongue of the gnomes. Le'lorinel paused at the base of a ladder, waiting for a response.

"E'kressa diknomin tue?" the elf asked again, louder and more insistently.

A response drifted through the air on unseen breezes.

"What adventures dark and fell, await the darker side of Le'lorinel?" came a high-pitched, but still gravelly voice, speaking in the common tongue. "When dark skin splashes blade with red, then shall insatiable

907

hunger be fed? When Le'lorinel has noble drow dead, will he smile, his anger fled?"

Le'lorinel did smile then, at the display of divination, and at the obvious errors.

"May I—?" the elf started to ask.

"Do come up," came a quick interruption, the tone and abrupt manner telling Le'lorinel that E'kressa wanted to make it clear that the question had been foreseen.

With a chuckle, Le'lorinel trotted up the stairs. At the top, the elf found a door of hanging blue beads, a soft glow coming from behind them. Pushing through brought Le'lorinel into E'kressa's main audience chamber, obviously, a place of many carpets and pillows for sitting, and with arcane runes and artifacts: a skull here, a gigantic bat wing there, a crystal ball set on a pedestal along the wall, a large mirror, its golden edges all of shaped and twisted design.

Never had Le'lorinel seen so many trite wizardly items all piled together in one place, and after years of working with Mahskevic the elf knew indeed that they were minor things, window dressing and nothing more—except, perhaps, for the crystal ball.

Le'lorinel hardly paid them any heed, though, for the elf was watching E'kressa. Dressed in robes of dark blue with red swirling patterns all about them, and a with a gigantic conical hat, the gnome seemed almost a caricature of the classic expectations of a wizard, except, of course, that instead of being tall and imposing, E'kressa barely topped three feet. A large gray beard and bushy eyebrows stuck out from under that hat, and E'kressa tilted his head back, face aimed in the general direction of Le'lorinel, but not as if looking at the elf.

Two pure white orbs showed under those bushy eyebrows.

Le'lorinel laughed out loud. "A blind seer? How perfectly typical."

"You doubt the powers of my magical sight?" E'kressa replied, raising his arms in threat like the wings of a crowning eagle.

"More than you could ever understand," Le'lorinel casually replied.

E'kressa held the pose for a long moment, but then, in the face of Le'lorinel's relaxed posture and ridiculing smirk, the gnome finally relented. With a shrug, E'kressa reached up and took the phony white lenses out of his sparkling gray eyes.

"Works for the peasants," the illusionist seer explained. "Amazes them, indeed! And they always seem more eager to drop an extra coin or two to a blind seer."

"Peasants are easily impressed," said Le'lorinel. "I am not."

"And yet I knew of you, and your quest," E'kressa was fast to point out.

"And you know of Mahskevic, too," the elf replied dryly.

E'kressa stomped a booted foot and assumed a petulant posture that lasted all of four heartbeats. "You brought payment?" the seer asked indignantly.

Le'lorinel tossed a bag of silver across the expanse to the eager gnome's waiting hands. "Why not just use your incredible powers of divination to get the count?" Le'lorinel asked, as the gnome started counting out the coins.

E'kressa's eyes narrowed so that they were lost beneath the tremendous eyebrows. The gnome waved his hand over the bag, muttered a spell, then a moment later, nodded and put the bag aside. "I should charge you more for making me do that," he remarked.

"For counting your payment?" Le'lorinel asked skeptically.

"For having to show you yet another feat of my great powers of seeing," the gnome replied. "For not making you wait while I counted them out."

"It took little magic to know that the coins would all be there," the elf responded. "Why would I come here if I had not the agreed upon price?"

"Another test?" the gnome asked.

Le'lorinel groaned.

"Impatience is the folly of humans, not of elves," E'kressa reminded. "I foresee that if you pursue your quest with such impatience, doom will befall you."

"Brilliant," came the sarcastic reply.

"You're not making this easy, you know," the gnome said in deadpan tones.

"And while I can assure you that I have all the patience I will need to be rid of Drizzt Do'Urden, I do not wish to waste my hours standing here," said Le'lorinel. "Too many preparations yet await me, E'kressa."

The gnome considered that for a moment, then gave a simple shrug. "Indeed. Well, let us see what the crystal ball will show to us. The course of your pursuit, we hope, and perhaps whether Le'lorinel shall win or whether he shall lose." He rambled down toward the center of the room, waddling like a duck, then veered to the crystal ball.

"The course, and nothing more," Le'lorinel corrected.

E'kressa stopped short and turned about slowly to regard this curious creature. "Most would desire to know the outcome," he said.

"And yet, I know, as do you, that any such outcome is not predetermined," Le'lorinel replied.

"There is a probability . . ."

"And nothing more than that. And what am I to do, O great seer, if you tell me I shall win my encounter with Drizzt Do'Urden, that I shall slay him as he deserves to be slain and wipe my bloodstained sword upon his white hair?"

"Rejoice?" E'kressa asked sarcastically.

"And what am I to do, O great seer, if you tell me that I shall lose this fight?" Le'lorinel went on. "Abandon that which I can not abandon? Forsake my people and suffer the drow to live?"

"Some people think he's a pretty nice guy."

"Illusions do fool some people, do they not?" Le'lorinel remarked.

909

E'kressa started to respond, but then merely sighed and shrugged and continued on his waddling way to the crystal ball. "Tell me your thoughts of the road before you," he instructed.

"The extra payment insures confidentiality?" Le'lorinel asked.

E'kressa regarded the elf as if that was a foolish question indeed. "Why would I inform this Drizzt character if ever I met him?" he asked. "And why would I ever meet him, with him being halfway across the world?"

"Then you have already spied him out?"

E'kressa picked up the cue that was the eagerness in the elf's voice, and that anxious pitch made him straighten his shoulders and puff out his chest with pride. "Might that I have," he said. "Might that I have."

Le'lorinel answered with a determined stride, moving to the crystal ball directly opposite the gnome. "Find him."

E'kressa began his casting. His little arms waved in high circles above his head while strange utterances in a language Le'lorinel did not know, and in a voice that hardly seemed familiar, came out of his mouth.

The gray eyes popped open. E'kressa bent forward intently. "Drizzt Do'Urden," he said quietly, but firmly. "The doomed drow, for there can be but one outcome of such tedious and careful planning.

"Drizzt Do'Urden," the gnome said again, the name running off his lips as rhythmically and enchantingly as had the arcane words of his spell. "I see . . . I see . . . I see . . ."

E'kressa paused and gave a "Hmm," then stood straighter. "I see the distorted face of an over-eager bald-headed ridiculously masked elf," he explained, bending to peer around the crystal ball and into Le'lorinel's wide-eyed face. "Do you think you might step back a bit?"

Le'lorinel's shoulders sagged, and a great sigh came forth, but the elf did as requested.

E'kressa rubbed his plump little hands together and muttered a continuance of the spell, then bent back in. "I see," he said again. "Winter blows and deep, deep snows. I hear wind . . . yes, yes, I hear wind in my ears and the running hooves of deers."

"Deers?" Le'lorinel interrupted.

E'kressa stood up straight and glared at the elf.

"Deers?" Le'lorinel said again. "Rhymes with 'ears,' right?"

"You are a troublesome one."

"And you are somewhat annoying," the elf replied. "Why must you speak in rhymes as soon as you fall into your divining? Is that a seer's rule, or something?"

"Or a preference!" the flustered gnome answered, again stamping his hard boot on the carpeted floor.

"I am no peasant to be impressed," Le'lorinel explained. "Save yourself the trouble and the silly words, for you'll get no extra coins for atmosphere, visual or audible."

E'kressa muttered a couple of curses under his breath and bent back down.

"Deers," Le'lorinel said again, with a snort.

"Mock me one more time and I will send you hunting Drizzt in the Abyss itself," the gnome warned.

"And from that place, too, I shall return, to repay you your favor," Le'lorinel replied without missing a beat. "And I assure you, I know an illusion from an enemy, a guard of manipulated light from that of substance, and possess a manner of secrecy that will escape your eyes."

"Ah, but I see all, foolish son of a foolish son!" E'kressa protested.

Le'lorinel merely laughed at that statement, and that proved to be as vigorous a response as any the elf might have offered, though E'kressa, of course, had no idea of the depth of irony in his boast.

Both elf and gnome sighed then, equally tired of the useless exchange, and with a shrug the gnome bent forward and peered again into the crystal ball.

"Word has been heard that Gandalug Battlehammer is not well," Le'lorinel offered.

E'kressa muttered some arcane phrases and waggled his little arms about the curve of the sphere.

"To Mithral Hall seeing eyes go roaming, to throne and curtained bed, shrouded in gloaming," the gnome began, but he stopped, hearing the impatient clearing of Le'lorinel's throat.

E'kressa stood up straight and regarded the elf. "Gandalug lays ill," the gnome confirmed, losing both the mysterious voice and the aggravating rhymes. "Aye, and dying at that."

"Priests in attendance?"

"Dwarf priests, yes," the gnome answered. "Which is to say, little of any healing powers that might be offered to the dying king. No gentle hands there.

"Nor would it matter," E'kressa went on, bending again to study the images, to absorb the *feel* of the scene as much as the actual display. "It is no wound, save the ravages of time, I fear, and no illness, save the one that fells all if nothing kills him sooner." E'kressa stood straight again and blew a fluffy eyebrow up from in front of one gray eye.

"Old age," the gnome explained. "The Ninth King of Mithral Hall is dying of old age."

Le'lorinel nodded, having heard as much. "And Bruenor Battlehammer?" the elf asked.

"The Ninth King lies on a bed of sorrow," the gnome said dramatically. "The Tenth King rises with the sun of the morrow!"

Le'lorinel crossed arms and assumed an irritated posture.

"Had to be said," the gnome explained.

"Better by you, then," the elf replied. "If it had to be."

"It did," said E'kressa, needing to get in the last word.

"Bruenor Battlehammer?" the elf asked.

The gnome spent a long time studying the scene in the crystal ball then, murmuring to himself, even at one point putting his ear flat against the smooth surface to better hear the events transpiring in the distant dwarf kingdom.

"He is not there," E'kressa said with some confidence soon after. "Good enough for you, too, for if he had returned, with the dark elf beside him, would you think to penetrate a dwarven stronghold?"

"I will do as I must," came the quiet and steady response.

E'kressa started to chuckle but stopped short when he saw the grim countenance worn by Le'lorinel.

"Better for you, then," the gnome said, waving away the images in the scrying ball and enacting another spell of divination. He closed his eyes, not bothering with the ball, as he continued the chant—the call to an otherworldly being for some sign, some guidance.

A curious image entered his thoughts, burning like glowing metal. Two symbols showed clearly, images that he knew, though he had never seen them thus entwined.

"Dumathoin and Clangeddin," he mumbled. "Dumathoin and Moradin."

"Three dwarf gods?" Le'lorinel asked, but E'kressa, standing very still, eyes fluttering, didn't seem to hear.

"But how?" the gnome asked quietly.

Before Le'lorinel could inquire as to what the seer might be speaking of, E'kressa's gray eyes popped open wide. "To find Drizzt, you must indeed find Bruenor," the gnome announced.

"To Mithral Hall, then," Le'lorinel reasoned.

"Not so!" shrieked the gnome. "For there is a place more urgent in the eyes of the dwarf, a place as a father and not a king."

"Riddles?"

E'kressa shook his hairy head vehemently. "Find the dwarf's most prized creation of his hands," the gnome explained, "to find the dwarf's most prized creation of the flesh—well, one of two, but it sounded better that way," the gnome admitted.

Le'lorinel's expression could not have been more puzzled.

"Bruenor Battlehammer made something once, something powerful and magical beyond his abilities as a craftsman," E'kressa explained. "He crafted it for someone he treasured greatly. That creation of metal will bring the dwarf more certainly than will the void on Mithral Hall's stone throne. And more, that creation will bring the dark elf running."

"What is it?" Le'lorinel asked, eagerness now evident. "Where is it?"

E'kressa bounded to his small desk and pulled forth a piece of parchment. With Le'lorinel rushing to join him, he enacted another spell, this one transforming the image that his previous spell had just burned into his thoughts to the parchment. He held up his handiwork, a perfect representation of the jumbled symbols of the dwarven gods.

"Find this mark, Le'lorinel, and you will find the end of your long road," he explained.

E'kressa went into his spellcasting again, this time bringing forth lines on the opposite side of the parchment.

"Or this one," he explained, holding the new image, one that looked very much like the old, up before Le'lorinel.

The elf took the parchment gently, staring at it wide-eyed.

"One is the mark of Clangeddin, covered by the mark of Dumathoin, the Keeper of Secrets Under the Mountain. The other is the mark of Moradin, similarly disguised."

Le'lorinel nodded, turning the page over gently and reverently, like some sage studying the writings of some long-lost civilization.

"Far to the west, I believe," the gnome explained before Le'lorinel could ask the question. "Waterdeep? Luskan? Somewhere in between? I can not be sure."

"But you believe this to be the region?" the elf asked. "Did your divination tell you this, or is it a logical hunch, considering that Icewind Dale is immediately north of these places?"

E'kressa considered the words for a while, then merely shrugged. "Does it matter?"

Le'lorinel stared at him hard.

"Have you a better course to follow?" the gnome asked.

"I paid you well," the elf reminded.

"And there, in your hands, you have the goods returned, tenfold," the gnome asserted, so obviously pleased by his performance this day.

Le'lorinel looked down at the parchment, the lines of the intertwining symbols burned indelibly into the brown paper.

"I know not the immediate connection," the gnome admitted. "I know not how this symbol, or the item holding it, will bring you to your obsession. But there lies the end of your road, so my spells have shown me. More than that, I do not know."

"And will this end of the road prove fruitful to Le'lorinel?" the elf asked, despite the earlier discounting of such prophecy.

"This I have not seen," the gnome replied smugly. "Shall I wager a guess?"

Le'lorinel, only then realizing the betrayal of emotions presented by merely asking the question, assumed a defensive posture. "Spare me," the elf said.

"I could do it in rhyme," the gnome offered with a superior smirk.

Le'lorinel thought to mention that a rhyme might be offered in return, a song actually, sung with eagerness as a delicate elven dagger removed a tongue from the mouth of a gloating gnome.

The elf said nothing, though, and the thought dissipated as the image on the parchment obscured all other notions.

913

Here it was, in Le'lorinel's hands, the destination of a lifetime's quest.

Given that, the elf had no anger left to offer.

Given that, the elf had too many questions to ponder, too many preparations to make, too many fears to overcome, and too many fantasies to entertain of seeing Drizzt Do'Urden, the imitation hero, revealed for the imposter he truly was.

*   *   *   *   *

Chogurugga lay back on five enormous pillows, stuffing great heaps of mutton into her fang-filled mouth. At eight and a half feet, the ogress wasn't very tall, but with legs the girth of ancient oaks and a round waist, she packed more than seven hundred pounds into her ample frame.

Many male attendants rushed about the central cavern, the largest in Golden Cove, keeping her fed and happy. Always they had been attentive of Chogurugga because of her unusual and exotic appearance. Her skin was light violet in color, not the normal yellow of her clan, perfectly complimenting her long and greasy bluish-black hair. Her eyes were caught somewhere between the skin and hair in hue, seeming deep purple or just a shade off true blue, depending on the lighting about her.

Chogurugga was indeed used to the twenty males of Clan Thump fawning over her, but since her new allegiance with the human pirates, an allegiance that had elevated the females of the clan to even higher stature, the males practically tripped over one another rushing to offer her food and fineries.

Except for Bloog, of course, the stern taskmaster of Golden Cove, the largest, meanest, ugliest ogre ever to walk these stretches of the Spine of the World. Many whispered that Bloog wasn't even a true ogre, that he had a bit of mountain giant blood in him, and since he stood closer to fifteen feet than to ten, with thick arms the size of Chogurugga's legs, it was a rumor not easily discounted.

Chogurugga, with the help of Sheila Kree, had become the brains of the ogre side of Golden Cove, but Bloog was the brawn, and, whenever he desired it to be so, the true boss. And he had become even meaner since Sheila Kree had come into their lives and had given to him a gift of tremendous power, a crafted warhammer that allowed Bloog to expand caverns with a single, mighty blow.

"Back again?" the ogress said when Sheila and Bellany strode into the cavern. "And what goodzies did yez bring fer Chogurugga this time?"

"A broken ship," the pirate leader replied sarcastically. "Think ye might be eating that?"

Bloog's chuckle from the side of the room rumbled like distant thunder.

Chogurugga cast a glower his way. "Me got Bathunk now," the female reminded. "Me no need Bloog."

Bloog furrowed his brow, which made it stick out far beyond his deep-set eyes, a scowl that would have been comical had it not been coming from a beast that was a ton of muscle. Bathunk, Chogurugga and Bloog's vicious son, was becoming quite an issue between the couple of late. Normally in ogre society, when the son of a chieftain was growing as strong and as mean as the father, and that father was still young, the elder brute would beat the child down, and repeatedly, to secure his own place in the tribe. If that didn't work, the son would be killed, or put out at least. But this was no ordinary group of ogres, Clan Thump was a matriarchy instead of the more customary patriarchy, and Chogurugga would tolerate none of that behavior from Bloog—not with Bathunk, anyway.

"We barely hit open water when a familiar sight appeared on our horizon," explained an obviously disgusted Bellany, who had no intention of witnessing another of Chogurugga and Bloog's legendary "Bathunk" battles.

"Chogurugga guesses three sails?" the ogress asked, taking the bait to change the subject and holding up four fingers.

Sheila Kree cast a disapproving glance Bellany's way—she didn't need to have the ogres' respect for her diminished in any way—then turned the same expression over Chogurugga. "He's a persistent one," she admitted. "One day, he'll even follow us to Golden Cove."

Bloog chuckled again, and so did Chogurugga, both of them reveling in the thought of some fresh man-flesh.

Sheila Kree, though she surely wasn't in a smiling mood, joined in, but soon after motioned for Bellany to follow and headed out the exit on the opposite side of the room, to the tunnels leading to their quarters higher up in the mountain.

Sheila's room was not nearly as large as the chamber shared by the ogre leaders, but it was almost hedonistic in its furnishings, with ornate lamps throwing soft light into every nook along the uneven walls, and fine carpets piled so high that the women practically bounced along as they crossed the place.

"I grow weary o' that Deudermont," Sheila said to the sorceress.

"He is likely hoping for that very thing," Bellany replied. "Perhaps we'll grow weary enough to stop running, weary of the run enough to confront *Sea Sprite* on the open waters."

Sheila looked at her most trusted companion, gave an agreeing smile, and nodded. Bellany was, in many ways, her better half, the crusty pirate knew. Always thinking, always looking ahead to the consequences, the wise and brilliant sorceress had been the greatest addition to *Bloody Keel*'s crew in decades. Sheila trusted her implicitly—Bellany had been the very first to wear the brand once Sheila had decided to use the intricate design on the side of Aegis-fang's mithral head in that manner.

Sheila even loved Bellany as her own sister, and, despite her overblown sense of pride, and the fact that she was always a bit too merciful and gentle-hearted toward their captives for Sheila's vicious tastes, Sheila knew better than to discount anything Bellany might say.

Three times in the last couple of months, Deudermont's ship had chased *Bloody Keel* off the high seas, though Sheila wasn't even certain *Sea Sprite* had seen them the first time and doubted that there had been any definite identification the other two. But perhaps Bellany was right. Perhaps that was Deudermont's way of catching elusive pirates. He'd chase them until they tired of running, and when they at last turned to fight. . . .

A shudder coursed Sheila Kree's spine as she thought of doing battle with *Sea Sprite* on the open waters.

"Not any bait we're soon to be taking," Sheila said, and the answering expression from Bellany, who had no desire to ever tangle with *Sea Sprite*'s devastating and legendary Robillard, was surely one of relief.

"Not out there," Sheila Kree went on, moving to the side of the chamber, to one of the few openings in the dark caverns of Golden Cove, a natural window overlooking the small bay and the reefs beyond. "But he's chasin' us from profits, and we've got to make him pay."

"Well, perhaps one day he'll be foolish enough to chase us into Golden Cove. We'll let Chogurugga's clan rain heavy stones down on his deck," Bellany replied.

But Sheila Kree, staring out at the cold waters, at the waves where she and *Bloody Keel* should now be sailing in pursuit of greater riches and fame, wasn't so certain she could maintain that kind of patience.

There were other ways to win such a personal war.

Chapter 4

The Brand

Now, this was the kind of council meeting Regis of Lonelywood most enjoyed. The halfling sat back in his cushioned chair, hands folded behind his head, his cherubic face a mask of contentment, as the prisoners taken from the road south of Bremen were paraded before the councilors. Two were missing, one recovering (perhaps) from a newly placed crease in his chest, and the other—the woman whom the friends had believed to be the leader of the rogue band—held in another room to be brought in separately.

"It must be wonderful having such mighty friends," Councilor Tamaroot of Easthaven, never a fan of the Lonelywood representative, said cynically and quietly in Regis's ear.

"Those two," the halfling replied more loudly, so that the other three councilors on his side of the room certainly heard him. The halfling paused just long enough to ensure that he had the attention of all four, and of a couple of the five from across the way, as well as the attention of Elderman Cassius, then pointed to the two thugs he'd battled—or that he'd forced to battle each other. "I took them both, without aid," the halfling finished.

Tamaroot bristled and sat back in his seat.

Regis smoothed his curly brown locks and put his hands behind his head again. He could not contain his smile.

After the introductions, and with no disputes from any of the others, Cassius imposed the expected sentence. "As you killed no one on the road—none that we know of, at least—so your own lives are not forfeit," he said.

"Unless the wound Bruenor's axe carved into the missing one puts him down," the councilor from Caer-Konig, the youngest and often crudest of the group, piped in. Despite the poor taste of the remark, a bit of muffled chortling did sound about the decorated room.

Cassius cleared his throat, a call for some solemnity. "But neither are your crimes dismissed," the elderman went on. "Thus you are indentured, for a period of ten years, to a boat of Councilor Kemp's choosing, to serve on the waters of Maer Dualdon. All of your catch shall be forfeited to the common fund of Ten-Towns, less Kemp's expenses for the boat and the guards, of course, and less only enough to see that you live in a measure of meager sustenance. That is the judgment of this council. Do you accept it?"

"And what choice are we given?" said one of the thugs, the large man Catti-brie had overwhelmed.

"More than you deserve," Kemp interjected before Cassius could reply. "Had you been captured by the Luskan authorities, you would have been paraded before Prisoner's Carnival and tortured to death in front of a screaming crowd of gleeful onlookers. We can arrange something similar, if that is your preference."

He looked to Cassius as he finished, and the elderman nodded his grim approval of the Targos councilor's imposing speech.

"So which shall it be?" Cassius asked the group.

The answer was rather predictable, and the grumbling group of men was paraded out of the room and out of Brynn Shander, on the way to Targos where their prison ship waited.

As soon as they had gone, Cassius called for the cheers of the council, a salute to Regis and the others for a job well done.

The halfling soaked it in.

"And I fear we may need the group, the Companions of the Hall, yet again, and soon enough," Cassius explained a moment later, and he motioned to the chamber's door sentries. One exited and returned with Jule Pepper, who cut a regal figure indeed, despite her capture and imprisonment.

Regis looked at her with a fair amount of respect. The tall woman's black hair shone, but no more than did her intelligent eyes. She stood straight, unbroken, as if this entire episode were no more than a nuisance, as if these pitiful creatures who had captured her could not really do anything long-lasting or devastating to her.

The functional tunic and leggings she had worn on the road were gone now, replaced by a simple gray dress, sleeveless and, since it was too short

918

for a woman of Jule's stature, worn low off the shoulder. It was a simple piece really, nearly formless, and yet, somehow, the woman beneath it managed to give it quite an alluring shape, bringing it down just enough to hint at her shapely and fairly large breasts. The dress was even torn on one side—Regis suspected that Jule had done that, and purposely—and through that slot, the woman did well to show one smooth and curvaceous leg.

"Jule Pepper," Cassius said curiously, and with a hint of sarcasm. "Of the Pepper family of . . . ?"

"Was I to be imprisoned in the name my parents chose for me?" the woman answered, her voice deep and resonant, and with a stiff eastern accent that seemed to shorten every word into a crisp, accentuated sound. "Am I not allowed to choose for myself the title I shall wear?"

"That would be the custom," Cassius said dryly.

"The custom of unremarkable people," Jule confidently replied. "The jewel sparkles, the pepper spices." She ended with a devastating grin, one that had several of the councilors—ten males, including the elderman, and only one woman—shifting uneasily in their seats.

Regis was no less flustered, but he tried to look beyond the impressive woman's obvious physical allure, taking even greater interest in Jule's manipulative cunning. She was one to be wary of, the halfling knew, and still, he could not deny he had more than a little curiosity about exploring this interesting creature more fully.

"May I ask why I am being held here against my choice and free will?" the woman remarked a moment later, after the group had settled again, with one even tugging at his collar, as if to let some heat out of his burning body.

Cassius snorted and waved a dismissive hand her way. "For crimes against Ten-Towns, obviously," he replied.

"List them then," Jule demanded. "I have done nothing."

"Your band—" Cassius started to respond.

"I have no band," Jule interrupted, her eyes flashing and narrowing. "I was on my way to Ten-Towns when I happened to cross paths with those rogues. I knew not who they were or why they were in that place at that time, but their fire was warm and their food acceptable, and any company seemed better than the murmuring of that endless wind."

"Ridiculous!" one of the councilors asserted. "You were speaking with them knowingly when the terrified pair returned to you—on the word of Drizzt Do'Urden himself, and I have come to trust in that dark elf!"

"Indeed," another councilor agreed.

"And pray tell me what I said, exactly," the woman answered, and her grin showed that she didn't fear any answers they might give. "I spoke to the fools knowingly about Drizzt and Catti-brie and Bruenor. Certainly, I am as versed on the subject as any wise person venturing to Icewind Dale would be. Did I not speak knowingly that the fools had done something stupid and had then been baited by the drow and his companions? No stretch of intelligence there, I would say."

The councilors began murmuring among themselves and Regis stared hard at Jule, his smile showing his respect for her cunning, if nothing else. He could tell already that with her devastating posture and shapeliness, combined with more than a measure of cunning and careful preparedness out on the road, she would likely slip through these bonds unscathed.

And Regis, knew, too, whatever she might say, that this one, Jule Pepper, was the leader of the highwayman band.

"We will discuss this matter," Cassius said soon after, the private conversations of the councilors escalating into heated debate, divisions becoming apparent.

Jule smiled knowingly at Cassius. "Then I am free to go?"

"You are invited to return to the room we have provided," the older and more comprehending elderman replied, and he waved to the guards.

They came up on either side of Jule, who gave Cassius one last perfectly superior look and turned to leave, swaying her shoulders in exactly the right manner to again set off the sweat of the male councilors.

Regis grinned at it all, thoroughly impressed, but his smile dropped into an open-mouthed stare a moment later, as Jule completed her turn, as he noticed a curious marking on the back of her right shoulder, a brand the halfling surely recognized.

"Wait!" the halfling cried and he hopped up from his seat and ducked low to scramble under the table rather than take the time to go around it.

The guards and Jule stopped, all turning about to regard the sudden commotion.

"Turn back," the halfling instructed. "Turn back!" He waved his hand at Jule as he spoke, and the woman just stared at him incredulously, her gaze shifting from curiosity to withering.

"Cassius, turn her back!" the halfling pleaded.

Cassius looked at him with no less incredulity than had Jule.

Regis didn't wait for him. The halfling ran up to Jule, grabbed her right arm and started pulling her around. She resisted for a moment, but the halfling, stronger than he appeared, gave a great tug that brought her around enough, briefly, to show the brand.

"There!" Regis said, poking an accusing finger.

Jule pulled away from him, but it was out now, the councilors all leaning in and Cassius coming forward, motioning for Jule to turn around, or for the guards to turn her if she didn't willingly comply.

With a disgusted shake of her head, the raven-haired woman finally turned.

Regis went up on a nearby chair to better see the brand, but he knew before the inspection that his keen eyes had not deceived him, that the brand on the woman's shoulder was of a design unique to Bruenor Battle-hammer, and more than that, a marking Bruenor had used only once, on the side of Aegis-fang. Moreover, the brand was exactly the right size for the warhammer's marking, as if a heated Aegis-fang had been pressed against her skin.

Regis nearly swooned. "Where did you get that?" he asked.

"A rogue's mark," Cassius remarked. "Common enough, I'd say, for any guild."

"Not common," Regis answered, shaking his head. "Not that mark."

"You know it?" the elderman inquired.

"My friends will speak with her," Regis answered. "At once."

"When we are done with her," Councilor Tamaroot insisted.

"At once," Regis insisted, turning to face the man. "Else you, good Tamaroot, can explain to King Bruenor the delay when his adopted son's life may likely hang in the balance."

That brought a myriad of murmurs in the room.

Jule Pepper just glared down at Regis, and he got the distinct feeling that she had little idea what he was talking about, little idea of the significance of the mark.

For her sake, the halfling knew, that better be the truth of it.

* * * * *

A few nights later, Drizzt found Bruenor atop a quiet and dark place called Bruenor's Climb, in the small rocky valley the dwarves mined to the northeast of Brynn Shander, between Maer Dualdon and the lake called Lac Dinneshire. Bruenor always had such private places as this, wherever he was, and he always named them Bruenor's Climb, as much to warn any intruders as out of any personal pride.

This was the dwarf's spot for reflection, his quiet place where he could ponder things beyond the everyday trials and tribulations of his station in life. This was the one place where practical and earthy Bruenor, on dark nights, could let go of his bonds a bit, could let his spirit climb to some place higher than the imagination of a dwarf. This was where Brue-nor could come to ponder the meaning of it all and the end of it all.

Drizzt had found Bruenor up on his personal climb back at Mithral Hall, looking very much the same as he did now, when the yochlol had taken Wulfgar, when they had all believed that his adopted son was dead.

Silent as the clouds flying beneath the stars, the drow walked up behind the dwarf and stood patiently.

"Ye'd think losin' him a second time would've been easier," Bruenor remarked at length. "Especially since he'd been such an orc-kin afore he left us."

"You do not know that you have lost him," the drow reminded.

921

"Ain't no mark in the world like it," Bruenor reasoned. "And the thief said she got it from a hammer's head."

Indeed, Jule had willingly surrendered much information to the imposing friends when they had spoken with her right after the confrontation in the council hall. She'd admitted that the brand was intentional, a marking given by a woman ship's captain. When pressed, Jule had admitted that this woman, Sheila Kree, was a pirate and that this particular brand was reserved by her for those most trusted within her small band.

Drizzt felt great pity for his friend. He started to remark on the fact that Jule had stated that the only physically large members of the pirate band were a clan of ogres Sheila Kree kept for tacking and steering. Wulfgar had not fallen in with the dogs, apparently. The drow held back the remarks, though, because the other implication, a clear one if Wulfgar was not in league with the pirates, was even more dire.

"Ye think this dog Kree killed me boy?" Bruenor asked, his thoughts obviously rolling along the same logic. "Or do ye think it was someone else, some dog who then sold the hammer to this one?"

"I do not think Wulfgar is dead at all," Drizzt stated without hesitation.

Bruenor turned a curious eye up at him.

"Wulfgar may have sold the hammer," Drizzt remarked, and Bruenor's look became even more skeptical. "He denied his past when he ran away from us," the drow reminded. "Perhaps relieving himself of that hammer was a further step along the road he saw before him."

"Yeah, or maybe he just needed the coin," Bruenor said with such sarcasm that Drizzt let his argument die silently.

In truth, the drow hadn't even convinced himself. He knew Wulfgar's bond with Aegis-fang, and knew the barbarian would no sooner willingly part with the warhammer than he would part with one of his own arms.

"Then a theft," Drizzt said after a pause. "If Wulfgar went to Luskan or to Waterdeep, as we believe, then he would likely find himself in the company of thieves."

"In the company of murderers," Bruenor remarked, and he looked back up at the starry sky.

"We can not know," Drizzt said to him quietly.

The dwarf merely shrugged, and when his shoulders came back down from that action, they seemed to Drizzt lower than ever.

The very next morning dark clouds rumbled up from the south off the winds of the Spine of the World, threatening to deluge the region with a torrent of rain that would turn the thawed ground into a quagmire. Still, Drizzt and Catti-brie set out from Ten-Towns, running fast for Luskan. Running fast for answers all four of the friends needed desperately to hear.

Chapter 5
The Honesty of Love

Wulfgar was the first off *Sea Sprite* when the pirate hunter returned to her berth at Waterdeep's long wharf. The barbarian leaped down to the dock before the ship had even been properly tied in, and his stride as he headed for shore was long and determined.

"Will you take him back out?" Robillard asked Deudermont, the two of them standing amidships, watching Wulfgar's departure.

"Your tone indicates to me that you do not wish me to," the captain answered, and he turned to face his trusted wizard friend.

Robillard shrugged.

"Because he interfered with your plan of attack?" Deudermont asked.

"Because he jeopardized the safety of the crew with his rash actions," the wizard replied, but there was little venom in his voice, just practicality. "I know you feel a debt to this one, Captain, though for what reason I cannot fathom. But Wulfgar is not Drizzt or Catti-brie. Those two were disciplined and understood how to play a role as part of our crew. This one is more like . . . more like Harkle Harpell, I say! He finds a course and runs down it without regard to the consequences for those he leaves behind. Yes, we fought two successful engagements on this venture, sank a pirate, and brought another one in—"

923

"And captured two crews nearly intact," Deudermont added.

"Still," the wizard argued, "in both of those fights, we walked a line of disaster." He knew he really didn't have to convince Deudermont, knew the captain understood as well as he did that Wulfgar's actions had been less than exemplary.

"We always walk that line," Deudermont said.

"Too close to the edge this time," the wizard insisted. "And with a long fall beside us."

"You do not wish me to invite Wulfgar back."

Again came the wizard's noncommittal shrug. "I wish to see the Wulfgar who took *Sea Sprite* through her trials at the Pirate Isles those years ago," Robillard explained. "I wish to fight beside the Wulfgar who made himself so valuable a member of the Companions of the Hall, or whatever that gang of Drizzt Do'Urden's was called. The Wulfgar who fought to reclaim Mithral Hall and who gave his life, so it had seemed, to save his friends when the dark elves attacked the dwarf kingdom. All these tales I have heard of this magnificent barbarian warrior, and yet the Wulfgar I have known is a man consorting with thieves the likes of Morik the Rogue, the Wulfgar who was indicted for trying to assassinate you."

"He had no part in that," Deudermont insisted, but the captain did wince even in denial, for the memory of the poison and of the Prisoner's Carnival was a painful one.

Deudermont had lost much in granting Wulfgar his reprieve from the vicious magistrate that day in Luskan. By association, by his generosity to those the magistrates believed were truly not deserving, Deudermont had sullied *Sea Sprite*'s reputation with the leaders of that important northern port. For Deudermont had stolen their show, had granted so unexpected a pardon, and all of that without any real proof that Wulfgar had not been involved in the attempt on his life.

"Perhaps not," Robillard admitted. "And Wulfgar's character on this voyage, whatever his shortcomings, has borne out your decision to grant the pardon, I admit. But his discretion on the open waters has not borne out your decision to take him aboard *Sea Sprite*."

Captain Deudermont let the wizard's honest and fair words sink in for a long while. Robillard could be a crotchety and judgmental sort, a curmudgeon in the extreme, and a merciless one concerning those he believed had brought their doom upon themselves. In this case, though, his words rang of honest truth, of simple and undeniable observation. That truth stung Deudermont. When he'd encountered Wulfgar in Luskan, a bouncer in a seedy tavern, he recognized the big man's fall from glory and had tried to entice Wulfgar away from that life. Wulfgar had denied him outright, had even refused to admit his own true identity to the captain. Then came the assassination attempt, with Wulfgar indicted while Deudermont lay unconscious and near death.

The captain still wasn't sure why he'd denied the magistrate his murderous fun at Prisoner's Carnival that day, why he'd gone with his gut instinct against the common belief and a fair amount of circumstantial evidence, as well. Even after that display of mercy and trust, Wulfgar had shown little gratitude or friendship.

Deudermont had been pained when they parted outside of Luskan's gate that day of the reprieve, when Wulfgar had again refused him his offer to sail with *Sea Sprite*. The captain had been fond of the man once and considered himself a good friend of Drizzt and Catti-brie, who had sailed with him honorably those years after Wulfgar's fall. Yes, he had dearly wanted to help Wulfgar climb back to grace, and so Deudermont had been overjoyed when Wulfgar had arrived in Waterdeep, at this same long wharf, a woman and child in tow, announcing that he wished to sail with Deudermont, that he was searching for his lost warhammer.

Deudermont had correctly read that as something much more, had known then as he did now that Wulfgar was searching for more than his lost weapon, that he was searching for his former self.

But Robillard's observations had been on the mark, as well. While Wulfgar had not been a problem in any way during the routine tendays of patrolling, in the two battles *Sea Sprite* had fought, the barbarian had not performed well. Courageously? Yes. Devastating to the enemy? Yes. But Wulfgar, wild and vicious, had not been part of the crew, had not allowed the more conventional and less risky tactics of using Robillard's wizardry to force submission from afar, the chance to work. Deudermont wasn't sure why Wulfgar had gone into this battle rage. The seasoned captain understood the inner heat of battle, the ferocious surge that any man needed to overcome his logical fears, but Wulfgar's explosions of rage seemed something beyond even that, seemed the stuff of barbarian legend—and not a legend that shone favorably on the future of *Sea Sprite*.

"I will speak with him before we sail," Deudermont offered.

"You already have," the wizard reminded.

Deudermont looked to him and gave a slight shrug. "Then I will again," he said.

Robillard's eyes narrowed.

"And if that is not effective, we will put Wulfgar to duty on the tiller," the captain explained before Robillard could begin his obviously forthcoming stream of complaints, "belowdecks and away from the fighting."

"Our steering crew is second to none," Robillard did say.

"And they will appreciate Wulfgar's unparalleled strength when executing the tightest of turns."

Robillard snorted, hardly seeming convinced. "He will probably ram us into the next pirate in line," the wizard grumbled quietly as he walked away.

Despite the gravity of the situation, Deudermont could not suppress a chuckle as he watched Robillard's typical, grumbling departure.

* * * * *

Wulfgar's surprise when he burst through the door to find Delly waiting for him was complete and overwhelming. He knew the woman, surely, with her slightly crooked smile and her light brown eyes, and yet he hardly recognized her. Wulfgar had known Delly as a barmaid living in squalor and as a traveling companion on a long and dirty road. Now, in the beautiful house of Captain Deudermont, with all his attendants and resources behind her, she hardly seemed the same person.

Before, she had almost always kept her dark brown hair pinned up, mostly because of the abundant lice she encountered in the Cutlass, but now her hair hung about her shoulders luxuriously, silken and shining and seeming darker. That, of course, only made her light brown eyes—remarkable eyes, Wulfgar realized—shine all the brighter. Before, Delly had worn plain and almost formless clothing, simple smocks and shifts, that had made her thin limbs seem spindly. But now she was dressed in a formed blue dress with a low-cut white blouse.

It occurred to the barbarian, just briefly (for other things were suddenly flooding his thoughts!) how much an advantage the wealthy women of Faerûn held over the peasant women in terms of beauty. When first he and Delly had arrived, Deudermont had thrown a party for many of Waterdeep's society folk. Delly had felt so out of place, and so had Wulfgar, but for the woman, it was much worse, as her meager resources for beauty had been called to attention at every turn.

Not so now, Wulfgar understood. If Deudermont held another of his many parties on this stay in port, then Delly Curtie would shine more beautifully than any woman there!

Wulfgar could hardly find his breath. He had always thought Delly comely, even pretty, and her beauty had only increased for him in their time on the road from Luskan, as he had come to appreciate the depth of the woman even more. Now, combining that honest respect and love with this physical image proved too much for the barbarian who had spent the last three months at sea.

He fell over her with a great, crushing hug, interrupting her words with kiss after kiss, lifting her with ease right from the ground and burying his face in that mane of brown hair, biting gently at her delicate—and now it seemed delicate and not just skinny—neck. How tiny Delly seemed in his arms, for Wulfgar stood a foot and a half taller than her and was nearly thrice her body weight.

With hardly an effort, Wulfgar scooped her more comfortably into his arms, spinning her to the side and sliding one arm under her knees.

He laughed, then, when he noted that she was barefoot, and even her feet looked prettier to him.

926

"Are ye making fun o' me?" Delly asked, and Wulfgar noted that her peasant accent seemed less than he remembered, with the woman articulating the "g" on the end of the word "making."

"Making fun of you?" Wulfgar asked, and he laughed again, all the louder. "I am making love to you," he corrected, and he kissed her again, then launched into a spinning dance, swinging her all about as he headed for the door of their private room.

They almost got past the threshold before Colson started crying.

* * * * *

The two did find some time alone together later that night, and made love again before the dawn. As the first slanted rays of morning shone through the eastern window of their room, Wulfgar lay on his side beside his lover, his hand gently tracing about her neck, face, and shoulders.

"Sure that it's good to have ye home," Delly said quietly, and she brought her small hand up to rub Wulfgar's muscular forearm. "Been a lonely time with ye out."

"Perhaps my days out with Deudermont are at their end," Wulfgar replied.

Delly looked at him curiously. "Did ye find yer hammer, then?" she asked. "And if ye did, then why'd ye wait for telling me?"

Wulfgar was shaking his head before she ever finished. "No word of it or of Sheila Kree," he answered. "For all I know, the pirate went to the bottom of the sea and took Aegis-fang with her."

"But ye're not knowing that."

Wulfgar fell to his back and rubbed both his hands over his face.

"Then how can ye be saying ye're done with Deudermont?" Delly asked.

"How can I not?" Wulfgar asked. "With you here, and Colson? This is my life now, and a fine one it is! Am I to risk it all in pursuit of a weapon I no longer need? No, if Deudermont and his crew hear of Sheila Kree, they'll hunt her down without my help, and I hold great faith that they will return the warhammer to me."

Now it was Delly's turn to come upon her elbows, the smooth sheets falling from her naked torso. She gave a frustrated shake to toss her tangled brown hair out of her face, then fixed Wulfgar with a glare of severe disapproval.

"What kind of a fool's words are spilling from yer mouth?" she asked.

"You would prefer that I leave?" Wulfgar asked, a bit of suspicion showing on his square-jawed face.

For so many years that face had held a boyish charm, an innocence that reflected in Wulfgar's sky blue eyes. No more, though. He had shaved all the stubble from his face before retiring with Delly, but somehow Wulfgar's face now seemed almost out of place without the blond beard.

927

The lines and creases, physical manifestation of honest emotional turmoil, were not the markings of a young man, though Wulfgar was only in his twenties.

"And more the fool do ye sound now!" Delly scolded. "Ye know I'm not wanting ye to go—ye know it! And ye know that no others are sharing me bed.

"But ye must be going," Delly continued solemnly, and she fell back on the bed. "What's to haunt ye, then, if Deudermont and his crew go out without ye and find the pirate and some o' them die trying to get yer hammer back? How're ye to feel when they bring ye the hammer and the news, and all the while, ye been sitting here safe while they did yer work for ye?"

Wulfgar looked at Delly hard, studying her face and recognizing that she was indeed pained to be speaking to him so.

"Stupid Josi Puddles for stealing the damn hammer and selling it out to the pirate," the woman finished.

"Some could die," Wulfgar agreed. "Sheila Kree is known to be a fierce one, and by all accounts she has surrounded herself with a formidable crew. By your own reasoning, then, none of us, not Deudermont and not Wulfgar, should go out in search of her and Aegis-fang."

"Not me own reasoning at all," Delly argued. "Deudermont and his crew're choosing the road of pirate hunting—that's not yer doing. It's their calling, and they'd be going after Sheila Kree even if she'd ne'er taken yer hammer."

"Then we are back where we started," Wulfgar reasoned with a chuckle. "Let Deudermont and his fine crew go out and find the hammer if they—"

"Not so!" Delly interrupted angrily. "Their calling is to go and hunt the pirates, to be sure, and yer own is to be with them until they're finding yer hammer. Yers is to find yer hammer and yerself, to get back where ye once were."

Wulfgar settled back on the bed and ran his huge, callused hands over his face again. "Perhaps I do not wish to be back there."

"Perhaps ye don't," said Delly. "But that's not a choice for ye to make until ye do get back there. When ye've found out again who ye were, me love, only then will ye be able to tell yerself honestly where ye're wanting to go. Until ye get it to where all is for the taking, then ye'll always be wondering and wanting."

She went quiet then, and Wulfgar had no response. He sighed many times and started to repudiate her many times, but every avenue he tried to explore proved inevitably to be a dead end.

"When did Delly Curtie become so wise in the course of life?" a defeated Wulfgar asked a short while later.

Delly snickered and rolled to face him. "Might that I always been," she answered playfully. "Or might not be at all. I'm just telling ye what

I'm thinking, and what I'm thinking is that ye got to get back to a certain place afore ye can climb higher. Ye need to be getting yerself back to where ye once were, and ye'll find the road ye most want to walk, and not just the road ye're thinking ye have to walk."

"I was back to that place," Wulfgar replied in all seriousness, and a cloud passed over his face. "I was with them in Icewind Dale again, as it had been before, and I left, of my own choice."

"Because of a better road calling?" Delly asked. "Or because ye weren't yet ready to be back? There's a bit o' difference there."

Wulfgar was out of answers, and he knew it. He wasn't sure that he agreed with Delly, but when the call from Deudermont and *Sea Sprite* came the next day, he answered it.

Chapter 6

The Paths of Doom

Le'lorinel worked defensively, as always, letting the opponent take the lead, his twin scimitars weaving a furious dance. The elf parried and backed, dodged easily and twirled aside, letting Tunevec's furious charge go right past.

Tunevec stumbled, and cursed under his breath, thinking the fight lost, thinking Le'lorinel would surely complain and moan about his deficiencies. He closed his eyes, waiting for the slap of a sword across his back, or his rump if Le'lorinel was feeling particularly petty this day.

No blow came.

Tunevec turned about to see the bald elf leaning against the wall, weapons put away.

"You do not even bother to finish the fight?" Tunevec asked.

Le'lorinel regarded him absently, as if it didn't matter. The elf stared up at the lone window on this side of the tower, the one to Mahskevic's study. Behind that window, Le'lorinel knew, the wizard was getting some more answers.

"Come!" Tunevec bade, and he clapped his scimitars in the air before him. "You paid me for one last fight, so let us fight!"

Le'lorinel eventually got around to looking at the impatient warrior. "We are done, now and forever."

"You paid for the last fight, and the last fight is not finished," Tunevec protested.

"But it is. Take your coins and be gone. I have no further need of your services."

Tunevec stared at the elf in abject disbelief. They had been sparring together for many months, and now to be dismissed so casually, so callously!

"Keep the scimitars," Le'lorinel remarked, not even looking at Tunevec anymore, but rather, staring up at that window.

Tunevec stood there for a long while, staring at the elf incredulously. Finally, having sorted it all out, the reality of the dismissal leaving a foul taste in his mouth, he tossed the scimitars to the ground at Le'lorinel's feet, turned about, and stormed off, muttering curses.

Le'lorinel didn't even bother to retrieve the scimitars or to glance Tunevec's way. The fighter had done his job—not very well, but he had served a useful purpose—and now that job was done.

In a matter of moments, Le'lorinel stood before the door of Mahskevic's study, hand up to knock, but hesitating. Mahskevic wasn't pleased by all of this, Le'lorinel knew, and had seemed quite sullen since the elf's return from E'kressa.

Before Le'lorinel could find the nerve to knock, the door swung open, as if of its own accord, affording the elf a view of Mahskevic sitting behind his desk, his tall and pointy blue wizard's cap bent halfway up and leaning to the left, several large tomes open on the oaken desk before him, including one penned by Talasay, the bard of Silverymoon, detailing the recent events of Mithral Hall, including the reclamation of the dwarves' homeland from the duergar and the shadow dragon Shimmergloom, the anointing of Bruenor as King, the coming of the dark elves bearing Gandalug Battlehammer—Bruenor's grandfather—and finally, after the great victory over the forces of the Underdark, Bruenor's abdication of the throne to Gandalug and his reputed return to Icewind Dale. Le'lorinel had paid dearly for that tome and knew every word in it very well.

Between the books on the wizard's desk, and partially beneath one of them, was spread a parchment that Le'lorinel had written out for the wizard, recounting the exact words E'kressa had used in his divination.

"I told you that I would call to you when I was done," Mahskevic, who seemed very surly this day, remarked without looking up. "Can you not find a bit of patience after all of these years?"

"Tunevec is gone," Le'lorinel answered. "Dismissed and departed."

Now Mahskevic did look up, his face a mask of concern. "You did not kill him?" the wizard asked.

Le'lorinel smiled. "Do you believe me to be such an evil creature?"

"I believe that you are obsessed beyond reason," the wizard answered bluntly. "Perhaps you fear to leave witnesses behind, that one might alert Drizzt Do'Urden of the pursuit."

"Then E'kressa would be dead, would he not?"

Mahskevic considered the words for a moment, then shrugged in acceptance of the simple logic. "But Tunevec has left?"

Le'lorinel nodded.

"A pity. I was just growing fond of the young and able warrior. As were you, I had thought."

"Not so fine a fighter," the elf answered, as if that was all that truly mattered.

"Not up to the standards you demanded of your sparring partner who was meant to emulate this notable dark elf," Mahskevic replied immediately. "But then, who would be?"

"What have you learned?" Le'lorinel asked.

"Intertwined symbols of Dumathoin, the Keeper of Secrets under the Mountain, and of Clangeddin, dwarf god of battle," the wizard explained. "E'kressa was correct."

"The symbol of Bruenor Battlehammer," Le'lorinel stated.

"Not really," Mahskevic answered. "A symbol used only once by Bruenor, as far as I can tell. He was quite an accomplished smith, you know."

As he spoke, he waved Le'lorinel over to his side, and when the elf arrived, he pointed out a few drawings in Talasay's work: unremarkable weapons and a breastplate.

"Bruenor's work," Mahskevic remarked, and indeed, the picture captions indicated that very thing. "Yet I see no marking similar to the one E'kressa gave to you. There," he explained, pointing to a small mark on the bottom corner of the breastplate. "There is Bruenor's mark, the mark of Clan Battlehammer with Bruenor's double 'B' on the mug."

Le'lorinel bent in low to regard the drawing and saw the foaming mug standard of the dwarven clan and Bruenor's particular brand, as Mahskevic had declared. Of course, the elf had already reviewed all of this, though it seemed Mahskevic was drawing clues where Le'lorinel had not.

"As far as I can tell, Bruenor used this common brand for all his work," the wizard explained.

"That is not what the seer told to me."

"Ah," the wizard remarked, holding up one crooked and bony finger, "but then there is this." As he finished, he flipped to a different page in the large tome, to another drawing, this one depicting in great detail a fabulous warhammer, Aegis-fang, set upon a pedestal.

"The artist copying the image was remarkable," Mahskevic explained. "Very detail-minded, that one!"

He lifted a circular glass about four inches in diameter and laid it upon the image, magnifying the warhammer. There, unmistakably, was the mark E'kressa had given to Le'lorinel.

"Aegis-fang," the elf said quietly.

"Made by Bruenor for one of his two adopted children," Mahskevic remarked, and that declaration made E'kressa's cryptic remarks come into clearer focus and seemed to give credence to the overblown and showy seer.

"Find the dwarf's most prized creation of his hands to find the dwarf's most prized creation of the flesh," the gnome diviner had said, and he had admitted that he was referring to one of two creations of the flesh, or, it now seemed obvious, children.

"Find Aegis-fang to find Wulfgar?" Le'lorinel asked skeptically, for as far as both of them knew, as far as the tome indicated, Wulfgar, the young man for whom Bruenor had created Aegis-fang, was dead, killed by a hand-maiden of Lolth, a yochlol, when the drow elves had attacked Mithral Hall.

"E'kressa did not name Wulfgar," Mahskevic replied. "Perhaps he was referring to Catti-brie."

"Find the hammer to find Catti-brie, to find Bruenor Battlehammer, to find Drizzt Do'Urden," Le'lorinel said with a frustrated sigh.

"Difficult crew to be fighting," Mahskevic said, and he gave a sly smile. "I would enjoy your continued company," he explained. "I have so much work yet to be done, and I am not a young man. I could use an apprentice, and you have shown remarkable insight and intelligence."

"Then you will have to wait until my business is finished," the stubborn elf said sternly. "If I live to return."

"Remarkable intelligence in most matters," the old wizard dryly clarified.

Le'lorinel snickered and took no offense.

"This group of friends surrounding Drizzt has earned quite a reputation," Mahskevic stated.

"I have no desire to fight Bruenor Battlehammer, or Catti-brie, or anyone else other than Drizzt Do'Urden," said the elf. "Though perhaps there would be a measure of justice in killing Drizzt's friends."

Mahskevic gave a great growl and slammed Talasay's tome shut, then shoved back from the desk and stood tall, staring down hard at the elf. "And that would be an unconscionable act by every measure of the word," he scolded. "Is your bitterness and hatred toward this dark elf so great that you would take innocent life to satisfy it?"

Le'lorinel stared at him coldly, lips very thin.

"If it is, then I beg you to reconsider your course even more seriously," the wizard added. "You claim righteousness on your side in this inexplicable pursuit of yours, and yet nothing—nothing I say—would justify such unrelated murder! Do you hear me, boy? Do my words sink through that stubborn wall of hatred for Drizzt Do'Urden that you have, for some unexplained reason, erected?"

"I was not serious in my remark concerning the woman or the dwarf," Le'lorinel admitted, and the elf visibly relaxed, features softening, eyes glancing downward.

"Can you not find a more constructive pursuit?" Mahskevic asked sincerely. "You are more a prisoner of your hatred for Drizzt than the dark elf could ever be."

"I am a prisoner because I know the truth," Le'lorinel agreed in that melodic alto voice. "And to hear tales of his heroism, even this far from Mithral Hall or Ten-Towns stabs profoundly at my heart."

"You do not believe in redemption?"

"Not for Drizzt, not for any dark elf."

"An uncompromising attitude," Mahskevic remarked, stroking a hand knowingly over his fluffy beard. "And one that you will likely one day regret."

"Perhaps I already regret that I know the truth," the elf replied. "Better to be ignorant, to sing bard songs of Drizzt the hero."

"Sarcasm is not becoming."

"Honesty is oft painful."

Mahskevic started to respond but just threw up his hands and gave a defeated laugh and a great shake of his shaggy head.

"Enough," he said. "Enough. This is a circular road we have ridden far too often. You know that I do not approve."

"Noted," the uncompromising Le'lorinel said. "And dismissed."

"Perhaps I was wrong," Mahskevic mused aloud. "Perhaps you do not have the qualities necessary to serve as an appropriate apprentice."

If his words were meant to wound Le'lorinel, they seemed to fail badly, for the elf merely turned around and calmly walked out of the room.

Mahskevic gave a great sigh and dropped his palms that he could lean on his desk. He had come to like Le'lorinel over the years, had come to think of the elf as an apprentice, even as a son, but he found this self-destructive single-mindedness disconcerting and disheartening, a shattering reality against his hopes and wishes.

Mahskevic had also spent more than a little effort in learning about this rogue drow that so possessed the elf's soul, and while information concerning Drizzt was scarce in these parts far to the east of Silverymoon, everything the wizard had heard marked the unusual dark elf as an honorable and decent sort. He wondered, then, if he should even allow Le'lorinel to begin this hunt, wondered if he would then be morally compromised through his inaction against what seemed a grave injustice.

He was still wondering that very thing the next morning, when Le'lorinel found him in his little spice garden on the small balcony halfway up his gray stone tower.

"You are versed in teleportation," the elf explained. "It will be an expensive spell for me to purchase, I presume, since you do not approve of my destination, but I am willing to work another two tendays, from before dawn to after dusk, in exchange for a magical journey to Luskan, on the Sword Coast."

935

Mahskevic didn't even look up from his spice plants, though he did stop his weeding long enough to consider the offer. "I do not approve, indeed," he said quietly. "Once again I beseech you to abandon this folly."

"And once again I tell you that it is none of your affair," the elf retorted. "Help me if you will. If not, I suspect I will easily enough find a wizard in Silverymoon who is willing to sell a simple teleport."

Mahskevic stood straight, even put his hand on the back of his hip for support and arched his back, stretching out the kinks. Then he turned, deliberately, and put an imposing glare over the confident elf.

"Will you indeed?" the wizard asked, his glare going to the elf's hand, to the onyx ring he had sold to Le'lorinel and into which he had placed the desired magical spells.

Le'lorinel had little trouble in following his gaze to discern the item that held his attention.

"And you will have enough coin, I expect," the wizard remarked. "For I have changed my mind concerning the ring I created and will buy it back."

Le'lorinel smiled. "There is not enough gold in all the world."

"Give it over," Mahskevic said, holding out his hand. "I will return your payment."

Le'lorinel turned around and walked off the balcony, moving right to the stairs and heading down.

An angry Mahskevic caught up just outside the tower.

"This is foolishness!" he declared, rushing around and blocking the smaller elf's progress. "You are consumed by a vengeance that goes beyond all reason and beyond all morality!"

"Morality?" Le'lorinel echoed incredulously. "Because I see a drow elf for what he truly is? Because I know the truth of Drizzt Do'Urden and will not suffer his glowing reputation? You are wise in many things, old wizard, and I am better for having tutored under you these years, but of this quest I have undertaken, you know nothing."

"I know you are likely to get yourself killed."

Le'lorinel shrugged, not disagreeing. "And if I abandon this, then I am already dead."

Mahskevic gave a shout and shook his head vigorously. "Insanity!" he cried. "This is naught but insanity. And I'll not have it!"

"And you can not stop it," said Le'lorinel, and the elf started around the old man, but Mahskevic was quick to shift, again blocking the way.

"Do not underestimate—" Mahskevic started to say, but he stopped short, the tip of a dagger suddenly pressing against his throat.

"Take your own advice," Le'lorinel threatened. "What spells have you prepared this day? Battle spells? Not likely, I know, and even if you have a couple in your present repertoire, do you believe you will ever get the chance to cast them? Think hard, wizard. A few seconds is a long time."

"Le'lorinel," Mahskevic said as calmly as he could muster.

"It is only because of our friendship that I will put my weapons aside," the elf said quietly, and Mahskevic breathed more easily as the dagger went away. "I had hoped you would help me on my way, but I knew that as the time drew near, your efforts to aid me would diminish. And so I forgive you your abandonment, but be warned, I will not tolerate interference from anybody. Too long have I waited, have I prepared, and now the day is upon me. Wish me well, for our years together, if for nothing else."

Mahskevic considered it for a while, then grimly nodded. "I do wish you well," he said. "I pray you will find a greater truth in your heart than this and a greater road to travel than one of blind hatred."

Le'lorinel just walked away.

"He is beyond reason," came a familiar voice behind Mahskevic a few moments later, with the wizard watching the empty road where Le'lorinel had already gone out of sight. Mahskevic turned to see Tunevec standing there, quite at ease.

"I had hoped to dissuade him, as well," Tunevec explained. "I believed the three of us could have carved out quite an existence here."

"The two of us, then?" Mahskevic asked, and Tunevec nodded, for he and the wizard had already spoken of his apprenticeship.

"Le'lorinel is not the first elf I have heard grumble about this Drizzt Do'Urden," Tunevec explained as the pair walked back to the tower. "On those occasions when the rogue drow visited Alustriel in Silverymoon, there were more than a few citizens openly offering complaints, the light-skinned elves foremost among them. The enmity between the elves, light and dark, can not be overstated."

Mahskevic gave one longing glance back over his shoulder at the road Le'lorinel had walked. "Indeed," he said, his heart heavy.

With a profound sigh, the old wizard let go of his friend, of a large part of the last few years of his life.

*　*　*　*　*

On a rocky road many hundreds of miles away, Sheila Kree stood before a quartet of her crewmen.

One of her most trusted compatriots, Gayselle Wayfarer, her deck commander for boarding parties, sat astride a small but strong chestnut mare. Though not nearly as thin or possessed of classic beauty as Bellany the Sorceress or the tall and willowy Jule Pepper, Gayselle was far from unattractive. Even though she kept her blond hair cropped short, there was a thickness and a luster to it that nicely complimented the softness of her blue eyes and her light complexion, a creaminess to her skin that remained despite the many days aboard ship. Gayselle, a short woman with the muscular stature to match her mount, was, perhaps, the most skilled with weapons of anyone aboard *Bloody Keel*, with the exception of

Sheila Kree herself. She favored a short sword and dagger. The latter she could throw as precisely as anyone who'd ever served with Sheila Kree.

"Bellany wouldn't agree with this," Gayselle said.

"If the task is completed, Bellany will be glad for it," Sheila Kree replied.

She looked around somewhat sourly at Gayselle's chosen companions, a trio of brutal half-ogres. These three would be running, not riding, for no horse would suffer one of them on its back. It hardly seemed as if it would slow Gayselle down on her journey to Luskan's docks, where a small rowboat would be waiting for them, for their ogre heritage gave them a long, swift stride and inhuman endurance.

"You have the potions?" the pirate captain asked.

Gayselle lifted one fold of her brown traveling cloak, revealing several small vials. "My companions will look human enough to walk through the gates of Luskan and off the docks of Waterdeep," the rider assured her captain.

"If *Sea Sprite* is in . . ."

"We go nowhere near Deudermont's house," Gayselle completed.

Sheila Kree started another remark but stopped and nodded, reminding herself that this was Gayselle, intelligent and dependable, the second of her crew after Bellany to wear the brand. Gayselle understood not only the desired course for this, but any alternate routes should the immediate plan not be possible. She would get the job done, and Captain Deudermont and the other fools of *Sea Sprite* would understand that their hounding of Sheila Kree might not be a wise course to continue.

Part 2

Tracking

It has often struck me how reckless human beings tend to be.

In comparison to the other goodly reasoning beings, I mean, for comparisons of humans to dark elves and goblins and other creatures of selfish and vicious ends make no sense. Menzoberranzan is no safe place, to be sure, and most dark elves die long before the natural expiration of their corporeal bodies, but that, I believe, is more a matter of ambition and religious zeal, and also a measure of hubris. Every dark elf, in his ultimate confidence, rarely envisions the possibility of his own death, and when he does, he often deludes himself into thinking that any death in the chaotic service of Lolth can only bring him eternal glory and paradise beside the Spider Queen.

The same can be said of the goblinkin, creatures who, for whatever misguided reasons, often rush headlong to their deaths.

Many races, humans included, often use the reasoning of godly service to justify dangerous actions, even warfare, and there is a good deal of truth to the belief that dying in the cause of a greater good must be an ennobling thing.

But aside from the fanaticism and the various cultures of warfare, I find that humans are often the most reckless of the goodly reasoning beings. I have witnessed many wealthy humans venturing to Ten-Towns

941

for holiday, to sail on the cold and deadly waters of Maer Dualdon, or to climb rugged Kelvin's Cairn, a dangerous prospect. They risk everything for the sake of minor accomplishment.

I admire their determination and trust in themselves.

I suspect that this willingness to risk is in part due to the short expected life span of the humans. A human of four decades risking his life could lose a score of years, perhaps two, perhaps three in extraordinary circumstances, but an elf of four decades would be risking several centuries of life! There is, then, an immediacy and urgency in being human that elves, light or dark, and dwarves will never understand.

And with that immediacy comes a zest for life beyond anything an elf or a dwarf might know. I see it, every day, in Catti-brie's fair face—this love of life, this urgency, this need to fill the hours and the days with experience and joy. In a strange paradox, I saw that urgency only increase when we thought that Wulfgar had died, and in speaking to Catti-brie about this, I came to know that such eagerness to experience, even at great personal risk, is often experienced by humans who have lost a loved one, as if the reminder of their own impending mortality serves to enhance the need to squeeze as much living as possible into the days and years remaining.

What a wonderful way to view the world, and sad, it seems, that it takes a loss to correct the often mundane path.

What course for me, then, who might know seven centuries of life, even eight, perhaps? Am I to take the easy trail of contemplation and sedentary existence, so common to the elves of Toril? Am I to dance beneath the stars every night, and spend the days in reverie, turning inward to better see the world about me? Both worthy pursuits, indeed, and dancing under the nighttime sky is a joy I would never forsake. But there must be more for me, I know. There must be the pursuit of adventure and experience. I take my cue from Catti-brie and the other humans on this, and remind myself of the fuller road with every beautiful sunrise.

The fewer the lost hours, the fuller the life, and a life of a few decades can surely, in some measures, be longer than a life of several centuries. How else to explain the accomplishments of a warrior such as Artemis Entreri, who could outfight many drow veterans ten times his age? How else to explain the truth that the most accomplished wizards in the world are not elves but humans, who spend decades, not centuries, pondering the complexities of the magical Weave?

I have been blessed indeed in coming to the surface, in finding a companion such as Catti-brie. For this, I believe, is the mission of my existence, not just the purpose, but the point of life itself. What opportunities might I find if I can combine the life span of my heritage with the intensity of humanity? And what joys might I miss if I follow the more patient and sedate road, the winding road dotted with signposts reminding me that I have too much to lose, the road that avoids mountain and valley alike, traversing the plain, sacrificing the heights for fear of the depths?

Often elves forsake intimate relationships with humans, denying love, because they know, logically, that it can not be, in the frame of elven time, a long-lasting partnership.

Alas, a philosophy doomed to mediocrity.

We need to be reminded sometimes that a sunrise lasts but a few minutes.

But its beauty can burn in our hearts eternally.

—Drizzt Do'Urden

Chapter 7

Unseemly Company

The guard blanched ridiculously, seeming as if he would simply fall over dead, when he noted the sylvan features and ebony skin of the visitor to Luskan's gate this rainy morning. He stuttered and stumbled, clenched his polearm so tightly in both hands that his knuckles turned as white as his face, and at last he managed to stammer out, "Halt!"

We're not moving," Catti-brie replied, looking at the man curiously. "Just standing here, watching yerself sweating."

The man gave what could have been either a growl or a whimper, then, as if finding his heart, called out for support and boldly stepped in front of the pair, presenting his polearm defensively. "Halt!" he said again, though neither of them had started moving.

"He figured out ye were a drow," Catti-brie said dryly.

"He does not recognize that even a high elf's skin might darken under the sun," Drizzt replied with a profound sigh. "The curse of fine summer weather."

The guard stared at him, perplexed by the foolish words. "What do you want?" he demanded. "Why are you here?"

To enter Luskan," said Catti-brie. "Can't ye be guessing that much yerself?"

Enough of your ridicule!" cried the guard, and he thrust the polearm threateningly in Catti-brie's direction.

A black hand snapped out before the sentry could even register the movement, catching his weapon just below its metal head.

"There is no need of any of this," Drizzt remarked, striding next to the trapped weapon to better secure his hold. "I, we, are no strangers to Luskan, nor, can I assure you, have we ever been less than welcomed."

"Well, Drizzt Do'Urden, bless my eyes!" came a call behind the startled sentry, a cry from one of a pair of soldiers rushing up to answer the man's cry. "And Catti-brie, looking less like a dwarf than e'er before!"

"Oh, put your weapon away, you fool, before this pair puts it away for you, in a holder you'd not expect and not much enjoy!" said the other of the newcomers. "Have you not heard of this duo before? Why, they sailed with *Sea Sprite* for years and brought more pirates in for trial than we've soldiers to guard them!"

The first sentry swallowed hard and, as soon as Drizzt let go of the polearm, hastily retracted it and skittered out of the way. "Your pardon," he said with an awkward bow. "I did not know . . . the sight of a . . ." He stopped there, obviously mortified.

"And how might you know?" Drizzt generously returned. "We have not been here in more than a year."

"I have only served for three months," the relieved sentry answered.

"And a pity to have to bury one so quickly," one of the soldiers behind him remarked with a hearty laugh. "Threatening Drizzt and Catti-brie! O, but that will get you in the ground right quick and make yer wife a weeping widow!"

Drizzt and Catti-brie accepted the compliments with a slight grin and a nod, trying to get past it. For the dark elf, compliments sat as uncomfortably as insults, and one of the natural side-products of hunting with Deudermont was a bit of notoriety in the port towns along the northern Sword Coast.

"So what blesses Luskan with your presence?" one of the more knowledgeable soldiers asked. His demeanor made both Drizzt and Catti-brie think they should know the man.

"Looking for an old friend," Drizzt answered. "We have reason to believe he might be in Luskan."

"Many folks in Luskan," the other seasoned soldier answered.

"A barbarian," Catti-brie explained. "A foot and more taller than me, with blond hair. If you saw him, you'd not likely forget him."

The closest of the soldiers nodded, but then a cloud crossed his face and he turned about to regard his companion.

"What's his name?" the other asked. "Wulfgar?"

Drizzt's excitement at hearing the confirmation was shallowed by the expressions worn by both soldiers, grave looks that made him think immediately that something terrible had befallen his friend.

"You have seen him," the drow stated, holding his arm out to calm Catti-brie, who had likewise noted the guards' concern.

"You'd best come with me, Master Drizzt," the older of the soldiers remarked.

"Is he in trouble?" Drizzt asked.

"Is he dead?" Catti-brie asked, stating the truth of what was on Drizzt's mind.

"*Was* in trouble, and I'd not be surprised one bit if he's now dead," the soldier answered. "Come along and I'll lead you to someone who can offer more answers."

They followed the soldier along Luskan's winding avenues, moving toward the center of the city, and, finally, into one of the largest buildings in all the city, which housed both the jail and most of the city officials. The soldier, apparently a man of some importance, led the way without challenge from any of the many guards posted at nearly every corridor, up a couple of flights of stairs and into an area where every door marked the office of a magistrate.

He stopped in front of one that identified the office of Magistrate Bardoun, then, with a concerned look back at the pair, knocked loudly.

"Enter," came a commanding reply.

Two black-robed men were in the room, on opposite sides of a huge desk cluttered with papers. The closest, standing, looked every bit the part of one of Luskan's notorious justice-bringers, with hawkish features and narrow eyes all but hidden beneath long gray eyebrows. The man sitting behind the desk, Bardoun, obviously, was much younger than his counterpart, no more than thirty, certainly, with thick brown hair and matching eyes and a clean-shaven, boyish face.

"Begging your pardon, Magistrate," the soldier asked, his voice showing a nervous edge, "but I have here two heroes, Drizzt Do'Urden and Catti-brie, daughter of dwarf King Bruenor Battlehammer himself, come back to Luskan in search of an old friend."

"Do enter," Bardoun said in a friendly tone. His standing partner, though, put a scrutinizing glare over the two, particularly over the dark elf.

"Drizzt and Catti-brie sailed with Deudermont—" the soldier started to remark, but Bardoun stopped him with an upraised hand.

"Their exploits are well known to us," the magistrate said. "You may leave us."

The soldier bowed, offered a wink to the pair then exited, closing the door behind him.

"My associate, Magistrate Callanan," Bardoun introduced, and he stood up, motioning for the pair to come closer. "We will be of any help we may, of course," he said. "Though Deudermont has fallen on some disfavor among some of the magistrates, many of us greatly appreciate the work he and his brave crew have done in clearing the waters about our fair city of some dreadful pirates."

Drizzt glanced at Catti-brie, both of them surprised to hear that Captain Deudermont, as fine a man as ever sailed the Sword Coast, a man given a prized three-masted schooner by the Lords of Waterdeep to aid in his gallant work, had fallen upon any disfavor at all from officers of the law.

"Your soldier indicated that you might be able to help us in locating an old friend," Drizzt explained. "Wulfgar, by name. A large northman of fair complexion and light hair. We have reason to believe . . ." The drow stopped in mid-sentence, caught by the cloud that crossed Bardoun's face and the scowl suddenly worn by Callanan.

"If you are friends of that one, then perhaps you should not be in Luskan," Callanan remarked with a derisive snort.

Bardoun composed himself and sat back down. "Wulfgar is well known to us indeed," he explained. "Too well known, perhaps."

He motioned for Drizzt and Catti-brie to take the seats along the side of the small office, then told them the story of Wulfgar's entanglement with Luskan's law, of how the barbarian had been accused and convicted of trying to murder Deudermont (which Catti-brie interrupted by saying, "Impossible!"), and had been facing execution at Prisoner's Carnival, barely moments from death, when Deudermont himself had pardoned the man.

"A foolish move by the good captain," Callanan added. "One that brought him disfavor. We do not enjoy seeing a guilty man walk free of the Carnival."

"I know what you enjoy," Drizzt said, more harshly than he had intended.

The drow was no fan of the brutal and sadistic Prisoner's Carnival, nor did he carry many kind words for the magistrates of Luskan. When he and Catti-brie had sailed with Deudermont and they had taken pirate prisoners on the high seas, the couple had always prompted the captain to turn for Waterdeep instead of Luskan, and Deudermont, no fan of the vicious Prisoner's Carnival himself, had often complied, even if the larger city was a longer sail.

Recognizing the harshness in his tone, Drizzt turned to the relatively gentle Bardoun and said, "Some of you, at least."

"You speak honestly," Bardoun returned. "I do respect that, even if I do not agree with you. Deudermont saved your friend from execution, but not from banishment. He, along with his little friend were cast out of Luskan, though rumor has it that Morik the Rogue has returned."

"And apparently with enough influence so that we are instructed not to go and bring him back to our dungeons for breaking the exile," Callanan said with obvious disgust.

"Morik the Rogue?" Catti-brie asked.

Bardoun waved his hand, indicating that this character was of no great importance. "A minor street thug," he explained.

"And he traveled with Wulfgar?"

"They were known associates, yes, and convicted together of the attempt upon Deudermont's life, along with a pair of pirates whose lives were not spared that day."

Callanan's wicked grin at Bardoun's remark was not lost on Drizzt, yet another confirmation to the dark elf of the barbarism that was Luskan's Prisoner's Carnival.

Drizzt and Catti-brie looked to each other again.

"Where can we find Morik?" the woman asked, her tone determined and offering no debate.

"In the gutter," Callanan answered. "Or the sewer, perhaps."

"You may try Half-Moon Street," Magistrate Bardoun added. "He has been known to frequent that area, particularly a tavern known as the Cutlass."

The name had a ring of familiarity to Drizzt, and he nodded as he remembered the place. He hadn't been there during his days with Deudermont, but well before that, he and Wulfgar had come through Luskan on their way to reclaim Mithral Hall. Together, they had gone into the Cutlass, where Wulfgar had started quite a brawl.

"That is where your friend Wulfgar made quite a reputation, as well," said Callanan.

Drizzt nodded, as did Catti-brie. "My thanks to you for the information," he said. "We will find our friend, I am sure." He bowed and started away, but stopped at the door as Bardoun called after him.

"If you do find Wulfgar, and in Luskan, do well by him and take him far, far away," the magistrate said. "Far away from here, and, for his own sake, far away from the rat, Morik the Rogue."

Drizzt turned and nodded, then left the room. He and Catti-brie went and got their own lodgings at a fine inn along one of the better avenues of Luskan, and spent the day walking about the city, reminiscing about old times and their previous journey through the city. The weather was fine for the season, with bright sun splashing about the leaves, beginning their autumnal color turn, and the city certainly had many places of great beauty. Together, then, walking and enjoying the sights and the weather, Drizzt and Catti-brie took no note of the gawks and the gasps, even the sight of several children running full speed away from the dark elf.

Drizzt couldn't be bothered by such things. Not with Catti-brie at his side.

The couple waited patiently for the fall of night, when they knew they had a better chance of finding someone like Morik the Rogue, and, it seemed, of finding someone like Wulfgar.

The Cutlass was not busy when the pair entered, soon after dusk, though it seemed to Drizzt as if a hundred sets of eyes had suddenly focused upon him, most notably, a glance both horrified and threatening from a skinny man seated at the bar, directly opposite the barkeep, whose rag stopped its movement completely as he, too, focused on the unexpected newcomer. When he had come into this place those years ago, Drizzt had remained off to the side, buried in the clamor and tumult of the busy, ill-lit tavern, his hood up and his head low.

Drizzt nodded to the barkeep and approached him directly. The skinny man gave a yelp and fell away, scrambling to the far end of the room.

"Greetings, good sir," Drizzt said to the barkeep. "I come here with no ill intentions, I assure you, despite the panic of your patron."

"Just Josi Puddles," the barkeep replied, though he, too, was obviously a bit shaken at the appearance of a dark elf in his establishment. "Don't pay him any attention." The man extended his hand, then retracted it quickly and wiped it on his apron before offering it again. "Arumn Gardpeck at your service."

"Drizzt Do'Urden," the drow replied, taking the hand in his own surprisingly strong grasp. "And my friend is Catti-brie."

Arumn looked at the pair curiously, his expression softening as if he came to truly recognize them.

"We seek someone," Drizzt started.

"Wulfgar," Arumn said with confidence, and he grinned at the wide-eyed expressions his response brought to the drow and the woman. "Aye, he told me of you. Both of you."

"Is he here?" Catti-brie asked.

"Been gone for a long time," the skinny man, Josi, said, daring to come forward. "Come back only once, to get Delly."

"Delly?"

"She worked here," Arumn explained. "Was always sweet on Wulfgar. He came back for her, and the three of them left Luskan—for Waterdeep, I'm guessing."

"Three?" Drizzt asked, thinking the third to be Morik.

"Wulfgar, Delly, and the baby," Josi explained.

"The baby?" both Drizzt and Catti-brie said together. They looked at each other incredulously. When they turned back to Arumn, he merely shrugged, having nothing to offer.

"That was months ago," Josi Puddles interjected. "Ain't heared a thing o' them since."

Drizzt paused, digesting it all. Apparently, Wulfgar would have quite a tale to tell when at last they found him—if he was still alive. "Actually, we came in here seeking one we were told might have information about Wulfgar," the drow explained. "A man named Morik."

There came a scuffle of scrambling feet from behind, and the pair turned to see a small, dark-cloaked figure moving swiftly out of the tavern.

"That'd be yer Morik," Arumn explained.

Drizzt and Catti-brie rushed outside, glancing up and down the nearly deserted Half-Moon Street, but Morik, obviously a master of shadows, was nowhere to be seen.

Drizzt bent down near the soft dirt just beyond the Cutlass's wooden porch, noting a boot print. He smiled at Catti-brie and pointed to the left, an easy trail for the skilled ranger to follow.

* * * * *

"Ye're a pretty laddie, ain't ye?" the grimy old lech said. He pushed Le'lorinel up against the wall, putting his smelly face right up against the elf's.

Le'lorinel looked past him, to the other four old drunkards, all of them howling with laughter as the old fool started fiddling with the rope he used as a belt.

He stopped abruptly and slowly sank to the floor before the elf, moving his suddenly trembling hands lower, to where the knee had just connected.

Le'lorinel came out from the wall, drawing a sword, putting the flat of it against the old wretch's head, and none too gently pushing him over to the floor.

"I came in asking a simple question," the elf explained to the others, who were not laughing any longer.

The old wretches, former sailors, former pirates, glanced nervously from one to the other.

"Ye be a good laddie," one bald-headed man said, climbing to stand on severely bowed legs. "Tookie, there, he was just funning with ye."

"A simple question," Le'lorinel said again.

The elf had come into this dirty tavern along Luskan's docks showing the illusionary images E'kressa had prepared, asking about the significance of the mark.

"Not so simple, mayhaps," the bald-headed sea dog replied. "Ye're askin' about a mark, and many're wearin' marks."

"And most who are wearin' marks ain't looking to show 'em," another of the old men said.

Le'lorinel heard a movement to the side and saw the man, Tookie, rising fast from the floor and coming in hard. A sweep and turn, swinging the sword down to the side, not to slash the man—though Le'lorinel thought he surely deserved it—but to force him into an awkward, off-balance dodge, followed by a simple duck and step maneuver had the elf behind the attacker. A firm shove against Tookie's back had him diving forward to skid down hard to the floor.

But two of the others were there, one brandishing a curved knife used for scaling fish, another a short gaff hook.

Le'lorinel's right hand presented the sword defensively, while the elf's left hand went to the right hip, then snapped out.

The man with the gaff hook fell back, wailing and wheezing, a dagger deep in his chest.

Le'lorinel lunged forward, and the other attacker leaped back, presented his hands up before him in surrender, and let the curved knife fall to the floor.

"A simple question," the elf reiterated through gritted teeth, and the look in Le'lorinel's blue and gold eyes left no doubt among any in the room that this warrior would leave them all dead with hardly a thought.

"I ain't never seen it," the man who'd been holding the knife replied.

"But you are going to go and find out about it for me, correct?" Le'lorinel remarked. "All of you."

"Oh, yes, laddie, we'll get ye yer answers," another said.

The one still lying on the floor and facing away from Le'lorinel scrambled up suddenly and bolted for the door, bursting through and out into the twilight. Another rose to follow, but Le'lorinel stepped to the side, tore the dagger free from the dying man's chest and cocked it back, ready to throw.

"A simple question," Le'lorinel said yet again. "Find me my answer and I will reward you. Fail me and. . . ." The elf finished by turning to look at the man propped against the wall, laboring for breath now, obviously suffering in the last moments of his life.

Le'lorinel walked for the open door, pausing only long enough to wipe the dagger on the tunic of the man who'd attacked with the curved blade, finishing by sliding the knife up teasingly toward the man's throat, up and over his shoulder as the elf walked by.

* * * * *

The small form came out of the alleyway in a blur of motion, spinning and swinging, a pair of silvery daggers in his hands.

His attack was nearly perfect, slicing in low at Drizzt's midsection with his left, then stopping short with a feint and launching a wide-arching chopping left, coming down at the side of the drow's neck.

Nearly perfect.

Drizzt saw the feint for what it was, ignored the first attack, and focused on the second. The dark elf caught Morik's hand in his own and as he did he turned the rogue's hand in so that Drizzt's fingers covered those of the rogue.

Morik neatly adjusted to the block, trying instead to finish his first stab, but Drizzt was too quick and too balanced, skittering with blazing speed, his already brilliant footwork enhanced by magical anklets. The drow went right under Morik's upraised arm, turning as he moved, then running right behind the rogue, twisting that arm and maneuvering out of the reach of the other stabbing dagger.

Morik, too, started to turn, but then Drizzt merely cupped the ends of his fingers and squeezed, compressing the top knuckles of Morik's hand and causing excruciating pain. The dagger fell to the ground, and Morik too went down to one knee.

Catti-brie had the rogue's other hand caught and held before he could even think of trying to retaliate again.

"Oh, please don't kill me," the rogue pleaded. "I did get the jewels . . . I told the assassin . . . I did follow Wulfgar . . . everything you said!"

Drizzt stared up at Catti-brie in disbelief, and he lessened his pressure on the man's hand and yanked Morik back to his feet.

"I did not betray Jarlaxle," Morik cried. "Never that!"

"Jarlaxle?" Catti-brie asked incredulously. "Who does he think we are?"

"A good question," Drizzt asked, looking to Morik for an answer.

"You are not agents of Jarlaxle?" the rogue asked. A moment later, his face beamed with obvious relief and he gave a little embarrassed chuckle. "But then, who . . ." He stopped short, his smile going wide. "You're Wulfgar's friends," he said, his smile nearly taking in his ears.

Drizzt let him go, and so did Catti-brie, and the man retrieved his fallen dagger and replaced both in his belt. "Well met!" he said exuberantly, reaching his hand toward them. "Wulfgar told me so much about the both of you!"

"It would appear that you and Wulfgar have a few tales of your own to tell," Drizzt remarked.

Morik chuckled again and shook his head. When it became apparent that neither the drow nor the woman were going to take the offered handshake, Morik brought his hand back in and wiped it on his hip. "Too many tales to tell!" he explained. "Stories of battle and love all the way from Luskan to Auckney."

"How do you know Jarlaxle?" Catti-brie asked. "And where is Wulfgar?"

"Two completely unrelated events, I assure you," Morik replied. "At least, they were when last I saw my large friend. He left Luskan some time ago, with Delly Curtie and the child he took from the foppish lord of Auckney."

"Kidnapped?" Drizzt asked skeptically.

"Saved," Morik replied. "A bastard child of a frightened young lady, certain to be killed by the fop or his nasty sister." He gave a great sigh. "It is a long and complicated tale. Better that you hear it from Wulfgar."

"He is alive?"

"Last I heard," Morik replied. "Alive and heading for . . . for Waterdeep, I believe. Trying to find Captain Deudermont, and hoping the captain would help him retrieve his lost warhammer."

Catti-brie blew a most profound and relieved sigh.

"How did he lose the warhammer?" Drizzt asked.

"The fool Josi Puddles stole it and sold it to Sheila Kree, a most disagreeable pirate," Morik answered. "Nasty sort, that pirate lady, but Wulfgar's found his heart again, I believe, and so I would not wish to be serving beside Sheila Kree!" He looked at Drizzt, who was staring at Catti-brie, and with both wearing their emotions in plain sight. "You thought he was dead," Morik stated.

"We found a highwayman, a highway*woman*, actually, wearing a brand that could only have come from Aegis-fang," Drizzt explained. "We know how dear that weapon was to Wulfgar and know that he was not in league with the bandit's former gang."

"Never did we think he'd have let the thing go, except from his dying grasp," Catti-brie admitted.

"I think we owe you a meal and a drink, at least," Drizzt said to Morik, whose face brightened at the prospect.

Together, the three walked back toward the Cutlass, Morik seeming quite pleased with himself.

"And you can tell us how you have come to know Jarlaxle," Drizzt remarked as they were entering, and Morik's shoulders visibly slumped.

The rogue did tell them of the coming of the dark elves to Luskan, of how he had been visited by henchmen of Jarlaxle and by the strange mercenary himself and told to shadow Wulfgar. He recounted his more recent adventures with the dark elves, after Wulfgar had departed Luskan and Morik's life, taking care to leave out the part about Jarlaxle's punishment once he had lost touch with the barbarian. Still, when he got to that particular part of the tale, Morik's hand went up reflexively for his face, which had been burned away by the nasty Rai-guy, a dark elf Morik despised with all his heart.

Catti-brie and Drizzt looked at each other throughout the tale with honest concern. If Jarlaxle was interested in their friend, perhaps Wulfgar was not so safe after all. Even more perplexing to them, though, was the question of why the dangerous Jarlaxle would be interested in Wulfgar in the first place.

Morik went on to assure the two that he'd had no dealings with Jarlaxle or his lieutenants in months and didn't expect to see any of them again. "Not since that human assassin showed up and told me to run away," Morik explained. "Which I did, and only recently came back. I'm smarter than to have that band after me, but I believe the human covered my trail well enough. He could not have gone back to them if they believed I was still alive, I would guess."

"Human assassin?" Drizzt asked, and he could guess easily enough who it might have been, though as to why Artemis Entreri would spare the life of anyone and risk the displeasure of mighty Bregan D'aerthe, the drow could not begin to guess. But that was a long tale, likely, and one that Drizzt hoped had nothing to do with Wulfgar.

"Where can we find Sheila Kree?" he asked, stopping Morik before he could really get going with his dark elf stories.

Morik stared at him for a few moments. "The high seas, perhaps," he answered. "She may have a favored and secret port—in fact, I believe I have heard rumors of one."

"You can find out for us?" Catti-brie asked.

"Such information will not come cheaply," Morik started to explain, but his words were lost in a great gulp when Drizzt, a friend of a rich dwarf king whose stake in Wulfgar's return was no less than his own, dropped a small bag bulging with coins on the table.

"Tomorrow night," the drow explained. "In here."

Morik took the purse, nodded, and went fast out of the Cutlass.

"Ye're thinking the rogue will return with information?" Catti-brie asked.

"He was an honest friend of Wulfgar's," Drizzt answered, "and he's too afraid of us to stay away."

"Sounds like our old friend got himself mixed up in a bit of trouble and adventure," Catti-brie remarked.

"Sounds like our old friend found his way out of the darkness," Drizzt countered, his smile beaming behind his dark features, his lavender eyes full of sparkling hope.

Chapter 8

Tearing at the Warrior's Soul

They found the merchant vessel listing badly, a fair portion of her sails torn away by chain-shot, and her crewmen—those who were still aboard—lying dead, sprawled across the deck. Deudermont and his experienced crew knew that others had been aboard. A ship such as this would normally carry a crew of at least a dozen and only seven bodies had been found. The captain held out little hope that any of the missing were still alive. An abundance of sharks could be seen in the water around the wounded caravel, and probably more than a few had their bellies full of human flesh.

"No more than a few hours," Robillard announced to the captain, catching up to Deudermont near to the damaged ship's tied-off wheel.

The pirates had wounded her, stripped her of her crew and her valuables, then set her on a tight course, circling in the water. In the stiff wind that had been blowing all day, Deudermont had been forced to order Robillard to further damage the merchant vessel, letting loose a lightning bolt to destroy the rudder, before he could allow *Sea Sprite* to even catch hold of the caravel.

"They would have taken a fair haul from her," Deudermont reasoned.

The remaining stocks in the merchant vessel's hold indicated that the ship, bound from Memnon, had been carrying a large cargo of fabrics, though the cargo log said nothing about any exotic or exceptional pieces.

"Minimal value goods," Robillard replied. "They had to take a substantial amount simply to make the scuttling and murder worth their time. If they filled their hold, they're obviously running for land." He paused and wetted a finger, then held it up. "And they've a favorable breeze for such a journey."

"No more favorable than our own," the captain said grimly. He called to one of his lieutenants, who was standing nearby ordering a last check for any survivors, to be followed by a hasty return to *Sea Sprite*.

The hunt was on.

* * * * *

Standing not so far away from Captain Deudermont and Robillard, Wulfgar heard every word. He agreed with the assessment that the atrocity was barely hours old. With the strong wind, the fleet *Sea Sprite*, her holds empty, would quickly overtake the laden pirate, even if the pirate was making all speed for safe harbor.

The barbarian closed his eyes and considered the forthcoming battle, his first action since *Sea Sprite* had put back out from Waterdeep. This would be a moment of truth for Wulfgar, a time when his determination and strength of will would have to take command from his faltering fortitude. He looked around at the murdered merchant sailors, men slaughtered by bloodthirsty pirates. Those killers deserved the harsh fate that would likely find them soon, deserved to be sent to a cold and lonely death in the dark waters, or to be captured and returned to Waterdeep, even to Luskan, for trial and execution.

Wulfgar told himself that it was his duty to avenge these innocent sailors, that it was his responsibility to use his gods-given prowess as a warrior to help bring justice to a wild world, to help bring security to helpless and innocent people.

Standing there on the deck of the broken merchant caravel, Wulfgar tried to consciously appeal to every ennobling characteristic, to every ideal. Standing there in that place of murder, Wulfgar appealed to his instincts of duty and responsibility, to the altruism of his former friends—to Drizzt, who would not hesitate to throw himself in harm's way for the sake of another.

But he kept seeing Delly and Colson, standing alone against the harshness of the world, broken in grief and poverty.

A prod in the side alerted the barbarian to the scene about him, to the fact that he and the lieutenant who had poked him were the only remaining crewmen on the wounded caravel. He followed the lieutenant to the boarding plank and noted that Robillard was watching his every step.

Stepping back onto *Sea Sprite*, the barbarian took one last glance at the grisly scene on the merchant ship and burned the images of the dead sailors into his consciousness that he might recall it when the time came for action.

He tried very hard to suppress the images of Delly and Colson as he did, tried to remind himself of who he was and of who he must be.

* * * * *

Using common sense and a bit of Robillard's magic, *Sea Sprite* had the pirate in sight soon after the next dawn. It seemed a formidable craft, a large three-master with a prominent second deck and catapult. Even from a distance, Deudermont could see many crewmen scrambling about the pirate's deck, bows in hand.

"Carling Badeen?" Robillard asked Deudermont, moving beside him near the prow of the swift-sailing schooner.

"It could be," the captain replied, turning to regard his thin friend.

Sea Sprite had been chasing Carling Badeen, one of the more notorious pirates of the Sword Coast, off and on for years. It appeared they'd finally caught up to the elusive cutthroat. By reputation, Badeen's ship was large but slow and formidably armored and armed, with a crack crew of archers and a pair of notorious wizards. The pirate Badeen himself was known to be one of the more bloodthirsty of the breed, and certainly the gruesome scene back at the merchant ship fit the pattern of Badeen's work.

"If it is, then we must be at our very best, or risk losing many crewmen," Robillard remarked.

Deudermont, his eye back against his spyglass, did not disagree.

"One error, like the many we have been making of late, could cost many of our crew their lives," the wizard pressed on.

Deudermont lowered the glass and regarded his cryptic friend, then followed Robillard's reasoning, and his sidelong glance, to Wulfgar, who stood at the starboard rail amidships.

"He has been shown his errors," Deudermont reminded.

"Errors that he logically understood he was making even as he was making them," Robillard countered. "Our large friend is not controlled by reason when these affairs begin, but rather by emotion, by fear and by rage. You appeal to his rational mind when you explain the errors to him, and on that level, your words do get through. But once the battle is joined, that rational mind, that level of logical progression, is replaced by something more primal and apparently uncontrollable."

Deudermont listened carefully, if somewhat defensively. Still, despite his hopes to the opposite, he could not deny his wizard friend's reasoning.

Neither could he ignore the implications for the rest of his crew should Wulfgar act irrationally, interrupting Robillard's progression of the battle. Badeen's ship, after all, carried two wizards and a healthy number of dangerous archers.

"We will win this fight by sailing circles around the lumbering craft," Robillard went on. "We will need to be quick and responsive, and strong on the turn."

Deudermont nodded, for indeed *Sea Sprite* had employed maneuverability as its main weapon against many larger ships, often putting a broadside along a pirate's stern for a devastating archer rake of the enemy decks. Robillard's words, then, seemed fairly obvious.

"Strong on the turn," the wizard reiterated, and Deudermont caught on to what the wizard was really saying.

"You wish me to assign Wulfgar to the rudder crew."

"I wish you to do that which is best for the safety of every man aboard *Sea Sprite*," Robillard answered. "We know how to defeat a ship such as this one, Captain. I only ask that you allow us to do so in our practiced manner, without adding a dangerous variable to the mix. I am not going to deny that our Wulfgar is a mighty warrior, but unlike his friends who once sailed with us, he is unpredictable."

Robillard made to continue, but Deudermont stopped him with an upraised hand and a slight nod, an admission of defeat in this debate. Wulfgar had indeed acted dangerously in previous encounters, and doing that now, against this formidable pirate, could bring disaster.

Was Deudermont willing to risk that for the sake of a friend's ego?

He looked more closely at Wulfgar, the big man standing at the rail staring intently at their quarry, fists clenched, blue eyes blazing with inner fires.

* * * * *

Wulfgar reluctantly climbed down into the hold—even more so when he realized he actually preferred to be down there. He had watched the captain's approach, coming to him from Robillard, but still Wulfgar had been surprised when Deudermont instructed him to go down into the aft hold where the battle rudder crew worked. Normally, *Sea Sprite*'s rudder worked off the wheel above, but when battle was joined the navigator at the wheel simply relayed his commands to the crew below, who more forcefully and reliably turned the ship as instructed.

Wulfgar had never worked the manual rudder before and hardly saw it as the optimal place to make use of his talents.

"Sour face," said Grimsley, the rudder crew chief. "Ye should be glad for bein' outta the way o' the wizards and bowmen."

Wulfgar hardly responded, just walked over and took up the heavy steering pole.

960

"He put ye down here for yer strength, I'm guessin'," Grimsley went on, and Wulfgar recognized that the grizzled old seaman was trying to spare his feelings.

The barbarian knew better. If Deudermont truly wanted to utilize his great strength in steering the ship, he would have put Wulfgar on the main tack lines above. Once, aboard the old *Sea Sprite* many years before, Wulfgar had brilliantly and mightily turned the ship, bringing her prow right out of the water, executing a seemingly impossible maneuver to win the day.

But now, it seemed, Deudermont would not even trust him at that task, would not allow him to even view the battle at all.

Wulfgar didn't like it—not one bit—but this was Deudermont's ship, he reminded himself. It was not his place to question the captain, especially with a battle looming before them.

The first shouts of alarm echoed down a few moments later. Wulfgar heard the concussion of a fireball exploding nearby.

"Pull her left to mark three!" Grimsley yelled.

Wulfgar and the one other man on the long pole tugged hard, lining the pole's front tip with the third mark on the wall to the left of center.

"Bring her back to left one!" Grimsley screamed.

The pair responded, and *Sea Sprite* cut back out of a steep turn.

Wulfgar heard the continuing shouts above, the hum of bowstrings, the swish of the catapult, and the blasts of wizardry. The sounds cut to the core of the noble barbarian's warrior identity.

Warrior?

How could Wulfgar rightly even call himself that when he could not be trusted to join in the battle, when he could not be allowed to perform the tasks he had trained for all his life? Who was he, then, he had to wonder, when companions—men of lesser fighting skill and strength than he—were doing battle right above him, while he acted the part of a mule and nothing more?

With a growl, Wulfgar responded to the next command of, "Two right!" then yanked back fiercely as Grimsley, following the frantic shouts from above, called for a dramatic cut to the left, as steep as *Sea Sprite* could make it.

The beams and rudder groaned in protest as Wulfgar forced the bar all the way to the left, and *Sea Sprite* leaned so violently that the man working the pole behind Wulfgar lost his balance.

"Easy! Easy!" Grimsley shouted at the mighty barbarian. "Ye're not to pitch the crew off the deck, ye fool!"

Wulfgar eased up a bit and accepted the scolding as deserved. He was hardly listening to Grimsley anyway, other than the specific commands the old sea dog was shouting. His attention was more to the sound of the battle above, the shrieks and the cries, the continuing roar of wizardry and catapult.

Other men were up there in danger, in his place.

"Bah, don't ye worry," Grimsley remarked, obviously noting the sour expression on Wulfgar's face, "Deudermont and his boys'll win the day, don't ye doubt!"

Indeed, Wulfgar didn't doubt that at all. Captain Deudermont and his crew had been successfully waging these battles since long before his arrival. But that wasn't what was tearing at Wulfgar's heart. He knew his place, and this wasn't it, but because of his own weakness of heart it was the only place Captain Deudermont could responsibly put him.

Above him, the fireballs boomed and the lightning crackled, the bowstrings hummed and the catapults launched their fiery loads with a great swish of sound. The battle went on for nearly an hour, and when the call was relayed through Grimsley that the crew could reattach the rudder to the wheel, the man working beside Wulfgar eagerly rushed up to the deck to survey the victory, right behind Grimsley.

Wulfgar stayed alone in the aft hold, sitting against the wall, too ashamed to show his face above, too fearful that someone had died in his stead.

He heard someone on the ladder a short while later and was surprised to see Robillard coming down, his dark blue robes hiked up so that he could manage the steps.

"Control is back with the wheel," the wizard said. "Do you not think you might be useful helping to salvage what we might from the pirate ship?"

Wulfgar stared at him hard. Even sitting, the barbarian seemed to tower over the wizard. Wulfgar was thrice the man's weight, with arms thicker than Robillard's skinny legs. By all appearances, Wulfgar could snap the wizard into pieces with hardly an effort.

If Robillard was the least bit intimidated by the barbarian, he never once showed it.

"You did this to me," Wulfgar remarked.

"Did what?"

"Your words put me here, not those of Captain Deudermont," Wulfgar clarified. "You did this."

"No, dear Wulfgar," Robillard said venomously. "You did."

Wulfgar lifted his chin, his stare defiant.

"In the face of a potentially difficult battle, Captain Deudermont had no choice but to relegate you to this place," the wizard was happy to explain. "Your own insolence and independence demanded nothing less of him. Do you think we would risk losing crewmen to satisfy your unbridled rage and high opinion of yourself?"

Wulfgar shifted forward and went up to his feet, into a crouch as if he meant to spring out and throttle the wizard.

"For what else but such an opinion, unless it is sheer stupidity itself, could possibly have guided your actions in the last battles?" Robillard went on, seeming hardly impressed or nervous. "We are a team, well-disciplined and each with a role to play. When one does not play his prescribed part, then we are a weakened team, working in spite of each other instead of in unison. That we can not tolerate. Not from you, not from anyone. So spare me your insults, your accusations and your empty threats, or you may find yourself swimming."

Wulfgar's eyes did widen a bit, betraying his intentionally stoic posture and stare.

"And I assure you, we are a long way from land," Robillard finished, and he started up the ladder. He paused, though, and looked back to Wulfgar. "If you did not enjoy this day's battle, then perhaps you would be wise to remain behind after our next docking in Waterdeep.

"Yes, perhaps that would be the best course," Robillard went on after a pause, after assuming a pensive posture. "Go back to the land, Wulfgar. You do not belong here."

The wizard left, but Wulfgar did not start after him. Rather, the barbarian slumped back to the wall, sliding to a sitting position once again, thinking of who he once had been, of who he now was—an awful truth he did not wish to face.

He couldn't even begin to look ahead, to consider who he wished to become.

Chapter 9

Paths Crossing . . . Almost

Le'lorinel stalked down Dollemand Street in Luskan, the elf's stride revealing anxiety and eagerness. The destination was a private apartment, where the elf was to meet with a representative of Sheila Kree. It all seemed to be falling into place now, the road to Drizzt Do'Urden, the road to justice.

The elf stopped abruptly and wheeled about as two cloaked figures came out of an alley. Hands going to sword and dagger, Le'lorinel had to pause and take a deep breath, recognizing that these two were no threat. They weren't even paying the elf any heed but were simply walking on their way back down the street in the opposite direction.

"Too anxious," the elf quietly chided, easing the sword and dagger back into their respective sheaths.

With a last look at the pair as they walked away, Le'lorinel gave a laugh and turned back toward the apartment, resuming the march down the road for Drizzt Do'Urden.

* * * * *

Walking the other way down Dollemand Street, Drizzt and Cattibrie didn't even notice Le'lorinel as the elf spun on them, thinking them to be a threat. Had Drizzt not been wearing the hood of his cloak, his distinctive long, thick white hair might have marked him clearly for the vengeful elf.

The couple's strides were no less eager than Le'lorinel's, carrying them in the opposite direction, to a meeting with Morik the Rogue and news of Wulfgar. They found the rogue in the appointed place, a back table in Arumn Gardpeck's Cutlass. He smiled at their approach and lifted his foaming mug of beer in toast to them.

"Ye've got our information, then?" Catti-brie asked, sliding into a seat opposite the rogue.

"As much as can be found," Morik replied. His smile dimmed and he lifted the bag of coins Drizzt had given him to the table. "You might want to take some of it back," Morik admitted, pushing it out toward the pair.

"We shall see," Drizzt said, pushing it right back.

Morik shrugged but didn't reach for the bag. "Not much to be learned of Sheila Kree," he began. "I will be honest with you in saying that I'm not overly fond of even asking anyone about her. The only ones who truly know about her are her many commanders, all of them women, and none of them fond of men. Men who go asking too much about Kree usually wind up dead or running, and I have no desire for either course."

"But ye said ye did learn a bit," the eager Catti-brie prompted.

Morik nodded and took a long draw on his beer. "It's been rumored that she operates her own private, secret port somewhere north of Luskan, probably nestled in one of the many coves along the end of the Spine of the World. That would make sense, since she's rarely seen in Luskan of late and has never been known to sail the waters to the south. I don't think her ship has ever been seen in Waterdeep."

Drizzt looked at Catti-brie, the two sharing silent agreement. They had chased pirates with Deudermont for some time, mostly to the south off the docks of Waterdeep, and neither had ever heard of the pirate, Kree.

"What's her ship's name?" Catti-brie asked.

"*Bloody Keel*," Morik replied. "Well-earned name. Sheila takes great enjoyment in keelhauling her victims." He shuddered visibly and took another drink. "That is all I have," he finished, and he again pushed the bag of coins back toward Drizzt.

"And more than I expected," the drow replied, pushing it right back. This time, after a quick pause and a confirming look, Morik took it up and slipped it away.

"There is one more thing," the rogue said as the couple stood to leave. "From all reports, Sheila has not been seen much of late. It may well be that she is in hiding, knowing Deudermont to be after her."

"With her reputation and Wulfgar's hammer, don't ye think she'd try to take *Sea Sprite* on?" Catti-brie asked.

Morik laughed aloud before she ever finished asking the question.

"Kree's no fool, and one would have to be a fool to go against *Sea Sprite* on the open waters. *Sea Sprite*'s got one purpose in being out there, and she and her crew do that task with perfect efficiency. Kree might have the warhammer, but Deudermont's got Robillard, and a nasty one he is! And Deudermont's got Wulfgar. No, Kree's laying low, and wise to be doing so. That might well work to your advantage, though."

He paused, making sure he had their attention, which he most certainly did.

"Kree knows the waters north of here better than anyone," Morik explained. "Better than Deudermont, certainly, who spends most of his time to the south. If she's in hiding the good captain will have a hard time finding her. I think it likely that *Sea Sprite* has many voyages ahead before they ever catch sight of *Bloody Keel*."

Again, Drizzt and Catti-brie exchanged curious looks. "Perhaps we should stay put in the city if we wish to find Wulfgar," the drow offered.

"*Sea Sprite* doesn't put in to Luskan much anymore," Morik interjected. "The ship's wizard is not so fond of the Hosttower of the Arcane."

"And Captain Deudermont has sullied his good name somewhat, has he not?" Catti-brie asked.

Morik's expression showed surprise. "Deudermont and his crew have been the greatest pirate hunters along the Sword Coast for longer than the memories of the eldest elves," he said.

"In freeing yerself and Wulfgar, I mean," Catti-brie clarified with an unintentional smirk. "We're hearing his action at Prisoner's Carnival wasn't looked on with favor by the magistrates."

"Idiots all," Morik mumbled. "But yes, Deudermont's reputation took a blow that day—the day he acted in the name of justice and not politics. He would have been better off personally in letting them kill us, but . . ."

"To his credit, he did not," Drizzt finished for him.

"Deudermont never liked the carnival," Catti-brie remarked.

"So it's likely that the captain has found a more favorable berth for his ship," Morik went on. "Waterdeep, I'd guess, since that's where he is best known—and known to keep a fairly fabulous house."

Drizzt looked to Catti-brie yet again. "We can be there in a tenday," he suggested, and the woman nodded her agreement.

"Well met, Morik, and thank you for your time," the drow said. He bowed and turned to leave.

"You are described in the same manner as a paladin might be, dark elf," Morik remarked, turning both friends back to him one last time. "Righteous and self-righteous. Does it not harm your reputation to do business with the likes of Morik the Rogue?"

Drizzt offered a smile that somehow managed to be warm, self-deprecating, and to show the ridiculousness of Morik's statement clearly, all at once. "You were a friend of Wulfgar's, by all I have heard. I name Wulfgar among my most trusted of companions."

"The Wulfgar you knew, or the one I knew?" Morik asked. "Perhaps they are not one and the same."

"Perhaps they are," Drizzt replied, and he bowed again, as did Catti-brie, and the pair departed.

* * * * *

Le'lorinel entered the small room at the back of the tavern tentatively, hands on dagger and sword. A woman—Sheila Kree's representative, Le'lorinel believed—sat across the room, not behind any desk, but simply against the wall, out in the open. Flanking her were two huge guards, brutes Le'lorinel figured had more than human blood running through their veins—a bit of orc, perhaps even ogre.

"Do come in," the woman said in a friendly and casual manner. She held up her hands to show the elf that she had no weapon. "You requested an audience, and so you have found one."

Le'lorinel relaxed, just a bit, one hand slipping down from the weapon hilt. A glance to the left and the right showed that no one was concealed in the small and sparsely furnished room, so the elf took a stride forward.

The right cross came out of nowhere, a heavy slug that caught the unsuspecting elf on the side of the jaw.

Only the far wall kept the staggering Le'lorinel from falling to the floor. The elf struggled against waves of dizziness and disorientation, fighting to find some center of balance.

The third guard, the largest of the trio, came visible, the concealing enchantment dispelled with the attack. Smiling evilly through a couple of crooked yellow teeth, the brute waded in with another heavy punch, this one blowing the air out of the stunned elf's lungs.

Le'lorinel went for dagger and sword, but the third punch, an uppercut, connected squarely under the elf's chin, lifting Le'lorinel into the air. The last thing Le'lorinel saw was the approach of the other two, one of them with its huge fists wrapped in chains.

A downward chop caught the elf on the side of the head, bringing a myriad of flashing explosions.

All went black.

* * * * *

"Information is not so high a price to pay," Val-Doussen said dramatically—as he said everything dramatically—waving his arms so that his voluminous sleeves seemed more like a raven's wings. "Is it so much that I ask of you?"

Drizzt dropped his head and ran his fingers through his thick white hair, glancing sidelong at Catti-brie as he did. The two had come to the Hosttower of the Arcane, Luskan's wizards guild, in hopes that they would find a mage traveling to Ten-Towns, one who might deliver a message to Bruenor. They knew the dwarf to be terribly worried, and the things they'd learned concerning Wulfgar, while not confirming that he was alive, certainly pointed in that positive direction.

They'd been directed to this black-robed eccentric, Val-Doussen, who'd been planning a trip to Icewind Dale for several tendays. They didn't think they were asking much of the wizard, though they were prepared to pay him, if necessary, but then the silver-haired and bearded wizard had taken a huge interest in Drizzt, particularly in the drow's origins.

He would deliver the information to Bruenor, as requested, but only if Drizzt would give him a dissertation on the dark elf society of Menzoberranzan.

"I have not the time," Drizzt said, yet again. "I am bound for the south, for Waterdeep."

"Might that our wizardly friend here can take us to Waterdeep in a hurry," Catti-brie put in on sudden inspiration, as Val-Doussen began to nervously tug at his beard.

Across the room, the other mage in attendance, one of the guild's leaders by the name of Cannabere, began waving his arms frantically, warding off the suggestion with a look of the purest alarm on his craggy old features.

"Well, well," Val-Doussen said, picking up on Catti-brie's suggestion. "Yes, that would require a bit of effort, but it can be done. For a price, of course, and a substantial one at that. Yes, let me think . . . I take you two to Waterdeep in exchange for a thousand gold coins and two days of tales of Menzoberranzan. Yes, yes, that might do well. And of course, I'll then go to Ten-Towns, as I had planned, and speak with Bruenor—but that for yet another day of dark elven tales."

He looked up at Drizzt, bright-eyed with eagerness, but the drow merely shook his head.

"I've no tales to tell," Drizzt remarked. "I left before I knew much of the place. In truth, I'm certain that many others, likely yourself included, know more of Menzoberranzan than I."

Val-Doussen's expression became a pout. "One day of stories, then, and I shall take your letter to Bruenor."

"No tales of Menzoberranzan," Drizzt replied firmly. He reached under the folds of his cloak and pulled forth the letter he'd prepared for Bruenor. "I will pay you twenty gold pieces—and that is a great sum for this small favor—for you to deliver this to a councilor in Brynn Shander, where you are going anyway, with the request that he relay it to Regis of Lonelywood."

"Small favor?" Val-Doussen asked dramatically.

"We have spent more time discussing this issue than it will take you to carry through with my request," Drizzt replied.

969

"I will have my stories!" the wizard insisted.

"From someone else," Drizzt answered. He rose to leave, Catti-brie right behind.

The couple nearly made it to the door before Cannabere called out, "He will do it."

Drizzt turned to regard the guildmaster, then the huffing Val-Doussen.

Cannabere looked to the flustered mage, as well, then nodded toward Drizzt. With a great sigh, Val-Doussen went over and took the note. As he began to hold out his hand for the payment, Cannabere added, "As a favor to you, Drizzt Do'Urden, and with our thanks for your work with *Sea Sprite.*"

Val-Doussen grumbled again, but he snapped up the note in his hand and spun away.

"Perhaps I will weave a tale or two for you when we meet again," Drizzt said to placate him, as the wizard stormed from the room.

The drow looked to the guildmaster, who merely bowed politely, and Drizzt and Catti-brie went on their way, bound for Luskan's southern gate and the road to Waterdeep.

* * * * *

Tight cords dug deep lines into Le'lorinel's wrists as the elf sat upright on a hard, high, straight-backed wooden chair. A leather band even went about Le'lorinel's neck, holding the elf firmly in place, forcing a grimace.

One eye didn't open all the way, bloated and bruised from the beating, and both shoulders ached and showed purplish bruises, for the elf was no longer wearing a tunic, was no longer wearing many clothes at all.

As the elf's eyes adjusted, Le'lorinel noted that the same four—three brutish guards and a brown-haired woman of medium build—remained in the room. The guards were standing to the side, the woman sitting directly across the way, staring hard at the prisoner.

"My Lady is not fond of having people inquiring about her in public," the woman remarked, her eyes roaming Le'lorinel's finely muscled frame.

"Your lady can not distinguish between friend and foe," Le'lorinel, ever defiant, replied.

"Some things are difficult to distinguish," the woman agreed, and she smiled as she continued her scan.

Le'lorinel gave a derisive snicker, and the woman nodded to the side. A brutish guard was beside the prisoner in a moment, offering a vicious smack across the face.

"Your attitude will get you killed," the woman calmly stated.

Now it was Le'lorinel's turn to stare hard.

"You have been all around Luskan asking about Sheila Kree," the woman went on after a few moments. "What is it about? Are you with the authorities? With that wretch Deudermont perhaps?"

"I am alone, and without friends west of Silverymoon," Le'lorinel replied with equal calm.

"But with the name of a hoped-for contact you carelessly utter to anyone who will listen."

"Not so," the elf answered. "I spoke of Kree only to the one group, and only because I believed they could lead me to her."

Again the woman nodded, and again the brute smacked Le'lorinel across the face.

"*Sheila* Kree," the woman corrected.

Le'lorinel didn't audibly respond but did give a slight, deferential nod.

"You should explain, then, here and now, and parse your words carefully," the woman explained. "Why do you so seek out my boss?"

"On the directions of a seer," Le'lorinel admitted. "The one who created the sketch for me."

As the elf finished, the woman lifted the parchment that held the symbol of Aegis-fang, the symbol that had become so connected to Sheila Kree's pirate band.

"I come in search of another, a dangerous foe, and one who will seek out Kr—Sheila Kree," Le'lorinel explained. "I know not the time nor the place, but by the words of the seer, I will complete my quest to do battle with this rogue when I am in the company of Sheila Kree, if it is indeed Sheila Kree who now holds the weapon bearing that insignia."

"A dangerous foe?" the woman slyly asked. "Captain Deudermont, perhaps?"

"Drizzt Do'Urden," Le'lorinel stated clearly, seeing no reason to hide the truth—especially since any ill-considered words now could prove disastrous for the quest and for the elf's very life. "A dark elf, and friend to the one who once owned that weapon."

"A drow?" the woman asked skeptically, showing no obvious recognition of the strange name.

"Indeed," Le'lorinel said with a huff. "Hero of the northland. Beloved by many in Icewind Dale—and other locales."

The woman's expression became curious, as if she might have heard of such a drow, but she merely shrugged it away. "And he seeks Sheila Kree?" she asked.

It was Le'lorinel's turn to shrug—had the tight binding allowed for such a movement. "I know only what the seer told to me and have traveled many hundreds of miles to find the vision fulfilled. I intend to kill this dark elf."

"And what, then, of any relationship you begin with my boss?" the woman asked. "Is she merely a pawn for your quest?"

"She . . . her home, or fortress, or ship, or wherever it is she resides, is merely my destination, yes," Le'lorinel admitted. "As of now, I have no relationship with your captain. Whether that situation changes or not will likely have more to do with her than with me, since . . ." The elf stopped and glanced at the bindings.

The woman spent a long while studying the elf and considering the strange tale, then nodded again to her brutish guards, offering a subtle, yet clear signal to them.

One moved fast for Le'lorinel, drawing a long, jagged knife. The elf thought that doom had come, but then the brute stepped behind the chair and cut the wrist bindings. Another of the brutish guards came out of the shadows at the side of the room, bearing Le'lorinel's clothing and belongings, except for the weapons and the enchanted ring.

Le'lorinel looked to the woman, trying hard to ignore the disappointed scowls of the three brutes, and noted that she was wearing the ring—the ring Le'lorinel so desperately needed to win a battle against Drizzt Do'Urden.

"Give back the weapons, as well," the woman instructed the guards, and all three paused and stared at her incredulously—or perhaps just stupidly.

"The road to Sheila Kree is fraught with danger," the woman explained. "You will likely need your blades. Do not disappoint me in this journey, and perhaps you will live long enough to tell your tale to Sheila Kree, though whether she listens to it in full or merely kills you for the fun of it, only time will tell."

Le'lorinel had to be satisfied with that. The elf gathered up the clothes and dressed, trying hard not to rush, trying hard to remain indignant toward the rude guards all the while.

Soon they, all five, were on the road, out of Luskan's north gate.

Chapter 10

Damn the Winter

"From Drizzt," Cassius explained, handing the parchment over to Regis. "Delivered by a most unfriendly fellow from Luskan. A wizard of great importance, by his own measure, at least."

Regis took the rolled and tied note and undid the bow holding it.

"You will be pleased, I believe," Cassius prompted.

The halfling looked up at him skeptically. "You read it?"

"The wizard from Luskan, Val-Doussen by name—and he of self-proclaimed great intellect—forgot the name of the person I was supposed to give it to," Cassius explained dryly. "So, yes, I perused it, and from its contents it seems obvious that it's either for you or for Bruenor Battlehammer or both."

Regis nodded as if satisfied, though in truth he figured Cassius could have reasoned as much without ever reading the note. Who else would Drizzt and Catti-brie be sending messages to, after all? The halfling let it go, though, too concerned with what Drizzt might have to say. He pulled open the note, his eyes scanning the words quickly.

A smile brightened his face.

"Perhaps the barbarian remains alive," Cassius remarked.

"So it would seem," said the halfling. "Or at least, the brand we found on the woman does not mean what we all feared it might."

Cassius nodded, but Regis couldn't help but note a bit of a cloud passing over his features.

"What is it?" the halfling asked.

"Nothing."

"More than nothing," Regis reasoned, and he considered his own words that had brought on the slight frown. "The woman," he reasoned. "What of the woman?"

"She is gone," Cassius admitted.

"Dead?"

"Escaped," the elderman corrected. "A tenday ago. Councilor Kemp put her on a Targos fishing ship for indenture—a different ship than that on which he placed the other ruffians, for he knew she was the most dangerous by far. She leaped from the deck soon after the ship put out."

"Then she died, frozen in Maer Dualdon," Regis reasoned, for he knew the lake well and knew that no one could survive for long in the cold waters even in midsummer, let alone at this time of the year.

"So the crew believed," Cassius said. "She must have had some enchantment upon her, for she was seen emerging from the water a short distance from the western reaches of Targos."

"Then she is lying dead of exposure along the lake's southern bank," the halfling said, "or is wandering in a near-dead stupor along the water's edge."

Cassius was shaking his head through every word. "Jule Pepper is a clever one, it would seem," he said. "She is nowhere to be found, and clothing was stolen from a farmhouse to the west of the city. Likely that one is long on the road out of Icewind Dale, and a glad farewell I offer her."

Regis wasn't thinking along those same lines. He wondered if Jule Pepper presented any threat to his friends. Jule knew of Drizzt, obviously and likely held a grudge against him. If she was returning to her old hunting band, perhaps she and the drow would cross paths once more.

Regis forced himself to calm down, remembering the two friends, Drizzt and Catti-brie, that he was fearing for. If Jule Pepper crossed paths with that pair, then woe to her, he figured, and he let it go at that.

"I must get to Bruenor," he said to Cassius. Regis snapped the parchment up tight in his hand and rushed out of the elderman's house, sprinting across Brynn Shander in the hopes that he might catch up to a merchant caravan he knew to be leaving for the dwarven mines that very morning.

Luck was with him, and he talked his way into a ride on a wagon full of grain bags. He slept nearly all the way.

Bruenor was in a foul mood when Regis finally caught up to him late that same night—a mood that had been common with the dwarf since Drizzt and Catti-brie had left Ten-Towns.

974

"Ye're bringing up weak stone!" the red-bearded dwarf king howled at a pair of young miners, their faces and beards black with dirt and dust. Bruenor held up one of the rock samples he had proffered from their small cart and crumbled it in one hand. "Ye're thinking there's ore worth taking in that?" he asked incredulously.

"A tough dig," remarked one of the younger dwarves, his black beard barely reaching the middle of his thick neck. "We're down the deepest hole, hanging upside down . . ."

"Bah, but ye're mixing me up for one who's caring to hear yer whining!" Bruenor roared. The dwarf king gritted his teeth, clenched his fists, and gave a great growl, trembling as if he was throwing all of the rage right out of his body.

"Me king!" the black-bearded dwarf exclaimed. "We'll go and get better stone!"

"Bah!" Bruenor snorted.

He turned and slammed his body hard against the laden cart, overturning it. As if that one explosion had released the tension, Bruenor stood there, staring at the overturned cart and the stones strewn about the corridor, stubby hands on hips. He closed his eyes.

"Ye're not needing to go back down there," he said calmly to the pair. "Ye go get yerselves cleaned and get yerselves some food. Ain't a thing wrong with most o' that ore—it's yer king who's needing a bit o' toughening, by me own eyes and ears."

"Yes, me king," both young dwarves said in unison.

Regis came up from the other side, then, and nodded to the pair, who turned and trotted away, mumbling.

The halfling walked up and put his hand on Bruenor's shoulder. The dwarf king nearly jumped out of his boots, spinning about, his face a mask of fury.

"Don't ye be doing that!" he roared, though he did calm somewhat when he saw that it was only Regis. "Ain't ye supposed to be in a council meeting?"

"They can get through it without me," the halfling replied, managing a smile. "I think you might need me more."

Bruenor looked at him curiously, so Regis just turned and led the dwarf's gaze down the corridor, to the departing pair. "Criminals?" the halfling asked sarcastically.

Bruenor kicked a stone, sending it flying against the wall, seeming again as if he was so full of rage and frustration that he would simply explode. The dark cloud passed quickly, though, replaced by a more general air of gloom, and the dwarf's shoulders slumped. He bowed his head and shook it slowly.

"I can't be losin' me boy again," he admitted.

Regis was beside him in an instant, one hand comfortingly placed on Bruenor's shoulder. As soon as the dwarf looked up at his buddy,

Regis offered a wide smile and held the parchment up before him. "From Drizzt," the halfling explained.

The words had barely left Regis's mouth before Bruenor grabbed the parchment away and pulled it open.

"He and Catti-brie found me boy!" the dwarf howled, but he stopped short as he read on.

"No, but they found out how Wulfgar got separated from Aegis-fang," Regis was quick to add, for that, after all, had been the primary source of their concern that the barbarian might be dead.

"We're goin'," Bruenor declared.

"Going?" Regis echoed. "Going where?"

"To find Drizzt and Catti-brie. To find me boy!" the dwarf roared. He stormed away down the corridor. "We're leaving tonight, Rumblebelly. Ye'd best get yerself ready."

"But . . ." Regis started to reply. He stuttered over the beginnings of a series of arguments, the primary of which was the fact that it was getting late in the season to be heading out of Ten-Towns. Autumn was fast on the wane, and Icewind Dale had never been known for especially long autumn seasons, with winter seeming ever hungry to descend upon the region.

"We'll get to Luskan, don't ye worry, Rumblebelly!" Bruenor howled.

"You should take dwarves with you," Regis stammered, skittering to catch up. "Yes, sturdy dwarves who can brave the winter snows, and who can fight. . . ."

"Don't need me kin," Bruenor assured him. "I've got yerself beside me, and I know ye wouldn't be missing the chance to help me find me boy."

It wasn't so much what Bruenor had said as it was the manner in which he had said it, a flat declaration that left no hint at all that he would even listen to contrary arguments.

Regis sputtered out a few undecipherable sounds, then just huffed through a resigned sigh. "All of my supplies for the road are in Lonelywood," the halfling did manage to complain.

"And anything ye'll be needin' is right here in me caves," Bruenor explained. "We'll put through Brynn Shander on our way so ye can apologize to Cassius—he'll see to yer house and yer possessions."

"Indeed," Regis mumbled under his breath, and in purely sarcastic tones, for the last time he had left the region, as in all the times he had wandered out of Icewind Dale, he had returned to find that he had nothing left waiting for him. The folk of Ten-Towns were honest enough as neighbors, but perfectly vulturelike when it came to picking clean abandoned houses—even if they were only supposed to be abandoned for a short time.

True to Bruenor's word, the halfling and the dwarf were on the road that very night, rambling along under crystalline skies and a cold wind, following the distant lights to Brynn Shander. They arrived just before the dawn, and though Regis begged for patience Bruenor led the way

976

straight to Cassius's house and banged hard on the door, calling out loudly enough to not only wake Cassius but a substantial number of his neighbors as well.

When a sleepy-eyed Cassius at last opened his door, the dwarf bellowed, "Ye got five minutes!" and shoved Regis through.

And when, by Bruenor's count, the appropriated time had passed, the dwarf barged through the door, collected the halfling by the scruff of his neck, offered a few insincere apologies to Cassius, and pulled Regis out the door. Bruenor prodded him along all the way across the city and out the western gate.

"Cassius informed me that the fishermen are expecting a gale," Regis said repeatedly, but if Bruenor even heard him, the determined dwarf wasn't showing it. "The wind and rain will be bad enough, but if it turns to snow and sleet. . . ."

"Just a storm," Bruenor said with a derisive snort. "Ain't no storm to stop me, Rumblebelly, nor yerself. I'll get ye there!"

"The yetis are out in force this time of year," Regis cautioned.

"Good enough for keeping me axe nice and sharp," Bruenor countered. "Hard-headed beasts."

The storm began that same night, a cold and biting, steady rain, pelting them more horizontally than vertically in the driving wind.

Thoroughly miserable and soaked to the bone, Regis complained continually, though he knew Bruenor, in the sheer volume of the wind, couldn't even hear him. The wind was directly behind them, at least, propelling them along at a great pace, which Bruenor pointed out often and with a wide smile.

But Regis knew better, and so did the dwarf. The storm was coming from the southeast, off the mountains, the most unlikely direction, and often the most ominous. In Icewind Dale, such storms, if they progressed as expected, were known as Nor'westers. If the gale made its way across the dale and to the sea, the cold northeasterly wind would hold it there, over the moving ice, sometimes for days on end.

The pair stopped at a farmhouse for the evening and were welcomed in, though told that they could sleep in the barn with the livestock and not in the main house. Huddled about a small fire, naked and with their clothes drying on a rafter above, Regis again appealed to Bruenor's common sense.

The halfling found that target a hard one to locate.

"Nor'wester," Regis explained. "Could storm for a tenday and could turn colder."

"Not a Nor'wester yet," the dwarf replied gruffly.

"We can wait it out. Stay here—or go to Bremen, perhaps. But to cross the dale in this could be the end of us!"

"Bah, it's just a bit o' rain," Bruenor grumbled. He bit a huge chunk off the piece of mutton their hosts had provided. "Seen worse—used to

977

play in worse when I was but a boy in Mithral Hall. Ye should've seen the snows in the mountains out there, Rumblebelly. Twice a dwarf's height in a single fall!"

"And a quarter of that will stop us cold on the road," Regis answered. "And leave us frozen and dead in a place where only the yetis will ever find us."

"Bah!" Bruenor snorted. "No snow'll stop me from me boy, or I'm a bearded gnome! Ye can turn about if ye're wantin'—ye should be able to get to Targos easy enough, and they'll get ye across the lake to yer home. But I'm for going on, soon as I get me sleep, and I'm not for stopping until I see Luskan's gate, until I find that tavern Drizzt wrote about, the Cutlass."

Regis tried to hide his frown and just nodded.

"I'm not holdin' a bit o' yer choices against ye," Bruenor said. "If ye ain't got the heart for it, then turn yerself about."

"But you are going on?" Regis asked.

"All the way."

What Regis didn't have the heart for, despite what his common sense was screaming out at him, was abandoning his friend to the perils of the road. When Bruenor left the next day, Regis was right beside him.

The only change that next day was that the wind was now from the northwest instead of the southeast, blowing the rain into their faces, which made them all the more miserable and slowed their progress considerably. Bruenor didn't complain, didn't say a word, just bent low into the gale and plowed on.

And Regis went with him, stoically, though the halfling did position himself somewhat behind and to the left of the dwarf, using Bruenor's wide body to block a bit of the rain and the wind.

The dwarf did concede to a more northerly route that day, one that would bring them to another farmhouse along the route, a homestead that was quite used to having visitors. In fact, when the dwarf and halfling arrived, they met with another group who had started on their way to Luskan. They had pulled in two days before, fearing that the mud would stop their wagon wheels dead in their tracks.

"Too early in the season," the lead driver explained to the duo. "Ground's not frozen up yet, so we've no chance of getting through."

"Seems as if we'll be wintering in Bremen," another of the group grumbled.

"Happened before, and'll happen again," the lead driver said. "We'll take ye on with us to Bremen, if ye want."

"Not going to Bremen," Bruenor explained between bites of another mutton dinner. "Going to Luskan."

Every member of the other group glanced incredulously at each other, and both Bruenor and Regis heard the word "Nor'wester" mumbled more than once.

"Got no wagons to get stuck in the mud," Bruenor explained.

"Mud that'll reach more than halfway up yer little legs," said another, with a chuckle that lasted only as long as it took Bruenor to fix him with a threatening scowl.

The other group, even the lead driver, appealed to the pair to be more sensible, but it was Regis, not Bruenor, who finally said, "We will see you on the road. Next spring. We'll be returning as you're leaving."

That brought a great belly laugh out of Bruenor, and sure enough, before dawn the next day, before any members of the farm family or the other group had even opened their eyes, the dwarf and the halfling were on the road, bending into the cold wind. They knew they'd spent their last comfortable night for a long while, knew they'd have a difficult time even finding enough shelter to start a fizzling fire, knew that deep mud awaited them and possibly with deep snow covering it.

But they knew, too, that Drizzt and Catti-brie waited for them, and, perhaps, so did Wulfgar.

Regis did not register a single complaint that third day, nor the fourth, nor the fifth, though they were out of dry clothes and the wind had turned decidedly colder, and the rain had become sleet and snow. They plowed on, single file, Bruenor's sheer strength and determination plowing a trail ahead of Regis, though the mud grabbed at his every stride and the snow was piling as deep as his waist.

The fifth night they built a dome of snow for shelter and Bruenor did manage a bit of a fire, but neither could feel their feet any longer. With the current pace of the snowfall they expected to wake up to find the white stuff as deep as the horn on Bruenor's helmet.

"I shouldn't have taked ye along," Bruenor admitted solemnly, as close to an admission of defeat as Regis had ever heard from the indomitable dwarf. "Should've trusted in Drizzt and Catti-brie to bring me boy back in the spring."

"We're almost out of the dale," Regis replied with as much enthusiasm as he could muster. It was true enough. Despite the weather, they had made great progress, and the mountain pass was in sight, though still a day's march away. "The storm has kept the yetis at bay."

"Only because the damn things're smarter than us," Bruenor grumbled. He put his toes practically into the fire, trying to thaw them.

They had a difficult time falling asleep that night, expecting the wind and the storm to collapse the dome atop them. In fact, when Regis awoke in the darkness, everything seeming perfectly still—too still! He knew in his heart that he was dead.

He lay there for what seemed like days, when finally the snow dome above him began to lighten and even glow.

Regis breathed a sigh of relief, but where was Bruenor? The halfling rolled to his side and propped himself up on his elbows, glancing all about. In the dim light, he finally made out Bruenor's bedroll, tossed asunder.

Before he could even begin to question the scene, he heard a commotion by the low tunnel to the igloo and sucked in his breath.

It was Bruenor coming through, and wearing less clothing than Regis had seen him in for several days.

"Sun's up," the dwarf said with a wide smile. "And the snow's fast melting. We best get our things and ourselves outta here afore the roof melts in on us!"

They didn't travel very far that day, for the warming weather fast melted the snows, making the mud nearly impossible to traverse. At least they weren't freezing anymore, though, and so they took the slowdown in good stride. Bruenor managed to find a dry spot for their camp, and they enjoyed a hearty meal and a fretful night filled with the sounds of wolves howling and yetis growling.

Still, they managed to find a bit of sleep, but when they awoke they had to wonder how good a thing that was. In the night a wolf, by the shape of the tracks, had come in and made off with a good deal of their supplies.

Despite loss and weariness, it was in good spirits that they made the beginning of the pass that day. No snow had fallen there, and the ground was stony and dry. They camped just within the protective walls of stone that night and were surprised when other lights appeared in the darkness. There was a camp of some sort higher up on the gorge's eastern wall.

"Well, go and see what that's all about," Bruenor bade Regis.

Regis looked at him skeptically.

"Ye're the sneak, ain't ye?" the dwarf said.

With a helpless chuckle, Regis picked himself up from the stone on which he had been enjoying his meal, gave a series of belches, and rubbed his full belly.

"Get all the wind outta ye afore ye try sneakin' up on our friends," the dwarf advised.

Regis burped again and patted his belly, then, with a resigned sigh (he always seemed to be doing that around Bruenor), he turned and started off into the dark night, leaving Bruenor to do the clean-up.

The smell of venison cooking as he neared the encampment, climbing quietly up a steep rock face, made the halfling think that perhaps Bruenor had been right in sending him out. Perhaps they would find a band of rangers willing to share the spoils of their hunt, or a band of merchants who had ridden out of the dale before them, and would be glad to hire them on as guards for the duration of the journey to Luskan.

Lost in fantasies of comfort, so eager to get his mouth on that beautiful-smelling venison, Regis nearly pulled himself full over the ledge with a big smile. Caution got the better of the halfling, though, and it was a good thing it did. As he pulled himself up slowly, lifting to just peek over the ledge, he saw that these were not rangers and were not merchants, but orcs. Big, smelly, ugly, nasty orcs. Fierce mountain orcs, wearing the skins of yetis, tearing at the hocks of venison with abandon, crunching cartilage and bone, swearing at each other and jostling for every piece they tore off the cooking carcass.

It took Regis a few moments to even realize that his arms had gone weak, and he had to catch himself before falling off the thirty-foot cliff. Slowly, trying hard not to scream out, trying hard not to breathe too loudly, he lowered himself back below the lip.

In times past, that would have been the end of it, with Regis scrambling back down then running to Bruenor to report that there was nothing to be gained. But now, bolstered by the confidence that had come through his efforts on the road over the last few months, where he had worked hard to play an important role in his friends' heroics, and still stung by the nearly constant dismissal others showed to him when speaking of the Companions of the Hall, Regis decided it was not yet time to turn back. Far from it.

The halfling would get himself a meal of venison and one for Bruenor, too. But how?

The halfling worked himself around to the side, just a bit. Once out of the illumination of the firelight, he peeked over the ledge again. The orcs remained engrossed in their meal. One fight nearly broke out as two reached for the same chunk of meat, the first one even trying to bite the arm of the second as it reached in.

In the commotion that ensued, Regis went up over the ledge, staying flat on his belly and crawling behind a rock. A few moments later, with another squabble breaking out at the camp, the halfling picked a course and moved closer, and closer again.

"O, but now I've done it," Regis silently mouthed. "I'll get myself killed, to be sure. Or worse, captured, and Bruenor will get himself killed coming to find me!"

The potential of that thought weighed heavily on the little halfling. The dwarf was a brutal foe, Regis knew, and these orcs would feel his wrath terribly, but they were big and tough, and there were six of them after all.

The thought that he might get his friend killed almost turned the halfling back.

Almost.

Eventually he was close enough to smell the ugly brutes, and, more importantly, to notice some of the particulars about them. Like the fact that one was wearing a fairly expensive bracelet of gold, with a clasp that Regis knew he could easily undo.

A plan began to take shape.

The orc with the bracelet had a huge chunk of deer, a rear leg, in that hand. The nasty creature brought it up to its chomping mouth, then brought it back down to its side, then up and down, repeatedly and predictably.

Regis waited patiently for the next struggle that orc had with the beast to its left, as he knew that it would, as they all were, one after the other. As the bracelet-wearing brute held the venison out to the right defensively, fending off the advance of the creature on its left, a small hand came up from the shadows, taking the bracelet with a simple flick of plump little fingers.

The halfling brought his hand down, but to the right and not back, taking his loot to the pocket of the orc sitting to the right of his victim. In it went, softly and silently, and Regis took care to hang the end of the chain out in open sight.

The halfling quickly went back behind his rock and waited.

He heard his victim start with surprise a moment later.

"Who taked it?" the orc asked in its own brutish tongue, some of which Regis understood.

"Take what?" blustered the orc to the left. "Yer got yerself the bestest piece, ye glutton!"

"Yer taked me chain!" the victimized orc growled. It brought the deer leg across, smacking the other orc hard on the head.

"Aw, now how's Tuko got it?" asked another of the group. Ironically, it was the one with the chain hanging out of its pocket. "Yer been keeping yer hand away from Tuko all night!"

Things calmed for a second. Regis held his breath.

"Yer right, ain't ye, Ginick?" asked the victimized orc, and from its sly tone, Regis knew that the dim-witted creature had spotted something.

A terrible row ensued, with Regis's victim leaping up and swinging the deer leg in both hands like a club, aiming for Ginick's head. The target orc blocked with a burly arm and came up hard, catching the other about the waist and bearing it right over poor Tuko the other way. Soon all six were into it—pulling each other's hair, clubbing, punching, and biting.

Regis crept away soon after, enough venison in hand to satisfy a hungry dwarf and a hungrier halfling.

And wearing on his left wrist a newly acquired gold bracelet, one that had conveniently dropped from the pocket of a falsely accused orc thief.

Chapter 11

Diverging Roads

We'd've found a faster road with a bit of wizard's magic," Catti-brie remarked. It wasn't the first time the woman had good-naturedly ribbed Drizzt about his refusal to accept Val-Doussen's offer. "We'd be well on our way back, I'm thinking, and with Wulfgar in tow."

"You sound more like a dwarf every day," Drizzt countered, using a stick to prod the fire upon which a fine stew was cooking. "You should begin to worry when you notice an aversion to open spaces, like the road we now travel.

"No, wait!" the drow sarcastically exclaimed, as if the truth had just come to him. "Are you not expressing just such an aversion?"

"Keep waggin' yer tongue, Drizzt Do'Urden," Catti-brie muttered quietly. "Ye might be fine with yer spinning blades, but how are ye with catching a few stinging arrows?"

"I have already cut your bowstring," the drow casually replied, leaning forward and taking a sip of the steaming stew.

Catti-brie actually started to look over at Taulmaril, lying unstrung at the side of the fallen log on which she now sat. She put on a smirk, though, and turned back to her sarcastic friend. "I'm just thinking we might have missed *Sea Sprite* as she put out for her last run o' the season," Catti-brie said, seriously, this time.

Indeed, the wind had taken on a bit of a bite over the last few days, autumn fast flowing past. Deudermont often took *Sea Sprite* out at this time of the year to haunt the waters off Waterdeep for a couple of tendays before turning south to warmer climes and more active pirates.

Drizzt knew it, too, as was evident by the frown that crossed his angular features. That little possibility had been troubling him since he and Catti-brie had left the Hosttower, and made him wonder if his refusal of Val-Doussen's offer had been too selfish an act.

"All the fool mage wanted was a bit of talking," the woman went on. "A few hours of yer time would've made him happy and would have saved us a tenday of walking—and no, I'm not fearing the road or even bothered by it, and ye know it! There's no place in the world I'd rather be than on the road beside ye, but we've got others to think of, and it'd be better for Bruenor, and for Wulfgar, if we find him before he gets into too much more trouble."

Drizzt started to respond with a reminder that Wulfgar, if he was indeed with Deudermont and the crew of *Sea Sprite*, was in fine hands, was among allies at least as powerful as the Companions of the Hall. He held the words, though, and considered Catti-brie's argument more carefully, truly hearing what she was saying instead of reflexively formulating a defensive answer.

He knew she was right, that Wulfgar, that all of them, would be better off if they were reunited. Perhaps he should have spent a few hours talking to Val-Doussen.

"So just tell me why ye didn't," Catti-brie gently prompted. "Ye could've got us to Waterdeep in the blink of a wizard's eye, and I'm knowing ye believe that to be a good thing. And yet ye didn't, so might ye be telling me why?"

"Val-Doussen is no scholar," Drizzt replied.

Catti-brie leaned in and took the spoon from him, then dipped it into the stew and, brushing her thick, long auburn hair back from her face, took a sip. She stared at Drizzt all the while, her inquisitive expression indicating that he should elaborate.

"His interest in Menzoberranzan is one of personal gain and nothing more," Drizzt remarked. "He had no desire for bettering the world, but only hoped that something I would tell him might offer him an advantage he could exploit."

Still Catti-brie stared at him, obviously not catching on. Even if Drizzt's words were true, why, given Drizzt's relationship with his wicked kin, did that even matter?

"He hoped I would unveil some of the mysteries of the drow," Drizzt continued, undaunted by his companion's expression.

"And even if ye did, from what I know of Menzoberranzan Val-Doussen couldn't be using yer words for anything more than his own doom," Catti-brie put in, and sincerely, for she had visited that exotic dark elf city, and she knew well the great power of the place.

Drizzt shrugged and reached for the spoon, but Catti-brie, smiling widely, pulled it away from him.

Drizzt sat back, staring at her, not sharing her smile. He was deep in concentration, needing to make his point. "Val-Doussen hoped to personally profit from my words, to use my tales for his own nefarious reasons, and at the expense of those my information delivered unto him. Be it my kin in Menzoberranzan, or Bruenor's in Mithral Hall, my actions would have been no less wicked."

"I'd not be comparing Clan Battlehammer to—" Catti-brie started.

"I am not," Drizzt assured her. "I speak of nothing more here than my own principles. If Val-Doussen sought information of a goblin settlement that he could lead a preemptive assault against them, I would gladly comply, because I trust that such a goblin settlement would soon enough cause tragedy to any living nearby."

"And didn't yer own kin come to Mithral Hall?" Catti-brie asked, following the logic.

"Once," Drizzt admitted. "But as far as I know, my kin are not on their way back to the surface world in search of plunder and mayhem."

"As far as ye know."

"Besides, anything I offered to Val-Doussen would not have prevented any dark elf raids in any case," Drizzt went on, stepping lightly so that Catti-brie could not catch him in a logic trap. "No, more likely, the fool would have gone to Menzoberranzan, alone or with others, in some attempt at grand thievery. That most likely would have done no more than to stir up the dark elves into murderous revenge."

Catti-brie started to ask another question, but just sat back instead, staring at her friend. Finally, she nodded and said, "Ye're making a bit o' assumptions there."

Drizzt didn't begin to disagree, audibly or with his body language.

"But I'm seeing yer point that ye shouldn't be mixing yerself up with those of less than honorable intent."

"You respect that?" Drizzt asked.

Catti-brie gave what might have been an agreeing nod.

"Then give me the spoon," the dark elf said more forcefully. "I'm starving!"

In response, Catti-brie moved forward and dipped the spoon into the pot, then lifted it toward Drizzt's waiting lips. At the last moment, the drow's lavender eyes closed against the steam, the woman pulled the spoon back to her own lips.

Drizzt's eyes popped open, his surprised and angry expression overwhelmed by the playful and teasing stare of Catti-brie. He went forward in a sudden burst, falling over the woman and knocking her right off the back of the log, then wrestling with her for the spoon.

Neither Drizzt nor Catti-brie could deny the truth that there was no place in all the world they would rather be.

* * * * *

The walls climbed up around the small party, a combination of dark gray-brown cliff facings and patches of steeply sloping green grass. A few trees dotted the sides of the gorge, small and thin things, really, unable to get firm footing or to send their roots very deep into the rocky ground.

The place was ripe for an ambush, Le'lorinel understood, but neither the elf nor the other four members of the party were the least bit worried of any such possibility. Sheila Kree and her ruffians owned this gorge. Le'lorinel had caught the group's leader, the brown-haired woman named Genny, offering a few subtle signals toward the peaks. Sentries were obviously in place there.

There would be no calls, though, for none would be heard beyond a few dozen strides. In the distance, Le'lorinel could hear the constant song of the river that had cut this gorge, flowing underground now, under the left-hand wall as they made their way to the south. Directly ahead, some distance away, the surf thundered against the rocky coast. The wind blew down from behind them, filling their ears. The chilling wind of Icewind Dale escaped the tundra through this mountain pass.

Le'lorinel felt strangely comfortable in this seemingly inhospitable and forlorn place. The elf felt a sense of freedom away from the clutter of society that had never held much interest. Perhaps there would be more to this relationship with Sheila Kree, Le'lorinel mused. Perhaps after the business with Drizzt Do'Urden was finished, Le'lorinel could stay on with Kree's band, serving as a sentry in this very gorge.

Of course, that all hinged on whether or not the elf remained alive after an encounter with the deadly dark elf, and in truth, unless Le'lorinel could find some way to get the enchanted ring back from Genny, that seemed a remote possibility indeed.

Without that ring, would Le'lorinel even dare to go against the dark elf?

A shudder coursed the elf's spine, one brought on by thoughts and not the chilly wind.

The party moved past several small openings, natural vents for the caverns that served as Kree's home in the three-hundred-foot mound to the left, a series of caves settled above the present-day river. Down around a bend in the gorge, they came to a wide natural alcove and a larger cave entrance, a place where the river had once cut its way out through the limestone rock.

A trio of guards sat among the crags to the right-hand wall within, huddled in the shadows, throwing bones and chewing near-raw mutton, their heavy weapons close at hand. Like the three who had accompanied Le'lorinel to this place, the guards were huge, obviously a product of mixed parentage, human and ogre, and favoring the ogre side indeed.

They bristled at the approach of the band but didn't seem too concerned, and Le'lorinel understood that the sentries along the gorge had likely warned them of the intruders.

"Where is the boss?" Genny asked.

"Chogurugga in her room," one soldier grunted in reply.

"Not Chogurugga," said Genny. "Sheila Kree. The real boss."

Le'lorinel didn't miss the scowl that came at the woman at that proclamation. The elf readily understood that there was some kind of power struggle going on here, likely between the pirates and the ogres.

One of the guards grunted and showed its nasty yellow teeth, then motioned toward the back of the cave.

The three accompanying soldiers took out torches and set them ablaze. On the travelers went, winding their way through a myriad of spectacular natural designs. At first, Le'lorinel thought running water was all around them, cascading down the sides of the tunnel in wide, graceful waterfalls, but as the elf looked closer the truth became evident. It was not water, but formations of rock left behind by the old river, limestone solidified into waterfall images still slick from the dripping that came with every rainfall.

Great tunnels ran off the main one, many winding up, spiraling into the mound, others branching off at this level often forming huge, boulder-filled chambers. So many shapes assaulted the elf's outdoor sensibilities! Images of animals and weapons, of lovers entwined and great forests, of whatever Le'lorinel's imagination allowed the elf to see! Le'lorinel was a creature of the forest, a creature of the moon, and had never before been underground. For the very first time, the elf gained some appreciation of the dwarves and the halflings, the gnomes and any other race that chose the subterranean world over that of the open sky.

No, not *any* other race, Le'lorinel promptly reminded. Not the drow, those ebon-skinned devils of lightless chambers. Certainly there was beauty here, but beauty only reflected in the light of the torches.

The party moved on in near silence, save the crackle of the torches, for the floor was of clay, smooth and soft. They descended for some time along the main chamber, the primary riverbed of ages past, and moved beyond several other guard stations, sometimes manned by half-ogres, once by a pair of true ogres, and once by normal-looking men—pirates, judging from their dress and from the company they kept.

Le'lorinel took it all in halfheartedly, too concerned with the forthcoming meeting, the all-important plea that had to be made to Sheila Kree. With Kree's assistance, Le'lorinel might find the end of a long, heart-wrenching road. Without Kree's favor, Le'lorinel would likely wind up dead and discarded in one of these side-passages.

And worse, to the elf's sensibilities, Drizzt Do'Urden would remain very much alive.

Genny turned aside suddenly, down a narrow side passage. Both Genny and Le'lorinel had to drop to all fours to continue on, crawling under a low overhang of solid stone. Their three larger companions had to get right down on their bellies and crawl. On the other side was a wide chamber of startling design, widening up and out to the left, its stalactite ceiling many, many feet above.

Genny didn't even look at it, though, but rather focused on a small hole in the floor, moving to a ladder that had been set into one wall. Down she went, followed by a guard, then Le'lorinel, then the other two.

Far down, perhaps a hundred steps, they came to another corridor and set off, arriving soon after in another cave. It was a huge cavern, open to the southwest, to the rocky bay and the sea beyond. Water poured in from many openings in the walls and ceiling, the river emptying into the sea.

In the cave sat *Bloody Keel*, moored to the western wall, with sailors crawling all over her repairing the rigging and hull damage.

"Now that you've seen this much, you would be wise to pray to whatever god you know that Sheila Kree accepts you," Genny whispered to the elf. "There are but two ways out of here: as a friend or as a corpse."

Looking at the ruffian crew scrambling all about the ship, cutthroats all, Le'lorinel didn't doubt those words for a moment.

Genny led the way out of another exit, this one winding back up into the mountain from the back of the docking cave. The passages smelled of smoke, and were torch-lit all the way, so the escorting guards doused their own torches and put them away. Higher and higher they climbed into the mountain, passing storerooms and barracks, crossing through an area that seemed to Le'lorinel to be reserved for the pirates, and another horribly smelly place that housed the ogre clan.

More than a few hungry gazes came the elf's way as they passed by the ravenous ogres, but none came close enough to even prod Le'lorinel. Their respect for Kree was tremendous, the elf recognized, simply from the fact that they weren't causing any trouble. Le'lorinel had enough experience with ogres to know that they were usually unruly and more than ready to make a meal of any smaller humanoid they encountered.

They came to the highest levels of the mound soon after, pausing in an open chamber lined by several doors. Genny motioned for the other four to wait there while she went to the center door of the room, knocked, and disappeared through the door. She returned a short while later.

"Come," she bade Le'lorinel.

When the three brutish guards moved to escort the elf, Genny held them at bay with an upraised hand. "Go get some food," the brown-haired woman instructed the half-ogres.

Le'lorinel glanced at the departing half-ogres curiously, not sure whether this signaled that Sheila Kree trusted Genny's word, or whether the pirate was simply too confident or too well-protected to care.

Le'lorinel figured it must be the latter.

Sheila Kree, dressed in nothing more than light breeches and a thin, sleeveless shirt, was standing in the room within, amongst piles of furs, staring out her window at the wide waters. She turned when Genny announced Le'lorinel, her smile bright on her freckled face, her green eyes shining under the crown of her tied-up red hair.

"I've been told ye're fearing for me life, elf," the pirate leader remarked. "I'm touched by yer concern."

Le'lorinel stared at her curiously.

"Ye've come to warn me of a dark elf, so says Genny," the pirate clarified.

"I have come to slay a dark elf," Le'lorinel corrected. "That my actions will benefit you as well is merely a fortunate coincidence."

Sheila Kree gave a great belly laugh and strode over to stand right in front of the elf, towering over Le'lorinel. The pirate's eyes roamed up and down Le'lorinel's slender, even delicate form. "Fortunate for yerself, or for me?"

"For both, I would guess," Le'lorinel answered.

"Ye must hate this drow more than a bit to have come here," Sheila Kree remarked.

"More than you can possibly imagine."

"And would ye tell me why?"

"It is a long tale," Le'lorinel said.

"Well, since winter's fast coming and *Bloody Keel*'s still in dock, it's looking like I've got the time," Sheila Kree said with another laugh. She swept her arm out toward some piles of furs, motioning for Le'lorinel to join her.

They talked for the rest of the afternoon, with Le'lorinel giving an honest, if slanted account of the many errors of Drizzt Do'Urden. Sheila Kree listened intently, as did Genny, as did a third woman, Bellany, who came in soon after the elf had begun the tale. All three seemed more than a little amused and interested, and as time went on, Le'lorinel relaxed even more.

When the tale was done, both Bellany and Genny applauded, but just for a moment stopping and looking to Sheila for a cue.

"A good tale," the pirate leader decided. "And I find that I believe yer words. Ye'll understand that we've much to check on afore we let ye have a free run."

"Of course," Le'lorinel agreed, giving a slight bow.

"Ye give over yer weapons, and we'll set ye in a room," Sheila explained. "I've no work for ye right now, so ye can get yer rest from the long road." As she finished, the pirate held out her hand.

Le'lorinel considered things for just a moment, then decided that Kree and her associates—especially the one named Bellany, who Le'lorinel had concluded was a spellcaster, likely a sorceress—in truth made surrendering the weapons nothing more than symbolic. With a smile at the fiery pirate, the elf turned over the dagger and sword.

* * * * *

"I suppose you consider this humorous," Drizzt said dryly, his tone interrupted only by the occasional wheeze as he tried to draw breath.

He was lying on the ground, facedown in the dirt, with six hundred pounds of panther draped over him. He had called up Guenhwyvar to do some hunting while he and Catti-brie continued their mock battle over the stew, but then the woman had whispered something in Guen's ear, and the cat, obviously gender loyal, had brought Drizzt down with a great flying tackle.

A few feet away, Catti-brie was thoroughly enjoying her stew.

"Ye do look a bit ridiculous," she admitted between sips.

Drizzt scrambled, and almost slipped out from under the panther. Guenhwyvar dropped a huge paw on his shoulder, extracting long claws and holding him fast.

"Ye keep on with yer fighting and Guen'll have herself a meal," Catti-brie remarked.

Drizzt's lavender eyes narrowed. "There remains a small matter of repayment," he said quietly.

Catti-brie gave a snort, then moved down close to him, on her knees. She lifted a spoon full of stew and blew on it gently, then moved it out toward Drizzt, slowly, teasingly. It almost reached his mouth when the woman pulled it back abruptly, the spoon disappearing into her mouth.

Her smile went away fast, though, as she saw Guenhwyvar dissipating into a gray mist. The cat protested, but the dismissal of her master, Drizzt, could not be ignored.

Catti-brie darted off into the woods with Drizzt in fast pursuit.

He caught her with a leaping tackle a short distance away, bearing her to the ground beneath him, then using his amazing agility and deceptive strength to roll her over and pin her. The firelight was lost behind the trees and shrubs, the starlight and the glow of a half moon alone highlighting the woman's beautiful features.

"Ye call this repayment?" the woman teased when Drizzt was atop her, straddling her and holding her arms to the ground above her head.

"Only beginning," he promised.

Catti-brie started to laugh, but stopped suddenly, her look to Drizzt becoming serious, even concerned.

"What is it?" the perceptive drow asked. He backed off a bit, letting go of her arms.

"With any luck, we'll be finding Wulfgar," Catti-brie said.

"That is our hope, yes," the drow agreed.

"How're ye feeling about that?" the woman asked bluntly.

Drizzt sat up straighter, staring at her hard. "How should I feel?"

"Are ye jealous?" Catti-brie asked. "Are ye fearing that Wulfgar's return—if he should return with us, I mean—will change some things in yer life that ye're not wanting changed?"

Drizzt gave a helpless chuckle, overwhelmed by Catti-brie's straight-forwardness and honesty. Something was beginning to burn between them, the drow knew, something long overdue yet still amazing and unexpected. Catti-brie had once loved Wulfgar, had even been engaged to marry him before his apparent demise in Mithral Hall, so what would happen if Wulfgar returned to them now—not the Wulfgar who had run away, the Wulfgar who had slapped Catti-brie hard—but the man they had once known, the man who had once taken Catti-brie's heart?

"Do I hope that Wulfgar's return will not affect our relationship in any negative way?" he asked. "Of course I do. And saying that, do I hope that Wulfgar returns to us? Of course I do. And I pray that he has climbed out of his darkness, back to the man we both once knew and loved."

Catti-brie settled comfortably and didn't interrupt, her interested expression prompting him to elaborate.

Drizzt began with a shrug. "I do not wish to live my life in a jealous manner," he said. "And I especially can not think in those terms with any of my true friends. My stake in Wulfgar's return is no less than your own. My happiness will be greater if once again the proud and noble barbarian I once adventured beside returns to my life.

"As for our friendship and what may come of it," Drizzt continued quietly, but with that same old self-assurance, that inner guidance that had walked the drow out of wicked Menzoberranzan and had carried him through so many difficult adventures and decisions ever since.

He gave a wistful smile and a shrug. "I live my life in the best manner I can," he said. "I act honestly and in good faith and with the hopes of good friendship, and I hope that things turn out for the best. I can only be this drow you see before you, whether or not Wulfgar returns to us. If in your heart and in mine, there is meant to be more between us, then it shall be. If not. . . ." He stopped and smiled and shrugged again.

"There ye go, with yer tongue wandering about again," Catti-brie said. "Did ye ever think ye should just shut up and kiss me?"

Chapter 12

The Lavender-eyed Statue

"Pull quiet, you oafs," Gayselle softly scolded as the small skiff approached the imposing lights of Waterdeep Harbor. "I hope to make shore without any notice at all."

The three oarsmen, half-ogres with burly muscles that lacked a gentle touch, grumbled amongst themselves but did try, with no success, to quiet the splash of the oars. Gayselle suffered through it, knowing they were doing the best they could. She would be glad when this business was ended, when she could be away from her present companions, whose names she did not know but who she'd nicknamed Lumpy, Grumpy, and Dumb-bunny.

She stayed up front of the skiff, trying to make out some markers along the shoreline that would guide her in. She had put into Waterdeep many, many times over the last few years and knew the place well. Most of all now, she wanted to avoid the long wharves and larger ships, wanted to get into the smaller, less observed and regulated docks, where a temporary berth could be bought for a few coins.

To her relief she noted that few of the guards were moving about the pier this dark evening. The skiff, even with the half-ogres' splashing, had little trouble gliding into the collection of small docks to the south of the long wharves.

Gayselle shifted back and reached to the nearest brute, Grumpy, holding out a satchel that held three small vials. "Drink and shift to human form," she explained. When Grumpy gave her a lewd smile as he took the satchel, she added, "A *male* human form. Sheila Kree would not suffer one of you to even briefly assume the form of a woman."

That brought some more grumbling from the brutes, but they each took a bottle and quaffed the liquid contents. One after another they transformed their physical features into those of human men.

Gayselle nodded with satisfaction and took a few long and steady breaths, considering the course before her. She knew the location of the target's house, of course. It was not far from the docks, set up on a hill above a rocky cove. They had to be done with this dark business quickly, she knew, for the polymorph potions would not last for very long, and the last thing Gayselle wanted was to be walking along Waterdeep's streets accompanied by a trio of half-ogres.

The woman made up her mind then and there that if the potions wore off and her companions became obvious as intruders, she would abandon them and go off on her own, deeper into the city, where she had friends who could get her back to Sheila Kree.

They set up the boat against one of the smaller docks, tying it off beside a dozen other similar boats quietly bumping the pier with the gentle ebb and flow of the tide. With no one about, Gayselle and her three "human" escorts moved with all speed to the north, off the docks and onto the winding avenues that would take them to Captain Deudermont's house.

* * * * *

Not so far away, Drizzt and Catti-brie walked through Waterdeep's northern gate, the drow easily brushing away the hard stares that came at him from nearly every sentry. One or two recognized him for who he was and said as much to their nervous companions, but it would take more than a few reassuring words to alleviate the average surface dweller's trepidation toward a drow elf.

It didn't bother Drizzt, for he had played through this scenario a hundred times before.

"They know ye, don't ye worry," Catti-brie whispered to him.

"Some," he agreed.

"Enough," the woman said flatly. "Ye canno' be expecting all the world to know yer name."

Drizzt gave a chuckle at that and shook his head in agreement. "And I know well enough that no matter what I may accomplish in my life, I will suffer their stares." He gave a sincere smile and a shrug. "Suffer is not the right word," he assured her. "Not any more."

Catti-brie started to respond but stopped short, her defiant words defeated by Drizzt's disarming smile. She had fought this battle for

994

acceptance beside her friend for all these years, in Icewind Dale, in Mithral Hall and Silverymoon, and even here in Waterdeep, and in every city and town along the Sword Coast during the years they sailed with Deudermont. In many ways, Catti-brie understood at that telling moment, she was more bothered by the stares than was Drizzt. She forced herself to take his lead this time, to let the looks slide off her shoulders, for surely Drizzt was doing just that. She could tell from the sincerity of his smile.

Drizzt stopped and spun about to face the guards, and the nearest couple jumped back in surprise.

"Is *Sea Sprite* in?" the drow asked.

"*S-Sea Sprite*?" one stammered in reply. "In where? What?"

An older soldier stepped by the flustered pair. "Captain Deudermont is not yet in," he explained. "Though he's expected for a last stop at least before the winter sets in."

Drizzt touched his hand to his forehead in a salute of thanks, then spun back and walked off with Catti-brie.

* * * * *

Delly Curtie was in fine spirits this evening. She had this feeling that Wulfgar would soon return with Aegis-fang and that she and her husband could finally get on with their lives.

Delly wasn't quite sure what that meant. Would they return to Luskan and life at the Cutlass with Arumn Gardpeck? She didn't think so. No, Delly understood that this hunt for Aegis-fang was about more than the retrieval of a warhammer—had it been just that, Delly would have discouraged Wulfgar from ever going out in search of the weapon.

This hunt was about Wulfgar finding himself, his past and his heart, and when that happened, Delly believed, he would also find his way back home—his true home, in Icewind Dale.

"And we will go there with him," she said to Colson, as she held the baby girl out at arms' length.

The thought of Icewind Dale appealed to Delly. She knew the hardships of the region, knew all about the tremendous snows and powerful winds, of the goblins and the yetis and other perils. But to Delly, who had grown up on the dirty streets of Luskan, there seemed something clean about Icewind Dale, something honest and pure, and in any case, she would be beside the man she loved, the man she loved more every day. She knew that when Wulfgar found himself, their relationship would only grow stronger.

She began to sing, then, dancing gracefully around the room, swinging Colson about as she turned and skittered, this way and that.

"Daddy will be home soon," she promised their daughter, and, as if understanding, Colson laughed.

And Delly danced.

And all the world seemed beautiful and full of possibilities.

* * * * *

Captain Deudermont's house was indeed palatial, even by Water-dhavian standards. It was two stories tall, with more than a dozen rooms. A great sweeping stairway dominated the foyer, which also sported a domed alcove that held two grand wooden double doors, each decorated with the carving of one half of a three-masted schooner. When the doors were closed, the image of *Sea Sprite* was clear to see. A second staircase in back led to the drawing room that overlooked the rocky cove and the sea.

This was Waterdeep, the City of Splendors, a city of laws. But despite the many patrols of the fabled Waterdhavian Watch and the general civil-ity of the populace, most of the larger houses, Deudermont's included, also employed personal guards.

Deudermont had hired two, former soldiers, former sailors, both of whom had actually served on *Sea Sprite* many years before. They were friends as much as hired hands, house guests as much as sentries. Though they took their job seriously, they couldn't help but be lax about their work. Every day was inevitably uneventful. Thus, the pair helped out with chores, working with Delly at repairing the shingles blown away by a sea wind, or with the nearly constant painting of the clapboards. They cooked and they cleaned. Sometimes they carried their weapons, and sometimes they did not, for they understood, and so did Deudermont, that they were there more as a preventative measure than anything else. The thieves of Waterdeep avoided homes known to house guards.

Thus the pair were perfectly unprepared for what befell the House of Deudermont that dark night.

Gayselle was the first to Deudermont's front door, accompanied by one of the brutes who, using the polymorph potion, was doing a pretty fair imitation of the physical traits of Captain Deudermont. So good, in fact, that Gayselle found herself wondering if she had misnamed the brute Dumb-bunny. With a look around to see that the streets were quiet, Gay-selle nodded to Lumpy, who was standing at the end of the walk, between the two hedgerows. Immediately, the brute began rubbing its feet on the stones, gaining traction and grinning wickedly.

One of the double doors opened to the knock, just three or four inches, for it was, as expected, secured with a chain. A clean-shaven, large man with short black hair and a brow so furrowed it seemed as if it could shield his eyes from a noonday sun, answered.

"Can I help you . . . ?"

His voice trailed off, though, as he scanned the man standing behind the woman, a man who surely resembled Captain Deudermont.

996

"I have brought the brother of Captain Deudermont," Gayselle answered. "Come to speak with his long-lost sibling."

The guard's eyes widened for just a moment, then he resumed his steely, professional demeanor. "Well met," he offered, "but I fear that your brother is not in Waterdeep at this time. Tell me where you will be staying and I will inform him as soon as he returns."

"Our funds are low," Gayselle answered quickly. "We have been on the road for a long time. We were hoping to find shelter here."

The guard thought it over for just a moment but then shook his head. His orders concerning such matters were uncompromising, despite this surprising twist, and especially so with a woman and her child as guests in the house. He started to explain, to tell them he was sorry, but that they could find shelter at one of several inns for a reasonable price.

Gayselle was hardly listening. She casually looked back down the walk, to the eager half-ogre. The pirate gave a slight nod, setting Lumpy into a charge.

"Perhaps you will then open your door for the third of my group," the woman said sweetly.

Again the guard shook his head. "I doubt—" he started to say, but then his words and his breath were stolen away as the half-ogre hit the doors in a dead run, splintering wood and tearing free the chain anchors. The guard was thrown back and to the floor, and the half-ogre stumbled in to land atop him.

In went Gayselle and the Deudermont impersonator, drawing weapons. The half-ogre willed away the illusionary image, dropping the human facade.

The guard on the floor started to call out, as he tried to scramble away from the half-ogre, but Gayselle was there, dagger in hand. With a swift and sure movement, she slashed open his throat.

The second guard came through the door at the side of the foyer. Then, his expression one of the purest horror, he sprinted for the stands.

Gayselle's dagger caught him in the back of the leg, hamstringing him. He continued on stubbornly, limping up the stairs and calling out. Dumb-bunny caught up to him and with fearful strength yanked him off the stairs and sent him flying back down to the bottom. The other half-ogre waited there.

Grumpy, still in human form, entered. He calmly closed the doors, though one no longer sat straight on its bent hinges.

* * * * *

Delly heard clearly the sour note from below that ended her song. Having grown up around ruffians, having seen and been involved in many, many brawls, the woman understood the gist of what was happening below.

997

"By the gods," she muttered, biting off a wail before it could give her and Colson away.

She hugged the child close to her and rushed to the door. She cracked it, peeked out, then swung it wide. She paused only long enough to kick off her hard shoes, knowing they would give her away, then padded quietly along the corridor between the wall and the banister. She hugged the wall, not wanting to be spotted from the foyer below, and that, she could tell from the noises—grunting and heavy punches—was where the intruders were. Had she been alone, she would have rushed down the stairs and joined in the fight, but with Colson in her arms, the woman's only thoughts were for the safety of her child.

Past the front stairs, Delly turned down a side passage and ran full out, cutting through Deudermont's personal suite to the back staircase. Down she went, holding her breath with every step, for she had no way of knowing if others might be in the house, perhaps even in the room below.

She heard a noise above her and understood that she had few options, so she pushed right through the door into the elaborate drawing room. One of the windows was open across the wide room. A chill breeze was blowing in, just catching the edge of one opened drape, fluttering it below the sash tie.

Delly considered the route. Those large windows overlooked a rocky drop to the cove. She cursed herself then for having discarded her shoes, but she knew in her heart that it made little difference. The climb was too steep and too treacherous—she doubted the intruders had gained access from that direction—and she didn't dare attempt it with Colson in her arms.

But where to go?

She turned for the room's main doors, leading to a corridor to the foyer. There were side rooms off that corridor, including the kitchen, which held a garbage chute. Thinking she and Colson could hide in there, she rushed to the doors and cracked them open—but slammed them immediately and dropped the locking bar across them when she saw the approach of hulking figures. She heard running steps on the other side, followed by a tremendous crash as someone hurled himself against the locked doors.

Delly glanced all around, to the stairs and the open window, not knowing where she should run. So flustered was she that she didn't even see another form slip into the room.

The doors got hit again and started to crack. Delly heard one powerful man pounding hard against the wood. The woman retreated.

Then came some running footsteps, and another threw himself against the doors. They burst open, a large hulking form going down atop the pile of kindling. A woman entered, flanked by one, and the second as the door-breaker stood up. They were two of the ugliest, most imposing brutes Delly Curtie had ever seen. She didn't know what they were, having had few experiences outside of Luskan, but from their splotchy greenish skin and sheer size she understood that they had to be some kind of giantkin.

"Well, well, pretty one," said the strange woman with a wicked smile. "You're not thinking of leaving before the party is over, are you?"

Delly turned for the stairs but didn't even start that way, seeing yet another of the brutes slowly descending, eyeing her lewdly with every step.

Delly considered the window behind her, the one that she and Wulfgar used to spend so many hours at, watching the setting sun or the reflection of the stars on the dark waters. She couldn't possibly get out and away without being caught, but she honestly considered that route anyway, thought of running full speed and throwing herself and Colson down onto the rocks, ending it quickly and mercifully.

Delly Curtie knew this type of ruffian and understood that she was surely doomed.

The woman and her two companions took a step toward her.

The window, Delly decided. She turned and fled, determined to leap far and wide to ensure a quick and painless end.

But the third giantkin had come down from the stairs by then, Delly's hesitation costing her the suicidal escape. The brute caught her easily with one huge arm, pinning her tightly to its massive chest.

It turned back, laughing, and was joined by the howls of its two ogre companions. The woman, though, seemed hardly amused. She stalked up to Delly, eyeing her every inch.

"You're Deudermont's woman, aren't you?" she asked.

"No," Delly answered honestly, but her sincerity was far from apparent in her tone, since she was trembling so with fear.

She wasn't so much afraid for herself as for Colson, though she knew that the next few moments of her life, likely the last few moments of her life, were going to be as horrible as anything she had ever known.

The strange woman calmly walked over to her, smiling. "Deudermont is your man?"

"No," Delly repeated, a bit more confidently.

The woman slapped her hard across the face, a blow that had Delly staggering back a step. A thug promptly pulled her forward, though, back into striking range.

"She's a tender one," the brute said with a lewd chuckle, and it gave Delly's arms a squeeze. "We plays with her 'fore we eats her!"

The other two in the room started laughing, one of them gyrating its hips crudely.

Delly felt her legs going weak beneath her, but she gritted her teeth and strengthened her resolve, realizing that she had a duty that went beyond the sacrifice that was soon to be forced upon her.

"Do as ye will with me," she said. "And I'll be making it good for ye, so long as ye don't hurt me baby."

The strange woman's eyes narrowed as Delly said that, the woman obviously not thrilled about Delly taking any kind of control at all. "You get your fun later," she said to her three companions, then she swiveled her head, scanning each in turn. "Now go and gather some loot. You wouldn't wish to face the boss without any loot, now would you?"

The brute holding Delly tensed at the words but didn't let her go. Its companions, however, scrambled wildly, falling all over each other in an attempt to satisfy their boss's demands.

"Please," Delly said to the woman. "I'm not a threat to ye and won't be any trouble. Just don't be hurting me babe. Ye're a woman, so ye know."

"Shut your mouth," the stranger interrupted harshly.

"Eats 'em both!" the giantkin holding Delly shouted, taking a cue from the woman's dismissive tone.

The woman came forward a step, hand upraised, and Delly flinched. But this slap went past her, striking the surprised brute. The woman stepped back, eyeing Delly once more.

"We will see about the baby," she said calmly.

"Please," Delly pleaded.

"For yourself, you're done with, and you know it," the woman went on, ignoring her. "But you tell us the best loot and we might take pity on the little one. I might even consider taking her in myself."

Delly tried hard not to wince at that wretched thought.

The stranger's smile widened as she leaned closer, regarding the child. "She can not be pointing us out to the watch, after all, now can she?"

Delly knew she should say something constructive at that point, knew that she should sort through the terror and the craziness of all of this and lead the woman on in the best direction for the sake of Colson. But it proved to be too much for her, a stymieing realization that she was soon to die, that her daughter was in mortal peril, and there was not a thing she could do about it. She stuttered and stammered and in the end said nothing at all.

The woman curled up her fist and punched Delly hard, right in the face. As Delly fell away, the stranger tore Colson from her arms.

Delly reached out even as she fell, trying to grab the baby back, but the big thug drove a heavy forearm across her chest, speeding her descent. She landed hard on her back, and the brute wasted no time in scrambling atop her.

A crash from the side granted her a temporary reprieve, all eyes turning to see one of the other brutes standing amidst a pile of broken dinnerware—very expensive dinnerware.

"Find something for carrying it, you fool!" the woman yelled at him. She glanced all about the room, finally settling her gaze on one of the heavy, long drapes, then motioned for the creature to be quick.

She gave a disgusted sigh, then stepped forward and kicked the brute that was still atop Delly hard in the ribs. "Just kill the witch and be done with it," she said.

The brute looked up at her, as defiant as any of them had yet been, and shook its head.

To Delly's dismay, the woman merely waved away the ugly creature, giving in.

Delly closed her eyes and tried to let her mind fly free of her body.

The thug that had dropped the dinnerware scrambled across the room to the drapery beside the open window and with one great tug, pulled it free. The brute started to turn back for the remaining dinnerware, but it stopped, regarding a curious sculpture revealed by removing the curtain. It was a full-sized elf figure, dressed in the garb of an adventurer and apparently made of some ebony material, black stone or wood. It stood with eyes closed and two ornate scimitars presented in a cross-chest pose.

"Huh?" the brute said.

"Huh?" it said again, reaching slowly to feel the smooth skin.

The eyes popped open, penetrating, lavender orbs that froze the giantkin in place, that seemed to tell the brute without the slightest bit of doubt that its time in this world was fast ending.

* * * * *

With a blur the creature hardly even registered, the "statue" exploded into motion, scimitars cutting left and right. Around spun the drow elf, gaining momentum for even mightier slashes. A double-cut, one scimitar following the other, opened the stunned half-ogre from shoulder to hip. A quick-step put the drow right beside the falling brute. He reversed his grip with his right hand and plunged one enchanted blade deeply into the half-ogre's back, severing its spine, then half-turned and hamstrung the beast—both legs—with a precise and devastating slash of the other blade.

Drizzt stepped aside as the dying half-ogre crumbled to the floor.

"You should probably get off of her," the drow said casually to the next brute, who was laying atop Delly, staring at Drizzt incredulously.

Before the pirate woman could even growl out, "Kill him!" the third half-ogre charged across the room at Drizzt, a course that brought it right past the opened window. Halfway across, a flying black form intercepted the brute. Six hundred pounds of snapping teeth and raking claws stopped dead the half-ogre's progress toward Drizzt and launched it back toward the center of the room.

The brute flailed wildly, but the panther had too many natural weapons and too much sheer strength. Guenhwyvar snapped one forearm in her maw, then ripped her head back and forth, shattering the bone and tearing the flesh. All the while, the panther's front paws clawed repeatedly at the frantic brute's face, too quick for the other arm to block. Guen's powerful back legs found holds on the half-ogre's legs and torso, claws digging in, then tearing straight back.

The surviving half-ogre rolled off of Delly and onto its feet. It lifted its weapon, a heavy broadsword, and rushed the drow, thinking to cut Drizzt in half with a single stroke.

The slashing sword met only air as the agile drow easily side-stepped the blow, then poked Twinkle into the brute's belly and danced another step away.

The half-ogre grabbed at the wound, but only for a moment. It came on fast with a straightforward thrust.

The scimitar Icingdeath, in Drizzt's left hand, easily turned the broadsword to the side. Drizzt stepped forward beside the lunging brute and poked it hard again with Twinkle, this time the scimitar's tip scratching off a thick rib.

The half-ogre roared and spun, slashing mightily as it went, expecting to cut Drizzt in half. Again the blade cut only air.

The half-ogre paused, dumbfounded, for its opponent was nowhere to be seen.

"Strong, but slow," came the drow's voice behind it. "Terrible combination."

The half-ogre howled in fear and leaped to the side, but Icingdeath was quicker, slashing in hard at the side of its neck. The half-ogre took three running strides, hand going up to its torn neck, then stumbled to one knee, then to the ground, writhing in agony.

Drizzt started toward it to finish it off but changed direction and stopped cold, staring hard at the woman who had backed to the wall beside the room's broken doors. The baby girl was in her arms, with a narrow, deadly dagger pressed up against the child's throat.

"What business does a dark elf have in Waterdeep?" the woman asked, trying to sound calm and confident, but obviously shaken. "If you wish the house as your own target, I will leave it to you. I assure you I have no interest in speaking with the authorities." The woman paused and stared hard at Drizzt, a smile of recognition at last coming over her.

"You are no drow come from the lightless depths as part of a raid," the woman remarked. "You sailed with Deudermont."

Drizzt bowed to her and didn't even bother trying to stop the last half-ogre he had grievously wounded as it crawled toward the woman. Across the room, Guenhwyvar stalked about the wall, flanking the woman, leaving the other half-ogre torn and dead in a puddle of its own blood and gore.

"And who are you who comes unbidden to the House of Deudermont?" Drizzt asked. "Along with some less-than-acceptable companions."

"Give me Colson!" pleaded the second woman—who must have been Delly Curtie. She was still on the floor, propped on her elbows. "Oh, please. She has done nothing."

"Silence!" the pirate roared at her. She looked back at Drizzt, pointedly turning that nasty dagger over and over against the child's throat. "She will get her child back, and alive," the woman explained. "Once I am out of here, running free."

"You bargain with that which you only think you possess," Drizzt remarked, coming forward a step.

The half-ogre had reached its boss by that time. With great effort, it worked itself into a kneeling position before her, climbing its arms up the wall and pulling itself to its knees.

Gayselle gave it one look, then her hand flashed, driving her dagger deep into the brute's throat. It fell away gasping, dying.

The woman, obviously no novice to battle, had the dagger back at the child's throat in an instant, a flashing movement that made Delly cry out and had both Drizzt and Guenhwyvar breaking for her briefly. But only briefly, for that dagger was in place too quickly, and there could be no doubt that she would put it to use.

"I could not take him with me and could not leave the big mouth behind," the woman explained as the drow looked at her dying half-ogre companion.

"As I can not let you leave with the child," the drow replied.

"But you can, for you have little choice," she announced. "I will leave this place, and I will send word as to where you can retrieve the uninjured babe."

"No," Drizzt corrected. "You will give the babe to her mother, then leave this place, never to return."

The woman laughed at the notion. "Your panther friend would catch me and pull me down before I made the street," she said.

"I give you my word," Drizzt offered.

Again, the woman laughed. "I am to take the word of a drow elf?"

"And I am to take the word of a thief and murderess?" Drizzt was quick to reply.

"But you have no choice, drow," the woman explained, lifting the baby closer to her face, looking at it with a strange, cold expression, and sliding the flat of the dagger back and forth over Colson's neck.

Delly Curtie whimpered again and buried her face in her hands.

"How are you to stop me, drow?" the woman teased.

Even as the words left her mouth, a streak like blue lightning shot across the room, over the prone form of Delly Curtie, cutting right beside the tender flesh of Colson, to nail the pirate woman right between the eyes, slamming her back against the wall and pinning her there.

Her arms flew out wide, jerking spasmodically, the baby falling from her grasp.

But not to the floor, for as soon as he heard that familiar bowstring, Drizzt dived into a forward roll, coming around right before the pinned woman and gently catching Colson in his outstretched hands. He stood up and stared at the pirate.

The woman was already dead. Her arms gave a few more jerking spasms, and she went limp, hanging there, skull pinned to the wall. She wasn't seeing or hearing anything of this world.

"Just like that," Drizzt told her anyway.

Chapter 13

Winter Settling

"Never much liked this place," Bruenor grumbled as he and Regis stood at the north gate of Luskan. They had been held up for a long, long time by the curious and suspicious guards.

"They'll let us in soon," Regis replied. "They always get like this as the weather turns—that's when the scum floats down from the mountains, after all. And when the highwaymen wander back into the city, pretending as if they belonged there all along."

Bruenor spat on the ground.

Finally, the guard who'd first stopped them returned, along with another, older soldier.

"My friend says you've come from Icewind Dale," the older man remarked. "And what goods have you brought to sell over the winter?"

"I bringed meself, and that oughta be enough for ye," Bruenor grumbled. The soldier eyed him dangerously.

"We've come to meet up with friends who are on the road," Regis was quick to interject, in a calmer tone.

He stepped between Bruenor and the soldier, trying to diffuse a potentially volatile situation—for any situation involving Bruenor

Battlehammer was volatile these days! The dwarf was anxious to find his lost son, and woe to any who hindered him on that road.

"I am a councilor in Ten-Towns," the halfling explained. "Regis of Lonelywood. Perhaps you have heard of me?"

The soldier, his bristles up from Bruenor's attitude, spat at the halfling's feet. "Nope."

"And my companion is Bruenor Battlehammer himself," Regis said, somewhat dramatically. "Leader of Clan Battlehammer in Ten-Towns. Once, and soon again to be, King of Mithral Hall."

"Never heard of that either."

"But oh, ye're gonna," Bruenor muttered. He started around Regis, and the halfling skittered to stay in his way.

"Tough one, aren't you?" the soldier said.

"Please, good sir, enough of this foolishness," Regis pleaded. "Bruenor is in a terrible way, for he has lost his son, who is rumored to be sailing with Captain Deudermont."

This brought a puzzled expression to the face of the old soldier. "Haven't heard of any dwarves sailing on *Sea Sprite*," he said.

"His son is no dwarf, but a warrior, proud and strong," Regis explained. "Wulfgar by name." The halfling thought that he was making progress here, but, at the mention of Wulfgar's name, the soldier took on a most horrified and outraged expression.

"If you're calling that oaf your son, then you are far from welcome in Luskan!" the soldier declared.

Regis sighed, knowing what was to come. The many-notched axe hit the ground at his feet. At least Bruenor wouldn't cut the man in half. The halfling tried to anticipate the dwarf's movements to keep between the two, but Bruenor casually picked him up and turned around, dropping Regis behind him.

"Ye stay right there," the dwarf instructed, wagging a gnarly, crooked finger in the halfling's face.

By the time the dwarf turned back around, the soldier had drawn his sword.

Bruenor regarded it and laughed. "Now, what was ye saying about me boy?" he asked.

"I said he was an oaf," the man said, after glancing around to make sure he had enough support in the area. "And there are a million other insults I could rightfully hurl at the one named Wulfgar, murderer and rogue among them!"

He almost finished the sentence.

He almost got his sword up in time to block Bruenor's missile—that missile being Bruenor's entire body.

* * * * *

Drizzt turned to see a ragged and dirty Catti-brie standing at the window, outside and leaning on the pane, grim-faced and with Taulmaril in hand.

"It took you long enough," the drow remarked, but his humor found no spot in Catti-brie—not so soon after the kill. She stared right past Drizzt, not even registering his words. Would such actions ever become less troubling to her?

A big part of the woman who was Catti-brie hoped they would not.

Delly Curtie sprang up from the floor and rushed at Drizzt, running to her crying child's call. The woman calmed as she neared, for the smiling dark elf held the unharmed, though obviously upset child out to her and gladly handed Colson over.

"It would have been easier if you came up right behind me," Drizzt said to Catti-brie. "We could have saved some trouble."

"Are these looking like elven-bred to ye?" the woman growled back, pointing to her eyes—human orbs far inferior in the low light of the Waterdeep night. "And are ye thinking this to be an easy climb?"

Drizzt shrugged, grinning still. After all, the rocky climb hadn't given him any trouble at all.

"Go back down, then," Catti-brie insisted. She threw one leg over the window and eased herself into the room, not moving quickly, for her pant leg was torn, her leg bleeding. "Come back up with yer eyes closed, and ye tell me how easy them wet rocks might be for climbing."

She stumbled into the room, moving forward a few steps before fully gaining her balance—and that put her right in front of Delly Curtie and the baby.

"Catti-brie," the woman said. Her tone, while friendly and grateful enough, showed that she was a bit uneasy with seeing Catti-brie here.

The woman from Icewind Dale gave a slight bow. "And ye're Delly Curtie, unless I'm missing me guess," she replied. "Me and me friend just came from Luskan, from the tavern of Arumn Gardpeck."

Delly gave a chuckle and seemed to breathe for the first time since the fighting began. She looked from Catti-brie to Drizzt, knowing them from the tales Wulfgar had told to her. "Never seen a drow elf before," she said. "But I've heard all about ye from me man."

Despite herself, Catti-brie started at that remark, her blue eyes widening. She looked at Drizzt and saw him regarding her knowingly. She just grinned, shook her head, and turned her sights back on Delly.

"From Wulfgar," Delly said evenly.

"Wulfgar is yer man?" Catti-brie asked bluntly.

"He's been," Delly admitted, chewing her bottom lip.

Catti-brie read the woman perfectly. She understood that Delly was afraid, not of any physical harm, but that the return of Catti-brie into Wulfgar's life would somehow endanger her relationship with him. But Delly was ambiguous, as well, Catti-brie understood, for she couldn't rightly be upset about the arrival of Catti-brie and Drizzt, considering the pair had just saved her and her baby from certain death.

"We have come to find him," Drizzt explained, "to see if it is time for him to come home, to Icewind Dale."

"He's not alone anymore, ye know," Delly said to the drow. "He's got . . ." She started to name herself, but stopped and presented Colson instead. "He's got a little one to take care of."

"So we heard, but a confusing tale, it seems," Catti-brie said, approaching. "Can I hold the girl?"

Delly pulled the still-crying child in closer. "She's afraid," she explained. "Best that she's with her ma."

Catti-brie smiled at her, offering an expression that was honestly warm.

Their joy at the rescue was muted somewhat when Drizzt left Delly and Catti-brie in the drawing room and confirmed just how bloodthirsty this band truly had been. He found the two house guards murdered in the foyer, one lying by the door, one on the stairs. He went out front of the house, then, and called out repeatedly, until there at last came a reply.

"Go and fetch the watch," Drizzt bade the neighbor. "A murder most terrible has occurred!"

The drow went back to Delly and Catti-brie. He found Delly sitting with the child, trying to stop her crying, while Catti-brie stood by the window, staring out, with Guenhwyvar curled up on the floor beside her.

"She's got quite a tale to tell us of our Wulfgar," Catti-brie said to Drizzt.

The drow looked at Delly Curtie.

"He's speaking of ye both often," Delly explained. "Ye should know the road he's walked."

"Soon enough, then," Drizzt replied. "But not now. The authorities should arrive momentarily." The dark elf glanced around the room as he finished, his gaze landing alternately on the bodies of the intruders. "Do you have any idea what might have precipitated this attack?" he asked Delly.

"Deudermont's made many enemies," Catti-brie reminded him from the window, not even turning about as she spoke.

"Nothing more than the usual," Delly agreed. "Lots who'd like Captain Deudermont's head, but nothing special is afoot that I'm knowing."

Drizzt paused before responding, thinking to ask Delly what she knew of this pirate who supposedly had Wulfgar's warhammer. He looked again at the fallen intruders, settling his gaze on the woman.

The pattern fit, he realized, given what he had learned from the encounter with Jule Pepper in Icewind Dale and from Morik the Rogue. He crossed the room, ignoring the noise of the authorities coming to the front door, and moved right beside the dead woman, who was still stuck upright against the wall, pinned by Catti-brie's arrow.

"What're ye doing?" Catti-brie asked as Drizzt tugged at the collar of the dead woman's bloody tunic. "Just pull the damned arrow out to drop her from the perch."

Catti-brie was obviously unnerved by the sight of the dead woman, the sight of her latest kill, but Drizzt wasn't trying to pull this one down. Far from it, her present angle afforded him the best view.

He took out one scimitar and used its fine edge to slice through the clothing a bit, enough so that he could pull the fabric down low over the back of the dead woman's shoulder.

The drow nodded, far from surprised.

"What is it?" Delly asked from her seat, where she had at last quieted Colson.

Catti-brie's expression showed that she was about to ask the same thing, but it shifted almost at once as she considered the angle with which Drizzt was viewing the woman and the knowing expression stamped upon his dark face. "She's branded," Catti-brie answered, though she remained across the room.

"The mark of Aegis-fang," Drizzt confirmed. "The mark of Sheila Kree."

"What does it mean?" asked a concerned Delly, and she rose out of her chair, moving toward the drow, hugging her child close like some living, emotional armor. "Does it mean that Wulfgar and Captain Deudermont have caught Sheila Kree, and so her friends're trying to hit back?" she asked, looking nervously from the drow to the woman at the window. "Or might it mean that Sheila's sunk *Sea Sprite* and now is coming to finish off everything connected with Captain Deudermont and his crew?" Her voice rose as she finished, an edge of anxiety bubbling over.

"Or it means nothing more than that the pirate has learned that Captain Deudermont is in pursuit of her, and she wished to strike the first blow," Drizzt replied, unconvincingly.

"Or it means nothing at all," Catti-brie added. "Just a coincidence."

The other two looked at her, but none, not even Catti-brie, believed that for a moment.

The door crashed open a moment later and a group of soldiers charged into the room. Some turned immediately for the dark elf, howling at the sight of a drow, but others recognized Drizzt, or at least recognized Delly Curtie and saw by her posture that the danger had passed. They held their companions at bay.

Catti-brie ushered Delly Curtie away, the woman bearing the child, and with Catti-brie calling Guenhwyvar to follow, while Drizzt gave the authorities a full account of what had occurred. The drow didn't stop at that, but went on to explain the likely personal feud heightening between Sheila Kree and Captain Deudermont.

After he had secured a net of soldiers to stand guard about the house, Drizzt went upstairs to join the women.

He found them in good spirits, with Catti-brie rocking Colson and Delly resting on the bed, a glass of wine in hand.

Catti-brie nodded to the woman, and without further word, Delly launched into her tale of Wulfgar, telling Drizzt and Catti-brie all about the barbarian's decline in Luskan, his trial at Prisoner's Carnival, his flight to the north with Morik and the circumstances that had brought him the child.

"Surprised was I when Wulfgar came back to the Cutlass," Delly finished. "For me!"

She couldn't help but glance at Catti-brie as she said that, somewhat nervously, somewhat superiorly. The auburn-haired woman's expression hardly changed, though.

"He came to apologize, and oh, but he owed it to us all," Delly went on. "We left, us three—me man and me child—to find Captain Deudermont, and for Wulfgar to find Aegis-fang. He's out there now," Delly ended, staring out the west-facing window. "So I'm hoping."

"Sheila Kree has not met up with *Sea Sprite* yet," Drizzt said to her. "Or if she has, then her ship is at the bottom of those cold waters, and Wulfgar is on his way back to Waterdeep."

"Ye can not know that," Delly said.

"But we will find out," a determined Catti-brie put in.

* * * * *

"The winter fast approaches," Captain Deudermont remarked to Wulfgar, the two of them standing at *Sea Sprite*'s rail as the ship sailed along at a great clip. They had seen no pirates over the past few tendays, and few merchant vessels save the last groups making the southern run out of Luskan.

Wulfgar, who had grown up in Icewind Dale and knew well the change of the season—a dramatic and swift change this far north—didn't disagree. He, too, had seen the signs, the noticeably chilly shift in the wind and the change of direction, flowing more from the northwest now, off the cold waters of the Sea of Moving Ice.

"We will not put in to Luskan, but sail straight for Waterdeep," Deudermont explained. "There, we will ready the ship for winter sailing."

"Then you do not intend to put in for the season," Wulfgar reasoned.

"No, but our route will be south out of Waterdeep harbor and not north," Deudermont pointedly explained. "Perhaps we will patrol off of Baldur's Gate, perhaps even farther south. Robillard has made it clear that he would prefer a busy winter and has mentioned the Pirate Isles to me many times."

Wulfgar nodded grimly, understanding more from Deudermont's leading tone than from his actual words. The captain was politely inviting him to debark in Waterdeep and remain there with Delly and Colson.

"You will need my strong arm," Wulfgar said, less than convincingly.

"We are not likely to find Sheila Kree south of Waterdeep," Deudermont said clearly. "*Bloody Keel* has never been known to sail south of the City of Splendors. She has a reputation for putting into dock, wherever that dock may be, for the winter months."

There, he had said it, plainly and bluntly. Wulfgar looked at him, trying hard to take no offense. Logically, he understood the captain's reasoning. He hadn't been of much help to *Sea Sprite*'s efforts of late, he had to admit. While that only made him want to get right back into battle, he understood that Deudermont had more to worry about than the sensibilities of one warrior.

Wulfgar found it hard to get the words out of his mouth, but he graciously said, "I will spend the winter with my family. If you would allow us the use of your house through the season."

"Of course," said Deudermont. He managed a smile and gently patted Wulfgar on the shoulder, which meant that he had to reach up a considerable distance. "Enjoy these moments with your family," he said quietly and with great compassion. "We will seek out Sheila Kree in the spring, on my word, and Aegis-fang will be returned to its rightful owner."

Every fiber within Wulfgar wanted to refuse this entire scenario, wanted to shout out at Deudermont that he was not a broken warrior, that he would find his way back to the battle, with all of the fury, and, more importantly, with all of the discipline demanded by a crack crew. He wanted to explain to the captain that he would find his way clear, to assure the man that the warrior who was Wulfgar, son of Beornegar, was waiting to be freed of this emotional prison to find his way back.

But Wulfgar held back the thoughts. In light of his recent, dangerous failures in battle, it was not his place to argue with Deudermont but rather to graciously accept the captain's polite excuse to get him off the ship.

They would be in Waterdeep in a tenday's time, and there Wulfgar would stay.

* * * * *

Delly Curtie found Drizzt and Catti-brie packing their belongings, preparing to leave Deudermont's house early the next morning.

"*Sea Sprite* will likely return soon," she explained to the duo.

"Likely," Drizzt echoed. "But I fear there might already be news of a confrontation between Kree and *Sea Sprite*, farther in the north. We will go to Luskan, where we are to meet with some friends and follow a trail that will take us to Kree, or to Wulfgar."

Delly thought about it for just a moment. "Give me some time to pack and to ready Colson," she said.

1011

Catti-brie was shaking her head before Delly ever finished the thought. "Ye'll slow us down," she said.

"If ye're going to Wulfgar, then me place is with yerself," the woman replied firmly.

"We're not knowing that we're going to Wulfgar," Catti-brie replied with all honesty and with measured calm. "It might well be that Wulfgar will soon enough be here, with *Sea Sprite*. If that's the truth, then better that ye're here to meet with him and tell him all that ye know."

"If you come with us, and *Sea Sprite* puts into Waterdeep, Wulfgar will be terribly worried about you," Drizzt explained. "You stay here—the watch will keep you and your child safe now."

Delly considered the pair for a few moments, her trepidation obvious on her soft features. Catti-brie caught it clearly and certainly understood.

"If we're first to Wulfgar, then we'll be coming with him back here," she said, and Delly relaxed visibly.

After a moment, the woman nodded her agreement.

Drizzt and Catti-brie left a short while later, after gaining assurances from the authorities that Deudermont's house, and Delly and Colson, would be guarded day and night.

"Our road's going back and forth," Catti-brie remarked to the drow as they made their way out of the great city's northern gate. "And all the while, Wulfgar's sailing out there, back and forth. We've just got to hope that our routes cross soon enough, though I'm thinking that he'll be landing in Waterdeep while we're walking into Luskan."

Drizzt didn't crack a smile at her humorous words and tone. He looked to her and stared intently, giving her a moment to reflect on the raid of the previous night, and the dangerous implications, then said grimly, "We've just got to hope that *Sea Sprite* is still afloat and that Wulfgar is still alive."

Part 3

The Bloody Trail

Once again Catti-brie shows me that she knows me better than I know myself. As we came to understand that Wulfgar was climbing out of his dark hole, was truly resurfacing into the warrior he had once been, I have to admit a bit of fear, a bit of jealousy. Would he come back as the man who once stole Catti-brie's heart? Or had he, in fact, ever really done that? Was their planned marriage more a matter of convenience on both parts, a logical joining of the only two humans, matched in age and beauty, among our little band?

I think it was a little of both, and hence my jealousy. For though I understand that I have become special to Catti-brie in ways I had never before imagined, there is a part of me that wishes no one else ever had. For though I am certain that we two share many feelings that are new and exciting to both of us, I do not like to consider the possibility that she ever shared such emotions with another, even one who is so dear a friend.

Perhaps especially one who is so dear a friend!

But even as I admit all this, I know that I must take a deep breath and blow all of my fears and jealousies away. I must remind myself that I love this woman, Catti-brie, and that this woman is who she is because of a combination of all the experiences that brought her to this point. Would I prefer that her human parents had never died? On the one hand, of course! But if they hadn't, Catti-brie would not have wound up as Bruenor's adopted daughter, would likely not have come to reside in Icewind Dale at all. Given that, it is unlikely that we would have ever met. Beyond that, if she had been raised in a traditional human manner, she never would have become the warrior that she now is, the person who can best share my sense of adventure, who can accept the hardships of the road with good humor and risk, and allow me to risk—everything!—when going against the elements and the monsters of the world.

Hindsight, I think, is a useless tool. We, each of us, are at a place in our lives because of innumerable circumstances, and we, each of us, have a responsibility (if we do not like where we are) to move along life's road, to find a better path if this one does not suit, or to walk happily along this one if it is indeed our life's way. Changing even the bad things that have gone before would fundamentally change who we now are, and whether or not that would be a good thing, I believe, is impossible to predict.

So I take my past experiences and let Catti-brie take hers and try to regret nothing for either. I just try to blend our current existence into something grander and more beautiful together.

What of Wulfgar, then? He has a new bride and a child who is neither his nor hers naturally. And yet, it was obvious from Delly Curtie's face, and from her willingness to give herself if only the child would be unharmed that she loves the babe as if it was her own. I think the same must be true for Wulfgar because, despite the trials, despite the more recent behaviors, I know who he is, deep down, beneath the crusted, emotionally hardened exterior.

I know from her words that he loves this woman, Delly Curtie, and yet I know that he once loved Catti-brie as well.

What of this mystery, love? What is it that brings about this most elusive of magic? So many times I have heard people proclaim that their partner is their only love, the only possible completion to their soul, and surely I feel that way about Catti-brie, and I expect that she feels the same about me. But logically, is that possible? Is there one other person out there who can complete the soul of another? Is it really one for one, or is it rather a matter of circumstance?

Or do reasoning beings have the capacity to love many, and situation instead of fate brings them together?

Logically, I know the answer to be the latter. I know that if Wulfgar, or Catti-brie, or myself resided in another part of the world, we would all likely find that special completion to our soul, and with another. Logically, in a world of varying races and huge populations, that must be the case, or how, then, would true lovers ever meet? I am a thinking creature, a rational being, and so I know this to be the truth.

Why is it, then, that when I look at Catti-brie, all of those logical arguments make little sense? I remember our first meeting, when she was barely a young woman—more a girl, actually—and I saw her on the side of Kelvin's Cairn. I remember looking into her blue eyes on that occasion, feeling the warmth of her smile and the openness of her heart—something I had not much encountered since coming to the surface world—and feeling a definite bond there, a magic I could not explain. And as I watched her grow, that bond only strengthened.

So was it situation or fate? I know what logic says.

But I know, too, what my heart tells me.

It was fate. She is the one.

Perhaps situation allows for some, even most, people to find a suitable partner, but there is much more to it than finding just that. Perhaps some people are just more fortunate than others.

When I look into Catti-brie's blue eyes, when I feel the warmth of her smile and the openness of her heart, I know that I am.

—Drizzt Do'Urden

Chapter 14

Confirmation

"Ye've been keeping yer eyes and ears on the elf?" Sheila Kree asked Bellany when the woman joined her in her private quarters that blustery autumn day.

"Le'lorinel is at work on *Bloody Keel*, attending to duties with little complaint or argument," the sorceress replied.

"Just what I'd be expectin' from a spy."

Bellany shrugged, brushing back her dark hair, her expression a dismissal of Sheila Kree's suspicions. "I have visited Le'lorinel privately and without permission. Magically, when Le'lorinel believed the room was empty. I have seen or heard nothing to make me doubt the elf's story."

"A dark elf," Sheila Kree remarked, going to the opening facing the sea, her red hair fluttering back from the whistling salty breeze that blew in. "A dark elf will seek us out, by Le'lorinel's own words." She half-turned to regard Bellany, who seemed as if she might believe anything at that moment.

"If this dark elf, this Drizzt Do'Urden, does seek us out, then we will be glad we have not disposed of that one," the sorceress reasoned.

Sheila Kree turned back to the sea, shaking her head as if it seemed impossible. "And how long should we be waitin' before we decide that Le'lorinel is a spy?" she asked.

"We can not keel-haul the elf while *Bloody Keel* is in dock anyway," Bellany said with a chuckle, and her reasoning brightened Sheila's mood as well. "The winter will not be so long, I expect."

It wasn't the first time these two had shared such a discussion. Ever since Le'lorinel had arrived with the wild tale of a dark elf and a dwarf king coming to retrieve the warhammer, which Sheila believed she had honestly purchased from the fool Josi Puddles, the boss and her sorceress advisor had spent countless hours and endless days debating the fate of this strange elf. And on many of those days, Bellany had left Sheila thinking that Le'lorinel would likely be dead before the next dawn.

And yet, the elf remained alive.

"A visitor, boss lady," came a guttural call from the door. A half-ogre guard entered, leading a tall and willowy black-haired woman, flanked by a pair of the half-ogre's kin. Both Sheila and Bellany gawked in surprise when they noted the newcomer.

"Jule Pepper," Sheila said incredulously. "I been thinking that ye must own half the Ten-Towns by now!"

The black-haired woman, obviously bolstered by the warm tone from her former boss, shook her arms free of the two brutes flanking her and walked across the room to share a hug with Sheila and one with Bellany.

"I was doing well," the highwaywoman purred. "I had a band of reasonable strength working under me, and on a scheme that seemed fairly secure. Or so I thought, until a certain wretched drow elf and his friends showed up to end the party."

Sheila Kree and Bellany turned to each other in surprise, the pirate boss giving an amazed snort. "A dark elf?" she asked Jule. "Wouldn't happen to be one named Drizzt Do'Urden, would it?"

* * * * *

Even without the aid of wizards and clerics, without their magic spells of divination and communication, word traveled fast along the northern stretches of the Sword Coast, particularly when the news concerned the people living outside the restrictions and sensibilities of the law, and even more particularly when the hero of the hour was of a race not known for such actions. From tavern to tavern, street to street, boat to boat, and port to port went the recounting of the events at the house of Captain Deudermont, of how a mysterious drow elf and his two companions, one a great cat, throttled a theft and murder plot against the good captain's house. Few made the connection between Drizzt and Wulfgar or even between Drizzt and Deudermont, though some did know that a dark elf once had sailed on *Sea Sprite*. It was a juicy tale bringing great interest on its own, but for the folks of the city bowels, ones who understood that such attempts against a noble and heroic citizen were rarely self-contained things, the interest was even greater. There were surely implications here that went beyond the events in the famous captain's house.

So the tale sped along the coast, and even at one point did encounter some wizardly assistance in moving it along, and so the news of the events at the house long preceded the arrival of Drizzt and Catti-brie in Luskan, and so the news spread even faster farther north.

Sheila Kree knew of the loss of Gayselle before the dark elf crossed through Luskan's southern gate.

The pirate stormed about her private rooms, overturning tables and swearing profusely. She called a pair of half-ogre sentries in so that she could yell at them and slap them, playing out her frustrations for a long, long while.

Finally, too exhausted to continue, the red-haired pirate dismissed the guards and picked up a chair so that she could fall into it, cursing still under her breath.

It made no sense to her. Who was this stupid dark elf—the same one who had foiled Jule Pepper's attempts to begin a powerful band in Ten-Towns—and how in the world did he happen to wind up at Captain Deudermont's house at the precise time to intercept Gayselle's band? Sheila Kree closed her eyes and let it all sink in.

"Redecorating?" came a question from the doorway, and Sheila opened her eyes to see Bellany, a bemused smile on her face, standing at the door.

"Ye heard o' Gayselle?" Sheila asked.

The sorceress shrugged as if it didn't matter. "She'll not be the last we lose."

"I'm thinkin' that I'm hearing too much about a certain drow elf of late," Sheila remarked.

"Seems we have made an enemy," Bellany agreed. "How fortunate that we have been forewarned."

"Where's the elf?"

"At work on the boat, as with every day. Le'lorinel goes about any duties assigned without a word of complaint."

"There's but one focus for that one."

"A certain dark elf," Bellany agreed. "Is it time for Le'lorinel to take a higher step in our little band?"

"Time for a talk, at least," Sheila replied, and Bellany didn't have to be told twice. She turned around with a nod and headed off for the lower levels to fetch the elf, whose tale had become so much more intriguing with the return of Jule Pepper and the news of the disaster in Waterdeep.

* * * * *

"When ye first came wandering in, I thought to kill ye dead and be done with ye," Sheila Kree remarked bluntly. The pirate nodded to her burly guards, and they rushed in close, grabbing Le'lorinel fast by the arms.

"I have not lied to you, have done nothing to deserve—" Le'lorinel started to protest.

"Oh, ye're to get what ye're deserving," Sheila Kree assured the elf. She walked over and grabbed a handful of shirt, and with a wicked grin and a sudden jerk, she tore the shirt away, stripping the elf to the waist.

The two half-ogres giggled. Sheila Kree motioned to the door at the back of the room, and the brutes dragged their captive off, through the door and into a smaller room, undecorated except for a hot fire pit near one wall and a block set at about waist height in the center.

"What are you doing?" Le'lorinel demanded in a tone that held its calm edge, despite the obvious trouble.

"It's gonna hurt," Sheila Kree promised as the half-ogres yanked the elf across the block, holding tight.

Le'lorinel struggled futilely against the powerful press.

"Now, ye tell me again about the drow elf, Drizzt Do'Urden," Sheila remarked.

"I told you everything, and honestly," Le'lorinel protested.

"Tell me again," said Sheila.

"Yes, do," came another voice, that of Bellany, who walked into the room. "Tell us about this fascinating character who has suddenly become so very important to us."

"I heard of the killings at Captain Deudermont's house," Le'lorinel remarked, grunting as the half-ogres pulled a bit too hard. "I warned you that Drizzt Do'Urden is a powerful enemy."

"But one ye're thinking ye can defeat," Sheila interjected.

"I have prepared for little else."

"And have ye prepared for the pain?" Sheila asked wickedly. Le'lorinel felt an intense heat.

"I do not deserve this!" the elf protested, but the sentence ended with an agonized scream as the glowing hot metal came down hard on Le'lorinel's back.

The sickly smell of burning skin permeated the room.

"Now, ye tell us all about Drizzt Do'Urden again," Sheila Kree demanded some time later, when Le'lorinel had come back to consciousness and sensibility. "Everything, including why ye're so damned determined to see him dead."

Still held over the block, Le'lorinel stared at the pirate long and hard.

"Ah, let the fool go," Sheila told the half-ogres. "And get ye gone, both of ye!"

The pair did as they were ordered, rushing out of the room. With great effort, Le'lorinel straightened.

Bellany thrust a shirt into the elf's trembling hands. "You might want to wait a while before you try to put that on," the sorceress explained.

Le'lorinel nodded and stretched repeatedly, trying to loosen the new scars.

"I'll be wanting to hear it all," Sheila said. "Ye're owing me that, now."

Le'lorinel looked at the pirate for a moment, then craned to see the new brand, the mark of Aegis-fang, the mark of acceptance and hierarchy in Sheila's band.

Eyes narrowed threateningly, teeth gritted with rage that denied the burning agony of the brand, the elf looked back at Sheila. "Everything, and you will come to trust that I will never rest until Drizzt Do'Urden is dead, slain by my own hands."

Later Sheila, Bellany, and Jule Pepper sat together in Sheila's room, digesting all that Le'lorinel had told them of Drizzt Do'Urden and his companions, who were apparently hunting Sheila in an effort to retrieve the warhammer.

"We are fortunate that Le'lorinel came to us," Bellany admitted.

"Ye thinking that the elf can beat the drow?" Sheila asked with a doubtful snort. "Damn drow. Never seen one. Never wanted to."

"I have no idea whether Le'lorinel has any chance at all against this dark elf or not," Bellany honestly answered. "I do know that the elf's hatred for Drizzt is genuine and deep, and whatever the odds, we can expect Le'lorinel to lead the charge if Drizzt Do'Urden comes against us. That alone is a benefit." As she finished, she turned a leading gaze over Jule Pepper, the only one of them to ever encounter Drizzt and his friends.

"I would hesitate to ever bet against that group," Jule said. "Their teamwork is impeccable, wrought of years fighting together, and each of them, even the runt halfling, is formidable."

"What o' these other ones, then?" the obviously nervous pirate leader asked. "What o' Bruenor the dwarf king? Think he'll bring an army against us?"

Neither Jule nor Bellany had any way of knowing. "Le'lorinel told us much," the sorceress said, "but the information is far from complete."

"In my encounter with them in Icewind Dale, the dwarf worked with his friends, but with no support from his clan whatsoever," Jule interjected. "If Bruenor knows the power of your band, though, he might decide to rouse the fury of Clan Battlehammer."

"And?" Sheila asked.

"Then we sail, winter storm or no," Bellany was quick to reply. Sheila started to scold her but noted that Jule was nodding her agreement, and in truth, the icy waters of the northern Sword Coast in winter seemed insignificant against the threat of an army of hostile dwarves.

"When Wulfgar was in Luskan, he was known to be working for Arumn Gardpeck at the Cutlass," Jule, who had been in Luskan in those days, offered.

" 'Twas Arumn's fool friend who sold me the warhammer," Sheila remarked.

"But his running companion was an old friend of mine," Jule went on. "A shadowy little thief known as Morik the Rogue."

Sheila and Bellany looked to each other and nodded. Sheila had heard of Morik, though not in any detail. Bellany, though, knew the man fairly well, or had known him, at least, back in her days as an apprentice at the Hosttower of the Arcane. She looked to Jule, considered what she personally knew of lusty Morik, and understood what the beautiful, sensuous woman likely meant by the phrase "an old friend."

"Oh, by the gods," Sheila Kree huffed a few moments later, her head sagging as so many things suddenly became clear to her.

Both of her companions looked at her curiously.

"Deudermont's chasing us," Sheila Kree explained. "What'd'ye think he's looking for?"

"Do we know that he's looking for anything at all?" Bellany replied, but she slowed down as she finished the sentence, as if starting to catch on.

"And now Drizzt and his girlfriend are waiting for us at Deudermont's house," Sheila went on.

"So Deudermont is after Aegis-fang, as well," reasoned Jule Pepper. "It's all connected. But Wulfgar is not—or at least was not—with Drizzt and the others from Icewind Dale, so . . ."

"Wulfgar might be with Deudermont," Bellany finished.

"I'll be paying Josi Puddles back for this, don't ye doubt," Sheila said grimly, settling back in her seat.

"We know not where Wulfgar might be," Jule Pepper put in. "We do know that Deudermont will not likely be sailing anywhere north of Waterdeep for the next season, so if Wulfgar is with Deudermont . . ."

She stopped as Sheila growled and leaped up from her seat, pounding a fist into an open palm. "We're not knowing enough to make any choices," she grumbled. "We're needing to learn more."

An uncomfortable silence followed, at last broken by Jule Pepper. "Morik," the woman said.

Bellany and Sheila looked at her curiously.

"Morik the Rogue, as well-connected as any rogue on Luskan's streets," Bellany explained. "And with a previous interest in Wulfgar, as you just said. He will have some answers for us, perhaps."

Sheila thought it over for a moment. "Bring him to me," she ordered Bellany, whose magical powers could take her quickly to Luskan, despite the season.

Bellany nodded, and without a word she rose and left the room.

"Dark elves and warhammers," Sheila Kree remarked when she and Jule were alone. "A mysterious and beautiful elf visitor . . ."

"Exotic, if not beautiful," Jule agreed. "And I admit I do like the look. Especially the black mask."

Sheila Kree laughed at the craziness of it all and shook her head vigorously, her wild red hair flying all about. "If Le'lorinel survives this, then I'll be naming an elf among me commanders," she explained.

"A most mysterious and beautiful and exotic elf," Jule agreed with a laugh. "Though perhaps a bit crazy."

Sheila considered her with an incredulous expression. "Ain't we all?"

Chapter 15

Sharing a Drink
With a Surly Dwarf

"I should've known better than to let the two of ye go running off on yer own," a blustering voice greeted loudly as Drizzt and Catti-brie entered the Cutlass in Luskan. Bruenor and Regis sat at the bar, across from Arumn Gardpeck, both looking a bit haggard still from their harrowing journey.

"I didn't think you would come out," Drizzt remarked, pulling a seat up beside his friends. "It is late in the season."

"Later than you think," Regis mumbled, and both Drizzt and Catti-brie turned to Bruenor for clarification.

"Bah, a little storm and nothing to fret about," the dwarf bellowed.

"Little to a mountain giant," Regis muttered quietly, and Bruenor gave a snort.

"Fix up me friend and me girl here with a bit o' the wine," Bruenor called to Arumn, who was already doing just that. As soon as the drinks were delivered and Arumn, with a nod to the pair, started away, the red-bearded dwarf's expression grew very serious.

"So where's me boy?" he asked.

"With Deudermont, sailing on *Sea Sprite*, as far as we can tell," Catti-brie answered.

"Not in port here," Regis remarked.

"Nor in Waterdeep, though they might put in before winter," Drizzt explained. "That would be Captain Deudermont's normal procedure, to properly stock the ship for the coming cold season."

"Then they'll likely sail south," Catti-brie added. "Not returning to Waterdeep until the spring."

Bruenor snorted again, but with a mouthful of ale, and wound up spitting half of it over Regis. "Then why're ye here?" he demanded. "If me boy's soon to be in Waterdeep, and not back for half a year, why ain't ye there seeing to him?"

"We left word," Drizzt explained.

"Word?" the dwarf echoed incredulously. "What word might that be? Hello? Well met? Keep warm through the winter? Ye durn fool elf, I was counting on ye to bring me boy back to us."

"It is complicated," Drizzt replied.

Only then did Catti-brie note that both Arumn Gardpeck and Josi Puddles were quietly edging closer, each craning an ear the way of the four friends. She didn't scold them, though, for she well understood their stake in all of this.

"We found Delly," she said, turning to regard the two of them in turn. "And the child, Colson."

"How fares my Delly?" asked Arumn, and Catti-brie didn't miss the fact that Josi Puddles was chewing his lip with anticipation. Likely that one was sweet on the girl, Catti-brie recognized.

"She does well, as does the little girl," Drizzt put in. "Though even as we arrived, we found them in peril."

All four of the listeners stared hard at those ominous words.

"Sheila Kree, the pirate, or so we believe," Drizzt explained. "For some reason that I do not yet know, she took it upon herself to send a raiding party to Waterdeep."

"Looking for me boy?" Bruenor asked.

"Or looking to back off Deudermont, who's been chasing her all season," remarked Arumn, who was well versed in such things, listening to much of the gossip from the many sailors who frequented his tavern.

"One or the other, and so we have returned to find out which," Drizzt replied.

"Do we even know that *Sea Sprite* is still afloat?" Regis asked.

The halfling's eyes went wide and he bit his lip as soon as he heard the words coming out of his mouth, his wince showing clearly that he had realized, too late, that such a possibility as the destruction of the ship would weigh very heavily on the shoulders of Bruenor.

Still, it was an honest question to ask, and one that Drizzt and Catti-brie had planned on asking Arumn long before they arrived in Luskan. Both looked questioningly to the tavern-keeper.

"Heard nothing to say it ain't," Arumn answered. "But if Sheila Kree got *Sea Sprite*, then it could well be months before we knowed it here. Can't believe she did, though. Word among the docks is that none'd take on *Sea Sprite* in the open water."

"See what you can find out, I beg you," Drizzt said to him.

The portly tavern-keeper nodded and motioned to Josi to likewise begin an inquiry.

"I strongly doubt that Sheila Kree got anywhere near to *Sea Sprite*," Drizzt echoed, for Bruenor's benefit, and with conviction. "Or if she did, then likely it was the remnants of her devastated band that staged the raid against Captain Deudermont's house, seeking one last bit of retribution for the destruction of Sheila's ship and the loss of her crew. I sailed with Captain Deudermont for five years, and I can tell you that I never encountered a single ship that could out-duel *Sea Sprite*."

"Or her wizard, Robillard," Catti-brie added.

Bruenor continued simply to stare at the two of them hard, the dwarf obviously on the very edge of anxiety for his missing son.

"And so we're to wait?" he asked a few moments later. It was obvious from his tone that he wasn't thrilled with that prospect.

"The winter puts *Sea Sprite* out of the hunt for Sheila Kree's ship," Drizzt explained, lowering his voice so that only the companions could hear. "And likely it puts Sheila Kree off the cold waters for the season. She has to be docked somewhere."

That seemed to appease Bruenor somewhat. "We'll find her, then," he said determinedly. "And get back me warhammer."

"And hopefully Wulfgar will join us," Catti-brie added. "That he might be holdin' Aegis-fang once again. That he might be finding where he belongs and where the hammer belongs."

Bruenor lifted his mug of ale in a toast to that hopeful sentiment, and all the others joined in, each understanding that Catti-brie's scenario had to be considered the most optimistic and that a far darker road likely awaited them all.

In the subsequent discussion, the companions decided to spend the next few days searching the immediate area around Luskan, including the docks. Arumn and Josi, and Morik the Rogue once they could find him, were to inquire where they might about *Sea Sprite* and Sheila Kree. The plan would give Wulfgar a chance to catch up with them, perhaps, if he got the news in Waterdeep and that was his intent. It was also possible that *Sea Sprite* would come through Luskan on its way to Waterdeep. If that was to happen, it would be very soon, Drizzt knew, for the season was getting late.

Drizzt ordered a round for all four, then held back the others before they could begin their drinking. He held his own glass up in a second toast, a reaffirmation of Bruenor's first one.

"The news is brighter than we could have expected when first we left Ten-Towns," he reminded them all. "By all accounts, our friend is alive and with good and reliable company."

"To Wulfgar!" said Regis, as Drizzt paused.

"And to Delly Curtie and to Colson," Catti-brie added with a smile aimed right at Bruenor and even more pointedly at Drizzt. "A fine wife our friend has found, and a child who'll grow strong under Wulfgar's watchful eye."

"He learned to raise a son from a master, I would say," Drizzt remarked, grinning at Bruenor.

"And too bad it is that that one didn't know as much about raising a girl," Catti-brie added, but she waited until precisely the moment that Bruenor began gulping his ale before launching the taunt.

Predictably, the dwarf spat and Regis got soaked again.

* * * * *

Morik the Rogue wore a curious and not displeased expression when he opened the door to his small apartment to find a petite, dark-haired woman waiting for him.

"Perhaps you have found the wrong door," Morik graciously offered, his dark eyes surveying the woman with more than a little interest. She was a comely one, and she held herself with perfect poise and a flicker of intelligence that Morik always found intriguing.

"Many people would call the door of Morik the Rogue the wrong door," the woman answered. "But no, this is where I intended to be." She gave a coy little smile and looked Morik over as thoroughly as he was regarding her. "You have aged well," she said.

The implication that this enticing creature had known Morik in his earlier years piqued the rogue's curiosity. He stared at her hard, trying to place her.

"Perhaps it would help if I cast spells to shake our bed," the woman remarked. "Or multicolored lights to dance about us as we make love."

"Bellany!" Morik cried suddenly. "Bellany Tundash! How many years have passed?"

Indeed, Morik hadn't seen the sorceress in several years, not since she was a minor apprentice in the Hosttower of the Arcane. She had been the wild one! Sneaking out from the wizards' guild nearly every night to come and play along the wilder streets of Luskan. And like so many pretty women who had come out to play, Bellany had inevitably found her way to Morik's side and Morik's bed for a few encounters.

Amazing encounters, Morik recalled.

"Not so many years, Morik," Bellany replied. "And here I thought I was more special than that to you." She gave a little pout, pursing her lips in such a way as to make Morik's knees go weak. "I believed you would recognize me immediately and sweep me into your arms for a great kiss."

"A situation I must correct!" said Morik, coming forward with his arms out wide, a bright and eager expression on his face.

* * * * *

Both Catti-brie and Regis retired early that night, but Drizzt stayed on in the tavern with Bruenor, suspecting that the dwarf needed to talk.

"When this business is finished, you and I must go to Waterdeep," the drow remarked. "It would do my heart good to hear Colson talk of her grandfather."

"Kid's talking?" Bruenor asked.

"No, not yet," Drizzt replied with a laugh. "But soon enough."

Bruenor merely nodded, seeming less than intrigued with it all.

"She has a good mother," Drizzt said after a while. "And we know the character of her father. Colson will be a fine lass."

"Colson," Bruenor muttered, and he downed half his mug of ale. "Stupid name."

"It is Elvish," Drizzt explained. "With two meanings, and seeming perfectly fitting. 'Col' means 'not', and so the name literally translates into 'not-son,' or 'daughter.' Put together, though, the name Colson means 'from the dark town'. A fitting name, I would say, given Delly Curtie's tale of how Wulfgar came by the child."

Bruenor huffed again and finished the mug.

"I would have thought you would be thrilled at the news," the drow dared to say. "You, who knows better than any the joy of finding a wayward child to love as your own."

"Bah," Bruenor snorted.

"And I suspect that Wulfgar will soon enough produce grandchildren for you from his own loins," Drizzt remarked, sliding another ale Bruenor's way.

"Grandchildren?" Bruenor echoed doubtfully, and he turned in his chair to face the drow directly. "Ain't ye assuming that Wulfgar's me own boy?"

"He is."

"Is he?" Bruenor asked. "Ye're thinking that a couple o' years apart mended me heart for his actions on Catti-brie." The dwarf snorted yet again, threw his hand up in disgust, then turned back to the bar, cradling his new drink below him, muttering, "Might be that I'm looking to find him so I can give him a big punch in the mouth for the way he treated me girl."

"Your worry has been obvious and genuine," Drizzt remarked. "You have forgiven Wulfgar, whether you admit it or not.

"As have I," Drizzt quickly added when the dwarf turned back on him, his eyes narrow and threatening. "As has Catti-brie. Wulfgar was in a

1031

dark place, but from all I've learned, it would seem that he has begun the climb back to the light."

Those words softened Bruenor's expression somewhat, and his ensuing snort was not as definitive this time.

"You will like Colson," Drizzt said with a laugh. "And Delly Curtie."

"Colson," Bruenor echoed, listening carefully to the name as he spoke it. He looked at Drizzt and shook his head, but if he was trying to continue to show his disapproval, he was failing miserably.

"So now I got a granddaughter from a son who's not me own, and a daughter o' his that's not his own," Bruenor said some time later, he and Drizzt having gone back to their respective drinks for a few reflective moments. "Ye'd think that one of us would've figured out that half the fun's in makin' the damn brats!"

"And will Bruenor one day sire his own son?" Drizzt asked. "A dwarf child?"

The dwarf turned and regarded Drizzt incredulously, but considered the words for a moment and shrugged. "I just might," he said. He looked back at his ale, his face growing more serious and a bit sad, Drizzt noticed. "I'm not a young one, ye know, elf?" he asked. "Seen the centuries come and go, and remember times when Catti-brie and Wulfgar's parents' parents' parents' parents hadn't felt the warming of their first dawn. And I feel old, don't ye doubt! Feel it in me bones."

"Centuries of banging stone will do that," Drizzt said dryly, but his levity couldn't penetrate the dwarf's mood at that moment.

"And I see me girl all grown, and me boy the same, and now he's got a little one . . ." Bruenor's voice trailed off and he gave a great sigh, then drained the rest of his mug, turning as he finished to face Drizzt squarely. "And that little one will grow old and die, and I'll still be here with me aching bones."

Drizzt understood, for he too, as a long-living creature, surely saw Bruenor's dilemma. When elves, dark or light, or dwarves befriended the shorter living races—humans, halflings, and gnomes—there came the expectancy that they would watch their friends grow old and die. Drizzt knew that one of the reasons elves and dwarves remained clannish to their own, whether they wanted to admit it or not, was because of exactly that—both races protecting themselves from the emotional tearing.

"Guess that's why we should be stickin' with our own kind, eh, elf?" Bruenor finished, looking slyly at Drizzt out of the corner of his eye.

Drizzt's expression went from sympathy to curiosity. Had Bruenor just warned him away from Catti-brie? That caught the drow off his guard, indeed! And rocked him right back in his seat, as he sat staring hard at Bruenor. Had he finally let himself see the truth of his feelings for Catti-brie just to encounter this dwarven roadblock? Or was Bruenor right, and was Drizzt being a fool?

The drow took a long, long moment to steady himself and collect his thoughts.

"Or perhaps those of us who hide from the pain will never know the joys that might lead to such profound pain," Drizzt finally said. "Better to—"

"To what?" Bruenor interrupted. "To fall in love with one of them? To marry one, elf?"

Drizzt still didn't know what Bruenor was up to. Was he telling Drizzt to back off, calling the drow a fool for even thinking of falling in love with Catti-brie?

But then Bruenor tipped his hand.

"Yeah, fall in love with one," he said with a derisive snort, but one Drizzt recognized that was equally aimed at himself. "Or maybe take one of 'em in to raise as yer own. Heck, maybe more than one!"

Bruenor glanced over at Drizzt, his toothy smile showing through his brilliant red whiskers. He lifted his mug toward Drizzt in a toast. "To the both of us, then, elf!" he boomed. "A pair o' fools, but smiling fools!"

Drizzt gladly answered that toast with a tap of his own glass. He understood then that Bruenor wasn't subtly trying to (in a dwarf sort of way) ward him off, but rather that the dwarf was merely making sure Drizzt understood the depth of what he had.

They went back to their drinking. Bruenor drained mug after mug, but Drizzt cradled that single glass of fine wine.

Many minutes passed before either spoke again, and it was Bruenor, cracking in a tone that seemed all seriousness, which made it all the funnier, "Hey, elf, me next grandkid won't be striped, will it?"

"As long as it doesn't have a red beard," Drizzt replied without missing a beat.

* * * * *

"I heard you were traveling with a great barbarian warrior named Wulfgar," Bellany said to Morik when the rogue finally woke up long after the following dawn.

"Wulfgar?" Morik echoed, rubbing the sleep from his dark eyes and running his fingers through his matted black hair. "I have not seen Wulfgar in many months."

He didn't catch on to the telling manner in which Bellany was scrutinizing him.

"He went south, to find Deudermont, I think," Morik went on, and he looked at Bellany curiously. "Am I not enough man for you?" he asked.

The dark-haired sorceress smirked in a neutral manner, pointedly not answering the rogue's question. "I ask only for a friend of mine," she said.

Morik's smile was perfectly crude. "Two of you, eh?" he asked. "Am I not man enough?"

Bellany gave a great sigh and rolled to the side of the bed, gathering up the bedclothes about her and dragging them free as she rose.

Only then, upon the back of her naked shoulder, did Morik take note of the curious brand.

"So you have not spoken with Wulfgar in months?" the woman asked, moving to her clothing.

"Why do you ask?"

The suspicious nature of the question had the sorceress turning about to regard Morik, who was still reclining on the bed, lying on his side and propped up on one elbow.

"A friend wishes to know of him," Bellany said, rather curtly.

"Seems like a lot of people are suddenly wanting to know about him," the rogue remarked. He fell to his back and threw one arm across his eyes.

"People like a dark elf?" Bellany asked.

Morik peeked out at her from under his arm, his expression answering the question clearly.

Wider went his eyes when the sorceress lifted the robe that was lying across one chair, and produced from beneath it a thin, black wand. Bellany didn't point it at him, but the threat was obvious.

"Get dressed, and quickly," Bellany said. "My lady will speak with you."

"Your lady?"

"I've not the time to explain things now," Bellany replied. "We've a long road ahead of us, and though I have spells to speed us along our way, it would be better if we were gone from Luskan within the hour."

Morik scoffed at her. "Gone to where?" he asked. "I have no plans to leave . . ."

His voice trailed off as Bellany came back over to the edge of the bed, placing one knee up on it in a sexy pose, and lowered her face, putting one finger across her pouting lips.

"There are two ways we can do this, Morik," she explained quietly and calmly—too calmly for the sensibilities of the poor, surprised rogue. "One will be quite pleasurable for you, I am sure, and will guarantee your safe return to Luskan, where your friends here will no doubt comment on the wideness and constancy of your smile."

Morik regarded the enticing woman for a few moments. "Don't even bother to tell me the other way," he agreed.

* * * * *

"Arumn Gardpeck has not seen him," Catti-brie reported, "nor have any of the other regulars at the Cutlass—and they see Morik the Rogue almost every day."

Drizzt considered the words carefully. It was possible, of course, that the absence of Morik—he was not at his apartment, nor in any of his familiar haunts—was nothing more than coincidence. A man like Morik was constantly on the move, from one deal to another, from one theft to another.

But more than a day had passed since the four friends had begun their search for the rogue, using all the assets at their disposal, including the Luskan town guard, with no sign of the man. Given what had happened in Waterdeep with the agents of Sheila Kree, and given that Morik was a known associate of Wulfgar, Drizzt was not pleased by this disappearance.

"You put word in at the Hosttower?" Drizzt asked Regis.

"Robbers to a wizard," the halfling replied. "But yes, they will send word to *Sea Sprite*'s wizard, Robillard, as soon as they can locate him. It took more than half a bag of gold to persuade them to do the work."

"I gave ye a whole bag to pay for the task," Bruenor remarked dryly.

"Even with my ruby pendant, it took more than half a bag of gold to persuade them to do the work," Regis clarified.

Bruenor just put his head down and shook it. "Well, that means ye got nearly half a bag o' me gold for safe-keeping, Rumblebelly," he took care to state openly, and before witnesses.

"Did the wizards say anything about the fate of *Sea Sprite*?" Catti-brie asked. "Do they know if she's still afloat?"

"They said they've seen nothing to indicate anything different," Regis answered. "They have contacts among the docks, including many pirates. If *Sea Sprite* went down anywhere near Luskan the celebration would be immediate and surely loud."

It wasn't much of a confirmation, really, but the other three took the words with great hope.

"Which brings us back to Morik," Drizzt said. "If the pirate Kree is trying to strike first to chase off Deudermont and Wulfgar, then perhaps Morik became a target."

"What connection would Deudermont hold with that rogue?" Catti-brie asked, a perfectly logical question and one that had Drizzt obviously stumped.

"Perhaps Morik is in league with Sheila Kree," Regis reasoned. "An informant?"

Drizzt was shaking his head before the halfling ever finished. From his brief meeting with Morik, he did not think that the man would do such a thing. Though, he had to admit, Morik was a man whose loyalties didn't seem hard to buy.

"What do we know of Kree?" the drow asked.

"We know she ain't nowhere near to here," Bruenor answered impatiently. "And we know that we're wasting time here, that bein' the case!"

"True enough," Catti-brie agreed.

"But the season is deepening up north," Regis put in. "Perhaps we should begin our search to the south."

"All signs are that Sheila Kree is put in up north," Drizzt was quick to answer. "The rumors we have heard, from Morik and from Josi Puddles, place her somewhere up there."

"Lotta coast between here and the Sea o' Moving Ice," Bruenor put in.

"So we should wait?" Regis quickly followed.

"So we should get moving!" Bruenor retorted just as quickly, and since both Drizzt and Catti-brie agreed with the dwarf's reasoning the four friends departed Luskan later that same day, only hours after Morik and Bellany had left the city. But the latter, moving with the enhancements of many magical spells, and knowing where they were going, were soon enough far, far away.

Chapter 16

Unexpected Friendship

As usual, Wulfgar was the first one to debark *Sea Sprite* when the schooner glided into dock at one of Waterdeep's many long wharves. There was little spring in the barbarian's step this day, despite his excitement at the prospect of seeing Delly and Colson again. Deudermont's last real discussion with him, more than a tenday before, had put many things into perspective for Wulfgar, had forced him to look into a mirror.

He did not like the reflection.

He knew Captain Deudermont was his friend, an honest friend and one who had spared his life despite evidence that he, along with Morik, had tried to murder the man. Deudermont had believed in Wulfgar when no others would. He'd rescued Wulfgar from Prisoner's Carnival without even a question, begging confirmation that Wulfgar had not been involved in any plot to kill him. Deudermont had welcomed Wulfgar aboard *Sea Sprite* and had altered the course of his pirate-hunting schooner many times in an effort to find the elusive Sheila Kree. Even with the anger bubbling within him from the image in the mirror Deudermont had pointedly held up before his eyes on the return journey to their home port, Wulfgar could not dispute the honesty embodied in that image.

Deudermont had told him the truth of who he had become, with as much tact as was possible.

Wulfgar couldn't ignore that truth now. He knew his days sailing with *Sea Sprite* were at their end, at least for the season. If *Sea Sprite* was going south, as was her usual winter route—and in truth, the only available winter route—then there was little chance of encountering Kree. And if the ship wasn't going to find Kree, then what point would there be in having Wulfgar aboard, especially if the barbarian warrior and his impulsive tactics were a detriment to the crew?

That was the crux of it, Wulfgar knew. That was the truth in the mirror. Never before had the proud son of Beornegar considered himself anything less than a warrior. Many times in his life, Wulfgar had done things of which he was not proud—nothing more poignantly than the occasion on which he had slapped Catti-brie. But even then, Wulfgar had one thing he could hold onto. He was a fighter, among the greatest ever to come out of Icewind Dale, among the most legendary to ever come out of the Tribe of the Elk, or any of the other tribes. He was the warrior who had united the tribes with strength of arm and conviction, the barbarian who had hurled his warhammer high to shatter the cavern's hold on the great icicle, dropping the natural spear onto the back of the great white wyrm, Icingdeath. He was the warrior who had braved the Calimport sun and the assassins, tearing through the guildhouse of a notorious ruffian to save his halfling friend. He was, above all else, the companion of Drizzt Do'Urden, a Companion of the Hall, part of a team that had fostered the talk of legend wherever it had gone.

But not now. Now he could not rightly hold claim to that title of mighty warrior, not after his disastrous attempts to battle pirates aboard *Sea Sprite*. Now his friend Deudermont—an honest and compassionate friend—had looked him in the eye and showed to him the truth, and a diminishing truth it was. Would Wulfgar find again the courageous heart that had guided him through his emotional crises? Would he ever again be that proud warrior who had united the tribes of Ten-Towns, who had helped reclaim Mithral Hall, who had chased a notorious assassin across Toril too rescue his halfling friend?

Or had Errtu stolen that from him forever? Had the demon truly broken that spirit deep within the son of Beornegar? Had the demon altered his identity forever?

As he walked across the city of Waterdeep, turning to the hillock containing Deudermont's house, Wulfgar could not truly deny the possibility that the man he had once been, the warrior he had once been, was now lost to him forever. He wasn't sure what that meant, however.

Who was he?

His thoughts remained inward until he almost reached the front door of Captain Deudermont's mansion, when the sharp, unfamiliar voice ordered him to halt and be counted.

Wulfgar looked up, his crystal-blue eyes scanning all about, noting the many soldiers standing about the perimeter of the house, noting the lighter colors of the splintered wood near the lock of the front doors.

Wulfgar felt his gut churning, his warrior instincts telling him clearly that something was terribly amiss, his heart telling him that danger had come to Delly and Colson. With a growl that was half rage and half terror, Wulfgar sprinted straight ahead for the house, oblivious to the trio of soldiers who rushed to bar the way with their great halberds.

"Let him pass!" came a shout at the last second, right before Wulfgar crashed through the blocking soldiers. "It's Wulfgar returned! *Sea Sprite* is in!"

The soldiers parted, the rearmost wisely rushing back to push open the door or Wulfgar would have surely shattered it to pieces. The barbarian charged through.

He skidded to an abrupt stop just in side the foyer, though, spotting Delly coming down the main stairway, holding Colson tight in her arms.

She stared at him, managing a weak smile until she reached the bottom of the stairs—and there she broke down, tears flowing freely, and she rushed forward, falling into Wulfgar's waiting arms and tender hug.

Time seemed to stop for the couple as they stood there, clenched, needing each other's support. Wulfgar could have stayed like that for hours, indeed, but then he heard the voice of Captain Deudermont's surprise behind him, followed by a stream of curses from Robillard.

Wulfgar gently pushed Delly back, and turned about as the pair entered. The three stood there, looking about blankly, and their stares were no less incredulous when Delly at last inserted some sense into the surreal scene by saying, simply, "Sheila Kree."

* * * * *

Deudermont caught up to Wulfgar later, alone, the barbarian staring out the window at the crashing waves far below. It was the same window through which Drizzt and Catti-brie had entered, to save Delly and Colson.

"Fine friends you left behind in Icewind Dale," the captain remarked, moving to stand beside Wulfgar and staring out rather than looking at the huge man. When Wulfgar didn't answer, Deudermont did glance his way, and noted that his expression was pained.

"Do you believe you should have been here, protecting Delly and the child?" the captain said bluntly. He looked up as Wulfgar looked down upon him, not scowling, but not looking very happy, either.

"You apparently believe so," the barbarian quipped.

"Why do you say that?" the captain asked. "Because I hinted that perhaps you should not take the next voyage out of Waterdeep with *Sea Sprite*? What would be the point? You joined with us to hunt Sheila Kree, and we'll not find her in the south, where surely we will go."

"Even now?" Wulfgar asked, seeming a bit surprised. "After Kree launched this attack against your own house? After your two friends lay cold in the ground, murdered by her assassins?"

"We can not sail to the north with the winter winds beginning to blow," Deudermont replied. "And thus, our course is south, where we will find many pirates the equal to Sheila Kree in their murders and mayhem. But do not think that I will forget this attack upon my house," the captain added with a dangerous grimace. "When the warm spring winds blow, *Sea Sprite* will return and sail right into the Sea of Moving Ice, if necessary, to find Kree and pay her her due."

Deudermont paused and stared at Wulfgar, holding the look until the barbarian reciprocated with a stare of his own. "Unless our dark elf friend beats us to the target, of course," the captain remarked.

Again Wulfgar winced, and looked back out to sea.

"The attack was nearly a month ago," Deudermont went on. "Drizzt is likely far north of Luskan by now, already on the hunt."

Wulfgar nodded, but didn't even blink at the proclamation, and the captain could see that the huge man was truly torn.

"I suspect the drow and Catti-brie would welcome the companionship of their old friend for this battle," he dared to say.

"Would you so curse Drizzt as to wish that upon him?" Wulfgar asked in all seriousness. He turned an icy glare upon Deudermont as he spoke the damning words, a look that showed a combination of sarcasm, anger, and just a bit of resignation.

Deudermont matched that stare for just a few short moments, taking a measure of the man. Then he just shrugged his shoulders and said, "As you wish. But I must tell you, Wulfgar of Icewind Dale, self pity does not become you."

With that, the captain turned and walked out of the room, leaving Wulfgar alone with some very unsettling thoughts.

* * * * *

"The captain said we can stay as long as we wish," Wulfgar explained to Delly that same night. "Through the winter and spring. I'll find some work—I am no stranger to a blacksmith's shop—and perhaps we can find our own home next year."

"In Waterdeep?" the woman asked, seeming quite concerned.

"Perhaps. Or Luskan, or anywhere else you believe would be best for Colson to grow strong."

"Icewind Dale?" the woman asked without hesitation, and Wulfgar's shoulders sagged.

"It is a difficult land, full of hardship," Wulfgar answered, trying to remain matter-of-fact.

"Full o' strong men," Delly added. "Full of heroes."

Wulfgar's expression showed clearly that he was through playing this game. "Full of cutthroats and thieves," he said sternly. "Full of folk running from the honest lands, and no place for a girl to grow to a woman."

"I know of one girl who grew quite strong and true up there," the indomitable Delly Curtie pressed.

Wulfgar glanced all around, seeming angry and tense, and Delly knew that she had put him into a box here. Given his increasingly surly expression, she had to wonder if that was a good thing, and was about to suggest that they stay in Waterdeep for the foreseeable future just to let him out of the trap.

But then Wulfgar admitted the truth, bluntly. "I will not return to Icewind Dale. That is who I was, not who I am, and I have no desire to ever see the place again. Let the tribes of my people find their way without me."

"Let yer friends find their way without ye, even when they're trying to find their way to help ye?"

Wulfgar stared at her for a long moment, grinding his teeth at her accusatory words. He turned and pulled off his shirt, as if the matter was settled, but Delly Curtie could not be put in her place so easily.

"And ye speak of honest work," she said after him, and though he didn't turn back, he did stop walking away. "Honest work like hunting pirates with Captain Deudermont? He'd give ye a fine pay, no doubt, and get ye yer hammer in the meantime."

Wulfgar turned slowly, ominously. "Aegis-fang is not mine," he announced, and Delly had to chew on her bottom lip so she didn't scream out at him. "It belonged to a man who is dead, to a warrior who is no more."

"Ye canno' be meaning that!" Delly exclaimed, moving right up to grab him in a hug.

But Wulfgar pushed her back to arms' length and answered her denial with an uncompromising glare.

"Do ye not even wish to find Drizzt and Catti-brie to offer yer thanks for their saving me and yer baby girl?" the woman, obviously wounded, asked. "Or is that no big matter to ye?"

Wulfgar's expression softened, and he brought Delly in and hugged her tightly. "It is everything to me," he whispered into her ear. "Everything. And if I ever cross paths with Drizzt and Catti-brie again, I will offer my thanks. But I'll not go to find them—there is no need. They know how I feel."

Delly Curtie just let herself enjoy the hug and let the conversation end there. She knew that Wulfgar was kidding himself, though. There was no way Drizzt and Catti-brie could know how he truly felt.

How could they, when Wulfgar didn't even know?

Delly didn't know her place here, to push the warrior back to his roots or to allow him this new identity he was apparently trying on. Would the return to who he once was break him in the process, or would he forever be haunted by that intimidating and heroic past if he settled into a more mundane life as a blacksmith?

Delly Curtie had no answers.

* * * * *

A foul mood followed Wulfgar throughout the next few days. He took his comfort with Delly and Colson, using them as armor against the emotional turmoil that now roiled within him, but he could plainly see that even Delly was growing frustrated with him. More than once, the woman suggested that perhaps he should convince Deudermont to take him with *Sea Sprite* when they put out for the south, an imminent event.

Wulfgar understood those suggestions for what they were: frustration on the part of poor Delly, who had to listen to his constant grumbling, who had to sit by and watch him get torn apart by emotions he could not control.

He went out of the house often those few days and even managed to find some work with one of the many blacksmiths operating in Waterdeep.

He was at that job on the day *Sea Sprite* sailed.

He was at that job the day after that when a very unexpected visitor walked in to see him.

"Putting those enormous muscles of yours to work, I see," said Robillard the wizard.

Wulfgar looked at the man incredulously, his expression shifting from surprise to suspicion. He gripped the large hammer he had been using tightly as he stood and considered the visitor, ready to throw the tool right through this one's face if he began any sort of spellcasting. For Wulfgar knew that *Sea Sprite* was long out of dock, and he knew, too, that Robillard was well enough known among the rabble of the pirate culture for other wizards to use magic to impersonate him. Given the previous attack on Deudermont's house, the barbarian wasn't about to take any chances.

"It is me, Wulfgar," Robillard said with a chuckle, obviously recognizing every doubt on the barbarian's face. "I will rejoin the captain and crew in a couple of days—a minor spell, really, to teleport me to a place I have set up on the ship for just such occasions."

"You have never done that before, to my knowledge," Wulfgar remarked, his suspicions holding strong, his grip as tight as ever on the hammer.

"Never before have I had to play nursemaid to a confused barbarian," Robillard countered.

"Here now," came a gruff voice. A grizzled man walked in, all girth and hair and beard, his skin as dark as his hair from all the soot. "What're ye looking to buy or get fixed?"

1042

"I am looking to speak with Wulfgar, and nothing more," Robillard said curtly.

The blacksmith spat on the floor, then wiped a dirty cloth across his mouth. "I ain't paying him to talk," he said. "I'm paying him to work!"

"We shall see," the wizard replied. He turned back to Wulfgar but the blacksmith stormed over, poking a finger the wizard's way and reiterating his point.

Robillard turned his bored expression toward Wulfgar, and the barbarian understood that if he did not calm his often-angry boss, he might soon be self-employed. He patted the blacksmith's shoulders gently, and with strength that mocked even that of the lifelong smith, Wulfgar guided the man away.

When Wulfgar returned to Robillard, his face was a mask of anger. "What do you want, wizard?" he asked gruffly. "Have you come here to taunt me? To inform me of how much better off *Sea Sprite* is with me here on land?"

"Hmm," said Robillard, scratching at his chin. "There is truth in that, I suppose."

Wulfgar's crystal-blue eyes narrowed threateningly.

"But no, my large, foolish . . . whatever you are," Robillard remarked, and if he was the least bit nervous about Wulfgar's dangerous posture, he didn't show it one bit. "I came here, I suppose, because I am possessed of a tender heart."

"Well hidden."

"Purposely so," the wizard replied without hesitation. "So tell me, are you planning to spend the entirety of the winter at Deudermont's house, working . . . here?" He finished the question with a derisive snort.

"Would you be pleased if I left the captain's house?" Wulfgar asked in reply. "Do you have plans for the house? Because if you do, then I will gladly leave, and at once."

"Calm down, angry giant," Robillard said in purely condescending tones. "I have no plans for the house, for as I already told you I will be rejoining *Sea Sprite* very soon, and I have no family to speak of left on shore. You should pay better attention."

"Then you simply want me out," Wulfgar concluded. "Out of the house and out of Deudermont's life."

"That is a completely different point," Robillard dryly responded. "Have I said that I want you out, or have I asked if you plan to stay?"

Tired of the word games, and tired of Robillard all together, Wulfgar gave a little growl and went back to his work, banging away on the metal with his heavy hammer. "The captain told me that I could stay," he said. "And so I plan to stay until I have earned enough coin to purchase living quarters of my own. I would leave now—I plan to hold no debts to any man—except that I have Delly and Colson to look after."

"Got that backward," Robillard muttered under his breath, but loud enough—and Wulfgar knew, intentionally so—so that Wulfgar could hear.

"Wonderful plan," the wizard said more loudly. "And you will execute it while your former friends run off, and perhaps get themselves killed, trying to retrieve the magical warhammer that you were too stupid to hold onto. Brilliant, young Wulfgar!"

Wulfgar stood up straight from his work, the hammer falling from his hand, his jaw dropping open in astonishment.

"It is the truth, is it not?" the unshakable wizard calmly asked.

Wulfgar started to respond, but had no practical words to use as armor against the brutal and straightforward attack. However he might parse his response, however he might speak the words to make himself feel better, the simple fact was that Robillard's observations were correct.

"I can not change that which has happened," the defeated barbarian said as he bent to retrieve his hammer.

"But you can work to right the wrongs you have committed," Robillard pointed out. "Who are you, Wulfgar of Icewind Dale? And more importantly, who do you wish to be?"

There was nothing friendly in Robillard's sharp tone or in his stiff and hawkish posture, his arms crossed defiantly over his chest, his expression one of absolute superiority. But still, the mere fact that the wizard was showing any interest in Wulfgar's plight at all came as a surprise to the barbarian. He had thought, and not without reason, that Robillard's only concern regarding him was to keep him off *Sea Sprite*.

Wulfgar's angry stare at Robillard gradually eased into a self-deprecating chuckle. "I am who you see before you," he said, and he presented himself with his arms wide, his leather smithy apron prominently displayed. "Nothing more, nothing less."

"A man who lives a lie will soon enough be consumed by it," Robillard remarked.

Wulfgar's smile became a sudden scowl.

"Wulfgar the smith?" Robillard asked skeptically, and he gave a snort. "You are no laborer, and you fool yourself if you think that this newest pursuit will allow you to hide from the truth. You were born a warrior, bred and trained a warrior, and have ever relished that calling. How many times has Wulfgar charged into battle, the song of Tempus on his lips?"

"Tempus," Wulfgar said with disdain. "Tempus deserted me."

"Tempus was with you, and your faith in the code of the warrior sustained you through your trials," Robillard strongly countered. "*All* of your trials."

"You can not know what I endured."

"I do not care what I endured," Robillard replied. His claim, and the sheer power in his voice, surely had Wulfgar back on his heels. "I care only for that which I see before me now, a man living a lie and bringing pain to all around him and to himself because he hasn't the courage to face the truth of his own identity."

"A warrior?" Wulfgar asked doubtfully. "And yet it is Robillard who keeps me from that very pursuit. It is Robillard who bids Captain Deudermont to put me off *Sea Sprite*."

"You do not belong on *Sea Sprite*, of that I am certain," the wizard calmly replied. "Not at this time, at least. *Sea Sprite* is no place for one who would charge ahead in pursuit of personal demons. We succeed because we each know our place against the pirates. But I know, too, that you do not belong here, working as a smith in a Waterdhavian shop. Take heed of my words here and now, Wulfgar of Icewind Dale. Your friends are walking into grave danger, and whether you admit it or not, they are doing so for your benefit. If you do not join with them now, or at least go and speak with them to alter their course, there will be consequences. If Drizzt Do'Urden and Catti-brie walk into peril in search of Aegis-fang, whatever the outcome, you will punish yourself for the rest of your life. Not for your stupidity in losing the hammer so much as your cowardice in refusing to join in with them."

The wizard ended abruptly and just stood staring at the barbarian, whose expression was blank as he digested the truth of the words.

"They have been gone nearly a month," Wulfgar said, his voice carrying far less conviction. "They could be anywhere."

"They passed through Luskan, to be sure," Robillard replied. "I can have you there this very day, and from there, I have contacts to guide our pursuit."

"You will join in the hunt?"

"For your former friends, yes," Robillard answered. "For Aegis-fang? We shall see, but it hardly seems my affair."

Wulfgar looked as if a gentle breeze could blow him right over. He rocked back and forth, from foot to foot, staring blankly.

"Do not refuse this opportunity," Robillard warned. "It is your one chance to answer the questions that so haunt you and your one chance to belay the guilt that will forever stoop your shoulders. I offer you this, but life's road is too wound with unexpected turns for you to dare hope that the opportunity will ever again be before you."

"Why?" Wulfgar asked quietly.

"I have explained my reasoning of your current state clearly enough, as well as my beliefs that you should now take the strides to correct your errant course," Robillard answered, but Wulfgar was shaking his head before the wizard finished the thought.

"No," the barbarian clarified. "Why you?" When Robillard didn't immediately answer, Wulfgar went on, "You offer to help me, though you have shown me little friendship and I have made no attempt to befriend you. Yet here you are, offering advice and assistance. Why?

Is it out of your previous friendship with Drizzt and Catti-brie? Or is it out of your desire to be rid of me, to have me far from your precious *Sea Sprite*?"

Robillard looked at him slyly. "Yes," he answered.

Chapter 17

Morik's View

"He's a bit forthcoming for a prisoner, I'd say," Sheila Kree remarked to Bellany after an exhausting three hours of interrogation during which Morik the Rogue had volunteered all he knew of Wulfgar, Drizzt, and Catti-brie. Sheila had listened carefully to every word about the dark elf in particular.

"Morik's credo is self-preservation," Bellany explained. "Nothing more than that. He would put a dagger into Wulfgar's heart himself, if his own life demanded it. Morik will not be glad if Drizzt and Wulfgar come against us. He may even find ways to stay out of the fight and not aid us as we destroy his former companion. but he'll not risk his own life going against us. Nor will he jeopardize the promise of a better future he knows we can offer to him. That's just not his way."

Sheila could accept the idea of personal gain over communal loyalty readily enough. It was certainly the source of any loyalty her cutthroat band held for her. They were a crew she kept together only by threat and promise—only because they all knew their best personal gains could be found under the command of Sheila Kree. They likewise knew that if they tried to leave, they would face the wrath of the deadly pirate leader and her elite group of commanders.

Sitting at the side of the room, Jule Pepper was even more convinced of Morik's authenticity, mostly because of his actions since he'd arrived with Bellany in Golden Cove. Everything Morik had said had been in complete agreement with all she'd learned of Drizzt during her short stay in Ten-Towns.

"If the drow and Catti-brie intend to come after the warhammer, then we can expect the dwarf, Bruenor, and the halfling, Regis, to join with them," she said. "And do not dismiss that panther companion Drizzt carries along."

"Won't forget any of it," Sheila Kree assured her. "Makes me glad Le'lorinel came to us."

"Le'lorinel's appearance here might prove to be the most fortunate thing of all," Bellany agreed.

"Morik's going to fight the elf now?" the pirate leader asked, for Le'lorinel, so obsessed with Drizzt, had requested some private time with this newest addition to the hide-out, one who had just suffered firsthand experience against the hated dark elf.

Jule Pepper laughed aloud at the question. Soon after Jule had arrived at Golden Cove, Le'lorinel had spent hour after hour with her, making her mimic every movement she'd seen Drizzt make, even those unrelated to battle. Le'lorinel wanted to know the length of his stride, the tilt of his head when he spoke, anything at all about the hated drow. Jule knew Morik would likely show the elf nothing of any value, but knew, too, that Le'lorinel would make him repeat his actions and words again and again. Never had Jule seen anyone so perfectly obsessed.

"Morik is likely beside Le'lorinel even now, no doubt reenacting the sequence that got him caught by Drizzt and Catti-brie," Bellany answered with a glance at the amused Jule.

"Ye be watchin' them with yer magic," Sheila instructed the sorceress. "Ye pay attention to every word Le'lorinel utters, to every movement made toward Morik."

"You still fear that our enemies might have sent the elf as a diversion?" Bellany asked.

"Le'lorinel's arrival was a bit too convenient," Jule remarked.

"What I'm fearin' even more is that the fool elf'll go finding Drizzt and his friends afore they're finding us," Sheila explained. "That group might be spendin' tendays wandering the mountains without any sign o' Minster Gorge or Golden Cove, and I'm preferring that to having enemies that powerful walkin' right in."

"I'd like to raise a beacon to guide them in," Jule said quietly. "I owe that group and intend to see them paid back in full."

"To say nothing of the many magical treasures they carry," Bellany agreed. "I believe I could get used to such a companion as Guenhwyvar, and wouldn't you look fine, Sheila, wearing the dark elf's reportedly fabulous scimitars strapped about your waist?"

Sheila Kree nodded and smiled wickedly. "But we got to get that group on our own terms and not theirs," she explained. "We'll bring 'em in when we're ready for 'em, after the winter's softened them up a bit. We'll get Le'lorinel the fight that's been doggin' the stubborn fool elf for all these years and hope that Drizzt falls hard then and there. And if not, there'll be fewer of us left to split the treasure."

"Speaking of that," Jule put in, "I note that many of our ogre friends have gone out and about, hunting the countryside. We would do well, I think, to keep them close until this business with Drizzt Do'Urden is finished."

"Only a few out at a time," Sheila Kree replied. "I telled as much to Chogurugga already."

Bellany left the room soon after, and she couldn't help but smile at the way things were playing out. Normally, the winters had been dreadfully uneventful, but now this one promised a good fight, better treasure, and more companionship in the person of Morik the Rogue than the young sorceress had known since her days as an apprentice back in Luskan.

It was going to be a fine winter.

But Bellany knew that Sheila Kree was right concerning Le'lorinel. If they weren't careful, the crazy elf's obsession with Drizzt could invite disaster.

Bellany went right to her chamber and gathered together the components she needed for some divination spells, tuning in to the wide and rocky chamber Sheila Kree had assigned to Le'lorinel, watching as the elf and Morik went at their weapon dance, Le'lorinel instructing Morik over and over again to tell everything he knew about this strange dark elf.

* * * * *

"How many times must I tell you that it was no fight?" Morik asked in exasperation, holding his arms out and down to the side, a dagger in each hand. "I had no desire to continue when I learned the prowess of the drow and his friend."

"No desire to continue," Le'lorinel pointedly echoed. "Which means that you began. And you just admitted that you learned of the dark elf's prowess. So show me, and now, else I will show you *my* prowess!"

Morik tilted his head and smirked at the elf, dismissing this upstart's threat. Or at least, appearing to. In truth, Le'lorinel had Morik quite unsettled. The rogue had survived many years on the tough streets by understanding his potential enemies and friends. He instinctively knew when to fight, when to bluff, and when to run away.

This encounter was fast shifting into the third category, for Morik could get no barometer on Le'lorinel. The elf's obsession was beyond readable, he recognized, drifting into something nearing insanity. He could see that clearly in the sheer intensity of the elf's blue and gold eyes, staring out at him through that ridiculous black mask. Would Le'lorinel really attack him if he didn't give the necessary information, and, apparently, in a manner that Le'lorinel could accept? He didn't doubt that for a moment, nor did he doubt that he might be overmatched. Drizzt Do'Urden had defeated his best attack routine with seeming ease, and had begun a counter that would have had Morik dead in seconds if the drow had so desired, and if Le'lorinel could pose an honest challenge to Drizzt . . .

"You wish him dead, but why?" the rogue asked.

"That is my affair and not your own," Le'lorinel answered curtly.

"You speak to me in anger, as if I can not or would not help you," Morik said, forcing a distinct level of calm into his voice. "Perhaps there's a way—"

"This is my fight and not your own," came the response, as sharp as Morik's daggers.

"Ah, but you alone, against Drizzt and his friends?" the rogue reasoned. "You may begin a brilliant and winning attack against the drow only to be shot dead by Catti-brie, standing calmly off to the side. Her bow—"

"I know all of Taulmaril and of Guenhwyvar and all the others," the elf assured him. "I will find Drizzt on my own terms and defeat him face to face, as justice demands."

Morik gave a laugh. "He is not such a bad fellow," he started to say, but the feral expression growing in Le'lorinel's eyes advised him to alter that course of reasoning. "Perhaps you should go and find a woman," the rogue added. "Elf or human—there seem to be many attractive ones about. Make love, my friend. That is justice!"

The expression that came back at Morik, though he had never expected agreement, caught him by surprise, so doubtful and incredulous did it seem.

"How old are you?" Morik pressed on. "Seventy? Fifty? Even less? It is so hard to tell with you elves, and yes, I am jealous of you for that. But you are undeniably handsome, a delicate beauty the women will enjoy. So find a lover, my friend. Find two! And do not risk the centuries of life you have remaining in this battle with Drizzt Do'Urden."

Le'lorinel came forward a step. Morik fast retreated, subtly twisting his hands to prepare to launch a dagger into the masked face of his opponent, should Le'lorinel continue.

"I can not live!" the elf cried angrily. "I will see justice done! The mere notion of a dark elf walking the surface, feigning friendship and goodness offends everything I am and everything I believe. This dupe that is Drizzt Do'Urden is an insult to all of my ancestors, who drove the drow from the surface world and into the lightless depths where they belong."

"And if Drizzt retreated into the lightless depths, would you then pursue him?" Morik asked, thinking he might have found a break in the elf's wall of reasoning.

"I would kill every drow if that power was in my hands," Le'lorinel sneered in response. "I would obliterate the entire race and be proud of the action. I would kill their matrons and their murderous raiders. I would drive my dagger into the heart of every drow child!"

The elf was advancing with every sentence, and Morik was wisely backing, staying out of dangerous range, holding his hands up before him, daggers still ready, and patting the air in an effort to calm this brewing storm.

Finally Le'lorinel stopped the approach and stood glaring at him. "Now, Morik, are you going to show me the action that occurred between you and Drizzt Do'Urden, or am I to test your battle mettle personally and use it as a measure of the prowess of Drizzt Do'Urden, given what I already know about your encounter?"

Morik gave a sigh and nodded his compliance. Then he positioned Le'lorinel as Drizzt had been that night in the Luskan alley and took the elf through the attack and defense sequence.

Over and over and over and over, at Le'lorinel's predictable insistence.

* * * * *

Bellany watched the entire exchange with more than a bit of amusement. She enjoyed watching Morik's fluid motions, though she couldn't deny that Le'lorinel was even more beautiful in battle than he, with greater skill and grace. Bellany laughed aloud at that, given Morik's errant perceptions.

When the pair at last finished the multiple dances, Bellany heard Morik dare to argue, "You are a fine fighter, a wonderful warrior. I do not question your abilities, friend. But I warn you that Drizzt Do'Urden is good, very good. Perhaps as good as anyone in all the northland. I know that not only from my brief encounter with him, but from the tales that Wulfgar told me during our time together. I see that your rage is an honest one, but I implore you to reconsider this course. Drizzt Do'Urden is very good, and his friends are powerful indeed. If you follow through with this course, he will kill you. And what a waste of centuries that would be!"

Morik bowed, turned, and quickly headed away, moving, Bellany suspected, toward her room. She liked that thought, for watching the play between Morik and Le'lorinel had surely excited her, and she decided she would not correct the rogue. Not soon, at least.

This was too much fun.

* * * * *

Morik did indeed consider going to see Bellany as he departed Le'lorinel's sparring chamber. The elf had more amused him than

1051

shaken him—Morik saw him as a complete fool, wasting every potential enjoyment and experience in life in seeking this bloody vow of vengeance against a dark elf better left alone. Whether Drizzt was a good sort or a bad one wasn't really the issue, in Morik's view. The simple measure of the worth of Le'lorinel's quest was the question of whether or not Drizzt was seeking the elf. If he was, then Le'lorinel would do well to strike first, but if he was not, then the elf was surely a fool.

Drizzt was not looking for the elf. Morik knew that instinctively. Drizzt had come seeking information about Wulfgar and about Aegis-fang but had said nothing about any elf named Le'lorinel, or about any elf at all. Drizzt wasn't hunting Le'lorinel, and likely, he didn't even know that Le'lorinel was hunting him.

Morik turned down a side corridor, moving to an awkwardly set wooden door. With great effort, he managed to push it open and moved through it to an outside landing high up on the cliff face, perhaps two hundred feet from the crashing waves far below.

Morik considered the path that wound down around the rocky spur that would take him to the floor of the gorge on the other side of the mound and to the trails that would lead him far away from Sheila Kree. He could probably get by the sentries watching the gorge with relative ease, could probably get far, far away with little effort.

Of course, the storm clouds were gathering in the northwest, over the Sea of Moving Ice, and the wind was cold. He'd have a hard time making Luskan before the season overwhelmed him, and it wouldn't be a pleasant journey even if he did make it. And of course, Bellany had already shown that she could find him in Luskan.

Morik grinned as he considered other possible routes. He wasn't exactly sure where he was—Bellany had used magic to bounce them from place to place on the way there—but he suspected he wasn't very far from a potential shelter against the winter.

"Ah, Lord Feringal, are you expecting visitors?" the rogue whispered, but he was laughing with every word, hardly considering the possibility of fleeing to Auckney—if he could even figure out where Aukney was, relative to Golden Cove. Without the proper attire, it would not be easy for the rogue Morik to assume again the identity of Lord Brandeburg of Waterdeep, an alias he had once used to dupe Lord Feringal of Auckney.

Morik was laughing at the thought of wandering away into the wintry mountains, and the notion was far from serious. It was just comforting for Morik to know he could likely get away if he so desired.

With that in mind, Morik wasn't surprised that the pirates had given him fairly free reign. If they offered to put him back in Luskan and never bother him again, he wasn't sure he would take them up on it. Life there was tough, even for one of Morik's cunning and reputation, but life in the cove seemed easy enough, and certainly Bellany was going out of her way to make it pleasant.

But what about Wulfgar? What about Drizzt Do'Urden and Catti-brie?

Morik looked out over the cold waters and seriously considered the debts he might owe to his former traveling companion. Yes, he did care about Wulfgar, and he made up his mind then and there, that if the barbarian did come against Golden Cove in an effort to regain Aegis-fang, then he would do all that he could to convince Sheila Kree and particularly Bellany to try to capture the man and not to destroy him.

That would be a more difficult task concerning Drizzt, Morik knew, considering his recent encounter with the crazy Le'lorinel, but Morik was able to shrug that possibility away easily enough.

In truth, what in the world did Morik the Rogue owe to Drizzt Do'Urden? Or to Catti-brie?

The little dark-haired thief stretched and hugged his arms close to his chest to ward the cold wind. He thought of Bellany and her warm bed and started off for her immediately.

*   *   *   *   *

Le'lorinel stood sullenly in the sparring chamber after Morik had gone, considering his last words.

Morik was wrong, Le'lorinel knew. The elf didn't doubt his assessment of Drizzt's fighting prowess. Le'lorinel knew well the tales of Drizzt's exploits. But Morik did not understand the years of preparation for this one fight, the great extremes to which Le'lorinel had gone to be in a position to defeat Drizzt Do'Urden.

But Le'lorinel could not easily dismiss Morik's warning. This fight with Drizzt would indeed happen, the elf repeated silently, fingering the ring that contained the necessary spells. Even if it went exactly as Le'lorinel had prepared and planned, it would likely end in two deaths, not one.

So be it.

Chapter 18

Where Trail and Smoke Combine

The four companions, wearing layers of fur and with blood thickened from years of living in the harshness of Icewind Dale, were not overly bothered by the wintry conditions they found waiting for them not so far north of Luskan. The snow was deep in some places, the trails icy in others, but the group plodded along. Bruenor led Catti-brie and Regis, plowing a trail with his stout body, with Drizzt guiding them from along the side.

Their progress was wonderful, given the season and the difficult terrain, but of course Bruenor found a reason to grumble. "Damn twinkly elf don't even break the crust!" he muttered, crunching through one snow drift that was more than waist high, while Drizzt skipped along on the crusty surface of the snow, half-skating, half-running. "Gotta get him to eat more and put some meat on them skinny limbs!"

Behind the dwarf, Catti-brie merely smiled. She knew, and so did Bruenor, that Drizzt's grace was more a measure of balance than of weight. The drow knew how to distribute his weight perfectly, and because he was always balanced, he could shift that weight to his other foot immediately if he felt the snow collapsing beneath him. Catti-brie was about Drizzt's height and was even a bit lighter than him, but there was no way she could possibly move as he did.

Because he was atop the snow instead of plowing through it, Drizzt was afforded a fine vantage point of the rolling white lands all around. He noted a trail not far to the side—a recent one, where someone or something had plodded along, much as Bruenor was doing now.

"Hold!" the drow called. Even as he spoke, Drizzt noted another curious sight, that of smoke up ahead, some distance away, rising in a thin line as if from a chimney. He considered it for just a moment, then glanced back to the trail, which seemed to be going in that general direction. He wondered if the two were somehow connected. A trapper's house, perhaps, or a hermit.

Figuring that the friends could all use a bit of rest, Drizzt made good speed for the trail. They had been out from Luskan for nearly a tenday, finding good shelter only twice, once with a farmer the first night and another night spent in a cave.

Drizzt wasn't as hopeful for shelter when he arrived at the line in the snow and saw footprints more than twice the size of his own.

"What'd'ye got, elf?" Bruenor called.

Drizzt motioned for the group to be quiet and for them to come and join him.

"Big orcs, perhaps," he remarked when they were all there. "Or small ogres."

"Or barbarians," Bruenor remarked. "Them folk got the biggest feet I ever seen on a human."

Drizzt examined one clear print more carefully, bending over to put his eyes only a few inches from it. He shook his head. "These are too heavy, and those who made them wore hard boots, not the doeskin Wulfgar's people would wear," he explained.

"Ogres, then," said Catti-brie. "Or big orcs."

"Plenty of those in these mountains," Regis put in.

"And heading for that line of smoke," Drizzt explained, pointing ahead to the thin plume.

"Might be their kinfolk making the smoke," Bruenor reasoned. With a wry grin, the dwarf turned to Regis. "Get to it, Rumblebelly."

Regis blanched, thinking then that perhaps he had done too well with that last orc camp, when he and Bruenor were making their way to Luskan. The halfling wasn't going to shy from his responsibilities, but if these were ogres, he'd be sorely overmatched. And Regis knew that ogres favored halfling as one of their most desired meals.

When Regis came out of his contemplation, he noted that Drizzt was looking at him, smiling knowingly, as if he'd read the halfling's every thought.

"This is no job for Regis," the dark elf said.

"He done it on the way to Luskan," Bruenor protested. "Done it well, too."

"But not in this snow," Drizzt replied. "No thief would be able to find appropriate shadows in this white-out. No, let us go in together to see what friends or enemies we might find."

"And if they are ogres?" Catti-brie asked. "Ye thinking we're overdue for a fight?"

Drizzt's expression showed clearly that the notion was not an unpleasant one, but he shook his head. "If they do not concern us, then better that we do not concern them," he said. "But let us learn what we might—it may be that we will find shelter and good food for the night."

Drizzt moved off to the side and a little ahead, and Bruenor led the way along the carved trail. The dwarf brought out his large axe, slapping its handle across his shield hand, and set his one-horned helmet firmly on his head, more than ready for a fight. Behind him, Catti-brie set an arrow to Taulmaril and tested the pull.

If these were ogres or orcs and they happened to have a decent shelter constructed, then Catti-brie fully expected to be occupying that shelter long before nightfall. She knew Bruenor Battlehammer too well to think that the dwarf would ever walk away from a fight with either of those beasts.

* * * * *

"Yer turn to get the firewood," Donbago snarled at his younger brother, Jeddith. He pushed the young man toward the tower door. "We'll all be frozen by morning if ye don't bring it!"

"Yeah, I know," the younger soldier grumbled, running a hand through his greasy hair and scratching at some lice. "Damn weather. Shouldn't be this cold yet."

The other two soldiers in the stone tower grumbled their agreement. Winter had come early, and with vigor, to the Spine of the World, sweeping down on an icy wind that cut right through the stones of the simple tower fortress to bite at the soldiers. They did have a fire burning in the hearth, but it was getting thin, and they didn't have enough wood to get through the night. There was plenty to be found, though, so none of them were worried.

"If ye help me, we'll bring enough to get it blazing," Jeddith observed, but Donbago grumbled about taking his turn on the tower top watch, and headed for the stairs even as Jeddith started for the outside door.

A breeze whistling in through the opened door pushed Donbago along as he made the landing to the second floor, to find the other two soldiers of the remote outpost.

"Well, who's up top?" Donbago scolded.

"No one," answered one of the pair, scaling the ladder running up from the center of the circular floor to the center of the ceiling. "The trapdoor's frozen stuck."

Donbago grumbled and moved to the base of the ladder, watching as his companion for the sentry duty banged at the metal trapdoor. It took them some time to break through the ice, and so Donbago wasn't on the

1057

rooftop and didn't have to watch helplessly as Jeddith, some thirty feet from the tower door, bent over to retrieve some deadwood, oblivious to the hulking ogre that stepped out from behind a tree and crushed his skull with a single blow from a heavy club.

Jeddith went down without a sound, and the marauder dragged him out of sight.

The brute working at the back of the tower was noisier, throwing a grapnel attached to a heavy rope at the tower's top lip, but its tumult was covered by the banging on the metal trapdoor.

Before Donbago and his companion had the door unstuck, the half-ogre grabbed the knotted rope in its powerful hands and walked itself right up the nearly thirty feet of the tower wall, heaving itself to the roof.

The brute turned about, reaching for a large axe it had strapped across its back, even as the door banged open and Donbago climbed through.

With a roar, the half-ogre leaped at him, but it wound up just bowling the man aside. Fortune was with Donbago, and the half-ogre's axe got hooked on the heavy strapping. Still, the man went flying down hard against the tower crenellation, his breath blasting away.

Gasping, Donbago couldn't even cry out a warning as his companion climbed onto the roof. The half-ogre tore its axe free.

Donbago winced and grimaced as the brute cut his companion nearly in half. Donbago drew his sword and forced himself to his feet and into a charge. He let his rage be his guide as he closed on the brute, saw his companion, his friend, half out of the trapdoor, squirming in the last moments of his life. A seasoned warrior, Donbago didn't let the image force him into any rash movements. He came in fast and furiously, but in a tempered manner, launching what looked like a wild swing then retracting the sword just enough so that the brute's powerful parry whistled past without hitting anything.

Now Donbago came forward with a stab, and another, driving the brute back and opening its gut.

The half-ogre wailed and tried to retreat, but lost its footing on the slippery stone and went down hard.

On came Donbago, leaping forward with a tremendous slash, but even as his sword descended, the half-ogre's great leg kicked up, connecting solidly and launching the man into a head-over-heels somersault. His blow still landed, though, and the ragged half-ogre had to work hard to regain its footing.

Donbago was up before it, stabbing and slashing. He kept looking from his target to his dead friend, letting the rage drive him on. Even as the ogre attacked he scored a deep strike. Still, in his offensive stance, he couldn't get aside, and he took a glancing blow from that awful axe. Then he took a heavy punch in the face, one that shattered his nose, cracked the bones in both his cheeks, and sent him skidding back hard into the wall.

He slumped there, telling himself that he had to shake the black spots out of his eyes, had to get up and in a defensive posture, telling himself that the brute was falling over him even then, and that he would be crushed and chopped apart.

With a growl that came from deep in his belly, the dazed and bleeding Donbago forced himself to his feet, his sword before him in a pitiful attempt to ward what he knew would be a killing blow.

But the half-ogre wasn't there. It stood, or rather knelt on one knee by the open trapdoor, clutching at its belly, holding in its entrails, the look on its ugly face one of pure incredulity and pure horror.

Not wanting to wait until the beast decided if the wound was mortal or not, Donbago rushed across the tower top and smashed his sword repeatedly on the half-ogre's upraised arm. When that arm was at last knocked aside, the man continued to bash with every ounce of strength and energy, again spurred on by the sight of his dead companion and by the sudden fear that his brother—

His brother!

Donbago cried out and bashed away, cracking the beast's skull, knocking it flat to the stone. He bashed away some more, long after the half-ogre stopped moving, turning its ugly head to pulp.

Then he got up and staggered to the open hatch, trying to pull his torn friend all the way through. When that didn't work, Donbago pushed the man inside instead, holding him as low as he could so that the fall wouldn't be too jarring to the torn corpse.

Sniffling away the horror and the tears, Donbago called out for the others to secure the tower, called out for someone to go and find his brother.

But he heard the fighting from below and knew that no one was hearing him.

Without the strength to rush down to join them, Donbago considered his other options and worried, too, that other brutes might be climbing up behind him.

He started to turn away from the trapdoor and the spectacle of his dead friend in the room below, but stopped as he saw another of the soldiers rush up the stairs to make the landing at the side of the second level.

"Ogres!" the man cried, stumbling for the ladder. He made it to the base, almost, but then a half-ogre appeared on the landing behind him and launched a grapnel secured to a chain. It hooked over the man's shoulder even as he grabbed the ladder.

Donbago yelled out and started to go down after him, but with a single mighty jerk, an inhumanly powerful tug, the half-ogre tore the man from the ladder, so instantly, so brutally, that Donbago had to blink away the illusion that the man had simply disappeared.

Or part of him had, at least, for still holding the ladder below him was the man's severed arm.

Donbago looked over to the landing just in time to see the man's last moments as the half-ogre pummeled him down to the stone floor. Then the brute looked up at Donbago, smiling wickedly.

The battered Donbago rolled away from the trapdoor and quickly turned the metal portal over and closed it, then rolled on top of it using his body as a locking bar.

A glance at the dead ogre on the tower top reminded him of his vulnerability up there. Hearing no noise from below other than the distant fighting, Donbago leaped up and ran to the back lip of the tower, pulling free the grapnel. He took it with him as he dived back to cover the trapdoor, pulling the rope up the tower's side from there.

A few moment's later, he felt the first jarring blow from beneath him, a thunderous report that shook the teeth in his mouth.

* * * * *

Drizzt noted that the tower door was ajar, and noted, too, the crimson stain on the snow near some trees not far away. Then he heard the shout from the tower top.

He motioned for his friends to be alert and ready, then sprinted off to the side, flanking the tower, trying to get a measure of what was happening and where he would best fit into the battle.

Catti-brie and Bruenor stayed on the ogre trail, but moved more cautiously then, motioning to Drizzt. To the drow's surprise, Regis did not remain with the pair. The halfling ran off to the left, flanking the tower the other way. He plowed through the snow, then finally reached a patch of wind-blown stone and sprinted off from shadow to shadow, keeping low and moving swiftly, heading around the back.

Drizzt couldn't suppress a grin, thinking that Regis was typically trying to find an out-of-the-way hiding spot.

That smile went away almost immediately, though, as the drow came to understand that the threat was imminent, that indeed battle was already underway. He saw a man, his tunic and face bloody, sprint out of the open tower door and rush off to the side, screaming for help.

A hulking form, a large and ugly ogre, chased after him in close pursuit, its already bloody club raised high.

The man had a few step lead, but that wouldn't last in the deep snow, Drizzt knew. The ogre's longer and stronger legs would close the gap fast, and that club. . . .

Drizzt turned away from the tower in pursuit of the pair. He managed to offer a quick hand signal to Bruenor and Catti-brie, showing them his intent and indicating that they should continue on to the tower. He ran on, his light steps keeping him atop the snow pack.

At first Drizzt feared that the ogre would get to the fleeing man first, but the man put on a burst of speed and dived headlong over the side of a ridge, tumbling away in the snow.

The ogre stopped at the ridge, and Drizzt yelled out. The brute seemed more than happy to spin about and fight this newest challenger. Of course, the eager gleam in the ogre's eye melted away, and the stupid grin became an expression of surprise indeed when the ogre recognized that this newest challenger was not another human, but a drow elf.

Drizzt went in hard, scimitars whirling, hoping to make a quick kill. Then he could see to the wounded man, and he could get back to the tower and help his friends.

But this brute was no ordinary ogre. This was a seasoned warrior, nine feet of muscle and bone with the agility to maneuver its heavy spiked club with surprising deftness.

Drizzt's eagerness nearly cost him dearly, for as he came ahead, scimitars twirling in oppositional arcs, the quick-footed ogre stepped back just out of range and brought its club across with a tremendous sweep, taking one scimitar along with it. Drizzt was barely able to keep a grip on the weapon. If he'd dropped it, he might never find it in the deep snow.

Drizzt managed not only to get his second blade, in his right hand, out of the way of the blow, but he got in a stab that bloodied the ogre's trailing forearm. The brute accepted the sting, though, in exchange for slipping through its real attack. Lifting its heavy leg and following the sweep of the club with a mighty kick, it caught Drizzt on the shoulder and launched him a dozen spinning feet through the air to crash down into the snow.

The drow recognized his error, then, and was only glad that he had made the error out in the open, where he could fast recover. If he had gotten kicked like that inside the tower, he figured he'd now be little more than a red stain on the stone wall.

* * * * *

They saw the drow's signal, but neither Bruenor nor Catti-brie were about to abandon Drizzt as he chased off after the ogre—until they heard the cry for help, as pitiful a wail as either had ever heard, coming from inside the tower.

"Ye keep yer damned shots higher than me head!" Bruenor yelled to his girl, and the dwarf bent his shoulders low and rambled on for the tower door, gaining speed, momentum, and fury.

Catti-brie worked hard to keep up, just a few feet behind, Taulmaril in hand, leveled and ready.

There was nothing subtle or quiet about the dwarf's charge, and predictably, Bruenor was met at the doorway by another hulking form. The dwarf's axe chopped hard. Catti-brie's arrow slammed the brute in the chest. Those two blows, combined with the sturdy dwarf's momentum, got Bruenor crashing into the main area of the tower's lowest floor.

This opponent, a half-ogre and a tough one at that, wasn't finished. It managed a counterstrike with its club, bouncing a mighty hit off Bruenor's shoulder.

"Ye got to do better than that!" the dwarf bellowed, though in truth, the blow hurt.

Smiling in spite of the pain, Bruenor swiped his axe across. The half-ogre stumbled out of reach but came back forward for a counter too soon. Bruenor's backhand caught it flat against the ribs, stealing its momentum and its intended attack.

The half-ogre staggered, giving Bruenor the time to set his feet properly and begin again. The next hit wasn't with the flat of the axe, but with the jagged, many-notched head, a swipe that cut a slice right down the battered brute's chest.

Before Bruenor could begin to celebrate the apparent victory, though, a second half-ogre leaped out from the stairway, slamming into its mortally wounded companion and taking both of them crashing over Bruenor, burying the dwarf beneath nearly a ton of flesh and bone.

The dwarf needed Catti-brie sorely at that point, but a call from above told him that, perhaps, so did someone else.

* * * * *

At the back of the tower, in close to the base of the wall and listening intently, Regis heard Bruenor's charge. He didn't have any great urge to go around with the dwarf, though, for Bruenor's tactics were straightforward, muscle against muscle, trading punch for punch.

Joining in that strategy against ogres, Regis wouldn't last beyond the first blow.

A cry from above jarred the halfling. He started to climb hand over hand, picking holds in the cold, cracked stone. By the time he was halfway up, his poor fingers were scraped and bleeding, but he kept going, moving with deceiving swiftness, picking his holds expertly and nearing the top.

He heard a yell and a crash, then some heavy scuffling. Up he went with all speed, and he nearly slipped and fell, catching himself at the very last moment—and with more than a little luck.

Finally he put his hand on the lip of the tower top and peeked over. What he saw almost made him want to leap right off.

* * * * *

Poor Donbago, crying out repeatedly, only wanted to hold the portal shut, to close his eyes and will all of this horror away. He was a seasoned fighter and had seen many battles and had lost many friends.

But not his brother.

He knew in his heart that Jeddith was down, and likely dead. He knew in his heart that the tower was lost, and that there would be no escape. Perhaps if he just lay there long enough, using his body to block the trapdoor, the brutes would go away. He knew, after all, that ogres were not known for persistence or for cunning.

Most were not, at least.

Donbago hardly noticed the warmth at first, though he did smell the burning leather. He didn't understand—until a sharp pain erupted in his back. Reflexively, the man rolled, but he stopped at once, realizing that he had to hold the door shut.

He tried going back, but the metal was hot—so hot!

The ogres below must have been heating it with torches.

Donbago jumped atop the door, hoping his boots would insulate him from the heat. He heard a scream as one of his companions exited the tower, and, a few moments later, a roar from below, by the front door.

He was hopping, his boots smoking. He looked around frantically, searching for something he could use to place over the door, a loose stone in the crenellation, perhaps.

He went flying away as an ogre below leveled a tremendous blow to the door. A second strike, before Donbago could scramble back, had the portal bouncing open. A brute came through with amazing speed, obviously boosted to the roof by a companion.

Donbago, waves of pain still spreading from his broken face, leaped into the fray immediately and furiously, thinking of his brother with every mad strike. He scored a couple of hits on the ogre, which seemed truly surprised by his ferocity, but then its companion was up beside it. Two heavy clubs swatted at him, back and forth.

He ducked, he dodged, he didn't even try to parry the too-powerful blows, and his desperate offensive posture allowed him to manage another serious stab at the first brute, sending it sprawling to the stone.

Donbago got hit, knocked to his back, his sword flying, and before he even realized what had happened, the valiant soldier felt a strong hand grab his ankle.

In an instant, he was scooped aloft, hanging upside down at the end of a mighty ogre's arm.

* * * * *

Drizzt rolled across the snow, not fighting the momentum but enhancing it, allowing the ogre's kick to take him as far from his formidable opponent as possible. He wanted to get up and face the ogre squarely, to take a better measure and put this fight back on more recognizable ground. He believed that his underestimation of his opponent alone had cost him that hit, that he had erred greatly.

He was surprised again when he at last tucked his feet under him and started to rise, to find that the ogre had kept up with him and was even then coming in for another furious attack.

The brute was moving too fast—too far beyond what Drizzt, no novice to battling ogres, would have expected from one of its lumbering kind.

In came the club, swatting down to the left, forcing the drow to dodge right. The ogre halted the swing quickly and put the club up and over, taking it up in both hands like someone splitting wood might, and slamming it straight down at the new position Drizzt was settling into, with more force than one of Drizzt's stature could possibly hope to block or even deflect.

Drizzt dived into a roll back to the left, coming up facing to the side and rushing fast in retreat, putting some ground between himself and the brute. He spun at the ready, almost expecting this surprising foe to be upon him once again.

This time, though, the ogre had remained in place. It grinned as it regarded Drizzt, then pulled a ceramic flask from its belt—a belt that already showed several open loops, Drizzt noted—and popped it into its mouth, chewing it up to get at the potion.

Almost immediately, the ogre's arms began to bulge with heightened strength, with the strength of a great giant.

Drizzt actually felt better now that he had sorted out the riddle. The ogre had taken a potion of speed, obviously, and now one of strength, and likely others of enhancing magical properties. Now the drow understood, and now the drow could better anticipate.

Drizzt lamented that Guenhwyvar had been with him the night before, that he had used up the magic of the figurine for the time being. He could not recall the panther, and now, it seemed, he could use the help.

In came the ogre, swatting its club all about, howling with rage and with the anticipation of this sweet kill. Drizzt had to drop low to his knees, else that victory would have come quickly for the brute.

But now Drizzt had a plan. The ogre was moving more quickly than it was used to moving, and its great strength would send its club out with tremendous, often unbreakable momentum. Drizzt could use that against the beast, perhaps, could utilize misdirection as a way of having the ogre off-balance and with apparent openings.

Up came the drow, skittering to the side—or seeming to—then cutting back and rushing straight ahead, scoring a solid hit on the ogre's leg as he waded past.

He continued and dived ahead, turning as he came up to face his foe, expecting to see the blood turning bright red near that torn leg.

The ogre was hardly bleeding, as if something other than its skin had absorbed the bulk of that wicked scimitar strike.

Drizzt's mind whirled through the possibilities. There were potions, he had heard, that could do such things, potions offering varying degrees of added heroism.

"Ah, Guen," the drow lamented, for he knew that he was in for quite a fight.

* * * * *

The dwarf wondered if he would simply suffocate under the press of the two heavy bodies, particularly the dead weight of the one he had defeated. He squirmed and tucked his legs, then worked to find some solid footing and pushed ahead with all his strength, his short, bunched muscles straining mightily.

He got his head out from under the fallen brute's hip, but then had to duck right back underneath as the second brute, still lying atop the dying one, slapped down at him with a powerful grasping hand.

The ogre finger-walked that hand underneath in pursuit of the dwarf, and with his own arms still pinned down beside him, Bruenor couldn't match the grab.

So he bit the hand instead, latching on like an angry dog, gnashing his teeth, and crunching the brute's knuckles.

The half-ogre howled and pulled back, but the dwarf's mighty jaw remained clamped. Bruenor held on ferociously. The brute crawled off its dying companion, twisting about to gain some leverage, then lifted the fallen ogre's hip and tugged hard, pulling the dwarf out on the end of its arm.

The brute lifted its other arm to smack at the dwarf, but once free, Bruenor didn't hesitate. He grabbed the trapped forearm in both hands and, still biting hard, ran straight back, turning about and twisting the arm as he went behind the half-ogre.

"Got one for ye!" the dwarf yelled, finally releasing his bite, for he had the half-ogre off-balance then, momentarily helpless and lined up for the open doorway. Bruenor drove ahead with all his strength and leverage, forcing the brute into a quick-step. With a great heave, the dwarf got the brute to the doorway and through it.

Where Catti-brie's arrow met it, square in the chest.

The half-ogre staggered backward, or started to, for as soon as he had let the thing go, Bruenor quick-stepped back a few steps, rubbed his heavy boots on the stone for traction, and rushed forward, leaping as the half-ogre staggered back to slam hard into the brute's lower back.

The brute stumbled out through the door, where another arrow hit it hard in the chest.

It fell to its knees grasping at the two shafts with trembling hands.

Catti-brie shot it again, right in the face.

"More on the stairs!" Bruenor yelled out to her. "Come on, girl, I need ye!"

Catti-brie started forward, ready to rush right in past the brute she had just felled, but then came another cry from above. She looked up to see a squirming, whimpering man hanging out over the tower's edge, a huge half-ogre holding him by the ankles.

Up came Taulmaril, leveling at the brute's face, for Catti-brie figured that the man might well survive the fall into the snow, which was piled pretty deep on this side of the tower, but knew that he had no chance of surviving his current captor.

But the half-ogre saw her as well, and, with a wicked grin, brought up its own weapon—a huge club—and lined up for a hit that would surely break the squirming man apart.

Catti-brie reflexively cried out.

* * * * *

At the back of the tower top, Regis heard that cry. Looking that way he understood that the poor soldier was in a precarious predicament. But the halfling couldn't get to the brute in time, and even if he did, what could he and his tiny mace do against something of that monster's bulk?

The second half-ogre, wounded by the soldier's valiant fight but not down, was on the move again to join its companion. It rushed across the tower top, oblivious to the halfling peering over the rim.

Purely on instinct—if he had thought about it, the halfling would have more likely simply passed out from fear than made the move—Regis pulled himself over the lip and scrambled forward half running, half diving, skidding low right between the running half-ogre's leading heel and trailing toe.

The brute tripped up, its kick as it stumbled forward jolting and battering the poor halfling and lifting Regis into a short flight.

Out of control, the half-ogre gained momentum, falling headlong into its companion's broad back.

* * * * *

Catti-brie saw no choice but to take her chances on the shot, much as she had done against the pirate holding Delly in Captain Deudermont's house.

The half-ogre apparently anticipated just that and delayed its swing at the man and ducked back instead, the arrow streaking harmlessly into the air before it.

Catti-brie winced, thinking the man surely doomed. Before she could even reach to set another arrow, though, the half-ogre came forward suddenly, way over the tower lip. It let go of the man, who dropped, screaming, into the snow. It too went over, hands flailing helplessly.

* * * * *

Gasping for his lost breath, his ribs sorely bruised, the battered halfling struggled to his feet and faced the half-ogre he had tripped even as the brute turned to regard him ominously. Its look was one of pure menace, promising a horrible death.

With a growl, it took a long step toward the halfling.

Regis considered his little mace, a perfectly insignificant weapon against the sheer mass and strength of this brute, then sighed and tossed it to the ground. With a tip of his hood, the halfling turned around and ran for the back of the tower, crying out with every running step. He understood the drop over that lip. It was a good thirty feet, and the back side of the tower, unlike the front, was nearly clear, wind-blown stone.

Still, the halfling never slowed. He leaped up and rolled over the edge. Without slowing, roaring in rage with every step, the half-ogre dived over right behind.

* * * * *

The lower vantage point for Bruenor proved an advantage as he charged at the half-ogre standing on the curving stairway. The brute slammed its club straight down at the dwarf but Bruenor got his fine shield—emblazoned with the "foaming mug" standard of Clan Battlehammer—up over his head and angled perfectly. The dwarf was strong enough of arm to accept and deflect the blow.

The half-ogre wasn't as fortunate against the counter, a mighty sweep of Bruenor's fine axe that cracked the brute's ankle, snapping bone and digging a deep, deep gash. The half-ogre howled in pain and reached down reflexively to grab at the torn limb. Bruenor moved against the wall and leaped up three steps, putting him one above the bending half-ogre. The dwarf turned and braced, planting his shield against the brute as it started to turn to face him. Bruenor shoved out with all his strength, his short, muscled legs driving hard.

The half-ogre went off the stairs. It wasn't a long fall, but one that proved disastrous, for as the brute tried to hold its balance it landed hard on the broken ankle. It fell over on its side with a howl.

Its blurry vision cleared a moment later, and it looked back to see a flying red-bearded dwarf coming its way, mouth opened in a primal roar, face twisted with eager rage, and that devilish axe gripped in both hands.

The dwarf snapped his body as he impacted, driving the axe in hard and heavy, cleaving the half-ogre's head in half.

"Bet that hurt," Bruenor grumbled, pulling himself to his feet.

He looked at the gore on his axe and winced, then just shrugged and wiped it on the dead beast's dirty fur tunic.

* * * * *

Drizzt skittered back against a tree, then ducked and rolled around it to avoid a thundering smash.

The ogre's club smacked hard against the young tree and proved the stronger, cracking the living wood apart.

Drizzt groaned aloud as he considered the toppling tree, picturing what his own slender form might have looked like had he not dodged aside. He had no time to ponder at length, though, for the ogre, moving with enhanced speed and wielding its heavy club with ease with its giant-strength muscles, was fast in pursuit. It leaped the falling tree and swung again.

Drizzt fell to the snow flat on his face, the club whistling right above him. With amazing speed and grace, the drow put his legs under him and leaped straight up over the ogre's fast backhand, which came down diagonally from the side to smack the spot where Drizzt had just been lying. In the air, the drow had little weight behind the strikes, but he worked his scimitars in rapid alternating stabs, popping their points into the ogre's broad chest.

The drow landed lightly and went right back into the air, twisting as he did so that he rolled over the side-cutting club. As he landed he reversed the momentum of his somersault and drove one blade hard into the ogre's belly. Again, he didn't score nearly as much of a wound as he would have expected, but he didn't pause to lament the fact. He spun around the ogre's hip, reversed his grip on the blade in his right hand, and stabbed it out and hard into the back of the ogre's treelike leg.

Drizzt sprinted straight ahead, leaping another fallen tree and spinning around a pair of oaks, turning to face his predictably charging opponent.

The ogre chased him around the two oaks, but Drizzt held an advantage, for he could cut between the close-growing trees while the huge brute had to circle both. He went to the outside through a couple of rotations, letting the ogre fall into a set pace, then darted between the trees and came around fast and hard before the brute could properly turn and set its defenses.

Again the drow scored a pair of hits, one a stab, the other a slash. As he came across with his right hand, he followed through with the motion, turning a complete circle then sprinting ahead once more, the howling ogre in fast pursuit.

And so it went for many minutes, Drizzt using a hit and retreat strategy, hoping to tire the ogre, hoping that the potions, likely temporary enhancements, would run their course.

Drizzt scored again and again with minor hits, but he knew that this was no contest of finesse, where the better fighter would be awarded the victory by some neutral judges. This was a battle to the end, and while he looked beautiful with his precision movements and strikes, the only hit that would matter would be the last one. Given the ogre's sheer power, given the images burned into the drow's mind as yet another tree splintered and toppled under the weight of the brute's blow, Drizzt understood that the first solid hit he took from the creature would likely be the last hit of the fight.

The drow went full speed over one snowy ridge, diving down in a roll on his back and sliding to the bottom. He came up fast, spinning to face the pursuit. The drow was looking to score another hit, perhaps, or more likely, in this unfavorable place, to simply run away.

But the ogre wasn't there, and Drizzt understood that it had used its heightened speed and heightened strength in a different manner when he heard the brute touch down behind him.

The ogre had leaped off the top of the ridge, right over the sliding and turning drow.

Drizzt realized his mistake.

* * * * *

The surprised half-ogre landed flat on its back a few feet out from the tower and from the captive it had dropped, but was moving immediately, hardly seeming hurt, scrambling to its feet.

Catti-brie led her charge with another streaking arrow, a gut shot, then she threw her bow aside and drew out Khazid'hea. The eager sword telepathically prompted her to cut the beast apart.

The brute clutched at its belly wound with one hand and reached out at her with the other, as if to try to catch her charge. The flash of Khazid'hea ended that possibility, sending stubby fingers flying all about.

Catti-brie went in with fury, taking the advantage and never offering it back, slashing her fine-edged sword to and fro and hardly slowing enough to even bother to line up her strikes.

She didn't have to; not with this sword.

The half-ogre's heavy clothing and hide armor parted as if it was thin paper, and bright lines of red striped the creature in a matter of moments.

The half-ogre managed one punch out at her, but Khazid'hea was there, intercepting the punch with its sharp edge, splitting the half-ogre's hand and riding that cut right up through its thick wrist.

How the beast howled!

But that cry was silenced a moment later when Catti-brie slashed Khazid'hea across up high, taking out the brute's throat. Down went the half-ogre, and Catti-brie leaped beside it, her sword slashing repeatedly.

"Girl!" Bruenor cried, half in terror and half in surprise when he exited the tower to see his adopted daughter covered in blood. He ran to her and nearly got cut in half as she swung around, Khazid'hea flashing.

"It's the damn sword!" Bruenor cried at her, falling back and throwing his arms up defensively.

Catti-brie stopped suddenly, staring at her fine blade with shock.

Bruenor was right. In her moment of anger and terror at seeing the man fall from the tower, in her moment of guilt blaming herself for the man's fall because of her missed bowshot, the viciously sentient sword Khazid'hea had found its way into her thoughts yet again, prodding her into a frenzy.

She laughed aloud, helplessly. Her white teeth looked ridiculous, shining out from her bloodied face. She slapped the sword's blade down into the snow.

"Girl?" Bruenor asked cautiously.

"I'm thinking that we could both use a bath," Catti-brie said to him, obviously in control again.

* * * * *

Regis, hanging on the edge of the tower top, wondered if the half-ogre even understood its mistake as it flew out over him, limbs flailing wildly on its fast descent to the stony ground. The brute hit with a muffled groan, and bounced once or twice.

The halfling pulled himself back over the tower top and looked down to see the half-ogre stubbornly trying to regain its footing. It stumbled once and went back down, but then tried to rise again.

Regis retrieved his little mace and took aim. He whistled down to the half-ogre as he let fly, timing it perfectly so that the brute looked up just in time to catch the falling weapon right in the face. There came a sharp report, like metal hitting stone, and the half-ogre stood there for a long while, staring up at Regis.

The halfling sucked in his breath, hardly believing that the mace, falling from thirty feet, hadn't done more damage.

But it had. The brute went down hard and didn't get up.

A shiver coursed up Regis's little spine, and he paused long enough to consider his actions in this battle, to consider that he had gotten involved at all when he really didn't have to. The halfling tried very hard not to look at things that way, tried to remind himself repeatedly that he had acted in accordance with the tenets of his group of friends, his dear, trusted companions, who would risk their lives without a second thought to help those in dire need.

Not for the first time, and not for the last, Regis wondered if he would be better off finding a new group of friends.

* * * * *

Drizzt could only guess from which direction the ogre's mighty swing would come, and he understood that if he guessed wrong, he'd be leaping

1070

right into the oncoming blow. In the split second he had to react, it all sorted out, his warrior instincts replaying the ogre's fighting style, telling him clearly that the ogre had initiated every attack with a right-to-left strike.

So Drizzt went left, his magical anklets speeding his feet into a desperate run.

And the club swatted in behind him, clipping him as he turned and leaped, launching him into a long, twisting tumble. The snow padded his fall, but when he came up he found that he was only holding one scimitar. His right arm had gone completely numb and his shoulder and side were exploding with pain. The drow glanced down and winced. His shoulder had clearly been dislocated, pushed back from its normal position.

Drizzt didn't have long, for the ogre was coming on in pursuit—though, the drow noted with some hope, not as quickly as it had been moving.

Drizzt skittered away, turning as he went and literally throwing himself backward into a tree, using the solidity of the tree to pop his shoulder back into place. The wave of agony turned his stomach and brought black spots spinning before his eyes. He nearly swooned, but knew that if he gave into that momentary weakness, the ogre would break him apart.

He rolled around the tree and stumbled away, buying himself more time. He knew then, by how easily he could distance himself from the brute, that at least one of the potions had worn off.

Every step was bringing some measure of relief to Drizzt. The ache in his shoulder had lessened already, and he found that he could feel his fingers again. He took a circuitous route that led him back to his fallen scimitar, with the dumb ogre, apparently thinking that it had the fight won, following fast in pursuit.

Drizzt stopped and turned, his lavender eyes boring into the approaching brute. Just before the combatants came together, their gazes met, and the ogre's confidence melted away.

There would be no underestimation by the dark elf this time.

Drizzt came ahead in a fury, holding the ogre's stare with his own. His scimitars worked as if of their own accord, in perfect harmony and with blazing speed—too quickly for the ogre, its magical speed worn away and its giant strength diminishing, to possibly keep up. The brute tried to take an offensive posture instead, swinging wildly, but Drizzt was behind it before it ever completed the blow. That other potion, the one that had someone made the ogre resistant to the drow's scimitar stings, was also dissipating.

This time, both Twinkle and Icingdeath dug in, one taking a kidney, the other hamstringing the brute.

Drizzt worked in a fury but with controlled precision, rushing all around his opponent, stabbing and slashing, and always at a vital area.

The victorious drow put his scimitars away soon after, his right arm going numb again now that the adrenaline of battle was subsiding.

Swaying with every step, and cursing himself for taking such an enemy as that for granted, he made his way back to the tower. There he found Bruenor and Regis sitting by the open door, both looking battered, and Catti-brie covered head to toe in blood, standing nearby, tending to a dazed and wounded man.

"A fine thing it'll be if we all wind up killed to death in battle afore we ever get to the pirate Kree," Bruenor grumbled.

Chapter 19

Wulfgar's Choice

He wasn't dead. Following Donbago's directions, after Jeddith had recovered his wits from the fall, Catti-brie and Regis found his brother behind some brush not far from the tower. His head was bloody and aching. They wrapped some bandages tight around the wound and tried to make him as comfortable as possible, but it became obvious that the dazed and delirious man would need to see a healer, and soon.

"He's alive," Catti-brie announced to the man as she and Regis ushered him back to where Donbago sat propped against the tower.

Tears streamed down Donbago's face. "Me thanks," he said over and over again. "Whoever ye are, me thanks for me brother's life and me own."

"Another one's alive inside the tower," Bruenor announced, coming out. "Ye finally waked up, eh?" he asked Donbago, who was nodding appreciatively.

"And we got one o' them stupid half-ogries alive," Bruenor added. "Ugly thing."

"We have to get this one to a healer, and quick," Catti-brie explained as she and Regis managed to ease the half-conscious Jeddith down beside his brother.

1073

"Auckney," Donbago insisted. "Ye got to get us to Auckney."

Drizzt came through the door and heard the man clearly. He and Catti-brie exchanged curious glances, knowing the name well from the tale Delly Curtie had told them of Wulfgar and the baby.

"How far a journey is Auckney?" the drow asked Donbago.

The man turned to regard Drizzt, and his eyes popped open wide. He seemed as if he would just fall over.

"He gets that a lot," Regis quipped, patting Donbago's shoulder. "He'll forgive you."

"Drow?" Donbago asked, trying to turn to regard Regis, but seeming unable to tear his eyes from the spectacle of a dark elf.

"Good drow," Regis explained. "You'll get to like him after a while."

"Bah, an elf's an elf!" Bruenor snorted.

"Yer pardon, good drow," Donbago stammered, obviously at a loss, his emotions torn between the fact that this group had just saved his life and his brother's, and all he'd ever known about the race of evil dark elves.

"No pardon is needed," Drizzt replied, "but an answer would be appreciated."

Donbago considered the statement for a few moments, then bobbed his head repeatedly. "Auckney," he echoed. "A few days and no more, if the weather holds."

"A few days if it don't," said Bruenor. "Good enough then. We got two to carry and a half-ogre to drag along by the crotch."

"I think the brute can walk," Drizzt remarked. "He's a bit heavy to drag."

Drizzt fashioned a pair of litters out of blankets and sticks he retrieved from nearby, and the group left soon after. As it turned out, the half-ogre wasn't too badly wounded. That was a good thing, for while Bruenor could drag along Jeddith, the drow's injured shoulder would not allow him the strength to pull the other litter. They made the prisoner do it, with Catti-brie walking right behind, Taulmaril strung and ready, an arrow set to its string.

The weather did hold, and the ragged band, battered as they were, made strong headway, arriving at the outskirts of Auckney in less than three days.

* * * * *

Wulfgar blinked repeatedly as the multicolored bubbles popped and dissipated in the air around him. Never fond of, and not very familiar with the ways of magic, the barbarian had to spend a long while reorienting himself to his new surroundings, for no longer was he in the grand city of Waterdeep. One structure, a uniquely designed tower whose branching arms made it look like a living tree, confirmed to Wulfgar that he was in Luskan now, as Robillard had promised.

1074

"I see doubt clearly etched upon your face," the wizard remarked sourly. "I thought we had agreed—"

"You agreed," Wulfgar interrupted, "with yourself."

"You do not believe this to be the best course for you, then?" Robillard asked skeptically. "You would prefer the company of Delly Curtie back in the safety of Waterdeep, back in the security of a blacksmith's shop?"

The words surely stung the barbarian, but it was Robillard's condescending tone that really made Wulfgar want to throttle the skinny man. He didn't look at the wizard, fearing that he would simply spit in Robillard's face. He wasn't really afraid of a fight with the formidable wizard, not when he was this close, but if one did ensue and he did break Robillard in half, he'd have a long walk indeed back to Waterdeep.

"I will not go through this again with you, Wulfgar of Icewind Dale," Robillard remarked. "Or Wulfgar of Waterdeep, or Wulfgar of wherever you think Wulfgar should be from. I have offered you more than you deserve from me already, and more than I would normally offer to one such as you. I must be in a fine and generous mood this day."

Wulfgar scowled at him, but that only made Robillard laugh aloud.

"You are in the exact center of the city," Robillard went on. "Through the south gate lies the road to Waterdeep and Delly, and your job as a smith. Through the north gate, the road back to your friends and what I believe to be your true home. I suspect that you'll find the south road an easier journey by far than the north, Wulfgar son of Beornegar."

Wulfgar didn't respond, didn't even return the measuring stare Robillard was now casting over him. He knew which road the wizard believed he should take.

"I have always found those who take the easier road, when they know they should be walking the more difficult one, to be cowards," Robillard remarked. "Haven't you?"

"It is not as easy as you make it sound," Wulfgar replied quietly.

"It is likely far more difficult than ever I could imagine," the wizard said. For the first time, Wulfgar detected a bit of sympathy in his voice. "I know nothing of that which you have endured, nothing of the pains that have so weakened your heart. But I know who you were, and know who you now are, and I can say with more than a little confidence that you are better off walking into darkness and dying than trying to hide behind the embers of a smithy's hearth.

"Those are your choices," the wizard finished. "Farewell, wherever you fare!" With that Robillard began waving his arms again, casting another spell.

Wulfgar, distracted and looking to the north, didn't notice until it was too late. He turned to see the multicolored bubbles already filling the air around the vanishing wizard. A sack appeared where the wizard had been standing, along with a large axelike bardiche. It was a rather unwieldy weapon, but one that resembled the great warhammer in design and style of fighting, at least, and one that could deal tremendous damage. He knew without even looking that the sack likely contained supplies for the road.

Wulfgar was alone, as much so as he had ever been, standing in the exact center of Luskan, and he remembered then that he was not supposed to be in this place. He was an outlaw in Luskan, or had been. He could only hope that the magistrates and the guards did not have so long a memory.

But which way to go, the barbarian wondered. He turned several circles. It was all too confusing, all too frightening, and Robillard's dire words haunted him with every turn.

Wulfgar of Icewind Dale exited Luskan's northern gate soon after, trudging off alone into the cold wilderness.

*　*　*　*　*

It was under the glare of one surprised and horrified expression after another that the friends made their way through the small village of Auckney and into the castle of Lord Feringal and Lady Meralda. Donbago, well enough to walk easily by that time, guided them in and warded away any who grabbed at weapons at the sight of the half-ogre, to say nothing of the dark elf.

Donbago talked them through a mob of soldiers led by a growling gnome guard at the door. The gnome put the others into efficient motion, helping Donbago scurry poor delirious Jeddith off to the healer and dragging the half-ogre down into the dungeons, beating the brute with every step.

The fierce gnome, Liam Woodgate, then led the five to an inner room and introduced them to an old, hawkish-looking man named Temigast.

"Drizzt Do'Urden," Temigast echoed, nodding with recognition as he spoke the name. "The ranger of Ten-Towns, I have heard. And you, good dwarf, are you not the King of Mithral Hall?"

"Was once and will be again, if me friends here don't get me killed to death," Bruenor replied.

"Might we meet with yer lord and lady?" Catti-brie asked. While Regis and Bruenor looked at her curiously, Drizzt, who also wanted to get a glimpse of this woman who had mothered the child Wulfgar was now raising as his own, smiled.

"Liam will show you to a place where you can properly clean and dress for your audience," Steward Temigast explained. "When you are ready, the audience with the Lord and Lady of Auckney will be arranged."

While Bruenor barely splashed some of the water over him, grumbling that he looked good enough for anyone, Drizzt and Regis thoroughly washed. In another room, Catti-brie not only took a most welcomed soapy bath, but then spent a long while trying on many of the gorgeous gowns that Lady Meralda had sent down to her.

Soon after, the four were in the grand audience hall of Castle Auck, standing before Lord Feringal, a man in his thirties with curly black hair and a thick, dark goatee, and Lady Meralda, younger and an undeniably beautiful woman, with raven hair and creamy skin and a smile that brightened the whole of the huge room.

And while the Lord of Auckney was scowling almost continually, Meralda's smile didn't dissipate for a moment.

"I suppose that you now desire a reward," asked the third in attendance, a shrewish, heavyset woman seated to Feringal's left and just a bit behind, which, in the tradition of the region, marked her as Feringal's sister.

Behind the four road-weary companions, Steward Temigast cleared his throat.

"Ye thinking ye got enough gold for us to even notice?" Bruenor growled back at her.

"We have no need of coin," Drizzt interjected, trying to keep things calm. Bruenor had just suffered a bath, after all, and that always put the already surly dwarf into an even more foul mood. "We came here merely to return Donbago and two wounded men to their homes, as well as to deliver the prisoner. We would ask, though, that if you garner any information from the brute that might concern a certain notorious pirate by the name of Sheila Kree, you would pass it along. It is Kree we are hunting."

"Of course we will share with ye whatever we might learn," the Lady Meralda replied, cutting short her husband, whatever he meant to say. "And more. Whatever ye're needing, we're owing."

Drizzt didn't miss the scowl from the woman at the side, and he knew it to be both her general surliness and the somewhat common manner in which the Lady of Auckney spoke.

"Ye can stay the winter through, if ye so choose," Meralda went on.

Feringal looked at her, at first with surprise, but then in agreement.

"We might find an empty house about the town for—" the woman behind started to say.

"We will put them up right here in the castle, Priscilla," the Lady of Auckney declared.

"I hardly think—" Priscilla started to argue.

"In yer own room if I hear another word from ye," Meralda said, and she threw a wink at the four friends.

"Feri!" Priscilla roared.

"Shut up, dear sister," said Feringal, in an exasperated tone that showed the friends clearly that he often had to extend such sentiments his troublesome sister's way. "Do not embarrass us before our most distinguished guests—guests who rescued three of my loyal soldiers and avenged our losses at the hands of the beastly ogres."

"Guests who've got tales to tell of faraway lands and dragon's hoards," Meralda added with a gleam in her green eyes.

"Only the night, I fear," said Drizzt. "Our road will be winding and long, no doubt. We are determined to find and punish the pirate Kree before the spring thaw—before she can put her ship back out into the safety of the open seas and bring more mischief to the waters off Luskan."

Meralda's disappointment was obvious, but Feringal nodded, seeming to hardly care whether they stayed or left.

The Lord and Lady of Auckney put on a splendid feast that night in honor of the heroes, and Donbago was able to attend as well, bringing with him the welcomed news that both his brother and the other man were faring better and seemed as if they would recover.

They ate (Bruenor and Regis more than all the others combined!) and they laughed. The companions, with so many miles beneath their weathered and well-worn boots, told tales of faraway lands as Lady Meralda had desired.

Much later, Catti-brie managed to toss a wink and nod to Drizzt, guiding him into a small side room where they could be alone. They fell onto a couch, side by side, beneath a bright tapestry cheaply sketched but with rich colors.

"Ye think we should tell her about the babe?" Catti-brie asked, her hand settling on Drizzt's slender, strong forearm.

"That would only bring her pain, after the initial relief, I fear," the drow replied. "One day, perhaps, but not now."

"Oh, ye must join us!" Meralda interrupted, coming through the door to stand beside the pair. "King Bruenor is telling the best o' tales, one of a dark dragon that stole his kingdom."

"One we're knowing all too well," Catti-brie replied with a smile.

"But it would be impolite not to hear it again," said Drizzt, rising. He took Catti-brie's hand and pulled her up, and the two started past Meralda.

"So do ye think ye'll find him?" the Lady of Auckney asked as they walked by.

The pair stopped and turned as one to regard her.

"The other one of yer group," Meralda explained. "The one who went to reclaim Mithral Hall with ye, by the dwarf's own words." She paused and stared hard at both of them. "The one ye call Wulfgar."

Drizzt and Catti-brie stood silent for a moment, the woman so obviously on the edge of her nerves here, biting her lip and looking to the drow for a cue.

"It is our hope to find him, and find him whole," Drizzt answered quietly, trying not to involve the whole room in this conversation.

"I've an interest . . ."

"We know all about it," Catti-brie interjected.

Lady Meralda stood very straight, obviously fighting to keep herself from swaying.

"The child grows strong and safe," Drizzt assured her.

"And what did they name her?"

"Colson."

Meralda sighed and steadied herself. A sadness showed in her green eyes, but she managed a smile a moment later. "Come," she said quietly. "Let us go and hear the dwarf's tale."

* * * * *

"The prisoner will be hung as soon as we find a rope strong enough to hold it," Lord Feringal assured the group early the next morning, when they had gathered at the foyer of Castle Auckney, preparing to leave.

"The beast fancies itself a strong one," the man went on with a snicker. "But how it whimpered last night!"

Drizzt winced, as did Catti-brie and Regis, but Bruenor merely nodded.

"The brute was indeed part of a larger band," Feringal explained. "Perhaps pirates, though the stupid creature didn't seem to understand the word."

"Perhaps Kree," the drow said. "Do you have any idea where the raiding band came from?"

"South coast of the mountain spur," Feringal answered. "We could not get the ogre to admit it openly, but we believe it knows something of Minster Gorge. It will be a difficult hike in winter, with the passes likely full of snow."

"Difficult, but one worth taking," Drizzt replied.

Lady Meralda entered the room then, seeming no less beautiful in the early morning light than she had the night before. She regarded Drizzt and Catti-brie each in turn, offering a grateful smile.

And both the woman and the drow noted, too, that Feringal couldn't hide his scowl at the silent exchange. The wounds here were still too raw, and Feringal had obviously recognized Wulfgar's name from Bruenor's tale the night before, and that recognition had pained him greatly.

No doubt, the frustrated Lord of Auckney had taken that anger out on the half-ogre prisoner.

The four friends left Castle Auckney and the kingdom that same morning, though clouds had gathered in the east. There was no fanfare, no cheers for the departing heroes.

Just Lady Meralda, standing atop the parapet between the gate towers, wrapped in a heavy fur coat, watching them go.

Even from that distance, Drizzt and Catti-brie could see the mixture of pain and hope in her green eyes.

Part 4

The Hunt
for Meaning

The weather was terrible, the cold biting at my fingers, the ice crusting my eyes until it pained me to see. Every pass was fraught with danger—an avalanche waiting to happen, a monster ready to spring. Every night was spent in the knowledge that we might get buried within whatever shelter we found (if we were even lucky enough to find shelter), unable to claw our way out, certain to die.

Not only was I in mortal danger, but so were my dearest friends.

Never in my life have I been more filled with joy.

For a purpose guided our steps, every one through the deep and driving snow. Our goal was clear, our course correct. In traversing the snowy mountains in pursuit of the pirate Kree and the warhammer Aegis-fang, we were standing for what we believed in, were following our hearts and our spirits.

Though many would seek short cuts to the truth, there is no way around the simplest of tenets: hardship begets achievement and achievement begets joy—true joy, and the sense of accomplishment that defines who we are as thinking beings. Often have I heard people lament that if only they had the wealth of the king, then they could be truly happy, and I take care not to argue the point, though I know they are surely wrong. There is a truth I will grant that, for the poorest, some measure of wealth can allow for some measure of happiness, but beyond filling the basic needs, the path to joy is not paved in gold, particularly in gold unearned.

Hardly that! The path to joy is paved in a sense of confidence and self-worth, a feeling that we have made the world a little bit better, perhaps, or that we fought on for our beliefs despite adversity. In my travels with Captain Deudermont, I dined with many of the wealthiest families of Waterdeep. I broke bread with many of the children of the very rich. Deudermont himself was among that group, his father being a prominent landowner in Waterdeep's southern district. Many of the current crop of young aristocrats would do well to hold Captain Deudermont up as an example, for he was unwilling to rest on the laurels of the previous generation. He spotted, very young, the entrapment of wealth without earning. And so the good captain decided at a young age the course of his own life, an existence following his heart and trying very hard to make the waters of the Sword Coast a better place for decent and honest sailors.

Captain Deudermont might die young because of that choice to serve, as I might because of my own, as Catti-brie might beside me. But the simple truth of it is that, had I remained in Menzoberranzan those decades ago, or had I chosen to remain safe and sound in Ten-Towns or Mithral Hall at this time, I would already, in so many ways, be dead.

No, give me the road and the dangers, give me the hope that I am striding purposefully for that which is right, give me the sense of accomplishment, and I will know joy.

So deep has my conviction become that I can say with confidence that even if Catti-brie were to die on the road beside me, I would not backtrack to that safer place. For I know that her heart is much as my own on this matter. I know that she will—that she must—pursue those endeavors, however dangerous, that point her in the direction of her heart and her conscience.

Perhaps that is the result of being raised by dwarves, for no race on all of Toril better understands this simple truth of happiness better than the growling, grumbling, bearded folk. Dwarf kings are almost always among the most active of the clan, the first to fight and the first to work. The first to envision a mighty underground fortress and the first to clear away the clay that blocks the cavern in which it will stand. The tough, hard-working dwarves long ago learned the value of accomplishment versus luxury, long ago came to understand that there are riches of spirit more valuable by far than gold—though they do love their gold!

So I find myself in the cold, windblown snow, and the treacherous passes surrounded by enemies, on our way to do battle with an undeniably formidable foe.

Could the sun shine any brighter?

—Drizzt Do'Urden

Chapter 20
Eviction Notice

The people of Faerûn's northern cities thought they understood the nature of snowstorms and the ferocity of winter but in reality, no person who hadn't walked the tundra of Icewind Dale or the passes of the Spine of the World during a winter blizzard could truly appreciate the raw power of nature unleashed.

Such a storm found the four friends as they traversed one high pass southeast of Auckney.

Driven by fierce and frigid winds that had them leaning far forward just to prevent being blown over, icy, stinging snow crashed against them more than fell over them. That driving wind shifted constantly among the alternating cliff faces, swirling and changing direction, denying them any chance of finding a shielding barricade, and always seeming to put snow in their faces no matter which way they turned. They each tried to formulate a plan and had to shout out their suggestions at the top of their lungs, putting lips right against the ear of the person with whom they were trying to communicate.

In the end, any hope of a plan for achieving some relief had to rely completely upon luck—the companions needed to find a cave, or at least a deep overhang with walls shielding them from the most pressing winds.

Drizzt bent low on the white trail and placed his black onyx figurine on the ground before him. With the same urgency he might have used if a tremendous battle loomed before him, the dark elf called to Guenhwyvar. Drizzt stepped back, but not too far, and waited for the gray mist to appear, swirling and gradually forming into the shape of the panther, then solidifying into the cat itself. The drow bent low and communicated his wishes, and the panther leaped away, padding off through the storm, searching the mountain walls and the many side passes that dipped down from the main trail.

Drizzt started away as well, on the same mission. The other three companions, though, remained tight together, defensively huddled from the wind and other potential dangers. That proximity alone prevented complete disaster when one great gust of wind roared up, knocking Catti-brie to one knee and blowing the poor halfling right over backward. Regis tumbled and scrambled, trying to find his balance, or at least find something to hold onto.

Bruenor, sturdy and steady, grabbed his daughter by the elbow and hoisted her up, then pushed her off in the direction of the scrambling halfling. Catti-brie reacted immediately, diving out over the lip of the trail's crest, pulling Taulmaril off her shoulder, falling flat to her belly and reaching the bow out toward the skidding, sliding halfling.

Regis caught the bow and held on a split second before he went tumbling over the side of the high trail, a spill that would have had him bouncing down hundreds of feet to a lower plateau and would have likely dropped an avalanche on his head right behind him. It only took a couple of minutes for Catti-brie to extract the halfling from the open face, but by the time she yanked him in he was covered white with snow and shivering terribly.

"We canno' stay out here," the woman yelled to Bruenor, who came stomping over. "The storm'll be the death of us!"

"The elf'll find us something!" the dwarf yelled. "Him or that cat o' his!"

Catti-brie nodded. Regis tried to nod as well, but his shivering only made the motion look ridiculous. All three knew that they were fast running out of options. All three understood that Drizzt and Guenhwyvar had better find them some shelter.

And soon.

* * * * *

Guenhwyvar's roar came as the most welcome sound Drizzt Do'Urden had heard in a long, long time. He peered through the blinding sheets of blowing white, to see the huge black panther atop a windblown jag of stone, ears flat back, face masked with icy white snow.

Drizzt half skipped and half fell along a diagonal course that kept the mighty wind somewhat behind him as he made his way to Guenhwyvar.

"What have you found?" he asked the cat when he arrived just below her, peering up.

Guenhwyvar roared again and leaped away. The drow rushed to follow, and a few hundred feet down a side trail piled deep with snow, the pair came under a long overhang of rock. Drizzt nodded, thinking that this would provide some shelter, at least, but then Guenhwyvar prodded him and growled. She moved into the shelter, toward the very back, which remained shadowed. The panther was moving and peering more intently, the drow understood, for there, in the back of the sheltered area, Drizzt spotted a fair-sized crack at the base of the stone wall.

The dark elf padded over, quickly and silently, and kneeled down to the crack, taking heart as his keen eyes revealed to him that there was indeed an even more sheltered area within, a cave or a passage. Hardly slowing, reminding himself that his friends were still out in the blizzard, Drizzt dived into the opening head first, squirming to get his feet under him as he came to a lower landing.

He was in a cave, large and with many rocky shelves and boulders. The floor was clay, mostly, and as he allowed his vision to shift into the heat-seeing spectrum of the Underdark dwellers, he did indeed note a heat source, a fire pit whose contents had been very recently extinguished.

So, the cave was not unoccupied, and given their locale and the tremendous storm blowing outside, Drizzt would have been honestly surprised if it had been.

He spotted the inhabitants a moment later, moving along the shadows of the far wall, their warmer bodies shining clearly to him. He knew at once that they were goblins, and he could well imagine that there were more than a few in this sheltered area.

Drizzt considered going back outside, retrieving his friends, and taking the cave as their own. Working with their typical efficiency, the companions should have little trouble with a small gang of goblins.

But the drow paused, and not out of fear for his friends. What of the morality involved? What of the companions walking into another creature's home and expelling it into the deadly weather? Drizzt recalled another goblin he had once met in his travels, long before and far away, a creature who was not evil. These goblins, so far out and so high up in nearly impassable mountains, might have never encountered a human, an elf, a dwarf, or any other of the goodly reasoning races. Was it acceptable, then, for Drizzt and his friends to wage war on them in an attempt to steal their home?

"Hail and well met," the drow called in the goblin tongue, which he had learned during his years in Menzoberranzan. Though the dialect of the goblins of the deep Underdark was vastly different from that of their surface cousins, he could communicate with them well enough.

The surprise on the goblin's face when it discovered that the intruder was not an elf, but a dark elf, was obvious indeed as the creature neared—

or started to approach, only to skitter back, its sickly yellowish eyes wide with shock.

"My friends and I need shelter from the storm," Drizzt explained, standing calm and confident, trying to show neither hostility nor fear. "May we join you?"

The goblin stuttered too badly to even begin a response. It turned around, panic-stricken, to regard one of its companions. This second goblin, larger by far and likely, Drizzt surmised from his understanding of goblin culture, a leader in the tribe, stepped out from the shadows.

"How many?" it croaked at Drizzt.

Drizzt regarded the goblin for a few moments, noted that its dress was better than that of its ugly fellows, with a tall lumberjack's cap and golden ear-cuffs on both ears.

"Five," the drow replied.

"You pay gold?"

"We pay gold."

The large goblin gave a croaking laugh, which Drizzt took as an agreement. The drow pulled himself back out of the cave, set Guenhwyvar as a sentry, and rushed off to find the others.

It wasn't hard for Drizzt to predict Bruenor's reaction when he told the dwarf of the arrangement with their new landlords.

"Bah!" the dwarf blustered. "If ye're thinking that I'm givin' one piece o' me gold coins to the likes o' smelly goblins, then ye're thinkin' with the brains of a thick rock, elf! Or worse yet, ye're thinking like a smelly goblin!"

"They have little understanding of wealth," Drizzt replied with all confidence. He pointedly led the group away as he continued the discussion, not wanting to waste any time at all out in the freezing cold. Regis in particular was starting to look worse for wear, and was constantly trembling, his teeth chattering. "A coin or two should suffice."

"Ye can put copper coins over their eyes when I cleave 'em down!" Bruenor roared in reply. "Some folks do that."

Drizzt stopped, and stared hard at the dwarf. "I have made an arrangement, rightly or wrongly, but it is one that I expect you to honor," he explained. "We do not know if these goblins are deserving of our wrath, and whatever the case if we simply walk in and put them out of their own home then are we any better than they?"

Bruenor laughed aloud. "Been drinking the holy water again, eh, elf?" he asked.

Drizzt narrowed his lavender eyes.

"Bah, I'll let ye lead on this one," the dwarf conceded. "But be knowing that me axe'll be right in me hand the whole time, and if any stupid goblin makes a bad move or says a stupid thing, the place'll get a new coat o' paint—*red* paint!"

Drizzt looked at Catti-brie, expecting support, but the expression he saw there surprised him. The woman, if anything, seemed to be favoring Bruenor's side of this debate. Drizzt had to wonder if he might be wrong, had to wonder if he and his friends should have just walked in and sent the goblins running.

The dark elf went back into the cave first, with Guenhwyvar right behind. While the sight of the huge panther set more than a few goblins back on their heels, the sight of the next visitor—a red-bearded dwarf— had many of the humanoid tribe howling in protest, pointing crooked fingers, waving their fists, and hopping up and down.

"You drow, no dwarf!" the big goblin protested.

"Duergar," Drizzt replied. "Deep dwarf." He nudged Bruenor and whispered out of the corner of his mouth, "Try to act gray."

Bruenor turned a skeptical look his way.

"Dwarf!" the goblin leader protested.

"Duergar," Drizzt retorted. "Do you not know the duergar? The deep dwarves, allies of the drow and the goblins of the Underdark?"

There was enough truth in the dark elf's statement to put the goblin leader off his guard. The deep dwarves of Faerûn, the duergar, often traded and sometimes allied with the drow. In the Underdark, the duergar had roughly the same relationship with the deep goblins as did the drow, not so much a friendship as tolerance. There were goblins in Menzoberranzan, many goblins. Someone had to do the cleaning, after all, or give a young matron a target that she might practice with her snake whip.

Regis was the next one in, and the goblin leader squealed again.

"Young duergar," Drizzt said before the protest could gain any momentum. "We use them as decoys to infiltrate halfling villages."

"Oh," came the response.

Last in was Catti-brie, and the sight of her, the sight of a human, brought a new round of whooping and stomping, finger-pointing and fist waving.

"Ah, prisoner!" the goblin leader said lewdly.

Drizzt's eyes widened at the word and the tone, at the goblin leader's obvious intentions toward the woman. The drow recognized his error. He had refused to accept that Nojheim, the exceptional goblin he'd met those years before, was something less than representative of his cruel race. Nojheim was a complete anomaly, unique indeed.

"What'd he say?" asked Bruenor, who wasn't very good at under- standing the goblin dialect.

"He said the deal is off," Drizzt replied. "He told us to get out."

Before Bruenor could begin to question what the drow wanted to do next, Drizzt had his scimitars in hand and began stalking across the uneven floor.

"Drizzt?" Catti-brie called to the drow. She looked to Bruenor, hardly seeing him in the dim light.

"Well, they started it!" the dwarf roared, but his bluster ended abruptly, and he called out to the dark elf, in less than certain terms, "Didn't they?"

"Oh, yes," came the drow's reply.

"Put up a torch for me girl, Rumblebelly!" Bruenor said with a happy howl, and he slapped his axe hard against his open hand and rushed forward. "Just shoot left, girl, until ye can see! Trust that I'll be keepin' meself to the right!"

A pair of goblins rushed in at Drizzt, one from either side. The drow skittered right, turned, and went into a sudden dip, thrusting both scimitars out that way. The goblin, holding a small spear, made a fine defensive shift and almost managed to parry one of the blades.

Drizzt retracted and swung back around the other way, turning right past his friends and letting his right hand lead in a vicious cross. He felt the throb in his injured shoulder, but that remark by the goblin leader, "prisoner," that inference that it would be happy to spend some time playing with Catti-brie, gave him the strength to ignore the pain.

The goblin coming in at him ducked the first blade and instinctively lifted its spear up to parry, should Drizzt dip that leading scimitar lower.

The second crossing scimitar took out its throat.

A third creature charged in on that goblin's heels and was suddenly lying atop its dead companion, taken down by a quick-step and thrust, the bloodied left-hand scimitar cutting a fast line to its heart, while Drizzt worked the right-hand blade in tight circles around the thrusting sword of a fourth creature.

"Damn elf, ye're taking all the fun!" Bruenor roared.

He rushed right past Drizzt, thinking to bury his axe into the skull of the goblin parrying back and forth with the dark elf. A black form flew past the dwarf, though, and launched the goblin away, pinning it under six hundred pounds of black fur and raking claws.

The cave lit suddenly with a sharp blue light, then another, as Catti-brie put her deadly bow to work, sending off a line of lightning-streaking arrows. The first shots burrowed into the stone wall to the cave's left side, but each offered enough illumination for her to sort out a target or two.

By the third shot, she got a goblin, and each successive shot either found a deadly mark or zipped in close enough to have goblins diving all about.

The three friends pressed on, cutting down goblins and sending dozens of the cowardly creatures running off before them.

Catti-brie kept up a stream of streaking arrows to the side, not really scoring any hits now, for all of the goblins over there were huddled under cover. Her efforts were not in vain, though, for she was keeping the creatures out of the main fight in the cave's center.

1090

Regis, meanwhile, made his way around the other wall, creeping past boulders and stalagmites and huddling goblins. He noted that the goblins were disappearing sporadically through a crack in the back of the cave and that the leader had already gone in.

Regis waited for a lull in the goblin line, then slipped into the deeper darkness of the inner tunnels.

The fight was over in a short time, for in truth, other than the initial three goblins' charge at Drizzt, it never was much of a fight. Goblins worked harder at running away than at defending themselves from the mighty intruders—some even threw their kinfolk into the path of the charging dwarf or leaping panther.

It ended with Drizzt and Bruenor simultaneously stabbing and chopping a goblin as it tried to exit at the back of the cave.

Bruenor yanked back on his axe, but the embedded blade didn't disengage and he wound up hoisting the limp goblin right over his shoulder.

"Big one got through," the dwarf grumbled, seeming oblivious to the fact that he was holding a dead goblin on the end of his axe. "Ye going after it?"

"Where is Regis?" came Catti-brie's call from the cave entrance.

The pair turned to see the woman crouching just before the entrance slope, lighting a torch.

"Rumblebelly ain't good at following directions," Bruenor griped. "I telled him to do that!"

"I didn't need it with me bow," Catti-brie explained. "But he ran off." She called out loudly, "Regis?"

"He ran away," Bruenor whispered to Drizzt, but that just didn't sound right—to either of them—after the halfling's brave work on the roads outside of Ten-Towns and his surprisingly good performance against the ogres. "I'm thinking them ogres scared the fight outta him."

Drizzt shook his head, slowly turning to scan the perimeter of the cave, fearing more that Regis had been cut down than that he had run off.

They heard their little friend a few moments later, whistling happily as he exited the goblin escape tunnel. He looked at Drizzt and Bruenor, who stared at him in blank amazement, then tossed something to Drizzt.

The drow caught it and regarded it, and his smile widened indeed.

A goblin ear, wearing a golden cuff.

The dwarf and the dark elf looked at the halfling incredulously.

"I heard what he said," Regis answered their stares. "And I do understand goblin." He snapped his little fingers in the air before the stunned pair and started across the cave toward Catti-brie. He stopped a few strides away, though, turned back, and tossed the second ear to Drizzt.

"What's gettin' into him?" Bruenor quietly asked the drow when Regis was far away.

"The adventurous spirit?" Drizzt asked more than stated.

"Ye could be right," said Bruenor. He spat on the ground. "He's gonna get us all killed, or I'm a bearded gnome."

The five, for Guenhwyvar remained throughout the night, waited out the rest of the storm in the goblin cave. They found a pile of kindling at the side of the cave, along with some rancid meat they didn't dare cook, and Bruenor set a blazing fire near the outside opening. Guenhwyvar stood sentry while Drizzt, Catti-brie, and Regis deposited the goblin bodies far down the passageway. They ate, and they huddled around the fire. They took turns on watch that night, sleeping two at a time, though they didn't really expect the cowardly goblins to return anytime soon.

* * * * *

Many miles to the south and east of the companions, another weary traveler didn't have the luxury of comrades who could stand watch while he slept. Still, not expecting that many enemies would be out and about on a stormy night such as this, Wulfgar did settle back against the rear wall of the covered nook he chose as his shelter and closed his eyes.

He had dug out this nook, and so he was flanked left and right by walls of solid snow, with the rock wall behind and a rising snow wall before him. He knew that even if no monsters or wild animals would likely find him, he had to take his sleep in short bursts, for if he didn't regularly clear some of the snow from the front, he ran the risk of being buried alive, and if he didn't occasionally throw another log on the fire, he'd likely freeze to death on this bitter night.

These were only minor inconveniences to the hearty barbarian, who had been raised from a babe on the open tundra of brutal Icewind Dale, who had been weaned with the bitter north wind singing in his ears.

And who had been hardened in the fiery swirls of Errtu's demonic home.

The wind sang a mournful song across the small opening of Wulfgar's rock and snow shelter, a long and melancholy note that opened the doorway to the barbarian's battered heart. In that cave, in that storm, and on that windy note, Wulfgar's thoughts were sent back across the span of time.

He recalled so many things about his childhood with the Tribe of the Elk, running the open and wild tundra, following the footsteps of his ancestors in hunts and rituals that had survived for hundreds of years.

He recalled the battle that had brought him to Ten-Towns, an aggressive attack by his warrior people upon the settlers of the villages. There an ill-placed blow on the head of a particularly hard-headed dwarf had led to young Wulfgar's defeat—and that defeat had landed young Wulfgar squarely in the tutelage and indenture of one Bruenor Battlehammer, the surly, gruff, golden-hearted dwarf who Wulfgar would soon enough come to know as a father. That defeat on the battlefield had brought Wulfgar to the side of Drizzt and Catti-brie, had set him on the road that had guided the later years of his youth and the early years of his adulthood. That same road, though, had landed Wulfgar in that most awful of all places, the lair of the demon Errtu.

Outside, the wind mourned and called to his soul, as if asking him to turn away now on his road of memories, to reject all thoughts of Errtu's hellish lair.

Warning him, warning him . . .

But Wulfgar, as tormented by his self-perception as he was by the tortures of Errtu, would not turn away. Not this time. He embraced the awful memories. He brought them into his consciousness and examined them fully and rationally, telling himself that this was as it had been. Not as it should have been, but a simple reality of his past, a memory that he would have to carry with him.

A place from which he should try to grow, and not one from which he should reflexively cower.

The wind wailed its dire warnings, calling to him that he might lose himself within that pit of horror, that he might be going to dark places better left at rest. But Wulfgar held on to the thoughts, carried them through to the final victory over Errtu, out on the Sea of Moving Ice.

With his friends beside him.

That was the rub, the forlorn barbarian knew. *With his friends beside him!* He had forsaken his former companions because he had believed that he must. He had run away from them, particularly from Catti-brie, because he could not let them come to see what he had truly become: a broken wretch, a shell of his former glory.

Wulfgar paused in his contemplation and tossed the last of his logs onto the fire. He adjusted the stones he had set under the blaze, rocks that would catch the heat and hold it for some time. He prodded one stone away from the fire and rolled it under his bedroll, then worked it down under the fabric so that he could comfortably rest atop it.

He did just that and felt the new heat rising beneath, but the new-found comfort could not eliminate or deflect the wall of questions.

"And where am I now?" the barbarian asked of the wind, but it only continued its melancholy wail.

It had no answers, and neither did he.

* * * * *

The next morning dawned bright and clear, with the brilliant sun climbing into a cloudless eastern sky, sending the temperatures to comfortable levels and beginning the melt of the previous day's blizzard.

Drizzt regarded the sight and the warmth with mixed feelings, for while he and all the others were glad to have some feeling returning to

1093

their extremities, they all knew the dangers that sunshine after a blizzard could bring to mountain passes. They would have to move extra carefully that day, wary of avalanches with every step.

The drow looked back to the cave, wherein slept his three companions, resting easily, hoping to continue on their way. With any luck, they might make the coast that very day and begin the search in earnest for Minster Gorge and Sheila Kree.

Drizzt looked around and realized they would need considerable luck. Already he could hear the distant rumblings of falling snow.

*   *   *   *   *

Wulfgar punched and thrashed his way out of the overhang that had become a cave, that had become a snowy tomb, crawling out and stretching in the brilliant morning sunlight.

The barbarian was right on the edge of the mountains, with the terrain sloping greatly down to the south toward Luskan and with towering, snow-covered peaks all along the northern horizon. He noted, too, with a snort of resignation, that he had apparently been on the edge of the rain/snow line of the blizzard's precipitation, for those sloping hillsides south of him seemed more wet than deep with snow, while the region north of him was clogged with powder.

It was as if the gods themselves were telling him to turn back.

Wulfgar nodded. Perhaps that was it. Or perhaps the storm had been no more than an analogy of the roads now facing him in his life. The easy way, as it would have been out of Luskan, was to the south. That road called to him clearly, showing him a path where he could avoid the difficult terrain.

The hearty barbarian laughed at the symbolism of it all, at the way nature herself seemed to be pushing him back toward that more peaceful and easy existence. He hoisted his pack and the unbalanced bardiche he carried in Aegis-fang's stead and trudged off to the north.

Chapter 21

Wasted Charms

"I have business to attend to in Luskan," Morik complained. "So many things I have set in place—connections and deals—and now, because of you and your friends, all of that will be for naught."

"But you will enjoy the long winter's night," Bellany said with a wicked grin. She curled seductively on the pile of furs.

"That is of no . . . well, there is that," Morik admitted, shaking his head. "And my protest has nothing to do with you—you do understand that."

"You talk way too much," the woman replied, reaching for the small man.

"I . . . I mean, no this cannot be! Not now. There is my business—"

"Later."

"Now!"

Bellany grinned, rolled over, and stretched. Morik's protests had to wait for some time. Later on, though, the rogue from Luskan was right back at it, complaining to Bellany that her little side trip here was going to cost him a king's treasure and more.

"Unavoidable," the sorceress explained. "I had to bring you here, and winter came early."

"And I am not allowed to leave?"

"Leave at your will," Bellany replied. "It is a long, cold road—do you think you'll survive all the way back to Luskan?"

"You brought me here, you take me back."

"Impossible," the sorceress said calmly. "I can not teleport such distances. That spell is beyond me. I could conjure the odd magical portal for short distances perhaps, but not enough to skip our way to Luskan. And I do not like the cold, Morik. Not at all."

"Then Sheila Kree will have to find a way to take me home," Morik declared, pulling his trousers on—or at least trying to. As he brought the pants up over his ankles, Bellany waved her hand and cast a simple spell to bring about a sudden breeze. The gust was strong enough to push the already off-balance Morik backward, causing him to trip and fall.

He rolled and put his feet under him, rising, stumbling back to his knees, then pulling himself up and turning an indignant stare over the woman.

"Very humorous," he said grimly, but as soon as he spoke the words, Morik noted the look on Bellany's face, one that showed little humor.

"You will go to Sheila Kree and demand that she take you home?" the sorceress asked.

"And if I do?"

"She will kill you," Bellany stated. "Sheila is not overly fond of you, my friend, and in truth she desires you gone from here as much as you desire to be gone. But she'll spare no resources to do that, unless it is the short journey for one of her pet ogres to toss your lifeless body into the frigid ocean waters.

"No, Morik, understand that you would do well to remain unobtrusive and quietly out of Sheila's way," Bellany went on. *"Bloody Keel* will sail in the spring, and likely along the coast. We'll put you ashore not so far from Luskan, perhaps even in port, if we can be certain Deudermont's not lying in wait for us there."

"I will be a pauper by then."

"Well, if you are still rich, and wish to die that way, then go to Sheila with your demands," the sorceress said with a laugh. She rolled over, wrapping herself in the furs, burying even her head to signal Morik that this conversation was at its end.

The rogue stood there staring at his lover for a long while. He liked Bellany—a lot—and believed that a winter of cuddling beside her wouldn't be so bad a thing. There were several other women there as well, including a couple of quite attractive ones, like Jule Pepper. Perhaps Morik might find a bit of challenge this season!

The rogue shook that thought out of his head. He had to be careful with such things, while in such tight and inescapable quarters beside such formidable companions. Woe to him if he angered Bellany by making a play for Jule. He winced as he considered the beating this beautiful sorceress might put on him. Morik had never liked wizards of any type, for they could see through his disguises and stealth and could blast him away before he ever got close to them. To Morik's way of thinking, wizards simply didn't fight fair.

Yes, he had to be careful not to evoke any jealousies.

Or perhaps that was it, Morik mused, considering Sheila's obvious disdain. Perhaps the fiery pirate didn't approve of Bellany's companion because she was trapped here as well, and with no one to warm her furs.

A wry smile grew on Morik's face as he watched the rhythmic breathing of sleeping Bellany.

"Ah, Sheila," he whispered, and he wondered if he would even want to go home after spending some time with the captain, wondered if he might not find an even greater prosperity right here.

* * * * *

Chogurugga stalked about her huge room angrily, throwing furniture and any of the smaller ogres and half-ogres who were too slow to get out of her way.

"Bathunk!" the ogress wailed repeatedly. "Bathunk, where you be?" The ogress's prized son had gone out from the home to lead a raiding party, an expedition that was supposed to last only three or four days, but now nearly a tenday had passed, with no word from the young beast.

"Snow deep," said a composed Bloog from the side of the room, lying back on a huge hammock—a gift from Sheila Kree—his massive legs hanging over, one on either side.

Chogurugga raced across the room, grabbed the side of the hammock, and dumped Bloog onto the stone floor. "If me learn that you hurt—"

"Bathunk go out," Bloog protested, keeping his calm, though whether that was because he didn't want to lash out at his beautiful wife or because he didn't want to laugh at her hysteria, the ogress could not tell. "Him come back or him not. Bloog not go out."

The logic, simple enough for even Chogurugga to grasp, did not calm the ogress, but turned her away from Bloog at least. She rushed across the room, wailing for Bathunk.

In truth, her son had been late in returning from raiding parties many times, but this time was different. It wasn't just the fierce storm that had come up. This time, Chogurugga sensed that something was terribly amiss. Disaster had befallen her beloved Bathunk.

He wouldn't be coming home.

The ogress just knew it.

* * * * *

Morik grinned widely and pulled a second goblet, another beautiful silver and glass piece, out of the small belt pouch on his right hip, placing it in front of Sheila Kree on the table between them.

Sheila regarded him with an amused expression and a nod, bidding him to continue.

Out of the pouch next came a bottle of Feywine—itself much too big to fit in the small pouch, let alone beside a pair of sizeable goblets.

"What else ye got in yer magical pouch, Morik the Rogue?" Sheila asked suspiciously. "Does Bellany know ye got that magic about ye?"

"Why would it concern her, dear, beautiful Sheila?" Morik asked, pouring a generous amount of the expensive liquor into Sheila's cup and a lesser amount into his own. "I am no threat to anyone here. A friend and no enemy."

Sheila smirked, then brought her goblet up so fast for a big swallow that some wine splashed out the sides of the drinking vessel and across her ruddy face. Hardly caring, the pirate banged the goblet back to the table, then ran an arm across her face.

"Would any enemy e'er say different?" she asked, simply. "Don't know o' many who'd be calling themselfs a foe when they're caught."

Morik chuckled. "You do not approve of Bellany bringing me here."

"Have I ever gived ye a different feeling?"

"Nor do you approve of Bellany's interest in my companionship," Morik dared to say.

When Sheila winced slightly and shifted in her seat, Morik knew he'd hit a nerve. Bolstered by the thought that Sheila's gruffness toward him might be nothing more than jealousy—and to confident Morik's way of thinking, why should it not be?—the rogue lifted his goblet out toward the pirate leader in toast.

"To a better understanding of each other's worth," he said, tapping Sheila's cup.

"And a better understanding of each other's desires," the pirate replied, her smirk even wider.

Morik grinned as well, considering how he might turn this one's fire into some wild pleasures.

He didn't get what he bargained for.

Morik staggered out of Sheila's room a short while later, his head throbbing from the left hook the pirate had leveled his way while still wearing that smirk of hers. Confused by Sheila's violent reaction to his advance—Morik had sidled up to her and gently brushed the back of his hand across her ruddy cheek—the rogue muttered a dozen different curses and stumbled across the way toward Bellany's room. Morik wasn't used to such treatment from the ladies, and his indignation was clear to the sorceress as she opened the door and stood there, blocking the way.

"Making love with a trapped badger?" the grinning Bellany asked.

"That would have been preferable," Morik replied and tried to enter the room. Bellany, though, kept her arm up before him, blocking the way.

Morik looked at her quizzically. "Surely you are not jealous."

"You seem to have a fair estimation of your worth to so definitely know that truth," she replied.

Morik started to respond, but then the insult registered, and he stopped and gave a little salute to the woman.

"Jealous?" Bellany asked skeptically. "Hardly that. I would have thought you'd have bedded Jule Pepper by now, at least. You do surprise me with your taste, though. I didn't think you were Sheila Kree's type, nor she yours."

"Apparently your suspicions are correct," the rogue remarked, rubbing his bruised temple. He started ahead again, and this time Bellany let him move past her and into the room. "I suspect *you* would have had more luck in wooing that one."

"Took you long enough to figure that one out," Bellany replied, closing the door as she entered behind the rogue.

Morik fell upon a bed of soft furs and rolled to cast a glance at the grinning sorceress. "A simple word of warning?" he asked. "You could not have done that for me beforehand?"

"And miss the fun?"

"You did not miss much," said Morik, and he held his arms out toward her.

"Do you need your wound massaged?" Bellany asked, not moving. "Or your pride?"

Morik considered the question for just a moment. "Both," he admitted, and, her smile widening even more, the sorceress approached.

"This is the last time I will warn you," she said, slipping onto the bed beside him. "Tangle with Sheila Kree, and she will kill you. If you are lucky, I mean. If not, she'll likely tell Chogurugga that you have amorous designs over her."

"The ogress?" asked a horrified Morik.

"And if your coupling with that one does not kill you, then Bloog surely will."

Bellany edged in closer, trying to kiss the man, but Morik turned away, any thoughts of passion suddenly flown.

"Chogurugga," he said, and a shudder coursed his spine.

Chapter 22
One Step at a Time

    With the freezing wind roaring in at him from the right, Wulfgar plodded along, ducking his shoulder and head against the constant icy press. He was on a high pass, and though he didn't like being out in the open, this windblown stretch was the route with by far the least remaining snow. He knew that enemies might spot him from a mile away, a dark spot against the whiteness, but knew he also that unless they were aerial creatures—and ones large enough to buck the wintry blow—they'd never get near to him.

    What he was hoping for was that his former companions might spot him. For how else might he find them in this vast, up-and-down landscape, where vision was ever limited by the next mountain peak and where distances were badly distorted? Sometimes the next mountain slope, where individual trees could be picked out, might seem to be a short march, but was in reality miles and miles away, and those with often insurmountable obstacles, a sharp ravine or unclimbable facing, preventing Wulfgar from getting there without a detour that would take days.

    How did I ever hope to find them? the barbarian asked himself, and not for the first, or even the hundredth time. He shook his head at his own

1101

foolishness in ever walking through Luskan's north gate on that fateful morning, and again at continuing into the mountains after the terrific storm when the south road seemed so much more accessible.

"And would I not be the fool if Drizzt and the others have sought out shelter, a town through which they can spend the winter?" the barbarian asked himself, and he laughed aloud.

Yes, this was about as hopeless as seemed possible, seeking his friends in a wilderness so vast and inhospitable, in conditions so wild that he might pass within a few yards of them without ever noticing them. But still, when he considered it in context, the barbarian realized he was not foolish, despite the odds, that he had done what he needed to do.

Wulfgar paused from that high vantage point and looked all around him at the valleys, at the peak looming before him, and at one expanse of fir trees, a dark green splash against the white-sided mountain, down to the right.

He decided he would go there, under the cover of those trees, making his way to the west until he came to the main mountain pass that would take him back into Icewind Dale. If he found his former companions along the way, then all the better. If not, he would continue along to Ten-Towns and stay there until Drizzt and the others came to him, or until the spring, if they did not arrive, when he could sign on with a caravan heading back to Waterdeep.

Wulfgar shielded his eyes from the glare and the blowing snow and picked his path. He'd have to continue across the open facing to the larger mountain, then make his way down its steep western side. At least there were trees along that slope, against which he could lean his weight and slow his descent. If he tried to go down from this barren area and got into a slide, he'd tumble a long way indeed.

Wulfgar put his head down again and plowed on, leaning into the wind.

That lean cost him when he stepped upon one stone, which sloped down to the right much more than it appeared. His furry boot found little traction on the icy surface, and the overbalanced Wulfgar couldn't compensate quickly enough to belay the skid. Out he went, feet first, to land hard on his rump. He was sliding, his arms flailing wildly in an effort to find a hold.

He let go of the large, unwieldy bardiche, tossing the weapon a bit to the side so it didn't tumble down onto his head behind him. He couldn't slow and was soon bouncing more than sliding, going into a headlong roll and clipping one large stone that turned him over sideways. The straps on his pack fell loose, one untying, the other tearing free. He left it behind, its flap opening and a line of his supplies spilling out behind it as it slid.

Wulfgar continued his twisting, bouncing descent and left the pack, the bardiche, and the top of the pass, far behind.

* * * * *

"He's hurt!" Captain Deudermont said, his voice rising with anxiety as he watched the barbarian's long and brutal tumble.

He and Robillard were in his private quarters aboard *Sea Sprite*, staring into a bowl of enchanted water the wizard was using to scrye out the wandering barbarian. Robillard was not fond of such divination spells, nor was he very proficient with them, but he had secretly placed a magical pin under the folds of Wulfgar's silver wolf-furred clothing. That pin, attuned to the bowl, allowed even Robillard, whose prowess was in evocation and not divination, to catch a glimpse of the distant man.

"Oaf," Robillard quietly remarked.

They watched silently, Deudermont chewing his lip, as Wulfgar climbed to his feet at the bottom of the long slide. The barbarian leaned over to one side, favoring an injured shoulder. As he walked about, obviously trying to sort out the best path back to his equipment, the pair noted a pronounced limp.

"He'll not make it back up without aid," Deudermont said.

"Oaf," Robillard said again.

"Look at him!" the captain cried. "He could have turned south, as you predicted, but he did not. No, he went out to the north and into the frozen mountains, a place where few would travel, even in the summer and even in a group, and fewer still would dare try alone."

"That is the way of nature," Robillard quipped. "Those who would try alone likely have and thus are all dead. Fools have a way of weeding themselves out of the bloodlines."

"You wanted him to go north," the captain pointedly reminded. "You said as much, and many times. And not so that he would fall and die. You insisted that if Wulfgar was a man deserving of such friends as Drizzt and Catti-brie, that he would go in search of them, no matter the odds.

"Look now, my curmudgeonly friend," Deudermont stated, waving his arm out toward the water bowl, to the image of stubborn Wulfgar.

Obviously in pain but just grimacing it away, the man was scrambling inch by inch to scale back up the mountainside. The barbarian didn't stop and cry out in rage, didn't punch his fist into the air. He just picked his path and clawed at it without complaint.

Deudermont eyed Robillard as intently as the wizard was then eyeing the scrying bowl. Finally, Robillard looked up. "Perhaps there is more to this Wulfgar than I believed," the wizard admitted.

"Are we to let him die out there, alone and cold?"

Robillard sighed, then growled and rubbed his hands forcefully across his face, so that his skinny features glowed bright red. "He has been nothing but trouble since the day he arrived on Waterdeep's long dock to speak with you!" Robillard snarled, and he shook his head. "Nay, even before that, in Luskan, when he tried to kill—"

"He did not!" Deudermont insisted, angry that Robillard had reopened that old wound. "That was neither Wulfgar nor the little one named Morik."

"So you say."

"He suffers hardships without complaint," the captain went on, again directing the wizard's eyes to the image in the bowl. "Though I hardly think Wulfgar considers such a storm as this even a hardship after the torments he likely faced at the hands of the demon Errtu."

"Then there is no problem here."

"But what now?" the captain pressed. "Wulfgar will never find his friends while wandering aimlessly through the wintry mountains."

Deudermont could tell by the ensuing sigh that Robillard understood him completely.

"We spotted a pirate just yesterday," the wizard remarked, a verbal squirm if Deudermont had ever heard one. "Likely we will do battle in the morning. You can not afford—"

"If we see the pirate again and you have not returned, or if you are not yet prepared for the fight, then we will shadow her. As we can outrun any ship when we are in pursuit, so we can when we are in retreat."

"I do not like teleporting to unfamiliar places," Robillard grumbled. "I may appear too high, and fall."

"Enact a spell of flying or floating before you go, then."

"Or too low," Robillard said grimly, for that was ever a possibility, and any wizard who wound up appearing at the other end of a teleport spell too low would find pieces of himself scattered amongst the rocks and dirt.

Deudermont had no answer for that other than a shrug, but it wasn't really a debate. Robillard was only complaining anyway, with every intention of going to the wounded man.

"Wait for me to return before engaging any pirates," the wizard grumbled, fishing through his many pockets for the components he would need to safely—as safely as possible, anyway—go to Wulfgar. "If I do return, that is."

"I have every confidence."

"Of course you do," said Robillard.

Captain Deudermont stepped back as Robillard moved to a side cabinet and flung it open, removing one of Deudermont's own items, a heavy woolen blanket. Grumbling continually, the wizard began his casting, first a spell that had him gently floating off of the floor, and another that seemed to tear the fabric of the air itself. Many multicolored bubbles surrounded the wizard until his form became blurred by their multitude—and he was gone, and there were only bubbles, gradually popping and flowing together so that the air seemed whole again.

Deudermont rushed forward and stared into the watery bowl, catching the last images of Wulfgar before Robillard's divining dweomer dissipated.

He saw a second form come onto the snowy scene.

* * * * *

Wulfgar started to slip yet again, but growled and fell flat, reaching his arm up and catching onto a jag in the little bare stone he could find. His pulled with his powerful arm, sliding himself upward.

"We will be here all afternoon if you continue at that pace," came a familiar voice from above.

The barbarian looked up to see Robillard standing atop the pass, a heavy brown blanket wrapped around him, over his customary wizard robes.

"What?" the astonished Wulfgar started to ask, but with his surprise came distraction, and he wound up sliding backward some twenty feet to crash heavily against a rocky outcrop.

The barbarian pulled himself to his feet and looked back up to see Robillard, the bardiche in hand, floating down the mountain slope. The wizard scooped a few of Wulfgar's other belongings on the way, dropped them to Wulfgar, and swooped about, flying magically back and forth until he had collected all of the spilled possessions. That job completed, he landed lightly beside the huge man.

"I hardly expected to see you here," said Wulfgar.

"No less than I expected to see you," Robillard answered. "I predicted that you would take the south road, not the north. Your surprising fortitude even cost me a wager I made with Donnark the oarsman."

"Should I repay you?" Wulfgar said dryly.

Robillard shrugged and nodded. "Another time, perhaps. I have no desire to remain in this godsforsaken wilderness any longer than is necessary."

"I have my possessions and am not badly injured," Wulfgar stated. He squared his massive shoulders and thrust out his chin defiantly, more than ready to allow the wizard to leave.

"But you have not found your friends," the wizard explained, "and have little chance of ever doing so without my help. And so I am here."

"Because you are my friend?"

"Because Captain Deudermont is," Robillard corrected, and with a huff to deny the wry grin that adorned the barbarian's ruddy and bristled face.

"You have spells to locate them?" Wulfgar asked.

"I have spells to make us fly up above the peaks," Robillard corrected, "and others to get us quickly from place to place. We will soon enough

1105

take account of every creature walking the region. We can only hope that your friends are among them."

"And if they are not?"

"Then I suggest that you return with me to Waterdeep."

"To *Sea Sprite*?"

"To Waterdeep," Robillard forcefully repeated.

Wulfgar shrugged, not wanting to argue the point—one that he hoped would be moot. He believed that Drizzt and the others had come in search of Aegis-fang, and if that was the case he expected that they would still be there, alive and well.

He still wasn't sure if he had chosen correctly that day back in Luskan, still wasn't sure if he was ready for this, if he wanted this. How would he react when he saw them again? What would he say to Bruenor, and what might he do if the dwarf, protective of Catti-brie to the end, simply leaped at him to throttle him? And what might he say to Catti-brie? How could he ever look into her blue eyes again after what he had done to her?

Those questions came up at him forcefully at that moment, now that it seemed possible that he would actually find the companions.

But he had no answers for those questions and knew that he would not be able to foresee the confrontation, even from his own sensibilities.

Wulfgar came out of his contemplation to see Robillard staring at him, the wizard wearing as close to an expression of empathy as Wulfgar had ever seen.

"How did you get this far?" Robillard asked.

Wulfgar's expression showed that he did not understand.

"One step at a time," Robillard answered his own question. "And that is how you will go on. One step at a time will Wulfgar trample his demons."

Robillard did something then that surprised the big man as profoundly as he had ever been: he reached up and patted Wulfgar on the shoulder.

Chapter 23
And In Walked . . .

"I'm thinking that we might be crawling back to that fool Lord Feringal and his little land o' Auckney," Bruenor grumbled when he crept back into the small cave the group had used for shelter that night after the storm had abated. The weather was better, to be sure, but Bruenor understood the dangers of avalanches, and the sheer volume of snow that had fallen the night before stunned him. "Snow's deeper than a giant's crotch!"

"Walk atop it," Drizzt remarked with a wry grin.

But in truth none of them, not even the drow, was much in the mood for smiling. The snow had piled high all through the mountains, and the day's travel had been shortened, as Drizzt had feared, by the specter of avalanches. Dozens cascaded down all around them, many blocking passes that would force the companions to wander far afield. This could mean a journey of hours, perhaps days, to circumvent a slide-filled pass that should have taken them but an hour to walk through.

"We ain't gonna find 'em, elf," Bruenor said bluntly. "They're deep underground, don't ye doubt, and not likely to stick their smelly heads above ground until the spring. We ain't for finding them in this."

"We always knew it would not be easy," Catti-brie reminded the dwarf.

"We found the group raiding the tower, and they pointed us in the right direction," Regis piped in. "We'll need some more luck, to be sure, but did we not know that all along?"

"Bah!" Bruenor snorted. He kicked a fairly large stone, launching it into a bouncing roll to crash into the side wall of the small cave.

"Surrender the hammer to them?" Drizzt asked Bruenor in all earnestness.

"Or get buried afore we e'er get near 'em?" the dwarf replied. "Great choices there, elf!"

"Or return to Auckney and wait out the winter," Regis offered. "Then try again in the spring."

"When *Bloody Keel* will likely be sailing the high seas," reminded Catti-brie. "With Sheila Kree and Aegis-fang long gone from these shores."

"We go south, then," reasoned Bruenor. "We find Deudermont and sign on to help with his pirate-killin' until we catch up to Kree. Then we take me hammer back and put the witch on the bottom o' those high seas—and good enough for her!"

A silence followed, profound and unbroken for a long, long time. Perhaps Bruenor was right. Perhaps hunting for the warhammer now wouldn't bring them anything but disaster. And if anyone among them had the right to call off the search for Aegis-fang, it was certainly Bruenor. He had crafted the hammer, after all, and had given it to Wulfgar. In truth, though, none of them, not even Regis, who was perhaps the most removed from the situation, wanted to let go of that warhammer, that special symbol of what Wulfgar had once been to all of them.

Perhaps it made sense to wait out the wintry season, but Drizzt couldn't accept the logical conclusion that the weather had made the journey simply too dangerous to continue. The drow wanted this done with, and soon. He wanted to finally catch up to Wulfgar, to retrieve both Aegis-fang and the lost symbol of all they had once been, and the thought of sitting around through several months of snow would not settle comfortably on his slender shoulders. Looking around, the drow realized that the others, even Bruenor—perhaps even particularly Bruenor, despite his typical blustering—were feeling much the same way.

The drow walked out of the cave, scrambling up the wall of snow that had drifted in front of the entrance. He ran to the highest vantage point he could find, and despite the glare that was surely stinging his light-sensitive eyes, he peered all around, seeking a course to the south, to the sea, seeking some way that they could continue.

He heard someone approaching from behind a short time later and from the sound of the footfalls knew it to be Catti-brie. She was walking with a stride that was somewhere between Drizzt's light-stepping and Bruenor's plowing technique.

"Lookin' as bad to me in going back as in going ahead," the woman said when she moved up beside Drizzt. "Might as well be going ahead, then, by me own thinking."

"And will Bruenor agree? Or Regis?"

"Rumblebelly's making much the same case to Bruenor inside right now," Catti-brie remarked, and Drizzt turned to regard her. Always before, Regis would have been the very first to abandon the road to adventure, the very first to seek a way back to warm comfort.

"Do you remember when Artemis Entreri impersonated Regis?" Drizzt asked, his tone a clear warning.

Catti-brie's blue eyes widened in shock for just a moment, until Drizzt's expression clearly conveyed that he was only kidding. Still, the point that something was very different with Regis was clearly made, and fully taken.

"Ye'd think that the goblin spear he caught on the river in the south would've put him even more in the fluffy chair," Catti-brie remarked.

"Without the magical aid from that most unlikely source, he would have lost his arm, at least," Drizzt reminded, and it was true enough.

When Regis had been stabbed in the shoulder, the friends simply could not stop the bleeding. Drizzt and Catti-brie were actually in the act of preparing Regis's arm for amputation, which they figured to be the only possible chance they had for keeping the halfling alive, when Jarlaxle's drow lieutenant, in the guise of Cadderly, had walked up and offered some magical healing.

Regis had been quiet through the remainder of that adventure, the road to Jarlaxle's crystal tower and Drizzt's fight with Entreri, and the long and sullen road all the way back to Icewind Dale. The friends had seen many adventures together, and in truth, that last one had seen the worst outcome of all. The Crystal Shard was lost to the dangerous leader of Bregan D'aerthe. It had also been easily the most painful and dangerous for Regis personally, and yet for some reason Drizzt and Catti-brie could not fathom, that last adventure had apparently sparked something within Regis. It had become evident almost immediately after their return to Ten-Towns. Not once had Regis tried to dodge out of the companions' policing of the dangerous roads in and out of the region, and on those few occasions when they had encountered monsters or highwaymen, Regis had refused to sit back and let his skilled friends handle the situation.

And here he was, trying to convince Bruenor to plow on through the inhospitable and deadly mountains, when the warm hearth of Lord Feringal's castle sat waiting behind them.

"Three against one, then," Catti-brie said at length. "We'll be going ahead, it seems."

"With Bruenor grumbling every step of the way."

"He'd be grumbling every step of the way if we turned back, as well."

"There is a dependability there."

"A reminder of times gone past and a signal of times to come," Catti-brie replied without missing a beat, and the pair shared a needed, heartfelt laugh.

When they went back into the deep, high cave they found Bruenor hard at work in packing up the camp, rolling blankets into tight bundles, while Regis stirred the pot over the still-blazing fire.

"Ye seein' a road worth trying?" Bruenor asked.

"Ahead or back . . . it is much the same," Drizzt answered.

"Except if we go ahead, we'll still have to come back," Bruenor reasoned.

"Go on, I say," Catti-brie offered. "We're not to find our answers in the sleepy town of Auckney, and I'm wanting answers before the spring thaw."

"What says yerself, elf?" Bruenor asked.

"We knew that the road would be dangerous and inhospitable before we ever set out from Luskan," Drizzt answered. "We knew the season then, and this snowfall is hardly unusual or unexpected."

"But we hoped to find the stupid pirate afore this," the dwarf put in.

"Hoped, but hardly expected," Drizzt was quick to reply. He looked to Catti-brie. "I, too, have little desire to spend the winter worrying about Wulfgar."

"On, then," Bruenor suddenly agreed. "And let the snow take us. And let Wulfgar spend the winter worrying about us!" The dwarf ended with a stream of curses, muttering under his breath in that typical Bruenor fashion. The other three in the cave shared a few knowing winks and smiles.

The low hum of Bruenor's grumbles shifted, though, into a more general humming noise that filled all the air and caught the attention of all four.

In the middle of the cave, a blue vertical line appeared, glowing to a height of about seven feet. Before the friends could begin to call out or react, that line split apart into two of equal height, and those two began drifting apart, a horizontal blue line atop them.

"Wizard door!" Regis cried, rolling to the side, scrambling for the shadows, and taking out his mace.

Drizzt dropped the figurine of Guenhwyvar to the floor, ready to call out to the panther. He drew forth his scimitars, moving beside Bruenor to face the growing portal directly, while Catti-brie slipped a few steps back and to the side, stringing and drawing her bow in one fluid motion.

The door formed completely, the area within the three defining lines buzzing with a lighter blue haze.

Out stepped a form, dressed in dark blue robes. Bruenor roared and lifted his many-notched axe, and Catti-brie pulled back, ready to let fly.

"Robillard!" Drizzt called, and Catti-brie echoed the name a split second later.

1110

"Deudermont's wizard friend?" Bruenor started to ask.

"What are you doing here?" the drow asked, but his words fell away as a second form came through the magical portal behind the wizard, a huge and hulking form.

Regis said it first, for the other three, especially Bruenor, couldn't seem to find a single voice among them. "Wulfgar?"

Chapter 24

Drow-sign

The unearthly wail, its notes primal and agonized, echoed off the stone walls of the cavern complex, reverberating into the very heart of the mountain itself.

The tips of Le'lorinel's sword and dagger dipped toward the floor. The elf stopped the training session and turned to regard the room's open door and the corridor beyond, where that awful cry was still echoing.

"What is it?" Le'lorinel asked as a form rushed by. Jule Pepper, the elf, who sprinted to catch up, guessed.

Down the winding way Le'lorinel went, pursuing Jule all the way to the complex of large chambers immediately below those of Sheila Kree and her trusted, brand-wearing compatriots, and into the lair of Chogurugga and Bloog.

Le'lorinel had to dodge aside upon entering, as a huge chair sailed by to smash against the stone. Again came that terrible cry—Chogurugga's shriek. Looking past the ogress, Le'lorinel understood it to be a wail of grief.

For there, in the middle of the floor, lay the bloated body of another ogre, a young and strong one. Sheila Kree and Bellany stood over the body beside another ogre who was kneeling, its huge, ugly head resting atop the corpse. At first, Le'lorinel figured it to be Bloog, but then the elf spotted the gigantic ogre leader, looking on from the wall behind them. It didn't take Le'lorinel long to figure out that the mask of anguish that Bloog wore was far from genuine.

It occurred to Le'lorinel that Bloog might have done this.

"Bathunk! Me baby!" Chogurugga shrieked with concern very atypical for a mother ogress. "Bathunk! Bathunk!"

Sheila Kree moved to talk to the ogress, perhaps to console her, but Chogurugga went into another flailing fit at that moment, lifting a rock from the huge fire pit and hurling it to smash against the wall—not so far from the ducking Bloog, Le'lorinel noted.

"They found Bathunk's body near an outpost to the north," Bellany explained to Jule and Le'lorinel, the sorceress walking over to them. "A few were killed, it seems. That one, Pokker, thought it prudent to bring back Bathunk's body." As she explained, she pointed to the ogre kneeling over the body.

"You sound as if he shouldn't have," Jule Pepper remarked.

Bellany shrugged as if it didn't matter. "Look at the wretch," she whispered, nodding her chin toward the wild Chogurugga. "She'll likely kill half the ogres in Golden Cove or get herself killed by Bloog."

"Or by Sheila," Jule observed, for it seemed obvious that Sheila Kree was fast losing patience with the ogress.

"There is always that possibility," Bellany deadpanned.

"How did it happen?" asked Le'lorinel.

"It is not so uncommon a thing," Bellany answered. "We lose a few ogres every year, particularly in the winter. The idiots simply can't allow good judgment to get in the way of their need to squash people. The soldiers of the Spine of the World communities are veterans all, and no easy mark, even for monsters as powerful and as well-outfitted as Chogurugga's ogres."

While Bellany was answering, Le'lorinel subtly moved toward Bathunk's bloated corpse. Noting that it seemed as if Sheila had Chogurugga momentarily under control then, the elf dared move even closer, bending low to examine the body.

Le'lorinel found breathing suddenly difficult. The cuts on the body were many, were beautifully placed and were, in many different areas, curving. Curving like the blades of a scimitar. Noting one bruise behind Bathunk's hip, the elf gently reached down and edged the corpse a bit to the side. The mark resembled the imprint of a delicately curving blade, much like the blades Le'lorinel had fashioned for Tunevec during his portrayal of a certain dark elf.

Le'lorinel looked up suddenly, trying to digest it all, recognizing clearly that no ordinary soldier had downed this mighty ogre.

The elf nearly laughed aloud then—a desire only enhanced when Le'lorinel noticed that Bloog was sniffling and wiping his eyes as if they were teary, which they most surely were not. But another roar from behind came as a clear reminder that a certain ogress might not enjoy anyone making light of this tragedy.

Le'lorinel rose quickly and walked back to Jule and Bellany, then kept right on moving out of the room, running back up the passageway to the safety of the upper level. There, the elf gasped and laughed heartily, at once thrilled and scared.

For Le'lorinel knew that Drizzt Do'Urden had done this thing, that the drow was in the area—not so far away if the ogre could carry Bathunk back in this wintry climate.

"My thanks, E'kressa," the elf whispered.

Le'lorinel's hands went instinctively for sword and dagger, then came together in front, the fingers of the right hand turning the enchanted ring about its digit on the left. After all these years, it was about to happen. After all the careful planning, the studying of Drizzt's style and technique, the training, the consultations with some of the finest swordsmen of northern Faerûn to find ways to counter the drow's maneuvers. After all the costs, the years of labor to pay for the ring, the partners, the information.

Le'lorinel could hardly draw breath. Drizzt was near. It had to have been that dangerous dark elf who had felled Bathunk.

The elf stalked about the room then went out into the corridor, stalking past Bellany's room and Sheila's, to the end of the hall and the small chamber where Jule Pepper had set up for the winter.

The three women arrived a few moments later, shaking their heads and making off-color jokes about Chogurugga's antics, with Sheila Kree doing a fair imitation of the crazed ogress.

"Quite an exit," Bellany remarked. "You missed the grandest show of all."

"Poor Chogurugga," said Jule with a grin.

"Poor Bloog, ye mean," Sheila was quick to correct, and the three had a laugh.

"All right, ye best be telling me what ye're knowing about it," Sheila said to Le'lorinel when the elf didn't join in the mirth, when the elf didn't crack the slightest of smiles, intensity burning behind those blue and gold orbs.

"I was here when Bathunk was killed, obviously," Le'lorinel reminded.

Bellany was the first to laugh. "You know something," the sorceress said. "As soon as you went to Bathunk's corpse . . ."

"Ye think it was that damned drow who did it to Bathunk," Sheila Kree reasoned.

Le'lorinel didn't answer, other than to keep a perfectly straight, perfectly grim countenance.

"Ye do!"

"The mountains are a big place, with many dangerous adversaries," Jule Pepper put in. "There are thousands who could have done this to the foolish young ogre."

Before Le'lorinel could counter, Bellany said, "Hmm," and walked out in front of the other two, one delicate hand up against her pursed lips. "But you saw the wounds," the sorceress reasoned.

"Curving wounds, like the cuts of a scimitar," Le'lorinel confirmed

"A sword will cut a wound like that if the target's falling when he gets it," Sheila put in. "The wounds don't tell ye as much as ye think."

"They tell me all I need to know," Le'lorinel replied.

"They were well placed," Jule reasoned. "No novice swordsman cut down Bathunk.

"And I know Chogurugga gave him many of the potions you delivered to her," she added to Bellany.

That made even Sheila lift her eyebrows in surprise. Bathunk was no ordinary ogre. He was huge, strong, and well trained, and some of those potions were formidable enhancements.

"It was Drizzt," Le'lorinel stated with confidence. "He is nearby and likely on his way to us."

"So said the diviner who delivered you here," said Bellany, who knew the story well.

"E'kressa the gnome. He sent me to find the mark of Aegis-fang, for that mark would bring Drizzt Do'Urden."

Jule and Bellany looked to each other, then turned to regard Sheila Kree, who was standing with her head down, deep in thought.

"Could've been the soldiers at the tower," the pirate leader said at length. "Could've been reinforcements from one of the smaller villages. Could've been a wandering band of heroes, or even other monsters, trying to claim the prize the ogres had taken."

"Could've been Drizzt Do'Urden," interjected Jule, who had first-hand experience with the dangerous drow and his heroic friends.

Sheila looked at the tall, willowy woman and nodded, then turned her gaze over Le'lorinel. "Ye ready for him—if it is him and if he is coming this way?"

The elf stood straight and tall, head back, chest out proudly. "I have prepared for nothing else in many years."

"If he can take down Bathunk, he'll be a tough fight, don't ye doubt," the pirate leader added.

"We will all be there to aid in the cause," Bellany pointed out, but Le'lorinel didn't seem thrilled at that prospect.

"I know him as well as he knows himself," the elf explained. "If Drizzt Do'Urden comes to us, then he will die."

"At the end of your blade," Bellany said with a grin.

"Or at the end of his own," the ever-cryptic Le'lorinel replied.

"Then we'll be hoping that it's Drizzit," Sheila agreed. "But ye canno' be knowing. The towers in the mountains are well guarded.

Many o' Chogurugga's kinfolk've been killed in going against them, or just in working the roads. Too many soldiers about and too many hero-minded adventurers. Ye canno' be knowing it's Drizzt or anyone else."

Le'lorinel let it go at that. Let Sheila think whatever Sheila wanted to think.

Le'lorinel, though, heard again the words of E'kressa.

Le'lorinel knew that it was Drizzt, and Le'lorinel was ready. Nothing else—not Sheila, not Drizzt's friends, not the ogres—mattered.

Chapter 25

Coming to Terms

"Wulfgar," Regis said again, when no one reacted at all to his first remark.

The halfling looked around to the others, trying to read their expressions. Catti-brie's was easy enough to discern. The woman looked like she could be pushed over by a gentle breeze, looked frozen in shock at the realization that Wulfgar was again standing before her.

Drizzt appeared much more composed, and it seemed to Regis as if the perceptive drow was consciously studying Wulfgar's every move, that he was trying to get some honest gauge as to who this man standing before him truly was. The Wulfgar of their earlier days, or the one who had slapped Catti-brie?

As for Bruenor, Regis wasn't sure if the dwarf wanted to run up and hug the man or run up and throttle him. Bruenor was trembling—though out of surprise, rage, or simple amazement, the halfling couldn't tell.

And Wulfgar, too, seemed to be trying to read some hint of the truth of Bruenor's expression and posture. The barbarian, his stern gaze never leaving the crusty and sour look of Bruenor Battlehammer, gave a deferential nod the halfling's way.

"We have been looking for you," Drizzt remarked. "All the way to Waterdeep and back."

Wulfgar nodded, his expression holding steady, as if he feared to change it.

"It may be that Wulfgar has been looking for Wulfgar, as well," Robillard interjected. The wizard arced an eyebrow when Drizzt turned to regard him directly.

"Well, we found you—or you found us," said Regis.

"But ye think ye found yerself?" Bruenor asked, a healthy skepticism in his tone.

Wulfgar's lips tightened to thin lines, his jaw clenching tightly. He wanted to cry out that he had—he prayed that he had. He looked to them all in turn, wanting to explode into a wild rush that would gather them all up in his arms.

But there he found a wall, as fluid and shifting as the smoke of Errtu's Abyss, and yet through which his emotions seemed not to be able to pass.

"Once again, it seems that I am in your debt," the barbarian managed to say, a perfectly stupid change of subject, he knew.

"Delly told us of your heroics," Robillard was quick to add. "All of us are grateful, needless to say. Never before has anyone so boldly gone against the house of Deudermont. I assure you that the perpetrators have brought the scorn of the Lords of Waterdeep upon those they represented."

The grand statement was diminished somewhat by the knowledge of all in the audience that the Lords of Waterdeep would not likely come to the north in search of those missing conspirators. The Lords of Waterdeep, like the lords of almost every large city, were better at making proclamations than at carrying through with action.

"Perhaps we can exact that vengeance for the Lords of Waterdeep, and for Captain Deudermont as well," Drizzt offered with a sly expression turned Robillard's way. "We hunt for Sheila Kree, and it was she who perpetrated the attack on the captain's house."

"I have delivered Wulfgar to you to join in that hunt."

Again all eyes fell over the huge barbarian, and again, his lips thinned with the tension. Drizzt saw it clearly and understood that this was not the time to burst the dam that was holding back Wulfgar's, and thus all of their feelings. The drow turned to regard Catti-brie, and the fact that she didn't blink for several long moments told him much about her fragile state of mind.

"But what of Robillard?" the dark elf asked suddenly, thinking to deflect, or at least delay the forthcoming flood. "Will he not use his talents to aid us?"

That caught the wizard off guard, and his eyes widened. "He already did!" he protested, but the weakness of the argument was reflected in his tone.

Drizzt nodded, accepting that. "And he can do so much more, and with ease."

"My place is with Captain Deudermont and *Sea Sprite*, who are already at sea hunting pirates, and were, in fact, in pursuit of one such vessel even as I flew off to collect Wulfgar," Robillard explained, but the drow's smile only widened.

"Your magical talents allow you to search far and wide in a short time," Drizzt explained. "We know the approximate location of our prey, but with the ups and downs of the snow-covered mountains, they could be just beyond the next rise without our ever knowing it."

"My skills have been honed for shipboard battles, Master Do'Urden," Robillard replied.

"All we ask of you is aid in locating the pirate clan, if they are, as we believe, holed up on the southwestern edge of the mountains. Certainly if they've put their ship into winter port, they're near the water. How much more area can you scout, and how much grander the vantage point, with enchantments of flying and the like?"

Robillard thought the words over for a few moments, brought a hand up, and rubbed the back of his neck. "The mountains are vast," he countered.

"We believe we know the general direction," Drizzt answered.

Robillard paused a bit longer, then nodded his head. "I will search out a very specific region, giving you just this one afternoon," he said. "Then I must return to my duties aboard *Sea Sprite*. We've a pirate in chase that I'll not let flee."

"Fair enough," Drizzt said with a nod.

"I will take one of you with me," the wizard said. He glanced around, his gaze fast settling on Regis, who was by far the lightest of the group. "You," he said, pointing to the halfling. "You will ride with me on the search, learn what you may, then guide your friends back to the pirates."

Regis agreed without the slightest hesitation, and Drizzt and Catti-brie looked at each other with continued surprise.

The preparations were swift indeed, with Robillard gathering up one of the empty packs and bidding Regis to follow him outside. He warned the halfling to don more layers of clothing to battle the cold winds and the great chill up high, then cast an enchantment upon himself.

"Do you know the region Drizzt spoke of?" he asked.

Regis nodded and the wizard cast a second spell, this one over the halfling, shrinking him down considerably in size. Robillard plucked the halfling up and set him in place in the open pack, and off the pair flew, into the bright daylight.

"Quarterling?" Bruenor asked with a chuckle.

"Lookin' more like an eighthling," Catti-brie answered, and the two laughed.

1121

The levity didn't seem to sink in to Wulfgar, nor to Drizzt who, now that the business with Robillard was out of the way, understood that it was time for them to deal with a much more profound issue, one they certainly could not ignore if they were to walk off together into danger with any hope of succeeding.

*   *   *   *   *

He saw the world as a bird might, soaring past below him as the wizard climbed higher and higher into the sky, finding wind currents that took them generally and swiftly in the desired direction, south and to the sea.

At first, Regis considered how vulnerable they were up there, black spots against a blue sky, but as they soared on the halfling lost himself in the experience. He watched the rolling landscape, coming over one ridge of a mountain, the ground beyond falling away so fast it took the halfling's breath away. He spotted a herd of deer below and took comfort in their tiny appearance, for if they were that small, barely distinguishable black spots, then how small he and Robillard must seem from the ground. How easy for them to be mistaken for a bird, Regis realized, especially given the wizard's trailing, flowing cape.

Of course, the sudden realization of how high they truly were soon incited other fears in Regis, and he grabbed on tightly to the wizard's shoulders.

"Lessen your pinching grasp!" Robillard shouted against the wind, and Regis complied, just a tiny bit.

Soon the pair were out over cold waters, and Robillard brought them down somewhat, beneath the line of the mountaintops. Below, white water thrashed over many looming rocks and waves thundered against the stony shore, a war that had been raging for millennia. Though they were lower in the sky, Regis couldn't help but tighten his grip again.

A thin line of smoke ahead alerted the pair to a campfire and Robillard immediately swooped back in toward shore, cutting up behind the closest peaks in an attempt to use them as a shield against the eyes of any potential sentries. To the halfling's surprise and relief, the wizard set down on a bare patch of stone.

"I must renew the spell of flying," Robillard explained, "and enact a couple more." The wizard fumbled in his pouch for various components, then began his spellcasting. A few seconds later, he disappeared.

Regis gave a little squeak of surprise and alarm.

"I am right here," Robillard's voice explained.

The halfling heard him begin casting again—the same spell, Regis recognized—and a moment later Regis was invisible too.

"You will have to feel your way back into my pack as soon as I am done renewing the spell of flying," the wizard's voice explained, and he began casting again.

Soon the pair were airborne once more, and though he knew logically that he was safer because he was invisible, Regis felt far less secure simply because he couldn't see the wizard supporting him in his flight. He clung with all his might as Robillard zoomed them around the mountains, finding lower passes that led in the general direction of the smoke they'd seen. Soon that smoke was back in sight yet again, only this time the pair were flying in from the northwest instead of the southwest.

As they approached, they came to see that it was indeed sentries. There was a pair of them, one a rough-looking human and the other a huge, muscled brute—a short ogre perhaps, or a creature of mixed human and ogre blood. The two huddled over a meager fire on a high ridge, rubbing their hands and hardly paying attention to their obvious duty overlooking a winding pass in a gorge just beyond their position.

"The prisoners we captured mentioned a gorge," Regis said to the wizard, loudly enough for Robillard to hear.

In response, Robillard swooped to the north and followed the ridge up to the end of the long gorge. Then he swung around and flew the halfling down the descending, swerving line of the ravine. It had obviously once been a riverbed that wound down toward the sea between two long walls of steep stone, two, maybe three hundred feet tall. The base was no more than a hundred feet wide at its widest point, the expanse widening as the walls rose so that from cliff top to cliff top was several hundred feet across in many locations.

They passed the position of the two sentries and noted another pair across the way, but the wizard didn't slow long enough for Regis to get a good look at this second duo.

Down the wizard and his unenthusiastic passenger went, soaring along, the gorge walls rolling past at a pace that had the poor halfling's thoughts whirling. Robillard spotted yet another ogre-looking sentry, but the halfling, too dizzy from the ride, didn't even look up to acknowledge the wizard's sighting.

The gorge rolled along for more than a thousand feet, and as they rounded one last bend, the pair came in sight of the wind-whipped sea. To the right, the ground broke away into various piles of boulders and outcroppings—a jagged, blasted terrain. To the left, at the base of the gorge, loomed a large mound perhaps four or five hundred feet high. There were openings along its rocky side, including a fairly large cave at ground level.

Robillard went past this, out to the sea, then turned a swift left to encircle the south side of the mound. Many great rocks dotted the seascape, a veritable maze of stone and danger for any ships that might dare it. Other mounds jutted out even more than this one all about the coast, further obscuring it from any seafaring eyes.

And there, in the south facing at sea level, loomed a cave large enough for a masted ship to enter.

Robillard went past it, rising as he continued to circle. Both he and Regis noted a pathway then, beginning to the side of the ocean level cavern and rising as it encircled the mountain to the east. Climbing up past the eastern face, the pair saw one door, and could easily imagine others along that often-shielded trail.

Robillard went up over the eastern face, continuing back to the north and cutting back down into the gorge. To the halfling's surprise and trepidation, the wizard put down at the base of the mound, right beside the cave opening, which was large enough for a pair of wagons to drive through side by side.

The wizard held onto the invisible halfling, pulling him along into the cave. They heard the gruff banter of three ogres as soon as they went in.

"There might be a better way into the complex for yourself and the drow," the wizard suggested in a whisper.

The halfling nearly jumped in the air at the sound of the voice right beside him. Regis composed himself quickly enough not to squeal out and alert the guards.

"Stay here," Robillard whispered, and he was gone.

And Regis was all alone, and though he was invisible he felt very small and very vulnerable indeed.

* * * * *

"You nearly killed me with the first throw of the warhammer!" Drizzt reminded, and he and Catti-brie both smiled when the drow's words brought a chuckle to Wulfgar's grim visage.

They were discussing old times, fond recollections initiated by Drizzt in an effort to break the ice and to draw Wulfgar out of his understandable shell. There was nothing comfortable about this reunion, as was evidenced by Bruenor's unrelenting scowl and Wulfgar's obvious tension.

They were recounting the tales of Drizzt and Wulfgar's first battle together, in the lair of a giant named Biggrin. The two had been training together, and they understood their relative styles, and at many junctures those styles had meshed into brilliance. But indeed, as Drizzt clearly admitted, at some points more luck than teamwork or skill had been involved.

Despite Bruenor's quiet and continuing scowl, the drow went on with tales of the old days in Icewind Dale, of the many adventures, of the forging of Aegis-fang (at which both Bruenor and Wulfgar winced noticeably), of the journey to Calimport to rescue Regis and the trip back to the north and east to find and reclaim Mithral Hall. Even Drizzt was surprised at the sheer volume of the tales, of the depth of the friendship that had been. He started to talk of the coming of the dark elves to Mithral Hall, the tragic encounter that had taken Wulfgar away from them, but he stopped, reconsidering his words.

"How could such bonds have been so fleeting?" the drow asked bluntly. "How could even the intervention of a demon have sundered that which we all spent so many years constructing?"

"It was not the demon Errtu," Wulfgar said, even as Catti-brie started to respond.

The other three stared at the huge man, for these were his first words since Drizzt had begun the tales.

"It was the demon Errtu implanted within me," Wulfgar explained. He paused and moved to the side, facing Catti-brie directly instead of Drizzt. He gently took the woman's hands in his own. "Or the demons that were there before . . ."

His voice broke apart, and he looked up, moisture gathering in his crystal-blue eyes. Stoically, Wulfgar blinked it away and looked back determinedly at the woman.

"I can only say that I am sorry," he said, his normally resonant voice barely a whisper.

Even as he spoke the words, Catti-brie reached up and wrapped him in a great hug, burying her face in his huge shoulder. Wulfgar returned that hug a thousand times over, bending his face into the woman's thick auburn hair.

Catti-brie turned her face to the side, to regard Drizzt, and the drow was smiling and nodding, as pleased as she that this first in what would likely be a long line of barriers to the normal resumption of their friendship had been so thrown down.

Catti-brie stepped back a moment later, wiping her own eyes and regarding Wulfgar with a warm smile. "Ye've a fine wife there in Delly," she said. "And a beautiful child, though she's not yer own."

Wulfgar nodded to both, seeming very pleased at that moment, seeming as if he had just taken a huge step in the right direction.

His grunt was as much in surprise as in pain, then, when he got slammed suddenly in the side. A heavy punch staggered him to the side. The barbarian turned to see a fuming Bruenor standing there, hands on hips.

"Ye ever hit me girl again and I'll be making a fine necklace outta yer teeth, boy! Ye want to be callin' yerself me son, and ye don't go hitting yer sister!"

The way he put it was perfectly ridiculous, of course, but as Bruenor stomped past them and out of the cave the three left behind heard a little sniffle and understood that the dwarf had reacted in the only way his proud sensibilities would allow, that he was as pleased by the reunion as the rest of them.

Catti-brie walked over to Drizzt, then, and casually but tellingly draped her arm across his back. Wulfgar at first seemed surprised, at least as much so as when Bruenor had slugged him. Gradually, though, that look of surprise melted into an expression completely accepting and approving, the barbarian offering a wistful smile.

"The road before us becomes muddled," Drizzt said. "If we are together, and contented, need we go to find Aegis-fang now, against these obstacles?"

Wulfgar looked at him as if he didn't believe what he was hearing. The barbarian's expression changed, though, and quickly, as he seemed to almost come to agree with the reasoning.

"Ye're bats," Catti-brie answered Drizzt, in no uncertain terms.

The drow turned a surprised and incredulous look over her, given her vehemence.

"Don't ye be taking me own word," the woman said. "Ask him." As she finished, she pointed back behind the drow, who turned to see Bruenor stomping back in.

"What?" the dwarf asked.

"Drizzt was thinking that we might be better off leaving the hammer for now," Catti-brie remarked.

Bruenor's eyes widened and for a moment it seemed as if he would launch himself at the drow. "How can ye . . . ye durn fool elf . . . why . . . w-what?" he stammered.

Drizzt patted his hand in the air and offered a slight grin, while subtly motioning for the dwarf to take a look at Wulfgar. Bruenor continued to sputter for a few more moments before catching on, but then he steadied himself, hands on hips, and turned on the barbarian.

"Well?" the dwarf bellowed. "What're ye thinking, boy?"

Wulfgar took a deep breath as the gazes of his four friends settled over him. They placed him squarely in the middle of it all, which was where he belonged, he understood, for it was his action that had cost him the hammer, and since it was his hammer his word should be the final say on the course before them.

But what a weight that decision carried.

Wulfgar's thoughts swirled through all the possibilities, many of them grim indeed. What if he led the companions to Sheila Kree only to have the pirate band wipe them out? Or even worse, he figured, suppose one or more of his friends died, but he survived? How could he possibly live with himself if that . . .

Wulfgar laughed aloud and shook his head, seeing the trap for what it was.

"I lost Aegis-fang through my own fault," he admitted, which of course everyone already knew. "And now I understand the error—my error. And so I will go after the warhammer as soon as I may, through sleet and snow, against dragons and pirates alike if need be. But I can not make you, any of you, join with me. I would not blame any who turned back now for Ten-Towns, or for one of the smaller towns nestled in the mountains. I will go. That is my duty and my responsibility."

"Ye think we'd let ye do it alone?" Catti-brie remarked, but Wulfgar cut her short.

"And I welcome any aid that you four might offer, though I feel that I am hardly deserving of it."

"Stupid words," Bruenor huffed. " 'Course we're going, ye big dope. Ye got yer face into the soup, and so we're pullin' it out."

"The dangers—" Wulfgar started to respond.

"Ogries and stupid pirates," said Bruenor. "Ain't nothing tough there. We'll kill a few and send a few more running, get yer hammer back, and be home afore the spring. And if there's a dragon there . . ." Bruenor paused and smiled wickedly. "Well, we'll let ye kill it yerself!"

The levity was perfectly timed, and all of the companions seemed to be just that again, four friends on a singular mission.

"And if ye ever lose Aegis-fang again," Bruenor roared on, pointing a stubby finger Wulfgar's way, "I'll be buryin' ye afore I go get it back!"

Bruenor's tirade seemed as if it would ramble on, but a voice from outside silenced him and turned all heads that way.

Robillard and Regis entered the small cave.

"We found them," Regis said before the wizard could begin. The halfling stuffed his stubby thumbs under the edges of his heavy woolen vest, assuming a proud posture. "We went right in, past the ogre guards and—"

"We don't know if it is Sheila Kree," Robillard interrupted, "but it seems as if we've found the source of the ogre raiding party—a large complex of tunnels and caverns down by the sea."

"With a cave on the water large enough for a ship to sail into," Regis was quick to add.

"You believe it to be Kree?" Drizzt asked, staring at the wizard as he spoke.

"I would guess," Robillard answered with only the slightest hesitation. "*Sea Sprite* has pursued what we think was Kree's ship into these waters on more than one occasion, then simply lost her. We always suspected that she had a hidden port, perhaps a cave. The complex at the end of that gorge to the south would support that."

"Then that is where we must go," Drizzt remarked.

"I can not carry you all," Robillard explained. "Certainly that one is too large to hang on my back as I fly." He pointed to Wulfgar.

"You know the way?" the drow asked Regis.

The halfling stood very straight, seeming as if he was about to salute the drow. "I can find it," he assured Drizzt and Robillard.

The wizard nodded. "A day's march, and no more," he said. "And thus, your way is clear to you. If . . ." He paused and looked at each of them in turn, his gaze at last settling on Wulfgar. "If you don't choose to pursue this now, *Sea Sprite* would welcome you all in the spring, when we might find a better opportunity to retrieve the lost item from Sheila Kree."

"We go now," Wulfgar said.

1127

"Won't be no Kree to chase, come spring," Bruenor snickered, and to accentuate his point, he pulled forth his battle-axe and slapped it across his open palm.

Robillard laughed and nodded his agreement.

"Good Robillard," Drizzt said, moving to stand before the wizard, "if you and *Sea Sprite* see *Bloody Keel* on the high seas, hail her before you sink her. It might well be us, bringing the pirateer into port."

Robillard laughed again, all the louder. "I do not doubt you," he said to Drizzt, patting the drow on the shoulder. "Pray, if we do meet on the open water, that you and your friends do not sink us!"

The good-natured humor was much appreciated, but it didn't last. Robillard walked past the dark elf to stand before Wulfgar.

"I have never come to like you," he said bluntly.

Wulfgar snorted—or started to, but he caught himself and let the wizard continue. Wulfgar expected a berating that perhaps he deserved, given his actions. The barbarian squared himself and set his shoulders back, but made no move to interrupt.

"But perhaps I have never really come to know you," Robillard admitted. "Perhaps the man you truly are is yet to be found. If so, and you do find the true Wulfgar, son of Beornegar, then do come back to sail with us. Even a crusty old wizard, who has seen too much sun and smelled too much brine, might change his mind."

Robillard turned to wave to the others, but looked back, turning a sly glance over Wulfgar. "If that matters to you at all, of course," he said, and he seemed to be joking.

"It does," Wulfgar said in all seriousness, a tone that stiffened the wizard and the friends with surprise.

An expression that showed startlement, and a pleasant one, widened on Robillard's face. "Farewell to you all, then," the wizard said with a great bow. He ended by launching directly and smoothly into a spell of teleportation, the air around him bubbling like multicolored boiling water, obscuring his form.

And he was gone, and it was just the five of them.

As it had once been.

Chapter 26

Leading With Their Faces

The sky had grayed again, threatening yet another wintry blast, but the friends, undaunted, started out from their latest resting spot full of hope and spirit, ready to do battle against whatever obstacles they might find. They were together again, and for the first time since Wulfgar's unexpected return from the Abyss it seemed comfortable to them all. It seemed . . . right.

When Wulfgar had first returned to them—in an icy cave on the Sea of Moving Ice in the midst of their raging battle against the demon Errtu—there had been elation, of course, but it had been an uncomfortable thing on many levels. It was a shock and a trial to readjust to this sudden new reality. Wulfgar had returned from the grave, and all the grief the other four friends had thought settled had suddenly been unearthed, resolution thrown aside.

Elation had led to many uncomfortable but much-needed adjustments as the friends had tried to get to know each other again. That led to disaster, to Wulfgar's moodiness, to Wulfgar's outrage, and to the subsequent disbanding of the Companions of the Hall. But now they were together again.

They fell into a comfortable rhythm in their determined march, with Bruenor leading the main group, plowing the trail with his sturdy body.

Regis came next, noting the mountain peaks and guiding the dwarf. Then came Wulfgar, the heavy bardiche on his shoulder, using his height to scan the trail ahead and to the sides.

Catti-brie, a short distance back, brought up the rear of the four, bow in hand, on the alert and keeping track of the drow who was constantly flanking them, first on one side and then the other. Drizzt had not brought up Guenhwyvar from the Astral Plane—in fact, he had handed the figurine controlling the panther over to Catti-brie—because the longer they could wait, the more rested the great cat would be. And the drow had a feeling he would be needing Guenhwyvar before this was ended.

Soon after noon, with the band making great progress and the snow still holding back, Catti-brie noted a hand signal from Drizzt, who was ahead and to the left.

"Hold," she whispered to Wulfgar, who relayed the command to the front.

Bruenor pulled up, breathing hard from his trudging. He lifted the axe off his back and dropped the head to the snow, leaning on the upright handle.

"Drizzt approaches," said Wulfgar, who could easily see over the snowy berm and the drifts on the path ahead.

"Another trail," the drow explained when he appeared above the berm. "Crossing this one and leading to the west."

"We should go straight south from here," Regis reminded.

Drizzt shook his head. "Not a natural trail," he explained.

"Tracks?" asked Bruenor, seeming quite eager. "More ogres?"

"Different," said Drizzt, and he motioned for them all to follow him.

Barely a hundred yards ahead, they came upon the second trail. It was a pressed area of snow cutting across their current path, moving along the sloping ground to the east. There, continuing across an expanse of deep, blown snow, the friends saw a lower area full of slush and with a bit of steam still rising from it.

"What in the Nine Hells done that?" asked Bruenor.

"Polar worm," Drizzt explained.

Bruenor spat, Regis shivered, and Catti-brie stood a bit straighter, suddenly on her guard. They all had some experience with the dreaded remorhaz, the great polar worms. Enough experience, certainly, to know that they each had little desire to battle one again.

"No foe I wish to leave behind us," the drow explained.

"So ye're thinking we should go and fight the damned thing?" Bruenor asked doubtfully.

Drizzt shook his head. "We should figure out where it is, at least. Whether or not we should kill the creature will depend on many things."

"Like how stupid we really are," Regis muttered under his breath. Only Catti-brie, who was standing near to him, heard. She looked at him with a smile and a wink, and the halfling only shrugged.

Hardly waiting for confirmation, Drizzt rushed up to take the point. He was far ahead, creeping along the easier path carved out by the strange and powerful polar worm, a beast that could superheat its spine to vaporize snow and, the drow reminded himself, vaporize flesh. They found the great beast only a few hundred yards off the main path, down in a shallow dell, devouring the last of a mountain goat it had caught in the deep snow. The mighty creature's back glowed from the excitement of the kill and feast.

"The beast will not bother with us," Wulfgar remarked. "They feed only rarely and once sated, they seek no further prey."

"True enough," Drizzt agreed, and he led them back to the main trail.

A few light flakes were drifting through the air by that point, but Regis bade them not to worry, for in the distance he noted a peculiar mountain peak that signaled the northern tip of Minster Gorge.

The snow was still light, no more than a flurry, when the five reached the trail on the side of the peak, with Minster Gorge winding away to the south before them. Regis took command, explaining the general layout of the winding run, pointing out the expected locations of sentries, left and right, and leading their gazes far, far to the south where the white-capped top of one larger mound could just be seen. Carefully, the halfling again diagrammed the place for the others, explaining the outer, ascending path running past the sea facing and around to the east on that distant mound. That path, he explained, led to at least one door set into the mound's side.

Regis looked to Drizzt, nodded, and said, "And there is another, more secret way inside."

"Ye thinking we'd be better splitting apart?" Bruenor asked the halfling doubtfully. He turned to aim his question at Drizzt as well, for it was obvious that Regis's reminder had the drow deep in thought.

Drizzt hesitated. Normally, the Companions of the Hall fought together, side by side, and usually to devastating effect. But this was no normal attack for them. This time, they were going against an entrenched fortress, a place no doubt secure and well defended. If he could take the inner corridors to some behind-the-lines vantage point, he might be able to help out quite a bit.

"Let us discern our course one step at a time," the drow finally said. "First we must deal with the sentries, if there are any."

"There were a few when I flew by with Robillard," said Regis. "A pair, at least, on either side of the gorge. They didn't seem to be in any hurry to leave."

"Then we must take alternate paths to avoid them," Wulfgar put in. "For if we strike at a band on one side, the band opposite will surely alert all the region before we ever get near to them."

"Unless Catti-brie can use her bow . . ." Regis started to say, but the woman was shaking her head, looking doubtfully at the expanse between the high gorge walls.

"We can not leave these potential enemies behind us," the drow decided. "I will go to the right, while the rest of you go to the left."

"Bah, there's a fool's notion," snorted Bruenor. "Ye might be killin' a pair o' half-ogres, elf—might even take out a pair o' full-ogres—but ye'd not do it in time to stop them from yelling for their friends."

"Then we have to disguise the truth of the attack across the way," Catti-brie said.

When the others turned to her, they found her wearing a most determined expression. The woman looked back to the north and west.

"Worm's not hungry," she explained. "But that don't mean we can't get the damn thing angry."

* * * * *

"Ettin?" one of the half-ogre guards on the eastern rim of the gorge asked.

Scratching its lice-ridden head, the half-ogre stared in amazement as the seven-foot-tall creature approached. It sported two heads, so it seemed to be of the ettin family, but one of those heads looked more akin to a human with blond hair, and the other had the craggy, wrinkled features and thick red hair and beard of a dwarf.

"Huh?" asked the second sentry, moving to join its companion.

"Ain't no ettins about," the third called from the warm area beside the fire.

"Well there's one coming," argued the first.

And indeed, the two-headed creature was coming on fast, though it presented no weapon and was not advancing in any threatening manner. The half-ogres lifted their respective weapons anyway and called for the curious creature to halt.

It did so, just a few strides away, staring at the sentries with a pair of positively smug smiles.

"What you about?" asked one half-ogre.

"About to get outta the way!" the red-haired head exclaimed.

The half-ogres' chins dropped considerably a moment later when the huge human—for it was indeed a human!—threw aside the blanket and the red-haired dwarf leaped off his shoulder, rolling to the left. The human, too, took off, sprinting to the right. Coming fast behind the splitting pair, bearing down on their original position, and thus bearing down on the stunned half-ogres, came a rolling line of steam.

The brutes screamed. The polar worm broke through the snow cap and reared, towering over them.

"That ain't no ettin, ye fools!" screeched the half-ogre by the fire. With typical loyalty for its wild nature, it leaped up and ran off to the south along the ravine edge and toward the cavern complex.

Or tried to, for three strides away, a blue-streaking arrow like a bolt of lightning slammed it in the hip, staggering it. The slowed beast, limping and squealing, didn't even see the next attack. The red-haired dwarf crashed in, body-slamming it, then chopping away with his nasty, many-notched axe. For good measure, the dwarf spun around and smashed his shield so hard into the slumping brute's face that he left an impression of a foaming mug on the half-ogre's cheek.

* * * * *

Regis heard the commotion behind him and took comfort in it as he worked his way along the side of the ravine across the way, working for handholds just below the rim, out of sight of the guards on that side. He and Drizzt had left the other three, picking their way to the western wall. Then Regis and the drow had split up, with the drow taking an inland route around the back of the sentry position. Regis, a plan in mind, had gone along the wall.

The halfling was well aware from the smirk Drizzt had given him when they'd split up, that Drizzt didn't expect much from him in the fight, that the drow believed he was just finding a place to hide. But Regis had a very definite plan in mind, and he was almost to the spot to execute it: a wide overhang of ice and snow.

He worked his way under it, staying against the stone wall, and began chipping away at the overhang's integrity with his small mace.

He glanced back across the gorge to see the polar worm rear again, a half-ogre thrashing about in its mouth. Regis winced in sympathy for the brute as the polar worm rolled its head back and let go of the half-ogre, rolling it over the horned head and down onto the glowing, superheated spine of the great creature. How the agonized half-ogre thrashed!

Further along, Regis spotted Bruenor, Wulfgar, and Catti-brie sprinting down to the south, getting as far away from the polar worm and the three wounded—and soon to be dead—half-ogres as possible.

The halfling paused, hearing commotion above. The guards on his side recognized the disaster across the way.

"Help!" Regis called out a moment later, and all above him went quiet.

"Help!" he called again.

He heard movement, heard the ice pack crunch a bit, and knew that one of the stupid brutes was moving out onto the overhang.

"Hey, yer little rat!" came the roar a moment later, as the half-ogre's head poked down. The creature was obviously lying flat atop the overhang, staring at Regis incredulously and reaching for him.

"Break . . . break," Regis demanded, smacking his mace up at the ice pack with all the strength he could muster. He had to stop the pounding and dodge aside when the brute's hand snapped at him, nearly getting him.

The half-ogre crept even lower. The ice pack creaked and groaned in protest.

"Gotcha!"

1133

The brute's declaration became a wail of surprise and terror as the ice pack broke free, taking the half-ogre with it down the side of the ravine.

"Do you now?" Regis asked the fast-departing beast.

"Yup," came an unexpected response from above, and Regis slowly looked up to see the second sentry glaring down at him, spear in hand, and with Regis well within stabbing distance. The halfling thought of letting go, then, of taking his chances on a bouncing ride down the side of the ravine, but the half-ogre stiffened suddenly and hopped forward, then tried to turn but got slashed across the face. Over it went, plummeting past the halfling, and Drizzt was in its stead, lying flat and reaching down for Regis.

The halfling grabbed the offered hand, and Drizzt pulled him up.

"Five down," said Regis, his excitement bubbling over from the victory his information had apparently delivered. "See? I had the count right. Four, maybe five—and right where I told you they would be!"

"Six," Drizzt corrected, leading the halfling's gaze back a ways to another brute lying dead in a widening pool of bright red blood. "You missed one."

Regis stared at it for a moment, mouth hanging open, and, deflated, he only shrugged.

Surveying the scene, the pair quickly surmised that none of these two groups would give them any further trouble. Across the way, the three were dead, the white worm tearing at their bodies, and the two that had gone over the edge had bounced, tumbled, and fallen a long, long way. One of them was lying very still at the bottom of the gorge. The other, undoubtedly nearby its broken companion, was buried under a deep pile of snow and ice.

"Our friends went running down the edge of the ravine," Regis explained, "but I don't know where they went."

"They had to move away from the gorge," Drizzt reasoned, seeming hardly concerned. They had discussed this very possibility before bringing the white worm from its feast. The drow pointed down along the gorge to where a sizeable number of huge ogres and half-ogres were running up the ravine. The companions had hoped to dispatch these sentries without alerting the main base, but they had understood from the beginning that such might be the case—that's why they had used the white worm.

"Come," Drizzt bade the halfling. "We will catch up with our friends, or they with us, in due time." He started away to the south, staying as near to the edge of the gorge as he safely could.

They heard the ogre posse pass beneath them soon after, and Drizzt veered back to the edge, then moved down a bit farther and went right over, picking his way down a less steep part of the ravine.

Regis huffed and puffed and worked hard but somehow managed to keep up. Soon, the halfling and the drow were standing on the floor of the gorge, the posse far away to the north, the mound that housed the main complex just to the south and with the cave opening quite apparent.

"Are you ready?" Drizzt asked Regis.

The halfling swallowed hard, not so thrilled about moving off with the dangerous Drizzt alone. He far preferred having Bruenor and Wulfgar standing strong before him and having Catti-brie covering him with that deadly bow of hers, but it was obvious that Drizzt wasn't about to let this opportunity to get right inside the enemies' lair go by.

"Lead on," Regis heard himself saying, though he could hardly believe the words as they came out of his mouth.

* * * * *

The four leaders of Sheila Kree's band all came out of their rooms together, hearing the shouts from below and from outside the mound complex.

"Chogurugga dispatched a group to investigate," Bellany informed the others. The sorceress's room faced north, the direction of the tumult, and included a door to the outside landing.

"Ye go and do the same," Sheila Kree told her. "Get yer scrying pool up and see what's coming against us."

"I heard yells about a white worm," the sorceress replied.

Sheila Kree shook her head, her fiery red hair flying wildly. "Too convenient," she muttered as she ran out of the room and down the curving, sloping passage leading to Chogurugga and Bloog's chamber, with Jule Pepper right behind her.

Le'lorinel made no move, though, just stood in the corridor, nodding knowingly.

"Is it the drow?" Bellany asked.

The elf smiled and retreated back into the private room, shutting the door.

Standing alone in the common area, Bellany just shook her head and took a deep breath and considered the possibilities if it turned out to be Drizzt Do'Urden and the Companions of the Hall who were now coming against them. The sorceress hoped it was indeed a white worm that had caused the commotion, whatever the cost of driving the monster away.

She went back into her chamber and set up for some divining spells, thinking to look out over the troubled area to the north and to look in on Morik, just to check on where his loyalties might truly lie.

* * * * *

A few moments later, Le'lorinel slipped back out and headed down the same way Sheila and Jule had gone.

Chogurugga's chamber was in complete chaos, with the ogress's two large attendants rushing around, strapping on armor pieces and hoisting heavy weapons. Chogurugga stood quietly on the side of the room in front of an opened wardrobe, its shelves filled with potion bottles. Chogurugga mulled them over one at a time, pocketing some and separating the others into two bunches.

At the back of the room, Bloog remained in the hammock, the ogre's huge legs hanging over, one on either side. If Bloog was the slightest bit worried by the commotion, the lazy brute didn't show it.

Le'lorinel went to him. "He will find you," the elf warned. "It was foreseen that the drow would come for the warhammer."

"Drow?" the big ogre asked. "No damn drow. White worm."

"Perhaps," Le'lorinel replied with a shrug and a look that told Bloog implicitly that the elf hardly believed all the commotion was being caused by such a creature as that.

"Drow?" the ogre asked, and Bloog suddenly seemed a bit less cocksure.

"He will find you."

"Bloog crunch him down!" the ogre shouted, rising, or at least trying to, though the movement nearly spilled him out of the unsteady hammock. "No take Bloog's new hammer! Crunch him down!"

"Crunch who?" Chogurugga called from across the way, and the ogress scowled, seeing Le'lorinel close to Bloog.

"Not as easy as that, mighty Bloog," the elf explained, pointedly taking no note of ugly Chogurugga. "Come, my friend. I will show you how to best defeat the dark elf."

Bloog looked from Le'lorinel to his scowling mate, then back to the delicate elf. With an expression that told Le'lorinel he was as interested in angering Chogurugga as he was in learning what he might about the drow, the giant ogre pulled himself out of the hammock and hoisted Aegis-fang to his shoulder. The mighty weapon was dwarfed by the creature's sheer bulk and muscle that it looked more like a carpenter's hammer.

With a final glance to Chogurugga, just to make sure the volatile ogress wasn't preparing a charge, Le'lorinel led Bloog out of the room and back up the ramp, going to the northern end of the next level and knocking hard on Bellany's door.

"What is he doing up here?" the sorceress asked when she answered the knock a few minutes later. "Sheila would not approve."

"What have you learned?" Le'lorinel asked.

A cloud passed over Bellany's face. "More than a white worm," she confirmed. "I have seen a dwarf and a large man moving close to our position, running hard."

"Bruenor Battlehammer and Wulfgar, likely," Le'lorinel replied. "What of the drow?"

Bellany shrugged and shook her head.

"If they have come, then so has Drizzt Do'Urden," Le'lorinel insisted. "The fight out there is likely a diversion. Look closer!"

Bellany scowled at the elf, but Le'lorinel didn't back down.

"Drizzt Do'Urden might already be in the complex," the elf added.

That took the anger off of Bellany's face, and she moved back into her room and shut the door. A moment later, Le'lorinel heard her casting a spell and watched with a smile as the wood on Bellany's door seemed to swell a bit, fitting the portal tightly into the jamb.

Fighting hard not to laugh out loud, as much on the edge of nerves as ever before, Le'lorinel motioned for Bloog to follow and moved to a different door.

* * * * *

Regis put his cherubic face up against the stone and didn't dare to breathe. He heard the rumble of the next pair of brutes, along with the snarl of a more human voice, as they came past his and Drizzt's position, heading up the gorge to check on their companions.

The halfling took some comfort in the fact that Drizzt was hiding right beside him—until he managed to turn his face that way to find that the drow was gone.

Panic welled in Regis. He could hear the cursing trio of enemies right behind him.

"Too bloody cold to be chasin' shadows!" the human snarled.

"Big wormie," said one of the ogres.

"And that makes it better?" the human asked sarcastically. "Leave the ugly thing alone, and it'll slither away!"

"Big worm killeded Bonko!" the other ogre said indignantly.

The human started to respond—likely to dismiss the importance of a dead ogre, Regis realized, but apparently he thought the better of it and just cursed under his breath.

They went right past the halfling's position, and if they'd come any closer, they surely would have brushed right against Regis's rear end.

The halfling didn't breathe easier until their voices had faded considerably, and still he stood there in the shadows, hugging the wall.

"Regis," came a whisper, and he looked up to see Drizzt on a ledge above him. "Come along and be quick. It's clear into the cave."

Mustering all the courage he could find, the halfling scrambled up, taking the drow's offered hand. The pair skittered along the thin ridge, behind a wall of blocking boulders to the corner of the large cave.

Drizzt peeked around, then skittered in, pulling Regis along behind him.

The cave narrowed into a tunnel soon after, running level and branching in two or three places. The air was smoky, with torches lining the walls at irregular intervals, their dancing flames illuminating the place with wildly elongating and shrinking shadows.

"This way," Regis said, slipping past the drow at one fork, and moving down to the left. He tried to recall everything Robillard had told him about the place, for the wizard had done a thorough scan of the area and had even found his way up into the complex a bit.

The ground sloped down in some places, up in others, though the pair were generally descending. They came through darker rooms where there was no torchlight, and other chambers filled with stalagmites breaking up the trail, and with stalactites leering down at them threateningly from above. Many shelves lined the walls, rolling back to marvelous rock formations or with sheets of water-smoothed rock that seemed to be flowing. Many smaller tunnels ran off at every conceivable angle.

Soon Regis slowed, the sound of guttural voices becoming audible ahead of them. The halfling turned on Drizzt, an alarmed expression on his face. He pointed ahead emphatically, to where the corridor circled left and back to the right, ascending gradually.

Drizzt caught the signal and motioned for Regis to wait a moment, then slipped ahead into the shadows, moving with such grace, speed, and silence that Regis blinked many times, wondering if his friend had just simply disappeared. As soon as his amazement diminished, though, the halfling remembered where he was and took note of the fact that he was now alone. He quickly skittered into the shadows off to the side.

The drow returned a short while later, to Regis's profound relief, and with a smile that showed he had found the desired area. Drizzt led him around a bend and up a short incline, then up a few steps that were part natural, part carved, into a chamber that widened off to the left along a broken, rocky plateau about chest high to the drow.

The voices were much closer now, just up ahead and around the next bend. Drizzt leaped up to the left, then reached back and pulled Regis up beside him.

"Lots of loose stone," the drow quietly explained. "Take great care."

They inched across the wider area, staying as tight to the wall as possible until they came to one area cleared of stony debris. Drizzt bent down against the wall there and stuck his hand into a small alcove, pulling it back out and rubbing his fingers together.

Regis nodded knowingly. Ash. This was a natural chimney, the one Robillard had described to him on the flight back to the friends, the one he had subsequently described to Drizzt.

The drow went in first, bending his body perfectly to slide up the narrow hole. Before he could even consider the course before him, before he could even pause to muster his courage, Regis heard the sound of many voices moving along the corridor back behind him.

In he went, into the absolute darkness, sliding his hands and finding holds, blindly propelling himself up behind the drow.

* * * * *

For Drizzt, it was suddenly as if he were back in the Underdark, back in the realm of the hunter, were all his senses had to be on the very edge of perfection if he was to have any chance of survival. He heard so many sounds then: the distant dripping of water; a grating of stone on stone; shouts from below and in the distance, leaking through cracks in the stone. He could *feel* that noise in his sensitive fingertips as he continued his climb, slowing only because he understood that Regis couldn't possibly keep up. Drizzt, a creature of the Underdark where natural chutes were common, where even a halfling's fine night vision would be perfectly useless, could move up this narrow chute as quickly as Regis could trot through a starlit meadow.

The drow marveled in the texture of the stone, feeling the life of this mound, once teeming with rushing water. The smoothness of the edges made the ascent more comfortable, and the walls were uneven enough so that the smoothness didn't much adversely affect climbing.

He moved along, silently, alertly.

"Drizzt," he heard whispered below, and he understood that Regis had come to an impasse.

The drow backed down, finally lowering his leg so that Regis could grab on.

"I should have stayed with the others," the halfling whispered when he at last got over the troublesome rise.

"Nonsense," the drow answered. "Feel the life of the mountain about you. We will find a way to be useful to our friends here, perhaps pivotal."

"We do not even know if the fight will come in here."

"Even if it does not, our enemies will not expect us in here, behind them. Come along."

And so they went, higher and higher inside the mountain. Soon they heard the booming voices of huge humanoids, growing louder and louder as they ascended.

A short, slightly descending tunnel branched off the chute, with some heat rising, and the booming voices coming in loud and clear with it.

Drizzt waited for Regis to get up level with him in this wider area, then he moved along the side passage, coming to an opening above the low-burning embers of a wide hearth.

The opening of that hearth was somewhat higher than the bottom of the angling tunnel, so Drizzt could see into the huge room beyond, where three ogres, one an exotic, violet-skinned female, were rushing around, strapping on belts and testing weapons.

To the side of the room, Drizzt clearly marked another well-worn passage, sloping upward. The drow backed up to where Regis was waiting.

"Up," he whispered.

He paused and pulled off his waterskin, wetted the top of his shirt and pulled it over the bottom half of his face to ward off the smoke. Helping Regis do likewise, Drizzt started away.

Barely thirty feet higher, the pair came to a hub of sorts. The main chute continued upward, but five side chambers broke off at various heights and angles, with heat and some smoke coming back at the pair. Also, these side tunnels were obviously hand cut, and fashioned by smaller hands than those of an ogre.

Drizzt motioned for Regis to slowly follow, then crept along the tunnel he figured was heading most directly to the north.

The fire in this hearth was burning brighter, though fortunately the wood was not very wet and not much smoke was coming up. Also, the angle of the chimney to the hearth was steeper, and so Drizzt could not see into the room beyond.

The drow spent a moment tying his long hair back and wetting it, then he knelt, took a deep breath, and went over head first, creeping like a spider down the side of the chute until he could poke his face out under the top lip of the hearth, the flames burning not far below him and with sparks rising up and stinging him.

This room appeared very different from the chamber of the ogres below. It was full of fine furniture and carpets, and with a lavish bed. A door stood across the way, partly opened and leading into another room. Drizzt couldn't make out much in there, but he did discern a few tables, covered with equipment like one might see in an alchemical workshop. Also, across that second room loomed another door, heavier in appearance, and with daylight creeping in around it.

Now he was intrigued, but out of time, for he had to retreat from the intense heat.

He got back to Regis at the hub and described what he had seen.

"We should go outside and try to spot the others," the halfling suggested, and Drizzt was nodding his agreement when they heard a loud voice echo along one of the other side passages.

"Bloog crunch! No take Bloog's new hammer!"

Off went the drow, Regis following right behind. They came to another steep chute at another hearth, this one hardly burning. Drizzt inverted and poked his head down.

There stood an ogre, a gigantic, ugly, and angry beast, swinging Aegis-fang easily at the end of one arm. Behind it, talking to the ogre in soothing tones, stood a slender elf swordsman.

Without even waiting for Regis, the drow flipped himself over to the fireplace, straddling the embers for a moment, then boldly striding out into the room.

* * * * *

The three friends ran along the ridge at full speed, veering away from the lip when they heard the ruckus of ogre reinforcements charging out from the mound below. They had to veer even farther from the straight path when a second group of beasts came off the mound above the ridge-line, charging up through the snow.

"Probably many more within," Catti-brie remarked.

"More the reason to go!" snarled Bruenor.

"Drizzt and Regis are likely already nearing the place, if not already in," Wulfgar added.

The woman, bow in hand, motioned forward.

"Ye gonna call up that cat?" Bruenor asked.

Catti-brie glanced at her belt, where she had set the figurine of Guen-hwyvar. "As we near," she answered. Bruenor only nodded, trusting her implicitly, and rushed off after Wulfgar.

Up ahead, Wulfgar ducked suddenly as another ogre leaped off the mound, across a short ravine to the sloping ridgeline, the brute coming at him with a great swing of a heavy club.

Easily dodging, Wulfgar kicked out and slashed, cutting a deep gash in back of the brute's shoulder. The ogre started to turn, but then lurched wildly as Bruenor came in hard, smashing his axe through the brute's kneecap.

Down it went, howling.

"Finish it, girl!" Bruenor demanded, running past, running for the mound. The dwarf skittered to a stop, though, foiled by the ravine separating the mound from the slope, which was too far across for him to jump.

Then Bruenor had to dive to the side as a rock sailed at him from a position along the side of that mound, just up above him.

Wulfgar came past, roaring "Tempus!" and making the leap across the ravine. The barbarian crashed along some rocks, but settled himself quickly onto a narrow trail winding its way up along the steep slope.

"Should've thrown me first," Bruenor grumbled, and he dived aside again as another rock crashed by.

The dwarf did pick out a path that would get him to the winding trail, but he knew he would be far behind Wulfgar by that point. "Girl! I need ye!" he howled.

He turned back to see the fallen ogre shudder again as another arrow buried itself deep into its skull.

Catti-brie rushed up, falling to one knee and setting off a stream of arrows at the concealed rock-thrower. The brute popped up once more, rock high over its head, but it fell away as an arrow sizzled past.

Catti-brie and Bruenor heard the roars of battle as Wulfgar reached the brute. Off ran the dwarf, while Catti-brie dropped the onyx figurine to the ground, called for the cat, then put her bow right back to work.

For on a ledge high above Wulfgar's position, a new threat had arrived, a group of archers firing bows instead of hurling boulders.

* * * * *

"Is it them?" Morik the Rogue asked, pushing against the unyielding door of Bellany's private chambers. He looked up at the swelled wood and understood that the sorceress had magically sealed it. "Bellany?"

In response, the door seemed to exhale and shrink to normal size, and Morik crept through.

"Bellany?"

"I believe your friend and his companions have come to retrieve the warhammer," came a voice from right in front of Morik. He nearly jumped out of his boots, for he could not see the woman standing before him.

"Wizards," he muttered as he settled down. "Where is Sheila Kree?"

There came no answer.

"Did you just shrug?" the rogue surmised.

Bellany's ensuing giggle told him she had.

"What of you, then?" Morik asked. "Are you to hide up here, or join in the fray?"

"Sheila instructed me to divine the source of the commotion, and so I have," the invisible sorceress answered.

A smile widened on Morik's face. He understood well what Bellany's cryptic answer meant. She was waiting to see who would win out before deciding her course. The rogue's respect for the sorceress heightened considerably at that moment.

"Have you another such enchantment?" he asked. "For me?"

Bellany was spellcasting before he ever finished the question. In a few moments Morik, too, vanished from sight.

"A minor enchantment only," Bellany explained. "It will not last for long."

"Long enough for me to find a dark hole to hide in," Morik answered, but he ended short, hearing sounds from outside, farther down the mountainside.

"They are fighting out along the trail," the sorceress explained.

A moment later, Bellany heard the creak from the other room and saw an increase in light as Morik moved through the outer door. The sorceress went to the side of the room, then heard a cry of surprise from across the way—from Le'lorinel's room.

1142

Chapter 27

Blind Vengeance

"Crunch! Crunch!" the huge ogre roared, speaking to the elf and waving Aegis-fang.

"Slash, slash," came a remark behind the brute, spinning it around in surprise.

"Huh?"

The elf moved out around the side of the ogre and froze in place, staring hard at the slender dark figure who had come into the room.

Slowly Drizzt reached up and pulled his wet shirt down from in front of his face.

The ogre staggered, eyes bulging, but the drow was no longer even looking at the brute. He was staring hard at the elf, at the pair of blue, gold-flecked eyes staring out at him from behind the holes in a thin black mask, regarding him with haunting familiarity and intense hatred.

The ogre stammered over a couple more words, finally blurting, "Drow!"

"And no friend," said the elf. "Crunch him."

Drizzt, his scimitars still sheathed, simply stared at the elf, trying to figure out where he had seen those eyes before, where he had seen this elf before. And how had this one known right away that he was an enemy, almost as if expecting him?

"He has come to take your hammer, Bloog," the elf said teasingly.

The ogre exploded into motion, its roar shaking the stone of the walls. It grabbed up the hammer in both hands and chopped mightily at the drow. Or tried to, for Aegis-fang arced up behind the brute to slam hard into the low ceiling, cracking free a chip that dropped onto Bloog's head.

Drizzt didn't move, didn't take his intense stare off the elf, who was making no move against him, or even toward him.

Bloog roared again and stooped a bit. He tried again to crush the drow flat, this time with the hammer clearing the low ceiling and coming over in a tremendous swat.

Drizzt, who was standing somewhat sideways to the brute, hopped and did a sidelong somersault at the ogre, inside the angle of the blow. Even as the drow came around, he drew out his scimitars then landed lightly and bore into Bloog, stabbing several times and offering one slash before skittering out to the side opposite the elf.

The ogre retracted Aegis-fang easily with one arm, while he tried to grab at the drow with his free hand.

Drizzt was too quick for that, and as Bloog reached out in pursuit, the drow, who was skittering backward and still looking at the ogre, launched a double slash at the exposed hand.

Bloog howled and pulled his bloody hand in, but came forward in a sudden and devastating rush, Aegis-fang whipping wildly.

Drizzt dropped down to the floor, scrambled forward, came back up and rolled around the ogre's bulk, scoring a vicious double slash against the back of Bloog's hip as he passed. He stopped short, though, and rushed back expecting a charge from the elf, who now held a fine sword and dagger.

But the elf only laughed at him, and continued to stare.

"Bloog crunch you down!" the stubborn ogre roared, bouncing off the wall with a turn and charging back at Drizzt.

Aegis-fang whipped out, right and left, but Drizzt was in his pure fighting mode now, certainly not underestimating this monster—not with Aegis-fang in his grasp and not after he had nearly lost to a smaller ogre out by the tower.

The drow ducked the first swing, then ducked the second, and both times the drow managed to score small stings against the ogre's huge forearms.

Bloog swung again, and again Drizzt dropped to the floor. Aegis-fang smashed against the stone of the hearth, bringing a surprised squeak from Regis—who was still inside the chimney—that made Drizzt wince in fear.

Drizzt went forward hard, but the ogre didn't back from the twin stabbing scimitars, accepting the hit in exchange for a clear shot at the drow's puny head.

The whipping backhand with Aegis-fang, coming across and down, almost got Drizzt, almost smashed his skull to little bits.

He stabbed again, and hard, and rushed out to the side, but the ogre hardly seemed hurt, though his blood was running from many wounds.

Drizzt had to wonder how many hits it would take to bring this monster down.

Drizzt had to wonder how much time he had before others rushed in to the ogre's aid.

Drizzt had to wonder when that elf, seeming so very confident, would decide to join in.

* * * * *

Screaming to Tempus, his god of battle, the former guiding light in his warrior existence, the son of Beornegar charged along the winding trail. Sometimes the path was open to his right and sometimes blocked by low walls of stone. Sometimes the mountain on his left was steep and sheer, other times it sloped gradually, affording him a wider view of the mound.

And affording archers hiding among the higher rocks clear shots at him.

But Wulfgar ran on, coming to a place where the path leveled out. Around a bend ahead, in a larger area, he heard the ogre rock-thrower. With a silent prayer to Tempus, the barbarian charged right in, howling when the brute saw him, ducking when the surprised ogre hurled its boulder at him.

Seeing the boulder fly above the mark, the ogre reached for a heavy club, but Wulfgar was too fast for the brute to get its weapon ready. And the barbarian was too enraged, too full of battle-lust, for the ogre to accept the bardiche hit. The weapon pounded home with tremendous force, driving deep into the ogre's chest, sending it back against the wall, where it slumped in the last moments of its life.

But as Wulfgar leaped back, he understood that he was in trouble. For in that mighty hit, he felt the bardiche handle crack apart. It didn't splinter completely, but Wulfgar knew that the integrity of the weapon had been severely compromised. Worse still, a rock at the back of the clearing, against the mountain, suddenly rolled aside, revealing a passageway. Out poured another half-ogre, roaring and charging. A small and ugly man came out beside it, with a red-haired, powerful-looking woman behind them.

An arrow skipped off the stone right beside the backing barbarian, and he understood that he had to stay closer to the mountain wall in this exposed place.

He bore in on the half-ogre, then stopped fast as the brute lowered its head and shoulder and tried to barrel over him. How glad Wulfgar was at that moment that he had been trained by Drizzt Do'Urden, that he had learned the subtleties and wisdom of angled deflection instead of just

1145

shrugging off every hit and responding in kind. He slipped to the side a single step, leaving his leg out in front of the overbalancing brute, then turned as the half-ogre stumbled past, planting the butt of his weapon behind the half-ogre's armpit and shoving with all his strength.

Wulfgar took some relief as the brute barreled forward, right over the lip of the front side of the clearing, tumbling over the rocks there. He didn't know how far down the mountainside the brute might be falling, but he understood that it was out of the fight for a while, at least.

And a good thing that was, for the human pirate was right there, stabbing with a nasty sword, and Wulfgar had to work furiously to keep that biting tip at bay. Worse, the red-haired woman bore in, her sword working magnificently, rolling around the blocking bardiche and forcing Wulfgar back with a devilish thrust.

She was good. Wulfgar recognized that at once. He knew it would take all his energy if he was to have any hope. So the barbarian took a chance, stepping forward suddenly and accepting a slight stab from the man on his side.

That stab had little energy, though, for as the man started to attack, Wulfgar let go of his weapon with his right hand and punched straight out, connecting on the pirate's face even as his smile started to widen. Before his sword could slip deeply into the barbarian's side, the pirate was flying away, crumpling to the stone.

Then it was Wulfgar and Sheila Kree—Wulfgar recognized that this was indeed the pirate leader. How he wished she was holding Aegis-fang instead of this fine-edged sword. How he would have loved to summon the warhammer from her hand at that moment, then turn it back against her!

As it was, the barbarian had to work furiously to keep the warrior pirate at bay, for Sheila was surely no novice to battle. She stabbed and slashed, spun a complete circle and dived her sword in at Wulfgar's neck. The barbarian found himself forced back out into the open and took another hit as an arrow slashed down across his shoulder.

Sheila's smile widened.

A large ogre came out of the opening in the mountainside. Another roar came from above, and yet another from behind Wulfgar and not so far down the mountain—the half-ogre he had tripped up, he knew, on its way back.

"I need you!" the desperate barbarian cried out to his friends, but the wind stole the momentum from that call.

He knew that Catti-brie and Bruenor, wherever they were, would not likely hear him. He felt the bardiche handle cracking even more in his hand, and believed that the weapon would break apart in his hands with the next hit.

He forced his way forward again, skipping to his left, trying to delay the ogre's entry into the fray for as long as possible. But then he saw yet another form come out of the opening, another human pirate, it seemed, and he knew that he was doomed.

*   *   *   *   *

Drizzt scored and scored again, using the tight quarters and the low ceiling against the huge ogre. This one would have proven a much tougher opponent outdoors, the drow knew, especially with Aegis-fang in hand. But in here, now that he had the ogre's speed sorted out, the drow was too quick and too experienced.

Wound after wound opened up on the howling Bloog, and the ogre started calling for the elf to jump in and help.

And that elf did come forward, and Drizzt prepared a new strategy he had just worked out for keeping the ogre between him and this newest opponent. Before the drow could implement that strategy, though, the ogre lurched suddenly. A new and deeper wound appeared behind Bloog's hip, and the elf smiled wickedly.

Drizzt looked at the elf with amazement, and so did the ogre.

And the elf promptly drove the sword in again. The ogre howled and spun, but Drizzt was right there, his scimitar taking the beast deep in the kidney.

Back and forth it went, the two skilled warriors picking away while poor Bloog turned back and forth, never recovering from that initial surprise and the deep wound.

Soon enough, the big ogre went down hard and lay still.

Drizzt stood staring at the elf from across the large body. His scimitar tips lowered toward the floor, but he had them ready, unsure of this one's motives and intent.

"Perhaps I am a friend," the elf said, in a tone that was mocking and insincere. "Or perhaps I just wanted to kill you myself and grew impatient with Bloog's pitiful efforts against you."

Drizzt was circling then, and so was the elf, moving about Bloog's body, keeping it between as a deterrent to the potential foe.

"It would seem as if only you can answer which of the possibilities it might be."

The elf snorted derisively. "I have waited for this moment for years, Drizzt Do'Urden," came the surprising response.

Drizzt took a deep breath. This was as challenger here, perhaps someone who had studied his abilities and reputation and had prepared against him. This was not one to take lightly—he had seen the warrior's graceful movements against Bloog—but the drow suddenly remembered that he had more at stake here than this one fight, that he had others counting on him.

"This is not the time for a personal challenge," he said.

"This is exactly the time," the elf answered. "As I have arranged!"

1147

"Regis!" Drizzt called.

The drow burst forward, putting both scimitars in one hand, grabbing Aegis-fang with the other, and tossing it into the hearth. The halfling leaped down to grab it up, pausing only to see the first exchange as the elf leaped in at Drizzt, sword and dagger flashing.

But Drizzt was away in the blink of an eye, scimitars out and ready, balanced in a perfect defensive posture.

Regis knew that he had no place in this titanic struggle, so he gathered up the warhammer and climbed back up the chimney, then moved down the other side passage toward the apparently empty room they had already scouted.

* * * * *

The wind was just right, and so Catti-brie heard Wulfgar's desperate call for help after all. She knew he was in trouble, could hear the fighting up above, could see the half-ogre scrambling, almost back to the ledge.

But the woman, who had leaped across the ravine to the winding trail, was held in place by a barrage of arrows coming down at her.

Guenhwyvar had finally taken form by then, but before Catti-brie could even offer a command to the panther, an arrow drove down into the cat. Guenhwyvar, with a great roar, leaped away.

Catti-brie worked furiously then, using every opportunity to pop back out from the mountainside and let fly a devastating missile. Her arrow blasted through stone, and given the cry of pain and surprise, apparently scored a hit on one of the archers. But they were many, and she was stuck and could not get to Wulfgar.

She did manage to slip out and let fly at the half-ogre that was stubbornly climbing back to Wulfgar's position, her missile slamming the creature in the hip and sending it into a slide back down the slope.

But Catti-brie took an arrow for her efforts, the missile biting into her forearm. She fell back against the wall with a cry. The woman clutched at the shaft gingerly, then steeled her gaze and her grip. Growling away the agony, she pushed the arrow through. Catti-brie reached for her pack, pulling forth a bandage and tightly wrapping the arm.

"Bruenor, where are you?" she said quietly, fighting against despair.

It occurred to her as more than a passing possibility that they had all come together again just to be sundered apart, and permanently.

"Oh, get to him, Guen," the woman quietly begged, tying off the bandage and wincing away the pain as she set another arrow.

* * * * *

He fought brilliantly, purely on instinct, without rage and without fear. But he got hit again and again, and though no one wound was serious, Wulfgar knew that it was only a matter of time—a very short amount of time—before they overcame him. He sang out to Tempus, thinking it fitting, hoping it acceptable to the god, that he be singing that name as he died.

For surely this was the end for the son of Beornegar, with the red-haired pirate and the ogre pressing him, with his weapon falling apart in his hands, with a third opponent swiftly moving in.

No one could get to him in time.

He was glad, at least, that he might die honorably, in battle.

He took a stinging hit from the red-haired pirate, then had to pivot fast to block the ogre, and knew even as he turned that it was over. He had just left an opening for Sheila Kree to cut him down.

He glanced back to see the fatal blow.

Wulfgar, content for the first time in so many years, smiled.

* * * * *

Shouts of surprise from above clued Catti-brie, and she dared to leap out into the open.

There, above her, mighty Guenhwyvar charged the archers' nest, taking arrow after stinging arrow, but never veering and never slowing. The archers were standing then, and so the woman wasted no time in putting an arrow into the side of one's head, then taking down another.

She took aim for a third, but held the shot, for Guenhwyvar leaped in among the nest then, scattering the band. One man tried to scramble up the back side, farther up the mountain, but a great black paw caught him in the back of his leg and tore him back down.

Another man leaped over the rim of the nest, falling and bouncing, preferring to the fall to the grim fate at the claws of the panther. He tried desperately to control his descent and finally managed to settle on a stone.

Right in Catti-brie's sights.

He died quickly, at least.

* * * * *

Sheila Kree had him dead, obviously so, and her sword dived in at Wulfgar's exposed flank.

But the pirate leader had to pull back before ever hitting the mark, for a pair of legs wrapped around her waist, and a pair of daggers stabbed in viciously at the sides of her neck.

The veteran pirate bent forward, flipping the cunning assassin over her.

"Morik, ye dog!" she cried as the rogue went into a roll that stood him up right beside Wulfgar, bloody daggers in hand.

1149

Sheila stumbled backward, taking some comfort as more of her fighters passed her by.

"Kill 'em both!" she screamed as she staggered back into the cave complex.

"Like old times, eh?" Morik said to the stunned Wulfgar, who was already back to fending the ogre attacker.

Wulfgar could hardly respond. He just shook his head at the unexpected reprieve.

"Like old times?" Morik said again, as he fell into a fight with a pair of dirty pirates.

"We didn't win many of the fights in the old times," Wulfgar poignantly reminded him, for the odds had far from evened.

* * * * *

Drizzt worked his scimitars in a flurry of spinning parries, gradually turning them and altering his angle, moving his defensive posture into one more offensive, and forcing the elf back.

"Well done," the elf congratulated, skipping over one of fallen Bloog's legs.

"I do not even know your name, yet you bear me this hatred," the drow remarked.

The elf laughed at him. "I am Le'lorinel. That is the only name you need to hear."

Drizzt shook his head, staring at those intense eyes, somewhat recognizing them, but unable to place them.

And he was back into the fray, as Le'lorinel leaped forward, blades working furiously.

A sword came at Drizzt's head and he picked it off with an upraised scimitar. Le'lorinel turned the sword under the drow's curving blade and came ahead with a left-hand thrust of the dagger, a brilliant move.

But Drizzt was better. He accepted the cunning turn of the blades and instead of trying to move his second blade in front to deflect the dagger, he rolled to his right, driving his scimitar in toward the center, pushing the sword across and forcing his opponent to shift and alter the dagger thrust.

The drow's second blade came around with a sweep, driving against the elf's side.

The blade bounced off. Drizzt might as well have tried to slash through stone.

The drow rushed out, eyeing the turning and smiling Le'lorinel. He knew the enchantment immediately, for he had seen wizards use it. Was this elf a spellsword, then, a warrior trained in both the arcane and martial arts?

Drizzt hopped fallen Bloog's bloody chest, making a fast retreat to the back of the room, near to the hearth.

Le'lorinel continued to smile and held up one hand, whispering something Drizzt did not hear. The ring flared, and the elf moved even faster, hastened by yet another enchantment.

Oh, yes, this one was indeed prepared.

* * * * *

Regis dropped Aegis-fang down onto the burning logs, then scrambled as low as he could, rolled over so that he was going down head first, and caught the lip of the hearth and swung himself out. He was glad, as his feet kicked through the flames, that he was wearing heavy winter boots instead of walking in his typical barefoot manner.

The halfling scanned the room, seeing it much as Drizzt had described. He reached back and pulled Aegis-fang from the fire, then started across the room, to the partially opened door.

He went through silently, coming into a smaller chamber, this one some sort of alchemical workshop. There loomed the other door, with daylight streaming in around it.

The halfling ran for it, grabbed the handle, and tugged it open.

Then he was hit by a series of stinging, burning bursts against his hip and back. With a squeal, Regis scrambled out onto a natural balcony, but one that left him nowhere to run. He saw the fighting almost directly below him, so he threw the warhammer as far as he could, which wasn't very far, and cried out for Wulfgar.

Regis scrambled back, not even watching the hammer's bouncing descent. He saw the sorceress then, her invisibility enchantment dispelled. She stared at him from the side of the room, her hands working in the midst of casting yet another spell.

Regis yelped and ran out of the room into the main chamber, heading first for the hearth, then veering for another door.

The air around him grew thick with drifting strands of sticky, stringlike material. The halfling changed course yet again, making for the hearth, hoping its flames would burn this magical webbing away. He never got close, though, his strides shortened, his momentum stolen.

He was caught, encased in magical webbing that was holding him fast and was so thick around him he couldn't even breathe.

And the sorceress was there, in front of him, on the outside of the webbing barely a few inches away. She lifted a hand, holding a shining dagger up to Regis's face.

* * * * *

Another archer went down. Ignoring the burning pain and tightness in her arm, Catti-brie set another arrow to her bow.

1151

More archers had appeared above Guenhwyvar. As the woman took aim on that position, she noted another movement in a more dangerous place, a ledge high up above where Wulfgar was fighting.

Catti-brie whirled and nearly fired.

It was Regis, falling back—and Aegis-fang, falling down!

Catti-brie held her breath, thinking that the warhammer would bounce all the way down to the sea, but it caught suddenly and held in place on a small ledge up above and to the side.

"Call for it!" she screamed repeatedly.

With a glance to the lower archer ledge, where she knew Guenhwyvar was still engaged, she ran along the trail.

* * * * *

Drizzt made the hearth and skidded down to one knee, dropping Icingdeath to the stone floor and reaching into the glowing fireplace. Out his arm pumped, then back in, then out again, launching a barrage of missiles at Le'lorinel. One hit, then another. The elf blocked a third, a spinning stick, but the missile broke apart across the elf's blade, each side spinning in to score a hit.

None of them were serious, none of them would have been even without the stoneskin defense, but every one, every strike upon the elf, removed a bit more of the defensive enchantment.

"Very wise, drow!" Le'lorinel congratulated, and on the elf warrior came, sword flashing for the stooping drow.

Drizzt grabbed his blade and started up, then dropped back to the floor and kicked out, his foot barely hitting Le'lorinel's shin.

Then Drizzt had to roll to the side and over backward to his feet, against the wall. His scimitars came up immediately, ringing with parry after parry as Le'lorinel launched a series of strong attacks his way.

* * * * *

The bardiche was falling apart in his hands by then, as Wulfgar worked against the ogre.

To the side, Morik, too, found himself hard-pressed by a pair of pirates, both wielding vicious-looking cutlasses.

"We can't win!" the rogue cried.

"Then why did you help me?" Wulfgar countered.

Morik found his next words caught in his throat. Why indeed had he gone against Sheila Kree? Even when he had come visible again, on the ramp descending from Chogurugga's chamber, it would not have been difficult for him to find a shadowy place to sit out the fight. Cursing himself for what he now had to consider a foolhardy decision, the rogue leaped ahead, daggers slashing. He landed in a turn that sent his dark cloak flying wide.

"Run away!" he cried out, leaving the cloak behind as a pair of slashing cutlasses came against it. He skittered behind Wulfgar, moving between a pair of huge boulders and heading up the trail.

Then he came back onto the small clearing, shouting, "Not that way!" Yet another ogre was in fast pursuit.

Wulfgar groaned as this new foe seemed to be entering the fray—and another, he noted, seeing movement beside Morik.

But that was no ogre.

Bruenor Battlehammer leaped up onto the rock as Morik passed underneath. Axe in both hands and down behind him, the dwarf took aim as the oblivious ogre came by in fast pursuit.

Crack!

The hit resounded like splitting stone, and everyone on the clearing stopped their fighting for just a moment to regard the wild-eyed red-haired dwarf standing atop the stone, his axe buried deeply into the skull of an ogre that was only still upright because the mighty dwarf was holding it there, trying to tug the axe back out.

"Ain't that a beautiful sound?" Bruenor called to Wulfgar.

Wulfgar shook his head and went back into defensive action against the ogre, and now with the two pirates joining in. "Took you long enough!" he replied.

"Quit yer bitchin'!" Bruenor yelled back. "Me girl's seen yer hammer, ye durn fool! Call for it, boy!"

The ogre in front of Wulfgar stepped back to get some charging room, roared defiantly, and lifted its club, coming on hard.

Wulfgar threw his ruined bardiche at the beast, who blocked it with its chest and arm and tossed the pieces aside.

"Oh, brilliant!" complained Morik, who was back behind Wulfgar, coming around to engage the two pirates.

But Wulfgar wasn't even listening to the complaint or to the threats from the enraged ogre. He was yelling out instead, trusting Bruenor's word.

"What you to do now, puny one?" the ogre said, though its expression changed considerably as it finished the question. A finely crafted warhammer appeared in Wulfgar's waiting grasp.

"Catch this one," the barbarian remarked, letting fly.

As it had with the cracked bardiche, the ogre tried to accept the blow with its chest and its arm, tried to just take the hit and push the warhammer aside.

But this was no cracked bardiche.

The ogre had no idea why it was sitting against the wall then, unable to draw breath.

His hand up high in the air, Wulfgar called out again for the hammer.

And there it was, in his grasp, warrior and weapon united.

A cutlass came in at him from the side, along with a cry of warning from Morik.

Wulfgar snapped his warhammer down, blasting the thrusting cutlass away. With perfect balance, as if the warhammer was an extension of his own arm, Wulfgar turned the weapon and swung it out hard.

The pirate flew away.

The other turned and ran, but Morik had him before he reached the opening, stabbing him down.

Another ogre exited the cave and glared threateningly at nearby Morik, but a blue streak cut between the barbarian and the rogue, knocking the brute back inside.

The friends turned to see Catti-brie standing there, bow in hand.

"Guen's got them up above," the woman explained.

"And Rumblebelly's up there too, and likely needin' us!" howled Bruenor, motioning for them.

They ran on up the path, winding farther around the mountain. They came to another level, wide area with a huge door facing them, set into the mountain.

"Not that one," Morik tried to explain. "Big ogres . . ."

The rogue shut up as Bruenor and Wulfgar fell over the door, hammer and axe chopping, splintering the wood to pieces.

In the pair went.

Chogurugga and her attendants were waiting.

* * * * *

Their weapons rang against each other repeatedly, a blur of motion, a constant sound. Hastened by the enchantment, Le'lorinel matched Drizzt's blinding speed, but unlike the drow, the elf was not used to such lightning reflexive action.

Scimitar right, scimitar left, scimitar straight ahead, and Drizzt scored a hard stab against Le'lorinel's chest that would have finished the elf had it not been for the stonelike dweomer.

"How many more will it stop?" the drow asked, growing more confident now as his routines slipped around Le'lorinel's defenses. "We need not do this."

But the elf showed no sign of letting up.

Drizzt slashed out with his right, then spun as Le'lorinel, parrying, went into a circuit to the right as well, both coming together out of their respective spins with a clash of four blades.

Drizzt turned his blade over the elf's, driving Le'lorinel's down. When the elf predictably stabbed ahead, the drow leaped into a somersault right over the attack, landing on his feet and falling low as the sword swished over his head. Drizzt slashed out, scoring on Le'lorinel's hip, then kicked out as the elf retreated, clipping a knee.

Le'lorinel squeaked in pain and stumbled back a few steps.

The enchantment was defeated. The next scimitar hit would draw blood.

"There is no need for this," Drizzt graciously said.

Le'lorinel glared at him, and smiled again. Up came the ring, and with a word from the elf, it flashed again.

Drizzt charged, wanting to beat whatever trick might be coming next.

But Le'lorinel was gone, vanished from sight.

Drizzt skidded to a stop, eyes widening with surprise. On instinct, he reached within himself to his own magical powers, his innate drow abilities, and summoned a globe of darkness about him, one that filled the room and put him back on even footing with the invisible warrior.

Just as Le'lorinel had expected he would. For now, with the ring's fourth enchantment—the most insidious of the group—the invisible elf's form was outlined again in glowing fires.

Drizzt moved in, spinning and launching slashing attack routines, as he had long ago learned when fighting blindly. Every attack was also a parry, his scimitars whirling out wide from his body.

And he listened, and he heard the shuffle of feet.

He was on the spot in an instant and took heart when his blade rang against a blocking sword, awkwardly held.

The elf had miscalculated, he believed, had altered the fight into one in which the experienced drow held a great advantage.

He struck with wide-reaching blows, coming in from the left and the right, keeping his opponent before him.

Right and left again, and Drizzt turned suddenly behind his second swing, spinning and slashing with the right as he came around.

The victory was his, he knew, from the position of the blocking sword and dagger, the elf caught flatfooted and without defense.

His scimitar drove against Le'lorinel's side, tearing flesh.

But at precisely the same instant, Drizzt, too, got hit in the side.

Unable to retract or slow his blow, Drizzt had to finish the move, the scimitar bouncing off of a rib, tearing a lung and cutting back out across the front of the elf's chest.

And the same wound burrowed across the drow's chest.

Even as the pain exploded within him, even as he stumbled back, tripping over Bloog's leg and falling hard to the floor against the wall, Drizzt understood what had happened, recognized the fire shield enchantment, a devilish spell that inflicted damage upon anyone striking the spell-user.

He lay there, one lung collapsing, his lifeblood running out freely.

Across the way, Le'lorinel, dying as Drizzt was dying, groaned.

Chapter 28

Not Without Loss

With equal intensity, Bruenor and Wulfgar charged into the large cave. Wulfgar headed to the side to intercept a pair of large, armored ogres while Bruenor went for the most exotic of the three, an ogress with light violet skin wearing a huge shining helmet and wielding an enormous scythe.

Morik came in behind the ferocious pair, tentatively, and making no definite strides to join the battle.

More eager behind him came Catti-brie. She had an arrow flying almost immediately, staggering one of the two ogres closing on Wulfgar.

That blast gave the barbarian all the momentum he needed. He drove hard against the other brute, Aegis-fang pounding repeatedly. The ogre blocked and blocked again, but the third chop hit it on the breastplate and sent it staggering backward.

Wulfgar bore in, smashing away.

The ogre's wounded companion tried to move back into the fight, but Catti-brie hit it with a second arrow, and a third. Howling with rage and pain, the brute turned and charged the door instead.

"Brilliant," Morik groaned, and he cried out as a large form brushed past him, sending him sprawling.

Guenhwyvar hit the charging, arrow-riddled ogre head on. She leaped onto its face, clawing, raking, and biting. The brute stood straight, its momentum lost, and staggered backward, its face erupting in fountains of blood.

"Good girl," said Catti-brie, and she turned and fired up above Bruenor, nailing the ogress, then drew out Khazid'hea. She paused and glanced back at Morik, who was standing against the wall, shaking his head.

"Well done," he muttered, in obvious disbelief.

They were indeed an efficient group!

* * * * *

The magical darkness lifted.

Drizzt sat against the wall. Across from him sat Le'lorinel, in almost the exact posture and with a wound identical to the drow's.

Drizzt stared at his fallen opponent, his eyes widening. Thin magical flames still licked at Le'lorinel's skin, but Drizzt hardly noted them. For the wound, torn through Le'lorinel's leather vest and across the front, revealed a breast—a female breast!

And Drizzt understood so very much, and knew those eyes so much better, and knew who this truly was even before Le'lorinel reached up and pulled the mask off her face.

An elf, a Moon elf, once a little child whom Drizzt had saved from drow raiders. An elf driven to rage by the devastation of the drow on that fateful, evil day, when she was bathed in the blood of her own murdered mother to convince the dark elves that she, too, was already dead.

"By the gods," the drow rasped, his voice weak for lack of air.

"You are dead, Drizzt Do'Urden," the elf said, her voice equally weak and faltering. "My family is avenged."

Drizzt tried to respond, but he could not begin to find the words. In this short time, how could he possibly explain to Le'lorinel that he had not participated in that murder, that he had saved her at great personal peril, and most importantly, that he was sorry, so very sorry, for what his evil kin had done.

He stared at Le'lorinel, bearing her no ill will, despite the fact that her misguided actions and blind vengeance had cost them both their very lives.

* * * * *

Chogurugga was doing well against the mighty Bruenor Battlehammer, her potion-enhanced muscles, potion-enhanced speed, and potion-enhanced defenses more than holding their own against the dwarf.

Bruenor just growled and cursed, swatting powerfully, taking hits that would fell most opponents and shrugging them off with dwarven toughness then boring on, his axe slashing in.

He was losing, though, and he knew it, but then Catti-brie's arrow sizzled in above him, driving into the ogress's chest and sending her staggering backward.

"Oh, good girl!" the dwarf roared, taking the advantage to charge forward and press the offensive.

But even as he got there the ogress had yet another vial in hand and up to her lips, swallowing its contents in one great gulp.

Even as Bruenor closed, starting the battle once more, the ogress's wounds began to bind.

The dwarf growled in protest. "Damn healing potion!" he howled, and he got a hit in against Chogurugga's thigh, opening a gash.

Immediately, Chogurugga had another vial, one similar to the last, off of her belt and moving up to her lips. Bruenor cursed anew.

A black form sailed above the dwarf, slamming into the ogress and latching on.

Chogurugga flailed as Guenhwyvar tore at her face, front claws holding fast, fangs biting and tearing, back claws raking wildly.

The ogress dropped the vial, which hit the floor but did not break, and dropped her weapon as well. The ogress grabbed at the cat with both hands, trying to pull Guenhwyvar away.

The panther's hooked claws held tight, which meant that throwing Guenhwyvar aside would mean tearing her face right off. And of course Bruenor was right there, smashing the ogress's legs and midsection with mighty, vicious chops.

Bruenor heard a crash to the side, and Catti-brie was beside him, her powerful sword slicing easily through Chogurugga's flesh and bone.

The ogress toppled to the floor.

The two companions and Guenhwyvar turned about just as Wulfgar's hammer caved in the last ogre's skull, the brute falling right over its dead partner.

"This way!" Morik called from an exit across the wide room, with a corridor beyond heading farther up into the complex.

Bruenor paused to wait for his girl as Catti-brie stooped to retrieve Chogurugga's fallen vial.

"When I find out who's selling this stuff to damn ogres, I'll chop him up!" the frustrated dwarf declared.

Across the room, Morik bit his lower lip. He knew who it was, for he had seen Bellany's alchemical room.

Up went the companions, to the level corridor with five doors that marked Sheila Kree's complex. A groan from the side brought them immediately to one door, which Bruenor barreled through with dwarven subtlety.

1159

There lay Drizzt, and there lay the elf, both mortally wounded.

Catti-brie came in right behind, moving immediately for Drizzt, but the drow stopped her with an upheld hand.

"Save her," he demanded, his voice very weak. "You must."

And he slumped.

* * * * *

Wulfgar stood at the door, horrified, but Morik didn't even slow at that particular room, but rather ran across the hall to Bellany's chambers. He burst through, and even as he was entering he prayed that the wizard hadn't trapped the portal.

The rogue skidded to a stop just inside the threshold, hearing a shriek. He turned to see a halfling extracting himself from a magical web.

"Who are you?" Regis asked, then quickly added, "See what I have?" He pulled open his shirt, lifting out a ruby pendant for Morik to see.

"Where is the sorceress?" Morik demanded, not even noticing the tantalizing gemstone.

Regis pointed to the open outer door and the balcony beyond, and Morik sprinted out. The halfling glanced down, then, at his enchanted ruby pendant and scratched his head, wondering why it hadn't had its usual charming effect. Regis was glad that this small man was too busy to be bothered with him.

* * * * *

Catti-brie paused, taken aback by the sincerity and demand in Drizzt's voice as he had given her the surprising instructions. The woman turned toward the fallen elf, whose breathing was as shallow as Drizzt's, who seemed, as did Drizzt, as if each breath might be her last.

"The Nine Hells ye will!" Bruenor roared, rushing to her and tearing the vial away.

Sputtering a string of curses, the dwarf went right to Drizzt and poured the healing liquid down his throat.

The drow coughed and almost immediately began to breathe easier.

"Damn it all!" Catti-brie cried, and she ran across the room to the fallen elf, lifting her head gently with her hands, staring into those eyes.

Empty eyes.

Even as Drizzt opened his eyes once more, Le'lorinel's spirit fled her body.

"Come quickly!" said Regis, arriving at the door. The halfling paused, though, when he saw Drizzt lying there so badly wounded.

"What'd'ye know, Rumblebelly?" Bruenor said after a moment's pause.

"S-sorceress," Regis stammered, still staring at Drizzt. "Um . . . Morik's chasing her." Never turning his eyes, he pointed across the way.

Wulfgar started off and Bruenor called to Catti-brie as she fell to her knees beside the drow, "Get yer bow out there! They'll be needing ye!"

The woman hesitated for a long while, staring helplessly at Drizzt, but Bruenor pushed her away.

"Go, and be quick!" he demanded. "I ain't one for killing wizards. Yer bow's better for that."

Catti-brie rose and ran out of the room.

"But holler if ye see another ogre!" the dwarf shouted behind her.

* * * * *

Bellany cursed under her breath as she gingerly picked her way along the mountainside to come in sight of the coast, only to see *Bloody Keel* riding the receding tide out of the cave. Her deck bristled with pirates, including, prominently, Sheila Kree, wounded but undaunted, shouting orders from the deck.

Bellany fell into her magical powers immediately, beginning to cast a spell that would transport her to the deck. She almost finished the casting, was uttering the very last words and making the final motions, when she was grabbed from behind.

Horrified, the sorceress turned her head to see Morik the Rogue, grim-faced and holding her fast.

"Let me go!" she demanded.

"Do not," Morik said, shaking his head. "Do not, I beg."

"You fool, they will kill me!" Bellany howled, trying hard to pull away. "I could have slain you, but I did not! I could have killed the halfling, but . . ."

Her voice trailed away over those last few words, though, for the huge form of a barbarian warrior came bounding around the mountainside.

"What have you done to me?" the defeated woman asked Morik.

"Did you not let the halfling live?" the rogue reasoned.

"More than that! I cut him out," Bellany answered defiantly. She went silent, for Wulfgar was there, towering over her.

"Who is this?" the enraged barbarian demanded.

"An observer," Morik answered, "and nothing more. She is innocent."

Wulfgar narrowed his eyes, staring hard at both Bellany and Morik, and his expression showed that he hardly believed the rogue.

But Morik had saved his life this day, and so he said nothing.

Wulfgar's eyes widened and he stepped forward as he noted the ship, sails unfurling, gliding out past the rocks. He leaped out to another rock, gaining a better vantage point, and lifted Aegis-fang as if he meant to hurl it at the departing ship.

But *Bloody Keel* was long out of even his range.

Catti-brie joined the group next, and wasted no time in putting up Taulmaril, leveling the bow at *Bloody Keel*'s deck.

"The red-haired one," Morik instructed. Bellany elbowed him hard in the ribs and scowled at him deeply.

Indeed, Catti-brie already had a bead drawn on Sheila Kree, the pirate easy to spot on the ship's deck.

But the woman paused and lifted her head from the bow for a wider view. She took note of the many waves breaking over submerged rocks, all about the escaping pirate, and understood well the skill needed to take a ship out through those dangerous waters.

Catti-brie leveled her bow again, scouring the deck.

When she found the wheel, and the crewman handling it, she let fly.

The pirate lurched forward, then slid down to the decking, taking the wheel over to the side as he went.

Bloody Keel cut a sharp turn, crewmen rushing desperately from every angle to grab the wheel.

Then came the crunch as the ship sailed over a jagged reef, and the wind in the sails kept her going, splintering the hull all the way.

Many were thrown from the ship with the impact. Others leaped into the icy waters, the ship disintegrating beneath them. Still others grabbed a rail or a mast and held on for dear life.

Amidst it all stood Sheila Kree. The fiery pirate looked up at the mountainside, up at Catti-brie, in defiance.

And she, too, went into the cold water, and *Bloody Keel* was no more than kindling, scattering in the rushing waters.

Few would escape that icy grip, and those who did, and those who never got onto the ship in the first place—ogre, half-ogre, and human alike—had no intention of engaging the mighty friends again.

The fight for Golden Cove was won.

Epilogue

They buried the elf who called herself Le'lorinel in the clay, in the cave complex, as near to the exit and the outside air and the starry night sky as possible.

Drizzt didn't help with the digging, for his vicious wound was far from healed, but he watched it, every moment. And when they had put the elf, Ellifain by her true name, in the cold ground and had covered her with damp and cold clay, Drizzt Do'Urden stood there, staring helplessly.

"It should not have been like this," the drow said quietly to Catti-brie, who was standing beside him, supporting him.

"I heard that in yer voice," the woman replied. "When ye told me to save her."

"And so I wish that you had."

"Ye durn fool!" came a rocky voice from the side. "Get yerself healed quick so I can pound yer face!"

Drizzt turned to Bruenor, matching the dwarf's scowl.

"Ye think we'd've done that?" Bruenor demanded. "Do ye really? Ye think we'd've let ye die to save the one that killed ye?"

"You do not understand . . ." Drizzt tried to explain, his lavender orbs wet with tears.

"And would ye have saved the damned elf instead of me?" the fiery dwarf bellowed. "Or instead of me girl? Ye say yes, elf, and I'll be wiping yer blood from me axe!"

The truth of that statement hit home to Drizzt, and he turned helplessly to Catti-brie.

"I would not have given her the potion," the woman said definitively. "Ye caught me by surprise, to be sure, but I'd've been back to ye with the brew in a moment."

Drizzt sighed and accepted the inevitable truth of that, but still, this whole thing seemed so very unfair to him, so very wrong. He had encountered Ellifain before this, and not so many years ago, in the Moonwood on his way back to the Underdark. The elf had come after him then with murderous rage, but her protective clan had held her back and had ushered Drizzt on his way. And Drizzt, though he knew that her anger was misplaced, could do nothing to persuade her or calm her.

And now this. She had come after him because of what his evil kin had done to her mother, to her family, to her.

Drizzt sighed at the irony of it all, his heart surely broken by this sad turn of fate. If Ellifain had revealed herself to him truly, he never would have found the strength to lift his blades against her, even if she came at him to kill him.

"I had no choice," Drizzt said to Catti-brie, his voice barely a whisper.

"The elf killed herself," the woman replied. Bruenor, coming over to join his friends, agreed wholeheartedly.

"She should be alive, and healing from those wounds she felt those decades ago," the drow said.

To the side, Bruenor gave a loud snort. "Yerself's the one who should be alive," the dwarf bellowed. "And so ye are."

Drizzt looked at him and shrugged.

"Ye'd have gived the potion to me," the dwarf insisted quietly, and Drizzt nodded.

"But it saddens me," the drow explained.

"If it didn't, ye'd be less a friend of mine," Bruenor assured him.

Catti-brie held Drizzt close and kissed him on the cheek.

He didn't look at her, though, just stood there staring at the new grave, his shoulders slumped with the weight of the world.

* * * * *

The five companions, along with Morik and Bellany, left Golden Cove a tenday later, when the weather broke clear.

They knew they were fighting time in trying to get out of the mountains, but with Bellany's magical help they made the main pass through the Spine of the World, leading north to Icewind Dale and south to Luskan, soon enough.

And there they parted ways, with Morik, Bellany, and Wulfgar heading south, and the other four turning north back for Ten-Towns.

Before they split apart, though, Wulfgar promised his friends that he would be home soon.

Home. Icewind Dale.

* * * * *

Spring was in full bloom before Wulfgar, Delly, and Colson came through Luskan again, heading north for Icewind Dale.

The family paid a visit to the Cutlass, to Arumn and Josi, and to Bellany and Morik, who had taken up together in Morik's apartment—one made more comfortable by far by the workings of the sorceress.

Wulfgar didn't stay long in Luskan, though, his wagon rolling out the front gate within two days. For the warrior, knowing again who he was, was indeed anxious to be home with his truest friends.

Delly, too, was anxious to see this new home, to raise Colson in the clear, crisp air of fabled Icewind Dale.

As night was settling over the land, the couple noted a blazing campfire in the distance, just off the road, and since there were farmhouses all around in this civilized region, they rolled up without fear.

They smelled the encampment's occupants before they could make out the individual forms, and though Delly whispered, "goblins," Wulfgar knew better.

"Dwarves," he corrected.

Since this particular group apparently hadn't bothered to set any sort of a sentry, Wulfgar and Delly moved right into their midst, near to the campfire, before any of the dwarves cried out in surprise or protest. After a moment's hesitation, with many vicious-looking, many-bladed, many-hooked weapons rising up in the air, the most unpleasant, smelly, and animated dwarf either of the humans had ever seen bounded up before them. He still wore his armor, though it was obvious that the camp had been set hours before, and what armor that was! Razor-sharp edges showed everywhere, along with many small spikes.

"Wulfie!" bellowed Thibbledorf Pwent, raucous leader of the famed Gutbuster Brigade of Mithral Hall. "I heared ye wasn't dead!" He gave a huge, gap-toothed grin as he finished and slugged Wulfgar hard. "Tougher than the stone, ain't ye?"

"Why are you here?" the surprised barbarian asked, not thrilled to see this particular old friend.

Wulfgar had lived beside Thibbledorf in Mithral Hall those years ago and had watched the amazing training of the famed Gutbusters, a group of wild and vicious thugs. One of Thibbledorf's infamous battle tactics was to leap onto a foe and begin shaking wildly, his nasty armor cutting the enemy to pieces.

"Going to Icewind Dale," Thibbledorf explained. "Got to get to King Bruenor."

Wulfgar started to ask for the dwarf to expand on that, but he held the words as the title Thibbledorf had just laid upon Bruenor's powerful shoulders hit him clearly.

"King?"

Thibbledorf lowered his eyes, a movement that had all the other Gutbusters, a dozen or so, leaping up and falling to one knee. All of them save the leader gave a deep, monotone intonation, a long and low hum.

"Praise Moradin in taking Gandalug Battlehammer," Thibbledorf said solemnly. "The King of Mithral Hall is no more. The king before him is king again—Bruenor Battlehammer of the clan that bears his name. Long life and good beer to King Bruenor!"

He ended with a shout, and all the Gutbusters leaped up into the air. They resembled a field of bouncing rocks, punching their fists, most covered with spiked gauntlets, into the air.

"King Bruenor!" they all roared.

"What's it mean?" Delly whispered to Wulfgar.

"It means we should not get too comfortable in Ten-Towns," the barbarian answered. "For we'll be on the road again, do not doubt. A long road to the east, to Mithral Hall."

Delly looked around at the Gutbusters, who were dancing in couples, chanting "King Bruenor!" and ending each call with a shallow hop and a short run that brought each couple crashing together.

"Well, at least our own road north'll be safer now," the woman remarked. "If a bit more fragrant."

Wulfgar started to nod, but then saw Thibbledorf crash together forehead to forehead with one poor Gutbuster, laying the dwarf out cold. Thibbledorf shook his head to clear the dizziness, his lips flapping wildly. When he saw what he'd done, he howled all the louder and charged at another—who took up the challenge and roared and charged.

And went flying away into the peaceful land of sleeping Gutbusters.

Thibbledorf howled all the louder and hopped about, looking for a third victim.

"Safer? We shall see," was all that Wulfgar could say to Delly.